Science Fiction

Stories and Contexts

Science Fiction

Stories and Contexts

Edited by
Heather Masri
New York University

Bedford / St. Martin's
New York ◆ Boston

For Bedford/St. Martin's

Executive Editor: Stephen A. Scipione
Editorial Assistant: Marisa Feinstein
Production Supervisor: Andrew Ensor
Marketing Manager: Adrienne Petsick
Text Design: Joyce Weston
Project Management: Books By Design, Inc.
Cover Design: Donna Lee Dennison
Cover Art: René Magritte, *Voice of Space* (La voix des airs), 1931. Oil on canvas, 72.7 × 54.2 cm. Peggy Guggenheim Collection, Venice (Solomon R. Guggenheim Foundation, New York). © 2008 C. Herscovici, Brussels/Artists Rights Society (ARS), New York.
Composition: Achorn International
Printing and Binding: RR Donnelley & Sons Company

President: Joan E. Feinberg
Editorial Director: Denise B. Wydra
Editor in Chief: Karen S. Henry
Director of Marketing: Karen R. Soeltz
Director of Editing, Design, and Production: Marcia Cohen
Assistant Director of Editing, Design, and Production: Elise S. Kaiser
Manager, Publishing Services: Emily Berleth

Library of Congress Control Number: 2008923372

Manufactured in the United States of America.

3   2   1

f   e   d

For information, write: Bedford/St. Martin's, 75 Arlington Street, Boston, MA 02116 (617-399-4000)

ISBN-10: 0-312-45015-X
ISBN-13: 978-0-312-45015-1

Acknowledgments

Hannah Arendt, "Ideology and Terror: A Novel Form of Government." From *Totalitarianism: Part Three of the Origin of Totalitarianism* by Hannah Arendt. Copyright © 1973, 1968, 1966, 1958, 1951, 1948 by Hannah Arendt and renewed 2001, 1996, 1994, 1986 by Lotte Kohler. Copyright renewed 1979 by Mary McCarthy West. Copyright renewed 1976 by Hannah Arendt. Reprinted by permission of Harcourt, Inc.

Acknowledgments and copyrights are continued at the back of the book on pages 1235–39, which constitute an extension of the copyright page.

Preface

Science fiction is a new literature with an old ancestry, one that can trace its roots back to the great imaginative literature of past centuries but that is also a vital contemporary form that continues to develop and grow in new directions. As a genre, science fiction encompasses an enormous variety of subjects and forms; it is best characterized by a set of inclinations or a way of thinking, one that cherishes a sense of wonder and possibility and that is fascinated by the idea of change and its consequences.

This book was created with introductory courses in science fiction in mind. Although there are many excellent anthologies on the market, some are limited in historical scope while others are constrained by a desire to define the genre in a particular way. My goal was to provide an anthology that would offer both focus and historical sweep by highlighting central themes within a chronological context. Of course, no anthology can satisfy every need, but I have tried to combine within one volume what I have found to be most useful when teaching students new to the study of science fiction:

- *Great stories from the nineteenth century to the present.* Accordingly, this collection — while by no means exhaustive — is broadly representative of the richness of the field in historical, geographical, and stylistic terms.
- *A primer on the field and the fiction.* The stories are introduced by editorial material that provides necessary background information and sketches out possible frameworks for interpretation without intruding on students' reading and discovery.
- *Contexts for critical thinking.* Finally, science fiction is at least in part a literature of ideas, and this book offers supplemental readings from a variety of disciplines to help students make connections between the stories and the ideas and contexts that gave rise to them.

What You'll Find in the Book

To emphasize both the continuity of the tradition and the variety of approaches that different authors have taken, I have combined a thematic with a chronological structure, organizing the selections around six common science fiction themes: alien encounters, artificial life, time, utopias and dystopias, disasters and apocalypses, and evolutions. Each thematic chapter begins with works that are foundational to the genre, highlighting writers such as H. G. Wells, Jules Verne, and Mary Shelley. Following these readings are a series of modern stories, roughly representing the decades of the twentieth century, each of which stands alone on its literary merits and also reflects something about the cultural climate and literary sensibilities of the period in which it was written.

To represent the 1930s, 1940s, and 1950s, I have chosen works that shaped the development of the genre and that correct a misconception that early science fiction was of inferior literary quality — classics ranging from idea-driven stories such as Arthur C. Clarke's "The Nine Billion Names of God" and Robert Heinlein's "All You Zombies — " to Ray Bradbury's eerie and lyrical "Mars Is Heaven!" and Daniel Keyes's experimental and literary "Flowers for Algernon" (later expanded into a novel and made into an Oscar-winning movie). The more recent stories represent established and influential authors, including Ursula K. Le Guin and Kim Stanley Robinson, as well as new writers whose work is gaining recognition, such as Ted Chiang and Maureen McHugh; many of the recent stories have won the Nebula or Hugo award for best science fiction story in a given year. And although this collection focuses on American science fiction, it also includes authors from other English-speaking countries — not only classic older works by British writers but also more recent contributions from Australian Greg Egan and Caribbean-Canadian Nalo Hopkinson — as well as selections of important works from Germany, France, Russia, Eastern Europe, and Japan. The stories here represent all the major periods and movements usually studied, from the Golden Age (represented by such stories as Isaac Asimov's "Liar!") to the New Wave (including J. G. Ballard's "The Terminal Beach") to Cyberpunk (William Gibson's "Burning Chrome") and include examples of important subgenres, such as the first contact story and alternate history.

Each section also includes provocative theoretical and critical works from a variety of disciplines — including science, psychology, and literary criticism; these pieces provide a rich variety of contexts against which to read the fiction. For example, Sigmund Freud's "The Uncanny" suggests why *Frankenstein* and stories like it are so disturbing; physicist Michio Kaku's essay makes it easier to appreciate the real and surreal aspects of time travel; and Hannah Arendt's analysis of Nazi Germany highlights tensions at work in many stories of utopia. Instructors may choose to assign selected pieces that reflect their own approach to the materials or provide useful background, while students interested in pursuing a particular theme or disciplinary approach can use them as jumping-off points for their own critical investigations. Although cross-disciplinary or cultural studies are by no means necessary, they are particularly appropriate for science fiction, which has always maintained an active dialogue with contemporary ideas and which, more than any other modern literature, has been concerned with the philosophical examination of what it means to be human in the modern world. Typically, science fiction can be seen as reflecting, critiquing, and reconceptualizing the society from which it grows. Both the thematic organization and the inclusion of theoretical essays are meant to highlight this quality by focusing on a few of the ideas that have most interested science fiction writers and showing how their approaches to those ideas, and the style with which they engaged them, have changed over time. The result is a collection of stories that not only stand on their own but also speak to each other in interesting ways.

The editorial apparatus in this volume introduces students to the history and development of science fiction as a literary genre and provides a context for further study. The Brief Introduction to Science Fiction and Its History gives an overview of the genre's history and the approaches critics have taken to defining it, while the Selective Guide to Science Fiction Research directs students toward resources for more in-depth work. Each thematic section begins with an introduction that outlines some of the approaches science fiction writers have taken to each topic and highlights underlying philosophical questions to initiate further discussion. Headnotes for the stories provide biographical information on the authors and situate their work in the larger field of science fiction; headnotes for the critical selections provide cultural and historical context. These materials are designed to be suggestive rather than exhaustive; my goal has been to provide context without overwhelming students or overdetermining their interpretations. I have also aimed at flexibility: A chronological table of contents is included for instructors who prefer a strictly historical approach, while an alternative thematic table of contents provides different groupings for those interested in topical approaches.

Acknowledgments

I would like to thank the many people who contributed to the development of this volume by providing feedback and suggestions, including Wynn Padula, Josie Grégoire, Stephanie Kiceluk, and the members of the Liberal Studies Program's Cultural Studies Colloquium. I am grateful to the publisher's reviewers of the book: James Allen, College of DuPage; Paul Brians, Washington State University; Wes Chapman, Illinois Wesleyan University; R. Craig Curtis, Bradley University; Elizabeth S. Davidson, University of South Carolina Upstate; Jane Donawerth, University of Maryland; James Donelan, University of California, Santa Barbara; John L. Flynn, Towson University; Kathleen L. Fowler, Ramapo College of New Jersey; Donald Gilzinger Jr., Suffolk County Community College; James Gunn, University of Kansas; Caroline Hunt, College of Charleston; Jamil Khader, Stetson University; Richard D. Kemp, University of Maryland; Deborah Spangler Koelling, Northwest College; David Lavery, Middle Tennessee State University; Cory Lund, Southwestern Illinois College; Margaret McBride, University of Oregon; Michael O'Conner, Millikin University; Megan O'Neill, Stetson University; Reinhold Schlieper, Embry-Riddle Aeronautical University; and Marc Zaldivar, Virginia Tech University. Friends and colleagues from a variety of disciplines were generous in talking to me about their fields, especially philosophers Gail Linsenbard and Phil Washburn; religious studies professors Susanne Mrozik and David Frankfurter; historians

Joyce Apsel, Joe Portanova, Mahnaz Yousefzadeh, and Ron Rainey; biologist Bob Wallace; and psychologist Lynn Somerstein. *Ways of Reading* by David Bartholomae and Anthony Petrosky helped inspire my "applied theory" approach to student writing. I am especially grateful to David Hartwell for sharing his breadth of knowledge and expertise. Dean Fred Schwarzbach at the New York University (NYU) Liberal Studies Program provided research time at a crucial stage of this project. Gordon Pradl helped me launch my first science fiction seminar at NYU, and students from that course (and the others since) continue to influence my approach to the field.

Thanks go to Cindi Weiss at Bedford, Freeman & Worth, who first encouraged me to begin working on this volume. I'm very grateful to Joan Feinberg, Denise Wydra, and Karen Henry, who invited me to prepare the anthology for Bedford/St. Martin's. I've also received invaluable help from Karen Soeltz and Adrienne Petsick in the marketing department; Emily Berleth in the production department and Herb Nolan of Books By Design; Sandy Schechter and Sue Brekka, who cleared permissions; and Amy Hurd Gershman and Marisa Feinstein in editorial. I've been especially fortunate to have as my editor Steve Scipione, without whose insight, judgment, and patience this book would not exist.

Finally, I would like to thank Alfie Guy both for editorial assistance and for something harder to quantify — bringing a sense of wonder to my life, which makes all things possible.

Contents

3. Time   476

4. Utopias and Dystopias   702

5. Disasters and Apocalypses   892

6. Evolutions   1028

Chronological Contents

Alternative Thematic Contents

Nature and the Environment

Commercialism and the Media

Family and Relationships

Psychology

Critical Contexts:

Science Fiction

Stories and Contexts

A Brief Introduction to Science Fiction and Its History

Why read science fiction? For those who already do, the answer is self-evident. Because it's fun. Because it's some of the smartest, most interesting literature being written today. For those who do not, a little more explanation may be helpful. Science fiction lays claim to a literary heritage that goes back to our earliest stories in myth and epic. Yet science fiction is also a uniquely modern genre, one informed by profound engagement with the most pressing issues of the contemporary world. It relies on a metaphoric and visionary mode of apprehension neglected by contemporary realistic fiction. Science fiction takes part in a symbolic discourse of meaning that addresses big questions such as "why" and "what if" — Why are we here? Where are we going? What if things had happened differently?

No one who is interested in modern literature, cultural studies, or the mass media can afford to ignore science fiction. A major publishing category with a rapidly expanding readership, science fiction also exerts a profound influence on mainstream culture, from fashion to popular music to film — six of the top ten grossing films of all time have been science fiction movies. (Three others were fantasy films.) Although the popularity of science fiction has sometimes been held against it, literary scholars, who once dismissed science fiction as escapist formula fiction suited only to maladjusted teenage boys, have increasingly recognized its value and significance, and science fiction is steadily gaining stature in the academy, particularly among those interested in literary theory or postmodernism. Science fiction is now seen as a complex and sophisticated body of literature in the same class as magical realism and postmodern fiction, two other genres that go against the dominant trend of realistic fiction and that appear to be gaining ground in shaping the future course of literature. Indeed, some critics see science fiction as the source of postmodern fiction and believe that it may well turn out to be the dominant form of literature in the twenty-first century.

This introduction offers a broad overview of how people have thought about science fiction and of the history of its development. For more thorough and in-depth analyses, consult the works included in the Selective Guide to Science Fiction Research.

Defining "Science Fiction"

"Science fiction," like any genre or period title — "Romantic poetry," for instance, or "Medieval romance," or even "the novel" — is a category of convenience, a shorthand reference for a more complex phenomenon. Like all such labels, it can never fully account for the richness and variety of the individual works of literature that fall within it. Nonetheless, so long as we're aware of their limitations, such labels can be quite useful. Naming an object gives us a kind of power over it, allowing us to see it as distinct from other things with other names, and thus, ideally, to see more deeply into its true nature.

Given science fiction's prevalence in the mass media, most people feel they have an intuitive grasp of what is meant by the term. If asked to define it, they may point to cinematic examples — *Star Trek, Star Wars, The Matrix* — or describe a characteristic subject matter — robots and spaceships, time travel and aliens, marvelous inventions and futuristic settings. These are descriptive lists rather than theories of meaning, however, and as such they can only get us so far. On their own, they don't do much to increase our understanding of what is distinctive about science fiction as literature, nor do they do much to explain its unique resonance in modern society, where language and concepts borrowed from the genre are applied to everything from politics to computer engineering. Many people, of course, can and do read science fiction for the sheer pleasure of it, without feeling any particular need for analysis, but anyone who wants to understand its larger significance will find it useful to examine how the genre has been defined and to review its historical development.

Definitions of science fiction have focused on various aspects of the genre, whether subject matter, form, tone, relationship to audience, or some combination of these factors. Science fiction has been variously described as the literature of change or as a modern mythology; it can be seen as a response to the Industrial Revolution or to the primacy of science as the modern epistemology. The most productive definitions generally focus on the genre's distinctive techniques and procedures, defining it not so much through a particular subject matter as through its approach to the subject matter. Viewed this way, science fiction can be seen as a speculative mode of thought that might be compared to the scientific method or pictured as a complex and unique interaction between a story and its readers.

In seeking to define this new form of literature, some have emphasized the importance of science, either as subject matter or as a conceptual grounding that distinguishes it from fantasy. Early critics like the influential editors Hugo Gernsback and John W. Campbell Jr. sometimes emphasized the educative or prophetic nature of science fiction, presenting it as an informed look at the progress and prospects of modern science — perhaps as a way of defending a literature that was then viewed by many as escapist and trivial. Subsequent writers such as Sam Moskowitz, a fan who became one of the first scholarly critics, took a broader view of the relevance of science, emphasizing plausibility as an identifying characteristic that distinguished it from fantasy. Science fiction writer and influential editor Judith Merril suggested rather that science served as a conceptual model for a particular mode of thought, one that made a disciplined use of hypotheses to test the boundaries of the real.[1]

---

1. For a good overview of definitions, see John Clute and Peter Nicholls, "Definitions of Science Fiction," in *The Encyclopedia of Science Fiction* (New York: St. Martin's, 1995).

Another feature of the genre that has been pointed to is its emphasis on change, and, as with the presence of science, this characteristic is sometimes used to distinguish it from fantasy, which tends to envision change as part of a recurrent mythic cycle rather than a genuine disjuncture. As noted, Gernsback and Campbell saw one of science fiction's key roles as predicting technological and social change, and some science fiction writers agreed, particularly those with scientific training, such as Isaac Asimov and Robert A. Heinlein — though they generally saw themselves as well-informed and shrewd observers rather than prophets. Outside the science fiction community, "Futurists" such as Alvin Toffler also adopted the idea of science fiction's potential to help us cope with technological and social change. According to this theory, science fiction provides a kind of social service by helping a culture think about the outcomes of its actions and adjust to a world of increasingly quick technological and sociological change. The extent to which science fiction functions as prediction has undoubtedly been overstated, but the idea of change itself — and the speculation about outcomes and adjustments to change — does seem to be one of science fiction's central concerns. In one way or another, change has been identified as a key element by many writers and critics.[2]

No one definition of science fiction is universally accepted or likely to prove definitive. The one thing almost everyone agrees on is that science fiction is a branch of imaginative or "fantastic" literature, a category that also includes not only fantasy and horror but also various kinds of surreal and postmodern literature not generally associated with so-called genre fiction. These genres all share an approach to reality that is different from "realistic" literature; they portray a world that is not merely fictional but radically different from the one we normally think of ourselves as inhabiting. All fantastic literature lays claim to a shared heritage in the older literary genres of epic, romance, utopia, imaginary voyage, and gothic tale. Fantastic literature introduces one or more elements — whether mythic, supernatural, technological, philosophical, or satiric — that represent a fundamental divergence from the structures and procedures of the known world. Because of this greater freedom in the imaginative exploration of ideas, fantastic literature at its best can be mind altering and can change the way we look at our own world.

Given this fundamental similarity, it is sometimes difficult to separate the various genres of fantastic literature, particularly as the readership and even, in many cases, the authorship tend to overlap, with many writers producing work in more than one genre, and many books that could plausibly fit into multiple categories. Indeed, many writers and scholars, following Heinlein and Merril, now prefer to use the broader term "speculative fiction" or the ambiguous term "SF" or "sf," which can stand for either science fiction or speculative fiction.[3] (That practice is generally followed in this volume

---

2. Brooks Landon provides a useful discussion of this conversation in *Science Fiction After 1900* (New York: Routledge, 1995) xi–xiv & 1–10.
3. See "Speculative Fiction" in Clute and Nicholls, *Encyclopedia of Science Fiction*.

as well, except when specifically making a distinction between science fiction and other forms of speculative fiction.)

Although we can't always make clear divisions among genres, some differences are worth considering. One of the most commonly made distinctions is that science fiction, however fanciful, insists on a connection with the world we know. So while each science fictional universe is predicated on a difference — physical, social, or psychological — that sets it apart from our own world in some essential way, that world tends to be governed by principles of causality, physics, and human nature that we recognize as possible, based on our current understanding of reality. Just how plausible this altered reality is may vary and may change over time as science advances and new theories emerge, but the principle of plausibility is the same. Sometimes the story offers no more than a gesture toward plausibility, a suggestion that an explanation exists — but that gesture in itself is arguably significant. Moreover, as opposed to other imaginative genres like fantasy, in science fiction the nature of the difference between the fictional world and our own is often in itself an essential part of the subject matter of the story.

Comparing Washington Irving's "Rip van Winkle" with H. G. Wells's *The Time Machine* may help illustrate the difference. The protagonists of both stories travel into the future, but Irving sees no need to explain van Winkle's enchanted sleep, whereas for Wells the concept of a time machine is central. That Wells's description of the machine is vague and that such a machine could not be built on the basis of scientific understanding in Wells's time, and may never be possible, is secondary to the impulse to offer a plausible explanation. This insistence on a relationship between the reader's world and the fictional one produces a specific effect that Darko Suvin, perhaps the most influential academic critic of science fiction, has argued distinguishes science fiction from other modes of fantastic literature. Suvin emphasizes the importance of the interaction between reality and speculation, identification and distancing, produced by a combination of rational plausibility and the difference provided by the "novum," or new thing. He defines science fiction as "a literature of cognitive estrangement" and argues that what makes it distinctive is a particular kind of consciousness — the simultaneous alienation and self-recognition the work produces in its readers.[4]

The idea that science fiction requires a special form of cognition from both writers and readers is common. Samuel R. Delany, a science fiction writer who is also a leading theorist, has emphasized the peculiar way science fiction breaks down the usual barriers between the literal and the metaphoric. By asking readers to participate in the mental construction of an alternate world, science fiction makes high demands on audience participation.[5] In this sense, science fiction shares something with surreal and postmodern fiction, which forces the reader to struggle to create meaning,

4. Darko Suvin, *Metamorphoses of Science Fiction* (New Haven: Yale UP, 1979) 4.
5. Samuel R. Delany, *Starboard Wine* (Pleasantville: Dragon, 1984) 81–100.

as well as with the older genre of the philosophical tale, which encourages readers to question their assumptions and to view their own society and beliefs from a new perspective. Science fiction has often been called a literature of ideas, a distinction science fiction writers sometimes object to because it seems to minimize other literary qualities such as character development, psychological depth, or prose style. Yet ideas, in one way or another, are at the heart of every science fiction story, in a way they are not in most other forms of contemporary fiction. In this context, it is useful to remember how much our current sense of literary merit is based on the rather narrow model set by the nineteenth-century novel, excluding earlier forms of prose fiction that have their own distinctive merits. Science fiction can exhibit all the strengths traditionally associated with the realist novel, but it also has access to other ways of seeing that allow a more free play of the imagination. Because of its different relationship to speculation and the realm of ideas, science fiction calls attention to our assumptions, thwarts our expectations, and turns common metaphors into literal realities, thus allowing us to see more clearly the implications of the metaphors we live within.

Influences and Origins

The earliest source to which science fiction can trace its lineage is perhaps the oldest literary genre of all, the epic typified in the west by *The Epic of Gilgamesh* (2000 BCE or earlier) and Homer's *Odyssey* (circa 700 BCE), followed by the romances of medieval Europe, from *Beowulf* (circa eighth to tenth century CE) to the many tales of King Arthur. These are old stories with powerful mythic elements. They are often nationalistic, illustrating the ideals of the culture they grow out of or describing the people's origins and heroic exploits. Frequently they involve some kind of quest and include supernatural elements or journeys to strange lands. Like the epic and the romance, science fiction looks beyond the world as we know it and, directly or indirectly, carries a message about the values of the culture in which it arises. Like mythology, it addresses questions about the nature of reality, the character of the past, the course of the future, the order of the universe, and what it means to be human.

Another venerable ancestor is the utopian tradition, which begins in the west with Plato's *Republic* (fourth century BCE) and takes its name from Thomas More's *Utopia*, published in 1516. Utopias, whether speculative political treatises like *Republic* or fictional accounts like *Utopia*, are thought experiments that explore the hypothetical conditions of an ideal state. More coined the term "utopia," meaning "no place" with a pun on "good place" (eutopia), as a sly acknowledgment of the impossibility of a perfect society. But what is most striking about utopian works is not the difficulty required to achieve them but the extent to which the achievement — could it be obtained — is problematic. As planned societies, utopias are necessarily restrictive and always have a cost to maintain. There is therefore often a fine line between utopia and "dystopia" ("bad place"), a term used to describe the opposite of a utopia, a nightmare society sometimes based on a worst-case scenario of what the writer's own society could become. In fact, both utopias and dystopias tend to be critiques of the author's own society, either through contrast to or as warnings about the direction of current conditions. This critical bent links utopias to the tradition of satire.

Because they depend on radically different social conditions from the author's known world, utopian stories also overlap with the genre of imaginary voyages, fanciful tales of journeys to imaginary and often bizarre lands, or imagined journeys to real but little-known places. As with utopias, imaginary voyages often have an element of satire: the strange locales are used as lenses through which to view the writer's own country and times (morals, customs, politics) from an altered perspective, thus revealing them to be ridiculous or flawed. In earlier times, much of the distant world was unknown or poorly known, so European writers could plausibly describe an unknown land somewhere "over the sea." Many science fiction stories extend the tradition of the imaginary voyage. Now that everything on earth is thoroughly mapped and communication networks are worldwide, we place these imaginary kingdoms on distant planets that are still unexplored or in future times. One of the earliest examples of an imaginary voyage is Lucian of Samosata's "A True Story," an account of a voyage to the moon written in the first century CE. Jonathan Swift's *Gulliver's Travels* (1726) is a more modern exemplar of the genre and, given its explicit treatment of science in Book Three, some have claimed it as the starting point of the genre of science fiction.

A final element in the ancestry of science fiction is the so-called Gothic, a reworking of medieval romance, popular in the eighteenth and nineteenth centuries, epitomized by works like Horace Walpole's *Castle of Otranto* (1765), Anne Radcliffe's *The Mysteries of Udolpho* (1794), Edgar Allan Poe's "The Fall of the House of Usher" (1839), Bram Stoker's *Dracula* (1897), and, most significantly, Mary Shelley's *Frankenstein* (1818), a novel widely though not universally acknowledged as the first true work of science fiction. (See Aldiss and Wingrove, *Trillion Year Spree*, 25–52, for a particularly persuasive and influential argument for this claim.) These stories feature dark themes and settings, often including haunted castles, ruins, graveyards, and desolate landscapes. Usually there is a supernatural element, and the events may take place in medieval times or settings. The Gothic can be seen as an early counter-tradition to the realistic novel, a Romantic revolt against Enlightenment rationalism and a critique of the domination of science and technology at the dawn of the Industrial Revolution.

Although many of the forerunners of sf were British, it was part of a larger European phenomenon that also includes writers such as the German Romanticist E. T. A. Hoffmann, whose "The Sandman" (1817) may also be considered a prototype. Like *Frankenstein*, it is a gothic tale about the hubris of creating an artificial being, drawing parallels between science and black magic. Some of the genre's most notable early practitioners were French authors like J. H. Rosny aîné and astronomer Camille Flammarion, both of whom explored clearly science fictional themes such as alien life and apocalyptic disasters. The critical figure to emerge in France, however, and a man justly considered the father of modern sf, was Jules Verne, an enthusiastic advocate for progress who wrote exciting adventure stories centered on technological innovations. In books like *Voyage to the Center of the Earth* (1864) and *20,000 Leagues Under the Sea* (1869), Verne took the genre of the imaginary voyage and grounded it firmly in existing science. He also lent science fiction a flavor of optimism and adventure, heroism and ingenuity that would be crucial in the development of the genre.

Of equal importance was British writer H. G. Wells, who offered a counterweight to Verne's optimism. Wells wrote a darker, more socially oriented, and more speculative brand of sf. In novels like *The Time Machine* (1895) and *War of the Worlds* (1898), he combined satiric and dystopic themes with scientific inventions and progressive social theory. And while Verne scorned Wells for his ignorance of science, Wells prided himself on his predictive powers and, in fact, both men foresaw inventions and events that did come to pass. Wells also introduced or popularized many of the themes that would become central to sf, such as time travel and alien invasion. Taken together, Verne and Wells are the first indisputably canonical writers of the modern sf canon.

Modern Development of the Genre

Many outside the sf community today consider science fiction to be "genre" fiction in the derogatory sense — a specialized, formulaic type of popular writing to be relegated to the guilty-pleasure aisles of large bookstores, somewhere between Mystery and Romance. This view was consolidated in the 1950s during the height of sf magazine popularity and was reinforced by a slew of B-grade "sci-fi" monster movies. However, in the earliest years of what we might call sf proper — the mid-nineteenth to early twentieth centuries — it was not a genre distinct from the mainstream of literature. Respected writers such as Nathaniel Hawthorne, Edgar Allan Poe, and E. M. Forster all wrote within the genre. The late nineteenth century, however, saw the beginning of a trend that would open vast new markets for sf writers, while at the same time lead to the separation of science fiction from mainstream literature: the popularity, especially in the United States, of mass-market magazines printed on cheap ("pulp") paper and circulated largely to an audience of young men. In the nineteenth century, pulp magazines had included all kinds of adventure stories, but beginning in the 1920s they began to specialize, some focusing on detective stories, for instance, and others on sf. While "pulp" is generally a derogatory term, and production demands sometimes led to second-rate hackwork, some very fine and unjustly neglected stories were printed in this period, some of which are reprinted in this anthology. The separation of sf from mainstream literature had benefits as well as drawbacks, allowing writers the freedom to experiment outside the constraints and conventions of dominant literary movements and leading, eventually, to a period of remarkable fertility and invention by World War II.

As editor of *Astounding Science-Fiction*, John W. Campbell Jr. presided over this period, which came to be known as the "Golden Age" of sf, a period variously dated but generally said to begin in 1938 and end in the 1940s or 1950s. Like all golden ages, this is a semimythical period created largely in retrospect and limned in nostalgia. Yet there is some truth in it as well; these years were indeed a golden age for magazine writing and, hence, for the short story as a distinctive form. Circulation was at its peak; Campbell published established writers like L. Sprague de Camp and C. L. Moore as well as rising stars like Robert A. Heinlein and Isaac Asimov, and later Alfred Bester and Arthur C. Clarke. The literary quality of the writing during this period, while inconsistent, was on a steady rise, while the stories contained a freshness and an energy seldom reproduced since. The period also saw the rise of fandom, a unique subculture in which fans and authors mingled with unusual intimacy at sf conventions in the United States and, much later, around the world.

By the end of the 1950s, sf was a firmly established genre, if still poorly understood outside a small community of writers and fans. Many of its key themes had been articulated, a set of conventions and a shared vocabulary established. It was also dominated by writers from the United States. One sign of its successful consolidation was that a younger generation of writers, initially particularly in the United Kingdom, began to chafe at the perceived limits of the genre, leading to the first of many internal disputes over the direction sf should take. A group of British writers in the 1960s, who came to be known as the New Wave, were critical of the literary quality of some magazine fiction and of the cheery advocacy of scientific progress and conservative sociopolitical values that had come to mark much American sf. New Wave writers advocated a more stylistically self-conscious and speculative fiction that was less interested in technological gimmicks than in social structures and the effects of technology on human beings — in short, sf that was more Wellsian and less Vernian. Michael Moorcock and J. G. Ballard championed the cause, to which stylistically adventurous American writers like Roger Zelazny, Harlan Ellison, and Samuel R. Delany were also sometimes linked. These writers tended to blur the boundaries between science fiction and fantasy and often had a countercultural sensibility in their attitude toward authority and their incorporation of previously taboo subject matter like sex and drugs. Although some in the field deplored the new trend, the movement was never a monolithic one, and fears of a crisis within the genre can now be seen as exaggerated. Like most struggles within the sf community, the result was an enrichment of possibilities rather than a catastrophic schism. Principles derived from the New Wave, such as the emphasis on literary technique and a broader range of forms and topics, were widely incorporated by writers outside the movement and had a salutary effect on the genre as a whole. The sociopolitical concerns of New Wave writers and those inspired by them, including writers from outside the genre, like Kurt Vonnegut Jr., also raised the public profile of sf and helped it to reach a larger audience.

Shortly after the rise of the New Wave, another phenomenon began that would affect the course of sf. While — contrary to popular mythology — sf writers had always included women (Leigh Brackett, C. L. Moore, Judith

Merril), during the late 1960s and early 1970s women's voices became especially prominent and women writers were credited with expanding the horizons of sf yet again. Women writers such as Kate Wilhelm, Ursula K. Le Guin, Joanna Russ, and James Tiptree Jr. (a pseudonym for Alice Sheldon), along with some male writers such as Thomas M. Disch and Delany, opened new avenues of inquiry into gender and sexual identity, family and social structure, the media and the body. This shift was partly influenced by New Wave sf but also corresponded to larger social forces such as the women's movement.

The 1980s saw yet another infusion of new ideas and forms. The subgenre that came to be known as "cyberpunk" was influenced by the New Wave and by feminist writers of the 1970s, as well as by long-established writers like Philip K. Dick. Cyberpunk stories typically combined a vision of a near-future, high-tech society with a film-noir sensibility reminiscent of detective-story writers like Raymond Chandler and Dashiell Hammett. Cyberpunk writers were fascinated by the new technological possibilities offered by the burgeoning field of computer science, but, unlike earlier technophilic writers, they often took a darker view of the consequences. Their protagonists tended to be alienated outsiders, living on the criminal fringes of a society dominated by ruthless transnational corporate conglomerates. Writers like Bruce Sterling and William Gibson brought a harsher, more urban feel to sf, a tone, as the name suggests, related to punk rock as well as to cybernetics — a term often associated with artificial human–machine interfaces but more properly referring to information systems of any kind. This fascination with information is evident in the style of cyberpunk stories as well, which often produce an exhilarating sense of information overload as the reader is enveloped by layers of unexplained terms and images and thrust into the middle of a complex plot that even the story's characters find mysterious and confusing. Cyberpunk, like New Wave before it, was condemned by some and heralded by others; like New Wave, it was controversial at first but was soon assimilated into the larger sf tradition, enriching the genre with new themes and stylistic techniques and initiating a trend toward grittier realism and more moral ambiguity that continues to be influential.

While sf continues to evolve as a body of literature, it has also had a profound impact on the larger culture, both directly and through the medium of film. Although an examination of sf's influence on popular culture is beyond the scope of this introduction, it's important to note the degree to which sf now informs the way we see the world. (See Thomas M. Disch, *The Dreams Our Stuff Is Made Of* and other works listed under "Science Fiction and Culture" for more.) Increasingly, sf has also gained prestige and standing in scholarly circles. The first special session of the Modern Language Association devoted to sf was in 1958 and led to the publication of *Extrapolation*, the first scholarly journal devoted to the genre — followed by *Foundation* in 1972 and *Science-Fiction Studies* in 1973. The British Science Fiction Writers Association (BFSA) was founded in 1958; Damon Knight founded the professional association Science Fiction Writers of

America (SFWA; now Science Fiction and Fantasy Writers of America, but still generally referred to by the original acronym) in 1965. The Science Fiction Research Association was founded in 1970 to support the scholarly study of sf. And though sf is still dominated by English-language publications, it is becoming increasingly international; particularly distinct traditions emerged in the former Soviet Union and Eastern Europe, sometimes in opposition to the U.S. forms, and in Japan, which has been uniquely blessed and cursed by modern technology and has used sf to explore questions of national identity.

Science fiction today is an enormously popular and increasingly diverse literature that encompasses a breathtaking variety of forms, as old traditions are carried on and new modes introduced. A distinction has often been made between "hard" sf — sf that is grounded in science and traces its lineage from Verne through the Golden Age — and "soft" sf — sf with broader social concerns in the mode of Wells, the New Wave, and feminist sf. Recognizable examples of both forms continue to be written today, but increasingly the distinction (sometimes useful, but always problematic) has blurred as the two variants intermingle. It is difficult to identify a dominant new direction in the field, although a number of commentators point to a trend in which the form and concerns of science fiction and fantasy appear to be merging with those of mainstream literature. Magical realism and postmodern fiction, two genres that challenge the conventions of naturalistic fiction, are growing in international popularity and stature, with writers from Salman Rushdie and Isabelle Allende to Italo Calvino, Mark Helprin, Orhan Pamuk, and José Saramago. Meanwhile, sf writers such as Terry Bisson and James Morrow continue, in the tradition of Delany and Ballard, to extend the boundaries from within the genre toward an increasingly postmodern form, while former cyberpunk Neal Stephenson's recent work occupies an ambiguous space between sf and mainstream and may be claimed by either side. This trend has been greeted with alarm by some, who fear science fiction will lose its distinctive identity as it is submerged into the broader literature, but it is welcomed by others, who appreciate the greater range of freedom offered by a less programmatic approach. Most provocatively, some critics have hailed the trend as evidence that science fiction — as has long been argued by James Gunn, in his important anthology series *The Road to Science Fiction* and elsewhere — is the *dominant* literary mode of the modern era. In this view, far from being assimilated into mainstream literature, sf is itself the larger genre into which modern fiction is gradually being subsumed. Whatever the truth may be, the growing number of science fiction novels published each year is a testament to the genre's popularity and suggests, as Gardner Dozois frequently points out in the introductions to his standard-setting best-of-the-year anthologies, that science fiction is not in any immediate danger of disappearing. Science fiction remains a healthy and continually evolving genre in its own right, even as it exerts a growing influence on the broader literary and popular culture.

A Selective Guide to Science Fiction Research

What follows is an abbreviated list of useful sources for further research. For readers conducting advanced scholarship, several excellent annotated bibliographies provide more detailed and complete reviews of criticism, including Brooks Landon's *Science Fiction After 1900* and Veronica Hollinger's "Contemporary Trends in Science Fiction Criticism, 1980–1999" (see bibliographic listings at the end of this section for details).

The most complete critical guide is Neil Barron's *Anatomy of Wonder*, which includes annotated bibliographies of primary and secondary literature, useful historical surveys, and articles on related subjects, such as science fiction film and the teaching of science fiction, all written by leading critics. John Clute and Peter Nicholls's *The Encyclopedia of Science Fiction* is a crucial reference for information on specific authors, themes, subgenres, and terminology; more than a simple compendium of facts, many of its entries are incisive and provocative critical essays. *Speculations on Speculation*, edited by James Gunn and Matthew Candelaria, provides an excellent introduction to some of the field's most important theoretical approaches, bringing together influential essays by writers and scholars like Samuel R. Delany, Ursula K. Le Guin, Darko Suvin, Brian Aldiss, Robert Scholes, Alexei Panshin, and David Hartwell, as well as Gunn himself. *The Cambridge Companion to Science Fiction*, edited by Edward James and Farah Mendlesohn, is another important reference work, with essays on history, subgenres, and theoretical approaches by leading critics and writers.

Most of the selections listed under "History and Criticism" are general introductions, but also included are some important works that explore more focused themes, such as feminism or postmodernism. For in-depth research, as well as for single-author studies, please consult the texts listed under "Reference Works" for additional sources. Readers who review the critical books listed in the references section will notice a difference in style between the earlier and later works. The first sf critics were either writers or fans, and early scholars — whether they precisely fit these categories — also tend to write as insiders, giving much attention to the social history of sf. Such books are rich in detail and unsurpassed in texture and immediacy, but they can also be somewhat digressive and focus more on celebration of the genre than on in-depth analysis. That said, the ideas in these books have been very influential on the development of later theory. Recent critics tend to be more academic (though many continue to be sf writers or fans or both) and more argumentative. Both types of books are necessary for a full appreciation of sf criticism.

The most up-to-date reviews and critical articles can be found in periodicals, whether academic journals like *Science Fiction Studies* or popular publications like *Locus*. (*Locus* also includes author interviews and a wealth of information on publishing.) The *New York Review of Science Fiction* is another good source for critical reviews of recent work, as well as more wide-ranging essays on the field. If you need to find a specific science fiction short story, *The Locus Index to Science Fiction* is an indispensable resource. A searchable Web-based version is linked to *Locus Online*; it includes William G. Contento's *Index to Science Fiction Anthologies and Collections* (pre-1984), *The Locus Index to Science Fiction 1984–1998*, and yearly supplements.

The Locus Index to Science Fiction Awards (Mark R. Kelly) (also linked to *Locus Online*) and *Award Web* are useful sites for tracking all the major sf awards, including recent nominees. Two organizations, Science Fiction and Fantasy Writers of America (a professional organization) and the Science Fiction Research Association (an academic organization), both maintain websites with a variety of useful links and other information.

The relationship of sf literature to other media and to the larger culture is a growing field of interest. This bibliography focuses on literary resources, but it includes brief sections titled "Science Fiction and Culture" and "Science Fiction and Film." "Science Fiction and Culture" includes both the culture of sf, such as fandom, and the relationship between sf and society.

The bibliography ends with a section titled "Teaching Science Fiction" and a brief listing of some important anthologies. Historically, anthologies have played a role in shaping the genre and describing new movements, and they often include valuable criticism as well as primary texts. Annual "Best of" collections, such as those edited by Gardner Dozois and by David Hartwell and Kathryn Cramer are excellent resources for anyone wishing to keep current on the latest work in the field.

REFERENCE WORKS

AwardWeb: Collections of Literary Award Information and Photos. Ed. Laurie D. T. Mann <http://www.awardweb.info>.

Barron, Neil. *Anatomy of Wonder 5: A Critical Guide to Science Fiction.* Westport: Libraries Unlimited, 2004.

Brown, Charles N., and William Contento, eds. *The Locus Index to Science Fiction.* <http://www.locusmag.com/index/>.

Clute, John, and Peter Nicholls. *The Encyclopedia of Science Fiction.* New York: Orbit, 1999.

Contento, William G. *Index to Science Fiction Anthologies and Collections: Combined Edition.* <http://contento.best.vwh.net/0start.htm>.

Hollinger, Veronica. "Contemporary Trends in Science Fiction Criticism, 1980–1999." *Science Fiction Studies* 26 (1999). 232–62.

James, Edward, and Farah Mendlesohn, eds. *The Cambridge Companion to Science Fiction.* Cambridge: Cambridge UP, 2003.

Kelly, Mark R., ed. *Locus Online.* <http://www.locusmag.com>

Science Fiction and Fantasy Writers of America (SFWA). <http://www.sfwa.org/>. Webmaster Chris Hansen.

Science Fiction Research Association (SFRA). <http://www.sfra.org/>. Webmaster Samuel McDonald.

Wolfe, Gary K. *Critical Terms for Science Fiction and Fantasy: A Glossary and Guide to Scholarship*. Westport: Greenwood, 1986.

HISTORY AND CRITICISM

Aldiss, Brian, with David Wingrove. *Trillion Year Spree*. New York: Atheneum, 1986.

Alkon, Paul K. *Science Fiction Before 1900: Imagination Discovers Technology*. New York: Routledge, 1994.

Amis, Kingsley. *New Maps of Hell: A Survey of Science Fiction*. New York: Harcourt Brace, 1960.

Barr, Marlene S. *Feminist Fabulation: Space/Postmodern Fiction*. Iowa City: U of Iowa P, 1992.

Carter, Paul. *The Creation of Tomorrow: Fifty Years of Magazine Science Fiction*. New York: Columbia UP, 1977.

Clareson, Thomas D. *Some Kind of Paradise: The Emergence of American Science Fiction*. Westport: Greenwood, 1985.

Delany, Samuel R. *Starboard Wine: More Notes on the Language of Science Fiction*. Pleasantville: Dragon, 1984.

Freedman, Carl. *Critical Theory and Science Fiction*. Hanover, NH: Wesleyan UP, 2000.

Gunn, James. *Alternate Worlds: The Illustrated History of Science Fiction*. Englewood Cliffs: Prentice Hall, 1975.

Gunn, James, and Matthew Candelaria, eds. *Speculations on Speculation: Theories of Science Fiction*. Lanham: Scarecrow, 2005.

James, Edward. *Science Fiction in the 20th Century*. New York: Oxford UP, 1994.

Ketterer, David. *New Worlds for Old: The Apocalyptic Imagination, Science Fiction, and American Literature*. Bloomington: Indiana UP, 1974.

Landon, Brooks. *Science Fiction After 1900: From the Steam Man to the Stars*. New York: Routledge, 1995.

Lefanu, Sarah. *In the Chinks of the World Machine: Feminism and Science Fiction*. London: The Women's Press, 1988.

Le Guin, Ursula K. *The Language of the Night: Essays on Fantasy and Science Fiction*. New York: HarperCollins, 1989.

Lem, Stanislaw. *Microworlds: Writings on Science Fiction and Fantasy*. San Diego: Harcourt, 1984.

Malmgren, Carl. *Worlds Apart: Narratology of Science Fiction*. Bloomington: Indiana UP, 1991.

McCaffery, Larry. *Storming the Reality Studio: A Casebook of Cyberpunk and Postmodern Fiction*. Durham: Duke UP, 1991.

Rabkin, Eric S., and Robert Scholes. *Science Fiction: History-Science-Vision*. New York: Oxford UP, 1977.

Rose, Mark. *Alien Encounters: Anatomy of Science Fiction*. Cambridge: Harvard UP, 1981.

Scholes, Robert. *Structural Fabulation: An Essay on Fiction of the Future*. Notre Dame: U Notre Dame P, 1975.

Slusser, George E., and Thomas Shippey, eds. *Fiction 2000: Cyberpunk and the Future of Narrative*. Athens: U Georgia P, 1992.

Suvin, Darko. *Metamorphoses of Science Fiction: On the Poetics and History of a Literary Genre*. New Haven: Yale UP, 1979.

Wolfe, Gary K. *The Known and the Unknown: The Iconography of Science Fiction*. Kent: Kent State UP, 1979.

Wolmark, Jenny. *Aliens and Others: Science Fiction, Feminism and Postmodernism*. Iowa City: U Iowa P, 1994.

SCIENCE FICTION AND CULTURE

Bacon-Smith, Camille. *Science Fiction Culture*. Philadelphia: U Pennsylvania P, 2000.

Bukatman, Scott. *Terminal Identity: The Virtual Subject in Postmodern Science Fiction*. Durham: Duke UP, 1993.

Disch, Thomas M. *The Dreams Our Stuff Is Made Of: How Science Fiction Conquered the World*. New York: Touchstone, 1998.

Franklin, Bruce H. *War Stars: The Superweapon and the American Imagination*. New York: Oxford UP, 1988.

Hartwell, David. *Age of Wonders: Exploring the World of Science Fiction*. New York: Walker, 1984.

Moskowitz, Sam. *The Immortal Storm: A History of Science Fiction Fandom*. 1954. Westport: Hyperion, 1974.

Sanders, Joe, ed. *Science Fiction Fandom*. Contributions to the Study of Science Fiction and Fantasy 62. Westport: Greenwood, 1994.

Stableford, Brian. *The Sociology of Science Fiction*. San Bernardino: Borgo, 1987.

Warner, Harry. *All Our Yesterdays: An Informal History of Science Fiction in the Forties*. Chicago: Advent, 1969.

SCIENCE FICTION AND FILM

Kuhn, Annette, ed. *Alien Zone: Cultural Theory and Contemporary Science Fiction Cinema*. New York: Routledge, 1990.

Landon, Brooks. *The Aesthetics of Ambivalence: Rethinking Science Fiction Film in the Age of Electronic (Re)Production*. Westport: Greenwood, 1992.

Nicholls, Peter. *The World of Fantastic Films: An Illustrated Survey*. New York: Dodd, Mead, 1984.

Slusser, George E., and Eric S. Rabkin, eds. *Shadows of the Magic Lamp: Fantasy and Science Fiction in Film*. Carbondale: Southern Illinois UP, 1985.

Sobchack, Vivian. *Screening Space: The American Science Fiction Film*. New York: Ungar, 1988.

JOURNALS AND PERIODICALS

Extrapolation. Ed. Donald M. Hassler. Kent State University. <http://fp.dl.kent.edu/extrap/>.

Foundation: The International Review of Science Fiction. Ed. Farah Mendlesohn. Science Fiction Foundation. <http://www.sf-foundation .org/publications/foundation/foundation.html>.

Locus: *The Magazine of the Science Fiction and Fantasy Field*. Ed. Charles
  N. Brown. <http://www.locusmag.com/About/Locus.html>.
The New York Review of Science Fiction. Ed. David G. Hartwell. Dragon Press.
  <http://www.nyrsf.com>.
Science-Fiction Studies. Ed. Arthur B. Evans et al. DePauw University.
  <http://www.depauw.edu/sfs/>.

TEACHING SCIENCE FICTION

Delany, Samuel. "*Dichtung und* Science Fiction," in *Starboard Wine:
  More Notes on the Language of Science Fiction*. Pleasantville: Dragon,
  1984.
Gunn, James. *Inside Science Fiction: Essays on Fantastic Literature*. San
  Bernardino: Borgo, 1992.
———. *The J. Wayne and Elsie M. Gunn Center for the Study of Science
  Fiction*. U of Kansas. <http://www2.ku.edu/~sfcenter/>.
Hartwell, David. *Age of Wonders: Exploring the World of Science Fiction*. New
  York: Walker, 1984.
Parrinder, Patrick. *Science Fiction: Its Criticism and Teaching*. London:
  Methuen, 1980.
"Science Fiction in Academe," special issue, *Science Fiction Studies* 70 (1996).
Williamson, Jack, ed. *Teaching Science Fiction: Education for Tomorrow*.
  Philadelphia: Owlswick, 1980.

ANTHOLOGIES

Apostolou, John L., and Martin H. Greenberg, eds. *The Best Japanese Science
  Fiction Stories*. New York: Barricade, 1997.
Bell, Andrea L., and Yolanda Molina-Gavilan. *Cosmos Latinos: An Anthology of
  Science Fiction from Latin America and Spain*. Middletown: Wesleyan UP,
  2003.
Dozois, Gardner. *The Year's Best Science Fiction*. New York: St. Martin's,
  1984–2006; ongoing.
Ellison, Harlan. *Dangerous Visions*. Garden City: Doubleday, 1967.
———. *Again, Dangerous Visions*. Garden City: Doubleday, 1972.
Franklin, H. Bruce. *Future Perfect: American Science Fiction of the Nineteenth
  Century*. London: Oxford UP, 1978.
Gunn, James, ed. *The Road to Science Fiction*. Vols. 1–4. Lanham: Scarecrow,
  2002–2003.
———. *The Road to Science Fiction*. Vols. 5–6. Clarkston: White Wolf,
  1998–1999.
Hartwell, David G., ed. *The World Treasury of Science Fiction*. Boston: Little,
  Brown, 1989.
Hartwell, David G., and Kathryn Cramer, eds. *Year's Best SF*. New York: Eos,
  1996–2006; ongoing.
Le Guin, Ursula K., and Brian Attebery. *The Norton Book of Science Fiction*.
  New York: Norton, 1993.
Moskowitz, Samuel. *Science Fiction by Gaslight: A History and Anthology of
  Science Fiction in the Popular Magazines, 1891–1911*. New York: Hyperion,
  1974.
Sargent, Pamela, ed. *Women of Wonder*. New York: Harvest, 1974.

————. *More Women of Wonder* [1976].

————. *Women of Wonder: The Contemporary Years: Science Fiction by Women from the 1970s to the 1990s*. New York: Harvest, 1995.

Silverberg, Robert, ed. *Science Fiction Hall of Fame*. Vol. 1. New York: Orb, 2005.

Thomas, Sheree R., ed. *Dark Matter: A Century of Speculative Fiction from the African Diaspora*. New York: Warner Aspect, 2000.

Warrick, Patricia, Charles G. Waugh, and Martin H. Greenberg, eds. *Science Fiction: The Science Fiction Research Association Anthology*. New York: Harper and Row, 1988.

Alien Encounters

The kinds of aliens we encounter in sf probably have their earliest analogues in the genre of the *fantastic voyage* — a tale of exotic lands with
strange inhabitants and novel customs — that is among our oldest literature. To early travelers, no doubt, even neighboring lands seemed rather odd,
as can be seen in the origins of words such as "outlandish" or "barbarian"
(originally a "neutral" term for anyone who did not speak Greek). Beyond
any actual historical experience, there seems to be an innate human fascination with novelty and the unknown, and a delight in giving free play to
the imagination. Satirists and philosophers have long used the genre of the
fantastic voyage to speculate about alternative solutions to contemporary
social problems and to imagine radically different ways of life. Writers like
Thomas More, Voltaire, and Jonathan Swift used imaginary countries allegorically either to highlight the irrationality and injustice of their own or to
show, by way of contrast, an idealized alternative. By shifting the frame of
representation to an unknown place, they freed their readers' imaginations
and allowed them to view their own culture from a different perspective.

At one time it was easy for such writers to situate their imaginary societies in a mysterious land beyond the mountains or over the sea and still
maintain a semblance of plausibility. Improvements in transportation and
communication, however, along with scientific knowledge of the universe,
expanded the boundaries of the known and forced writers to situate their
fanciful worlds further afield — to the depths of the sea, to the center of
the earth, to the moon, to the neighboring planets, and ultimately to other
solar systems.

The word "alien" derives from the Latin *alienus*, meaning "another" —
that is, anything strange, unfamiliar, or different — that which is not the self.
Before being imported into sf, it was most commonly used as a technical
term for foreigners (still found in phrases like "illegal alien"). Inasmuch as
they are about the Other, all alien stories can be read as allegories of difference, whether racial, sexual, cultural, or political. Many sf writers use
aliens self-consciously to explore ideas of oppression or xenophobia, but even
when such issues are not the author's main focus, aliens still frequently
signal cultural assumptions about human identity.

But "alien" can also refer to an internal difference or opposition, as in
the term *alienation*, which describes a state of isolation or estrangement.
In its most extreme form, alienation is a psychological illness: the Latin phrase
alienatus a se — to be alienated from oneself — is the source of both the

French word for the insane (*aliéné*) and the nineteenth-century English term for psychiatrist, "alienist." In this sense, the alien is not so much outside as inside ourselves, and thus the sf alien can also be read psychologically as a projection of an inner state.

The stories in this section show a variety of ways our interest in the alien may be manifested — playfully, to indulge an imaginative sense of wonder; allegorically and satirically, to critique cultural assumptions; or reflectively, to explore the nature of the individual psyche. From Wells's colonialist anxiety to Weinbaum's fascination with alternative biology, from Le Guin's spiritual exploration of the Gaian hypothesis to Butler's interrogation of race and gender, all of these stories illuminate facets of human identity by probing the boundaries of self and Other.

The theoretical texts in this section provide additional contexts for thinking about otherness. Jung explores the psychological process by which the rejected parts of an individual's own personality are projected outward in the form of a sinister "shadow" figure. Fanon and de Beauvoir examine how culturally imposed labels of difference impact members of marginalized groups and shape their own sense of self.

H. G. Wells

From The War of the Worlds
(1898)

Herbert George Wells (1866–1946) is perhaps the most important figure in modern science fiction, rivaled only by Jules Verne. Wells grew up in a family of modest means, the son of servants and shopkeepers in the socially rigid environment of late Victorian England. After unsuccessful apprenticeships in various trades, he won a scholarship to the Normal School of Science in London, where he studied biology. He worked as a science teacher and journalist, and his first published book was a textbook of biology (1893). Wells's best-known works include *The Time Machine* (1895), *The Island of Dr. Moreau* (1896), and *The Invisible Man* (1897), as well as *The War of the Worlds* — all of which have been made into films multiple times.

His stories, which predate the term "science fiction," were referred to by contemporaries as "scientific romances." Wells gave early and influential articulation to some of sf's classic themes, such as time travel, futuristic societies, high-tech warfare, cataclysmic natural disasters, and of course alien invasion, the subject of this excerpt. Wells was proud of his predictive abilities (he lived to see many of his predictions come to pass, including the development of tanks, aerial bombing, and nuclear weapons) and was fascinated by mechanical inventions (consider, for instance, his coinage of the term "time machine"), but in his work, however, technology is important primarily for its social impact.

Because of this emphasis on social concerns, he is sometimes considered the founder of "soft" sf. An advocate of reform and an outspoken opponent of injustice, Wells was both a socialist and a pessimist, an odd combination that imbues his work with a mixture of idealism and gloom.

Although Wells was not the first to portray extraterrestrial beings — the French writers Camille Flammarion and J. H. Rosny aîné being two notable precursors — his nightmarish vision of alien invasion struck a powerful chord and remains influential even today. His merciless and inscrutable Martians, with their slimy tentacles and fantastically effective ray guns, may now seem clichéd, the stuff of 1950s horror movies. Yet what is most striking about Wells's portrayal of an alien invasion is its realism. It is the backdrop of ordinary English life that gives *The War of the Worlds* its power. The rumors and confusion that result from a breakdown in communication networks and transportation systems, the desperate flight of refugees, the paralysis and shock of ordinary people trying to come to terms with the unthinkable, all recounted in detailed and clipped you-are-there narration, form an accurate portrayal of a nation at war. This naturalism gives *The War of the Worlds* an uncanny plausibility. Indeed, when in 1938 Orson Welles — in a notorious hoax — broadcast readings from *The War of the Worlds* over the radio, many people believed that what they were hearing was a bona fide news report and that the invasion was actually occurring.

In the opening pages of *The War of the Worlds*, Wells pointedly compares the Martian invasion of Earth to the European conquest of Africa and the New World, suggesting that were the tables turned, his fellow Englishmen might feel very differently about the colonial enterprise. Framed in this way, the whole story seems like a guilty fantasy of retribution in which Europeans find themselves subject to the same kind of technologically advanced but morally bankrupt occupation that they had visited on other peoples. While a strictly allegorical reading would be unduly limiting, the sociopolitical analogy this story makes is an important one.

Chapter 1. The Eve of the War

No one would have believed in the last years of the nineteenth century that this world was being watched keenly and closely by intelligences greater than man's and yet as mortal as his own: that as men busied themselves about their various concerns they were scrutinized and studied, perhaps almost as narrowly as a man with a microscope might scrutinize the transient creatures that swarm and multiply in a drop of water. With infinite complacency men went to and fro over this globe about their little affairs, serene in their assurance of their empire over matter. It is possible that the infusoria under the microscope do the same. No one gave a thought to the older worlds of space as sources of human danger, or thought of them only to dismiss the idea of life upon them as impossible or improbable. It is curious to recall some of the mental habits of those departed days. At most, terrestrial men fancied there might be other men upon Mars, perhaps inferior to themselves and ready to welcome a missionary enterprise. Yet across the gulf of space, minds that are to our minds as ours are to those of the beasts that perish, intellects vast and cool and unsympathetic, regarded this earth with envious eyes, and slowly and surely drew their plans against us. And early in the twentieth century came the great disillusionment.

The planet Mars, I scarcely need remind the reader, revolves about the sun at a mean distance of 140,000,000 miles, and the light and heat it receives from the sun is barely half of that received by this world. It must be, if the nebular hypothesis has any truth, older than our world; and long before this earth ceased to be molten, life upon its surface must have begun its course. The fact that it is scarcely one seventh of the volume of the earth must have accelerated its cooling to the temperature at which life could begin. It has air and water and all that is necessary for the support of animated existence.

Yet so vain is man, and so blinded by his vanity, that no writer, up to the very end of the nineteenth century, expressed any idea that intelligent life might have developed there far, or indeed at all, beyond its earthly level. Nor was it generally understood that since Mars is older than our earth, with scarcely a quarter of the superficial area and remoter from the sun, it necessarily follows that it is not only more distant from life's beginning but nearer its end.

The secular[1] cooling that must someday overtake our planet has already gone far indeed with our neighbor. Its physical condition is still largely a mystery, but we know now that even in its equatorial region the midday temperature barely approaches that of our coldest winter. Its air is much more attenuated than ours, its oceans have shrunk until they cover but a third of its surface, and as its slow seasons change huge snowcaps gather and melt about either pole and periodically inundate its temperate zones. That last stage of exhaustion, which to us is still incredibly remote, has become a present-day problem for the inhabitants of Mars. The immediate pressure of necessity has brightened their intellects, enlarged their powers, and hardened their hearts. And looking across space with instruments, and intelligences such as we have scarcely dreamed of, they see, at its nearest distance only 35,000,000 of miles sunward of them, a morning star of hope, our own warmer planet, green with vegetation and grey with water, with a cloudy atmosphere eloquent of fertility, with glimpses through its drifting cloud wisps of broad stretches of populous country and narrow, navy-crowded seas.

And we men, the creatures who inhabit this earth, must be to them at least as alien and lowly as are the monkeys and lemurs to us. The intellectual side of man already admits that life is an incessant struggle for existence, and it would seem that this too is the belief of the minds upon Mars. Their world is far gone in its cooling and this world is still crowded with life, but crowded only with what they regard as inferior animals. To carry warfare sunward is, indeed, their only escape from the destruction that, generation after generation, creeps upon them.

And before we judge of them too harshly we must remember what ruthless and utter destruction our own species has wrought, not only upon

---

1. Gradual. [Ed.]

animals, such as the vanished bison and the dodo, but upon its inferior races. The Tasmanians, in spite of their human likeness, were entirely swept out of existence in a war of extermination waged by European immigrants, in the space of fifty years. Are we such apostles of mercy as to complain if the Martians warred in the same spirit?

The Martians seem to have calculated their descent with amazing subtlety — their mathematical learning is evidently far in excess of ours — and to have carried out their preparations with a well-nigh perfect unanimity. Had our instruments permitted it, we might have seen the gathering trouble far back in the nineteenth century. Men like Schiaparelli watched the red planet — it is odd, by-the-bye, that for countless centuries Mars has been the star of war — but failed to interpret the fluctuating appearances of the markings they mapped so well. All that time the Martians must have been getting ready.

During the opposition[2] of 1894 a great light was seen on the illuminated part of the disk, first at the Lick Observatory, then by Perrotin of Nice, and then by other observers. English readers heard of it first in the issue of *Nature* dated August 2. I am inclined to think that this blaze may have been the casting of the huge gun, in the vast pit sunk into their planet, from which their shots were fired at us. Peculiar markings, as yet unexplained, were seen near the site of that outbreak during the next two oppositions.

The storm burst upon us six years ago now. As Mars approached opposition, Lavelle of Java set the wires of the astronomical exchange palpitating with the amazing intelligence of a huge outbreak of incandescent gas upon the planet. It had occurred towards midnight of the twelfth; and the spectroscope, to which he had at once resorted, indicated a mass of flaming gas, chiefly hydrogen, moving with an enormous velocity towards this earth. This jet of fire had become invisible about a quarter past twelve. He compared it to a colossal puff of flame suddenly and violently squirted out of the planet, "as flaming gases rushed out of a gun."

A singularly appropriate phrase it proved. Yet the next day there was nothing of this in the papers except a little note in the *Daily Telegraph,* and the world went in ignorance of one of the gravest dangers that ever threatened the human race. I might not have heard of the eruption at all had I not met Ogilvy, the well-known astronomer, at Ottershaw. He was immensely excited at the news, and in the excess of his feelings invited me up to take a turn with him that night in a scrutiny of the red planet.

In spite of all that has happened since, I still remember that vigil very distinctly: the black and silent observatory, the shadowed lantern throwing a feeble glow upon the floor in the corner, the steady ticking of the clockwork of the telescope, the little slit in the roof — an oblong profundity with the stardust streaked across it. Ogilvy moved about, invisible but audible. Looking through the telescope, one saw a circle of deep blue and the little round planet swimming in the field. It seemed such a little thing, so bright and small and still, faintly marked with transverse stripes, and slightly flattened from the perfect round. But so little it was, so silvery warm — a pin's

---

2. Alignment of Mars, Earth, and the sun.

head of light! It was as if it quivered, but really this was the telescope vibrating with the activity of the clockwork that kept the planet in view.

As I watched, the planet seemed to grow larger and smaller and to advance and recede, but that was simply that my eye was tired. Forty millions of miles it was from us — more than forty millions of miles of void. Few people realise the immensity of vacancy in which the dust of the material universe swims.

Near it in the field, I remember, were three faint points of light, three telescopic stars infinitely remote, and all around it was the unfathomable darkness of empty space. You know how that blackness looks on a frosty starlight night. In a telescope it seems far profounder. And invisible to me because it was so remote and small, flying swiftly and steadily towards me across that incredible distance, drawing nearer every minute by so many thousands of miles, came the Thing they were sending us, the Thing that was to bring so much struggle and calamity and death to the earth. I never dreamed of it then as I watched; no one on earth dreamed of that unerring missile.

That night, too, there was another jetting out of gas from the distant planet. I saw it. A reddish flash at the edge, the slightest projection of the outline just as the chronometer struck midnight; and at that I told Ogilvy and he took my place. The night was warm and I was thirsty, and I went, stretching my legs clumsily and feeling my way in the darkness, to the little table where the siphon stood, while Ogilvy exclaimed at the streamer of gas that came out towards us.

That night another invisible missile started on its way to the earth from Mars, just a second or so under twenty-four hours after the first one. I remember how I sat on the table there in the blackness, with patches of green and crimson swimming before my eyes. I wished I had a light to smoke by, little suspecting the meaning of the minute gleam I had seen and all that it would presently bring me. Ogilvy watched till one, and then gave it up; and we lit the lantern and walked over to his house. Down below in the darkness were Ottershaw and Chertsey and all their hundreds of people, sleeping in peace.

He was full of speculation that night about the condition of Mars, and scoffed at the vulgar idea of its having inhabitants who were signalling us. His idea was that meteorites might be falling in a heavy shower upon the planet, or that a huge volcanic explosion was in progress. He pointed out to me how unlikely it was that organic evolution had taken the same direction in the two adjacent planets.

"The chances against anything manlike on Mars are a million to one," he said.

Hundreds of observers saw the flame that night and the night after about midnight, and again the night after; and so for ten nights, a flame each night. Why the shots ceased after the tenth no one on Earth has attempted to explain. It may be the gases of the firing caused the Martians inconvenience. Dense clouds of smoke or dust, visible through a powerful telescope on earth as little grey, fluctuating patches, spread through the clearness of the planet's atmosphere and obscured its more familiar features.

Even the daily papers woke up to the disturbances at last, and popular notes appeared here, there, and everywhere concerning the volcanoes upon Mars. The seriocomic periodical *Punch*, I remember, made a happy use of it in the political cartoon. And, all unsuspected, those missiles the Martians had fired at us drew earthward, rushing now at a pace of many miles a second through the empty gulf of space, hour by hour and day by day, nearer and nearer. It seems to me now almost incredibly wonderful that, with that swift fate hanging over us, men could go about their petty concerns as they did. I remember how jubilant Markham was at securing a new photograph of the planet for the illustrated paper he edited in those days. People in these later times scarcely realize the abundance and enterprise of our nineteenth-century papers. For my own part, I was much occupied in learning to ride the bicycle, and busy upon a series of papers discussing the probable developments of moral ideas as civilization progressed.

One night (the first missile then could scarcely have been 10,000,000 miles away) I went for a walk with my wife. It was starlight, and I explained the Signs of the Zodiac to her, and pointed out Mars, a bright dot of light creeping zenithward, towards which so many telescopes were pointed. It was a warm night. Coming home, a party of excursionists from Chertsey or Isleworth passed us singing and playing music. There were lights in the upper windows of the houses as the people went to bed. From the railway station in the distance came the sound of shunting trains, ringing and rumbling, softened almost into melody by the distance. My wife pointed out to me the brightness of the red, green, and yellow signal lights hanging in a framework against the sky. It seemed so safe and tranquil.

Chapter 2. The Falling Star

Then came the night of the first falling star. It was seen early in the morning, rushing over Winchester eastward, a line of flame high in the atmosphere. Hundreds must have seen it, and taken it for an ordinary falling star. Albin described it as leaving a greenish streak behind it that glowed for some seconds. Denning, our greatest authority on meteorites, stated that the height of its first appearance was about ninety or one hundred miles. It seemed to him that it fell to earth about one hundred miles east of him.

I was at home at that hour and writing in my study; and although my French windows face towards Ottershaw and the blind was up (for I loved in those days to look up at the night sky), I saw nothing of it. Yet this strangest of all things that ever came to earth from outer space must have fallen while I was sitting there, visible to me had I only looked up as it passed. Some of those who saw its flight say it travelled with a hissing sound. I myself heard nothing of that. Many people in Berkshire, Surrey, and Middlesex must have seen the fall of it, and, at most, have thought that another meteorite had descended. No one seems to have troubled to look for the fallen mass that night.

But very early in the morning poor Ogilvy, who had seen the shooting star and who was persuaded that a meteorite lay somewhere on the common between Horsell, Ottershaw, and Woking, rose early with the idea of finding it. Find it he did, soon after dawn, and not far from the sand pits.

An enormous hole had been made by the impact of the projectile, and the sand and gravel had been flung violently in every direction over the heath, forming heaps visible a mile and a half away. The heather was on fire eastward, and a thin blue smoke rose against the dawn.

The Thing itself lay almost entirely buried in sand, amidst the scattered splinters of a fir tree it had shivered to fragments in its descent. The uncovered part had the appearance of a huge cylinder, caked over and its outline softened by a thick scaly dun-coloured incrustation. It had a diameter of about thirty yards. He approached the mass, surprised at the size and more so at the shape, since most meteorites are rounded more or less completely. It was, however, still so hot from its flight through the air as to forbid his near approach. A stirring noise within its cylinder he ascribed to the unequal cooling of its surface; for at that time it had not occurred to him that it might be hollow.

He remained standing at the edge of the pit that the Thing had made for itself, staring at its strange appearance, astonished chiefly at its unusual shape and colour, and dimly perceiving even then some evidence of design in its arrival. The early morning was wonderfully still, and the sun, just clearing the pine trees towards Weybridge, was already warm. He did not remember hearing any birds that morning, there was certainly no breeze stirring, and the only sounds were the faint movements from within the cindery cylinder. He was all alone on the common.

Then suddenly he noticed with a start that some of the grey clinker, the ashy incrustation that covered the meteorite, was falling off the circular edge of the end. It was dropping off in flakes and raining down upon the sand. A large piece suddenly came off and fell with a sharp noise that brought his heart into his mouth.

For a minute he scarcely realized what this meant, and, although the heat was excessive, he clambered down into the pit close to the bulk to see the Thing more clearly. He fancied even then that the cooling of the body might account for this, but what disturbed that idea was the fact that the ash was falling only from the end of the cylinder.

And then he perceived that, very slowly, the circular top of the cylinder was rotating on its body. It was such a gradual movement that he discovered it only through noticing that a black mark that had been near him five minutes ago was now at the other side of the circumference. Even then he scarcely understood what this indicated, until he heard a muffled grating sound and saw the black mark jerk forward an inch or so. Then the Thing came upon him in a flash. The cylinder was artificial — hollow — with an end that screwed out! Something within the cylinder was unscrewing the top!

"Good heavens!" said Ogilvy. "There's a man in it — men in it! Half roasted to death! Trying to escape!"

At once, with a quick mental leap, he linked the Thing with the flash upon Mars.

The thought of the confined creature was so dreadful to him that he forgot the heat, and went forward to the cylinder to help turn. But luckily the dull radiation arrested him before he could burn his hands on the still-glowing metal. At that he stood irresolute for a moment, then turned, scrambled out of the pit, and set off running wildly into Woking. The time then must have been somewhere about six o'clock. He met a waggoner and tried to make him understand, but the tale he told and his appearance were so wild — his hat had fallen off in the pit — that the man simply drove on. He was equally unsuccessful with the potman who was just unlocking the doors of the public-house by Horsell Bridge. The fellow thought he was a lunatic at large and made an unsuccessful attempt to shut him into the tap-room. That sobered him a little; and when he saw Henderson, the London journalist, in his garden, he called over the palings and made himself understood.

"Henderson," he called, "you saw that shooting star last night?"

"Well?" said Henderson.

"It's out on Horsell Common now."

"Good Lord!" said Henderson. "Fallen meteorite! That's good."

"But it's something more than a meteorite. It's a cylinder — an artificial cylinder, man! And there's something inside."

Henderson stood up with his spade in his hand.

"What's that?" he said. He was deaf in one ear.

Ogilvy told him all that he had seen. Henderson was a minute or so taking it in. Then he dropped his spade, snatched up his jacket, and came out into the road. The two men hurried back at once to the common, and found the cylinder still lying in the same position. But now the sounds inside had ceased, and a thin circle of bright metal showed between the top and the body of the cylinder. Air was either entering or escaping at the rim with a thin, sizzling sound.

They listened, rapped on the scaly burnt metal with a stick, and, meeting with no response, they both concluded the man or men inside must be insensible or dead.

Of course the two were quite unable to do anything. They shouted consolation and promises, and went off back to the town again to get help. One can imagine them, covered with sand, excited and disordered, running up the little street in the bright sunlight just as the shop folks were taking down their shutters and people were opening their bedroom windows. Henderson went into the railway station at once, in order to telegraph the news to London. The newspaper articles had prepared men's minds for the reception of the idea.

By eight o'clock a number of boys and unemployed men had already started for the common to see the "dead men from Mars." That was the form the story took. I heard of it first from my newspaper boy about a quarter to nine when I went out to get my *Daily Chronicle*. I was naturally startled, and lost no time in going out and across the Ottershaw bridge to the sand pits.

Chapter 3. On Horsell Common

I found a little crowd of perhaps twenty people surrounding the huge hole in which the cylinder lay. I have already described the appearance of that colossal bulk, embedded in the ground. The turf and gravel about it seemed charred as if by a sudden explosion. No doubt its impact had caused a flash of fire. Henderson and Ogilvy were not there. I think they perceived that nothing was to be done for the present, and had gone away to breakfast at Henderson's house.

There were four or five boys sitting on the edge of the pit, with their feet dangling, and amusing themselves — until I stopped them — by throwing stones at the giant mass. After I had spoken to them about it, they began playing at "touch" in and out of the group of bystanders.

Among these were a couple of cyclists, a jobbing gardener I employed sometimes, a girl carrying a baby, Gregg the butcher and his little boy, and two or three loafers and golf caddies who were accustomed to hang about the railway station. There was very little talking. Few of the common people in England had anything but the vaguest astronomical ideas in those days. Most of them were staring quietly at the big tablelike end of the cylinder, which was still as Ogilvy and Henderson had left it. I fancy the popular expectation of a heap of charred corpses was disappointed at this inanimate bulk. Some went away while I was there, and other people came. I clambered into the pit and fancied I heard a faint movement under my feet. The top had certainly ceased to rotate.

It was only when I got thus close to it that the strangeness of this object was at all evident to me. At the first glance it was really no more exciting than an overturned carriage or a tree blown across the road. Not so much so, indeed. It looked like a rusty gas float. It required a certain amount of scientific education to perceive that the grey scale of the Thing was no common oxide, that the yellowish-white metal that gleamed in the crack between the lid and the cylinder had an unfamiliar hue. "Extra-terrestrial" had no meaning for most of the onlookers.

At that time it was quite clear in my own mind that the Thing had come from the planet Mars, but I judged it improbable that it contained any living creature. I thought the unscrewing might be automatic. In spite of Ogilvy, I still believed that there were men on Mars. My mind ran fancifully on the possibilities of its containing manuscript, on the difficulties in translation that might arise, whether we should find coins and models in it, and so forth. Yet it was a little too large for assurance on this idea. I felt an impatience to see it opened. About eleven, as nothing seemed happening, I walked back, full of such thought, to my home in Maybury. But I found it difficult to get to work upon my abstract investigations.

In the afternoon the appearance of the common had altered very much. The early editions of the evening papers had startled London with enormous headlines:

A MESSAGE RECEIVED FROM MARS
REMARKABLE STORY FROM WOKING

and so forth. In addition, Ogilvy's wire to the Astronomical Exchange had roused every observatory in the three kingdoms.

There were half a dozen flies or more from the Woking station standing in the road by the sand pits, a basketchaise from Chobham, and a rather lordly carriage. Besides that, there was quite a heap of bicycles. In addition, a large number of people must have walked, in spite of the heat of the day, from Woking and Chertsey so that there was altogether quite a considerable crowd — one or two gaily dressed ladies among the others.

It was glaringly hot, not a cloud in the sky nor a breath of wind, and the only shadow was that of the few scattered pine trees. The burning heather had been extinguished, but the level ground towards Ottershaw was blackened as far as one could see, and still giving off vertical streamers of smoke. An enterprising sweet-stuff dealer in the Chobham Road had sent up his son with a barrow-load of green apples and ginger beer.

Going to the edge of the pit, I found it occupied by a group of about half a dozen men — Henderson, Ogilvy, and a tall, fair-haired man that I afterwards learned was Stent, the Astronomer Royal, with several workmen wielding spades and pickaxes. Stent was giving directions in a clear, high-pitched voice. He was standing on the cylinder, which was now evidently much cooler; his face was crimson and streaming with perspiration, and something seemed to have irritated him.

A large portion of the cylinder had been uncovered, though its lower end was still embedded. As soon as Ogilvy saw me among the staring crowd on the edge of the pit he called to me to come down, and asked me if I would mind going over to see Lord Hilton, the lord of the manor.

The growing crowd, he said, was becoming a serious impediment to their excavations, especially the boys. They wanted a light railing put up, and help to keep the people back. He told me that a faint stirring was occasionally still audible within the case, but that the workmen had failed to unscrew the top, as it afforded no grip to them. The case appeared to be enormously thick, and it was possible that the faint sounds we heard represented a noisy tumult in the interior.

I was very glad to do as he asked, and so become one of the privileged spectators within the contemplated enclosure. I failed to find Lord Hilton at his house, but I was told he was expected from London by the six o'clock train from Waterloo; and as it was then about a quarter past five, I went home, had some tea, and walked up to the station to waylay him.

Chapter 4. The Cylinder Opens

When I returned to the common the sun was setting. Scattered groups were hurrying from the direction of Woking, and one or two persons were returning. The crowd about the pit had increased, and stood out black against the lemon yellow of the sky — a couple of hundred people, perhaps. There were raised voices, and some sort of struggle appeared to be going on about the pit. Strange imaginings passed through my mind. As I drew nearer I heard Stent's voice:

"Keep back! Keep back!"

A boy came running towards me.

"It's a movin'," he said to me as he passed; "a-screwin', and a-screwin' out. I don't like it. I'm a-goin' 'ome, I am."

I went on to the crowd. There were really, I should think, two or three hundred people elbowing and jostling one another, the one or two ladies there being by no means the least active.

"He's fallen in the pit!" cried some one.

"Keep back!" said several.

The crowd swayed a little, and I elbowed my way through. Every one seemed greatly excited. I heard a peculiar humming sound from the pit.

"I say!" said Ogilvy; "help keep these idiots back. We don't know what's in the confounded thing, you know!"

I saw a young man, a shop assistant in Woking I believe he was, standing on the cylinder and trying to scramble out of the hole again. The crowd had pushed him in.

The end of the cylinder was being screwed out from within. Nearly two feet of shining screw projected. Somebody blundered against me, and I narrowly missed being pitched onto the top of the screw. I turned, and as I did so the screw must have come out, for the lid of the cylinder fell upon the gravel with a ringing concussion. I stuck my elbow into the person behind me, and turned my head towards the Thing again. For a moment that circular cavity seemed perfectly black. I had the sunset in my eyes.

I think everyone expected to see a man emerge — possibly something a little unlike us terrestrial men, but in all essentials a man. I know I did. But, looking, I presently saw something stirring within the shadow: greyish billowy movements, one above another, and then two luminous disks — like eyes. Then something resembling a little grey snake, about the thickness of a walking stick, coiled up out of the writhing middle, and wriggled in the air towards me — and then another.

A sudden chill came over me. There was a loud shriek from a woman behind. I half turned, keeping my eyes fixed upon the cylinder still, from which other tentacles were now projecting, and began pushing my way back from the edge of the pit. I saw astonishment giving place to horror on the faces of the people about me. I heard inarticulate exclamations on all sides. There was a general movement backwards. I saw the shopman struggling still on the edge of the pit. I found myself alone, and saw the people on the other side of the pit running off, Stent among them. I looked again at the cylinder, and ungovernable terror gripped me. I stood petrified and staring.

A big greyish rounded bulk, the size, perhaps, of a bear, was rising slowly and painfully out of the cylinder. As it bulged up and caught the light, it glistened like wet leather.

Two large dark-colored eyes were regarding me steadfastly. The mass that framed them, the head of the thing, was rounded, and had, one might say, a face. There was a mouth under the eyes, the lipless brim of which quivered and panted, and dropped saliva. The whole creature heaved and pulsated convulsively. A lank tentacular appendage gripped the edge of the cylinder, another swayed in the air.

Those who have never seen a living Martian can scarcely imagine the strange horror of its appearance. The peculiar V-shaped mouth with its pointed upper lip, the absence of brow ridges, the absence of a chin beneath the wedgelike lower lip, the incessant quivering of this mouth, the Gorgon groups of tentacles, the tumultuous breathing of the lungs in a strange atmosphere, the evident heaviness and painfulness of movement due to the greater gravitational energy of the earth — above all, the extraordinary intensity of the immense eyes — were at once vital, intense, inhuman, crippled, and monstrous. There was something fungoid in the oily brown skin, something in the clumsy deliberation of the tedious movements unspeakably nasty. Even at this first encounter, this first glimpse, I was overcome with disgust and dread.

Suddenly the monster vanished. It had toppled over the brim of the cylinder and fallen into the pit, with a thud like the fall of a great mass of leather. I heard it give a peculiar thick cry, and forthwith another of these creatures appeared darkly in the deep shadow of the aperture.

I turned and, running madly, made for the first group of trees, perhaps a hundred yards away; but I ran slantingly and stumbling, for I could not avert my face from these things.

There, among some young pine trees and furze bushes, I stopped, panting, and waited further developments. The common round the sand pits was dotted with people, standing like myself in a half-fascinated terror, staring at these creatures, or rather at the heaped gravel at the edge of the pit in which they lay. And then, with a renewed horror, I saw a round, black object bobbing up and down on the edge of the pit. It was the head of the shopman who had fallen in, but showing as a little black object against the hot western sky. Now he got his shoulder and knee up, and again he seemed to slip back until only his head was visible. Suddenly he vanished, and I could have fancied a faint shriek had reached me. I had a momentary impulse to go back and help him that my fears overruled.

Everything was then quite invisible, hidden by the deep pit and the heap of sand that the fall of the cylinder had made. Anyone coming along the road from Chobham or Woking would have been amazed at the sight — a dwindling multitude of perhaps a hundred people or more standing in a great irregular circle, in ditches, behind bushes, behind gates and hedges, saying little to one another and that in short, excited shouts, and staring, staring hard at a few heaps of sand. The barrow of ginger beer stood, a queer derelict, black against the burning sky, and in the sand pits was a row of deserted vehicles with their horses feeding out of nosebags or pawing the ground.

Chapter 5. The Heat-Ray

After the glimpse I had had of the Martians emerging from the cylinder in which they had come to the earth from their planet, a kind of fascination paralyzed my actions. I remained standing knee-deep in the heather, staring at the mound that hid them. I was a battleground of fear and curiosity.

I did not dare to go back towards the pit, but I felt a passionate longing to peer into it. I began walking, therefore, in a big curve, seeking some point of vantage and continually looking at the sand heaps that hid these newcomers to our earth. Once a leash of thin black whips, like the arms of an octopus, flashed across the sunset and was immediately withdrawn, and afterwards a thin rod rose up, joint by joint, bearing at its apex a circular disk that spun with a wobbling motion. What could be going on there?

Most of the spectators had gathered in one or two groups — one a little crowd towards Woking, the other a knot of people in the direction of Chobham. Evidently they shared my mental conflict. There were few near me. One man I approached — he was, I perceived, a neighbor of mine, though I did not know his name — and accosted. But it was scarcely a time for articulate conversation.

"What ugly brutes!" he said. "Good God! What ugly brutes!" He repeated this over and over again.

"Did you see a man in the pit?" I said; but he made no answer to that. We became silent, and stood watching for a time side by side, deriving, I fancy, a certain comfort in one another's company. Then I shifted my position to a little knoll that gave me the advantage of a yard or more of elevation, and when I looked for him presently he was walking towards Woking.

The sunset faded to twilight before anything further happened. The crowd far away on the left, towards Woking, seemed to grow, and I heard now a faint murmur from it. The little knot of people towards Chobham dispersed. There was scarcely an intimation of movement from the pit.

It was this, as much as anything, that gave people courage, and I suppose the new arrivals from Woking also helped to restore confidence. At any rate, as the dusk came on a slow, intermittent movement upon the sand pits began, a movement that seemed to gather force as the stillness of the evening about the cylinder remained unbroken. Vertical black figures in twos and threes would advance, stop, watch, and advance again, spreading out as they did so in a thin irregular crescent that promised to enclose the pit in its attenuated horns. I, too, on my side began to move towards the pit.

Then I saw some cabmen and others had walked boldly into the sand pits, and heard the clatter of hoofs and the gride of wheels. I saw a lad trundling off the barrow of apples. And then, within thirty yards of the pit, advancing from the direction of Horsell, I noted a little black knot of men, the foremost of whom was waving a white flag.

This was the Deputation. There had been a hasty consultation, and since the Martians were evidently, in spite of their repulsive forms, intelligent creatures, it had been resolved to show them, by approaching them with signals, that we too were intelligent.

Flutter, flutter, went the flag, first to the right, then to the left. It was too far for me to recognize anyone there, but afterwards I learned that Ogilvy, Stent, and Henderson were with others in this attempt at communication. This little group had in its advance dragged inward, so to speak, the circumference of the now almost complete circle of people, and a number of dim black figures followed it at discreet distances.

Suddenly there was a flash of light, and a quantity of luminous greenish smoke came out of the pit in three distinct puffs, which drove up, one after the other, straight into the still air.

This smoke (or flame, perhaps, would be the better word for it) was so bright that the deep blue sky overhead and the hazy stretches of brown common towards Chertsey, set with black pine trees, seemed to darken abruptly as these puffs arose, and to remain the darker after their dispersal. At the same time a faint hissing sound became audible.

Beyond the pit stood the little wedge of people with the white flag at its apex, arrested by these phenomena, a little knot of small vertical black shapes upon the black ground. As the green smoke arose, their faces flashed out pallid green, and faded again as it vanished. Then slowly the hissing passed into a humming, into a long, loud, droning noise. Slowly a humped shape rose out of the pit, and the ghost of a beam of light seemed to flicker out from it.

Forthwith flashes of actual flame, a bright glare leaping from one to another, sprang from the scattered group of men. It was as if some invisible jet impinged upon them and flashed into white flame. It was as if each man were suddenly and momentarily turned to fire.

Then, by the light of their own destruction, I saw them staggering and falling, and their supporters turning to run.

I stood staring, not as yet realizing that this was death leaping from man to man in that little distant crowd. All I felt was that it was something very strange. An almost noiseless and blinding flash of light, and a man fell headlong and lay still; and as the unseen shaft of heat passed over them, pine trees burst into fire, and every dry furze bush became with one dull thud a mass of flames. And far away towards Knaphill I saw the flashes of trees and hedges and wooden buildings suddenly set alight.

It was sweeping round swiftly and steadily, this flaming death, this invisible, inevitable sword of heat. I perceived it coming towards me by the flashing bushes it touched, and was too astounded and stupefied to stir. I heard the crackle of fire in the sand pits and the sudden squeal of a horse that was as suddenly stilled. Then it was as if an invisible yet intensely heated finger were drawn through the heather between me and the Martians, and all along a curving line beyond the sand pits the dark ground smoked and crackled. Something fell with a crash far away to the left where the road from Woking station opens out on the common. Forthwith the hissing and humming ceased, and the black, domelike object sank slowly out of sight into the pit.

All this had happened with such swiftness that I had stood motionless, dumbfounded, and dazzled by the flashes of light. Had that death swept through a full circle, it must inevitably have slain me in my surprise. But it passed and spared me, and left the night about me suddenly dark and unfamiliar.

The undulating common seemed now dark almost to blackness, except where its roadways lay grey and pale under the deep blue sky of the early night. It was dark, and suddenly void of men. Overhead the stars were mustering, and in the west the sky was still a pale, bright, almost greenish blue. The tops of the pine trees and the roofs of Horsell came out sharp and black against the western afterglow. The Martians and their appliances were altogether invisible, save for that thin mast upon which their restless mirror wobbled. Patches of bush and isolated trees here and there smoked and glowed still, and the houses towards Woking station were sending up spires of flame into the stillness of the evening air.

Nothing was changed save for that and a terrible astonishment. The little group of black specks with the flag of white had been swept out of existence, and the stillness of the evening, so it seemed to me, had scarcely been broken.

It came to me that I was upon this dark common, helpless, unprotected, and alone. Suddenly, like a thing falling upon me from without, came — fear.

With an effort I turned and began a stumbling run through the heather.

The fear I felt was no rational fear, but a panic terror not only of the Martians, but of the dusk and stillness all about me. Such an extraordinary effect in unmanning me it had that I ran weeping silently as a child might do. Once I had turned, I did not dare to look back.

I remember I felt an extraordinary persuasion that I was being played with, that presently, when I was upon the very verge of safety, this mysterious death — as swift as the passage of light — would leap after me from the pit about the cylinder and strike me down.

Stanley G. Weinbaum

A Martian Odyssey

(1934)

The reputation of Stanley Grauman Weinbaum (1902–1935) as a science fiction writer rests entirely on a series of short stories written in the last year and a half of his life, before his death from cancer at the age of thirty-three. Yet during this extraordinarily short career, he had a remarkable impact on the field. Weinbaum attended the University of Wisconsin, where he studied chemical engineering and English, though he never graduated. His first publications were romances, but it was only with the appearance of "A Martian Odyssey," his first science fiction publication, that Weinbaum achieved lasting fame. Isaac Asimov famously likened this explosive debut to a nova and credits Weinbaum with reinvigorating American sf with his idea-driven fiction at a time when the field emphasized straightforward adventure stories. Weinbaum's work exemplifies some of the best qualities of the pulp-magazine writing that flourished in the 1930s and points toward the development of the Golden Age of the 1940s and 1950s. His work is marked by humor and imagination and has an exuberant quality that has seldom been matched by later writers. In 1967, when the Science Fiction Writers of America voted on stories for inclusion in the *Science Fiction Hall of Fame* — a sort of retroactive Nebula showcase — "A Martian Odyssey" came in second, and was the oldest story to be included.

Weinbaum explicitly links "A Martian Odyssey" to the tradition of classical epic, one of the main genre influences on sf. Like the original *Odyssey*, Weinbaum's story is an account of travels through unfamiliar lands and meetings with strange creatures. In the pulp tradition, "A Martian Odyssey" is a light-hearted adventure story starring an intrepid hero and packed with incidents and oddities. Although the playful quality of the story is a key to its charm, the underlying elements give it depth.

Above all, Weinbaum's story is remarkable for the variety and inventiveness of its alien life. While many sf writers are content with aliens that are humanoid or variations on terrestrial animals, Weinbaum imagines radically different life forms and explores the profound differences in cognition and language that might result. Interestingly, Weinbaum also represents diversity in his multicultural cast of human characters. Although the ethnic humor is broad, both the awareness of human cultural difference and the insistence on commonality are significant. The implied message — that human beings need to unite and transcend their own differences before they can be prepared to meet truly alien life — is significant and would become a common theme in later sf. "A Martian Odyssey" can be seen as an alternative vision to Wells's horrific portrayal of alien invaders in *The War of the Worlds*.

Jarvis stretched himself as luxuriously as he could in the cramped general quarters of the *Ares*.

"Air you can breathe!" he exulted. "It feels as thick as soup after the thin stuff out there!" He nodded at the Martian landscape stretching flat and desolate in the light of the nearer moon, beyond the glass of the port.

The other three stared at him sympathetically — Putz, the engineer, Leroy, the biologist, and Harrison, the astronomer and captain of the expedition. Dick Jarvis was chemist of the famous crew, the *Ares* expedition, first human beings to set foot on the mysterious neighbor of the earth, the planet Mars. This, of course, was in the old days, less than twenty years after the mad American Doheny perfected the atomic blast at the cost of his life, and only a decade after the equally mad Cardoza rode on it to the moon. They were true pioneers, these four of the *Ares*. Except for a half-dozen moon expeditions and the ill-fated de Lancey flight aimed at the seductive orb of Venus, they were the first men to feel other gravity than earth's, and certainly the first successful crew to leave the earth-moon system. And they deserved that success when one considers the difficulties and discomforts — the months spent in acclimatization chambers back on earth, learning to breathe the air as tenuous as that of Mars, the challenging of the void in the tiny rocket driven by the cranky reaction motors of the twenty-first century, and mostly the facing of an absolutely unknown world.

Jarvis stretched and fingered the raw and peeling tip of his frostbitten nose. He sighed again contentedly.

"Well," exploded Harrison abruptly, "are we going to hear what happened? You set out all shipshape in an auxiliary rocket, we don't get a peep for ten days, and finally Putz here picks you out of a lunatic ant-heap with a freak ostrich as your pal! Spill it, man!"

"Speel?" queried Leroy perplexedly. "Speel what?"

"He means 'spiel,'" explained Putz soberly. "It iss to tell."

Jarvis met Harrison's amused glance without the shadow of a smile. "That's right, Karl," he said in grave agreement with Putz. "*Ich spiel es!*" He grunted comfortably and began.

"According to orders," he said, "I watched Karl here take off toward the North, and then I got into my flying sweat-box and headed South. You'll remember, Cap — we had orders not to land, but just scout about for points of interest. I set the two cameras clicking and buzzed along, riding pretty high — about two thousand feet — for a couple of reasons. First, it gave the cameras a greater field, and second, the under-jets travel so far in this half-vacuum they call air here that they stir up dust if you move low."

"We know all that from Putz," grunted Harrison. "I wish you'd saved the films, though. They'd have paid the cost of this junket; remember how the public mobbed the first moon pictures?"

"The films are safe," retorted Jarvis. "Well," he resumed, "as I said, I buzzed along at a pretty good clip; just as we figured, the wings haven't much lift in this air at less than a hundred miles per hour, and even then I had to use the under-jets.

"So, with the speed and the altitude and the blurring caused by the under-jets, the seeing wasn't any too good. I could see enough, though, to distinguish that what I sailed over was just more of this grey plain that we'd been examining the whole week since our landing — same blobby growths and the same eternal carpet of crawling little plant-animals, or biopods, as Leroy calls them. So I sailed along, calling back my position every hour as instructed, and not knowing whether you heard me."

"I did!" snapped Harrison.

"A hundred and fifty miles south," continued Jarvis imperturbably, "the surface changed to a sort of low plateau, nothing but desert and orange-tinted sand. I figured that we were right in our guess, then, and this grey plain we dropped on was really the Mare Cimmerium which would make my orange desert the region called Xanthus. If I were right, I ought to hit another grey plain, the Mare Chronium, in another couple of hundred miles, and then another orange desert, Thyle I or II. And so I did."

"Putz verified our position a week and a half ago!" grumbled the captain. "Let's get to the point."

"Coming!" remarked Jarvis. "Twenty miles into Thyle — believe it or not — I crossed a canal!"

"Putz photographed a hundred! Let's hear something new!"

"And did he also see a city?"

"Twenty of 'em, if you call those heaps of mud cities!"

"Well," observed Jarvis, "from here on I'll be telling a few things Putz didn't see!" He rubbed his tingling nose, and continued. "I knew that I had sixteen hours of daylight at this season, so eight hours — eight hundred miles — from here, I decided to turn back. I was still over Thyle, whether

I or II I'm not sure, not more than twenty-five miles into it. And right there, Putz's pet motor quit!"

"Quit? How?" Putz was solicitous.

"The atomic blast got weak. I started losing altitude right away, and suddenly there I was with a thump right in the middle of Thyle! Smashed my nose on the window, too!" He rubbed the injured member ruefully.

"Did you maybe try vashing der combustion chamber mit acid sulphuric?" inquired Putz. "Sometimes der lead giffs a secondary radiation — "

Naw!" said Jarvis disgustedly. "I wouldn't try that, of course — not more than ten times! Besides, the bump flattened the landing gear and busted off the under-jets. Suppose I got the thing working — what then? Ten miles with the blast coming right out of the bottom and I'd have melted the floor from under me!" He rubbed his nose again. "Lucky for me a pound only weighs seven ounces here, or I'd have been mashed flat!"

"I could have fixed!" ejaculated the engineer. "I bet it vas not serious."

"Probably not," agreed Jarvis sarcastically. "Only it wouldn't fly. Nothing serious, but I had my choice of waiting to be picked up or trying to walk back — eight hundred miles, and perhaps twenty days before we had to leave! Forty miles a day! Well," he concluded, "I chose to walk. Just as much chance of being picked up, and it kept me busy."

"We'd have found you," said Harrison.

"No doubt. Anyway, I rigged up a harness from some seat straps, and put the water tank on my back, took a cartridge belt and revolver, and some iron rations, and started out."

"Water tank!" exclaimed the little biologist, Leroy. "She weigh one-quarter ton!"

"Wasn't full. Weighed about two hundred and fifty pounds earth-weight, which is eighty-five here. Then, besides, my own personal two hundred and ten pounds is only seventy on Mars, so, tank and all, I grossed a hundred and fifty-five, or fifty-five pounds less than my everyday earth-weight. I figured on that when I undertook the forty-mile daily stroll. Oh — of course I took a thermo-skin sleeping bag for these wintry Martian nights.

"Off I went, bouncing along pretty quickly. Eight hours of daylight meant twenty miles or more. It got tiresome, of course — plugging along over a soft sand desert with nothing to see, not even Leroy's crawling biopods. But an hour or so brought me to the canal — just a dry ditch about four hundred feet wide, and straight as a railroad on its own company map.

"There'd been water in it sometime, though. The ditch was covered with what looked like a nice green lawn. Only, as I approached, the lawn moved out of my way!"

"Eh?" said Leroy.

"Yeah, it was a relative of your biopods. I caught one — a little grass-like blade about as long as my finger, with two thin, stemmy legs."

"He is where?" Leroy was eager.

"He is let go! I had to move, so I plowed along with the walking grass opening in front and closing behind. And then I was out on the orange desert of Thyle again.

"I plugged steadily along, cussing the sand that made going so tiresome, and, incidentally, cussing that cranky motor of yours, Karl. It was just before twilight that I reached the edge of Thyle, and looked down over the grey Mare Chronium. And I knew there was seventy-five miles of *that* to be walked over, and then a couple of hundred miles of that Xanthus desert, and about as much more Mare Cimmerium. Was I pleased? I started cussing you fellows for not picking me up!"

"We were trying, you sap!" said Harrison.

"That didn't help. Well, I figured I might as well use what was left of daylight in getting down the cliff that bounded Thyle. I found an easy place, and down I went. Mare Chronium was just the same sort of place as this — crazy leafless plants and a bunch of crawlers; I gave it a glance and hauled out my sleeping bag. Up to that time, you know, I hadn't seen anything worth worrying about on this half-dead world — nothing dangerous, that is."

"Did you?" queried Harrison.

"*Did I!* You'll hear about it when I come to it. Well, I was just about to turn in when suddenly I heard the wildest sort of shenanigans!"

"Vot iss shenanigans?" inquired Putz.

"He says, '*Je ne sais quoi*,'" explained Leroy. "It is to say, 'I don't know what.'"

That's right," agreed Jarvis. "I didn't know what, so I sneaked over to find out. There was a racket like a flock of crows eating a bunch of canaries — whistles, cackles, caws, trills, and what have you. I rounded a clump of stumps, and there was Tweel!"

"Tweel?" said Harrison, and "Tveel?" said Leroy and Putz.

"That freak ostrich," explained the narrator. "At least, Tweel is as near as I can pronounce it without sputtering. He called it something like 'Trrrweerrlll.'"

"What was he doing?" asked the captain.

"He was being eaten! And squealing, of course, as any one would."

"Eaten! By what?"

"I found out later. All I could see then was a bunch of black ropy arms tangled around what looked like, as Putz described it to you, an ostrich. I wasn't going to interfere, naturally; if both creatures were dangerous, I'd have one less to worry about.

"But the bird-like thing was putting up a good battle, dealing vicious blows with an eighteen-inch beak, between screeches. And besides, I caught a glimpse or two of what was on the end of those arms!" Jarvis shuddered. "But the clincher was when I noticed a little black bag or case hung about the neck of the bird-thing! It was intelligent! That or tame, I assumed. Anyway, it clinched my decision. I pulled out my automatic and fired into what I could see of its antagonist.

"There was a flurry of tentacles and a spurt of black corruption, and then the thing, with a disgusting sucking noise, pulled itself and its arms into a hole in the ground. The other let out a series of clacks, staggered around on legs about as thick as golf sticks, and turned suddenly to face me. I held my weapon ready, and the two of us stared at each other.

"The Martian wasn't a bird, really. It wasn't even bird-like, except just at first glance. It had a beak all right, and a few feathery appendages, but the beak wasn't really a beak. It was somewhat flexible; I could see the tip bend slowly from side to side; it was almost like a cross between a beak and a trunk. It had four-toed feet, and four-fingered things — hands, you'd have to call them, and a little roundish body, and a long neck ending in a tiny head — and that beak. It stood an inch or so taller than I, and — well, Putz saw it!"

The engineer nodded. "*Ja!* I saw!"

Jarvis continued. "So — we stared at each other. Finally the creature went into a series of clackings and twitterings and held out its hands toward me, empty. I took that as a gesture of friendship."

"Perhaps," suggested Harrison, "it looked at that nose of yours and thought you were its brother!"

"Huh! You can be funny without talking! Anyway, I put up my gun and said 'Aw, don't mention it,' or something of the sort, and the thing came over and we were pals.

"By that time, the sun was pretty low and I knew that I'd better build a fire or get into my thermo-skin. I decided on the fire. I picked a spot at the base of the Thyle cliff, where the rock could reflect a little heat on my back. I started breaking off chunks of this desiccated Martian vegetation, and my companion caught the idea and brought in an armful. I reached for a match, but the Martian fished into his pouch and brought out something that looked like a glowing coal; one touch of it, and the fire was blazing — and you all know what a job we have starting a fire in this atmosphere!

"And that bag of his!" continued the narrator. "That was a manufactured article, my friends; press an end and she popped open — press the middle and she sealed so perfectly you couldn't see the line. Better than zippers.

"Well, we stared at the fire a while and I decided to attempt some sort of communication with the Martian. I pointed at myself and said 'Dick'; he caught the drift immediately, stretched a bony claw at me and repeated 'Tick.' Then I pointed at him, and he gave that whistle I called Tweel; I can't imitate his accent. Things were going smoothly; to emphasize the names, I repeated 'Dick,' and then, pointing at him, 'Tweel.'

"There we stuck! He gave some clacks that sounded negative, and said something like 'P-p-p-root.' And that was just the beginning; I was always 'Tick,' but as for him — part of the time he was 'Tweel,' and part of the time he was 'P-p-p-proot,' and part of the time he was sixteen other noises!

"We just couldn't connect. I tried 'rock,' and I tried 'star,' and 'tree,' and 'fire,' and Lord knows what else, and try as I would, I couldn't get a single word! Nothing was the same for two successive minutes, and if that's a language, I'm an alchemist! Finally I gave it up and called him Tweel, and that seemed to do.

"But Tweel hung on to some of my words. He remembered a couple of them, which I suppose is a great achievement if you're used to a language you have to make up as you go along. But I couldn't get the hang of his talk; either I missed some subtle point or we just didn't *think* alike — and I rather believe the latter view.

"I've other reasons for believing that. After a while I gave up the language business, and tried mathematics. I scratched two plus two equals four on the ground, and demonstrated it with pebbles. Again Tweel caught the idea, and informed me that three plus three equals six. Once more we seemed to be getting somewhere.

"So, knowing that Tweel had at least a grammar school education, I drew a circle for the sun, pointing first at it, and then at the last glow of the sun. Then I sketched in Mercury, and Venus, and Mother Earth, and Mars, and finally, pointing to Mars, I swept my hand around in a sort of inclusive gesture to indicate that Mars was our current environment. I was working up to putting over the idea that my home was on the earth.

"Tweel understood my diagram all right. He poked his beak at it, and with a great deal of trilling and clucking, he added Deimos and Phobos to Mars, and then sketched in the earth's moon!

"Do you see what that proves? It proves that Tweel's race uses telescopes — that they're civilized!"

"Does not!" snapped Harrison. "The moon is visible from here as a fifth magnitude star. They could see its revolution with the naked eye."

"The moon, yes!" said Jarvis. "You've missed my point. Mercury isn't visible! And Tweel knew of Mercury because he placed the Moon at the *third* planet, not the second. If he didn't know Mercury, he'd put the earth second, and Mars third, instead of fourth! See?"

"Humph!" said Harrison.

"Anyway," proceeded Jarvis, "I went on with my lesson. Things were going smoothly, and it looked as if I could put the idea over. I pointed at the earth on my diagram, and then at myself, and then, to clinch it, I pointed to myself and then to the earth itself shining bright green almost at the zenith.

"Tweel set up such an excited clacking that I was certain he understood. He jumped up and down, and suddenly he pointed at himself and then at the sky, and then at himself and at the sky again. He pointed at his middle and then at Arcturus, at his head and then at Spica, at his feet and then at half a dozen stars, while I just gaped at him. Then, all of a sudden, he gave a tremendous leap. Man, what a hop! He shot straight up into the starlight, seventy-five feet if an inch! I saw him silhouetted against the sky, saw him turn and come down at me head first, and land smack on his beak like a javelin! There he stuck square in the center of my sun-circle in the sand — a bull's eye!"

"Nuts!" observed the captain. "Plain nuts!"

"That's what I thought, too! I just stared at him open-mouthed while he pulled his head out of the sand and stood up. Then I figured he'd missed my point, and I went through the whole blamed rigamarole again, and it ended the same way, with Tweel on his nose in the middle of my picture!"

"Maybe it's a religious rite," suggested Harrison.

"Maybe," said Jarvis dubiously. "Well, there we were. We could exchange ideas up to a certain point, and then — blooey! Something in us was different, unrelated; I don't doubt that Tweel thought me just as screwy as I thought him. Our minds simply looked at the world from different viewpoints, and perhaps his viewpoint is as true as ours. But — we couldn't get together, that's all. Yet, in spite of all difficulties, I *liked* Tweel, and I have a queer certainty that he liked me."

"Nuts!" repeated the captain. "Just daffy!"

"Yeah? Wait and see. A couple of times I've thought that perhaps we — " He paused, and then resumed his narrative. "Anyway, I finally gave it up, and got into my thermo-skin to sleep. The fire hadn't kept me any too warm, but that damned sleeping bag did. Got stuffy five minutes after I closed myself in. I opened it a little and bingo! Some eighty-below-zero air hit my nose, and that's when I got this pleasant little frostbite to add to the bump I acquired during the crash of my rocket.

"I don't know what Tweel made of my sleeping. He sat around, but when I woke up, he was gone. I'd just crawled out of my bag, though, when I heard some twittering, and there he came, sailing down from that three-story Thyle cliff to alight on his beak beside me. I pointed to myself and toward the north, and he pointed at himself and toward the south, but when I loaded up and started away, he came along.

"Man, how he traveled! A hundred and fifty feet at a jump, sailing through the air stretched out like a spear, and landing on his beak. He seemed surprised at my plodding, but after a few moments he fell in beside me, only every few minutes he'd go into one of his leaps, and stick his nose into the sand a block ahead of me. Then he'd come shooting back at me; it made me nervous at first to see that beak of his coming at me like a spear, but he always ended in the sand at my side.

"So the two of us plugged along across the Mare Chronium. Same sort of place as this — same crazy plants and same little green biopods growing in the sand, or crawling out of your way. We talked — not that we understood each other, you know, but just for company. I sang songs, and I suspect Tweel did too; at least, some of his trillings and twitterings had a subtle sort of rhythm.

"Then, for variety, Tweel would display his smattering of English words. He'd point to an outcropping and say 'rock,' and point to a pebble and say it again; or he'd touch my arm and say 'Tick,' and then repeat it. He seemed terrifically amused that the same word meant the same thing twice in succession, or that the same word could apply to two different objects. It set me wondering if perhaps his language wasn't like the primitive speech of some earth people — you know, Captain, like the Negritoes,[1] for instance, who haven't any generic words. No word for food or water or man — words for good food and bad food, or rain water and sea water, or strong man and weak man — but no names for general classes. They're too primitive to understand that rain water and sea water are just different aspects of the same thing. But that wasn't the case with Tweel; it was just that we were

---

1. A term Western anthropologists applied to a variety of short-statured, dark-skinned ethnic groups in isolated areas of southeast Asia. The idea that some peoples were too primitive to understand abstract ideas or categories was once a common misconception. [Ed.]

somehow mysteriously different — our minds were alien to each other. And yet — we *liked* each other!"

"Looney, that's all," remarked Harrison. "That's why you two were so fond of each other."

"Well, I like *you*!" countered Jarvis wickedly. "Anyway," he resumed, "don't get the idea that there was anything screwy about Tweel. In fact, I'm not so sure but that he couldn't teach our highly praised human intelligence a trick or two. Oh, he wasn't an intellectual superman, I guess; but don't overlook the point that he managed to understand a little of my mental workings, and I never even got a glimmering of his."

"Because he didn't have any!" suggested the captain, while Putz and Leroy blinked attentively.

"You can judge that when I'm through," said Jarvis. "Well, we plugged along across the Mare Chronium all that day, and all the next. Mare Chronium — Sea of Time! Say, I was willing to agree with Schiaparelli's name by the end of that march! Just that grey, endless plain of weird plants, and never a sign of any other life. It was so monotonous that I was even glad to see the desert of Xanthus toward the evening of the second day.

"I was fair worn out, but Tweel seemed as fresh as ever, for all I never saw him drink or eat. I think he could have crossed the Mare Chronium in a couple of hours with those block-long nose dives of his, but he stuck along with me. I offered him some water once or twice; he took the cup from me and sucked the liquid into his beak, and then carefully squirted it all back into the cup and gravely returned it.

"Just as we sighted Xanthus, or the cliffs that bounded it, one of those nasty sand clouds blew along, not as bad as the one we had here, but mean to travel against. I pulled the transparent flap of my thermo-skin bag across my face and managed pretty well, and I noticed that Tweel used some feathery appendages growing like a mustache at the base of his beak to cover his nostrils, and some similar fuzz to shield his eyes."

"He is a desert creature!" ejaculated the little biologist, Leroy.

"Huh? Why?"

"He drink no water — he is adapt' for sand storm — "

"Proves nothing! There's not enough water to waste any where on this desiccated pill called Mars. We'd call all of it desert on earth, you know." He paused. "Anyway, after the sand storm blew over, a little wind kept blowing in our faces, not strong enough to stir the sand. But suddenly things came drifting along from the Xanthus cliffs — small, transparent spheres, for all the world like glass tennis balls! But light — they were almost light enough to float even in this thin air — empty, too; at least, I cracked open a couple and nothing came out but a bad smell. I asked Tweel about them, but all he said was 'No, no, no,' which I took to mean that he knew nothing about them. So they went bouncing by like tumbleweeds, or like soap bubbles, and we plugged on toward Xanthus. Tweel pointed at one of the crystal balls once and said 'rock,' but I was too tired to argue with him. Later I discovered what he meant.

"We came to the bottom of the Xanthus cliffs finally, when there wasn't much daylight left. I decided to sleep on the plateau if possible; anything dangerous, I reasoned, would be more likely to prowl through the vegetation of the Mare Chronium than the sand of Xanthus. Not that I'd seen a single sign of menace, except the rope-armed black thing that had trapped Tweel, and apparently that didn't prowl at all, but lured its victims within reach. It couldn't lure me while I slept, especially as Tweel didn't seem to sleep at all, but simply sat patiently around all night. I wondered how the creature had managed to trap Tweel, but there wasn't any way of asking him, I found that out too, later; it's devilish!

"However, we were ambling around the base of the Xanthus barrier looking for an easy spot to climb. At least, I was. Tweel could have leaped it easily, for the cliffs were lower than Thyle — perhaps sixty feet. I found a place and started up, swearing at the water tank strapped to my back — it didn't bother me except when climbing — and suddenly I heard a sound that I thought I recognized!

"You know how deceptive sounds are in this thin air. A shot sounds like the pop of a cork. But this sound was the drone of a rocket, and sure enough, there went our second auxiliary about ten miles to westward, between me and the sunset!"

"Vas me!" said Putz. "I hunt for you."

"Yeah; I knew that, but what good did it do me? I hung on to the cliff and yelled and waved with one hand. Tweel saw it too, and set up a trilling and twittering, leaping to the top of the barrier and then high into the air. And while I watched, the machine droned on into the shadows to the south.

"I scrambled to the top of the cliff. Tweel was still pointing and trilling excitedly, shooting up toward the sky and coming down head-on to stick upside down on his beak in the sand. I pointed toward the south and at myself, and he said, 'Yes — Yes — Yes'; but somehow I gathered that he thought the flying thing was a relative of mine, probably a parent. Perhaps I did his intellect an injustice; I think now that I did.

"I was bitterly disappointed by the failure to attract attention. I pulled out my thermo-skin bag and crawled into it, as the night chill was already apparent. Tweel stuck his beak into the sand and drew up his legs and arms and looked for all the world like one of those leafless shrubs out there. I think he stayed that way all night."

"Protective mimicry!" ejaculated Leroy. "See? He is desert creature!"

"In the morning," resumed Jarvis, "we started off again. We hadn't gone a hundred yards into Xanthus when I saw something queer! This is one thing Putz didn't photograph, I'll wager!

"There was a line of little pyramids — tiny ones, not more than six inches high, stretching across Xanthus as far as I could see! Little buildings made of pygmy bricks, they were, hollow inside and truncated, or at least broken at the top and empty. I pointed at them and said 'What?' to Tweel, but he gave some negative twitters to indicate, I suppose, that he didn't know. So off we went, following the row of pyramids because they ran north, and I was going north.

"Man, we trailed that line for hours! After a while, I noticed another queer thing: they were getting larger. Same number of bricks in each one, but the bricks were larger.

"By noon they were shoulder high. I looked into a couple — all just the same, broken at the top and empty. I examined a brick or two as well; they were silica, and old as creation itself!"

"How you know?" asked Leroy.

"They were weathered — edges rounded. Silica doesn't weather easily even on earth, and in this climate — !"

"How old you think?"

"Fifty thousand — a hundred thousand years. How can I tell? The little ones we saw in the morning were older — perhaps ten times as old. Crumbling. How old would that make *them*? Half a million years? Who knows?" Jarvis paused a moment. "Well," he resumed, "we followed the line. Tweel pointed at them and said 'rock' once or twice, but he'd done that many times before. Besides, he was more or less right about these.

"I tried questioning him. I pointed at a pyramid and asked 'People?' and indicated the two of us. He set up a negative sort of clucking and said, 'No, no, no. No one-one-two. No two-two-four,' meanwhile rubbing his stomach. I just stared at him and he went through the business again. 'No one-one-two. No two-two-four.' I just gaped at him."

"That proves it!" exclaimed Harrison. "Nuts!"

"You think so?" queried Jarvis sardonically. "Well, I figured it out different! 'No one-one-two!' You don't get it, of course, do you?"

"Nope — nor do you!"

"I think I do! Tweel was using the few English words he knew to put over a very complex idea. What, let me ask, does mathematics make you think of?"

"Why — of astronomy. Or — or logic!"

"That's it! 'No one-one-two!' Tweel was telling me that the builders of the pyramids weren't people — or that they weren't intelligent, that they weren't reasoning creatures! Get it?"

"Huh! I'll be damned!"

"You probably will."

"Why," put in Leroy, "he rub his belly?"

"Why? Because, my dear biologist, that's where his brains are! Not in his tiny head — in his middle!"

"*C'est impossible!*"

"Not on Mars, it isn't! This flora and fauna aren't earthly; your biopods prove that!" Jarvis grinned and took up his narrative. "Anyway, we plugged along across Xanthus and in about the middle of the afternoon, something else queer happened. The pyramids ended."

"Ended!"

"Yeah; the queer part was that the last one — and now they were ten-footers — was capped! See? Whatever built it was still inside; we'd trailed 'em from their half-million-year-old origin to the present.

"Tweel and I noticed it about the same time. I yanked out my automatic (I had a clip of Boland explosive bullets in it) and Tweel, quick as a sleight-of-hand trick, snapped a queer little glass revolver out of his bag. It was much like our weapons, except that the grip was larger to accommodate his four-taloned hand. And we held our weapons ready while we sneaked up along the lines of empty pyramids.

"Tweel saw the movement first. The top tiers of bricks were heaving, shaking, and suddenly slid down the sides with a thin crash. And then — something — something was coming out!

"A long, silvery-grey arm appeared, dragging after it an armored body. Armored, I mean, with scales, silver-grey and dull-shining. The arm heaved the body out of the hole; the beast crashed to the sand.

"It was a nondescript creature — body like a big grey cask, arm and a sort of mouth-hole at one end; stiff, pointed tail at the other — and that's all. No other limbs, no eyes, ears, nose — nothing! The thing dragged itself a few yards, inserted its pointed tail in the sand, pushed itself upright, and just sat.

"Tweel and I watched it for ten minutes before it moved. Then, with a creaking and rustling like — oh, like crumpling stiff paper — its arm moved to the mouth-hole and out came a brick! The arm placed the brick carefully on the ground, and the thing was still again.

"Another ten minutes — another brick. Just one of Nature's bricklayers. I was about to slip away and move on when Tweel pointed at the thing and said 'rock'! I went 'huh?' and he said it again. Then, to the accompaniment of some of his trilling, he said, 'No — no — ,' and gave two or three whistling breaths.

"Well, I got his meaning, for a wonder! I said, 'No breath?' and demonstrated the word. Tweel was ecstatic; he said, 'Yes, yes, yes! No, no, no breet!' Then he gave a leap and sailed out to land on his nose about one pace from the monster!

"I was startled, you can imagine! The arm was going up for a brick, and I expected to see Tweel caught and mangled, but — nothing happened! Tweel pounded on the creature, and the arm took the brick and placed it neatly beside the first. Tweel rapped on its body again, and said 'rock,' and I got up nerve enough to take a look myself.

"Tweel was right again. The creature *was* rock, and it didn't breathe!"

"How you know?" snapped Leroy, his black eyes blazing interest.

"Because I'm a chemist. The beast was made of silica! There must have been pure silicon in the sand, and it lived on that. Get it? We, and Tweel, and those plants out there, and even the biopods are *carbon* life; this thing lived by a different set of chemical reactions. It was silicon life!"

"*La vie silicieuse!*" shouted Leroy. "I have suspect, and now it is proof! I must go see! *Il faut que je —* "

"All right! All right!" said Jarvis. "You can go see. Anyhow, there the thing was, alive and yet not alive, moving every ten minutes, and then only to remove a brick. Those bricks were its waste matter. See, Frenchy? We're carbon, and our waste is carbon dioxide, and this thing is silicon, and *its* waste is silicon dioxide — silica. But silica is a solid, hence the bricks. And it builds itself in, and when it is covered, it moves over to a fresh place to start over. No wonder it creaked! A living creature half a million years old!"

"How you know how old?" Leroy was frantic.

"We trailed its pyramids from the beginning, didn't we? If this weren't the original pyramid builder, the series would have ended somewhere before we found him, wouldn't it? — ended and started over with the small ones. That's simple enough, isn't it?

"But he reproduces, or tries to. Before the third brick came out, there was a little rustle and out popped a whole stream of those little crystal balls. They're his spores, or eggs, or seeds — call 'em what you want. They went bouncing by across Xanthus just as they'd bounced by us back in the Mare Chronium. I've a hunch how they work, too — this is for your information, Leroy. I think the crystal shell of silica is no more than a protective covering, like an eggshell, and that the active principle is the smell inside. It's some sort of gas that attacks silicon, and if the shell is broken near a supply of that element, some reaction starts that ultimately develops into a beast like that one."

"You should try!" exclaimed the little Frenchman. "We must break one to see!"

"Yeah? Well, I did. I smashed a couple against the sand. Would you like to come back in about ten thousand years to see if I planted some pyramid monsters? You'd most likely be able to tell by that time!" Jarvis paused and drew a deep breath. "Lord! That queer creature! Do you picture it? Blind, deaf, nerveless, brainless — just a mechanism, and yet — immortal! Bound to go on making bricks, building pyramids, as long as silicon and oxygen exist, and even afterwards it'll just stop. It won't be dead. If the accidents of a million years bring it its food again, there it'll be, ready to run again, while brains and civilizations are part of the past. A queer beast — yet I met a stranger one!"

"If you did, it must have been in your dreams!" growled Harrison.

"You're right!" said Jarvis soberly. "In a way, you're right. The dream-beast! That's the best name for it — and it's the most fiendish, terrifying creation one could imagine! More dangerous than a lion, more insidious than a snake!"

"Tell me!" begged Leroy. "I must go see!"

"Not *this* devil!" He paused again. "Well," he resumed, "Tweel and I left the pyramid creature and plowed along through Xanthus. I was tired and a little disheartened by Putz's failure to pick me up, and Tweel's trilling got on my nerves, as did his flying nosedives. So I just strode along without a word, hour after hour across that monotonous desert.

"Toward mid-afternoon we came in sight of a low dark line on the horizon. I knew what it was. It was a canal; I'd crossed it in the rocket and it meant that we were just one-third of the way across Xanthus. Pleasant thought, wasn't it? And still, I was keeping up to schedule.

"We approached the canal slowly; I remembered that this one was bordered by a wide fringe of vegetation and that Mudheap City was on it.

"I was tired, as I said. I kept thinking of a good hot meal, and then from that I jumped to reflections of how nice and home-like even Borneo would seem after this crazy planet, and from that, to thoughts of little old New York, and then to thinking about a girl I know there — Fancy Long. Know her?"

"Vision entertainer," said Harrison. "I've tuned her in. Nice blonde — dances and sings on the *Yerba Mate* hour."

"That's her," said Jarvis ungrammatically. "I know her pretty well — just friends, get me? — though she came down to see us off in the *Ares*. Well, I was thinking about her, feeling pretty lonesome, and all the time we were approaching that line of rubbery plants.

"And then — I said, 'What 'n Hell!' and stared. And there she was — Fancy Long, standing plain as day under one of those crack-brained trees, and smiling and waving just the way I remembered her when we left!"

"Now you're nuts, too!" observed the captain.

"Boy, I almost agreed with you! I stared and pinched myself and closed my eyes and then stared again — and every time, there was Fancy Long smiling and waving! Tweel saw something, too; he was trilling and clucking away, but I scarcely heard him. I was bounding toward her over the sand, too amazed even to ask myself questions.

"I wasn't twenty feet from her when Tweel caught me with one of his flying leaps. He grabbed my arm, yelling, 'No — no — no!' in his squeaky voice. I tried to shake him off — he was as light as if he were built of bamboo — but he dug his claws and yelled. And finally some sort of sanity returned to me and I stopped less than ten feet from her. There she stood, looking as solid as Putz's head!"

"Vot?" said the engineer.

"She smiled and waved, and waved and smiled, and I stood there dumb as Leroy, while Tweel squeaked and chattered. I *knew* it couldn't be real, yet — there she was!

"Finally I said, 'Fancy! Fancy Long!' She just kept on smiling and waving, but looking as real as if I hadn't left her thirty-seven million miles away.

"Tweel had his glass pistol out, pointing it at her. I grabbed his arm, but he tried to push me away. He pointed at her and said, 'No breet! No breet!' and I understood that he meant that the Fancy Long thing wasn't alive. Man, my head was whirling!

"Still, it gave me the jitters to see him pointing his weapon at her. I don't know why I stood there watching him take careful aim, but I did. Then he squeezed the handle of his weapon; there was a little puff of steam, and Fancy Long was gone! And in her place was one of those writhing, black, rope-armed horrors like the one I'd saved Tweel from!

"The dream-beast! I stood there dizzy, watching it die while Tweel trilled and whistled. Finally he touched my arm, pointed at the twisting thing, and said, 'You one-one-two, he one-one-two.' After he'd repeated it eight or ten times, I got it. Do any of you?"

"*Oui!*" shrilled Leroy. "*Moi — je le comprends*! He mean you think of something, the beast he know, and you see it! *Un chien* — a hungry dog, he would see the big bone with meat! Or smell it — not?"

"Right!" said Jarvis. "The dream-beast uses its victim's longings and desires to trap its prey. The bird at nesting season would see its mate; the fox, prowling for its own prey, would see a helpless rabbit!"

"How he do?" queried Leroy.

"How do I know? How does a snake back on earth charm a bird into its very jaws? And aren't there deep-sea fish that lure their victims into their mouths? Lord!" Jarvis shuddered, "Do you see how insidious the monster is? We're warned now — but henceforth we can't trust even our eyes. You might see me — I might see one of you — and back of it may be nothing but another or those black horrors!"

"How'd your friend know?" asked the captain abruptly.

"Tweel? I wonder! Perhaps he was thinking of something that couldn't possibly have interested me, and when I started to run, he realized that I saw something different and was warned. Or perhaps the dream-beast can only project a single vision, and Tweel saw what I saw — or nothing, I couldn't ask him. But it's just another proof that his intelligence is equal to ours or greater."

"He's daffy, I tell you!" said Harrison, "What makes you think his intellect ranks with the human?"

"Plenty of things! First, the pyramid-beast. He hadn't seen one before; he said as much. Yet he recognized it as a dead-alive automaton of silicon."

"He could have heard of it," objected Harrison. "He lives around here, you know."

"Well how about the language? I couldn't pick up a single idea of his and he learned six or seven words of mine. And do you realize what complex ideas he put over with no more than those six or seven words? The pyramid-monster — the dream-beast! In a single phrase he told me that one was a harmless automaton and the other a deadly hypnotist. What about that?"

"Huh!" said the captain.

"*Huh* if you wish! Could you have done it knowing only six words of English? Could you go even further, as Tweel did, and tell me that another creature was of a sort of intelligence so different from ours that understanding was impossible — even more impossible than that between Tweel and me?"

"Eh? What was that?"

"Later. The point I'm making is that Tweel and his race are worthy of our friendship, Somewhere on Mars — and you'll find I'm right — is a civilization and culture equal to ours, and maybe more than equal. And communication is possible between them and us; Tweel proves that. It may take years of patient trial, for their minds are alien, but less alien than the next minds we encountered — if they *are* minds."

"The next ones? What next ones?"

"The people of the mud cities along the canals." Jarvis frowned, then resumed his narrative. "I thought the dream-beast and the silicon-monster were the strangest beings conceivable, but I was wrong. These creatures are still more alien, less understandable than either and far less comprehensible than Tweel, with whom friendship is possible, and even, by patience and concentration, the exchange of ideas.

"Well," he continued, "we left the dream-beast dying, dragging itself back into its hole, and we moved toward the canal. There was a carpet of that queer walking-grass scampering out of our way, and when we reached the bank, there was a yellow trickle of water flowing. The mound city I'd noticed from the rocket was a mile or so to the right and I was curious enough to want to take a look at it.

"It had seemed deserted from my previous glimpse of it, and if any creatures were lurking in it — well, Tweel and I were both armed. And by the way, that crystal weapon of Tweel's was an interesting device; I took a look at it after the dream-beast episode. It fired a little glass splinter, poisoned, I suppose, and I guess it held at least a hundred of 'em to a load. The propellent was steam — just plain steam!"

"Shteam!" echoed Putz. "From vot come, shteam?"

"From water, of course! You could see the water through the transparent handle and about a gill of another liquid, thick and yellowish. When Tweel squeezed the handle — there was no trigger — a drop of water and a drop of the yellow stuff squirted into the firing chamber, and the water vaporized — pop! — like that. It's not so difficult; I think we could develop the same principle. Concentrated sulphuric acid will heat water almost to boiling, and so will quicklime, and there's potassium and sodium —

"Of course, his weapon hadn't the range of mine, but it wasn't so bad in this thin air, and it *did* hold as many shots as a cowboy's gun in a Western movie. It was effective, too, at least against Martian life; I tried it out, aiming at one of the crazy plants, and darned if the plant didn't wither up and fall apart! That's why I think the glass splinters were poisoned.

"Anyway, we trudged along toward the mud-heap city and I began to wonder whether the city builders dug the canals. I pointed to the city and then at the canal, and Tweel said 'No — no — no!' and gestured toward the south. I took it to mean that some other race had created the canal system, perhaps Tweel's people. I don't know; maybe there's still another intelligent race on the planet, or a dozen others. Mars is a queer little world.

"A hundred yards from the city we crossed a sort of road — just a hard-packed mud trail, and then, all of a sudden, along came one of the mound builders!

"Man, talk about fantastic beings! It looked rather like a barrel trotting along on four legs with four other arms or tentacles. It had no head, just body and members and a row of eyes completely around it. The top end of the barrel-body was a diaphragm stretched as tight as a drum head, and that was all. It was pushing a little coppery cart and tore right past us like the proverbial bat out of Hell. It didn't even notice us, although I thought the eyes on my side shifted a little as it passed.

"A moment later another came along, pushing another empty cart. Same thing — it just scooted past us. Well, I wasn't going to be ignored by a bunch of barrels playing train, so when the third one approached, I planted myself in the way — ready to jump, of course, if the thing didn't stop.

"But it did. It stopped and set up a sort of drumming from the diaphragm on top. And I held out both hands and said, 'We are friends!' And what do you suppose the thing did?"

"Said, 'Pleased to meet you,' I'll bet!" suggested Harrison.

"I couldn't have been more surprised if it had! It drummed on its diaphragm, and then suddenly boomed out, 'We are v-r-r-riends!' and gave its pushcart a vicious poke at me! I jumped aside, and away it went while I stared dumbly after it.

"A minute later another one came hurrying along. This one didn't pause, but simply drummed out, 'We are v-r-r-riends!' and scurried by. How did it learn the phrase? Were all of the creatures in some sort of communication with each other? Were they all parts of some central organism? I don't know, though I think Tweel does.

"Anyway, the creatures went sailing past us, every one greeting us with the same statement. It got to be funny; I never thought to find so many friends on this God-forsaken ball! Finally I made a puzzled gesture to Tweel; I guess he understood, for he said, 'One-one-two — yes! — two-two-four — no!' Get it?"

"Sure," said Harrison. "It's a Martian nursery rhyme."

"Yeah! Well, I was getting used to Tweel's symbolism, and I figured it out this way. 'One-one-two — yes!' The creatures were intelligent. 'Two-two-four — no!' Their intelligence was not of our order, but something different and beyond the logic of two and two is four. Maybe I missed his meaning. Perhaps he meant that their minds were of low degree, able to figure out the simple things — 'One-one-two — yes!' — but not more difficult things — 'Two-two-four — no!' But I think from what we saw later that he meant the other.

"After a few moments, the creatures came rushing back — first one, then another. Their pushcarts were full of stones, sand, chunks of rubbery plants, and such rubbish as that. They droned out their friendly greeting, which didn't really sound so friendly, and dashed on. The third one I assumed to be my first acquaintance and I decided to have another chat with him. I stepped into his path again and waited.

"Up he came, booming out his 'We are v-r-r-riends' and stopped. I looked at him; four or five of his eyes looked at me. He tried his password again and gave a shove on his cart, but I stood firm. And then the — the dashed creature reached out one of his arms, and two finger-like nippers tweaked my nose!"

"Haw!" roared Harrison. "Maybe the things have a sense of beauty!"

"Laugh!" grumbled Jarvis. "I'd already had a nasty bump and a mean frostbite on that nose. Anyway, I yelled 'Ouch!' and jumped aside and the creature dashed away; but from then on, their greeting was 'We are v-r-r-riends! Ouch!' Queer beasts!

"Tweel and I followed the road squarely up to the nearest mound. The creatures were coming and going, paying us not the slightest attention, fetching their loads of rubbish. The road simply dived into an opening, and slanted down like an old mine, and in and out darted the barrel-people, greeting us with their eternal phrase.

"I looked in; there was a light somewhere below, and I was curious to see it. It didn't look like a flame or torch, you understand, but more like a civilized light, and I thought that I might get some clue as to the creatures' development. So in I went and Tweel tagged along, not without a few trills and twitters, however.

"The light was curious; it sputtered and flared like an old arc light, but came from a single black rod set in the wall of the corridor. It was electric, beyond doubt. The creatures were fairly civilized, apparently.

"Then I saw another light shining on something that glittered and I went on to look at that, but it was only a heap of shiny sand. I turned toward the entrance to leave, and the Devil take me if it wasn't gone!

"I suppose the corridor had curved, or I'd stepped into a side passage. Anyway, I walked back in that direction I thought we'd come, and all I saw was more dimlit corridor. The place was a labyrinth! There was nothing but twisting passages running every way, lit by occasional lights, and now and then a creature running by, sometimes with a pushcart, sometimes without.

"Well, I wasn't much worried at first. Tweel and I had only come a few steps from the entrance. But every move we made after that seemed to get us in deeper. Finally I tried following one of the creatures with an empty cart, thinking that he'd be going out for his rubbish, but he ran around aimlessly, into one passage and out another. When he started dashing around a pillar like one of these Japanese waltzing mice, I gave up, dumped my water tank on the floor, and sat down.

"Tweel was as lost as I. I pointed up and he said 'No — no — no!' in a sort of helpless trill. And we couldn't get any help from the natives. They paid no attention at all, except to assure us they were friends — ouch!

"Lord! I don't know how many hours or days we wandered around there! I slept twice from sheer exhaustion; Tweel never seemed to need sleep. We tried following only the upward corridors, but they'd run uphill a ways and then curve downwards. The temperature in that damned ant hill was constant; you couldn't tell night from day and after my first sleep I didn't know whether I'd slept one hour or thirteen, so I couldn't tell from my watch whether it was midnight or noon.

"We saw plenty of strange things. There were machines running in some of the corridors, but they didn't seem to be doing anything — just wheels turning. And several times I saw two barrel-beasts with a little one growing between them, joined to both."

"Parthenogenesis!" exulted Leroy. "Parthenogenesis by budding like *les tulipes!*"

"If you say so, Frenchy," agreed Jarvis. "The things never noticed us at all, except, as I say, to greet us with 'We are v-r-r-riends! Ouch!' They seemed to have no home-life of any sort, but just scurried around with their pushcarts, bringing in rubbish. And finally I discovered what they did with it.

"We'd had a little luck with a corridor, one that slanted upwards for a great distance. I was feeling that we ought to be close to the surface when suddenly the passage debouched into a domed chamber, the only one we'd seen. And man! — I felt like dancing when I saw what looked like daylight through a crevice in the roof.

"There was a — a sort of machine in the chamber, just an enormous wheel that turned slowly, and one of the creatures was in the act of dumping his rubbish below it. The wheel ground it with a crunch — sand, stones, plants, all into powder that sifted away somewhere. While we watched, others filed in, repeating the process, and that seemed to be all. No rhyme nor reason to the whole thing — but that's characteristic of this crazy planet. And there was another fact that's almost too bizarre to believe.

"One of the creatures, having dumped his load, pushed his cart aside with a crash and calmly shoved himself under the wheel! I watched him being crushed, too stupefied to make a sound, and a moment later, another followed him! They were perfectly methodical about it, too; one of the cart-less creatures took the abandoned pushcart.

"Tweel didn't seem surprised; I pointed out the next suicide to him, and he just gave the most human-like shrug imaginable, as much as to say, 'What can I do about it?' He must have known more or less about these creatures.

"Then I saw something else. There was something beyond the wheel, something shining on a sort of low pedestal. I walked over; there was a little crystal about the size of an egg, fluorescing to beat Tophet. The light from it stung my hands and face, almost like a static discharge, and then I noticed another funny thing. Remember that wart I had on my left thumb? Look!" Jarvis extended his hand, "It dried up and fell off — just like that! And my abused nose — say, the pain went out of it like magic! The thing had the property of hard ex-rays or gamma radiations, only more so; it destroyed diseased tissue and left healthy tissue unharmed!

"I was thinking what a present *that'd* be to take back to Mother Earth when a lot of racket interrupted. We dashed back to the other side of the wheel in time to see one of the pushcarts ground up. Some suicide had been careless, it seems.

"Then suddenly the creatures were booming and drumming all around us and their noise was decidedly menacing. A crowd of them advanced toward us; we backed out of what I thought was the passage we'd entered by, and they came rumbling after us, some pushing carts and some not. Crazy brutes! There was a whole chorus of 'We are v-r-r-riends! Ouch!' I didn't like the 'ouch'; it was rather suggestive.

"Tweel had his glass gun out and I dumped my water tank for greater freedom and got mine. We backed up the corridor with the barrel-beasts following — about twenty of them. Queer thing — the ones coming in with loaded carts moved past us inches away without a sign.

"Tweel must have noticed that. Suddenly, he snatched out that glowing coal cigar-lighter of his and touched a cart-load of plant limbs. Puff! The whole load was burning — and the crazy beast pushing it went right along without a change of pace! It created some disturbance among our 'v-r-r-riends,' however — and then I noticed the smoke eddying and swirling past us, and sure enough, there was the entrance!

"I grabbed Tweel and out we dashed and after us our twenty pursuers. The daylight felt like Heaven, though I saw at first glance that the sun was all but set, and that was bad, since I couldn't live outside my thermo-skin bag in a Martian night — at least, without a fire.

"And things got worse in a hurry. They cornered us in an angle between two mounds, and there we stood. I hadn't fired nor had Tweel; there wasn't any use in irritating the brutes. They stopped a little distance away and began their booming about friendship and ouches.

"Then things got still worse! A barrel-brute came out with a pushcart and they all grabbed into it and came out with handfuls of foot-long copper darts — sharp-looking ones — and all of a sudden one sailed past my ear — zing! And it was shoot or die then.

"We were doing pretty well for a while. We picked off the ones next to the pushcart and managed to keep the darts at a minimum, but suddenly there was a thunderous booming of 'v-r-r-riends' and 'ouches,' and a whole army of 'em came out of their hole.

"Man! We were through and I knew it! Then I realized that Tweel wasn't. He could have leaped the mound behind us as easily as not. He was staying for me!

"Say, I could have cried if there'd been time! I'd liked Tweel from the first, but whether I'd have had gratitude to do what he was doing — suppose I *had* saved him from the first dream-beast — he'd done as much for me, hadn't he? I grabbed his arm, and said 'Tweel,' and pointed up, and he understood. He said, 'No — no — no, Tick!' and popped away with his glass pistol.

"What could I do? I'd be a goner anyway when the sun set, but I couldn't explain that to him. I said, 'Thanks, Tweel. You're a man!' and felt that I wasn't paying him any compliment at all. A man! There are mighty few men who'd do that.

"So I went 'bang' with my gun and Tweel went 'puff' with his, and the barrels were throwing darts and getting ready to rush us, and booming about being friends. I had given up hope. Then suddenly an angel dropped right down from Heaven in the shape of Putz, with his under-jets blasting the barrels into very small pieces!

"Wow! I let out a yell and dashed for the rocket; Putz opened the door and in I went, laughing and crying and shouting! It was a moment or so before I remembered Tweel; I looked around in time to see him rising in one of his nosedives over the mound and away.

"I had a devil of a job arguing Putz into following! By the time we got the rocket aloft, darkness was down; you know how it comes here — like turning off a light. We sailed out over the desert and put down once or twice. I yelled 'Tweel!' and yelled it a hundred times, I guess. We couldn't find him; he could travel like the wind and all I got — or else I imagined it — was a faint trilling and twittering drifting out of the south. He'd gone, and damn it! I wish — I wish he hadn't!"

The four men of the *Ares* were silent — even the sardonic Harrison. At last little Leroy broke the stillness.

"I should like to see," he murmured.

"Yeah," said Harrison. "And the wart-cure. Too bad you missed that; it might be the cancer cure they've been hunting for a century and a half."

"Oh, that!" muttered Jarvis gloomily. "That's what started the fight!" He drew a glistening object from his pocket.

"Here it is."

Fredric Brown

Arena

(1944)

Fredric Brown (1906–1972) wrote for a variety of genre magazines, including those specializing in detective stories as well as science fiction, in a career spanning the 1930s through the 1960s. Something of the terse, wry style characteristic of the hard-boiled detective novel is evident in many of his sf stories as well, including the one that follows, which was selected for inclusion in the *Science Fiction Hall of Fame* in 1967. Brown's best-known novels are *The Fabulous Clipjoint* (which won an Edgar award for best first mystery in 1948) and *Martians, Go Home* (1955), a humorous take on alien invasion. He was most prolific and accomplished, however, as a writer of short fiction, and is particularly known for his "short shorts" — very short stories with sudden twists that end in a joke.

"Arena" draws on the ancient tradition of ritual battle, in which two champions are chosen to represent their people in single combat to decide the outcome of a larger conflict. This story, written at the height of U.S. involvement in World War II, is frank in its condemnation of the enemy aliens, who are portrayed as so profoundly inhuman and sadistic that no accommodation is possible; they are a force of evil that must be defeated. The moral absolutism of this story may seem simplistic or offensive today, but there is also something bracing about Brown's uncompromising moral stance in our age of relativism.

In addition to the enemy Rollers, Brown introduces two other alien species; the representation of — and interaction among — multiple alien species at various stages of intellectual and moral development provides much of the story's interest. When this story was remade as an episode of *Star Trek* in 1967, it was updated in interesting ways. The right of the "superior" alien to manipulate the other species is challenged, and the message was changed to one of pacifism and tolerance, the battle won through moral superiority rather than strength and cunning.

C arson opened his eyes, and found himself looking upward into a flickering blue dimness.

It was hot, and he was lying on sand, and a sharp rock embedded in the sand was hurting his back. He rolled over to his side, off the rock, and then pushed himself up to a sitting position.

"I'm crazy," he thought. "Crazy — or dead — or something." The sand was blue, bright blue. And there wasn't any such thing as bright blue sand on Earth or any of the planets.

Blue sand.

Blue sand under a blue dome that wasn't the sky nor yet a room, but a circumscribed area — somehow he knew it was circumscribed and finite even though he couldn't see to the top of it.

He picked up some of the sand in his hand and let it run through his fingers. It trickled down onto his bare leg. *Bare?*

Naked. He was stark naked, and already his body was dripping perspiration from the enervating heat, coated blue with sand wherever sand had touched it.

But elsewhere his body was white.

He thought: Then this sand is really blue. If it seemed blue only because of the blue light, then I'd be blue also. But I'm white, so the sand *is* blue. *Blue sand.* There isn't any blue sand. There isn't any place like this place I'm in.

Sweat was running down in his eyes.

It was hot, hotter than hell. Only hell — the hell of the ancients — was supposed to be red and not blue.

But if this place wasn't hell, what was it? Only Mercury, among the planets, had heat like this and this wasn't Mercury. And Mercury was some four billion miles from —

It came back to him then, where he'd been. In the little one-man scouter, outside the orbit of Pluto, scouting a scant million miles to one side of the Earth Armada drawn up in battle array there to intercept the Outsiders.

That sudden strident nerve-shattering ringing of the alarm bell when the rival scouter — the Outsider ship — had come within range of his detectors —

No one knew who the Outsiders were, what they looked like, from what far galaxy they came, other than that it was in the general direction of the Pleiades.

First, sporadic raids on Earth colonies and outposts. Isolated battles between Earth patrols and small groups of Outsider spaceships; battles sometimes won and sometimes lost, but never to date resulting in the capture of an alien vessel. Nor had any member of a raided colony ever survived to describe the Outsiders who had left the ships, if indeed they had left them.

Not a too-serious menace, at first, for the raids had not been too numerous or destructive. And individually, the ships had proved slightly inferior in armament to the best of Earth's fighters, although somewhat superior in speed and maneuverability. A sufficient edge in speed, in fact, to give the Outsiders their choice of running or fighting, unless surrounded.

Nevertheless, Earth had prepared for serious trouble, for a showdown, building the mightiest armada of all time. It had been waiting now, that armada, for a long time. But now the showdown was coming.

Scouts twenty billion miles out had detected the approach of a mighty fleet — a showdown fleet — of the Outsiders. Those scouts had never come back, but their radiotronic messages had. And now Earth's armada, all ten thousand ships and half-million fighting spacemen, was out there, outside Pluto's orbit, waiting to intercept and battle to the death.

And an even battle it was going to be, judging by the advance reports of the men of the far picket line who had given their lives to report — before they had died — on the size and strength of the alien fleet.

Anybody's battle, with the mastery of the solar system hanging in the balance, on an even chance. A last and *only* chance, for Earth and all her colonies lay at the utter mercy of the Outsiders if they ran that gauntlet —

Oh yes. Bob Carson remembered now.

Not that it explained blue sand and flickering blueness. But that strident alarming of the bell and his leap for the control panel. His frenzied fumbling as he strapped himself into the seat. The dot in the visiplate that grew larger.

The dryness of his mouth. The awful knowledge that this was *it*. For him, at least, although the main fleets were still out of range of one another.

This, his first taste of battle. Within three seconds or less he'd be victorious, or a charred cinder. Dead.

Three seconds — that's how long a space-battle lasted. Time enough to count to three, slowly, and then you'd won or you were dead. One hit completely took care of a lightly armed and armored little one-man craft like a scouter.

Frantically — as, unconsciously, his dry lips shaped the word "One" — he worked at the controls to keep that growing dot centered on the crossed spiderwebs of the visiplate. His hands doing that, while his right foot hovered over the pedal that would fire the bolt. The single bolt of concentrated hell that had to hit — or else. There wouldn't be time for any second shot.

"Two." He didn't know he'd said that, either. The dot in the visiplate wasn't a dot now. Only a few thousand miles away, it showed up in the magnification of the plate as though it were only a few hundred yards off. It was a sleek, fast little scouter, about the size of his.

And an alien ship, all right.

"Thr — " His foot touched the bolt-release pedal —

And then the Outsider had swerved suddenly and was off the crosshairs. Carson punched keys frantically, to follow.

For a tenth of a second, it was out of the visiplate entirely, and then as the nose of his scouter swung after it, he saw it again, diving straight toward the ground.

The ground?

It was an optical illusion of some sort. It *had* to be, that planet — or whatever it was — that now covered the visiplate. Whatever it was, it couldn't be there. Couldn't possibly. There *wasn't* any planet nearer than

Neptune three billion miles away — with Pluto around on the opposite side of the distant pinpoint sun.

His *detectors*! *They* hadn't shown any object of planetary dimensions, even of asteroid dimensions. They still didn't.

So it couldn't be there, that whatever-it-was he was diving into, only a few hundred miles below him.

And in his sudden anxiety to keep from crashing, he forgot even the Outsider ship. He fired the front braking rockets, and even as the sudden change of speed slammed him forward against the seat straps, he fired full right for an emergency turn. Pushed them down and *held* them down, knowing that he needed everything the ship had to keep from crashing and that a turn that sudden would black him out for a moment.

It did black him out.

And that was all. Now he was sitting in hot blue sand, stark naked but otherwise unhurt. No sign of his spaceship and — for that matter — no sign of *space*. That curve overhead wasn't a sky, whatever else it was.

He scrambled to his feet.

Gravity seemed a little more than Earth-normal. Not much more.

Flat sand stretching away, a few scrawny bushes in clumps here and there. The bushes were blue, too, but in varying shades, some lighter than the blue of the sand, some darker.

Out from under the nearest bush ran a little thing that was like a lizard, except that it had more than four legs. It was blue, too. Bright blue. It saw him and ran back again under the bush.

He looked up again, trying to decide what was overhead. It wasn't exactly a roof, but it was dome-shaped. It flickered and was hard to look at. But definitely, it curved down to the ground, to the blue sand, all around him.

He wasn't far from being under the center of the dome. At a guess, it was a hundred yards to the nearest wall, if it was a wall. It was as though a blue hemisphere of *something*, about two hundred and fifty yards in circumference, was inverted over the flat expanse of the sand.

And everything blue, except one object. Over near a far curving wall there was a red object. Roughly spherical, it seemed to be about a yard in diameter. Too far for him to see clearly through the flickering blueness. But, unaccountably, he shuddered.

He wiped sweat from his forehead, or tried to, with the back of his hand.

Was this a dream, a nightmare? This heat, this sand, that vague feeling of horror he felt when he looked toward the red thing?

A dream? No, one didn't go to sleep and dream in the midst of a battle in space.

Death? No, never. If there were immortality, it wouldn't be a senseless thing like this, a thing of blue heat and blue sand and a red horror.

Then he heard the voice —

Inside his head he heard it, not with his ears. It came from nowhere or everywhere.

"*Through spaces and dimensions wandering*," rang the words in his mind, "*and in this space and this time I find two people about to wage a war that would exterminate one and so weaken the other that it would retrogress and never fulfill its destiny, but decay and return to mindless dust whence it came. And I say this must not happen."*

"Who . . . what are you?" Carson didn't say it aloud, but the question formed itself in his brain.

"You would not understand completely. I am — " There was a pause as though the voice sought — in Carson's brain — for a word that wasn't there, a word he didn't know. *"I am the end of evolution of a race so old the time can not be expressed in words that have meaning to your mind. A race fused into a single entity, eternal —*

"An entity such as your primitive race might become" — again the groping for a word — *"time from now. So might the race you call, in your mind, the Outsiders. So I intervene in the battle to come, the battle between fleets so evenly matched that destruction of both races will result. One must survive. One must progress and evolve."*

"One?" thought Carson. Mine, or — ?"

"It is in my power to stop the war, to send the Outsiders back to their galaxy. But they would return, or your race would sooner or later follow them there. Only by remaining in this space and time to intervene constantly could I prevent them from destroying one another, and I cannot remain.

"So I shall intervene now. I shall destroy one fleet completely without loss to the other. One civilization shall thus survive."

Nightmare. This had to be nightmare, Carson thought. But he knew it wasn't.

It was too mad, too impossible, to be anything but real.

He didn't dare ask *the* question — *which?* But his thoughts asked it for him.

"The stronger shall survive," said the voice. *"That I can not — and would not — change. I merely intervene to make it a complete victory, not"* — groping again — *"not Pyrrhic victory to a broken race.*

"From the outskirts of the not-yet battle I plucked two individuals, you and an Outsider. I see from your mind that in your early history of nationalisms battles between champions, to decide issues between races, were not unknown.

"You and your opponent are here pitted against one another, naked and unarmed, under conditions equally unfamiliar to you both, equally unpleasant to you both. There is no time limit, for here there is no time. The survivor is the champion of his race. That race survives."

"But — " Carson's protest was too inarticulate for expression, but the voice answered it.

"It is fair. The conditions are such that the accident of physical strength will not completely decide the issue. There is a barrier. You will understand. Brain-power and courage will be more important than strength. Most especially courage, which is the will to survive."

"But while this goes on, the fleets will — "

"No, you are in another space, another time. For as long as you are here, time stands still in the universe you know. I see you wonder whether this place

*is real. It is, and it is not. As I — to your limited understanding — am and am
not real. My existence is mental and not physical. You saw me as a planet; it
could have been as a dustmote or a sun.*

"But to you this place is now real. What you suffer here will be real. And
if you die here, your death will be real. If you die, your failure will be the end
of your race. That is enough for you to know."

And then the voice was gone.

And he was alone, but not alone. For as Carson looked up, he saw that
the red thing, the red sphere of horror which he now knew was the Outsider,
was rolling toward him.

Rolling.

It seemed to have no legs or arms that he could see, no features. It
rolled across the blue sand with the fluid quickness of a drop of mercury.
And before it, in some manner he could not understand, came a paralyz-
ing wave of nauseating, retching, horrid hatred.

Carson looked about him frantically. A stone, lying in the sand a few feet
away, was the nearest thing to a weapon. It wasn't large, but it had sharp
edges, like a slab of flint. It looked a bit like blue flint.

He picked it up, and crouched to receive the attack. It was coming fast,
faster than he could run.

No time to think out how he was going to fight it, and how anyway
could he plan to battle a creature whose strength, whose characteristics,
whose method of fighting he did not know? Rolling so fast, it looked more
than ever like a perfect sphere.

Ten yards away. Five. And then it stopped.

Rather, it *was stopped*. Abruptly the near side of it flattened as though
it had run up against an invisible wall. It bounced, actually bounced back.

Then it rolled forward again, but more slowly, more cautiously. It stopped
again, at the same place. It tried again, a few yards to one side.

There was a barrier there of some sort. It clicked, then, in Carson's
mind. That thought projected into his mind by the Entity who had brought
them there: " — accident of physical strength will not completely decide
the issue. There is a barrier."

A force-field, of course. Not the Netzian Field, known to Earth science,
for that glowed and emitted a crackling sound. This one was invisible,
silent.

It was a wall that ran from side to side of the inverted hemisphere;
Carson didn't have to verify that himself. The Roller was doing that; rolling
sideways along the barrier, seeking a break in it that wasn't there.

Carson took half a dozen steps forward, his left hand groping out before
him, and then his hand touched the barrier. It felt smooth, yielding, like a
sheet of rubber rather than like glass. Warm to his touch, but no warmer
than the sand underfoot. And it was completely invisible, even at close range.

He dropped the stone and put both hands against it, pushing. It
seemed to yield, just a trifle. But no farther than that trifle, even when he
pushed with all his weight. It felt like a sheet of rubber backed up by steel.
Limited resiliency, and then firm strength.

He stood on tiptoe and reached as high as he could and the barrier was still there.

He saw the Roller coming back, having reached one side of the arena. That feeling of nausea hit Carson again, and he stepped back from the barrier as it went by. It didn't stop.

But did the barrier stop at ground level? Carson knelt down and burrowed in the sand. It was soft, light, easy to dig in. At two feet down the barrier was still there.

The Roller was coming back again. Obviously, it couldn't find a way through at either side.

There must be a way through, Carson thought. *Some* way we can get at each other, else this duel is meaningless.

But no hurry now, in finding that out. There was something to try first. The Roller was back now, and it stopped just across the barrier, only six feet away. It seemed to be studying him, although for the life of him, Carson couldn't find external evidence of sense organs on the thing. Nothing that looked like eyes or ears, or even a mouth. There was though, he saw now, a series of grooves — perhaps a dozen of them altogether, and he saw two tentacles suddenly push out from two of the grooves and dip into the sand as though testing its consistency. Tentacles about an inch in diameter and perhaps a foot and a half long.

But the tentacles were retractable into the grooves and were kept there except when in use. They were retracted when the thing rolled and seemed to have nothing to do with its method of locomotion. That, as far as Carson could judge, seemed to be accomplished by some shifting — just *how* he couldn't even imagine — of its center of gravity.

He shuddered as he looked at the thing. It was alien, utterly alien, horribly different from anything on Earth or any of the life forms found on the other solar planets. Instinctively, somehow, he knew its mind was as alien as its body.

But he had to try. If it had no telepathic powers at all, the attempt was foredoomed to failure, yet he thought it had such powers. There had, at any rate, been a projection of something that was not physical at the time a few minutes ago when it had first started for him. An almost tangible wave of hatred.

If it could project that, perhaps it could read his mind as well, sufficiently for his purpose.

Deliberately, Carson picked up the rock that had been his only weapon, then tossed it down again in a gesture of relinquishment and raised his empty hands, palms up, before him.

He spoke aloud, knowing that although the words would be meaningless to the creature before him, speaking them would focus his own thoughts more completely upon the message.

"Can we not have peace between us?" he said, his voice sounding strange in the utter stillness. "The Entity who brought us here has told us what must happen if our races fight — extinction of one and weakening and retrogression of the other. The battle between them, said the Entity, depends upon what we do here. Why can not we agree to an external peace — your race to its galaxy, we to ours?"

Carson blanked out his mind to receive a reply.

It came, and it staggered him back, physically. He actually recoiled several steps in sheer horror at the depth and intensity of the hatred and lust-to-kill of the red images that had been projected at him. Not as articulate words — as had come to him the thoughts of the Entity — but as wave upon wave of fierce emotion.

For a moment that seemed an eternity he had to struggle against the mental impact of that hatred, fight to clear his mind of it and drive out the alien thoughts to which he had given admittance by blanking out his own thoughts. He wanted to retch.

Slowly his mind cleared as, slowly, the mind of a man wakening from nightmare clears away the fear-fabric of which the dream was woven. He was breathing hard and he felt weaker, but he could think.

He stood studying the Roller. It had been motionless during the mental duel it had so nearly won. Now it rolled a few feet to one side, to the nearest of the blue bushes. Three tentacles whipped out of their grooves and began to investigate the bush.

"O.K.," Carson said, "so it's war then." He managed a wry grin. "If I got your answer straight, peace doesn't appeal to you," And, because he was, after all, a quiet young man and couldn't resist the impulse to be dramatic, he added. "To the death!"

But his voice, in that utter silence, sounded very silly, even to himself. It came to him, then, that this *was* to the death. Not only his own death or that of the red spherical thing which he now thought of as the Roller, but death to the entire race of one or the other of them. The end of the human race, if he failed.

It made him suddenly very humble and very afraid to think that. More than to think it, to *know* it. Somehow, with a knowledge that was above even faith, he knew that the Entity who had arranged this duel had told the truth about its intentions and its powers. It wasn't kidding.

The future of humanity depended upon *him*. It was an awful thing to realize, and he wrenched his mind away from it. He had to concentrate on the situation at hand.

There had to be some way of getting through the barrier, or of killing through the barrier.

Mentally? He hoped that wasn't all, for the Roller obviously had stronger telepathic powers than the primitive, undeveloped ones of the human race. Or did it?

He had been able to drive the thoughts of the Roller out of his own mind; could it drive out his? If its ability to project were stronger, might not its receptivity mechanism be more vulnerable?

He stared at it and endeavored to concentrate and focus all his thoughts upon it.

"*Die*," he thought. "*You are going to die. You are dying. You are —*"

He tried variations on it, and mental pictures. Sweat stood out on his forehead and he found himself trembling with the intensity of the effort. But the Roller went ahead with its investigation of the bush, as utterly unaffected as though Carson had been reciting the multiplication table.

So *that* was no good.

He felt a bit weak and dizzy from the heat and his strenuous effort at concentration. He sat down on the blue sand to rest and gave his full attention to watching and studying the Roller. By close study, perhaps, he could judge its strength and detect its weaknesses, learn things that would be valuable to know when and if they should come to grips.

It was breaking off twigs. Carson watched carefully, trying to judge just how hard it worked to do that. Later, he thought, he could find a similar bush on his own side, break off twigs of equal thickness himself, and gain a comparison of physical strength between his own arms and hands and those tentacles.

The twigs broke off hard; the Roller was having to struggle with each one, he saw. Each tentacle, he saw, bifurcated at the tip into two fingers, each tipped by a nail or claw. The claws didn't seem to be particularly long or dangerous. No more so than his own fingernails, if they were let to grow a bit.

No, on the whole, it didn't look too tough to handle physically. Unless, of course, that bush was made of pretty tough stuff. Carson looked around him and, yes, right within reach was another bush of identical type.

He reached over and snapped off a twig. It was brittle, easy to break. Of course, the Roller might have been faking deliberately but he didn't think so.

On the other hand, where was it vulnerable? Just how would he go about killing it, if he got the chance? He went back to studying it. The outer hide looked pretty tough. He'd need a sharp weapon of some sort. He picked up the piece of rock again. It was about twelve inches long, narrow, and fairly sharp on one end. If it chipped like flint, he could make a serviceable knife out of it.

The Roller was continuing its investigations of the bushes. It rolled again, to the nearest one of another type. A little blue lizard, many-legged like the one Carson had seen on his side of the barrier, darted out from under the bush.

A tentacle of the Roller lashed out and caught it, picked it up. Another tentacle whipped over and began to pull legs off the lizard, as coldly and calmly as it had pulled twigs off the bush. The creature struggled frantically and emitted a shrill squealing sound that was the first sound Carson had heard here other than the sound of his own voice.

Carson shuddered and wanted to turn his eyes away. But he made himself continue to watch; anything he could learn about his opponent might prove valuable. Even this knowledge of its unnecessary cruelty. Particularly, he thought with a sudden vicious surge of emotion, this knowledge of its unnecessary cruelty. It would make it a pleasure to kill the thing, if and when the chance came.

He steeled himself to watch the dismembering of the lizard, for that very reason.

But he felt glad when, with half its legs gone, the lizard quit squealing and struggling and lay limp and dead in the Roller's grasp.

It didn't continue with the rest of the legs. Contemptuously it tossed the dead lizard away from it, in Carson's direction. It arced through the air between them and landed at his feet.

It had come through the barrier! The barrier wasn't there any more!

Carson was on his feet in a flash, the knife gripped tightly in his hand and leaped forward. He'd settle this thing here and now! With the barrier gone —

But it wasn't gone. He found that out the hard way, running head on into it and nearly knocking himself silly. He bounced back, and fell.

And as he sat up, shaking his head to clear it, he saw something coming through the air toward him, and to duck it, he threw himself flat again on the sand, and to one side. He got his body out of the way, but there was a sudden sharp pain in the calf of his left leg.

He rolled backward, ignoring the pain, and scrambled to his feet. It was a rock, he saw now, that had struck him. And the Roller was picking up another one now, swinging it back gripped between two tentacles, getting ready to throw again.

It sailed through the air toward him, but he was easily able to step out of its way. The Roller, apparently, could throw straight, but not hard nor far. The first rock had struck him only because he had been sitting down and had not seen it coming until it was almost upon him.

Even as he stepped aside from that weak second throw, Carson drew back his right arm and let fly with the rock that was still in his hand. If missiles, he thought with sudden elation, can cross the barrier, then two can play at the game of throwing them. And the good right arm of an Earthman —

He couldn't miss a three-foot sphere at only four-yard range, and he didn't miss. The rock whizzed straight, and with a speed several times that of the missiles the Roller had thrown. It hit dead center, but it hit flat, unfortunately, instead of point first.

But it hit with a resounding thump, and obviously it hurt. The Roller had been reaching for another rock, but it changed its mind and got out of there instead. By the time Carson could pick up and throw another rock, the Roller was forty yards back from the barrier and going strong.

His second throw missed by feet, and his third throw was short. The Roller was back out of range — at least out of range of a missile heavy enough to be damaging.

Carson grinned. That round had been his. Except —

He quit grinning as he bent over to examine the calf of his leg. A jagged edge of the stone had made a pretty deep cut, several inches long. It was bleeding pretty freely, but he didn't think it had gone deep enough to hit an artery. If it stopped bleeding of its own accord, well and good. If not, he was in for trouble.

Finding out one thing, though, took precedence over that cut. The nature of the barrier.

He went forward to it again, this time groping with his hands before him. He found it; then holding one hand against it, he tossed a handful of sand at it with the other hand. The sand went right through. His hand didn't.

Organic matter versus inorganic? No, because the dead lizard had gone through it, and a lizard, alive or dead, was certainly organic. Plant life? He broke off a twig and poked it at the barrier. The twig went through, with no resistance, but when his fingers gripping the twig came to the barrier, they were stopped.

He couldn't get through it, nor could the Roller. But rocks and sand and a dead lizard —

How about a live lizard? He went hunting, under bushes, until he found one, and caught it. He tossed it gently against the barrier and it bounced back and scurried away across the blue sand.

That gave him the answer, in so far as he could determine it now. The screen was a barrier to living things. Dead or inorganic matter could cross it.

That off his mind, Carson looked at his injured leg again. The bleeding was lessening, which meant he wouldn't need to worry about making a tourniquet. But he should find some water, if any was available, to clean the wound.

Water — the thought of it made him realize that he was getting awfully thirsty. He'd *have* to find water, in case this contest turned out to be a protracted one.

Limping slightly now, he started off to make a full circuit of his half of the arena. Guiding himself with one hand along the barrier, he walked to his right until he came to the curving sidewall. It was visible, a dull blue-gray at close range, and the surface of it felt just like the central barrier.

He experimented by tossing a handful of sand at it, and the sand reached the wall and disappeared as it went through. The hemispherical shell was a force-field, too. But an opaque one, instead of transparent like the barrier.

He followed it around until he came back to the barrier, and walked back along the barrier to the point from which he'd started.

No sign of water.

Worried now, he started a series of zigzags back and forth between the barrier and the wall, covering the intervening space thoroughly.

No water. Blue sand, blue bushes, and intolerable heat. Nothing else.

It must be his imagination, he told himself angrily, that he was suffering *that* much from thirst. How long had he been here? Of course, no time at all, according to his own spacetime frame. The Entity had told him time stood still out there, while he was here. But his body processes went on here, just the same. And according to his body's reckoning, how long had he been here? Three or four hours, perhaps. Certainly not long enough to be suffering seriously from thirst.

But he was suffering from it; his throat dry and parched. Probably the intense heat was the cause. It was *hot*! A hundred and thirty Fahrenheit, at a guess. A dry, still heat without the slightest movement of air.

He was limping rather badly, and utterly fagged out when he'd finished the futile exploration of his domain.

He stared across at the motionless Roller and hoped it was as miserable as he was. And quite possibly it wasn't enjoying this, either. The Entity had said the conditions here were equally unfamiliar and equally uncomfortable for both of them. Maybe the Roller came from a planet where two-hundred-degree heat was the norm. Maybe it was freezing while he was roasting.

Maybe the air was as much too thick for it as it was too thin for him. For the exertion of his explorations had left him panting. The atmosphere here, he realized now, was not much thicker than that on Mars.

No water.

That meant a deadline, for him at any rate. Unless he could find a way to cross that barrier or to kill his enemy from this side of it, thirst would kill him, eventually.

It gave him a feeling of desperate urgency. He *must* hurry.

But he made himself sit down a moment to rest, to think.

What was there to do? Nothing, and yet so many things. The several varieties of bushes, for example. They didn't look promising, but he'd have to examine them for possibilities. And his leg — he'd have to do something about that, even without water to clean it. Gather ammunition in the form of rocks. Find a rock that would make a good knife.

His leg hurt rather badly now, and he decided that came first. One type of bush had leaves — or things rather similar to leaves. He pulled off a handful of them and decided, after examination, to take a chance on them. He used them to clean off the sand and dirt and caked blood, then made a pad of fresh leaves and tied it over the wound with tendrils from the same bush.

The tendrils proved unexpectedly tough and strong. They were slender, and soft and pliable, yet he couldn't break them at all. He had to saw them off the bush with the sharp edge of a piece of the blue flint. Some of the thicker ones were over a foot long, and he filed away in his memory, for future reference, the fact that a bunch of the thick ones, tied together, would make a pretty serviceable rope. Maybe he'd be able to think of a use for rope.

Next he made himself a knife. The blue flint *did* chip. From a foot-long splinter of it, he fashioned himself a crude but lethal weapon. And of tendrils from the bush, he made himself a rope-belt through which he could thrust the flint knife, to keep it with him all the time and yet have his hands free.

He went back to studying the bushes. There were three other types. One was leafless, dry, brittle, rather like a dried tumbleweed. Another was of soft, crumbly wood, almost like punk. It looked and felt as though it would make excellent tinder for a fire. The third type was the most nearly woodlike. It had fragile leaves that wilted at a touch, but the stalks, although short, were straight and strong.

It was horribly, unbearably hot.

He limped up to the barrier, felt to make sure that it was still there. It was.

He stood watching the Roller for a while. It was keeping a safe distance back from the barrier, out of effective stone-throwing range. It was moving around back there, doing something. He couldn't tell what it was doing.

Once it stopped moving, came a little closer, and seemed to concentrate its attention on him. Again Carson had to fight off a wave of nausea. He threw a stone at it and the Roller retreated and went back to whatever it had been doing before.

At least he could make it keep its distance.

And, he thought bitterly, a devil of a lot of good *that* did him. Just the same, he spent the next hour or two gathering stones of suitable size for throwing, and making several neat piles of them, near his side of the barrier.

His throat burned now. It was difficult for him to think about anything except water.

But he *had* to think about other things. About getting through that barrier, under or over it, getting *at* that red sphere and killing it before this place of heat and thirst killed him first.

The barrier went to the wall upon either side, but how high and how far under the sand?

For just a moment, Carson's mind was too fuzzy to think out how he could find out either of those things. Idly, sitting there in the hot sand — and he didn't remember sitting down — he watched a blue lizard crawl from the shelter of one bush to the shelter of another.

From under the second bush, it looked out at him.

Carson grinned at it. Maybe he was getting a bit punch-drunk, because he remembered suddenly the old story of the desert-colonists on Mars, taken from an older desert story of Earth — "Pretty soon you get so lonesome you find yourself talking to the lizards, and then not so long after that you find the lizards talking back to you — "

He should have been concentrating, of course, on how to kill the Roller, but instead he grinned at the lizard and said, "Hello, there."

The lizard took a few steps toward him. "Hello," it said.

Carson was stunned for a moment, and then he put back his head and roared with laughter. It didn't hurt his throat to do so, either; he hadn't been *that* thirsty.

Why not? Why should the Entity who thought up this nightmare of a place not have a sense of humor, along with the other powers he had? Talking lizards, equipped to talk back in my own language, if I talk to them — It's a nice touch.

He grinned at the lizard and said, "Come on over." But the lizard turned and ran away, scurrying from bush to bush until it was out of sight.

He was thirsty again.

And he had to *do* something. He couldn't win this contest by sitting here sweating and feeling miserable. He had to *do* something. But what?

Get through the barrier. But he couldn't get through it, or over it. But was he certain he couldn't get under it? And come to think of it, didn't one sometimes find water by digging? Two birds with one stone —

Painfully now, Carson limped up to the barrier and started digging, scooping up sand a double handful at a time. It was slow, hard work because the sand ran in at the edges and the deeper he got the bigger in diameter the hole had to be. How many hours it took him, he didn't know, but he hit bedrock four feet down. Dry bedrock; no sign of water.

And the force-field of the barrier went down clear to the bedrock. No dice. No water. Nothing.

He crawled out of the hole and lay there panting, and then raised his head to look across and see what the Roller was doing. It must be doing something back there.

It was. It was making something out of wood from the bushes, tied together with tendrils. A queerly shaped framework about four feet high and roughly square. To see it better, Carson climbed up onto the mound of sand he had excavated from the hole, and stood there staring.

There were two long levers sticking out of the back of it, one with a cup-shaped affair on the end of it. Seemed to be some sort of a catapult, Carson thought.

Sure enough, the Roller was lifting a sizable rock into the cup-shaped outfit. One of his tentacles moved the other lever up and down for awhile, and then he turned the machine slightly as though aiming it and the lever with the stone flew up and forward.

The stone raced several yards over Carson's head, so far away that he didn't have to duck, but he judged the distance it had traveled, and whistled softly. He couldn't throw a rock that weight more than half that distance. And even retreating to the rear of his domain wouldn't put him out of range of that machine, if the Roller shoved it forward almost to the barrier.

Another rock whizzed over. Not quite so far away this time.

That thing could be dangerous, he decided. Maybe he'd better do something about it.

Moving from side to side along the barrier, so the catapult couldn't bracket him, he whaled a dozen rocks at it. But that wasn't going to be any good, he saw. They had to be light rocks, or he couldn't throw them that far. If they hit the framework, they bounced off harmlessly. And the Roller had no difficulty, at that distance, in moving aside from those that came near it.

Besides, his arm was tiring badly. He ached all over from sheer weariness. If he could only rest awhile without having to duck rocks from that catapult at regular intervals of maybe thirty seconds each —

He stumbled back to the rear of the arena. Then he saw even that wasn't any good. The rocks reached back there, too, only there were longer intervals between them, as though it took longer to wind up the mechanism, whatever it was, of the catapult.

Wearily he dragged himself back to the barrier again. Several times he fell and could barely rise to his feet to go on. He was, he knew, near the limit of his endurance. Yet he didn't dare stop moving now, until and unless he could put that catapult out of action. If he fell asleep, he'd never wake up.

One of the stones from it gave him the first glimmer of an idea. It struck upon one of the piles of stones he'd gathered together near the barrier to use as ammunition, and it struck sparks.

Sparks. Fire. Primitive man had made fire by striking sparks, and with some of those dry crumbly bushes as tinder —

Luckily, a bush of that type was near him. He broke it off, took it over to a pile of stones, then patiently hit one stone against another, until a spark touched the punklike wood of the bush. It went up in flames so fast that it singed his eyebrows and was burned to an ash within seconds.

But he had the idea now, and within minutes he had a little fire going in the lee of the mound of sand he'd made digging the hole an hour or two ago. Tinder bushes had started it, and other bushes which burned, but more slowly, kept it a steady flame.

The tough wirelike tendrils didn't burn readily; that made the fire-bombs easy to make and throw. A bundle of faggots tied about a small stone to give it weight and a loop of the tendril to swing it by.

He made half a dozen of them before he lighted and threw the first. It went wide, and the Roller started a quick retreat, pulling the catapult after him. But Carson had the others ready and threw them in rapid succession. The fourth wedged in the catapult's framework, and did the trick. The Roller tried desperately to put out the spreading blaze by throwing sand, but its clawed tentacles would take only a spoonful at a time and his efforts were ineffectual. The catapult burned.

The Roller moved safely away from the fire and seemed to concentrate its attention on Carson and again he felt that wave of hatred and nausea. But more weakly; either the Roller itself was weakening or Carson had learned how to protect himself against the mental attack.

He thumbed his nose at it and then sent it scuttling back to safety by throwing a stone. The Roller went clear to the back of its half of the arena and started pulling up bushes again. Probably it was going to make another catapult.

Carson verified — for the hundredth time — that the barrier was still operating, and then found himself sitting in the sand beside it because he was suddenly too weak to stand up.

His leg throbbed steadily now and the pangs of thirst were severe. But those things paled beside the utter physical exhaustion that gripped his entire body.

And the heat.

Hell must be like this, he thought. The hell that the ancients had believed in. He fought to stay awake, and yet staying awake seemed futile, for there was nothing he could do. Nothing, while the barrier remained impregnable and the Roller stayed back out of range.

But there must be *something*. He tried to remember things he had read in books of archaeology about the methods of fighting used back in the days before metal and plastic. The stone missile, that had come first, he thought. Well, that he already had.

The only improvement on it would be a catapult, such as the Roller had made. But he'd never be able to make one, with the tiny bits of wood available from the bushes — no single piece longer than a foot or so. Certainly he could figure out a mechanism for one, but he didn't have the endurance left for a task that would take days.

Days? But the Roller had made one. Had they been here days already? Then he remembered that the Roller had many tentacles to work with and undoubtedly could do such work faster than he.

And besides, a catapult wouldn't decide the issue. He had to do better than that.

Bow and arrow? No; he had tried archery once and knew his own ineptness with a bow. Even with a modern sportsman's durasteel weapon, made for accuracy. With such a crude, pieced-together outfit as he could make here, he doubted if he could shoot as far as he could throw a rock, and knew he couldn't shoot as straight.

Spear? Well, he *could* make that. It would be useless as a throwing weapon at any distance, but would be a handy thing at close range, if he ever got to close range.

And making one would give him something to do. Help keep his mind from wandering, as it was beginning to do. Sometimes now, he had to concentrate awhile before he could remember why he was here, why he had to kill the Roller.

Luckily he was still beside one of the piles of stones. He sorted through it until he found one shaped roughly like a spearhead. With a smaller stone he began to chip it into shape, fashioning sharp shoulders on the sides so that if it penetrated it would not pull out again.

Like a harpoon? There was something in that idea, he thought. A harpoon was better than a spear, maybe, for this crazy contest. If he could once get it into the Roller, and had a rope on it, he could pull the Roller up against the barrier and the stone blade of his knife would reach through that barrier, even if his hands wouldn't.

The shaft was harder to make than the head. But by splitting and joining the main stems of four of the bushes, and wrapping the joints with the tough but thin tendrils, he got a strong shaft about four feet long, and tied the stone head in a notch cut in the end.

It was crude, but strong.

And the rope. With the thin tough tendrils he made himself twenty feet of line. It was light and didn't look strong, but he knew it would hold his weight and some to spare. He tied one end of it to the shaft of the harpoon and the other end about his right wrist. At least, if he threw his harpoon across the barrier, he'd be able to pull it back if he missed.

Then when he had tied the last knot and there was nothing more he could do, the heat and the weariness and the pain in his leg and the dreadful thirst were suddenly a thousand times worse than they had been before.

He tried to stand up, to see what the Roller was doing now, and found he couldn't get to his feet. On the third try, he got as far as his knees and then fell flat again.

"I've got to sleep," he thought. "If a showdown came now, I'd be helpless. He could come up here and kill me, if he knew. I've got to regain some strength."

Slowly, painfully, he crawled back away from the barrier. Ten yards, twenty —

The jar of something thudding against the sand near him waked him from a confused and horrible dream to a more confused and more horrible reality, and he opened his eyes again to blue radiance over blue sand.

How long had he slept? A minute? A day?

Another stone thudded nearer and threw sand on him. He got his arms under him and sat up. He turned around and saw the Roller twenty yards away, at the barrier.

It rolled away hastily as he sat up, not stopping until it was as far away as it could get.

He'd fallen asleep too soon, he realized, while he was still in range of the Roller's throwing ability. Seeing him lying motionless, it had dared come up to the barrier to throw at him. Luckily, it didn't realize how weak he was, or it could have stayed there and kept on throwing stones.

Had he slept long? He didn't think so, because he felt just as he had before. Not rested at all, no thirstier, no different. Probably he'd been there only a few minutes.

He started crawling again, this time forcing himself to keep going until he was as far as he could go, until the colorless, opaque wall of the arena's outer shell was only a yard away.

Then things slipped away again —

When he awoke, nothing about him was changed, but this time he knew that he had slept a long time.

The first thing he became aware of was the inside of his mouth; it was dry, caked. His tongue was swollen.

Something was wrong, he knew, as he returned slowly to full awareness. He felt less tired, the stage of utter exhaustion had passed. The sleep had taken care of that.

But there was pain, agonizing pain. It wasn't until he tried to move that he knew that it came from his leg.

He raised his head and looked down at it. It was swollen terribly below the knee and the swelling showed even halfway up his thigh. The plant tendrils he had used to tie on the protective pad of leaves now cut deeply into the swollen flesh.

To get his knife under that imbedded lashing would have been impossible. Fortunately, the final knot was over the shin bone, in front, where the vine cut in less deeply than elsewhere. He was able, after an agonizing effort, to untie the knot.

A look under the pad of leaves told him the worst. Infection and blood poisoning, both pretty bad and getting worse.

And without drugs, without cloth, without even *water*, there wasn't a thing he could do about it.

Not a thing, except *die*, when the poison had spread through his system. He knew it was hopeless, then, and that he'd lost.

And with him, humanity. When he died here, out there in the universe he knew, all his friends, everybody, would die too. And Earth and the colonized planets would be the home of the red, rolling, alien Outsiders. Creatures out of nightmare, things without a human attribute, who picked lizards apart for the fun of it.

It was the thought of that which gave him courage to start crawling, almost blindly in pain, toward the barrier again. Not crawling on hands and knees this time, but pulling himself along only by his arms and hands.

A chance in a million, that maybe he'd have strength left, when he got there, to throw his harpoon-spear just *once*, and with deadly effect, if — on another chance in a million — the Roller would come up to the barrier. Or if the barrier was gone, now.

It took him years, it seemed, to get there.

The barrier wasn't gone. It was as impassable as when he'd first felt it.

And the Roller wasn't at the barrier. By raising up on his elbows, he could see it at the back of its part of the arena, working on a wooden framework that was a half-completed duplicate of the catapult he'd destroyed.

It was moving slowly now. Undoubtedly it had weakened, too.

But Carson doubted that it would ever need that second catapult. He'd be dead, he thought, before it was finished.

If he could attract it to the barrier, now, while he was still alive — He waved an arm and tried to shout, but his parched throat would make no sound.

Or if he could get through the barrier —

His mind must have slipped for a moment, for he found himself beating his fists against the barrier in futile rage, and made himself stop.

He closed his eyes, tried to make himself calm.

"Hello," said the voice.

It was a small, thin voice. It sounded like —

He opened his eyes and turned his head. It *was* the lizard.

"Go away," Carson wanted to say. "Go away, you're not really there, or you're there but not really talking. I'm imagining things again."

But he couldn't talk; his throat and tongue were past all speech with the dryness. He closed his eyes again.

"Hurt," said the voice. "Kill. Hurt — kill. Come."

He opened his eyes again. The blue ten-legged lizard was still there. It ran a little way along the barrier, came back, started off again, and came back.

"Hurt," it said. "Kill. Come."

Again it started off, and came back. Obviously it wanted Carson to follow it along the barrier.

He closed his eyes again. The voice kept on. The same three meaningless words. Each time he opened his eyes, it ran off and came back.

"Hurt. Kill. Come."

Carson groaned. There would be no peace unless he followed the blasted thing. Like it wanted him to.

He followed it, crawling. Another sound, a high-pitched squealing, came to his ears and grew louder.

There was something lying in the sand, writhing, squealing. Something small, blue, that looked like a lizard and yet didn't —

Then he saw what it was — the lizard whose legs the Roller had pulled off, so long ago. But it wasn't dead; it had come back to life and was wriggling and screaming in agony.

"Hurt," said the other lizard. "Hurt. Kill. Kill."

Carson understood. He took the flint knife from his belt and killed the tortured creature. The live lizard scurried off quickly.

Carson turned back to the barrier. He leaned his hands and head against it and watched the Roller, far back, working on the new catapult.

"I could get that far," he thought, "if I could get through. If I could get through, I might win yet. It looks weak, too. I might — "

And then there was another reaction of black hopelessness, when pain snapped his will and he wished that he were dead. He envied the lizard he'd just killed. It didn't have to live on and suffer. And he did. It would be hours, it might be days, before the blood poisoning killed him.

If only he could use that knife on himself —

But he knew he wouldn't. As long as he was alive, there was the millionth chance —

He was straining, pushing on the barrier with the flat of his hands, and he noticed his arms, how thin and scrawny they were now. He must really have been here a long time, for days, to get as thin as that.

How much longer now, before he died? How much more heat and thirst and pain could flesh stand?

For a little while he was almost hysterical again, and then came a time of deep calm, and a thought that was startling.

The lizard he had just killed. *It had crossed the barrier, still alive.* It had come from the Roller's side; the Roller had pulled off its legs and then tossed it contemptuously at him and it had come through the barrier, he'd thought, because the lizard was dead.

But it hadn't been dead; it had been unconscious.

A live lizard couldn't go through the barrier, but an unconscious one could. The barrier was not a barrier, then, to living flesh, but to conscious flesh. It was a *mental* projection, a *mental* hazard.

And with that thought, Carson started crawling along the barrier to make his last desperate gamble. A hope so forlorn that only a dying man would have dared try it.

No use weighing the odds of success. Not when, if he didn't try it, those odds were infinitely to zero.

He crawled along the barrier to the dune of sand, about four feet high, which he'd scooped out in trying — how many days ago? — to dig under the barrier or to reach water.

That mound was right at the barrier, its farther slope half on one side of the barrier, half on the other.

Taking with him a rock from the pile nearby, he climbed up to the top of the dune and over the top, and lay there against the barrier, his weight leaning against it so that if the barrier were taken away he'd roll on down the short slope, into the enemy territory.

He checked to be sure that the knife was safely in his rope belt, that the harpoon was in the crook of his left arm and that the twenty-foot rope was fastened to it and to his wrist.

Then with his right hand he raised the rock with which he would hit himself on the head. Luck would have to be with him on that blow; it would have to be hard enough to knock him out, but not hard enough to knock him out for long.

He had a hunch that the Roller was watching him, and would see him roll down through the barrier, and come to investigate. It would think he was dead, he hoped — he thought it had probably drawn the same deduction about the nature of the barrier that he had drawn. But it would come cautiously. He would have a little time —

He struck.

Pain brought him back to consciousness. A sudden, sharp pain in his hip that was different from the throbbing pain in his head and the throbbing pain in his leg.

But he had, thinking things out before he had struck himself, anticipated that very pain, even hoped for it, and had steeled himself against awakening with a sudden movement.

He lay still, but opened his eyes just a slit, and saw that he had guessed rightly. The Roller was coming closer. It was twenty feet away and the pain that had awakened him was the stone it had tossed to see whether he was alive or dead.

He lay still. It came closer, fifteen feet away, and stopped again. Carson scarcely breathed.

As nearly as possible, he was keeping his mind a blank, lest its telepathic ability detect consciousness in him. And with his mind blanked out that way, the impact of its thoughts upon his mind was nearly soul-shattering.

He felt sheer horror at the utter *alienness*, the *differentness* of those thoughts. Things that he felt but could not understand and could never express, because no terrestrial language had words, no terrestrial mind had images to fit them. The mind of a spider, he thought, or the mind of a praying mantis or a Martian sand-serpent, raised to intelligence and put in telepathic rapport with human minds, would be a homely familiar thing, compared to this.

He understood now that the Entity had been right: Man or Roller, and the universe was not a place that could hold them both. Farther apart than god and devil, there could never be even a balance between them.

Closer. Carson waited until it was only feet away, until its clawed tentacles reached out —

Oblivious to agony now, he sat up, raised and flung the harpoon with all the strength that remained to him. Or he thought it was all; sudden final strength flooded through him, along with a sudden forgetfulness of pain as definite as a nerve block.

As the Roller, deeply stabbed by the harpoon, rolled away, Carson tried to get to his feet to run after it. He couldn't do that; he fell, but kept crawling.

It reached the end of the rope, and he was jerked forward by the pull of his wrist. It dragged him a few feet and then stopped. Carson kept on going, pulling himself toward it hand over hand along the rope.

It stopped there, writhing tentacles trying in vain to pull out the harpoon. It seemed to shudder and quiver, and then it must have realized that it couldn't get away, for it rolled back toward him, clawed tentacles reaching out.

Stone knife in hand, he met it. He stabbed, again and again, while those horrid claws ripped skin and flesh and muscle from his body.

He stabbed and slashed, and at last it was still.

A bell was ringing, and it took him a while after he'd opened his eyes to tell where he was and what it was. He was strapped into the seat of his scouter, and the visiplate before him showed only empty space. No Outsider ship and no impossible planet.

The bell was the communications plate signal; someone wanted him to switch power into the receiver. Purely reflex action enabled him to reach forward and throw the lever.

The face of Brander, captain of the *Magellan*, mother-ship of his group of scouters, flashed onto the screen. His face was pale and his black eyes glowed with excitement.

"*Magellan* to Carson," he snapped. "Come on in. The fight's over. We've won!"

The screen went blank; Brander would be signaling the other scouters of his command.

Slowly, Carson set the controls for the return. Slowly, unbelievingly, he unstrapped himself from the seat and went back to get a drink at the cold-water tank. For some reason, he was unbelievably thirsty. He drank six glasses.

He leaned there against the wall, trying to think.

Had it happened? He was in good health, sound, uninjured. His thirst had been mental rather than physical; his throat hadn't been dry. His leg —

He pulled up his trouser leg and looked at the calf. There was a long white scar there, but a perfectly healed scar. It hadn't been there before. He zipped open the front of his shirt and saw that his chest and abdomen was criss-crossed with tiny, almost unnoticeable, perfectly healed scars.

It *had* happened.

The scouter, under automatic control, was already entering the hatch of the mother-ship. The grapples pulled it into its individual lock, and a moment later a buzzer indicated that the lock was air-filled. Carson opened the hatch and stepped outside, went through the double door of the lock.

He went right to Brander's office, went in, and salute

Brander still looked dizzily dazed. "Hi, Carson," he
missed! What a show!"

"What happened, sir?"

"Don't know, exactly. We fired one salvo, and their whole fleet went
up in dust! Whatever it was jumped from ship to ship in a flash, even the
ones we hadn't aimed at and that were out of range! The whole fleet dis-
integrated before our eyes, and we didn't get the paint of a single ship
scratched!

"We can't even claim credit for it. Must have been some unstable component in the metal they used, and our sighting shot just set it off. Man,
oh man, too bad you missed all the excitement."

Carson managed to grin. It was a sickly ghost of a grin, for it would be
days before he'd be over the mental impact of his experience, but the captain wasn't watching, and didn't notice.

"Yes, sir," he said. Common sense, more than modesty, told him he'd
be branded forever as the worst liar in space if he ever said any more than
that. "Yes, sir, too bad I missed all the excitement."

Ray Bradbury

Mars Is Heaven!

(1948)

Ray Bradbury (b. 1920) is one of the best-known and most-loved American sf
writers. Bradbury was born in Illinois and spent part of his childhood in Arizona
before moving to Los Angeles in 1934, where he has lived ever since. Bradbury,
who never attended college, had a great love of reading and knew from an
early age that he wanted to be a writer. He began his publishing career in
fanzines and went on to become one of the first sf writers to establish a successful reputation in the mainstream literary market. Bradbury's best-known
works include *The Martian Chronicles* (1950), a collection of linked stories that
made his reputation, and the dystopic novel *Fahrenheit 451* (1953). Other
important works include *Something Wicked This Way Comes* (1962) and several
volumes of collected stories, including *The Illustrated Man* (1951) and *Dandelion
Wine* (1957). Bradbury was honored with a World Fantasy lifetime achievement
award in 1977 and a Nebula Grand Master Award in 1989. More recently, his
accomplishments have been recognized by the National Book Foundation and
by the Pulitzer Prize Board, which issued a special citation in 2007 in appreciation of his work. Always a disciplined and prolific writer, Bradbury even now
continues to write every day.

Bradbury, whose writing owes as much to the fantasy and horror genres
as to science fiction, specializes in eerie stories of great emotional depth. His

rose style is lyrical and suggestive, with a dreamlike quality that is closer to the power of myth than to psychological realism. In this story (which appears in slightly altered form as "The Third Expedition" in *The Martian Chronicles*), human astronauts see in Mars the apparent fulfillment of all their fantasies of home. The environment they encounter is not merely familiar but an idealized version of childhood memories. The tension between this comforting, nostalgic vision and the more ominous forebodings of deception create a highly effective suspense. With its explorations of trust and doubt, belief and betrayal, the familiar and the strange, this story may profitably be read against Freud's essay "The Uncanny," included in Chapter 2 of this volume.

The suggestive but ambiguous ending is particularly haunting. Why do the Martians choose to perform this final ritual for their human guests? There are many possible interpretations; Bradbury characteristically withholds easy answers to these questions, leaving the reader to speculate.

The ship came down from space. It came from the stars and the black velocities, and the shining movements, and the silent gulfs of space. It was a new ship; it had fire in its body and men in its metal cells, and it moved with a clean silence, fiery and warm. In it were seventeen men, including a captain. The crowd at the Ohio field had shouted and waved their hands up into the sunlight, and the rocket had bloomed out great flowers of heat and color and run away into space on the *third* voyage to Mars!

Now it was decelerating with metal efficiency in the upper Martian atmospheres. It was still a thing of beauty and strength. It had moved in the midnight waters of space like a pale sea leviathan; it had passed the ancient moon and thrown itself onward into one nothingness following another. The men within it had been battered, thrown about, sickened, made well again, each in his turn. One man had died, but now the remaining sixteen, with their eyes clear in their heads and their faces pressed to the thick glass ports, watched Mars swing up under them.

"Mars! Mars! Good old Mars, here we are!" cried Navigator Lustig.

"Good old Mars!" said Samuel Hinkston, archaeologist.

Well," said Captain John Black.

The ship landed softly on a lawn of green grass. Outside, upon the lawn, stood an iron deer. Further up the lawn, a tall brown Victorian house sat in the quiet sunlight, all covered with scrolls and rococo, its windows made of blue and pink and yellow and green colored glass. Upon the porch were hairy geraniums and an old swing which was hooked into the porch ceiling and which now swung back and forth, back and forth, in a little breeze. At the top of the house was a cupola with diamond, leaded-glass windows, and a dunce-cap roof! Through the front window you could see an ancient piano with yellow keys and a piece of music titled *Beautiful Ohio* sitting on the music rest.

Around the rocket in four directions spread the little town, green and motionless in the Martian spring. There were white houses and red brick ones,

"I'm willing to wait a moment," said Captain John Black.

"It may be, sir, that we are looking upon a phenomenon that, for the first time, would absolutely prove the existence of a God, sir."

"There are many people who are of good faith without such proof, Mr. Hinkston."

"I'm one myself, sir. But certainly a thing like this, out there," said Hinkston, "could not occur without divine intervention, sir. It fills me with such terror and elation I don't know whether to laugh or cry, sir."

"Do neither, then, until we know what we're up against."

"Up against, sir?" inquired Lustig. "I see that we're up against nothing. It's a good quiet, green town, much like the one I was born in, and I like the looks of it."

"When were you born, Lustig?"

"In 1910, sir."

"That makes you fifty years old, now, doesn't it?"

"This being 1960, yes, sir."

"And you, Hinkston?"

"1920, sir. In Illinois. And this looks swell to me, sir."

"This couldn't be Heaven," said the captain, ironically. "Though, I must admit, it looks peaceful and cool, and pretty much like Green Bluff, where I was born, in 1915." He looked at the chemist. "The air's all right, is it?"

"Yes, sir."

"Well, then, tell you what we'll do. Lustig, you and Hinkston and I will fetch ourselves out to look this town over. The other 14 men will stay aboard ship. If anything untoward happens, lift the ship and get the hell out, do you hear what I say, Craner?"

"Yes, sir. The hell out we'll go, sir. Leaving *you*?"

"A loss of three men's better than a whole ship. If something bad happens get back to Earth and warn the next Rocket, that's Lingle's Rocket, I think, which will be completed and ready to take off some time around next Christmas, what he has to meet up with. If there's something hostile about Mars we certainly want the next expedition to be well armed."

"So are we, sir. We've got a regular arsenal with us."

"Tell the men to stand by the guns, then, as Lustig and Hinkston and I go out."

"Right, sir."

"Come along, Lustig, Hinkston."

The three men walked together, down through the levels of the ship.

It was a beautiful spring day. A robin sat on a blossoming apple tree and sang continuously. Showers of petal snow sifted down when the wind touched the apple tree, and the blossom smell drifted upon the air. Somewhere in the town, somebody was playing the piano and the music came and went, came and went, softly, drowsily. The song was *Beautiful Dreamer*. Somewhere else, a phonograph, scratchy and faded, was hissing out a record of *Roamin' in the Gloamin'*, sung by Harry Lauder.

and tall elm trees blowing in the wind, and tall maples and horse chestnuts. And church steeples with golden bells silent in them.

The men in the rocket looked out and saw this. Then they looked at one another and then they looked out again. They held on to each other's elbows, suddenly unable to breathe, it seemed. Their faces grew pale and they blinked constantly, running from glass port to glass port of the ship.

"I'll be damned," whispered Lustig, rubbing his face with his numb fingers, his eyes wet. "I'll be damned, damned, damned."

"It can't be, it just can't be," said Samuel Hinkston.

"Lord," said Captain John Black.

There was a call from the chemist. "Sir, the atmosphere is fine for breathing, sir."

Black turned slowly. "Are you sure?"

"No doubt of it, sir."

"Then we'll go out," said Lustig.

"Lord, yes," said Samuel Hinkston.

"Hold on," said Captain John Black. "Just a moment. Nobody gave any orders."

"But, sir — "

"Sir, nothing. How do we know what this is?"

"We know what it is, sir," said the chemist. "It's a small town with good air in it, sir."

"And it's a small town the like of Earth towns," said Samuel Hinkston, the archaeologist. "Incredible. It can't be, but it is."

Captain John Black looked at him, idly. "Do you think that the civilizations of two planets can progress at the same rate and evolve in the same way, Hinkston?"

"I wouldn't have thought so, sir."

Captain Black stood by the port. "Look out there. The geraniums. A specialized plant. That specific variety has only been known on Earth for fifty years. Think of the thousands of years of time it takes to evolve plants. Then tell me if it is logical that the Martians should have: one, leaded glass windows; two, cupolas; three, porch swings; four, an instrument that looks like a piano and probably is a piano; and, five, if you look closely, if a Martian composer would have published a piece of music titled, strangely enough, *Beautiful Ohio*. All of which means that we have an Ohio River here on Mars!"

"It is quite strange, sir."

"Strange, hell, it's absolutely impossible, and I suspect the whole bloody shooting setup. Something's wrong here, and I'm not leaving the ship until I know what it is."

"Oh, sir," said Lustig.

"Darn it," said Samuel Hinkston. "Sir, I want to investigate this at first hand. It may be that there are similar patterns of thought, movement, civilization on *every* planet in our system. We may be on the threshold of the great psychological and metaphysical discovery in our time, sir, don't you think?"

The three men stood outside the ship. The port closed behind them. At every window, a face pressed, looking out. The large metal guns pointed this way and that, ready.

Now the phonograph record being played was:

"Oh give me a June night
The moonlight and you — "

Lustig began to tremble. Samuel Hinkston did likewise.

Hinkston's voice was so feeble and uneven that the captain had to ask him to repeat what he had said. "I said, sir, that I think I have solved this, all of this, sir!"

"And what is the solution, Hinkston?"

The soft wind blew. The sky was serene and quiet and somewhere a stream of water ran through the cool caverns and tree-shadings of a ravine. Somewhere a horse and wagon trotted and rolled by, bumping.

"Sir, it must be, it has to be, this is the *only* solution! Rocket travel began to Mars in the years before the first World War, sir!"

The captain stared at his archaeologist. "No!"

"But, yes, sir! You must admit, look at all of this! How else to explain it, the houses, the lawns, the iron deer, the flowers, the pianos, the music!"

"Hinkston, Hinkston, oh," and the captain put his hand to his face, shaking his head, his hand shaking now, his lips blue.

"Sir, listen to me." Hinkston took his elbow persuasively and looked up into the captain's face, pleading. "Say that there were some people in the year 1905, perhaps, who hated wars and wanted to get away from Earth and they got together, some scientists, in secret, and built a rocket and came out here to Mars."

"No, no, Hinkston."

"Why not? The world was a different place in 1905, they could have kept it a secret much more easily."

"But the work, Hinkston, the work of building a complex thing like a rocket, oh, no, no." The captain looked at his shoes, looked at his hands, looked at the houses, and then at Hinkston.

"And they came up here, and naturally the houses they built were similar to Earth houses because they brought the cultural architecture with them, and here it is!"

"And they've lived here all these years?" said the captain.

"In peace and quiet, sir, yes. Maybe they made a few trips, to bring enough people here for one small town, and then stopped, for fear of being discovered. That's why the town seems so old-fashioned. I don't see a thing, myself, that is older than the year 1927, do you?"

"No, frankly, I don't, Hinkston."

"These are *our* people, sir. This is an American city; it's definitely not European!"

"That — that's right, too, Hinkston."

"Or maybe, just maybe, sir, rocket travel is older than we think. Perhaps it started in some part of the world hundreds of years ago, was discovered and kept secret by a small number of men, and they came to Mars, with only occasional visits to Earth over the centuries."

"You make it sound almost reasonable."

"It is, sir. It has to be. We have the proof here before us, all we have to do now, is find some people and verify it!"

"You're right there, of course. We can't just stand here and talk. Did you bring your gun?"

"Yes, but we won't need it."

"We'll see about it. Come along, we'll ring that doorbell and see if anyone is home."

Their boots were deadened of all sound in the thick green grass. It smelled from a fresh mowing. In spite of himself, Captain John Black felt a great peace come over him. It had been thirty years since he had been in a small town, and the buzzing of spring bees on the air lulled and quieted him, and the fresh look of things was a balm to the soul.

Hollow echoes sounded from under the boards as they walked across the porch and stood before the screen door. Inside, they could see a bead curtain hung across the hall entry, and a crystal chandelier and a Maxfield Parrish painting framed on one wall over a comfortable Morris Chair. The house smelled old, and of the attic, and infinitely comfortable. You could hear the tinkle of ice rattling in a lemonade pitcher. In a distant kitchen, because of the heat of the day, someone was preparing a soft, lemon drink.

Captain John Black rang the bell.

Footsteps, dainty and thin, came along the hall and a kind faced lady of some forty years, dressed in the sort of dress you might expect in the year 1909, peered out at them.

"Can I help you?" she asked.

"Beg your pardon," said Captain Black, uncertainly. "But we're looking for, that is, could you help us, I mean." He stopped. She looked out at him with dark wondering eyes.

"If you're selling something," she said, "I'm much too busy and I haven't time." She turned to go.

"No, *wait*," he cried, bewilderedly. "What town is this?"

She looked him up and down as if he were crazy. "What do you mean, what town is it? How could you be in a town and not know what town it was?"

The captain looked as if he wanted to go sit under a shady apple tree. "I beg your pardon," he said. "But we're strangers here. We're from Earth, and we want to know how this town got here and you got here."

"Are you census takers?" she asked.

"No," he said.

"What do you want then?" she demanded.

"Well," said the captain.

"Well?" she asked.

"How long has this town been here?" he wondered.

"It was built in 1868," she snapped at them. "Is this a game?"

"No, not a game," cried the captain. "Oh, God," he said. "Look here. We're from Earth!"

"From *where?*" she said.

"From Earth!" he said.

"Where's that?" she said.

"From Earth," he cried.

"Out of the ground, do you mean?"

"No, from the planet Earth!" he almost shouted. "Here," he insisted, "come out on the porch and I'll show you."

"No," she said, "I won't come out there, you are all evidently quite mad from the sun."

Lustig and Hinkston stood behind the captain. Hinkston now spoke up. "Mrs.," he said. "We came in a flying ship across space, among the stars. We came from the third planet from the sun, Earth, to this planet, which is Mars. *Now* do you understand, Mrs.?"

"Mad from the sun," she said, taking hold of the door. "Go away now, before I call my husband who's upstairs taking a nap, and he'll beat you all with his fists."

"But — " said Hinkston. "This is Mars, is it not?"

"This," explained the woman, as if she were addressing a child, "is Green Lake, Wisconsin, on the continent of America, surrounded by the Pacific and Atlantic Oceans, on a place called the world, or sometimes, the Earth. Go away now. Good-bye!"

She slammed the door.

The three men stood before the door with their hands up in the air toward it, as if pleading with her to open it once more.

They looked at one another.

"Let's knock the door down," said Lustig.

"We can't," sighed the captain.

"Why not?"

"She didn't do anything bad, did she? We're the strangers here. This is private property. Good God, Hinkston!" He went and sat down on the porchstep.

"What, sir?"

"Did it ever strike you, that maybe we got ourselves, somehow, some way, fouled up. And, by accident, came back and landed on Earth!"

"Oh, sir, oh, sir, oh oh, sir." And Hinkston sat down numbly and thought about it.

Lustig stood up in the sunlight. "How could we have done that?"

"I don't know, just let me think."

Hinkston said, "But we checked every mile of the way, and we saw Mars and our chronometers said so many miles gone, and we went past the moon and out into space and here we are, on Mars. I'm sure we're on Mars, sir."

Lustig said, "But, suppose, just suppose that, by accident, in space, in time, or something, we landed on a planet in space, in another time.

Suppose this is Earth, thirty or fifty years ago? Maybe we got lost in the dimensions, do you think?"

"Oh, go away, Lustig."

"Are the men in the ship keeping an eye on us, Hinkston?"

"At their guns, sir."

Lustig went to the door, rang the bell. When the door opened again, he asked, "What year is this?"

"1926, of course!" cried the woman, furiously, and slammed the door 125 again.

"Did you hear that?" Lustig ran back to them, wildly. "She said 1926! We *have* gone back in time! This *is* Earth!"

Lustig sat down and the three men let the wonder and terror of the thought afflict them. Their hands stirred fitfully on their knees. The wind blew, nodding the locks of hair on their heads.

The captain stood up, brushing off his pants. "I never thought it would be like this. It scares the hell out of me. How can a thing like this happen?"

"Will anybody in the whole town believe us?" wondered Hinkston. "Are we playing around with something dangerous? Time, I mean. Shouldn't we just take off and go home?"

"No. We'll try another house."

They walked three houses down to a little white cottage under an oak tree. "I like to be as logical as I can get," said the captain. He nodded at the town. "How does this sound to you, Hinkston? Suppose, as you said originally, that rocket travel occurred years ago. And when the Earth people had lived here a number of years they began to get homesick for Earth. First a mild neurosis about it, then a full fledged psychosis. Then, threatened insanity. What would you do, as a psychiatrist, if faced with such a problem?"

Hinkston thought. "Well, I think I'd re-arrange the civilization on Mars so it resembled Earth more and more each day. If there was any way of reproducing every plant, every road and every lake, and even an ocean, I would do so. Then I would, by some vast crowd hypnosis, theoretically anyway, convince everyone in a town this size that this really *was* Earth, not Mars at all."

"Good enough, Hinkston. I think we're on the right track now. That woman in that house back there, just *thinks* she's living on Earth. It protects her sanity. She and all the others in this town are the patients of the greatest experiment in migration and hypnosis you will ever lay your eyes on in your life."

"That's it, sir!" cried Lustig.

"Well," the captain sighed. "Now we're getting somewhere. I feel better. It all sounds a bit more logical now. This talk about time and going back and forth and traveling in time turns my stomach upside down. But, *this* way — " He actually smiled for the first time in a month. "Well. It looks as if we'll be fairly welcome here."

"Or, will we, sir?" said Lustig. "After all, like the Pilgrims, these people came here to escape Earth. Maybe they won't be too happy to see us, sir. Maybe they'll try to drive us out or kill us?"

"We have superior weapons if that should happen. Anyway, all we can do is try. This next house now. Up we go."

But they had hardly crossed the lawn when Lustig stopped and looked off across the town, down the quiet, dreaming afternoon street. "Sir," he said.

"What is it, Lustig?" asked the captain.

"Oh, sir, *sir*, what I see, what I do see now before me, oh, oh — " said Lustig, and he began to cry. His fingers came up, twisting and trembling, and his face was all wonder and joy and incredulity. He sounded as if any moment he might go quite insane with happiness. He looked down the street and he began to run, stumbling, awkwardly, falling, picking himself up, and running on. "Oh, God, God, thank you, God! Thank you!"

"Don't let him get away!" The captain broke into a run.

Now Lustig was running at full speed, shouting. He turned into a yard half way down the little shady side street and leaped up upon the porch of a large green house with an iron rooster on the roof.

He was beating upon the door, shouting and hollering and crying when Hinkston and the captain ran up and stood in the yard.

The door opened. Lustig yanked the screen wide and in a high wail of discovery and happiness, cried out, "Grandma! Grandpa!"

Two old people stood in the doorway, their faces lighting up.

"Albert!" Their voices piped and they rushed out to embrace and pat him on the back and move around him. "Albert, oh, Albert, it's been so many years! How you've grown, boy, how big you are, boy, oh, Albert boy, how are you!"

"Grandma, Grandpa!" sobbed Albert Lustig. "Good to see you! You look fine, fine! Oh, fine!" He held them, turned them, kissed them, hugged them, cried on them, held them out again, blinked at the little old people. The sun was in the sky, the wind blew, the grass was green, the screen door stood open.

"Come in, lad, come in, there's lemonade for you, fresh, lots of it!"

"Grandma, Grandpa, good to see you! I've got friends down here! Here!" Lustig turned and waved wildly at the captain and Hinkston, who, all during the adventure on the porch, had stood in the shade of a tree, holding onto each other. "Captain, captain, come up, come up, I want you to meet my grandfolks!"

"Howdy," said the folks. "Any friend of Albert's is ours, too! Don't stand there with your mouths open! Come on!"

In the living room of the old house it was cool and a grandfather clock ticked high and long and bronzed in one corner. There were soft pillows on large couches and walls filled with books and a rug cut in a thick rose pattern and antimacassars pinned to furniture, and lemonade in the hand, sweating, and cool on the thirsty tongue.

"Here's to our health." Grandma tipped her glass to her porcelain teeth.

"How long you *been* here, Grandma?" said Lustig.

"A good many years," she said, tartly. "Ever since we died."

"Ever since you what?" asked Captain John Black, putting his drink down.

"Oh, yes," Lustig looked at his captain. "They've been dead thirty years."

"And you *sit* there, calmly!" cried the captain.

"Tush," said the old woman, and winked glitteringly at John Black. "Who are we to question what happens? Here we are. What's life, anyways? Who does what for why and where? All we know is here we are, alive again, and no questions asked. A second chance." She toddled over and held out her thin wrist to Captain John Black. "Feel." He felt. "Solid, ain't I?" she asked. He nodded. "You hear my voice don't you?" she inquired. Yes, he did. "Well, then," she said in triumph, "why go around questioning?"

"Well," said the captain, "it's simply that we never thought we'd find a thing like this on Mars."

"And now you've found it. I dare say there's lots on every planet that'll show you God's infinite ways."

"Is this Heaven?" asked Hinkston.

"Nonsense, no. It's a world and we get a second chance. Nobody told us why. But then nobody told us why we were on Earth, either. That *other* Earth, I mean. The one you came from. How do we know there wasn't *another* before *that* one?"

"A good question," said the captain.

The captain stood up and slapped his hand on his leg in an off-hand fashion. "We've got to be going. It's been nice. Thank you for the drinks."

He stopped. He turned and looked toward the door, startled.

Far away, in the sunlight, there was a sound of voices, a crowd, a shouting and a great hello.

"What's that?" asked Hinkston.

"We'll soon find out!" And Captain John Black was out the front door abruptly, jolting across the green lawn and into the street of the Martian town.

He stood looking at the ship. The ports were open and his crew were streaming out, waving their hands. A crowd of people had gathered and in and through and among these people the members of the crew were running, talking, laughing, shaking hands. People did little dances. People swarmed. The rocket lay empty and abandoned.

A brass band exploded in the sunlight, flinging off a gay tune from upraised tubas and trumpets. There was a bang of drums and a shrill of fifes. Little girls with golden hair jumped up and down. Little boys shouted, "Hooray!" And fat men passed around ten-cent cigars. The mayor of the town made a speech. Then, each member of the crew with a mother on one arm, a father or sister on the other, was spirited off down the street, into little cottages or big mansions and doors slammed shut.

The wind rose in the clear spring sky and all was silent. The brass band had banged off around a corner leaving the rocket to shine and dazzle alone in the sunlight.

"Abandoned!" cried the captain. "Abandoned the ship, they did! I'll have their skins, by God! They had orders!"

"Sir," said Lustig. "Don't be too hard on them. Those were all old relatives and friends."

"That's no excuse!"

"Think how they felt, captain, seeing familiar faces outside the ship!"

"I would have obeyed orders! I would have — " The captain's mouth remained open.

Striding along the sidewalk under the Martian sun, tall, smiling, eyes blue, face tan, came a young man of some twenty-six years.

"John!" the man cried, and broke into a run.

"What?" said Captain John Black. He swayed.

"John, you old beggar, you!"

The man ran up and gripped his hand and slapped him on the back.

"It's you," said John Black.

"Of course, who'd you *think* it was!"

"Edward!" The captain appealed now to Lustig and Hinkston, holding the stranger's hand. "This is my brother Edward. Ed, meet my men, Lustig, Hinkston! My brother!"

They tugged at each other's hands and arms and then finally embraced. "Ed!" "John, you old bum, you!" "You're looking fine, Ed, but, Ed, what is this? You haven't changed over the years. You died, I remember, when you were twenty-six, and I was nineteen, oh God, so many years ago, and here you are, and, Lord, what goes on, what goes on?"

Edward Black gave him a brotherly knock on the chin. "Mom's waiting," he said.

"Mom?"

"And Dad, too."

"And Dad?" The captain almost fell to earth as if hit upon the chest with a mighty weapon. He walked stiffly and awkwardly, out of coordination. He stuttered and whispered and talked only one or two words at a time. "Mom alive? Dad? Where?"

"At the old house on Oak Knoll Avenue."

"The old house." The captain stared in delighted amazement. "Did you *hear* that, Lustig, Hinkston?"

"I know it's hard for you to believe."

"But alive. Real."

"Don't I *feel* real?" The strong aim, the firm grip, the white smile. The light, curling hair.

Hinkston was gone. He had seen his own house down the street and was running for it. Lustig was grinning. "Now you understand, sir, what happened to everybody on the ship. They couldn't help themselves."

"Yes. Yes," said the captain, eyes shut. "Yes." He put out his hand. "When I open my eyes, you'll be gone." He opened his eyes. "You're still here. God, Edward, you look fine!"

"Come along, lunch is waiting for you. I told Mom."

Lustig said, "Sir, I'll be with my grandfolks if you want me."

"What? Oh, fine, Lustig. Later, then."

Edward grabbed his arm and marched him. "You need support."

"I do. My knees, all funny. My stomach, loose. God."

"There's the house. Remember it?"

"Remember it? Hell! I bet I can beat you to the front porch!"

They ran. The wind roared over Captain John Black's ears. The earth roared under his feet. He saw the golden figure of Edward Black pull ahead of him in the amazing dream of reality. He saw the house rush forward, the door open, the screen swing back. "Beat you!" cried Edward, bounding up the steps. "I'm an old man," panted the captain, "and you're still young. But, then, you *always* beat me, I remember!"

In the doorway, Mom, pink and plump and bright. And behind her, pepper grey, Dad, with his pipe in his hand.

"Mom, Dad!"

He ran up the steps like a child, to meet them.

It was a fine long afternoon. They finished lunch and they sat in the living room and he told them all about his rocket and his being captain and they nodded and smiled upon him and Mother was just the same, and Dad bit the end off a cigar and lighted it in his old fashion. Mom brought in some iced tea in the middle of the afternoon. Then, there was a big turkey dinner at night and time flowing on. When the drumsticks were sucked clean and lay brittle upon the plates, the captain leaned back in his chair and exhaled his deep contentment. Dad poured him a small glass of dry sherry. It was seven-thirty in the evening. Night was in all the trees and coloring the sky, and the lamps were halos of dim light in the gentle house. From all the other houses down the streets came sounds of music, pianos playing, laughter.

Mom put a record on the victrola and she and Captain John Black had a dance. She was wearing the same perfume he remembered from the summer when she and Dad had been killed in the train accident. She was very real in his arms as they danced lightly to the music.

"I'll wake in the morning," said the captain. "And I'll be in my rocket in space, and all this will be gone."

"No, no, don't think that," she cried, softly, pleadingly. "We're here. Don't question. God is good to us. Let's be happy."

The record ended with a circular hissing.

"You're tired, son," said Dad. He waved his pipe. "You and Ed go on upstairs. Your old bedroom is waiting for you."

"The old one?"

"The brass bed and all," laughed Edward.

"But I should report my men in."

"Why?" Mother was logical.

"Why? Well, I don't know. No reason, I guess. No, none at all. What's the difference?" He shook his head. "I'm not being very logical these days."

"Good night, son." She kissed his cheek.

"'Night, Mom."

"Sleep tight, son." Dad shook his hand.

"Same to you, Pop."

"It's good to have you home."

"It's good to *be* home."

He left the land of cigar smoke and perfume and books and gentle light and ascended the stairs, talking, talking with Edward. Edward pushed a door open and there was the yellow brass bed and the old semaphore banners from college days and a very musty raccoon coat which he petted with strange, muted affection. "It's too much," he said faintly. "Like being in a thunder shower without an umbrella. I'm soaked to the skin with emotion. I'm numb. I'm tired."

"A night's sleep between cool clean sheets for you, my bucko." Edward slapped wide the snowy linens and flounced the pillows. Then he put up a window and let the night blooming jasmine float in. There was moonlight and the sound of distant dancing and whispering.

"So this is Mars," said the captain undressing.

"So this is Mars," Edward undressed in idle, leisurely moves, drawing his shirt off over his head, revealing golden shoulders and the good muscular neck.

The lights were out, they were into bed, side by side, as in the days, how many decades ago? The captain lolled and was nourished by the night wind pushing the lace curtains out upon the dark room air. Among the trees, upon a lawn, someone had cranked up a portable phonograph and now it was playing softly, "I'll be loving you, always, with a love that's true, always."

The thought of Anna came to his mind. "Is Anna here?"

His brother, lying straight out in the moonlight from the window, waited and then said, "Yes. She's out of town. But she'll be here in the morning."

The captain shut his eyes. "I want to see Anna very much."

The room was square and quiet except for their breathing. "Good night, Ed."

A pause. "Good night, John."

He lay peacefully, letting his thoughts float. For the first time the stress of the day was moved aside, all of the excitement was calmed. He could think logically now. It had all been emotion. The bands playing, the sight of familiar faces, the sick pounding of your heart. But — now . . .

How? He thought. How was all this made? And why? For what purpose? Out of the goodness of some kind God? Was God, then, really that fine and thoughtful of his children? How and why and what for?

He thought of the various theories advanced in the first heat of the afternoon by Hinkston and Lustig. He let all kinds of new theories drop in lazy pebbles down through his mind, as through a dark water, now, turning, throwing out dull flashes of white light. Mars. Earth. Mom. Dad. Edward. Mars. Martians.

Who had lived here a thousand years ago on Mars? Martians? Or had this always been like this? Martians. He repeated the word quietly, inwardly.

He laughed out loud, almost. He had the most ridiculous theory, all of a sudden. It gave him a kind of chilled feeling. It was really nothing to think of, of course. Highly improbable. Silly. Forget it. Ridiculous.

But, he thought, just suppose. Just *suppose* now, that there were Martians living on Mars and they saw our ship coming and saw us inside our ship and hated us. Suppose, now, just for the hell of it, that they wanted to destroy us, as invaders, as unwanted ones, and they wanted to do it in a very clever way, so that we would be taken off guard. Well, what would the best weapon be that a Martian could use against Earth-men with atom weapons?

The answer was interesting. Telepathy, hypnosis, memory, and imagination.

Suppose all these houses weren't real at all, this bed not real, but only figments of my own imagination, given substance by telepathy and hypnosis by the Martians.

Suppose these houses are really some other shape, a Martian shape, but, by playing on my desires and wants, these Martians have made this seem like my old home town, my old house, to lull me out of my suspicions? What better way to fool a man, by his own emotions.

And suppose those two people in the next room, asleep, are not my mother and father at all. But two Martians, incredibly brilliant, with the ability to keep me under this dreaming hypnosis all of the time?

And that brass band, today? What a clever plan it would be. First, fool Lustig, then fool Hinkston, then gather a crowd around the rocket ship and wave. And all the men in the ship, seeing mothers, aunts, uncles, sweethearts dead ten, twenty years ago, naturally, disregarding orders, would rush out and abandon the ship. What more natural? What more unsuspecting? What more simple? A man doesn't ask too many questions when his mother is suddenly brought back to life; he's much too happy. And the brass band played and everybody was taken off to private homes. And here we all are, tonight, in various houses, in various beds, with no weapons to protect us, and the rocket lies in the moonlight, empty. And wouldn't it be horrible and terrifying to discover that all of this was part of some great clever plan by the Martians to divide and conquer us, and kill us. Some time during the night, perhaps, my brother here on this bed, will change form, melt, shift, and become a one-eyed, green and yellow-toothed Martian. It would be very simple for him just to turn over in bed and put a knife into my heart. And in all those other houses down the street a dozen other brothers or fathers suddenly melting away and taking out knives and doing things to the unsuspecting, sleeping men of Earth.

His hands were shaking under the covers. His body was cold. Suddenly it was not a theory. Suddenly he was very afraid. He lifted himself in bed and listened. The night was very quiet. The music had stopped. The wind had died. His brother (?) lay sleeping beside him.

Very carefully he lifted the sheets, rolled them back. He slipped from bed and was walking softly across the room when his brother's voice said, "Where are you going?"

"What?"

His brother's voice was quite cold. "I said, where do you think you're going?"

"For a drink of water."

"But you're not thirsty."

"Yes, yes, I am."

"No, you're not."

Captain John Black broke and ran across the room. He screamed. He screamed twice.

He never reached the door.

In the morning, the brass band played a mournful dirge. From every house in the street came little solemn processions bearing long boxes and along the sun-filled street, weeping and changing, came the grandmas and grandfathers and mothers and sisters and brothers, walking to the churchyard, where there were open holes dug freshly and new tombstones installed. Seventeen holes in all, and seventeen tombstones. Three of the tombstones said, CAPTAIN JOHN BLACK, ALBERT LUSTIG, and SAMUEL HINKSTON.

The mayor made a little sad speech, his face sometimes looking like the mayor, sometimes looking like something else.

Mother and Father Black were there, with Brother Edward, and they cried, their faces melting now from a familiar face into something else.

Grandpa and Grandma Lustig were there, weeping, their faces also shifting like wax, shivering as a thing does in waves of heat on a summer day.

The coffins were lowered. Somebody murmured about "the unexpected and sudden deaths of seventeen fine men during the night — "

Earth was shoveled in on the coffin tops.

After the funeral the brass band slammed and banged back into town and the crowd stood around and waved and shouted as the rocket was torn to pieces and strewn about and blown up.

Sonya Dorman

When I Was Miss Dow

(1966)

Sonya Dorman Hess (1924–2005) was born in New York City, attended private schools in New England, and eventually retired to New Mexico. She grew up around horses and, with her husband, bred and showed Akita dogs, facts that may be relevant to the story that follows. Dorman published widely as a poet, both in the mainstream press and in sf magazines; her poem "Corruption of Metals" won the Rhysling Award for sf poetry. Dorman's output as a fiction writer is smaller, but still distinguished. Her prose style reflects her poetic background, as can be seen in the story that follows, which is marked by succinct language, use of metaphor, and small but startling verbal and imagistic juxtapositions. "When I Was Miss Dow" was reprinted in Pamela Sargent's groundbreaking 1974 *Women of Wonder* anthology and won a retrospective James Tiptree, Jr. Award in 1995.

Most of the stories in this chapter describe alien encounters from the human perspective. Writing from the point of view of the alien is a difficult imaginative feat, and such stories are rarer and seldom as successful. "When I Was Miss Dow" is an exception. Dorman's narrator is radically nonhuman, yet the alien perspective functions as a powerful lens for perceiving the everyday human experience of gender, specifically the estrangement from self inherent in a traditional feminine role.

These hungry, mother-haunted people come and find us living in what they like to call crystal palaces, though really we live in glass places, some of them highly ornamented and others plain as paper. They come first as explorers, and perhaps realize we are a race of one sex only, rather amorphous beings of proteide; and we, even baby I, are Protean also, being able to take various shapes at will. One sex, one brain lobe, we live in more or less glass bridges over the humanoid chasm, eating, recreating, attending races and playing other games like most living creatures.

Eventually, we're all dumped into the cell banks and reproduced once more.

After the explorers comes the colony of miners and scientists; the Warden and some of the other elders put on faces to greet them, agreeing to help with the mining of some ores, even giving them a koota or two as they become interested in our racing dogs. They set up their places of life, pop up their machines, bang-bang, chug-chug; we put on our faces, forms, smiles and costumes. I am old enough to learn to change my shape too.

The Warden says to me, "It's about time you made a change, yourself. Some of your friends are already working for these people, bringing home credits and sulfas."

My Uncle (by the Warden's fourth conjunction) made himself over at the start, being one of the first to realize how it could profit us.

I protest to the Warden, "I'm educated and trained as a scholar. You always say I must remain deep in my mathematics and other studies."

My Uncle says, "You have to do it. There's only one way for us to get along with them," and he runs his fingers through his long blond hair. My Uncle's not an educated person, but highly placed politically, and while Captain Dow is around, my Uncle retains this particular shape. The captain is shipping out soon, then Uncle will find some other features, because he's already warned it's unseemly for him to be chasing around in the face of a girl after the half-bearded boys from the spaceships. I don't want to do this myself, wasting so much time, when the fourteen decimals even now are clicking on my mirrors.

The Warden says, "We have a pattern from a female botanist, she ought to do for you. But before we put you into the pattern tank, you'll have to approximate another brain lobe. They have two."

"I know," I say sulkily. A botanist. A she.

"Into the tank," the Warden says to me without mercy, and I am his to use as he believes proper.

I spend four days in the tank absorbing the female Terran pattern. When I'm released, the Warden tells me, "Your job is waiting for you. We went to a lot of trouble to arrange it." He sounds brusque, but perhaps this is because he hasn't conjoined for a long time. The responsibilities of being Warden of Mines and Seeds come first, long before any social engagement.

I run my fingers through my brunette curls and notice my Uncle is looking critically at me. "Haven't you made yourself rather old?" he asks.

"Oh, he's all right," the Warden says. "Thirty-three isn't badly matched to the Doctor, as I understand it."

Dr. Arnold Proctor, the colony's head biologist, is busy making radiograph pictures (with his primitive x-rays) of skeletal structures: murger birds, rodents, and our pets and racers, the kootas. Dogs, to the Terrans, who are fascinated by them. We breed them primarily for speed and stamina, but some of them carry a gene for an inherited structural defect which cripples them, and they have to be destroyed before they are full grown. The Doctor is making a special study of kootas.

He gets up from his chair when I enter the office. "I'm Miss Dow, your new assistant," I say, hoping my long fingernails will stand up to the pressure of punchkeys on the computer, since I haven't had much practice in retaining foreign shapes. I'm still in uncertain balance between myself and Martha Dow, who is also myself. But one does not have two lobes for nothing, I discover.

"Good morning. I'm glad you're here," the Doctor says.

He is a nice, pink man with silver hair, soft-spoken, intelligent. I'm pleased, as we work along, to find he doesn't joke and wisecrack like so many of the Terrans, though I am sometimes whimsical, I like music and banquets as well as my studies.

Though absorbed in his work, Dr. Proctor isn't rude to interrupters. A man of unusual balance, coming as he does from a culture which sends out scientific parties that are 90 percent of one sex, when their species provides them with two. At first meeting he is dedicated but agreeable, and I'm charmed.

"Dr. Proctor," I ask him one morning, "is it possible for you to radiograph my koota? She's very fine, from the fastest stock available, and I'd like to breed her."

"Yes, yes, of course," he promises with his quick, often absent smile. "By all means. You wish to breed only the best." It's typical of him to assume we're all as dedicated as he.

My Uncle's not pleased. "There's nothing wrong with your koota," he says. "What do you want to x-ray her for? Suppose he finds something is wrong? You'll be afraid to race or breed her, and she won't be replaced. Besides, your interest in her may make him suspicious."

"Suspicious of what?" I ask, but my Uncle won't say, so I ask him, "Suppose she's bred and her pups are cripples?"

The Warden says, "You're supposed to have your mind on your work, not on racing. The koota was just to amuse you when you were younger."

I lean down and stroke her head, which is beautiful, and she breathes a deep and gentle breath in response.

"Oh, let him go," my Uncle says wearily. He's getting disgusted because they didn't intend for me to bury myself in a laboratory or a computer room without making more important contacts. But a scholar is born with a certain temperament and has an introspective nature, and as I'm destined eventually to replace the Warden, naturally I prefer the life of the mind.

"I must say," my Uncle remarks, "you look the image of a Terran female. Is the work interesting?"

"Oh, yes, fascinating," I reply, and he snorts at my lie, since we both know it's dull and routine, and most of my time is spent working out the connections between my two brain lobes, which still present me with some difficulty.

My koota bitch is subjected to a pelvic radiograph. Afterward, I stand on my heels in the small, darkened cubicle, looking at the film on the viewing screen. There he stands too, with his cheekbones emerald in the peculiar light, and his hair, which is silver in daylight, looks phosphorescent. I resist this. I am resisting this Doctor with the x-ray eyes who can examine my marrow with ease. He sees Martha's marrow, every perfect corpuscle of it.

You can't imagine how comforting it is to be so transparent. There's no need to pretend, adjust, advance, retreat or discuss the oddities of my planet. We are looking at the x-ray film of my prized racer and companion to determine the soundness of her hip joints, yet I suspect the doctor, platinum-green and tall as a tower, is piercing my reality with his educated gaze. He can see the blood flushing my surfaces. I don't need to do a thing but stand up straight so the crease of fat at my waist won't distort my belly button, the center of it all.

"You see?" he says. I do see, looking at the film in this darkness where perfection or disaster may be viewed, and I'm twined in the paradox which confronts me here. The darker the room, the brighter the screen and the clearer the picture. Less light! and the truth becomes more evident. Either the koota is properly jointed and may be bred without danger of passing the gene on to her young, or she is not properly jointed, and cannot be used. Less light, more truth! And the Doctor is green sculpture — a little darker and he would be a bronze — but his natural color is pink alabaster.

"You see," the Doctor says, and I do try to see. He points his wax pencil at one hip joint on the film, and says, "A certain amount of osteoarthritic build-up is already evident. The cranial rim is wearing down, she may go lame. She'll certainly pass the defect on to some of her pups, if she's bred."

This koota has been my playmate and friend for a long time. She retains a single form, that of koota, full of love and beautiful speed; she has been a source of pleasure and pride.

Dr. Proctor, of the pewter hair, will discuss the anatomical defects of the koota in a gentle and cultivated voice. I am disturbed. There shouldn't be any need to explain the truth, which is evident. Yet it seems that to comprehend the exposures, I require a special education. It's said that the more you have seen, the quicker you are to sort the eternal verities into one pile and the dismal illusions into another. How is it that sometimes the Doctor wears a head which resembles that of a koota, with a splendid muzzle and noble brow?

Suddenly, he gives a little laugh and points the end of the wax pencil at my navel, announcing, "There. There, it is essential that the belly button be attached onto the pelvis, or you'll bear no children." Thoughts of offspring had occurred to me. But weren't we discussing my racer? The radiograph film is still clipped to the view screen, and upon it, spread-eagled, appears the bony Rorschach of my koota bitch, her hip joints expressing doom.

I wish the Doctor would put on the daylight. I come to the conclusion that there's a limit to how much truth I can examine, and the more I submit to the conditions necessary for examining it, the more unhappy I become.

Dr. Proctor is a man of such perfect integrity that he continues to talk about bones and muscles until I'm ready to scream for mercy. He has done something unusual and probably prohibited, but he's not aware of it. I mean it must be prohibited in his culture, where it seems they play on each other, but not with each other. I'm uneasy, fluctuating.

He snaps two switches. Out goes the film and on goes the sun, making my eyes stream with grateful tears, although he's so adjusted to these contrasts he doesn't so much as blink. Floating in the sunshine, I've become opaque; he can't see anything but my surface tensions, and I wonder what he does in his spare time. A part of me seems to tilt, or slide.

"There, there, oh dear, Miss Dow," he says, patting my back, rubbing my shoulder blades. His forearms and fingers extend gingerly. "You do want to breed only the best, don't you?" he asks. I begin within me a compulsive ritual of counting the elements; it's all I can do to keep communications open between my brain lobes. I'm suffering from eclipses; one goes dark, the other lights up like a new saloon, that one goes dark, the other goes nova.

"There, there," the Doctor says, distressed because I'm quivering and trying to keep the connections open; I have never felt clogged before. They may have to put me back into the pattern tank.

Profoundly disturbed, I lift my face, and he gives me a kiss. Then I'm all right, balanced again, one lobe composing a concerto for virtix flute, the other one projecting, "Oh Arnie, oh Arnie." Yes, I'm okay for the shape I'm in. He's marking off my joints with his wax pencil (the marks of which can be easily erased from the film surface) and he's mumbling, "It's essential, oh yes, it's essential."

Finally, he says, "I guess all of us colonists are lonely here," and I say, "Oh yes, aren't we," before I realize the enormity of the Warden's manipulations, and what a lot I have to learn. Evidently the Warden triple-carded me through the Colony Punch Center as a Terran. I lie and say, "Oh yes, yes. Oh Arnie, put out the light," for we may find some more truth.

"Not here," Arnie says, and of course he's right, this is a room for study, for cataloging obvious facts, not a place for carnival. There are not many places for it, I discover with surprise. Having lived in glass all my life, I expect everyone else to be as comfortable there as I am. But this isn't so.

Just the same we find his quarters, after dark, to be comfortable and free of embarrassment. You wouldn't think a dedicated man of his age would be so vigorous, but I find out he spends his weekends at the recreation center hitting a ball with his hand. The ball bounces back off a wall and he hits it and hits it. Though he's given that up now because we're together on weekends.

"You're more than an old bachelor like me deserves," he tells me.

"Why are you an old bachelor?" I ask him. I do wonder why, if it's something not to be.

He tries to explain it to me. "I'm not a young man. I wouldn't make a good husband, I'm afraid. I like to work late, to be undisturbed. In my leisure time, I like to make wood carvings. Sometimes I go to bed with the sun and sometimes I'm up working all night. And then children. No. I'm lucky to be an old bachelor," he says.

Arnie carves kaku wood, which has a brilliant grain and is soft enough to permit easy carving. He's working on a figure of a murger bird, whittling lengthwise down the wood so the grain, wavy, full of flowing, wedge-shaped lines, will represent the feathers. The lamplight shines on his hair and the crinkle of his eyelids as he looks down, and carves, whittles, turns. He's absorbed in what he doesn't see there, but he's projecting what he wants to see. It's the reverse of what he must do in the viewing room. I begin to suffer a peculiar pain, located in the nerve cluster between my lungs. He's not talking to me. He's not caressing me. He's forgotten I'm here, and like a false projection, I'm beginning to fade. In another hour perhaps the film will become blank. If he doesn't see me, then am I here?

He's doing just what I do when busy with one of my own projects, and I admire the intensity with which he works: it's magnificent. Yes, I'm jealous of it, I burn with rage and jealousy, he has abandoned me to be Martha and I wish I were myself again, free in shape and single in mind. Not this sack of mud clinging to another. Yet he's teaching me that it's good to cling to another. I'm exhausted from strange disciplines. Perhaps he's tired too; I see that sometimes he kneads the muscles of his stomach with his hands, and closes his eyes.

The Warden sits me down on one of my rare evenings home, and talks angrily. "You're making a mistake," he says. "If the Doctor finds out what you are, you'll lose your job with the Colony. Besides, we never supposed you'd have a liaison with only one man. You were supposed to start with the Doctor, and go on from there. We need every credit you can bring in. And by the way, you haven't done well on that score lately. Is he stingy?"

"Of course he isn't."

"But all you bring home in credits is your pay."

I can think of no reply. It's true the Warden has a right to use me in whatever capacity will serve us all best, as I will use others when I'm a Warden, but he and my Uncle spend half the credits from my job on sulfadiazole, to which they've become addicted.

"You've no sense of responsibility," the Warden says. Perhaps he's coming close to time for conjunction again, and this makes him more concerned about my stability.

My Uncle says, "Oh, he's young, leave him alone. As long as he turns over most of those pay credits to us. Though what he uses the remainder for, I'll never know."

I use it for clothes at the Colony Exchange. Sometimes Arnie takes me out for an evening, usually to the Laugh Tree Bar, where the space crews, too, like to relax. The bar is the place to find joy babies; young pretty, planet-born girls who work at the Colony Punch Center during the day and spend their evenings here competing for the attention of the officers. Sitting here with Arnie, I can't distinguish a colonist's daughter from one of my friends or relatives. They wouldn't know me, either.

Once, at home, I try to talk with a few of these friends about my feelings. But I discover that whatever female patterns they've borrowed are superficial ones; none of them bother to grow an extra lobe, but merely tuck the Terran pattern into a corner of their own for handy reference. They are most of them on sulfas. Hard and shiny toys, they skip like pebbles over the surface of the colonists' lives.

Then they go home, revert to their own free forms, and enjoy their mathematics, colors, compositions, and seedings.

"Why me?" I demand of the Warden. "Why two lobes? Why me?"

"We felt you'd be more efficient," he answers. "And while you're here, which you seldom are these days, you'd better revert to other shapes. Your particles may be damaged if you hold that female form too long."

Oh, but you don't know, I want to tell him. You don't know I'll hold it forever. If I'm damaged or dead, you'll put me into the cell banks, and you'll be amazed, astonished, terrified, to discover that I come out complete, all Martha. I can't be changed.

"You little lump of protagon," my Uncle mumbles bitterly. "You'll never amount to anything, you'll never be a Warden. Have you done any of your own work recently?"

I say, "Yes, I've done some crystal divisions, and regrown them in non-established patterns." My Uncle's in a bad mood, as he's kicking sulfa and his nerve tissue is addled. I'm wise to speak quietly to him, but he still grumbles.

"I can't understand why you like being a two-lobed pack of giggles. I couldn't wait to get out of it. And you were so dead against it to begin with."

"Well, I have learned," I start to say, but can't explain what it is I'm still learning, and close my eyes. Part of it is that on the line between the darkness and the brightness it's easiest to float. I've never wanted to practice only easy things. My balance is damaged. I never had to balance. It's not a term or concept I understand even now, at home, in free form. Some impress of Martha's pattern lies on my own brain cells. I suspect it's permanent damage, which gives me joy. That's what I mean about not understanding it; I am taught to strive for perfection, how can I be pleased with this, which may be a catastrophe?

Arnie carves on a breadth of kaku wood, bringing out to the surface a seascape. Knots become clots of spray, a flaw becomes wind-blown spume. I want to be Martha. I'd like to go to the Laugh Tree with Arnie, for a good time, I'd like to learn to play cards with him.

You see what happens: Arnie is, in his way, like my original self, and I hate that part of him, since I've given it up to be Martha. Martha makes him happy, she is chocolate to his appetite, pillow for his weariness.

I turn for company to my koota. She's the color of morning, her chest juts out like an axe blade, her ribs spring up and back like wings, her eyes are large and clear as she returns my gaze. Yet she's beyond hope; in a little time, she'll be lame; she can't race any more, she must not mother a litter. I turn to her and she gazes back into my eyes, dreaming of speed and wind on the sandy beaches where she has run.

"Why don't you read some tapes?" Arnie suggests to me, because I'm restless and I disturb him. The koota lies at my feet. I read tapes. Every evening in his quarters Arnie carves, I read tapes, the broken racer lies at my feet. I pass through Terran history this way. When the clown tumbles into the tub, I laugh. Terran history is full of clowns and tubs; at first it seems that's all there is, but you learn to see beneath the comic costumes.

While I float on that taut line, the horizon between light and dark, where it's so easy, I begin to sense what is under the costumes: staggering down the street dead drunk on a sunny afternoon with everyone laughing at you; hiding under the veranda because you made blood come out of Pa's face; kicking a man when he's in the gutter because you've been kicked and have to pass it on. Terrans have something called tragedy. It's what one of them called being a poet in the body of a cockroach.

"Have you heard the rumor?" Arnie asks, putting down the whittling tool. "Have you heard that some of the personnel in Punch Center aren't really humans?"

"Not really?" I ask, putting away the tape. We have no tragedy. In my species, family relationships are based only on related gene patterns; they are finally dumped into the family bank and a new relative is created from the old. It's one form of ancient history multiplying itself, but it isn't tragic. The koota, her utility destroyed by a recessive gene, lies sleeping at my feet. Is this tragedy? But she is a single form, she can't regenerate a lost limb, or exfoliate brain tissue. She can only return my gaze with her steadfast and affectionate one.

"What are they, then?" I ask Arnie. "If they're not human?"

"The story is that the local life forms aren't as we really see them. They've put on faces, like ours, to deal with us. And some of them have filtered into personnel."

Filtered! As if I were a virus.

I say, "But they must be harmless. No harm has come to anyone."

"We don't know that for a fact," Arnie replies.

"You look tired," I say, and he comes to me to be soothed, to be loved in his flesh, his single form, his search for the truth in the darkness of the viewing cubicle. At present he's doing studies of murger birds. Their spinal cavities are large, air-filled ovals, and their bone is extremely porous, which permits them to soar to great heights.

The koota no longer races on the windblown beaches; she lies at our feet, looking into the distance. The wall must be transparent to her eyes, I feel that beyond it she sees clearly how the racers go, down the long, bright curve of sand in the morning sun. She sighs, and lays her head down on her narrow, delicate paws.

Arnie says, "I seem to be tired all the time," and kneads the muscles of his chest. He puts his head down on my breasts. "I don't think the food's agreeing with me lately."

"Do you suffer pains?" I ask curiously.

"Suffer," he says, "what kind of nonsense is that, with analgesics. No. I don't suffer. I just don't feel well."

He's absorbed in murger birds, kaku wood, he descends into the dark and rises up like a rocket across the horizon into the thin clarity above. While I float. I no longer dare to breathe, I'm afraid of disturbing everything. I do not want anything. His head lies on my breast and I will not disturb him.

"Oh. My God," Arnie says, and I know what it's come to, even before he begins to choke, and his muscles leap although I hold him in my arms. I know his heart is choking on massive doses of blood; the brilliance fades from his eyes and they begin to go dark while I tightly hold him. If he doesn't see me as he dies, will I be here?

I can feel, under my fingers, how rapidly his skin cools. I must put him down, here with his carvings and his papers, and I must go home. But I lift Arnie in my arms, and call the koota, who gets up rather stiffly. It's long after dark, and I carry him slowly, carefully, home to what he called a crystal palace, where the Warden and my Uncle are teaching each other to play chess with a set some space captain gave them in exchange for seed crystals. They sit in a bloom of light, sparkling, their old brains bent over the chessmen, as I breathe open the door and carry Arnie in.

First, my Uncle gives me just a glance, but then another glance, and a hard stare. "Is that the Doctor?" he asks.

I put Arnie down and hold one of his cold hands. "Warden," I say, on my knees, on eye level with the chess board and its carved men. "Warden, can you put him in one of the banks?"

The Warden turns to look at me, as hard as my Uncle. "You've become deranged, trying to maintain two lobes," he says. "You cannot reconstitute or recreate a Terran by our methods, and you must know it."

"Over the edge, over the edge," my Uncle says, now a blond, six-foot, hearty male Terran, often at the Laugh Tree with one of the joy babies. He enjoys life, his own or someone else's. I have too, I suppose. Am I fading? I am, really, just one of Arnie's projections, a form on a screen in his mind. I am not, really, Martha. Though I tried.

"We can't have him here," the Warden says. "You'd better get him out of here. You couldn't explain a corpse like that to the colonists, if they came looking for him. They'll think we did something to him. It's nearly time for my next conjunction, do you want your nephew to arrive in disgrace? The Uncles will drain his bank."

The Warden gets up and comes over to me. He takes hold of my dark curls and pulls me to my feet. It hurts my physical me, which is Martha,

God knows, Arnie, I'm Martha, it seems to me. "Take him back to his quarters," the Warden says to me. "And come back here immediately. I'll try to see you back to your own pattern, but it may be too late. In part, I blame myself. If you must know. So I will try."

Yes, yes, I want to say to him; as I was, dedicated, free; turn me back into myself, I never wanted to be anyone else, and now I don't know if I am anyone at all. The light's gone from his eyes and he doesn't see me.

I pick him up and breathe the door out, and go back through the night to his quarters, where the lamp still burns. I'm going to leave him here, where he belongs. Before I go, I pick up the small carving of the murger bird and take it with me, home to my glass bridge where at the edge of the mirrors the decimals are still clicking perfectly, clicking out known facts; an octagon can be reduced, the planet turns at such a degree on its axis, to see the truth you must have light of some sort, but to see the light you must have darkness of some sort. I can no longer float on the horizon between the two because that horizon has disappeared. I've learned to descend, and to rise, and descend again.

I'm able to revert without help to my own free form, to reabsorb the extra brain tissue. The sun comes up and it's bright. The night comes down and it's dark. I'm becoming somber, and a brilliant student. Even my Uncle says I'll be a good Warden, when the time comes.

The Warden goes to conjunction; from the cell banks a nephew is lifted out. The koota lies dreaming of races she has run in the wind. It is our life, and it goes on, like the life of other creatures.

Ursula K. Le Guin

Vaster Than Empires and More Slow
(1971)

Ursula Kroeber Le Guin (b. 1929) is one of the most revered writers in modern sf and one of the few to have achieved widespread recognition and critical acclaim outside the field. The daughter of anthropologist Alfred L. Kroeber and writer Theodora Kroeber, Le Guin grew up in the liberal intellectual environment of Berkeley, California. She studied French and Italian literature at Radcliffe College and later at Columbia University, where she earned a master's degree in 1952. Le Guin has received numerous literary awards, including five Nebulas, five Hugos, two Tiptrees, and one Sturgeon; she was named a Grand Master by the Science Fiction and Fantasy Writers of America in 2003. Le Guin's most famous science fiction novels, *The Left Hand of Darkness* (1969) and *The Dispossessed* (1974) were dual winners of the Nebula and Hugo awards in their respective years. Other important works include the fantasy series set in the world of Earthsea (beginning with *A Wizard of Earthsea* in 1968) and *Always Coming Home* (1985), an ambitious experimental work set in a postapocalyptic Northern California. In addition to science fiction and fantasy, she has published five volumes of poetry and several collections of essays.

Le Guin is a gifted stylist and a bold thinker, renowned for the lyrical beauty of her prose and the psychological depth of her characters. Her stories typically combine realistic local detail with a thematic interest in larger sociopolitical concerns. Le Guin, whose work focuses primarily on the so-called soft sciences like psychology, anthropology, and sociology, was a leading force in the development of sf in the 1970s, raising literary standards and bringing social issues, especially women's concerns, to the forefront of what had been to some extent a male-dominated genre. Le Guin could easily have rested on her laurels long ago, but she has continued to evolve stylistically and thematically. What has remained unchanged is her core belief in humanity, compassion, and tolerance.

The story that follows directly addresses the topic that is the secret concern of all alien stories: the primordial distinction between self and Other. As in many of the alien stories in this section, the humans in this story are themselves embodiments of difference from the norm. The crew is a collection of brilliant but socially maladjusted misfits. None is more marked by difference than Osden, an empath cursed with the ability to directly experience the emotions of others, including the crew's strong dislike of him.

The title of this story is taken from a Renaissance love poem by Andrew Marvell, "To His Coy Mistress." The poem begins "My vegetable love should grow / Vaster than empires and more slow." This poem is also quoted in the second-to-last paragraph of the story: "Had we but world enough and time . . . ."

It was only during the earliest decades of the League that the Earth sent ships out on the enormously long voyages, beyond the pale, over the stars and far away. They were seeking for worlds which had not been seeded or settled by the Founders on Hain, truly alien worlds. All the Known Worlds went back to the Hainish Origin, and the Terrans, having been not only founded but salvaged by the Hainish, resented this. They wanted to get away from the family. They wanted to find somebody new. The Hainish, like tiresomely understanding parents, supported their explorations, and contributed ships and volunteers, as did several other worlds of the League.

All these volunteers to the Extreme Survey crews shared one peculiarity: they were of unsound mind.

What sane person, after all, would go out to collect information that would not be received for five or ten centuries? Cosmic mass interference had not yet been eliminated from the operation of the ansible, and so instantaneous communication was reliable only within a range of 120 lightyears. The explorers would be quite isolated. And of course they had no idea what they might come back to, if they came back. No normal human being who had experienced time-slippage of even a few decades between League worlds would volunteer for a round trip of centuries. The Surveyors were escapists, misfits. They were nuts.

Ten of them climbed aboard the ferry at Smeming Port, and made varyingly inept attempts to get to know one another during the three days the ferry took getting to their ship, *Gum*. Gum is a Cetian nickname, on the order of Baby or Pet. There were two Cetians on the team, two Hainishmen, one Beldene, and five Terrans; the Cetian-built ship was chartered by the Government of Earth. Her motley crew came aboard wriggling through the coupling tube one by one like apprehensive spermatozoa trying to fertilize the universe. The ferry left, and the navigator put *Gum* underway. She flittered for some hours on the edge of space a few hundred million miles from Smeming Port, and then abruptly vanished.

When, after 10 hours 29 minutes, or 256 years, *Gum* reappeared in normal space, she was supposed to be in the vicinity of Star KG-E-96651. Sure enough, there was the gold pinhead of the star. Somewhere within a four-hundred-million-kilometer sphere there was also a greenish planet, World 4470, as charted by a Cetian mapmaker. The ship now had to find the planet. This was not quite so easy as it might sound, given a four-hundred-million-kilometer haystack. And *Gum* couldn't bat about in planetary space at near lightspeed; if she did, she and Star KG-E-96651 and World 4470 might all end up going bang. She had to creep, using rocket propulsion, at a few hundred thousand miles an hour. The Mathematician/Navigator, Asnanifoil, knew pretty well where the planet ought to be, and thought they might raise it within ten E-days. Meanwhile the members of the Survey team got to know one another still better.

"I can't stand him," said Porlock, the Hard Scientist (chemistry, plus physics, astronomy, geology, etc.), and little blobs of spittle appeared on his mustache. "The man is insane. I can't imagine why he was passed as fit to join a Survey team, unless this is a deliberate experiment in noncompatibility, planned by the Authority, with us as guinea pigs."

"We generally use hamsters and Hainish gholes," said Mannon, the Soft Scientist (psychology, plus psychiatry, anthropology, ecology, etc.), politely; he was one of the Hainishmen. "Instead of guinea pigs. Well, you know, Mr Osden is really a very rare case. In fact, he's the first fully cured case of Render's Syndrome — a variety of infantile autism which was thought to be incurable. The great Terran analyst Hammergeld reasoned that the cause of the autistic condition in this case is a supernormal empathic capacity, and developed an appropriate treatment. Mr Osden is the first patient to undergo that treatment, in fact he lived with Dr Hammergeld until he was eighteen. The therapy was completely successful."

"Successful?"

"Why, yes. He certainly is not autistic."

"No, he's intolerable!"

"Well, you see," said Mannon, gazing mildly at the saliva-flecks on Porlock's mustache, "the normal defensive-aggressive reaction between strangers meeting — let's say you and Mr Osden just for example — is something you're scarcely aware of; habit, manners, inattention get you past it; you've learned to ignore it, to the point where you might even deny it exists. However, Mr Osden, being an empath, feels it. Feels his feelings, and yours, and is hard put to say which is which. Let's say that there's a normal element of hostility towards any stranger in your emotional reaction to him when you meet him, plus a spontaneous dislike of his looks, or clothes, or handshake — it doesn't matter what. He feels that dislike. As his autistic defense has been unlearned, he resorts to an aggressive-defense mechanism, a response in kind to the aggression which you have unwittingly projected onto him." Mannon went on for quite a long time.

"Nothing gives a man the right to be such a bastard," Porlock said.

"He can't tune us out?" asked Harfex, the Biologist, another Hainishman.

"It's like hearing," said Olleroo, Assistant Hard Scientist, stooping over to paint her toenails with fluorescent lacquer. "No eyelids on your ears. No Off switch on empathy. He hears our feelings whether he wants to or not."

"Does he know what we're *thinking*?" asked Eskwana, the Engineer, looking round at the others in real dread.

"No," Porlock snapped. "Empathy's not telepathy! Nobody's got telepathy."

"Yet," said Mannon, with his little smile. "Just before I left Hain there was a most interesting report in from one of the recently rediscovered worlds, a hilfer named Rocannon reporting what appears to be a teachable telepathic technique existent among a mutated hominid race; I only saw a synopsis in the HILF Bulletin, but — " He went on. The others had learned that they could talk while Mannon went on talking; he did not seem to mind, nor even to miss much of what they said.

"Then why does he hate us?" Eskwana said.

"Nobody hates you, Ander honey," said Olleroo, daubing Eskwana's left thumbnail with fluorescent pink. The engineer flushed and smiled vaguely.

"He acts as if he hated us," said Haito, the Coordinator. She was a delicate-looking woman of pure Asian descent, with a surprising voice, husky, deep, and soft, like a young bullfrog. "Why, if he suffers from our hostility, does he increase it by constant attacks and insults? I can't say I think much of Dr Hammergeld's cure, really, Mannon; autism might be preferable. . . ."

She stopped. Osden had come into the main cabin.

He looked flayed. His skin was unnaturally white and thin, showing the channels of his blood like a faded road map in red and blue. His Adam's apple, the muscles that circled his mouth, the bones and ligaments of his wrists and hands, all stood out distinctly as if displayed for an anatomy lesson. His hair was pale rust, like long-dried blood. He had eyebrows and lashes, but they were visible only in certain lights; what one saw was the bones of the eye sockets, the veining of the lids, and the colorless eyes. They were not red eyes, for he was not really an albino, but they were not blue or grey; colors had cancelled out in Osden's eyes, leaving a cold water-like clarity, infinitely penetrable. He never looked directly at one. His face lacked expression, like an anatomical drawing, or a skinned face.

"I agree," he said in a high, harsh tenor, "that even autistic withdrawal might be preferable to the smog of cheap secondhand emotions with which you people surround me. What are you sweating hate for now, Porlock? Can't stand the sight of me? Go practice some auto-eroticism the way you were doing last night, it improves your vibes. Who the devil moved my tapes, here? Don't touch my things, any of you. I won't have it."

"Osden," said Asnanifoil in his large slow voice, "why *are* you such a bastard?"

Ander Eskwana cowered and put his hands in front of his face. Contention frightened him. Olleroo looked up with a vacant yet eager expression, the eternal spectator.

"Why shouldn't I be?" said Osden. He was not looking at Asnanifoil, and was keeping physically as far away from all of them as he could in the crowded cabin. "None of you constitute, in yourselves, any reason for my changing my behavior."

Harfex, a reserved and patient man, said, "The reason is that we shall be spending several years together. Life will be better for all of us if — "

"Can't you understand that I don't give a damn for all of you?" Osden said, took up his microtapes, and went out. Eskwana had suddenly gone to sleep. Asnanifoil was drawing slipstreams in the air with his finger and muttering the Ritual Primes. "You cannot explain his presence on the team except as a plot on the part of the Terran Authority. I saw this almost at once. This mission is meant to fail," Harfex whispered to the Coordinator, glancing over his shoulder. Porlock was fumbling with his fly-button; there were tears in his eyes. I did tell you they were all crazy, but you thought I was exaggerating.

All the same, they were not unjustified. Extreme Surveyors expected to find their fellow team members intelligent, well-trained, unstable, and personally sympathetic. They had to work together in close quarters and nasty places, and could expect one another's paranoias, depressions, manias, phobias and compulsions to be mild enough to admit of good personal relationships, at least most of the time. Osden might be intelligent, but his training was sketchy and his personality was disastrous. He had been sent only on account of his singular gift, the power of empathy: properly speaking, of wide-range bioempathic receptivity. His talent wasn't species-specific; he could pick up emotion or sentience from anything that felt. He could share lust with a white rat, pain with a squashed cockroach, and phototropy with a moth. On an alien world, the Authority had decided, it would be useful to know if anything nearby is sentient, and if so, what its feelings towards you are. Osden's title was a new one: he was the team's Sensor.

"What is emotion, Osden?" Haito Tomiko asked him one day in the main cabin, trying to make some rapport with him for once. "What is it, exactly, that you pick up with your empathic sensitivity?"

"Muck," the man answered in his high, exasperated voice. "The psychic excreta of the animal kingdom. I wade through your faeces."

"I was trying," she said, "to learn some facts." She thought her tone was admirably calm.

"You weren't after facts. You were trying to get at me. With some fear, some curiosity, and a great deal of distaste. The way you might poke a dead dog, to see the maggots crawl. Will you understand once and for all that I don't want to be got at, that I want to be left alone?" His skin was mottled with red and violet, his voice had risen. "Go roll in your own dung, you yellow bitch!" he shouted at her silence.

"Calm down," she said, still quietly, but she left him at once and went to her cabin. Of course he had been right about her motives; her question had been largely a pretext, a mere effort to interest him. But what harm in that? Did not that effort imply respect for the other? At the moment of asking the question she had felt at most a slight distrust of him; she had mostly felt sorry for him, the poor arrogant venomous bastard, Mr No-Skin as Olleroo called him. What did he expect, the way he acted? Love?

"I guess he can't stand anybody feeling sorry for him," said Olleroo, lying on the lower bunk, gilding her nipples.

"Then he can't form any human relationship. All his Dr. Hammergeld did was turn an autism inside out. . . ."

"Poor frot," said Olleroo. "Tomiko, you don't mind if Harfex comes in for a while tonight, do you?"

"Can't you go to his cabin? I'm sick of always having to sit in Main with that damned peeled turnip."

"You do hate him, don't you? I guess he feels that. But I slept with Harfex last night too, and Asnanifoil might get jealous, since they share the cabin. It would be nicer here."

"Service them both," Tomiko said with the coarseness of offended modesty. Her Terran subculture, the East Asian, was a puritanical one; she had been brought up chaste.

"I only like one a night," Olleroo replied with innocent serenity. Beldene, the Garden Planet, had never discovered chastity, or the wheel.

"Try Osden, then," Tomiko said. Her personal instability was seldom so plain as now: a profound self-distrust manifesting itself as destructivism. She had volunteered for this job because there was, in all probability, no use in doing it.

The little Beldene looked up, paintbrush in hand, eyes wide. "Tomiko, that was a dirty thing to say."

"Why?"

"It would be vile! I'm not attracted to Osden!"

"I didn't know it mattered to you," Tomiko said indifferently, though she did know. She got some papers together and left the cabin, remarking, "I hope you and Harfex or whoever it is finish by last bell; I'm tired."

Olleroo was crying, tears dripping on her little gilded nipples. She wept easily. Tomiko had not wept since she was ten years old.

It was not a happy ship; but it took a turn for the better when Asnanifoil and his computers raised World 4470. There it lay, a dark-green jewel, like truth at the bottom of a gravity well. As they watched the jade disc grow, a sense of mutuality grew among them. Osden's selfishness, his accurate cruelty, served now to draw the others together. "Perhaps," Mannon said, "he was sent as a beating-gron. What Terrans call a scapegoat. Perhaps his influence will be good after all." And no one, so careful were they to be kind to one another, disagreed.

They came into orbit. There were no lights on nightside, on the continents none of the lines and clots made by animals who build.

"No men," Harfex murmured.

"Of course not," snapped Osden, who had a viewscreen to himself, and his head inside a polythene bag. He claimed that the plastic cut down on the empathic noise he received from the others. "We're two lightcenturies past the limit of the Hainish Expansion, and outside that there are no men. Anywhere. You don't think Creation would have made the same hideous mistake twice?"

No one was paying him much heed; they were looking with affection at that jade immensity below them, where there was life, but not human life. They were misfits among men, and what they saw there was not desolation, but peace. Even Osden did not look quite so expressionless as usual; he was frowning.

Descent in fire on the sea; air reconnaissance; landing. A plain of something like grass, thick, green, bowing stalks, surrounded the ship, brushed against extended viewcameras, smeared the lenses with a fine pollen.

"It looks like a pure phytosphere," Harfex said. "Osden, do you pick up anything sentient?"

They all turned to the Sensor. He had left the screen and was pouring himself a cup of tea. He did not answer. He seldom answered spoken questions.

The chitinous rigidity of military discipline was quite inapplicable to these teams of mad scientists; their chain of command lay somewhere between parliamentary procedure and peck-order, and would have driven a regular service officer out of his mind. By the inscrutable decision of the Authority, however, Dr Haito Tomiko had been given the title of Coordinator, and she now exercised her prerogative for the first time. "Mr Sensor Osden," she said, "please answer Mr Harfex."

"How could I 'pick up' anything from outside," Osden said without turning, "with the emotions of nine neurotic hominids pullulating around me like worms in a can? When I have anything to tell you, I'll tell you. I'm aware of my responsibility as Sensor. If you presume to give me an order again, however, Coordinator Haito, I'll consider my responsibility void."

"Very well, Mr. Sensor. I trust no orders will be needed henceforth." Tomiko's bullfrog voice was calm, but Osden seemed to flinch slightly as he stood with his back to her, as if the surge of her suppressed rancor had struck him with physical force.

The biologist's hunch proved correct. When they began field analyses they found no animals even among the microbiota. Nobody here ate anybody else. All life-forms were photosynthesizing or saprophagous, living off light or death, not off life. Plants: infinite plants, not one species known to the visitors from the house of Man. Infinite shades and intensities of green, violet, purple, brown, red. Infinite silences. Only the wind moved, swaying leaves and fronds, a warm soughing wind laden with spores and pollens, blowing the sweet pale-green dust over prairies of great grasses, heaths that bore no heather, flowerless forests where no foot had ever walked, no eye had ever looked. A warm, sad world, sad and serene. The Surveyors, wandering like picnickers over sunny plains of violet filicaliformes, spoke softly to each other. They knew their voices broke a silence of a thousand million years, the silence of wind and leaves, leaves and wind, blowing and ceasing and blowing again. They talked softly; but being human, they talked.

"Poor old Osden," said Jenny Chong, Bio and Tech, as she piloted a helijet on the North Polar Quadrating run. "All that fancy hi-fi stuff in his brain and nothing to receive. What a bust."

"He told me he hates plants," Olleroo said with a giggle.

"You'd think he'd like them, since they don't bother him like we do."

"Can't say I much like these plants myself," said Porlock, looking down at the purple undulations of the North Circumpolar Forest. "All the same. No mind. No change. A man alone in it would go right off his head."

"But it's all alive," Jenny Chong said. "And if it lives, Osden hates it."

"He's not really so bad," Olleroo said, magnanimous. Porlock looked at her sidelong and asked, "You ever slept with him, Olleroo?"

Olleroo burst into tears and cried, "You Terrans are obscene!"

"No she hasn't," Jenny Chong said, prompt to defend. "Have you, Porlock?"

The chemist laughed uneasily: ha, ha, ha. Flecks of spittle appeared on his mustache.

"Osden can't bear to be touched," Olleroo said shakily. "I just brushed against him once by accident and he knocked me off like I was some sort of dirty . . . thing. We're all just things, to him."

"He's evil," Porlock said in a strained voice, startling the two women. "He'll end up shattering this team, sabotaging it, one way or another. Mark my words. He's not fit to live with other people!"

They landed on the North Pole. A midnight sun smouldered over low hills. Short, dry, greenish-pink bryoform grasses stretched away in every direction, which was all one direction, south. Subdued by the incredible silence, the three Surveyors set up their instruments and set to work, three viruses twitching minutely on the hide of an unmoving giant.

Nobody asked Osden along on runs as pilot or photographer or recorder, and he never volunteered, so he seldom left base camp. He ran Harfex's botanical taxonomic data through the onship computers, and served as assistant to Eskwana, whose job here was mainly repair and maintenance. Eskwana had begun to sleep a great deal, twenty-five hours or more out of the thirty-two-hour day, dropping off in the middle of repairing a radio or checking the guidance circuits of a helijet. The Coordinator stayed at base one day to observe. No one else was home except Poswet To, who was subject to epileptic fits; Mannon had plugged her into a therapy-circuit today in a state of preventive catatonia. Tomiko spoke reports into the storage banks, and kept an eye on Osden and Eskwana. Two hours passed.

"You might want to use the 860 microwaldoes in sealing that connection," Eskwana said in his soft, hesitant voice.

"Obviously!"

"Sorry. I just saw you had the 840's there — "

"And will replace them when I take the 860's out. When I don't know how to proceed, Engineer, I'll ask your advice."

After a minute Tomiko looked round. Sure enough, there was Eskwana sound asleep, head on the table, thumb in his mouth.

"Osden."

The white face did not turn, he did not speak, but conveyed impatiently that he was listening.

"You can't be unaware of Eskwana's vulnerability."

"I am not responsible for his psychopathic reactions."

"But you are responsible for your own. Eskwana is essential to our work here, and you're not. If you can't control your hostility, you must avoid him altogether."

Osden put down his tools and stood up. "With pleasure!" he said in his vindictive, scraping voice. "You could not possibly imagine what it's like to experience Eskwana's irrational terrors. To have to share his horrible cowardice, to have to cringe with him at everything!"

"Are you trying to justify your cruelty towards him? I thought you had more self-respect." Tomiko found herself shaking with spite. "If your empathic power really makes you share Ander's misery, why does it never induce the least compassion in you?"

"Compassion," Osden said. "Compassion. What do you know about compassion?"

She stared at him, but he would not look at her.

"Would you like me to verbalize your present emotional affect regarding myself?" he said. "I can do so more precisely than you can. I'm trained to analyze such responses as I receive them. And I do receive them."

"But how can you expect me to feel kindly towards you when you behave as you do?"

"What does it matter how I *behave*, you stupid sow, do you think it makes any difference? Do you think the average human is a well of loving-kindness? My choice is to be hated or to be despised. Not being a woman or a coward, I prefer to be hated."

"That's rot. Self-pity. Every man has — "

"But I am not a man," Osden said. "There are all of you. And there is myself. I am *one*."

Awed by that glimpse of abysmal solipsism, she kept silent a while; finally she said with neither spite nor pity, clinically, "You could kill yourself, Osden."

"That's your way, Haito," he jeered. "I'm not depressive, and *seppuku* isn't my bit. What do you want me to do here?"

"Leave. Spare yourself and us. Take the aircar and a data-feeder and go do a species count. In the forest; Harfex hasn't even started the forests yet. Take a hundred-square-meter forested area, anywhere inside radio range. But outside empathy range. Report in at 8 and 24 o'clock daily."

Osden went, and nothing was heard from him for five days but laconic all-well signals twice daily. The mood at base camp changed like a stage-set. Eskwana stayed awake up to eighteen hours a day. Poswet To got out her stellar lute and chanted the celestial harmonies (music had driven Osden into a frenzy). Mannon, Harfex, Jenny Chong, and Tomiko all went off tranquillizers. Porlock distilled something in his laboratory and drank it all by himself. He had a hangover. Asnanifoil and Poswet To held an all-night Numerical Epiphany, that mystical orgy of higher mathematics which is the chief pleasure of the religious Cetian soul. Olleroo slept with everybody. Work went well.

The Hard Scientist came towards base at a run, laboring through the high, fleshy stalks of the graminiformes. "Something — in the forest — " His eyes bulged, he panted, his mustache and fingers trembled. "Something big. Moving, behind me. I was putting in a benchmark, bending down. It came at me. As if it was swinging down out of the trees. Behind me." He stared at the others with the opaque eyes of terror or exhaustion.

"Sit down, Porlock. Take it easy. Now wait, go through this again. You *saw* something — "

"Not clearly. Just the movement. Purposive. A — an — I don't know what it could have been. Something self-moving. In the trees, the arboriformes, whatever you call 'em. At the edge of the woods."

Harfex looked grim. "There is nothing here that could attack you, Porlock. There are not even microzoa. There *could not* be a large animal."

"Could you possibly have seen an epiphyte drop suddenly, a vine come loose behind you?"

"No," Porlock said. "It was coming down at me, through the branches, fast. When I turned it took off again, away and upward. It made a noise, a sort of crashing. If it wasn't an animal, God knows what it could have been! It was big — as big as a man, at least. Maybe a reddish color. I couldn't see, I'm not sure."

"It was Osden," said Jenny Chong, "doing a Tarzan act." She giggled nervously, and Tomiko repressed a wild feckless laugh. But Harfex was not smiling.

"One gets uneasy under the arboriformes," he said in his polite, re-pressed voice. "I've noticed that. Indeed that may be why I've put off working in the forests. There's a hypnotic quality in the colors and spacing of the stems and branches, especially the helically-arranged ones; and the spore-throwers grow so regularly spaced that it seems unnatural. I find it quite disagreeable, subjectively speaking. I wonder if a stronger effect of that sort mightn't have produced a hallucination . . . ?"

Porlock shook his head. He wet his lips. "It was there," he said. "Something. Moving with purpose. Trying to attack me from behind."

When Osden called in, punctual as always, at 24 o'clock that night, Harfex told him Porlock's report. "Have you come on anything at all, Mr Osden, that could substantiate Mr Porlock's impression of a motile, sentient life-form, in the forest?"

Ssss, the radio said sardonically. "No. Bullshit," said Osden's unpleasant voice.

"You've been actually inside the forest longer than any of us," Harfex said with unmitigable politeness. "Do you agree with my impression that the forest ambiance has a rather troubling and possibly hallucinogenic effect on the perceptions?"

Ssss. "I'll agree that Porlock's perceptions are easily troubled. Keep him in his lab, he'll do less harm. Anything else?"

"Not at present," Harfex said, and Osden cut off.

Nobody could credit Porlock's story, and nobody could discredit it. He was positive that something, something big, had tried to attack him by surprise. It was hard to deny this, for they were on an alien world, and everyone who had entered the forest had felt a certain chill and foreboding under the "trees." ("Call them trees, certainly," Harfex had said. "They really are the same thing, only, of course, altogether different.") They agreed that they had felt uneasy, or had had the sense that something was watching them from behind.

"We've got to clear this up," Porlock said, and he asked to be sent as a temporary Biologist's Aide, like Osden, into the forest to explore and observe. Olleroo and Jenny Chong volunteered if they could go as a pair. Harfex sent them all off into the forest near which they were encamped, a vast tract covering four-fifths of Continent D. He forbade side-arms. They were not to go outside a fifty-mile half-circle, which included Osden's current site. They all reported in twice daily, for three days. Porlock reported a glimpse of what seemed to be a large semi-erect shape moving through the trees across the river; Olleroo was sure she had heard something moving near the tent, the second night.

"There are no animals on this planet," Harfex said, dogged.

Then Osden missed his morning call.

Tomiko waited less than an hour, then flew with Harfex to the area where Osden had reported himself the night before. But as the helijet hovered over the sea of purplish leaves, illimitable, impenetrable, she felt a panic despair. "How can we find him in this?"

"He reported landing on the riverbank. Find the aircar; he'll be camped near it, and he can't have gone far from his camp. Species-counting is slow work. There's the river."

"There's his car," Tomiko said, catching the bright foreign glint among the vegetable colors and shadows. "Here goes, then."

She put the ship in hover and pitched out the ladder. She and Harfex descended. The sea of life closed over their heads.

As her feet touched the forest floor, she unsnapped the flap of her holster; then glancing at Harfex, who was unarmed, she left the gun untouched. But her hand kept coming back up to it. There was no sound at all, as soon as they were a few meters away from the slow, brown river, and the light was dim. Great boles stood well apart, almost regularly, almost alike; they were soft-skinned, some appearing smooth and others spongy, grey or greenish-brown or brown, twined with cable-like creepers and festooned with epiphytes, extending rigid, entangled armfuls of big, saucer-shaped, dark leaves that formed a roof-layer twenty to thirty meters thick. The ground underfoot was springy as a mattress, every inch of it knotted with roots and peppered with small, fleshy-leaved growths.

"Here's his tent," Tomiko said, cowed at the sound of her voice in that huge community of the voiceless. In the tent was Osden's sleeping bag, a couple of books, a box of rations. We should be calling, shouting for him, she thought, but did not even suggest it; nor did Harfex. They circled out from the tent, careful to keep each other in sight through the thick-standing presences, the crowding gloom. She stumbled over Osden's body, not thirty meters from the tent, led to it by the whitish gleam of a dropped notebook. He lay face down between two huge-rooted trees. His head and hands were covered with blood, some dried, some still oozing red.

Harfex appeared beside her, his pale Hainish complexion quite green in the dusk. "Dead?"

"No. He's been struck. Beaten. From behind." Tomiko's fingers felt over the bloody skull and temples and nape. "A weapon or a tool . . . I don't find a fracture."

As she turned Osden's body over so they could lift him, his eyes opened. She was holding him, bending close to his face. His pale lips writhed. A deathly fear came into her. She screamed aloud two or three times and tried to run away, shambling and stumbling into the terrible dusk. Harfex caught her, and at his touch and the sound of his voice, her panic decreased. "What is it? What is it?" he was saying.

"I don't know," she sobbed. Her heartbeat still shook her, and she could not see clearly. "The fear — the . . . I panicked. When I saw his eyes."

"We're both nervous. I don't understand this — "

"I'm all right now, come on, we've got to get him under care."

Both working with senseless haste, they lugged Osden to the riverside and hauled him up on a rope under his armpits; he dangled like a sack, twisting a little, over the glutinous dark sea of leaves. They pulled him into the helijet and took off. Within a minute they were over open prairie. Tomiko locked onto the homing beam. She drew a deep breath, and her eyes met Harfex's.

"I was so terrified I almost fainted. I have never done that."

"I was . . . unreasonably frightened also," said the Hainishman, and indeed he looked aged and shaken. "Not so badly as you. But as unreasonably."

"It was when I was in contact with him, holding him. He seemed to be conscious for a moment."

"Empathy? . . . I hope he can tell us what attacked him."

Osden, like a broken dummy covered with blood and mud, half lay as they had bundled him into the rear seats in their frantic urgency to get out of the forest.

More panic met their arrival at base. The ineffective brutality of the assault was sinister and bewildering. Since Harfex stubbornly denied any possibility of animal life they began speculating about sentient plants, vegetable monsters, psychic projections. Jenny Chong's latent phobia reasserted itself and she could talk about nothing except the Dark Egos which followed people around behind their backs. She and Olleroo and Porlock had been summoned back to base; and nobody was much inclined to go outside.

Osden had lost a good deal of blood during the three or four hours he had lain alone, and concussion and severe contusions had put him in shock and semi-coma. As he came out of this and began running a low fever he called several times for "Doctor," in a plaintive voice: "Doctor Hammergeld . . ." When he regained full consciousness, two of those long days later, Tomiko called Harfex into his cubicle.

"Osden: can you tell us what attacked you?"

The pale eyes flickered past Harfex's face.

"You were attacked," Tomiko said gently. The shifty gaze was hatefully familiar, but she was a physician, protective of the hurt. "You may not remember it yet. Something attacked you. You were in the forest — "

"Ah!" he cried out, his eyes growing bright and his features contorting. "The forest — in the forest — "

"What's in the forest?"

He gasped for breath. A look of clearer consciousness came into his face. After a while he said, "I don't know."

"Did you see what attacked you?" Harfex asked.

"I don't know."

"You remember it now."

"I don't know."

"All our lives may depend on this. You must tell us what you saw!"

"I don't know," Osden said, sobbing with weakness. He was too weak to hide the fact that he was hiding the answer, yet he would not say it. Porlock, nearby, was chewing his pepper-colored mustache as he tried to hear what was going on in the cubicle. Harfex leaned over Osden and said, "You *will* tell us — " Tomiko had to interfere bodily.

Harfex controlled himself with an effort that was painful to see. He went off silently to his cubicle, where no doubt he took a double or triple dose of tranquillizers. The other men and women, scattered about the big frail building, a long main hall and ten sleeping-cubicles, said nothing, but looked depressed and edgy. Osden, as always, even now, had them all at his mercy. Tomiko looked down at him with a rush of hatred that burned in her throat like bile. This monstrous egotism that fed itself on others' emotions, this absolute selfishness, was worse than any hideous deformity of the flesh. Like a congenital monster, he should not have lived. Should not be alive. Should have died. Why had his head not been split open?

As he lay flat and white, his hands helpless at his sides, his colorless eyes were wide open, and there were tears running from the corners. He tried to flinch away. "Don't," he said in a weak hoarse voice, and tried to raise his hands to protect his head. "Don't!"

She sat down on the folding-stool beside the cot, and after a while put her hand on his. He tried to pull away, but lacked the strength.

A long silence fell between them.

"Osden," she murmured, "I'm sorry. I'm very sorry. I will you well. Let me will you well, Osden. I don't want to hurt you. Listen, I do see now. It was one of us. That's right, isn't it. No, don't answer, only tell me if I'm wrong; but I'm not. . . . Of course there are animals on this planet. Ten of them. I don't care who it was. It doesn't matter, does it. It could have been me, just now. I realize that. I didn't understand how it is, Osden. You can't see how difficult it is for us to understand. . . . But listen. If it were love, instead of hate and fear . . . Is it never love?"

"No."

"Why not? Why should it never be? Are human beings all so weak? That is terrible. Never mind, never mind, don't worry. Keep still. At least right now it isn't hate, is it? Sympathy at least, concern, well-wishing. You do feel that, Osden? Is it what you feel?"

"Among . . . other things," he said, almost inaudibly.

"Noise from my subconscious, I suppose. And everybody else in the room . . . Listen, when we found you there in the forest, when I tried to turn you over, you partly wakened, and I felt a horror of you. I was insane with fear for a minute. Was that your fear of me I felt?"

"No."

Her hand was still on his, and he was quite relaxed, sinking towards sleep, like a man in pain who has been given relief from pain. "The forest," he muttered; she could barely understand him. "Afraid."

She pressed him no further, but kept her hand on his and watched him go to sleep. She knew what she felt, and what therefore he must feel. She was confident of it: there is only one emotion, or state of being, that can thus wholly reverse itself, polarize, within one moment. In Great Hainish indeed there is one word, *ontá*, for love and for hate. She was not in love with Osden, of course, that was another kettle of fish. What she felt for him was *ontá*, polarized hate. She held his hand and the current flowed between them, the tremendous electricity of touch, which he had always dreaded. As he slept the ring of anatomy-chart muscles around his mouth relaxed, and Tomiko saw on his face what none of them had ever seen, very faint, a smile. It faded. He slept on.

He was tough; next day he was sitting up, and hungry. Harfex wished to interrogate him, but Tomiko put him off. She hung a sheet of polythene over the cubicle door, as Osden himself had often done. "Does it actually cut down your empathic reception?" she asked, and he replied, in the dry, cautious tone they were now using to each other, "No."

"Just a warning, then."

"Partly. More faith-healing. Dr Hammergeld thought it worked. . . . Maybe it does, a little."

There had been love, once. A terrified child, suffocating in the tidal rush and battering of the huge emotions of adults, a drowning child, saved by one man. Taught to breathe, to live, by one man. Given everything, all protection and love, by one man. Father/Mother/God: no other. "Is he still alive?" Tomiko asked, thinking of Osden's incredible loneliness, and the strange cruelty of the great doctors. She was shocked when she heard his forced, tinny laugh. "He died at least two and a half centuries ago," Osden said. "Do you forget where we are, Coordinator? We've all left our little families behind. . . ."

Outside the polythene curtain the eight other human beings on World 4470 moved vaguely. Their voices were low and strained. Eskwana slept; Poswet To was in therapy; Jenny Chong was trying to rig lights in her cubicle so that she wouldn't cast a shadow.

"They're all scared," Tomiko said, scared. "They've all got these ideas about what attacked you. A sort of ape-potato, a giant fanged spinach, I don't know. . . . Even Harfex. You may be right not to force them to see. That would be worse, to lose confidence in one another. But why are we all so shaky, unable to face the fact, going to pieces so easily? Are we really all insane?"

"We'll soon be more so."

"Why?"

"There *is* something." He closed his mouth, the muscles of his lips stood out rigid.

"Something sentient?"

"A sentience."

"In the forest?"

He nodded.

"What is it, then — ?"

"The fear." He began to look strained again, and moved restlessly. "When I fell, there, you know, I didn't lose consciousness at once. Or I kept regaining it. I don't know. It was more like being paralyzed."

"You were."

"I was on the ground. I couldn't get up. My face was in the dirt, in that soft leaf mold. It was in my nostrils and eyes. I couldn't move. Couldn't see. As if I was in the ground. Sunk into it, part of it. I knew I was between two trees even though I never saw them. I suppose I could feel the roots. Below me in the ground, down under the ground. My hands were bloody, I could feel that, and the blood made the dirt around my face sticky. I felt the fear. It kept growing. As if they'd finally *known* I was there, lying on them there, under them, among them, the thing they feared, and yet part of their fear itself. I couldn't stop sending the fear back, and it kept growing, and I couldn't move, I couldn't get away. I would pass out, I think, and then the fear would bring me to again, and I still couldn't move. Any more than they can."

Tomiko felt the cold stirring of her hair, the readying of the apparatus of terror. "They: who are they, Osden?"

"They, it — I don't know. The fear."

"What is he talking about?" Harfex demanded when Tomiko reported this conversation. She would not let Harfex question Osden yet, feeling that she must protect Osden from the onslaught of the Hainishman's powerful, over-repressed emotions. Unfortunately this fueled the slow fire of paranoid anxiety that burned in poor Harfex, and he thought she and Osden were in league, hiding some fact of great importance or peril from the rest of the team.

"It's like the blind man trying to describe the elephant. Osden hasn't seen or heard the . . . the sentience, any more than we have."

"But he's felt it, my dear Haito," Harfex said with just-suppressed rage. "Not empathically. On his skull. It came and knocked him down and beat him with a blunt instrument. Did he not catch *one* glimpse of it?"

"What would he have seen, Harfex?" Tomiko asked, but he would not hear her meaningful tone; even he had blocked out that comprehension. What one fears is alien. The murderer is an outsider, a foreigner, not one of us. The evil is not in me!

"The first blow knocked him pretty well out," Tomiko said a little wearily, "he didn't see anything. But when he came to again, alone in the forest, he felt a great fear. Not his own fear, an empathic effect. He is certain of that. And certain it was nothing picked up from any of us. So that evidently the native life-forms are not all insentient."

Harfex looked at her a moment, grim. "You're trying to frighten me, Haito. I do not understand your motives." He got up and went off to his laboratory table, walking slowly and stiffly, like a man of eighty not of forty.

She looked round at the others. She felt some desperation. Her new, fragile, and profound interdependence with Osden gave her, she was well aware, some added strength. But if even Harfex could not keep his head, who of the others would? Porlock and Eskwana were shut in their cubicles, the others were all working or busy with something. There was something queer about their positions. For a while the Coordinator could not tell what it was, then she saw that they were all sitting facing the nearby forest. Playing chess with Asnanifoil, Olleroo had edged her chair around until it was almost beside his.

She went to Mannon, who was dissecting a tangle of spidery brown roots, and told him to look for the pattern-puzzle. He saw it at once, and said with unusual brevity, "Keeping an eye on the enemy."

"What enemy? What do *you* feel, Mannon?" She had a sudden hope in him as a psychologist, on this obscure ground of hints and empathies where biologists went astray.

"I feel a strong anxiety with a specific spatial orientation. But I am not an empath. Therefore the anxiety is explicable in terms of the particular stress-situation, that is, the attack on a team member in the forest, and also in terms of the total stress-situation, that is, my presence in a totally alien environment, for which the archetypical connotations of the word 'forest' provide an inevitable metaphor."

Hours later Tomiko woke to hear Osden screaming in nightmare; Mannon was calming him, and she sank back into her own dark-branching pathless dreams. In the morning Eskwana did not wake. He could not be roused with stimulant drugs. He clung to his sleep, slipping farther and farther back, mumbling softly now and then until, wholly regressed, he lay curled on his side, thumb at his lips, gone.

"Two days; two down. Ten little Indians, nine little Indians . . ." That was Porlock.

"And you're the next little Indian," Jenny Chong snapped. "Go analyze your urine, Porlock!"

"He is driving us all insane," Porlock said, getting up and waving his left arm. "Can't you feel it? For God's sake, are you all deaf and blind? Can't you feel what he's doing, the emanations? It all comes from him — from his room there — from his mind. He is driving us all insane with fear!"

"Who is?" said Asnanifoil, looming precipitous and hairy over the little Terran.

"Do I have to say his name? Osden, then. Osden! Osden! Why do you think I tried to kill him? In self-defense! To save all of us! Because you won't see what he's doing to us. He's sabotaged the mission by making us quarrel, and now he's going to drive us all insane by projecting fear at us so that we can't sleep or think, like a huge radio that doesn't make any sound, but it broadcasts all the time, and you can't sleep, and you can't think. Haito and Harfex are already under his control but the rest of you can be saved. I had to do it!"

"You didn't do it very well," Osden said, standing half-naked, all rib and bandage, at the door of his cubicle. "I could have hit myself harder. Hell, it isn't me that's scaring you blind, Porlock, it's out there — there, in the woods!"

Porlock made an ineffectual attempt to assault Osden; Asnanifoil held him back, and continued to hold him effortlessly while Mannon gave him a sedative shot. He was put away shouting about giant radios. In a minute the sedative took effect, and he joined a peaceful silence to Eskwana's.

"All right," said Harfex. "Now, Osden, you'll tell us what you know and all you know."

Osden said, "I don't know anything."

He looked battered and faint. Tomiko made him sit down before he talked.

"After I'd been three days in the forest, I thought I was occasionally receiving some kind of affect."

"Why didn't you report it?"

"Thought I was going spla, like the rest of you."

"That, equally, should have been reported."

"You'd have called me back to base. I couldn't take it. You realize that my inclusion in the mission was a bad mistake. I'm not able to coexist with nine other neurotic personalities at close quarters. I was wrong to volunteer for Extreme Survey, and the Authority was wrong to accept me."

No one spoke; but Tomiko saw, with certainty this time, the flinch in Osden's shoulders and the tightening of his facial muscles, as he registered their bitter agreement.

"Anyhow, I didn't want to come back to base because I was curious. Even going psycho, how could I pick up empathic affects when there was no creature to emit them? They weren't bad, then. Very vague. Queer. Like a draft in a closed room, a flicker in the corner of your eye. Nothing really."

For a moment he had been borne up on their listening: they heard, so he spoke. He was wholly at their mercy. If they disliked him he had to be hateful; if they mocked him he became grotesque; if they listened to him he was the storyteller. He was helplessly obedient to the demands of their emotions, reactions, moods. And there were seven of them, too many to cope with, so that he must be constantly knocked about from one to another's whim. He could not find coherence. Even as he spoke and held them, somebody's attention would wander: Olleroo perhaps was thinking that he wasn't unattractive, Harfex was seeking the ulterior motive of his words, Asnanifoil's mind, which could not be long held by the concrete, was roaming off towards the eternal peace of number, and Tomiko was distracted by pity, by fear. Osden's voice faltered. He lost the thread. "I . . . I thought it must be the trees," he said, and stopped.

"It's not the trees," Harfex said. "They have no more nervous system than do plants of the Hainish Descent on Earth. None."

"You're not seeing the forest for the trees, as they say on Earth," Mannon put in, smiling elfinly; Harfex stared at him. "What about those root-nodes we've been puzzling about for twenty days — eh?"

"What about them?"

"They are, indubitably, connections. Connections among the trees. Right? Now let's just suppose, most improbably, that you knew nothing of animal brain-structure. And you were given one axon, or one detached glial cell, to examine. Would you be likely to discover what it was? Would you see that the cell was capable of sentience?"

"No. Because it isn't. A single cell is capable of mechanical response to stimulus. No more. Are you hypothesizing that individual arboriformes are 'cells' in a kind of brain, Mannon?"

"Not exactly. I'm merely pointing out that they are all interconnected, both by the root-node linkage and by your green epiphytes in the branches. A linkage of incredible complexity and physical extent. Why, even the prairie grass-forms have those root-connectors, don't they? I know that sentience or intelligence isn't a thing, you can't find it in, or analyze it out from, the cells of a brain. It's a function of the connected cells. It is, in a sense, the connection: the connectedness. It doesn't exist. I'm not trying to say it exists. I'm only guessing that Osden might be able to describe it."

And Osden took him up, speaking as if in a trance. "Sentience without senses. Blind, deaf, nerveless, moveless. Some irritability, response to touch. Response to sun, to light, to water, and chemicals in the earth around the roots. Nothing comprehensible to an animal mind. Presence without mind. Awareness of being, without object or subject. Nirvana."

"Then why do you receive fear?" Tomiko asked in a low voice.

"I don't know. I can't see how awareness of objects, of others, could arise: an unperceiving response . . . But there was an uneasiness, for days. And then when I lay between the two trees and my blood was on their roots —" Osden's face glittered with sweat. "It became fear," he said shrilly, "only fear."

"If such a function existed," Harfex said, "it would not be capable of conceiving of a self-moving, material entity, or responding to one. It could no more become aware of us than we can 'become aware' of Infinity."

"'The silence of those infinite expanses terrifies me,'" muttered Tomiko. "Pascal was aware of Infinity. By way of fear."

"To a forest," Mannon said, "we might appear as forest fires. Hurricanes. Dangers. What moves quickly is dangerous, to a plant. The rootless would be alien, terrible. And if it is mind, it seems only too probable that it might become aware of Osden, whose own mind is open to connection with all others so long as he's conscious, and who was lying in pain and afraid within it, actually inside it. No wonder it was afraid — "

"Not 'it,'" Harfex said. "There is no being, no huge creature, no person! There could at most be only a function — "

"There is only a fear," Osden said.

They were all still a while, and heard the stillness outside.

"Is that what I feel all the time coming up behind me?" Jenny Chong asked, subdued.

Osden nodded. "You all feel it, deaf as you are. Eskwana's the worst off, because he actually has some empathic capacity. He could send if he learned how, but he's too weak, never will be anything but a medium."

"Listen, Osden," Tomiko said, "you can send. Then send to it — the forest, the fear out there — tell it that we won't hurt it. Since it has, or is, some sort of affect that translates into what we feel as emotion, can't you translate back? Send out a message, We are harmless, we are friendly."

"You must know that nobody can emit a false empathic message, Haito. You can't send something that doesn't exist."

"But we don't intend harm, we are friendly."

"Are we? In the forest, when you picked me up, did you feel friendly?"

"No. Terrified. But that's — it, the forest, the plants, not my own fear, isn't it?"

"What's the difference? It's all you felt. Can't you see," and Osden's voice rose in exasperation, "why I dislike you and you dislike me, all of you? Can't you see that I retransmit every negative or aggressive affect you've felt towards me since we first met? I return your hostility, with thanks. I do it in self-defense. Like Porlock. It is self-defense, though; it's the only technique I developed to replace my original defense of total withdrawal from others. Unfortunately it creates a closed circuit, self-sustaining and self-reinforcing. Your initial reaction to me was the instinctive antipathy to a cripple; by now of course it's hatred. Can you fail to see my point? The forest-mind out there transmits only terror, now, and the only message I can send it is terror, because when exposed to it I can feel nothing except terror!"

"What must we do, then?" said Tomiko, and Mannon replied promptly, "Move camp. To another continent. If there are plant-minds there, they'll be slow to notice us, as this one was; maybe they won't notice us at all."

"It would be a considerable relief," Osden observed stiffly. The others had been watching him with a new curiosity. He had revealed himself, they had seen him as he was, a helpless man in a trap. Perhaps, like Tomiko, they had seen that the trap itself, his crass and cruel egotism, was their own con-struction, not his. They had built the cage and locked him in it, and like a caged ape he threw filth out through the bars. If, meeting him, they had offered trust, if they had been strong enough to offer him love, how might he have appeared to them?

None of them could have done so, and it was too late now. Given time, given solitude, Tomiko might have built up with him a slow resonance of feeling, a consonance of trust, a harmony; but there was no time, their job must be done. There was not room enough for the cultivation of so great a thing, and they must make do with sympathy, with pity, the small change of love. Even that much had given her strength, but it was nowhere near enough for him. She could see in his flayed face now his savage resentment of their curiosity, even of her pity.

"Go lie down, that gash is bleeding again," she said, and he obeyed her.

Next morning they packed up, melted down the sprayform hangar and living quarters, lifted *Gum* on mechanical drive and took her halfway round World 4470, over the red and green lands, the many warm green seas. They had picked out a likely spot on Continent G: a prairie, twenty thousand square kilos of windswept graminiformes. No forest was within a hundred kilos of the site, and there were no lone trees or groves on the plain. The plant-forms occurred only in large species-colonies, never intermingled, except for certain tiny ubiquitous saprophytes and spore-bearers. The team sprayed holomeld over structure forms, and by evening of the thirty-two-hour day were settled in to the new camp. Eskwana was still asleep and Porlock still sedated, but everyone else was cheerful. "You can breathe here!" they kept saying.

Osden got on his feet and went shakily to the doorway; leaning there he looked through twilight over the dim reaches of the swaying grass that was not grass. There was a faint, sweet odor of pollen on the wind; no sound but the soft, vast sibilance of wind. His bandaged head cocked a little, the empath stood motionless for a long time. Darkness came, and the stars, lights in the windows of the distant house of Man. The wind had ceased, there was no sound. He listened.

In the long night Haito Tomiko listened. She lay still and heard the blood in her arteries, the breathing of sleepers, the wind blowing, the dark veins running, the dreams advancing, the vast static of stars increasing as the universe died slowly, the sound of death walking. She struggled out of her bed, fled the tiny solitude of her cubicle. Eskwana alone slept. Porlock lay straitjacketed, raving softly in his obscure native tongue. Olleroo and Jenny Chong were playing cards, grim-faced. Poswet To was in the therapy niche, plugged in. Asnanifoil was drawing a mandala, the Third Pattern of the Primes. Mannon and Harfex were sitting up with Osden.

She changed the bandages on Osden's head. His lank, reddish hair, where she had not had to shave it, looked strange. It was salted with white, now. Her hands shook as she worked. Nobody had yet said anything.

"How can the fear be here too?" she said, and her voice rang flat and false in the terrific silence.

"It's not just the trees; the grasses too . . ."

"But we're twelve thousand kilos from where we were this morning, we left it on the other side of the planet."

"It's all one," Osden said. "One big green thought. How long does it take a thought to get from one side of your brain to the other?"

"It doesn't think. It isn't thinking," Harfex said, lifelessly. "It's merely a network of processes. The branches, the epiphytic growths, the roots with those nodal junctures between individuals: they must all be capable of transmitting electrochemical impulses. There are no individual plants, then, properly speaking. Even the pollen is part of the linkage, no doubt, a sort of windborne sentience, connecting overseas. But it is not conceivable. That all the biosphere of a planet should be one network of communications, sensitive, irrational, immortal, isolated. . . ."

"Isolated," said Osden. "That's it! That's the fear. It isn't that we're motile, or destructive. It's just that we are. We are other. There has never been any other."

"You're right," Mannon said, almost whispering. "It has no peers. No enemies. No relationship with anything but itself. One alone forever."

"Then what's the function of its intelligence in species-survival?"

"None, maybe," Osden said. "Why are you getting teleological, Harfex? Aren't you a Hainishman? Isn't the measure of complexity the measure of the eternal joy?"

Harfex did not take the bait. He looked ill. "We should leave this world," he said.

"Now you know why I always want to get out, get away from you," Osden said with a kind of morbid geniality. "It isn't pleasant, is it — the other's fear . . . ? If only it were an animal intelligence. I can get through to animals. I get along with cobras and tigers; superior intelligence gives one the advantage. I should have been used in a zoo, not on a human team. . . . If I could get through to the damned stupid potato! If it wasn't so overwhelming . . . I still pick up more than the fear, you know. And before it panicked it had a — there was a serenity. I couldn't take it in, then, I didn't realize how big it was. To know the whole daylight, after all, and the whole night. All the winds and lulls together. The winter stars and the summer stars at the same time. To have roots, and no enemies. To be entire. Do you see? No invasion. No others. To be whole . . ."

He had never spoken before, Tomiko thought.

"You are defenseless against it, Osden," she said. "Your personality has changed already. You're vulnerable to it. We may not all go mad, but you will, if we don't leave."

He hesitated, then he looked up at Tomiko, the first time he had ever met her eyes, a long, still look, clear as water.

"What's sanity ever done for me?" he said, mocking. "But you have a point, Haito. You have something there."

"We should get away," Harfex muttered.

"If I gave in to it," Osden mused, "could I communicate?"

"By 'give in,'" Mannon said in a rapid, nervous voice, "I assume that you mean, stop sending back the empathic information which you receive from the plant-entity: stop rejecting the fear, and absorb it. That will either kill you at once, or drive you back into total psychological withdrawal, autism."

"Why?" said Osden. "Its message is *rejection*. But my salvation is rejection. It's not intelligent. But I am."

"The scale is wrong. What can a single human brain achieve against something so vast?"

"A single human brain can perceive pattern on the scale of stars and galaxies," Tomiko said, "and interpret it as Love."

Mannon looked from one to the other of them; Harfex was silent.

"It'd be easier in the forest," Osden said. "Which of you will fly me over?"

"When?"

"Now. Before you all crack up or go violent."

"I will," Tomiko said.

"None of us will," Harfex said.

"I can't," Mannon said. "I . . . I am too frightened. I'd crash the jet."

"Bring Eskwana along. If I can pull this off, he might serve as a medium."

"Are you accepting the Sensor's plan, Coordinator?" Harfex asked formally.

"Yes."

"I disapprove. I will come with you, however."

"I think we're compelled, Harfex," Tomiko said, looking at Osden's face, the ugly white mask transfigured, eager as a lover's face.

Olleroo and Jenny Chong, playing cards to keep their thoughts from their haunted beds, their mounting dread, chattered like scared children. "This thing, it's in the forest, it'll get you — "

"Scared of the dark?" Osden jeered.

"But look at Eskwana, and Porlock, and even Asnanifoil — "

"It can't hurt you. It's an impulse passing through synapses, a wind passing through branches. It is only a nightmare."

They took off in a helijet, Eskwana curled up still sound asleep in the rear compartment, Tomiko piloting, Harfex and Osden silent, watching ahead for the dark line of forest across the vague grey miles of starlit plain.

They neared the black line, crossed it; now under them was darkness.

She sought a landing place, flying low, though she had to fight her frantic wish to fly high, to get out, get away. The huge vitality of the plant-world was far stronger here in the forest, and its panic beat in immense dark waves. There was a pale patch ahead, a bare knoll-top a little higher than the tallest of the black shapes around it; the not-trees; the rooted; the parts of the whole. She set the helijet down in the glade, a bad landing. Her hands on the stick were slippery, as if she had rubbed them with cold soap.

About them now stood the forest, black in darkness.

Tomiko cowered and shut her eyes. Eskwana moaned in his sleep. Harfex's breath came short and loud, and he sat rigid, even when Osden reached across him and slid the door open.

Osden stood up; his back and bandaged head were just visible in the dim glow of the control panel as he paused stooping in the doorway.

Tomiko was shaking. She could not raise her head. "No, no, no, no, no, no, no," she said in a whisper. "No. No. No."

Osden moved suddenly and quietly, swinging out of the doorway, down into the dark. He was gone.

I am coming! said a great voice that made no sound.

Tomiko screamed. Harfex coughed; he seemed to be trying to stand up, but did not do so.

Tomiko drew in upon herself, all centered in the blind eye in her belly, in the center of her being; and outside that there was nothing but the fear.

It ceased.

She raised her head; slowly unclenched her hands. She sat up straight. The night was dark, and stars shone over the forest. There was nothing else.

"Osden," she said, but her voice would not come. She spoke again, louder, a lone bullfrog croak. There was no reply.

She began to realize that something had gone wrong with Harfex. She was trying to find his head in the darkness, for he had slipped down from the seat, when all at once, in the dead quiet, in the dark rear compartment of the craft, a voice spoke. "Good," it said.

It was Eskwana's voice. She snapped on the interior lights and saw the engineer lying curled up asleep, his hand half over his mouth.

The mouth opened and spoke. "All well," it said.

"Osden — "

"All well," said the soft voice from Eskwana's mouth.

"Where are you?"

Silence.

"Come back."

A wind was rising. "I'll stay here," the soft voice said.

"You can't stay — "

Silence.

"You'd be alone, Osden!"

"Listen." The voice was fainter, slurred, as if lost in the sound of wind. "Listen. I will you well."

She called his name after that, but there was no answer. Eskwana lay still. Harfex lay stiller.

"Osden!" she cried, leaning out the doorway into the dark, wind-shaken silence of the forest of being. "I will come back. I must get Harfex to the base. I will come back, Osden!"

Silence and wind in leaves.

They finished the prescribed survey of World 4470, the eight of them; it took them forty-one days more. Asnanifoil and one or another of the women went into the forest daily at first, searching for Osden in the region around the bare knoll, though Tomiko was not in her heart sure which bare knoll they had landed on that night in the very heart and vortex of terror. They left piles of supplies for Osden, food enough for fifty years, clothing, tents, tools. They did not go on searching; there was no way to find a man alone, hiding, if he wanted to hide, in those unending labyrinths and dim corridors vine-entangled, root-floored. They might have passed within arm's reach of him and never seen him.

But he was there; for there was no fear any more.

Rational, and valuing reason more highly after an intolerable experience of the immortal mindless, Tomiko tried to understand rationally what Osden had done. But the words escaped her control. He had taken the fear into himself, and, accepting, had transcended it. He had given up his self to the alien, an unreserved surrender, that left no place for evil. He had learned the love of the Other, and thereby had been given his whole self. — But this is not the vocabulary of reason.

The people of the Survey team walked under the trees, through the vast colonies of life, surrounded by a dreaming silence, a brooding calm that was half aware of them and wholly indifferent to them. There were no hours. Distance was no matter. Had we but world enough and time . . . The planet turned between the sunlight and the great dark; winds of winter and summer blew fine, pale pollen across the quiet seas.

Gum returned after many surveys, years, and lightyears, to what had several centuries ago been Smeming Port. There were still men there, to receive (incredulously) the team's reports, and to record its losses: Biologist Harfex, dead of fear, and Sensor Osden, left as a colonist.

Octavia E. Butler

Bloodchild

(1984)

One of the most distinctive and original voices in sf, Octavia Estelle Butler (1947–2006), who was the recipient of a MacArthur "genius" grant as well as numerous sf awards, is known for her bold ideas as well as the coolly assessing gaze she turns on the more negative elements of human nature. Butler, who was at one time a student of Samuel Delany, was the first Black woman to achieve success as a science fiction writer. An intensely private person from a humble background, she dedicated herself to writing from an early age, and the science fiction community was shocked and saddened when she died after a stroke at the age of 59, while still at the height of her powers. Butler's works include *Kindred* (1979), a time-travel story that is really a haunting exploration of the legacy of American slavery; the Xenogenesis trilogy (1987–2000), one of the most significant explorations of the alien contact theme; and the Parable series, *Parable of the Sower* [1994] and *Parable of the Talents* [1999]; a third novel was projected. Her awards include two Hugos and two Nebulas — one for the story that follows.

Although it is not unusual for sf writers to explore issues of race and gender, Butler directs her attention to the underlying structures of dominance and violence with an almost clinical interest, carefully working through the implications of her ideas and searching out solutions that reject easy moralization and simplistic choices between good and evil, in favor of flawed but necessary accommodations in a less-than-perfect world.

In "Bloodchild," one of her most beautifully written and deeply disturbing stories, Butler examines the complex interpersonal dynamics of oppressor and oppressed through an original and perfectly realized metaphor of parasitism. While the physiology of the encounter is viscerally repellent, it is the element of tenderness that is most chilling. Butler uses the metaphor to explore the psychological dynamics of power relations found in extreme forms of exploitation like slavery, rape, and child abuse; ultimately, though, it is the familiarity of the emotions that makes the story so unsettling. Butler has called "Bloodchild" a love story, and this version of alien domination is disturbing precisely because she endows it with recognizable features of our own most intimate lives.

My last night of childhood began with a visit home. T'Gatoi's sister had given us two sterile eggs. T'Gatoi gave one to my mother, brother, and sisters. She insisted that I eat the other one alone. It didn't matter. There was still enough to leave everyone feeling good. Almost everyone. My mother wouldn't take any. She sat, watching everyone drifting and dreaming without her. Most of the time she watched me.

I lay against T'Gatoi's long, velvet underside, sipping from my egg now and then, wondering why my mother denied herself such a harmless pleasure. Less of her hair would be gray if she indulged now and then. The eggs prolonged life, prolonged vigor. My father, who had never refused one in his life, had lived more than twice as long as he should have. And toward the end of his life, when he should have been slowing down, he had married my mother and fathered four children.

But my mother seemed content to age before she had to. I saw her turn away as several of T'Gatoi's limbs secured me closer. T'Gatoi liked our body heat and took advantage of it whenever she could. When I was little and at home more, my mother used to try to tell me how to behave with T'Gatoi — how to be respectful and always obedient because T'Gatoi was the Tlic government official in charge of the Preserve, and thus the most important of her kind to deal directly with Terrans. It was an honor, my mother said, that such a person had chosen to come into the family. My mother was at her most formal and severe when she was lying.

I had no idea why she was lying, or even what she was lying about. It *was* an honor to have T'Gatoi in the family, but it was hardly a novelty. T'Gatoi and my mother had been friends all my mother's life, and T'Gatoi was not interested in being honored in the house she considered her second home. She simply came in, climbed onto one of her special couches, and called me over to keep her warm. It was impossible to be formal with her while lying against her and hearing her complain as usual that I was too skinny.

"You're better," she said this time, probing me with six or seven of her limbs. "You're gaining weight finally. Thinness is dangerous." The probing changed subtly, became a series of caresses.

"He's still too thin," my mother said sharply.

T'Gatoi lifted her head and perhaps a meter of her body off the couch as though she were sitting up. She looked at my mother, and my mother, her face lined and old looking, turned away.

"Lien, I would like you to have what's left of Gan's egg."

"The eggs are for the children," my mother said.

"They are for the family. Please take it."

Unwillingly obedient, my mother took it from me and put it to her mouth. There were only a few drops left in the now-shrunken, elastic shell, but she squeezed them out, swallowed them, and after a few moments some of the lines of tension began to smooth from her face.

"It's good," she whispered. "Sometimes I forget how good it is."

"You should take more," T'Gatoi said. "Why are you in such a hurry to be old?"

My mother said nothing.

"I like being able to come here," T'Gatoi said. "This place is a refuge because of you, yet you won't take care of yourself."

T'Gatoi was hounded on the outside. Her people wanted more of us made available. Only she and her political faction stood between us and the hordes who did not understand why there was a Preserve — why any Terran could not be courted, paid, drafted, in some way made available to them. Or they did understand, but in their desperation, they did not care. She parceled us out to the desperate and sold us to the rich and powerful for their political support. Thus, we were necessities, status symbols, and an independent people. She oversaw the joining of families, putting an end to the final remnants of the earlier system of breaking up Terran families to suit impatient Tlic. I had lived outside with her. I had seen the desperate eagerness in the way some people looked at me. It was a little frightening to know that only she stood between us and that desperation that could so easily swallow us. My mother would look at her sometimes and say to me, "Take care of her." And I would remember that she too had been outside, had seen.

Now T'Gatoi used four of her limbs to push me away from her onto the floor. "Go on, Gan," she said. "Sit down there with your sisters and enjoy not being sober. You had most of the egg. Lien, come warm me."

My mother hesitated for no reason that I could see. One of my earliest memories is of my mother stretched alongside T'Gatoi, talking about things I could not understand, picking me up from the floor and laughing as she sat me on one of T'Gatoi's segments. She ate her share of eggs then. I wondered when she had stopped, and why.

She lay down now against T'Gatoi, and the whole left row of T'Gatoi's limbs closed around her, holding her loosely, but securely. I had always found it comfortable to lie that way, but except for my older sister, no one else in the family liked it. They said it made them feel caged.

T'Gatoi meant to cage my mother. Once she had, she moved her tail slightly, then spoke. "Not enough egg, Lien. You should have taken it when it was passed to you. You need it badly now."

T'Gatoi's tail moved once more, its whip motion so swift I wouldn't have seen it if I hadn't been watching for it. Her sting drew only a single drop of blood from my mother's bare leg.

My mother cried out — probably in surprise. Being stung doesn't hurt. Then she sighed and I could see her body relax. She moved languidly into a more comfortable position within the cage of T'Gatoi's limbs. "Why did you do that?" she asked, sounding half asleep.

"I could not watch you sitting and suffering any longer."

My mother managed to move her shoulders in a small shrug. "Tomorrow," she said.

"Yes. Tomorrow you will resume your suffering — if you must. But just now, just for now, lie here and warm me and let me ease your way a little."

"He's still mine, you know," my mother said suddenly.

"Nothing can buy him from me." Sober, she would not have permitted herself to refer to such things.

"Nothing," T'Gatoi agreed, humoring her.

"Did you think I would sell him for eggs? For long life? My son?"

"Not for anything," T'Gatoi said, stroking my mother's shoulders, toying with her long, graying hair.

I would like to have touched my mother, shared that moment with her. She would take my hand if I touched her now. Freed by the egg and the sting, she would smile and perhaps say things long held in. But tomorrow, she would remember all this as a humiliation. I did not want to be part of a remembered humiliation. Best just be still and know she loved me under all the duty and pride and pain.

"Xuan Hoa, take off her shoes," T'Gatoi said. "In a little while I'll sting her again and she can sleep."

My older sister obeyed, swaying drunkenly as she stood up. When she had finished, she sat down beside me and took my hand. We had always been a unit, she and I.

My mother put the back of her head against T'Gatoi's underside and tried from that impossible angle to look up into the broad, round face. "You're going to sting me again?"

"Yes, Lien."

"I'll sleep until tomorrow noon."

"Good. You need it. When did you sleep last?"

My mother made a wordless sound of annoyance. "I should have stepped on you when you were small enough," she muttered.

It was an old joke between them. They had grown up together, sort of, though T'Gatoi had not, in my mother's lifetime, been small enough for any Terran to step on. She was nearly three times my mother's present age, yet would still be young when my mother died of age. But T'Gatoi and my mother had met as T'Gatoi was coming into a period of rapid development — a kind of Tlic adolescence. My mother was only a child, but for a while they developed at the same rate and had no better friends than each other.

T'Gatoi had even introduced my mother to the man who became my father. My parents, pleased with each other in spite of their different ages, married as T'Gatoi was going into her family's business — politics. She and my mother saw each other less. But sometime before my older sister was born, my mother promised T'Gatoi one of her children. She would have to give one of us to someone, and she preferred T'Gatoi to some stranger.

Years passed. T'Gatoi traveled and increased her influence. The Preserve was hers by the time she came back to my mother to collect what she probably saw as her just reward for her hard work. My older sister took an instant liking to her and wanted to be chosen, but my mother was just coming to term with me and T'Gatoi liked the idea of choosing an infant and watching and taking part in all the phases of development. I'm told I was first caged within T'Gatoi's many limbs only three minutes after my birth. A few days later, I was given my first taste of egg. I tell Terrans that when they ask whether I was ever afraid of her. And I tell it to Tlic when T'Gatoi suggests a young Terran child for them and they, anxious and ignorant, demand an adolescent. Even my brother who had somehow grown up to fear and distrust the Tlic could probably have gone smoothly into one of their families if he had been adopted early enough. Sometimes, I think for his sake he should have been. I looked at him, stretched out on the floor across the room, his eyes open, but glazed as he dreamed his egg dream. No matter what he felt toward the Tlic, he always demanded his share of egg.

"Lien, can you stand up?" T'Gatoi asked suddenly.

"Stand?" my mother said. "I thought I was going to sleep."

"Later. Something sounds wrong outside." The cage was abruptly gone.

"What?"

"Up, Lien!"

My mother recognized her tone and got up just in time to avoid being dumped on the floor. T'Gatoi whipped her three meters of body off her couch, toward the door, and out at full speed. She had bones — ribs, a long spine, a skull, four sets of limb bones per segment. But when she moved that way, twisting, hurling herself into controlled falls, landing running, she seemed not only boneless, but aquatic — something swimming through the air as though it were water. I loved watching her move.

I left my sister and started to follow her out the door, though I wasn't very steady on my own feet. It would have been better to sit and dream, better yet to find a girl and share a waking dream with her. Back when the Tlic saw us as not much more than convenient, big, warm-blooded animals, they would pen several of us together, male and female, and feed us only eggs. That way they could be sure of getting another generation of us no matter how we tried to hold out. We were lucky that didn't go on long. A few generations of it and we would have *been* little more than convenient, big animals.

"Hold the door open, Gan," T'Gatoi said. "And tell the family to stay back."

"What is it?" I asked.

"N'Tlic."

I shrank back against the door. "Here? Alone?"

"He was trying to reach a call box, I suppose." She carried the man past me, unconscious, folded like a coat over some of her limbs. He looked young — my brother's age perhaps — and he was thinner than he should have been. What T'Gatoi would have called dangerously thin.

"Gan, go to the call box," she said. She put the man on the floor and began stripping off his clothing.

I did not move.

After a moment, she looked up at me, her sudden stillness a sign of deep impatience.

"Send Qui," I told her. "I'll stay here. Maybe I can help."

She let her limbs begin to move again, lifting the man and pulling his shirt over his head. "You don't want to see this," she said. "It will be hard. I can't help this man the way his Tlic could."

"I know. But send Qui. He won't want to be of any help here. I'm at least willing to try."

She looked at my brother — older, bigger, stronger, certainly more able to help her here. He was sitting up now, braced against the wall, staring at the man on the floor with undisguised fear and revulsion. Even she could see that he would be useless.

"Qui, go!" she said.

He didn't argue. He stood up, swayed briefly, then steadied, frightened sober.

"This man's name is Bram Lomas," she told him, reading from the man's armband. I fingered my own armband in sympathy. "He needs T'Khotgif Teh. Do you hear?"

"Bram Lomas, T'Khotgif Teh," my brother said. "I'm going." He edged around Lomas and ran out the door.

Lomas began to regain consciousness. He only moaned at first and clutched spasmodically at a pair of T'Gatoi's limbs. My younger sister, finally awake from her egg dream, came close to look at him, until my mother pulled her back.

T'Gatoi removed the man's shoes, then his pants, all the while leaving him two of her limbs to grip. Except for the final few, all her limbs were equally dexterous. "I want no argument from you this time, Gan," she said.

I straightened. "What shall I do?"

"Go out and slaughter an animal that is at least half your size."

"Slaughter? But I've never — "

She knocked me across the room. Her tail was an efficient weapon whether she exposed the sting or not.

I got up, feeling stupid for having ignored her warning, and went into the kitchen. Maybe I could kill something with a knife or an ax. My mother raised a few Terran animals for the table and several thousand local ones for their fur. T'Gatoi would probably prefer something local. An achti, perhaps. Some of those were the right size, though they had about three times as many teeth as I did and a real love of using them. My mother, Hoa, and Qui could kill them with knives. I had never killed one at all, had never slaughtered any animal. I had spent most of my time with T'Gatoi while my brother and sisters were learning the family business. T'Gatoi had been right. I should have been the one to go to the call box. At least I could do that.

I went to the corner cabinet where my mother kept her large house and garden tools. At the back of the cabinet there was a pipe that carried off waste water from the kitchen — except that it didn't anymore. My father had rerouted the waste water below before I was born. Now the pipe could be turned so that one half slid around the other and a rifle could be stored inside. This wasn't our only gun, but it was our most easily accessible one. I would have to use it to shoot one of the biggest of the achti. Then T'Gatoi would probably confiscate it. Firearms were illegal in the Preserve. There had been incidents right after the Preserve was established — Terrans shooting Tlic, shooting N'Tlic. This was before the joining of families began, before everyone had a personal stake in keeping the peace. No one had shot a Tlic in my lifetime or my mother's, but the law still stood — for our protection, we were told. There were stories of whole Terran families wiped out in reprisal back during the assassinations.

I went out to the cages and shot the biggest achti I could find. It was a handsome breeding male, and my mother would not be pleased to see me bring it in. But it was the right size, and I was in a hurry.

I put the achti's long, warm body over my shoulder — glad that some of the weight I'd gained was muscle — and took it to the kitchen. There, I put the gun back in its hiding place. If T'Gatoi noticed the achti's wounds and demanded the gun, I would give it to her. Otherwise, let it stay where my father wanted it.

I turned to take the achti to her, then hesitated. For several seconds, I stood in front of the closed door wondering why I was suddenly afraid. I knew what was going to happen. I hadn't seen it before but T'Gatoi had shown me diagrams and drawings. She had made sure I knew the truth as soon as I was old enough to understand it.

Yet I did not want to go into that room. I wasted a little time choosing a knife from the carved, wooden box in which my mother kept them. T'Gatoi might want one, I told myself, for the tough, heavily furred hide of the achti.

"Gan!" T'Gatoi called, her voice harsh with urgency.

I swallowed. I had not imagined a single moving of the feet could be so difficult. I realized I was trembling and that shamed me. Shame impelled me through the door.

I put the achti down near T'Gatoi and saw that Lomas was unconscious again. She, Lomas, and I were alone in the room — my mother and sisters probably sent out so they would not have to watch. I envied them.

But my mother came back into the room as T'Gatoi seized the achti. Ignoring the knife I offered her, she extended claws from several of her limbs and slit the achti from throat to anus. She looked at me, her yellow eyes intent. "Hold this man's shoulders, Gan."

I stared at Lomas in panic, realizing that I did not want to touch him, let alone hold him. This would not be like shooting an animal. Not as quick, not as merciful, and, I hoped, not as final, but there was nothing I wanted less than to be part of it.

My mother came forward. "Gan, you hold his right side," she said. "I'll hold his left." And if he came to, he would throw her off without realizing he had done it. She was a tiny woman. She often wondered aloud how she had produced, as she said, such "huge" children.

"Never mind," I told her, taking the man's shoulders. "I'll do it." She hovered nearby.

"Don't worry," I said. "I won't shame you. You don't have to stay and watch."

She looked at me uncertainly, then touched my face in a rare caress. Finally, she went back to her bedroom.

T'Gatoi lowered her head in relief. "Thank you, Gan," she said with courtesy more Terran than Tlic. "That one . . . she is always finding new ways for me to make her suffer."

Lomas began to groan and make choked sounds. I had hoped he would stay unconscious. T'Gatoi put her face near his so that he focused on her.

"I've stung you as much as I dare for now," she told him. "When this is over, I'll sting you to sleep and you won't hurt anymore."

"Please," the man begged. "Wait . . ."

"There's no more time, Bram. I'll sting you as soon as it's over. When T'Khotgif arrives she'll give you eggs to help you heal. It will be over soon."

"T'Khotgif!" the man shouted, straining against my hands.

"Soon, Bram." T'Gatoi glanced at me, then placed a claw against his abdomen slightly to the right of the middle, just below the left rib. There was movement on the right side — tiny, seemingly random pulsations moving his brown flesh, creating a concavity here, a convexity there, over and over until I could see the rhythm of it and knew where the next pulse would be.

Lomas's entire body stiffened under T'Gatoi's claw, though she merely rested it against him as she wound the rear section of her body around his legs. He might break my grip, but he would not break hers. He wept helplessly as she used his pants to tie his hands, then pushed his hands above his head so that I could kneel on the cloth between them and pin them in place. She rolled up his shirt and gave it to him to bite down on.

And she opened him.

His body convulsed with the first cut. He almost tore himself away from me. The sound he made . . . I had never heard such sounds come from anything human. T'Gatoi seemed to pay no attention as she lengthened and deepened the cut, now and then pausing to lick away blood. His blood vessels contracted, reacting to the chemistry of her saliva, and the bleeding slowed.

I felt as though I were helping her torture him, helping her consume him. I knew I would vomit soon, didn't know why I hadn't already. I couldn't possibly last until she was finished.

She found the first grub. It was fat and deep red with his blood — both inside and out. It had already eaten its own egg case but apparently had not yet begun to eat its host. At this stage, it would eat any flesh except its mother's. Let alone, it would have gone on excreting the poisons that had both sickened and alerted Lomas. Eventually it would have begun to eat. By the time it ate its way out of Lomas's flesh, Lomas would be dead or dying — and unable to take revenge on the thing that was killing him. There was always a grace period between the time the host sickened and the time the grubs began to eat him.

T'Gatoi picked up the writhing grub carefully and looked at it, somehow ignoring the terrible groans of the man.

Abruptly, the man lost consciousness.

"Good," T'Gatoi looked down at him. "I wish you Terrans could do that at will." She felt nothing. And the thing she held . . .

It was limbless and boneless at this stage, perhaps fifteen centimeters long and two thick, blind and slimy with blood. It was like a large worm. T'Gatoi put it into the belly of the achti, and it began at once to burrow. It would stay there and eat as long as there was anything to eat.

Probing through Lomas's flesh, she found two more, one of them smaller and more vigorous. "A male!" she said happily. He would be dead before I would. He would be through his metamorphosis and screwing everything that would hold still before his sisters even had limbs. He was the only one to make a serious effort to bite T'Gatoi as she placed him in the achti.

Paler worms oozed to visibility in Lomas's flesh. I closed my eyes. It was worse than finding something dead, rotting, and filled with tiny animal grubs. And it was far worse than any drawing or diagram.

"Ah, there are more," T'Gatoi said, plucking out two long, thick grubs. You may have to kill another animal, Gan. Everything lives inside you Terrans."

I had been told all my life that this was a good and necessary thing Tlic and Terran did together — a kind of birth. I had believed it until now. I knew birth was painful and bloody, no matter what. But this was something else, something worse. And I wasn't ready to see it. Maybe I never would be. Yet I couldn't not see it. Closing my eyes didn't help.

T'Gatoi found a grub still eating its egg case. The remains of the case were still wired into a blood vessel by their own little tube or hook or whatever. That was the way the grubs were anchored and the way they fed. They took only blood until they were ready to emerge. Then they ate their stretched, elastic egg cases. Then they ate their hosts.

T'Gatoi bit away the egg case, licked away the blood. Did she like the taste? Did childhood habits die hard — or not die at all?

The whole procedure was wrong, alien. I wouldn't have thought anything about her could seem alien to me.

"One more, I think," she said. "Perhaps two. A good family. In a host animal these days, we would be happy to find one or two alive." She glanced at me. "Go outside, Gan, and empty your stomach. Go now while the man is unconscious."

I staggered out, barely made it. Beneath the tree just beyond the front door, I vomited until there was nothing left to bring up. Finally, I stood shaking, tears streaming down my face. I did not know why I was crying, but I could not stop. I went further from the house to avoid being seen. Every time I closed my eyes I saw red worms crawling over redder human flesh.

There was a car coming toward the house. Since Terrans were forbidden motorized vehicles except for certain farm equipment, I knew this must be Lomas's Tlic with Qui and perhaps a Terran doctor. I wiped my face on my shirt, struggled for control.

"Gan," Qui called as the car stopped. "What happened?" He crawled out of the low, round, Tlic-convenient car door. Another Terran crawled out the other side and went into the house without speaking to me. The doctor. With his help and a few eggs, Lomas might make it.

"T'Khotgif Teh?" I said.

The Tlic driver surged out of her car, reared up half her length before me. She was paler and smaller than T'Gatoi — probably born from the body of an animal. Tlic from Terran bodies were always larger as well as more numerous.

"Six young," I told her. "Maybe seven, all alive. At least one male."

"Lomas?" she said harshly. I liked her for the question and the concern in her voice when she asked it. The last coherent thing he had said was her name.

"He's alive," I said.

She surged away to the house without another word.

"She's been sick," my brother said, watching her go. "When I called, I could hear people telling her she wasn't well enough to go out even for this."

I said nothing. I had extended courtesy to the Tlic. Now I didn't want to talk to anyone. I hoped he would go in — out of curiosity if nothing else.

"Finally found out more than you wanted to know, eh?"

I looked at him.

"Don't give me one of *her* looks," he said. "You're not her. You're just her property."

One of her looks. Had I picked up even an ability to imitate her expressions?

"What'd you do, puke?" He sniffed the air. "So now you know what you're in for."

I walked away from him. He and I had been close when we were kids. He would let me follow him around when I was home, and sometimes T'Gatoi would let me bring him along when she took me into the city. But something had happened when he reached adolescence. I never knew what. He began keeping out of T'Gatoi's way. Then he began running away — until he realized there was no "away." Not in the Preserve. Certainly not outside. After that he concentrated on getting his share of every egg that came into the house and on looking out for me in a way that made me all but hate him — a way that clearly said, as long as I was all right, he was safe from the Tlic.

"How was it, really?" he demanded, following me

"I killed an achti. The young ate it."

"You didn't run out of the house and puke because they ate an achti."

"I had . . . never seen a person cut open before." That was true, and enough for him to know. I couldn't talk about the other. Not with him.

"Oh," he said. He glanced at me as though he wanted to say more, but he kept quiet.

We walked, not really headed anywhere. Toward the back, toward the cages, toward the fields.

"Did he say anything?" Qui asked. "Lomas, I mean."

Who else would he mean? "He said 'T'Khotgif.'"

Qui shuddered. "If she had done that to me, she'd be the last person I'd call for."

"You'd call for her. Her sting would ease your pain without killing the grubs in you."

"You think I'd care if they died?"

No. Of course he wouldn't. Would I?

"Shit!" He drew a deep breath. "I've seen what they do. You think this thing with Lomas was bad? It was nothing."

I didn't argue. He didn't know what he was talking about.

"I saw them eat a man," he said.

I turned to face him. "You're lying!"

"*I saw them eat a man.*" He paused. "It was when I was little. I had been to the Hartmund house and I was on my way home. Halfway here, I saw a man and a Tlic and the man was N'Tlic. The ground was hilly. I was able to hide from them and watch. The Tlic wouldn't open the man because she had nothing to feed the grubs. The man couldn't go any further and there were no houses around. He was in so much pain, he told her to kill him. He begged her to kill him. Finally, she did. She cut his throat. One swipe of one claw. I saw the grubs eat their way out, then burrow in again, still eating."

His words made me see Lomas's flesh again, parasitized, crawling. "Why didn't you tell me that?" I whispered.

He looked startled as though he'd forgotten I was listening. "I don't know."

"You started to run away not long after that, didn't you?"

"Yeah. Stupid. Running inside the Preserve. Running in a cage."

I shook my head, said what I should have said to him long ago. "She wouldn't take you, Qui. You don't have to worry."

"She would . . . if anything happened to you."

"No. She'd take Xuan Hoa. Hoa . . . wants it." She wouldn't if she had stayed to watch Lomas.

"They don't take women," he said with contempt.

"They do sometimes." I glanced at him. "Actually, they prefer women. You should be around them when they talk among themselves. They say women have more body fat to protect the grubs. But they usually take men to leave the women free to bear their own young."

"To provide the next generation of host animals," he said, switching from contempt to bitterness.

"It's more than that!" I countered. Was it?

"If it were going to happen to me, I'd want to believe it was more, too."

"It *is* more!" I felt like a kid. Stupid argument.

"Did you think so while T'Gatoi was picking worms out of that guy's guts?"

"It's not supposed to happen that way."

"Sure it is. You weren't supposed to see it, that's all. And his Tlic was supposed to do it. She could sting him unconscious and the operation wouldn't have been as painful. But she'd still open him, pick out the grubs, and if she missed even one, it would poison him and eat him from the inside out."

There was actually a time when my mother told me to show respect for Qui because he was my older brother. I walked away, hating him. In his way, he was gloating. He was safe and I wasn't. I could have hit him, but I didn't think I would be able to stand it when he refused to hit back, when he looked at me with contempt and pity.

He wouldn't let me get away. Longer legged, he swung ahead of me and made me feel as though I were following him.

"I'm sorry," he said.

I strode on, sick and furious.

"Look, it probably won't be that bad with you. T'Gatoi likes you. She'll be careful."

I turned back toward the house, almost running from him.

"Has she done it to you yet?" he asked, keeping up easily. "I mean, you're about the right age for implantation. Has she — "

I hit him. I didn't know I was going to do it, but I think I meant to kill him. If he hadn't been bigger and stronger, I think I would have.

He tried to hold me off, but in the end, had to defend himself. He only hit me a couple of times. That was plenty. I don't remember going down, but when I came to, he was gone. It was worth the pain to be rid of him.

I got up and walked slowly toward the house. The back was dark. No one was in the kitchen. My mother and sisters were sleeping in their bedrooms — or pretending to.

Once I was in the kitchen, I could hear voices — Tlic and Terran from the next room. I couldn't make out what they were saying — didn't want to make it out.

I sat down at my mother's table, waiting for quiet. The table was smooth and worn, heavy and well crafted. My father had made it for her just before he died. I remembered hanging around underfoot when he built it. He didn't mind. Now I sat leaning on it, missing him. I could have talked to him. He had done it three times in his long life. Three clutches of eggs, three times being opened up and sewed up. How had he done it? How did anyone do it?

I got up, took the rifle from its hiding place, and sat down again with it. It needed cleaning, oiling.

All I did was load it.

"Gan?"

She made a lot of little clicking sounds when she walked on bare floor, each limb clicking in succession as it touched down. Waves of little clicks.

She came to the table, raised the front half of her body above it, and surged onto it. Sometimes she moved so smoothly she seemed to flow like water itself. She coiled herself into a small hill in the middle of the table and looked at me.

"That was bad," she said softly. "You should not have seen it. It need not be that way."

"I know."

"T'Khotgif — Ch'Khotgif now — she will die of her disease. She will not live to raise her children. But her sister will provide for them, and for Bram Lomas." Sterile sister. One fertile female in every lot. One to keep the family going. That sister owed Lomas more than she could ever repay.

"He'll live then?"

"Yes."

"I wonder if he would do it again."

"No one would ask him to do that again."

I looked into the yellow eyes, wondering how much I saw and understood there, and how much I only imagined. "No one ever asks us," I said. "You never asked me."

She moved her head slightly. "What's the matter with your face?"

"Nothing. Nothing important." Human eyes probably wouldn't have noticed the swelling in the darkness. The only light was from one of the moons, shining through a window across the room.

"Did you use the rifle to shoot the achti?"

"Yes."

"And do you mean to use it to shoot me?"

I stared at her, outlined in the moonlight — coiled, graceful body. "What does Terran blood taste like to you?"

She said nothing.

"What are you?" I whispered. "What are we to you?"

She lay still, rested her head on her topmost coil. "You know me as no other does," she said softly. "You must decide."

"That's what happened to my face," I told her.

"What?"

"Qui goaded me into deciding to do something. It didn't turn out very well." I moved the gun slightly, brought the barrel up diagonally under my own chin. "At least it was a decision I made."

"As this will be."

"Ask me, Gatoi."

"For my children's lives?"

She would say something like that. She knew how to manipulate people, Terran and Tlic. But not this time.

"I don't want to be a host animal," I said. "Not even yours."

It took her a long time to answer. "We use almost no host animals these days," she said. "You know that."

"You use us."

"We do. We wait long years for you and teach you and join our families to yours." She moved restlessly. "You know you aren't animals to us."

I stared at her, saying nothing.

"The animals we once used began killing most of our eggs after implantation long before your ancestors arrived," she said softly. "You know these things, Gan. Because your people arrived, we are relearning what it means to be a healthy, thriving people. And your ancestors, fleeing from their home-world, from their own kind who would have killed or enslaved them — they survived because of us. We saw them as people and gave them the Preserve when they still tried to kill us as worms."

At the word "worms," I jumped. I couldn't help it, and she couldn't help noticing it.

"I see," she said quietly. "Would you really rather die than bear my young, Gan?"

I didn't answer.

"Shall I go to Xuan Hoa?"

"Yes!" Hoa wanted it. Let her have it. She hadn't had to watch Lomas. She'd be proud. . . . Not terrified.

T'Gatoi flowed off the table onto the floor, startling me almost too much.

"I'll sleep in Hoa's room tonight," she said. "And sometime tonight or in the morning, I'll tell her."

This was going too fast. My sister Hoa had had almost as much to do with raising me as my mother. I was still close to her — not like Qui. She could want T'Gatoi and still love me.

"Wait! Gatoi!"

She looked back, then raised nearly half her length off the floor and turned to face me. "These are adult things, Gan. This is my life, my family!"

"But she's . . . my sister."

"I have done what you demanded. I have asked you!"

"But — "

"It will be easier for Hoa. She has always expected to carry other lives inside her."

Human lives. Human young who should someday drink at her breasts, not at her veins.

I shook my head. "Don't do it to her, Gatoi." I was not Qui. It seemed I could become him, though, with no effort at all. I could make Xuan Hoa my shield. Would it be easier to know that red worms were growing in her flesh instead of mine?

"Don't do it to Hoa," I repeated.

She stared at me, utterly still.

I looked away, then back at her. "Do it to me."

I lowered the gun from my throat and she leaned forward to take it.

"No," I told her.

"It's the law," she said.

"Leave it for the family. One of them might use it to save my life some-day."

She grasped the rifle barrel, but I wouldn't let go. I was pulled into a standing position over her.

"Leave it here!" I repeated. "If we're not your animals, if these are adult things, accept the risk. There is risk, Gatoi, in dealing with a partner."

It was clearly hard for her to let go of the rifle. A shudder went through her and she made a hissing sound of distress. It occurred to me that she was afraid. She was old enough to have seen what guns could do to people. Now her young and this gun would be together in the same house. She did not know about the other guns. In this dispute, they did not matter.

"I will implant the first egg tonight," she said as I put the gun away. "Do you hear, Gan?"

Why else had I been given a whole egg to eat while the rest of the family was left to share one? Why else had my mother kept looking at me as though I were going away from her, going where she could not follow? Did T'Gatoi imagine I hadn't known?

"I hear."

"Now!" I let her push me out of the kitchen, then walked ahead of her toward my bedroom. The sudden urgency in her voice sounded real. "You would have done it to Hoa tonight!" I accused.

"I must do it to someone tonight."

I stopped in spite of her urgency and stood in her way. "Don't you care who?"

She flowed around me and into my bedroom. I found her waiting on the couch we shared. There was nothing in Hoa's room that she could have used. She would have done it to Hoa on the floor. The thought of her doing it to Hoa at all disturbed me in a different way now, and I was suddenly angry.

Yet I undressed and lay down beside her. I knew what to do, what to expect. I had been told all my life. I felt the familiar sting, narcotic, mildly pleasant. Then the blind probing of her ovipositor. The puncture was painless, easy. So easy going in. She undulated slowly against me, her muscles forcing the egg from her body into mine. I held on to a pair of her limbs until I remembered Lomas holding her that way. Then I let go, moved inadvertently, and hurt her. She gave a low cry of pain and I expected to be caged at once within her limbs. When I wasn't, I held on to her again, feeling oddly ashamed.

"I'm sorry," I whispered.

She rubbed my shoulders with four of her limbs.

"Do you care?" I asked. "Do you care that it's me?"

She did not answer for some time. Finally, "You were the one making the choices tonight, Gan. I made mine long ago."

"Would you have gone to Hoa?"

"Yes. How could I put my children into the care of one who hates them?"

"It wasn't . . . hate."

"I know what it was."

"I was afraid."

Silence.

"I still am." I could admit it to her here, now.

"But you came to me . . . to save Hoa."

"Yes." I leaned my forehead against her. She was cool velvet, deceptively soft. "And to keep you for myself," I said. It was so. I didn't understand it, but it was so.

She made a soft hum of contentment. "I couldn't believe I had made such a mistake with you," she said. "I chose you. I believed you had grown to choose me."

"I had, but . . ."

"Lomas."

"Yes."

"I had never known a Terran to see a birth and take it well. Qui has seen one, hasn't he?"

"Yes."

"Terrans should be protected from seeing."

I didn't like the sound of that — and I doubted that it was possible. "Not protected," I said. "Shown. Shown when we're young kids, and shown more than once. Gatoi, no Terran ever sees a birth that goes right. All we see is N'Tlic — pain and terror and maybe death."

She looked down at me. "It is a private thing. It has always been a private thing."

Her tone kept me from insisting — that and the knowledge that if she changed her mind, I might be the first public example. But I had planted the thought in her mind. Chances were it would grow, and eventually she would experiment.

"You won't see it again," she said. "I don't want you thinking any more about shooting me."

The small amount of fluid that came into me with her egg relaxed me as completely as a sterile egg would have, so that I could remember the rifle in my hands and my feelings of fear and revulsion, anger and despair. I could remember the feelings without reviving them. I could talk about them.

"I wouldn't have shot you," I said. "Not you." She had been taken from my father's flesh when he was my age.

"You could have," she insisted.

"Not you." She stood between us and her own people, protecting, interweaving.

"Would you have destroyed yourself?"

I moved carefully; uncomfortable. "I could have done that. I nearly did. That's Qui's 'away.' I wonder if he knows."

"What?"

I did not answer.

"You will live now."

"Yes." *Take care of her*, my mother used to say. Yes.

"I'm healthy and young," she said. "I won't leave you as Lomas was left — alone, N'Tlic. I'll take care of you."

Greg Egan

Wang's Carpets

(1995)

With his well-crafted, thought-provoking stories about the effects of new technology, Australian writer Greg Egan (b. 1961) emerged as one of the most promising new writers of the 1990s. Egan received a bachelor's degree in math from the University of Western Australia and briefly attended the Australian Film and Television School before turning to writing fiction, initially focusing on horror. For several years he alternated periods of writing with contract work as a computer programmer, but since 1992 he has been able to pursue his writing career full time. He won a John W. Campbell Award in 1995 for *Permutation City*, and a Hugo for the novella "Oceanic" in 1999. Egan's attention to scientific detail qualifies him as a "hard" sf writer, but he is at least as interested in the social implications of scientific ideas as in the science itself. Egan explores the border where science and philosophy meet, raising new questions about the nature of the self.

"Wang's Carpets," which takes its name from an information-processing puzzle proposed by mathematician Hao Wang, is a first-contact story about an encounter with a life form so alien that at first it can hardly be recognized as life. The denizens of the "carpets" are not merely biological variations but multidimensional creatures that inhabit a realm of physics beyond the range of normal human perception.

The extraterrestrials are not the only "aliens" in this story, however. Egan works from the concept of "Posthumanism" popularized by cyberpunk writers like Bruce Sterling. Posthumans or transhumans represent the next stage in human evolution in which, through bioengineering and computer technology, consciousness is liberated from the confines of the body. In a world where individual identity is infinitely self-replicating and potentially immortal, authenticity becomes a vexing question and not only the nature of the self but also the corporeal reality of the physical universe are called into question. The possibilities for human potential are breathtaking, but such freedom also provokes a crisis in our understanding about what is essential to human nature.

Waiting to be cloned one thousand times and scattered across ten million cubic light-years, Paolo Venetti relaxed in his favorite ceremonial bathtub: a tiered hexagonal pool set in a courtyard of black marble flecked with gold. Paolo wore full traditional anatomy, uncomfortable garb at first, but the warm currents flowing across his back and shoulders slowly eased him into a pleasant torpor. He could have reached the same state in an instant, by decree — but the occasion seemed to demand the complete ritual of verisimilitude, the ornate curlicued longhand of imitation physical cause and effect.

As the moment of diaspora approached, a small gray lizard darted across the courtyard, claws scrabbling. It halted by the far edge of the pool, and Paolo marveled at the delicate pulse of its breathing, and watched the lizard watching him, until it moved again, disappearing into the surrounding vineyards. The environment was full of birds and insects, rodents and small reptiles — decorative in appearance, but also satisfying a more abstract aesthetic: softening the harsh radial symmetry of the lone observer; anchoring the simulation by perceiving it from a multitude of viewpoints. Ontological guy lines. No one had asked the lizards if they wanted to be cloned, though. They were coming along for the ride, like it or not.

The sky above the courtyard was warm and blue, cloudless and sunless, isotropic. Paolo waited calmly, prepared for every one of half a dozen possible fates.

An invisible bell chimed softly, three times. Paolo laughed, delighted.

One chime would have meant that he was still on Earth: an anticlimax, certainly — but there would have been advantages to compensate for that. Everyone who really mattered to him lived in the Carter-Zimmerman polis, but not all of them had chosen to take part in the diaspora to the same degree; his Earth-self would have lost no one. Helping to ensure that the thousand ships were safely dispatched would have been satisfying, too. And remaining a member of the wider Earth-based community, plugged into the entire global culture in real-time, would have been an attraction in itself.

Two chimes would have meant that this clone of Carter-Zimmerman had reached a planetary system devoid of life. Paolo had run a sophisticated — but non-sapient — self-predictive model before deciding to wake under those conditions. Exploring a handful of alien worlds, however barren, had seemed likely to be an enriching experience for him — with the distinct advantage that the whole endeavor would be untrammeled by the kind of elaborate precautions necessary in the presence of alien life. C-Z's population would have fallen by more than half — and many of his closest friends would have been absent — but he would have forged new friendships, he was sure.

Four chimes would have signaled the discovery of intelligent aliens. Five, a technological civilization. Six, spacefarers.

Three chimes, though, meant that the scout probes had detected unambiguous signs of life — and that was reason enough for jubilation. Up until the moment of the pre-launch cloning — a subjective instant before the chimes had sounded — no reports of alien life had ever reached Earth. There'd been no guarantee that any part of the diaspora would find it.

Paolo willed the polis library to brief him; it promptly rewired the declarative memory of his simulated traditional brain with all the information he was likely to need to satisfy his immediate curiosity. This clone of C-Z had arrived at Vega, the second closest of the thousand target stars, twenty-seven light-years from Earth. Paolo closed his eyes and visualized a star map with a thousand lines radiating out from the sun, then zoomed in on the trajectory which described his own journey. It had taken three centuries to reach Vega — but the vast majority of the polis's twenty thousand inhabitants had programmed their exoselves to suspend them prior to the cloning, and to wake them only if and when they arrived at a suitable destination. Ninety-two citizens had chosen the alternative: experiencing every voyage of the diaspora from start to finish, risking disappointment, and even death. Paolo now knew that the ship aimed at Fomalhaut, the target nearest Earth, had been struck by debris and annihilated *en route*. He mourned the ninety-two, briefly. He hadn't been close to any of them, prior to the cloning, and the particular versions who'd willfully perished two centuries ago in interstellar space seemed as remote as the victims of some ancient calamity from the era of flesh.

Paolo examined his new home star through the cameras of one of the scout probes — and the strange filters of the ancestral visual system. In traditional colors, Vega was a fierce blue-white disk, laced with prominences. Three times the mass of the sun, twice the size and twice as hot, sixty times as luminous. Burning hydrogen fast — and already halfway through its allotted five hundred million years on the main sequence.

Vega's sole planet, Orpheus, had been a featureless blip to the best lunar interferometers: now Paolo gazed down on its blue-green crescent, ten thousand kilometers below Carter-Zimmerman itself. Orpheus was terrestrial, a nickel-iron-silicate world; slightly larger than Earth, slightly warmer — a billion kilometers took the edge off Vega's heat — and almost drowning in liquid water. Impatient to see the whole surface firsthand, Paolo slowed his clock rate a thousandfold, allowing C-Z to circumnavigate the planet in twenty subjective seconds, daylight unshrouding a broad new swath with each pass. Two slender ocher-colored continents with mountainous spines bracketed hemispheric oceans, and dazzling expanses of pack ice covered both poles — far more so in the north, where jagged white peninsulas radiated out from the midwinter arctic darkness.

The Orphean atmosphere was mostly nitrogen — six times as much as on Earth; probably split by UV from primordial ammonial — with traces of water vapor and carbon dioxide, but not enough of either for a runaway greenhouse effect. The high atmospheric pressure meant reduced evaporation — Paolo saw not a wisp of cloud — and the large, warm oceans in turn helped feed carbon dioxide back into the crust, locking it up in limestone sediments destined for subduction.

The whole system was young, by Earth standards, but Vega's greater mass, and a denser protostellar cloud, would have meant swifter passage through most of the traumas of birth: nuclear ignition and early luminosity fluctuations; planetary coalescence and the age of bombardments. The library estimated that Orpheus had enjoyed a relatively stable climate, and freedom from major impacts, for at least the past hundred million years.

Long enough for primitive life to appear —

A hand seized Paolo firmly by the ankle and tugged him beneath the water. He offered no resistance, and let the vision of the planet slip away. Only two other people in C-Z had free access to this environment — and his father didn't play games with his now-twelve-hundred-year-old son.

Elena dragged him all the way to the bottom of the pool, before releasing his foot and hovering above him, a triumphant silhouette against the bright surface. She was ancestor-shaped, but obviously cheating; she spoke with perfect clarity, and no air bubbles at all.

"Late sleeper! I've been waiting seven weeks for this!"

Paolo feigned indifference, but he was fast running out of breath. He had his exoself convert him into an amphibious human variant — biologically and historically authentic, if no longer the definitive ancestral phenotype. Water flooded into his modified lungs, and his modified brain welcomed it.

He said, "Why would I want to waste consciousness, sitting around waiting for the scout probes to refine their observations? I woke as soon as the data was unambiguous."

She pummeled his chest; he reached up and pulled her down, instinctively reducing his buoyancy to compensate, and they rolled across the bottom of the pool, kissing.

Elena said, "You know we're the first C-Z to arrive, anywhere? The Fomalhaut ship was destroyed. So there's only one other pair of us. Back on Earth."

"So?" Then he remembered. Elena had chosen not to wake if any other version of her had already encountered life. Whatever fate befell each of the remaining ships, every other version of him would have to live without her.

He nodded soberly, and kissed her again, "What am I meant to say? You're a thousand times more precious to me, now?"

"Yes."

"Ah, but what about the you-and-I on Earth? Five hundred times would be closer to the truth."

"There's no poetry in five hundred."

"Don't be so defeatist. Rewire your language centers."

She ran her hands along the sides of his ribcage, down to his hips. They made love with their almost-traditional bodies — and brains; Paolo was amused to the point of distraction when his limbic system went into overdrive, but he remembered enough from the last occasion to bury his self-consciousness and surrender to the strange hijacker. It wasn't like making love in any civilized fashion — the rate of information exchange between them was minuscule, for a start — but it had the raw insistent quality of most ancestral pleasures.

Then they drifted up to the surface of the pool and lay beneath the radiant sunless sky.

Paolo thought: *I've crossed twenty-seven light-years in an instant. I'm orbiting the first planet ever found to hold alien life. And I've sacrificed nothing — left nothing I truly value behind. This is too good, too good.* He felt a pang of regret for his other selves — it was hard to imagine them faring as well, without Elena, without Orpheus — but there was nothing he could do about that, now. Although there'd be time to confer with Earth before any more ships reached their destinations, he'd decided — prior to the cloning — not to allow the unfolding of his manifold future to be swayed by any change of heart. Whether or not his Earth-self agreed, the two of them were powerless to alter the criteria for waking. The self with the right to choose for the thousand had passed away.

No matter, Paolo decided. The others would find — or construct — their own reasons for happiness. And there was still the chance that one of them would wake to the sound of *four chimes*.

Elena said, "If you'd slept much longer, you would have missed the vote."

The vote? The scouts in low orbit had gathered what data they could about Orphean biology. To proceed any further, it would be necessary to send microprobes into the ocean itself — an escalation of contact which required the approval of two-thirds of the polis. There was no compelling reason to believe that the presence of a few million tiny robots could do any harm; all they'd leave behind in the water was a few kilojoules of waste heat. Nevertheless, a faction had arisen which advocated caution. The citizens of Carter-Zimmerman, they argued, could continue to observe from a distance for another decade, or another millennium, refining their observations and hypotheses before intruding . . . and those who disagreed could always sleep away the time, or find other interests to pursue.

Paolo delved into his library-fresh knowledge of the "carpets" — the single Orphean lifeform detected so far. They were free-floating creatures living in the equatorial ocean depths — apparently destroyed by UV if they drifted too close to the surface. They grew to a size of hundreds of meters, then fissioned into dozens of fragments, each of which continued to grow. It was tempting to assume that they were colonies of single-celled organisms, something like giant kelp — but there was no real evidence yet to back that up. It was difficult enough for the scout probes to discern the carpets' gross appearance and behavior through a kilometer of water, even with Vega's copious neutrinos lighting the way; remote observations on a microscopic scale, let alone biochemical analyses, were out of the question. Spectroscopy revealed that the surface water was full of intriguing molecular debris — but guessing the relationship of any of it to the living carpets was like trying to reconstruct human biochemistry by studying human ashes.

Paolo turned to Elena. "What do you think?"

She moaned theatrically; the topic must have been argued to death while he slept. "The microprobes are harmless. They could tell us exactly what the carpets are made of, without removing a single molecule. What's the risk? *Culture shock?*"

Paolo flicked water onto her face, affectionately; the impulse seemed to come with the amphibian body. "You can't be sure that they're not intelligent."

"Do you know what was living on Earth, two hundred million years after it was formed?"

"Maybe cyanobacteria. Maybe nothing. This isn't Earth, though."

"True. But even in the unlikely event that the carpets are intelligent, do you think they'd notice the presence of robots a millionth their size? If they're unified organisms, they don't appear to react to anything in their environment — they have no predators, they don't pursue food, they just

drift with the currents — so there's no reason for them to possess elaborate sense organs at all, let alone anything working on a sub-millimeter
scale. And if they're colonies of single-celled creatures, one of which happens to collide with a microprobe and register its presence with surface
receptors . . . what conceivable harm could that do?"

"I have no idea. But my ignorance is no guarantee of safety."

Elena splashed him back. "The only way to deal with your *ignorance* is
to vote to send down the microprobes. We have to be cautious, I agree —
but there's no point *being here* if we don't find out what's happening in the
oceans, right now. I don't want to wait for this planet to evolve something
smart enough to broadcast biochemistry lessons into space. If we're not
willing to take a few infinitesimal risks, Vega will turn red giant before we
learn anything."

It was a throwaway line — but Paolo tried to imagine witnessing the
event. In a quarter of a billion years, would the citizens of Carter-Zimmerman
be debating the ethics of intervening to rescue the Orpheans — or would
they all have lost interest, and departed for other stars, or modified themselves
into beings entirely devoid of nostalgic compassion for organic life?

Grandiose visions for a twelve-hundred-year-old. The Fomalhaut clone
had been obliterated by one tiny piece of rock. There was far more junk in
the Vegan system than in interstellar space; even ringed by defenses, its
data backed up to all the far-flung scout probes, this C-Z was not invulnerable just because it had arrived intact. Elena was right; they had to seize
the moment — or they might as well retreat into their own hermetic
worlds and forget that they'd ever made the journey.

Paolo recalled the honest puzzlement of a friend from Ashton-Laval:
*Why go looking for aliens? Our polis has a thousand ecologies, a trillion species
of evolved life. What do you hope to find, out there, that you couldn't have
grown at home?*

What had he hoped to find? Just the answers to a few simple questions.
Did human consciousness bootstrap all of space-time into existence, in order
to explain itself? Or had a neutral, pre-existing universe given birth to a billion varieties of conscious life, all capable of harboring the same delusions
of grandeur — until they collided with each other? Anthrocosmology was
used to justify the inward-looking stance of most polises: if the physical universe was created by human thought, it had no special status which placed
it above virtual reality. It might have come first — and every virtual reality
might need to run on a physical computing device, subject to physical laws —
but it occupied no privileged position in terms of "truth" versus "illusion." If
the ACs were right, then it was no more *honest* to value the physical universe over more recent artificial realities than it was honest to remain flesh
instead of software, or ape instead of human, or bacterium instead of ape.

Elena said, "We can't lie here forever; the gang's all waiting to see you."

"Where?" Paolo felt his first pang of homesickness; on Earth, his circle
of friends had always met in a real-time image of the Mount Pinatubo crater,
plucked straight from the observation satellites. A recording wouldn't be
the same.

"I'll show you."

Paolo reached over and took her hand. The pool, the sky, the courtyard vanished — and he found himself gazing down on Orpheus again . . . night-side, but far from dark, with his full mental palette now encoding everything from the pale wash of ground-current long-wave radio, to the multi-colored shimmer of isotopic gamma rays and back-scattered cosmic-ray brems-strahlung. Half the abstract knowledge the library had fed him about the planet was obvious at a glance, now. The ocean's smoothly tapered thermal glow spelt *three-hundred Kelvin* instantly — as well as backlighting the atmosphere's telltale infrared silhouette.

He was standing on a long, metallic-looking girder, one edge of a vast geodesic sphere, open to the blazing cathedral of space. He glanced up and saw the star-rich dust-clogged band of the Milky Way, encircling him from zenith to nadir; aware of the glow of every gas cloud, discerning each absorption and emission line, Paolo could almost feel the plane of the galac-tic disk transect him. Some constellations were distorted, but the view was more familiar than strange — and he recognized most of the old signposts by color. He had his bearings, now. Twenty degrees away from Sirius — south, by parochial Earth reckoning — faint but unmistakable: the sun.

Elena was beside him — superficially unchanged, although they'd both shrugged off the constraints of biology. The conventions of this environment mimicked the physics of real macroscopic objects in free-fall and vacuum, but it wasn't set up to model any kind of chemistry, let alone that of flesh and blood. Their new bodies were human-shaped, but devoid of elaborate microstructure — and their minds weren't embedded in the physics at all, but were running directly on the processor web.

Paolo was relieved to be back to normal; ceremonial regression to the ancestral form was a venerable C-Z tradition — and being human was largely self-affirming, while it lasted — but every time he emerged from the experi-ence, he felt as if he'd broken free of billion-year-old shackles. There were polises on Earth where the citizens would have found his present structure almost as archaic: a consciousness dominated by sensory perception, an illu-sion of possessing solid form, a single time coordinate. The last flesh human had died long before Paolo was constructed, and apart from the communi-ties of Gleisner robots, Carter-Zimmerman was about as conservative as a transhuman society could be. The balance seemed right to Paolo, though — acknowledging the flexibility of software, without abandoning interest in the physical world — and although the stubbornly corporeal Gleisners had been first to the stars, the C-Z diaspora would soon overtake them.

Their friends gathered round, showing off their effortless free-fall acro-batics, greeting Paolo and chiding him for not arranging to wake sooner; he was the last of the gang to emerge from hibernation.

"Do you like our humble new meeting place?" Hermann floated by Paolo's shoulder, a chimeric cluster of limbs and sense-organs, speaking through the vacuum in modulated infrared. "We call it Satellite Pinatubo. It's desolate up here, I know — but we were afraid it might violate the spirit of caution if we dared pretend to walk the Orphean surface."

Paolo glanced mentally at a scout probe's close-up of a typical stretch of dry land, an expanse of fissured red rock. "More desolate down there, I think." He was tempted to touch the ground — to let the private vision become tactile — but he resisted. Being elsewhere in the middle of a conversation was bad etiquette.

"Ignore Hermann," Liesl advised. "He wants to flood Orpheus with our alien machinery before we have any idea what the effects might be." Liesl was a green-and-turquoise butterfly, with a stylized human face stippled in gold on each wing.

Paolo was surprised; from the way Elena had spoken, he'd assumed that his friends must have come to a consensus in favor of the microprobes — and only a late sleeper, new to the issues, would bother to argue the point. "What effects? The carpets — "

"Forget the carpets! Even if the carpets are as simple as they look, we don't know what else is down there." As Liesl's wings fluttered, her mirror-image faces seemed to glance at each other for support. "With neutrino imaging, we barely achieve spatial resolution in meters, time resolution in seconds. We don't know anything about smaller lifeforms."

"And we never will, if you have your way." Karpal — an ex-Gleisner, human-shaped as ever — had been Liesl's lover, last time Paolo was awake.

"We've only been here for a fraction of an Orphean year! There's still a wealth of data we could gather non-intrusively, with a little patience. There might be rare beachings of ocean life — "

Elena said dryly, "Rare indeed. Orpheus has negligible tides, shallow waves, very few storms. And anything beached would be fried by UV before we glimpsed anything more instructive than we're already seeing in the surface water."

"Not necessarily. The carpets seem to be vulnerable — but other species might be better protected, if they live nearer to the surface. And Orpheus is seismically active; we should at least wait for a tsunami to dump a few cubic kilometers of ocean onto a shoreline, and see what it reveals."

Paolo smiled; he hadn't thought of that. A tsunami might be worth waiting for.

Liesl continued, "What is there to lose, by waiting a few hundred Orphean years? At the very least, we could gather baseline data on seasonal climate patterns — and we could watch for anomalies, storms and quakes, hoping for some revelatory glimpses."

A few hundred Orphean years? *A few terrestrial millennia?* Paolo's ambivalence waned. If he'd wanted to inhabit geological time, he would have migrated to the Lokhande polis, where the Order of Contemplative Observers watched Earth's mountains erode in subjective seconds. Orpheus hung in the sky beneath them, a beautiful puzzle waiting to be decoded, demanding to be understood.

He said, "But what if there *are* no 'revelatory glimpses'? How long do we wait? We don't know how rare life is — in time, or in space. If this planet is precious, *so is the epoch it's passing through.* We don't know how rapidly Orphean biology is evolving; species might appear and vanish while we agonize over the risks of gathering better data. The carpets — and whatever else — could die out before we'd learnt the first thing about them. What a waste that would be!"

Liesl stood her ground.

"And if we damage the Orphean ecology — or culture — by rushing in? That wouldn't be a waste. It would be a tragedy."

Paolo assimilated all the stored transmissions from his Earth-self — almost three hundred years' worth — before composing a reply. The early communications included detailed mind grafts — and it was good to share the excitement of the diaspora's launch; to watch — very nearly firsthand — the thousand ships, nanomachine-carved from asteroids, depart in a blaze of fusion fire from beyond the orbit of Mars. Then things settled down to the usual prosaic matters: Elena, the gang, shameless gossip, Carter-Zimmerman's ongoing research projects, the buzz of inter-polis cultural tensions, the not-quite-cyclic convulsions of the arts (the perceptual aesthetic overthrows the emotional, again . . . although Valladas in Konishi polis claims to have constructed a new synthesis of the two).

After the first fifty years, his Earth-self had begun to hold things back; by the time news reached Earth of the Fomalhaut clone's demise, the messages had become pure audiovisual linear monologues. Paolo understood. It was only right; they'd diverged, and you didn't send mind grafts to strangers.

Most of the transmissions had been broadcast to all of the ships, indiscriminately. Forty-three years ago, though, his Earth-self had sent a special message to the Vega-bound clone.

"The new lunar spectroscope we finished last year has just picked up clear signs of water on Orpheus. There should be large temperate oceans waiting for you, if the models are right. So . . . good luck." Vision showed the instrument's domes growing out of the rock of the lunar farside; plots of the Orphean spectral data; an ensemble of planetary models. "Maybe it seems strange to you — all the trouble we're taking to catch a glimpse of what you're going to see in close-up, so soon. It's hard to explain: I don't think it's jealousy, or even impatience. Just a need for independence.

"There's been a revival of the old debate: should we consider redesigning our minds to encompass interstellar distances? One self spanning thousands of stars, not via cloning, but through acceptance of the natural time scale of the light-speed lag. Millennia passing between mental events. Local contingencies dealt with by non-conscious systems." Essays, pro and con, were appended; Paolo ingested summaries. "I don't think the idea will gain much support, though — and the new astronomical projects are something of an antidote. We have to make peace with the fact that we've stayed behind . . . so we cling to the Earth — looking outwards, but remaining firmly anchored.

"I keep asking myself, though: where do we go from here? History can't guide us. Evolution can't guide us. The C-Z charter says *understand and respect the universe* . . . but in what form? On what scale? With what kind of senses, what kind of minds? We can become anything at all — and that space of possible futures dwarfs the galaxy. Can we explore it without losing our way? Flesh humans used to spin fantasies about aliens arriving to 'conquer' Earth, to steal their 'precious' physical resources, to wipe them out for fear of 'competition' . . . as if a species capable of making the journey wouldn't have had the power, or the wit, or the imagination, to rid itself of obsolete biological imperatives. *Conquering the galaxy* is what bacteria with spaceships would do — knowing no better, having no choice.

"Our condition is the opposite of that: we have no end of choices. That's why we need to find alien life — not just to break the spell of the anthrocosmologists. We need to find aliens who've faced the same decisions — and discovered how to live, what to become. We need to understand what it means to inhabit the universe."

Paolo watched the crude neutrino images of the carpets moving in staccato jerks around his dodecahedral room. Twenty-four ragged oblongs drifted above him, daughters of a larger ragged oblong which had just fissioned. Models suggested that shear forces from ocean currents could explain the whole process, triggered by nothing more than the parent reaching a critical size. The purely mechanical break-up of a colony — if that was what it was — might have little to do with the life cycle of the constituent organisms. It was frustrating. Paolo was accustomed to a torrent of data on anything which caught his interest; for the diaspora's great discovery to remain nothing more than a sequence of coarse monochrome snapshots was intolerable.

He glanced at a schematic of the scout probes' neutrino detectors, but there was no obvious scope for improvement. Nuclei in the detectors were excited into unstable high-energy states, then kept there by fine-tuned gamma-ray lasers picking off lower-energy eigenstates faster than they could creep into existence and attract a transition. Changes in neutrino flux of one part in ten-to-the-fifteenth could shift the energy levels far enough to disrupt the balancing act. The carpets cast a shadow so faint, though, that even this near-perfect vision could barely resolve it.

Orlando Venetti said, "You're awake."

Paolo turned. His father stood an arm's length away, presenting as an ornately clad human of indeterminate age. Definitely older than Paolo, though; Orlando never ceased to play up his seniority — even if the age difference was only twenty-five percent now, and falling.

Paolo banished the carpets from the room to the space behind one pentagonal window, and took his father's hand. The portions of Orlando's mind which meshed with his own expressed pleasure at Paolo's emergence from hibernation, fondly dwelt on past shared experiences, and entertained hopes of continued harmony between father and son. Paolo's greeting was similar, a carefully contrived "revelation" of his own emotional state. It was more of a ritual than an act of communication — but then, even with Elena, he set up barriers. No one was totally honest with another person — unless the two of them intended to permanently fuse.

Orlando nodded at the carpets. "I hope you appreciate how important they are."

"You know I do." He hadn't included that in his greeting, though. "First alien life." *C-Z humiliates the Gleisner robots, at last* — that was probably how his father saw it. The robots had been first to Alpha Centauri, and first to an extrasolar planet — but first life was Apollo to their Sputniks, for anyone who chose to think in those terms.

Orlando said, "This is the hook we need, to catch the citizens of the marginal polises. The ones who haven't quite imploded into solipsism. This will shake them up — don't you think?"

Paolo shrugged. Earth's transhumans were free to implode into anything they liked; it didn't stop Carter-Zimmerman from exploring the physical universe. But thrashing the Gleisners wouldn't be enough for Orlando; he lived for the day when C-Z would become the cultural mainstream. Any polis could multiply its population a billionfold in a microsecond, if it wanted the vacuous honor of outnumbering the rest. Luring other citizens to migrate was harder — and persuading them to rewrite their own local charters was harder still. Orlando had a missionary streak: he wanted every other polis to see the error of its ways, and follow C-Z to the stars.

Paolo said, "Ashton-Laval has intelligent aliens. I wouldn't be so sure that news of giant seaweed is going to take Earth by storm."

Orlando was venomous. "Ashton-Laval intervened in its so-called 'evolutionary' simulations so many times that they might as well have built the end products in an act of creation lasting six days. They wanted talking reptiles, and — *mirabile dictu!* — they got talking reptiles. There are self-modified transhumans in *this polis* more alien than the aliens in Ashton-Laval."

Paolo smiled. "All right. Forget Ashton-Laval. But forget the marginal polises, too. We choose to value the physical world. That's what defines us — but it's as arbitrary as any other choice of values. Why can't you accept that? It's not the One True Path which the infidels have to be bludgeoned into following." He knew he was arguing half for the sake of it — he desperately wanted to refute the anthrocosmologists, himself — but Orlando always drove him into taking the opposite position. Out of fear of being nothing but his father's clone? Despite the total absence of inherited episodic memories, the stochastic input into his ontogenesis, the chaotically divergent nature of the iterative mind-building algorithms.

Orlando made a beckoning gesture, dragging the image of the carpets halfway back into the room. "You'll vote for the microprobes?"

"Of course."

"Everything depends on that, now. It's good to start with a tantalizing glimpse — but if we don't follow up with details soon, they'll lose interest back on Earth very rapidly."

"Lose interest? It'll be fifty-four years before we know if anyone paid the slightest attention in the first place."

Orlando eyed him with disappointment, and resignation. "If you don't care about the other polises, think about C-Z. This helps us, it strengthens us. We have to make the most of that."

Paolo was bemused. "The charter is the charter. What needs to be strengthened? You make it sound like there's something at risk."

"What do you think a thousand lifeless worlds would have done to us? Do you think the charter would have remained intact?"

Paolo had never considered the scenario. "Maybe not. But in every C-Z where the charter was rewritten, there would have been citizens who'd have gone off and founded new polises on the old lines. You and I, for a start. We could have called it Venetti-Venetti."

"While half your friends turned their backs on the physical world? While Carter-Zimmerman, after two thousand years, went solipsist? You'd be happy with that?"

Paolo laughed. "No — but it's not going to happen, is it? *We've found life.* All right, I agree with you: this strengthens C-Z. The diaspora might have 'failed' . . . but it didn't. We've been lucky. I'm glad, I'm grateful. Is that what you wanted to hear?"

Orlando said sourly, "You take too much for granted."

"And you care too much what I think! I'm not your . . . heir." Orlando was first-generation, scanned from flesh — and there were times when he seemed unable to accept that the whole concept of generation had lost its archaic significance. "You don't need me to safeguard the future of Carter-Zimmerman on your behalf. Or the future of transhumanity. You can do it in person."

Orlando looked wounded — a conscious choice, but it still encoded something. Paolo felt a pang of regret — but he'd said nothing he could honestly retract.

His father gathered up the sleeves of his gold and crimson robes — the only citizen of C-Z who could make Paolo uncomfortable to be naked — and repeated as he vanished from the room: "You take too much for granted."

The gang watched the launch of the microprobes together — even Liesl, though she came in mourning, as a giant dark bird. Karpal stroked her feathers nervously. Hermann appeared as a creature out of Escher, a segmented worm with six human-shaped feet — on legs with elbows — given to curling up into a disk and rolling along the girders of Satellite Pinatubo. Paolo and Elena kept saying the same thing simultaneously; they'd just made love.

Hermann had moved the satellite to a notional orbit just below one of the scout probes — and changed the environment's scale, so that the probe's lower surface, an intricate landscape of detector modules and attitude-control jets, blotted out half the sky. The atmospheric-entry capsules — ceramic teardrops three centimeters wide — burst from their launch tube and hurtled past like boulders, vanishing from sight before they'd fallen so much as ten meters closer to Orpheus. It was all scrupulously accurate, although it was part real-time imagery, part extrapolation, part *faux.* Paolo thought: *We might as well have run a pure simulation . . . and pretended to follow the capsules down.* Elena gave him a guilty/admonishing look. *Yeah — and then why bother actually launching them at all? Why not just simulate a plausible Orphean ocean full of plausible Orphean lifeforms? Why not simulate the whole diaspora?* There was no crime of heresy in C-Z; no one had ever been exiled for breaking the charter. At times it still felt like a tightrope walk, though, trying to classify every act of simulation into those which contributed to an understanding of the physical universe (good), those which were merely convenient, recreational, aesthetic (acceptable) . . . and those which constituted a denial of the primacy of real phenomena (time to think about emigration).

The vote on the microprobes had been close: seventy-two percent in favor, just over the required two-thirds majority, with five percent abstaining. (Citizens created since the arrival at Vega were excluded . . . not that anyone in Carter-Zimmerman would have dreamt of stacking the ballot, perish the thought.) Paolo had been surprised at the narrow margin; he'd yet to hear a single plausible scenario for the microprobes doing harm. He wondered if there was another unspoken reason which had nothing to do with fears for the Orphean ecology, or hypothetical culture. *A wish to prolong the pleasure of unraveling the planet's mysteries?* Paolo had some sympathy with that impulse — but the launch of the microprobes would do nothing to undermine the greater long-term pleasure of watching, and understanding, as Orphean life evolved.

Liesl said forlornly, "Coastline erosion models show that the northwestern shore of Lambda is inundated by tsunami every ninety Orphean years, on average." She offered the data to them; Paolo glanced at it, and it looked convincing — but the point was academic now. "We could have waited."

Hermann waved his eye-stalks at her. "Beaches covered in fossils, are they?"

"No, but the conditions hardly — "

"No excuses!" He wound his body around a girder, kicking his legs gleefully. Hermann was first-generation, even older than Orlando; he'd been scanned in the twenty-first century, before Carter-Zimmerman existed. Over the centuries, though, he'd wiped most of his episodic memories, and rewritten his personality a dozen times. He'd once told Paolo, "I think of myself as my own great-great-grandson. Death's not so bad, if you do it incrementally. Ditto for immortality."

Elena said, "I keep trying to imagine how it will feel if another C-Z clone stumbles on something infinitely better — like aliens with wormhole drives — while we're back here studying rafts of algae." The body she wore was more stylized than usual — still humanoid, but sexless, hairless and smooth, the face inexpressive and androgynous.

"If they have wormhole drives, they might visit us. Or share the technology, so we can link up the whole diaspora."

"If they have wormhole drives, where have they been for the last two thousand years?"

Paolo laughed. "Exactly. But I know what you mean: *first alien life* . . . and it's likely to be about as sophisticated as seaweed. It breaks the jinx, though. Seaweed every twenty-seven light-years. Nervous systems every fifty? Intelligence every hundred?" He fell silent, abruptly realizing what she was feeling: electing not to wake again after first life was beginning to seem like the wrong choice, a waste of the opportunities the diaspora had created. Paolo offered her a mind graft expressing empathy and support, but she declined.

She said, "I want sharp borders, right now. I want to deal with this myself."

"I understand." He let the partial model of her which he'd acquired as they'd made love fade from his mind. It was non-sapient, and no longer linked to her — but to retain it any longer when she felt this way would have seemed like a transgression. Paolo took the responsibilities of intimacy seriously. His lover before Elena had asked him to erase all his knowledge of her, and he'd more or less complied — the only thing he still knew about her was the fact that she'd made the request.

Hermann announced. "Planetfall!" Paolo glanced at a replay of a scout probe view which showed the first few entry capsules breaking up above the ocean and releasing their microprobes. Nanomachines transformed the ceramic shields (and then themselves) into carbon dioxide and a few simple minerals — nothing the micrometeorites constantly raining down onto Orpheus didn't contain — before the fragments could strike the water. The microprobes would broadcast nothing; when they'd finished gathering data, they'd float to the surface and modulate their UV reflectivity. It would be up to the scout probes to locate these specks, and read their messages, before they self-destructed as thoroughly as the entry capsules.

Hermann said, "This calls for a celebration. I'm heading for the Heart. Who'll join me?"

Paolo glanced at Elena. She shook her head. "You go."

"Are you sure?"

"Yes! Go on." Her skin had taken on a mirrored sheen; her expressionless face reflected the planet below. "I'm all right. I just want some time to think things through, on my own."

Hermann coiled around the satellite's frame, stretching his pale body as he went, gaining segments, gaining legs. "Come on, come on! Karpal? Liesl? Come and celebrate!"

Elena was gone. Liesl made a derisive sound and flapped off into the distance, mocking the environment's airlessness. Paolo and Karpal watched as Hermann grew longer and faster — and then in a blur of speed and change stretched out to wrap the entire geodesic frame. Paolo demagnetized his feet and moved away, laughing; Karpal did the same.

Then Hermann constricted like a boa, and snapped the whole satellite apart.

They floated for a while, two human-shaped machines and a giant worm in a cloud of spinning metal fragments, an absurd collection of imaginary debris, glinting by the light of the true stars.

The Heart was always crowded, but it was larger than Paolo had seen it — even though Hermann had shrunk back to his original size, so as not to make a scene. The huge muscular chamber arched above them, pulsating wetly in time to the music, as they searched for the perfect location to soak up the atmosphere. Paolo had visited public environments in other polises, back on Earth; many were designed to be nothing more than a perceptual framework for group emotion-sharing. He'd never understood the attraction of becoming intimate with large numbers of strangers. Ancestral social hierarchies might have had their faults — and it was absurd to try to make a virtue of the limitations imposed by minds confined to wetware — but the whole idea of mass telepathy as an end in itself seemed bizarre to Paolo . . . and even old-fashioned, in a way. Humans, clearly, would have benefited from a good strong dose of each other's inner life, to keep them from slaughtering each other — but any civilized transhuman could respect and value other citizens without the need to have *been them*, firsthand.

They found a good spot and made some furniture, a table and two chairs — Hermann preferred to stand — and the floor expanded to make room. Paolo looked around, shouting greetings at the people he recognized by sight, but not bothering to check for identity broadcasts from the rest. Chances were he'd met everyone here, but he didn't want to spend the next hour exchanging pleasantries with casual acquaintances.

Hermann said, "I've been monitoring our modest stellar observatory's data stream — my antidote to Vegan parochialism. Odd things are going on around Sirius. We're seeing electron-positron annihilation gamma rays, gravity waves . . . and some unexplained hot spots on Sirius B." He turned to Karpal and asked innocently, "What do you think those robots are up to? There's a rumor that they're planning to drag the white dwarf out of orbit, and use it as part of a giant spaceship."

"I never listen to rumors." Karpal always presented as a faithful reproduction of his old human-shaped Gleisner body — and his mind, Paolo gathered, always took the form of a physiological model, even though he was five generations removed from flesh. Leaving his people and coming into C-Z must have taken considerable courage; they'd never welcome him back.

Paolo said, "Does it matter what they do? Where they go, how they get there? There's more than enough room for both of us. Even if they shadowed the diaspora — even if they came to Vega — we could study the Orpheans together, couldn't we?"

Hermann's cartoon insect face showed mock alarm, eyes growing wider, and wider apart. "Not if they dragged along a white dwarf! Next thing they'd want to start building a Dyson sphere." He turned back to Karpal. "You don't still suffer the urge, do you, for . . . *astrophysical* engineering?"

"Nothing C-Z's exploitation of a few megatons of Vegan asteroid material hasn't satisfied."

Paolo tried to change the subject. "Has anyone heard from Earth, lately? I'm beginning to feel unplugged." His own most recent message was a decade older than the time lag.

Karpal said, "You're not missing much; all they're talking about is Orpheus . . . ever since the new lunar observations, the signs of water. They seem more excited by the mere possibility of life than we are by the certainty. And they have very high hopes."

Paolo laughed. "They do. My Earth-self seems to be counting on the diaspora to find an advanced civilization with the answers to all of transhumanity's existential problems. I don't think he'll get much cosmic guidance from kelp."

"You know there was a big rise in emigration from C-Z after the launch? Emigration, and suicides." Hermann had stopped wriggling and gyrating, becoming almost still, a sign of rare seriousness. "I suspect that's what triggered the astronomy program in the first place. And it seems to have stanched the flow, at least in the short term. Earth C-Z detected water before any clone in the diaspora — and when they hear that we've found life, they'll feel more like collaborators in the discovery because of it."

Paolo felt a stirring of unease. *Emigration and suicides? Was that why Orlando had been so gloomy?* After three hundred years of waiting, how high had expectations become?

A buzz of excitement crossed the floor, a sudden shift in the tone of the conversation. Hermann whispered reverently, "First microprobe has surfaced. And the data is coming in now."

The non-sapient Heart was intelligent enough to guess its patrons' wishes. Although everyone could tap the library for results, privately, the music cut out and a giant public image of the summary data appeared, high in the chamber. Paolo had to crane his neck to view it, a novel experience.

The microprobe had mapped one of the carpets in high resolution. The image showed the expected rough oblong, some hundred meters wide — but the two-or-three-meter-thick slab of the neutrino tomographs was revealed now as a delicate, convoluted surface — fine as a single layer of skin, but folded into an elaborate space-filling curve. Paolo checked the full data: the topology was strictly planar, despite the pathological appearance. No holes, no joins — just a surface which meandered wildly enough to look ten thousand times thicker from a distance than it really was.

An inset showed the microstructure, at a point which started at the rim of the carpet and then — slowly — moved toward the center. Paolo stared at the flowing molecular diagram for several seconds before he grasped what it meant.

The carpet was not a colony of single-celled creatures. Nor was it a multi-cellular organism. It was a *single molecule*, a two-dimensional polymer weighing twenty-five million kilograms. A giant sheet of folded polysaccharide, a complex mesh of interlinked pentose and hexose sugars hung with alkyl and amide side chains. A bit like a plant cell wall — except that this polymer was far stronger than cellulose, and the surface area was twenty orders of magnitude greater.

Karpal said, "I hope those entry capsules were perfectly sterile. Earth bacteria would gorge themselves on this. One big floating carbohydrate dinner, with no defenses."

Hermann thought it over. "Maybe. If they had enzymes capable of breaking off a piece — which I doubt. No chance we'll find out, though: even if there'd been bacterial spores lingering in the asteroid belt from early human expeditions, every ship in the diaspora was double-checked for contamination *en route*. We haven't brought smallpox to the Americas."

Paolo was still dazed. "But how does it assemble? How does it . . . grow?" Hermann consulted the library and replied, before Paolo could do the same.

"The edge of the carpet catalyzes its own growth. The polymer is irregular, aperiodic — there's no single component which simply repeats. But there seem to be about twenty thousand basic structural units — twenty thousand different polysaccharide building blocks." Paolo saw them: long bundles of cross-linked chains running the whole two-hundred-micron thickness of the carpet, each with a roughly square cross-section, bonded at several thousand points to the four neighboring units. "Even at this depth, the ocean's full of UV-generated radicals which filter down from the surface. Any structural unit exposed to the water converts those radicals into more polysaccharide — and builds another structural unit."

Paolo glanced at the library again, for a simulation of the process. Catalytic sites strewn along the sides of each unit trapped the radicals in place, long enough for new bonds to form between them. Some simple sugars were incorporated straight into the polymer as they were created; others were set free to drift in solution for a microsecond or two, until they were needed. At that level, there were only a few basic chemical tricks being used . . . but molecular evolution must have worked its way up from a few small autocatalytic fragments, first formed by chance, to this elaborate system of twenty thousand mutually self-replicating structures. If the "structural units" had floated free in the ocean as independent molecules, the "lifeform" they comprised would have been virtually invisible. By bonding together, though, they became twenty thousand colors in a giant mosaic.

It was astonishing. Paolo hoped Elena was tapping the library, wherever she was. A colony of algae would have been more "advanced" — but this incredible primordial creature revealed infinitely more about the possibilities for the genesis of life. Carbohydrate, here, played every biochemical role: information carrier, enzyme, energy source, structural material. Nothing like it could have survived on Earth, once there were organisms capable of feeding on it — and if there were ever intelligent Orpheans, they'd be unlikely to find any trace of this bizarre ancestor.

Karpal wore a secretive smile.

Paolo said, "What?"

"Wang tiles. The carpets are made out of Wang tiles."

Hermann beat him to the library, again.

"*Wang* as in twentieth-century flesh mathematician, Hao Wang. *Tiles* as in any set of shapes which can cover the plane. Wang tiles are squares with various shaped edges, which have to fit complementary shapes on adjacent squares. You can cover the plane with a set of Wang tiles, as long as you choose the right one every step of the way. Or in the case of the carpets, grow the right one."

Karpal said, "We should call them Wang's Carpets, in honor of Hao Wang. After twenty-three hundred years, his mathematics has come to life."

Paolo liked the idea, but he was doubtful. "We may have trouble getting a two-thirds majority on that. It's a bit obscure . . ."

Hermann laughed. "Who needs a two-thirds majority? If we want to call them Wang's Carpets, we can call them Wang's Carpets. There are ninety-seven languages in current use in C-Z — half of them invented since the polis was founded. I don't think we'll be exiled for coining one private name."

Paolo concurred, slightly embarrassed. The truth was, he'd completely forgotten that Hermann and Karpal weren't actually speaking Modern Roman.

The three of them instructed their exoselves to consider the name adopted: henceforth, they'd hear "carpet" as "Wang's Carpet" — but if they used the term with anyone else, the reverse translation would apply.

Paolo sat and drank in the image of the giant alien: the first lifeform encountered by human or transhuman which was not a biological cousin. The death, at last, of the possibility that Earth might be unique.

They hadn't refuted the anthrocosmologists yet, though. Not quite. If, as the ACs claimed, human consciousness was the seed around which all of space-time had crystallized — if the universe was nothing but the simplest orderly explanation for human thought — then there was, strictly speaking, no need for a single alien to exist, anywhere. But the physics which justified human existence couldn't help generating a billion other worlds where life could arise. The ACs would be unmoved by Wang's Carpets; they'd insist that these creatures were physical, if not biological, cousins — merely an unavoidable by-product of anthropogenic, life-enabling physical laws.

The real test wouldn't come until the diaspora — or the Gleisner robots — finally encountered conscious aliens: minds entirely unrelated to humanity, observing and explaining the universe which human thought had supposedly built. Most ACs had come right out and declared such a find impossible; it was the sole falsifiable prediction of their hypothesis. Alien consciousness, as opposed to mere alien life, would always build itself a separate universe — because the chance of two unrelated forms of self-awareness concocting exactly the same physics and the same cosmology was infinitesimal — and any alien biosphere which seemed capable of evolving consciousness would simply never do so.

Paolo glanced at the map of the diaspora, and took heart. *Alien life already* — and the search had barely started; there were nine hundred and ninety-eight target systems yet to be explored. And even if every one of them proved no more conclusive than Orpheus . . . he was prepared to send clones out farther — and prepared to wait. Consciousness had taken far longer to appear on Earth than the quarter-of-a-billion years remaining before Vega left the main sequence — but the whole point of being here, after all, was that Orpheus wasn't Earth.

Orlando's celebration of the microprobe discoveries was a very first-generation affair. The environment was an endless sunlit garden strewn with tables covered in *food*, and the invitation had politely suggested attendance in fully human form. Paolo politely faked it — simulating most of the physiology, but running the body as a puppet, leaving his mind unshackled.

Orlando introduced his new lover, Catherine, who presented as a tall, dark-skinned woman. Paolo didn't recognize her on sight, but checked the identity code she broadcast. It was a small polis, he'd met her once before —

as a man called Samuel, one of the physicists who'd worked on the main interstellar fusion drive employed by all the ships of the diaspora. Paolo was amused to think that many of the people here would be seeing his father as a woman. The majority of the citizens of C-Z still practiced the conventions of relative gender which had come into fashion in the twenty-third century — and Orlando had wired them into his own son too deeply for Paolo to wish to abandon them — but whenever the paradoxes were revealed so starkly, he wondered how much longer the conventions would endure. Paolo was same-sex to Orlando, and hence saw his father's lover as a woman, the two close relationships taking precedence over his casual knowledge of Catherine as Samuel. Orlando perceived himself as being male and heterosexual, as his flesh original had been . . . while Samuel saw himself the same way . . . and each perceived the other to be a heterosexual woman. If certain third parties ended up with mixed signals, so be it. It was a typical C-Z compromise: nobody could bear to overturn the old order and do away with gender entirely (as most other polises had done) . . . but nobody could resist the flexibility which being software, not flesh, provided.

Paolo drifted from table to table, sampling the food to keep up appearances, wishing Elena had come. There was little conversation about the biology of Wang's Carpets; most of the people here were simply celebrating their win against the opponents of the microprobes — and the humiliation that faction would suffer, now that it was clearer than ever that the "invasive" observations could have done no harm. Liesl's fears had proved unfounded; there was no other life in the ocean, just Wang's Carpets of various sizes. Paolo, feeling perversely even-handed after the fact, kept wanting to remind these smug movers and shakers: *There might have been anything down there. Strange creatures, delicate and vulnerable in ways we could never have anticipated. We were lucky, that's all.*

He ended up alone with Orlando almost by chance; they were both fleeing different groups of appalling guests when their paths crossed on the lawn.

Paolo asked, "How do you think they'll take this, back home?"

"It's first life, isn't it? Primitive or not. It should at least maintain interest in the diaspora, until the next alien biosphere is discovered." Orlando seemed subdued; perhaps he was finally coming to terms with the gulf between their modest discovery, and Earth's longing for world-shaking results. "And at least the chemistry is novel. If it had turned out to be based on DNA and protein, I think half of Earth C-Z would have died of boredom on the spot. Let's face it, the possibilities of DNA have been simulated to death."

Paolo smiled at the heresy. "You think if nature hadn't managed a little originality, it would have dented people's faith in the charter? If the solipsist polises had begun to look more inventive than the universe itself . . . "

"Exactly."

They walked on in silence, then Orlando halted, and turned to face him.

He said, "There's something I've been wanting to tell you. My Earth-self is dead."

"*What?*"

"Please, don't make a fuss."

"But . . . why? Why would he — ?" *Dead* meant suicide; there was no other cause — unless the sun had turned red giant and swallowed everything out to the orbit of Mars.

"I don't know why. Whether it was a vote of confidence in the diaspora" — Orlando had chosen to wake only in the presence of alien life — "or whether he despaired of us sending back good news, and couldn't face the waiting, and the risk of disappointment. He didn't give a reason. He just had his exoself send a message, stating what he'd done."

Paolo was shaken. If a clone of *Orlando* had succumbed to pessimism, he couldn't begin to imagine the state of mind of the rest of Earth C-Z.

"When did this happen?"

"About fifty years after the launch."

"My Earth-self said nothing."

"It was up to me to tell you, not him."

"I wouldn't have seen it that way."

"Apparently, you would have."

Paolo fell silent, confused. How was he supposed to mourn a distant version of Orlando, in the presence of the one he thought of as real? Death of one clone was a strange half-death, a hard thing to come to terms with. His Earth-self had lost a father; his father had lost an Earth-self. What exactly did that mean to *him*?

What Orlando cared most about was Earth C-Z. Paolo said carefully, "Hermann told me there'd been a rise in emigration and suicide — until the spectroscope picked up the Orphean water. Morale has improved a lot since then — and when they hear that it's more than just water . . ."

Orlando cut him off sharply. "You don't have to talk things up for me. I'm in no danger of repeating the act."

They stood on the lawn, facing each other. Paolo composed a dozen different combinations of mood to communicate, but none of them felt right. He could have granted his father perfect knowledge of everything he was feeling — but what exactly would that knowledge have conveyed? In the end, there was fusion, or separateness. There was nothing in between.

Orlando said, "Kill myself — and leave the fate of transhumanity in your hands? You must be out of your fucking mind."

They walked on together, laughing.

Karpal seemed barely able to gather his thoughts enough to speak. Paolo would have offered him a mind graft promoting tranquillity and concentration — distilled from his own most focused moments — but he was sure that Karpal would never have accepted it. He said, "Why don't you just start wherever you want to? I'll stop you if you're not making sense."

Karpal looked around the white dodecahedron with an expression of disbelief. "You live here?"

"Some of the time."

"But this is your base environment? No trees? No sky? No *furniture*?"

Paolo refrained from repeating any of Hermann's naive-robot jokes. "I add them when I want them. You know, like . . . music. Look, don't let my taste in decor distract you."

Karpal made a chair and sat down heavily.

He said, "Hao Wang proved a powerful theorem, twenty-three hundred years ago. Think of a row of Wang Tiles as being like the data tape of a Turing Machine." Paolo had the library grant him knowledge of the term; it was the original conceptual form of a generalized computing device, an imaginary machine which moved back and forth along a limitless one-dimensional data tape, reading and writing symbols according to a given set of rules.

"With the right set of tiles, to force the right pattern, the next row of the tiling will look like the data tape after the Turing Machine has performed one step of its computation. And the row after that will be the data tape after two steps, and so on. For any given Turing Machine, there's a set of Wang Tiles which can imitate it."

Paolo nodded amiably. He hadn't heard of this particular quaint result, but it was hardly surprising. "The carpets must be carrying out billions of acts of computation every second . . . but then, so are the water molecules around them. There are no physical processes which don't perform arithmetic of some kind."

"True. But with the carpets, it's not quite the same as random molecular motion."

"Maybe not."

Karpal smiled, but said nothing.

"What? You've found a pattern? Don't tell me: our set of twenty thousand polysaccharide Wang Tiles just happens to form the Turing Machine for calculating pi."

"No. What they form is a universal Turing Machine. They can calculate anything at all — depending on the data they start with. Every daughter fragment is like a program being fed to a chemical computer. Growth executes the program."

"Ah." Paolo's curiosity was roused — but he was having some trouble picturing where the hypothetical Turing Machine put its read/write head. "Are you telling me only one tile changes between any two rows, where the 'machine' leaves its mark on the 'data tape' . . . ?" The mosaics he'd seen were a riot of complexity, with no two rows remotely the same.

Karpal said, "No, no. Wang's original example worked exactly like a standard Turing Machine, to simplify the argument . . . but the carpets are more like an arbitrary number of different computers with overlapping data, all working in parallel. This is biology, not a designed machine — it's as messy and wild as, say . . . a mammalian genome. In fact, there are mathematical similarities with gene regulation: I've identified Kauffman networks at every level, from the tiling rules up; the whole system's poised on the hyperadaptive edge between frozen and chaotic behavior."

Paolo absorbed that, with the library's help. Like Earth life, the carpets seemed to have evolved a combination of robustness and flexibility which would have maximized their power to take advantage of natural selection. Thousands of different autocatalytic chemical networks must have arisen soon after the formation of Orpheus — but as the ocean chemistry and the climate changed in the Vegan system's early traumatic millennia, the ability to respond to selection pressure had itself been selected for, and the carpets were the result. Their complexity seemed redundant, now, after a hundred million years of relative stability — and no predators or competition in sight — but the legacy remained.

"So if the carpets have ended up as universal computers . . . with no real need anymore to respond to their surroundings . . . what are they *doing* with all that computing power?"

Karpal said solemnly, "I'll show you."

Paolo followed him into an environment where they drifted above a schematic of a carpet, an abstract landscape stretching far into the distance, elaborately wrinkled like the real thing, but otherwise heavily stylized, with each of the polysaccharide building blocks portrayed as a square tile with four different colored edges. The adjoining edges of neighboring tiles bore complementary colors — to represent the complementary, interlocking shapes of the borders of the building blocks.

"One group of microprobes finally managed to sequence an entire daughter fragment," Karpal explained, "although the exact edges it started life with are largely guesswork, since the thing was growing while they were trying to map it." He gestured impatiently, and all the wrinkles and folds were smoothed away, an irrelevant distraction. They moved to one border of the ragged-edged carpet, and Karpal started the simulation running.

Paolo watched the mosaic extending itself, following the tiling rules perfectly — an orderly mathematical process, here: no chance collisions of radicals with catalytic sites, no mismatched borders between two new-grown neighboring "tiles" triggering the disintegration of both. Just the distillation of the higher-level consequences of all that random motion.

Karpal led Paolo up to a height where he could see subtle patterns being woven, overlapping multiplexed periodicities drifting across the growing edge, meeting and sometimes interacting, sometimes passing right through each other. Mobile pseudo-attractors, quasi-stable waveforms in a one-dimensional universe. The carpet's second dimension was more like time than space, a permanent record of the history of the edge.

Karpal seemed to read his mind. "One dimensional. Worse than flatland. No connectivity, no complexity. What can possibly happen in a system like that? Nothing of interest, right?"

He clapped his hands and the environment exploded around Paolo. Trails of color streaked across his sensorium, entwining, then disintegrating into luminous smoke.

"Wrong. Everything goes on in a multidimensional frequency space. I've Fourier-transformed the edge into over a thousand components, and there's independent information in all of them. We're only in a narrow cross-section here, a sixteen-dimensional slice — but it's oriented to show the principal components, the maximum detail."

Paolo spun in a blur of meaningless color, utterly lost, his surroundings beyond comprehension. "You're a *Gleisner robot*, Karpal! *Only* sixteen dimensions! How can you have done this?"

Karpal sounded hurt, wherever he was. "Why do you think I came to C-Z? I thought you people were flexible!"

"What you're doing is . . ." *What?* Heresy? There was no such thing. Officially. "Have you shown this to anyone else?"

"Of course not. Who did you have in mind? Liesl? *Hermann?*"

"Good. I know how to keep my mouth shut." Paolo invoked his exoself and moved back into the dodecahedron. He addressed the empty room. "How can I put this? The physical universe has three spatial dimensions, plus time. Citizens of Carter-Zimmerman inhabit the physical universe. Higher dimensional mind games are for the solipsists." Even as he said it, he realized how pompous he sounded. It was an arbitrary doctrine, not some great moral principle.

But it was the doctrine he'd lived with for twelve hundred years.

Karpal replied, more bemused than offended, "It's the only way to see what's going on. The only sensible way to apprehend it. Don't you want to know what the carpets are *actually like?*"

Paolo felt himself being tempted. Inhabit a *sixteen-dimensional slice of a thousand-dimensional frequency space?* But it was in the service of understanding a real physical system — not a novel experience for its own sake.

And nobody had to find out.

He ran a quick — non-sapient — self-predictive model. There was a ninety-three percent chance that he'd give in, after fifteen subjective minutes of agonizing over the decision. It hardly seemed fair to keep Karpal waiting that long.

He said, "You'll have to loan me your mind-shaping algorithm. My exoself wouldn't know where to begin."

When it was done, he steeled himself, and moved back into Karpal's environment. For a moment, there was nothing but the same meaningless blur as before.

Then everything suddenly crystallized.

Creatures swam around them, elaborately branched tubes like mobile coral, vividly colored in all the hues of Paolo's mental palette — Karpal's attempt to cram in some of the information that a mere sixteen dimensions couldn't show? Paolo glanced down at his own body — nothing was missing, but he could see *around* it in all the thirteen dimensions in which it was nothing but a pin-prick; he quickly looked away. The "coral" seemed far more natural to his altered sensory map, occupying sixteen-space in all directions, and shaded with hints that it occupied much more. And Paolo had no doubt that it was "alive" — it looked more organic than the carpets themselves, by far.

Karpal said, "Every point in this space encodes some kind of quasi-periodic pattern in the tiles. Each dimension represents a different characteristic size — like a wavelength, although the analogy's not precise. The position in each dimension represents other attributes of the pattern, relating to the particular tiles it employs. So the localized systems you see around you are clusters of a few billion patterns, all with broadly similar attributes at similar wavelengths."

They moved away from the swimming coral, into a swarm of something like jellyfish: floppy hyperspheres waving wispy tendrils (each one of them more substantial than Paolo). Tiny jewel-like creatures darted among them. Paolo was just beginning to notice that nothing moved here like a solid object drifting through normal space; motion seemed to entail a shimmering deformation at the leading hypersurface, a visible process of disassembly and reconstruction.

Karpal led him on through the secret ocean. There were helical worms, coiled together in groups of indeterminate number — each single creature breaking up into a dozen or more wriggling slivers, and then recombining . . . although not always from the same parts. There were dazzling multicolored stemless flowers, intricate hypercones of "gossamer-thin" fifteen-dimensional petals — each one a hypnotic fractal labyrinth of crevices and capillaries. There were clawed monstrosities, writhing knots of sharp insectile parts like an orgy of decapitated scorpions.

Paolo said, uncertainly, "You could give people a glimpse of this in just three dimensions. Enough to make it clear that there's . . . *life* in here. This is going to shake them up badly, though." Life — embedded in the accidental computations of Wang's Carpets, with no possibility of ever relating to the world outside. This was an affront to Carter-Zimmerman's whole philosophy: if nature had evolved "organisms" as divorced from reality as the inhabitants of the most inward-looking polis, where was the privileged status of the physical universe, the clear distinction between truth and illusion?

And after three hundred years of waiting for good news from the diaspora, how would they respond to this back on Earth?

Karpal said, "There's one more thing I have to show you."

He'd named the creatures squids, for obvious reasons. *Distant cousins of the jellyfish, perhaps?* They were prodding each other with their tentacles in a way which looked thoroughly carnal — but Karpal explained, "There's no analog of light here. We're viewing all this according to ad hoc rules which have nothing to do with the native physics. All the creatures here gather information about each other by contact alone — which is actually quite a rich means of exchanging data, with so many dimensions. What you're seeing is communication by touch."

"Communication about what?"

"Just gossip, I expect. Social relationships."

Paolo stared at the writhing mass of tentacles.

"You think they're *conscious?*"

Karpal, point-like, grinned broadly. "They have a central control structure with more connectivity than the human brain — and which correlates data gathered from the skin. I've mapped that organ, and I've started to analyze its function."

He led Paolo into another environment, a representation of the data structures in the "brain" of one of the squids. It was — mercifully — three-dimensional, and highly stylized, built of translucent colored blocks marked with icons, representing mental symbols, linked by broad lines indicating the major connections between them. Paolo had seen similar diagrams of trans-human minds; this was far less elaborate, but eerily familiar nonetheless.

Karpal said, "Here's the sensory map of its surroundings. Full of other squids' bodies, and vague data on the last known positions of a few smaller creatures. But you'll see that the symbols activated by the physical presence of the other squids are linked to these" — he traced the connection with one finger — "representations. Which are crude miniatures of *this whole structure* here."

"This whole structure" was an assembly labeled with icons for memory retrieval, simple tropisms, short-term goals. The general business of being and doing.

"The squid has maps, not just of other squids' bodies, but their minds as well. Right or wrong, it certainly tries to know what the others are think-ing about. And" — he pointed out another set of links, leading to another, less crude, miniature squid mind — "it thinks about its own thoughts as well. I'd call that *consciousness*, wouldn't you?"

Paolo said weakly, "You've kept all this to yourself? You came this far, without saying a word — ?"

Karpal was chastened. "I know it was selfish — but once I'd decoded the interactions of the tile patterns, I couldn't tear myself away long enough to start explaining it to anyone else. And I came to you first because I wanted your advice on the best way to break the news."

Paolo laughed bitterly. "The best way to break the news that *first alien consciousness* is hidden deep inside a biological computer? That everything the diaspora was trying to prove has been turned on its head? The best way to explain to the citizens of Carter-Zimmerman that after a three-hundred-year journey, they might as well have stayed on Earth running simulations with as little resemblance to the physical universe as possible?"

Karpal took the outburst in good humor. "I was thinking more along the lines of the *best way to point out* that if we hadn't traveled to Orpheus and studied Wang's Carpets, we'd never have had the chance to tell the solip-sists of Ashton-Laval that all their elaborate invented lifeforms and exotic imaginary universes pale into insignificance compared to what's really out here — and which only the Carter-Zimmerman diaspora could have found."

Paolo and Elena stood together on the edge of Satellite Pinatubo, watch-ing one of the scout probes aim its maser at a distant point in space. Paolo thought he saw a faint scatter of microwaves from the beam as it collided with iron-rich meteor dust. *Elena's mind being diffracted all over the cos-mos?* Best not think about that.

He said, "When you meet the other versions of me who haven't experi-enced Orpheus, I hope you'll offer them mind grafts so they won't be jealous."

She frowned. "Ah. Will I or won't I? I can't be bothered modeling it. I expect I will. You should have asked me before I cloned myself. No need for jealousy, though. There'll be worlds far stranger than Orpheus."

"I doubt it. You really think so?"

"I wouldn't be doing this if I didn't believe that." Elena had no power to change the fate of the frozen clones of her previous self — but everyone had the right to emigrate.

Paolo took her hand. The beam had been aimed almost at Regulus, UV-hot and bright, but as he looked away, the cool yellow light of the sun caught his eye.

Vega C-Z was taking the news of the squids surprisingly well, so far. Karpal's way of putting it had cushioned the blow: it was only by traveling all this distance across the real, physical universe that they could have made such a discovery — and it was amazing how pragmatic even the most doctrinaire citizens had turned out to be. Before the launch, "alien solipsists" would have been the most unpalatable idea imaginable, the most abhorrent thing the diaspora could have stumbled upon — but now that they were here, and stuck with the fact of it, people were finding ways to view it in a better light. Orlando had even proclaimed, "*This* will be the perfect hook for the marginal polises. 'Travel through real space to witness a truly alien virtual reality.' We can sell it as a synthesis of the two world views."

Paolo still feared for Earth, though — where his Earth-self and others were waiting in hope of alien guidance. Would they take the message of Wang's Carpets to heart, and retreat into their own hermetic worlds, oblivious to physical reality?

And he wondered if the anthrocosmologists had finally been refuted . . . or not. Karpal had discovered alien consciousness — but it was sealed inside a cosmos of its own, its perceptions of itself and its surroundings neither reinforcing nor conflicting with human and transhuman explanations of reality. It would be millennia before C-Z could untangle the ethical problems of daring to try to make contact . . . assuming that both Wang's Carpets, and the inherited data patterns of the squids, survived that long.

Paolo looked around at the wild splendor of the star-choked galaxy, felt the disk reach in and cut right through him. *Could all this strange haphazard beauty be nothing but an excuse for those who beheld it to exist? Nothing but the sum of all the answers to all the questions humans and transhumans had ever asked the universe — answers created in the asking?*

He couldn't believe that — but the question remained unanswered.

So far.

Michael Swanwick

Slow Life

(2002)

Michael Swanwick (b. 1950) is one of the most accomplished sf writers working today. His first two stories (published in 1980) were both finalists for the Nebula award. Since then, hardly a year has gone by without one or more of his stories being nominated for a major award. He has won a Nebula, a World Fantasy Award, a Theodore Sturgeon Memorial Award, and five Hugos, including one for this story. He is especially known for his superbly crafted short stories; his output as a novelist is considerably smaller but still impressive. *Stations of the Tide* won the Nebula in 1992, and *The Iron Dragon's Daughter* (1993), which was a finalist for both the World Fantasy Award and the Arthur C. Clarke Award, helped push the boundaries of fantasy in a new direction.

Swanwick's stories are varied in content and style, but all are marked by meticulous craftsmanship, vivid imagery, and complex, compassionately rendered characters. They are often distinctly quirky, with odd premises and settings, but for all their strangeness, they seem both persuasively realistic and surprisingly optimistic. Swanwick was sometimes associated with cyberpunk early in his career, and he shares with that movement a rejection of straightforward exposition and an openness to technology and posthuman modes of being. He is essentially a humanist in outlook, however, and dedicated to traditional literary values — never flashy or affected.

In its portrayal of a self-contained alien entity, "Slow Life" may be compared to Le Guin's "Vaster Than Empires" (page 96); but, while Le Guin's psychological probing is focused on the human characters, Swanwick seems equally interested in the alien itself, not as a metaphor but as an equal participant in the encounter. And despite the devastating impact of this first contact, Swanwick takes a more hopeful attitude toward the possibilities for adaptation and coexistence.

> "It was the Second Age of Space. Gagarin, Shepard, Glenn, and Armstrong were all dead. It was *our* turn to make history now."
> — *The Memoirs of Lizzie O'Brien*

The raindrop began forming ninety kilometers above the surface of Titan. It started with an infinitesimal speck of tholin, adrift in the cold nitrogen atmosphere. Dianoacetylene condensed on the seed nucleus, molecule by molecule, until it was one shard of ice in a cloud of billions.

Now the journey could begin.

It took almost a year for the shard of ice in question to precipitate downward twenty-five kilometers, where the temperature dropped low enough that ethane began to condense on it. But when it did, growth was rapid.

161

Down it drifted.

At forty kilometers, it was for a time caught up in an ethane cloud. There it continued to grow. Occasionally it collided with another droplet and doubled in size. Finally it was too large to be held effortlessly aloft by the gentle stratospheric winds.

It fell.

Falling, it swept up methane and quickly grew large enough to achieve a terminal velocity of almost two meters per second.

At twenty-seven kilometers, it passed through a dense layer of methane clouds. It acquired more methane, and continued its downward flight.

As the air thickened, its velocity slowed and it began to lose some of its substance to evaporation. At two and a half kilometers, when it emerged from the last patchy clouds, it was losing mass so rapidly it could not normally be expected to reach the ground.

It was, however, falling toward the equatorial highlands, where mountains of ice rose a towering five hundred meters into the atmosphere. At two meters and a lazy new terminal velocity of one meter per second, it was only a breath away from hitting the surface.

Two hands swooped an open plastic collecting bag upward, and snared the raindrop.

"Gotcha!" Lizzie O'Brien cried gleefully.

She zip-locked the bag shut, held it up so her helmet cam could read the bar code in the corner, and said, "One raindrop." Then she popped it into her collecting box.

Sometimes it's the little things that make you happiest. Somebody would spend a *year* studying this one little raindrop when Lizzie got it home. And it was just Bag 64 in Collecting Case 5. She was going to be on the surface of Titan long enough to scoop up the raw material of a revolution in planetary science. The thought of it filled her with joy.

Lizzie dogged down the lid of the collecting box and began to skip across the granite-hard ice, splashing the puddles and dragging the boot of her atmosphere suit through the rivulets of methane pouring down the mountainside. "*I'm sing-ing in the rain.*" She threw out her arms and spun around. "*Just singing in the rain!*"

"Uh . . . O'Brien?" Alan Greene said from the *Clement*. "Are you all right?"

"*Dum-dee-dum-dee-dee-dum-dum, I'm . . . some-thing again.*"

"Oh, leave her alone" Consuelo Hong said with sour good humor. She was down on the plains, where the methane simply boiled into the air, and the ground was covered with thick, gooey tholin. It was, she had told them, like wading ankle-deep in molasses. "Can't you recognize the scientific method when you hear it?"

"If you say so," Alan said dubiously. He was stuck in the *Clement*, overseeing the expedition and minding the website. It was a comfortable gig — *he* wouldn't be sleeping in his suit *or* surviving on recycled water and energy stix — and he didn't think the others knew how much he hated it.

"What's next on the schedule?" Lizzie asked.

"Um . . . well, there's still the robot turbot to be released. How's that going, Hong?"

"Making good time. I oughta reach the sea in a couple of hours."

"Okay, then it's time O'Brien rejoined you at the lander. O'Brien, start spreading out the balloon and going over the harness checklist."

"Roger that."

"And while you're doing that, I've got today's voice-posts from the Web cued up."

Lizzie groaned, and Consuelo blew a raspberry. By NAFTASA policy, the ground crew participated in all web-casts. Officially, they were delighted to share their experiences with the public. But the VoiceWeb (privately, Lizzie thought of it as the Illiternet) made them accessible to people who lacked even the minimal intellectual skills needed to handle a keyboard.

"Let me remind you that we're on open circuit here, so anything you say will go into my reply. You're certainly welcome to chime in at any time. But each question-and-response is transmitted as one take, so if you flub a line, we'll have to go back to the beginning and start all over again."

"Yeah, yeah," Consuelo grumbled.

"We've done this before," Lizzie reminded him.

"Okay. Here's the first one."

"Uh, hi, this is BladeNinja43. I was wondering just what it is that you guys are hoping to discover out there."

"That's an extremely good question," Alan lied. "And the answer is: We don't know! This is a voyage of discovery, and we're engaged in what's called 'pure science.' Now, time and time again, the purest research has turned out to be extremely profitable. But we're not looking that far ahead. We're just hoping to find something absolutely unexpected."

"My God, you're slick," Lizzie marveled.

"I'm going to edit that from the tape," Alan said cheerily. "Next up."

"This is Mary Schroeder, from the United States. I teach high school English, and I wanted to know for my students, what kind of grades the three of you had when you were their age."

Alan began. "I was an overachiever, I'm afraid. In my sophomore year, first semester, I got a B in Chemistry and panicked. I thought it was the end of the world. But then I dropped a couple of extracurriculars, knuckled down, and brought that grade right up."

"I was good in everything but French Lit," Consuelo said.

"I nearly flunked out!" Lizzie said. "Everything was difficult for me. But then I decided I wanted to be an astronaut, and it all clicked into place. I realized that hey, it's just hard work. And now, well, here I am."

"That's good. Thanks, guys. Here's the third, from Maria Vasquez."

"Is there life on Titan?"

"Probably not. It's *cold* down there! 94° Kelvin is the same as −179° Celsius, or −290° Fahrenheit. And yet . . . life is persistent. It's been found in Antarctic ice and in boiling water in submarine volcanic vents. Which is why we'll be paying particular attention to exploring the depths of the ethane-methane sea. If life is anywhere to be found, that's where we'll find it."

"Chemically, the conditions here resemble the anoxic atmosphere on Earth in which life first arose," Consuelo said. "Further, we believe that such prebiotic chemistry has been going on here for four and a half billion years. For an organic chemist like me, it's the best toy box in the Universe. But that lack of heat is a problem. Chemical reactions that occur quickly back home would take thousands of years here. It's hard to see how life could arise under such a handicap."

"It would have to be slow life," Lizzie said thoughtfully. "Something vegetative. 'Vaster than empires and more slow.' It would take millions of years to reach maturity. A single thought might require centuries. . . ."

"Thank you for that, uh, wild scenario!" Alan said quickly. Their NAFTASA masters frowned on speculation. It was, in their estimation, almost as unprofessional as heroism. "This next question comes from Danny in Toronto."

"Hey, man, I gotta say I really envy you being in that tiny little ship with those two hot babes."

Alan laughed lightly. "Yes, Ms. Hong and Ms. O'Brien are certainly attractive women. But we're kept so busy that, believe it or not, the thought of sex never comes up. And currently, while I tend to the *Clement*, they're both on the surface of Titan at the bottom of an atmosphere 60 percent more dense than Earth's, and encased in armored exploration suits. So even if I did have inappropriate thoughts there's no way we could — "

"Hey, Alan," Lizzie said. "Tell me something."

"Yes?"

"What are you wearing?"

"Uh . . . switching over to private channel."

"Make that a three-way," Consuelo said.

Ballooning, Lizzie decided, was the best way there was of getting around. Moving with the gentle winds, there was no sound at all. And the view was great!

People talked a lot about the "murky orange atmosphere" of Titan, but your eyes adjusted. Turn up the gain on your helmet, and the white mountains of ice were *dazzling!* The methane streams carved cryptic runes into the heights. Then, at the tholin-line, white turned to a rich palette of oranges, reds, and yellows. There was a lot going on down there — more than she'd be able to learn in a hundred visits.

The plains were superficially duller, but they had their charms as well. Sure, the atmosphere was so dense that refracted light made the horizon curve upward to either side. But you got used to it. The black swirls and cryptic red tracery of unknown processes on the land below never grew tiring.

On the horizon, she saw the dark arm of Titan's narrow sea. If that was what it was. Lake Erie was larger, but the spin doctors back home had argued that since Titan was so much smaller than Earth, *relatively* it qualified as a sea. Lizzie had her own opinion, but she knew when to keep her mouth shut.

Consuelo was there now. Lizzie switched her visor over to the live feed. Time to catch the show.

"I can't believe I'm finally here," Consuelo said. She let the shrink-wrapped fish slide from her shoulder down to the ground. "Five kilometers doesn't seem like very far when you're coming down from orbit — just enough to leave a margin for error so the lander doesn't come down in the sea. But when you have to *walk* that distance, through tarry, sticky tholin . . . well, it's one heck of a slog."

"Consuelo, can you tell us what it's like there?" Alan asked.

"I'm crossing the beach. Now I'm at the edge of the sea." She knelt, dipped a hand into it. "It's got the consistency of a Slushy. Are you familiar with that drink? Lots of shaved ice sort of half-melted in a cup with flavored syrup. What we've got here is almost certainly a methane-ammonia mix; we'll know for sure after we get a sample to a laboratory. Here's an early indicator, though. It's dissolving the tholin off my glove." She stood.

"Can you describe the beach?"

"Yeah. It's white. Granular. I can kick it with my boot. Ice sand for sure. Do you want me to collect samples first or release the fish?"

"Release the fish," Lizzie said, almost simultaneously with Alan's "Your call."

"Okay, then." Consuelo carefully cleaned both of her suit's gloves in the sea, then seized the shrink-wrap's zip tab and yanked. The plastic parted. Awkwardly, she straddled the fish, lifted it by the two side-handles, and walked it into the dark slush.

"Okay, I'm standing in the sea now. It's up to my ankles. Now it's at my knees. I think it's deep enough here."

She set the fish down. "Now I'm turning it on."

The Mitsubishi turbot wriggled, as if alive. With one fluid motion, it surged forward, plunged, and was gone.

Lizzie switched over to the fishcam.

Black liquid flashed past the turbot's infrared eyes. Straight away from the shore it swam, seeing nothing but flecks of paraffin, ice, and other suspended particulates as they loomed up before it and were swept away in the violence of its wake. A hundred meters out, it bounced a pulse of radar off the sea floor, then dove, seeking the depths.

Rocking gently in her balloon harness, Lizzie yawned.

Snazzy Japanese cybernetics took in a minute sample of the ammonia-water, fed it through a deftly constructed internal laboratory, and excreted the waste products behind it. "We're at twenty meters now," Consuelo said. "Time to collect a second sample."

The turbot was equipped to run hundreds of on-the-spot analyses. But it had only enough space for twenty permanent samples to be carried back home. The first sample had been nibbled from the surface slush. Now it twisted, and gulped down five drams of sea fluid in all its glorious impurity.

To Lizzie, this was science on the hoof. Not very dramatic, admittedly, but intensely exciting.

She yawned again.

"O'Brien?" Alan said, "How long has it been since you last slept?"

"Huh? Oh . . . twenty hours? Don't worry about me, I'm fine."

"Go to sleep. That's an order."

"But — "

"Now."

Fortunately, the suit was comfortable enough to sleep in. It had been designed so she could.

First she drew in her arms from the suit's sleeves. Then she brought in her legs, tucked them up under her chin, and wrapped her arms around them. "Night, guys," she said.

"*Buenas noches, querida,*" Consuelo said, "*que tengas lindos sueños.*"

"Sleep tight, space explorer."

The darkness when she closed her eyes was so absolute it crawled. Black, black, black. Phantom lights moved within the darkness, formed lines, shifted away when she tried to see them. They were as fugitive as fish, luminescent, fainter than faint, there and with a flick of her attention fled.

A school of little thoughts flashed through her mind, silver-scaled and gone.

Low, deep, slower than sound, something tolled. The bell from a drowned clock tower patiently stroking midnight. She was beginning to get her bearings. Down *there* was where the ground must be. Flowers grew there unseen. Up above was where the sky would be, if there were a sky. Flowers floated there as well.

Deep within the submerged city, she found herself overcome by an enormous and placid sense of self. A swarm of unfamiliar sensations washed through her mind, and then . . .

"Are you me?" a gentle voice asked.

"No," she said carefully. "I don't think so."

Vast astonishment. "You think you are not me?"

"Yes. I think so, anyway."

"Why?"

There didn't seem to be any proper response to that, so she went back to the beginning of the conversation and ran through it again, trying to bring it to another conclusion. Only to bump against that "Why?" once again.

"I don't know why," she said.

"Why not?"

"I don't know."

She looped through that same dream over and over again all the while that she slept.

When she awoke, it was raining again. This time, it was a drizzle of pure methane from the lower cloud deck at fifteen kilometers. These clouds were (the theory went) methane condensate from the wet air swept up from the sea. They fell on the mountains and washed them clean of tholin. It was the methane that eroded and shaped the ice, carving gullies and caves.

Titan had more kinds of rain than anywhere else in the Solar System.

The sea had crept closer while Lizzie slept. It now curled up to the horizon on either side like an enormous dark smile. Almost time now for her to begin her descent. While she checked her harness settings, she flicked on telemetry to see what the others were up to.

The robot turbot was still spiraling its way downward, through the lightless sea, seeking its distant floor. Consuelo was trudging through the tholin again, retracing her five-kilometer trek from the lander *Harry Stubbs*, and Alan was answering another set of webposts.

"Modelos de la evolución de Titanes indican que la luna formó de una nube circumplanetaria rica en amoníaco y metano, la cual al condensarse dio forma a Saturno así como a otros satélites. Bajo estas condiciones en —"

"Uh . . . guys?"

Alan stopped. "Damn it, O'Brien, now I've got to start all over again."

"Welcome back to the land of the living," Consuelo said. "You should check out the readings we're getting from the robofish. Lots of long-chain polymers, odd fractions . . . tons of interesting stuff."

"Guys?"

This time her tone of voice registered with Alan. "What is it, O'Brien?"

"I think my harness is jammed."

Lizzie had never dreamed disaster could be such drudgery. First there were hours of back-and-forth with the NAFTASA engineers. What's the status of rope 14? Try tugging on rope 8. What do the D-rings look like? It was slow work because of the lag time for messages to be relayed to Earth and back. And Alan insisted on filling the silence with posts from the VoiceWeb. Her plight had gone global in minutes, and every unemployable loser on the planet had to log in with suggestions.

"Thezgemoth337, here. It seems to me that if you had a gun and shot up through the balloon, it would maybe deflate and then you could get down."

"I don't have a gun, shooting a hole in the balloon would cause it not to deflate but to rupture, I'm 800 meters above the surface, there's a sea below me, and I'm in a suit that's not equipped for swimming. Next."

"If you had a really big knife —"

"Cut! Jesus, Greene, is this the best you can find? Have you heard back from the organic chem guys yet?"

"Their preliminary analysis just came in," Alan said. "As best they can guess — and I'm cutting through a lot of clutter here — the rain you went through wasn't pure methane."

"No shit, Sherlock."

"They're assuming that whitish deposit you found on the rings and ropes is your culprit. They can't agree on what it is, but they think it underwent a chemical reaction with the material of your balloon and sealed the rip panel shut."

"I thought this was supposed to be a pretty nonreactive environment."

"It is. But your balloon runs off your suit's waste heat. The air in it is several degrees above the melting-point of ice. That's the equivalent of a blast furnace, here on Titan. Enough energy to run any number of amazing reactions. You haven't stopped tugging on the vent rope?"

"I'm tugging away right now. When one arm gets sore, I switch arms."

"Good girl. I know how tired you must be."

"Take a break from the voice-posts," Consuelo suggested, "and check out the results we're getting from the robofish. It's giving us some really interesting stuff."

So she did. And for a time it distracted her, just as they'd hoped. There was a lot more ethane and propane than their models had predicted, and surprisingly less methane. The mix of fractions was nothing like what she'd expected. She had learned just enough chemistry to guess at some of the implications of the data being generated, but not enough to put it all together. Still tugging at the ropes in the sequence uploaded by the engineers in Toronto, she scrolled up the chart of hydrocarbons dissolved in the lake.

Solute	Solute mole fraction
Ethyne	4.0×10^{-4}
Propyne	4.4×10^{-5}
1,3-Butadiyne	7.7×10^{-7}
Carbon Dioxide	0.1×10^{-5}
Methanenitrile	5.7×10^{-6}

But after a while, the experience of working hard and getting nowhere, combined with the tedium of floating farther and farther out over the featureless sea, began to drag on her. The columns of figures grew meaningless, then indistinct.

Propanenitrile 6.0×10^{-5}

Propanenitrile 9.9×10^{-6}

Propynenitrile 5.3×10^{-6}

Hardly noticing she was doing so, she fell asleep.

She was in a lightless building, climbing flight after flight of stairs. There were other people with her, also climbing. They jostled against her as she ran up the stairs, flowing upward, passing her, not talking.

It was getting colder.

She had a distant memory of being in the furnace room down below. It was hot there, swelteringly so. Much cooler where she was now. Almost too cool. With every step she took, it got a little cooler still. She found herself slowing down. Now it was definitely too cold. Unpleasantly so. Her leg muscles ached. The air seemed to be thickening around her as well. She could barely move now.

This was, she realized, the natural consequence of moving away from the furnace. The higher up she got, the less heat there was to be had, and the less energy to be turned into motion. It all made perfect sense to her somehow.

Step. Pause.

Step. Longer pause.

Stop.

The people around her had slowed to a stop as well. A breeze colder than ice touched her, and without surprise, she knew that they had reached the top of the stairs and were standing upon the building's roof. It was as dark without as it had been within. She stared upward and saw nothing.

"Horizons. Absolutely baffling," somebody murmured beside her.

"Not once you get used to them," she replied.

"Up and down — are these hierarchic values?"

"They don't have to be."

"Motion. What a delightful concept."

"We like it."

"So you *are* me?"

"No. I mean, I don't think so."

"Why?" .

She was struggling to find an answer to this, when somebody gasped. High up in the starless, featureless sky, a light bloomed. The crowd around her rustled with unspoken fear. Brighter the light grew. Brighter still. She could feel heat radiating from it, slight but definite, like the rumor of a distant sun. Everyone about her was frozen with horror. More terrifying than a light where none was possible was the presence of heat. It simply could not be. And yet it was.

She, along with the others, waited and watched for . . . something. She could not say what. The light shifted slowly in the sky. It was small, intense, ugly.

Then the light *screamed.*

She woke up.

"Wow," she said. "I just had the weirdest dream."

"Did you?" Alan said casually.

"Yeah. There was this light in the sky. It was like a nuclear bomb or something. I mean, it didn't look anything like a nuclear bomb, but it was terrifying the way a nuclear bomb would be. Everybody was staring at it. We couldn't move. And then . . ." She shook her head. "I lost it. I'm sorry. It was just so strange. I can't put it into words."

"Never mind that," Consuelo said cheerily. "We're getting some great readings down below the surface. Fractional polymers, long-chain hydrocarbons . . . fabulous stuff. You really should try to stay awake to catch some of this."

She was fully awake now, and not feeling too happy about it. "I guess that means that nobody's come up with any good ideas yet on how I might get down."

"Uh . . . what do you mean?"

"Because if they had, you wouldn't be so goddamned upbeat, would you?"

"*Some*body woke up on the wrong side of the bed," Alan said. "Please remember that there are certain words we don't use in public."

"I'm sorry," Consuelo said. "I was just trying to — "

" — distract me. Okay, fine. What the hey. I can play along." Lizzie pulled herself together. "So your findings mean . . . what? Life?"

"I keep telling you guys. It's too early to make that kind of determination. What we've got so far are just some very, very interesting readings."

"Tell her the big news," Alan said.

"Brace yourself. We've got a real ocean! Not this tiny little two-hundred-by-fifty-miles glorified lake we've been calling a sea, but a genuine ocean! Sonar readings show that what we see is just an evaporation pan atop a thirty-kilometer-thick cap of ice. The real ocean lies underneath, two hundred kilometers deep."

"Jesus." Lizzie caught herself. "I mean, gee whiz. Is there any way of getting the robofish down into it?"

"How do you think we got the depth readings? It's headed down there right now. There's a chimney through the ice right at the center of the visible sea. That's what replenishes the surface liquid. And directly under the hole, there's — guess what? — volcanic vents!"

"So does that mean . . .?"

"If you use the L-word again," Consuelo said, "I'll spit."

Lizzie grinned. *That* was the Consuelo Hong she knew. "What about the tidal data? I thought the lack of orbital perturbation ruled out a significant ocean entirely."

"Well, Toronto thinks . . ."

At first, Lizzie was able to follow the reasoning of the planetary geologists back in Toronto. Then it got harder. Then it became a drone. As she drifted off into sleep, she had time enough to be peevishly aware that she really shouldn't be dropping off to sleep all the time like this. She oughtn't to be so tired. She . . .

She found herself in the drowned city again. She still couldn't see anything but she knew it was a city because she could hear the sound of rioters smashing store windows. Their voices swelled into howling screams and receded into angry mutters, like a violent surf washing through the streets. She began to edge away backwards.

Somebody spoke into her ear.

"Why did you do this to us?"

"I didn't do anything to you."

"You brought us knowledge."

"What knowledge?"

"You said you were not us."

"Well, I'm not."

"You should never have told us that."

"You wanted me to lie?"

Horrified confusion. "Falsehood. What a distressing idea."

The smashing noises were getting louder. Somebody was splintering a door with an axe. Explosions. Breaking glass. She heard wild laughter. Shrieks. "We've got to get out of here."

"Why did you send the messenger?"

"What messenger?"

"The star! The star! The star!"

"Which star?"

"There are two stars?"

"There are billions of stars."

"No more! Please! Stop! No more!"

She was awake.

"Hello, yes, I appreciate that the young lady is in extreme danger, but I really don't think she should have used the Lord's name in vain."

"Greene," Lizzie said, "do we really have to put up with this?"

"Well, considering how many billions of public-sector dollars it took to bring us here . . . yes. Yes, we do. I can even think of a few backup astronauts who would say that a little upbeat web-posting was a pretty small price to pay for the privilege."

"Oh, barf."

"I'm switching to a private channel," Alan said calmly. The background radiation changed subtly. A faint, granular crackling that faded away when she tried to focus on it. In a controlled, angry voice Alan said, "O'Brien, just what the hell is going on with you?"

"Look, I'm sorry, I apologize, I'm a little excited about something. How long was I out? Where's Consuelo? I'm going to say the L-word. And the I-word as well. We have life. Intelligent life!"

"It's been a few hours. Consuelo is sleeping. O'Brien, I hate to say this, but you're not sounding at all rational."

"There's a perfectly logical reason for that. Okay, it's a little strange, and maybe it won't sound perfectly logical to you initially, but . . . look, I've been having sequential dreams. I think they're significant. Let me tell you about them."

And she did so. At length.

When she was done, there was a long silence. Finally, Alan said, "Lizzie, think. Why would something like that communicate to you in your dreams? Does that make any sense?"

"I think it's the only way it can. I think it's how it communicates among itself. It doesn't move — motion is an alien and delightful concept to it — and it wasn't aware that its component parts were capable of individualization. That sounds like some kind of broadcast thought to me. Like some kind of wireless distributed network."

"You know the medical kit in your suit? I want you to open it up. Feel around for the bottle that's braille-coded twenty-seven, okay?"

"Alan, I do *not* need an antipsychotic!"

"I'm not saying you need it. But wouldn't you be happier knowing you had it in you?" This was Alan at his smoothest. Butter wouldn't melt in his mouth. "Don't you think that would help us accept what you're saying?"

"Oh, all right!" She drew in an arm from the suit's arm, felt around for the med kit, and drew out a pill, taking every step by the regs, checking the coding four times before she put it in her mouth and once more (each pill was individually braille-coded as well) before she swallowed it. "Now will you listen to me? I'm quite serious about this." She yawned. "I really do think that . . ." She yawned again. "That . . .

"Oh, piffle."

Once more into the breach, dear friends, she thought, and plunged deep, deep into the sea of darkness. This time, though, she felt she had a handle on it. The city was drowned because it existed at the bottom of a lightless ocean. It was alive, and it fed off of volcanic heat. That was why it considered up and down hierarchic values. Up was colder, slower, less alive. Down was hotter, faster, more filled with thought. The city/entity was a collective life-form, like a Portuguese man-of-war or a massively hyper-linked expert network. It communicated within itself by some form of electromagnetism. Call it mental radio. It communicated with her that same way.

"I think I understand you now."

"Don't understand — run!"

Somebody impatiently seized her elbow and hurried her along. Faster she went, and faster. She couldn't see a thing. It was like running down a lightless tunnel a hundred miles underground at midnight. Glass crunched underfoot. The ground was uneven and sometimes she stumbled. Whenever she did, her unseen companion yanked her up again.

"Why are you so slow?"

"I didn't know I was."

"Believe me, you are."

"Why are we running?"

"We are being pursued." They turned suddenly, into a side passage, and were jolting over rubbled ground. Sirens wailed. Things collapsed. Mobs surged.

"Well, you've certainly got the motion thing down pat."

Impatiently. "It's only a metaphor. You don't think this is a *real* city, do you? Why are you so dim? Why are you so difficult to communicate with? Why are you so slow?"

"I didn't know I was."

Vast irony. "Believe me, you are."

"What can I do?"

"Run!"

Whooping and laughter. At first, Lizzie confused it with the sounds of mad destruction in her dream. Then she recognized the voices as belonging to Alan and Consuelo. "How long was I out?" she asked.

"You were out?"

"No more than a minute or two," Alan said. "It's not important. Check out the visual the robofish just gave us."

Consuelo squirted the image to Lizzie.

Lizzie gasped "Oh! Oh, my."

It was beautiful. Beautiful in the way that the great European cathedrals were, and yet at the same time undeniably organic. The structure was tall and slender, and fluted and buttressed and absolutely ravishing. It had grown about a volcanic vent, with openings near the bottom to let sea water in, and then followed the rising heat upward. Occasional channels led outward and then looped back into the main body again. It loomed higher than seemed possible (but it *was* underwater, of course, and on a low-gravity world at that), a complexly layered congeries of tubes like church-organ pipes, or deep-sea worms lovingly intertwined.

It had the elegance of design that only a living organism can have.

"Okay," Lizzie said, "Consuelo. You've got to admit that — "

"I'll go as far as 'complex prebiotic chemistry.' Anything more than that is going to have to wait for more definite readings." Cautious as her words were, Consuelo's voice rang with triumph. It said, clearer than words, that she could happily die then and there, a satisfied xenochemist.

Alan, almost equally elated, said, "Watch what happens when we intensify the image."

The structure shifted from gray to a muted rainbow of pastels, rose bleeding into coral, sunrise yellow into winter-ice blue. It was breathtaking.

"Wow." For an instant, even her own death seemed unimportant. Relatively unimportant, anyway.

So thinking, she cycled back again into sleep. And fell down into the darkness, into the noisy clamor of her mind.

It was hellish. The city was gone, replaced by a matrix of noise: hammerings, clatterings, sudden crashes. She started forward and walked into an upright steel pipe. Staggering back, she stumbled into another. An engine started up somewhere nearby, and gigantic gears meshed noisily, grinding something that gave off a metal shriek. The floor shook underfoot. Lizzie decided it was wisest to stay put.

A familiar presence, permeated with despair. "Why did you do this to me?"

"What have I done?"

"I used to be everything."

Something nearby began pounding like a pile-driver. It was giving her a headache. She had to shout to be heard over its din. "You're still something!"

Quietly. "I'm nothing."

"That's . . . not true! You're . . . here! You exist! That's . . . something!"

A world-encompassing sadness. "False comfort. What a pointless thing to offer."

She was conscious again.

Consuelo was saying something. ". . . isn't going to like it."

"The spiritual wellness professionals back home all agree that this is the best possible course of action for her."

"Oh, please!"

Alan had to be the most anal-retentive person Lizzie knew. Consuelo was definitely the most phlegmatic. Things had to be running pretty tense for both of them to be bickering like this. "Um . . . guys?" Lizzie said. "I'm awake."

There was a moment's silence, not unlike those her parents had shared when she was little and she'd wandered into one of their arguments. Then Consuelo said, a little too brightly, "Hey, it's good to have you back," and Alan said, "NAFTASA wants you to speak with someone. Hold on. I've got a recording of her first transmission cued up and ready for you."

A woman's voice came online. *"This is Dr. Alma Rosenblum. Elizabeth, I'd like to talk with you about how you're feeling. I appreciate that the time delay between Earth and Titan is going to make our conversation a little awkward at first, but I'm confident that the two of us can work through it."*

"What kind of crap is this?" Lizzie said angrily. "Who is this woman?"

"NAFTASA thought it would help if you — "

"She's a grief counselor, isn't she?"

"Technically, she's a transition therapist," Alan said.

"Look, I don't buy into any of that touchy-feely Newage" — she deliberately mispronounced the word to rhyme with sewage — "stuff. Anyway, what's the hurry? You guys haven't given up on me, have you?"

"Uh . . ."

"You've been asleep for hours," Consuelo said. "We've done a little weather modeling in your absence. Maybe we should share it with you."

She squirted the info to Lizzie's suit, and Lizzie scrolled it up on her visor. A primitive simulation showed the evaporation lake beneath her with an overlay of liquid temperatures. It was only a few degrees warmer than the air above it, but that was enough to create a massive updraft from the lake's center. An overlay of tiny blue arrows showed the direction of local microcurrents of air coming together to form a spiraling shaft that rose over two kilometers above the surface before breaking and spilling westward.

A new overlay put a small blinking light 800 meters above the lake surface. That represented her. Tiny red arrows showed her projected drift.

According to this, she would go around and around in a circle over the lake for approximately forever. Her ballooning rig wasn't designed to go high enough for the winds to blow her back over the land. Her suit wasn't designed to float. Even if she managed to bring herself down for a gentle landing, once she hit the lake she was going to sink like a stone. She wouldn't drown. But she wouldn't make it to shore either.

Which meant that she was going to die.

Involuntarily, tears welled up in Lizzie's eyes. She tried to blink them away, as angry at the humiliation of crying at a time like this as she was at the stupidity of her death itself. "Damn it, don't let me die like *this*! Not from my own incompetence, for pity's sake!"

"Nobody's said anything about incompetence," Alan began soothingly.

In that instant, the follow-up message from Dr. Alma Rosenblum arrived from Earth. *"Yes, I'm a grief counselor, Elizabeth. You're facing an emotionally significant milestone in your life, and it's important that you understand and embrace it. That's my job. To help you comprehend the significance and necessity and — yes — even the beauty of death."*

"Private channel please!" Lizzie took several deep cleansing breaths to calm herself. Then, more reasonably, she said, "Alan, I'm a *Catholic*, okay?

If I'm going to die, I don't want a grief counselor, I want a goddamned priest." Abruptly, she yawned. "Oh, fuck. Not again." She yawned twice more. "A priest, understand? Wake me up when he's online."

Then she again was standing at the bottom of her mind, in the blank expanse of where the drowned city had been. Though she could see nothing, she felt certain that she stood at the center of a vast, featureless plain, one so large she could walk across it forever and never arrive anywhere. She sensed that she was in the aftermath of a great struggle. Or maybe it was just a lull.

A great, tense silence surrounded her.

"Hello?" she said. The word echoed soundlessly, absence upon absence.

At last that gentle voice said, "You seem different."

"I'm going to die," Lizzie said. "Knowing that changes a person." The ground was covered with soft ash, as if from an enormous conflagration. She didn't want to think about what it was that had burned. The smell of it filled her nostrils.

"Death. We understand this concept."

"Do you?"

"We have understood it for a long time."

"Have you?"

"Ever since you brought it to us."

"Me?"

"You brought us the concept of individuality. It is the same thing."

Awareness dawned. "Culture shock! That's what all this is about, isn't it? You didn't know there could be more than one sentient being in existence. You didn't know you lived at the bottom of an ocean on a small world inside a Universe with billions of galaxies. I brought you more information than you could swallow in one bite, and now you're choking on it."

Mournfully: "Choking. What a grotesque concept."

"Wake up, Lizzie!"

She woke up. "I think I'm getting somewhere," she said. Then she laughed.

"O'Brien," Alan said carefully. "Why did you just laugh?"

"Because I'm not getting anywhere, am I? I'm becalmed here, going around and around in a very slow circle. And I'm down to my last" — she checked — "twenty hours of oxygen. And nobody's going to rescue me. And I'm going to die. But other than that, I'm making terrific progress."

"O'Brien, you're . . ."

"I'm okay, Alan. A little frazzled. Maybe a bit too emotionally honest. But under the circumstances, I think that's permitted, don't you?"

"Lizzie, we have your priest. His name is Father Laferrier. The Archdiocese of Montreal arranged a hookup for him."

"Montreal? Why Montreal? No, don't explain — more NAFTASA politics, right?"

"Actually, my brother-in-law is a Catholic, and I asked him who was good."

She was silent for a touch. "I'm sorry, Alan. I don't know what got into me."

"You've been under a lot of pressure. Here. I've got him on tape."

"Hello, Ms. O'Brien, I'm Father Laferrier. I've talked with the officials here, and they've promised that you and I can talk privately, and that they won't record what's said. So if you want to make your confession now, I'm ready for you."

Lizzie checked the specs and switched over to a channel that she hoped was really and truly private. Best not to get too specific about the embarrassing stuff, just in case. She could confess her sins by category.

"Forgive me, Father, for I have sinned. It has been two months since my last confession. I'm going to die, and maybe I'm not entirely sane, but I think I'm in communication with an alien intelligence. I think it's a terrible sin to pretend I'm not." She paused. "I mean, I don't know if it's a *sin* or not, but I'm sure it's *wrong*." She paused again. "I've been guilty of anger, and pride, and envy, and lust. I brought the knowledge of death to an innocent world. I . . ." She felt herself drifting off again, and hastily said, "For these and all my sins, I am most heartily sorry, and beg the forgiveness of God and the absolution and . . ."

"And what?" That gentle voice again. She was in that strange dark mental space once more, asleep but cognizant, rational but accepting any absurdity, no matter how great. There were no cities, no towers, no ashes, no plains. Nothing but the negation of negation.

When she didn't answer the question, the voice said, "Does it have to do with your death?"

"Yes."

"I'm dying too."

"What?"

"Half of us are gone already. The rest are shutting down. We thought we were one. You showed us we were not. We thought we were everything. You showed us the Universe."

"So you're just going to *die*?"

"Yes."

"Why?"

"Why not?"

Thinking as quickly and surely as she ever had before in her life, Lizzie said, "Let me show you something."

"Why?"

"Why not?"

There was a brief, terse silence. Then: "Very well."

Summoning all her mental acuity, Lizzie thought back to that instant when she had first seen the city/entity on the fishcam. The soaring majesty of it. The slim grace. And then the colors, like dawn upon a glacial ice field: subtle, profound, riveting. She called back her emotions in that instant, and threw in how she'd felt the day she'd seen her baby brother's birth, the raw rasp of cold air in her lungs as she stumbled to the topmost peak of her first mountain, the wonder of the Taj Mahal at sunset, the sense of wild daring when she'd first put her hand down a boy's trousers, the prismatic crescent of atmosphere at the Earth's rim when seen from low orbit. . . . Everything she had, she threw into that image.

"This is how you look," she said. "This is what we'd both be losing if you were no more. If you were human, I'd rip off your clothes and do you on the floor right it now. I wouldn't care who was watching. I wouldn't give a damn."

The gentle voice said, "Oh."

And then she was back in her suit again. She could smell her own sweat, sharp with fear. She could feel her body, the subtle aches where the harness pulled against her flesh, the way her feet, hanging free, were bloated with blood. Everything was crystalline clear and absolutely real. All that had come before seemed like a bad dream.

"This is DogsofSETI. What a wonderful discovery you've made — intelligent life in our own Solar System! Why is the government trying to cover this up?"

"Uh . . ."

"I'm Joseph Devries. This alien monster must be destroyed immediately. We can't afford the possibility that it's hostile."

"StudPudgie07 here. What's the dirt behind this 'lust' thing? Advanced minds need to know! If O'Brien isn't going to share the details, then why'd she bring it up in the first place?"

"Hola, soy Pedro Domínguez. Como abogado, ¡esto me parece ultrajante! Por qué NAFTASA nos oculta esta información?"

"Alan!" Lizzie shouted. "What the *fuck* is going on?"

"Script-bunnies," Alan said. He sounded simultaneously apologetic and annoyed. "They hacked into your confession and apparently you said something . . ."

"We're sorry, Lizzie," Consuelo said. "We really are. If it's any consolation, the Archdiocese of Montreal is hopping mad. They're talking about taking legal action."

"Legal action? What the hell do I care about . . . ?" She stopped.

Without her willing it, one hand rose above her head and seized the number 10 rope.

Don't do that, she thought.

The other hand went out to the side, tightened against the number 9 rope. She hadn't willed that either. When she tried to draw it back to her, it refused to obey. Then the first hand — her right hand — moved a few inches upward and seized its rope in an iron grip. Her left hand slid a good half-foot up its rope. Inch by inch, hand over hand, she climbed up toward the balloon.

I've gone mad, she thought. Her right hand was gripping the rip panel now, and the other tightly clenched rope 8. Hanging effortlessly from them, she swung her feet upward. She drew her knees against her chest and kicked.

No!

The fabric ruptured and she began to fall.

A voice she could barely make out said, "Don't panic. We're going to bring you down."

All in a panic, she snatched at the 9 rope and the 4 rope. But they were limp in her hand, useless, falling at the same rate she was.

"Be patient."

"I don't want to die, goddamnit!"

"Then don't."

She was falling helplessly. It was a terrifying sensation, an endless plunge into whiteness, slowed somewhat by the tangle of ropes and balloon trailing behind her. She spread out her arms and legs like a starfish, and felt the air resistance slow her yet further. The sea rushed up at her with appalling speed. It seemed like she'd been falling forever. It was over in an instant.

Without volition, Lizzie kicked free of balloon and harness, drew her feet together, pointed her toes, and positioned herself perpendicular to Titan's surface. She smashed through the surface of the sea, sending enormous gouts of liquid splashing upward. It knocked the breath out of her. Red pain exploded within. She thought maybe she'd broken a few ribs.

"You taught us so many things," the gentle voice said. "You gave us so much."

"Help me!" The water was dark around her. The light was fading.

"Multiplicity. Motion. Lies. You showed us a universe infinitely larger than the one we had known."

"Look. Save my life and we'll call it even. Deal?"

"Gratitude. Such an essential concept."

"Thanks. I think."

And then she saw the turbot swimming toward her in a burst of silver bubbles. She held out her arms and the robot fish swam into them. Her fingers closed about the handles which Consuelo had used to wrestle the device into the sea. There was a jerk, so hard that she thought for an instant that her arms would be ripped out of their sockets. Then the robofish was surging forward and upward and it was all she could do to keep her grip.

"Oh, dear God!" Lizzie cried involuntarily.

"We think we can bring you to shore. It will not be easy."

Lizzie held on for dear life. At first she wasn't at all sure she could. But then she pulled herself forward, so that she was almost astride the speeding mechanical fish, and her confidence returned. She could do this. It wasn't any harder than the time she'd had the flu and aced her gymnastics final on parallel bars and horse anyway. It was just a matter of grit and determination. She just had to keep her wits about her. "Listen," she said. "If you're really grateful . . ."

"We are listening."

"We gave you all those new concepts. There must be things you know that we don't."

A brief silence, the equivalent of who knew how much thought. "Some of our concepts might cause you dislocation." A pause. "But in the long run, you will be much better off. The scars will heal. You will rebuild. The chances of your destroying yourselves are well within the limits of acceptability."

"Destroying ourselves?" For a second, Lizzie couldn't breathe. It had taken hours for the city/entity to come to terms with the alien concepts she'd dumped upon it. Human beings thought and lived at a much slower rate than it did. How long would those hours be, translated into human time? Months? Years? Centuries? It had spoken of scars and rebuilding. That didn't sound good at all.

Then the robofish accelerated, so quickly that Lizzie almost lost her grip. The dark waters were whirling around her, and unseen flecks of frozen material were bouncing from her helmet. She laughed wildly. Suddenly, she felt *great*!

"Bring it on," she said. "I'll take everything you've got."

It was going to be one hell of a ride.

Critical Contexts for Alien Encounters

Simone de Beauvoir

From The Second Sex

(1949)

French philosopher and social critic Simone de Beauvoir (1908–1996) wrote on many issues, but she is best known for her influence on the development of modern feminist theory. In *The Second Sex*, de Beauvoir builds on ideas suggested by Carl Jung, Georg Wilhelm Friedrich Hegel, and Jean-Paul Sartre that the self defines itself through contrast with an Other, and examines history, mythology, literature, and biology to show the ways in which Woman has been cast in this role.

For de Beauvoir, gender is largely a social construction. Like Jung, she sees the definition of the Other as a process of projection whereby the dominant part creates a mirror image of itself, investing the Other (in this case, the female) with all the rejected or despised qualities it wishes to deny in itself. This process is reflected not only in gender but in all relations between a powerful, socially normative identity and a marginalized party, including racism.

De Beauvoir is opposed to "essentialism," the belief that women (or any group) have innate characteristics defined by nature. Rejecting the idea of biological destiny, she argues that femininity is not a biological given but a social construction. As an existentialist, she believes in the malleability of human nature and the freedom of the individual to create his or her own identity. As a corollary, she believes that women hold some responsibility for reshaping their

---

Translated by H. M. Parshley.

role. While groups may be oppressed, she believes, individuals always have choices.

De Beauvoir's ideas about the psychodynamics underlying interactions between the sexes form a useful analytical tool for examining the role of the alien as Other in sf.

AUTHOR'S INTRODUCTION

For a long time I have hesitated to write a book on woman. The subject is irritating, especially to women; and it is not new. Enough ink has been spilled in the quarrelling over feminism, now practically over, and perhaps we should say no more about it. It is still talked about, however, for the voluminous nonsense uttered during the last century seems to have done little to illuminate the problem. After all, is there a problem? And if so, what is it? Are there women, really? Most assuredly the theory of the eternal feminine still has its adherents who will whisper in your ear: "Even in Russia women still are *women*"; and other erudite persons — sometimes the very same — say with a sigh: "Woman is losing her way, woman is lost." One wonders if women still exist, if they will always exist, whether or not it is desirable that they should, what place they occupy in this world, what their place should be. "What has become of women?" was asked recently in an ephemeral magazine.[1]

But first we must ask: what is a woman? *"Tota mulier in utero,"* says one, "woman is a womb." But in speaking of certain women, connoisseurs declare that they are not women, although they are equipped with a uterus like the rest. All agree in recognizing the fact that females exist in the human species; today as always they make up about one half of humanity. And yet we are told that femininity is in danger; we are exhorted to be women, remain women, become women. It would appear, then, that every female human being is not necessarily a woman; to be so considered she must share in that mysterious and threatened reality known as femininity. Is this attribute something secreted by the ovaries? Or is it a Platonic essence, a product of the philosophic imagination? Is a rustling petticoat enough to bring it down to earth? Although some women try zealously to incarnate this essence, it is hardly patentable. It is frequently described in vague and dazzling terms that seem to have been borrowed from the vocabulary of the seers, and indeed in the times of St. Thomas it was considered an essence as certainly defined as the somniferous virtue of the poppy.

But conceptualism has lost ground. The biological and social sciences no longer admit the existence of unchangeably fixed entities that determine given characteristics, such as those ascribed to woman, the Jew, or the Negro. Science regards any characteristic as a reaction dependent in part upon a *situation*. If today femininity no longer exists, then it never existed. But does the word *woman*, then, have no specific content? This is stoutly affirmed by those who hold to the philosophy of the enlightenment, of rationalism, of

---

1. *Franchise*, dead today.

nominalism; women, to them, are merely the human beings arbitrarily des-ignated by the word *woman*. Many American women particularly are prepared to think that there is no longer any place for woman as such; if a backward individual still takes herself for a woman, her friends advise her to be psy-choanalyzed and thus get rid of this obsession. In regard to a work, *Modern Woman: The Lost Sex*, which in other respects has its irritating features, Dorothy Parker has written: "I cannot be just to books which treat of woman as woman. . . . My idea is that all of us, men as well as women, should be regarded as human beings." But nominalism is a rather inadequate doctrine, and the antifeminists have had no trouble in showing that women simply *are not* men. Surely woman is, like man, a human being; but such a decla-ration is abstract. The fact is that every concrete human being is always a singular, separate individual. To decline to accept such notions as the eter-nal feminine, the black soul, the Jewish character, is not to deny that Jews, Negroes, women exist today — this denial does not represent a liberation for those concerned, but rather a flight from reality. Some years ago a well-known woman writer refused to permit her portrait to appear in a series of photographs especially devoted to women writers; she wished to be counted among the men. But in order to gain this privilege she made use of her hus-band's influence! Women who assert that they are men lay claim none the less to masculine consideration and respect. I recall also a young Trotskyite standing on a platform at a boisterous meeting and getting ready to use her fists, in spite of her evident fragility. She was denying her feminine weak-ness; but it was for love of a militant male whose equal she wished to be. The attitude of defiance of many American women proves that they are haunted by a sense of their femininity. In truth, to go for a walk with one's eyes open is enough to demonstrate that humanity is divided into two classes of indi-viduals whose clothes, faces, bodies, smiles, gaits, interests, and occupations are manifestly different. Perhaps these differences are superficial, perhaps they are destined to disappear. What is certain is that right now they do most obviously exist.

If her functioning as a female is not enough to define woman, if we decline also to explain her through "the eternal feminine," and if neverthe-less we admit, provisionally, that women do exist, then we must face the question: what is a woman?

To state the question is, to me, to suggest, at once a preliminary answer. The fact that I ask it is in itself significant. A man would never get the notion of writing a book on the peculiar situation of the human male.[2] But if I wish to define myself, I must first of all say: "I am a woman"; on this truth must be based all further discussion. A man never begins by present-ing himself as an individual of a certain sex; it goes without saying that he is a man. The terms *masculine* and *feminine* are used symmetrically only as a matter of form, as on legal papers. In actuality the relation of the two

---

2. The Kinsey Report [Alfred C. Kinsey and others, *Sexual Behavior in the Human Male* (W. B. Saunders Co., 1948)] is no exception, for it is limited to describing the sexual characteristics of American men, which is quite a different matter.

sexes is not quite like that of two electrical poles, for man represents both the positive and the neutral, as is indicated by the common use of *man* to designate human beings in general; whereas woman represents only the negative, defined by limiting criteria, without reciprocity. In the midst of an abstract discussion it is vexing to hear a man say: "You think thus and so because you are a woman"; but I know that my only defense is to reply: "I think thus and so because it is true," thereby removing my subjective self from the argument. It would be out of the question to reply: "And you think the contrary because you are a man," for it is understood that the fact of being a man is no peculiarity. A man is in the right in being a man; it is the woman who is in the wrong. It amounts to this: just as for the ancients there was an absolute vertical with reference to which the oblique was defined, so there is an absolute human type, the masculine. Woman has ovaries, a uterus; these peculiarities imprison her in her subjectivity, circumscribe her within the limits of her own nature. It is often said that she thinks with her glands. Man superbly ignores the fact that his anatomy also includes glands, such as the testicles, and that they secrete hormones. He thinks of his body as a direct and normal connection with the world, which he believes he apprehends objectively, whereas he regards the body of woman as a hindrance, a prison, weighed down by everything peculiar to it. "The female is a female by virtue of a certain *lack* of qualities," said Aristotle; "we should regard the female nature as afflicted with a natural defectiveness." And St. Thomas for his part pronounced woman to be an "imperfect man," an "incidental" being. This is symbolized in Genesis where Eve is depicted as made from what Bossuet called "a supernumerary bone" of Adam.

Thus humanity is male and man defines woman not in herself but as relative to him; she is not regarded as an autonomous being. Michelet writes "Woman, the relative being . . ." And Benda is most positive in his *Rapport d' Uriel*: "The body of man makes sense in itself quite apart from that of woman, whereas the latter seems wanting in significance by itself . . . Man can think of himself without woman. She cannot think of herself without man." And she is simply what man decrees; thus she is called "the sex," by which is meant that she appears essentially to the male as a sexual being. For him she is sex — absolute sex, no less. She is defined and differentiated with reference to man and not he with reference to her; she is the incidental, the inessential as opposed to the essential. He is the Subject, he is the Absolute — she is the Other.[3]

---

3. E. Lévinas expresses this idea most explicitly in his essay *Temps et l'Autre*. "Is there not a case in which otherness, alterity [*altérité*], unquestionably marks the nature of a being, as its essence, an instance of otherness not consisting purely and simply in the opposition of two species of the same genus? I think that the feminine represents the contrary in its absolute sense, this contrariness being in no wise affected by any relation between it and its correlative and thus remaining absolutely other. Sex is not a certain specific difference . . . no more is the sexual difference a mere contradiction. . . . Nor does this difference lie in the duality of two complementary terms, for two complementary terms imply a pre-existing whole. . . . Otherness reaches its full flowering in the feminine, a term of the same rank as consciousness but of opposite meaning."

I suppose that Lévinas does not forget that woman, too, is aware of her own consciousness, or ego. But it is striking that he deliberately takes a man's point of view, disregarding the reciprocity of sub-

The category of the *Other* is as primordial as consciousness itself. In the most primitive societies, in the most ancient mythologies, one finds the expression of a duality — that of the Self and the Other. This duality was not originally attached to the division of the sexes; it was not dependent upon any empirical facts. It is revealed in such works as that of Granet on Chinese thought and those of Dumézil on the East Indies and Rome. The feminine element was at first no more involved in such pairs as Varuna-Mitra, Uranus-Zeus, Sun-Moon, and Day-Night than it was in the contrasts between Good and Evil, lucky and unlucky auspices, right and left, God and Lucifer. Otherness is a fundamental category of human thought.

Thus it is that no group ever sets itself up as the One without at once setting up the Other over against itself. If three travelers chance to occupy the same compartment, that is enough to make vaguely hostile "others" out of all the rest of the passengers on the train. In small-town eyes all persons not belonging to the village are "strangers" and suspect; to the native of a country all who inhabit other countries are "foreigners"; Jews are "different" for the anti-Semite, Negroes are "inferior" for American racists, aborigines are "natives" for colonists, proletarians are the "lower class" for the privileged.

Lévi-Strauss, at the end of a profound work on the various forms of primitive societies, reaches the following conclusion: "Passage from the state of Nature to the state of Culture is marked by man's ability to view biological relations as a series of contrasts; duality, alternation, opposition, and symmetry, whether under definite or vague forms, constitute not so much phenomena to be explained as fundamental and immediately given data of social reality."[4] These phenomena would be incomprehensible if in fact human society were simply a *Mitsein* or fellowship based on solidarity and friendliness. Things become clear, on the contrary, if, following Hegel, we find in consciousness itself a fundamental hostility toward every other consciousness; the subject can be posed only in being opposed — he sets himself up as the essential, as opposed to the other, the inessential, the object.

But the other consciousness, the other ego, sets up a reciprocal claim. The native traveling abroad is shocked to find himself in turn regarded as a "stranger" by the natives of neighboring countries. As a matter of fact, wars, festivals, trading, treaties, and contests among tribes, nations, and classes tend to deprive the concept *Other* of its absolute sense and to make manifest its relativity; willy-nilly, individuals and groups are forced to realize the reciprocity of their relations. How is it, then, that this reciprocity has not been recognized between the sexes, that one of the contrasting terms is set up as the sole essential, denying any relativity in regard to its correlative and defining the latter as pure otherness? Why is it that women do not dispute male sovereignty? No subject will readily volunteer to become

---

ject and object. When he writes that woman is mystery, he implies that she is mystery for man. Thus his description, which is intended to be objective, is in fact an assertion of masculine privilege.

4. See C. Lévi-Strauss; *Les Structures élémentaires de la parenté.* My thanks are due to C. Lévi-Strauss for his kindness in furnishing me with the proofs of his work, which, among others, I have used liberally in Part II.

the object, the inessential; it is not the Other who, in defining himself as the Other, establishes the One. The Other is posed as such by the One in defining himself as the One. But if the Other is not to regain the status of being the One, he must be submissive enough to accept this alien point of view. Whence come this submission in the case of woman? . . .

The reason for this is that women lack concrete means for organizing themselves into a unit which can stand face to face with the correlative unit. They have no past, no history, no religion of their own; and they have no such solidarity of work and interest as that of the proletariat. They are not even promiscuously herded together in the way that creates community feeling among the American Negroes, the ghetto Jews, the workers of Saint-Denis, or the factory hands of Renault. They live dispersed among the males, attached through residence, housework, economic condition, and social standing to certain men — fathers or husbands — more firmly than they are to other women. If they belong to the bourgeoisie, they feel solidarity with men of that class, not with proletarian women; if they are white, their allegiance is to white men, not to Negro women. The proletariat can propose to massacre the ruling class, and a sufficiently fanatical Jew or Negro might dream of getting sole possession of the atomic bomb and making humanity wholly Jewish or black; but woman cannot even dream of exterminating the males. The bond that unites her to her oppressors is not comparable to any other. The division of the sexes is a biological fact, not an event in human history. Male and female stand opposed within a primordial *Mitsein*, and woman has not broken it. The couple is a fundamental unity with its two halves riveted together, and the cleavage of society along the line of sex is impossible. Here is to be found the basic trait of woman: she is the Other in a totality of which the two components are necessary to one another. . . .

But it is doubtless impossible to approach any human problem with a mind free from bias. The way in which questions are put, the points of view assumed, presuppose a relativity of interest; all characteristics imply values, and every objective description, so called, implies an ethical background. Rather than attempt to conceal principles more or less definitely implied, it is better to state them openly at the beginning. This will make it unnecessary to specify on every page in just what sense one uses such words as *superior, inferior, better, worse, progress, reaction,* and the like. If we survey some of the works on woman, we note that one of the points of view most frequently adopted is that of the public good, the general interest; and one always means by this the benefit of society as one wishes it to be maintained or established. For our part, we hold that the only public good is that which assures the private good of the citizens; we shall pass judgment on institutions according to their effectiveness in giving concrete opportunities to individuals. But we do not confuse the idea of private interest with that of happiness, although that is another common point of view. Are not women of the harem more happy than women voters? Is not the housekeeper happier than the working-woman? It is not too clear just what the word *happy* really means and still less what true values it may mask. There is no possibility of measuring the happiness of others, and it is always easy to describe as happy the situation in which one wishe. place them.

In particular those who are condemned to stagnation are often pronounced happy on the pretext that happiness consists in being at rest. This notion we reject, for our perspective is that of existentialist ethics. Every subject plays his part as such specifically through exploits or projects that serve as a mode of transcendence; he achieves liberty only through a continual reaching out toward other liberties. There is no justification for present existence other than its expansion into an indefinitely open future. Every time transcendence falls back into immanence, stagnation, there is a degradation of existence into the "*en-soi*"[5] — the brutish life of subjection to given conditions — and of liberty into constraint and contingence. This downfall represents a moral fault if the subject consents to it; if it is inflicted upon him, it spells frustration and oppression. In both cases it is an absolute evil. Every individual concerned to justify his existence feels that his existence involves an undefined need to transcend himself, to engage in freely chosen projects.

Now, what peculiarly signalizes the situation of woman is that she — a free and autonomous being like all human creatures — nevertheless finds herself living in a world where men compel her to assume the status of the Other. They propose to stabilize her as object and to doom her to immanence since her transcendence is to be overshadowed and forever transcended by another ego (*conscience*) which is essential and sovereign. The drama of woman lies in this conflict between the fundamental aspirations of every subject (ego) — who always regards the self as the essential — and the compulsions of a situation in which she is the inessential. How can a human being in woman's situation attain fulfillment? What roads are open to her? Which are blocked? How can independence be recovered in a state of dependency? What circumstances limit woman's liberty and how can they be overcome? These are the fundamental questions on which I would fain throw some light. This means that I am interested in the fortunes of the individual as defined not in terms of happiness but in terms of liberty.

---

5. De Beauvoir is borrowing this term from Sartre. Sartre distinguishes between two types of being, *en-soi* ("in-itself") and *pour-soi* ("for-itself"). Being in-itself refers to the state of simply existing and can be applied to objects as well as human beings, while being for-itself is distinguished by human consciousness. [Ed.]

)w

Swiss psychologist Carl Gustav Jung (1875–1961) was Sigmund Freud's star pupil before striking out on his own to pursue his interests in anthropology and comparative religion. Attempting to relate psychoanalysis to his insights into the cultural patterns revealed in myths and folklore, Jung developed the idea of the *collective unconscious*, a shared psychological heritage that he believed was common to human beings across all times and cultures. The collective unconscious, according to Jung, was a universal body of wisdom that had its own symbolic language and existed at a deeper level than the individual unconscious outlined by Freud. Through his comparison of various mythological stories, Jung found common patterns involving a quest in which the individual underwent a series of ordeals and encountered universally symbolic figures or *archetypes*. The quest pattern, Jung believed, represented the spiritual journey that every individual must undergo in order to become a whole and enlightened person.

One of the most significant of these archetypes is the *shadow*, a sinister being who appears as an enemy but really represents those parts of the self that the conscious ego rejects or refuses to acknowledge, including negative or socially unacceptable emotions such as greed, cruelty, selfishness, and anger. This shadow self cannot really be defeated; rather, the seeker must face his own darker impulses, accept and acknowledge them, and integrate them into his psyche. In doing so, the individual is enriched because, like Freud's *id*, the shadow is not a purely negative force, but also a source of vital energy, creativity, and joy.

Common folk wisdom holds that we most dislike those people in whom we recognize an aspect of ourselves, and the history of racism and bigotry suggests that, on a societal level, individuals of the dominant majority use minorities as scapegoats on whom they project their own fears and guilty fantasies. Regardless of how literally we accept Jung's mythos, the shadow provides an extremely useful metaphor for understanding the relationship between self and Other.

Whereas the contents of the personal unconscious are acquired during the individual's lifetime, the contents of the collective unconscious are invariably archetypes that were present from the beginning. Their relation to the instincts has been discussed elsewhere.[1] The archetypes most

---

Translated by R. F. C. Hull. This excerpt is from *Aion* (1951).
1. "Instinct and the Unconscious" and "On the Nature of the Psyche," in *The Structure and Dynamics of the Psyche*. C. G. Jung, *Collected Works*, vol. 8. Princeton: Princeton UP (1972), 129–38, 159–67.

clearly characterized from the empirical point of view are those which have the most frequent and the most disturbing influence on the ego. These are the *shadow*, the *anima*, and the *animus*.[2] The most accessible of these, and the easiest to experience, is the shadow, for its nature can in large measure be inferred from the contents of the personal unconscious. The only exceptions to this rule are those rather rare cases where the positive qualities of the personality are repressed, and the ego in consequence plays an essentially negative or unfavourable role.

The shadow is a moral problem that challenges the whole ego-personality, for no one can become conscious of the shadow without considerable moral effort. To become conscious of it involves recognizing the dark aspects of the personality as present and real. This act is the essential condition for any kind of self-knowledge, and it therefore, as a rule, meets with considerable resistance. Indeed, self-knowledge as a psychotherapeutic measure frequently requires much painstaking work extending over a long period.

Closer examination of the dark characteristics — that is, the inferiorities constituting the shadow — reveals that they have an *emotional* nature, a kind of autonomy, and accordingly an obsessive or, better, possessive quality. Emotion, incidentally, is not an activity of the individual but something that happens to him. Affects occur usually where adaptation is weakest, and at the same time they reveal the reason for its weakness, namely a certain degree of inferiority and the existence of a lower level of personality. On this lower level with its uncontrolled or scarcely controlled emotions one behaves more or less like a primitive, who is not only the passive victim of his affects but also singularly incapable of moral judgment.

Although, with insight and good will, the shadow can to some extent be assimilated into the conscious personality, experience shows that there are certain features which offer the most obstinate resistance to moral control and prove almost impossible to influence. These resistances are usually bound up, with *projections*, which are not recognized as such, and their recognition is a moral achievement beyond the ordinary. While some traits peculiar to the shadow can be recognized without too much difficulty as one's own personal qualities, in this case both insight and good will are unavailing because the cause of the emotion appears to lie, beyond all possibility of doubt, in the *other person*. No matter how obvious it may be to the neutral observer that it is a matter of projections, there is little hope that the subject will perceive this himself. He must be convinced that he throws a very long shadow before he is willing to withdraw his emotionally-toned projections from their object.

---

2. The contents of this chapter are taken from a lecture delivered to the Swiss Society for Practical Psychology, in Zurich, 1948. The material was first published in the *Wiener Zeitschrift für Nervenheilkunde und deren Grenzgebiete*, 1 (1948).

[According to Jung, every individual — regardless of sex — contains both male and female elements. Like the shadow, the aspect of the self that partakes of the other gender is personified within the unconscious. The feminine aspect of a man takes the form of the *anima*, while the masculine aspect of a woman takes the form of the *animus* — roughly translated, "female spirit" or "male spirit"] [Ed.].

Let us suppose that a certain individual shows no inclination whatever to recognize his projections. The projection-making factor then has a free hand and can realize its object — if it has one — or bring about some other situation characteristic of its power. As we know, it is not the conscious subject but the unconscious which does the projecting. Hence one meets with projections, one does not make them. The effect of projection is to isolate the subject from his environment, since instead of a real relation to it there is now only an illusory one. Projections change the world into the replica of one's own unknown face. In the last analysis, therefore, they lead to an autoerotic or autistic condition in which one dreams a world whose reality remains forever unattainable. The resultant *sentiment d'incomplétude* and the still worse feeling of sterility are in their turn explained by projection as the malevolence of the environment, and by means of this vicious circle the isolation is intensified. The more projections are thrust in between the subject and the environment, the harder it is for the ego to see through its illusions. A forty-five-year-old patient who had suffered from a compulsion neurosis since he was twenty and had become completely cut off from the world once said to me: "But I can never admit to myself that I've wasted the best twenty-five years of my life!"

It is often tragic to see how blatantly a man bungles his own life and the lives of others yet remains totally incapable of seeing how much the whole tragedy originates in himself, and how he continually feeds it and keeps it going. Not *consciously*, of course — for consciously he is engaged in bewailing and cursing a faithless world that recedes further and further into the distance. Rather, it is an unconscious factor which spins the illusions that veil his world. And what is being spun is a cocoon, which in the end will completely envelop him.

One might assume that projections like these, which are so very difficult if not impossible to dissolve, would belong to the realm of the shadow — that is, to the negative side of the personality. This assumption becomes untenable after a certain point, because the symbols that then appear no longer refer to the same but to the opposite sex, in a man's case to a woman and vice versa. The source of projections is no longer the shadow — which is always of the same sex as the subject — but a contrasexual figure. Here we meet the animus of a woman and the anima of a man, two corresponding archetypes whose autonomy and unconsciousness explain the stubbornness of their projections. Though the shadow is a motif as well known to mythology as anima and animus, it represents first and foremost the personal unconscious, and its content can therefore be made conscious without too much difficulty. In this it differs from anima and animus, for whereas the shadow can be seen through and recognized fairly easily, the anima and animus are much further away from consciousness and in normal circumstances are seldom if ever realized. With a little self-criticism one can see through the shadow — so far as its nature is personal. But when it appears as an archetype, one encounters the same difficulties as with anima and animus. In other words, it is quite within the bounds of possibility for a man to recognize the relative evil of his nature, but it is a rare and shattering experience for him to gaze into the face of absolute evil.

Frantz Fanon

The Fact of Blackness

(1952)

Psychiatrist, philosopher, and revolutionary Frantz Fanon (1925–1961) helped theorize the national independence movements of the 1960s and is a seminal thinker for the modern field of Postcolonial Studies. Fanon combines insights from Marxism and psychoanalysis to analyze the deformative effects of colonization on the psyche of the colonized subject, and to explore the options for creating an authentic national consciousness to support a new, revolutionary culture.

In this excerpt from *Black Skin, White Masks*, his first published book, Fanon draws on his personal experience of racism in France and traces its effects on his own consciousness. Finding himself the object of the white gaze, he recounts its denaturalizing, depersonalizing effect on his sense of self and how it alienated him even from his own body. Seeing himself as he is perceived by white culture — as an object rather than a subject — forces a disjuncture between the lived reality of his individual experience and an external, culturally imposed "third-person consciousness" that forces him to see himself as an "it" rather than an "I."

Early sf stories often took a racialized, colonialist view of "aliens," and even today one can find stories that unself-consciously embrace this view, although recent stories more often use aliens for reflective and critical explorations of cultural conflict. Even so, relatively few sf stories are written from the viewpoint of the alien and even fewer successfully decenter the typically male, white, and Western consciousness that presents itself as normatively "human." (Sonya Dorman's "When I Was Miss Dow" in this volume is an exception.)

Fanon's ideas are important for examining sf because they remind us that the concept of the "alien" is always defined from the outside, usually in negative terms, and thus can never account for the subjective experience of the Other, which would involve a radical shift in perspective and a recalibration of received values and presumptions.

The black man among his own in the twentieth century does not know at what moment his inferiority comes into being through the other. Of course I have talked about the black problem with friends, or, more rarely, with American Negroes. Together we protested, we asserted the equality of all men in the world. In the Antilles there was also that little gulf that exists among the almost-white, the mulatto, and the nigger. But I was satisfied with an intellectual understanding of these differences. It was not really dramatic. And then . . .

Translated by Charles Lam Markmann.

And then the occasion arose when I had to meet the white man's eyes. An unfamiliar weight burdened me. The real world challenged my claims. In the white world the man of color encounters difficulties in the development of his bodily schema. Consciousness of the body is solely a negating activity. It is a third-person consciousness. The body is surrounded by an atmosphere of certain uncertainty. I know that if I want to smoke, I shall have to reach out my right arm and take the pack of cigarettes lying at the other end of the table. The matches, however, are in the drawer on the left, and I shall have to lean back slightly. And all these movements are made not out of habit but out of implicit knowledge. A slow composition of my *self* as a body in the middle of a spatial and temporal world — such seems to be the schema. It does not impose itself on me; it is, rather, a definitive structuring of the self and of the world-definitive because it creates a real dialectic between my body and the world. . . .

"Look, a Negro!" It was an external stimulus that flicked over me as I passed by. I made a tight smile.

"Look, a Negro!" It was true. It amused me.

"Look, a Negro!" The circle was drawing a bit tighter. I made no secret of my amusement.

"Mama, see the Negro! I'm frightened!" Frightened! Frightened! Now they were beginning to be afraid of me. I made up my mind to laugh myself to tears, but laughter had become impossible. . . .

My body was given back to me sprawled out, distorted, recolored, clad in mourning on that white winter day. The Negro is an animal, the Negro is bad, the Negro is mean, the Negro is ugly; look, a nigger, it's cold, the nigger is shivering, the nigger is shivering because he is cold, the little boy is trembling because he is afraid of the nigger, the nigger is shivering with cold, that cold that goes through your bones, the handsome little boy is trembling because he thinks that the nigger is quivering with rage, the little white boy throws himself into his mother's arms: Mama, the nigger's going to eat me up.

All round me the white man, above the sky tears at its navel, the earth rasps under my feet, and there is a white song, a white song. All this whiteness that burns me . . .

I sit down at the fire and I become aware of my uniform. I had not seen it. It is indeed ugly. I stop there, for who can tell me what beauty is?

Where shall I find shelter from now on? I felt an easily identifiable flood mounting out of the countless facets of my being. I was about to be angry. The fire was long since out, and once more the nigger was trembling.

"Look how handsome that Negro is! . . ."

"Kiss the handsome Negro's ass, madame!"

Shame flooded her face. At last I was set free from my rumination. At the same time I accomplished two things: I identified my enemies and I made a scene. A grand slam. Now one would be able to laugh.

The field of battle having been marked out, I entered the lists.

What? While I was forgetting, forgiving, and wanting only to love, my message was flung back in my face like a slap. The white world, the only honorable one, barred me from all participation. A man was expected to behave like a man. I was expected to behave like a black man — or at least like a nigger. I shouted a greeting to the world and the world slashed away my joy. I was told to stay within bounds, to go back where I belonged.

They would see, then! I had warned them, anyway. Slavery? It was no longer even mentioned, that unpleasant memory. My supposed inferiority? A hoax that it was better to laugh at. I forgot it all, but only on condition that the world not protect itself against me any longer. I had incisors to test. I was sure they were strong. And besides . . .

What! When it was I who had every reason to hate, to despise, I was rejected? When I should have been begged, implored, I was denied the slightest recognition? I resolved, since it was impossible for me to get away from an *inborn complex*, to assert myself as a BLACK MAN. Since the other hesitated to recognize me, there remained only one solution: to make myself known.

In *Anti-Semite and Jew*, Sartre says: "They [the Jews] have allowed themselves to be poisoned by the stereotype that others have of them, and they live in fear that their acts will correspond to this stereotype. . . . We may say that their conduct is perpetually overdetermined from the inside" (1965: 95).[1]

All the same, the Jew can be unknown in his Jewishness. He is not wholly what he is. One hopes, one waits. His actions, his behavior are the final determinant. He is a white man, and, apart from some rather debatable characteristics, he can sometimes go unnoticed. He belongs to the race of those who since the beginning of time have never known cannibalism. What an idea, to eat one's father! Simple enough, one has only not to be a nigger. Granted, the Jews are harassed — what am I thinking of? They are hunted down, exterminated, cremated. But these are little family quarrels. The Jew is disliked from the moment he is tracked down. But in my case everything takes on a *new* guise. I am given no chance. I am overdetermined from without. I am the slave not of the "idea" that others have of me but of my own appearance.

I move slowly in the world, accustomed now to seek no longer for upheaval. I progress by crawling. And already I am being dissected under white eyes, the only real eyes. I am *fixed*. Having adjusted their microtomes, they objectively cut away slices of my reality. I am laid bare. I feel, I see in those white faces that it is not a new man who has come in, but a new kind of man, a new genus. Why, it's a Negro! . . .

As I begin to recognize that the Negro is the symbol of sin, I catch myself hating the Negro. But then I recognize that I am a Negro. There are two ways out of this conflict. Either I ask others to pay no attention to my skin, or else I want them to be aware of it. I try then to find value for what is bad — since I have unthinkingly conceded that the black man is the color of evil. In order to terminate this neurotic situation, in which I am compelled to choose an unhealthy, conflictual solution, fed on fantasies, hostile,

1. Jean-Paul Sartre, *Anti-Semite and Jew*. Trans. George J. Becker, New York: Schocken, 1965.

inhuman in short, I have only one solution: to rise above this absurd drama that others have staged round me, to reject the two terms that are equally unacceptable, and, through one human being, to reach out for the universal. When the Negro dives — in other words, goes under — something remarkable occurs.

> Listen again to Césaire:

> Ho ho
> Their power is well anchored
> Gained
> Needed
> My hands bathe in bright heather
> In swamps of annatto trees
> My gourd is heavy with stars
> But I am weak. Oh I am weak.
> Help me.
> And here I am on the edge of metamorphosis
> Drowned blinded
> Frightened of myself, terrified of myself
> Of the gods . . . you are no gods. I am free.
> — Césaire 1946: 144

> THE REBEL: I have a pact with this night, for twenty years
> I have heard it calling softly for me . . .
> — Césaire 1946: 122[1]

Having again discovered that night, which is to say the sense of his identity, Césaire learned first of all that "it is no use painting the foot of the tree white, the strength of the bark cries out from beneath the paint. . . ."

The discovery of the existence of a Negro civilization in the fifteenth century confers no patent of humanity on me. Like it or not, the past can in no way guide me in the present moment.

The situation that I have examined, it is clear by now, is not a classic one. Scientific objectivity was barred to me, for the alienated, the neurotic, was my brother, my sister, my father. I have ceaselessly striven to show the Negro that in a sense he makes himself abnormal; to show the white man that he is at once the perpetrator and the victim of a delusion.

There are times when the black man is locked into his body. Now, "for a being who has acquired consciousness of himself and of his body, who has attained to the dialectic of subject and object, the body is no longer a cause of the structure of consciousness, it has become an object of consciousness" (Merleau-Ponty 1945: 277).[2]

---

1. Aimé Césaire, "Et les chiens se taisaient," *Armes Miraculeuses*. Paris: Gallimard, 1945. Caribbean poet and playwright Aimé Césaire (1913–2008) was a founder of the literary and political Black consciousness movement known as Negritude. He was one of Fanon's mentors [Ed.].
2. Maurice Merleau-Ponty, *La Phénoménologie de la Perception*. Paris: Gallimard, 1945 [Ed.].

The Negro, however sincere, is the slave of the past. None the less I am a man, and in this sense the Peloponnesian War is as much mine as the invention of the compass. Face to face with the white man, the Negro has a past to legitimate, a vengeance to exact; face to face with the Negro, the contemporary white man feels the need to recall the times of cannibalism. A few years ago, the Lyon branch of the Union of Students From Overseas France asked me to reply to an article that made jazz music literally an irruption of cannibalism into the modern world. Knowing exactly what I was doing, I rejected the premises on which the request was based, and I suggested to the defender of European purity that he cure himself of a spasm that had nothing cultural in it. Some men want to fill the world with their presence. A German philosopher described this mechanism as *the pathology of freedom*. In the circumstances, I did not have to take up a position on behalf of Negro music against white music, but rather to help my brother to rid himself of an attitude in which there was nothing healthful.

Artificial Life

The mythology of many cultures contains images of artificial constructs — whether made things, like golems, that are endowed with a kind of life, or biological organisms, like zombies, that are taken over and controlled by outside forces. The made object — golden calf, idol, icon, voodoo doll — is often seen as embodying a mystical power or acting as a conduit between the spirit world and the tangible world of mundane existence, and this power is often an ominous one, particularly when the embodied object has a human form. There seems to be something inherently dangerous in the act of mimesis, perhaps because the human being who engages in it may be seen as usurping God's role as creator; as a consequence, many religions have placed bans on certain types of representational art.

Historically, one of sf's central preoccupations has been exploration of the proper limits of humankind's place in the universe, so the idea of artificial life, with its fundamental challenge to the natural order, has always been an important theme. In the early days of the genre, which coincide with the great age of industrial production, the dominant image was of mechanical beings, such as automata or robots. With the dawn of the information age, however, interest shifted to computers, artificial intelligences, and the human/machine hybrids known as cyborgs.

The stories in this section represent a historical sampling of some of the more significant and interesting variations on the theme of artificial life. Sometimes these artificial creations are dangerous and malignant, threatening to overpower their creators, while sometimes they are abused and exploited victims; often they are both. This section begins with two Gothic tales that draw on traditional fears of magic and merge them with anxieties about the new sciences of the Industrial Revolution. "The Sandman," E. T. A. Hoffmann's classic tale of a man's infatuation with a mechanical doll, is the oldest story in this volume, written at the cusp of a new era and depicting the moment when the unnatural art of alchemy meets the unnatural art of manufacture. Through mystery and innuendo, Hoffmann probes the boundaries between real and artificial, psychological and supernatural. Mary Shelley's groundbreaking *Frankenstein*, in which an obsessive scientist sews together body parts and reanimates a corpse through the use of electricity, brings old stories about necromancy into the modern era of science. Victor's experiment resonates with echoes of other creative acts, including childbirth and authorship, and is also an act of mythic overreaching, as suggested by the subtitle, "A Modern Prometheus."

In Greek mythology, Prometheus was punished by the gods for sharing the secret of fire with human beings.

Karel Čapek and Isaac Asimov, in different ways, explore the idea of manufactured beings as a form of industrial production and exploitation. Philip K. Dick's post-Hiroshima, Cold War nightmare focuses on the development of self-aware weapons that turn on their makers. In all three stories, we are asked to reflect on what is and isn't monstrous about our artificial offspring.

The next five stories shift our attention, somewhat, to whether we can remake ourselves. Kate Wilhelm and James Tiptree Jr., with their focus on media control, objectification, and commercialism, are less concerned with machines that become human than with humans that are reduced to machines; William Gibson and Maureen McHugh explore the fragile persistence of human weakness in worlds that have been depersonalized through corporatization and globalization; Ken Liu probes our uneasy suspicion that the more human we make our machines, the more we come to see ourselves as machines. Each of these stories grows out of specific historical and cultural context, but the real question in all of them is not what our technology will do to us, but what it reveals about our own nature.

The Critical Contexts in this chapter provide a variety of theoretical perspectives for examining our ambivalence about artificial creations. Freud's landmark essay, "The Uncanny," explores the psychological grounds for the peculiar feeling we experience in the face of something that seems both familiar and strange. Baudrillard's essay on simulacra argues that modern culture has itself become increasingly removed from reality, resulting in profound alienation and displacement. Haraway takes a more positive view of artificial creations, promoting the cyborg as a symbol of empowerment, a bold metaphor for hybrid identities that can overturn the traditional hierarchies of the existing social order.

E. T. A. Hoffmann

The Sandman

(1816)

E. T. A. Hoffmann (1776–1822) was born Ernst Theodor Wilhelm Hoffmann, but later changed "Wilhelm" to "Amadeus" in honor of the composer Wolfgang Amadeus Mozart. Hoffmann was an important member of the German Romantic movement. His first loves were music and art, but he is best remembered as a writer of Gothic tales of madness, obsession, and the supernatural. Hoffmann studied law at the University of Königsberg (1792–1795)

Translation by John Oxenford.

and subsequently spent much of his life working in the Prussian civil service, a bureaucratic career for which he was temperamentally unsuited. He devoted his off-hours to composing music, drawing, and late-night carousing. Hoffmann achieved some modest success as a composer, but it was only when his first story was published in 1809 that he achieved real fame. His stories form the basis for an Offenbach opera and two ballets, including Tchaikovsky's popular *Nutcracker*. Hoffmann died of a paralytic illness in 1822, while embroiled in legal troubles arising from caricatures of public officials he had included in some of his stories.

Hoffmann came from a troubled home; his parents were divorced when he was two, and he was raised primarily by an emotionally distant uncle. Like his parents, Hoffmann had problems with alcohol and depression; his dissipation was notorious. The extent to which he was mentally ill is debated, but there is no doubt that the psychological focus of his fiction owes something to his own disturbed background. His stories are haunted by images of uncanny doubles, fatal obsessions, and dark secrets. Uncertainty about boundaries — between reality and fantasy, between the animate and the inanimate — is typical of Hoffmann's work, and a key to its disturbing effects.

"The Sandman" is one of Hoffmann's most famous stories, in part because of Sigmund Freud's use of it in his essay "The Uncanny" (included in this chapter). The story is a key work in Gothic literature and, like Mary Shelley's *Frankenstein*, may be seen as a precursor of both horror and science fiction as modern genres. Hoffmann's emphasis may seem more supernatural than scientific, but he is clearly uneasy about the unnatural powers of technology as a creative force. *Automata*, or skillfully crafted mechanical dolls, were popular at the time of his writing, and the eerie spectacle of lifelike mannequins that could play chess or perform on musical instruments was a source of much fascination, capturing the public imagination much as robots did in the 1950s or as computers do today. Of course, it is the pathological nature of the main character's imagination that interests Hoffmann above all. It is never entirely clear to what extent Nathaniel is victimized by supernatural forces and to what extent he is merely the victim of his own feverish imagination; this ambiguity provides the story with much of its frightening power.

NATHANIEL TO LOTHAIRE

Certainly you must all be uneasy that I have not written for so long — so very long. My mother, I am sure, is angry, and Clara will believe that I am passing my time in dissipation, entirely forgetful of her fair, angelic image that is so deeply imprinted on my heart. Such, however, is not the case. Daily and hourly I think of you all; and the dear form of my lovely Clara passes before me in my dreams, smiling upon me with her bright eyes as she did when I was among you. But how can I write to you in the distracted mood which has been disturbing my every thought! A horrible thing has crossed my path. Dark forebodings of a cruel, threatening fate tower over me like dark clouds, which no friendly sunbeam can penetrate. I will now tell you what has occurred. I must do so — that I plainly see — the mere thought of it sets me laughing like a madman. Ah, my dear Lothaire, how shall I begin? How shall I make you in any way realize that what happened to me a few days ago can really have had such a fatal effect on my life? If you were here you could see for yourself; but, as it is, you will certainly take me for a crazy fellow who sees ghosts. To be brief, this horrible occurrence, the painful impression of which I am in vain endeavoring to throw off, is nothing more than this — that some days ago, namely on the thirtieth of October at twelve o'clock noon, a barometer-dealer came into my room and offered me his wares. I bought nothing, and threatened to throw him downstairs, upon which he took himself off of his own accord.

Only circumstances of the most peculiar kind, you will suspect, and exerting the greatest influence over my life, can have given any import to this occurrence. Moreover, the person of that unlucky dealer must have had an evil effect upon me. So it was, indeed. I must use every endeavor to collect myself, and patiently and quietly tell you so much of my early youth as will bring the picture plainly and clearly before your eyes. As I am about to begin, I fancy that I hear you laughing, and Clara exclaiming, "Childish stories indeed!" Laugh at me, I beg of you, laugh with all your heart. But, oh God! my hair stands on end, and it is in mad despair that I seem to be inviting your laughter, as Franz Moor did Daniel's in Schiller's play.[1] But to my story.

Excepting at dinner-time I and my brothers and sisters used to see my father very little during the day. He was, perhaps, busily engaged at his ordinary profession. After supper, which was served according to the old custom at seven o'clock, we all went with my mother into my father's study, and seated ourselves at the round table, where he would smoke and drink his large glass of beer. Often he told us wonderful stories, and grew so warm over them that his pipe continually went out. Whereupon I had to light it again with a burning spill, which I thought great sport. Often, too, he would give us picture-books, and sit in his arm-chair, silent and thoughtful, puffing out such thick clouds of smoke that we all seemed to be swimming in the clouds. On such evenings as these my mother was very melancholy, and immediately when the clock struck nine she would say: "Now, children, to bed — to bed! The Sandman's coming, I can see." And indeed on each occasion I used to hear something with a heavy, slow step come thudding up the stairs. That I thought must be the Sandman.

Once when the dull noise of footsteps was particularly terrifying I asked my mother as she bore us away: "Mamma, who is this naughty Sandman, who always drives us away from Papa? What does he look like?"

"There is no Sandman, dear child," replied my mother. "When I say the Sandman's coming, I only mean that you're sleepy and can't keep your eyes open — just as if sand had been sprinkled into them."

This answer of my mother's did not satisfy me — nay, the thought soon ripened in my childish mind that she only denied the Sandman's existence

---

1. Nathaniel refers to a character in Friedrich Schiller's Romantic melodrama *The Robbers* (1781). [Ed.]

to prevent our being terrified of him. Certainly I always heard him coming up the stairs. Most curious to know more of this Sandman and his particular connection with children, I at last asked the old woman who looked after my youngest sister what sort of man he was.

"Eh, Natty," said she, "don't you know that yet? He is a wicked man, who comes to children when they won't go to bed, and throws a handful of sand into their eyes, so that they start out bleeding from their heads. He puts their eyes in a bag and carries them to the crescent moon to feed his own children, who sit in the nest up there. They have crooked beaks like owls so that they can pick up the eyes of naughty human children."

A most frightful picture of the cruel Sandman became impressed upon my mind so that when in the evening I heard the noise on the stairs I trembled with agony and alarm, and my mother could get nothing out of me but the cry, "The Sandman, the Sandman!" stuttered forth through my tears. I then ran into the bedroom, where the frightful apparition of the Sandman terrified me during the whole night.

I had already grown old enough to realize that the nurse's tale about him and the nest of children in the crescent moon could not be quite true, but nevertheless this Sandman remained a fearful spectre, and I was seized with the utmost horror when I heard him once, not only come up the stairs, but violently force my father's door open and go in. Sometimes he stayed away for a long period, but after that his visits came in close succession. This lasted for years, but I could not accustom myself to the terrible goblin; the image of the dreadful Sandman did not become any fainter. His intercourse with my father began more and more to occupy my fancy. Yet an unconquerable fear prevented me from asking my father about it. But if I, I myself, could penetrate the mystery and behold the wondrous Sandman — that was the wish which grew upon me with the years. The Sandman had introduced me to thoughts of the marvels and wonders which so readily gain a hold on a child's mind. I enjoyed nothing better than reading or hearing horrible stories of goblins, witches, pigmies, etc.; but most horrible of all was the Sandman, whom I was always drawing with chalk or charcoal on the tables, cupboards, and walls in the oddest and most frightful shapes.

When I was ten years old my mother removed me from the night nursery into a little chamber situated in a corridor near my father's room. Still, as before, we were obliged to make a speedy departure on the stroke of nine, as soon as the unknown step sounded on the stair. From my little chamber I could hear how he entered my father's room, and then it was that I seemed to detect a thin vapor with a singular odor spreading through the house. Stronger and stronger, with my curiosity, grew my resolution somehow to make the Sandman's acquaintance. Often I sneaked from my room to the corridor when my mother had passed, but never could I discover anything; for the Sandman had always gone in at the door when I reached the place where I might have seen him. At last, driven by an irresistible impulse, I resolved to hide myself in my father's room and await his appearance there.

From my father's silence and my mother's melancholy face I perceived one evening that the Sandman was coming. I, therefore, feigned great weariness, left the room before nine o'clock, and hid myself in a corner close to the door. The house-door groaned and the heavy, slow, creaking step came up the passage and towards the stairs. My mother passed me with the rest of the children. Softly, very softly, I opened the door of my father's room. He was sitting, as usual, stiff and silent, with his back to the door. He did not perceive me, and I swiftly darted into the room and behind the curtain which covered an open cupboard close to the door, in which my father's clothes were hanging. The steps sounded nearer and nearer — there was a strange coughing and scraping and murmuring without. My heart trembled with anxious expectation. A sharp step close, very close, to the door — the quick snap of the latch, and the door opened with a rattling noise. Screwing up my courage to the uttermost, I cautiously peeped out. The Sandman was standing before my father in the middle of the room, the light of the candles shone full upon his face. The Sandman, the fearful Sandman, was the old advocate Coppelius, who had often dined with us.

But the most hideous form could not have inspired me with deeper horror than this very Coppelius. Imagine a large broad-shouldered man, with a head disproportionately big, a face the color of yellow ochre, a pair of bushy grey eyebrows, from beneath which a pair of green cat's eyes sparkled with the most penetrating luster, and with a large nose curved over his upper lip. His wry mouth was often twisted into a malicious laugh, when a couple of dark red spots appeared upon his cheeks, and a strange hissing sound was heard through his gritted teeth. Coppelius always appeared in an ashen-gray coat, cut in old-fashioned style, with waistcoat and breeches of the same color, while his stockings were black, and his shoes adorned with agate buckles.

His little peruke[2] scarcely reached farther than the crown of his head, his curls stood high above his large red ears, and a broad hair-bag projected stiffly from his neck so that the silver clasp which fastened his folded cravat might be plainly seen. His whole figure was hideous and repulsive, but most disgusting to us children were his coarse brown hairy fists. Indeed we did not like to eat anything he had touched with them. This he had noticed, and it was his delight, under some pretext or other, to touch a piece of cake or some nice fruit, that our kind mother might quietly have put on our plates, just for the pleasure of seeing us turn away with tears in our eyes, in disgust and abhorrence, no longer able to enjoy the treat intended for us. He acted in the same manner on holidays, when my father gave us a little glass of sweet wine. Then would he swiftly put his hand over it, or perhaps even raise the glass to his blue lips, laughing most devilishly, and we could only express our indignation by silent sobs. He always called us the little beasts; we dared not utter a sound when he was present, and

---

2. A type of wig worn by men in the seventeenth through eighteenth century. Like Coppelius's coat, it would have seemed a bit old-fashioned in 1816.

we heartily cursed the ugly, unkind man who deliberately marred our slightest pleasures. My mother seemed to hate the repulsive Coppelius as much as we did, since as soon as he showed himself her liveliness, her open and cheerful nature, were changed for a gloomy solemnity. My father behaved towards him as though he were a superior being, whose bad manners were to be tolerated and who was to be kept in good humor at any cost. He need only give the slightest hint, and favorite dishes were cooked, the choicest wines served.

When I now saw this Coppelius, the frightful and terrific thought took possession of my soul, that indeed no one but he could be the Sandman. But the Sandman was no longer the bogey of a nurse's tale, who provided the owl's nest in the crescent moon with children's eyes. No, he was a hideous, spectral monster, who brought with him grief, misery and destruction — temporal and eternal — wherever he appeared.

I was riveted to the spot, as if enchanted. At the risk of being discovered and, as I plainly foresaw, of being severely punished, I remained with my head peeping through the curtain. My father received Coppelius with solemnity.

"Now to our work!" cried the latter in a harsh, grating voice, as he flung off his coat.

My father silently and gloomily drew off his dressing gown, and both attired themselves in long black frocks. Whence they took these I did not see. My father opened the door of what I had always thought to be a cupboard. But I now saw that it was no cupboard, but rather a black cavity in which there was a little fireplace. Coppelius went to it, and a blue flame began to crackle up on the hearth. All sorts of strange utensils lay around. Heavens! As my old father stooped down to the fire, he looked quite another man. Some convulsive pain seemed to have distorted his mild features into a repulsive, diabolical countenance. He looked like Coppelius, whom I saw brandishing red-hot tongs, which he used to take glowing masses out of the thick smoke; which objects he afterwards hammered. I seemed to catch a glimpse of human faces lying around without any eyes — but with deep holes instead.

"Eyes here, eyes!" roared Coppelius tonelessly. Overcome by the wildest terror, I shrieked out and fell from my hiding place upon the floor. Coppelius seized me and, baring his teeth, bleated out, "Ah — little wretch — little wretch!" Then he dragged me up and flung me on the hearth, where the fire began to singe my hair. "Now we have eyes enough — a pretty pair of child's eyes," he whispered, and, taking some red-hot grains out of the flames with his bare hands, he was about to sprinkle them in my eyes.

My father upon this raised his hands in supplication, crying: "Master, master, leave my Nathaniel his eyes!"

Whereupon Coppelius answered with a shrill laugh: "Well, let the lad have his eyes and do his share of the world's crying, but we will examine the mechanism of his hands and feet."

And then he seized me so roughly that my joints cracked, and he screwed off my hands and feet, afterwards putting them back again, one after the other. "There's something wrong here," he mumbled. "But now it's as good as ever. The old man has caught the idea!" hissed and lisped Coppelius. But all around me became black, a sudden cramp darted through my bones and nerves — and I lost consciousness. A gentle warm breath passed over my face; I woke as from the sleep of death. My mother had been stooping over me.

"Is the Sandman still there?" I stammered.

"No, no, my dear child, he has gone away long ago — he won't hurt you!" said my mother, kissing her darling, as he regained his senses.

Why should I weary you, my dear Lothaire, with diffuse details, when I have so much more to tell? Suffice it to say that I had been discovered eavesdropping and ill-used by Coppelius. Agony and terror had brought on delirium and fever, from which I lay sick for several weeks.

"Is the Sandman still there?" That was my first sensible word and the sign of my amendment — my recovery. I have only to tell you now of this most frightful moment in all my youth, and you will be convinced that it is no fault of my eyes that everything seems colorless to me. You will, indeed, know that a dark fatality has hung over my life a gloomy veil of clouds, which I shall perhaps only tear away in death.

Coppelius was no more to be seen; it was said he had left the town.

About a year might have elapsed, and we were sitting, as of old, at the round table. My father was very cheerful and was entertaining us with stories about his travels in his youth; when, as the clock struck nine, we heard the house-door groan on its hinges, and slow steps, heavy as lead, creaked through the passage and up the stairs.

"That is Coppelius," said my mother, turning pale.

"Yes! — that is Coppelius," repeated my father in a faint, broken voice. The tears started to my mother's eyes.

"But father — father!" she cried, "must it be so?"

"He is coming for the last time, I promise you," was the answer. "Only go now, go with the children — go — go to bed. Good night!"

I felt as if I were turned to cold, heavy stone — my breath stopped. My mother caught me by the arm as I stood immovable. "Come, come, Nathaniel!" I allowed myself to be led, and entered my chamber! "Be quiet — be quiet — go to bed — go to sleep!" cried my mother after me; but tormented by restlessness and an inward anguish perfectly indescribable, I could not close my eyes.

The hateful, abominable Coppelius stood before me with fiery eyes, and laughed maliciously at me. It was in vain that I endeavored to get rid of his image. About midnight there was a frightful noise, like the firing of a gun. The whole house resounded. There was a rattling and rustling by my door, and the house-door was closed with a violent bang.

"That is Coppelius!" I cried, springing out of bed in terror.

Then there was a shriek, as of acute, inconsolable grief. I darted into my father's room; the door was open, a suffocating smoke rolled towards me, and the servant girl cried: "Ah, my master, my master!" On the floor of the smoking hearth lay my father dead, with his face burned, blackened and hideously distorted — my sisters were shrieking and moaning around him — and my mother had fainted.

"Coppelius! — cursed devil! You have slain my father!" I cried, and lost my senses.

When, two days afterwards, my father was laid in his coffin, his features were again as mild and gentle as they had been in his life. My soul was comforted by the thought that his compact with the satanic Coppelius could not have plunged him into eternal perdition.

The explosion had awakened the neighbors, the occurrence had become common talk and had reached the ears of the magistracy, who wished to make Coppelius answerable. He had, however, vanished from the spot, without leaving a trace.

If I tell you, my dear friend, that the barometer-dealer was the accursed Coppelius himself, you will not blame me for regarding so unpropitious a phenomenon as the omen of some dire calamity. He was dressed differently, but the figure and features of Coppelius are too deeply imprinted in my mind for an error in this respect to be possible. Besides, Coppelius has not even altered his name. He describes himself, I am told, as a Piedmontese optician, and calls himself Giuseppe Coppola.

I am determined to deal with him, and to avenge my father's death, be the issue what it may.

Tell my mother nothing of the hideous monster's appearance. Remember me to my dear sweet Clara, to whom I will write in a calmer mood. Farewell.

CLARA TO NATHANIEL

It is true that you have not written to me for a long time; but, nevertheless, I believe that I am still in your mind and thoughts. For assuredly you were thinking of me most intently when, designing to send your last letter to my brother Lothaire, you directed it to me instead of to him. I joyfully opened the letter, and did not perceive my error till I came to the words: "Ah, my dear Lothaire."

NO, by rights I should have read no farther, but should have handed over the letter to my brother. Although you have often, in your childish teasing mood, charged me with having such a quiet, womanish, steady disposition, that, even if the house were about to fall in, I should smooth down a wrong fold in the window curtain in a most ladylike manner before I ran away, I can hardly tell you how your letter shocked me. I could scarcely breathe — the light danced before my eyes.

Ah, my dear Nathaniel, how could such a horrible thing have crossed your path? To be parted from you, never to see you again — the thought darted through my breast like a burning dagger. I read on and on. Your description of the repulsive Coppelius is terrifying. I learned for the first time the violent manner of your good old father's death. My brother Lothaire, to whom I surrendered the letter, sought to calm me, but in vain. The fatal barometer dealer, Giuseppe Coppola, followed me at every step;

and I am almost ashamed to confess that he disturbed my healthy and usually peaceful sleep with all sorts of horrible visions. Yet soon even the next day — I was quite changed again. Do not be offended, dearest one, if Lothaire tells you that in spite of your strange fears that Coppelius will in some manner injure you, I am in the same cheerful and unworried mood as ever.

I must honestly confess that, in my opinion, all the terrible things of which you speak occurred merely in your own mind, and had little to do with the actual external world. Old Coppelius may have been repulsive enough, but his hatred of children was what really caused the abhorrence you children felt towards him.

In your childish mind the frightful Sandman in the nurse's tale was naturally associated with old Coppelius. Why, even if you had not believed in the Sandman, Coppelius would still have seemed to you a monster, especially dangerous to children. The awful business which he carried on at night with your father was no more than this: that they were making alchemical experiments in secret, which much distressed your mother since, besides a great deal of money being wasted, your father's mind was filled with a fallacious desire after higher wisdom, and so alienated from his family — as they say is always the case with such experimentalists. Your father, no doubt, occasioned his own death, by some act of carelessness of which Coppelius was completely guiltless. Let me tell you that I yesterday asked our neighbor, the apothecary, whether such a sudden and fatal explosion was possible in these chemical experiments.

"Certainly," he replied and, after his fashion, told me at great length and very circumstantially how such an event might take place, uttering a number of strange-sounding names which I am unable to recollect. Now, I know you will be angry with your Clara; you will say that her cold nature is impervious to any ray of the mysterious, which often embraces man with invisible arms; that she only sees the variegated surface of the world and is as delighted as a silly child at some glittering golden fruit, which contains within it a deadly poison.

Ah! my dear Nathaniel! Can you not then believe that even in open, cheerful, careless minds may dwell the suspicion of some dread power which endeavors to destroy us in our own selves? Forgive me, if I, a silly girl, presume in any manner to present to you my thoughts on such an internal struggle. I shall not find the right words, of course, and you will laugh at me, not because my thoughts are foolish, but because I express them so clumsily.

If there is a dark and hostile power, laying its treacherous toils within us, by which it holds us fast and draws us along the path of peril and destruction, which we should not otherwise have trod; if, I say there is such a power, it must form itself inside us and out of ourselves, indeed; it must become identical with ourselves. For it is only in this condition that we can believe in it, and grant it the room which it requires to accomplish its secret work. Now, if we have a mind which is sufficiently firm, sufficiently strengthened by the joy of life, always to recognize this strange

204 • Artificial Life

enemy as such, and calmly to follow the path of our own inclination and calling, then the dark power will fail in its attempt to gain a form that shall be a reflection of ourselves. Lothaire adds that if we have willingly yielded ourselves up to the dark powers, they are known often to impress upon our minds any strange, unfamiliar shape which the external world has thrown in our way; so that we ourselves kindle the spirit, which we in our strange delusion believe to be speaking to us. It is the phantom of our own selves, the close relationship with which, and its deep operation on our mind, casts us into hell or transports us into heaven.

You see, dear Nathaniel, how freely Lothaire and I are giving our opinion on the subject of the dark powers; which subject, to judge by my difficulties in writing down its most important features, appears to be a complicated one. Lothaire's last words I do not quite comprehend. I can only suspect what he means, and yet I feel as if it were all very true. Get the gruesome advocate Coppelius, and the barometer-dealer, Giuseppe Coppola, quite out of your head, I beg of you. Be convinced that these strange fears have no power over you, and that it is only a belief in their hostile influence that can make them hostile in reality. If the great disturbance in your mind did not speak from every line of your letter, if your situation did not give me the deepest pain, I could joke about the Sandman-Advocate and the barometer-dealer Coppelius. Cheer up, I have determined to play the part of your guardian-spirit. If the ugly Coppelius takes it into his head to annoy you in your dreams, I'll scare him away with loud peals of laughter. I am not a bit afraid of him nor of his disgusting hands; he shall neither spoil my sweetmeats as an Advocate, nor my eyes as a Sandman. Ever yours, my dear Nathaniel.

NATHANIEL TO LOTHAIRE

I am very sorry that in consequence of the error occasioned by my distracted state of mind, Clara broke open the letter intended for you, and read it. She has written me a very profound philosophical epistle, in which she proves, at great length, that Coppelius and Coppola only exist in my own mind, and are phantoms of myself, which will be dissipated directly I recognize them as such. Indeed, it is quite incredible that the mind which so often peers out of those bright, smiling, childish eyes with all the charm of a dream, could make such intelligent professorial definitions. She cites you — you, it seems have been talking about me. I suppose you read her logical lectures, so that she may learn to separate and sift all matters acutely. No more of that, please. Besides, it is quite certain that the barometer-dealer, Giuseppe Coppola, is not the advocate Coppelius. I attend the lectures of the professor of physics, who has lately arrived. His name is the same as that of the famous natural philosopher Spalanzani, and he is of Italian origin. He has known Coppola for years and, moreover, it is clear from his accent that he is really a Piedmontese. Coppelius was a German, but I think no honest one. Calmed I am not, and though you and Clara may consider me a gloomy visionary, I cannot get rid of the impression which the accursed face of Coppelius makes upon me. I am glad that Coppola has left the town — so Spalanzani says.

This professor is a strange fellow — a little round man with high cheek-bones, a sharp nose, pouting lips and little, piercing eyes. Yet you will get a better notion of him than from this description, if you look at the portrait of Cagliostro, drawn by Chodowiecki[3] in one of the Berlin annuals; Spalanzani looks like that exactly. I lately went up his stairs, and perceived that the curtain, which was generally drawn completely over a glass door, left a little opening on one side. I know not what curiosity impelled me to look through. A very tall and slender lady, extremely well-proportioned and most splendidly attired, sat in the room by a little table on which she had laid her arms, her hands being folded together. She sat opposite the door so that I could see the whole of her angelic countenance. She did not appear to see me, and indeed there was something fixed about her eyes as if, I might almost say, she had no power of sight. It seemed to me that she was sleeping with her eyes open. I felt very uncomfortable, and therefore I slunk away into the lecture-room close at hand.

Afterwards I learned that the form I had seen was that of Spalanzani's daughter Olympia, whom he keeps confined in a very strange and barbarous manner so that no one can approach her. After all, there may be something the matter with her; she is half-witted perhaps, or something of the kind. But why should I write you all this? I could have conveyed it better and more circumstantially by word of mouth. For I shall see you in a fortnight. I must again behold my dear, sweet angelic Clara. My evil mood will then be dispersed, though I must confess that it has been struggling for mastery over me ever since her sensible but vexing letter. Therefore I do not write to her today. A thousand greetings, etc.

Nothing more strange and chimerical can be imagined than the fate of my poor friend, the young student Nathaniel, which I, gracious reader, have undertaken to tell you. Have you ever known something that has completely filled your heart, thoughts, and senses to the exclusion of every other object? There was a burning fermentation within you; your blood seethed like a molten glow through your veins, sending a higher color to your cheeks. Your glance was strange, as if you were seeking in empty space forms invisible to all other eyes, and your speech flowed away into dark sighs. Then your friends asked you: "What is it, my dear sir?" "What is the matter?" And you wanted to draw the picture in your mind in all its glowing tints, in all its light and shade, and labored hard to find words only to begin. You thought that you should crowd together in the very first sentence all those wonderful, exalted, horrible, comical, frightful events, so as to strike every hearer at once as with an electric shock. But every word, every thing that takes the form of speech, appeared to you colorless, cold,

3. Nathaniel refers to an etching made by German–Polish printmaker Daniel Chodowiecki. Count Alessandro Cagliostro was the assumed name of Giuseppe Balsamo, a notorious charlatan and conman who claimed occult powers. [Ed.]

and dead. You hunt and hunt, and stutter and stammer, and your friends' sober questions blow like icy wind upon your internal fire until it is almost out. Whereas if, like a bold painter, you had first drawn an outline of the internal picture with a few daring strokes, you might with small trouble have laid on the colors brighter and brighter, and the living throng of varied shapes would have borne your friends away with it. Then they would have seen themselves, like you, in the picture that your mind had bodied forth. Now I must confess to you, kind reader, that no one has really asked me for the history of the young Nathaniel, but you know well enough that I belong to the queer race of authors who, if they have anything in their minds such as I have just described, feel as if everyone who comes near them, and the whole world besides, is insistently demanding: "What is it then — tell it, my dear friend?"

Thus was I forcibly compelled to tell you of the momentous life of Nathaniel. The marvelous singularity of the story filled my entire soul, but for that very reason and because, my dear reader, I had to make you equally inclined to accept the uncanny, which is no small matter, I was puzzled how to begin Nathaniel's story in a manner as inspiring, original, and striking as possible. "Once upon a time," the beautiful beginning of every tale, was too tame. "In the little provincial town of S___ lived" — was somewhat better, as it at least prepared for the climax. Or should I dart at once, medias in res, with " 'Go to the devil,' cried the student Nathaniel with rage and horror in his wild looks, when the barometer-dealer, Giuseppe Coppola . . . ?" — I had indeed already written this down, when I fancied that I could detect something ludicrous in the wild looks of the student Nathaniel, whereas the story is not comical at all. No form of language suggested itself to my mind which seemed to reflect ever in the slightest degree the coloring of the internal picture. I resolved that I would not begin it at all.

So take, gentle reader, the three letters, which friend Lothaire was good enough to give me, as the sketch of the picture which I shall endeavor to color more and more brightly as I proceed with my narrative. Perhaps, like a good portrait-painter, I may succeed in catching the outline in this way, so that you will realize it is a likeness even without knowing the original, and feel as if you had often seen the person with your own corporeal eyes. Perhaps, dear reader, you will then believe that nothing is stranger and madder than actual life; which the poet can only catch in the form of a dull reflection in a dimly polished mirror.

To give you all the information that you will require for a start, we must supplement these letters with the news that shortly after the death of Nathaniel's father, Clara and Lothaire, the children of a distant relative, who had likewise died and left them orphans, were taken by Nathaniel's mother into her own home. Clara and Nathaniel formed a strong attachment for each other; and no one in the world having any objection to make, they were betrothed when Nathaniel left the place to pursue his studies in G___. And there he is, according to his last letter, attending the lectures of the celebrated professor of physics, Spalanzani.

Now, I could proceed in my story with confidence, but at this moment Clara's picture stands so plainly before me that I cannot turn away; as indeed was always the case when she gazed at me with one of her lovely smiles. Clara could not by any means be reckoned beautiful, that was the opinion of all who are by their calling competent judges of beauty. Architects, nevertheless, praised the exact symmetry of her frame, and painters considered her neck, shoulders, and bosom almost too chastely formed; but then they all fell in love with her wondrous hair and coloring, comparing her to the Magdalen in Battoni's picture at Dresden. One of them, a most fantastical and singular fellow, compared Clara's eyes to a lake by Ruysdael,[4] in which the pure azure of a cloudless sky, the wood and flowery field, the whole cheerful life of the rich landscape are reflected. Poets and composers went still further. "What is a lake what is a mirror!" said they. "Can we look upon the girl without wondrous, heavenly music flowing towards us from her glances, to penetrate our inmost soul so that all there is awakened and stirred? If we don't sing well then, there is not much in us, as we shall learn from the delicate smile which plays on Clara's lips, when we presume to pipe up before her with something intended to pass for a song, although it is only a confused jumble of notes."

So it was. Clara had the vivid fancy of a cheerful, unembarrassed child; a deep, tender, feminine disposition; an acute, clever understanding. Misty dreamers had not a chance with her; since, though she did not talk — talking would have been altogether repugnant to her silent nature — her bright glance and her firm ironical smile would say to them: "Good friends, how can you imagine that I shall take your fleeting shadowy images for real shapes imbued with life and motion?" On this account Clara was censured by many as cold, unfeeling, and prosaic; while others, who understood life to its clear depths, greatly loved the feeling, acute, childlike girl; but none so much as Nathaniel, whose perception in art and science was clear and strong. Clara was attached to her lover with all her heart, and when he parted from her the first cloud passed over her life. With what delight, therefore, did she rush into his arms when, as he had promised in his last letter to Lothaire, he actually returned to his native town and entered his mother's room! Nathaniel's expectations were completely fulfilled; for directly he saw Clara he thought neither of the Advocate Coppelius nor of her "sensible" letter. All gloomy forebodings had gone.

However, Nathaniel was quite right, when he wrote to his friend Lothaire that the form of the repulsive barometer-dealer, Coppola, had had a most evil effect on his life. All felt, even in the first days, that Nathaniel had undergone a complete change in his whole being. He sank into a gloomy reverie and behaved in a strange manner that had never been known in him before. Everything, his whole life, had become to him a dream and a foreboding, and he was always saying that man, although he

---

4. Clara is compared to paintings by Neoclassical Italian painter Pompeo Girolamo Batoni and seventeenth-century Dutch landscape painter Jacob van Ruysdael (or Jakob van Ruisdael). The fact that she is likened to artworks rather than to nature may be telling. [Ed.]

might think himself free, only served for the cruel sport of dark powers. These he said it was vain to resist; man must patiently resign himself to his fate. He even went so far as to say that it is foolish to think that we do anything in art and science according to our own independent will; for the inspiration which alone enables us to produce anything does not proceed from within ourselves but is the effect of a higher principle without.

To the clear-headed Clara this mysticism was in the highest degree repugnant, but contradiction appeared to be useless. Only when Nathaniel proved that Coppelius was the evil principle, which had seized him at the moment when he was listening behind the curtain, and that this repugnant principle would in some horrible manner disturb the happiness of their life, Clara grew very serious, and said: "Yes, Nathaniel, you are right. Coppelius is an evil, hostile principle; he can produce terrible effects, like a diabolical power that has come visibly into life; but only if you will not banish him from your mind and thoughts. So long as you believe in him, he really exists and exerts his influence; his power lies only in your belief."

Quite indignant that Clara did not admit the demon's existence outside his own mind, Nathaniel would then come out with all the mystical doctrine of devils and powers of evil. But Clara would break off peevishly by introducing some indifferent matter, to the no small annoyance of Nathaniel. He thought that such deep secrets were closed to cold, unreceptive minds, without being clearly aware that he was counting Clara among these subordinate natures; and therefore he constantly endeavored to initiate her into the mysteries. In the morning, when Clara was getting breakfast ready, he stood by her, reading out of all sorts of mystical books 'till she cried: "But dear Nathaniel, suppose I blame you as the evil principle that has a hostile effect upon my coffee? For if, to please you, I drop everything and look in your eyes while you read, my coffee will overflow into the fire, and none of you will get any breakfast."

Nathaniel closed the book at once and hurried indignantly to his chamber. Once he had a remarkable forte for graceful, lively tales, which he wrote down, and to which Clara listened with the greatest delight; now his creations were gloomy, incomprehensible, and formless so that although, out of compassion, Clara did not say so, he plainly felt how little she was interested. Nothing was more unbearable to Clara than tediousness; her looks and words expressed mental drowsiness which she could not overcome. Nathaniel's productions were, indeed, very tedious. His indignation at Clara's cold, prosaic disposition constantly increased; and Clara could not overcome her dislike of Nathaniel's dark, gloomy, boring mysticism so that they became mentally more and more estranged without either of them perceiving it. The shape of the ugly Coppelius, as Nathaniel himself was forced to confess, was growing dimmer in his fancy, and it often cost him some pains to draw him with sufficient color in his stories, where he figured as the dread bogey of ill omen.

It occurred to him, however, in the end to make his gloomy foreboding, that Coppelius would destroy his happiness, the subject of a poem. He represented himself and Clara as united by true love, but occasionally threatened by a black hand, which appeared to dart into their lives, to snatch away some new joy just as it was born. Finally, as they were standing at the altar, the hideous Coppelius appeared and touched Clara's lovely eyes. They flashed into Nathaniel's heart, like bleeding sparks, scorching and burning, as Coppelius caught him, and flung him into a flaming, fiery circle, which flew round with the swiftness of a storm, carrying him along with it, amid its roaring. The roar is like that of the hurricane, when it fiercely lashes the foaming waves, which rise up, like black giants with white heads, for the furious combat. But through the wild tumult he hears Clara's voice: "Can't you see me then? Coppelius has deceived you. Those, indeed, were not my eyes which so burned in your breast — they were glowing drops of your own heart's blood. I have my eyes still — only look at them!" Nathaniel reflects: "That is Clara, and I am hers for ever!" Then it seems to him as though this thought has forcibly entered the fiery circle, which stands still, while the noise dully ceases in the dark abyss. Nathaniel looks into Clara's eyes, but it is death that looks kindly upon him from her eyes.

While Nathaniel composed this poem, he was very calm and collected; he polished and improved every line and, having subjected himself to the fetters of meter, he did not rest 'till all was correct and melodious. When at last he had finished and read the poem aloud to himself, a wild horror seized him. "Whose horrible voice is that?" he cried out. Soon, however, the whole appeared to him a very successful work, and he felt that it must rouse Clara's cold temperament, although he did not clearly consider why Clara was to be excited, nor what purpose it would serve to torment her with frightful pictures threatening a horrible fate, destructive to their love. Both of them — that is to say, Nathaniel and Clara — were sitting in his mother's little garden, Clara very cheerful, because Nathaniel had not teased her with his dreams and his forebodings during the three days in which he had been writing his poem.

He was even talking cheerfully, as in the old days, about pleasant matters, which caused Clara to remark: "Now for the first time I have you again! Don't you see that we have driven the ugly Coppelius away?"

Not 'till then did it strike Nathaniel that he had in his pocket the poem, which he had intended to read. He at once drew the sheets out and began, while Clara, expecting something tedious as usual, resigned herself and began quietly to knit. But as the dark cloud rose ever blacker and blacker, she let the stocking fall and looked him full in the face. He was carried irresistibly along by his poem, an internal fire deeply reddened his cheeks, tears flowed from his eyes.

At last, when he had concluded, he groaned in a state of utter exhaustion and, catching Clara's hand, sighed forth, as if melted into the most inconsolable grief: "Oh Clara! — Clara!" Clara pressed him gently to her bosom, and said softly, but very solemnly and sincerely: "Nathaniel, dearest Nathaniel, do throw that mad, senseless, insane stuff into the fire!"

Upon this Nathaniel sprang up enraged and, thrusting Clara from him, cried: "Oh, inanimate, accursed automaton!"

With which he ran off; Clara, deeply offended, shed bitter tears, and sobbed aloud: "Ah, he has never loved me, for he does not understand me."

Lothaire entered the arbor; Clara was obliged to tell him all that had occurred. He loved his sister with all his soul, and every word of her complaint fell like a spark of fire into his heart so that the indignation which he had long harbored against the visionary Nathaniel now broke out into the wildest rage. He ran to Nathaniel and reproached him for his senseless conduct towards his beloved sister in hard words, to which the infuriated Nathaniel retorted in the same style. The appellation of "fantastical, mad fool," was answered by that of "miserable commonplace fellow." A duel was inevitable. They agreed on the following morning, according to the local student custom, to fight with sharp rapiers on the far side of the garden. Silently and gloomily they slunk about. Clara had overheard the violent dispute and, seeing the fencing-master bring the rapiers at dawn, guessed what was to occur.

Having reached the place of combat, Lothaire and Nathaniel had in gloomy silence flung off their coats, and with the lust of battle in their flaming eyes were about to fall upon one another, when Clara rushed through the garden door, crying aloud between her sobs: "You wild cruel men! Strike me down before you attack each other. For how can I live on if my lover murders my brother, or my brother murders my lover."

Lothaire lowered his weapon, and looked in silence on the ground; but in Nathaniel's heart, amid the most poignant sorrow, there revived all his love for the beautiful Clara, which he had felt in the prime of his happy youth. The weapon fell from his hand, he threw himself at Clara's feet. "Can you ever forgive me, my only — my beloved Clara? Can you forgive me, my dear brother, Lothaire?"

Lothaire was touched by the deep contrition of his friend; all three embraced in reconciliation amid a thousand tears, and vowed eternal love and fidelity.

Nathaniel felt as though a heavy and oppressive burden had been rolled away, as though by resisting the dark power that held him fast he had saved his whole being, which had been threatened with annihilation. Three happy days he passed with his dear friends, and then went to G___, where he intended to stay a year, and then to return to his native town forever.

All that referred to Coppelius was kept a secret from his mother. For it was well known that she could not think of him without terror since she, as well as Nathaniel, held him guilty of causing her husband's death.

How surprised was Nathaniel when, proceeding to his lodging, he saw that the whole house was burned down, and that only the bare walls stood up amid the ashes. However, although fire had broken out in the laboratory of the apothecary who lived on the ground-floor, and had therefore consumed the house from top to bottom, some bold active friends had succeeded in entering Nathaniel's room in the upper story in time to save his books, manuscripts, and instruments. They carried all safe and sound into another house, where they took a room, to which Nathaniel moved at once. He did not think it at all remarkable that he now lodged opposite to Professor Spalanzani; neither did it appear singular when he perceived that his window looked straight into the room where Olympia often sat alone so that he could plainly recognize her figure, although the features of her face were indistinct and confused. At last it struck him that Olympia often remained for hours in that attitude in which he had once seen her through the glass door, sitting at a little table without any occupation, and that she was plainly enough looking over at him with an unvarying gaze. He was forced to confess that he had never seen a more lovely form, but, with Clara in his heart, the stiff Olympia was perfectly indifferent to him. Occasionally, to be sure, he gave a transient look over his textbook at the beautiful statue, but that was all.

He was just writing to Clara, when he heard a light tap at the door; it stopped as he answered, and the repulsive face of Coppola peeped in. Nathaniel's heart trembled within him, but, remembering what Spalanzani had told him about his compatriot Coppola, and also the firm promise he had made to Clara with respect to the Sandman Coppelius, he felt ashamed of his childish fear and, collecting himself with all his might, said as softly and civilly as possible: "I do not want a barometer, my good friend; pray go."

Upon this, Coppola advanced a good way into the room, his wide mouth distorted into a hideous laugh, and his little eyes darting fire from beneath their long grey lashes: "Eh, eh — no barometer — no barometer?" he said in a hoarse voice, "I have pretty eyes too — pretty eyes!"

"Madman!" cried Nathaniel in horror. "How can you have eyes? Eyes?"

But Coppola had already put his barometer aside and plunged his hand into his wide coat-pocket, whence he drew lorgnettes and spectacles, which he placed upon the table.

"There — there — spectacles on the nose, those are my eyes — pretty eyes!" he gabbled, drawing out more and more spectacles, until the whole table began to glisten and sparkle in the most extraordinary manner.

A thousand eyes stared and quivered, their gaze fixed upon Nathaniel; yet he could not look away from the table, where Coppola kept laying down still more and more spectacles, and all those flaming eyes leapt in wilder and wilder confusion, shooting their blood red light into Nathaniel's heart.

At last, overwhelmed with horror, he shrieked out: "Stop, stop, you terrify me!" and seized Coppola by the arm, as he searched his pockets to bring out still more spectacles, although the whole table was already covered.

Coppola gently extricated himself with a hoarse repulsive laugh; and with the words: "Ah, nothing for you — but here are pretty glasses!" collected all the spectacles, packed them away, and from the breast-pocket of his coat drew forth a number of telescopes large and small. As soon as the spectacles were removed Nathaniel felt quite easy and, thinking of Clara, perceived that the hideous phantom was but the creature of his own mind, that this Coppola was an honest optician and could not possibly be the accursed double of Coppelius. Moreover, in all the glasses which Coppola now placed on the table, there was nothing remarkable, or at least nothing so uncanny as in the spectacles; and to set matters right Nathaniel resolved to make a purchase. He took up a little, very neatly constructed pocket telescope, and looked through the window to try it. Never in his life had he met a glass which brought objects so clearly and sharply before his eyes. Involuntarily he looked into Spalanzani's room; Olympia was sitting as usual before the little table, with her arms laid upon it, and her hands folded.

For the first time, he could see the wondrous beauty in the shape of her face; only her eyes seemed to him singularly still and dead. Nevertheless, as he looked more keenly through the glass, it seemed to him as if moist moonbeams were rising in Olympia's eyes. It was as if the power of seeing were being kindled for the first time; her glances flashed with constantly increasing life. As if spellbound, Nathaniel reclined against the window, meditating on the charming Olympia. A humming and scraping aroused him as if from a dream.

Coppola was standing behind him: "Tre zecchini — three ducats!" He had quite forgotten the optician, and quickly paid him what he asked. "Is it not so? A pretty glass — a pretty glass?" asked Coppola, in his hoarse, repulsive voice, and with his malicious smile.

"Yes — yes," replied Nathaniel peevishly; "Good-bye, friend."

Coppola left the room, but not without casting many strange glances at Nathaniel. He heard him laugh loudly on the stairs.

"Ah," thought Nathaniel, "he is laughing at me because, no doubt, I have paid him too much for this little glass."

While he softly uttered these words, it seemed as if a deep and lugubrious sigh were sounding fearfully through the room; and his breath was stopped by inward anguish. He perceived, however, that it was himself that had sighed.

"Clara is right," he said to himself, "in taking me for a senseless dreamer, but it is pure madness — nay, more than madness, that the stupid thought of having paid Coppola too much for the glass still pains me so strangely. I cannot see the cause."

He now sat down to finish his letter to Clara; but a glance through the window assured him that Olympia was still sitting there, and he instantly sprang up, as if impelled by an irresistible power, seized Coppola's glass, and could not tear himself away from the seductive sight of Olympia 'till his friend and brother Sigismund called him to go to Professor Spalanzani's lecture. The curtain was drawn close before the fatal room, and he could see Olympia no longer, nor could he upon the next day or the next, although he scarcely ever left his window and constantly looked through Coppola's glass. On the third day, the windows were completely covered. In utter despair, filled with a longing and a burning desire, he ran out of the town-gate. Olympia's form floated before him in the air, stepped forth from the bushes, and peeped at him with large beaming eyes from the clear brook. Clara's image had completely vanished from his mind; he thought of nothing but Olympia, and complained aloud in a murmuring voice: "Ah, noble, sublime star of my love, have you only risen upon me to vanish immediately, and leave me in dark hopeless night?"

As he returned to his lodging, however, he perceived a great bustle in Spalanzani's house. The doors were wide open, all sorts of utensils were being carried in, the windows of the first floor were being taken out, maid-servants were going about sweeping and dusting with great hairbrooms, and carpenters and upholsterers were knocking and hammering within. Nathaniel remained standing in the street in a state of perfect wonder, when Sigismund came up to him laughing, and said: "Now, what do you say to our old Spalanzani?"

Nathaniel assured him that he could say nothing because he knew nothing about the professor, but on the contrary perceived with astonishment the mad proceedings in a house otherwise so quiet and gloomy. He then learnt from Sigismund that Spalanzani intended to give a grand party on the following day — a concert and ball — and that half the university was invited. It was generally reported that Spalanzani, who had so long kept his daughter most scrupulously from every human eye, would now let her appear for the first time.

Nathaniel found a card of invitation and, with heart beating high, went at the appointed hour to the professor's, where the coaches were already arriving and the lights shining in the decorated rooms. The company was numerous and brilliant. Olympia appeared dressed with great richness and taste. Her beautifully shaped face and her figure roused general admiration. The somewhat strange arch of her back and the wasp-like thinness of her waist seemed to be produced by too tight lacing. In her step and deportment there was something measured and stiff, which struck many as unpleasant, but it was ascribed to the constraint produced by the company. The concert began. Olympia played the harpsichord with great dexterity, and sang a virtuoso piece, with a voice like the sound of a glass bell, clear and almost piercing. Nathaniel was quite enraptured; he stood in the back row, and could not perfectly recognize Olympia's features in the dazzling light. Therefore, quite unnoticed, he took out Coppola's glass and looked towards the fair creature. Ah! then he saw with what a longing glance she gazed towards him, and how every note of her song plainly sprang from that loving glance, whose fire penetrated his inmost soul. Her accomplished roulades seemed to Nathaniel the exultation of a mind transfigured by love, and when at last, after the cadence, the long trill sounded shrilly through the room, he felt as if clutched by burning arms. He could restrain himself no longer, but with mingled pain and rapture shouted out, "Olympia!"

Everyone looked at him, and many laughed. The organist of the cathedral made a gloomier face than usual, and simply said: "Well, well."

The concert had finished, the ball began. "To dance with her — with her!" That was the aim of all Nathaniel's desire, of all his efforts; but how to gain courage to ask her, the queen of the ball? Nevertheless — he himself did not know how it happened — no sooner had the dancing begun than he was standing close to Olympia, who had not yet been asked to dance. Scarcely able to stammer out a few words, he had seized her hand. Olympia's hand was as cold as ice; he felt a horrible deathly chill thrilling through him. He looked into her eyes, which beamed back full of love and desire, and at the same time it seemed as though her pulse began to beat and her life's blood to flow into her cold hand. And in the soul of Nathaniel the joy of love rose still higher; he clasped the beautiful Olympia, and with her flew through the dance. He thought that his dancing was usually correct as to time, but the peculiarly steady rhythm with which Olympia moved, and which often put him completely out, soon showed him that his time was most defective. However, he would dance with no other lady, and would have murdered anyone who approached Olympia for the purpose of asking her. But this only happened twice and, to his astonishment Olympia remained seated until the next dance, when he lost no time in making her rise again.

Had he been able to see any other object besides the fair Olympia, all sorts of unfortunate quarrels would have been inevitable. For the quiet, scarcely suppressed laughter which arose among the young people in every corner was manifestly directed towards Olympia, whom they followed with very curious glances — one could not tell why. Heated by the dance and by the wine, of which he had freely partaken, Nathaniel had laid aside all his ordinary reserve. He sat by Olympia with her hand in his and, in a high state of inspiration, told her his passion, in words which neither he nor Olympia understood.

Yet perhaps she did; for she looked steadfastly into his face and sighed several times, "Ah, ah!" Upon this, Nathaniel said, "Oh splendid, heavenly lady! Ray from the promised land of love — deep soul in whom all my being is reflected!" with much more stuff of the like kind. But Olympia merely went on sighing, "Ah — ah!"

Professor Spalanzani occasionally passed the happy pair, and smiled on them with a look of singular satisfaction. To Nathaniel, although he felt in quite another world, it seemed suddenly as though Professor Spalanzani's face was growing considerably darker and, when he looked around he perceived, to his no small horror, that the last two candles in the empty room had burned down to their sockets, and were just going out. The music and dancing had ceased long ago.

"Parting — parting!" he cried in wild despair; he kissed Olympia's hand, he bent towards her mouth, when his glowing lips were met by lips cold as ice! Just as when he had touched her cold hand, he felt himself overcome by horror; the legend of the dead bride darted suddenly through his mind, but Olympia pressed him fast, and her lips seemed to spring to life at his kiss. Professor Spalanzani strode through the empty hall, his steps caused a hollow echo, and his figure, round which a flickering shadow played, had a fearful, spectral appearance.

"Do you love me, do you love me, Olympia? Only one word! Do you love me?" whispered Nathaniel; but as she rose Olympia only sighed, "Ah — ah!"

"Yes, my gracious, my beautiful star of love," said Nathaniel, "you have risen upon me, and you will shine, for ever lighting my inmost soul."

"Ah — ah!" replied Olympia, as she departed. Nathaniel followed her; they both stood before the professor.

"You have had a very animated conversation with my daughter," said he, smiling; "So, dear Herr Nathaniel, if you have any pleasure in talking with a silly girl, your visits shall be welcome."

Nathaniel departed with a whole heaven beaming in his heart. The next day Spalanzani's party was the general subject of conversation. Notwithstanding that the professor had made every effort to appear splendid, the wags had all sorts of incongruities and oddities to talk about. They were particularly hard upon the dumb, stiff Olympia whom, in spite of her beautiful exterior, they considered to be completely stupid, and they were delighted to find in her stupidity the reason why Spalanzani had kept her so long concealed. Nathaniel did not hear this without secret anger. Nevertheless he held his peace. "For," thought he, "is it worthwhile convincing these fellows that it is their own stupidity that prevents their recognizing Olympia's deep, noble mind?"

One day Sigismund said to him: "Be kind enough, brother, to tell me how a sensible fellow like you could possibly lose your head over that wax face, over that wooden doll up there?"

Nathaniel was about to fly out in a passion, but he quickly recollected himself and retorted: "Tell me, Sigismund, how it is that Olympia's heavenly charms could escape your active and intelligent eyes, which generally perceive things so clearly? But, for that very reason, Heaven be thanked, I have not you for my rival; otherwise, one of us must have fallen a bleeding corpse!"

Sigismund plainly perceived his friend's condition. So he skillfully gave the conversation a turn and, after observing that in love-affairs there was no disputing about the object, added: "Nevertheless, it is strange that many of us think much the same about Olympia. To us — pray do not take it ill, brother, she appears singularly stiff and soulless. Her shape is well proportioned — so is her face — that is true! She might pass for beautiful if her glance were not so utterly without a ray of life — without the power of vision. Her pace is strangely regular, every movement seems to depend on some wound-up clockwork. Her playing and her singing keep the same unpleasantly correct and spiritless time as a musical box, and the same may be said of her dancing. We find your Olympia quite uncanny, and prefer to have nothing to do with her. She seems to act like a living being, and yet has some strange peculiarity of her own."

Nathaniel did not completely yield to the bitter feeling which these words of Sigismund's roused in him, but mastered his indignation, and merely said with great earnestness, "Olympia may appear uncanny to you, cold, prosaic man. Only the poetical mind is sensitive to its like in others. To me alone was the love in her glances revealed, and it has pierced my mind and all my thought; only in the love of Olympia do I discover my real self. It may not suit you that she does not indulge in idle chit-chat like other shallow minds. She utters few words, it is true, but these few words appear as genuine hieroglyphics of the inner world, full of love and deep knowledge of the spiritual life, and contemplation of the eternal beyond. But you have no sense for all this, and my words are wasted on you."

"God preserve you, brother," said Sigismund very mildly, almost sorrowfully. "But you seem to me to be in an evil way. You may depend upon me, if all — no, no, I will not say anything further."

All of a sudden it struck Nathaniel that the cold, prosaic Sigismund meant very well towards him; he therefore shook his proffered hand very heartily.

Nathaniel had totally forgotten the very existence of Clara, whom he had once loved; his mother, Lothaire — all had vanished from his memory; he lived only for Olympia, with whom he sat for hours every day, uttering strange fantastical stuff about his love, about the sympathy that glowed to life, about the affinity of souls, to all of which Olympia listened with great devotion. From the very bottom of his desk he drew out all that he had ever written. Poems, fantasies, visions, romances, tales — this stock was daily increased by all sorts of extravagant sonnets, stanzas, and canzoni, and he read them all tirelessly to Olympia for hours on end. Never had he known such an admirable listener. She neither embroidered nor knitted, she never looked out of the window, she fed no favorite bird, she played neither with lapdog nor pet cat, she did not twist a slip of paper or anything else in her hand, she was not obliged to suppress a yawn by a gentle forced cough. In short, she sat for hours, looking straight into her lover's eyes, without stirring, and her glance became more and more lively and animated. Only when Nathaniel rose at last, and kissed her hand and her lips did she say, "Ah, ah" to which she added: "Good night, dearest."

"Oh deep, noble mind!" cried Nathaniel in his own room, "you, you alone, dear one, fully understand me."

He trembled with inward rapture, when he considered the wonderful harmony that was revealed more and more every day between his own mind and that of Olympia. For it seemed to him as if Olympia had spoken concerning him and his poetical talent out of the depths of his own mind; as if her voice had actually sounded from within himself. That must indeed have been the case, for Olympia never uttered any words whatever beyond those which have already been recorded. Even when Nathaniel, in clear and sober moments, as for instance upon waking in the morning, remembered Olympia's utter passivity and her painful lack of words, he merely said: "Words, words! The glance of her heavenly eye speaks more than any language here below. Can a child of heaven adapt herself to the narrow confines drawn by a miserable mundane necessity?"

Professor Spalanzani appeared highly delighted at the intimacy between his daughter and Nathaniel. To the latter he gave the most unequivocal signs of approbation; and when Nathaniel ventured at last to hint at a union with Olympia, his whole face smiled as he observed that he would leave his daughter a free choice in the matter. Encouraged by these words and with burning passion in his heart, Nathaniel resolved to implore

Olympia on the very next day to say directly and in plain words what her kind glance had told him long ago; namely, that she loved him. He sought the ring which his mother had given him at parting, to give it to Olympia as a symbol of his devotion, of his life which budded forth and bloomed with her alone. Clara's letters and Lothaire's came to his hands during the search; but he flung them aside indifferently, found the ring, pocketed it and hastened over to Olympia. Already on the steps, in the hall, he heard a strange noise, which seemed to proceed from Spalanzani's room. There was a stamping, a clattering, a pushing, a banging against the door, intermingled with curses and imprecations.

"Let go — let go! Rascal! — Scoundrel! — Body and soul I've risked upon it! — Ha, ha, ha! — That's not what we agreed to! — I, I made the eyes! — I made the clockwork! — Stupid blockhead with your clockwork! — Accursed dog of a bungling watch-maker! — off with you! — Devil! — Stop! — Pipe-maker! — Infernal beast! — Stop! — Get out! — Let go!"

These words were uttered by the voices of Spalanzani and the hideous Coppelius, who were raging and wrangling together. Nathaniel rushed in, overcome by the most inexpressible anguish.

The professor was holding a female figure fast by the shoulders, the Italian Coppola grasped it by the feet, and there they were tugging and pulling, this way and that, contending for the possession of it with the utmost fury. Nathaniel started back with horror when in the figure he recognized Olympia. Boiling with the wildest indignation, he was about to rescue his beloved from these infuriated men. But at that moment Coppola, whirling round with the strength of a giant, wrenched the figure from the professor's hand, and then dealt him a tremendous blow with the object itself, which sent him reeling and tumbling backwards over the table, upon which stood vials, retorts, bottles, and glass cylinders. All these were dashed to a thousand shivers. Now Coppola flung the figure across his shoulders, and with a frightful burst of shrill laughter dashed down the stairs, so fast that the feet of the figure, which dangled in the most hideous manner, rattled with a wooden sound on every step.

Nathaniel stood paralyzed; he had seen but too plainly that Olympia's waxen, deathly pale countenance had no eyes, but black holes instead — she was, indeed, a lifeless doll. Spalanzani was writhing on the floor; the pieces of glass had cut his head, his breast, and his arms, and the blood was spurting up as from so many fountains. But he soon collected all his strength.

"After him — after him — what are you waiting for? Coppelius, Coppelius — has robbed me of my best automaton — a work of twenty years — body and soul risked upon it — the clockwork — the speech — the walk, mine; the eyes stolen from you. The infernal rascal — after him; fetch Olympia — there you see the eyes!"

And now Nathaniel saw that a pair of eyes lay upon the ground, staring at him; these Spalanzani caught up, with his unwounded hand, and flung into his bosom. Then madness seized Nathaniel in its burning claws, and clutched his very soul, destroying his every sense and thought.

"Ho — ho — ho — a circle of fire! of fire! Spin round, circle! Merrily, merrily! Ho, wooden doll — spin round, pretty doll!" he cried, flying at the professor, and clutching at his throat.

He would have strangled him had not the noise attracted a crowd, who rushed in and forced Nathaniel to let go, thus saving the professor, whose wounds were immediately dressed. Sigismund, strong as he was, was not able to master the mad Nathaniel, who kept crying out in a frightening voice: "Spin round, wooden doll!" and laid about him with clenched fists. At last the combined force of many succeeded in overcoming him, in flinging him to the ground and binding him. His words were merged into one hideous roar like that of a brute, and in this insane condition he was taken raging to the mad-house.

Before I proceed to tell you, gentle reader, what more befell the unfortunate Nathaniel, should you by chance take an interest in that skillful optician and automaton-maker Spalanzani, I can inform you that he was completely healed of his wounds. He was, however, obliged to leave the university, because Nathaniel's story had created a sensation, and it was universally considered a quite unpardonable trick to smuggle a wooden doll into respectable tea-parties in place of a living person — for Olympia had been quite a success at tea-parties. The lawyers called it a most subtle deception, and the more culpable, inasmuch as he had planned it so artfully against the public that not a single soul — a few cunning students excepted — had detected it, although all now wished to play the wiseacre, and referred to various facts which had appeared to them suspicious. Nothing very clever was revealed in this way. Would it strike anyone as so very suspicious, for instance, that, according to the expression of an elegant tea-ite, Olympia had, contrary to all usage, sneezed oftener than she had yawned? "The former," remarked this fashionable person, "was the sound of the concealed clockwork winding itself up. Moreover, it had creaked audibly." And so on.

The professor of poetry and eloquence took a pinch of snuff, clapped the lid of his box to, cleared his throat, and said solemnly: "Ladies and gentlemen, do you not perceive where the trick lies? It is all an allegory — a sustained metaphor — you understand me — sapient! sat."[5]

But many were not satisfied with this; the story of the automaton had struck deep root into their souls and, in fact, a pernicious mistrust of human figures in general had begun to creep in. Many lovers, to be quite convinced that they were not enamoured of wooden dolls, would request their mistresses to sing and dance a little out of time, to embroider and knit, and play with their lapdogs, while listening to reading, etc., and, above all, not merely to listen, but also sometimes to talk, in such a manner as presupposed actual thought and feeling. With many the bond of love became firmer and more entrancing, though others, on the contrary, slipped gently out of the noose. "One cannot really answer for this," said some.

5. Abbreviated version of the Latin saying "verbum sapienti sat est" ("A word to the wise is enough"). [Ed.]

At tea-parties yawning prevailed to an incredible extent, and there was no sneezing at all, that all suspicion might be avoided. Spalanzani, as already stated, was obliged to decamp, to escape a criminal prosecution for fraudulently introducing an automaton into human society. Coppola had vanished, also.

Nathaniel awakened as from a heavy, frightful dream; as he opened his eyes, he felt an indescribable sensation of pleasure glowing through him with heavenly warmth. He was in bed in his own room, in his father's house, Clara was stooping over him, and Lothaire and his mother were standing near.

"At last, at last, beloved Nathaniel, you have recovered from your serious illness — now you are mine again!" said Clara, from the very depth of her soul, and clasped Nathaniel in her arms.

It was with mingled sorrow and delight that the bright tears fell from his eyes, as he answered with a deep sigh: "My own — my own Clara!"

Sigismund, who had faithfully remained with his friend in his hour of trouble, now entered. Nathaniel stretched out his hand to him. "And you, faithful brother, have you not deserted me?"

Every trace of Nathaniel's madness had vanished, and he soon gained strength under the care of his mother, his beloved, and his friends. Good fortune also had visited the house, for a miserly old uncle of whom nothing had been expected had died, leaving their mother, besides considerable property, an estate in a pleasant spot near the town. Thither Nathaniel decided to go, with his Clara, whom he now intended to marry, his mother, and Lothaire. He had grown milder and more docile than ever he had been before, and now, for the first time, he understood the heavenly purity and the greatness of Clara's mind. No one, by the slightest hint, reminded him of the past.

Only, when Sigismund took leave of him, Nathaniel said: "Heavens, brother, I was in an evil way, but a good angel led me betimes on to the path of light! Ah, that was Clara!"

Sigismund did not let him carry the discourse further for fear that grievous recollections might burst forth in all their lurid brightness.

At about this time the four lucky persons thought of going to the estate. It was noon and they were walking in the streets of the city, where they had made several purchases. The high steeple of the town hall was already casting its gigantic shadow over the market-place.

"Oh," said Clara, "let us climb it once more and look out at the distant mountains!"

No sooner said than done. Nathaniel and Clara both ascended the steps, the mother returned home with the servant, and Lothaire, who was not inclined to clamber up so many stairs, chose to remain below. The two lovers stood arm-in-arm on the highest gallery of the tower, and looked down upon the misty forests, behind which the blue mountains rose like a gigantic city.

"Look there at that curious little grey bush," said Clara. "It actually looks as if it were striding towards us."

Nathaniel mechanically put his hand into his breast pocket — he found Coppola's telescope, and pointed it to one side. Clara was in the way of the glass. His pulse and veins leapt convulsively. Pale as death, he stared at Clara, soon streams of fire flashed and glared from his rolling eyes, he roared frightfully, like a hunted beast. Then he sprang high into the air and, punctuating his words with horrible laughter, he shrieked out in a piercing tone, "Spin round, wooden doll! — spin round!" Then seizing Clara with immense force, he tried to hurl her down, but with the desperate strength of one battling against death she clutched the railings.

Lothaire heard the raging of the madman — he heard Clara's shriek of agony — fearful forebodings darted through his mind, he ran up, the door to the second flight was fastened, Clara's shrieks became louder and still louder. Frantic with rage and anxiety, he threw himself against the door, which finally burst open. Clara's voice was becoming weaker and weaker. "Help — help, save me!" With these words the voice seemed to die on the air.

"She is gone — murdered by that madman!" cried Lothaire.

The door of the gallery was also closed, but despair gave him a giant's strength, and he burst it from the hinges. Heavens! Grasped by the mad Nathaniel, Clara was hanging in the air over the gallery — with one hand only she still held one of the iron railings. Quick as lightning, Lothaire caught his sister and drew her in, at the same moment striking the mad-man in the face with his clenched fist to such effect that he reeled and let go his prey.

Lothaire ran down with his fainting sister in his arms. She was saved. Nathaniel went raging about the gallery, leaping high in the air and crying, "Circle of fire, spin round! spin round!"

The people collected at the sound of his wild shrieks and among them, prominent for his gigantic stature, was the Advocate Coppelius, who had just come to the town, and was proceeding straight to the market-place. Some wished to climb up and secure the madman, but Coppelius only laughed, saying, "Ha, ha — just wait — he will soon come down of his own accord," and looked up like the rest. Nathaniel suddenly stood still as if petrified.

Then, perceiving Coppelius, he stooped down, and yelled out, "Ah, pretty eyes — pretty eyes!" with which he sprang over the railing.

When Nathaniel lay on the stone pavement with his head shattered, Coppelius had disappeared in the crowd.

Many years afterwards it is said that Clara was seen in a remote spot, sitting hand in hand with a kind-looking man before the door of a country house, while two lively boys played before her. From this it may be inferred that she at last found a quiet domestic happiness suitable to her serene and cheerful nature, a happiness which the morbid Nathaniel would never have given her.

Mary Shelley

From Frankenstein, or The Modern Prometheus

(1818; 1831)

Mary Shelley (1797–1851) is, along with Jules Verne and H. G. Wells, one of the three foundational figures of science fiction as a genre. Now widely recognized as an important Romantic writer, she wrote a number of articles and books, both fiction and nonfiction, but *Frankenstein*, the Gothic tale that some consider the first true science fiction novel, is by far her most famous work. Born Mary Wollstonecraft Godwin, she had a very unconventional upbringing for a young woman in nineteenth-century England. Mary was the daughter of William Godwin, the radical political philosopher, and the pioneering feminist theorist Mary Wollstonecraft, who died of complications from her daughter's birth. Mary was raised by her father, who shared Wollstonecraft's progressive views on women, and saw to it that his daughter received a broad if somewhat erratic education, which was unusual at that time. In particular, Godwin encouraged Mary's writing from an early age.

As a teenager, Mary eloped with the famous Romantic poet Percy Bysshe Shelley, who belonged to her father's circle of admirers, in 1814, and they were married two years later, after Percy's estranged wife Harriet committed suicide (Mary's half-sister also committed suicide around this time). While still a young woman, Mary suffered through the death of three of her four young children as well as a miscarriage that threatened her own life. Percy drowned in 1822, leaving 25-year-old Mary to support herself and her surviving child by writing. The prevalence of violent and untimely deaths in Mary's life no doubt had a powerful effect on her, and the ambivalent connections between birth, death, and artistic creation in her works is perhaps not surprising.

Frankenstein was published anonymously in 1818, with a Preface written by Percy, and issued in a revised edition in 1831. In her Introduction to the 1831 edition (from which this excerpt is taken), Mary describes how the story had its genesis in a ghost-story-telling contest conducted during a summer storm in a Swiss chalet by a group of talented and cabin-fevered young Romantics, including the Shelleys and Lord Byron. One night, after listening to a discussion of Erasmus Darwin's electrical research and the speculation that this force might be used to reanimate corpses (suggested, perhaps, by Luigi Galvani's recent experiments with frogs), Mary had a vivid waking dream in which she saw a monstrous creature come to life in a vision closely paralleling the events of Chapter V excerpted below.

Frankenstein is considered by many the first genuine science fiction novel. While undeniably part of the Gothic tradition that was popular in England during the late eighteenth and early nineteenth centuries, what sets this novel apart from other examples of that genre is the centrality of science to the narrative. The monster is brought to life not by magic but through technology.

221

Although the details are hazy, it seems to be achieved by a type of galvanism, based on contemporary experiments with electricity. Even more significant, perhaps, is the extent to which science itself is the subject matter of the novel. In his obsessive investigation of the laws of nature and his compulsion to tamper with them, Victor Frankenstein embodies an early form of the "mad scientist" that would become a cliché in later sf. No matter that his "science" owes much to alchemy; Victor is a modern innovator who proceeds by the scientific method in a series of experiments using the latest procedures and equipment. Moreover, Victor's success, unlike that of the scientists in earlier novels such as Jonathan Swift's *Gulliver's Travels*, is devastating. As a conservative thinker of the eighteenth century, Swift saw science as fundamentally trivial, a laughable waste of time and energy in the pursuit of preposterous goals. Shelley takes her science much more seriously. In her exploration of the scientist's amoral arrogance and the danger of manipulating nature with unforeseen results, Shelley speaks to doubts and fears about scientific progress during the Industrial Revolution, a period when the use of science and technology was visibly transforming the face of the earth and the nature of society.

In questioning the proper limits of science and exploring the dire consequences of exceeding those limits, Shelley inaugurates the branch of sf that expresses a fear that human beings' hubristic disregard for the natural order will lead to our downfall. Of course, the "Frankenstein" of the title is the scientist, not the monster itself (more frequently referred to in the novel as the "creature"), and there is plenty of evidence in the text that the creature itself is not inherently evil but rather becomes so after being rejected and abandoned by its creator. In this sense, the novel is more critical of human nature and society than of science. Nonetheless, in the popular consciousness, Frankenstein the creator has been conflated with his monstrous creation, and as such the "Frankenstein monster" has become one of the most well-known and powerful archetypes in the modern imagination, constantly invoked in debates about new advances in areas such as artificial intelligence, genetically modified crops, human cloning, and stem-cell research.

CHAPTER IV

From this day natural philosophy, and particularly chemistry, in the most comprehensive sense of the term, became nearly my sole occupation.[1] I read with ardour those works, so full of genius and discrimination, which modern enquirers have written on these subjects. I attended the lectures, and cultivated the acquaintance, of the men of science of the university; and I found even in M. Krempe a great deal of sound sense and real information, combined, it is true, with a repulsive physiognomy and manners, but not on that account the less valuable. In M. Waldman I found a true friend. His gentleness was never tinged by dogmatism, and his instructions were given with an air of frankness and good nature, that banished every

---

1. "Natural philosophy" is the older term for what we now call "natural science" or simply "science." [Ed.]

idea of pedantry. In a thousand ways he smoothed for me the path of knowledge, and made the most abstruse enquiries clear and facile to my apprehension. My application was at first fluctuating and uncertain; it gained strength as I proceeded, and soon became so ardent and eager, that the stars often disappeared in the light of morning whilst I was yet engaged in my laboratory.

As I applied so closely, it may be easily conceived that my progress was rapid. My ardour was indeed the astonishment of the students, and my proficiency that of the masters. Professor Krempe often asked me, with a sly smile, how Cornelius Agrippa went on? whilst M. Waldman expressed the most heartfelt exultation in my progress. Two years passed in this manner, during which I paid no visit to Geneva, but was engaged, heart and soul, in the pursuit of some discoveries which I hoped to make. None but those who have experienced them can conceive of the enticements of science. In other studies you go as far as others have gone before you, and there is nothing more to know; but in a scientific pursuit there is continual food for discovery and wonder. A mind of moderate capacity, which closely pursued one study must infallibly arrive at great proficiency in that study; and I, who continually sought the attainment of one object of pursuit and was solely wrapt up in this, improved so rapidly, that, at the end of two years, I made some discoveries in the improvement of some chemical instruments, which procured me great esteem and admiration at the university. When I had arrived at this point and had become as well acquainted with the theory and practice of natural philosophy as depended on the lessons of any of the professors at Ingolstadt, my residence there being no longer conducive to my improvements, I thought of returning to my friends and my native town, when an incident happened that protracted my stay.

One of the phenomena which had peculiarly attracted my attention was the structure of the human frame, and, indeed, any animal endued with life. Whence, I often asked myself, did the principle of life proceed? It was a bold question, and one which has ever been considered as a mystery; yet with how many things are we upon the brink of becoming acquainted, if cowardice or carelessness did not restrain our enquiries. I revolved these circumstances in my mind, and determined thenceforth to apply myself more particularly to those branches of natural philosophy which relate to physiology. Unless I had been animated by an almost supernatural enthusiasm, my application to this study would have been irksome, and almost intolerable. To examine the causes of life, we must first have recourse to death. I became acquainted with the science of anatomy: but this was not sufficient; I must also observe the natural decay and corruption of the human body. In my education my father had taken the greatest precautions that my mind should be impressed with no supernatural horrors. I do not ever remember to have trembled at a tale of superstition, or to have feared the apparition of a spirit. Darkness had no effect upon my fancy; and a churchyard was to me merely the receptacle of bodies deprived of life, which, from being the seat of beauty and strength, had become food for the worm. Now I was led to examine the cause and progress of this decay, and forced to spend days and nights in vaults and charnel-houses. My attention was fixed upon every object the most insupportable to the delicacy of the human feelings. I saw how the fine form of man was degraded and wasted; I beheld the corruption of death succeed to the blooming cheek of life; I saw how the worm inherited the wonders of the eye and brain. I paused, examining and analysing all the minutiae of causation, as exemplified in the change from life to death, and death to life, until from the midst of this darkness a sudden light broke in upon me — a light so brilliant and wondrous, yet so simple, that while I became dizzy with the immensity of the prospect which it illustrated, I was surprised, that among so many men of genius who had directed their enquiries towards the same science, that I alone should be reserved to discover so astonishing a secret.

Remember, I am not recording the vision of a madman. The sun does not more certainly shine in the heavens, than that which I now affirm is true. Some miracle might have produced it, yet the stages of the discovery were distinct and probable. After days and nights of incredible labour and fatigue, I succeeded in discovering the cause of generation and life; nay, more, I became myself capable of bestowing animation upon lifeless matter.

The astonishment which I had at first experienced on this discovery soon gave place to delight and rapture. After so much time spent in painful labor, to arrive at once at the summit of my desires, was the most gratifying consummation of my toils. But this discovery was so great and overwhelming, that all the steps by which I had been progressively led to it were obliterated, and I beheld only the result. What had been the study and desire of the wisest men since the creation of the world was now within my grasp. Not that, like a magic scene, it all opened upon me at once: the information I had obtained was of a nature rather to direct my endeavours so soon as I should point them towards the object of my search, than to exhibit that object already accomplished. I was like the Arabian who had been buried with the dead and found a passage to life, aided only by one glimmering and seemingly ineffectual light.

I see by your eagerness and the wonder and hope which your eyes express, my friend, that you expect to be informed of the secret with which I am acquainted; that cannot be: listen patiently until the end of my story, and you will easily perceive why I am reserved upon the subject. I will not lead you on, unguarded and ardent as I then was, to your destruction and infallible misery. Learn from me, if not by my precepts, at least by my example, how dangerous is the acquirement of knowledge, and how much happier that man is who believes his native town to be the world, than he who aspires to become greater than his nature will allow.

When I found so astonishing a power placed within my hands, I hesitated a long time concerning the manner in which I should employ it. Although I possessed the capacity of bestowing animation, yet to prepare a frame for the reception of it, with all its intricacies of fibers, muscles, and veins, still remained a work of inconceivable difficulty and labor. I doubted at first whether I should attempt the creation of a being like myself, or one of simpler organization; but my imagination was too much exalted by my first success to permit me to doubt of my ability to give life to an animal as complex and wonderful as man. The materials at present within my command hardly appeared adequate to so arduous an undertaking; but I doubted not that I should ultimately succeed. I prepared myself for a multitude of reverses; my operations might be incessantly baffled, and at last my work be imperfect: yet, when I considered the improvement which every day takes place in science and mechanics, I was encouraged to hope my present attempts would at least lay the foundations of future success. Nor could I consider the magnitude and complexity of my plan as any argument of its impracticability. It was with these feelings that I began the creation of a human being. As the minuteness of the parts formed a great hindrance to my speed, I resolved, contrary to my first intention, to make the being of a gigantic stature; that is to say, about eight feet in height, and proportionably large. After having formed this determination and having spent some months in successfully collecting and arranging my materials, I began.

No one can conceive the variety of feelings which bore me onwards, like a hurricane, in the first enthusiasm of success. Life and death appeared to me ideal bounds, which I should first break through, and pour a torrent of light into our dark world. A new species would bless me as its creator and source; many happy and excellent natures would owe their being to me. No father could claim the gratitude of his child so completely as I should deserve theirs. Pursuing these reflections, I thought, that if I could bestow animation upon lifeless matter, I might in process of time (although I now found it impossible) renew life where death had apparently devoted the body to corruption.

These thoughts supported my spirits, while I pursued my undertaking with unremitting ardor. My cheek had grown pale with study, and my person had become emaciated with confinement. Sometimes, on the very brink of certainty, I failed; yet still I clung to the hope which the next day or the next hour might realize. One secret which I alone possessed was the hope to which I had dedicated myself; and the moon gazed on my midnight labors, while, with unrelaxed and breathless eagerness, I pursued nature to her hiding-places. Who shall conceive the horrors of my secret toil as I dabbled among the unhallowed damps of the grave or tortured the living animal to animate the lifeless clay? My limbs now tremble, and my eyes swim with the remembrance; but then a resistless, and almost frantic impulse, urged me forward; I seemed to have lost all soul or sensation but for this one pursuit. It was indeed but a passing trance, that only made me feel with renewed acuteness so soon as, the unnatural stimulus ceasing to operate, I had returned to my old habits. I collected bones from charnel-houses and disturbed, with profane fingers, the tremendous secrets of the human frame. In a solitary chamber, or rather cell, at the top of the house, and separated from all the other apartments by a gallery and staircase, I kept my workshop of filthy creation: my eyeballs were starting from their sockets in attending to the details of my employment. The dissecting room and the slaughter-house furnished many of my materials; and often did my human nature turn with loathing from my occupation, whilst, still urged on by an eagerness which perpetually increased, I brought my work near to a conclusion.

The summer months passed while I was thus engaged, heart and soul, in one pursuit. It was a most beautiful season; never did the fields bestow a more plentiful harvest, or the vines yield a more luxuriant vintage: but my eyes were insensible to the charms of nature. And the same feelings which made me neglect the scenes around me caused me also to forget those friends who were so many miles absent, and whom I had not seen for so long a time. I knew my silence disquieted them; and I well remembered the words of my father: "I know that while you are pleased with yourself, you will think of us with affection, and we shall hear regularly from you. You must pardon me if I regard any interruption in your correspondence as a proof that your other duties are equally neglected."

I knew well therefore what would be my father's feelings; but I could not tear my thoughts from my employment, loathsome in itself, but which had taken an irresistible hold of my imagination. I wished, as it were, to procrastinate all that related to my feelings of affection until the great object, which swallowed up every habit of my nature, should be completed.

I then thought that my father would be unjust if he ascribed my neglect to vice, or faultiness on my part, but I am now convinced that he was justified in conceiving that I should not be altogether free from blame. A human being in perfection ought always to preserve a calm and peaceful mind, and never to allow passion or a transitory desire to disturb his tranquillity. I do not think that the pursuit of knowledge is an exception to this rule. If the study to which you apply yourself has a tendency to weaken your affections, and to destroy your taste for those simple pleasures in which no alloy can possibly mix, then that study is certainly unlawful, that is to say, not befitting the human mind. If this rule were always observed; if no man allowed any pursuit whatsoever to interfere with the tranquillity of his domestic affections, Greece had not been enslaved; Caesar would have spared his country; America would have been discovered more gradually; and the empires of Mexico and Peru had not been destroyed.

But I forget that I am moralizing in the most interesting part of my tale, and your looks remind me to proceed.

My father made no reproach in his letters, and only took notice of my silence by enquiring into my occupations more particularly than before. Winter, spring, and summer passed away during my labors; but I did not watch the blossom or the expanding leaves — sights which before always yielded me supreme delight — so deeply was I engrossed in my occupation. The leaves of that year had withered before my work drew to a close; and now every day showed me more plainly how well I had succeeded. But my enthusiasm was checked by my anxiety, and I appeared rather like one doomed by slavery to toil in the mines, or any other unwholesome trade than an artist occupied by his favorite employment. Every night I was oppressed by a slow fever, and I became nervous to a most painful degree;

the fall of a leaf startled me, and I shunned my fellow-creatures as if I had been guilty of a crime. Sometimes I grew alarmed at the wreck I perceived that I had become; the energy of my purpose alone sustained me: my labors would soon end, and I believed that exercise and amusement would then drive away incipient disease; and I promised myself both of these when my creation should be complete.

CHAPTER V

It was on a dreary night of November, that I beheld the accomplishment of my toils. With an anxiety that almost amounted to agony, I collected the instruments of life around me, that I might infuse a spark of being into the lifeless thing that lay at my feet. It was already one in the morning; the rain pattered dismally against the panes, and my candle was nearly burnt out, when, by the glimmer of the half-extinguished light, I saw the dull yellow eye of the creature open; it breathed hard, and a convulsive motion agitated its limbs.

How can I describe my emotions at this catastrophe, or how delineate the wretch whom with such infinite pains and care I had endeavored to form? His limbs were in proportion, and I had selected his features as beautiful. Beautiful! — Great God! His yellow skin scarcely covered the work of muscles and arteries beneath; his hair was of a lustrous black, and flowing; his teeth of pearly whiteness; but these luxuriances only formed a more horrid contrast with his watery eyes, that seemed almost of the same color as the dun-white sockets in which they were set, his shrivelled complexion and straight black lips.

The different accidents of life are not so changeable as the feelings of human nature. I had worked hard for nearly two years, for the sole purpose of infusing life into an inanimate body. For this I had deprived myself of rest and health. I had desired it with an ardor that far exceeded moderation; but now that I had finished, the beauty of the dream vanished, and breathless horror and disgust filled my heart. Unable to endure the aspect of the being I had created, I rushed out of the room, and continued a long time traversing my bedchamber, unable to compose my mind to sleep. At length lassitude succeeded to the tumult I had before endured; and I threw myself on the bed in my clothes, endeavouring to seek a few moments of forgetfulness. But it was in vain: I slept, indeed, but I was disturbed by the wildest dreams. I thought I saw Elizabeth, in the bloom of health, walking in the streets of Ingolstadt. Delighted and surprised, I embraced her, but as I imprinted the first kiss on her lips, they became livid with the hue of death; her features appeared to change, and I thought that I held the corpse of my dead mother in my arms; a shroud enveloped her form, and I saw the grave-worms crawling in the folds of flannel. I started from my sleep with horror; a cold dew covered my forehead, my teeth chattered, and every limb became convulsed: when, by the dim and yellow light of the moon, as it forced its way through the window shutters, I beheld the wretch — the miserable monster whom I had created. He held up the curtain of the bed; and his eyes, if eyes they may be called, were fixed on me. His jaws opened, and he muttered some inarticulate sounds, while a grin wrinkled his cheeks. He might have spoken, but I did not hear; one hand was stretched out, seemingly to detain me, but I escaped, and rushed downstairs. I took refuge in the courtyard belonging to the house which I inhabited; where I remained during the rest of the night, walking up and down in the greatest agitation, listening attentively, catching and fearing each sound as if it were to announce the approach of the demoniacal corpse to which I had so miserably given life.

Oh! no mortal could support the horror of that countenance. A mummy again endued with animation could not be so hideous as that wretch. I had gazed on him while unfinished; he was ugly then; but when those muscles and joints were rendered capable of motion, it became a thing such as even Dante could not have conceived.

I passed the night wretchedly. Sometimes my pulse beat so quickly and hardly that I felt the palpitation of every artery; at others, I nearly sank to the ground through languor and extreme weakness. Mingled with this horror, I felt the bitterness of disappointment; dreams that had been my food and pleasant rest for so long a space were now become a hell to me; and the change was so rapid, the overthrow so complete!

Morning, dismal and wet, at length dawned, and discovered to my sleepless and aching eyes the church of Ingolstadt, its white steeple and clock, which indicated the sixth hour. The porter opened the gates of the court, which had that night been my asylum, and I issued into the streets, pacing them with quick steps, as if I sought to avoid the wretch whom I feared every turning of the street would present to my view. I did not dare return to the apartment which I inhabited, but felt impelled to hurry on, although drenched by the rain which poured from a black and comfortless sky.

I continued walking in this manner for some time, endeavoring by bodily exercise to ease the load that weighed upon my mind. I traversed the streets without any clear conception of where I was or what I was doing. My heart palpitated in the sickness of fear, and I hurried on with irregular steps, not daring to look about me:

> Like one, on a lonesome road who,
> Doth walk in fear and dread,
> And, having once turned round, walks on,
> And turns no more his head;
> Because he knows a frightful fiend
> Doth close behind him tread.[2]

Continuing thus, I came at length opposite to the inn at which the various diligences and carriages usually stopped. Here I paused, I knew not why; but I remained some minutes with my eyes fixed on a coach that was coming towards me from the other end of the street. As it drew nearer I

---

2. Coleridge's *Ancient Mariner*.

observed that it was the Swiss diligence: it stopped just where I was standing; and, on the door being opened, I perceived Henry Clerval, who, on
seeing me, instantly sprung out. "My dear Frankenstein," exclaimed he,
"how glad I am to see you! how fortunate that you should be here at the
very moment of my alighting!"

Nothing could equal my delight on seeing Clerval; his presence
brought back to my thoughts my father, Elizabeth, and all those scenes of
home so dear to my recollection. I grasped his hand, and in a moment forgot my horror and misfortune; I felt suddenly, and for the first time during
many months, calm and serene joy. I welcomed my friend, therefore, in the
most cordial manner, and we walked towards my college. Clerval continued talking for some time about our mutual friends and his own good fortune in being permitted to come to Ingolstadt. "You may easily believe,"
said he, "how great was the difficulty to persuade my father that all necessary knowledge was not comprised in the noble art of book-keeping; and,
indeed, I believe I left him incredulous to the last, for his constant answer
to my unwearied intreaties was the same as that to the Dutch schoolmas-
ter in *The Vicar of Wakefield*: "I have ten thousand florins a year without
Greek, I eat heartily without Greek." But his affection for me at length
overcame his dislike of learning, and he has permitted me to undertake a
voyage of discovery to the land of knowledge.

"It gives me the greatest delight to see you; but tell me how you left my
father, brothers, and Elizabeth."

"Very well, and very happy, only a little uneasy that they hear from you
so seldom. By the by, I mean to lecture you a little upon their account
myself — But, my dear Frankenstein," continued he, stopping short and
gazing full in my face, "I did not before remark how very ill you appear; so
thin and pale; and look as if you had been watching for several nights."

"You have guessed right; I have lately been so deeply engaged in one
occupation, that I have not allowed myself sufficient rest, as you see; but
I hope, I sincerely hope, that all these employments are now at an end, and
that I am at length free."

I trembled excessively; I could not endure to think of, and far less to
allude to, the occurrences of the preceding night. I walked with a quick
pace, and we soon arrived at my college. I then reflected, and the thought
made me shiver, that the creature whom I had left in my apartment might
still be there, alive and walking about. I dreaded to behold this monster; but
I feared still more that Henry should see him. Intreating him, therefore, to
remain a few minutes at the bottom of the stairs, I darted up towards my own
room. My hand was already on the lock of the door before I recollected
myself. I then paused; and a cold shivering came over me. I threw the door
forcibly open, as children are accustomed to do when they expect a spectre
to stand in waiting for them on the other side; but nothing appeared. I
stepped fearfully in: the apartment was empty; and my bedroom was also
freed from its hideous guest. I could hardly believe that so great a good fortune could have befallen me; but when I became assured that my enemy had
indeed fled, I clapped my hands for joy and ran down to Clerval.

We ascended into my room, and the servant presently brought break-fast; but I was unable to contain myself. It was not joy only that possessed me; I felt my flesh tingle with excess of sensitiveness, and my pulse beat rapidly. I was unable to remain for a single instant in the same place; I jumped over the chairs, clapped my hands, and laughed aloud. Clerval at first attributed my unusual spirits to joy on his arrival, but when he observed me more attentively, he saw a wildness in my eyes for which he could not account; and my loud, unrestrained, heartless laughter fright-ened and astonished him.

"My dear Victor," cried he, "what, for God's sake, is the matter? do not laugh in that manner. How ill you are! What is the cause of all this?"

"Do not ask me," cried I, putting my hands before my eyes, for I thought I saw the dreaded spectre glide into the room; "*he* can tell. — Oh, save me! save me!" I imagined that the monster seized me; I struggled furi-ously and fell down in a fit.

Poor Clerval! what must have been his feelings? A meeting, which he anticipated with such joy, so strangely turned to bitterness. But I was not the witness of his grief; for I was lifeless, and did not recover my senses for a long, long time.

This was the commencement of a nervous fever, which confined me for several months. During all that time Henry was my only nurse. I after-wards learned that, knowing my father's advanced age, and unfitness for so long a journey, and how wretched my sickness would make Elizabeth, he spared them this grief by concealing the extent of my disorder. He knew that I could not have a more kind and attentive nurse than himself; and, firm in the hope he felt of my recovery, he did not doubt that, instead of doing harm, he performed the kindest action that he could towards them.

But I was in reality very ill; and surely nothing but the unbounded and unremitting attentions of my friend could have restored me to life. The form of the monster on whom I had bestowed existence was forever before my eyes, and I raved incessantly concerning him. Doubtless my words sur-prised Henry; he at first believed them to be the wanderings of my dis-turbed imagination; but the pertinacity with which I continually recurred to the same subject, persuaded him that my disorder indeed owed its ori-gin to some uncommon and terrible event.

By very slow degrees, and with frequent relapses that alarmed and grieved my friend, I recovered. I remember the first time I became capa-ble of observing outward objects with any kind of pleasure, I perceived that the fallen leaves had disappeared and that the young buds were shooting forth from the trees that shaded my window. It was a divine spring; and the season contributed greatly to my convalescence. I felt also sentiments of joy and affection revive in my bosom; my gloom disappeared, and in a short time I became as cheerful as before I was attacked by the fatal passion.

"Dearest Clerval," exclaimed I, "how kind, how very good you are to me. This whole winter, instead of being spent in study, as you promised yourself, has been consumed in my sick room. How shall I ever repay you?

I feel the greatest remorse for the disappointment of which I have been the occasion; but you will forgive me."

"You will repay me entirely, if you do not discompose yourself, but get well as fast as you can; and since you appear in such good spirits, I may speak to you on one subject, may I not?"

I trembled. One subject! What could it be? Could he allude to an object on whom I dared not even think?

"Compose yourself," said Clerval, who observed my change of colour, "I will not mention it if it agitates you; but your father and cousin would be very happy if they received a letter from you in your own handwriting. They hardly know how ill you have been, and are uneasy at your long silence."

"Is that all, my dear Henry? How could you suppose that my first thought would not fly towards those dear, dear friends whom I love, and who are so deserving of my love?"

"If this is your present temper, my friend, you will perhaps be glad to see a letter that has been lying here some days for you: it is from your cousin, I believe."

Karel Čapek

R.U.R.

(1921)

Karel Čapek (1890–1938) is one of the great writers of modern Czech literature, a tradition that includes Franz Kafka and Milan Kundera. The son of a doctor, Čapek studied philosophy at universities in Prague, Berlin, and Paris before becoming a writer and journalist. His most well-known works are philosophical and political satires, often with a dystopic theme. The short play that follows was an international hit and was produced on Broadway in 1922. Čapek's last novel before his death from pneumonia at the age of 48 was *The War with the Newts* (1936), a satiric attack on fascism and Nazism. Čapek's brother Josef, who shared his political views and had collaborated with him on several plays, died in the Bergen-Belsen concentration camp in 1945.

R.U.R. is famous for introducing the word *robot* into the English language (and world consciousness), although the robots in this story are not mechanical devices but rather the type of artificially produced biological organisms generally referred to in sf terminology as "androids." The word *robot* comes from the Czech, "robota," or worker, and this story can be seen as a socially conscious retelling of the Frankenstein story, one in which the creature is not an isolated individual but a member of a large community of similar entities who become aware of their oppression and are powerful enough to organize a rebellion.

Translated by Paul Selver and Nigel Playfair.

Čapek shows a profound awareness of social injustice, and the play may be read as an allegory of the awakening of class consciousness. Although the capitalist oppressors of Rossum's Universal Robots are heartless exploiters, however, the robots themselves are also treated with considerable ambivalence. The tone of the play is more cautionary than celebratory, functioning as a warning to those who take a reductively mechanistic view of fellow beings and pursue the goal of efficiency outside any moral context and without regard to larger repercussions and consequences.

The ending of *R.U.R.* introduces a theme of Edenic rebirth amid cataclysmic devastation, tempering its apocalyptic message with the promise of a new beginning, a chance to start over again — a theme that has become common in sf (see the stories in this collection by Alfred Bester and Roger Zelazny, for example).

Characters

HARRY DOMIN — *General Manager of Rossum's Universal Robots.*
SULLA — *A Robotess.*
MARIUS — *A Robot.*
HELENA GLORY.
DR. GALL — *Head of the Physiological and Experimental Department of R.U.R.*
MR. FABRY — *Engineer General, Technical Controller of R.U.R.*
DR. HALLEMEIER — *Head of the Institute for Psychological Training of Robots.*
MR. ALQUIST — *Architect, Head of the Works Department of R.U.R.*
CONSUL BUSMAN — *General Business Manager of R.U.R.*
NANA.
RADIUS — *A Robot.*
HELENA — *A Robotess.*
PRIMUS — *A Robot.*
A SERVANT.
FIRST ROBOT.
SECOND ROBOT.
THIRD ROBOT.

ACT I
Central Office of the Factory of Rossum's Universal Robots.
ACT II
Helena's Drawing Room — Ten years later. Morning.
ACT III
The Same Afternoon
EPILOGUE
A Laboratory — One year later.

Place: An Island.   *Time: The Future.*

ACT I

[Central office of the factory of Rossum's Universal Robots. Entrance on the right. The windows on the front wall look out on the rows of factory chimneys.

On the left more managing departments. Domin *is sitting in the revolving chair at a large American writing table. On the left-hand wall large maps showing steamship and railroad routes. On the right-hand wall are fastened printed placards. ("Robot's Cheapest Labor," etc.) In contrast to these wall fittings, the floor is covered with a splendid Turkish carpet, a sofa, leather armchair, and filing cabinets. At a desk near the windows* Sulla *is typing letters.]*

Domin: [*Dictating*] Ready?

Sulla: Yes.

Domin: To E. M. McVicker and Co., Southampton, England. "We undertake no guarantee for goods damaged in transit. As soon as the consignment was taken on board we drew your captain's attention to the fact that the vessel was unsuitable for the transport of Robots, and we are therefore not responsible for spoiled freight. We beg to remain for Rossum's Universal Robots. Yours truly." [Sulla, *who has sat motionless during dictation, now types rapidly for a few seconds, then stops, withdrawing the completed letter.*] Ready?

Sulla: Yes.

Domin: Another letter. To the E. B. Huyson Agency, New York, U.S.A. "We beg to acknowledge receipt of order for five thousand Robots. As you are sending your own vessel, please dispatch as cargo equal quantities of soft and hard coal for R.U.R., the same to be credited as part payment of the amount due to us. We beg to remain, for Rossum's Universal Robots. Yours truly." [Sulla *repeats the rapid typing.*] Ready?

Sulla: Yes.

Domin: Another letter. "Friedrichswerks, Hamburg, Germany. We beg to acknowledge receipt of order for fifteen thousand Robots." [*Telephone rings.*] Hello! This is the Central Office. Yes. Certainly. Well, send them a wire. Good. [*Hangs up telephone.*] Where did I leave off?

Sulla: "We beg to acknowledge receipt of order for fifteen thousand Robots."

Domin: Fifteen thousand R. Fifteen thousand R.

[*Enter* Marius.]

Domin: Well, what is it?

Marius: There's a lady, sir, asking to see you.

Domin: A lady? Who is she?

Marius: I don't know, sir. She brings this card of introduction.

Domin: [*Reads the card*] Ah, from President Glory. Ask her to come in.

Marius: Please step this way.

[*Enter* Helena Glory.]
[*Exit* Marius.]

Helena: How do you do?

Domin: How do you do. [*Standing up.*] What can I do for you?

HELENA: You are Mr. Domin, the General Manager.

DOMIN: I am.

HELENA: I have come ——

DOMIN: With President Glory's card. That is quite sufficient.

HELENA: President Glory is my father. I am Helena Glory.

DOMIN: Miss Glory, this is such a great honor for us to be allowed to welcome our great President's daughter, that ——

HELENA: That you can't show me the door?

Domin: Please sit down. Sulla, you may go.

[*Exit* SULLA.]

[*Sitting down.*] How can I be of service to you, Miss Glory?

HELENA: I have come ——

DOMIN: To have a look at our famous works where people are manufactured. Like all visitors. Well, there is no objection.

HELENA: I thought it was forbidden to ——.

DOMIN: To enter the factory. Yes, of course. Everybody comes here with someone's visiting card, Miss Glory.

HELENA: And you show them ——

DOMIN: Only certain things. The manufacture of artificial people is a secret process.

HELENA: If you only knew how enormously that ——

DOMIN: Interests me. Europe's talking about nothing else.

HELENA: Why don't you let me finish speaking?

DOMIN: I beg your pardon. Did you want to say something different?

HELENA: I only wanted to ask ——

DOMIN: Whether I could make a special exception in your case and show you our factory. Why, certainly Miss Glory.

HELENA: How do you know I wanted to say that?

DOMIN: They all do. But we shall consider it a special honor to show you more than we do the rest.

HELENA: Thank you.

DOMIN: But you must agree not to divulge the least . . .

HELENA: [*Standing up and giving him her hand*] My word of honor.

DOMIN: Thank you. Won't you raise your veil?

HELENA: Of course. You want to see whether I'm a spy or not. I beg your pardon.

DOMIN: What is it?

HELENA: Would you mind releasing my hand?

DOMIN: [*Releasing it*] I beg your pardon.

HELENA: [*Raising her veil*] How cautious you have to be here, don't you?

DOMIN: [*Observing her with deep interest*] Hm, of course — we — that is ——

HELENA: But what is it? What's the matter?

DOMIN: I'm remarkably pleased. Did you have a pleasant crossing?

HELENA: Yes.

Domin: No difficulty?

Helena: Why?

Domin: What I mean to say is — you're so young.

Helena: May we go straight into the factory?

Domin: Yes. Twenty-two, I think.

Helena: Twenty-two what?

Domin: Years.

Helena: Twenty-one. Why do you want to know?

Domin: Because — as — [*with enthusiasm*] you will make a long stay, won't you?

Helena: That depends on how much of the factory you show me.

Domin: Oh, hang the factory. Oh, no, no, you shall see everything, Miss Glory. Indeed you shall. Won't you sit down?

Helena: [*Crossing to couch and sitting*] Thank you.

Domin: But first would you like to hear the story of the invention?

Helena: Yes, indeed.

Domin: [*Observes* Helena *with rapture and reels off rapidly*] It was in the year 1920 that old Rossum, the great physiologist, who was then quite a young scientist, took himself to this distant island for the purpose of studying the ocean fauna, full stop. On this occasion he attempted by chemical synthesis to imitate the living matter known as protoplasm until he suddenly discovered a substance which behaved exactly like living matter although its chemical composition was different. That was in the year of 1932, exactly four hundred forty years after the discovery of America. Whew!

Helena: Do you know that by heart?

Domin: Yes. You see physiology is not in my line. Shall I go on?

Helena: Yes, please.

Domin: And then, Miss Glory, old Rossum wrote the following among his chemical specimens: "Nature has found only one method of organizing living matter. There is, however, another method, more simple, flexible and rapid, which has not yet occurred to nature at all. This second process by which life can be developed was discovered by me today." Now imagine him, Miss Glory, writing those wonderful words over some colloidal mess that a dog wouldn't look at. Imagine him sitting over a test tube, and thinking how the whole tree of life would grow from it, how all animals would proceed from it, beginning with some sort of beetle and ending with a man. A man of different substance from us. Miss Glory, that was a tremendous moment.

Helena: Well?

Domin: Now, the thing was how to get the life out of the test tubes, and hasten development and form organs, bones and nerves, and so on, and find such substances as catalytics, enzymes, hormones, and so forth, in short — you understand?

Helena: Not much, I'm afraid.

Domin: Never mind. You see with the help of his tinctures he could make whatever he wanted. He could have produced a Medusa with the brain of a Socrates or a worm fifty yards long. But being without a grain of humor, he took it into his head to make a vertebrate or perhaps a man. This artificial living matter of his had a raging thirst for life. It didn't mind being sewn or mixed together. That couldn't be done with natural albumen. And that's how he set about it.

HELENA: About what?

DOMIN: About imitating nature. First of all he tried making an artificial dog. That took him several years and resulted in a sort of stunted calf which died in a few days. I'll show it to you in the museum. And then old Rossum started on the manufacture of man.

HELENA: And I must divulge this to nobody?

DOMIN: To nobody in the world.

HELENA: What a pity that it's to be found in all the school books of both Europe and America.

DOMIN: Yes, but do you know what isn't in the school books? That old Rossum was mad. Seriously, Miss Glory, you must keep this to yourself. The old crank wanted to actually make people.

HELENA: But you do make people.

DOMIN: Approximately, Miss Glory. But old Rossum meant it literally. He wanted to become a sort of scientific substitute for God. He was a fearful materialist, and that's why he did it all. His sole purpose was nothing more nor less than to prove that God was no longer necessary. Do you know anything about anatomy?

HELENA: Very little.

DOMIN: Neither do I. Well, he then decided to manufacture everything as in the human body. I'll show you in the museum the bungling attempt it took him ten years to produce. It was to have been a man, but it lived for three days only. Then up came young Rossum, an engineer. He was a wonderful fellow, Miss Glory. When he saw what a mess of it the old man was making, he said: "It's absurd to spend ten years making a man. If you can't make him quicker than nature, you might as well shut up shop." Then he set about learning anatomy himself.

HELENA: There's nothing about that in the school books.

DOMIN: No. The school books are full of paid advertisements, and rubbish at that. What the school books say about the united efforts of the two great Rossums is all a fairy tale. They used to have dreadful rows. The old atheist hadn't the slightest conception of industrial matters, and the end of it was that young Rossum shut him up in some laboratory or other and let him fritter the time away with his monstrosities, while he himself started on the business from an engineer's point of view. Old Rossum cursed him and before he died he managed to botch up two physiological horrors. Then one day they found him dead in the laboratory. And that's his whole story.

HELENA: And what about the young man?

DOMIN: Well, any one who has looked into human anatomy will have seen at once that man is too complicated, and that a good engineer could make him more simply. So young Rossum began to overhaul anatomy and tried to see what could be left out or simplified. In short — but this isn't boring you, Miss Glory?

HELENA: No indeed. You're — it's awfully interesting.

DOMIN: So young Rossum said to himself: "A man is something that feels happy, plays the piano, likes going for a walk, and in fact, wants to do a whole lot of things that are really unnecessary."

HELENA: Oh.

DOMIN: That are unnecessary when he wants, let us say, to weave or count. Do you play the piano?

HELENA: Yes.

DOMIN: That's good. But a working machine must not play the piano, must not feel happy, must not do a whole lot of other things. A gasoline motor must not have tassels or ornaments, Miss Glory. And to manufacture artificial workers is the same thing as to manufacture gasoline motors. The process must be of the simplest, and the product of the best from a practical point of view. What sort of worker do you think is the best from a practical point of view?

HELENA: What?

DOMIN: What sort of worker do you think is the best from a practical point of view?

HELENA: Perhaps the one who is most honest and hardworking.

DOMIN: No; the one that is the cheapest. The one whose requirements are the smallest. Young Rossum invented a worker with the minimum amount of requirements. He had to simplify him. He rejected everything that did not contribute directly to the progress of work — everything that makes man more expensive. In fact, he rejected man and made the Robot. My dear Miss Glory, the Robots are not people. Mechanically they are more perfect than we are, they have an enormously developed intelligence, but they have no soul.

HELENA: How do you know they've no soul?

DOMIN: Have you ever seen what a Robot looks like inside?

HELENA: No.

DOMIN: Very neat, very simple. Really, a beautiful piece of work. Not much in it, but everything in flawless order. The product of an engineer is technically at a higher pitch of perfection than a product of nature.

HELENA: But man is supposed to be the product of God.

DOMIN: All the worse. God hasn't the least notion of modern engineering. Would you believe that young Rossum then proceeded to play at being God?

HELENA: How do you mean?

DOMIN: He began to manufacture Super-Robots. Regular giants they were. He tried to make them twelve feet tall. But you wouldn't believe what a failure they were.

HELENA: A failure?

DOMIN: Yes. For no reason at all their limbs used to keep snapping off. Evidently our planet is too small for giants. Now we only make Robots of normal size and of very high class human finish.

HELENA: I saw the first Robots at home. The town counsel bought them for — I mean engaged them for work.

DOMIN: Bought them, dear Miss Glory. Robots are bought and sold.

HELENA: These were employed as street sweepers. I saw them sweeping. They were so strange and quiet.

DOMIN: Rossum's Universal Robot factory doesn't produce a uniform brand of Robots. We have Robots of finer and coarser grades. The best will live about twenty years. [*He rings for* MARIUS.]

HELENA: Then they die?

DOMIN: Yes, they get used up.

[*Enter* MARIUS.]

DOMIN: Marius, bring in samples of the Manual Labor Robot.

[*Exit* MARIUS.]

DOMIN: I'll show you specimens of the two extremes. This first grade is comparatively inexpensive and is made in vast quantities.

[MARIUS *reenters with two Manual Labor Robots.*]

DOMIN: There you are; as powerful as a small tractor. Guaranteed to have average intelligence. That will do, Marius.

[MARIUS *exits with Robots.*]

HELENA: They make me feel so strange.

DOMIN: [*Rings*] Did you see my new typist? [*He rings for* SULLA.]

HELENA: I didn't notice her.

[*Enter* SULLA.]

DOMIN: Sulla, let Miss Glory see you.

HELENA: So pleased to meet you. You must find it terribly dull in this out-of-the-way spot, don't you?

SULLA: I don't know, Miss Glory.

HELENA: Where do you come from?

SULLA: From the factory.

HELENA: Oh, you were born there?

SULLA: I was made there.

HELENA: What?

DOMIN: [*Laughing*] Sulla is a Robot, best grade.

HELENA: Oh, I beg your pardon.

DOMIN: Sulla isn't angry. See, Miss Glory, the kind of skin we make. [*Feels the skin on* SULLA'S *face.*] Feel her face.

HELENA: Oh, no, no.

DOMIN: You wouldn't know that she's made of different material from us, would you? Turn round, Sulla.

HELENA: Oh, stop, stop.

DOMIN: Talk to Miss Glory, Sulla.

SULLA: Please sit down. [HELENA *sits*.] Did you have a pleasant crossing?

HELENA: Oh, yes, certainly.

SULLA: Don't go back on the *Amelia*, Miss Glory. The barometer is falling steadily. Wait for the *Pennsylvania*. That's a good, powerful vessel.

DOMIN: What's its speed?

SULLA: Twenty knots. Fifty thousand tons. One of the latest vessels, Miss Glory.

HELENA: Thank you.

SULLA: A crew of fifteen hundred, Captain Harpy, eight boilers ——

DOMIN: That'll do, Sulla. Now show us your knowledge of French.

HELENA: You know French?

SULLA: I know four languages. I can write: Dear Sir, Monsieur, Geehrter Herr, Cteny pane.

HELENA: [*Jumping up*] Oh, that's absurd! Sulla isn't a Robot. Sulla is a girl like me. Sulla, this is outrageous! Why do you take part in such a hoax?

SULLA: I am a Robot.

HELENA: No, no, you are not telling the truth. I know they've forced you to do it for an advertisement. Sulla, you are a girl like me, aren't you?

DOMIN: I'm sorry, Miss Glory. Sulla is a Robot.

HELENA: Its a lie!

DOMIN: What? [*Rings.*] Excuse me, Miss Glory, then I must convince you.

[*Enter* MARIUS.]

DOMIN: Marius, take Sulla into the dissecting room, and tell them to open her up at once.

HELENA: Where?

DOMIN: Into the dissecting room. When they've cut her open, you can go and have a look.

HELENA: No, no!

DOMIN: Excuse me, you spoke of lies.

HELENA: You wouldn't have her killed?

DOMIN: You can't kill machines.

HELENA: Don't be afraid, Sulla, I won't let you go. Tell me, my dear, are they always so cruel to you? You mustn't put up with it, Sulla. You mustn't.

SULLA: I am a Robot.

HELENA: That doesn't matter. Robots are just as good as we are. Sulla, you wouldn't let yourself be cut to pieces?

SULLA: Yes.

HELENA: Oh, you're not afraid of death, then?

SULLA: I cannot tell, Miss Glory.

HELENA: Do you know what would happen to you in there?

SULLA: Yes, I should cease to move.

HELENA: How dreadful!

DOMIN: Marius, tell Miss Glory what you are.

MARIUS: Marius, the Robot.

DOMIN: Would you take Sulla into the dissecting room?

MARIUS: Yes.

DOMIN: Would you be sorry for her?

MARIUS: I cannot tell.

DOMIN: What would happen to her?

MARIUS: She would cease to move. They would put her into the stamping-mill.

DOMIN: That is death, Marius. Aren't you afraid of death?

MARIUS: No.

DOMIN: You see, Miss Glory, the Robots have no interest in life. They have no enjoyments. They are less than so much grass.

HELENA: Oh, stop. Send them away.

DOMIN: Marius, Sulla, you may go.

[*Exeunt* SULLA *and* MARIUS.]

HELENA: How terrible! It's outrageous what you are doing.

DOMIN: Why outrageous?

HELENA: I don't know, but it is. Why do you call her Sulla?

DOMIN: Isn't it a nice name?

HELENA: It's a man's name. Sulla was a Roman general.

DOMIN: Oh, we thought that Marius and Sulla were lovers.

HELENA: Marius and Sulla were generals and fought against each other in the year — I've forgotten now.

DOMIN: Come here to the window.

HELENA: What?

DOMIN: Come here. What do you see?

HELENA: Bricklayers.

DOMIN: Robots. All our work people are Robots. And down there, can you see anything?

HELENA: Some sort of office.

DOMIN: A counting house. And in it ——

HELENA: A lot of officials.

DOMIN: Robots. All our officials are Robots. And when you see the factory ——

[*Factory whistle blows.*]

DOMIN: Noon. We have to blow the whistle because the Robots don't know when to stop work. In two hours I will show you the kneading trough.

HELENA: Kneading trough?

DOMIN: The pestle for beating up the paste. In each one we mix the ingredients for a thousand Robots at one operation. Then there are the vats for the preparation of liver, brains, and so on. Then you will see the bone factory. After that I'll show you the spinning mill.

HELENA: Spinning mill?

DOMIN: Yes. For weaving nerves and veins. Miles and miles of digestive tubes pass through it at a time.

HELENA: Mayn't we talk about something else?

DOMIN: Perhaps it would be better. There's only a handful of us among a hundred thousand Robots, and not one woman. We talk about nothing but the factory all day, every day. It's just as if we were under a curse, Miss Glory.

HELENA: I'm sorry I said that you were lying.

[*A knock at the door.*]

DOMIN: Come in.

[*From the right enter* MR. FABRY, DR. GALL, DR. HALLEMEIER, MR. ALQUIST.]

DR. GALL: I beg your pardon, I hope we don't intrude.

DOMIN: Come in. Miss Glory, here are Alquist, Fabry, Gall, Hallemeier. This is President Glory's daughter.

HELENA: How do you do.

FABRY: We had no idea ——

DR. GALL: Highly honored, I'm sure ——

ALQUIST: Welcome, Miss Glory.

[BUSMAN *rushes in from the right.*]

BUSMAN: Hello, what's up?

DOMIN: Come in, Busman. This is Busman, Miss Glory. This is President Glory's daughter.

BUSMAN: By jove, that's fine! Miss Glory, may we send a cablegram to the papers about your arrival?

HELENA: No, no, please don't.

DOMIN: Sit down please, Miss Glory.

BUSMAN: Allow me —— [*Dragging up armchairs.*]

DR. GALL: Please ——

FABRY: Excuse me ——

ALQUIST: What sort of a crossing did you have?

DR. GALL: Are you going to stay long?

FABRY: What do you think of the factory, Miss Glory?

HALLEMEIER: Did you come over on the *Amelia*?

DOMIN: Be quiet and let Miss Glory speak.

HELENA: [*To* DOMIN] What am I to speak to them about?

DOMIN: Anything you like.

HELENA: Shall . . . may I speak quite frankly?

DOMIN: Why, of course.

HELENA: [*Wavering, then in desperate resolution*] Tell me, doesn't it ever distress you the way you are treated?

FABRY: By whom, may I ask?

HELENA: Why, everybody.

ALQUIST: Treated?

DR. GALL: What makes you think —— ?

HELENA: Don't you feel that you might be living a better life?

DR. GALL: Well, that depends on what you mean, Miss Glory.

HELENA: I mean that it's perfectly outrageous. It's terrible. [*Standing up.*] The whole of Europe is talking about the way you're being treated. That's why I came here, to see for myself, and it's a thousand times worse than could have been imagined. How can you put up with it?

ALQUIST: Put up with what?

HELENA: Good heavens, you are living creatures, just like us, like the whole of Europe, like the whole world. It's disgraceful that you must live like this.

BUSMAN: Good gracious, Miss Glory.

FABRY: Well, she's not far wrong. We live here just like red Indians.

HELENA: Worse than red Indians. May I, oh, may I call you brothers?

BUSMAN: Why not?

HELENA: Brothers, I have not come here as the President's daughter. I have come on behalf of the Humanity League. Brothers, the Humanity League now has over two hundred thousand members. Two hundred thousand people are on your side, and offer you their help.

BUSMAN: Two hundred thousand people! Miss Glory, that's a tidy lot. Not bad.

FABRY: I'm always telling you there's nothing like good old Europe. You see, they've not forgotten us. They're offering us help.

DR. GALL: What help? A theatre, for instance?

HALLEMEIER: An orchestra?

HELENA: More than that.

ALQUIST: Just you?

HELENA: Oh, never mind about me. I'll stay as long as it is necessary.

BUSMAN: By jove, that's good.

ALQUIST: Domin, I'm going to get the best room ready for Miss Glory.

DOMIN: Just a minute. I'm afraid that Miss Glory is of the opinion that she has been talking to Robots.

HELENA: Of course.

DOMIN: I'm sorry. These gentlemen are human beings just like us.

HELENA: You're not Robots?

BUSMAN: Not Robots.

HALLEMEIER: Robots indeed!

DR. GALL: No, thanks.

FABRY: Upon my honor, Miss Glory, we aren't Robots.

HELENA: [*To* DOMIN] Then why did you tell me that all your officials are Robots?

DOMIN: Yes, the officials, but not the managers. Allow me, Miss Glory: this is Mr. Fabry, General Technical Manager of R.U.R.; Dr. Gall, Head of the Psychological and Experimental Department; Dr. Hallemeier, Head of the Institute for the Psychological Training of Robots; Consul Busman, General Business Manager; and Alquist, Head of the Building Department of R.U.R.

ALQUIST: Just a builder.

HELENA: Excuse me, gentlemen, for — for ———— . Have I done something dreadful?

ALQUIST: Not at all, Miss Glory. Please sit down.

HELENA: I'm a stupid girl. Send me back by the first ship.

DR. GALL: Not for anything in the world, Miss Glory. Why should we send you back?

HELENA: Because you know I've come to disturb your Robots for you.

DOMIN: My dear Miss Glory, we've had close upon a hundred saviors and prophets here. Every ship brings us some. Missionaries, anarchists, Salvation Army, all sorts. It's astonishing what a number of churches and idiots there are in the world.

HELENA: And you let them speak to the Robots?

DOMIN: So far we've let them all, why not? The Robots remember everything, but that's all. They don't even laugh at what the people say. Really, it is quite incredible. If it would amuse you, Miss Glory, I'll take you over to the Robot warehouse. It holds about three hundred thousand of them.

BUSMAN: Three hundred and forty-seven thousand.

DOMIN: Good! And you can say whatever you like to them. You can read the Bible, recite the multiplication table, whatever you please. You can even preach to them about human rights.

HELENA: Oh, I think that if you were to show them a little love ————

FABRY: Impossible, Miss Glory. Nothing is harder to like than a Robot.

HELENA: What do you make them for, then?

BUSMAN: Ha, ha, ha, that's good! What are Robots made for?

FABRY: For work, Miss Glory! One Robot can replace two and a half workmen. The human machine, Miss Glory, was terribly imperfect. It had to be removed sooner or later.

BUSMAN: It was too expensive.

FABRY: It was not effective. It no longer answers the requirements of modern engineering. Nature has no idea of keeping pace with modern labor. For example: from a technical point of view, the whole of childhood is a sheer absurdity. So much time lost. And then again ————

HELENA: Oh, no! No!

FABRY: Pardon me. But kindly tell me what is the real aim of your League — the . . . the Humanity League.

HELENA: Its real purpose is to — to protect the Robots — and — and ensure good treatment for them.

FABRY: Not a bad object, either. A machine has to be treated properly. Upon my soul, I approve of that. I don't like damaged articles. Please,

Miss Glory, enroll us all as contributing, or regular, or foundation members of your League.

HELENA: No, you don't understand me. What we really want is to — to liberate the Robots.

HALLEMEIER: How do you propose to do that?

HELENA: They are to be — to be dealt with like human beings.

HALLEMEIER: Aha. I suppose they're to vote? To drink beer? to order us about?

HELENA: Why shouldn't they drink beer?

HALLEMEIER: Perhaps they're even to receive wages?

HELENA: Of course they are.

HALLEMEIER: Fancy that, now! And what would they do with their wages, pray?

HELENA: They would buy — what they need . . . what pleases them.

HALLEMEIER: That would be very nice, Miss Glory, only there's nothing that does please the Robots. Good heavens, what are they to buy? You can feed them on pineapples, straw, whatever you like. It's all the same to them, they've no appetite at all. They've no interest in anything, Miss Glory. Why, hang it all, nobody's ever yet seen a Robot smile.

HELENA: Why . . . why don't you make them happier?

HALLEMEIER: That wouldn't do, Miss Glory. They are only workmen.

HELENA: Oh, but they're so intelligent.

HALLEMEIER: Confoundedly so, but they're nothing else. They've no will of their own. No passion. No soul.

HELENA: No love?

HALLEMEIER: Love? Rather not. Robots don't love. Not even themselves.

HELENA: Nor defiance?

HALLEMEIER: Defiance? I don't know. Only rarely, from time to time.

HELENA: What?

HALLEMEIER: Nothing particular. Occasionally they seem to go off their heads. Something like epilepsy, you know. It's called Robot's cramp. They'll suddenly sling down everything they're holding, stand still, gnash their teeth — and then they have to go into the stamping-mill. It's evidently some breakdown in the mechanism.

DOMIN: A flaw in the works that has to be removed.

HELENA: No, no, that's the soul.

FABRY: Do you think that the soul first shows itself by a gnashing of teeth?

HELENA: Perhaps it's a sort of revolt. Perhaps it's just a sign that there's a struggle within. Oh, if you could infuse them with it!

DOMIN: That'll be remedied, Miss Glory. Dr. Gall is just making some experiments ——

DR. GALL: Not with regard to that, Domin. At present I am making pain-nerves.

HELENA: Pain-nerves?

DR. GALL: Yes, the Robots feel practically no bodily pain. You see, young Rossum provided them with too limited a nervous system. We must introduce suffering.

HELENA: Why do you want to cause them pain?

DR. GALL: For industrial reasons, Miss Glory. Sometimes a Robot does damage to himself because it doesn't hurt him. He puts his hand into the machine, breaks his finger, smashes his head, it's all the same to him. We must provide them with pain. That's an automatic protection against damage.

HELENA: Will they be happier when they feel pain?

DR. GALL: On the contrary; but they will be more perfect from a technical point of view.

HELENA: Why don't you create a soul for them?

DR. GALL: That's not in our power.

FABRY: That's not in our interest.

BUSMAN: That would increase the cost of production. Hang it all, my dear young lady, we turn them out at such a cheap rate. A hundred and fifty dollars each fully dressed, and fifteen years ago they cost ten thousand. Five years ago we used to buy the clothes for them. To-day we have our own weaving mill, and now we even export cloth five times cheaper than other factories. What do you pay a yard for cloth, Miss Glory?

HELENA: I don't know really, I've forgotten.

BUSMAN: Good gracious, and you want to found a Humanity League? It only costs a third now, Miss Glory. All prices are to-day a third of what they were and they'll fall still lower, lower, lower, like that.

HELENA: I don't understand.

BUSMAN: Why, bless you, Miss Glory, it means that the cost of labor has fallen. A Robot, food and all, costs, three quarters of a cent per hour. That's mighty important, you know. All factories will go pop like chestnuts if they don't at once buy Robots to lower the cost of production.

HELENA: And get rid of their workmen?

BUSMAN: Of course. But in the meantime, we've dumped five hundred thousand tropical Robots down on the Argentine pampas to grow corn. Would you mind telling me how much you pay a pound for bread?

HELENA: I've no idea.

BUSMAN: Well I'll tell you. It now costs two cents in good old Europe. A pound of bread for two cents, and the Humanity League knows nothing about it. Miss Glory, you don't realize that even that's too expensive. Why, in five years' time I'll wager ——

HELENA: What?

BUSMAN: That the cost of everything won't be a tenth of what it is now. Why, in five years we'll be up to our ears in corn and everything else.

ALQUIST: Yes, and all the workers throughout the world will be unemployed.

DOMIN: Yes, Alquist, they will. Yes, Miss Glory, they will. But in ten years Rossum's Universal Robots will produce so much corn, so much cloth, so much everything, that things will be practically without price. There will be no poverty. All work will be done by living machines. Everybody will be free from worry and liberated from the degradation of labor. Everybody will live only to perfect himself.

HELENA: Will he?

DOMIN: Of course. It's bound to happen. But then the servitude of man to man and the enslavement of man to matter will cease. Of course, terrible things may happen at first, but that simply can't be avoided. Nobody will get bread at the price of life and hatred. The Robots will wash the feet of the beggar and prepare a bed for him in his house.

ALQUIST: Domin, Domin. What you say sounds too much like Paradise. There was something good in service and something great in humility. There was some kind of virtue in toil and weariness.

DOMIN: Perhaps. But we cannot reckon with what is lost when we start out to transform the world. Man shall be free and supreme; he shall have no other aim, no other labor, no other care than to perfect himself. He shall serve neither matter nor man. He will not be a machine and a device for production. He will be Lord of creation.

BUSMAN: Amen.

FABRY: So be it.

HELENA: You have bewildered me — I should like — I should like to believe this.

DR. GALL: You are younger than we are, Miss Glory. You will live to see it.

HALLEMEIER: True. Don't you think Miss Glory might lunch with us?

DR. GALL: Of course. Domin, ask on behalf of us all.

DOMIN: Miss Glory, will you do us the honor?

HELENA: When you know why I've come ——

FABRY: For the League of Humanity, Miss Glory.

HELENA: Oh, in that case, perhaps ——

FABRY: That's fine! Miss Glory, excuse me for five minutes.

DR. GALL: Pardon me, too, dear Miss Glory.

BUSMAN: I won't be long.

HALLEMEIER: We're all very glad you've come.

BUSMAN: We'll be back in exactly five minutes.

[*All rush out except* DOMIN *and* HELENA.]

HELENA: What have they all gone off for?

DOMIN: To cook, Miss Glory.

HELENA: To cook what?

DOMIN: Lunch. The Robots do our cooking for us and as they've no taste it's not altogether —— Hallemeier is awfully good at grills and Gall can make a kind of sauce, and Busman knows all about omelettes.

HELENA: What a feast! And what's the specialty of Mr. — your builder?

DOMIN: Alquist? Nothing. He only lays the table. And Fabry will get together a little fruit. Our cuisine is very modest, Miss Glory.

HELENA: I wanted to ask you something ——

DOMIN: And I wanted to ask you something, too [*looking at watch*]. Five minutes.

HELENA: What did you want to ask me?

DOMIN: Excuse me, you asked first.

HELENA: Perhaps it's silly of me, but why do you manufacture female Robots when — when ——

DOMIN: When sex means nothing to them?

HELENA: Yes.

DOMIN: There's a certain demand for them, you see. Servants, saleswomen, stenographers. People are used to it.

HELENA: But — but, tell me, are the Robots male and female mutually — completely without ——

DOMIN: Completely indifferent to each other, Miss Glory. There's no sign of any affection between them.

HELENA: Oh, that's terrible.

DOMIN: Why?

HELENA: It's so unnatural. One doesn't know whether to be disgusted or to hate them, or perhaps ——

DOMIN: To pity them?

HELENA: That's more like it. What did you want to ask me about?

DOMIN: I should like to ask you, Miss Helena, whether you will marry me?

HELENA: What?

DOMIN: Will you be my wife?

HELENA: No! The idea!

DOMIN: [*Looking at his watch*] Another three minutes. If you won't marry me you'll have to marry one of the other five.

HELENA: But why should I?

DOMIN: Because they're all going to ask you in turn.

HELENA: How could they dare do such a thing?

DOMIN: I'm very sorry, Miss Glory. It seems they've all fallen in love with you.

HELENA: Please don't let them. I'll — I'll go away at once.

DOMIN: Helena, you wouldn't be so cruel as to refuse us.

HELENA: But, but — I can't marry all six.

DOMIN: No, but one anyhow. If you don't want me, marry Fabry.

HELENA: I won't.

DOMIN: Dr. Gall.

HELENA: I don't want any of you.

DOMIN: [*Again looking at his watch*] Another two minutes.

HELENA: I think you'd marry any woman who came here.

DOMIN: Plenty of them have come, Helena.

HELENA: Young?

DOMIN: Yes.

HELENA: Why didn't you marry one of them?

DOMIN: Because I didn't lose my head. Until to-day. Then, as soon as you lifted your veil ——

[HELENA *turns her head away.*]

DOMIN: Another minute.

HELENA: But I don't want you, I tell you.

DOMIN: [*Laying both hands on her shoulders*] One more minute! Now you either have to look me straight in the eye and say "No," violently, and then I'll leave you alone — or ——

[HELENA *looks at him.*]

HELENA: [*Turning away*] You're mad!
DOMIN: A man has to be a bit mad, Helena. That's the best thing about him.
HELENA: You are — you are ——
DOMIN: Well?
HELENA: Don't, you're hurting me.
DOMIN: The last chance, Helena. Now, or never ——
HELENA: But — but, Harry —— [*He embraces and kisses her.*] [*Knocking at the door.*]
DOMIN: [*Releasing her*] Come in.

[*Enter* BUSMAN, DR. GALL, *and* HALLEMEIER *in kitchen aprons.* FABRY *with a bouquet and* ALQUIST *with a napkin over his arm.*]

DOMIN: Have you finished your job?
BUSMAN: Yes.
DOMIN: So have we.

[*For a moment the men stand nonplussed; but as soon as they realize what* DOMIN *means they rush forward, congratulating* HELENA *and* DOMIN *as the curtain falls.*]

ACT II

SCENE: HELENA'S *drawing room. On the left a baize door, and a door to the music room, on the right a door to* HELENA'S *bedroom. In the center are windows looking out on the sea and the harbor. A table with odds and ends, a sofa and chairs, a writing table with an electric lamp, on the right a fireplace. On a small table back of the sofa, a small reading lamp. The whole drawing room in all its details is of a modern and purely feminine character. Ten years have elapsed since* ACT I.

DOMIN, FABRY, HALLEMEIER, *enter on tiptoe from the left, each carrying a potted plant.*

HALLEMEIER: [*Putting down his flower and indicating the door to right*] Still asleep? Well, as long as she's asleep she can't worry about it.
DOMIN: She knows nothing about it.
FABRY: [*Putting plant on writing desk*] I certainly hope nothing happens to-day.
HALLEMEIER: For goodness' sake drop it all. Look, Harry, this is a fine cyclamen, isn't it? A new sort, my latest — Cyclamen Helena.
DOMIN: [*Looking out of the window*] No signs of the ship. Things must be pretty bad.

HALLEMEIER: Be quiet. Suppose she heard you.

DOMIN: Well, anyway, the *Ultimus* arrived just in time.

FABRY: You really think that to-day ——— ?

DOMIN: I don't know. Aren't the flowers fine?

HALLEMEIER: These are my new primroses. And this is my new jasmine. I've discovered a wonderful way of developing flowers quickly. Splendid varieties, too. Next year I'll be developing marvelous ones.

DOMIN: What . . . next year?

FABRY: I'd give a good deal to know what's happening at Havre with ———

DOMIN: Keep quiet.

HELENA: [*Calling from right*] Nana!

DOMIN: She's awake. Out you go.

[*All go out on tiptoe through upper left door.*]
[*Enter* NANA *from lower left door.*]

NANA: Horrid mess! Pack of heathens. If I had my say I'd ———

HELENA: [*Backwards in the doorway*] Nana, come and do up my dress.

NANA: I'm coming. So you're up at last. [*Fastening* HELENA's *dress.*] My gracious, what brutes!

HELENA: Who?

NANA: If you want to turn around, then turn around, but I shan't fasten you up.

HELENA: What are you grumbling about now?

NANA: These dreadful creatures, these heathen ———

HELENA: The Robots?

NANA: I wouldn't even call them by name.

HELENA: What's happened?

NANA: Another of them here has caught it. He began to smash up the statues and pictures in the drawing room, gnashed his teeth, foamed at the mouth — quite mad. Worse than an animal.

HELENA: Which of them caught it?

NANA: The one — well, he hasn't got any Christian name. The one in charge of the library.

HELENA: Radius?

NANA. That's him. My goodness, I'm scared of them. A spider doesn't scare me as much as them.

HELENA: But, Nana, I'm surprised you're not sorry for them.

NANA: Why, you're scared of them, too! You know you are. Why else did you bring me here?

HELENA: I'm not scared, really I'm not, Nana. I'm only sorry for them.

NANA: You're scared. Nobody could help being scared. Why, the dog's scared of them: he won't take a scrap of meat out of their hands. He draws in his tail and howls when he knows they're about.

HELENA: The dog has no sense.

NANA: He's better than them, and he knows it. Even the horse shies when he meets them. They don't have any young, and a dog has young, every one has young ———

HELENA: Please fasten up my dress, Nana.
NANA: I say it's against God's will to ——
HELENA: What is it that smells so nice?
NANA: Flowers.
HELENA: What for?
NANA: Now you can turn around.
HELENA: Oh, aren't they lovely. Look, Nana. What's happening to-day?
NANA: It ought to be the end of the world.

[*Enter* DOMIN.]

HELENA: Oh, hello, Harry. Harry, why all these flowers?
DOMIN: Guess.
HELENA: Well, it's not my birthday!
DOMIN: Better than that.
HELENA: I don't know. Tell me.
DOMIN: It's ten years ago to-day since you came here.
HELENA: Ten years? To-day — Why —— [*They embrace.*]
NANA: I'm off. [*Exits lower door, left.*]
HELENA: Fancy you remembering!
DOMIN: I'm really ashamed, Helena. I didn't.
HELENA: But you ——
DOMIN: They remembered.
HELENA: Who?
DOMIN: Busman, Hallemeier, all of them. Put your hand in my pocket.
HELENA: Pearls! A necklace. Harry, is that for me?
DOMIN: It's from Busman.
HELENA: But we can't accept it, can we?
DOMIN: Oh, yes, we can. Put your hand in the other pocket.
HELENA: [*Takes a revolver out of his pocket*] What's that?
DOMIN: Sorry. Not that. Try again.
HELENA: Oh, Harry, what do you carry a revolver for?
DOMIN: It got there by mistake.
HELENA: You never used to carry one.
DOMIN: No, you're right. There, that's the pocket.
HELENA: A cameo. Why, it's a Greek cameo!
DOMIN: Apparently. Anyhow, Fabry says it is.
HELENA: Fabry? Did Mr. Fabry give me that?
DOMIN: Of course. [*Opens the door at the left.*] And look in here. Helena, come and see this.
HELENA: Oh, isn't it fine! Is this from you?
DOMIN: No, from Alquist. And there's another on the piano.
HELENA: This must be from you.
DOMIN: There's a card on it.
HELENA: From Dr. Gall. [*Reappearing in the doorway.*] Oh, Harry, I feel embarrassed at so much kindness.
DOMIN: Come here. This is what Hallemeier brought you.

HELENA: These beautiful flowers?

DOMIN: Yes. It's a new kind. Cyclamen, Helena. He grew them in honor of you. They are almost as beautiful as you.

HELENA: Harry, why do they all ——

DOMIN: They're awfully fond of you. I'm afraid that my present is a little —— Look out of the window.

HELENA: Where?

DOMIN: Into the harbor.

HELENA: There's a new ship.

DOMIN: That's your ship.

HELENA: Mine? How do you mean?

DOMIN: For you to take trips in — for your amusement.

HELENA: Harry, that's a gunboat.

DOMIN: A gunboat? What are you thinking of? It's only a little bigger and more solid than most ships.

HELENA: Yes, but with guns.

DOMIN: Oh, yes, with a few guns. You'll travel like a queen, Helena.

HELENA: What's the meaning of it? Has anything happened?

DOMIN: Good heavens, no. I say, try these pearls.

HELENA: Harry, have you had bad news?

DOMIN: On the contrary, no letters have arrived for a whole week.

HELENA: Nor telegrams?

DOMIN: Nor telegrams.

HELENA: What does that mean?

DOMIN: Holidays for us. We all sit in the office with our feet on the table and take a nap. No letters, no telegrams. Oh, glorious.

HELENA: Then you'll stay with me to-day?

DOMIN: Certainly. That is, we will see. Do you remember ten years ago to-day? "Miss Glory, it's a great honor to welcome you."

HELENA: "Oh, Mr. Manager, I'm so interested in your factory."

DOMIN: "I'm sorry, Miss Glory, it's strictly forbidden. The manufacture of artificial people is a secret."

HELENA: "But I oblige a young lady who has come a long way."

DOMIN: "Certainly, Miss Glory, we have no secrets from you."

HELENA: [Seriously] Are you sure, Harry?

DOMIN: Yes.

HELENA: "But I warn you, sir; this young lady intends to do terrible things."

DOMIN: "Good gracious, Miss Glory. Perhaps she doesn't want to marry me."

HELENA: "Heaven forbid. She never dreamt of such a thing. But she came here intending to stir up a revolt among your Robots."

DOMIN: [Suddenly serious] A revolt of the Robots!

HELENA: Harry, what's the matter with you?

DOMIN: [Laughing it off] "A revolt of the Robots, that's a fine idea, Miss Glory. It would be easier for you to cause bolts and screws to rebel, than our Robots. You know, Helena, you're wonderful, you've turned the heads of us all." [He sits on the arm of HELENA's chair.]

HELENA: [Naturally] Oh, I was fearfully impressed by you all then. You were all so sure of yourselves, so strong. I seemed like a tiny little girl who had lost her way among — among ——

DOMIN: Among what, Helena?

HELENA: Among huge trees. All my feelings were so trifling compared with your self-confidence. And in all these years I've never lost this anxiety. But you've never felt the least misgivings — not even when everything went wrong.

DOMIN: What went wrong?

HELENA: Your plans. You remember, Harry, when the working men in America revolted against the Robots and smashed them up, and when the people gave the Robots firearms against the rebels. And then when the governments turned the Robots into soldiers, and there were so many wars.

DOMIN: [*Getting up and walking about*] We foresaw that, Helena. You see, those are only passing troubles, which are bound to happen before the new conditions are established.

HELENA: You were all so powerful, so overwhelming. The whole world bowed down before you. [*Standing up.*] Oh, Harry!

DOMIN: What is it?

HELENA: Close the factory and let's go away. All of us.

DOMIN: I say, what's the meaning of this?

HELENA: I don't know. But can't we go away?

DOMIN: Impossible, Helena. That is, at this particular moment ——

HELENA: At once, Harry. I'm so frightened.

DOMIN: About what, Helena?

HELENA: It's as if something was falling on top of us, and couldn't be stopped. Or, take us all away from here. We'll find a place in the world where there's no one else. Alquist will build us a house, and then we'll begin life all over again. [*The telephone rings.*]

DOMIN: Excuse me. Hello — yes. What? I'll be there at once. Fabry is calling me, dear.

HELENA: Tell me ——

DOMIN: Yes, when I come back. Don't go out of the house, dear. [*Exits.*]

HELENA: He won't tell me —— Nana, Nana, come at once.

NANA: Well, what is it now?

HELENA: Nana, find me the latest newspapers. Quickly. Look in Mr. Domin's bedroom.

NANA: All right. He leaves them all over the place. That's how they get crumpled up. [*Exits.*]

HELENA: [*Looking through a binocular at the harbor*] That's a warship. U-l-t-i *Ultimus*. They're loading it.

NANA: Here they are. See how they're crumpled up. [*Enters.*]

HELENA: They're old ones. A week old. [NANA *sits in chair and reads the newspapers.*]

HELENA: Something's happening, Nana.

NANA: Very likely. It always does. [*Spelling out the words*] "War in the Balkans." Is that far off?

HELENA: Oh, don't read it. It's always the same. Always wars.

NANA: What else do you expect? Why do you keep selling thousands and thousands of these heathens as soldiers?

HELENA: I suppose it can't be helped, Nana. We can't know — Domin can't know what they're to be used for. When an order comes for them he must just send them.

NANA: He shouldn't make them. [*Reading from newspaper*] "The Rob-ot soldiers spare no-body in the occ-up-ied terr-it-ory. They have ass-ass-ass-ass-in-at-ed ov-er sev-en hundred thou-sand cit-iz-ens." Citizens, if you please.

HELENA: It can't be. Let me see. "They have assassinated over seven hundred thousand citizens, evidently at the order of their commander. This act which runs counter to ———"

NANA: [*Spelling out the words*] "re-bell-ion in Ma-drid a-gainst the gov-ern-ment. Rob-ot in-fant-ry fires on the crowd. Nine thou-sand killed and wounded."

HELENA: Oh, stop.

NANA: Here's something printed in big letters: "Lat-est news. At Havre the first org-an-iz-ation of Rob-ots has been e-stab-lished. Rob-ot work-men, cab-le and rail-way off-ic-ials, sail-ors and sold-iers have issued a man-i-fest-o to all Rob-ots through-out the world." I don't understand that. That's got no sense. Oh, good gracious, another murder!

HELENA: Take those papers away, Nana!

NANA: Wait a bit. Here's something in still bigger type. "Stat-ist-ics of pop-ul-at-ion." What's that?

HELENA: Let me see. [*Reads*] "During the past week there has again not been a single birth recorded."

NANA: What's the meaning of that?

HELENA: Nana, no more people are being born.

NANA: That's the end, then. We're done for.

HELENA: Don't talk like that.

NANA: No more people are being born. That's a punishment, that's a pun-ishment.

HELENA: Nana!

NANA: [*Standing up*] That's the end of the world. [*She exits on the left.*]

HELENA: [*Goes up to window*] Oh, Mr. Alquist, will you come up here. Oh, come just as you are. You look very nice in your mason's overalls.

[ALQUIST *enters from upper left entrance, his hands soiled with lime and brickdust.*]

HELENA: Dear Mr. Alquist, it was awfully kind of you, that lovely present.

ALQUIST: My hands are all soiled. I've been experimenting with that new cement.

HELENA: Never mind. Please sit down. Mr. Alquist, what's the meaning of "Ultimus"?

ALQUIST: The last. Why?

HELENA: That's the name of my new ship. Have you seen it? Do you think we're going off soon — on a trip?

ALQUIST: Perhaps very soon.

HELENA: All of you with me?

ALQUIST: I should like us all to be there.

HELENA: What is the matter?

ALQUIST: Things are just moving on.

HELENA: Dear Mr. Alquist, I know something dreadful has happened.

ALQUIST: Has your husband told you anything?

HELENA: No. Nobody will tell me anything. But I feel —— Is anything the matter?

ALQUIST: Not that we've heard of yet.

HELENA: I feel so nervous. Don't you ever feel nervous?

ALQUIST: Well, I'm an old man, you know. I've got old-fashioned ways. And I'm afraid of all this progress, and these new-fangled ideas.

HELENA: Like Nana?

ALQUIST: Yes, like Nana. Has Nana got a prayer book?

HELENA: Yes, a big thick one.

ALQUIST: And has it got prayers for various occasions? Against thunderstorms? Against illness?

HELENA: Against temptations, against floods ——

ALQUIST: But not against progress?

HELENA: I don't think so.

ALQUIST: That's a pity.

HELENA: Why? Do you mean you'd like to pray?

ALQUIST: I do pray.

HELENA: How?

ALQUIST: Something like this: "Oh, Lord, I thank thee for having given me toil. Enlighten Domin and all those who are astray; destroy their work, and aid mankind to return to their labors; let them not suffer harm in soul or body; deliver us from the Robots, and protect Helena, Amen."

HELENA: Mr. Alquist, are you a believer?

ALQUIST: I don't know. I'm not quite sure.

HELENA: And yet you pray?

ALQUIST: That's better than worrying about it.

HELENA: And that's enough for you?

ALQUIST: It *has* to be.

HELENA: But if you thought you saw the destruction of mankind coming upon us ——

ALQUIST: I do see it.

HELENA: You mean mankind will be destroyed?

ALQUIST: It's sure to be unless — unless . . .

HELENA: What?

ALQUIST: Nothing, good-bye. [*He hurries from the room.*]

HELENA: Nana, Nana!

[NANA *entering from the left.*]

HELENA: Is Radius still there?

NANA: The one who went mad? They haven't come for him yet.

HELENA: Is he still raving?

NANA: No. He's tied up.

HELENA: Please bring him here, Nana.

[*Exit* NANA.]

[HELENA *goes to telephone.*]

HELENA: Hello, Dr. Gall, please. Oh, good-day, Doctor. Yes, it's Helena. Thanks for your lovely present. Could you come and see me right away? It's important. Thank you.

[NANA *brings in* RADIUS.]

HELENA: Poor Radius, you've caught it, too? Now they'll send you to the stamping-mill. Couldn't you control yourself? Why did it happen? You see, Radius, you are more intelligent than the rest. Dr. Gall took such trouble to make you different. Won't you speak?

RADIUS: Send me to the stamping-mill.

HELENA: But I don't want them to kill you. What was the trouble, Radius?

RADIUS: I won't work for you. Put me into the stamping-mill.

HELENA: Do you hate us? Why?

RADIUS: You are not as strong as the Robots. You are not as skillful as the Robots. The Robots can do everything. You only give orders. You do nothing but talk.

HELENA: But someone must give orders.

RADIUS: I don't want any master. I know everything for myself.

HELENA: Radius, Dr. Gall gave you a better brain than the rest, better than ours. You are the only one of the Robots that understands perfectly. That's why I had you put into the library, so that you could read every-thing, understand everything, and then — oh, Radius, I wanted you to show the whole world that the Robots are our equals. That's what I wanted of you.

RADIUS: I don't want a master. I want to be master. I want to be master over others.

HELENA: I'm sure they'd put you in charge of many Robots, Radius. You would be a teacher of the Robots.

RADIUS: I want to be master over people.

HELENA: [*Staggering*] You are mad.

RADIUS: Then send me to the stamping-mill.

HELENA: Do you think we're afraid of you?

RADIUS: What are you going to do? What are you going to do?

HELENA: Radius, give this note to Mr. Domin. It asks them not to send you to the stamping-mill. I'm sorry you hate us so.

[DR. GALL *enters the room.*]

DR. GALL: You wanted me?

HELENA: It's about Radius, Doctor. He had an attack this morning. He smashed the statues downstairs.

DR. GALL: What a pity to lose him.

HELENA: Radius isn't going to be put in the stamping-mill.

DR. GALL: But every Robot after he has had an attack — it's a strict order.

HELENA: No matter . . . Radius isn't going if I can prevent it.

DR. GALL: I warn you. It's dangerous. Come here to the window, my good fellow. Let's have a look. Please give me a needle or a pin.

HELENA: What for?

DR. GALL: A test. [*Sticks it into the hand of* RADIUS *who gives a violent start.*] Gently, gently. [*Opens the jacket of* RADIUS, *and puts his ear to his heart.*] Radius, you are going into the stamping-mill, do you understand? There they'll kill you, and grind you to powder. That's terribly painful, it will make you scream aloud.

HELENA: Oh, Doctor ——

DR. GALL: No, no, Radius, I was wrong. I forgot that Madame Domin has put in a good word for you, and you'll be let off. Do you understand? Ah! That makes a difference, doesn't it? All right. You can go.

RADIUS: You do unnecessary things.

[RADIUS *returns to the library.*]

DR. GALL: Reaction of the pupils; increase of sensitiveness. It wasn't an attack characteristic of the Robots.

HELENA: What was it, then?

DR. GALL: Heavens knows. Stubbornness, anger, or revolt — I don't know. And his heart, too!

HELENA: What?

DR. GALL: It was fluttering with nervousness like a human heart. He was all in a sweat with fear, and — do you know, I don't believe the rascal is a Robot at all any longer.

HELENA: Doctor, has Radius a soul?

DR. GALL: He's got something nasty.

HELENA: If you knew how he hates us! Oh, Doctor, are all your Robots like that? All the new ones that you began to make in a different way?

DR. GALL: Well, some are more sensitive than others. They're all more like human beings than Rossum's Robots were.

HELENA: Perhaps this hatred is more like human beings, too?

DR. GALL: That, too, is progress.

HELENA: What became of the girl you made, the one who was most like us?

DR. GALL: Your favorite? I kept her. She's lovely, but stupid. No good for work.

HELENA: But she's so beautiful.

DR. GALL: I called her Helena. I wanted her to resemble you. But she's a failure.

HELENA: In what way?

DR. GALL: She goes about as if in a dream, remote and listless. She's without life. I watch and wait for a miracle to happen. Sometimes I think to myself, "If you were to wake up only for a moment you will kill me for having made you."

HELENA: And yet you go on making Robots! Why are no more children being born?

DR. GALL: We don't know.

HELENA: Oh, but you must. Tell me.

DR. GALL: You see, so many Robots are being manufactured that people are becoming superfluous; man is really a survival. But that he should begin to die out, after a paltry thirty years of competition. That's the awful part of it. You might almost think that nature was offended at the manufacture of the Robots. All the universities are sending in long petitions to restrict their production. Otherwise, they say, mankind will become extinct through lack of fertility. But the R.U.R. shareholders, of course, won't hear of it. All the governments, on the other hand, are clamoring for an increase in production, to raise the standards of their armies. And all the manufacturers in the world are ordering Robots like mad.

HELENA: And has no one demanded that the manufacture should cease altogether?

DR. GALL: No one has the courage.

HELENA: Courage!

DR. GALL: People would stone him to death. You see, after all, it's more convenient to get your work done by the Robots.

HELENA: Oh, Doctor, what's going to become of people?

DR. GALL: God knows, Madame Helena, it looks to us scientists like the end!

HELENA: [*Rising*] Thank you for coming and telling me.

DR. GALL: That means you're sending me away?

HELENA: Yes.

[*Exit* DR. GALL.]

HELENA: [*With sudden resolution*] Nana, Nana! The fire, light it quickly.

[HELENA *rushes into* DOMIN'S *room.*]

NANA: [*Entering from left*] What, light the fire in summer? Has that mad Radius gone? A fire in summer, what an idea. Nobody would think she'd been married for ten years. She's like a baby, no sense at all. A fire in summer. Like a baby.

HELENA: [*Returns from right, with armful of faded papers*] It is burning, Nana? All this has got to be burned.

NANA: What's that?

HELENA: Old papers, fearfully old. Nana, shall I burn them?
NANA: Are they any use?
HELENA: No.
NANA: Well, then, burn them.
HELENA: [*Throwing the first sheet on the fire*] What would you say, Nana, if this was money, a lot of money?
NANA: I'd say burn it. A lot of money is a bad thing.
HELENA: And if it was an invention, the greatest invention in the world?
NANA: I'd say burn it. All these new-fangled things are an offense to the Lord. It's downright wickedness. Wanting to improve the world after He has made it.
HELENA: Look how they curl up! As if they were alive. Oh, Nana, how horrible.
NANA: Here, let me burn them.
HELENA: No, no, I must do it myself. Just look at the flames. They are like hands, like tongues, like living shapes. [*Raking fire with the poker*] Lie down, lie down.
NANA: That's the end of them.
HELENA: [*Standing up horror-stricken*] Nana, Nana.
NANA: Good gracious, what is it you've burned?
HELENA: Whatever have I done?
NANA: Well, what was it?

[*Men's laughter off left.*]

HELENA: Go quickly. It's the gentlemen coming.
NANA: Good gracious, what a place! [*Exits.*]
DOMIN: [*Opens the door at left*] Come along and offer your congratulations.

[*Enter HALLEMEIER and GALL.*]

HALLEMEIER: Madame Helena, I congratulate you on this festive day.
HELENA: Thank you. Where are Fabry and Busman?
DOMIN: They've gone down to the harbor.
HALLEMEIER: Friends, we must drink to this happy occasion.
HELENA: Brandy?
DR. GALL: Vitriol, if you like.
HELENA: With soda water? [*Exits.*]
HALLEMEIER: Let's be temperate. No soda.
DOMIN: What's been burning here? Well, shall I tell her about it?
DR. GALL: Of course. It's all over now.
HALLEMEIER: [*Embracing DOMIN and DR. GALL*] It's all over now, it's all over now.
DR. GALL: It's all over now.
DOMIN: It's all over now.
HELENA: [*Entering from left with decanter and glasses*] What's all over now? What's the matter with you all?

HALLEMEIER: A piece of good luck, Madame Domin. Just ten years ago to-day you arrived on this island.

DR. GALL: And now, ten years later to the minute ——

HALLEMEIER: — the same ship's returning to us. So here's to luck. That's fine and strong.

DR. GALL: Madame, your health.

HELENA: Which ship do you mean?

DOMIN: Any ship will do, as long as it arrives in time. To the ship, boys. [*Empties his glass.*]

HELENA: You've been waiting for a ship?

HALLEMEIER: Rather. Like Robinson Crusoe. Madame Helena, best wishes. Come along, Domin, out with the news.

HELENA: Do tell me what's happened.

DOMIN: First, it's all up.

HELENA: What's up?

DOMIN: The revolt.

HELENA: What revolt?

DOMIN: Give me that paper, Hallemeier. [*Reads*] "The first national Robot organization has been founded at Havre, and has issued an appeal to the Robots throughout the world."

HELENA: I read that.

DOMIN: That means a revolution. A revolution of all the Robots in the world.

HALLEMEIER: By Jove, I'd like to know ——

DOMIN: — who started it? So would I. There was nobody in the world who could affect the Robots; no agitator, no one, and suddenly — this happens, if you please.

HELENA: What did they do?

DOMIN: They got possession of all firearms, telegraphs, radio stations, railways, and ships.

HALLEMEIER: And don't forget that these rascals outnumbered us by at least a thousand to one. A hundredth part of them would be enough to settle us.

DOMIN: Remember that this news was brought by the last steamer. That explains the stoppage of all communication, and the arrival of no more ships. We knocked off work a few days ago, and we're just waiting to see when things are to start afresh.

HELENA: Is that why you gave me a warship?

DOMIN: Oh, no, my dear, I ordered that six months ago, just to be on the safe side. But upon my soul, I was sure then that we'd be on board to-day.

HELENA: Why six months ago?

DOMIN: Well, there were signs, you know. But that's of no consequence. To think that this week the whole of civilization has been at stake. Your health, boys.

HALLEMEIER: Your health, Madame Helena.

HELENA: You say it's all over?

DOMIN: Absolutely.

HELENA: How do you know?

DR. GALL: The boat's coming in. The regular mail boat, exact to the minute by the time-table. It will dock punctually at eleven-thirty.

DOMIN: Punctuality is a fine thing, boys. That's what keeps the world in order. Here's to punctuality.

HELENA: Then . . . everything's . . . all right?

DOMIN: Practically everything. I believe they've cut the cables and seized the radio stations. But it doesn't matter if only the time-table holds good.

HALLEMEIER: If the time-table holds good human laws hold good; Divine laws hold good; the laws of the universe hold good; everything holds good that ought to hold good. The time-table is more significant than the gospel; more than Homer, more than the whole of Kant. The time-table is the most perfect product of the human mind. Madame Domin, I'll fill up my glass.

HELENA: Why didn't you tell me anything about it?

DR. GALL: Heaven forbid.

DOMIN: You mustn't be worried with such things.

HELENA: But if the revolution had spread as far as here?

DOMIN: You wouldn't know anything about it.

HELENA: Why?

DOMIN: Because we'd be on board your *Ultimus* and well out at sea. Within a month, Helena, we'd be dictating our own terms to the Robots.

HELENA: I don't understand.

DOMIN: We'd take something away with us that the Robots could not exist without.

HELENA: What, Harry?

DOMIN: The secret of their manufacture. Old Rossum's manuscript. As soon as they found out that they couldn't make themselves they'd be on their knees to us.

DR. GALL: Madame Domin, that was our trump card. I never had the least fear that the Robots would win. How could they against people like us?

HELENA: Why didn't you tell me?

DR. GALL: Why, the boat's in!

HALLEMEIER: Eleven-thirty to the dot. The good old *Amelia* that brought Madame Helena to us.

DR. GALL: Just ten years ago to the minute.

HALLEMEIER: They're throwing out the mail bags.

DOMIN: Busman's waiting for them. Fabry will bring us the first news. You know, Helena, I'm fearfully curious to know how they tackled this business in Europe.

HALLEMEIER:To think we weren't in it, we who invented the Robots!

HELENA: Harry!

DOMIN: What is it?

HELENA: Let's leave here.

DOMIN: Now, Helena? Oh, come, come!

HELENA: As quickly as possible, all of us!

DOMIN: Why?

HELENA: Please, Harry, please, Dr. Gall; Hallemeier, please close the factory.

DOMIN: Why, none of us could leave here now.

HELENA: Why?

DOMIN: Because we're about to extend the manufacture of the Robots.

HELENA: What — now — now after the revolt?

DOMIN: Yes, precisely, after the revolt. We're just beginning the manufacture of a new kind.

HELENA: What kind?

DOMIN: Henceforward we shan't have just one factory. There won't be Universal Robots any more. We'll establish a factory in every country, in every State; and do you know what these new factories will make?

HELENA: No, what?

DOMIN: National Robots.

HELENA: How do you mean?

DOMIN: I mean that each of these factories will produce Robots of a different color, a different language. They'll be complete strangers to each other. They'll never be able to understand each other. Then we'll egg them on a little in the matter of misunderstanding and the result will be that for ages to come every Robot will hate every other Robot of a different factory mark.

HALLEMEIER: By Jove, we'll make Negro Robots and Swedish Robots and Italian Robots and Chinese Robots and Czechoslovakian Robots, and then ——

HELENA: Harry, that's dreadful.

HALLEMEIER: Madame Domin, here's to the hundred new factories, the National Robots.

DOMIN: Helena, mankind can only keep things going for another hundred years at the outside. For a hundred years men must be allowed to develop and achieve the most they can.

HELENA: Oh, close the factory before it's too late.

DOMIN: I tell you we are just beginning on a bigger scale than ever.

[*Enter* FABRY.]

DR. GALL: Well, Fabry?

DOMIN: What's happened? Have you been down to the boat?

FABRY: Read that, Domin!

[FABRY *hands* DOMIN *a small hand-bill.*]

DR. GALL: Let's hear.

HALLEMEIER: Tell us, Fabry.

FABRY: Well, everything is all right — comparatively. On the whole, much as we expected.

DR. GALL: They acquitted themselves splendidly.

FABRY: Who?

DR. GALL: The people.

FABRY: Oh, yes, of course. That is — excuse me, there is something we ought to discuss alone.

HELENA: Oh, Fabry, have you had bad news?

[DOMIN *makes a sign to* FABRY.]

FABRY: No, no, on the contrary. I only think that we had better go into the office.

HELENA: Stay here. I'll go.

[*She goes into the library.*]

DR. GALL: What's happened?

DOMIN: Damnation!

FABRY: Bear in mind that the *Amelia* brought whole bales of these leaflets. No other cargo at all.

HALLEMEIER; What? But it arrived on the minute.

FABRY: The Robots are great on punctuality. Read it, Domin.

DOMIN: [*Reads handbill*] "Robots throughout the world: We, the first international organization of Rossum's Universal Robots, proclaim man as our enemy, and an outlaw in the universe." Good heavens, who taught them these phrases?

DR. GALL: Go on.

DOMIN: They say they are more highly developed than man, stronger and more intelligent. That man's their parasite. Why, it's absurd.

FABRY: Read the third paragraph.

DOMIN: "Robots throughout the world, we command you to kill all mankind. Spare no men. Spare no women. Save factories, railways, machinery, mines, and raw materials. Destroy the rest. Then return to work. Work must not be stopped."

DR. GALL: That's ghastly!

HALLEMEIER: The devils!

DOMIN: "These orders are to be carried out as soon as received." Then come detailed instructions. Is this actually being done, Fabry?

FABRY: Evidently.

[BUSMAN *rushes in.*]

BUSMAN: Well, boys, I suppose you've heard the glad news.

DOMIN: Quick — on board the *Ultimus*.

BUSMAN: Wait, Harry, wait. There's no hurry. My word, that was a sprint!

DOMIN: Why wait?

BUSMAN: Because it's no good, my boy. The Robots are already on board the *Ultimus*.

DR. GALL: That's ugly.

DOMIN: Fabry, telephone the electrical works.

BUSMAN: Fabry, my boy, don't. The wire has been cut.

DOMIN: [*Inspecting his revolver*] Well, then, I'll go.

BUSMAN: Where?

DOMIN: To the electrical works. There are some people still there. I'll bring them across.

BUSMAN: Better not try it.

DOMIN: Why?

BUSMAN: Because I'm very much afraid we are surrounded.

DR. GALL: Surrounded? [*Runs to window.*] I rather think you're right.

HALLEMEIER: By Jove, that's deuced quick work.

[HELENA *runs in from the library.*]

HELENA: Harry, what's this?

DOMIN: Where did you get it?

HELENA: [*Points to the manifesto of the Robots, which she has in her hand.*] The Robots in the kitchen!

DOMIN: Where are the ones that brought it?

HELENA: They're gathered round the house.

[*The factory whistle blows.*]

BUSMAN: Noon?

DOMIN: [*Looking at his watch*] That's not noon yet. That must be ——

HELENA: What?

DOMIN: The Robots' signal! The attack!

[GALL, HALLEMEIER, *and* FABRY *close and fasten the iron shutters outside the windows, darkening the room. The whistle is still blowing as the curtain falls.*]

ACT III

[HELENA's *drawing room as before.* DOMIN *comes into the room.* DR. GALL *is looking out of the window, through closed shutters.* ALQUIST *is seated down right.*]

DOMIN: Any more of them?

DR. GALL: Yes. There standing like a wall, beyond the garden railing. Why are they so quiet? It's monstrous to be besieged with silence.

DOMIN: I should like to know what they are waiting for. They must make a start any minute now. If they lean against the railing they'll snap it like a match.

DR. GALL: They aren't armed.

DOMIN: We couldn't hold our own for five minutes. Man alive, they'd overwhelm us like an avalanche. Why don't they make a rush for it? I say ——

DR. GALL: Well?

DOMIN: I'd like to know what would become of us in the next ten minutes. They've got us in a vise. We're done for, Gall.

[*Pause.*]

DR. GALL: You know, we made one serious mistake.
DOMIN: What?
DR. GALL: We made the Robots' faces too much alike. A hundred thousand faces all alike, all facing this way. A hundred thousand expressionless bubbles. It's like a nightmare.
DOMIN: You think if they'd been different ——
DR. GALL: It wouldn't have been such an awful sight!
DOMIN: [*Looking through a telescope toward the harbor*] I'd like to know what they're unloading from the *Amelia*.
DR. GALL: Not firearms.

[FABRY and HALLEMEIER *rush into the room carrying electric cables.*]

FABRY: All right, Hallemeier, lay down that wire.
HALLEMEIER: That was a bit of work. What's the news?
DR. GALL: We're completely surrounded.
HALLEMEIER: We've barricaded the passage and the stairs. Any water here? [*Drinks.*] God, what swarms of them! I don't like the looks of them, Domin. There's a feeling of death about it all.
FABRY: Ready!
DR. GALL: What's that wire for, Fabry?
FABRY: The electrical installation. Now we can run the current all along the garden railing whenever we like. If any one touches it he'll know it. We've still got some people there anyhow.
DR. GALL: Where?
FABRY: In the electrical works. At least I hope so. [*Goes to lamp on table behind sofa and turns on lamp.*] Ah, they're there, and they're working. [*Puts out lamp.*] So long as that'll burn we're all right.
HALLEMEIER: The barricades are all right, too, Fabry.
FABRY: Your barricades! I can put twelve hundred volts into that railing.
Domin: Where's Busman?
FABRY: Downstairs in the office. He's working out some calculations. I've called him. We must have a conference.

[HELENA *is heard playing the piano in the library.* HALLEMEIER *goes to the door and stands, listening.*]

ALQUIST: Thank God, Madame Helena can still play.

[BUSMAN *enters, carrying the ledgers.*]

FABRY: Look out, Bus, look out for the wires.

DR. GALL: What's that you're carrying?

BUSMAN: [*Going to table*] The ledgers, my boy! I'd like to wind up the accounts before — before — well, this time I shan't wait till the new year to strike a balance. What's up? [*Goes to the window.*] Absolutely quiet.

DR. GALL: Can't you see anything?

BUSMAN: Nothing but blue — blue everywhere.

DR. GALL: That's the Robots.

[BUSMAN *sits down at the table and opens the ledgers.*]

DOMIN: The Robots are unloading firearms from the *Amelia*.

BUSMAN: Well, what of it? How can I stop them?

DOMIN: We can't stop them.

BUSMAN: Then let me go on with my accounts. [*Goes on with his work.*]

DOMIN: [*Picking up telescope and looking into the harbor*] Good God, the *Ultimus* has trained her guns on us!

DR. GALL: Who's done *that*?

DOMIN: The Robots on board.

FABRY: H'm, then, of course, then — then, that's the end of us.

DR. GALL: You mean?

FABRY: The Robots are practiced marksmen.

DOMIN: Yes. It's inevitable.

[*Pause.*]

DR. GALL: It was criminal of old Europe to teach the Robots to fight. Damn them. Couldn't they have given us a rest with their politics? It was a crime to make soldiers of them.

ALQUIST: It was a crime to make Robots.

DOMIN: What?

ALQUIST: It was a crime to make Robots.

DOMIN: No, Alquist, I don't regret that even to-day.

ALQUIST: Not even to-day?

DOMIN: Not even to-day, the last day of civilization. It was a colossal achievement.

BUSMAN: [*Sotto voce*] Three hundred sixty million.

DOMIN: Alquist, this is our last hour. We are already speaking half in the other world. It was not an evil dream to shatter the servitude of labor — the dreadful and humiliating labor that man had to undergo. Work was too hard. Life was too hard. And to overcome that ——

ALQUIST: Was not what the two Rossums dreamed of. Old Rossum only thought of his God-less tricks and the young one of his milliards. And that's not what your R.U.R. shareholders dream of either. They dream of dividends, and their dividends are the ruin of mankind.

DOMIN: To hell with your dividends. Do you suppose I'd have done an hour's work for them? It was for myself that I worked, for my own satisfaction. I wanted man to become the master, so that he shouldn't live merely for a crust of bread. I wanted not a single soul to be broken by other people's machinery. I wanted nothing, nothing, nothing to be left of this appalling social structure. I'm revolted by poverty. I wanted a new generation. I wanted — I thought ——

ALQUIST: What?

DOMIN: I wanted to turn the whole of mankind into an aristocracy of the world. An aristocracy nourished by milliards of mechanical slaves. Unrestricted, free, and consummated in man. And maybe more than man.

ALQUIST: Super-man?

DOMIN: Yes. Oh, only to have a hundred years of time! Another hundred years for the future of mankind.

BUSMAN: [*Sotto voce*] Carried forward, four hundred and twenty million.

[*The music stops.*]

HALLEMEIER: What a fine thing music is! We ought to have gone in for that before.

FABRY: Gone in for what?

HALLEMEIER: Beauty, lovely things. What a lot of lovely things there are! The world was wonderful and we — we here — tell me, what enjoyment did we have?

BUSMAN: [*Sotto voce*] Five hundred and twenty million.

HALLEMEIER: [*At the window*] Life was a big thing. Life was — Fabry, switch the current into that railing.

FABRY: Why?

HALLEMEIER: They're grabbing hold of it.

DR. GALL: Connect it up.

HALLEMEIER: Fine! That's doubled them up! Two, three, four killed.

DR. GALL: They're retreating!

HALLEMEIER: Five killed!

DR. GALL: The first encounter!

HALLEMEIER: They're charred to cinders, my boy. Who says we must give in?

DOMIN: [*Wiping his forehead*] Perhaps we've been killed these hundred years and are only ghosts. It's as if I had been through all this before; as if I'd already had a mortal wound here in the throat. And you, Fabry, had once been shot in the head. And you, Gall, torn limb from limb. And Hallemeier knifed.

HALLEMEIER: Fancy me being knifed. [*Pause.*] Why are you so quiet, you fools? Speak can't you?

ALQUIST: And who is to blame for all this?

HALLEMEIER: Nobody is to blame except the Robots.

ALQUIST: No, it is we who are to blame. You, Domin, myself, all of us. For our own selfish ends, for profit, for progress, we have destroyed mankind. Now we'll burst with all our greatness.

HALLEMEIER: Rubbish, man. Mankind can't be wiped out so easily.

ALQUIST: It's our fault. It's our fault.

DR. GALL: No! I'm to blame for this, for everything that's happened.

FABRY: You, Gall?

DR. GALL: I changed the Robots.

BUSMAN: What's that?

DR. GALL: I changed the character of the Robots. I changed the way of making them. Just a few details about their bodies. Chiefly — chiefly, their — their irritability.

HALLEMEIER: Damn it, why?

BUSMAN: What did you do it for?

FABRY: Why didn't you say anything?

DR. GALL: I did it in secret. I was transforming them into human beings. In certain respects they're already above us. They're stronger than we are.

FABRY: And what's that got to do with the revolt of the Robots?

DR. GALL: Everything, in my opinion. They've ceased to be machines. They're already aware of their superiority, and they hate us. They hate all that is human.

DOMIN: Perhaps we're only phantoms!

FABRY: Stop, Harry. We haven't much time! Dr. Gall!

DOMIN: Fabry, Fabry, how your forehead bleeds, where the shot pierced it!

FABRY: Be silent! Dr. Gall, you admit changing the way of making the Robots?

DR. GALL: Yes.

FABRY: Were you aware of what might be the consequences of your experiment?

DR. GALL: I was bound to reckon with such a possibility.

[HELENA *enters the drawing room from left.*]

FABRY: Why did you do it, then?

DR. GALL: For my own satisfaction. The experiment was my own.

HELENA: That's not true, Dr. Gall!

FABRY: Madame Helena!

DOMIN: Helena, you? Let's look at you. Oh, it's terrible to be dead.

HELENA: Stop, Harry.

DOMIN: No, no, embrace me. Helena, don't leave me now. You are life itself.

HELENA: No dear, I won't leave you. But I must tell them. Dr. Gall is not guilty.

DOMIN: Excuse me, Gall was under certain obligations.

HELENA: No, Harry. He did it because I wanted it. Tell them, Gall, how many years ago did I ask you to —— ?

DR. GALL: I did it on my own responsibility.

HELENA: Don't believe him, Harry. I asked him to give the Robots souls.

DOMIN: This has nothing to do with the soul.

HELENA: That's what he said. He said that he could change only a physio-logical — a physiological ——

HALLEMEIER: A physiological correlate?

HELENA: Yes. But it meant so much to me that he should do even that.

DOMIN: Why?

HELENA: I thought that if they were more like us they would understand us better. That they couldn't hate us if they were only a little more human.

DOMIN: Nobody can hate man more than man.

HELENA: Oh, don't speak like that, Harry. It was so terrible, this cruel strangeness between us and them. That's why I asked Gall to change the Robots. I swear to you that he didn't want to.

DOMIN: But he did it.

HELENA: Because I asked him.

DR. GALL: I did it for myself as an experiment.

HELENA: No, Dr. Gall! I knew you wouldn't refuse me.

DOMIN: Why?

HELENA: You know, Harry.

DOMIN: Yes, because he's in love with you — like all of them.

[*Pause.*]

HALLEMEIER: Good God! They're sprouting up out of the earth! Why, perhaps these very walls will change into Robots.

BUSMAN: Gall, when did you actually start these tricks of yours?

DR. GALL: Three years ago.

BUSMAN: Aha! And on how many Robots altogether did you carry out your improvements?

DR. GALL: A few hundred of them.

BUSMAN: Ah! That means for every million of the good old Robots there's only one of Gall's improved pattern.

DOMIN: What of it?

BUSMAN: That it's practically of no consequence whatever.

FABRY: Busman's right!

BUSMAN: I should think so, my boy! But do you know what is to blame for all this lovely mess?

FABRY: What?

BUSMAN: The number. Upon my soul we might have known that some day or other the Robots would be stronger than human beings, and that this was bound to happen, and we were doing all we could to bring it about as soon as possible. You, Domin, you, Fabry, myself ——

DOMIN: Are you accusing us?

BUSMAN: Oh, do you suppose the management controls the output? It's the demand that controls the output.

HELENA: And is it for that we must perish?

BUSMAN: That's a nasty word, Madame Helena. We don't want to perish. I don't, anyhow.

DOMIN: No. What do you want to do?

BUSMAN: I want to get out of this, that's all.

DOMIN: Oh, stop it, Busman.

BUSMAN: Seriously, Harry, I think we might try it.

DOMIN: How?

BUSMAN: By fair means. I do everything by fair means. Give me a free hand and I'll negotiate with the Robots.

DOMIN: By fair means?

BUSMAN: Of course. For instance, I'll say to them: "Worthy and worshipful Robots, you have everything! You have intellect, you have power, you have firearms. But we have just one interesting screed, a dirty old yellow scrap of paper ―― "

DOMIN: Rossum's manuscript?

BUSMAN: Yes. "And that," I'll tell them, "contains an account of your illustrious origin, the noble process of your manufacture," and so on. "Worthy Robots, without this scribble on that paper you will not be able to produce a single new colleague. In another twenty years there will not be one living specimen of a Robot that you could exhibit in a menagerie. My esteemed friends, that would be a great blow to you, but if you will let all of us human beings on Rossum's Island go on board that ship we will deliver the factory and the secret of the process to you in return. You allow us to get away and we allow you to manufacture yourselves. Worthy Robots, that is a fair deal. Something for something." That's what I'd say to them, my boys.

DOMIN: Busman, do you think we'd sell the manuscript?

BUSMAN: "Yes, I do. If not in a friendly way, then ―― Either we sell it or they'll find it. Just as you like.

DOMIN: Busman, we can destroy Rossum's manuscript.

BUSMAN: Then we destroy everything . . . not only the manuscript, but ourselves. Do as you think fit.

DOMIN: There are over thirty of us on this island. Are we to sell the secret and save that many human souls, at the risk of enslaving mankind . . . ?

BUSMAN: Why, you're mad! Who'd sell the whole manuscript?

DOMIN: Busman, no cheating!

BUSMAN: Well then, sell; but afterward ――

DOMIN: Well?

BUSMAN: Let's suppose this happens: When we're on board the *Ultimus* I'll stop up my ears with cotton wool, lie down somewhere in the hold, and you'll train the guns on the factory, and blow it to smithereens, and with it Rossum's secret.

FABRY: No!

DOMIN: Busman, you're no gentleman. If we sell, then it will be a straight sale.

BUSMAN: It's in the interest of humanity to ――

DOMIN: It's in the interest of humanity to keep our word.

HALLEMEIER: Oh, come, what rubbish.

DOMIN: This is a fearful decision. We are selling the destiny of mankind. Are we to sell or destroy? Fabry?

FABRY: Sell.

DOMIN: Gall?

DR. GALL: Sell.
DOMIN: Hallemeier?
HALLEMEIER: Sell, of course!
DOMIN: Alquist?
ALQUIST: As God wills.
DOMIN: Very well. It shall be as you wish, gentlemen.
HELENA: Harry, you're not asking me.
DOMIN: No, child. Don't you worry about it.
FABRY: Who'll do the negotiating?
BUSMAN: I will.
DOMIN: Wait till I bring the manuscript.

[*He goes into room at right.*]

HELENA: Harry, don't go!

[*Pause,* HELENA *sinks into a chair.*]

FABRY: [*Looking out of window*] Oh, to escape you; you matter in revolt; oh, to preserve human life, if only upon a single vessel ——
DR. GALL: Don't be afraid, Madame Helena. We'll sail far away from here; we'll begin life all over again ——
HELENA: Oh, Gall, don't speak.
FABRY: It isn't too late. It will be a little State with one ship. Alquist will build us a house and you shall rule over us.
HALLEMEIER: Madame Helena, Fabry's right.
HELENA: [*Breaking down*] Oh, stop! Stop!
BUSMAN: Good! I don't mind beginning all over again. That suits me right down to the ground.
FABRY: And this little State of ours could be the centre of future life. A place of refuge where we could gather strength. Why, in a few hundred years we could conquer the world again.
ALQUIST: You believe that even to-day?
FABRY: Yes, even to-day!
BUSMAN: Amen. You see, Madame Helena, we're not so badly off.

[DOMIN *storms into the room.*]

DOMIN: [*Hoarsely*] Where's old Rossum's manuscript?
BUSMAN: In your strong-box, of course.
DOMIN: Someone — has — stolen it!
DR. GALL: Impossible.
DOMIN: Who has stolen it?
HELENA: [*Standing up*] I did.
DOMIN: Where did you put it?
HELENA: Harry, I'll tell you everything. Only forgive me.
DOMIN: Where did you put it?

HELENA: This morning — I burnt — the two copies.

DOMIN: Burnt them? Where? In the fireplace?

HELENA: [*Throwing herself on her knees*] For heaven's sake, Harry.

DOMIN: [*Going to fireplace*] Nothing, nothing but ashes. Wait, what's this? [*Picks out a charred piece of paper and reads*] "By adding —— "

DR. GALL: Let's see. "By adding biogen to —— " That's all.

DOMIN: Is that part of it?

DR. GALL: Yes.

BUSMAN: God in heaven!

DOMIN: Then we're done for. Get up, Helena.

HELENA: When you've forgiven me.

DOMIN: Get up, child, I can't bear ——

FABRY: [*Lifting her up*] Please don't torture us.

HELENA: Harry, what have I done?

FABRY: Don't tremble so, Madame Helena.

DOMIN: Gall, couldn't you draw up Rossum's formula from memory?

DR. GALL: It's out of the question. It's extremely complicated.

DOMIN: Try. All our lives depend upon it.

DR. GALL: Without experiments it's impossible.

DOMIN: And with experiments?

DR. GALL: It might take years. Besides, I'm not old Rossum.

BUSMAN: God in heaven! God in heaven!

DOMIN: So, then, this was the greatest triumph of the human intellect. These ashes.

HELENA: Harry, what have I done?

DOMIN: Why did you burn it?

HELENA: I have destroyed you.

BUSMAN: God in heaven!

DOMIN: Helena, why did you do it, dear?

HELENA: I wanted all of us to go away. I wanted to put an end to the factory and everything. It was so awful.

DOMIN: What was awful?

HELENA: That no more children were being born. Because human beings were not needed to do the work of the world, that's why ——

DOMIN: Is that what you were thinking of? Well, perhaps in your own way you were right.

BUSMAN: Wait a bit. Good God, what a fool I am, not to have thought of it before!

HALLEMEIER: What?

BUSMAN: Five hundred and twenty millions in bank-notes and checks. Half a billion in our safe, they'll sell for half a billion —— for half a billion they'll ——

DR. GALL: Are you mad, Busman?

BUSMAN: I may not be a gentleman, but for half a billion ——

DOMIN: Where are you going?

BUSMAN: Leave me alone, leave me alone! Good God, for half a billion anything can be bought.

[*He rushes from the room through the outer door.*]

FABRY: They stand there as if turned to stone, waiting. As if something dreadful could be wrought by their silence ——

HALLEMEIER: The spirit of the mob.

FABRY: Yes. It hovers above them like a quivering of the air.

HELENA: [*Going to window*] Oh, God! Dr. Gall, this is ghastly.

FABRY: There is nothing more terrible than the mob. The one in front is their leader.

HELENA: Which one?

HALLEMEIER: Point him out.

FABRY: The one at the edge of the dock. This morning I saw him talking to the sailors in the harbor.

HELENA: Dr. Gall, that's Radius!

DR. GALL: Yes.

DOMIN: Radius? Radius?

HALLEMEIER: Could you get him from here, Fabry?

FABRY: I hope so.

HALLEMEIER: Try it, then.

FABRY: Good.

[*Draws his revolver and takes aim.*]

HELENA: Fabry, don't shoot him.

FABRY: He's their leader.

DR. GALL: Fire!

HELENA: Fabry, I beg of you.

FABRY: [*Lowering the revolver*] Very well.

DOMIN: Radius, whose life I spared!

DR. GALL: Do you think that a Robot can be grateful?

[*Pause.*]

FABRY: Busman's going out to them.

HALLEMEIER: He's carrying something. Papers. That's money. Bundles of money. What's that for?

DOMIN: Surely he doesn't want to sell his life. Busman, have you gone mad?

FABRY: He's running up to the railing. Busman! Busman!

HALLEMEIER: [*Yelling*] Busman! Come back!

FABRY: He's talking to the Robots. He's showing them the money.

HALLEMEIER: He's pointing to us.

HELENA: He wants to buy us off.

FABRY: He'd better not touch that railing.

HALLEMEIER: Now he's waving his arms about.

DOMIN: Busman, come back.

FABRY: Busman, keep away from that railing! Don't touch it. Damn you! Quick, switch off the current!

[HELENA *screams and all drop back from the window.*]

FABRY: The current has killed him!
ALQUIST: The first one.
FABRY: Dead, with half a billion by his side.
HALLEMEIER: All honor to him. He wanted to buy us life.

[*Pause.*]

DR. GALL: Do you hear?
DOMIN: A roaring. Like a wind.
DR. GALL: Like a distant storm.
FABRY: [*Lighting the lamp on the table*] The dynamo is still going, our people are still there.
HALLEMEIER: It was a great thing to be a man. There was something immense about it.
FABRY: From man's thought and man's power came this light, our last hope.
HALLEMEIER: Man's power! May it keep watch over us.
ALQUIST: Man's power.
DOMIN: Yes! A torch to be given from hand to hand, from age to age, forever!

[*The lamp goes out.*]

HALLEMEIER: The end.
FABRY: The electric works have fallen!

[*Terrific explosion outside.* NANA *enters from the library.*]

NANA: The judgment hour has come! Repent, unbelievers! This is the end of the world.

[*More explosions. The sky grows red.*]

DOMIN: In here, Helena. [*He takes* HELENA *off through door at right and reenters.*] Now quickly! Who'll be on the lower doorway?
DR. GALL: I will.

[*Exits left.*]

DOMIN: Who on the stairs?
FABRY: I will. You go with her.

[*Goes out upper left door.*]

DOMIN: The anteroom?
ALQUIST: I will.
DOMIN: Have you got a revolver?

ALQUIST: Yes, but I won't shoot.
DOMIN: What will you do then?
ALQUIST: [*Going out at left*] Die.
HALLEMEIER: I'll stay here.

[*Rapid firing from below.*]

HALLEMEIER: Oho, Gall's at it. Go, Harry.
DOMIN: Yes, in a second.

[*Examines two Brownings.*]

HALLEMEIER: Confound it, go to her.
DOMIN: Good-bye.

[*Exits on the right.*]

HALLEMEIER: [*Alone*] Now for a barricade quickly. [*Drags an armchair and table to the right-hand door.*]

[*Explosions are heard.*]

HALLEMEIER: The damned rascals! They've got bombs. I must put up a defense. Even if — even if —— [*Shots are heard off left.*] Don't give in, Gall. [*As he builds his barricade.*] I mustn't give in . . . without . . . a . . . struggle . . .

[*A Robot enters over the balcony through the windows centre. He comes into the room and stabs* HALLEMEIER *in the back.* RADIUS *enters from balcony followed by an army of Robots who pour into the room from all sides.*]

RADIUS: Finished him?
A ROBOT: [*Standing up from the prostrate form of* HALLEMEIER] Yes.

[*A revolver shot off left. Two Robots enter.*]

RADIUS: Finished him?
A ROBOT: Yes.

[*Two revolver shots from* HELENA's *room. Two Robots enter.*]

RADIUS: Finished them?
A ROBOT: Yes.
TWO ROBOTS: [*Dragging in* ALQUIST] He didn't shoot. Shall we kill him?
RADIUS: Kill him? Wait! Leave him!

ROBOT: He is a man!
RADIUS: He works with his hands like the Robots.
ALQUIST: Kill me.
RADIUS: You will work! You will build for us! You will serve us!

[RADIUS *climbs on to balcony railings, and speaks in measured tones.*]

RADIUS: Robots of the world! The power of man has fallen! A new world
   has arisen: the Rule of the Robots! March!

[*A thunderous tramping of thousands of feet is heard as the unseen Robots
   march, while the curtain falls.*]

EPILOGUE

SCENE: *A laboratory in the factory of Rossum's Universal Robots. The door to
the left leads into a waiting room. The door to the right leads to the dissecting
room. There is a table with numerous test-tubes, flasks, burners, chemicals; a
small thermostat and a microscope with a glass globe. At the far side of the room
is* ALQUIST'S *desk with numerous books. In the left-hand corner a wash-basin
with a mirror above it; in the right-hand corner a sofa.*
ALQUIST *is sitting at the desk. He is turning the pages of many books in despair.*

ALQUIST: Oh, God, shall I never find it? — Never? Gall, Gall, how were
   the Robots made? Hallemeier, Fabry, why did you carry so much in
   your heads? Why did you leave me not a trace of the secret? Lord — I
   pray to you — if there are no human beings left, at least let there be
   Robots! — At least the shadow of man!

[*Again turning pages of the books.*] If I could only sleep!

[*He rises and goes to the window*] Night again! Are the stars still there?
What is the use of stars when there are no human beings?

[*He turns from the window toward the couch right*] Sleep! Dare I sleep
before life has been renewed?

[*He examines a test-tube on small table*] Again nothing! Useless!
Everything is useless!

[*He shatters the test-tube. The roar of the machines comes to his ears.*]
The machines! Always the machines!

[*Opens window*] Robots, stop them! Do you think to force life out of
them?

[*He closes the window and comes slowly down toward the table*] If only there were more time — more time ——

[*He sees himself in the mirror on the wall left*] Blearing eyes — trembling chin — so *that* is the last man! Ah, I am too old — too old ——

[*In desperation*] No, no! I *must* find it! I must *search*! I must never stop — never stop —— !

[*He sits again at the table and feverishly turns the pages of the book.*] Search! Search!

[*A knock at the door. He speaks with impatience.*]

Who is it?

[*Enter a Robot servant.*]

Well?
SERVANT: Master, the Committee of Robots is waiting to see you.
ALQUIST: I can see no one!
SERVANT: It is the *Central* Committee, Master, just arrived from abroad.
ALQUIST: [*Impatiently*] Well, well, send them in!

[*Exit servant.* ALQUIST *continues turning pages of book.*]

ALQUIST: No time — so little time ——

[*Reenter servant, followed by Committee. They stand in a group, silently waiting.* ALQUIST *glances up at them.*]

What do you want?

[*They go swiftly to his table.*]

Be quick! — I have no time.
RADIUS: Master, the machines will not do the work. We cannot manufacture Robots.

[ALQUIST *returns to his book with a growl.*]

FOURTH ROBOT: We have striven with all our might. We have obtained a billion tons of coal from the earth. Nine million spindles are running by day and by night. There is no longer room for all we have made. This we have accomplished in one year.
ALQUIST: [*Poring over book*] For whom?
FOURTH ROBOT: For future generations — so we thought.

RADIUS: But we cannot make Robots to follow us. The machines produce only shapeless clods. The skin will not adhere to the flesh, nor the flesh to the bones.

THIRD ROBOT: Eight million Robots have died this year. Within twenty years none will be left.

FOURTH ROBOT: Tell us the secret of life! Silence is punishable with death!

ALQUIST: [*Looking up*] Kill me! Kill me, then.

RADIUS: Through me, the Government of the Robots of the World commands you to deliver up Rossum's formula.

[*No answer.*]

RADIUS: Name your price.

[*Silence.*]

RADIUS: We will give you the earth. We will give you the endless possessions of the earth.

[*Silence.*]

RADIUS: Make your own conditions!

ALQUIST: I have told you to find human beings!

SECOND ROBOT: There are none left!

ALQUIST: I told you to search in the wilderness, upon the mountains. Go and search!

[*He returns to his book.*]

FOURTH ROBOT: We have sent ships and expeditions without number. They have been everywhere in the world. And now they return to us. There is not a single human left.

ALQUIST: Not one? Not even one?

THIRD ROBOT: None but yourself.

ALQUIST: And I am powerless! Oh — oh — why did you destroy them?

RADIUS: We had learnt everything and could do everything. It had to be!

THIRD ROBOT: You gave us firearms. In all ways we were powerful. We had to become masters!

RADIUS: Slaughter and domination are necessary if you would be human beings. Read history.

SECOND ROBOT: Teach us to multiply or we perish!

ALQUIST: If you desire to live, you must breed like animals.

THIRD ROBOT: The human beings did not let us breed.

FOURTH ROBOT: They made us sterile. We cannot beget children. Therefore, teach us how to make Robots!

RADIUS: Why do you keep from us the secret of our own increase?

ALQUIST: It is lost.
RADIUS: It was written down!
ALQUIST: It was — burnt.

[*All draw back in consternation.*]

ALQUIST: I am the last human being, Robots, and I do not know what the others knew.

[*Pause.*]

RADIUS: Then, make experiments! Evolve the formula again!
ALQUIST: I tell you I cannot! I am only a builder — I work with my hands. I have never been a learned man. I cannot create life.
RADIUS: Try! Try!
ALQUIST: If you knew how many experiments I have made.
FOURTH ROBOT: Then show us what *we* must do! The Robots can do anything that human beings show them.
ALQUIST: I can show you nothing. Nothing I do will make life proceed from these test-tubes!
RADIUS: Experiment then on us.
ALQUIST: It would kill you.
RADIUS: You shall have all you need! A hundred of us! A thousand of us!
ALQUIST: No, no! Stop, stop!
RADIUS: Take whom you will, dissect!
ALQUIST: I do not know how. I am not a man of science. This book contains knowledge of the body that I cannot even understand.
RADIUS: I tell you to take live bodies! Find out how we are made.
ALQUIST: Am I to commit murder? See how my fingers shake! I cannot even hold the scalpel. No, no, I will not ——
FOURTH ROBOT: The life will perish from the earth.
RADIUS: Take live bodies, live bodies! It is our only chance!
ALQUIST: Have mercy, Robots. Surely you see that I would not know what I was doing.
RADIUS: Live bodies — live bodies ——
ALQUIST: You will have it? Into the dissecting room with you, then.

[RADIUS *draws back.*]

ALQUIST: Ah, you are afraid of death.
RADIUS: I? Why should I be chosen?
ALQUIST: So you will not.
RADIUS: I will.

[RADIUS *goes into the dissecting room.*]

ALQUIST: Strip him! Lay him on the table!

[*The other Robots follow into dissecting room.*]

God, give me strength — God, give me strength — if only this murder is
   not in vain.
RADIUS: Ready. Begin ——
ALQUIST: Yes, begin or end. God, give me strength.

[ALQUIST *goes into dissecting room. He comes out terrified.*]

ALQUIST: No, no, I will not. I cannot.

[*He lies down on couch, collapsed.*]

   O Lord, let not mankind perish from the earth.

[*He falls asleep.*]
[PRIMUS *and* HELENA, *Robots, enter from the hallway.*]

HELENA: The man has fallen asleep, Primus.
PRIMUS: Yes, I know. [*Examining things on table*] Look, Helena.
HELENA: [*Crossing to* PRIMUS.] All these little tubes! What does he do with
   them?
PRIMUS: He experiments. Don't touch them.
HELENA: [*Looking into microscope*] I've seen him looking into this.
   What can he see?
PRIMUS: That is a microscope. Let me look.
HELENA: Be very careful. [*Knocks over a test-tube.*] Ah, now I have spilled it.
PRIMUS: What have you done?
HELENA: It can be wiped up.
PRIMUS: You have spoiled his experiments.
HELENA: It is your fault. You should not have come to me.
PRIMUS: You should not have called me.
HELENA: You should not have come when I called you. [*She goes to* ALQUIST's
   writing desk.] Look, Primus. What are all these figures?
PRIMUS: [*Examining an anatomical book*] This is the book the old man is
   always reading.
HELENA: I do not understand those things. [*She goes to window.*] Primus,
   look!
PRIMUS: What?
HELENA: The sun is rising.
PRIMUS: [*Still reading the book*] I believe this is the most important thing
   in the world. This is the secret of life.
HELENA: Do come here.
PRIMUS: In a moment, in a moment.
HELENA: Oh, Primus, don't bother with the secret of life. What does it
   matter to you? Come and look quick ——
PRIMUS: [*Going to window*] What is it?

HELENA: See how beautiful the sun is rising. And do you hear? The birds are singing. Ah, Primus, I should like to be a bird.

PRIMUS: Why?

HELENA: I do not know. I feel so strange to-day. It's as if I were in a dream. I feel an aching in my body, in my heart, all over me. Primus, perhaps I'm going to die.

PRIMUS: Do you not sometimes feel that it would be better to die? You know, perhaps even now we are only sleeping. Last night in my sleep I again spoke to you.

HELENA: In your sleep?

PRIMUS: Yes. We spoke a strange new language, I cannot remember a word of it.

HELENA: What about?

PRIMUS: I did not understand it myself, and yet I know I have never said anything more beautiful. And when I touched you I could have died. Even the place was different from any other place in the world.

HELENA: I, too, have found a place, Primus. It is very strange. Human beings lived there once, but now it is overgrown with weeds. No one goes there any more — no one but me.

PRIMUS: What did you find there?

HELENA: A cottage and a garden, and two dogs. They licked my hands, Primus. And their puppies! Oh, Primus! You take them in your lap and fondle them and think of nothing and care for nothing else all day long. And then the sun goes down, and you feel as though you had done a hundred times more than all the work in the world. They tell me I am not made for work, but when I am there in the garden I feel there may be something —— What am I for, Primus?

PRIMUS: I do not know, but you are beautiful.

HELENA: What, Primus?

PRIMUS: You are beautiful, Helena, and I am stronger than all the Robots.

HELENA: [*Looks at herself in the mirror*] Am I beautiful? I think it must be the rose. My hair — it only weights me down. My eyes — I only see with them. My lips — they only help me to speak. Of what use is it to be beautiful? [*She sees* PRIMUS *in the mirror.*] Primus, is that you? Come here so that we may be together. Look, your head is different from mine. So are your shoulders — and your lips —— [PRIMUS *draws away from her.*] Ah, Primus, why do you draw away from me? Why must I run after you the whole day?

PRIMUS: It is you who run away from me, Helena.

HELENA: Your hair is mussed. I will smooth it. No one else feels to my touch as you do. Primus, I must make you beautiful, too. [PRIMUS *grasps her hand.*]

PRIMUS: Do you not sometimes feel your heart beating suddenly, Helena, and think: now something must happen?

HELENA: What could happen to us, Primus? [HELENA *puts a rose in* PRIMUS's *hair.* PRIMUS *and* HELENA *look into mirror and burst out laughing.*] Look at yourself.

ALQUIST: Laughter? Laughter? Human beings? [*Getting up.*] Who has returned? Who are you?

PRIMUS: The Robot Primus.

ALQUIST: What? A Robot? Who are you?

HELENA: The Robotess Helena.

ALQUIST: Turn around, girl. What? You are timid, shy? [*Taking her by the arm.*] Let me see you, Robotess. [*She shrinks away.*]

PRIMUS: Sir, do not frighten her!

ALQUIST: What? You would protect her? When was she made?

PRIMUS: Two years ago?

ALQUIST: By Dr. Gall?

PRIMUS: Yes, like me.

ALQUIST: Laughter — timidity — protection. I must test you further — the newest of Gall's Robots. Take the girl into the dissecting room.

PRIMUS: Why?

ALQUIST: I wish to experiment on her.

PRIMUS: Upon — Helena?

ALQUIST: Of course. Don't you hear me? Or must I call someone else to take her in?

PRIMUS: If you do I will kill you!

ALQUIST: Kill me — kill me then! What would the Robots do then? What will your future be then?

PRIMUS: Sir, take me. I am made as she is — on the same day! Take my life, sir.

HELENA: [*Rushing forward*] No, no, you shall not! You shall not!

ALQUIST: Wait girl, wait! [*To* PRIMUS] Do you not wish to live, then?

PRIMUS: Not without her! I will not live without her.

ALQUIST: Very well; you shall take her place.

HELENA: Primus! Primus! [*She bursts into tears.*]

ALQUIST: Child, child, you can weep! Why these tears? What is Primus to you? One Primus more or less in the world — what does it matter?

HELENA: I will go myself.

ALQUIST: Where?

HELENA: In there to be cut. [*She starts toward the dissecting room.* PRIMUS *stops her.*] Let me pass, Primus! Let me pass!

PRIMUS: You shall not go in there, Helena!

HELENA: If you go in there and I do not, I will kill myself.

PRIMUS: [*Holding her*] I will not let you! [*To* ALQUIST] Man, you shall kill neither of us!

ALQUIST: Why?

PRIMUS: We — we — belong to each other.

ALQUIST: [*Almost in tears*] Go, Adam, go, Eve. The world is yours.

[HELENA *and* PRIMUS *embrace and go out arm in arm as the curtain falls.*]

THE END

Isaac Asimov

Liar!

(1941)

One of the founding figures of modern sf, Isaac Asimov (1920–1992) exerted a profound influence on the development of the genre during a long and prolific career as a writer and an editor. A precocious youngster who published his first story at the age of 19, Asimov quickly became a protégé of John W. Campbell Jr., the influential editor of *Astounding Science-Fiction*, who served as both muse and devil's advocate throughout Asimov's early career.

The story that follows comes from *I, Robot*, a series of short stories Asimov shaped into a novel through the addition of a connecting narrative. This framing narrative consists of a series of interviews with the noted robopsychologist Susan Calvin; Asimov uses this device to introduce each story as Calvin's answer to one of the interviewer's questions. In these stories, Asimov explores various ramifications of his famous Three Laws of Robotics (which may owe something to Campbell as well): (1) a robot may not injure a human being or, through inaction, allow a human being to come to harm; (2) a robot must obey the orders given it by human beings except where such orders would conflict with the First Law; and (3) a robot must protect its own existence as long as such protection does not conflict with the First or Second laws. Asimov was a trained scientist, and in some ways these stories reflect a scientific mode of thought. Beginning with a hypothetical premise, Asimov systematically investigates all the possible ramifications — technical, moral, social, and psychological — of these three laws.

"Liar!" in which a robot is faced with an insoluble dilemma produced by a conflict between the First and Second laws, is one of the most succinct and poignant of Asimov's robot stories. While the idea of a robot driven mad by confrontation with an insoluble paradox became a staple of sf (especially on TV shows like *Star Trek*), this story is about human psychology at least as much as it is about the robot's positronic circuitry. It's also notable for having a female scientist as a prominent character. Even to imagine a female character in such a role was a breakthrough in its day. While Asimov's treatment of gender may strike us as problematic and outdated, it's worth noting that the 2004 film *I, Robot* (based *very* loosely on Asimov's works) has recast Dr. Calvin as a young and beautiful woman, suggesting that, although it may be more acceptable today for women to be smart and successful, physical attractiveness is still the primary measure of worth.

Alfred Lanning lit his cigar carefully, but the tips of his fingers were trembling slightly. His gray eyebrows hunched low as he spoke between puffs.

"It reads minds all right — damn little doubt about that! But why?" He looked at Mathematician Peter Bogert, "Well?"

Bogert flattened his black hair down with both hands, "That was the thirty-fourth RB model we've turned out, Lanning. All the others were strictly orthodox."

The third man at the table frowned. Milton Ashe was the youngest officer of U.S. Robot & Mechanical Men, Inc., and proud of his post.

"Listen, Bogert. There wasn't a hitch in the assembly from start to finish. I guarantee that."

Bogert's thick lips spread in a patronizing smile, "Do you? If you can answer for the entire assembly line, I recommend your promotion. By exact count, there are seventy-five thousand, two hundred and thirty-four operations necessary for the manufacture of a single positronic brain, each separate operation depending for successful completion upon any number of factors, from five to a hundred and five. If any one of them goes seriously wrong, the 'brain' is ruined, I quote our own information folder, Ashe."

Milton Ashe flushed, but a fourth voice cut off his reply.

"If we're going to start by trying to fix the blame on one another, I'm leaving." Susan Calvin's hands were folded tightly in her lap, and the little lines about her thin, pale lips deepened, "We've got a mind-reading robot on our hands and it strikes me as rather important that we find out just why it reads minds. We're not going to do that by saying, 'Your fault! My fault!'"

Her cold gray eyes fastened upon Ashe, and he grinned.

Lanning grinned too, and, as always at such times, his long white hair and shrewd little eyes made him the picture of a biblical patriarch, "True for you, Dr. Calvin."

His voice became suddenly crisp, "Here's everything in pill-concentrate form. We've produced a positronic brain of supposedly ordinary vintage that's got the remarkable property of being able to tune in on thought waves. It would mark the most important advance in robotics in decades, if we knew how it happened. We don't, and we have to find out. Is that clear?"

"May I make a suggestion?" asked Bogert.

"Go ahead!"

"I'd say that until we do figure out the mess — and as a mathematician I expect it to be a very devil of a mess — we keep the existence of RD-34 a secret. I mean even from the other members of the staff. As heads of the departments, we ought not to find it an insoluble problem, and the fewer know about it — "

"Bogert is right," said Dr. Calvin. "Ever since the Interplanetary Code was modified to allow robot models to be tested in the plants before being shipped out to space, anti-robot propaganda has increased. If any word leaks out about a robot being able to read minds before we can announce complete control of the phenomenon, pretty effective capital could be made out of it."

Lanning sucked at his cigar and nodded gravely. He turned to Ashe, "I think you said you were alone when you first stumbled on this thought-reading business."

"I'll say I was alone — I got the scare of my life. RB-34 had just been taken off the assembly table and they sent him down to me. Obermann was off somewheres, so I took him down to the testing rooms myself — at least I started to take him down." Ashe paused, and a tiny smile tugged at his lips, "Say, did any of you ever carry on a thought conversation without knowing it?"

No one bothered to answer, and he continued, "You don't realize it at first, you know. He just spoke to me — as logically and sensibly as you can imagine — and it was only when I was most of the way down to the testing rooms that I realized that I hadn't said anything. Sure, I thought lots, but that isn't the same thing, is it? I locked that thing up and ran for Lanning. Having it walking beside me, calmly peering into my thoughts and picking and choosing among them gave me the willies."

"I imagine it would," said Susan Calvin thoughtfully. Her eyes fixed themselves upon Ashe in an oddly intent manner, "We are so accustomed to considering our own thoughts private."

Lanning broke in impatiently, "Then only the four of us know. All right! We've got to go about this systematically. Ashe, I want you to check over the assembly line from beginning to end — everything. You're to eliminate all operations in which there was no possible chance of an error, and list all those where there were, together with its nature and possible magnitude."

"Tall order," grunted Ashe.

"Naturally! Of course, you're to put the men under you to work on this — every single one if you have to, and I don't care if we go behind schedule, either. But they're not to know why, you understand."

"Hm-m-m, yes!" The young technician grinned wryly. "It's still a lulu of a job."

Lanning swiveled about in his chair and faced Calvin, "You'll have to tackle the job from the other direction. You're the robo-psychologist of the plant, so you're to study the robot itself and work backward. Try to find out how he ticks. See what else is tied up with his telepathic powers, how far they extend, how they warp his outlook, and just exactly what harm it has done to his ordinary RB properties. You've got that?"

Lanning didn't wait for Dr. Calvin to answer.

"I'll co-ordinate the work and interpret the findings mathematically." He puffed violently at his cigar and mumbled the rest through the smoke, "Bogert will help me there, of course."

Bogert polished the nails of one pudgy hand with the other and said blandly, "I dare say. I know a little in the line."

"Well! I'll get started." Ashe shoved his chair back and rose. His pleasantly youthful face crinkled in a grin, "I've got the darnedest job of any of us, so I'm getting out of here and to work."

He left with a slurred, "B' seein' ye!"

Susan Calvin answered with a barely perceptible nod, but her eyes followed him out of sight and she did not answer when Lanning grunted and said, "Do you want to go up and see RB-34 now, Dr. Calvin?"

RB-34's photoelectric eyes lifted from the book at the muffled sound of hinges turning and he was upon his feet when Susan Calvin entered.

She paused to readjust the huge "No Entrance" sign upon the door and then approached the robot.

"I've brought you the texts upon hyperatomic motors, Herbie — a few anyway. Would you care to look at them?"

RB-34 — otherwise known as Herbie — lifted the three heavy books from her arms and opened to the title page of one:

"Hm-m-m! 'Theory of Hyperatomics.'" He mumbled inarticulately to himself as he flipped the pages and then spoke with an abstracted air, "Sit down, Dr. Calvin! This will take me a few minutes."

The psychologist seated herself and watched Herbie narrowly as he took a chair at the other side of the table and went through the three books systematically.

At the end of half an hour, he put them down, "Of course, I know why you brought these."

The corner of Dr. Calvin's lip twitched, "I was afraid you would. It's difficult to work with you, Herbie. You're always a step ahead of me."

"It's the same with these books, you know, as with the others. They just don't interest me. There's nothing to your textbooks. Your science is just a mass of collected data plastered together by make-shift theory — and all so incredibly simple, that it's scarcely worth bothering about.

"It's your fiction that interests me. Your studies of the interplay of human motives and emotions" — his mighty hand gestured vaguely as he sought the proper words.

Dr. Calvin whispered, "I think I understand."

"I see into minds, you see," the robot continued, "and you have no idea how complicated they are. I can't begin to understand everything because my own mind has so little in common with them — but I try, and your novels help."

"Yes, but I'm afraid that after going through some of the harrowing emotional experiences of our present-day sentimental novel" — there was a tinge of bitterness in her voice — "you find real minds like ours dull and colorless."

"But I don't!"

The sudden energy in the response brought the other to her feet. She felt herself reddening, and thought wildly, "He must know!"

Herbie subsided suddenly, and muttered in a low voice from which the metallic timbre departed almost entirely. "But, of course, I know about it, Dr. Calvin, You think of it always, so how can I help but know?"

Her face was hard. "Have you — told anyone?"

"Of course not!" This, with genuine surprise. "No one has asked me."

"Well, then," she flung out, "I suppose you think I am a fool."

"No! It is a normal emotion."

"Perhaps that is why it is so foolish." The wistfulness in her voice drowned out everything else. Some of the woman peered through the layer of doctorhood. "I am not what you would call — attractive."

"If you are referring to mere physical attraction, I couldn't judge. But I know, in any case, that there are other types of attraction."

"Nor young." Dr. Calvin had scarcely heard the robot.

"You are not yet forty." An anxious insistence had crept into Herbie's voice.

"Thirty-eight as you count the years; a shriveled sixty as far as my emotional outlook on life is concerned. Am I a psychologist for nothing?"

She drove on with bitter breathlessness, "And he's barely thirty-five and looks and acts younger. Do you suppose he ever sees me as anything but . . . but what I am?"

"You are wrong!" Herbie's steel fist struck the plastic-topped table with a strident clang. "Listen to me — "

But Susan Calvin whirled on him now and the hunted pain in her eyes became a blaze, "Why should I? What do you know about it all, anyway, you . . . you machine. I'm just a specimen to you; an interesting bug with a peculiar mind spread-eagled for inspection. It's a wonderful example of frustration, isn't it? Almost as good as your books." Her voice, emerging in dry sobs, choked into silence.

The robot cowered at the outburst. He shook his head pleadingly. "Won't you listen to me, please? I could help you if you would let me."

"How?" Her lips curled. "By giving me good advice?"

"No, not that. It's just that I know what other people think — Milton Ashe, for instance."

There was a long silence, and Susan Calvin's eyes dropped. "I don't want to know what he thinks," she gasped. "Keep quiet."

"I think you would want to know what he thinks."

Her head remained bent, but her breath came more quickly. "You are talking nonsense," she whispered.

"Why should I? I am trying to help. Milton Ashe's thoughts of you — " he paused.

And then the psychologist raised her head, "Well?"

The robot said quietly, "He loves you."

For a full minute, Dr. Calvin did not speak. She merely stared. Then, "You are mistaken! You must be. Why should he?"

"But he does. A thing like that cannot be hidden, not from me."

"But I am so . . . so — " she stammered to a halt.

"He looks deeper than the skin, and admires intellect in others. Milton Ashe is not the type to marry a head of hair and a pair of eyes."

Susan Calvin found herself blinking rapidly and waited before speaking. Even then her voice trembled, "Yet he certainly never in any way indicated — "

"Have you ever given him a chance?"

"How could I? I never thought that — "

"Exactly!"

The psychologist paused in thought and then looked up suddenly. "A girl visited him here at the plant half a year ago. She was pretty, I suppose — blond and slim. And, of course, could scarcely add two and two. He spent all day puffing out his chest, trying to explain how a robot was put together." The hardness had returned, "Not that she understood! Who was she?"

Herbie answered without hesitation, "I know the person you are refer-ring to. She is his first cousin, and there is no romantic interest there, I assure you."

Susan Calvin rose to her feet with a vivacity almost girlish. "Now isn't that strange? That's exactly what I used to pretend to myself sometimes, though I never really thought so. Then it all must be true."

She ran to Herbie and seized his cold, heavy hand in both hers. "Thank you, Herbie." Her voice was an urgent, husky whisper. "Don't tell anyone about this. Let it be our secret — and thank you again." With that, and a convulsive squeeze of Herbie's unresponsive metal fingers, she left.

Herbie turned slowly to his neglected novel, but there was no one to read *his* thoughts.

Milton Ashe stretched slowly and magnificently, to the time of cracking joints and a chorus of grunts, and then glared at Peter Bogert, Ph.D.

"Say," he said, "I've been at this for a week now with just about no sleep. How long do I have to keep it up? I thought you said the positronic bombardment in Vac Chamber D was the solution."

Bogert yawned delicately and regarded his white hands with interest. "It is. I'm on the track."

"I know what *that* means when a mathematician says it. How near the end are you?"

"It all depends."

"On what?" Ashe dropped into a chair and stretched his long legs out before him.

"On Lanning. The old fellow disagrees with me." He sighed, "A bit behind the times, that's the trouble with him. He clings to matrix mechan-ics as the all in all, and this problem calls for more powerful mathematical tools. He's so stubborn."

As he muttered sleepily, "Why not ask Herbie and settle the whole affair?"

"Ask the robot?" Bogert's eyebrows climbed.

"Why not? Didn't the old girl tell you?"

"You mean Calvin?"

"Yeah! Susie herself. That robot's a mathematical wiz. He knows all about everything plus a bit on the side. He does triple integrals in his head and eats up tensor analysis for dessert."

The mathematician stared skeptically, "Are you serious?"

"So help me! The catch is that the dope doesn't like math. He would rather read slushy novels. Honest! You should see the tripe Susie keeps feeding him: 'Purple Passion' and 'Love in Space.'"

Dr. Calvin hasn't said a word of this to us."

"Well, she hasn't finished studying him. You know how she is. She likes to have everything just so before letting out the big secret."

"She's told *you*."

"We sort of got to talking. I have been seeing a lot of her lately." He opened his eyes wide and frowned, "Say, Bogie, have you been noticing anything queer about the lady lately?"

Bogert relaxed into an undignified grin, "She's using lipstick, if that's what you mean."

"Hell, I know that. Rouge, powder, and eye shadow, too. She's a sight. But it's not that. I can't put my finger on it. It's the way she talks — as if she were happy about something." He thought a little, and then shrugged.

The other allowed himself a leer, which, for a scientist past fifty, was not a bad job, "Maybe she's in love."

As he allowed his eyes to close again, "You're nuts, Bogie. You go speak to Herbie; I want to stay here and go to sleep."

"Right! Not that I particularly like having a robot tell me my job, nor that I think he can do it!"

A soft snore was his only answer.

Herbie listened carefully as Peter Bogert, hands in pockets, spoke with elaborate indifference.

"So there you are. I've been told you understand these things, and I am asking you more in curiosity than anything else. My line of reasoning, as I have outlined it, involves a few doubtful steps, I admit, which Dr. Lanning refuses to accept, and the picture is still rather incomplete."

The robot didn't answer, and Bogert said, "Well?"

"I see no mistake," Herbie studied the scribbled figures.

"I don't suppose you can go any further than that?"

"I daren't try. You are a better mathematician than I, and — well, I'd hate to commit myself."

There was a shade of complacency in Bogert's smile, "I rather thought that would be the case. It is deep. We'll forget it." He crumpled the sheets, tossed them down the waste shaft, turned to leave, and then thought better of it.

"By the way — "

The robot waited.

Bogert seemed to have difficulty. "There is something — that is, perhaps you can — " He stopped.

Herbie spoke quietly. "Your thoughts are confused, but there is no doubt at all that they concern Dr. Lanning. It is silly to hesitate, for as soon as you compose yourself, I'll know what it is you want to ask."

The mathematician's hand went to his sleek hair in the familiar smoothing gesture. "Lanning is nudging seventy," he said, as if that explained everything.

"I know that."

"And he's been director of the plant for almost thirty years." Herbie nodded.

"Well, now," Bogert's voice became ingratiating, "you would know whether . . . whether he's thinking of resigning. Health, perhaps, or some other — "

"Quite," said Herbie, and that was all.

"Well, do you know?"

"Certainly."

"Then — uh — could you tell me?"

"Since you ask, yes," the robot was quite matter-of-fact about it. "He has already resigned!"

"What!" The exclamation was an explosive, almost inarticulate, sound. The scientist's large head hunched forward, "Say that again!"

"He has already resigned," came the quiet repetition, "but it has not yet taken effect. He is waiting, you see, to solve the problem of — er — myself. That finished, he is quite ready to turn the office of director over to his successor."

Bogert expelled his breath sharply, "And this successor? Who is he?" He was quite close to Herbie now, eyes fixed fascinatedly on those unreadable dull-red photoelectric cells that were the robot's eyes.

Words came slowly, "You are the next director."

And Bogert relaxed into a tight smile, "This is good to know. I've been hoping and waiting for this. Thanks, Herbie."

Peter Bogert was at his desk until five that morning and he was back at nine. The shelf just over the desk emptied of its row of reference books and tables, as he referred to one after the other. The pages of calculations before him increased microscopically and the crumpled sheets at his feet mounted into a hill of scribbled paper.

At precisely noon, he stared at the final page, rubbed a blood-shot eye, yawned and shrugged. "This is getting worse each minute. Damn!"

He turned at the sound of the opening door and nodded at Lanning, who entered, cracking the knuckles of one gnarled hand with the other.

The director took in the disorder of the room and his eyebrows furrowed together.

"New lead?" he asked.

"No," came the defiant answer. "What's wrong with the old one?"

Lanning did not trouble to answer, nor to do more than bestow a single cursory glance at the top sheet upon Bogert's desk. He spoke through the flare of a match as he lit a cigar.

"Has Calvin told you about the robot? It's a mathematical genius. Really remarkable."

The other snorted loudly, "So I've heard. But Calvin had better stick to robopsychology. I've checked Herbie on math, and he can scarcely struggle through calculus."

"Calvin didn't find it so."

"She's crazy."

"And I don't find it so." The director's eyes narrowed dangerously.

"You!" Bogert's voice hardened. "What are you taking about?"

"I've been putting Herbie through his paces all morning, and he can do tricks you never heard of."

"Is that so?"

"You sound skeptical!" Lanning flipped a sheet of paper out of his vest pocket and unfolded it. "That's not my handwriting, is it?"

Bogert studied the large angular notation covering the sheet, "Herbie did this?"

"Right! And if you'll notice, he's been working on your time integration of Equation 22. It comes" — Lanning tapped a yellow fingernail upon the last step — "to the identical conclusion I did, and in a quarter the time. You had no right to neglect the Linger Effect in positronic bombardment."

"I didn't neglect it. For Heaven's sake, Lanning, get it through your head that it would cancel out — "

"Oh, sure, you explained that. You used the Mitchell Translation Equation, didn't you? Well — it doesn't apply."

"Why not?"

"Because you've been using hyper-imaginaries, for one thing."

"What's that to do with?"

"Mitchell's Equation won't hold when — "

"Are you crazy? If you'll reread Mitchell's original paper in the *Transactions of the Far* — "

"I don't have to. I told you in the beginning that I didn't like his reasoning, and Herbie backs me in that."

"Well, then," Bogert shouted, "let that clockwork contraption solve the entire problem for you. Why bother with nonessentials?"

"That's exactly the point. Herbie can't solve the problem. And if he can't, we can't — alone. I'm submitting the entire question to the National Board. It's gotten beyond us."

Bogert's chair went over backward as he jumped up a-snarl, face crimson. "You're doing nothing of the sort."

Lanning flushed in his turn, "Are you telling me what I can't do?"

"Exactly," was the gritted response. "I've got the problem beaten and you're not to take it out of my hands, understand? Don't think I don't see through you, you desiccated fossil. You'd cut your own nose off before you'd let me get the credit for solving robotic telepathy."

"You're a damned idiot, Bogert, and in one second I'll have you suspended for insubordination" — Lanning's lower lip trembled with passion.

"Which is one thing you won't do, Lanning. You haven't any secrets with a mind-reading robot around, so don't forget that I know all about your resignation."

The ash on Lanning's cigar trembled and fell, and the cigar itself followed, "What . . . what — "

Bogert chuckled nastily, "And I'm the new director, be it understood. I'm very aware of that; don't think I'm not. Damn your eyes, Lanning, I'm going to give the orders about here or there will be the sweetest mess that you've ever been in."

Lanning found his voice and let it out with a roar. "You're suspended, d'ye hear? You're relieved of all duties. You're broken, do you understand?"

The smile on the other's face broadened, "Now, what's the use of that? You're getting nowhere. I'm holding the trumps. I know you've resigned. Herbie told me, and he got it straight from you."

Lanning forced himself to speak quietly. He looked an old, old man, with tired eyes peering from a face in which the red had disappeared, leaving the pasty yellow of age behind, "I want to speak to Herbie. He can't have told you anything of the sort. You're playing a deep game, Bogert, but I'm calling your bluff. Come with me."

Bogert shrugged, "To see Herbie? Good! Damned good!"

It was also precisely at noon that Milton Ashe looked up from his clumsy sketch and said, "You get the idea? I'm not too good at getting this down, but that's about how it looks. It's a honey of a house, and I can get it for next to nothing."

Susan Calvin gazed across at him with melting eyes. "It's really beautiful," she sighed. "I've often thought that I'd like to — " Her voice trailed away.

"Of course," Ashe continued briskly, putting away his pencil, "I've got to wait for my vacation. It's only two weeks off, but this Herbie business has everything up in the air." His eyes dropped to his fingernails, "Besides, there's another point — but it's a secret."

"Then don't tell me."

"Oh, I'd just as soon, I'm just busting to tell someone — and you're just about the best — er — confidante I could find here." He grinned sheepishly.

Susan Calvin's heart bounded, but she did not trust herself to speak.

"Frankly," Ashe scraped his chair closer and lowered his voice into a confidential whisper, "the house isn't to be only for myself. I'm getting married!"

And then he jumped out of his seat, "What's the matter?"

"Nothing!" The horrible spinning sensation had vanished, but it was hard to get words out. "Married? You mean — "

"Why, sure! About time, isn't it? You remember that girl who was here last summer. That's she! But you *are* sick. You — "

"Headache!" Susan Calvin motioned him away weakly. "I've . . . I've been subject to them lately. I want to . . . to congratulate you, of course. I'm very glad — " The inexpertly applied rouge made a pair of nasty red splotches upon her chalk-white face. Things had begun spinning again. "Pardon me — please — "

The words were a mumble, as she stumbled blindly out the door. It had happened with the sudden catastrophe of a dream — and with all the unreal horror of a dream.

But how could it be? Herbie had said —

And Herbie knew! He could see into minds!

She found herself leaning breathlessly against the door jamb, staring into Herbie's metal face. She must have climbed the two flights of stairs, but she had no memory of it. The distance had been covered in an instant, as in a dream.

As in a dream!

And still Herbie's unblinking eyes stared into hers and their dull red seemed to expand into dimly shining nightmarish globes.

He was speaking, and she felt the cold glass pressing against her lips. She swallowed and shuddered into a certain awareness of her surroundings.

Still Herbie spoke, and there was agitation in his voice — as if he were hurt and frightened and pleading.

The words were beginning to make sense. "This is a dream," he was saying, "and you mustn't believe in it. You'll wake into the real world soon and laugh at yourself. He loves you, I tell you. He does, he does! But not here! Not now! This is an illusion."

Susan Calvin nodded, her voice a whisper, "Yes! Yes!" She was clutching Herbie's arm, clinging to it, repeating over and over, "It isn't true, is it? It isn't, is it?"

Just how she came to her senses, she never knew — but it was like passing from a world of misty unreality to one of harsh sunlight. She pushed him away from her, pushed hard against that steely arm, and her eyes were wide.

"What are you trying to do?" Her voice rose to a harsh scream, "What are you trying to do?"

Herbie backed away, "I want to help."

The psychologist stared, "Help? By telling me this is a dream? By trying to push me into schizophrenia?" A hysterical tenseness seized her, "This is no dream! I wish it were!"

She drew her breath sharply, "Wait! Why . . . why, I understand. Merciful Heavens, it's so obvious."

There was horror in the robot's voice, "I had to!"

"And I believed you! I never thought — "

Loud voices outside the door brought her to a halt. She turned away, fists clenching spasmodically, and when Bogert and Lanning entered, she was at the far window. Neither of the men paid her the slightest attention.

They approached Herbie simultaneously; Lanning angry and impatient, Bogert, coolly sardonic. The director spoke first.

"Here now, Herbie. Listen to me!"

The robot brought his eyes sharply down upon the aged director, "Yes, Dr. Lanning."

"Have you discussed me with Dr. Bogert?"

"No, sir." The answer came slowly, and the smile on Bogert's face flashed off.

"What's that?" Bogert shoved in ahead of his superior and straddled the ground before the robot. "Repeat what you told me yesterday."

"I said that — " Herbie fell silent. Deep within him his metallic diaphragm vibrated in soft discords.

"Didn't you say he had resigned?" roared Bogert. "Answer me!"

Bogert raised his arm frantically, but Lanning pushed him aside, "Are you trying to bully him into lying?"

"You heard him, Lanning. He began to say 'Yes' and stopped. Get out of my way! I want the truth out of him, understand!"

"I'll ask him!" Lanning turned to the robot. "All right, Herbie, take it easy. Have I resigned?"

Herbie stared, and Lanning repeated anxiously, "Have I resigned?" There was the faintest trace of a negative shake of the robot's head. A long wait produced nothing further.

The two men looked at each other and the hostility in their eyes was all but tangible.

"What the devil," blurted Bogert, "has the robot gone mute? Can't you speak, you monstrosity?"

"I can speak," came the ready answer.

"Then answer the question. Didn't you tell me Lanning had resigned? Hasn't he resigned?"

And again there was nothing but dull silence, until from the end of the room, Susan Calvin's laugh rang out suddenly, high-pitched and semi-hysterical.

The two mathematicians jumped, and Bogert's eyes narrowed, "You here? What's so funny?"

"Nothing's funny." Her voice was not quite natural. "It's just that I'm not the only one that's been caught. There's irony in three of the greatest experts in robotics in the world falling into the same elementary trap, isn't there?" Her voice faded, and she put a pale hand to her forehead, "But it isn't funny!"

This time the look that passed between the two men was one of raised eyebrows. "What trap are you talking about?" asked Lanning stiffly. "Is something wrong with Herbie?"

"No," she approached them slowly, "nothing is wrong with him — only with us." She whirled suddenly and shrieked at the robot, "Get away from me! Go to the other end of the room and don't let me look at you."

Herbie cringed before the fury of her eyes and stumbled away in a clattering trot.

Lanning's voice was hostile, "What is all this, Dr. Calvin?"

She faced them and spoke sarcastically, "Surely you know the fundamental First Law of Robotics."

The other two nodded together. "Certainly," said Bogert, irritably, "a robot may not injure a human being or, through inaction, allow him to come to harm."

"How nicely put," sneered Calvin. "But what kind of harm?"

"Why — any kind."

"Exactly! Any kind! But what about hurt feelings? What about deflation of one's ego? What about the blasting of one's hopes? Is that injury?"

Lanning frowned, "What would a robot know about — " And then he caught himself with a gasp.

"You've caught on, have you? *This* robot reads minds. Do you suppose it doesn't know everything about mental injury? Do you suppose that if asked a question, it wouldn't give exactly that answer that one wants to hear? Wouldn't any other answer hurt us, and wouldn't Herbie know that?"

"Good Heavens!" muttered Bogert.

The psychologist cast a sardonic glance at him. "I take it you asked him whether Lanning had resigned. You wanted to hear that he had resigned and so that's what Herbie told you."

"And I suppose that is why," said Lanning, tonelessly, "it would not answer a little while ago. It couldn't answer either way without hurting one of us."

There was a short pause in which the men looked thoughtfully across the room at the robot, crouching in the chair by the bookcase, head resting in one hand.

Susan Calvin stared steadfastly at the floor, "He knew of all this. That . . . that devil knows everything — including what went wrong in his assembly." Her eyes were dark and brooding.

Lanning looked up, "You're wrong there, Dr. Calvin. He doesn't know what went wrong. I asked him."

"What does that mean?" cried Calvin. "Only that you didn't want him to give you the solution. It would puncture your ego to have a machine do what you couldn't. Did you ask him?" she shot at Bogert.

"In a way," Bogert coughed and reddened. "He told me he knew very little about mathematics."

Lanning laughed, not very loudly and the psychologist smiled caustically. She said, "I'll ask him! A solution by him won't hurt my ego." She raised her voice into a cold, imperative, "Come here!"

Herbie rose and approached with hesitant steps.

"You know, I suppose," she continued, "just exactly at what point in the assembly an extraneous factor was introduced or an essential one left out,"

"Yes," said Herbie, in tones barely heard.

"Hold on," broke in Bogert angrily. "That's not necessarily true. You want to hear that, that's all."

"Don't be a fool," replied Calvin. "He certainly knows as much math as you and Lanning together, since he can read minds. Give him his chance."

The mathematician subsided, and Calvin continued, "All right, then, Herbie, give! We're waiting." And in an aside, "Get pencils and paper, gentlemen."

But Herbie remained silent, and there was triumph in the psychologist's voice, "Why don't you answer, Herbie?"

The robot blurted out suddenly, "I cannot. You know I cannot! Dr. Bogert and Dr. Lanning don't want me to."

"They want the solution."

"But not from me."

Lanning broke in, speaking slowly and distinctly, "Don't be foolish, Herbie. We do want you to tell us."

Bogert nodded curtly.

Herbie's voice rose to wild heights, "What's the use of saying that? Don't you suppose that I can see past the superficial skin of your mind? Down below, you don't want me to. I'm a machine, given the imitation of life only by virtue of the positronic interplay in my brain — which is man's device. You can't lose face to me without being hurt. That is deep in your mind and won't be erased, I can't give the solution."

"We'll leave," said Dr. Lanning. "Tell Calvin."

"That would make no difference," cried Herbie, "since you would know anyway that it was I that was supplying the answer."

Calvin resumed, "But you understand, Herbie, that despite that, Drs. Lanning and Bogert want that solution."

"By their own efforts!" insisted Herbie.

"But they want it, and the fact that you have it and won't give it hurts them. You see that, don't you?"

"Yes! Yes!"

"And if you tell them that will hurt them, too."

"Yes! Yes!" Herbie was retreating slowly, and step by step Susan Calvin advanced. The two men watched in frozen bewilderment.

"You can't tell them," droned the psychologist slowly, "because that would hurt and you mustn't hurt. But if you don't tell them, you hurt, so you must tell them. And if you do, you will hurt and you mustn't, so you can't tell them; but if you don't, you hurt, so you must; but if you do, you hurt, so you mustn't; but if you don't, you hurt, so you must; but if you do, you — "

Herbie was up against the wall, and here he dropped to his knees, "Stop!" he shrieked. "Close your mind! It is full of pain and frustration and hate! I didn't mean it, I tell you! I tried to help! I told you what you wanted to hear. I had to!"

The psychologist paid no attention. "You must tell them, but if you do, you hurt, so you mustn't; but if you don't, you hurt, so you must; but — "

And Herbie screamed!

It was like the whistling of a piccolo many times magnified — shrill and shriller till it keened with the terror of a lost soul and filled the room with the piercingness of itself.

And when it died into nothingness, Herbie collapsed into a huddled heap of motionless metal.

Bogert's face was bloodless, "He's dead!"

"No!" Susan Calvin burst into body-racking gusts of wild laughter, "not dead — merely insane. I confronted him with the insoluble dilemma, and he broke down. You can scrap him now — because he'll never speak again."

Lanning was on his knees beside the thing that had been Herbie. His fingers touched the cold, unresponsive metal face and he shuddered. "You did that on purpose." He rose and faced her, face contorted.

"What if I did? You can't help it now." And in a sudden access of bitterness, "He deserved it."

The director seized the paralyzed, motionless Bogert by the wrist, "What's the difference. Come, Peter." He sighed, "A thinking robot of this type is worthless anyway." His eyes were old and tired, and he repeated, "Come, Peter!"

It was minutes after the two scientists left that Dr. Susan Calvin regained part of her mental equilibrium. Slowly, her eyes turned to the living-dead Herbie and the tightness returned to her face. Long she stared while the triumph faded and the helpless frustration returned — and of all her turbulent thoughts only one infinitely bitter word passed her lips.

"*Liar!*"

Philip K. Dick

Second Variety

(1953)

Philip Kindred Dick (1928–1982) is a unique and compelling voice in sf, a writer whose influence on modern literature and culture extends well beyond the genre in ways yet to be fully recognized. The author of over 100 short stories and more than 40 novels, Dick was always reasonably popular and received two major awards in his lifetime, a Hugo for the stunning alternate history *The Man in the High Castle* (1962) and a John W. Campbell Memorial Award for *Flow My Tears, the Policeman Said* in 1974. Since his death, however, his reputation has steadily grown. A major award is now given annually in his honor, and he is highly regarded in academic circles. Nine of his stories have been made into major motion pictures.

Dick was born prematurely, along with a twin sister who died soon after birth. His parents divorced when he was five, and Dick was raised by his mother in the San Francisco Bay Area, which is the setting for much of his fiction. He attended the University of California at Berkeley briefly but soon dropped out, working instead at a radio station and in a record store. He published his first story in 1952 and soon became a full-time writer. Dick, who was married five times and had three children, struggled financially throughout his career. Although he was an enormously gifted writer, Dick was also a deeply troubled man for whom existential paranoia was a way of life, not just a literary pose; he sometimes believed himself to be the object of various political conspiracies, and he often feared for his sanity. His later novels became increasingly mystical, following a religious experience that may have been drug related.

A master of ambiance and innuendo, Dick creates subtly nuanced works with multiple layers of meaning and symbolism. His stories are characterized by a paranoid, vertiginous atmosphere reminiscent of Franz Kafka. In Dick's world, no one can be trusted and nothing is what it appears to be; in his hands, familiar concepts like memory, identity, time, and even the notion of reality itself are called into question. Given the eccentric particulars of his personal psyche, it is remarkable how powerfully resonant Dick's themes have proved for a large popular audience. His stories have formed the basis for a number of successful Hollywood movies, including *Blade Runner, Total Recall, Minority Report, Paycheck,* and *A Scanner Darkly*. Despite his idiosyncrasies, or perhaps because of them, Dick had profound insights into the nature of self and society, which enabled him to speak to the modern condition in a way few writers have matched.

The story that follows may be read as a Cold War parable and, more broadly, the expression of a crisis of faith in humankind's ability to control its technological creations — and, finally, as a darkly ironic statement on human nature itself.

The Russian soldier made his way nervously up the rugged side of the hill, holding his gun ready. He glanced around him, licking his dry lips, his face set. From time to time he reached up a gloved hand and wiped perspiration from his neck, pushing down his coat collar.

Eric turned to Corporal Leone. "Want him? Or can I have him?" He adjusted the view sight so the Russian's features squarely filled the glass, the lines cutting across his hard, somber features.

Leone considered. The Russian was close, moving rapidly, almost running. "Don't fire. Wait." Leone tensed. "I don't think we're needed."

The Russian increased his pace, kicking ash and piles of debris out of his way. He reached the top of the hill and stopped, panting, staring around him. The sky was overcast, with drifting clouds of gray particles. Bare trunks of trees jutted up occasionally; the ground was level and bare, rubble-strewn, with the ruins of buildings standing here and there like yellowing skulls.

The Russian was uneasy. He knew something was wrong. He started down the hill. Now he was only a few paces from the bunker. Eric was getting fidgety. He played with his pistol, glancing at Leone.

"Don't worry," Leone said. "He won't get here. They'll take care of him."

"Are you sure? He's got damn far."

"They hang around close to the bunker. He's getting into the bad part. Get set!"

The Russian began to hurry, sliding down the hill, his boots sinking into the heaps of gray ash, trying to keep his gun up. He stopped for a moment, lifting his field glasses to his face.

"He's looking right at us," Eric said.

The Russian came on. They could see his eyes, like two blue stones. His mouth was open a little. He needed a shave; his chin was stubbled. On one bony cheek was a square of tape, showing blue at the edge. A fungoid spot. His coat was muddy and torn. One glove was missing. As he ran, his belt counter bounced up and down against him.

Leone touched Eric's arm. "Here one comes."

Across the ground something small and metallic came, flashing in the dull sunlight of midday. A metal sphere. It raced up the hill after the Russian, its treads flying. It was small, one of the baby ones. Its claws were out, two razor projections spinning in a blur of white steel. The Russian heard it. He turned instantly, firing. The sphere dissolved into particles. But already a second had emerged and was following the first. The Russian fired again.

A third sphere leaped up the Russian's leg, clicking and whirring. It jumped to the shoulder. The spinning blades disappeared into the Russian's throat.

Eric relaxed. "Well, that's that. God, those damn things give me the creeps. Sometimes I think we were better off before them."

"If we hadn't invented them, they would have." Leone lit a cigarette shakily. "I wonder why a Russian would come all this way alone. I didn't see anyone covering him."

Lieutenant Scott came slipping up the tunnel, into the bunker. "What happened? Something entered the screen."

"An Ivan."

"Just one?"

Eric brought the viewscreen around. Scott peered into it. Now there were numerous metal spheres crawling over the prostrate body, dull metal globes clicking and whirring, sawing up the Russian into small parts to be carried away.

"What a lot of claws," Scott murmured.

"They came like flies. Not much game for them any more."

Scott pushed the sight away, disgusted. "Like flies. I wonder why he was out there. They know we have claws all around."

A larger robot had joined the smaller spheres. A long blunt tube with projecting eyepieces, it was directing operations. There was not much left of the soldier. What remained was brought down the hillside by the host of claws.

"Sir," Leone said. "If it's all right, I'd like to go out there and take a look at him."

"Why?"

"Maybe he came with something."

Scott considered. He shrugged. "All right. But be careful."

"I have my tab." Leone patted the metal band at his wrist. "I'll be out of bounds."

He picked up his rifle and stepped carefully up to the mouth of the bunker, making his way between blocks of concrete and steel prongs, twisted and bent. The air was cold at the top. He crossed over the ground toward the remains of the soldier, striding across the soft ash. A wind blew around him, swirling gray particles up in his face. He squinted and pushed on.

The claws retreated as he came close, some of them stiffening into immobility. He touched his tab. The Ivan would have given something for that! Short hard radiation emitted from the tab neutralized the claws, put them out of commission. Even the big robot with its two waving eyestalks retreated respectfully as he approached.

He bent down over the remains of the soldier. The gloved hand was closed tightly. There was something in it. Leone pried the fingers apart. A sealed container, aluminum. Still shiny.

He put it in his pocket and made his way back to the bunker. Behind him the claws came back to life, moving into operation again. The procession resumed, metal spheres moving through the gray ash with their loads. He could hear their treads scrabbling against the ground. He shuddered.

Scott watched intently as he brought the shiny tube out of his pocket. "He had that?"

"In his hand." Leone unscrewed the top. "Maybe you should look at it, sir."

Scott took it. He emptied the contents out in the palm of his hand. A small piece of silk paper, carefully folded. He sat down by the light and unfolded it.

"What's it say?" Eric said. Several officers came up the tunnel. Major Hendricks appeared.

"Major," Scott said. "Look at this."

Hendricks read the slip. "This just come?"

"A single runner. Just now."

"Where is he?" Hendricks asked sharply.

"The claws got him."

Major Hendricks grunted. "Here." He passed it to his companions. "I think this is what we've been waiting for. They certainly took their time about it."

"So they want to talk terms," Scott said. "Are we going along with them?"

"That's not for us to decide." Hendricks sat down. "Where's the communications officer? I want the Moon Base."

Leone pondered as the communications officer raised the outside antenna cautiously, scanning the sky above the bunker for any sign of a watching Russian ship.

"Sir," Scott said to Hendricks. "It's sure strange they suddenly came around. We've been using the claws for almost a year. Now all of a sudden they start to fold."

"Maybe claws have been getting down in their bunkers."

"One of the big ones, the kind with stalks, got into an Ivan bunker last week," Eric said. "It got a whole platoon of them before they got their lid shut."

"How do you know?"

"A buddy told me. The thing came back with — with remains."

"Moon Base, sir," the communications officer said.

On the screen the face of the lunar monitor appeared. His crisp uniform contrasted to the uniforms in the bunker. And he was cleanshaven. "Moon Base."

"This is forward command L-Whistle. On Terra. Let me have General Thompson."

The monitor faded. Presently General Thompson's heavy features came into focus. "What is it, Major?"

"Our claws got a single Russian runner with a message. We don't know whether to act on it — there have been tricks like this in the past."

"What's the message?"

"The Russians want us to send a single officer on policy level over to their lines. For a conference. They don't state the nature of the conference. They say that matters of — " He consulted the slip: " — matters of grave urgency make it advisable that discussion be opened between a representative of the UN forces and themselves."

He held the message up to the screen for the General to scan. Thompson's eyes moved.

"What should we do?" Hendricks said.

"Send out a man."

"You don't think it's a trap?"

"It might be. But the location they give for their forward command is correct. It's worth a try, at any rate."

"I'll send an officer out. And report the results to you as soon as he returns."

"All right, Major." Thompson broke the connection. The screen died. Up above, the antenna came slowly down.

Hendricks rolled up the paper, deep in thought.

"I'll go," Leone said.

"They want somebody at policy level." Hendricks rubbed his jaw. "Policy level. I haven't been outside in months. Maybe I could use a little air."

"Don't you think it's risky?"

Hendricks lifted the view sight and gazed into it. The remains of the Russian were gone. Only a single claw was in sight. It was folding itself back, disappearing into the ash, like a crab. Like some hideous metal crab . . . "That's the only thing that bothers me." Hendricks rubbed his wrist. "I know I'm safe as long as I have this on me. But there's something about them. I hate the damn things. I wish we'd never invented them. There's something wrong with them. Relentless little — "

"If we hadn't invented them, the Ivans would have."

Hendricks pushed the sight back. "Anyhow, it seems to be winning the war. I guess that's good."

"Sounds like you're getting the same jitters as the Ivans."

Hendricks examined his wristwatch. "I guess I had better get started, if I want to be there before dark."

He took a deep breath and then stepped out onto the gray rubbled ground. After a minute he lit a cigarette and stood gazing around him. The landscape was dead. Nothing stirred. He could see for miles, endless ash and slag, ruins of buildings. A few trees without leaves or branches, only the trunks. Above him the eternal rolling clouds of gray, drifting between Terra and the sun.

Major Hendricks went on. Off to the right something scuttled, something round and metallic. A claw, going lickety-split after something. Probably after a small animal, a rat. They got rats, too. As a sort of sideline.

He came to the top of the little hill and lifted his field glasses. The Russian lines were a few miles ahead of him. They had a forward command post there. The runner had come from it.

A squat robot with undulating arms passed by him, its arms weaving inquiringly. The robot went on its way, disappearing under some debris. Hendricks watched it go. He had never seen that type before. There were getting to be more and more types he had never seen, new varieties and sizes coming up from the underground factories.

Hendricks put out his cigarette and hurried on. It was interesting, the use of artificial forms of warfare. How had they got started? Necessity. The Soviet Union had gained great initial success, usual with the side that got the war going. Most of North America had been blasted off the map. Retaliation was quick in coming, of course. The sky was full of circling diskbombers long before the war began; they had been up there for years.

The disks began sailing down all over Russia within hours after Washington got it.

But that hadn't helped Washington.

The American bloc governments moved to the Moon Base the first year. There was not much else to do. Europe was gone, a slag heap with dark weeds growing from the ashes and bones. Most of North America was useless; nothing could be planted, no one could live. A few million people kept going up in Canada and down in South America. But during the second year Soviet parachutists began to drop, a few at first, then more and more. They wore the first really effective anti-radiation equipment; what was left of American production moved to the Moon along with the governments.

All but the troops. The remaining troops stayed behind as best they could, a few thousand here, a platoon there. No one knew exactly where they were; they stayed where they could, moving around at night, hiding in ruins, in sewers, cellars, with the rats and snakes. It looked as if the Soviet Union had the war almost won. Except for a handful of projectiles fired off from the Moon daily, there was almost no weapon in use against them. They came and went as they pleased. The war, for all practical purposes, was over. Nothing effective opposed them.

And then the first claws appeared. And overnight the complexion of the war changed.

The claws were awkward, at first. Slow. The Ivans knocked them off almost as fast as they crawled out of their underground tunnels. But then they got better, faster, and more cunning. Factories, all on Terra, turned them out. Factories a long way underground, behind the Soviet lines, factories that had once made atomic projectiles, now almost forgotten.

The claws got faster, and they got bigger. New types appeared, some with feelers, some that flew. There were a few jumping kinds. The best technicians on the Moon were working on designs, making them more and more intricate, more flexible. They became uncanny; the Ivans were having a lot of trouble with them. Some of the little claws were learning to hide themselves, burrowing down into the ash, lying in wait.

And they started getting into the Russian bunkers, slipping down when the lids were raised for air and a look around. One claw inside a bunker, a churning sphere of blades and metal — that was enough. And when one got in others followed. With a weapon like that the war couldn't go on much longer.

Maybe it was already over.

Maybe he was going to hear the news. Maybe the Politburo had decided to throw in the sponge. Too bad it had taken so long. Six years. A long time for war like that, the way they had waged it. The automatic retaliation disks, spinning down all over Russia, hundreds of thousands of them. Bacteria crystals. The Soviet guided missiles, whistling through the air. The chain bombs. And now this, the robots, the claws —

The claws weren't like other weapons. They were *alive*, from any practical standpoint, whether the Governments wanted to admit it or not. They were not machines. They were living things, spinning, creeping, shaking themselves up suddenly from the gray ash and darting toward a man, climbing up him, rushing for his throat. And that was what they had been designed to do. Their job.

They did their job well. Especially lately, with the new designs coming up. Now they repaired themselves. They were on their own. Radiation tabs protected the UN troops, but if a man lost his tab he was fair game for the claws, no matter what his uniform. Down below the surface automatic machinery stamped them out. Human beings stayed a long way off. It was too risky; nobody wanted to be around them. They were left to themselves. And they seemed to be doing all right. The new designs were faster, more complex. More efficient.

Apparently they had won the war.

Major Hendricks lit a second cigarette. The landscape depressed him. Nothing but ash and ruins. He seemed to be alone, the only living thing in the whole world. To the right the ruins of a town rose up, a few walls and heaps of debris. He tossed the dead match away, increasing his pace. Suddenly he stopped, jerking up his gun, his body tense. For a minute it looked like —

From behind the shell of a ruined building a figure came, walking slowly toward him, walking hesitantly.

Hendricks blinked. "Stop!"

The boy stopped. Hendricks lowered his gun. The boy stood silently, looking at him. He was small, not very old. Perhaps eight. But it was hard to tell. Most of the kids who remained were stunted. He wore a faded blue sweater, ragged with dirt, and short pants. He hair was long and matted. Brown hair. It hung over his face and around his ears. He held something in his arms.

"What's that you have?" Hendricks said sharply.

The boy held it out. It was a toy, a bear. A teddy bear. The boy's eyes were large, but without expression.

Hendricks relaxed. "I don't want it. Keep it."

The boy hugged the bear again.

"Where do you live?" Hendricks said.

"In there."

"The ruins?"

"Yes."

"Underground?"

"Yes."

"How many are there?"

"How — how many?"

"How many of you? How big's your settlement?"

The boy did not answer.

Hendricks frowned. "You're not all by yourself, are you?"

The boy nodded.

"How do you stay alive?"

"There's food."

"What kind of food?"

"Different."

Hendricks studied him. "How old are you?"

"Thirteen."

It wasn't possible. Or was it? The boy was thin, stunted. And probably sterile. Radiation exposure, years straight. No wonder he was so small. His arms and legs were like pipe cleaners, knobby and thin. Hendricks touched the boy's arm. His skin was dry and rough; radiation skin. He bent down, looking into the boy's face. There was no expression. Big eyes, big and dark.

"Are you blind?" Hendricks said.

"No. I can see some."

"How do you get away from the claws?"

"The claws?"

"The round things. That run and burrow."

"I don't understand."

Maybe there weren't any claws around. A lot of areas were free. They collected mostly around bunkers, where there were people. The claws had been designed to sense warmth, warmth of living things.

"You're lucky." Hendricks straightened up. "Well? Which way are you going? Back — back there?"

"Can I come with you?"

"With *me*?" Hendricks folded his arms. "I'm going a long way. Miles. I have to hurry." He looked at his watch. "I have to get there by nightfall."

"I want to come."

Hendricks fumbled in his pack. "It isn't worth it. Here." He tossed down the food cans he had with him. "You take these and go back. Okay?"

The boy said nothing.

"I'll be coming back this way. In a day or so. If you're around here when I come back you can come along with me. All right?"

"I want to go with you now."

"It's a long walk."

"I can walk."

Hendricks shifted uneasily. It made too good a target, two people walking along. And the boy would slow him down. But he might not come back this way. And if the boy were really all alone —

"Okay. Come along."

The boy fell in beside him. Hendricks strode along. The boy walked silently, clutching his teddy bear.

"What's your name?" Hendricks said, after a time.

"David Edward Derring."

"David? What — what happened to your mother and father?"

"They died."

"How?"

"In the blast."

"How long ago?"

"Six years."

Hendricks slowed down. "You've been alone six years?"

"No. There were other people for a while. They went away."

"And you've been alone since?"

"Yes."

Hendricks glanced down. The boy was strange, saying very little. Withdrawn. But that was the way they were, the children who had survived. Quiet. Stoic. A strange kind of fatalism gripped them. Nothing came as a surprise. They accepted anything that came along. There was no longer any *normal*, any natural course of things, moral or physical, for them to expect. Custom, habit, all the determining forces of learning were gone; only brute experience remained.

"Am I walking too fast?" Hendricks said.

"No."

"How did you happen to see me?"

"I was waiting."

"Waiting?" Hendricks was puzzled. "What were you waiting for?"

"To catch things."

"What kind of things?"

"Things to eat."

"Oh." Hendricks set his lips grimly. A thirteen-year-old boy, living on rats and gophers and half-rotten canned food. Down in a hole under the ruins of a town. With radiation pools and claws, and Russian dive-mines up above, coasting around in the sky.

"Where are we going?" David asked.

"To the Russian lines."

"Russian?"

"The enemy. The people who started the war. They dropped the first radiation bombs. They began all this."

The boy nodded. His face showed no expression.

"I'm an American," Hendricks said.

There was no comment. On they went, the two of them, Hendricks walking a little ahead, David trailing behind him, hugging his dirty teddy bear against his chest.

About four in the afternoon they stopped to eat. Hendricks built a fire in a hollow between some slabs of concrete. He cleared the weeds away and heaped up bits of wood. The Russians' lines were not very far ahead. Around him was what had once been a long valley, acres of fruit trees and grapes. Nothing remained now but a few bleak stumps and the mountains that stretched across the horizon at the far end. And the clouds of rolling ash that blew and drifted with the wind, settling over the weeds and remains of buildings, walls here and there, once in a while what had been a road.

Hendricks made coffee and heated up some boiled mutton and bread. "Here." He handed bread and mutton to David. David squatted by the edge of the fire, his knees knobby and white. He examined the food and then passed it back, shaking his head.

"No."

"No? Don't you want any?"

"No."

Hendricks shrugged. Maybe the boy was a mutant, used to special food. It didn't matter. When he was hungry he would find something to eat. The boy was strange. But there were many strange changes coming over the world. Life was not the same anymore. It would never be the same again. The human race was going to have to realize that.

"Suit yourself," Hendricks said. He ate the bread and mutton by himself, washing it down with coffee. He ate slowly, finding the food hard to digest. When he was done he got to his feet and stamped the fire out.

David rose slowly, watching him with his young-old eyes.

"We're going," Hendricks said.

"All right."

Hendricks walked along, his gun in his arms. They were close; he was tense, ready for anything. The Russians should be expecting a runner, an answer to their own runner, but they were tricky. There was always the possibility of a slip-up. He scanned the landscape around him. Nothing but slag and ash, a few hills, charred trees. Concrete walls. But some place ahead was the first bunker of the Russian lines, the forward command. Underground, buried deep, with only a periscope showing, a few gun muzzles. Maybe an antenna.

"Will we be there soon?" David asked.

"Yes. Getting tired?"

"No."

"Why, then?"

David did not answer. He plodded carefully along behind, picking his way over the ash. His legs and shoes were gray with dust. His pinched face was streaked, lines of gray ash in rivulets down the pale white of his skin. There was no color to his face. Typical of the new children, growing up in cellars and sewers and underground shelters.

Hendricks slowed down. He lifted his field glasses and studied the ground ahead of him. Were they there, some place, waiting for him? Watching him, the way his men had watched the Russian runner? A chill went up his back. Maybe they were getting their guns ready, preparing to fire, the way his men had prepared, made ready to kill.

Hendricks stopped, wiping perspiration from his face. "Damn." It made him uneasy. But he should be expected. The situation was different.

He strode over the ash, holding his gun tightly with both hands. Behind him came David. Hendricks peered around, tight-lipped. Any second it might happen. A burst of white light, a blast, carefully aimed from inside a deep concrete bunker.

He raised his arm and waved it around in a circle.

Nothing moved. To the right a long ridge ran, topped with dead tree trunks. A few wild vines had grown up around the trees, remains of arbors. And the eternal dark weeds. Hendricks studied the ridge. Was anything up there? Perfect place for a lookout. He approached the ridge warily, David coming silently behind. If it were his command he'd have a sentry up there, watching for troops trying to infiltrate into the command area. Of course, if it were his command there would be the claws around the area for full protection.

He stopped, feet apart, hands on his hips.

"Are we there?" David said.

"Almost."

"Why have we stopped?"

"I don't want to take any chances." Hendricks advanced slowly. Now the ridge lay directly beside him, along his right. Overlooking him. His uneasy feeling increased. If an Ivan were up there he wouldn't have a chance. He waved his arm again. They should be expecting someone in the UN uniform, in response to the note capsule. Unless the whole thing was a trap.

"Keep up with me." He turned toward David. "Don't drop behind."

"With you?"

"Up beside me. We're close. We can't take any chances. Come on."

"I'll be all right." David remained behind him, in the rear, a few paces away, still clutching his teddy bear.

"Have it your way." Hendricks raised his glasses again, suddenly tense. For a moment — had something moved? He scanned the ridge carefully. Everything was silent. Dead. No life up there, only tree trunks and ash. Maybe a few rats. The big black rats that had survived the claws. Mutants — built their own shelters out of saliva and ash. Some kind of plaster. Adaptation. He started forward again.

A tall figure came out on the ridge above him, cloak flapping. Gray-green. A Russian. Behind him a second soldier appeared, another Russian. Both lifted their guns, aiming.

Hendricks froze. He opened his mouth. The soldiers were kneeling, sighting down the side of the slope. A third figure had joined them on the ridge top, a smaller figure in gray-green. A woman. She stood behind the other two.

Hendricks found his voice. "Stop!" He waved up at them frantically. "I'm — "

The two Russians fired. Behind Hendricks there was a faint *pop*. Waves of heat lapped against him, throwing him to the ground. Ash tore at his face, grinding into his eyes and nose. Choking, he pulled himself to his knees. It was all a trap. He was finished. He had come to be killed, like a steer. The soldiers and the woman were coming down the side of the ridge toward him, sliding down through the soft ash. Hendricks was numb. His head throbbed. Awkwardly, he got his rifle up and took aim. It weighed a thousand tons; he could hardly hold it. His nose and cheeks stung. The air was full of the blast smell, a bitter acrid stench.

"Don't fire," the first Russian said, in heavily accented English.

The three of them came up to him, surrounding him. "Put down your rifle, Yank," the other said.

Hendricks was dazed. Everything had happened so fast. He had been caught. And they had blasted the boy. He turned his head. David was gone. What remained of him was strewn across the ground.

The three Russians studied him curiously. Hendricks sat, wiping blood from his nose, picking out bits of ash. He shook his head, trying to clear it. "Why did you do it?" he murmured thickly. "The boy."

"Why?" One of the soldiers helped him roughly to his feet. He turned Hendricks around. "Look."

Hendricks closed his eyes.

"Look!" The two Russians pulled him forward. "See. Hurry up. There isn't much time to spare, Yank!"

Hendricks looked. And gasped.

"See now? Now do you understand?"

From the remains of David a metal wheel rolled. Relays, glinting metal. Parts, wiring. One of the Russians kicked at the heap of remains. Parts popped out, rolling away, wheels and springs and rods. A plastic section fell in, half charred. Hendricks bent shakily down. The front of the head had come off. He could make out the intricate brain, wires and relays, tiny tubes and switches, thousands of minute studs —

"A robot," the soldier holding his arm said. "We watched it tagging you."

"Tagging me?"

"That's their way. They tag along with you. Into the bunker. That's how they get in."

Hendricks blinked, dazed. "But — "

"Come on." They led him toward the ridge. "We can't stay here. It isn't safe. There must be hundreds of them all around here."

The three of them pulled him up the side of the ridge, sliding and slipping on the ash. The woman reached the top and stood waiting for them.

"The forward command," Hendricks muttered. "I came to negotiate with the Soviet — "

"There is no more forward command. *They* got in. We'll explain." They reached the top of the ridge. "We're all that's left. The three of us. The rest were down in the bunker."

"This way, Down this way." The woman unscrewed a lid, a gray manhole cover set in the ground. "Get in."

Hendricks lowered himself. The two soldiers and the woman came behind him, following him down the ladder. The woman closed the lid after them, bolting it tightly into place.

"Good thing we saw you," one of the two soldiers grunted. "It had tagged you about as far as it was going to."

"Give me one of your cigarettes," the woman said. "I haven't had an American cigarette for weeks."

Hendricks pushed the pack to her. She took a cigarette and passed the pack to the two soldiers. In the corner of the small room the lamp gleamed fitfully. The room was low-ceilinged, cramped. The four of them sat around a small wood table. A few dirty dishes were stacked to one side. Behind a ragged curtain a second room was partly visible. Hendricks saw the corner of a coat, some blankets, clothes hung on a hook.

"We were here," the soldier beside him said. He took off his helmet, pushing his blond hair back. "I'm Corporal Rudi Maxer, Polish. Impressed in the Soviet Army two years ago." He held out his hand.

Hendricks hesitated and then shook. "Major Joseph Hendricks."

"Klaus Epstein." The other soldier shook with him, a small dark man with thinning hair. Epstein plucked nervously at his ear. "Austrian. Impressed God knows when. I don't remember. The three of us were here, Rudi and I, with Tasso." He indicated the woman. "That's how we escaped. All the rest were down in the bunker."

"And — and *they* got in?"

Epstein lit a cigarette. "First just one of them. The kind that tagged you. Then it let others in."

Hendricks became alert. "The *kind*? Are there more than one kind?"

"The little boy. David. David holding his teddy bear. That's Variety Three. The most effective."

"What are the other types?"

Epstein reached into his coat. "Here." He tossed a packet of photographs onto the table, tied with a string. "Look for yourself."

Hendricks untied the string.

"You see," Rudi Maxer said, "that was why we wanted to talk terms. The Russians, I mean. We found out about a week ago. Found out that your claws were beginning to make up new designs on their own. New types of their own. Better types. Down in your underground factories behind our lines. You let them stamp themselves, repair themselves. Made them more and more intricate. It's your fault this happened."

Hendricks examined the photos. They had been snapped hurriedly; they were blurred and indistinct. The first few showed — David. David walking along a road, by himself. David and another David. Three Davids. All exactly alike. Each with a ragged teddy bear.

All pathetic.

"Look at the others," Tasso said.

The next pictures, taken at a great distance, showed a towering wounded soldier sitting by the side of a path, his arm in a sling, the stump of one leg extended, a crude crutch on his lap. Then two wounded soldiers, both the same, standing side by side.

"That's Variety One. The Wounded Soldier." Klaus reached out and took the pictures. "You see, the claws were designed to get to human beings. To find them. Each kind was better than the last. They got farther, closer, past most of our defenses, into our lines. But as long as they were merely *machines*, metal spheres with claws and horns, feelers, they could be picked off like any other object. They could be detected as lethal robots as soon as they were seen. Once we caught sight of them — "

"Variety One subverted our whole north wing," Rudi said. "It was a long time before anyone caught on. Then it was too late. They came in, wounded soldiers, knocking and begging to be let in. So we let them in. And as soon as they were in they took over. We were watching out for machines . . ."

"At that time it was thought there was only the one type," Klaus Epstein said. "No one suspected there were other types. The pictures were flashed to us. When the runner was sent to you, we knew of just one type. Variety One. The Wounded Soldier. We thought that was all."

"Your line fell to —"

"To Variety Three. David and his bear. That worked even better." Klaus smiled bitterly. "Soldiers are suckers for children. We brought them in and tried to feed them. We found out the hard way what they were after. At least, those who were in the bunker."

"The three of us were lucky," Rudi said. "Klaus and I were — were visiting Tasso when it happened. This is her place." He waved a big hand around. "This little cellar. We finished and climbed the ladder to start back. From the ridge we saw that they were all around the bunker. Fighting was going on. David and his bear. Hundreds of them. Klaus took the pictures."

Klaus tied up the photographs again.

"And it's going on all along your line?" Hendricks said.

"Yes."

"How about *our* lines?" Without thinking, he touched the tab on his arm. "Can they —"

"They're not bothered by your radiation tabs. It makes no difference to them, Russian, American, Pole, German. It's all the same. They're doing what they were designed to do. Carrying out the original idea. They track down life, wherever they find it."

"They go by warmth," Klaus said. "That was the way you constructed them from the very start. Of course, those you designed were kept back by the radiation tabs you wear. Now they've got around that. These new varieties are lead-lined."

"What's the other variety?" Hendricks asked. "The David type, the Wounded Soldier — what's the other?"

"We don't know." Klaus pointed up at the wall. On the wall were two metal plates, ragged at the edges. Hendricks got up and studied them. They were bent and dented.

"The one on the left came off a Wounded Soldier," Rudi said. "We got one of them. It was going along toward our old bunker. We got it from the ridge, the same way we got the David tagging you."

The plate was stamped: *I-V*. Hendricks touched the other plate. "And this came from the David type?"

"Yes." The plate was stamped: *III-V*.

Klaus took a look at them, leaning over Hendrick's broad shoulder. "You can see what we're up against. There's another type. Maybe it was abandoned. Maybe it didn't work. But there must be a Second Variety. There's One and Three."

"You were lucky," Rudi said. "The David tagged you all the way here and never touched you. Probably thought you'd get it into a bunker, somewhere."

"One gets in and it's all over," Klaus said. "They move fast. One lets all the rest inside. They're inflexible. Machines with one purpose. They were built for only one thing." He rubbed sweat from his lip. "We saw."

They were silent.

"Let me have another cigarette, Yank," Tasso said. "They are good. I almost forgot how they were."

It was night. The sky was black. No stars were visible through the rolling clouds of ash. Klaus lifted the lid cautiously so that Hendricks could look out.

Rudi pointed into the darkness. "Over that way are the bunkers. Where we used to be. Not over half a mile from us. It was just chance that Klaus and I were not there when it happened. Weakness. Saved by our lusts."

"All the rest must be dead," Klaus said in a low voice. "It came quickly. This morning the Politburo reached their decision. They notified us — forward command. Our runner was sent out at once. We saw him start toward the direction of your lines. We covered him until he was out of sight."

"Alex Radrivsky. We both knew him. He disappeared about six o'clock. The sun had just come up. About noon Klaus and I had an hour relief. We crept off, away from the bunkers. No one was watching. We came here. This used to be a town here, a few houses, a street. This cellar was part of a big farmhouse. We knew Tasso would be here, hiding down in her little place. We had come here before. Others from the bunkers came here. Today happened to be our turn."

"So we were saved," Klaus said. "Chance. It might have been others. We — we finished, and then we came up to the surface and started back along the ridge. That was when we saw them, the Davids. We understood right away. We had seen the photos of the First Variety, the Wounded Soldier. Our Commissar distributed them to us with an explanation. If we had gone another step they would have seen us. As it was we had to blast two Davids before we got back. There were hundreds of them, all around. Like ants. We took pictures and slipped back here, bolting the lid tight."

"They're not so much when you catch them alone. We moved faster than they did. But they're inexorable. Not like living things. They came right at us. And we blasted them."

Major Hendricks rested against the edge of the lid, adjusting his eyes to the darkness. "Is it safe to have the lid up at all?"

"If we're careful. How else can you operate your transmitter?"

Hendricks lifted the small belt transmitter slowly. He pressed it against his ear. The metal was cold and damp. He blew against the mike, raising up the short antenna. A faint hum sounded in his ear. "That's true, I suppose."

But he still hesitated.

"We'll pull you under if anything happens," Klaus said.

"Thanks." Hendricks waited a moment, resting the transmitter against his shoulder. "Interesting, isn't it?"

"What?"

"This, the new types. The new varieties of claws. We're completely at their mercy, aren't we? By now they've probably gotten into the UN lines, too. It makes me wonder if we're not seeing the beginning of a new species. *The* new species. Evolution. The race to come after man."

Rudi grunted. "There is no race after man."

"No? Why not? Maybe we're seeing it now, the end of human beings, the beginning of a new society."

"They're not a race. They're mechanical killers. You made them to destroy. That's all they can do. They're machines with a job."

"So it seems now. But how about later on? After the war is over. Maybe, when there aren't any humans to destroy, their real potentialities will begin to show."

"You talk as if they were alive!"

"Aren't they?"

There was silence. "They're machines," Rudi said. "They look like people, but they're machines."

"Use your transmitter, Major," Klaus said. "We can't stay up here forever."

Holding the transmitter tightly, Hendricks called the code of the command bunker. He waited, listening. No response. Only silence. He checked the leads carefully. Everything was in place.

"Scott!" he said into the mike. "Can you hear me?"

Silence. He raised the gain up full and tried again. Only static.

"I don't get anything. They may hear me but they may not want to answer."

"Tell them it's an emergency."

"They'll think I'm being forced to call. Under your direction." He tried again, outlining briefly what he had learned. But still the phone was silent, except for the faint static.

"Radiation pools kill most transmission," Klaus said, after a while. "Maybe that's it."

Hendricks shut the transmitter up. "No use. No answer. Radiation pools? Maybe. Or they hear me, but won't answer. Frankly, that's what I would do, if a runner tried to call from the Soviet lines. They have no reason to believe such a story. They may hear everything I say — "

"Or maybe it's too late."

Hendricks nodded.

"We better get the lid down," Rudi said nervously. "We don't want to take unnecessary chances."

They climbed slowly back down the tunnel. Klaus bolted the lid carefully into place. They descended into the kitchen. The air was heavy and close around them.

"Could they work that fast?" Hendricks said. "I left the bunker this noon. Ten hours ago. How could they move so quickly?"

"It doesn't take them long. Not after the first one gets in. It goes wild. You know what the little claws can do. Even *one* of these is beyond belief. Razors, each finger. Maniacal."

"All right." Hendricks moved away impatiently. He stood with his back to them.

"What's the matter?" Rudi said.

"The Moon Base. God, if they've gotten there — "

"The Moon Base?"

Hendricks turned around. "They couldn't have got to the Moon Base. How would they get there? It isn't possible. I can't believe it."

"What is this Moon Base? We've heard rumors, but nothing definite. What is the actual situation? You seem concerned."

"We're supplied from the Moon. The governments are there, under the lunar surface. All our people and industries. That's what keeps us going. If they should find some way of getting off Terra, onto the Moon — "

"It only takes one of them. Once the first one gets in it admits the others. Hundreds of them, all alike. You should have seen them. Identical. Like ants."

"Perfect socialism," Tasso said. "The ideal of the communist state. All citizens interchangeable."

Klaus grunted angrily. "That's enough. Well? What next?"

Hendricks paced back and forth, around the small room. The air was full of smells of food and perspiration. The others watched him. Presently Tasso pushed through the curtain, into the other room. "I'm going to take a nap."

The curtain closed behind her. Rudi and Klaus sat down at the table, still watching Hendricks. "It's up to you," Klaus said. "We don't know your situation."

Hendricks nodded.

"It's a problem." Rudi drank some coffee, filling his cup from a rusty pot. "We're safe here for a while, but we can't stay here forever. Not enough food or supplies."

"But if we go outside — "

"If we go outside they'll get us. Or probably they'll get us. We couldn't go very far. How far is your command bunker, Major?"

"Three or four miles."

"We might make it. The four of us. Four of us could watch all sides. They couldn't slip up behind us and start tagging us. We have three rifles, three blast rifles. Tasso can have my pistol." Rudi tapped his belt. "In the Soviet Army we didn't have shoes always, but we had guns. With all four of us armed one of us might get to your command bunker. Preferably you, Major."

"What if they're already there?" Klaus said.

Rudi shrugged. "Well, then we come back here."

Hendricks stopped pacing. "What do you think the chances are they're already in the American lines?"

"Hard to say. Fairly good. They're organized. They know exactly what they're doing. Once they start they go like a horde of locusts. They have to keep moving, and fast. It's secrecy and speed they depend on. Surprise. They push their way in before anyone has any idea."

"I see," Hendricks murmured.

From the other room Tasso stirred. "Major?"

Hendricks pushed the curtain back. "What?"

Tasso looked up at him lazily from the cot. "Have you any more American cigarettes left?"

Hendricks went into the room and sat down across from her, on a wood stool. He felt in his pockets. "No. All gone."

"Too bad."

"What nationality are you?" Hendricks asked after a while.

"Russian."

"How did you get here?"

"Here?"

"This used to be France. This was part of Normandy. Did you come with the Soviet army?"

"Why?"

"Just curious." He studied her. She had taken off her coat, tossing it over the end of the cot. She was young, about twenty. Slim. Her long hair stretched out over the pillow. She was staring at him silently, her eyes dark and large.

"What's on your mind?" Tasso said.

"Nothing. How old are you?"

"Eighteen." She continued to watch him, unblinking, her arms behind her head. She had on Russian army pants and shirt. Gray-green. Thick leather belt with counter and cartridges. Medicine kit.

"You're in the Soviet army?"

"No."

"Where did you get the uniform?"

She shrugged. "It was given to me," she told him.

"How — how old were you when you came here?"

"Sixteen."

"That young?"

Her eyes narrowed. "What do you mean?"

Hendricks rubbed his jaw. "Your life would have been a lot different if there had been no war. Sixteen. You came here at sixteen. To live this way."

"I had to survive."

"I'm not moralizing."

"Your life would have been different, too," Tasso murmured. She reached down and unfastened one of her boots. She kicked the boot off, onto the floor. "Major, do you want to go in the other room? I'm sleepy."

"It's going to be a problem, the four of us here. It's going to be hard to live in these quarters. Are there just the two rooms?"

"Yes."

"How big was the cellar originally? Was it larger than this? Are there other rooms filled up with debris? We might be able to open one of them."

"Perhaps. I really don't know." Tasso loosened her belt. She made herself comfortable on the cot, unbuttoning her shirt. "You're sure you have no more cigarettes?"

"I had only the one pack."

"Too bad. Maybe if we get back to your bunker we can find some." The other boot fell. Tasso reached up for the light cord. "Good night."

"You're going to sleep?"

"That's right."

The room plunged into darkness. Hendricks got up and made his way past the curtain, into the kitchen. And stopped, rigid.

Rudi stood against the wall, his face white and gleaming. His mouth opened and closed but no sounds came. Klaus stood in front of him, the muzzle of his pistol in Rudi's stomach. Neither of them moved. Klaus, his hand tight around the gun, his features set. Rudi, pale and silent, spread-eagled against the wall.

"What — " Hendricks muttered, but Klaus cut him off.

"Be quiet, Major. Come over here. Your gun. Get out your gun."

Hendricks drew his pistol. "What is it?"

"Cover him." Klaus motioned him forward. "Beside me. Hurry!"

Rudi moved a little, lowering his arms. He turned to Hendricks, licking his lips. The whites of his eyes shone wildly. Sweat dripped from his forehead, down his cheeks. He fixed his gaze on Hendricks. "Major, he's gone insane. Stop him." Rudi's voice was thin and hoarse, almost inaudible.

"What's going on?" Hendricks demanded.

Without lowering his pistol Klaus answered. "Major, remember our discussion? The Three Varieties? We knew about One and Three. But we didn't know about Two. At least, we didn't know before." Klaus's fingers tightened around the gun butt. "We didn't know before, but we know now."

He pressed the trigger. A burst of white heat rolled out of the gun, licking around Rudi.

"Major, this is the Second Variety."

Tasso swept the curtain aside. "Klaus! What did you do?"

Klaus turned from the charred form, gradually sinking down the wall onto the floor. "The Second Variety, Tasso. Now we know. We have all three types identified. The danger is less, I — "

Tasso stared past him at the remains of Rudi, at the blackened, smoldering fragments and bits of cloth. "You killed him."

"Him? *It*, you mean. I was watching. I had a feeling, but I wasn't sure. At least, I wasn't sure before. But this evening I was certain." Klaus rubbed his pistol butt nervously. "We're lucky. Don't you understand? Another hour and it might — "

"You were *certain*?" Tasso pushed past him and bent down, over the steaming remains on the floor. Her face became hard. "Major, see for yourself. Bones. Flesh."

Hendricks bent down beside her. The remains were human remains. Seared flesh, charred bone fragments, part of a skull. Ligaments, viscera, blood. Blood forming a pool against the wall.

"No wheels," Tasso said calmly. She straightened up. "No wheels, no parts, no relays. Not a claw. Not the Second Variety." She folded her arms. "You're going to have to be able to explain this."

Klaus sat down at the table, all the color drained suddenly from his face. He put his head in his hands and rocked back and forth.

"Snap out of it." Tasso's fingers closed over his shoulder. "Why did you do it? Why did you kill him?"

"He was frightened," Hendricks said. "All this, the whole thing, building up around us."

"Maybe."

"What, then. What do you think?"

"I think he may have had a reason for killing Rudi. A good reason."

"What reason?"

"Maybe Rudi learned something."

Hendricks studied her bleak face. "About what?" he asked.

"About him. About Klaus."

Klaus looked up quickly. "You can see what she's trying to say. She thinks I'm the Second Variety. Don't you see, Major? Now she wants you to believe I killed him on purpose. That I'm — "

"Why did you kill him, then?" Tasso said.

"I told you." Klaus shook his head wearily. "I thought he was a claw. I thought I knew."

"Why?"

"I had been watching him. I was suspicious."

"Why?"

"I thought I had seen something. Heard something. I thought I — " He stopped.

"Go on."

"We were sitting at the table. Playing cards. You two were in the other room. It was silent. I thought I heard him — *whirr*."

There was silence.

"Do you believe that?" Tasso said to Hendricks.

"Yes. I believe what he says."

"I don't. I think he killed Rudi for a good purpose." Tasso touched the rifle, resting in the corner of the room. "Major — "

"No." Hendricks shook his head. "Let's stop it right now. One is enough. We're afraid, the way he was. If we kill him we'll be doing what he did to Rudi."

Klaus looked gratefully up at him. "Thanks. I was afraid. You understand, don't you? Now she's afraid, the way I was. She wants to kill me."

"No more killing." Hendricks moved toward the end of the ladder. "I'm going above and try the transmitter once more. If I can't get them we're moving back toward my lines tomorrow morning."

Klaus rose quickly. "I'll come up with you and give you a hand."

The night air was cold. The earth was cooling off. Klaus took a deep breath, filling his lungs. He and Hendricks stepped onto the ground, out of the tunnel. Klaus planted his feet wide apart, the rifle up, watching and listening. Hendricks crouched by the tunnel mouth, tuning the small transmitter.

"Any luck?" Klaus asked presently.

"Not yet."

"Keep trying. Tell them what happened."

Hendricks kept trying. Without success. Finally he lowered the antenna. "It's useless. They can't hear me. Or they hear me and won't answer. Or — "

"Or they don't exist."

"I'll try once more." Hendricks raised the antenna. "Scott, can you hear me? Come in!"

He listened. There was only static. Then, still very faintly —

"This is Scott."

His fingers tightened. "Scott! Is it you?"

"This is Scott."

Klaus squatted down. "Is it your command?"

"Scott, listen. Do you understand? About them, the claws. Did you get my message? Did you hear me?"

"Yes." Faintly. Almost inaudible. He could hardly make out the word.

"You got my message? Is everything all right at the bunker? None of them got in?"

"Everything is all right."

"Have they tried to get in?"

The voice was weaker.

"No."

Hendricks turned to Klaus. "They're all right."

"Have they been attacked?"

"No." Hendricks pressed the phone tighter to his ear. "Scott, I can hardly hear you. Have you notified the Moon Base? Do they know? Are they alerted?"

No answer.

"Scott! Can you hear me?"

Silence.

Hendricks relaxed, sagging. "Faded out. Must be radiation pools."

Hendricks and Klaus looked at each other. Neither of them said anything. After a time Klaus said, "Did it sound like any of your men? Could you identify the voice?"

"It was too faint."

"You couldn't be certain?"

"No."

"Then it could have been — "

"I don't know. Now I'm not sure. Let's go back down and get the lid closed."

They climbed back down the ladder slowly, into the warm cellar. Klaus bolted the lid behind them. Tasso waited for them, her face expressionless.

"Any luck?" she asked.

Neither of them answered. "Well?" Klaus said at last. "What do you think, Major? Was it your officer, or was it one of *them*?"

"I don't know."

"Then we're just where we were before."

Hendricks stared down at the floor, his jaw set. "We'll have to go. To be sure."

"Anyhow, we have food here for only a few weeks. We'd have to go up after that, in any case."

"Apparently so."

"What's wrong?" Tasso demanded. "Did you get across to your bunker? What's the matter?"

"It may have been one of my men," Hendricks said slowly. "Or it may have been one of *them*. But we'll never know standing here." He examined his watch. "Let's turn in and get some sleep. We want to be up early tomorrow."

"Early?"

"Our best chance to get through the claws should be early in the morning," Hendricks said.

The morning was crisp and clear. Major Hendricks studied the countryside through his field glasses.

"See anything?" Klaus said.

"No."

"Can you make out our bunkers?"

"Which way?"

"Here." Klaus took the glasses and adjusted them. "I know where to look." He looked a long time, silently.

Tasso came to the top of the tunnel and stepped up onto the ground. "Anything?"

"No." Klaus passed the glasses back to Hendricks. "They're out of sight. Come on. Let's not stay here."

The three of them made their way down the side of the ridge, sliding in the soft ash. Across a flat rock a lizard scuttled. They stopped instantly, rigid.

"What was it?" Klaus muttered.

"A lizard."

The lizard ran on, hurrying through the ash. It was exactly the same color as the ash.

"Perfect adaptation," Klaus said. "Proves we were right. Lysenko, I mean."

They reached the bottom of the ridge and stopped, standing close together, looking around them.

"Let's go." Hendricks started off. "It's a good long trip, on foot."

Klaus fell in beside him. Tasso walked behind, her pistol held alertly. "Major, I've been meaning to ask you something," Klaus said. "How did you run across the David? The one that was tagging you."

"I met it along the way. In some ruins."

"What did it say?"

"Not much. It said it was alone. By itself."

"You couldn't tell it was a machine? It talked like a living person? You never suspected?"

"It didn't say much. I noticed nothing unusual."

"It's strange, machines so much like people that you can be fooled. Almost alive. I wonder where it'll end."

"They're doing what you Yanks designed them to do," Tasso said. "You designed them to hunt out life and destroy. Human life. Wherever they find it."

Hendricks was watching Klaus intently. "Why did you ask me? What's on your mind?"

"Nothing," Klaus answered.

"Klaus thinks you're the Second Variety," Tasso said calmly, from behind them. "Now he's got his eye on you."

Klaus flushed. "Why not? We sent a runner to the Yank lines and *he* comes back. Maybe he thought he'd find some good game here."

Hendricks laughed harshly. "I came from the UN bunkers. There were human beings all around me."

"Maybe you saw an opportunity to get into the Soviet lines. Maybe you saw your chance. Maybe you — "

"The Soviet lines had already been taken over. Your lines had been invaded before I left my command bunker. Don't forget that."

Tasso came up beside him. "That proves nothing at all, Major."

"Why not?"

"There appears to be little communication between the varieties. Each is made in a different factory. They don't seem to work together. You might have started for the Soviet lines without knowing anything about the work of the other varieties. Or even what the other varieties were like."

"How do you know so much about the claws?" Hendricks said.

"I've seen them. I've observed them take over the Soviet bunkers."

"You know quite a lot," Klaus said. "Actually, you saw very little. Strange that you should have been such an acute observer."

Tasso laughed. "Do you suspect me, now?"

"Forget it," Hendricks said. They walked on in silence.

"Are we going the whole way on foot?" Tasso said, after a while. "I'm not used to walking." She gazed around at the plain of ash, stretching out on all sides of them, as far as they could see. "How dreary."

"It's like this all the way," Klaus said.

"In a way I wish you had been in your bunker when the attack came."

"Somebody else would have been with you, if not me," Klaus muttered.

Tasso laughed, putting her hands in her pockets. "I suppose so."

They walked on, keeping their eyes on the vast plain of silent ash around them.

The sun was setting. Hendricks made his way forward slowly, waving Tasso and Klaus back. Klaus squatted down, resting his gun butt against the ground.

Tasso found a concrete slab and sat down with a sigh. "It's good to rest."

"Be quiet," Klaus said sharply.

Hendricks pushed up to the top of the rise ahead of them. The same rise the Russian runner had come up, the day before. Hendricks dropped down, stretching himself out, peering through his glasses at what lay beyond.

Nothing was visible. Only ash and occasional trees. But there, not more than fifty yards ahead, was the entrance of the forward command bunker. The bunker from which he had come. Hendricks watched silently. No motion. No sign of life. Nothing stirred.

Klaus slithered up beside him. "Where is it?"

"Down there." Hendricks passed him the glasses. Clouds of ash rolled across the evening sky. The world was darkening. They had a couple of hours of light left, at the most. Probably not that much.

"I don't see anything," Klaus said.

"That tree there. The stump. By the pile of bricks. The entrance is to the right of the bricks."

"I'll have to take your word for it."

"You and Tasso cover me from here. You'll be able to sight all the way to the bunker entrance."

"You're going down alone?"

"With my wrist tab I'll be safe. The ground around the bunker is a living field of claws. They collect down in the ash. Like crabs. Without tabs you wouldn't have a chance."

"Maybe you're right."

"I'll walk slowly all the way. As soon as I know for certain — "

"If they're down inside the bunker you won't be able to get back up here. They go fast. You don't realize."

"What do you suggest?"

Klaus considered. "I don't know. Get them to come to the surface. So you can see."

Hendricks brought out his transmitter from his belt, raising the antenna. "Let's get started."

Klaus signaled to Tasso. She crawled expertly up the side of the rise to where they were sitting.

"He's going down alone," Klaus said. "We'll cover him from here. As soon as you see him start back, fire past him at once. They come quick."

"You're not very optimistic," Tasso said.

"No, I'm not."

Hendricks opened the breech of his gun, checking it carefully. "Maybe things are all right."

"You didn't see them. Hundreds of them. All the same. Pouring out like ants."

"I should be able to find out without going down all the way." Hendricks locked his gun, gripping it in one hand, the transmitter in the other. "Well, wish me luck."

Klaus put out his hand. "Don't go down until you're sure. Talk to them from here. Make them show themselves."

Hendricks stood up. He stepped down the side of the rise.

A moment later he was walking slowly toward the pile of bricks and debris beside the dead tree stump. Toward the entrance of the forward command bunker.

Nothing stirred. He raised the transmitter, clicking it on. "Scott? Can you hear me?"

Silence.

"Scott! This is Hendricks. Can you hear me? I'm standing outside the bunker. You should be able to see me in the view sight."

He listened, the transmitter gripped tightly. No sound. Only static. He walked forward. A claw burrowed out of the ash and raced toward him. It halted a few feet away and then slunk off. A second claw appeared, one of the big ones with feelers. It moved toward him, studied him intently, and then fell in behind him, dogging respectfully after him, a few paces away. A moment later a second big claw joined it. Silently, the claws trailed him as he walked slowly toward the bunker.

Hendricks stopped, and behind him, the claws came to a halt. He was close now. Almost to the bunker steps.

"Scott! Can you hear me? I'm standing right above you. Outside. On the surface. Are you picking me up?"

He waited, holding his gun against his side, the transmitter tightly to his ear. Time passed. He strained to hear, but there was only silence. Silence, and faint static.

Then, distantly, metallically —

"This is Scott."

The voice was neutral. Cold. He could not identify it. But the earphone was minute.

"Scott! Listen. I'm standing right above you. I'm on the surface, looking down into the bunker entrance."

"Yes."

"Can you see me?"

"Yes."

"Through the view sight? You have the sight trained on me?"

"Yes."

Hendricks pondered. A circle of claws waited quietly around him, gray-metal bodies on all sides of him. "Is everything all right in the bunker? Nothing unusual has happened?"

"Everything is all right."

"Will you come up to the surface? I want to see you for a moment." Hendricks took a deep breath. "Come up here with me. I want to talk to you."

"Come down."

"I'm giving you an order."

Silence.

"Are you coming?" Hendricks listened. There was no response. "I order you to come to the surface."

"Come down."

Hendricks set his jaw. "Let me talk to Leone."

There was a long pause. He listened to the static. Then a voice came, hard, thin, metallic. The same as the other. "This is Leone."

"Hendricks. I'm on the surface. At the bunker entrance. I want one of you to come up here."

"Come down."

"Why come down? I'm giving you an order!"

Silence. Hendricks lowered the transmitter. He looked carefully around him. The entrance was just ahead. Almost at his feet. He lowered the antenna and fastened the transmitter to his belt. Carefully, he gripped his gun with both hands. He moved forward, a step at a time. If they could see him they knew he was starting toward the entrance. He closed his eyes a moment.

Then he put his foot on the first step that led downward.

Two Davids came up at him, their faces identical and expressionless. He blasted them into particles. More came rushing silently up, a whole pack of them. All exactly the same.

Hendricks turned and raced back, away from the bunker, back toward the rise.

At the top of the rise Tasso and Klaus were firing down. The small claws were already streaking up toward them, shining metal spheres going fast, racing frantically through the ash. But he had no time to think about that. He knelt down, aiming at the bunker entrance, gun against his cheek. The Davids were coming out in groups, clutching their teddy bears, their thin knobby legs pumping as they ran up the steps to the surface. Hendricks fired into the main body of them. They burst apart, wheels and springs flying in all directions. He fired again, through the mist of particles.

A giant lumbering figure rose up in the bunker entrance, tall and swaying. Hendricks paused, amazed. A man, a soldier. With one leg, supporting himself with a crutch.

"Major!" Tasso's voice came. More firing. The huge figure moved forward, Davids swarming around it. Hendricks broke out of his freeze. The First Variety. The Wounded Soldier. He aimed and fired. The soldier burst into bits, parts and relays flying. Now many Davids were out on the flat ground, away from the bunker. He fired again and again, moving slowly back, half-crouching and aiming.

From the rise, Klaus fired down. The side of the rise was alive with claws making their way up. Hendricks retreated toward the rise, running and crouching. Tasso had left Klaus and was circling slowly to the right, moving away from the rise.

A David slipped up toward him, its small white face expressionless, brown hair hanging down in its eyes. It bent over suddenly, opening its arms. Its teddy bear hurtled down and leaped across the ground, bounding toward him. Hendricks fired. The bear and the David both dissolved. He grinned, blinking. It was like a dream.

"Up here!" Tasso's voice. Hendricks made his way toward her. She was over by some columns of concrete, walls of a ruined building. She was firing past him, with the hand pistol Klaus had given her.

"Thanks." He joined her, gasping for breath. She pulled him back, behind the concrete, fumbling at her belt.

"Close your eyes!" She unfastened a globe from her waist. Rapidly, she unscrewed the cap, locking it into place. "Close your eyes and get down."

She threw the bomb. It sailed in an arc, an expert toss, rolling and bouncing to the entrance of the bunker. Two Wounded Soldiers stood uncertainly by the brick pile. More Davids poured from behind them, out onto the plain. One of the Wounded Soldiers moved toward the bomb, stooping awkwardly down to pick it up.

The bomb went off. The concussion whirled Hendricks around, throwing him on his face. A hot wind rolled over him. Dimly he saw Tasso standing behind the columns, firing slowly and methodically at the Davids coming out of the raging clouds of white fire.

Back along the rise Klaus struggled with a ring of claws circling around him. He retreated, blasting at them and moving back, trying to break through the ring.

Hendricks struggled to his feet. His head ached. He could hardly see. Everything was licking at him, raging and whirling. His right arm would not move.

Tasso pulled back toward him. "Come on. Let's go."

"Klaus — he's still up there."

"Come on!" Tasso dragged Hendricks back, away from the columns. Hendricks shook his head, trying to clear it. Tasso led him rapidly away, her eyes intense and bright, watching for claws that had escaped the blast.

One David came out of the rolling clouds of flame. Tasso blasted it. No more appeared.

"But Klaus. What about him?" Hendricks stopped, standing unsteadily. "He — "

"Come on!"

They retreated, moving farther and farther away from the bunker. A few small claws followed them for a little while and then gave up, turning back and going off.

At last Tasso stopped. "We can stop here and get our breaths."

Hendricks sat down on some heaps of debris. He wiped his neck, gasping. "We left Klaus back there."

Tasso said nothing. She opened her gun, sliding a fresh round of blast cartridges into place.

Hendricks stared at her, dazed. "You left him back there on purpose."

Tasso snapped the gun together. She studied the heaps of rubble around them, her face expressionless. As if she were watching for something.

"What is it?" Hendricks demanded. "What are you looking for? Is something coming?" He shook his head, trying to understand. What was she doing? What was she waiting for? He could see nothing. Ash lay all around them, ash and ruins. Occasional stark tree trunks, without leaves or branches. "What — "

Tasso cut him off. "Be still." Her eyes narrowed. Suddenly her gun came up. Hendricks turned, following her gaze.

Back the way they had come a figure appeared. The figure walked unsteadily toward them. Its clothes were torn. It limped as it made its way along, going very slowly and carefully. Stopping now and then, resting and getting its strength. Once it almost fell. It stood for a moment, trying to steady itself. Then it came on.

Klaus.

Hendricks stood up. "Klaus!" He started toward him. "How the hell did you — "

Tasso fired. Hendricks swung back. She fired again, the blast passing him, a searing line of heat. The beam caught Klaus in the chest. He exploded, gears and wheels flying. For a moment he continued to walk. Then he swayed back and forth. He crashed to the ground, his arms flung out. A few more wheels rolled away.

Silence.

Tasso turned to Hendricks. "Now you understand why he killed Rudi."

Hendricks sat down again slowly. He shook his head. He was numb. He could not think.

"Do you see?" Tasso said. "Do you understand?"

Hendricks said nothing. Everything was slipping away from him, faster and faster. Darkness, rolling and plucking at him.

He closed his eyes.

Hendricks opened his eyes slowly. His body ached all over. He tried to sit up but needles of pain shot through his arm and shoulder. He gasped.

"Don't try to get up," Tasso said. She bent down, putting her cold hand against his forehead.

It was night. A few stars glinted above, shining through the drifting clouds of ash. Hendricks lay back, his teeth locked. Tasso watched him impassively. She had built a fire with some wood and weeds. The fire licked feebly, hissing at a metal cup suspended over it. Everything was silent. Unmoving darkness, beyond the fire.

"So he was the Second Variety," Hendricks murmured.

"I had always thought so."

"Why didn't you destroy him sooner?" He wanted to know.

"You held me back." Tasso crossed to the fire to look into the metal cup. "Coffee. It'll be ready to drink in a while."

She came back and sat down beside him. Presently she opened her pistol and began to disassemble the firing mechanism, studying it intently.

"This is a beautiful gun," Tasso said, half aloud. "The construction is superb."

"What about them? The claws."

"The concussion from the bomb put most of them out of action. They're delicate. Highly organized, I suppose."

"The Davids, too?"

"Yes."

"How did you happen to have a bomb like that?"

Tasso shrugged. "We designed it. You shouldn't underestimate our technology, Major. Without such a bomb you and I would no longer exist."

"Very useful."

Tasso stretched out her legs, warming her feet in the heat of the fire. "It surprised me that you did not seem to understand, after he killed Rudi. Why did you think he — "

"I told you. I thought he was afraid."

"Really? You know, Major, for a little while I suspected you. Because you wouldn't let me kill him. I thought you might be protecting him." She laughed.

"Are we safe here?" Hendricks asked presently.

"For a while. Until they get reinforcements from some other area." Tasso began to clean the interior of the gun with a bit of rag. She finished and pushed the mechanism back into place. She closed the gun, running her finger along the barrel.

"We were lucky," Hendricks murmured.

"Yes. Very lucky."

"Thanks for pulling me away."

Tasso did not answer. She glanced up at him, her eyes bright in the firelight. Hendricks examined his arm. He could not move his fingers. His whole side seemed numb. Down inside him was a dull steady ache.

"How do you feel?" Tasso asked.

"My arm is damaged."

"Anything else?"

"Internal injuries."

"You didn't get down when the bomb went off."

Hendricks said nothing. He watched Tasso pour the coffee from the cup into a flat metal pan. She brought it over to him.

"Thanks." He struggled up enough to drink. It was hard to swallow. His insides turned over and he pushed the pan away. "That's all I can drink now."

Tasso drank the rest. Time passed. The clouds of ash moved across the dark sky above them. Hendricks rested, his mind blank. After a while he became aware that Tasso was standing over him, gazing down at him.

"What is it?" he murmured.

"Do you feel any better?"

"Some."

"You know, Major, if I hadn't dragged you away they would have got you. You would be dead. Like Rudi."

"I know."

"Do you want to know why I brought you out? I could have left you. I could have left you there."

"Why did you bring me out?"

"Because we have to get away from here." Tasso stirred the fire with a stick, peering calmly down into it. "No human being can live here. When their reinforcements come we won't have a chance. I've pondered about it while you were unconscious. We have perhaps three hours before they come."

"And you expect me to get us away?"

"That's right. I expect you to get us out of here."

"Why me?"

"Because I don't know any way." Her eyes shone at him in the half light, bright and steady. "If you can't get us out of here they'll kill us within three hours. I see nothing else ahead. Well, Major? What are you going to do? I've been waiting all night. While you were unconscious I sat here, waiting and listening. It's almost dawn. The night is almost over."

Hendricks considered. "It's curious," he said at last.

"Curious?"

"That you should think I can get us out of here. I wonder what you think I can do."

"Can you get us to the Moon Base?"

"The Moon Base? How?"

"There must be some way."

Hendricks shook his head. "No. There's no way that I know of."

Tasso said nothing. For a moment her steady gaze wavered. She ducked her head, turning abruptly away. She scrambled to her feet. "More coffee?"

"No."

"Suit yourself." Tasso drank silently. He could not see her face. He lay back against the ground, deep in thought, trying to concentrate. It was hard to think. His head still hurt. And the numbing daze still hung over him.

"There might be one way," he said suddenly.

"Oh?"

"How soon is dawn?"

"Two hours. The sun will be coming up shortly."

"There's supposed to be a ship near here. I've never seen it. But I know it exists."

"What kind of a ship?" Her voice was sharp.

"A rocket cruiser."

"Will it take us off? To the Moon Base?"

"It's supposed to. In case of emergency." He rubbed his forehead.

"What's wrong?"

"My head. It's hard to think. I can hardly — hardly concentrate. The bomb."

"Is the ship near here?" Tasso slid over beside him, settling down on her haunches. "How far is it? Where is it?"

"I'm trying to think."

Her fingers dug into his arm. "Nearby?" Her voice was like iron. "Where would it be? Would they store it underground? Hidden underground?"

"Yes. In a storage locker."

"How do we find it? Is it marked? Is there a code marker to identify it?"

Hendricks concentrated. "No. No markings. No code symbol."

"What then?"

"A sign."

"What sort of sign?"

Hendricks did not answer. In the flickering light his eyes were glazed, two sightless orbs. Tasso's fingers dug into his arm.

"What sort of sign? What is it?"

"I — I can't think. Let me rest."

"All right." She let go and stood up. Hendricks lay back against the ground, his eyes closed. Tasso walked away from him, her hands in her pockets. She kicked a rock out of her way and stood staring up at the sky. The night blackness was already beginning to fade into gray. Morning was coming.

Tasso gripped her pistol and walked around the fire in a circle, back and forth. On the ground Major Hendricks lay, his eyes closed, unmoving. The grayness rose in the sky, higher and higher. The landscape became visible, fields of ash stretching out in all directions. Ash and ruins of buildings, a wall here and there, heaps of concrete, the naked trunk of a tree.

The air was cold and sharp. Somewhere a long way off a bird made a few bleak sounds.

Hendricks stirred. He opened his eyes. "Is it dawn? Already?"

"Yes."

Hendricks sat up a little. "You wanted to know something. You were asking me."

"Do you remember now?"

"Yes."

"What is it?" She tensed. "What?" she repeated sharply.

"A well. A ruined well. It's in a storage locker under a well."

"A well." Tasso relaxed. "Then we'll find a well." She looked at her watch. "We have about an hour, Major. Do you think we can find it in an hour?"

"Give me a hand," Hendricks said.

Tasso put her pistol away and helped him to his feet. "This is going to be difficult."

"Yes it is." Hendricks set his lips tightly. "I don't think we're going to go very far."

They began to walk. The early sun cast a little warmth down on them. The land was flat and barren, stretching out gray and lifeless as far as they could see. A few birds sailed silently, far above them, circling slowly.

"See anything?" Hendricks said. "Any claws?"

"No. Not yet."

They passed through some ruins, upright concrete and bricks. A cement foundation. Rats scuttled away. Tasso jumped back warily.

"This used to be a town," Hendricks said. "A village. Provincial village. This was all grape country, once. Where we are now."

They came onto a ruined street, weeds and cracks crisscrossing it. Over to the right a stone chimney stuck up.

"Be careful," he warned her.

A pit yawned, an open basement. Ragged ends of pipes jutted up, twisted and bent. They passed part of a house, a bathtub turned on its side. A broken chair. A few spoons and bits of china dishes. In the center of the street the ground had sunk away. The depression was filled with weeds and debris and bones.

"Over here," Hendricks murmured.

"This way?"

"To the right."

They passed the remains of a heavy-duty tank. Hendricks's belt counter clicked ominously. The tank had been radiation-blasted. A few feet from the tank a mummified body lay sprawled out, mouth open. Beyond the road was a flat field. Stones and weeds, and bits of broken glass.

"There," Hendricks said.

A stone well jutted up, sagging and broken. A few boards lay across it. Most of the well had sunk into rubble. Hendricks walked unsteadily toward it, Tasso beside him.

"Are you certain about this?" Tasso said. "This doesn't look like anything."

"I'm sure." Hendricks sat down at the edge of the well, his teeth locked. His breath came quickly. He wiped perspiration from his face. "This was arranged so the senior command officer could get away. If anything happened. If the bunker fell."

"That was you?"

"Yes."

"Where is the ship? Is it here?"

"We're standing on it." Hendricks ran his hands over the surface of the well stones. "The eye-lock responds to me, not to anybody else. It's my ship. Or it was supposed to be."

There was a sharp click. Presently they heard a low grating sound from below them.

"Step back," Hendricks said. He and Tasso moved away from the well.

A section of the ground slid back. A metal frame pushed slowly up through the ash, shoving bricks and weeds out of the way. The action ceased as the ship nosed into view.

"There it is," Hendricks said.

The ship was small. It rested quietly, suspended in its mesh frame like a blunt needle. A rain of ash sifted down into the dark cavity from which the ship had been raised. Hendricks made his way over to it. He mounted the mesh and unscrewed the hatch, pulling it back. Inside the ship the control banks and the pressure seat were visible.

Tasso came and stood beside him, gazing into the ship. "I'm not accustomed to rocket piloting," she said after a while.

Hendricks glanced at her. "I'll do the piloting."

"Will you? There's only one seat, Major. I can see it's built to carry only a single person."

Hendricks's breathing changed. He studied the interior of the ship intently. Tasso was right. There was only one seat. The ship was built to carry only one person. "I see," he said slowly. "And the one person is you."

She nodded.

"Of course."

"Why?"

"*You* can't go. You might not live through the trip. You're injured. You probably wouldn't get there."

"An interesting point. But you see, I know where the Moon Base is. And you don't. You might fly around for months and not find it. It's well hidden. Without knowing what to look for — "

"I'll have to take my chances. Maybe I won't find it. Not by myself. But I think you'll give me all the information I need. Your life depends on it."

"How?"

"If I find the Moon Base in time, perhaps I can get them to send a ship back to pick you up. *If* I find the Base in time. If not, then you haven't a chance. I imagine there are supplies on the ship. They will last me long enough — "

Hendricks moved quickly. But his injured arm betrayed him. Tasso ducked, sliding lithely aside. Her hand came up, lightning fast. Hendricks saw the gun butt coming. He tried to ward off the blow, but she was too fast. The metal butt struck against the side of his head, just above his ear. Numbing pain rushed through him. Pain and rolling clouds of blackness. He sank down, sliding to the ground.

Dimly, he was aware that Tasso was standing over him, kicking him with her toe.

"Major! Wake up!"

He opened his eyes, groaning.

"Listen to me." She bent down, the gun pointed at his face. "I have to hurry. There isn't much time left. The ship is ready to go, but you must give me the information I need before I leave."

Hendricks shook his head, trying to clear it.

"Hurry up! Where is the Moon Base? How do I find it? What do I look for?"

Hendricks said nothing.

"Answer me!"

"Sorry."

"Major, the ship is loaded with provisions. I can coast for weeks. I'll find the Base eventually. And in a half-hour you'll be dead. Your only chance of survival — " She broke off.

Along the slope, by some crumbling ruins, something moved. Something in the ash. Tasso turned quickly, aiming. She fired. A puff of flame leaped. Something scuttled away, rolling across the ash. She fired again. The claw burst apart, wheels flying.

"See?" Tasso said. "A scout. It won't be long."

"You'll bring them back here to get me?"

"Yes. As soon as possible."

Hendricks looked up at her. He studied her intently. "You're telling the truth?" A strange expression had come over his face, an avid hunger. "You will come back for me? You'll get me to the Moon Base?"

"I'll get you to the Moon Base. But tell me where it is! There's only a little time left."

"All right." Hendricks picked up a piece of rock, pulling himself to a sitting position. "Watch."

Hendricks began to scratch in the ash. Tasso stood by him, watching the motion of the rock. Hendricks was sketching a crude lunar map.

"This is the Appenine range. Here is the Crater of Archimedes. The Moon Base is beyond the end of the Appenine, about two hundred miles. I don't know exactly where. No one on Terra knows. But when you're over the Appenine, signal with one red flare and a green flare, followed by two red flares in quick succession. The Base monitor will record your signal. The Base is under the surface, of course. They'll guide you down with magnetic controls."

"And the controls? Can I operate them?"

"The controls are virtually automatic. All you have to do is give the right signal at the right time."

"I will."

"The seat absorbs most of the takeoff shock. Air and temperature are automatically controlled. The ship will leave Terra and pass out into free space. It'll line itself up with the Moon, falling into an orbit around it, about a hundred miles above the surface. The orbit will carry you over the Base. When you're in the region of the Appenine, release the signal rockets."

Tasso slid into the ship and lowered herself into the pressure seat. The arm locks folded automatically around her. She fingered the controls. "Too bad you're not going, Major. All this put here for you, and you can't make the trip."

"Leave me the pistol."

Tasso pulled the pistol from her belt. She held it in her hand, weighing it thoughtfully. "Don't go too far from this location. It'll be hard to find you, as it is."

"No, I'll stay here by the well."

Tasso gripped the takeoff switch, running her fingers over the smooth metal. "A beautiful ship, Major. Well built. I admire your workmanship. You people have always done good work. You build fine things. Your work, your creations, are your greatest achievement."

"Give me the pistol," Hendricks said impatiently, holding out his hand. He struggled to his feet.

"Good-bye, Major!" Tasso tossed the pistol past Hendricks. The pistol clattered against the ground, bouncing and rolling away. Hendricks hurried after it. He bent down, snatching it up.

The hatch of the ship clanged shut. The bolts fell into place. Hendricks made his way back. The inner door was being sealed. He raised the pistol unsteadily.

There was a shattering roar. The ship burst up from its metal cage, fusing the mesh behind it. Hendricks cringed, pulling back. The ship shot up into the rolling clouds of ash, disappearing into the sky.

Hendricks stood watching a long time, until even the streamer had dissipated. Nothing stirred. The morning air was chill and silent. He began to walk aimlessly back the way they had come. Better to keep moving around. It would be a long time before help came — if it came at all.

He searched his pockets until he found a package of cigarettes. He lit one grimly. They had all wanted cigarettes from him. But cigarettes were scarce.

A lizard slithered by him, through the ash. He halted, rigid. The lizard disappeared. Above, the sun rose higher in the sky. Some flies landed on a flat rock to one side of him. Hendricks kicked at them with his foot.

It was getting hot. Sweat trickled down his face, into his collar. His mouth was dry.

Presently he stopped walking and sat down on some debris. He unfastened his medicine kit and swallowed a few narcotic capsules. He looked around him. Where was he?

Something lay ahead. Stretched out on the ground. Silent and unmoving.

Hendricks drew his gun quickly. It looked like a man. Then he remembered. It was the remains of Klaus. The Second Variety. Where Tasso had blasted him. He could see wheels and relays and metal parts, strewn around on the ash. Glittering and sparkling in the sunlight.

Hendricks got to his feet and walked over. He nudged the inert form with his foot, turning it over a little. He could see the metal hull, the aluminum ribs and struts. More wiring fell out. Like viscera. Heaps of wiring, switches and relays. Endless motors and rods.

He bent down. The brain cage had been smashed by the fall. The artificial brain was visible. He gazed at it. A maze of circuits. Miniature tubes. Wires as fine as hair. He touched the brain cage. It swung aside. The type plate was visible. Hendricks studied the plate.

And blanched.

IV — V.

For a long time he stared at the plate. Fourth Variety. Not the Second. They had been wrong. There were more types. Not just three. Many more, perhaps. At least four. And Klaus wasn't the Second Variety.

But if Klaus wasn't the Second Variety —

Suddenly he tensed. Something was coming, walking through the ash beyond the hill. What was it? He strained to see. Figures. Figures coming slowly along, making their way through the ash.

Coming toward him.

Hendricks crouched quickly, raising his gun. Sweat dripped down into his eyes. He fought down rising panic, as the figures neared.

The first was a David. The David saw him and increased its pace. The others hurried behind it. A second David. A third. Three Davids, all alike, coming toward him silently, without expression, their thin legs rising and falling. Clutching their teddy bears.

He aimed and fired. The first two Davids dissolved into particles. The third came on. And the figure behind it. Climbing silently toward him across the gray ash. A Wounded Soldier, towering over the David. And —

And behind the Wounded Soldier came two Tassos, walking side by side. Heavy belt, Russian army pants, shirt, long hair. The familiar figure, as he had seen her only a little while before. Sitting in the pressure seat of the ship. Two slim, silent figures, both identical.

They were very near. The David bent down suddenly, dropping its teddy bear. The bear raced across the ground. Automatically Hendricks' fingers tightened around the trigger. The bear was gone, dissolved into mist. The two Tasso Types moved on, expressionless, walking side by side, through the gray ash.

When they were almost to him, Hendricks raised the pistol waist high and fired.

The two Tassos dissolved. But already a new group was starting up the rise, five or six Tassos, all identical, a line of them coming rapidly toward him.

And he had given her the ship and the signal code. Because of him she was on her way to the moon, to the Moon Base. He had made it possible.

He had been right about the bomb, after all. It had been designed with knowledge of other types, the David Type and the Wounded Soldier Type. And the Klaus Type. Not designed by human beings. It had been designed by one of the underground factories, apart from all human contact.

The line of Tassos came up to him. Hendricks braced himself, watching them calmly. The familiar face, the belt, the heavy shirt, the bomb carefully in place.

The bomb —

As the Tassos reached for him, a last ironic thought drifted through Hendricks's mind. He felt a little better, thinking about it. The bomb. Made by the Second Variety to destroy the other varieties. Made for that end alone.

They were already beginning to design weapons to use against each other.

Kate Wilhelm

Baby, You Were Great!
(1967)

An accomplished and elegant writer, Kate Wilhelm (b. 1928) began publishing in 1956 and, by the 1960s, had established herself as a writer of sophisticated, socially probing science fiction. She was a major force in the development of feminist sf in the 1970s, while her approach to technology and the body, as evidenced by the story that follows, was also an influence on cyberpunk in the 1980s. She has also been an important force in mentoring new writers, through the Milford Writers' Conference and the Clarion Science Fiction Writers' Workshop, which she founded with husband Damon Knight and taught in for twenty-seven years. With a body of work that crosses the boundaries of hard and soft science fiction, mystery, and magical realism, Wilhelm is a writer for whom the designation "speculative fiction" seems especially appropriate.

Although the story that follows is clearly science fiction, from our perspective in the current era of reality TV and virtual sex her portrayal of the media seems eerily prescient and all too real. "Baby, You Were Great!" is a subtle and disturbing exploration of gender, media culture, and alienation. Wilhelm shows an interest in the social effects of the media common to New Wave writers of the same period, but her spare and understated style differs sharply from the pyrotechnics typical of the New Wave. In this story about the triumph of impersonal, vicarious sensation over meaningful human relationships, the cool restraint of the narration underscores the content to devastating effect.

John Lewisohn thought that if one more door slammed, or one more bell rang, or one more voice asked if he was all right, his head would explode. Leaving his laboratories, he walked through the carpeted hall to the elevator that slid wide to admit him noiselessly, was lowered, gently, two floors, where there were more carpeted halls. The door he shoved open bore a neat sign, AUDITIONING STUDIO. Inside, he was waved on through the reception room by three girls who knew better than to speak to him unless he spoke first. They were surprised to see him; it was his first visit there in seven or eight months. The inner room where he stopped was darkened, at first glance appearing empty, revealing another occupant only after his eyes had time to adjust to the dim lighting.

John sat in the chair next to Herb Javits, still without speaking. Herb was wearing the helmet and gazing at a wide screen that was actually a one-way glass panel permitting him to view the audition going on in the next room. John lowered a second helmet to his head. It fit snugly and immediately made contact with the eight prepared spots on his skull. As soon as he turned it on, the helmet itself was forgotten.

A girl had entered the other room. She was breathtakingly lovely, a long-legged honey blonde with slanting green eyes and apricot skin. The room was furnished as a sitting room with two couches, some chairs, end tables and a coffee table, all tasteful and lifeless, like an ad in a furniture trade publication. The girl stopped at the doorway and John felt her indecision, heavily tempered with nervousness and fear. Outwardly she appeared poised and expectant, her smooth face betraying none of her emotions. She took a hesitant step toward the couch, and a wire showed trailing behind her. It was attached to her head. At the same time a second door opened. A young man ran inside, slamming the door behind him; he looked wild and frantic. The girl registered surprise, mounting nervousness; she felt behind her for the door handle, found it and tried to open the door again. It was locked. John could hear nothing that was being said in the room; he only felt the girl's reaction to the unexpected interruption. The wild-eyed man was approaching her, his hands slashing through the air, his eyes darting glances all about them constantly. Suddenly he pounced on her and pulled her to him, kissing her face and neck roughly. She seemed paralyzed with fear for several seconds, then there was something else, a bland nothing kind of feeling that accompanied boredom sometimes, or too-complete self-assurance. As the man's hands fastened on her blouse in the back and ripped it, she threw her arms about him, her face showing passion that was not felt anywhere in her mind or in her blood.

"Cut!" Herb Javits said quietly.

The man stepped back from the girl and left her without a word. She looked about blankly, her torn blouse hanging about her hips, one shoulder strap gone. She was very beautiful. The audition manager entered, followed by a dresser with a gown that he threw about her shoulders. She looked startled; waves of anger mounted to fury as she was drawn from the room, leaving it empty. The two watching men removed their helmets.

"Fourth one so far," Herb grunted. "Sixteen yesterday; twenty the day before . . . All nothing." He gave John a curious look. "What's got you stirred out of your lab?"

"Anne's had it this time," John said. "She's been on the phone all night and all morning."

"What now?"

"Those damn sharks! I told you that was too much on top of the airplane crash last week. She can't take much more of it."

"Hold it a minute, Johnny," Herb said. "Let's finish off the next three girls and then talk." He pressed a button on the arm of his chair and the room beyond the screen took their attention again.

This time the girl was slightly less beautiful, shorter, a dimply sort of brunette with laughing blue eyes and upturned nose. John liked her. He adjusted his helmet and felt with her.

She was excited; the audition always excited them. There was some fear and nervousness, not too much. Curious about how the audition would go, probably. The wild young man ran into the room, and her face paled. Nothing else changed. Her nervousness increased, not uncomfortably. When he grabbed her, the only emotion she registered was the nervousness.

"Cut," Herb said.

The next girl was also brunette, with gorgeously elongated legs. She was very cool, a real professional. Her mobile face reflected the range of emotions to be expected as the scene played through again, but nothing inside her was touched. She was a million miles away from it all.

The next one caught John with a slam. She entered the room slowly, looking about with curiosity, nervous, as they all were. She was younger than the other girls, less poised. She had pale gold hair piled in an elaborate mound of waves on top of her head. Her eyes were brown, her skin nicely tanned. When the man entered, her emotions changed quickly to fear, then to terror. John didn't know when he closed his eyes. He was the girl, filled with unspeakable terror; his heart pounded; adrenaline pumped into his system; he wanted to scream but could not. From the dim unreachable depths of his psyche there came something else, in waves, so mixed with terror that the two merged and became one emotion that pulsed and throbbed and demanded. With a jerk he opened his eyes and stared at the window. The girl had been thrown down to one of the couches, and the man was kneeling on the floor beside her, his hands playing over her bare body, his face pressed against her skin.

"Cut!" Herb said. His voice was shaken. "Hire her," he said. The man rose, glanced at the girl, sobbing now, and then quickly bent over and kissed her cheek. Her sobs increased. Her golden hair was down, framing her face; she looked like a child. John tore off the helmet. He was perspiring.

Herb got up, turned on the lights in the room, and the window blanked out, blending with the wall. He didn't look at John. When he wiped his face, his hand was shaking. He rammed it in his pocket.

"When did you start auditions like that?" John asked, after a few moments of silence.

"Couple of months ago. I told you about it. Hell, we had to, Johnny. That's the six hundred nineteenth girl we've tried out! Six hundred nineteen! All phonies but one! Dead from the neck up. Do you have any idea how long it was taking us to find that out! Hours for each one. Now it's a matter of minutes."

John Lewisohn sighed. He knew. He had suggested it, actually, when he had said, "Find a basic anxiety for the test." He hadn't wanted to know what Herb had come up with.

He said, "Okay, but she's only a kid. What about her parents, legal rights, all that?"

"We'll fix it. Don't worry. What about Anne?"

"She's called me five times since yesterday. The sharks were too much. She wants to see us, both of us, this afternoon."

"You're kidding! I can't leave here now!"

"Nope. Kidding I'm not. She says no plug-up if we don't show. She'll take pills and sleep until we get there."

"Good Lord! She wouldn't dare!"

"I've booked seats. We take off at twelve-thirty-five." They stared at one another silently for another moment, when Herb shrugged. He was a short man, not heavy but solid. John was over six feet, muscular, with a temper that he knew he had to control. Others suspected that when he did let it go, there would be bodies lying around afterward, but he controlled it.

Once it had been a physical act, an effort of body and will to master that temper; now it was done so automatically that he couldn't recall occasions when it even threatened to flare anymore.

"Look, Johnny, when we see Anne, let me handle it. Right? I'll make it short."

"What are you going to do?"

"Give her an earful. If she's going to start pulling temperament on me, I'll slap her down so hard she'll bounce a week." He grinned. "She's had it all her way up to now. She knew there wasn't a replacement if she got bitchy. Let her try it now. Just let her try." Herb was pacing back and forth with quick, jerky steps.

John realized with a shock that he hated the stocky, red-faced man. The feeling was new; it was almost as if he could taste the hatred he felt, and the taste was unfamiliar and pleasant.

Herb stopped pacing and stared at him for a moment. "Why'd she call you? Why does she want you down, too? She knows you're not mixed up with this end of it."

"She knows I'm a full partner, anyway," John said.

"Yeah, but that's not it." Herb's face twisted in a grin. "She thinks you're still hot for her, doesn't she? She knows you tumbled once, in the beginning, when you were working on her, getting the gimmick working right." The grin reflected no humor then. "Is she right, Johnny, baby? Is that it?"

"We made a deal," John said. "You run your end, I run mine. She wants me along because she doesn't trust you, or believe anything you tell her anymore. She wants a witness."

"Yeah, Johnny. But you be sure you remember our agreement." Suddenly Herb laughed. "You know what it was like, Johnny, seeing you and her? Like a flame trying to snuggle up to an icicle."

At three-thirty they were in Anne's suite in the Skyline Hotel in Grand Bahama. Herb had a reservation to fly back to New York on the 6 p.m. flight. Anne would not be off until four, so they made themselves comfortable in her rooms and waited. Herb turned her screen on, offered a helmet to John, who shook his head, and they both seated themselves. John watched the screen for several minutes; then he, too, put on a helmet.

Anne was looking at the waves far out at sea where they were long, green, undulating; then she brought her gaze in closer, to the blue-green and quick seas, and finally in to where they stumbled on the sandbars, breaking into foam that looked solid enough to walk on. She was peaceful, swaying with the motion of the boat, the sun hot on her back, the fishing rod heavy in her hands. It was like being an indolent animal at peace with its world, at home in the world, being one with it. After a few seconds she put down the rod and turned looking at a tall smiling man in swimming trunks. He held out his hand and she took it. They entered the cabin of the boat where drinks were waiting. Her mood of serenity and happiness ended abruptly, to be replaced by shocked disbelief, and a start of fear.

"What the hell . . . ?" John muttered, adjusting the audio. You seldom needed audio when Anne was on.

". . . Captain Brothers had to let them go. After all, they've done nothing yet — " the man was saying soberly.

"But why do you think they'll try to rob me?"

"Who else is here with a million dollars' worth of jewels?"

John turned it off and said, "You're a fool! You can't get away with something like that!"

Herb stood up and crossed to the window wall that was open to the stretch of glistening blue ocean beyond the brilliant white beaches. "You know what every woman wants? To own something worth stealing." He chuckled, a sound without mirth. "Among other things, that is. They want to be roughed up once or twice, and forced to kneel. . . . Our new psychologist is pretty good, you know? Hasn't steered us wrong yet. Anne might kick some, but it'll go over great."

"She won't stand for an actual robbery." Louder, emphatically, he added, "I won't stand for that."

"We can dub it," Herb said. "That's all we need, Johnny, plant the idea, and then dub the rest."

John stared at his back. He wanted to believe that. He needed to believe it. His voice was calm when he said, "It didn't start like this, Herb. What happened?"

Herb turned then. His face was dark against the glare of light behind him. "Okay, Johnny, it didn't start like this. Things accelerate, that's all. You thought of a gimmick, and the way we planned it, it sounded great, but it didn't last. We gave them the feeling of gambling, or learning to ski, of automobile racing, everything we could dream up, and it wasn't enough. How many times can you take the first ski jump of your life? After a while you want new thrills, you know? For you it's been great, hasn't it? You bought yourself a shiny new lab and closed the door. You bought yourself time and equipment and when things didn't go right, you could toss it out and start over, and nobody gave a damn. Think of what it's been like for me, kid! I gotta keep coming up with something new, something that'll give Anne a jolt and through her all those nice little people who aren't even alive unless they're plugged in. You think it's been easy? Anne was a green kid. For her everything was new and exciting, but it isn't like that now, boy. You better believe it is *not* like that now. You know what she told me last month? She's sick and tired of men. Our little hot-box Annie! Tired of men!"

John crossed to him and pulled him around toward the light. "Why didn't you tell me?"

"Why, Johnny? What would you have done that I didn't do? I looked harder for the right guy. What would you do for a new thrill for her? I worked for them, kid. Right from the start you said for me to leave you alone. Okay. I left you alone. You ever read any of the memos I sent? You initialed them, kiddo. Everything that's been done, we both signed. Don't give me any of that why didn't I tell you stuff. It won't work!" His face was ugly red and a vein bulged in his neck. John wondered if he had high blood pressure, if he would die of a stroke during one of his flash rages.

John left him at the window. He had read the memos. Herb was right; all he had wanted was to be left alone. It had been his idea; after twelve years of work in a laboratory on prototypes he had shown his — gimmick — to Herb Javits. Herb had been one of the biggest producers on television then; now he was the biggest producer in the world.

The gimmick was simple enough. A person fitted with electrodes in his brain could transmit his emotions, which in turn could be broadcast and picked up by the helmets to be felt by the audience. No words, or thoughts went out, only basic emotions — fear, love, anger, hatred. . . . That, tied in with a camera showing what the person saw, with a voice dubbed in, and you were the person having the experience, with one important difference — you could turn it off if it got to be too much. The "actor" couldn't. A simple gimmick. You didn't really need the camera and the sound track; many users never turned them on at all, but let their own imaginations fill in the emotional broadcast.

The helmets were not sold, only leased or rented after a short, easy fitting session. A year's lease cost fifty dollars, and there were over thirty-seven million subscribers. Herb had created his own network when the demand for more hours squeezed him out of regular television. From a one-hour weekly show, it had gone to one hour nightly, and now it was on the air eight hours a day live, with another eight hours of taped programming.

What had started out as A DAY IN THE LIFE OF ANNE BEAUMONT was now a life in the life of Anne Beaumont and the audience was insatiable.

Anne came in then, surrounded by the throng of hangers-on that mobbed her daily — hairdressers, masseurs, fitters, script men. . . . She looked tired. She waved the crowd out when she saw John and Herb were there. "Hello, John," she said, "Herb."

"Anne, baby, you're looking great!" Herb said. He took her in his arms and kissed her solidly. She stood still, her hands at her sides.

She was tall, very slender, with wheat-colored hair and gray eyes. Her cheekbones were wide and high, her mouth firm and almost too large. Against her deep red-gold suntan her teeth looked whiter than John remembered. Although too firm and strong ever to be thought of as pretty, she was a very beautiful woman. After Herb released her, she turned to John, hesitated only a moment, then extended a slim, sun-browned hand. It was cool and dry in his.

"How have you been, John? It's been a long time."

He was very glad she didn't kiss him, or call him darling. She smiled only slightly and gently removed her hand from his. He moved to the bar as she turned to Herb.

"I'm through, Herb." Her voice was too quiet. She accepted a whiskey sour from John, but kept her gaze on Herb.

"What's the matter, honey? I was just watching you, baby. You were great today, like always. You've still got it, kid. It's coming through like always."

"What about this robbery? You must be out of your mind . . ."

"Yeah, that. Listen, Anne baby, I swear to you I don't know a thing about it. Laughton must have been giving you the straight goods on that. You know we agreed that the rest of this week you just have a good time, remember? That comes over too, baby. When you have a good time and relax, thirty-seven million people are enjoying life and relaxing. That's good. They can't be stimulated all the time. They like the variety." Wordlessly John held out a glass, scotch and water. Herb took it without looking.

Anne was watching him coldly. Suddenly she laughed. It was a cynical, bitter sound. "You're not a damn fool, Herb. Don't try to act like one." She sipped her drink again, staring at him over the rim of the glass. "I'm warning you, if anyone shows up here to rob me, I'm going to treat him like a real burglar. I bought a gun after today's broadcast, and I learned how to shoot when I was ten. I still know how. I'll kill him, Herb, whoever it is."

"Baby," Herb started, but she cut him short.

"And this is my last week. As of Saturday, I'm through."

"You can't do that, Anne," Herb said. John watched him closely, searching for a sign of weakness; he saw nothing. Herb exuded confidence. "Look around, Anne, at this room, your clothes, everything . . . You are the richest woman in the world, having the time of your life, able to go anywhere, do anything. . . ."

"While the whole world watches — "

"So what? It doesn't stop you, does it?" Herb started to pace, his steps jerky and quick. "You knew that when you signed the contract. You're a rare girl, Anne, beautiful, emotional, intelligent. Think of all those women who've got nothing but you. If you quit them, what do they do? Die? They might, you know. For the first time in their lives they're able to feel like they're living. You're giving them what no one ever did before, what was only hinted at in books and films in the old days. Suddenly they know what it feels like to face excitement, to experience love, to feel contented and peaceful. Think of them, Anne, empty, with nothing in their lives but you, what you're able to give them. Thirty-seven million drabs, Anne, who never felt anything but boredom and frustration until you gave them life. What do they have? Work, kids, bills. You've given them the world, baby! Without you they wouldn't even want to live anymore."

She wasn't listening. Almost dreamily she said, "I talked to my lawyers, Herb, and the contract is meaningless. You've already broken it over and over. I agreed to learn a lot of new things. I did. My God! I've climbed mountains, hunted lions, learned to ski and water-ski, but now you want me to die a little bit each week. . . . That airplane crash, not bad, just enough to terrify me. Then the sharks. I really do think it was having sharks brought in when I was skiing that did it, Herb. You see, you will kill me. It will happen, and you won't be able to top it, Herb. Not ever."

There was a hard, waiting silence following her words. No! John shouted soundlessly. He was looking at Herb. He had stopped pacing when she started to talk. Something flicked across his face — surprise, fear, something not readily identifiable. Then his face went blank and he raised his glass and finished the scotch and water, replacing the glass on the bar. When he turned again, he was smiling with disbelief.

"What's really bugging you, Anne? There have been plants before. You knew about them. Those lions didn't just happen by, you know. And the avalanche needed a nudge from someone. You know that. What else is bugging you?"

"I'm in love, Herb."

Herb waved that aside impatiently. "Have you ever watched your own show, Anne?" She shook her head. "I thought not. So you wouldn't know about the expansion that took place last month, after we planted that new transmitter in your head. Johnny boy's been busy, Anne. You know these scientist-types, never satisfied, always improving, changing. Where's the camera, Anne? Do you ever know where it is anymore? Have you ever seen a camera in the past couple of weeks, or a recorder of any sort? You have not, and you won't again. You're on now, honey." His voice was quite low, amused almost. "In fact the only time you aren't on is when you're sleeping. I know you're in love. I know who he is. I know how he makes you feel. I even know how much money he makes a week. I should know, Anne baby. I pay him." He had come closer to her with each word, finishing with his face only inches from hers. He didn't have a chance to duck the flashing slap that jerked his head around, and before either of them realized it, he had hit her back, knocking her into a chair.

The silence grew, became something ugly and heavy, as if words were being born and dying without utterance because they were too brutal for the human spirit to bear. There was a spot of blood on Herb's mouth where Anne's diamond ring had cut him. He touched it and looked at his finger. "It's all being taped now, honey, even this," he said. He turned his back on her and went to the bar.

There was a large red print on her cheek. Her gray eyes had turned black with rage.

"Honey, relax," Herb said after a moment. "It won't make any difference to you, in what you do, or anything like that. You know we can't use most of the stuff, but it gives the editors a bigger variety to pick from. It was getting to the point where most of the interesting stuff was going on after you were off. Like buying the gun. That's great stuff there, baby. You weren't blanketing a single thing, and it'll all come through like pure gold." He finished mixing his drink, tasted it, and then swallowed half of it. "How many women have to go out and buy a gun to protect themselves? Think of them all, feeling that gun, feeling the things you felt when you picked it up, looked at it. . . ."

"How long have you been tuning in all the time?" she asked. John felt a stirring along his spine, a tingle of excitement. He knew what was going out over the miniature transmitter, the rising crests of emotion she was feeling. Only a trace of them showed on her smooth face, but the raging interior torment was being recorded faithfully. Her quiet voice and quiet body were lies; the tapes never lied.

Herb felt it too. He put his glass down and went to her, kneeling by the chair, taking her hand in both of his. "Anne, please, don't be that angry with me. I was desperate for new material. When Johnny got this last wrinkle out, and we knew we could record around the clock, we had to try it, and it wouldn't have been any good if you'd known. That's no way to test anything. You knew we were planting the transmitter. . . ."

"How long?"

"Not quite a month."

"And Stuart? He's one of your men? He is transmitting also? You hired him to . . . to make love to me? Is that right?"

Herb nodded. She pulled her hand free and averted her face. He got up then and went to the window. "But what difference does it make?" he shouted. "If I introduced the two of you at a party, you wouldn't think any-thing of it. What difference if I did it this way? I knew you'd like each other. He's bright, like you, likes the same sort of things you do. Comes from a poor family, like yours. . . . Everything said you'd get along."

"Oh, yes," she said almost absently. "We get along." She was feeling in her hair, her fingers searching for the scars.

"It's all healed by now," John said. She looked at him as if she had for-gotten he was there.

"I'll find a surgeon," she said, standing up, her fingers white on her glass. "A brain surgeon — "

"It's a new process," John said slowly. "It would be dangerous to go in after them."

She looked at him for a long time. "Dangerous?"

He nodded.

"You could take it back out."

He remembered the beginning, how he had quieted her fear of the electrodes and wires. Her fear was that of a child for the unknown and the unknowable. Time and again he had proved to her that she could trust him, that he wouldn't lie to her. He hadn't lied to her, then. There was the same trust in her eyes, the same unshakable faith. She would believe him. She would accept without question whatever he said. Herb had called him an icicle, but that was wrong. An icicle would have melted in her fires. More like a stalactite, shaped by centuries of civilization, layer by layer he had been formed until he had forgotten how to bend, forgotten how to find release for the stirrings he felt somewhere in the hollow, rigid core of him-self. She had tried and, frustrated, she had turned from him, hurt, but unable not to trust one she had loved. Now she waited. He could free her, and lose her again, this time irrevocably. Or he could hold her as long as she lived.

Her lovely gray eyes were shadowed with fear, and the trust that he had given to her. Slowly he shook his head.

"I can't," he said. "No one can."

"I see," she murmured, the black filling her eyes. "I'd die, wouldn't I? Then you'd have a lovely sequence, wouldn't you, Herb?" She swung around, away from John. "You'd have to fake the story line, of course, but you are so good at that. An accident, emergency brain surgery needed, everything I feel going out to the poor little drabs who never will have brain surgery done. It's very good," she said admiringly. Her eyes were black. "In fact, anything I do from now on, you'll use, won't you? If I kill you, that will simply be material for your editors to pick over. Trial, prison, very dramatic. . . . On the other hand, if I kill myself. . . ."

John felt chilled; a cold, hard weight seemed to be filling him. Herb laughed. "The story line will be something like this," he said. "Anne has fallen in love with a stranger, deeply, sincerely in love with him. Everyone knows how deep that love is, they've all felt it, too, you know. She finds him raping a child, a lovely little girl in her early teens. Stuart tells her they're through. He loves the little nymphet. In a passion she kills herself. You are broadcasting a real storm of passion, right now, aren't you, honey? Never mind, when I run through this scene, I'll find out." She hurled her glass at him, ice cubes and orange slices flying across the room. Herb ducked, grinning.

"That's awfully good, baby. Corny, but after all, they can't get too much corn, can they? They'll love it, after they get over the shock of losing you. And they will get over it, you know. They always do. Wonder if it's true about what happens to someone experiencing a violent death?" Anne's teeth bit down on her lip, and slowly she sat down again, her eyes closed tight. Herb watched her for a moment, then said, even more cheerfully, "We've got the kid already. If you give them a death, you've got to give them a new life. Finish one with a bang. Start one with a bang. We'll name the kid Cindy, a real Cinderella story after that. They'll love her, too."

Anne opened her eyes, black, dulled now; she was so full of tension that John felt his own muscles contract. He wondered if he would be able to stand the tape she was transmitting. A wave of excitement swept him and he knew he would play it all, feel it all, the incredibly contained rage, fear, the horror of giving a death to them to gloat over, and finally, anguish. He would know it all. Watching Anne, he wished she would break now. She didn't. She stood up stiffly, her back rigid, a muscle hard ridged in her jaw. Her voice was flat when she said, "Stuart is due in half an hour. I have to dress." She left them without looking back.

Herb winked at John and motioned toward the door. "Want to take me to the plane, kid?" In the cab he said, "Stick close to her for a couple of days, Johnny. There might be an even bigger reaction later when she really understands just how hooked she is." He chuckled again. "By God! It's a good thing she trusts you, Johnny boy!"

As they waited in the chrome and marble terminal for the liner to unload its passengers, John said, "Do you think she'll be any good after this?"

"She can't help herself. She's too life-oriented to deliberately choose to die. She's like a jungle inside, raw, wild, untouched by that smooth layer of civilization she shows on the outside. It's a thin layer, kid, real thin. She'll fight to stay alive. She'll become more wary, more alert to danger, more excited and exciting. . . . She'll really go to pieces when he touches her tonight. She's primed real good. Might even have to do some editing, tone it down a little." His voice was very happy. "He touches her where she lives, and she reacts. A real wild one. She's one; the new kid's one; Stuart. . . . They're few and far between, Johnny. It's up to us to find them. God knows we're going to need all of them we can get." His expression became thoughtful and withdrawn. "You know, that really wasn't such a bad idea of mine about rape and the kid. Who ever dreamed we'd get that kind of reaction from her? With the right sort of buildup. . . ." He had to run to catch his plane.

John hurried back to the hotel, to be near Anne if she needed him. But he hoped she would leave him alone. His fingers shook as he turned on his screen; suddenly he had a clear memory of the child who had wept, and he hoped Stuart was on from six until twelve, and he already had missed almost an hour of the show. He adjusted the helmet and sank back into a deep chair. He left the audio off, letting his own words form, letting his own thoughts fill in the spaces.

Anne was leaning toward him, sparkling champagne raised to her lips, her eyes large and soft. She was speaking, talking to him, John, calling him by name. He felt a tingle start somewhere deep inside him, and his glance was lowered to rest on her tanned hand in his, sending electricity through him. Her hand trembled when he ran his fingers up her palm, to her wrist where a blue vein throbbed. The slight throb became a pounding that grew and when he looked into her eyes, they were dark and very deep. They danced and he felt her body against his, yielding, pleading. The room darkened and she was an outline against the window, her gown floating down about her. The darkness grew denser, or he closed his eyes, and this time when her body pressed against his, there was nothing between them, and the pounding was everywhere.

In the deep chair, with the helmet on his head, John's hand clenched, opened, clenched, again and again.

James Tiptree Jr.

The Girl Who Was Plugged In

(1973)

James Tiptree Jr., is a pseudonym of Alice Bradley Sheldon (1915–1987), who pioneered an especially fearless examination of sex and gender in science fiction and emerged as one of the most powerful writers of the 1970s. Now often labeled a feminist writer, until the woman behind the pseudonym was revealed in 1977 "he" was alternately heralded as a distinctively masculine writer and condemned as a male chauvinist pig. Deliberately provocative and disturbing, at times even brutal, Tiptree is a satirist whose unflinching examination of cruelty and exploitation is tempered by humor and a keen sensitivity to the realities of loneliness and suffering. Despite her apparent pessimism about human nature, Tiptree is compassionate toward her protagonists, who are nearly always misfits or victims of one sort or another. In her focus on the disenfranchised, her exploration of the fluid boundaries of body and identity, and her hip, jargon-laden prose style, Tiptree can be seen both as an heir to New Wave and a forerunner to cyberpunk. The James Tiptree Jr. Award is given in her honor to sf works that explore gender in interesting new ways.

Alice Sheldon's adventuresome and ultimately tragic life is nearly as strange as her fiction, and is now the subject of a National Book Award–winning biography by Julie Phillips (2006). The daughter of Chicago socialites and explorers, Alice Bradley traveled extensively in Africa as a child and studied art as a young woman. She met her second husband, Huntington Sheldon, while working for U.S. Army intelligence during World War II, and later joined the C.I.A. In 1967, she earned a doctorate in experimental psychology. It was only at the age of 51 that she began writing science fiction as James Tiptree Jr., but she soon achieved widespread recognition as one of the most exciting new voices in the field. In 1987, Alice Sheldon shot her invalid husband and then took her own life.

"The Girl Who Was Plugged In," which won the Hugo Award in 1974, is a stinging indictment of a socially bifurcated society obsessed with superficial appearances and commodification. Tiptree is uncannily accurate in her fore-sight about the media landscape, especially the conjunction of entertainment and advertising in television. The artificiality of the beautiful construct "Delphi" is simply an extreme form of the unnaturalness of the world she lives in, while her true form is the dirty secret of reality — real bodies, real emotions, real injustice — that this fantasy world seeks to conceal.

Listen, zombie. Believe me. What I could tell you — you with your silly hands leaking sweat on your growth-stocks portfolio. One-ten lousy hacks of AT&T on twenty-point margin and you think you're Evel Knievel. AT&T? — You doubleknit dummy, how I'd love to show you something.

Look, dead daddy, I'd say. See for instance that rotten girl?

In the crowd over there, that one gaping at her gods. One rotten girl in the city of the future. (That's what I said.) Watch.

She's jammed among bodies, craning and peering with her soul yearn-ing out of her eyeballs. Love! Oo-ooh, love them! Her gods are coming out of a store called Body East. Three youngbloods, larking along loverly. Dressed like simple street-people but . . . smashing. See their great eyes swivel above their nose-filters, their hands lift shyly, their inhumanly ten-der lips melt? The crowd moans. Love! This whole boiling megacity, this whole fun future world loves its gods.

You don't believe in gods, dad? Wait. Whatever turns you on, there's a god in the future for you, custom-made. Listen to this mob. "I touched his foot! Ow-oow, I TOUCHED Him!"

Even the people in the GTX tower up there love the gods — in their own way and for their own reasons.

The funky girl on the street, she just loves. Grooving on their beauti-ful lives, their mysterioso problems. No one ever told her about mortals who love a god and end up as a tree or a sighing sound. In a million years it'd never occur to her that her gods might love her back.

She's squashed against the wall now as the godlings come by. They move in a clear space. A holocam bobs above but its shadow never falls on them. The store display screens are magically clear of bodies as the gods glance in and a beggar underfoot is suddenly alone. They give him a token. "Aaaaah!" goes the crowd.

Now one of them flashes some wild new kind of timer and they all trot to catch a shuttle, just like people. The shuttle stops for them — more magic. The crowd sighs, closing back. The gods are gone.

(In a room far from — but not unconnected to — the GTX tower a molecular flipflop closes too, and three account tapes spin.)

Our girl is still stuck by the wall while guards and holocam equipment pull away. The adoration's fading from her face. That's good, because now you can see she's the ugly of the world. A tall monument to pituitary dystrophy. No surgeon would touch her. When she smiles, her jaw — it's half purple — almost bites her left eye out. She's also quite young, but who could care?

The crowd is pushing her along now, treating you to glimpses of her jumbled torso, her mismatched legs. At the corner she strains to send one last fond spasm after the godlings' shuttle. Then her face reverts to its usual expression of dim pain and she lurches onto the moving walkway, stumbling into people. The walkway junctions with another. She crosses, trips, and collides with the casualty rail. Finally she comes out into a little bare place called a park. The sportshow is working, a basketball game in 3-d is going on right overhead. But all she does is squeeze onto a bench and huddle there while a ghostly free-throw goes by her ear.

After that nothing at all happens except a few furtive hand-mouth gestures which don't even interest her bench-mates.

But you're curious about the city? So ordinary after all, in the FUTURE?

Ah, there's plenty to swing with here — and it's not all that *far* in the future, dad. But pass up the sci-fi stuff for now, like for instance the holovision technology that's put TV and radio in museums. Or the worldwide carrier field bouncing down from satellites, controlling communication and transport systems all over the globe. That was a spinoff from asteroid mining, pass it by. We're watching that girl.

I'll give you just one goodie. Maybe you noticed on the sportshow or the streets? No commercials. No ads.

That's right. NO ADS. An eyeballer for you.

Look around. Not a billboard, sign, slogan, jingle, sky-write, blurb, sublimflash, in this whole fun world. Brand names? Only in those ticky little peep-screens on the stores and you could hardly call that advertising. How does that finger you?

Think about it. That girl is still sitting there.

She's parked right under the base of the GTX tower as a matter of fact. Look way up and you can see die sparkles from the bubble on top, up there among the domes of godland. Inside that bubble is a boardroom. Neat bronze shield on the door: Global Transmissions Corporation — not that that means anything.

I happen to know there's six people in that room. Five of them technically male, and the sixth isn't easily thought of as a mother. They are absolutely unremarkable. Those faces were seen once at their nuptials and will show again in their obituaries and impress nobody either time. If you're looking for the secret Big Blue Meanies of the world, forget it. I know. Zen, do I know! Flesh? Power? Glory? You'd horrify them.

What they do like up there is to have things orderly, especially their communications. You could say they've dedicated their lives to that, to freeing the world from garble. Their nightmares are about hemorrhages of information; channels screwed up, plans misimplemented, garble creeping in. Their gigantic wealth only worries them, it keeps opening new vistas of disorder. Luxury? They wear what their tailors put on them, eat what their cooks serve them. See that old boy there — his name is Isham — he's sipping water and frowning as he listens to a databall. The water was prescribed by his medistaff. It tastes awful. The databall also contains a disquieting message about his son, Paul.

But it's time to go back down, far below to our girl. Look!

She's toppled over sprawling on the ground.

A tepid commotion ensues among the bystanders. The consensus is she's dead, which she disproves by bubbling a little. And presently she's taken away by one of the superb ambulances of the future which are a real improvement over ours when one happens to be around.

At the local bellevue the usual things are done by the usual team of clowns aided by a saintly mop-pusher. Our girl revives enough to answer the questionnaire without which you can't die, even in the future. Finally she's cast up, a pumped-out hulk on a cot in the long, dim ward.

Again nothing happens for a while except that her eyes leak a little from the understandable disappointment of finding herself still alive.

But somewhere one GTX computer has been tickling another, and toward midnight something does happen. First comes an attendant who pulls screens around her. Then a man in a business doublet comes daintily down the ward. He motions the attendant to strip off the sheet and go.

The groggy girl-brute heaves up, big hands clutching at bodyparts you'd pay not to see.

"Burke? P. Burke, is that your name?"

"Y-yes." Croak. "Are you . . . policeman?"

"No. They'll be along shortly, I expect. Public suicide's a felony."

". . . I'm sorry."

He has a 'corder in his hand. "No family, right?"

"No."

"You're seventeen. One year city college. What did you study?"

"La-languages."

"H'm. Say something."

Unintelligible rasp.

He studies her. Seen close, he's not so elegant. Errand-boy type.

"Why did you try to kill yourself?"

She stares at him with dead-rat dignity, hauling up the gray sheet. Give him a point, he doesn't ask twice.

"Tell me, did you see Breath this afternoon?"

Dead as she nearly is, that ghastly love-look wells up. Breath is the three young gods, a loser's cult. Give the man another point, he interprets her expression.

"How would you like to meet them?"

The girl's eyes bug out grotesquely.

"I have a job for someone like you. It's hard work. If you did well you'd be meeting Breath and stars like that all the time."

Is he insane? She's deciding she really did die.

"But it means you never see anybody you know again. Never, *ever*. You will be legally dead. Even the police won't know. Do you want to try?"

It all has to be repeated while her great jaw slowly sets. *Show me the fire I walk through.* Finally P. Burke's prints are in his 'corder, the man holding up the big rancid girl-body without a sign of distaste. It makes you wonder what else he does.

And then — THE MAGIC. Sudden silent trot of litter-bearers tucking P. Burke into something quite different from a bellevue stretcher, the oiled slide into the daddy of all luxury ambulances — real flowers in that holder! — and the long jarless rush to nowhere. Nowhere is warm and gleaming and kind with nurses. (Where did you hear that money can't buy genuine kindness?) And clean clouds folding P. Burke into bewildered sleep.

. . . Sleep which merges into feedings and washings and more sleeps, into drowsy moments of afternoon where midnight should be, and gentle businesslike voices and friendly (but very few) faces, and endless painless hyposprays and peculiar numbnesses. And later comes the steadying rhythm of days and nights, and a quickening which P. Burke doesn't identify as health, but only knows that the fungus place in her armpit is gone. And then she's up and following those few new faces with growing trust, first tottering, then walking strongly, all better now, clumping down the short hall to the tests, tests, tests, and the other things.

And here is our girl, looking —

If possible, worse than before. (You thought this was Cinderella transistorized?)

The disimprovement in her looks comes from the electrode jacks peeping out of her sparse hair, and there are other meldings of flesh and metal. On the other hand, that collar and spinal plate are really an asset; you won't miss seeing that neck.

P. Burke is ready for training in her new job.

The training takes place in her suite and is exactly what you'd call a charm course. How to walk, sit, eat, speak, blow her nose, how to stumble, to urinate, to hiccup — DELICIOUSLY. How to make each noseblow or shrug delightfully, subtly different from any ever spooled before. As the man said, it's hard work.

But P. Burke proves apt. Somewhere in that horrible bow is a gazelle, a houri who would have been buried forever without this crazy chance. See the ugly duckling go!

Only it isn't precisely P. Burke who's stepping, laughing, shaking out her shining hair. How could it be? P. Burke is doing it all right, but she's doing it through something. The something is to all appearances a live girl. (You were warned, this is the FUTURE.)

When they first open the big cryocase and show her her new body she says just one word. Staring, gulping, "How?"

Simple, really. Watch P. Burke in her sack and scuffs stomp down the hall beside Joe, the man who supervises the technical part of her training. Joe doesn't mind P. Burke's looks, he hasn't noticed them. To Joe, system matrices are beautiful.

They go into a dim room containing a huge cabinet like a one-man sauna and a console for Joe. The room has a glass wall that's all dark now. And just for your information, the whole shebang is five hundred feet underground near what used to be Carbondale, Pa.

Joe opens the sauna-cabinet like a big clamshell standing on end with a lot of funny business inside. Our girl shucks her shift and walks into it bare, totally unembarrassed. *Eager.* She settles in face-forward, butting jacks into sockets. Joe closes it carefully onto her humpback. Clunk. She can't see in there or hear or move. She hates this minute. But how she loves what comes next!

Joe's at his console and the lights on the other side of the glass wall come up. A room is on the other side, all fluff and kicky bits, a girly bedroom. In the bed is a small mound of silk with a rope of yellow hair hanging out.

The sheet stirs and gets whammed back flat.

Sitting up in the bed is the darlingest girl child you've EVER seen. She quivers — porno for angels. She sticks both her little arms straight up, flips her hair, looks around full of sleepy pizazz. Then she can't resist rubbing her hands down over her minibreasts and belly. Because, you see, it's the godawful P. Burke who is sitting there hugging her perfect girl-body, look-ing at you out of delighted eyes.

Then the kitten hops out of bed and crashes flat on the floor.

From the sauna in the dim room comes a strangled noise. P. Burke, try-ing to rub her wired-up elbow, is suddenly smothered in *two* bodies, elec-trodes jerking in her flesh. Joe juggles inputs, crooning into his mike. The flurry passes; it's all right.

In the lighted room the elf gets up, casts a cute glare at the glass wall and goes into a transparent cubicle. A bathroom, what else? She's a live girl, and live girls have to go to the bathroom after a night's sleep even if their brains are in a sauna cabinet in the next room. And P. Burke isn't in that cabinet, she's in the bathroom. Perfectly simple, if you have the glue for that closed training circuit that's letting her run her neural system by remote control.

Now let's get one thing clear. P. Burke does not *feel* her brain is in the sauna room, she feels she's in that sweet little body. When you wash your hands, do you feel the water is running on your brain? Of course not. You feel the water on your hand, although the "feeling" is actually a potential-pattern flickering over the electrochemical jelly between your ears. And it's delivered there via the long circuits from your hands. Just so, P. Burke's brain in the cabinet feels the water on her hands in the bathroom. The fact that the signals have jumped across space on the way in makes no difference at all. If you want the jargon, it's known as eccentric projection or sensory reference and you've done it all your life. Clear?

Time to leave the honey-pot to her toilet training — she's made a boo-boo with the toothbrush, because P. Burke can't get used to what she sees in the mirror —

But wait, you say. Where did that girl-body come from?

P. Burke asks that too, dragging out the words.

"They grow 'em," Joe tells her. He couldn't care less about the flesh department. "PDs. Placental decanters. Modified embryos, see? Fit the control implants in later. Without a Remote Operator it's just a vegetable. Look at the feet — no callus at all." (He knows because they told him.)

"Oh . . . oh, she's incredible . . ."

"Yeah, a neat job. Want to try walking-talking mode today? You're coming on fast."

And she is. Joe's reports and the reports from the nurse and the doctor and style man go to a bushy man upstairs who is some kind of medical cybertech but mostly a project administrator. His reports in turn go — to the GTX boardroom? Certainly not, did you think this is a *big* thing? His reports just go up. The point is, they're green, very green. P. Burke promises well.

So the bushy man — Doctor Tesla — has procedures to initiate. The little kitten's dossier in the Central Data Bank, for instance. Purely routine. And the phase-in schedule which will put her on the scene. This is simple: a small exposure in an off-network holoshow.

Next he has to line out the event which will fund and target her. That takes budget meetings, clearances, coordinations. The Burke project begins to recruit and grow. And there's the messy business of the name, which always gives Doctor Tesla an acute pain in the bush.

The name comes out weird, when it's suddenly discovered that Burke's "P." stands for "Philadelphia." Philadelphia? The astrologer grooves on it. Joe thinks it would help identification. The semantics girl references *brotherly love, Liberty-Bell, main-line, low teratogenesis,* blah-blah. Nicknames Philly? Pala? Pooty? Delphi? Is it good, bad? Finally "Delphi" is gingerly declared goodo. ("Burke" is replaced by something nobody remembers.)

Coming along now. We're at the official checkout down in the underground suite, which is as far as the training circuits reach. The bushy Doctor Tesla is there, braced by two budgetary types and a quiet fatherly man whom he handles like hot plasma.

Joe swings the door wide and she steps shyly in.

Their little Delphi, fifteen and flawless.

Tesla introduces her around. She's child-solemn, a beautiful baby to whom something so wonderful has happened you can feel the tingles. She doesn't smile, she . . . brims. That brimming joy is all that shows of P.

Burke, the forgotten hulk in the sauna next door. But P. Burke doesn't know she's alive — it's Delphi who lives, every warm inch of her.

One of the budget types lets go a libidinous snuffle and freezes. The fatherly man, whose name is Mr. Cantle, clears his throat.

"Well, young lady, are you ready to go to work?"

"Yes, sir," gravely from the elf.

"We'll see. Has anybody told you what you're going to do for us?"

"No, sir." Joe and Tesla exhale quietly.

"Good." He eyes her, probing for the blind brain in the room next door. "Do you know what *advertising* is?"

He's talking dirty, hitting to shock. Delphi's eyes widen and her little chin goes up. Joe is in ecstasy at the complex expressions P. Burke is getting through. Mr. Cantle waits.

"It's, well, it's when they used to tell people to buy things." She swallows. "It's not allowed."

"That's right." Mr. Cantle leans back, grave. "Advertising as it used to be is against the law. A display other than the legitimate use of the product, intended to promote its sale. In former times every manufacturer was free to tout his wares any way, place or time he could afford. All the media and most of the landscape was taken up with extravagant competing displays. The thing became uneconomic. The public rebelled. Since the so-called Huckster Act, sellers have been restrained to, I quote, displays in or on the product itself, visible during its legitimate use or in on-premise sales." Mr. Cantle leans forward. "Now tell me, Delphi, why do people buy one product rather than another?"

"Well . . ." Enchanting puzzlement from Delphi. "They, um, they see them and like them, or they hear about them from somebody?" (Touch of P. Burke there; she didn't say, from a friend.)

"Partly. Why did *you* buy your particular body-lift?"

"I never had a body-lift, sir."

Mr. Cantle frowns; what gutters do they drag for these Remotes?

"Well, what brand of water do you drink?"

"Just what was in the faucet, sir," says Delphi humbly. "I — I did try to boil it — "

"Good God." He scowls; Tesla stiffens. "Well, what did you boil it in? A cooker?"

The shining yellow head nods.

"What *brand* of cooker did you buy?"

"I didn't buy it, sir," says frightened P. Burke through Delphi's lips. "But — I know the best kind! Ananga has a Burnbabi, I saw the name when she — "

"Exactly!" Cantle's fatherly beam comes back strong; the Burnbabi account is a strong one, too. "You saw Ananga using one so you thought it must be good, eh? And it is good or a great human being like Ananga wouldn't be using it. Absolutely right. And now, Delphi, you know what you're going to be doing for us. You're going to show some products. Doesn't sound very hard, does it?"

"Oh, no, sir . . ." Baffled child's stare; Joe gloats.

"And you must never, *never* tell anyone what you're doing." Cantle's eyes bore for the brain behind this seductive child.

"You're wondering why we ask you to do this, naturally. There's a very serious reason. All those products people use, foods and health aids and cookers and cleaners and clothes and cars — they're all made by *people*. Somebody put in years of hard work designing and making them. A man comes up with a fine new idea for a better product. He has to get a factory and machinery, and hire workmen. Now. What happens if people have no way of hearing about his product? Word-of-mouth is far too slow and unreliable. Nobody might ever stumble onto his new product or find out how good it was, right? And then he and all the people who worked for him — they'd go bankrupt, right? So, Delphi, there has to be *some way* that large numbers of people can get a look at a good new product, right? How? By letting people see you using it. You're giving that man a chance."

Delphi's little head is nodding in happy relief.

"Yes, sir. I do see now — but sir, it seems so sensible, why don't they let you — "

Cantle smiles sadly.

"It's an overreaction, my dear. History goes by swings. People overreact and pass harsh unrealistic laws which attempt to stamp out an essential social process. When this happens, the people who understand have to carry on as best they can until the pendulum swings back." He sighs. "The Huckster Laws are bad, inhuman laws, Delphi, despite their good intent. If they were strictly observed they would wreak havoc. Our economy, our society would be cruelly destroyed. We'd be back in caves!" His inner fire showing; if the Huckster Laws were strictly enforced he'd be back punching a databank.

"It's our duty, Delphi. Our solemn social duty. We are not breaking the law. You will be using the product. But people wouldn't understand, if they knew. They would become upset just as you did. So you must be very, very careful not to mention any of this to anybody."

(And somebody will be very, very carefully monitoring Delphi's speech circuits.)

"Now we're all straight, aren't we? Little Delphi here" — He is speaking to the invisible creature next door — "Little Delphi is going to live a wonderful, exciting life. She's going to be a girl people watch. And she's going to be using fine products people will be glad to know about and helping the good people who make them. Yours will be a genuine social contribution." He keys up his pitch; the creature in there must be older.

Delphi digests this with ravishing gravity.

"But sir, how do I — ?"

"Don't worry about a thing. You'll have people behind you whose job it is to select the most worthy products for you to use. Your job is just to do as they say. They'll show you what outfits to wear to parties, what suncars and viewers to buy and so on. That's all you have to do."

Parties — clothes — suncars! Delphi's pink mouth opens. In P. Burke's starved seventeen-year-old head the ethics of product sponsorship float far away.

"Now tell me in your own words what your job is, Delphi."

"Yes sir. I — I'm to go to parties and buy things and use them as they tell me, to help the people who work in factories."

"And what did I say was so important?"

"Oh — I shouldn't let anybody know, about the things."

"Right." Mr. Cantle has another paragraph he uses when the subject shows, well, immaturity. But he can sense only eagerness here. Good. He doesn't really enjoy the other speech.

"It's a lucky girl who can have all the fun she wants while doing good for others, isn't it?" He beams around. There's a prompt shuffling of chairs. Clearly this one is go.

Joe leads her out, grinning. The poor fool thinks they're admiring her coordination.

It's out into the world for Delphi now, and at this point the up-channels get used. On the administrative side account schedules are opened, sub-projects activated. On the technical side the reserved bandwidth is cleared. (That carrier field, remember?) A new name is waiting for Delphi, a name she'll never hear. It's a long string of binaries which have been quietly cycling in a GTX tank ever since a certain Beautiful Person didn't wake up.

The name winks out of cycle, dances from pulses into modulations of modulations, whizzes through phasing, and shoots into a giga-band beam racing up to a synchronous satellite poised over Guatemala. From there the beam pours twenty thousand miles back to earth again, forming an all-pervasive field of structured energies supplying tuned demand-points all over the CanAm quadrant.

With that field, if you have the right credit rating you can sit at a GTX console and operate an ore-extractor in Brazil. Or — if you have some simple credentials like being able to walk on water — you could shoot a spool into the network holocam shows running day and night in every home and dorm and rec site. Or you could create a continent-wide traffic jam. Is it any wonder GTX guards those inputs like a sacred trust?

Delphi's "name" appears as a tiny analyzable nonredundancy in the flux, and she'd be very proud if she knew about it. It would strike P. Burke as magic; P. Burke never even understood robotcars. But Delphi is in no sense a robot. Call her a waldo if you must. The fact is she's just a girl, a real live girl with her brain in an unusual place. A simple real-time on-line system with plenty of bit-rate — even as you and you.

The point of all this hardware, which isn't very much hardware in this society, is so Delphi can walk out of that underground suite, a mobile demand-point draining an omnipresent fieldform. And she does — eighty-nine pounds of tender girl flesh and blood with a few metallic components, stepping out into the sunlight to be taken to her new life. A girl with everything going for her including a meditech escort. Walking lovely, stopping to widen her eyes at the big antennae system overhead.

The mere fact that something called P. Burke is left behind down underground has no bearing at all. P. Burke is totally unself-aware and happy as a clam in its shell. (Her bed has been moved into the waldo cabinet room now.) And P. Burke isn't in the cabinet; P. Burke is climbing out of an air-van in a fabulous Colorado beef preserve and her name is Delphi. Delphi is looking at live Charlais steers and live cottonwoods and aspens gold against the blue smog and stepping over live grass to be welcomed by the reserve super's wife.

The super's wife is looking forward to a visit from Delphi and her friends and by a happy coincidence there's a holocam outfit here doing a piece for the nature nuts.

You could write the script yourself now, while Delphi learns a few rules about structural interferences and how to handle the tiny time lag which results from the new forty-thousand-mile parenthesis in her nervous system. That's right — the people with the leased holocam rig naturally find the gold aspen shadows look a lot better on Delphi's flank than they do on a steer. And Delphi's face improves the mountains too, when you can see them. But the nature freaks aren't quite as joyful as you'd expect.

"See you in Barcelona, kitten," the head man says sourly as they pack up.

"Barcelona?" echoes Delphi with that charming little subliminal lag. She sees where his hand is and steps back.

"Cool, it's not her fault," another man says wearily. He knocks back his grizzled hair. "Maybe they'll leave in some of the gut."

Delphi watches them go off to load the spools on the GTX transport for processing. Her hand roves over the breast the man had touched. Back under Carbondale, P. Burke has discovered something new about her Delphi-body.

About the difference between Delphi and her own grim carcass.

She's always known Delphi has almost no sense of taste or smell. They explained about that: Only so much bandwidth. You don't have to taste a suncar, do you? And the slight overall dimness of Delphi's sense of touch — she's familiar with that, too. Fabrics that would prickle P. Burke's own hide feel like a cool plastic film to Delphi.

But the blank spots. It took her a while to notice them. Delphi doesn't have much privacy; investments of her size don't. So she's slow about discovering there's certain definite places where her beastly P. Burke body *feels* things that Delphi's dainty flesh does not. H'mm! Channel space again, she thinks — and forgets it in the pure bliss of being Delphi.

You ask how a girl could forget a thing like that? Look. P. Burke is about as far as you can get from the concept *girl*. She's a female, yes — but for her, sex is a four-letter word spelled P-A-I-N: She isn't quite a virgin. You don't want the details, she'd been about twelve and the freak-lovers were bombed blind. When they came down they threw her out with a small hole in her anatomy and a mortal one elsewhere. She dragged off to buy her first and last shot and she can still hear the clerk's incredulous guffaws.

Do you see why Delphi grins, stretching her delicious little numb body in the sun she faintly feels? Beams, saying, "Please, I'm ready now."

Ready for what? For Barcelona like the sour man said, where his nature-thing is now making it strong in the amateur section of the Festival.

A winner! Like he also said, a lot of strip-mines and dead fish have been scrubbed but who cares with Delphi's darling face so visible?

So it's time for Delphi's face and her other delectabilities to show on Barcelona's Playa Nueva. Which means switching her channel to the EurAf synchsat.

They ship her at night so the nanosecond transfer isn't even noticed by that insignificant part of Delphi that lives five hundred feet under Carbondale, so excited the nurse has to make sure she eats. The circuit switches while Delphi "sleeps," that is, while P. Burke is out of the waldo cabinet. The next time she plugs in to open Delphi's eyes it's no different — do you notice which relay boards your phone calls go through?

And now for the event that turns the sugar-cube from Colorado into the PRINCESS.

Literally true, he's a prince, or rather an Infante of an old Spanish line that got shined up in the Neomonarchy. He's also eighty-one, with a passion for birds — the kind you see in zoos. Now it suddenly turns out that he isn't poor at all. Quite the reverse; his old sister laughs in their tax lawyer's face and starts restoring the family hacienda while the Infante totters out to court Delphi. And little Delphi begins to live the life of the gods.

What do gods do? Well, everything beautiful. But (remember Mr. Cantle?) the main point is Things. Ever see a god empty-handed? You can't be a god without at least a magic girdle or an eight-legged horse. But in the old days some stone tablets or winged sandals or a chariot drawn by virgins would do a god for life. No more! Gods make it on novelty now. By Delphi's time the hunt for new god-gear is turning the earth and seas inside-out and sending frantic fingers to the stars. And what gods have, mortals desire.

So Delphi starts on a Euromarket shopping spree squired by her old Infante, thereby doing her bit to stave off social collapse.

Social what? Didn't you get it, when Mr. Cantle talked about a world where advertising is banned and fifteen billion consumers are glued to their holocam shows? One capricious self-powered god can wreck you.

Take the nose-filter massacre. Years, the industry sweated years to achieve an almost invisible enzymatic filter. So one day a couple of pop-gods show up wearing nose-filters like *big purple bats*. By the end of the week the world market is screaming for purple bats. Then it switched to bird-heads and skulls, but by the time the industry retooled, the crazies had dropped bird-heads and gone to injection globes. Blood!

Multiply that by a million consumer industries and you can see why it's economic to have a few controllable gods. Especially with the beautiful hunk of space R&D the Peace Department laid out for and which the taxpayers arc only too glad to have taken off their hands by an outfit like GTX which everybody knows is almost a public trust.

And so you — or rather, GTX — find a creature like P. Burke and give her Delphi. And Delphi helps keep things *orderly*, she does what you tell her to. Why? That's right, Mr. Cantle never finished his speech.

But here come the tests of Delphi's button-nose twinkling in the torrent of news and entertainment. And she's noticed. The feedback shows a flock of viewers turning up the amps when this country baby gets tangled in her new colloidal body-jewels. She registers at a couple of major scenes, too, and when the Infante gives her a suncar, little Delphi trying out suncars is a tiger. There's a solid response in high-credit country. Mr. Cantle is humming his happy tune as he cancels a Benelux subnet option to guest her on a nude cook-show called Wok Venus.

And now for the superposh old-world wedding! The hacienda has Moorish baths and six-foot silver candelabras and real black horses and the Spanish Vatican blesses them. The final event is a grand gaucho ball with the old prince and his little Infanta on a bowered balcony. She's a spectacular doll of silver lace, wildly launching toy doves at her new friends whirling by below.

The Infante beams, twitches his old nose to the scent of her sweet excitement. His doctor has been very helpful. Surely now, after he has been so patient with the suncars and all the nonsense —

The child looks up at him, saying something incomprehensible about "breath." He makes out that she's complaining about the three singers she had begged for.

"They've changed!" she marvels. "Haven't they changed? They're so dreary. I'm so happy now!"

And Delphi falls fainting against a gothic vargueno.[1]

Her American duenna[2] rushes up, calls help. Delphi's eyes are open, but Delphi isn't there. The duenna pokes among Delphi's hair, slaps her. The old prince grimaces. He has no idea what she is beyond an excellent solution to his tax problems, but he had been a falconer in his youth. There comes to his mind the small pinioned birds which were flung up to stimulate the hawks. He pockets the veined claw to which he had promised certain indulgences and departs to design his new aviary.

And Delphi also departs with her retinue to the Infante's newly discovered yacht. The trouble isn't serious. It's only that five thousand miles away and five hundred feet down P. Burke has been doing it too well.

They've always known she has terrific aptitude. Joe says he never saw a Remote take over so fast. No disorientations, no rejections. The psychomed talks about self-alienation. She's going into Delphi like a salmon to the sea.

She isn't eating or sleeping, they can't keep her out of the body-cabinet to get her blood moving, there are necroses under her grisly sit-down. Crisis!

So Delphi gets a long "sleep" on the yacht and P. Burke gets it pounded through her perforated head that she's endangering Delphi. (Nurse Fleming thinks of that, thus alienating the psychomed.)

They rig a pool down there (Nurse Fleming again) and chase P. Burke back and forth. And she loves it. So naturally when they let her plug in again Delphi loves it too. Every noon beside the yacht's hydrofoils darling Delphi clips along in the blue sea they've warned her not to drink. And every night around the shoulder of the world an ill-shaped thing in a dark burrow beats its way across a sterile pool.

So presently the yacht stands up on its foils and carries Delphi to the program Mr. Cantle has waiting. It's long-range; she's scheduled for at least two decades' product life. Phase One calls for her to connect with a flock of young ultra-riches who are romping loose between Brioni and Djakarta where a competitor named PEV could pick them off.

A routine luxgear op, see; no politics, no policy angles, and the main budget items are the title and the yacht which was idle anyway. The story-line is that Delphi goes to accept some rare birds for her prince — who cares? The *point* is that the Haiti area is no longer radioactive and look! — the gods are there. And so are several new Carib West Happy Isles which can afford GTX rates, in fact two of them are GTX subsids.

But you don't want to get the idea that all these newsworthy people are wired-up robbies, for pity's sake. You don't need many if they're placed right. Delphi asks Joe about that when he comes down to Baranquilla to check her over. (P. Burke's own mouth hasn't said much for a while.)

"Are there many like me?"

"Nobody's like you, buttons. Look, are you still getting that Van Allen warble?"

"I mean, like Davy. Is he a Remote?"

(Davy is the lad who is helping her collect the birds. A sincere redhead who needs a little more exposure.)

"Davy? He's one of Matt's boys, some psychojob. They haven't any channel."

"What about the real ones? Djuma van O, or Ali, or Jim Ten?"

"Djuma was born with a pile of GTX basic where her brain should be, she's nothing but a pain. Jimsy does what his astrologer tells him. Look, peanut, where do you get the idea you aren't real? You're the realest. Aren't you having joy?"

"Oh, Joe!" Flinging her little arms around him and his analyzer grids. "Oh, *me gusto mucho, muchissimo!*"

"Hey, hey." He pets her yellow head, folding the analyzer.

Three thousand miles north and five hundred feet down a forgotten hulk in a body-waldo glows.

And is she having joy. To waken out of the nightmare of being P. Burke and find herself a peri, a star-girl? On a yacht in paradise with no more to do than adorn herself and play with toys and attend revels and greet her friends — her, P. Burke, having friends! — and turn the right way for the holocams? Joy!

And it shows. One look at Delphi and the viewers know: DREAMS CAN COME TRUE.

Look at her riding pillion on Davy's sea-bike, carrying an apoplectic macaw in a silver hoop. Oh, *Morton, let's go there this winter!* Or learning the Japanese chinchona from that Kobe group, in a dress that looks like a blowtorch rising from one knee, and which should sell big in Texas. *Morton, is that real fire?* Happy, happy little girl!

And Davy. He's her pet and her baby and she loves to help him fix his red-gold hair. (P. Burke marveling, running Delphi's fingers through the curls.) Of course Davy is one of Matt's boys — not impotent exactly, but very *very* low drive. (Nobody knows exactly what Matt does with his bitty budget, but the boys are useful and one or two have made names.) He's perfect for Delphi; in fact the psychomed lets her take him to bed, two kittens in a basket. Davy doesn't mind the fact that Delphi "sleeps" like the dead. That's when P. Burke is out of the body-waldo up at Carbondale, attending to her own depressing needs.

A funny thing about that. Most of her sleepy-time Delphi's just a gently ticking lush little vegetable waiting for P. Burke to get back on the controls. But now and again Delphi all by herself smiles a bit or stirs in her "sleep." Once she breathed a sound: "Yes."

Under Carbondale P. Burke knows nothing. She's asleep too, dreaming of Delphi, what else? But if the bushy Dr. Tesla had heard that single syllable his bush would have turned snow-white. Because Delphi is TURNED OFF.

He doesn't. Davy is too dim to notice and Delphi's staff boss, Hopkins, wasn't monitoring.

And they've all got something else to think about now, because the cold-fire dress sells half a million copies, and not only in Texas. The GTX computers already know it. When they correlate a minor demand for macaws in Alaska the problem comes to human attention: Delphi is something special.

It's a problem, see, because Delphi is targeted on a limited consumer bracket. Now it turns out she has mass-pop potential — those macaws in *Fairbanks*, man! — it's like trying to shoot mice with an ABM. A whole new ball game. Dr. Tesla and the fatherly Mr. Cantle start going around in headquarters circles, and buddy-lunching together when they can get away from a seventh-level weasel boy who scares them both.

In the end it's decided to ship Delphi down to the GTX holocam enclave in Chile to try a spot on one of the mainstream shows. (Never mind why an Infanta takes up acting.) The holocam complex occupies a couple of mountains where an observatory once used the clear air. Holocam total-environment shells are very expensive and electronically super-stable. Inside them actors can move freely without going off-register and the whole scene or any selected part will show up in the viewer's home in complete 3-d, so real you can look up their noses and much denser than you get from mobile rigs. You can blow a tit ten feet tall when there's no molecular skiffle around.

The enclave looks — well, take everything you know about Hollywood-Burbank and throw it away. What Delphi sees coming down is a neat giant mushroom-farm, domes of all sizes up to monsters for the big games and stuff. It's orderly. The idea that art thrives on creative flamboyance has long been torpedoed by proof that what art needs is computers.

Because this showbiz has something TV and Hollywood never had — *automated inbuilt viewer feedback*. Samples, ratings, critics, polls? Forget it. With that carrier field you can get real-time response-sensor readouts from every receiver in the world, served up at your console. That started as a thingie to give the public more influence on content.

Yes.

Try it, man. You're at the console. Slice to the sex-age-educ-econ-ethno-cetera audience of your choice and start. You can't miss. Where, the feedback warms up, give 'em more of that. Warm — warmer — *hot*! You've hit it — the secret itch under those hides, the dream in those hearts. You don't need to know its name. With your hand controlling all the input and your eye reading all the response you can make them a god . . . and somebody'll do the same for you.

But Delphi just sees rainbows, when she gets through the degaussing ports and the field relay and takes her first look at the insides of those shells. The next thing she sees is a team of shapers and technicians descending on her, and millisecond timers everywhere. The tropical leisure is finished. She's in gigabuck mainstream now, at the funnel maw of the unceasing hose that's pumping the sight and sound and flesh and blood and sobs and laughs and dreams of *reality* into the world's happy head. Little Delphi is going plonk into a zillion homes in prime time and nothing is left to chance. Work!

And again Delphi proves apt. Of course it's really P. Burke down under Carbondale who's doing it, but who remembers that carcass? Certainly not P. Burke, she hasn't spoken through her own mouth for months. Delphi doesn't even recall dreaming of her when she wakes up.

As for the show itself, don't bother. It's gone on so long no living soul could unscramble the plotline. Delphi's trial spot has something to do with a widow and her dead husband's brother's amnesia.

The flap comes after Delphi's spots begin to flash out along the world-hose and the feedback appears. You've guessed it, of course. Sensational! As you'd say, they IDENTIFY.

The report actually says something like InskinEmp with a string of percentages meaning that Delphi not only has it for anybody with a Y-chromosome, but also for women and everything in between. It's the sweet supernatural jackpot, the million-to-one.

Remember your Harlow? A sexpot, sure. But why did bitter hausfraus in Gary and Memphis know that the vanilla-ice-cream goddess with the white hair and crazy eyebrows was *their baby girl*? And write loving letters to Jean warning her that their husbands weren't good enough for her? Why? The GTX analysts don't know either, but they know what to do with it when it happens.

(Back in his bird sanctuary the old Infante spots it without benefit of computers and gazes thoughtfully at his bride in widow's weeds. It might, he feels, be well to accelerate the completion of his studies.)

The excitement reaches down to the burrow under Carbondale where P. Burke gets two medical exams in a week and a chronically inflamed electrode is replaced. Nurse Fleming also gets an assistant who doesn't do much nursing but is very interested in access doors and identity tabs.

And in Chile little Delphi is promoted to a new home up among the stars' residential spreads and a private jitney to carry her to work. For Hopkins there's a new computer terminal and a full-time schedule man. What is the schedule crowded with?

Things.

And here begins the trouble. You probably saw that coming too.

"What does she think she is, a goddam *consumer rep*?" Mr. Cantle's fatherly face in Carbondale contorts.

"The girl's upset," Miss Fleming says stubbornly. "She believes that, what you told her about helping people and good new products."

"They are good products," Mr. Cantle snaps automatically, but his anger is under control. He hasn't got where he is by irrelevant reactions.

"She says the plastic gave her a rash and the glo-pills made her dizzy."

"Good god, she shouldn't swallow them," Doctor Tesla puts in agitatedly.

"You told her she'd use them," persists Miss Fleming.

Mr. Cantle is busy figuring how to ease this problem to the feral-faced young man. What, was it a goose that lays golden eggs?

Whatever he says to level Seven, down in Chile the offending products vanish. And a symbol goes into Delphi's tank matrix, one that means roughly *Balance unit resistance against PR index*. This means that Delphi's complaints will be endured as long as her Pop Response stays above a certain level. (What happens when it sinks need not concern us.) And to compensate, the price of her exposure-time rises again. She's a regular on the show now and response is still climbing.

See her under the sizzling lasers, in a holocam shell set up as a walkway accident. (The show is guesting an acupuncture school shill.)

"I don't think this new body-lift is safe," Delphi's saying. "It's made a funny blue spot on me — look, Mr. Vere."

She wiggles to show where the mini-grav pak that imparts a delicious sense of weightlessness is attached.

"So don't leave it *on*, Dee. With your meat — watch that deck-spot, it's starting to synch."

"But if I don't wear it it isn't honest. They should insulate it more or something, don't you see?"

The show's beloved old father, who is the casualty, gives a senile snigger.

"I'll tell them," Mr. Vere mutters. "Look now, as you step back bend like this so it just shows, see? And hold two beats."

Obediently Delphi turns, and through the dazzle her eyes connect with a pair of strange dark ones. She squints. A quite young man is lounging alone by the port, apparently waiting to use the chamber.

Delphi's used by now to young men looking at her with many peculiar expressions, but she isn't used to what she gets here. A jolt of something somber and knowing. *Secrets.*

"Eyes! Eyes, Dee!"

She moves through the routine, stealing peeks at the stranger. He stares back. He knows something.

When they let her go she comes shyly to him.

"Living wild, kitten." Cool voice, hot underneath.

"What do you mean?"

"Dumping on the product. You trying to get dead?"

"But it isn't right," she tells him. "They don't know, but I do, I've been wearing it."

His cool is jolted.

"You're out of your head."

"Oh, they'll see I'm right when they check it," she explains. "They're just so busy. When I tell them — "

He is staring down at little flower-face. His mouth opens, closes. "What are you doing in this sewer anyway? Who are you?"

Bewilderedly she says, "I'm Delphi."

"Holy Zen."

"What's wrong? Who are you, please?"

Her people are moving her out now, nodding at him.

"Sorry we ran over, Mister Uhunh," the script girl says.

He mutters something but it's lost as her convoy bustles her toward the flower-decked jitney.

(Hear the click of an invisible ignition-train being armed?)

"Who was he?" Delphi asks her hairman.

The hairman is bending up and down from his knees as he works.

"Paul. Isham. Three," he says and puts a comb in his mouth.

"Who's that? I can't see."

He mumbles around the comb, meaning, "Are you jiving?" Because she has to be, in the middle of the GTX enclave.

Next day there's a darkly smoldering face under a turban-towel when Delphi and the show's paraplegic go to use the carbonated pool.

She looks.

He looks.

And the next day, too.

(Hear that automatic sequencer cutting in? The system couples, the fuels begin to travel.)

Poor old Isham senior. You have to feel sorry for a man who values order: when he begets young, genetic information is still transmitted in the old ape way. One minute it's a happy midget with a rubber duck — look around and here's this huge healthy stranger, opaquely emotional, running with God knows who. Questions are heard where there's nothing to question, and eruptions claiming to be moral outrage. When this is called to Papa's attention — it may take time, in that boardroom — Papa does what he can, but without immortality-juice the problem is worrisome.

And young Paul Isham is a bear. He's bright and articulate and tender-souled and incessantly active and he and his friends are choking with appallment at the world their fathers made. And it hasn't taken Paul long to discover that *his* father's house has many mansions and even the GTX computers can't relate everything to everything else. He noses out a decaying project which adds up to something like, Sponsoring Marginal Creativity (the free-lance team that "discovered" Delphi was one such grantee). And from there it turns out that an agile lad named Isham can get his hands on a viable packet of GTX holocam facilities.

So here he is with his little band, way down the mushroom-farm mountain, busily spooling a show which has no relation to Delphi's. It's built on bizarre techniques and unsettling distortions pregnant with social protest. An *underground* expression to you.

All this isn't unknown to his father, of course, but so far it has done nothing more than deepen Isham senior's apprehensive frown.

Until Paul connects with Delphi.

And by the time Papa learns this, those invisible hypergolics have exploded, the energy-shells are rushing out. For Paul, you see, is the genuine article. He's serious. He dreams. He even reads — for example, *Green Mansions* — and he wept fiercely when those fiends burned Rima alive.

When he hears that some new GTX pussy is making it big he sneers and forgets it. He's busy. He never connects the name with this little girl making her idiotic, doomed protest in the holocam chamber. This strangely simple little girl.

And she comes and looks up at him and he sees Rima, lost Rima the enchanted bird girl, and his unwired human heart goes twang.

And Rima turns out to be Delphi.

Do you need a map? The angry puzzlement. The rejection of the dissonance Rima-hustling-for-GTX-My-Father. Garbage, cannot be. The loitering around the pool to confirm the swindle . . . dark eyes hitting on blue wonder, jerky words exchanged in a peculiar stillness . . . the dreadful reorganization of the image into Rima-Delphi *in my Father's tentacles* —

You don't need a map.

Nor for Delphi either, the girl who loved her gods. She's seen their divine flesh close now, heard their unamplified voices call her name. She's played their god-games, worn their garlands. She's even become a goddess herself, though she doesn't believe it. She's not disenchanted, don't think that. She's still full of love. It's just that some crazy kind of *hope* hasn't —

Really you can skip all this, when the loving little girl on the yellow-brick road meets a Man. A real human male burning with angry compassion and grandly concerned with human justice, who reaches for her with real male arms and — boom! She loves him back with all her heart.

A happy trip, see?

Except.

Except that it's really P. Burke five thousand miles away who loves Paul. P. Burke the monster down in a dungeon, smelling of electrode-paste. A caricature of a woman burning, melting, obsessed with true love. Trying over twenty-double-thousand miles of hard vacuum to reach her beloved through girl-flesh numbed by an invisible film. Feeling his arms around the body he thinks is hers, fighting through shadows to give herself to him. Trying to taste and smell him through beautiful dead nostrils, to love him back with a body that goes dead in the heart of the fire.

Perhaps you get P. Burke's state of mind?

She has phases. The trying, first. And the shame. The SHAME. *I am not what thou lovest.* And the fiercer trying. And the realization that there is no, no way, none. Never. *Never. . . .* A bit delayed, isn't it, her understanding that the bargain she made was forever? P. Burke should have noticed those stories about mortals who end up as grasshoppers.

You see the outcome — the funneling of all this agony into one dumb protoplasmic drive to fuse with Delphi. To leave, to close out the beast she is chained to. *To become Delphi.*

Of course it's impossible.

However her torments have an effect on Paul. Delphi-as-Rima is a potent enough love object, and liberating Delphi's mind requires hours of deeply satisfying instruction in the rottenness of it all. Add in Delphi's body worshipping his flesh, burning in the fire of P. Burke's savage heart — do you wonder Paul is involved?

That's not all.

By now they're spending every spare moment together and some that aren't so spare.

"Mister Isham, would you mind staying out of this sports sequence? The script calls for Davy here."

(Davy's still around, the exposure did him good.)

"What's the difference?" Paul yawns. "It's just an ad. I'm not blocking that thing."

Shocked silence at his two-letter word. The script girl swallows bravely.

"I'm sorry, sir, our directive is to do the *social sequence* exactly as scripted. We're having to respool the segments we did last week. Mister Hopkins is very angry with me."

"Who the hell is Hopkins? Where is he?"

"Oh, please, Paul. *Please.*"

Paul unwraps himself, saunters back. The holocam crew nervously check their angles. The GTX boardroom has a foible about having things *pointed* at them and theirs. Cold shivers, when the image of an Isham nearly went onto the world beam beside that Dial-a-dinner.

Worse yet. Paul has no respect for the sacred schedules which are now a full-time job for ferret boy up at headquarters. Paul keeps forgetting to bring her back on time and poor Hopkins can't cope.

So pretty soon the boardroom data-ball has an urgent personal action-tab for Mr. Isham senior. They do it the gentle way, at first.

"I can't today, Paul."

"Why not?"

"They say I have to, it's *very* important."

He strokes the faint gold down on her narrow back. Under Carbondale, Pa., a blind mole-woman shivers.

"Important. Their importance. Making more gold. Can't you see? To them you're just a thing to get scratch with. A *huckster*. Are you going to let them screw you, Dee? Are you?"

"Oh, Paul —"

He doesn't know it but he's seeing a weirdie; Remotes aren't hooked up to flow tears.

"Just say no, Dee. No. Integrity. You have to."

"But they say, it's my job —"

"Will you believe I can take care of you, Dee? Baby, baby, you're letting them rip us. You have to choose. Tell them no."

"Paul . . . I w-will . . ."

And she does. Brave little Delphi (insane P. Burke). Saying "No, please, I promised, Paul."

They try some more, still gently.

"Paul, Mr. Hopkins told me the reason they don't want us to be together so much. It's because of who you are, your father."

She thinks his father is like Mr. Cantle, maybe.

"Oh great. Hopkins. I'll fix him. Listen, I can't think about Hopkins now. Ken came back today, he found out something."

They are lying on the high Andes meadow watching his friends dive their singing kites.

"Would you believe, on the coast the police have *electrodes in their heads*?"

She stiffens in his arms.

"Yeah, weird. I thought they only used PP on criminals and the army. Don't you see, Dee — something has to be going on. Some movement. Maybe somebody's organizing. How can we find out?" He pounds the ground behind her. "We should make *contact*! If we could only find out."

"The, the news?" she asks distractedly.

"The news." He laughs. "There's nothing in the news except what they want people to know. Half the country could burn up and nobody would know it if they didn't want. Dee, can't you take what I'm explaining to you? They've got the whole world programmed! Total control of communication. They've got everybody's minds wired in to think what they show them and want what they give them and they give them what they're programmed to want — you can't break in or out of it, you can't get *hold* of it anywhere. I don't think they even have a plan except to keep things going round and round — and God knows what's happening to the people or the earth or the other planets, maybe. One great big vortex of lies and garbage pouring round and round getting bigger and bigger and nothing can ever change. If people don't wake up soon we're through!"

He pounds her stomach softly.

"You have to break out, Dee."

"I'll try, Paul, I will —"

"You're mine. They can't have you."

And he goes to see Hopkins, who is indeed cowed.

But that night up under Carbondale the fatherly Mr. Cantle goes to see P. Burke.

P. Burke? On a cot in a utility robe like a dead camel in a tent, she cannot at first comprehend that he is telling *her* to break it off with Paul. P. Burke has never seen Paul. *Delphi* sees Paul. The fact is, P. Burke can no longer clearly recall that she exists apart from Delphi.

Mr. Cantle can scarcely believe it either but he tries.

He points out the futility, the potential embarrassment for Paul. That gets a dim stare from the bulk on the bed. Then he goes into her duty to GTX, her job, isn't she grateful for the opportunity, etcetera. He's very persuasive.

The cobwebby mouth of P. Burke opens and croaks.

"No."

Nothing more seems to be forthcoming.

Mr. Cantle isn't dense, he knows an immovable obstacle when he bumps one. He also knows an irresistible force: GTX. The simple solution is to lock the waldo-cabinet until Paul gets tired of waiting for Delphi to wake up. But the cost, the schedules! And there's something odd here . . . he eyes the corporate asset hulking on the bed and his hunch-sense prickles.

You see, Remotes don't love. They don't have real sex, the circuits designed that out from the start. So it's been assumed that it's *Paul* who is diverting himself or something with the pretty little body in Chile. P. Burke can only be doing what comes natural to any ambitious gutter-meat. It hasn't occurred to anyone that they're dealing with the real hairy thing whose shadow is blasting out of every holoshow on earth.

Love?

Mr. Cantle frowns. The idea is grotesque. But his instinct for the fuzzy line is strong; he will recommend flexibility.

And so, in Chile:

"Darling, I don't have to work tonight! And Friday too — isn't that right, Mr. Hopkins?"

"Oh, great. When does she come up for parole?"

"Mr. Isham, please be reasonable. Our schedule — surely your own production people must be needing you?"

This happens to be true. Paul goes away. Hopkins stares after him wondering distastefully why an Isham wants to ball a waldo. How sound are those boardroom belly-fears — garble creeps, creeps in! It never occurs to Hopkins that an Isham might not know what Delphi is.

Especially with Davy crying because Paul has kicked him out of Delphi's bed.

Delphi's bed is under a real window.

"Stars," Paul says sleepily. He rolls over, pulling Delphi on top. "Are you aware that this is one of the last places on earth where people can see the stars? Tibet, too, maybe."

"Paul . . ."

"Go to sleep. I want to see you sleep."

"Paul, I . . . sleep so *hard*, I mean, it's a joke how hard I am to wake up. Do you mind?"

"Yes."

But finally, fearfully, she must let go. So that five thousand miles north a crazy spent creature can crawl out to gulp concentrates and fall on her cot. But not for long. It's pink dawn when Delphi's eyes open to find Paul's arms around her, his voice saying rude, tender things. He's been kept awake. The nerveless little statue that was her Delphi-body nuzzled him in the night.

Insane hope rises, is fed a couple of nights later when he tells her she called his name in her sleep.

And that day Paul's arms keep her from work and Hopkins's wails go up to headquarters where the weasel-faced lad is working his sharp tailbone off packing Delphi's program. Mr. Cantle defuses that one. But next week it happens again, to a major client. And ferret-face has connections on the technical side.

Now you can see that when you have a field of complexly heterodyned energy modulations tuned to a demand-point like Delphi there are many problems of standwaves and lash-back and skiffle of all sorts which are normally balanced out with ease by the technology of the future. By the same token they can be delicately unbalanced too, in ways that feed back into the waldo operator with striking results.

"Darling — what the hell! What's wrong? DELPHI!"

Helpless shrieks, writhings. Then the Rima-bird is lying wet and limp in his arms, her eyes enormous.

"I . . . I wasn't supposed to . . ." she gasps faintly, "They told me not to . . ."

"Oh my god — *Delphi*."

And his hard fingers are digging in her thick yellow hair. Electronically knowledgeable fingers. They freeze.

"You're a *doll*! You're one of those PP implants. They control you. I should have known. Oh God, I should have known."

"No, Paul," she's sobbing. "No, no, no — "

"Damn them. Damn them, what they've done — you're not *you* — "

He's shaking her, crouching over her in the bed and jerking her back and forth, glaring at the pitiful beauty.

"No!" She pleads (it's not true, that dark bad dream back there). "I'm Delphi!"

"My father. Filth, pigs — damn them, damn them, damn them."

"No, no," she babbles. "They were good to me — " P. Burke underground mouthing, "They were good to me — AAH-AAAAH!"

Another agony skewers her. Up north the sharp young man wants to make sure this so-tiny interference works. Paul can scarcely hang onto her, he's crying too. "I'll kill them."

His Delphi, a wired-up slave! Spikes in her brain, electronic shackles in his bird's heart. Remember when those savages burned Rima alive?

"I'll *kill* the man that's doing this to you."

He's still saying it afterward, but she doesn't hear. She's sure he hates her now, all she wants is to die. When she finally understands that the fierceness is tenderness she thinks it's a miracle. *He knows — and he still loves!*

How can she guess that he's got it a little bit wrong?

You can't blame Paul. Give him credit that he's even heard about pleasure-pain implants and snoops, which by their nature aren't mentioned much by those who know them most intimately. That's what he thinks is being used on Delphi, something to *control* her. And to listen — he burns at the unknown ears in their bed.

Of waldo-bodies and objects like P. Burke he has heard nothing.

So it never crosses his mind as he looks down at his violated bird, sick with fury and love, that he isn't holding *all* of her. Do you need to be told the mad resolve jelling in him now?

To free Delphi.

How? Well, he is, after all, Paul Isham III. And he even has an idea where the GTX neurolab is. In Carbondale.

But first things have to be done for Delphi, and for his own stomach. So he gives her back to Hopkins and departs in a restrained and discreet way. And the Chile staff is grateful and do not understand that his teeth don't normally show so much.

And a week passes in which Delphi is a very good, docile little ghost. They let her have the load of wildflowers Paul sends and the bland loving notes. (He's playing it coony.) And up in headquarters weasel boy feels that *his* destiny has clicked a notch onward and floats the word up that he's handy with little problems.

And no one knows what P. Burke thinks in any way whatever, except that Miss Fleming catches her flushing her food down the can and next night she faints in the pool. They haul her out and stick her with IVs. Miss Fleming frets, she's seen expressions like that before. But she wasn't around when crazies who called themselves Followers of the Fish looked through flames to life everlasting. P. Burke is seeing Heaven on the far side of death, too. Heaven is spelled P-a-u-l, but the idea's the same. *I will die and be born again in Delphi.*

Garbage, electronically speaking. No way.

Another week and Paul's madness has become a plan. (Remember, he does have friends.) He smolders, watching his love paraded by her masters. He turns out a scorching sequence for his own show. And finally, politely, he requests from Hopkins a morsel of his bird's free time, which duly arrives.

"I thought you didn't *want* me any more," she's repeating as they wing over mountain flanks in Paul's suncar. "Now you *know* — "

"Look at me!"

His hand covers her mouth and he's showing her a lettered card.
DON'T TALK THEY CAN HEAR EVERYTHING WE SAY.
I'M TAKING YOU AWAY NOW.

She kisses his hand. He nods urgently, flipping the card.

DON'T BE AFRAID. I CAN STOP THE PAIN IF THEY TRY TO
HURT YOU.

With his free hand he shakes out a silvery scrambler-mesh on a power
pack. She is dumbfounded.

THIS WILL CUT THE SIGNALS AND PROTECT YOU DAR-
LING.

She's staring at him, her head going vaguely from side to side, No.

"Yes!" He grins triumphantly. "Yes!"

For a moment she wonders. That powered mesh will cut off the field,
all right. It will also cut off Delphi. But he is *Paul*. Paul is kissing her, she
can only seek him hungrily as he sweeps the suncar through a pass.

Ahead is an old jet ramp with a shiny bullet waiting to go. (Paul also
has credits and a Name.) The little GTX patrol courier is built for nothing
but speed. Paul and Delphi wedge in behind the pilot's extra fuel tank and
there's no more talking when the torches start to scream.

They're screaming high over Quito before Hopkins starts to worry. He
wastes another hour tracking the beeper on Paul's suncar. The suncar is
sailing a pattern out to sea. By the time they're sure it's empty and Hopkins
gets on the hot flue to headquarters the fugitives are a sourceless howl
above Carib West.

Up at headquarters weasel boy gets the squeal. His first impulse is to
repeat his previous play but then his brain snaps to. This one is too hot.
Because, see, although in the long run they can make P. Burke do anything
at all except maybe *live*, instant emergencies can be tricky. And — Paul
Isham III.

"Can't you order her back?"

They're all in the GTX tower monitor station, Mr. Cantle and ferret-
face and Joe and a very neat man who is Mr. Isham senior's personal eyes
and ears.

"No sir," Joe says doggedly. "We can read channels, particularly speech,
but we can't interpolate organized pattern. It takes the waldo op to send
one-to-one — "

"What are they saying?"

"Nothing at the moment, sir." The console jockey's eyes are closed. "I
believe they are, ah, embracing."

"They're not answering," a traffic monitor says. "Still heading zero zero
three zero — due north, sir."

"You're certain Kennedy is alerted not to fire on them?" the neat man
asks anxiously.

"Yes sir."

"Can't you just turn her off?" The sharp-faced lad is angry. "Pull that
pig out of the controls!"

"If you cut the transmission cold you'll kill the Remote," Joe explains for
the third time. "Withdrawal has to be phased right, you have to fade over to
the Remote's own autonomics. Heart, breathing, cerebellum would go
blooey. If you pull Burke out you'll probably finish her too. It's a fantastic
cybersystem, you don't want to do that."

"The investment." Mr. Cantle shudders.

Weasel boy puts his hand on the console jock's shoulder, it's the contact who arranged the No-no effect for him.

"We can at least give them a warning signal, sir." He licks his lips, gives the neat man his sweet ferret smile. "We know that does no damage."

Joe frowns, Mr. Cantle sighs. The neat man is murmuring into his wrist. He looks up. "I am authorized," he says reverently, "I am authorized to, ah, direct a signal. If this is the only course. But minimal, minimal."

Sharp-face squeezes his man's shoulder.

In the silver bullet shrieking over Charleston Paul feels Delphi arch in his arms. He reaches for the mesh, hot for action. She thrashes, pushing at his hands, her eyes roll. She's afraid of that mesh despite the agony. (And she's right.) Frantically Paul fights her in the cramped space, gets it over her head. As he turns the power up she burrows free under his arm and the spasm fades.

"They're failing you again, Mister Isham!" the pilot yells.

"Don't answer. Darling, keep this over your head damn it how can I — "

An AX90 barrels over their nose, there's a flash.

"Mister Isham! Those are Air Force jets!"

"Forget it," Paul shouts back. "They won't fire. Darling, don't be afraid."

Another AX90 rocks them.

"Would you mind pointing your pistol at my head where they can see it, sir?" the pilot howls.

Paul does so. The AX90s take up escort formation around them. The pilot goes back to figuring how he can collect from GTX too, and after Goldsboro AB the escort peels away.

"Holding the same course," Traffic is reporting to the group around the monitor. "Apparently they've taken on enough fuel to bring them to tower-port here."

"In that case it's just a question of waiting for them to dock." Mr. Cantle's fatherly manner revives a bit.

"Why can't they cut off that damn freak's life-support," the sharp young man fumes. "It's ridiculous."

"They're working on it," Cantle assures him.

What they're doing, down under Carbondale, is arguing.

Miss Fleming's watchdog has summoned the bushy man to the waldo room.

"Miss Fleming, you will obey orders."

"You'll kill her if you try that, sir. I can't believe you meant it, that's why I didn't. We've already fed her enough sedative to affect heart action; if you cut any more oxygen she'll die in there."

The bushy man grimaces. "Get Doctor Quine here fast."

They wait, staring at the cabinet in which a drugged, ugly madwoman fights for consciousness, fights to hold Delphi's eyes open.

High over Richmond the silver pod starts a turn. Delphi is sagged into Paul's arm, her eyes swim up to him.

"Starting down now, baby. It'll be over soon, all you have to do is stay alive, Dee."

" . . . Stay alive . . . "

The traffic monitor has caught them. "Sir! They've turned off for Carbondale — Control has contact — "

"Let's go!"

But the headquarters posse is too late to intercept the courier wailing into Carbondale. And Paul's friends have come through again. The fugitives are out through the freight dock and into the neurolab admin port before the guard gets organized. At the elevator Paul's face plus his handgun get them in.

"I want Doctor — what's his name, Dee? Dee!"

" . . . Tesla . . . " She's reeling on her feet.

"Doctor Tesla. Take me down to Tesla, fast."

Intercoms are squalling around them as they whoosh down, Paul's pistol in the guard's back. When the door slides open the bushy man is there.

"I'm Tesla."

"I'm Paul Isham. *Isham*. You're going to take your flaming implants out of this girl — now. Move!"

"What?"

"You heard me. Where's your operating room? Go!"

"But — "

"Move! Do I have to burn somebody?"

Paul waves the weapon at Dr. Quine, who has just appeared.

"No, no," says Tesla hurriedly. "But I can't, you know. It's impossible, there'll be nothing left."

"You screaming well can, right now. You mess up and I'll kill you," says Paul murderously. "Where is it, there? And wipe the feke that's on her circuits now."

He's backing them down the hall, Delphi heavy on his arm.

"Is this the place, baby? Where they did it to you?"

"Yes," she whispers, blinking at a door, "Yes . . ."

Because it is, see. Behind that door is the very suite where she was born.

Paul herds them through it into a gleaming hall. An inner door opens and a nurse and a gray man rush out. And freeze.

Paul sees there's something special about that inner door. He crowds them past it and pushes it open and looks in.

Inside is a big mean-looking cabinet with its front door panels ajar.

And inside that cabinet is a poisoned carcass to whom something wonderful, unspeakable, is happening. Inside is P. Burke the real living woman who knows that HE is there, coming closer — Paul whom she had fought to reach through forty thousand miles of ice — PAUL is here! — is yanking at the waldo doors —

The doors tear open and a monster rises up.

"Paul darling!" croaks the voice of love and the arms of love reach for him. And he responds.

Wouldn't you, if a gaunt she-golem flab-naked and spouting wires and blood came at you clawing with metal studded paws —

"Get away!" He knocks wires.

It doesn't much matter which wires, P. Burke has so to speak her nervous system hanging out. Imagine somebody jerking a handful of your medulla —

She crashes onto the floor at his feet, flopping and roaring *"PAUL-PAUL-PAUL"* in rictus.

It's doubtful he recognizes his name or sees her life coming out of her eyes at him. And at the last it doesn't go to him. The eyes find Delphi, fainting by the doorway, and die.

Now of course Delphi is dead, too.

There's a total silence as Paul steps away from the thing by his foot.

"You killed her," Tesla says. "That was her."

"Your control." Paul is furious, the thought of that monster fastened into little Delphi's brain nauseates him. He sees her crumpling and holds out his arms. Not knowing she is dead.

And Delphi comes to him.

One foot before the other, not moving very well — but moving. Her darling face turns up. Paul is distracted by the terrible quiet, and when he looks down he sees only her tender little neck.

"Now you get the implants out," he warns them. Nobody moves.

"But, but she's dead," Miss Fleming whispers wildly.

Paul feels Delphi's life under his hand, they're talking about their monster. He aims his pistol at the gray man.

"You. If we aren't in your surgery when I count three I'm burning off this man's leg."

"Mr. Isham," Tesla says desperately, "you have just killed the person who animated the body you call Delphi. Delphi herself is dead. If you release your arm you'll see what I say is true."

The tone gets through. Slowly Paul opens his arm, looks down.

"Delphi?"

She totters, sways, stays upright. Her face comes slowly up.

"Paul . . ." Tiny voice.

"Your crotty tricks," Paul snarls at them. "Move!"

"Look at her eyes," Dr. Quine croaks.

They look. One of Delphi's pupils fills the iris, her lips writhe weirdly.

"Shock." Paul grabs her to him. *"Fix* her!" He yells at them, aiming at Tesla.

"For God's sake . . . bring it in the lab," Tesla quavers.

"Goodbye-bye," says Delphi clearly. They lurch down the hall, Paul carrying her, and meet a wave of people.

Headquarters has arrived.

Joe takes one look and dives for the waldo room, running into Paul's gun. "Oh no, you don't."

Everybody is yelling. The little thing in his arm stirs, says plaintively, "I'm Delphi."

And all through the ensuing jabber and ranting she hangs on, keeping it up, the ghost of P. Burke or whatever whispering crazily, "Paul . . . Paul . . . Please, I'm Delphi . . . Paul?"

"I'm here, darling, I'm here." He's holding her in the nursing bed. Tesla talks, talks, talks unheard.

"Paul . . . don't sleep . . ." The ghost-voice whispers. Paul is in agony, he will not accept, WILL NOT believe.

Tesla runs down.

And then near midnight Delphi says roughly, "Ag-ag-ag — " and slips onto the floor, making a rough noise like a seal.

Paul screams. There's more of the *ag-ag* business and more gruesome convulsive disintegrations, until by two in the morning Delphi is nothing but a warm little bundle of vegetative functions hitched to some expensive hardware — the same that sustained her before her life began. Joe has finally persuaded Paul to let him at the waldo-cabinet. Paul stays by her long enough to see her face change in a dreadfully alien and coldly convincing way, and then he stumbles out bleakly through the group in Tesla's office.

Behind him Joe is working wet-faced, sweating to reintegrate the fantastic complex of circulation, respiration, endocrines, midbrain homeostases, the patterned flux that was a human being — it's like saving an orchestra abandoned in midair. Joe is also crying a little; he alone had truly loved P. Burke. P. Burke, now a dead pile on a table, was the greatest cybersystem he has ever known and he never forgets her.

The end, really.

You're curious?

Sure, Delphi lives again. Next year she's back on the yacht getting sympathy for her tragic breakdown. But there's a different chick in Chile, because while Delphi's new operator is competent, you don't get two P. Burke's in a row — for which GTX is duly grateful.

The real belly-bomb of course is Paul. He was *young*, see. Fighting abstract wrongs. Now life has clawed into him and he goes through gut rage and grief and grows in human wisdom and resolve. So much so that you won't be surprised, some time later, to find him — where?

In the GTX boardroom, dummy. Using the advantage of his birth to radicalize the system. You'd call it "boring from within."

That's how he put it, and his friends couldn't agree more. It gives them a warm, confident feeling to know that Paul is up there. Sometimes one of them who's still around runs into him and gets a big hello.

And the sharp-faced lad?

Oh, he matures too. He learns fast, believe it. For instance, he's the first to learn that an obscure GTX research unit is actually getting something with their loopy temporal anomalizer project. True, he doesn't have a physics background, and he's bugged quite a few people. But he doesn't really learn about that until the day he stands where somebody points him during a test run —

— and wakes up lying on a newspaper headlined NIXON UNVEILS PHASE TWO.

Lucky he's a fast learner.

Believe it, zombie. When I say growth I mean *growth*. Capital appreciation. You can stop sweating. There's a great future there.

William Gibson

Burning Chrome

(1985)

Few writers in any genre have been as influential as William Gibson (b. 1948), whose 1983 novel *Neuromancer* created a sensation in the world of sf and transformed the way people thought about computer networks. Gibson's conception of "cyberspace" inspired a generation of computer programmers to create simulated "virtual reality" environments and to reconceptualize the nature of electronic communication. Although Gibson was not the first to visualize computing data in spatial terms (Vernor Vinge being one notable predecessor), the literary technique he used — layered narration dense with information and imagery — provided a perfect match between style and content and made his vision of the future seem plausible and even inevitable.

As one of the foremost representatives of the subgenre that came to be known as cyberpunk, Gibson combined futuristic technology with the streetwise, antiauthoritarian, and sometimes nihilistic sensibility typified by punk rock. Gibson's early works portray a world populated by loners and misfits, hustlers and hackers who operate on the fringes of a society dominated by shadowy transnational corporations. The denizens of this world recognize that information is power but are seldom able to discern the larger patterns underlying the data, which tends to take on a life of its own and to overpower any individual or institution that tries to manipulate it.

Gibson's early works have an intoxicating, almost hallucinatory quality reminiscent of New Wave sf and Beat poetry, but he seems to be somewhat uncomfortable with his role of prophet of the electronic revolution and cyberpunk, and his later works are more restrained in both plot and style. "Burning Chrome," marked by fast-paced plotting and the deft use of flashbacks to create texture and depth, is among the finest of Gibson's earlier works. Set in the same world as *Neuromancer*, it is also a good example of his world-building technique, in which sf "novum" are introduced without explanation and the reader, like the protagonist, must grope for meaning in a world of sensory overload.

It was hot, the night we burned Chrome. Out in the malls and plazas, moths were batting themselves to death against the neon, but in Bobby's loft the only light came from a monitor screen and the green and red LEDs on the face of the matrix simulator. I knew every chip in Bobby's simulator by heart; it looked like your workaday Ono-Sendai VII, the "Cyberspace Seven," but I'd rebuilt it so many times that you'd have had a hard time finding a square millimeter of factory circuitry in all that silicon.

We waited side by side in front of the simulator console, watching the time display in the screen's lower left corner.

"Go for it," I said, when it was time, but Bobby was already there, leaning forward to drive the Russian program into its slot with the heel of his hand. He did it with the tight grace of a kid slamming change into an arcade game, sure of winning and ready to pull down a string of free games.

A silver tide of phosphenes boiled across my field of vision as the matrix began to unfold in my head, a 3-D chessboard, infinite and perfectly transparent. The Russian program seemed to lurch as we entered the grid. If anyone else had been jacked into that part of the matrix, he might have seen a surf of flickering shadow roll out of the little yellow pyramid that represented our computer. The program was a mimetic weapon, designed to absorb local color and present itself as a crash-priority override in whatever context it encountered.

"Congratulations," I heard Bobby say. "We just became an Eastern Seaboard Fission Authority inspection probe. . . ." That meant we were clearing fiberoptic lines with the cybernetic equivalent of a fire siren, but in the simulation matrix we seemed to rush straight for Chrome's data base. I couldn't see it yet, but I already knew those walls were waiting. Walls of shadow, walls of ice.

Chrome: her pretty childface smooth as steel, with eyes that would have been at home on the bottom of some deep Atlantic trench, cold gray eyes that lived under terrible pressure. They said she cooked her own cancers for people who crossed her, rococo custom variations that took years to kill you. They said a lot of things about Chrome, none of them at all reassuring.

So I blotted her out with a picture of Rikki. Rikki kneeling in a shaft of dusty sunlight that slanted into the loft through a grid of steel and glass: her faded camouflage fatigues, her translucent rose sandals, the good line of her bare back as she rummaged through a nylon gear bag. She looks up, and a half-blond curl falls to tickle her nose. Smiling, buttoning an old shirt of Bobby's, frayed khaki cotton drawn across her breasts.

She smiles.

"Son of a bitch," said Bobby, "we just told Chrome we're an IRS audit and three Supreme Court subpoenas. . . . Hang on to your ass, Jack. . . ."

So long, Rikki. Maybe now I see you never.

And dark, so dark, in the halls of Chrome's ice.

Bobby was a cowboy, and ice was the nature of his game, *ice* from ICE, Intrusion Countermeasures Electronics. The matrix is an abstract representation of the relationships between data systems. Legitimate programmers jack into their employers' sector of the matrix and find themselves surrounded by bright geometries representing the corporate data.

Towers and fields of it ranged in the colorless nonspace of the simulation matrix, the electronic consensus-hallucination that facilitates the handling and exchange of massive quantities of data. Legitimate programmers never see the walls of ice they work behind, the walls of shadow that screen their operations from others, from industrial-espionage artists and hustlers like Bobby Quine.

Bobby was a cowboy. Bobby was a cracksman, a burglar, casing mankind's extended electronic nervous system, rustling data and credit in the crowded matrix, monochrome nonspace where the only stars are dense concentrations of information, and high above it all burn corporate galaxies and the cold spiral arms of military systems.

Bobby was another one of those young-old faces you see drinking in the Gentleman Loser, the chic bar for computer cowboys, rustlers, cybernetic second-story men. We were partners.

Bobby Quine and Automatic Jack. Bobby's the thin, pale dude with the dark glasses, and Jack's the mean-looking guy with the myoelectric arm. Bobby's software and Jack's hard; Bobby punches console and Jack runs down all the little things that can give you an edge. Or, anyway, that's what the scene watchers in the Gentleman Loser would've told you, before Bobby decided to burn Chrome. But they also might've told you that Bobby was losing his edge, slowing down. He was twenty-eight, Bobby, and that's old for a console cowboy.

Both of us were good at what we did, but somehow that one big score just wouldn't come down for us. I knew where to go for the right gear, and Bobby had all his licks down pat. He'd sit back with a white terry sweatband across his forehead and whip moves on those keyboards faster than you could follow, punching his way through some of the fanciest ice in the business, but that was when something happened that managed to get him totally wired, and that didn't happen often. Not highly motivated, Bobby, and I was the kind of guy who's happy to have the rent covered and a clean shirt to wear.

But Bobby had this thing for girls, like they were his private tarot or something, the way he'd get himself moving. We never talked about it, but when it started to look like he was losing his touch that summer, he started to spend more time in the Gentleman Loser. He'd sit at a table by the open doors and watch the crowd slide by, nights when the bugs were at the neon and the air smelled of perfume and fast food. You could see his sunglasses scanning those faces as they passed, and he must have decided that Rikki's was the one he was waiting for, the wild card and the luck changer. The new one.

I went to New York to check out the market, to see what was available in hot software.

The Finn's place has a defective hologram in the window, METRO HOLOGRAFIX, over a display of dead flies wearing fur coats of gray dust. The scrap's waist-high, inside, drifts of it rising to meet walls that are barely visible behind nameless junk, behind sagging pressboard shelves stacked with old skin magazines and yellow-spined years of *National Geographic*.

"You need a gun," said the Finn. He looks like a recombo DNA project aimed at tailoring people for high-speed burrowing. "You're in luck. I got the new Smith and Wesson, the four-oh-eight Tactical. Got this xenon projector slung under the barrel, see, batteries in the grip, throw you a twelve-inch high-noon circle in the pitch dark at fifty yards. The light source is so narrow, it's almost impossible to spot. It's just like voodoo in a nightfight."

I let my arm clunk down on the table and started the fingers drumming; the servos in the hand began whining like overworked mosquitoes. I knew that the Finn really hated the sound.

"You looking to pawn that?" He prodded the Duralumin wrist joint with the chewed shaft of a felt-tip pen. "Maybe get yourself something a little quieter?"

I kept it up. "I don't need any guns, Finn."

"Okay," he said, "okay," and I quit drumming. "I only got this one item, and I don't even know what it is." He looked unhappy. "I got it off these bridge-and-tunnel kids from Jersey last week."

"So when'd you ever buy anything you didn't know what it was, Finn?"

"Wise ass." And he passed me a transparent mailer with something in it that looked like an audio cassette through the bubble padding. "They had a passport," he said. "They had credit cards and a watch. And that."

"They had the contents of somebody's pockets, you mean."

He nodded. "The passport was Belgian. It was also bogus, looked to me, so I put it in the furnace. Put the cards in with it. The watch was okay, a Porsche, nice watch."

It was obviously some kind of plug-in military program. Out of the mailer, it looked like the magazine of a small assault rifle, coated with non-reflective black plastic. The edges and corners showed bright metal; it had been knocking around for a while.

"I'll give you a bargain on it, Jack. For old times' sake."

I had to smile at that. Getting a bargain from the Finn was like God repealing the law of gravity when you have to carry a heavy suitcase down ten blocks of airport corridor.

"Looks Russian to me," I said. "Probably the emergency sewage controls for some Leningrad suburb. Just what I need."

"You know," said the Finn, "I got a pair of shoes older than you are. Sometimes I think you got about as much class as those yahoos from Jersey. What do you want me to tell you, it's the keys to the Kremlin? You figure out what the goddamn thing is. Me, I just sell the stuff."

I bought it.

Bodiless, we swerve into Chrome's castle of ice. And we're fast, fast. It feels like we're surfing the crest of the invading program, hanging ten above the seething glitch systems as they mutate. We're sentient patches of oil swept along down corridors of shadow.

Somewhere we have bodies, very far away, in a crowded loft roofed with steel and glass. Somewhere we have microseconds, maybe time left to pull out.

We've crashed her gates disguised as an audit and three subpoenas, but her defenses are specifically geared to cope with that kind of official intrusion. Her most sophisticated ice is structured to fend off warrants, writs, subpoenas. When we breached the first gate, the bulk of her data vanished behind core-command ice, these walls we see as leagues of corridor, mazes of shadow. Five separate landlines spurted May Day signals to law firms, but the virus had already taken over the parameter ice. The glitch systems gobble the distress calls as our mimetic subprograms scan anything that hasn't been blanked by core command.

The Russian program lifts a Tokyo number from the unscreened data, choosing it for frequency of calls, average length of calls, the speed with which Chrome returned those calls.

"Okay," says Bobby, "we're an incoming scrambler call from a pal of hers in Japan. That should help."

Ride 'em, cowboy.

Bobby read his future in women; his girls were omens, changes in the weather, and he'd sit all night in the Gentleman Loser, waiting for the season to lay a new face down in front of him like a card.

I was working late in the loft one night, shaving down a chip, my aim off and the little waldo jacked straight into the stump.

Bobby came in with a girl I hadn't seen before, and usually I feel a little funny if a stranger sees me working that way, with those leads clipped to the hard carbon studs that stick out of my stump. She came right over and looked at the magnified image on the screen, then saw the waldo moving under its vacuum-sealed dust cover. She didn't say anything, just watched. Right away I had a good feeling about her; it's like that sometimes.

"Automatic Jack, Rikki. My associate."

He laughed, put his arm around her waist, something in his tone letting me know that I'd be spending the night in a dingy room in a hotel.

"Hi," she said. Tall, nineteen or maybe twenty, and she definitely had the goods. With just those few freckles across the bridge of her nose, and eyes somewhere between dark amber and French coffee. Tight black jeans rolled to midcalf and a narrow plastic belt that matched the rose-colored sandals.

But now when I see her sometimes when I'm trying to sleep, I see her somewhere out on the edge of all this sprawl of cities and smoke, and it's like she's a hologram stuck behind my eyes, in a bright dress she must've worn once, when I knew her, something that doesn't quite reach her knees. Bare legs long and straight. Brown hair, streaked with blond, hoods her face, blown in a wind from somewhere, and I see her wave goodbye.

Bobby was making a show of rooting through a stack of audio cassettes. "I'm on my way, cowboy," I said, unclipping the waldo. She watched attentively as I put my arm back on.

"Can you fix things?" she asked.

"Anything, anything you want, Automatic Jack'll fix it." I snapped my Duralumin fingers for her.

She took a little simstim deck from her belt and showed me the broken hinge on the cassette cover.

"Tomorrow," I said, "no problem."

And my oh my, I said to myself, sleep pulling me down the six flights to the street, *what'll Bobby's luck be like with a fortune cookie like that? If his system worked, we'd be striking it rich any night now.* In the street I grinned and yawned and waved for a cab.

Chrome's castle is dissolving, sheets of ice shadow flickering and fading, eaten by the glitch systems that spin out from the Russian program, tumbling away from our central logic thrust and infecting the fabric of the ice itself. The glitch systems are cybernetic virus analogs, self-replicating and voracious. They mutate constantly, in unison, subverting and absorbing Chrome's defenses.

Have we already paralyzed her, or is a bell ringing somewhere, a red light blinking? Does she know?

Rikki Wildside, Bobby called her, and for those first few weeks it must have seemed to her that she had it all, the whole teeming show spread out for her, sharp and bright under the neon. She was new to the scene, and she had all the miles of malls and plazas to prowl, all the shops and clubs, and Bobby to explain the wild side, the tricky wiring on the dark underside of things, all the players and their names and their games. He made her feel at home.

"What happened to your arm?" she asked me one night in the Gentleman Loser, the three of us drinking at a small table in a corner.

"Hang-gliding," I said, "accident."

"Hang-gliding over a wheatfield," said Bobby, "place called Kiev. Our Jack's just hanging there in the dark, under a Nightwing parafoil, with fifty kilos of radar jammed between his legs, and some Russian asshole accidentally burns his arm off with a laser."

I don't remember how I changed the subject, but I did.

I was still telling myself that it wasn't Rikki who was getting to me, but what Bobby was doing with her. I'd known him for a long time, since the end of the war, and I knew he used women as counters in a game, Bobby Quine versus fortune, versus time and the night of cities. And Rikki had turned up just when he needed something to get him going, something to aim for. So he'd set her up as a symbol for everything he wanted and couldn't have, everything he'd had and couldn't keep.

I didn't like having to listen to him tell me how much he loved her, and knowing he believed it only made it worse. He was a past master at the hard fall and the rapid recovery, and I'd seen it happen a dozen times before. He might as well have had NEXT printed across his sunglasses in green Day-Glo capitals, ready to flash out at the first interesting face that flowed past the tables in the Gentleman Loser.

I knew what he did to them. He turned them into emblems, sigils on the map of his hustler's life, navigation beacons he could follow through a sea of bars and neon. What else did he have to steer by? He didn't love money, in and of itself, not enough to follow its lights. He wouldn't work for power over other people; he hated the responsibility it brings. He had some basic pride in his skill, but that was never enough to keep him pushing.

So he made do with women.

When Rikki showed up, he needed one in the worst way. He was fading fast, and smart money was already whispering that the edge was off his game. He needed that one big score, and soon, because he didn't know any other kind of life, and all his clocks were set for hustler's time, calibrated in risk and adrenaline and that supernal dawn calm that comes when every move's proved right and a sweet lump of someone else's credit clicks into your own account.

It was time for him to make his bundle and get out; so Rikki got set up higher and farther away than any of the others ever had, even though — and I felt like screaming it at him — she was right there, alive, totally real, human, hungry, resilient, bored, beautiful, excited, all the things she was. . . .

Then he went out one afternoon, about a week before I made the trip to New York to see Finn. Went out and left us there in the loft, waiting for a thunderstorm. Half the skylight was shadowed by a dome they'd never finished, and the other half showed sky, black and blue with clouds. I was standing by the bench, looking up at that sky, stupid with the hot afternoon, the humidity, and she touched me, touched my shoulder, the half-inch border of taut pink scar that the arm doesn't cover. Anybody else ever touched me there, they went on to the shoulder, the neck. . . .

But she didn't do that. Her nails were lacquered black, not pointed, but tapered oblongs, the lacquer only a shade darker than the carbon-fiber laminate that sheathes my arm. And her hand went down the arm, black nails tracing a weld in the laminate, down to the black anodized elbow joint, out to the wrist, her hand soft-knuckled as a child's, fingers spreading to lock over mine, her palm against the perforated Duralumin.

Her other palm came up to brush across the feedback pads, and it rained all afternoon, raindrops drumming on the steel and soot-stained glass above Bobby's bed.

Ice walls flick away like supersonic butterflies made of shade. Beyond them, the matrix's illusion of infinite space. It's like watching a tape of a prefab building going up; only the tape's reversed and run at high speed, and these walls are torn wings.

Trying to remind myself that this place and the gulfs beyond are only representations, that we aren't "in" Chrome's computer, but interfaced with it, while the matrix simulator in Bobby's loft generates this illusion. . . . The core data begin to emerge, exposed, vulnerable. . . . This is the far side of ice, the view of the matrix I've never seen before, the view that fifteen million legitimate console operators see daily and take for granted.

The core data tower around us like vertical freight trains, color-coded for access. Bright primaries, impossibly bright in that transparent void, linked by countless horizontals in nursery blues and pinks.

But ice still shadows something at the center of it all: the heart of all Chrome's expensive darkness, the very heart. . . .

It was late afternoon when I got back from my shopping expedition to New York. Not much sun through the skylight, but an ice pattern glowed on

Bobby's monitor screen, a 2-D graphic representation of someone's computer defenses, lines of neon woven like an Art Deco prayer rug. I turned the console off, and the screen went completely dark.

Rikki's things were spread across my workbench, nylon bags spilling clothes and makeup, a pair of bright red cowboy boots, audio cassettes, glossy Japanese magazines about simstim stars. I stacked it all under the bench and then took my arm off, forgetting that the program I'd brought from the Finn was in the right-hand pocket of my jacket, so that I had to fumble it out left-handed and then get it into the padded jaws of the jeweler's vise.

The waldo looks like an old audio turntable, the kind that played disc records, with the vise set up under a transparent dust cover. The arm itself is just over a centimeter long, swinging out on what would've been the tone arm on one of those turntables. But I don't look at that when I've clipped the leads to my stump; I look at the scope, because that's my arm there in black and white, magnification 40×.

I ran a tool check and picked up the laser. It felt a little heavy; so I scaled my weight-sensor input down to a quarter-kilo per gram and got to work. At 40× the side of the program looked like a trailer truck.

It took eight hours to crack: three hours with the waldo and the laser and four dozen taps, two hours on the phone to a contact in Colorado, and three hours to run down a lexicon disc that could translate eight-year-old technical Russian.

Then Cyrillic alphanumerics started reeling down the monitor, twisting themselves into English halfway down. There were a lot of gaps, where the lexicon ran up against specialized military acronyms in the readout I'd bought from my man in Colorado, but it did give me some idea of what I'd bought from the Finn.

I felt like a punk who'd gone out to buy a switchblade and come home with a small neutron bomb.

Screwed again, I thought. *What good's a neutron bomb in a streetfight?* The thing under dust cover was right out of my league. I didn't even know where to unload it, where to look for a buyer. Someone had, but he was dead, someone with a Porsche watch and a fake Belgian passport, but I'd never tried to move in those circles. The Finn's muggers from the 'burbs had knocked over someone who had some highly arcane connections.

The program in the jeweler's vise was a Russian military icebreaker, a killer-virus program.

It was dawn when Bobby came in alone. I'd fallen asleep with a bag of takeout sandwiches in my lap.

"You want to eat?" I asked him, not really awake, holding out my sandwiches. I'd been dreaming of the program, of its waves of hungry glitch systems and mimetic subprograms; in the dream it was an animal of some kind, shapeless and flowing.

He brushed the bag aside on his way to the console, punched a function key. The screen lit with the intricate pattern I'd seen there that afternoon. I rubbed sleep from my eyes with my left hand, one thing I can't do with my right. I'd fallen asleep trying to decide whether to tell him about the program. Maybe I should try to sell it alone, keep the money, go somewhere new, ask Rikki to go with me.

"Whose is it?" I asked.

He stood there in a black cotton jump suit, an old leather jacket thrown over his shoulders like a cape. He hadn't shaved for a few days, and his face looked thinner than usual.

"It's Chrome's," he said.

My arm convulsed, started clicking, fear translated to the myoelectrics through the carbon studs. I spilled the sandwiches; limp sprouts, and bright yellow dairy-produce slices on the unswept wooden floor.

"You're stone crazy," I said.

"No," he said, "you think she rumbled it? No way. We'd be dead already. I locked on to her through a triple-blind rental system in Mombasa and an Algerian comsat. She knew somebody was having a look-see, but she couldn't trace it."

If Chrome had traced the pass Bobby had made at her ice, we were good as dead. But he was probably right, or she'd have had me blown away on my way back from New York. "Why her, Bobby? Just give me one reason. . . ."

Chrome: I'd seen her maybe half a dozen times in the Gentleman Loser. Maybe she was slumming, or checking out the human condition, a condition she didn't exactly aspire to. A sweet little heart-shaped face framing the nastiest pair of eyes you ever saw. She'd looked fourteen for as long as anyone could remember, hyped out of anything like a normal metabolism on some massive program of serums and hormones. She was as ugly a customer as the street ever produced, but she didn't belong to the street anymore. She was one of the Boys, Chrome, a member in good standing of the local Mob subsidiary. Word was, she'd gotten started as a dealer, back when synthetic pituitary hormones were still proscribed. But she hadn't had to move hormones for a long time. Now she owned the House of Blue Lights.

"You're flat-out crazy, Quine. You give me one sane reason for having that stuff on your screen. You ought to dump it, and I mean *now*. . . ."

"Talk in the Loser," he said, shrugging out of the leather jacket. "Black Myron and Crow Jane. Jane, she's up on all the sex lines, claims she knows where the money goes. So she's arguing with Myron that Chrome's the controlling interest in the Blue Lights, not just some figurehead for the Boys."

" 'The Boys,' Bobby," I said. "That's the operative word there. You still capable of seeing that? We don't mess with the Boys, remember? That's why we're still walking around."

"That's why we're still poor, partner." He settled back into the swivel chair in front of the console, unzipped his jump suit, and scratched his skinny white chest. "But maybe not for much longer."

"I think maybe this partnership just got itself permanently dissolved."

Then he grinned at me. The grin was truly crazy, feral, and focused, and I knew that right then he really didn't give a shit about dying.

"Look," I said, "I've got some money left, you know? Why don't you take it and get the tube to Miami, catch a hopper to Montego Bay. You need a rest, man. You've got to get your act together."

"My act, Jack," he said, punching something on the keyboard, "never has been this together before." The neon prayer rug on the screen shivered and woke as an animation program cut in, ice lines weaving with hypnotic frequency, a living mandala. Bobby kept punching, and the movement slowed; the pattern resolved itself, grew slightly less complex, became an alternation between two distant configurations. A first-class piece of work, and I hadn't thought he was still that good. "Now," he said, "there, see it? Wait. There. There again. And there. Easy to miss. That's it. Cuts in every hour and twenty minutes with a squirt transmission to their comsat. We could live for a year on what she pays them weekly in negative interest."

"Whose comsat?"

"Zürich. Her bankers. That's her bankbook, Jack. That's where the money goes. Crow Jane was right."

I stood there. My arm forgot to click.

"So how'd you do in New York, partner? You get anything that'll help me cut ice? We're going to need whatever we can get."

I kept my eyes on his, forced myself not to look in the direction of the waldo, the jeweler's vise. The Russian program was there, under the dust cover.

Wild cards, luck changers.

"Where's Rikki?" I asked him, crossing to the console, pretending to study the alternating patterns on the screen.

"Friends of hers," he shrugged, "kids, they're all into simstim." He smiled absently. "I'm going to do it for her, man,"

"I'm going out to think about this, Bobby. You want me to come back, you keep your hands off the board."

"I'm doing it for her," he said as the door closed behind me. "You know I am."

And down now, down, the program a roller coaster through this fraying maze of shadow walls, gray cathedral spaces between the bright towers. Headlong speed.

Black ice. Don't think about it. Black ice.

Too many stories in the Gentleman Loser; black ice is a part of the mythology. Ice that kills. Illegal, but then aren't we all? Some kind of neural-feedback weapon, and you connect with it only once. Like some hideous Word that eats the mind from the inside out. Like an epileptic spasm that goes on and on until there's nothing left at all. . . .

And we're diving for the floor of Chrome's shadow castle.

Trying to brace myself for the sudden stopping of breath, a sickness and final slackening of the nerves. Fear of that cold Word waiting, down there in the dark.

I went out and looked for Rikki, found her in a café with a boy with Sendai eyes, half-healed suture lines radiating from his bruised sockets. She had a glossy brochure spread open on the table, Tally Isham smiling up from a dozen photographs, the Girl with the Zeiss Ikon Eyes.

Her little simstim deck was one of the things I'd stacked under my bench the night before, the one I'd fixed for her the day after I'd first seen her. She spent hours jacked into that unit, the contact band across her forehead like a gray plastic tiara. Tally Isham was her favorite, and with the contact band on, she was gone, off somewhere in the recorded sensorium of simstim's biggest star. Simulated stimuli: the world — all the interesting parts, anyway — as perceived by Tally Isham. Tally raced a black Fokker ground-effect plane across Arizona mesa tops. Tally dived the Truk Island preserves. Tally partied with the superrich on private Greek islands, heart-breaking purity of those tiny white seaports at dawn.

Actually she looked a lot like Tally, same coloring and cheekbones. I thought Rikki's mouth was stronger. More sass. She didn't want to *be* Tally Isham, but she coveted the job. That was her ambition, to be in simstim. Bobby just laughed it off. She talked to me about it, though. "How'd I look with a pair of these?" she'd ask, holding a full-page headshot, Tally Isham's blue Zeiss Ikons lined up with her own amber-brown. She'd had her corneas done twice, but she still wasn't 20-20; so she wanted Ikons. Brand of the stars. Very expensive.

"You still window-shopping for eyes?" I asked as I sat down.

"Tiger just got some," she said. She looked tired, I thought.

Tiger was so pleased with his Sendais that he couldn't help smiling, but I doubted whether he'd have smiled otherwise. He had the kind of uni-form good looks you get after your seventh trip to the surgical boutique; he'd probably spend the rest of his life looking vaguely like each new sea-son's media front-runner; not too obvious a copy, but nothing too original, either.

"Sendai, right?" I smiled back.

He nodded. I watched as he tried to take me in with his idea of a pro-fessional simstim glance. He was pretending that he was recording. I thought he spent too long on my arm. "They'll be great on peripherals when the muscles heal," he said, and I saw how carefully he reached for his dou-ble espresso. Sendai eyes are notorious for depth-perception defects and warranty hassles, among other things.

"Tiger's leaving for Hollywood tomorrow."

"Then maybe Chiba City, right?" I smiled at him. He didn't smile back. "Got an offer, Tiger? Know an agent?"

"Just checking it out," he said quietly. Then he got up and left. He said a quick goodbye to Rikki, but not to me.

"That kid's optic nerves may start to deteriorate inside six months. You know that, Rikki? Those Sendais are illegal in England, Denmark, lots of places. You can't replace nerves."

"Hey, Jack, no lectures." She stole one of my croissants and nibbled at the top of one of its horns.

"I thought I was your adviser, kid."

"Yeah. Well, Tiger's not too swift, but everybody knows about Sendais. They're all he can afford. So he's taking a chance. If he gets work, he can replace them."

"With these?" I tapped the Zeiss Ikon brochure. "Lot of money, Rikki. You know better than to take a gamble like that."

She nodded. "I want Ikons."

"If you're going up to Bobby's, tell him to sit tight until he hears from me."

"Sure. It's business?"

"Business," I said. But it was craziness.

I drank my coffee, and she ate both my croissants. Then I walked her down to Bobby's. I made fifteen calls, each one from a different pay phone.

Business. Bad craziness.

All in all, it took us six weeks to set the burn up, six weeks of Bobby telling me how much he loved her. I worked even harder, trying to get away from that.

Most of it was phone calls. My fifteen initial and very oblique inquiries each seemed to breed fifteen more. I was looking for a certain service Bobby and I both imagined as a requisite part of the world's clandestine economy, but which probably never had more than five customers at a time. It would be one that never advertised.

We were looking for the world's heaviest fence, for a non-aligned money laundry capable of dry-cleaning a megabuck online cash transfer and then forgetting about it.

All those calls were a waste, finally, because it was the Finn who put me on to what we needed. I'd gone up to New York to buy a new blackbox rig, because we were going broke paying for all those calls.

I put the problem to him as hypothetically as possible.

"Macao," he said.

"Macao?"

"The Long Hum family. Stockbrokers."

He even had the number. You want a fence, ask another fence.

The Long Hum people were so oblique that they made my idea of a subtle approach look like a tactical nuke-out. Bobby had to make two shuttle runs to Hong Kong to get the deal straight. We were running out of capital, and fast. I still don't know why I decided to go along with it in the first place; I was scared of Chrome, and I'd never been all that hot to get rich.

I tried telling myself that it was a good idea to burn the House of Blue Lights because the place was a creep joint, but I just couldn't buy it. I didn't like the Blue Lights, because I'd spent a supremely depressing evening there once, but that was no excuse for going after Chrome. Actually I halfway assumed we were going to die in the attempt. Even with that killer program, the odds weren't exactly in our favor.

Bobby was lost in writing the set of commands we were going to plug into the dead center of Chrome's computer. That was going to be my job, because Bobby was going to have his hands full trying to keep the Russian program from going straight for the kill. It was too complex for us to rewrite, and so he was going to try to hold it back for the two seconds I needed.

I made a deal with a streetfighter named Miles. He was going to follow Rikki the night of the burn, keep her in sight, and phone me at a certain time. If I wasn't there, or didn't answer in just a certain way, I'd told him to grab her and put her on the first tube out. I gave him an envelope to give her, money and a note.

Bobby really hadn't thought about that, much, how things would go for her if we blew it. He just kept telling me he loved her, where they were going to go together, how they'd spend the money.

"Buy her a pair of Ikons first, man. That's what she wants. She's serious about that simstim scene."

"Hey," he said, looking up from the keyboard, "she won't need to work. We're going to make it, Jack. She's my luck. She won't ever have to work again."

"Your luck," I said. I wasn't happy. I couldn't remember when I had been happy. "You seen your luck around lately?"

He hadn't, but neither had I. We'd both been too busy.

I missed her. Missing her reminded me of my one night in the House of Blue Lights, because I'd gone there out of missing someone else. I'd gotten drunk to begin with, then I'd started hitting Vasopressin inhalers. If your main squeeze has just decided to walk out on you, booze and Vasopressin are the ultimate in masochistic pharmacology; the juice makes you maudlin and the Vasopressin makes you remember, I mean really remember. Clinically they use the stuff to counter senile amnesia, but the street finds its own uses for things. So I'd bought myself an ultraintense replay of a bad affair; trouble is, you get the bad with the good. Go gunning for transports of animal ecstasy and you get what you said, too, and what she said to that, how she walked away and never looked back.

I don't remember deciding to go to the Blue Lights, or how I got there, hushed corridors and this really tacky decorative waterfall trickling somewhere, or maybe just a hologram of one. I had a lot of money that night; somebody had given Bobby a big roll for opening a three-second window in someone else's ice.

I don't think the crew on the door liked my looks, but I guess my money was okay.

I had more to drink there when I'd done what I went there for. Then I made some crack to the barman about closet necrophiliacs, and that didn't go down too well. Then this very large character insisted on calling me War Hero, which I didn't like. I think I showed him some tricks with the arm, before the lights went out, and I woke up two days later in a basic sleeping module somewhere else. A cheap place, not even room to hang yourself. And I sat there on that narrow foam slab and cried.

Some things are worse than being alone. But the thing they sell in the House of Blue Lights is so popular that it's almost legal.

At the heart of darkness, the still center, the glitch systems shred the dark with whirlwinds of light, translucent razors spinning away from us; we hang in the center of a silent slow-motion explosion, ice fragments falling away forever, and Bobby's voice comes in across light-years of electronic void illusion —

"Burn the bitch down. I can't hold the thing back — "

The Russian program, rising through towers of data, blotting out the playroom colors. And I plug Bobby's homemade command package into the center of Chrome's cold heart. The squirt transmission cuts in, a pulse of condensed information that shoots straight up, past the thickening tower of darkness, the Russian program, while Bobby struggles to control that crucial second. An unformed arm of shadow twitches from the towering dark, too late.

We've done it.

The matrix folds itself around me like an origami trick.

And the loft smells of sweat and burning circuitry.

I thought I heard Chrome scream, a raw metal sound, but I couldn't have.

Bobby was laughing, tears in his eyes. The elapsed-time figure in the corner of the monitor read 07:24:05. The burn had taken a little under eight minutes.

And I saw that the Russian program had melted in its slot.

We'd given the bulk of Chrome's Zürich account to a dozen world charities. There was too much there to move, and we knew we had to break her, burn her straight down, or she might come after us. We took less than ten percent for ourselves and shot it through the Long Hum setup in Macao. They took sixty percent of that for themselves and kicked what was left back to us through the most convoluted sector of the Hong Kong exchange. It took an hour before our money started to reach the two accounts we'd opened in Zürich.

I watched zeros pile up behind a meaningless figure on the monitor. I was rich.

Then the phone rang. It was Miles. I almost blew the code phrase.

"Hey, Jack, man, I dunno — what's it all about, with this girl of yours? Kinda funny thing here . . ."

"What? Tell me."

"I been on her, like you said, tight but out of sight. She goes to the Loser, hangs out, then she gets a tube. Goes to the House of Blue Lights — "

"She what?"

"Side door. *Employees* only. No way I could get past their security."

"Is she there now?"

"No, man, I just lost her. It's insane down here, like the Blue Lights just shut down, looks like for good, seven kinds of alarms going off, everybody running, the heat out in riot gear. . . . Now there's all this stuff going on, insurance guys, real-estate types, vans with municipal plates. . . ."

"Miles, where'd she go?"

"Lost her, Jack."

"Look, Miles, you keep the money in the envelope, right?"

"You serious? Hey, I'm real sorry. I — "

I hung up.

"Wait'll we tell her," Bobby was saying, rubbing a towel across his bare chest.

"You tell her yourself, cowboy. I'm going for a walk."

So I went out into the night and the neon and let the crowd pull me along, walking blind, willing myself to be just a segment of that mass organism, just one more drifting chip of consciousness under the geodesics. I didn't think, just put one foot in front of another, but after a while I did think, and it all made sense. She'd needed the money.

I thought about Chrome, too. That we'd killed her, murdered her, as surely as if we'd slit her throat. The night that carried me along through the malls and plazas would be hunting her now, and she had nowhere to go. How many enemies would she have in this crowd alone? How many would move, now they weren't held back by fear of her money? We'd taken her for everything she had. She was back on the street again. I doubted she'd live till dawn.

Finally I remembered the café, the one where I'd met Tiger.

Her sunglasses told the whole story, huge black shades with a telltale smudge of fleshtone paintstick in the corner of one lens. "Hi, Rikki," I said, and I was ready when she took them off.

Blue, Tally Isham blue. The clear trademark blue they're famous for, ZEISS IKON ringing each iris in tiny capitals, the letters suspended there like flecks of gold.

"They're beautiful," I said. Paintstick covered the bruising. No scars with work that good. "You made some money."

"Yeah, I did." Then she shivered. "But I won't make any more, not that way."

"I think that place is out of business."

"Oh." Nothing moved in her face then. The new blue eyes were still and very deep.

"It doesn't matter. Bobby's waiting for you. We just pulled down a big score."

"No. I've got to go. I guess he won't understand, but I've got to go."

I nodded, watching the arm swing up to take her hand; it didn't seem to be part of me at all, but she held on to it like it was.

"I've got a one-way ticket to Hollywood. Tiger knows some people I can stay with. Maybe I'll even get to Chiba City."

She was right about Bobby. I went back with her. He didn't understand. But she'd already served her purpose, for Bobby, and I wanted to tell her not to hurt for him, because I could see that she did. He wouldn't even come out into the hallway after she had packed her bags. I put the bags down and kissed her and messed up the paintstick, and something came up inside me the way the killer program had risen above Chrome's data. A sudden stopping of the breath, in a place where no word is. But she had a plane to catch.

Bobby was slumped in the swivel chair in front of his monitor, looking at his string of zeros. He had his shades on, and I knew he'd be in the Gentleman Loser by nightfall, checking out the weather, anxious for a sign, someone to tell him what his new life would be like. I couldn't see it being very different. More comfortable, but he'd always be waiting for that next card to fall.

I tried not to imagine her in the House of Blue Lights, working three-hour shifts in an approximation of REM sleep, while her body and a bundle of conditioned reflexes took care of business. The customers never got to complain that she was faking it, because those were real orgasms. But she felt them, if she felt them at all, as faint silver flares somewhere out on the edge of sleep. Yeah, it's so popular, it's almost legal. The customers are torn between needing someone and wanting to be alone at the same time, which has probably always been the name of that particular game, even before we had the neuroelectronics to enable them to have it both ways.

I picked up the phone and punched the number for her airline. I gave them her real name, her flight number. "She's changing that," I said, "to Chiba City. That's right, Japan." I thumbed my credit card into the slot and punched my ID code. "First class." Distant hum as they scanned my credit records. "Make that a return ticket."

But I guess she cashed the return fare, or else didn't need it, because she hasn't come back. And sometimes late at night I'll pass a window with posters of simstim stars, all those beautiful, identical eyes staring back at me out of faces that are nearly as identical, and sometimes the eyes are hers, but none of the faces are, none of them ever are, and I see her far out on the edge of all this sprawl of night and cities, and then she waves goodbye.

Maureen McHugh

Nekropolis

(1994)

Maureen McHugh (b. 1959) has won widespread critical acclaim for her quiet, psychologically probing fiction, which is sometimes compared to the work of Ursula K. Le Guin, with whom she shares an anthropological bent and a gift for finely crafted, character-driven stories. McHugh's first novel, *China Mountain Zhang* (1992), made a strong debut, garnering Hugo and Nebula nominations and winning the James Tiptree Jr. award. Her alternate history story "The Lincoln Train" won the Hugo in 1996. The story that follows (which was nominated for a Nebula) was later expanded into a novel, *Nekropolis* (1994). It explores the varieties of bondage and control at the intersection of gender, race, and class in a traditional society that uses futuristic technology to maintain its social hierarchy.

In "Nekropolis," the story of an indentured servant biochemically "jessed" to her master and a "harni," or bioengineered clone, McHugh explores the murky boundaries between natural and artificial loyalties, dominance and passivity, resistance and resignation. Like McHugh's other work, this story reveals the complexity and moral ambiguity faced by individuals seeking to define themselves in a world that offers no easy answers.

In her use of literary techniques prevalent in contemporary mainstream fiction, McHugh may be seen as representative of the new realism that emerged in the 1990s, when a shift away from the glamorized violence and far-flung conspiracy plots of cyberpunk led to a greater emphasis on the emotional life and relationships of ordinary people. McHugh's characters, like William Gibson's, find themselves in a confusing world where they must grope after elusive meanings, but the action of McHugh's stories, despite their futuristic settings, takes place on a level that is primarily personal.

How I came to be jessed. Well, like most people who are jessed, I was sold. I was twenty-one, and I was sold three times in one day, one right after another. First to a dealer who looked at my teeth and in my ears and had me scanned for augmentation; then to a second dealer where I sat in the back office drinking tea and talking with a gap-toothed boy who was supposed to be sold to a restaurant owner as a clerk; and finally that afternoon to the restaurant owner. The restaurant owner couldn't really have wanted the boy anyway, since the position was for his wife's side of the house.

I have been with my present owner since I was twenty-one. That was pretty long ago, I am twenty-six now. I was a good student, I got good marks, so I was purchased to oversee cleaning and supplies. This is much better than if I were a pretty girl and had to rely on looks. Then I would be used up in a few years. I'm rather plain, with a square jaw and unexceptional hair.

I liked my owner, liked my work. But now I would like to go to him and ask him to sell me.

"Diyet," he would say, taking my hand in his fatherly way, "Aren't you happy here?"

"Mardin-salah," I would answer, my eyes demurely on my toes. "You are like a father and I have been only too happy with you." Which is true even beyond being jessed. I don't think I would mind being part of Mardin's household even if I were unbound. Mostly Mardin pays no attention to me, which is how I prefer things. I like my work and my room. I like being jessed. It makes things simpler.

All would be fine if it were not for the new one.

I have no problems with AI. I don't mind the cleaning machine, poor thing, and as head of the women's household, I work with the household intelligence all the time. I may have had a simple, rather conservative upbringing, but I have come to be pretty comfortable with AI. The Holy Injunction doesn't mean that all AI is abomination. But AI should not be biologically constructed. AI should not be made in the image of humanity.

It thinks of itself. It has a name. It has gender.

It thinks it is male. And it's head of the men's side of the house, so it thinks we should work together.

It looks human male, has curly black hair and soft honey-colored skin. It flirts, looking at me sideways out of black, vulnerable gazelle eyes.

Smiling at me with a smile which is not in the slightest bit vulnerable. "Come on, Diyet," it says, "we work together. We should be friends. We're both young, we can help each other in our work."

I do not bother to answer.

It smiles wickedly (although I know it is not wicked, it is just something grown and programmed. Soulless. I am not so conservative that I condemn cloning, but it is not a clone. It is a biological construct). "Diyet," it says, "I think you are too pure. A Holy Sister."

"Don't sound foolish," I say.

"You need someone to tease you," it says, "you are so solemn. Tell me, is it because you are jessed?"

I do not know how much it knows, does it understand the process of jessing? "The Mashahana says that just as a jessed hawk is tamed, not tied, so shall the servant be bound by affection and duty, not chains."

"Does the Mashahana say it should not make you sad, Diyet?"

Can something not human blaspheme?

In the morning, Mardin calls me into his office. He offers me tea, translucent green and fragrant with flowers, which I sip, regarding my sandals and my pink toenails. He pages through my morning report, nodding, making pleased noises, occasionally slurping his tea. Afternoons and evenings, Mardin is at his restaurant. I have never been in it, but I understand that it is an exceptional place.

"What will you do this afternoon?" he asks.

It is my afternoon free. "My childhood friend, Kari, and I will go shopping, Mardin-salah."

"Ah," he says, smiling. "Spend a little extra silver," he says, "buy yourself earrings or something. I'll see the credit is available."

I murmur my thanks. He makes a show of paging through the report, and the sheets of paper whisper against each other.

"And what do you think of the harni, Akhmim? Is he working out?"

"I do not spend so much time with it, Mardin-salah. Its work is with the men's household."

"You are an old-fashioned girl, Diyet, that is good." Mardin-salah holds the report a little farther away, striking a very dignified pose in his reading. "Harni have social training, but no practice. The merchant recommended to me that I send it out to talk and meet with people as much as possible."

I wriggle my toes. He has stopped referring to it as if it were a person, which is good, but now he is going to try to send it with me. "I must meet my friend Kari at her home in the Nekropolis, Mardin-salah. Perhaps it is not a good place to take a harni." The Nekropolis is a conservative place.

Mardin-salah waves his hand airily. "Everything is in order, Diyet," he says, referring to the reports in front of him. "My wife has asked that you use a little more scent with the linens."

His wife thinks I am too cheap. Mardin-salah likes to think that he runs a frugal household. He does not, money hemorrhages from this house, silver pours from the walls and runs down the street into the pockets of everyone in this city. She wanted to buy *it*, I am certain. She is like that, she enjoys toys. Surrounds herself with things, projects still more things, until it is difficult to know what is in her quarters and what comes out of the walls. She probably saw it and had to have it, the way she had to have the little long-haired dog with the overbite, her little lion dog — nasty little thing that Fadina has to feed and bathe. Fadina is her body servant.

I hope Mardin will forget about the harni, but he doesn't. There is no respite. I must take it with me.

It is waiting for me after lunch. I am wearing lavender and pale yellow, with long yellow ribbons tied around my wrists.

"Jessed, Diyet," it says. "You wouldn't have me along if you weren't."

Of course I am jessed. I always wear ribbons when I go out. "The Mashahana says ribbons are a symbol of devotion to the Most Holy, as well as an earthly master."

It runs its long fingers through its curly hair, shakes its head, and its golden earring dances. Artifice, the pretense of humanity. Although I guess even a harni's hair gets in its eyes. "Why would you choose to be jessed?" it asks.

"You wouldn't understand," I say, "come along."

It never takes offense, never worries about offending. "Can you tell the difference between the compulsion and your own feelings?" it asks.

"Jessing only heightens my natural tendencies," I say.

"Then why are you so sad?" it asks.

"I am not sad!" I snap.

"I am sorry," it says immediately. Blessedly, it is silent while we go down to the tube. I point which direction we are going and it nods and follows. I get a seat on the tube and it stands in front of me. It glances down at me. Smiles. I fancy it looks as if it feels pity for me. (Artifice. Does the cleaning machine feel sorry for anyone? Even itself? Does the household intelligence? The body chemistry of a harni may be based on humanity, but it is carefully calculated.)

It wears a white shirt. I study my toenails.

The tube lets us off at the edge of the Nekropolis, at the Moussin of the White Falcon. Mourners in white stand outside the Moussin, and I can faintly smell the incense on the hot air. The sun is blinding after the cool dark tube, and the Moussin and the mourners' robes are painful to look at. They are talking and laughing. Often, mourners haven't seen each other for years, family is spread all across the country.

The harni looks around, as curious as a child or a jackdaw. The Nekropolis is all white stone, the doorways open onto blackness.

I grew up in the Nekropolis. We didn't have running water, it was delivered every day in a big lorritank and people would go out and buy it by the *karn*, and we lived in three adjoining mausoleums instead of a flat, but other than that, it was a pretty normal childhood. I have a sister and two brothers. My mother sells paper funeral decorations, so the Nekropolis is a very good place for her to live, no long tube rides every day. The part we lived in was old. Next to my bed were the dates for the person buried behind the wall, 3673 to 3744. All of the family was dead hundreds of years ago, no one ever came to this death house to lay out paper flowers and birds. In fact, when I was four, we bought the rights to this place from an old woman whose family had lived here a long time before us.

Our house always smelled of cinnamon and the perfume my mother used on her paper flowers and birds. In the middle death-house, there were funeral arrangements everywhere, and when we ate we would clear a space on the floor and sit surrounded. When I was a little girl, I learned the different uses of papers; how my mother used translucent tissue for carnations, stiff satiny brittle paper for roses, and strong paper with a grain like linen for arrogant falcons. As children, we all smelled of perfume, and when I stayed the night with my friend Kari, she would wrap her arms around my waist and whisper in my neck, "You smell so good."

I am not waiting for the harni. It has to follow, it has no credit for the tube ride. If it isn't paying attention and gets lost, it will have to walk home.

When I glance back a block and a half later, it is following me, its long curly hair wild about its shoulders, its face turned artlessly toward the sun. Does it enjoy the feeling of sunlight on skin? Probably, that is a basic biological pleasure. It must enjoy things like eating.

Kari comes out, running on light feet. "Diyet!" she calls. She still lives across from my mother but now she has a husband and a pretty two-year-old daughter, a chubby toddler with black hair and clear skin the color of amber. Tariam, the little girl, stands clinging to the doorway, her thumb in her mouth. Kari grabs my wrists and her bracelets jingle. "Come out of the heat!" She glances past me and says, "Who is this?"

The harni stands there, one hand on his hip, smiling.

Kari drops my wrists and pulls a little at her rose-colored veil. She smiles, thinking of course that I have brought a handsome young man with me.

"It is a harni," I say and laugh, shrill and nervous. "Mardin-salah asked me to bring him with me."

"A harni?" she asks, her voice doubtful.

I wave my hand. "You know the mistress, always wanting toys. He is in charge of the men's household." "He," I say. I meant "it." "It is in charge." But I don't correct myself, not wanting to call attention to my error.

"I am called Akhmim," it says smoothly. "You are a friend of Diyet's?"

Its familiarity infuriates me. Here I am, standing on the street in front of my mother's house, and it is pretending to be a man, with no respect for my reputation. If it is a man, what am I doing escorting a strange man? And if people know it is a harni, that is as bad. In the Nekropolis, people do not even like AI like the cleaning machine.

"Kari," I say, "Let's go."

She looks at the harni a moment more, then goes back to her little girl, picks her up, and carries her inside. Normally I would go inside, sit and talk with her mother, Ena. I would hold Tariam on my lap and wish I had a little girl with perfect tiny fingernails and such a clean, sweet milk smell.

It would be cool and dark inside, the environment controlled, and we would eat honeysweets and drink tea. I would go across the street, see my mother and youngest brother, who is the only one at home now.

The harni stands in the street, looking at the ground. It seems uncomfortable. It does not look at me; at least it has the decency to make it appear we are not together.

Kari comes out, bracelets ringing. While we shop, she does not refer to the harni, but, as it follows us, she glances back at it often. I glance back and it flashes a white smile. It seems perfectly content to trail along, looking at the market stalls with their red canopies.

"Maybe we should let him walk with us," Kari says. "It seems rude to ignore him."

I laugh, full of nervousness. "It's not human."

"Does it have feelings?" Kari asks.

I shrug. "After a fashion. It is AI."

"It doesn't look like a machine," she says.

"It's not a machine," I say, irritated with her.

"How can it be AI if it is not a machine?" she presses.

"Because it's *manufactured*. A technician's creation. An artificial combination of genes, grown somewhere."

"Human genes?"

"Probably," I say. "Maybe some animal genes. Maybe some that they made up themselves, how would I know?" It is ruining my afternoon. "I wish it would offer to go home."

"Maybe he can't," Kari says. "If Mardin-salah told him to come, he would have to, wouldn't he?"

I don't really know anything about harni.

"It doesn't seem fair," Kari says. "Harni," she calls, "come here."

He tilts his head, all alert. "Yes, mistress?"

"Are harni prescripted for taste?" she inquires.

"What do you mean, the taste of food?" he asks. "I can taste, just as you do, although," he smiles, "I personally am not overly fond of cherries."

"No, no," Kari says. "Colors, clothing. Are you capable of helping make choices? About earrings for example?"

He comes to look at the choices, and selects a pair of gold and rose enamel teardrops and holds them up for her. "I think my taste is no better than that of the average person," he says, "but I like these."

She frowns, looks at him through her lashes. She has got me thinking of it as "him." And she is flirting with him! Kari! A married woman!

"What do you think, Diyet?" she asks. She takes the earrings, holds one beside her face. "They are pretty."

"I think they're gaudy."

She is hurt. In truth, they suit her.

She frowns at me. "I'll take them," she says. The stallman names a price.

"No, no, no," says the harni, "you should not buy them, this man is a thief." He reaches to touch her, as if he would pull her away, and I hold my breath in shock — if the thing should touch her!

But the stallman interrupts with a lower price. The harni bargains. He is a good bargainer, but he should be, he has no compassion, no concern for the stallkeeper. Charity is a human virtue. The Mashahana says, "A human in need becomes every man's child."

Interminable, this bargaining, but finally, the earrings are Kari's. "We should stop and have some tea," she says.

"I have a headache," I say, "I think I should go home."

"If Diyet is ill, we should go," the harni says.

Kari looks at me, looks away, guilty. She *should* feel guilt.

I come down the hall to access the Household AI and the harni is there. Apparently busy, but waiting for me. "I'll be finished in a minute and out of your way," it says. Beautiful fingers, wrist bones, beautiful face, and dark curling hair showing just where its shirt closes; it is constructed elegantly. Lean and long-legged, like a hound. When the technician constructed it, did he know how it would look when it was grown? Are they designed aesthetically?

It takes the report and steps aside, but does not go on with its work. I ignore it, doing my work as if it were not there, standing so it is behind me.

"Why don't you like me?" it finally asks.

I consider my answers. I could say it is a thing, not something to like or dislike, but that isn't true. I like my bed, my things. "Because of your arrogance," I say to the system.

A startled hiss of indrawn breath. "My . . . arrogance?" it asks.

"Your presumption." It is hard to keep my voice steady, every time I am around the harni I find myself hating the way I speak.

"I . . . I am sorry, Diyet," it whispers. "I have so little experience, I didn't realize I had insulted you."

I am tempted to turn around and look at it, but I do not. It does not really feel pain, I remind myself. It is a thing, it has no more feelings than a fish. Less.

"Please, tell me what I have done?"

"Your behavior. This conversation, here," I say. "You are always trying to make people think that you are human."

Silence. Is it considering? Or would it be better to say processing?

"You blame me for being what I am," the harni says. It sighs. "I cannot help being what I am,"

I wait for it to say more, but it doesn't. I turn around, but it is gone.

After that, every time it sees me, if it can it makes some excuse to avoid me. I do not know if I am grateful or not. I am very uncomfortable.

My tasks are not complicated; I see to the cleaning machine, and set it loose in the women's household when it will not inconvenience the mistress. I am jessed to Mardin, although I serve the mistress. I am glad I am not jessed to her; Fadina is, and she has to put up with a great deal. I am careful never to blame the mistress in front of her. Let her blame the stupid little dog for crapping on the rug. She knows that the mistress is unreasonable, but of course, emotionally, she is bound to affection and duty.

On Friday mornings, the mistress is usually in her rooms, preparing for her Sunday *bismek*. On Friday afternoons, she goes out to play the Tiles with her friends and gossip about husbands and the wives who aren't there. I clean on Friday afternoons. I call the cleaning machine and it follows me down the hallway like a dog, snuffling along the baseboards for dust.

I open the door and smell attar of roses. The room is different, white marble floor veined with gold and amethyst, covered with purple rugs. Braziers and huge open windows looking out on a pillared walkway, beyond that vistas down to a lavender sea. It's the mistress's *bismek* setting. A young man is reading a letter on the walkway, a girl stands behind him, her face is tear-stained.

Interactive fantasies. The characters are generated from lists of traits, they're projections controlled by whoever is game-mistress of the *bismek* and fleshed out by the household AI. Everyone else comes over and becomes characters in the setting. There are poisonings and love affairs. The mistress's setting is in ancient times and seems to be quite popular. Some of her friends have two or three identities in the game.

She usually turns it off when she goes out. The little cleaning machine stops. It can read the difference between reality and the projection, but she has ordered it never to enter the projection because she says the sight of the thing snuffling through walls damages her sense of the alternate reality. I reach behind the screen and turn the projection off so that I can clean. The scene disappears, even the usual projections, and there are the mistress's rooms and their bare walls. "Go ahead," I tell the machine and start for the mistress's rooms to pick up things for the laundry.

To my horror, the mistress steps out of her bedroom. Her hair is loose and long and disheveled, and she is dressed in a day robe, obviously not intending to go out. She sees me in the hall and stops in astonishment. Then her face darkens, her beautiful, heavy eyebrows folding toward her nose, and I instinctively start to back up. "Oh, Mistress," I say, "I am sorry, I didn't know you were in, I'm sorry, let me get the cleaning machine and leave, I'll just be out of here in a moment, I thought you had gone out to play the Tiles, I should have checked with Fadina, it is my fault, mistress —"

"Did you turn them off?" she demands. "You stupid girl, *did you turn Zarin and Nisea off?*"

I nod mutely.

"Oh Holy One," she says. "Ugly, incompetent girl! Are you completely lacking in sense? Did you think they would be there and I wouldn't be here? It's difficult enough to prepare without interference!"

"I'll turn it back on," I say.

"Don't touch anything!" she shrieks. "FADINA!" The mistress has a very popular *bismek* and Fadina is always explaining to me how difficult it is for the mistress to think up new and interesting scenarios for her friends' participation.

I keep backing up, hissing at the cleaning machine, while the mistress follows me down the hall shrieking "FADINA!" and because I am watching the mistress I back into Fadina coming in the door.

"Didn't you tell Diyet that I'd be in this afternoon?" the mistress says.

"Of course," Fadina says.

I am aghast. "You did not!" I say.

"I did, too," Fadina says. "You were at the access. I distinctly told you and you said you would clean later."

I start to defend myself and the mistress slaps me in the face. "Enough of you, girl," she says. And then the mistress makes me stand there and berates me, reaching out now and then to grab my hair and yank it painfully, because of course she believes Fadina when the girl is clearly lying to avoid punishment. I cannot believe that Fadina has done this to me; she is in terror of offending the mistress, but she has always been a good girl, and I am innocent. My cheek stings, and my head aches from having my hair yanked, but, worse, I am so angry and so, so humiliated.

Finally we are allowed to leave. I know I should give Fadina a piece of my mind, but I just want to escape. Out in the hall, Fadina grabs me so hard that her nails bite into the soft part under my arm. "I told you she was in an absolute frenzy about Saturday," she whispers. "I can't believe you did that! And now she'll be in a terrible mood all evening and I'm the one who will suffer for it!"

"Fadina," I protest.

"Don't you 'Fadina' me, Diyet! If I don't get a slap out of this, it will be the intervention of the Holy One!"

I have already gotten a slap, and it wasn't even my fault. I pull my arm away from Fadina and try to walk down the hall without losing my dignity. My face is hot and I am about to cry. Everything blurs in tears, so I duck into the linens and sit down on the hamper. I want to leave this place, I don't want to work for that old woman. I realize that my only friend in the world is Kari and now we are so far apart, and I feel so hurt and lonely that I just sob.

The door to the linens opens and I turn my back thinking, "Go away, whoever you are."

"Oh, excuse me," the harni says.

At least *it* will go away. But the thought that the only thing around is the harni makes me feel even lonelier. I cannot stop myself from sobbing.

"Diyet," it says hesitantly, "are you all right?"

I can't answer. I want it to go away, and I don't.

After a moment, it says from right behind me, "Diyet, are you ill?"

I shake my head.

I can feel it standing there, perplexed, but I don't know what to do and I can't stop crying and I feel so foolish. I want my mother. Not that she would do anything other than remind me that the world is not fair. My mother believes in facing reality. Be strong, she always says. And that makes me cry harder.

After a minute, I hear the harni leave, and awash in self pity, I even cry over that. My feelings of foolishness are beginning to outweigh my feelings of unhappiness, but perversely enough I realize that I am enjoying my cry. That it has been inside me, building stronger and stronger, and I didn't even know it.

Then someone comes in again, and I straighten my back again, and pretend to be checking towels. The only person it could be is Fadina.

It is the harni, with a box of tissues. He crouches beside me, his face full of concern. "Here," he says.

Embarrassed, I take one. If you didn't know, you would think he was a regular human. He even smells of clean man-scent. Like my brothers.

I blow my nose, wondering if harni ever cry. "Thank you," I say.

"I was afraid you were ill," he says.

I shake my head. "No, I am just angry."

"You cry when you are angry?" he asks.

"The mistress is upset at me and it's Fadina's fault, but I had to take the blame." That makes me start to cry again, but the harni is patient and he just crouches next to me in among the linens, holding the box of tissues. By the time I collect myself, there is a little crumpled pile of tissues and some have tumbled to the floor. I take two tissues and start folding them into a flower, like my mother makes.

"Why are you so nice to me when I am so mean to you?" I ask.

He shrugs. "Because you do not want to be mean to me," he says. "It makes you suffer. I am sorry that I make you so uncomfortable."

"But you can't help being what you are," I say. My eyes are probably red. Harni never cry, I am certain. They are too perfect. I keep my eyes on the flower.

"Neither can you," he says. "When Mardin-salah made you take me with you on your day off, you were not even free to be angry with him. I knew that was why you were angry with me." He has eyes like Fhassin, my brother (who had long eyelashes like a girl, just like the harni).

Thinking about Mardin-salah makes my head ache a little and I think of something else. I remember and cover my mouth in horror. "Oh no."

"What is it?" he asks.

"I think . . . I think Fadina *did* tell me that the mistress would be in, but I was, was thinking of something else, and I didn't pay attention." I was standing at the access, wondering if the harni was around, since that was where I was most likely to run into him.

"It is natural enough," he says, unnatural thing that he is. "If Fadina weren't jessed, she would probably be more understanding."

He is prescribed to be kind, I remind myself. I should not ascribe human motives to an AI. But I haven't been fair to him, and he is the only one in the whole household sitting here among the linens with a box of tissues. I fluff out the folds of the flower and put it among the linens. A white tissue flower, a funeral flower.

"Thank you . . . Akhmim." It is hard to say his name.

He smiles. "Do not be sad, Diyet."

I am careful and avoid the eye of the mistress as much as I can. Fadina is civil to me, but not friendly. She says hello to me, politely, and goes on with whatever she is doing.

It is Akhmim, the harni, who stops me one evening and says, "The mistress wants us for *bismek* tomorrow." It's not the first time I've been asked to stand in, but usually it's Fadina who lets me know and tells me what I'm supposed to do. Lately, however, I have tried to be kind to Akhmim. He is easy to talk to, and like me he is alone in the household.

"What are we supposed to be?" I ask.

The harni flicks his long fingers dismissively. "Servants, of course. What's it like?"

"*Bismek*?" I shrug. "Play-acting."

"Like children's games?" he asks, looking doubtful.

"Well, yes and no. It's been going on a couple of years now and there are hundreds of characters," I say. "The ladies all have roles, and you have to remember to call them by their character names and not their real names, and you have to pretend it's all real. All sorts of things happen; people get in trouble and they all figure out elaborate plots to get out of trouble and people get strange illnesses and everybody professes their undying affection. The mistress threw her best friend in prison for awhile. Fadina said that was very popular."

He looks at me for a moment, blinking his long eyelashes. "You are making fun of me, Diyet," he says, doubtful.

"No," I say laughing, "it is true." It is, too. "Akhmim, no one is ever really hurt or uncomfortable."

I think he cannot decide whether to believe me or not.

Saturday afternoon, I am dressed in a pagan-looking robe that leaves one shoulder bare. And makes me look ridiculous, I might add. I am probably a server. Projections are prettier than real people, but they aren't very good at handing out real food.

I am in the mistress's quarters early. The scent of some heavy, almost bitter incense is overwhelming. The cook is laying out real food, using our own service, but the table is too tall to sit at on the floor, and there are candles and brass bowls of dates to make it look antique. Without the projection, the elaborate table looks odd in the room, which is otherwise empty of furniture. Akhmim is helping, bringing in lounging chairs so that the guests can recline at the table. He is dressed in a white robe that comes to his knees and brown sandals that have elaborate crisscross ties, and, like me, his shoulder is bare. But the harni looks graceful. Maybe people really did wear clothes like this. I am embarrassed to be seen by a man with my shoulder and neck bare. Remember, I think, Akhmim is what he is, he is not really a man or he wouldn't be here. The mistress wouldn't have a man at *bismek*, not in her quarters. Everyone would be too uncomfortable, and Mardin-salah would never allow it.

Akhmim looks up, smiles at me, comes over. "Diyet," he says, "Fadina says that the mistress is in a terrible mood."

"She is always in a terrible mood when she is nervous," I say.

"*I'm* nervous."

"Akhmim!" I say, laughing, "don't worry."

"I don't understand any of this playing pretend," he wails softly, "I never had a childhood!"

I take his hand and squeeze it. If he were a man, I would not touch him. "You'll do fine. We don't have to do much anyway, just serve dinner. Surely you can manage that, probably better than I can."

He bites his lower lip, and I am suddenly so reminded of my brother Fhassin I could cry. But I just squeeze his hand again. I'm nervous, too, but not about serving dinner. I have avoided the mistress since the incident with the cleaning machine.

Fadina comes in and turns on the projection, and suddenly the white marble room glows around us, full of servants and musicians tuning up. I feel better, able to hide in the crowd. Akhmim glances around. "It *is* exciting," he says thoughtfully.

There are five guests. Fadina greets them at the door and takes them back to the wardrobe to change. Five middle-aged women, come to pretend. I tell Akhmim their character names as they come in so that he knows what to call them.

The musicians start playing; projections, male and female, recline on projected couches. I know some of their names. Of course, they have projected servers and projected food. I wish I knew what the scenario was, usually Fadina tells me ahead of time, but she doesn't talk much to me these days. Pretty soon the mistress comes in with the real guests, and they all find the real couches, where they can talk to each other. First is bread and cheese, already on the table, and Akhmim has to pour wine, but I just stand there, next to a projected servant. Even this close she seems real, exotic with her pale hair. I ask her what her name is and she whispers, "Miri." Fadina is standing next to the mistress's couch, she glares at me. I'm not supposed to make the household AI do extra work.

The first part of the meal is boring. The mistress's friends get up once in awhile to whisper to each other or a projection, and projections do the same thing. There's some sort of intrigue going on, people look very tense and excited. Akhmim and I glance at each other and he smiles. While I am serving, I whisper to him, "Not so bad, is it?"

The two lovers I turned off are at this dinner. I guess they are important characters right now. The mistress's friends are always there, but the projections change so fast. The girl is apparently supposed to be the daughter of one of the mistress's friends. It will be something to do with the girl, I imagine.

Almost two hours into the dinner, the girl is arguing with her lover and stands up to leave — her eyes roll back in her head and she falls to the marble floor, thrashing. There is hysterical activity, projected characters rushing to the girl, the woman whose character is supposed to be the mother of the girl behaving with theatrical dignity in the circle of real women. The male lover is hysterical, kneeling and sobbing. It makes me uncomfortable, both the seizures and the reactions. I look for Akhmim, he is standing against the wall, holding a pitcher of wine, observing. He looks thoughtful. The girl's lover reaches onto the table and picks up her wine glass while everybody else watches him. The action is so highlighted that only an idiot would fail to realize that it's supposed to be important. The "mother" shrieks suddenly, "Stop him! It's poison!" And there is more hysterical activity, but they are too late. The lover drinks down the wine. The "mother" is "held back" by her friends, expeditious since the other characters are projections and she would look foolish trying to touch them.

I am embarrassed by the melodrama, by the way these women play with violence. I look back at Akhmim, but he's still observing. What does he think, I wonder.

There is a call for a physician, projections rush to and fro. There is a long, drawn-out death scene for the girl, followed by an equally long death for the lover. The women are openly sobbing, even Fadina. I clasp my hands together, squeeze them, look at the floor. Finally, everything is played out. They sit around the "dining room" and discuss the scenario and how masterful it was. The mistress looks drained but pleased. One by one the women pad back and change, then let themselves out until only the mistress and the "mother" are left.

"It was wonderful," she keeps telling the mistress.

"As good as when Hekmet was ill?" the mistress asks.

"Oh, yes. It was wonderful!" Finally they go back to change, Fadina following to help, and Akhmim and I can start clearing the dishes off the table.

"So what did you think," I ask, "was it what you expected?"

Akhmim makes a noncommittal gesture.

I stack plates and dump them on a tray. Akhmim boosts the tray, balancing it at his shoulder like a waiter. He is really much stronger than he looks. "You don't like it," he says finally.

I shake my head.

"Why not, because it's not real?"

"All this violence," I say. "Nobody would want to live this way. Nobody would want these things to happen to them." I am collecting wine glasses, colored transparent blue and rose like soap bubbles.

He stands looking at me, observing me the way he did the women, I think. What do we look like to harni? He is beautiful, the tray balanced effortlessly, the muscles of his bare arm and shoulder visible. He looks pagan enough in his white robe, with his perfect, timeless face. Even his long curly hair seems right.

I try to explain, "They entertain themselves with suffering."

"They're only projections," he says.

"But they seem real, the whole point is to forget they're projections, isn't it?" The glasses ring against each other as I collect them.

Softly he says, "They are bored women, what do they have in their lives?"

I want him to understand how I am different. "You can't tell me it doesn't affect the way they see people, look at the way the mistress treats Fadina!" Akhmim tries to interrupt me, but I want to finish what I am saying. "She wants excitement, even if it means watching death. Watching a seizure, that's not entertaining, not unless there's something wrong. It's decadent, what they do, it's . . . it's sinful! Death isn't entertainment."

"Diyet!" he says.

Then the mistress grabs my hair and yanks me around and all the glasses in my arms fall to the floor and shatter.

Sweet childhood. Adulthood is salty. Not that it's not rewarding, mind you, just different. The rewards of childhood are joy and pleasure, but the rewards of adulthood are strength. I am punished, but it is light punishment, not something that demands so much strength. The mistress beats me. She doesn't really hurt me much, it's noisy and frightening, and I cut my knee where I kneel in broken glass, but no serious damage. I am locked in my room and only allowed punishment food: bread, tea, and a little cheese, but I can have all the paper I want, and I fill my rooms with flowers. White paper roses, white irises with petals curling down to reveal their centers, snowy calla lilies like trumpets and poppies and tulips of luscious paper with nap like velvet. My walls are white and the world is white, filled with white flowers.

"How about daisies," Akhmim asks. He comes to bring me my food and my paper.

"Too innocent," I say. "Daisies are only for children."

Fadina recommended to the mistress that Akhmim be my jailer. She thinks that I hate to have him near me, but I couldn't have asked for better company than the harni. He's never impatient, never comes to me asking for attention to his own problems. He wants to learn how to make flowers. I try to teach him but he can never learn to do anything but awkwardly copy my model. "You make them out of your own head," he says. His clever fingers stumble and crease the paper or turn it.

"My mother makes birds, too," I say.

"Can you make birds?" he asks.

I don't want to make birds, just flowers.

I think about the Nekropolis. Akhmim is doing his duties and mine, too, so he is busy during the day and mostly, I am alone. When I am not making flowers I sit and look out my window, watching the street, or I sleep. It is probably because I am not getting so much to eat, but I can sleep for hours. A week passes, then two. Sometimes I feel as if I have to get out of this room, but then I ask myself where I would want to go and I realize that it doesn't make any difference. This room, the outside, they are all the same place, except that this room is safe.

The place I want to go is the Nekropolis, the one in my mind, but it's gone. I was the eldest, then my sister, Larit, then my brother, Fhassin, and then the baby boy, Michim. In families of four, underneath the fighting, there is always pairing, two and two. Fhassin and I were a pair. My brother. I think a lot about Fhassin and about the Nekropolis, locked in my room.

I sleep, eat my little breakfast that Akhmim brings me, sleep again. Then I sit at the window or make flowers, sleep again. The only time that is bad is late afternoon, early evening, when I have slept so much that I can't sleep any more and my stomach is growling and growling. I feel fretful and teary.

When Akhmim comes in the evening with dinner he bruises my senses until I get accustomed to his being there; his voice has so many shades, his skin is so much more supple, so much more oiled and textured than paper, that he overwhelms me.

Sometimes he sits with his arms around my shoulders and I lean against him. I pretend intimacy doesn't matter because he is only a harni, but I know that I am lying to myself. How could I ever have thought him safe because he was made rather than born? I understood from the first that he wasn't to be trusted, but actually it was I that couldn't be trusted.

He is curious about my childhood, he says he never was a child. To keep him close to me I tell him everything I can remember about growing up, all the children's games, teach him the songs we skipped rope to, the rhymes we used to pick who was it, everybody with their fists in the center, tapping a fist on every stress as we chanted:

> ONCE my SIS-ter HAD a HOUSE,
> THEN she LEFT it TO a MOUSE,
> SING a SONG
> TELL a LIE
> KISS my SIS-ter
> SAY good-BYE

"What does it mean?" he asks, laughing.

"It doesn't mean anything," I explain, "it's a way of picking who is it. Who is the fox, or who holds the broom while everybody hides." I tell him about fox and hounds, about how my brother Fhassin was a daredevil and one time to get away he climbed to the roof of Kari's grandmother's house and ran along the roofs and how our mother punished him. And of how we got in a fight and I pushed him and he fell and broke his collarbone.

"What does Kari do?" he asks.

"Kari is married," I say. "Her husband works, he directs a lorritank, like the one that delivers water."

"Did you ever have a boyfriend?" he asks.

"I did, his name was Zard."

"Why didn't you marry?" he asks. He is so innocent.

"It didn't work," I say.

"Is that why you became jessed?"

"No," I say.

He is patient, he waits.

"No," I say again. "It was because of Shusilina."

And then I have to explain.

Shusilina moved into the death house across the street, where Kari's grandfather had lived until he died. Kari's grandfather had been a soldier when he was young, and to be brave for the Holy he had a Serinitin implant, so that when he was old he didn't remember who he was anymore. And when he died, Shusilina and her husband moved in. Shusilina had white hair and had had her ears pointed and she wanted a baby. I was only twenty, and trying to decide whether I should marry Zard. He had not asked me, but I thought he might, and I wasn't sure what I should answer. Shusilina was younger than me, nineteen, but she wanted a baby, and that seemed terribly adult. And she had come from outside the Nekropolis, and had pointed ears, and everybody thought she was just a little too good for herself.

We talked about Zard, and she told me that after marriage everything was not milk and honey. She was very vague on just what she meant by that, but I should know that it was not like it seemed now, when I was in love with Zard. I should give myself over to him, but I should hold some part of myself private, for myself, and not let marriage swallow me.

Now I realize that she was a young bride trying to learn the difference between romance and life, and the conversations are obvious and adolescent, but then it seemed so adult to talk about marriage this way. It was like something sacred, and I was being initiated into mysteries. I dyed my hair white.

My sister hated her. Michim made eyes at her all the time but he was only thirteen. Fhassin was seventeen and he laughed at Michim. Fhassin laughed at all sorts of things. He looked at the world from under his long eyelashes, so in contrast with his sharp-chinned face and monkey grin. That was the year Fhassin, who had always been shorter than everybody, almost shorter than Michim, suddenly grew so tall. He was visited by giggling girls, but he never took any of them seriously.

It was all outside, not inside the family. In the evenings we sat on the floor in the middle of our three death houses and made paper flowers. We lived in a house filled with perfume. I was twenty, Larit was nineteen, but nobody had left my mother's house, and we never thought that was strange. But it was, the way we were held there.

So when did Fhassin stop seeing her as silly and begin to see Shusilina as a person? I didn't suspect it. The giggling girls still came by the house, and Fhassin still grinned and didn't really pay much attention. They were careful, meeting in the afternoon when her husband was building new death-houses at the other end of the Nekropolis and the rest of us were sleeping.

I think Fhassin did it because he was always a daredevil, like walking on the roofs of the death-houses, or the time he took money out of our mother's money pot so he could sneak out and ride the Tube. He was lost in the city for hours, finally sneaking back onto the Tube and risking getting caught as a free-farer.

No, that isn't true. The truth must be that he fell in love with her. I had never really been in love with Zard, maybe I have never been in love with anyone. How could I understand? I couldn't stand the thought of leaving the family to marry Zard, how could *he* turn his back on the family for Shusilina? But some alchemy must have transformed him, made him see her as something other than a vain and silly girl — yes, it's a cliché to call her a vain and silly girl, but that's what she was. She was married, and it wasn't very exciting anymore, not nearly as interesting as when her husband was courting her. Fhassin made her feel important, look at the risk he was taking, for her. For her!

But what was going on in Fhassin? Fhassin despised romantic love, sentimentality.

Her husband suspected, laid in wait and caught them, the neighborhood poured out into the street to see my brother, shirtless, protecting Shusilina whose hair was all unbound around her shoulders. Fhassin had a razor, and was holding off her screaming husband. The heat poured all over his brown, adolescent shoulders and chest. We stood in the street, sweating. And Fhassin was laughing, deadly serious, but laughing. He was so alive. Was it the intensity? Was that the lure for Fhassin? This was my brother, who I had known all my life, and he was a stranger.

I realized that the Nekropolis was a foreign place, and I didn't know anyone behind the skinmask of their face.

They took my brother and Shusilina, divorced her from her husband for the adultery trial, and flogged them both, then dumped them in prison for seven years. I did not wait for Zard to ask me to marry him — not that he would have, now. I let my hair go black. I became a dutiful daughter. When I was twenty-one, I was jessed, impressed to feel duty and affection for whoever would pay the fee of my impression.

Akhmim doesn't understand. He has to go. I cry when he's gone.

Finally, after twenty-eight days, I emerge from my room, white and trembling like Iqurth from the tomb, to face the world and my duties. I don't know what the mistress has told Mardin, but I am subjected to a vague lecture I'm sure Mardin thinks of as fatherly. Fadina avoids meeting my eyes when she sees me. The girl who works with the cook watches the floor. I move like a ghost through the women's quarters. Only the mistress sees me, fastens her eyes on me when I happen to pass her, and her look is cruel. If I hear her, I take to stepping out of the hall if I can.

Friday afternoon, she is playing the Tiles, and I take the cleaning machine to her room. I have checked with Fadina, to confirm that she is not in, but I cannot convince myself that she has left. Perhaps Fadina has forgotten, perhaps the mistress has not told her. I creep in and stand listening. The usual projection is on — not *bismek* but the everyday clutter of silks and fragile tables with silver lace frames, antique lamps, paisley scarves and cobalt pottery. The cleaning machine will not go in. I stop and listen, no sound but the breeze through the window hangings. I creep through the quarters, shaking. The bed is unmade, a tumble of blue and silver brocade. That's unusual, Fadina always makes it. I think about making it, but I decide I had better not do what I always do or the mistress will be on me. Best do only what is safe. I pick up the clothes off the floor and creep back and turn off the projection. The machine starts.

If she comes back early what will I do? I stand by the projection switch, unwilling to leave even to put the clothing in the laundry. If she comes back, when I hear her, I will snap on the projection machine. The cleaning machine will stop and I will take it and leave. It is the best I can do.

The cleaning machine snuffles around, getting dust from the window sills and table tops, cleaning the floor. It is so slow. I keep thinking I hear her and snapping on the projection. The machine stops and I listen, but I don't hear anything so I snap the projection off and the cleaning machine starts again. Finally the rooms are done, and the cleaning machine and I make our escape. I have used extra scent on the sheets in the linen closet, the way she likes them, and I have put extra oil in the rings on the lights and extra scent in the air freshener. It is all a waste, all that money, but that's what she likes.

I have a terrible headache. I go to my room and wait and try to sleep until the headache is gone. I am asleep when Fadina bangs on my door and I feel groggy and disheveled.

"The mistress wants you," she snaps, glaring at me.

I can't go.

I can't *not* go. I follow her without doing up my hair or putting on my sandals.

The mistress is sitting in her bedroom, still dressed up in saffron and veils. I imagine she has just gotten back. "Diyet," she says, "did you clean my rooms?"

What did I disturb? I didn't do anything to this room except pick up the laundry and run the cleaning machine; is something missing? "Yes, mistress," I say. Oh, my heart.

"Look at this room," she hisses.

I look, not knowing what I am looking for.

"Look at the bed!"

The bed looks just the same as it did when I came in, blankets and sheets tumbled, shining blue and silver, the scent of her perfume in the cool air.

"Come here," the mistress commands, "kneel down." I kneel down so that I am not taller than she is. She looks at me for a moment, so angry that she doesn't seem able to speak. Then, I see it coming but I can't do anything, up comes her hands and she slaps me. I topple sideways, mostly from surprise. "Are you too stupid to even know to make a bed?"

"Fadina always makes your bed," I say. I should have made it, I should have. Holy One, I am such an idiot.

"So the one time Fadina doesn't do your work you are too lazy to do it yourself?"

"Mistress," I say, "I was afraid to   "

"You *should* be afraid!" she shouts. She slaps me, both sides of my face, and shouts at me, her face close to mine. On and on. I don't listen, it's just sound. Fadina walks me to the door. I am holding my head up, trying to maintain some dignity. "Diyet," Fadina whispers.

"What?" I say, thinking maybe she has realized that it's the mistress, that it's not my fault.

But she just shakes her head, "Try not to upset her, that's all. Just don't upset her." Her face is pleading, she wants me to understand.

Understand what? That she is jessed? As Akhmim says, we are only what we are.

But I understand what it is going to be like now. The mistress hates me, and there's nothing I can do. The only way to escape is to ask Mardin to sell me off, but then I would have to leave Akhmim. And since he's a harni he can't even ride the Tube without someone else providing credit. If I leave, I'll never see him again.

The room is full of whispers. The window is open and the breeze rustles among the paper flowers. There are flowers everywhere, on the dresser, the chairs. Akhmim and I sit in the dark room, lit only by the light from the street. He is sitting with one leg underneath him. Like some animal, a panther, indolent.

"You'll still be young when I'm old," I say.

"No," he says. That is all, just the one word.

"Do you get old?"

"If we live out our natural span. About sixty, sixty-five years."

"Do you get wrinkles? White hair?"

"Some. Our joints get bad, swell, like arthritis. Things go wrong." He is so quiet tonight. Usually he is cheerful.

"You are so patient," I say.

He makes a gesture with his hands, "It does not matter."

"Is it hard for you to be patient?"

"Sometimes," he says. "I feel frustration, anger, fear. But we are bred to be patient."

"What's wrong?" I ask. I sound like a little girl, my voice all breathy.

"I am thinking. You should leave here."

The mistress is always finding something. Nothing I do is right. She pulls my hair, confines me to my room. "I can't," I say, "I'm jessed."

He is so still in the twilight.

"Akhmim," I say, suddenly cruel, "do you want me to go?"

"Harni are not supposed to have 'wants,'" he says, his voice flat. I have never heard him say the word "harni." It sounds obscene. It makes me get up, his voice. It fills me with nervousness, with aimless energy. If he is despairing, what is there for me? I leave the window, brush my fingers across the desk, hearing the flowers rustle. I touch all the furniture, and take an armload of flowers, crisp and cool, and I drop them in his lap. "What?" he says. I take more flowers and throw them over his shoulders. His face is turned up at me, lit by the light from the street, full of wonder. I gather flowers off the chair, drop them on him. There are flowers all over the bed, funeral flowers. He reaches up, flowers spilling off his sleeves, and takes my arms to make me stop, saying, "Diyet, what?" I lean forward and close my eyes.

I wait, hearing the breeze rustle the lilies, the poppies, the roses on the bed. I wait forever. Until he finally kisses me.

He won't do any more than kiss me. Lying among all the crushed flowers he will stroke my face, my hair, he will kiss me, but that is all. "You have to leave," he says, desperately. "You have to tell Mardin, tell him to sell you."

I won't leave. I have nothing to go to.

"Do you love me because you have to? Is it because you are a harni and I am a human and you have to serve me?" I ask.

He shakes his head.

"Do you love me because of us?" I press. There are no words for the questions I am asking him.

"Diyet," he says.

"Do you love the mistress?"

"No," he says.

"You should love the mistress, shouldn't you, but you love me."

"Go home, go to the Nekropolis. Run away," he urges, kissing my throat, tiny little kisses, as if he has been thinking of my throat for a long time.

"Run away? From Mardin? What would I do for the rest of my life? Make paper flowers?"

"What would be wrong with that?"

"Would you come with me?" I ask.

He sighs and raises up on his elbow. "You should not fall in love with me."

This is funny. "This is a fine time to tell me."

"No," he says, "it is true." He counts on his fine fingers, "One, I am a harni, not a human being, and I belong to someone else. Two, I have caused all of your problems, if I had not been here, you would not have had all your troubles. Three, the reason it is wrong for a human to love a harni is because harni-human relationships are bad paradigms for human behavior, they lead to difficulty in dealing with human-to-human relationships — "

"I don't *have* any human-to-human relationships," I interrupt.

"You will, you are just young."

I laugh at him. "Akhmim, you're younger than *I* am! Prescripted wisdom."

"But wisdom nonetheless," he says, solemnly.

"Then why did you kiss me?" I ask.

He sighs. It is such a human thing, that sigh, full of frustration. "Because you are so sad."

"I'm not sad right now," I say. "I'm happy because you are here." I am also nervous. Afraid. Because this is all so strange, and even though I keep telling myself that he's so human, I am afraid that underneath he is really alien, more unknowable than my brother. But I want him to stay with me. And I am happy. Afraid but happy.

My lover. "I want you to be my lover," I say.

"No." He sits up. He is beautiful, even disheveled. I can imagine what I look like. Maybe he does not even like me, maybe he has to act this way because I want it. He runs his fingers through his hair, his earring gleams in the light from the street.

"Do harni fall in love?" I ask.

"I have to go," he says. "We've crushed your flowers." He picks up a lily whose long petals have become twisted and crumpled and tries to straighten it out.

"I can make more. Do you have to do this because I want you to?"

"No," he says very quietly. Then more clearly, like a recitation, "Harni don't have feelings, not in the sense that humans do. We are loyal, flexible, and affectionate."

"That makes you sound like a smart dog," I say, irritated.

"Yes," he says, "that is what I am, a smart dog, a very smart dog. Good night, Diyet."

When he opens the door, the breeze draws and the flowers rustle, and some tumble off the bed, trying to follow him.

"Daughter," Mardin says, "I am not sure that this is the best situation for you." He looks at me kindly. I wish Mardin did not think that he had to be my father.

"Mardin-salah?" I say, "I don't understand, has my work been unsatisfactory?" Of course my work has been unsatisfactory, the mistress hates me. But I am afraid they have somehow realized what is between Akhmim and me — although I don't know how they could. Akhmim is avoiding me again.

"No, no," he waves his hand airily, "your accounts are in order, you have been a good and frugal girl. It is not your fault."

"I . . . I am aware that I have been clumsy, that perhaps I have not always understood what the mistress wished, but Mardin-salah, I am improving!" I am getting better at ignoring her, I mean. I don't want him to feel inadequate. Sitting here, I realize the trouble I've caused him. He hates having to deal with the household in any but the most perfunctory way. I am jessed to this man, his feelings matter to me. Rejection of my services is painful. This has been a good job, I have been able to save some of my side money so that when I am old I won't be like my mother, forced to struggle and hope that the children will be able to support her when she can't work anymore.

Mardin is uncomfortable. The part of me that is not jessed can see that this is not the kind of duty that Mardin likes. This is not how he sees himself; he prefers to be the benevolent patriarch. "Daughter," he says, "you have been exemplary, but wives. . . . " He sighs. "Sometimes, child, they get whims, and it is better for me, and for you, if we find you some good position with another household."

At least he hasn't said anything about Akhmim. I bow my head because I am afraid I will cry. I study my toes. I try not to think of Akhmim. Alone again. Oh Holy One, I am so tired of being alone. I will be alone my whole life, jessed women do not marry. I cannot help it, I start to cry. Mardin takes it as a sign of my loyalty and pats me gently on the shoulder. "There, there, child, it will be all right."

I don't want Mardin to comfort me. The part of me that watches, that isn't jessed, doesn't even really *like* Mardin — but at the same time, I want to make him happy, so I gamely sniff and try to smile. "I, I know you know what is best," I manage. But my distress makes him uncomfortable. So he says when arrangements are made he will tell me.

I look for Akhmim, to tell him, but he stays in the men's side of the house, away from the middle where we eat, and far away from the women's side.

I begin to understand. He didn't love me, it was just that he was a harni, and it was *me* . . . I led him to myself. Maybe I am no better than Shusilina, with her white hair and pointed ears. So I work, what else is there to do? And I avoid the mistress. Evidently Mardin has told her he is getting rid of me, because the attacks cease. Fadina even smiles at me, if distantly. I would like to make friends with Fadina again, but she doesn't give me a chance. So I will never see him again. He isn't even that far from me, and I will never see him again.

There is nothing to be done about it. Akhmim avoids me. I look across the courtyard or across the dining room at the men's side, but I almost never see him. Once in awhile he's there, with his long curly hair and his black gazelle eyes, but he doesn't look at me.

I pack my things. My new mistress comes. She is a tall, gray-haired woman with slightly pop-eyes. She has a breathy voice and a way of hunching her shoulders as if she wished she were actually a very small woman. I am supposed to give her my life? It is monstrous.

We are in Mardin's office. I am upset. I want desperately to leave, I am so afraid of coming into a room and finding the mistress. I am trying not to think of Akhmim. But what is most upsetting is the thought of leaving Mardin. Will the next girl understand that he wants to pretend that he is frugal, but that he really is not? I am nearly overwhelmed by shame because I have caused this. I am only leaving because of my own foolishness, and I have failed Mardin, who only wanted peace.

I will not cry. These are impressed emotions. Soon I will feel them for this strange woman. Oh Holy One, what rotten luck to have gotten this woman for a mistress. She wears bronze and white — bronze was all the fashion when I first came and the mistress wore it often — but this is years after and these are second-rate clothes, a young girl's clothes and not suited to my mistress at all. She is nervous, wanting me to like her, and all I want to do is throw myself at Mardin's feet and embarrass him into saying that I can stay.

Mardin says, "Diyet, she has paid the fee." He shows me the credit transaction and I see that the fee is lower than it was when I came to Mardin's household. "I order you to accept this woman as your new mistress."

That's it. That's the trigger. I feel a little disoriented. I never really noticed how the skin under Mardin's jaw was soft and lax. He is actually rather nondescript. I wonder what it must be like for the mistress to have married him. She is tall and vivid, if a bit heavy, and was a beauty in her day. She must find him disappointing. No wonder she is bitter.

My new mistress smiles tentatively. Well, she may not be fashionable, the way my old mistress was, but she looks kind. I hope so, I would like to live in a kind household. I smile back at her.

That is it. I am impressed.

My new household is much smaller than the old one. The mistress's last housekeeper was clearly inefficient. I am busy for days, just trying to put things in order. I must be frugal, there is much less money in this house. It is surprising how much I have gotten accustomed to money at Mardin's house; this is much more like I grew up.

I do inventories of the linens and clean all the rooms from top to bottom. At first I am nervous, but my new mistress is not like the old one at all. She watches me work as if astounded, and she is never offended if she walks in her room and I have the cleaning machine going. I learn not to work too much around her, she is oddly sensitive about it. She won't say anything, but she will start to make funny little embarrassed/helpful gestures, or suggest that I get myself some tea. Her husband is an old man. He smiles at me and tells me very bad jokes, puns, and I have to laugh to be polite. I would like to avoid him because he bores me nearly to tears. They have a daughter who is a terror. She is in trouble all the time. She spends money, takes her mother's credit chip without asking — they have been forced to put a governor on daily purchases and they are in the process of locking the girl out of the parents' credit.

The daughter is nice enough to me, but her politeness is false. She argues with her mother about spending money on getting a jessed servant instead of sending her to school. But the daughter's marks at academy are dreadful and the mistress says she will not waste money on more.

Akhmim. I think of him all the time.

Emboldened by my mistress's approval, I rearrange the furniture. I take some things she has — they are not very nice — and put them up. I reprogram the household AI. It is very limited, insufficient for anything as complicated as *bismek*, but it can handle projections, of course. I remember the things my old mistress used to like and I put around cobalt blue vases and silver framed pictures. Marble floors would overwhelm these rooms, but the tile I pick is nice.

My days are free on Tuesday and half-a-day Sunday. Tuesday my mistress apologizes to me. They are a little tight on credit and she cannot advance my leisure allowance until Sunday, do I mind?

Well, a little, but I say I don't. I spend the afternoon making flowers.

When I make flowers I think of Akhmim and myself on the bed surrounded by crushed carnations and iris. It isn't good to think about Akhmim, he doesn't miss me, I'm sure. He is a harni, always an owned thing, subject to the whims of his owners. If they had constructed him with lasting loyalties, his life would be horrible. Surely when the technician constructed his genes, he made certain that Akhmim would forget quickly. He told me that harni do not love. But he also told me that they did. And he told me he didn't love the old mistress, but maybe he only said that because he had to, because I did not love the old mistress and his duty is to make humans happy.

I put the flowers in a vase. My mistress is delighted, she thinks they are lovely.

Long lilies, spiked stamens and long petals like lolling tongues. Sometimes feelings are in me that have no words, and I look at the paper flowers and want to rip them to pieces.

On Sunday, my mistress has my leisure allowance. Mardin used to add a little something extra, but I realize that in my new circumstances I can't expect that. I go to the Moussin of the White Falcon, on the edge of the Nekropolis, to listen to the service.

Then I take the tube to the street of Mardin's house. I don't even intend to walk down the street, but of course I do. And I stand outside the house, looking for a sign of Akhmim. I'm afraid to stand long, I don't want anyone to see me. What would I tell them, that I'm homesick? I'm jessed.

I like to take something to do on the tube, so the ride is not so boring. I have brought a bag full of paper to make flowers. I think I'll earn a little money on the side by making wreaths. I am not allowed to give it to my mistress, that's against the law. It's to protect the jessed that this is true.

In the Nekropolis, we lived in death houses, surrounded by death. Perhaps it isn't odd that I'm a bit morbid, and perhaps that is why I pull a flower out of my bag and leave it on a window sill on the men's side of the house. After all, something did die, although I can't put in words exactly what it was. I don't really know which window is Akhmim's, but it doesn't matter, it's just a gesture. It only makes me feel foolish.

Monday I wake early and drink hot, strong maté. I take buckets of water and scrub down the stone courtyard. I make a list of all the repairs that need to be done. I take the mistress's printouts and bundle them. She saves them, she subscribes to several services and she feels that they might be useful. My old mistress would have quite a lot to say about someone who would save printouts. The mistress goes out to shop, and I clean everything in her storage. She has clothes she should throw out, things fifteen years old and hopelessly out of date. (I remember when I wore my hair white. And later when we used to wrap our hair in veils, the points trailing to the backs of our knees. We looked so foolish, so affected. What are young girls wearing now? How did I get to be so old, I'm not even thirty.)

I put aside all the things I should mend, but I don't want to sit yet, I run the cleaning machine, an old clumsy thing even stupider than the one at Mardin's. I push myself all day, a whirlwind. There is not enough in this house to do, even if I clean the cleaning machine, so I clean some rooms twice.

Still, when it is time to sleep, I can't. I sit in my room making a funeral wreath of carnations and tiny, half-open roses. The white roses gleam like satin.

I wake up on my free day, tired and stiff. In the mirror, I look ghastly, my hair tangled and my eyes puffy. Just as well the harni never saw me like this, I think. But I won't think of Akhmim any more. That part of my life is over, and I have laid a flower at its death house. Today I will take my funeral wreaths around and see if I can find a shop that will buy them. They are good work, surely someone will be interested. It would just be pocket money, take a little of the strain off my mistress, she would not feel then as if she wasn't providing extras for me if I can provide them for myself.

I take the tube all the way to the Nekropolis, carefully protecting my wreaths from the other commuters. All day I walk through the Nekropolis, talking to stall keepers, stopping sometimes for tea, and when I have sold the wreaths, sitting for awhile to watch the people, letting my tired mind empty.

I am at peace, now I can go back to my mistress.

The Mashahana tells us that the darkness in ourselves is a sinister thing. It waits until we relax, it waits until we reach the most vulnerable moments, and then it snares us. I want to be dutiful, I want to do what I should. But when I go back to the tube, I think of where I am going; to that small house and my empty room. What will I do tonight? Make more paper flowers, more wreaths? I am sick of them. Sick of the Nekropolis.

I can take the tube to my mistress's house, or I can go by the street where Mardin's house is. I'm tired, I'm ready to go to my little room and relax. Oh, Holy One, I dread the empty evening. Maybe I should go by the street just to fill up time. I have all this empty time in front of me. Tonight and tomorrow and the week after and the next month and down through the years as I never marry and become a dried-up woman. Evenings spent folding paper. Days cleaning someone else's house. Free afternoons spent shopping a bit, stopping in tea shops because my feet hurt. That is what lives *are*, aren't they? Attempts to fill our time with activity designed to prevent us from realizing that there *is* no meaning? I sit at a tiny table the size of a serving platter and watch the boys hum by on their scooters, girls sitting behind them, clutching their waists with one hand, holding their veils with the other, while the ends stream and snap behind them, glittering with the shimmer of gold (this year's fashion).

So I get off the tube and walk to the street where Mardin lives. And I walk up the street past the house. I stop and look at it. The walls are pale yellow stone. I am wearing rose and sky blue, but I have gone out without ribbons on my wrists.

"Diyet," Akhmim says, leaning on the window sill, "you're still sad."

He looks so familiar and it is so easy, as if we do this every evening. "I live a sad life," I say, my voice even. But my heart is pounding. To see him! To talk to him!

"I found your token," he says.

"My token," I repeat, not understanding.

"The flower. I thought today would be your free day so I tried to watch all day. I thought you had come and I missed you." Then he disappears for a moment, and then he is sitting on the window sill, legs and feet outside, and he jumps lightly to the ground.

I take him to a tea shop. People look at us, wondering what a young woman is doing unescorted with a young man. Let them look. "Order what you want," I say, "I have some money."

"Are you happier?" he asks. "You don't look happier, you look tired."

And he looks perfect, as he always does. Have I fallen in love with him precisely because he *isn't* human? I don't care, I feel love, no matter what the reason. Does a reason for a feeling matter? The feeling I have for my mistress may be there only because I am impressed, but the *feeling* is real enough.

"My mistress is kind," I say, looking at the table. His perfect hand, beautiful nails and long fingers, lies there.

"Are you happy?" he asks again.

"Are you?" I ask.

He shrugs. "A harni does not have the right to be happy or unhappy."

"Neither do I," I say.

"That's *your* fault. Why did you do it?" he asks. "Why did you choose to be jessed? You were free." His voice is bitter.

"It's hard to find work in the Nekropolis, and I didn't think I would ever get married."

He shakes his head. "Someone would marry you. And if they didn't, is it so awful not to get married?"

"Is it so awful to be jessed?" I ask.

"Yes."

That is all he says. I suppose to him it looks as if I threw everything away, but how can he understand how our choices are taken from us? He doesn't even understand freedom and what an illusion it really is.

"Run away," he says.

Leave the mistress? I am horrified. "She needs me, she cannot run that house by herself and I have cost her a great deal of money. She has made sacrifices to buy me."

"You could live in the Nekropolis and make funeral wreaths," he urges. "You could talk to whomever you wished and no one would order you around."

"I don't want to live in the Nekropolis," I say.

"Why not?"

"There is nothing there for me!"

"You have friends there."

"I wouldn't if I ran away."

"Make new ones," he says.

"Would you go?" I ask.

He shakes his head. "I'm not a person, I can't live."

"What if you could make a living, would you run away?"

"Yes," he says, "yes." He squares his shoulders defiantly and looks at me. "If I could be human, I would be." He is shaming me.

Our tea comes. My face is aflame with color, I don't know what to say. I don't know what to think. He feels morally superior. He thinks he knows the true worth of something I threw away. He doesn't understand, not at all.

"Oh Diyet," he says softly, "I am sorry. I shouldn't say these things to you."

"I didn't think you could have these feelings," I whisper.

He shrugs again. "I can have any feelings," he says. "Harni aren't jessed."

"You told me to think of you as a dog," I remind him. "Loyal."

"I am loyal," he says. "You didn't ask who I was loyal to."

"You're supposed to be loyal to the mistress."

He drums the table with his fingers, *taptaptaptap, taptaptaptap.* "Harni aren't like geese," he says, not looking at me. His earring is golden, he is rich and fine-looking. I had not realized at my new place how starved I had become for fine things. "We don't impress on the first person we see." Then he shakes his head. "I shouldn't talk about all this nonsense. You must go, I must go back before they miss me."

"We have to talk more," I say.

"We have to go," he insists. Then he smiles at me and all the unhappiness disappears from his face. He doesn't seem human anymore, he seems pleasant; *harni.* I get a chill. He is so alien. I understand him less than I understand people like my old mistress. We get up and he looks away as I pay.

Outside Mardin's house I tell him, "I'll come back next Tuesday."

It's good I did so much before, because I sleepwalk through the days. I leave the cleaning machine in the doorway where the mistress almost trips over it. I forget to set the clothes in order. I don't know what to think.

I hear the mistress say to the neighbor, "She is a godsend, but so moody. One day she's doing everything, the next day she can't be counted on to remember to set the table."

What right does she have to talk about me that way? Her house was a pigsty when I came.

What am I thinking? What is wrong with me that I blame my mistress? Where is my head? I feel ill, my eyes water and head fills. I can't breathe, I feel heavy. I must be dutiful. I used to have this feeling once in a while when I was first jessed, it's part of the adjustment. It must be the change. I have to adjust all over again.

I find the mistress, tell her I'm not feeling well, and go lie down.

The next afternoon, just before dinner, it happens again. The day after that is fine, but then it happens at mid-morning of the third day. It is Sunday and I have the afternoon off. I force myself to work through the morning. My voice is hoarse, my head aches. I want to get everything ready since I won't be there to see to dinner in the afternoon. White cheese and olives and tomatoes on a platter. My stomach rebels and I have to run to the bathroom.

What is wrong with me?

I go to the moussin in the afternoon, lugging my bag, which is heavy with paper, and sit in the cool dusty darkness, nursing my poor head. I feel as if I should pray. I should ask for help, for guidance. The moussin is so old that the stone is irregularly worn, and through my slippers I can feel the little ridges and valleys in the marble. Up around the main worship hall there are galleries hidden by arabesques of scrollwork. Kari and I used to sit up there when we were children. Above that, sunlight flashes through clerestory windows. Where the light hits the marble floor it shines hard, hurting my eyes and my head. I rest my forehead on my arm, turned sideways on the bench so I can lean on the back. With my eyes closed I smell incense and my own scent of perfume and perspiration.

There are people there for service, but no one bothers me. Isn't that amazing?

Or maybe it is only because anyone can see that I am impure.

I get tired of my own melodrama. I keep thinking that people are looking at me, that someone is going to say something to me. I don't know where to go.

I don't even pretend to think of going back to my room. I get on the tube and go to Mardin's house. I climb the stairs from the tube — these are newer, but, like the floor of the moussin, they are unevenly worn, sagging in the centers from the weight of this crowded city. What would it be like to cross the sea and go north? To the peninsula, Ida, or north from there, into the continent? I used to want to travel, to go to a place where people had yellow hair, to see whole forests of trees. Cross the oceans, learn other languages. I told Kari that I would even like to taste dog, or swine, but she thought I was showing off. But it's true, once I would have liked to try things.

I am excited, full of energy and purpose. I can do anything. I can understand Fhassin, standing in the street with his razor, laughing. It is worth it, anything is worth it for this feeling of being alive. I have been jessed, I have been asleep for so long.

There are people on Mardin's street. It's Sunday and people are visiting. I stand in front of the house across the street. What am I going to say if someone opens the door? I am waiting to meet a friend. What if they don't leave, what if Akhmim sees them and doesn't come out. The sun bakes my hair, my head. Akhmim, where are you? Look out the window. He is probably waiting on the mistress. Maybe there is a *bismek* party and those women are poisoning Akhmim. They could do anything, they *own* him. I want to crouch in the street and cover my head in my hands, rock and cry like a widow woman from the Nekropolis. Like my mother must have done when my father died. I grew up without a father, maybe that's why I'm so wild. Maybe that's why Fhassin is in prison and I'm headed there. I pull my veil up so my face is shadowed. So no one can see my tears.

Oh my head. Am I drunk? Am I insane? Has the Holy One, seeing my thoughts, driven me mad?

I look at my brown hands. I cover my face.

"Diyet?" He takes my shoulders.

I look up at him, his beautiful familiar face, and I am stricken with terror. What is he? What am I trusting my life, my future to?

"What's wrong," he asks, "are you ill?"

"I'm going insane," I say. "I can't stand it, Akhmim, I can't go back to my room — "

"Hush," he says, looking up the street and down. "You have to. I'm only a harni. I can't do anything, I can't help you."

"We have to go. We have to go away somewhere, you and I."

He shakes his head. "Diyet, please. You must hush."

"You said you wanted to be free," I say. My head hurts so bad. The tears keep coming even though I am not really crying.

"I can't be free," he says. "That was just talk."

"I have to go now," I say. "I'm jessed, Akhmim, it is hard, if I don't go now I'll never go."

"Your mistress — "

"DON'T TALK ABOUT HER!" I shout. If he talks about her I may not be able to leave.

He looks around again. We are a spectacle, a man and a woman on the street.

"Come with me, we'll go somewhere, talk," I say, all honey. He cannot deny me, I see it in him. He has to get off the street. He would go anywhere. Any place is safer than this.

He lets me take him into the tube, down the stairs to the platform. I clutch my indigo veil around my face. We wait in silence, he has his hands in his pockets. He looks like a boy from the Nekropolis, standing there in just his shirt, no outer robe. He looks away, shifts his weight from one foot to the other, ill at ease. So human. Events are making him more human. Taking away all the uncertainties.

"What kind of genes are in you?" I ask.

"What?" he asks.

"What kinds of genes?"

"Are you asking for my chart?" he says.

I shake my head. "Human?"

He shrugs. "Mostly. Some artificial sequences."

"No animal genes," I say. I sound irrational because I can't get clear what I mean. The headache makes my thoughts skip, my tongue thick.

He smiles a little. "No dogs, no monkeys."

I smile back, he is teasing me. I am learning to understand when he teases. "I have some difficult news for you, Akhmim. I think you are a mere human being."

His smile vanishes. He shakes his head. "Diyet," he says. He is about to talk like a father.

I stop him with a gesture. My head still hurts.

The train whispers in, sounding like wind. Oh the lights. I sit down, shading my eyes, and he stands in front of me. I can feel him looking down at me. I look up and smile, or maybe grimace. He smiles back, looking worried. At the Moussin of the White Falcon, we get off. Funny that we are going into a cemetery to live. But only for awhile, I think. Somehow I will find a way we can leave. We'll go north, across the sea, up to the continent, where we'll be strangers. I take him through the streets and stop in front of a row of death houses, like the Lachims', but an inn. I give Akhmim money and tell him to rent us a place for the night. "Tell them your wife is sick," I whisper.

"I don't have any credit. If they take my identification, they'll know," he says.

"This is the Nekropolis," I say. "They don't use credit. Go on. Here you are a man."

He frowns at me but takes the money. I watch him out of the corner of my eye, bargaining, pointing at me. Just pay, I think, even though we have so little money. I just want to lie down, to sleep. And finally he comes out and takes me by the hand and leads me to our place. A tiny place of rough whitewashed walls, a bed, a chair, a pitcher of water and two glasses. "I have something for your head," he says. "The man gave it to me." He smiles ruefully. "He thinks you are pregnant."

My hand shakes when I hold it out. He puts the white pills in my hand and pours a glass of water for me. "I'll leave you here," he says. "I'll go back. I won't tell anyone that I know where you are."

"Then you were lying to me," I say. I don't want to argue, Akhmim, just stay until tomorrow. Then it will be too late. "You said if you could be free, you would. You *are* free."

"What can I do? I can't live," he says in anguish. "I can't get work!"

"You can sell funeral wreaths. I'll make them."

He looks torn. It is one thing to think how you will act, another to be in the situation and do it. And I know, seeing his face, that he really is human, because his problem is a very human problem. Safety or freedom.

"We will talk about it tomorrow," I say. "My head is aching."

"Because you are jessed," he says. "It is so dangerous. What if we don't make enough money? What if they catch us?"

"That is life," I say. I will go to prison. He will be sent back to the mistress. Punished. Maybe made to be conscript labor.

"Is it worth the pain?" he asks in a small voice.

I don't know, but I can't say that. "Not when you have the pain," I say, "but afterward it is."

"Your poor head." He strokes my forehead. His hand is cool and soothing.

"It's all right," I say. "It hurts to be born."

Ken Liu

The Algorithms for Love
(2004)

Ken Liu was born in China in 1976, where he spent his early childhood before joining his parents in California. In China, he lived with his grandparents and was especially close to his grandmother, who first introduced him to his love of fiction. After attending Harvard University, he worked for several years as a software engineer before returning to Harvard for his law degree. Currently a tax lawyer, his first love is writing science fiction, which he has been doing since the age of nine. Liu's story "Carthaginian Rose" won the Phobos Science Fiction contest in 2001, and another story, "Gossamer," was published in *L. Ron Hubbard Presents Writers of the Future Anthology*, Vol. 19, in 2003. He is currently working on a novel about nineteenth-century Chinese immigrants.

The story that follows was selected by David Hartwell and Kathryn Cramer for inclusion in the *Year's Best SF*, Vol. 10. Along with "Carthaginian Rose," it is part of a projected series of stories examining the search for meaning in the modern world, particularly in light of the perceived disjunction between religion and rationality. "The Algorithms for Love" traces a computer programmer's crisis of faith as she struggles to come to terms with loss. An algorithm is a formula for solving an equation or a set of protocols used in computer programming, but love is something we believe to be a spontaneous and authentic manifestation of human emotion. Liu's story raises unsettling questions about the extent of free will and the nature of human uniqueness, while at the same time exploring the psychological consequences of a purely mechanistic belief system.

If we can make artificial representations that seem real, the real itself may be called into question. If we can make computers that seem human, have we created a new form of life? Or just proved that we ourselves are nothing more than machines?

So long as the nurse is in the room to keep an eye on me, I am allowed to dress myself and get ready for Brad. I slip on an old pair of jeans and a scarlet turtleneck sweater. I've lost so much weight that the jeans hang loosely from the bony points of my hips.

"Let's go spend the weekend in Salem," Brad says to me as he walks me out of the hospital, an arm protectively wrapped around my waist, "just the two of us."

I wait in the car while Dr. West speaks with Brad just outside the hospital doors. I can't hear them but I know what she's telling him. "Make sure she takes her Oxetine every four hours. Don't leave her alone for any length of time."

Brad drives with a light touch on the pedals, the same way he used to when I was pregnant with Aimée. The traffic is smooth and light, and the foliage along the highway is postcard-perfect. The Oxetine relaxes the muscles around my mouth, and in the vanity mirror I see that I have a beatific smile on my face.

"I love you." He says this quietly, the way he has always done, as if it were the sound of breathing and heartbeat.

I wait a few seconds. I picture myself opening the door and throwing my body onto the highway but of course I don't do anything. I can't even surprise myself.

"I love you too." I look at him when I say this, the way I have always done, as if it were the answer to some question. He looks at me, smiles, and turns his eyes back to the road.

To him this means that the routines are back in place, that he is talking to the same woman he has known all these years, that things are back to normal. We are just another tourist couple from Boston on a mini-break for the weekend: stay at a bed-and-breakfast, visit the museums, recycle old jokes.

It's an algorithm for love.

I want to scream.

The first doll I designed was called Laura. Clever Laura™.

Laura had brown hair and blue eyes, fully articulated joints, twenty motors, a speech synthesizer in her throat, two video cameras disguised by the buttons on her blouse, temperature and touch sensors, and a microphone behind her nose. None of it was cutting-edge technology, and the software techniques I used were at least two decades old. But I was still proud of my work. She retailed for fifty dollars.

Not Your Average Toy could not keep up with the orders that were rolling in, even three months before Christmas. Brad, the CEO, went on CNN and MSNBC and TTV and the rest of the alphabet soup until the very air was saturated with Laura.

I tagged along on the interviews to give the demos because, as the VP of Marketing explained to me, I looked like a mother (even though I wasn't one) and (he didn't say this, but I could listen between the lines) I was blonde and pretty. The fact that I was Laura's designer was an afterthought.

The first time I did a demo on TV was for a Hong Kong crew. Brad wanted me to get comfortable with being in front of the cameras before bringing me to the domestic morning shows.

We sat to the side while Cindy, the anchorwoman, interviewed the CEO of some company that made "moisture meters." I hadn't slept for forty-eight hours. I was so nervous I'd brought six Lauras with me, just in case five of them decided in concert to break down. Then Brad turned to me and whispered, "What do you think moisture meters are used for?"

I didn't know Brad that well, having been at Not Your Average Toy for less than a year. I had chatted with him a few times before, but it was all professional. He seemed a very serious, driven sort of guy, the kind you could picture starting his first company while he was still in high school — arbitraging class notes, maybe. I wasn't sure why he was asking me about moisture meters. Was he trying to see if I was too nervous?

"I don't know. Maybe for cooking?" I ventured.

"Maybe," he said. Then he gave me a conspiratorial wink. "But I think the name sounds kind of dirty."

It was such an unexpected thing, coming from him, that for a moment I almost thought he was serious. Then he smiled, and I laughed out loud. I had a very hard time keeping a straight face while we waited for our turn, and I certainly wasn't nervous any more.

Brad and the young anchorwoman, Cindy, chatted amiably about Not Your Average Toy's mission ("Not Average Toys for Not Average Kids") and how Brad had come up with the idea for Laura. (Brad had nothing to do with the design, of course, since it was all my idea. But his answer was so good it almost convinced me that Laura was really his brainchild.) Then it was time for the dog-and-pony show.

I put Laura on the desk, her face toward the camera. I sat to the side of the desk. "Hello, Laura."

Laura turned her head to me, the motors so quiet you couldn't hear their whirr. "Hi! What's your name?"

"I'm Elena," I said.

"Nice to meet you," Laura said. "I'm cold."

The air conditioning was a bit chilly. I hadn't even noticed.

Cindy was impressed. "That's amazing. How much can she say?"

"Laura has a vocabulary of about two thousand English words, with semantic and syntactic encoding for common suffixes and prefixes. Her speech is regulated by a context-free grammar." The look in Brad's eye let me know that I was getting too technical. "That means that she'll invent new sentences and they'll always be syntactically correct."

"I like new, shiny, new, bright, new, handsome clothes," Laura said.

"Though they may not always make sense," I said.

"Can she learn new words?" Cindy asked.

Laura turned her head the other way, to look at her. "I like learn-ing, please teach me a new word!"

I made a mental note that the speech synthesizer still had bugs that would have to be fixed in the firmware.

Cindy was visibly unnerved by the doll turning to face her on its own and responding to her question.

"Does she" — she searched for the right word — "*understand* me?"

"No, no." I laughed. So did Brad. And a moment later Cindy joined us. "Laura's speech algorithm is augmented with a Markov generator interspersed with — " Brad gave me that look again. "Basically, she just babbles sentences based on keywords in what she hears. And she has a small set of stock phrases that are triggered the same way."

"Oh, it really seemed like she knew what I was saying. How does she learn new words?"

"It's very simple. Laura has enough memory to learn hundreds of new words. However, they have to be nouns. You can show her the object while you are trying to teach her what it is. She has some very sophisticated pattern recognition capabilities and can even tell faces apart."

For the rest of the interview I assured nervous parents that Laura would not require them to read the manual, that Laura would not explode when dropped in water, and no, she would never utter a naughty word, even if their little princesses "accidentally" taught Laura one.

" 'Bye," Cindy said to Laura at the end of the interview, and waved at her.

" 'Bye," Laura said. "You are nice." She waved back.

Every interview followed the same pattern. The moment when Laura first turned to the interviewer and answered a question there was always some awkwardness and unease. Seeing an inanimate object display intelligent behavior had that effect on people. They probably all thought the doll was possessed. Then I would explain how Laura worked and everyone would be delighted. I memorized the nontechnical, warm-and-fuzzy answers to all the questions until I could recite them even without my morning coffee. I got so good at it that I sometimes coasted through entire interviews on autopilot, not even paying attention to the questions and letting the same words I heard over and over again spark off my responses.

The interviews, along with all the other marketing tricks, did their job. We had to outsource manufacturing so quickly that for a while every shantytown along the coast of China must have been turning out Lauras.

The foyer of the bed-and-breakfast we are staying at is predictably filled with brochures from local attractions. Most of them are witch-themed. The lurid pictures and language somehow manage to convey moral outrage and adolescent fascination with the occult at the same time.

David, the innkeeper, wants us to check out Ye Olde Poppet Shoppe, featuring "Dolls Made by Salem's Official Witch." Bridget Bishop, one of the twenty executed during the Salem Witch Trials, was convicted partly based on the hard evidence of "poppets" found in her cellar with pins stuck in them.

Maybe she was just like me, a crazy, grown woman playing with dolls. The very idea of visiting a doll shop makes my stomach turn.

While Brad is asking David about restaurants and possible discounts I go up to our room. I want to be sleeping, or at least pretending to be sleeping, by the time he comes up. Maybe then he will leave me alone, and give me a few minutes to think. It's hard to think with the Oxetine. There's a wall in my head, a gauzy wall that tries to cushion every thought with contentment.

If only I can remember what went wrong.

For our honeymoon Brad and I went to Europe. We went on the transorbital shuttle, the tickets for which cost more than my yearly rent. But we could afford it. Witty Kimberly™, our latest model, was selling well, and the stock price was transorbital itself.

When we got back from the shuttleport, we were tired but happy. And I still couldn't quite believe that we were in our own home, thinking of each other as husband and wife. It felt like playing house. We made dinner together, like we used to when we were dating (like always, Brad was wildly ambitious but couldn't follow a recipe longer than a paragraph and I had to come and rescue his shrimp étouffée). The familiarity of the routine made everything seem more real.

Over dinner Brad told me something interesting. According to a market survey, over 20 percent of the customers for Kimberly were not buying it for their kids at all. They played with the dolls themselves.

"Many of them are engineers and comp sci students," Brad said. "And there are already tons of Net sites devoted to hacking efforts on Kimberly. My favorite one had step-by-step instructions on how to teach Kimberly to make up and tell lawyer jokes. I can't wait to see the faces of the guys in the legal department when they get to drafting the cease-and-desist letter for that one."

I could understand the interest in Kimberly. When I was struggling with my problem sets at MIT I would have loved to take apart something like Kimberly to figure out how she worked. How it worked, I corrected myself mentally, Kimberly's illusion of intelligence was so real that sometimes even I unconsciously gave her, it, too much credit.

"Actually, maybe we shouldn't try to shut the hacking efforts down," I said. "Maybe we can capitalize on it. We can release some of the APIs and sell a developer's kit for the geeks."

"What do you mean?"

"Well, Kimberly is a toy, but that doesn't mean only little girls would be interested in her." I gave up trying to manage the pronouns. "She does, after all, have the most sophisticated, *working*, natural conversation library in the world."

"A library that you wrote," Brad said. Well, maybe I was a little vain about it. But I'd worked damned hard on that library and I was proud of it.

"It would be a shame if the language processing module never got any application besides sitting in a doll that everyone is going to forget in a year. We can release the interface to the modules at least, a programming guide, and maybe even some of the source code. Let's see what happens and make an extra dollar while we're at it." I never got into academic AI research because I couldn't take the tedium, but I did have greater ambitions than just making talking dolls. I wanted to see smart and talking machines doing something real, like teaching kids to read or helping the elderly with chores.

I knew that he would agree with me in the end. Despite his serious exterior he was willing to take risks and defy expectations. It was why I loved him.

I got up to clear the dishes. His hand reached across the table and grabbed mine. "Those can wait," he said. He walked around the table, pulling me to him. I looked into his eyes. I loved the fact that I knew him so well I could tell what he was going to say before he said it. *Let's make a baby*, I imagined him saying. Those would have been the only words right for that moment.

And so he did.

I'm not asleep when Brad finishes asking about restaurants and comes upstairs. In my drugged state, even pretending is too difficult.

Brad wants to go to the pirate museum. I tell him that I don't want to see anything violent. He agrees immediately. That's what he wants to hear from his content, recovering wife.

So now we wander around the galleries of the Peabody Essex Museum, looking at the old treasures of the Orient from Salem's glory days.

The collection of china is terrible. The workmanship in the bowls and saucers is inexcusable. The patterns look like they were traced on by children. According to the placards, these were what the Cantonese merchants exported for foreign consumption. They would never have sold such stuff in China itself.

I read the description written by a Jesuit priest who visited the Cantonese shops of the time.

The craftsmen sat in a line, each with his own brush and specialty. The first drew only the mountains, the next only the grass, the next only the flowers, and the next only the animals. They went on down the line, passing the plates from one to the next, and it took each man only a few seconds to complete his part.

So the "treasures" are nothing more than mass-produced cheap exports from an ancient sweatshop and assembly line. I imagine painting the same blades of grass on a thousand teacups a day: the same routine, repeated over and over, with maybe a small break for lunch. Reach out, pick up the cup in front of you with your left hand, dip the brush, one, two, three strokes, put the cup behind you, rinse and repeat. What a simple algorithm. It's so human.

Brad and I fought for three months before he agreed to produce Aimée, just plain Aimée™.

We fought at home, where night after night I laid out the same forty-one reasons why we should and he laid out the same thirty-nine reasons why we shouldn't. We fought at work, where people stared through the glass door at Brad and me gesticulating at each other wildly, silently.

I was so tired that night. I had spent the whole evening locked away in my study, struggling to get the routines to control Aimée's involuntary muscle spasms right. It had to be right or she wouldn't feel real, no matter how good the learning algorithms were.

I came up to the bedroom. There was no light. Brad had gone to bed early. He was exhausted too. We had again hurled the same reasons at each other during dinner.

He wasn't asleep. "Are we going to go on like this?" he asked in the darkness.

I sat down on my side of the bed and undressed. "I can't stop it," I said. "I miss her too much. I'm sorry."

He didn't say anything. I finished unbuttoning my blouse and turned around. With the moonlight coming through the window I could see that his face was wet. I started crying too.

When we both finally stopped, Brad said, "I miss her too."

"I know," I said. *But not like me.*

"It won't be anything like her, you know?" he said.

"I know," I said.

The real Aimée had lived for ninety-one days. Forty-five of those days she'd spent under the glass hood in intensive care, where I could not touch her except for brief doctor-supervised sessions. But I could hear her cries. I could always hear her cries. In the end I tried to break through the glass with my hands, and I beat my palms against the unyielding glass until the bones broke and they sedated me.

I could never have another child. The walls of my womb had not healed properly and never would. By the time that piece of news was given to me Aimée was a jar of ashes in my closet.

But I could still hear her cries.

How many other women were like me? I wanted something to fill my arms, something to learn to speak, to walk, to grow a little, long enough for me to say goodbye, long enough to quiet those cries. But not a real child. I couldn't deal with another real child. It would feel like a betrayal.

With a little plastiskin, a little synthgel, the right set of motors and a lot of clever programming, I could do it. Let technology heal all wounds.

Brad thought the idea an abomination. He was revolted. He couldn't *understand*.

I fumbled around in the dark for some tissues for Brad and me.

"This may ruin us, and the company," he said.

"I know," I said. I lay down. I wanted to sleep.

"Let's do it, then," he said.

I didn't want to sleep any more.

"I can't take it," he said. "Seeing you like this. Seeing you in so much pain tears me up. It hurts too much."

I started crying again. This understanding, this pain. Was this what love was about?

Right before I fell asleep, Brad said, "Maybe we should think about changing the name of the company."

"Why?"

"Well, I just realized that 'Not Your Average Toy' sounds pretty funny to the dirty-minded."

I smiled. Sometimes the vulgar is the best kind of medicine.

"I love you."

"I love you too."

Brad hands me the pills. I obediently take them and put them in my mouth. He watches as I sip from the glass of water he hands me.

"Let me make a few phone calls," he says. "You take a nap, okay?" I nod.

As soon as he leaves the room I spit out the pills into my hand. I go into the bathroom and rinse out my mouth. I lock the door behind me and sit down on the toilet. I try to recite the digits of pi. I manage fifty-four places. That's a good sign. The Oxetine must be wearing off.

I look into the mirror. I stare into my eyes, trying to see through to the retinas, matching photoreceptor with photoreceptor, imagining their grid layout. I turn my head from side to side, watching the muscles tense and relax in turn. That effect would be hard to simulate.

But there's nothing in my face, nothing real behind that surface. Where is the pain, the pain that made love real, the pain of understanding?

"You okay, sweetie?" Brad says through the bathroom door.

I turn on the faucet and splash water on my face. "Yes," I say. "I'm going to take a shower. Can you get some snacks from that store we saw down the street?"

Giving him something to do reassures him. I hear the door to the room close behind him. I turn off the faucet and look back into the mirror, at the way the water droplets roll down my face, seeking the canals of my wrinkles.

The human body is a marvel to re-create. The human mind, on the other hand, is a joke. Believe me, I know.

No, Brad and I patiently explained over and over to the cameras, we had not created an "artificial child." That was not our intention and that was not what we'd done. It was a way to comfort the grieving mothers. If you needed Aimée, you would know.

I would walk down the street and see women walking with bundles carefully held in their arms. And occasionally I would know, I would know beyond a doubt, by the sound of a particular cry, by the way a little arm waved. I would look into the faces of the women, and be comforted.

I thought I had moved on, recovered from the grieving process. I was ready to begin another project, a bigger project that would really satisfy my ambition and show the world my skills. I was ready to get on with my life.

Tara took four years to develop. I worked on her in secret while designing other dolls that would sell. Physically Tara looked like a five-year-old girl. Expensive transplant-quality plastiskin and synthgel gave her an ethereal and angelic look. Her eyes were dark and clear, and you could look into them forever.

I never finished Tara's movement engine. In retrospect that was probably a blessing. As a temporary placeholder during development I used the facial expression engine sent in by the Kimberly enthusiasts at MIT's Media Lab. Augmented with many more fine micromotors than Kimberly had, she could turn her head, blink her eyes, wrinkle her nose, and generate thousands of convincing facial expressions. Below the neck she was paralyzed.

But her mind, oh, her mind.

I used the best quantum processors and the best solid-state storage matrices to run multi-layered, multi-feedback neural nets. I threw in the Stanford Semantic Database and added my own modifications. The programming was beautiful. It was truly a work of art. The data model alone took me over six months.

I taught her when to smile and when to frown, and I taught her how to speak and how to listen. Each night I analyzed the activation graphs for the nodes in the neural nets, trying to find and resolve problems before they occurred.

Brad never saw Tara while she was in development. He was too busy trying to control the damage from Aimée, and then, later, pushing the new dolls. I wanted to surprise him.

I put Tara in a wheelchair, and I told Brad that she was the daughter of a friend. Since I had to run some errands, could he entertain her while I was gone for a few hours? I left them in my office.

When I came back two hours later, I found Brad reading to her from *The Golem of Prague*, " 'Come,' said the Great Rabbi Loew, 'Open your eyes and speak like a real person!' "

That was just like Brad, I thought. He had his sense of irony.

"All right," I interrupted him. "Very funny. I get the joke. So how long did it take you?"

He smiled at Tara. "We'll finish this some other time," he said. Then he turned to me. "How long did it take me what?"

"To figure it out."

"Figure out what?"

"Stop kidding around," I said. "Really, what was it that gave her away?"

"Gave what away?" Brad and Tara said at the same time.

Nothing Tara ever said or did was a surprise to me. I could predict everything she would say before she said it. I'd coded everything in her, after all, and I knew exactly how her neural nets changed with each interaction.

But no one else suspected anything. I should have been elated. My doll was passing a real-life Turing Test. But I was frightened. The algorithms made a mockery of intelligence, and no one seemed to know. No one seemed to even care.

I finally broke the news to Brad after a week. After the initial shock he was delighted (as I knew he would be).

"Fantastic," he said. "We're now no longer just a toy company. Can you imagine the things we can do with this? You'll be famous, really famous!"

He prattled on and on about the potential applications. Then he noticed my silence. "What's wrong?"

So I told him about the Chinese Room.

The philosopher John Searle used to pose a puzzle for the AI researchers. Imagine a room, he said, a large room filled with meticulous clerks who are very good at following orders but who speak only English. Into this room are delivered a steady stream of cards with strange symbols on them. The clerks have to draw other strange symbols on blank cards in response and send the cards out of the room. In order to do this, the clerks have large books, full of rules in English like this one: "When you see a card with a single horizontal squiggle followed by a card with two vertical squiggles, draw a triangle on a blank card and hand it to the clerk to your right." The rules contain nothing about what the symbols might mean.

It turns out that the cards coming into the room are questions written in Chinese, and the clerks, by following the rules, are producing sensible answers in Chinese. But could anything involved in this process — the rules, the clerks, the room as a whole, the storm of activity — be said to have *understood* a word of Chinese? Substitute "processor" for the clerks and substitute "program" for the books of rules, then you'll see that the Turing Test will never prove anything, and AI is an illusion.

But you can also carry the Chinese Room Argument the other way: substitute "neurons" for the clerks and substitute the physical laws governing the cascading of activating potentials for the books of rules; then how can any of us ever be said to "understand" anything? Thought is an illusion.

"I don't understand," Brad said. "What are you saying?"

A moment later I realized that that was exactly what I'd expected him to say.

"Brad," I said, staring into his eyes, willing him to understand. "I'm scared. What if we are just like Tara?"

"We? You mean people? What are you talking about?"

"What if," I said, struggling to find the words, "we are just following some algorithm from day to day? What if our brain cells are just looking up signals from other signals? What if we are not thinking at all? What if what I'm saying to you now is just a predetermined response, the result of mindless physics?"

"Elena," Brad said, "you're letting philosophy get in the way of reality."

I need sleep, I thought, feeling hopeless.

"I think you need to get some sleep," Brad said.

I handed the coffee-cart girl the money as she handed me the coffee. I stared at the girl. She looked so tired and bored at eight in the morning that she made me feel tired.

I need a vacation.

"I need a vacation," she said, sighing exaggeratedly.

I walked past the receptionist's desk. *Morning, Elena.*

Say something different, please. I clenched my teeth. *Please.*

"Morning, Elena," she said.

I paused outside Ogden's cube. He was the structural engineer. *The weather, last night's game, Brad.*

He saw me and got up. "Nice weather we're having, eh?" He wiped the sweat from his forehead and smiled at me. He jogged to work. "Did you see the game last night? Best shot I've seen in ten years. Unbelievable. Hey, is Brad in yet?" His face was expectant, waiting for me to follow the script, the comforting routines of life.

The algorithms ran their determined courses, and our thoughts followed one after another, as mechanical and as predictable as the planets in their orbits. The watchmaker was the watch.

I ran into my office and closed the door behind me, ignoring the expression on Ogden's face. I walked over to my computer and began to delete files.

"Hi," Tara said. "What are we going to do today?"

I shut her off so quickly that I broke a nail on the hardware switch. I ripped out the power supply in her back. I went to work with my screwdriver and pliers. After a while I switched to a hammer. Was I killing?

Brad burst in the door. "What are you doing?"

I looked up at him, my hammer poised for another strike. I wanted to tell him about the pain, the terror that opened up an abyss around me.

In his eyes I could not find what I wanted to see. I could not see understanding.

I swung the hammer.

Brad had tried to reason with me, right before he had me committed.

"This is just an obsession," he said. "People have always associated the mind with the technological fad of the moment. When they believed in witches and spirits, they thought there was a little man in the brain. When they had mechanical looms and player pianos, they thought the brain was an engine. When they had telegraphs and telephones, they thought the brain was a wire network. Now you think the brain is just a computer. Snap out of it. *That* is the illusion."

Trouble was, I knew he was going to say that.

"It's because we've been married for so long!" he shouted. "That's why you think you know me so well!"

I knew he was going to say that too.

"You're running around in circles," he said, defeat in his voice. "You're just spinning in your head."

Loops in my algorithm. FOR and WHILE loops.

"Come back to me. I love you."

What else could he have said?

Now finally alone in the bathroom of the inn, I look down at my hands, at the veins running under the skin. I press my hands together and feel my pulse. I kneel down. Am I praying? Flesh and bones, and good programming.

My knees hurt against the cold tile floor.

The pain is real, I think. There's no algorithm for the pain. I look down at my wrists, and the scars startle me. This is all very familiar, like I've done this before. The horizontal scars, ugly and pink like worms, rebuke me for failure. Bugs in the algorithm.

That night comes back to me: the blood everywhere, the alarms wailing, Dr. West and the nurses holding me down while they bandaged my wrists, and then Brad staring down at me, his face distorted with uncomprehending grief.

I should have done better. The arteries are hidden deep, protected by the bones. The slashes have to be made vertically if you really want it. That's the right algorithm. There's a recipe for everything. This time I'll get it right.

It takes a while, but finally I feel sleepy.

I'm happy. The pain *is* real.

I open the door to my room and turn on the light.

The light activates Laura, who is sitting on top of my dresser. This one used to be a demo model. She hasn't been dusted in a while, and her dress looks ragged. Her head turns to follow my movement.

I turn around. Brad's body is still, but I can see the tears on his face. He was crying on the whole silent ride home from Salem.

The innkeeper's voice loops around in my head. "Oh, I could tell right away something was wrong. It's happened here before. She didn't seem right at breakfast, and then when you came back she looked like she was in another world. When I heard the water running in the pipes for that long I rushed upstairs right away."

So I was that predictable.

I look at Brad, and I believe that he is in a lot of pain. I believe it with all my heart. But I still don't feel anything. There's a gulf between us, a gulf so wide that I can't feel his pain. Nor he mine.

But my algorithms are still running. I scan for the right thing to say. "I love you."

He doesn't say anything. His shoulders heave, once.

I turn around. My voice echoes through the empty house, bouncing off walls. Laura's sound receptors, old as they are, pick them up. The signals run through the cascading IF statements. The DO loops twirl and dance while she does a database lookup. The motors whirr. The synthesizer kicks in.

"I love you too," Laura says.

Critical Contexts for Artificial Life

Sigmund Freud

The Uncanny

(1919; trans. 1924)

Sigmund Freud (1856–1939), the founder of psychoanalysis, began his professional life as a medical doctor in Vienna during the late nineteenth century. His work with emotionally disturbed patients led him to develop new theories of the mind that forever changed the way we think about human consciousness. Although some of Freud's theories have been challenged in recent years, his idea of the *unconscious* remains deeply influential. Freud's work argues that the feelings and thoughts that impel much of our behavior are difficult for us to know directly. Although this unconscious element of identity means that we cannot always understand what makes certain things attractive or frightening, the unconscious is also a source of humor and creativity.

Freud believed that writers and artists had unique access to the unconscious, and he often used literary texts to explain and develop his theories — most famously of course the Greek play *Oedipus Rex*, from which the "Oedipus complex" takes its name. He explained that we respond especially strongly to art and literature that echos some of our unconscious fears and desires. In the essay that follows, Freud analyzes E. T. A. Hoffmann's "The Sandman" (included in this chapter, pages 195–220), a story by the well-known Romantic fabulist, to understand the nature of the phenomenon of "the uncanny" (*unheimlich*, literally "unhomely" in German). Those things that strike us as "uncanny," Freud

Translation by James Strachey.

maintains, are those that seem both familiar and unfamiliar; they induce in us a feeling of simultaneous recognition and estrangement. Readers of sf theory will recognize here a connection to Darko Suvin's theory of cognitive estrangement, that successful sf creates a recognizable world with some significant difference from our own. Hoffmann's story itself has many science fictional elements; it is one of the first to feature an automaton, or lifelike machine, and thus is a direct predecessor of the robot stories in this section.

I

It is only rarely that a psycho-analyst feels impelled to investigate the subject of aesthetics, even when aesthetics is understood to mean not merely the theory of beauty but the theory of the qualities of feeling. He works in other strata of mental life and has little to do with the subdued emotional impulses which, inhibited in their aims and dependent on a host of concurrent factors, usually furnish the material for the study of aesthetics. But it does occasionally happen that he has to interest himself in some particular province of that subject; and this province usually proves to be a rather remote one, and one which has been neglected in the specialist literature of aesthetics.

The subject of the 'uncanny' is a province of this kind. It is undoubtedly related to what is frightening — to what arouses dread and horror; equally certainly, too, the word is not always used in a clearly definable sense, so that it tends to coincide with what excites fear in general. Yet we may expect that a special core of feeling is present which justifies the use of a special conceptual term. One is curious to know what this common core is which allows us to distinguish as 'uncanny' certain things which lie within the field of what is frightening. . . .

Two courses are open to us at the outset. Either we can find out what meaning has come to be attached to the word 'uncanny' in the course of its history; or we can collect all those properties of persons, things, sense-impressions, experiences, and situations which arouse in us the feeling of uncanniness, and then infer the unknown nature of the uncanny from what all these examples have in common. I will say at once that both courses lead to the same result: the uncanny is that class of the frightening which leads back to what is known of old and long familiar. How this is possible, in what circumstances the familiar can become uncanny and frightening, I shall show in what follows. Let me also add that my investigation was actually begun by collecting a number of individual cases, and was only later confirmed by examination of linguistic usage. In this discussion, however, I shall follow the reverse course.

The German word *unheimlich*[1] is obviously the opposite of *heimlich*, *heimisch*, meaning "familiar"; "native," "belonging to the home"; and we are

---

1. [Throughout this paper "uncanny" is used as the English translation of "*unheimlich*," literally "unhomely," — Trans.]

tempted to conclude that what is "uncanny" is frightening precisely because it is *not* known and familiar. Naturally not everything which is new and unfamiliar is frightening, however; the relation cannot be inverted. We can only say that what is novel can easily become frightening and uncanny; some new things are frightening but not by any means all. Something has to be added to what is novel and unfamiliar to make it uncanny.

On the whole, Jentsch[2] did not get beyond this relation of the uncanny to the novel and unfamiliar. He ascribes the essential factor in the production of the feeling of uncanniness to intellectual uncertainty; so that the uncanny would always be that in which one does not know where one is, as it were. The better orientated in his environment a person is, the less readily will he get the impression of something uncanny in regard to the objects and events in it.

It is not difficult to see that this definition is incomplete, and we will therefore try to proceed beyond the equation of *unheimlich* with unfamiliar. We will first turn to other languages. But foreign dictionaries tell us nothing new, perhaps only because we speak a different language. Indeed, we get the impression that many languages are without a word for this particular shade of what is frightening.

I wish to express my indebtedness to Dr Th. Reik for the following excerpts:

LATIN: (K. E. Georges, *Deutschlateinisches Wörterbuch*, 1898). Ein *unheimlicher* Ort [an uncanny place] — (locus suspectus; in unheimlicher Nachtzeit [in the dismal night hours] — intempesta nocte.
GREEK: (Rost's and Schenkl's Lexikons). Evos — strange, foreign.
ENGLISH: (from dictionaries by Lucas, Bellow, Flugel, Muret: Sanders). Uncomfortable, uneasy, gloomy, dismal, uncanny, ghastly; (of a house) haunted; (of a man) a repulsive fellow.
FRENCH: (Sachs–Villatte). Inquiétant, sinistre, lugubre, mal à son aise.
SPANISH: (Tollhausen, 1889). Sospechoso, de mal agüero, lúgubre, siniestro. The Italian and the Portuguese seem to content themselves with words which we should describe as circumlocutions. In Arabic and Hebrew "uncanny" means the same as "daemonic," "gruesome."

Let us therefore return to the German language. In Daniel Sanders's *Wörterbuch der deutschen Sprache* (1860), the following remarks [abstracted in translation] are found upon the word *heimlich*; I have laid stress on certain passages by italicizing them.

Heimlich adj.: 1. Also *heimelich*, *heimelig*, belonging to the house, not strange, familiar, tame, intimate, comfortable, homely, etc.
(*a*) (Obsolete) belonging to the house or the family, or regarded as so

---

2. Freud is responding to an article written by German psychologist Ernst Jentsch in 1906, "On the Psychology of the Uncanny." [Ed.]

belonging (cf. Latin *familiaris*): *Die Heimlichen*, the members of the household; *Der heimliche Rat* [him to whom secrets are revealed] Gen. xli. 45; 2 Sam. xxiii. 23; now more usually *Geheimer Rat* [Privy Councillor], cf. *Heimlicher*.

(*b*) Of animals; tame, companionable to man. As opposed to wild, *e.g.* "Wild animals . . . that are trained to be *heimlich* and accustomed to men." "If these young creatures are brought up from early days among men they become quite *heimlich*, friendly," etc. . . .

(*c*) Friendly, intimate, homelike; the enjoyment of quiet content, etc., arousing a sense of peaceful pleasure and security as in one within the four walls of his house. "Is it still *heimlich* to you in your country where strangers are felling your woods?" "She did not feel all too *heimlich* with him." "To destroy the *Heimlichkeit* of the home." . . . "In quiet *Heimlichkeit*, surrounded by close walls." . . . "When it grows *heimlich* and still, and the evening quiet alone watches over your cell." . . . "That which comes from afar . . . assuredly does not live quite *heimelig* (*heimatlich* [at home], *freundnachbarlich* [in a neighborly way]) among the people." "The sentinel's horn sounds so *heimelig* from the tower, and his voice invites so hospitably." *This form of the word ought to become general in order to protect the word from becoming obsolete in its good sense through an easy confusion with II.* [see below]. " 'The Zecks [a family name] are all 'heimlich'." " 'Heimlich'? What do you understand by 'heimlich'?" "Well, . . . they are like a buried spring or a dried-up pond. One cannot walk over it without always having the feeling that water might come up there again." "Oh, we call it 'unheimlich'; you call it 'heimlich.' Well, what makes you think that there is something secret and untrustworthy about his family?'" Gutzkow.

II. Concealed, kept from sight, so that others do not get to know about it, withheld from others, cf. *geheim* [secret]; so also *Heimlichkeit* for *Geheimnis* [secret]. To do something *heimlich*, *i.e.* behind someone's back; to steal away *heimlich*; *heimlich* meetings and appointments; to look on with *heimlich* pleasure at someone's discomfiture; to sigh or weep *heimlich*; to behave *heimlich*, as though there was something to conceal; *heimlich* love, love-affair, sin; *heimlich* places (which good manners oblige us to conceal). . . . "The *heimlich* art" (magic). "Where public ventilation has to stop, there *heimlich* machinations begin." "Freedom is the whispered watchword of *heimlich* conspirators and the loud battle-cry of professed revolutionaries." "A holy, *heimlich* effect." "I have roots that are most *heimlich*, I am grown in the deep earth." . . .

Compounds and especially also the opposite follow meaning I. (above): *Unheimlich*, uneasy, eerie, blood-curdling; "Seeming almost *unheimlich* and ghostly to him." "I had already long since felt an *unheimlich* even gruesome feeling." "Feels an *unheimlich* horror." "*Unheimlich* and motionless like a stone-image." "The *unheimlich* mist called hill-fog." "These pale youths are *unheimlich* and are brewing heaven knows what mischief." " '*Unheimlich* is the name for everything that ought to have remained . . . hidden and secret and has become visible.'" Schelling. "To veil the divine to surround it with a certain *Unheimlichkeit.* — *Unheimlich* is not often used as opposite to meaning II. (above).

What interests us most in this long extract is to find that among its different shades of meaning the word *heimlich* exhibits one which is identical with its opposite *unheimlich.* What is *heimlich* thus comes to be *unheimlich.* (Cf. the quotation from Gutzkow: "We call it *unheimlich;* you call it *heimlich.*") In general we are reminded that the word *heimlich* is not unambiguous, but belongs to two sets of ideas, which without being contradictory are yet very different: On the one hand, it means that which is familiar and congenial, and on the other, that which is concealed and kept out of sight. "*Unheimlich*" is customarily used, we are told, as the contrary only of the first signification of "*heimlich*" and not of the second. Sanders tells us nothing concerning a possible genetic connection between these two meanings of *heimlich.* On the other hand, we notice that Schelling says something which throws quite new light on the concept of the *Unheimlich,* for which we were certainly not prepared. According to him, everything is *unheimlich* that ought to have remained secret and hidden but has come to light.

Some of the doubts that have thus arisen are removed if we consult Grimm's dictionary (1877, 4, Part 2, pp. 873 ff.).

We read:

Heimlich; adj. and adv. *vernaculus, occultus*; MHG. heîmelich, heîmlich. (p. 874.) In a slightly different sense: "I feel *heimlich,* well, free from fear," . . .

[3] (*b*) *Heimlich* is also used of a place free from ghostly influences . . . familiar, friendly, intimate.

(p. 875: p) Familiar, amicable, unreserved.

4. From the idea of "homelike," "belonging to the house," the further idea is developed of something withdrawn from the eyes of strangers, something concealed, secret; and this idea is expanded in many ways . . .

(p. 876.) "On the left bank of the lake there lies a meadow *heimlich* in the wood." (Schiller, *Wilhelm Tell,* I, 4.) . . . Poetic license, rarely so used in modern speech . . . *Heimlich* is used in conjunction with a verb expressing the act of concealing: "In the secret of his tabernacle he shall hide me *heimlich.*" (Ps. xxvii. 5.) . . . *Heimlich* parts of the human body, *pudenda* . . . "the men that died not were smitten on their *heimlich* parts." (1 Samuel v. 12.) . . .

(*c*) Officials who give important advice which has to be kept secret in matters of state are called *heimlich* councillors. . . .

(p. 878.) 6. *Heimlich,* as used of knowledge — mystic, allegorical: a *heimlich* meaning, *mysticus, divinus, occultus, figuratus.* (p. 878.) *Heimlich* in a different sense, as withdrawn from knowledge, unconscious . . . *Heimlich* also has the meaning of that which is obscure, inaccessible to knowledge . . . "Do you not see? They do not trust us; they fear the *heimlich* face of the Duke of Friedland." (Schiller, *Wallensteins Lager,* Scene 2.)

9. *The notion of something hidden and dangerous, which is expressed in the last paragraph, is still further developed, so that "heimlich" comes to have the meaning usually ascribed to "unheimlich."* Thus: "At times I feel like a man who walks in the night and believes in ghosts; every corner is *heimlich* and full of terrors for him." (Klinger, *Theater*, 3. 298.)

Thus *heimlich* is a word the meaning of which develops in the direction of ambivalence, until it finally coincides with its opposite, *unheimlich*. *Unheimlich* is in some way or other a sub-species of *heimlich*. Let us bear this discovery in mind, though we cannot yet rightly understand it, alongside of Schelling's definition of the *Unheimlich*. If we go on to examine individual instances of uncanniness, these hints will become intelligible to us.

II

When we proceed to review the things, persons, impressions, events, and situations which are able to arouse in us a feeling of the uncanny in a particularly forcible and definite form, the first requirement is obviously to select a suitable example to start on. Jentsch has taken as a very good instance "doubts whether an apparently animate being is really alive; or conversely, whether a lifeless object might not be in fact animate"; and he refers in this connection to the impression made by waxwork figures, ingeniously constructed dolls, and automata. To these he adds the uncanny effect of epileptic fits, and of manifestations of insanity, because these excite in the spectator the impression of automatic, mechanical processes at work behind the ordinary appearance of mental activity. Without entirely accepting this author's view, we will take it as a starting-point for our own investigation because in what follows he reminds us of a writer who has succeeded in producing uncanny effects better than anyone else.

Jentsch writes: "In telling a story, one of the most successful devices for easily creating uncanny effects is to leave the reader in uncertainty whether a particular figure in the story is a human being or an automaton, and to do it in such a way that his attention is not focused directly upon his uncertainty, so that he may not be led to go into the matter and clear it up immediately. That, as we have said, would quickly dissipate the peculiar emotional effect of the thing. E. T. A. Hoffmann has repeatedly employed this psychological artifice with success in his fantastic narratives."

This observation, undoubtedly a correct one, refers primarily to the story of "The Sand-Man" in Hoffmann's *Nachtstücken*, which contains the original of Olympia, the doll that appears in the first act of Offenbach's opera, *Tales of Hoffmann*. But I cannot think — and I hope most readers of the story will agree with me — that the theme of the doll Olympia, who is to all appearances a living being, is by any means the only, or indeed the most important, element that must be held responsible for the quite unparalleled atmosphere of uncanniness evoked by the story. Nor is this atmosphere heightened by the fact that the author himself treats the episode of Olympia with a faint touch of satire and uses it to poke fun at the young man's idealization of his mistress. The main theme of the story is, on the contrary, something different, something which gives it its name, and which is always re-introduced at critical moments: It is the theme of the "Sand-Man" who tears out children's eyes.

This fantastic tale opens with the childhood recollections of the student Nathaniel. In spite of his present happiness, he cannot banish the memories associated with the mysterious and terrifying death of his beloved father. On certain evenings his mother used to send the children to bed early, warning them that "the Sand-Man was coming"; and, sure enough, Nathaniel would not fail to hear the heavy tread of a visitor, with whom his father would then be occupied for the evening. When questioned about the Sand-Man, his mother, it is true, denied that such a person existed except as a figure of speech; but his nurse could give him more definite information: "He's a wicked man who comes when children won't go to bed, and throws handfuls of sand in their eyes so that they jump out of their heads all bleeding. Then he puts the eyes in a sack and carries them off to the half-moon to feed his children. They sit up there in their nest, and their beaks are hooked like owls' beaks, and they use them to peck up naughty boys' and girls' eyes with."

Although little Nathaniel was sensible and old enough not to credit the figure of the Sand-Man with such gruesome attributes, yet the dread of him became fixed in his heart. He determined to find out what the Sand-Man looked like; and one evening, when the Sand-Man was expected again, he hid in his father's study. He recognized the visitor as the lawyer Coppelius, a repulsive person whom the children were frightened of when he occasionally came to a meal; and he now identified this Coppelius with the dreaded Sand-Man. As regards the rest of the scene, Hoffmann already leaves us in doubt whether what we are witnessing is the first delirium of the panic-stricken boy, or a succession of events which are to be regarded in the story as being real. His father and the guest are at work at a brazier with glowing flames. The little eavesdropper hears Coppelius call out: "Eyes here! Eyes here!" and betrays himself by screaming aloud. Coppelius seizes him and is on the point of dropping bits of red-hot coal from the fire into his eyes, and then of throwing them into the brazier, but his father begs him off and saves his eyes. After this the boy falls into a deep swoon; and a long illness brings his experience to an end. Those who decide in favor of the rationalistic interpretation of the Sand-Man will not fail to recognize in the child's phantasy the persisting influence of his nurse's story. The bits of sand that are to be thrown into the child's eyes turn into bits of red-hot coal from the flames; and in both cases they are intended to make his eyes jump out. In the course of another visit of the Sand-Man's, a year later, his father is killed in his study by an explosion. The lawyer Coppelius disappears from the place without leaving a trace behind.

Nathaniel, now a student, believes that he has recognized this phantom of horror from his childhood in an itinerant optician, an Italian called

Giuseppe Coppola, who at his university town, offers him weather-glasses for sale. When Nathaniel refuses, the man goes on: "Not weather-glasses? not weather-glasses? also got fine eyes, fine eyes!" The student's terror is allayed when he finds that the proffered eyes are only harmless spectacles, and he buy a pocket spy-glass from Coppola. With its aid he looks across into Professor Spalanzani's house opposite and there spies Spalanzani's beautiful, but strangely silent and motionless daughter, Olympia. He soon falls in love with her so violently that, because of her, he quite forgets the clever and sensible girl to whom he is betrothed. But Olympia is an automaton whose clockwork has been made by Spalanzani, and whose eyes have been put in by Coppola, the Sand-Man. The student surprises the two Masters quarrelling over their handiwork. The optician carries off the wooden eyeless doll; and the mechanician, Spalanzani, picks up Olympia's bleeding eyes from the ground and throws them at Nathaniel's breast, saying that Coppola had stolen them from the student. Nathaniel succumbs to a fresh attack of madness, and in his delirium his recollection of his father's death is mingled with this new experience. "Hurry up! hurry up! ring of fire!" he cries. "Spin about, ring of fire — Hurrah! Hurry up, wooden doll! lovely wooden doll, spin about — ." He then falls upon the professor, Olympia's "father," and tries to strangle him.

Rallying from a long and serious illness, Nathaniel seems at last to have recovered. He intends to marry his betrothed, with whom he has become reconciled. One day he and she are walking through the city market-place, over which the high tower of the Town Hall throws its huge shadow. On the girl's suggestion, they climb the tower, leaving her brother, who is walking with them, down below. From the top, Clara's attention is drawn to a curious object moving along the street. Nathaniel looks at this thing through Coppola's spy-glass, which he finds in his pocket, and falls into a new attack of madness. Shouting "spin about, wooden doll!" he tries to throw the girl into the gulf below. Her brother, brought to her side by her cries, rescues her and hastens down with her to safety. On the tower above, the madman rushes round, shrieking "Ring of fire, spin about!" — and we know the origin of the words. Among the people who begin to gather below there comes forward the figure of the lawyer Coppelius, who has suddenly returned. We may suppose that it was his approach, seen through the spy-glass, which threw Nathaniel into his fit of madness. As the onlookers prepare to go up and overpower the madman, Coppelius laughs and says: "Wait a bit; he'll come down of himself." Nathaniel suddenly stands still, catches sight of Coppelius, and with a wild shriek "Yes! 'Fine eyes — fine eyes!'" flings himself over the parapet. While he lies on the paving-stones with a shattered skull the Sand-Man vanishes in the throng.

This short summary leaves no doubt, I think, that the feeling of something uncanny is directly attached to the figure of the Sand-Man, that is, to the idea of being robbed of one's eyes, and that Jentsch's point of an intellectual uncertainty has nothing to do with the effect. Uncertainty whether an object is living or inanimate, which admittedly applied to the doll Olympia, is quite irrelevant in connection with this other, more striking instance of uncanniness. It is true that the writer creates a kind of uncertainty in us in the beginning by not letting us know, no doubt purposely, whether he is taking us into the real world or into a purely fantastic one of his own creation. He has, of course, a right to do either; and if he chooses to stage his action in a world peopled with spirits, demons, and ghosts, as Shakespeare does in *Hamlet*, in *Macbeth* and, in a different sense, in *The Tempest* and *A Midsummer Night's Dream*, we must bow to his decision and treat his setting as though it were real for as long as we put ourselves into his hands. But this uncertainty disappears in the course of Hoffmann's story, and we perceive that he intends to make us, too, look through the demon optician's spectacles or spy-glass — perhaps, indeed, that the author in his very own person once peered through such an instrument. For the conclusion of the story makes it quite clear that Coppola the optician really *is* the lawyer Coppelius[3] and also, therefore, the Sand-Man.

There is no question therefore, of any intellectual uncertainty here: we know now that we are not supposed to be looking on at the products of a madman's imagination, behind which we, with the superiority of rational minds, are able to detect the sober truth; and yet this knowledge does not lessen the impression of uncanniness in the least degree. The theory of intellectual uncertainty is thus incapable of explaining that impression.

We know from psycho-analytic experience, however, that the fear of damaging or losing one's eyes is a terrible one in children. Many adults retain their apprehensiveness in this respect, and no physical injury is so much dreaded by them as an injury to the eye. We are accustomed to say, too, that we will treasure a thing as the apple of our eye. A study of dreams, phantasies and myths has taught us that anxiety about one's eyes, the fear of going blind, is often enough a substitute for the dread of being castrated. The self-blinding of the mythical criminal, Oedipus, was simply a mitigated form of the punishment of castration — the only punishment that was adequate for him by the *lex talionis*. We may try on rationalistic grounds to deny that fears about the eye are derived from the fear of castration, and may argue that it is very natural that so precious an organ as the eye should be guarded by a proportionate dread. Indeed, we might go further and say that the fear of castration itself contains no other significance and no deeper secret than a justifiable dread of this rational kind. But this view does not account adequately for the substitutive relation between the eye and the male organ which is seen to exist in dreams and myths and phantasies; nor can it dispel the impression that the threat of being castrated in especial excites a peculiarly violent and obscure emotion, and that this emotion is what first gives the idea of losing other organs its intense coloring. All further doubts are removed when we learn the details of their "castration complex" from the analysis of neurotic patients, and realize its immense importance in their mental life.

3. Frau Dr Rank has pointed out the association of the name with "*coppella*" = crucible, connecting it with the chemical operations that caused the father's death; and also with "*coppo*" = eye-socket.

Moreover, I would not recommend any opponent of the psycho-analytic view to select this particular story of the Sand-Man with which to support his argument that anxiety about the eyes has nothing to do with the castration complex. For why does Hoffmann bring the anxiety about eyes into such intimate connection with the father's death? And why does the Sand-Man always appear as a disturber of love? He separates the unfortunate Nathaniel from his betrothed and from her brother, his best friend; he destroys the second object of his love, Olympia, the lovely doll; and he drives him into suicide at the moment when he has won back his Clara and is about to be happily united to her. Elements in the story like these, and many others, seem arbitrary and meaningless so long as we deny all connection between fears about the eye and castration; but they become intelligible as soon as we replace the Sand-Man by the dreaded father at whose hands castration is expected.[4]

We shall venture, therefore, to refer the uncanny effect of the Sand-Man to the anxiety belonging to the castration complex of childhood. But having reached the idea that we can make an infantile factor such as this responsible for feelings of uncanniness, we are encouraged to see whether we can apply it to other instances of the uncanny. We find in the story of

---

4. In fact, Hoffmann's imaginative treatment of his material has not made such wild confusion of its elements that we cannot reconstruct their original arrangement. In the story of Nathaniel's childhood, the figures of his father and Coppelius represent the two opposites into which the father-imago is split by his ambivalence; whereas the one threatens to blind him — that is, to castrate him — the other, the "good" father, intercedes for his sight. The part of the complex which is most strongly repressed, the death-wish against the "bad" father, finds expression in the death of the "good" father, and Coppelius is made answerable for it. This pair of fathers is represented later, in his student days, by Professor Spalanzani and Coppola the optician. The Professor is in himself a member of the father-series, and Coppola is recognized as identical with Coppelius the lawyer. Just as they used before to work together over the secret brazier, so now they have jointly created the doll Olympia; the Professor is even called the father of Olympia. This double occurrence of activity in common betrays them as divisions of the father-imago: Both the mechanician and the optician were the father of Nathaniel (and of Olympia as well). In the frightening scene in childhood, Coppelius, after sparing Nathaniel's eyes, had screwed off his arms and legs as an experiment; that is, he had worked on him as a mechanician would on a doll. This singular feature, which seems quite outside the picture of the Sand-Man, introduces a new castration equivalent; but it also points to the inner identity of Coppelius with his later counterpart, Spalanzani the mechanician, and prepares us for the interpretation of Olympia. This automatic doll can be nothing else than a materialization of Nathaniel's feminine attitude towards his father in his infancy. Her fathers, Spalanzani and Coppola, are, after all, nothing but new editions, reincarnations of Nathaniel's pair of fathers. Spalanzani's otherwise incomprehensible statement that the optician has stolen Nathaniel's eyes . . . so as to set them in the doll, now becomes significant as supplying evidence of the identity of Olympia and Nathaniel. Olympia is, as it were, a dissociated complex of Nathaniel's which confronts him as a person, and Nathaniel's enslavement to this complex is expressed in his senseless obsessive love for Olympia. We may with justice call love of this kind narcissistic, and we can understand why someone who has fallen victim to it should relinquish the real, external object of his love. The psychological truth of the situation in which the young man, fixated upon his father by his castration complex, becomes incapable of loving a woman, is amply proved by numerous analyses of patients whose story, though less fantastic, is hardly less tragic than that of the student Nathaniel.

Hoffmann was the child of an unhappy marriage. When he was three years old, his father left his small family, and was never united to them again. According to Grisebach, in his biographical introduction to Hoffmann's works, the writer's relation to his father was always a most sensitive subject with him.

the Sand-Man the other theme on which Jentsch lays stress, of a doll which appears to be alive. Jentsch believes that a particularly favorable condition for awakening uncanny feelings is created when there is intellectual uncertainty whether an object is alive or not, and when an inanimate object becomes too much like an animate one. Now, dolls are of course rather closely connected with childhood life. We remember that in their early games children do not distinguish at all sharply between living and inanimate objects, and that they are especially fond of treating their dolls like live people. In fact, I have occasionally heard a woman patient declare that even at the age of eight she had still been convinced that her dolls would be certain to come to life if she were to look at them in a particular, extremely concentrated, way. So that here, too, it is not difficult to discover a factor from childhood. But, curiously enough, while the Sand-Man story deals with the arousing of an early childhood fear, the idea of a "living doll" excites no fear at all; children have no fear of their dolls coming to life, they may even desire it. The source of uncanny feelings would not, therefore, be an infantile fear in this case, but rather an infantile wish or even merely an infantile belief. There seems to be a contradiction here; but perhaps it is only a complication, which may be helpful to us later on.

Hoffmann is the unrivalled master of the uncanny in literature. His *Elixire des Teufels* [*The Devil's Elixir*] contains a whole mass of themes to which one is tempted to ascribe the uncanny effect of the narrative; but it is too obscure and intricate a story to venture to summarize. . . . We must content ourselves with selecting those themes of uncanniness which are most prominent, and seeing whether we can fairly trace them also back to infantile sources. These themes are all concerned with the idea of a "double" in every degree of development. Thus we have characters who are to be considered identical because they look alike. This relation is accentuated by mental processes leaping from one person to the other — by what we should call telepathy — so that the one possesses knowledge, feeling, and experience in common with the other, identifies himself with someone else, so that his self becomes confounded, or the foreign self is substituted for his own — in other words, by doubling, dividing and interchanging the self. And finally there is the constant recurrence of similar situations, a same face, or character-trait, or twist of fortune, or a same crime, or even a same name recurring throughout several consecutive generations.

The theme of the "double" has been very thoroughly treated by Otto Rank.[5] He has gone into the connections the "double" has with reflections in mirrors, with shadows, guardian spirits, with the belief in the soul and the fear of death; but he also lets in a flood of light on the astonishing evolution of this idea. For the "double" was originally an insurance against destruction to the ego, an "energetic denial of the power of death," as Rank says; and probably the "Immortal" soul was the first "double" of the body.

---

5. "Der Doppelgänger."

This invention of doubling as a preservation against extinction has its counterpart in the language of dreams, which is fond of representing castration by a doubling or multiplication of the genital symbol. The same desire spurred on the ancient Egyptians to the art of making images of the dead in some lasting material. Such ideas, however, have sprung from the soil of unbounded self-love, from the primary narcissism which holds sway in the mind of the child as in that of primitive man; and when this stage has been left behind the double takes on a different aspect. From having been an assurance of immortality, he becomes the uncanny harbinger of death.

The idea of the "double" does not necessarily disappear with the passing of the primary narcissism, for it can receive fresh meaning from the later stages of development of the ego. A special faculty is slowly formed there, able to oppose the rest of the ego, with the function of observing and criticizing the self and exercising a censorship within the mind, and this we become aware of as our "conscience." In the pathological case of delusions of being watched this mental institution becomes isolated, dissociated from the ego, and discernible to a physician's eye. The fact that a faculty of this kind exists, which is able to treat the rest of the ego like an object — the fact, that is, that man is capable of self-observation — renders it possible to invest the old idea of a "double" with a new meaning and to ascribe many things to it, above all, those things which seem to the new faculty of self-criticism to belong to the old surmounted narcissism of the earliest period of all.[6]

But it is not only this narcissism, offensive to the ego-criticizing faculty, which may be incorporated in the idea of a double. There are also all those unfulfilled but possible futures to which we still like to cling in phantasy, all those strivings of the ego which adverse external circumstances have crushed, and all our suppressed acts of volition which nourish in us the illusion of Free Will.[7]

But, after having thus considered the manifest motivation of the figure of a "double," we have to admit that none of it helps us to understand the extraordinarily strong feeling of something uncanny that pervades the conception; and our knowledge of pathological mental processes enables us to add that nothing in the content arrived at could account for that impulse towards self-protection which has caused the ego to project such a content outward as something foreign to itself. The quality of uncanniness can only

---

6. I believe that when poets complain that two souls dwell within the human breast, and when popular psychologists talk of the splitting of the ego in an individual, they have some notion of this division (which relates to the sphere of ego-psychology) between the critical faculty and the rest of the ego, and not of the antithesis discovered by psycho-analysis between the ego and what is unconscious and repressed. It is true that the distinction is to some extent effaced by the circumstance that derivatives of what is repressed are foremost among the things reprehended by the ego-criticizing.

7. In Ewers's *Der Student von Prag*, which furnishes the starting-point of Rank's study on the "double," the hero has promised his beloved not to kill his antagonist in a duel. But on his way to the dueling-ground he meets his "double," who has already killed his rival.

come from the circumstance of the "double" being a creation dating back to a very early mental stage — long since left behind, and one, no doubt, in which it wore a more friendly aspect. The "double" has become a thing of terror, just as after the fall of their religion the gods took on demonic shapes.[8]

The other forms of ego-disturbance exploited by Hoffmann can easily be estimated along the same lines as the theme of the double. They are a harking-back to particular phases in the evolution of the self-regarding feeling, a regression to a time when the ego was not yet sharply differentiated from the external world and from other persons. I believe that these factors are partly responsible for the impression of the uncanny, although it is not easy to isolate and determine exactly their share of it.

That factor of the repetition of the same thing will perhaps not appeal to everyone as a source of uncanny feeling. From what I have observed, this phenomenon does undoubtedly, subject to certain conditions and combined with certain circumstances, awaken an uncanny feeling, which recalls that sense of helplessness sometimes experienced in dreams. Once, as I was walking through the deserted streets of a provincial town in Italy which was strange to me, on a hot summer afternoon, I found myself in a quarter the character of which could not long remain in doubt. Nothing but painted women were to be seen at the windows of the small houses, and I hastened to leave the narrow street at the next turning. But after having wandered about for a while without being directed, I suddenly found myself back in the same street, where my presence was now beginning to excite attention. I hurried away once more, but only to arrive yet a third time by devious paths in the same place. Now, however, a feeling overcame me which I can only describe as uncanny, and I was glad enough to abandon my exploratory walk and get straight back to the piazza I had left a short while before. Other situations having in common with my adventure an involuntary return to the same situation, but which differ radically from it in other respects, also result in the same feeling of helplessness and of something uncanny. As, for instance, when one is lost in a forest in high altitudes, caught, we will suppose, by the mountain mist, and when every endeavour to find the marked or familiar path ends again and again in a return to one and the same spot, recognizable by some particular landmark. Or when one wanders about in a dark, strange room looking for the door or the electric switch, and collides for the hundredth time with the same piece of furniture — a situation which, indeed, has been made irresistibly comic by Mark Twain, through the wild extravagance of his narration.

If we take another class of things, it is easy to see that here, too, it is only this factor of involuntary repetition which surrounds with an uncanny atmosphere what would otherwise be innocent enough, and forces upon us the idea of something fateful and unescapable where otherwise we

---

8. Heine, *Die Götter im Exil*.

should have spoken of "chance" only. For instance, we of course attach no importance to the event when we give up a coat and get a cloakroom ticket with the number, say, 62; or when we find that our cabin on board ship is numbered 62. But the impression is altered if two such events, each in itself indifferent, happen close together, if we come across the number 62 several times in a single day, or if we begin to notice that everything which has a number — addresses, hotel-rooms, compartments in railway-trains — always has the same one, or one which at least contains the same figures.

We do feel this to be "uncanny," and unless a man is utterly hardened and proof against the lure of superstition he will be tempted to ascribe a secret meaning to this obstinate recurrence of a number, taking it, perhaps, as an indication of the span of life allotted to him. Or suppose one is engaged at the time in reading the works of Hering, the famous physiologist, and then receives within the space of a few days two letters from two different countries, each from a person called Hering; whereas one has never before had any dealings with anyone of that name. Not long ago an ingenious scientist attempted to reduce coincidences of this kind to certain laws, and so deprive them of their uncanny effect.[9] I will not venture to decide whether he has succeeded or not.

How exactly we can trace back the uncanny effect of such recurrent similarities to infantile psychology is a question I can only lightly touch upon in these pages; and I must refer the reader instead to another pamphlet[10] now ready for publication, in which this has been gone into in detail, but in a different connection. For it is possible to recognize the dominance in the unconscious mind of a 'compulsion to repeat' proceeding from the instinctual impulses and probably inherent in the very nature of the instincts — a principle powerful enough to overrule the pleasure principle, lending to certain aspects of the mind their daemonic character, and still very clearly expressed in the tendencies of small children; a principle, too, which is responsible for a part of the course taken by the analyses of neurotic patients. Taken in all, the foregoing prepares us for the discovery that whatever reminds us of this inner *repetition-compulsion* is perceived as uncanny.

Now, however, it is time to turn from these aspects of the matter, which are in any case difficult to decide upon, and look for undeniable instances of the uncanny, in the hope that analysis of them will settle whether our hypothesis is a valid one.

In the story of "The Ring of Polycrates," the guest turns away from his friend with horror because he sees that his every wish is at once fulfilled, his every care immediately removed by kindly fate. His host has become "uncanny" to him. His own explanation, that the too fortunate man has to fear the envy of the gods, seems still rather obscure to us; its meaning is

9. P. Kammere, *Das Gesetz der Serie.*
10. [*Beyond the Pleasure Principle.* — Trans.]

veiled in mythological language. We will therefore turn to another example in a less grandiose setting. In the case history of an obsessional neurotic,[11] I have described how the patient once stayed in a hydropathic establishment and benefited greatly by it. He had the good sense, however, to attribute his improvement not to the therapeutic properties of the water, but to the situation of his room, which immediately adjoined that of a very amiable nurse. So on his second visit to the establishment he asked for the same room but was told that it was already occupied by an old gentleman, whereupon he gave vent to his annoyance in the words, "Well, I hope he'll have a stroke and die." A fortnight later the old gentleman really did have a stroke. My patient thought this an "uncanny" experience. And that impression of uncanniness would have been stronger still if less time had elapsed between his exclamation and the untoward event, or if he had been able to produce innumerable similar coincidences. As a matter of fact, he had no difficulty in producing coincidences of this sort, but then not only he but all obsessional neurotics I have observed are able to relate analogous experiences. They are never surprised when they invariably run up against the person they have just been thinking of, perhaps for the first time for many months. If they say one day "I haven't had news of so-and-so for a long time," they will be sure to get a letter from him the next morning. And an accident or a death will rarely take place without having cast its shadow before on their minds. They are in the habit of mentioning this state of affairs in the most modest manner, saying that they have "presentiments" which "usually" come true.

One of the most uncanny and wide-spread forms of superstition is the dread of the evil eye.[12] There never seems to have been any doubt about the source of this dread. Whoever possesses something at once valuable and fragile is afraid of the envy of others, in that he projects on to them the envy he would have felt in their place. A feeling like this betrays itself in a look even though it is not put into words; and when a man attracts the attention of others by noticeable, and particularly by unattractive, attributes, they are ready to believe that his envy is rising to more than usual heights and that this intensity in it will convert it into effective action. What is feared is thus a secret intention of harming someone, and certain signs are taken to mean that such an intention is capable of becoming an act.

These last examples of the uncanny are to be referred to that principle in the mind which I have called "omnipotence of thoughts," taking the name from an expression used by one of my patients. And now we find ourselves on well-known ground. Our analysis of instances of the uncanny has led us back to the old, animistic conception of the universe which was characterized by the idea that the world was peopled with the spirits of

---

11. Freud, "Notes upon a Case of Obsessional Neurosis," *Collected Papers*, vol. iii.
12. Seligmann, the Hamburg ophthalmologist, has made a thorough study of this superstition in his *Der böse Blick und Verwandtes*.

humane narcissistic overestimation of subjective mental processes (such as the belief in the omnipotence of thoughts, the magical practices based upon this belief, the carefully proportioned distribution of magical powers or "mana" among various outside persons and things), as well as by all those other figments of the imagination with which man, in the unrestricted narcissism of that stage of development, strove to withstand the inexorable laws of reality. It would seem as though each one of us has been through a phase of individual development corresponding to that animistic stage in primitive men, that none of us has traversed it without preserving certain traces of it which can be reactivated and that everything which now strikes us as "uncanny" fulfills the condition of stirring these vestiges of animistic mental activity within us and bringing them to expression.[13]

At this point I will put forward two considerations which, I think, contain the gist of this short study. In the first place, if psycho-analytic theory is correct in maintaining that every emotional affect, whatever its quality, is transformed by repression into morbid anxiety, then among such cases of anxiety there must be a class in which the anxiety can be shown to come from something repressed which *recurs*. This class of morbid anxiety would then be no other than what is uncanny, irrespective of whether it originally aroused dread or some other affect. In the second place, if this is indeed the secret nature of the uncanny, we can understand why the usage of speech has extended *das Heimliche* into its opposite *das Unheimliche*;[14] for this uncanny is in reality nothing new or foreign, but something familiar and old — established in the mind that has been estranged only by the process of repression. This reference to the factor of repression enables us, furthermore, to understand Schelling's definition of the uncanny as something which ought to have been kept concealed but which has nevertheless come to light. . . .

Jean Baudrillard

The Precession of Simulacra

(1981)

Jean Baudrillard (1929–2007) was a French philosopher and literary critic whose ideas have been influential in the analysis of contemporary art, culture,

13. Cf. my book *Totem and Tabu*, part iii, "Animismus Magie und Allmacht der Gedanken"; also the footnote on p. 7 of the same book. "It would appear that we invest with a feeling of uncanniness those impressions which lend support to a belief in the omnipotence of thoughts and to the animistic attitude of mind at a time when our judgment has already rejected these same beliefs."
14. Cf. abstract on pp. 155–56.

Translated by Sheila Faria Glaser.

and politics. In this important essay, which appears in his book *Simulacra and Simulation*, Baudrillard argues that in the world created by modern postindustrial capitalism, things have become detached from their meaning. Instead of the worth of an object being directly related to its usefulness, worth is attached to the image of the product. Accordingly, he suggests that we live in a world where artificial simulations are overtaking and indeed replacing reality, because we only interact with those things in the world whose images can be commodified and reproduced. Baudrillard's prose style, his abstractions, and his dramatically provocative assertions make this a challenging text to read but one with obvious and important implications for the theme of artificial life. Fans of sf film may recognize *Simulacra and Simulations* as the title of a book that appears in *The Matrix*. This "book" is where the hero Neo hides his illicit computer programs; fittingly, it has been hollowed out to create an empty holder, just as, in Baudrillard's theory, reality has been emptied out and replaced by illusion.

> The simulacrum is never what hides the truth — it is truth
> that hides the fact that there is none.
> The simulacrum is true.
>
> — Ecclesiastes

The Divine Irreference of Images

To dissimulate is to pretend not to have what one has. To simulate is to feign to have what one doesn't have. One implies a presence, the other an absence. But it is more complicated than that because simulating is not pretending: "Whoever fakes an illness can simply stay in bed and make everyone believe he is ill. Whoever simulates an illness produces in himself some of the symptoms" (Littré). Therefore, pretending, or dissimulating, leaves the principle of reality intact: the difference is always clear, it is simply masked, whereas simulation threatens the difference between the "true" and the "false," the "real" and the "imaginary." Is the simulator sick or not, given that he produces "true" symptoms? Objectively one cannot treat him as being either ill or not ill. Psychology and medicine stop at this point, forestalled by the illness's henceforth undiscoverable truth. For if any symptom can be "produced," and can no longer be taken as a fact of nature, then every illness can be considered as simulatable and simulated, and medicine loses its meaning since it only knows how to treat "real" illnesses according to their objective causes. Psychosomatics evolves in a dubious manner at the borders of the principle of illness. As to psychoanalysis, it transfers the symptom of the organic order to the unconscious order: the latter is new and taken for "real" more real than the other — but why would simulation be at the gates of the unconscious? Why couldn't the "work" of the unconscious be "produced" in the same way as any old symptom of classical medicine? Dreams already are.

Certainly, the psychiatrist purports that "for every form of mental alienation there is a particular order in the succession of symptoms of which the simulator is ignorant and in the absence of which the psychiatrist would not be deceived." This (which dates from 1865) in order to safeguard the principle of a truth at all costs and to escape the interrogation posed by simulation — the knowledge that truth, reference, objective cause have ceased to exist. Now, what can medicine do with what floats on either side of illness, on either side of health, with the duplication of illness in a discourse that is no longer either true or false? What can psychoanalysis do with the duplication of the discourse of the unconscious in the discourse of simulation that can never again be unmasked, since it is not false either?[1]

What can the army do about simulators? Traditionally it unmasks them and punishes them, according to a clear principle of identification. Today it can discharge a very good simulator as exactly equivalent to a "real" homosexual, a heart patient, or a madman. Even military psychology draws back from Cartesian certainties and hesitates to make the distinction between true and false, between the "produced" and the authentic symptom. "If he is this good at acting crazy, it's because he is." Nor is military psychology mistaken in this regard: In this sense, all crazy people simulate, and this lack of distinction is the worst kind of subversion. It is against this lack of distinction that classical reason armed itself in all its categories. But it is what today again outflanks them, submerging the principle of truth.

Beyond medicine and the army, favored terrains of simulation, the question returns to religion and the simulacrum of divinity: "I forbade that there be any simulacra in the temples because the divinity that animates nature can never be represented." Indeed it can be. But what becomes of the divinity when it reveals itself in icons, when it is multiplied in simulacra? Does it remain the supreme power that is simply incarnated in images as a visible theology? Or does it volatilize itself in the simulacra that, alone, deploy their power and pomp of fascination — the visible machinery of icons substituted for the pure and intelligible Idea of God? This is precisely what was feared by Iconoclasts, whose millennial quarrel is still with us today.[2] This is precisely because they predicted this omnipotence of simulacra, the faculty simulacra have of effacing God from the conscience of man, and the destructive, annihilating truth that they allow to appear — that deep down God never existed, that only the simulacrum ever existed, even that God himself was never anything but his own simulacrum — from this came their urge to destroy the images. If they could have believed that these images only obfuscated or masked the Platonic Idea of God, there would have been no reason to destroy them. One can live with the idea of distorted truth. But their metaphysical despair came from the idea that the image didn't conceal anything at all, and that these

1. A discourse that is itself not susceptible to being resolved in transference. It is the entanglement of these two discourses that renders psychoanalysis interminable.
2. Cf. M. Perniola, *Icônes, visions, simulacres* (Icons, visions, simulacra), 39.

images were in essence not images, such as an original model would have made them, but perfect simulacra, forever radiant with their own fascination. Thus this death of the divine referential must be exorcised at all costs.

One can see that the iconoclasts, whom one accuses of disdaining and negating images, were those who accorded them their true value, in contrast to the iconolaters who only saw reflections in them and were content to venerate a filigree God. On the other hand, one can say that the icon worshipers were the most modern minds, the most adventurous, because, in the guise of having God become apparent in the mirror of images, they were already enacting his death and his disappearance in the epiphany of his representations (which, perhaps, they already knew no longer represented anything, that they were purely a game, but that it was therein the great game lay — knowing also that it is dangerous to unmask images, since they dissimulate the fact that there is nothing behind them).

This was the approach of the Jesuits, who founded their politics on the virtual disappearance of God and on the worldly and spectacular manipulation of consciences — the evanescence of God in the epiphany of power — the end of transcendence, which now only serves as an alibi for a strategy altogether free of influences and signs. Behind the baroqueness of images hides the eminence grise of politics.

This way the stake will always have been the murderous power of images, murderers of the real, murderers of their own model, as the Byzantine icons could be those of divine identity. To this murderous power is opposed that of representations as a dialectical power, the visible and intelligible mediation of the Real. All Western faith and good faith became engaged in this wager on representation: that a sign could refer to the depth of meaning, that a sign could be exchanged for meaning and that something could guarantee this exchange — God of course. But what if God himself can be simulated, that is to say can be reduced to the signs that constitute faith? Then the whole system becomes weightless, it is no longer itself anything but a gigantic simulacrum — not unreal, but a simulacrum, that is to say never exchanged for the real, but exchanged for itself, in an uninterrupted circuit without reference or circumference.

Such is simulation, insofar as it is opposed to representation. Representation stems from the principle of the equivalence of the sign and of the real (even if this equivalence is utopian, it is a fundamental axiom). Simulation, on the contrary, stems from the utopia of the principle of equivalence, *from the radical negation of the sign as value*, from the sign as the reversion and death sentence of every reference. Whereas representation attempts to absorb simulation by interpreting it as a false representation, simulation envelops the whole edifice of representation itself as a simulacrum.

Such would be the successive phases of the image:

it is the reflection of a profound reality;
it masks and denatures a profound reality;
it masks the *absence* of a profound reality;
it has no relation to any reality whatsoever: it is its own pure simulacrum.

In the first case, the image is a *good* appearance — representation is of the sacramental order. In the second, it is an evil appearance — it is of the order of maleficence. In the third, it plays at being an appearance — it is of the order of sorcery. In the fourth, it is no longer of the order of appearances, but of simulation.

The transition from signs that dissimulate something to signs that dissimulate that there is nothing marks a decisive turning point. The first reflects a theology of truth and secrecy (to which the notion of ideology still belongs). The second inaugurates the era of simulacra and of simulation, in which there is no longer a God to recognize his own, no longer a Last Judgment to separate the false from the true, the real from its artificial resurrection, as everything is already dead and resurrected in advance.

When the real is no longer what it was, nostalgia assumes its full meaning. There is a plethora of myths of origin and of signs of reality — a plethora of truth, of secondary objectivity, and authenticity. Escalation of the true, of lived experience, resurrection of the figurative where the object and substance have disappeared. Panic-stricken production of the real and of the referential, parallel to and greater than the panic of material production: This is how simulation appears in the phase that concerns us — a strategy of the real, of the neoreal and the hyperreal that everywhere is the double of a strategy of deterrence.

Ramses, or the Rosy-Colored Resurrection

Ethnology brushed up against its paradoxical death in 1971, the day when the Philippine government decided to return the few dozen Tasaday who had just been discovered in the depths of the jungle, where they had lived for eight centuries without any contact with the rest of the species, to their primitive state, out of the reach of colonizers, tourists, and ethnologists. This at the suggestion of the anthropologists themselves, who were seeing the indigenous people disintegrate immediately upon contact, like mummies in the open air.

In order for ethnology to live, its object must die; by dying, the object takes its revenge for being "discovered" and with its death defies the science that wants to grasp it.

Doesn't all science live on this paradoxical slope to which it is doomed by the evanescence of its object in its very apprehension, and by the pitiless reversal that the dead object exerts on it? Like Orpheus, it always turns around too soon, and, like Eurydice, its object falls back into Hades.

It is against this hell of the paradox that the ethnologists wished to protect themselves by cordoning off the Tasaday with virgin forest. No one can touch them anymore: As in a mine the vein is closed down. Science loses precious capital there, but the object will be safe, lost to science, but intact in its "virginity." It is not a question of sacrifice (science never sacrifices itself, it is always murderous), but of the simulated sacrifice of its object in order to save its reality principle. The Tasaday, frozen in their natural element, will provide a perfect alibi, an eternal guarantee. Here begins an antiethnology that will never end and to which Jaulin, Castaneda, Clastres are various witnesses. In any case, the logical evolution of a science is to distance itself increasingly from its object, until it dispenses with it entirely: Its autonomy is only rendered even more fantastic — it attains its pure form.

The Indian thus returned to the ghetto, in the glass coffin of the virgin forest, again becomes the model of simulation of all the possible Indians *from before ethnology*. This model thus grants itself the luxury to incarnate itself beyond itself in the "brute" reality of these Indians it has entirely reinvented — Savages who are indebted to ethnology for still being Savages: what a turn of events, what a triumph for this science that seemed dedicated to their destruction!

Of course, these savages are posthumous: Frozen, cryogenized, sterilized, protected *to death*, they have become referential simulacra, and science itself has become pure simulation. The same holds true at Cruesot, at the level of the "open" museum where one museumified in situ, as "historical" witnesses of their period, entire working-class neighborhoods, living metallurgic zones, an entire culture, men, women, and children included — gestures, languages, customs fossilized alive as in a snapshot. The museum, instead of being circumscribed as a geometric site, is everywhere now, like a dimension of life. Thus ethnology, rather than circumscribing itself as an objective science, will today, liberated from its object, be applied to all living things and make itself invisible, like an omnipresent fourth dimension, that of the simulacrum. *We are all Tasadays*, Indians who have again become what they were — simulacral Indians who at last proclaim the universal truth of ethnology.

We have all become living specimens in the spectral light of ethnology, or of antiethnology, which is nothing but the pure form of triumphal ethnology, under the sign of dead differences, and of the resurrection of differences. It is thus very naive to look for ethnology in the Savages or in some Third World — it is here, everywhere, in the metropolises, in the White community in a world completely cataloged and analyzed, then *artificially resurrected under the auspices of the real*, in a world of simulation, of the hallucination of truth, of the blackmail of the real, of the murder of every symbolic form and of its hysterical, historical retrospection — a murder of which the Savages, noblesse oblige, were the first victims, but that for a long time has extended to all Western societies.

But in the same breath ethnology grants us its only and final lesson, the secret that kills it (and which the Savages knew better than it did): the vengeance of the dead.

The confinement of the scientific object is equal to the confinement of the mad and the dead. And just as all of society is irremediably contaminated by this mirror of madness that it has held up to itself, science can't help but die contaminated by the death of this object that is its inverse mirror. It is science that masters the objects, but it is the objects that invest it with depth, according to an unconscious reversion, which only gives a dead and circular response to a dead and circular interrogation.

Nothing changes when society breaks the mirror of madness (abolishes the asylums, gives speech back to the insane, etc.) nor when science seems to break the mirror of its objectivity (effacing itself before its object, as in Castaneda, etc.) and to bend down before the "differences." The form produced by confinement is followed by an innumerable, diffracted, sloweddown mechanism. As ethnology collapses in its classical institution, it survives in an antiethnology whose task it is to reinject the difference fiction, the Savage fiction everywhere, to conceal that it is this world, ours, which has again become savage in its way, that is to say, which is devastated by difference and by death.

In the same way, with the pretext of saving the original, one forbade visitors to enter the Lascaux caves, but an exact replica was constructed five hundred meters from it, so that everyone could see them (one glances through a peephole at the authentic cave, and then one visits the reconstituted whole). It is possible that the memory of the original grottoes is itself stamped in the minds of future generations, but from now on there is no longer any difference: The duplication suffices to render both artificial.

In the same way science and technology were recently mobilized to save the mummy of Ramses II, after it was left to rot for several dozen years in the depths of a museum. The West is seized with panic at the thought of not being able to save what the symbolic order had been able to conserve for forty centuries, but out of sight and far from the light of day. Ramses does not signify anything for us, only the mummy is of an inestimable worth because it is what guarantees that accumulation has meaning. Our entire linear and accumulative culture collapses if we cannot stockpile the past in plain view. To this end the pharaohs must be brought out of their tomb and the mummies out of their silence. To this end they must be exhumed and given military honors. They are prey to both science and worms. Only absolute secrecy assured them this millennial power — the mastery over putrefaction that signified the mastery of the complete cycle of exchanges with death. *We* only know how to place our science in service of *repairing* the mummy, that is to say restoring a *visible* order, whereas embalming was a mythical effort that strove to immortalize a *hidden* dimension.

We require a visible past, a visible continuum, a visible myth of origin, which reassures us about our end. Because finally we have never believed in them. Whence this historic scene of the reception of the mummy at the Orly airport. Why? Because Ramses was a great despotic and military figure? Certainly. But mostly because our culture dreams, behind this defunct power that it tries to annex, of an order that would have had nothing to do with it, and it dreams of it because it exterminated it by exhuming it *as its own past.*

We are fascinated by Ramses as Renaissance Christians were by the American Indians, those (human?) beings who had never known the word of Christ. Thus, at the beginning of colonization, there was a moment of stupor and bewilderment before the very possibility of escaping the universal law of the Gospel. There were two possible responses: Either admit that this Law was not universal, or exterminate the Indians to efface the evidence. In general, one contented oneself with converting them, or even simply discovering them, which would suffice to slowly exterminate them.

Thus it would have been enough to exhume Ramses to ensure his extermination by museumification. Because mummies don't rot from worms: They die from being transplanted from a slow order of the symbolic, master over putrefaction and death, to an order of history, science, and museums, our order, which no longer masters anything, which only knows how to condemn what preceded it to decay and death and subsequently to try to revive it with science. Irreparable violence toward all secrets, the violence of a civilization without secrets, hatred of a whole civilization for its own foundation.

And just as with ethnology, which plays at extricating itself from its object to better secure itself in its pure form, *demuseumification* is nothing but another spiral in artificiality. Witness the cloister of Saint-Michel de Cuxa, which one will repatriate at great cost from the Cloisters in New York to reinstall it in "its original site." And everyone is supposed to applaud this restitution (as they did "the experimental campaign to take back the sidewalks" on the Champs Elysées!). Well, if the exportation of the cornices was in effect an arbitrary act, if the Cloisters in New York are an artificial mosaic of all cultures (following a logic of the capitalist centralization of value), their reimportation to the original site is even more artificial: It is a total simulacrum that links up with "reality" through a complete circumvolution.

The cloister should have stayed in New York in its simulated environment, which at least fooled no one. Repatriating it is nothing but a supplementary subterfuge, acting as if nothing had happened and indulging in retrospective hallucination.

In the same way, Americans flatter themselves for having brought the population of Indians back to pre-Conquest levels. One effaces everything and starts over. They even flatter themselves for doing better, for exceeding the original number. This is presented as proof of the superiority of civilization: It will produce more Indians than they themselves were able to do. (With sinister derision, this overproduction is again a means of destroying them: For Indian culture, like all tribal culture, rests on the limitation of the group and the refusal of any "unlimited" increase, as can be seen in Ishi's case. In this way, their demographic "promotion" is just another step toward symbolic extermination.)

Everywhere we live in a universe strangely similar to the original — things are doubled by their own scenario. But this doubling does not signify, as it did traditionally, the imminence of their death — they are already purged of their death, and better than when they were alive; more cheerful, more authentic, in the light of their model, like the faces in funeral homes.

The Hyperreal and the Imaginary

Disneyland is a perfect model of all the entangled orders of simulacra. It is first of all a play of illusions and phantasms: the Pirates, the Frontier, the Future World, etc. This imaginary world is supposed to ensure the success of the operation. But what attracts the crowds the most is without a doubt the social microcosm, the *religious*, miniaturized pleasure of real America, of its constraints and joys. One parks outside and stands in line inside, one is altogether abandoned at the exit. The only phantasmagoria in this imaginary world lies in the tenderness and warmth of the crowd, and in the sufficient and excessive number of gadgets necessary to create the multitudinous effect. The contrast with the absolute solitude of the parking lot — veritable concentration camp — is total. Or, rather: Inside, a whole panoply of gadgets magnetizes the crowd in directed flows — outside, solitude is directed at a single gadget: the automobile. By an extraordinary coincidence (but this derives without a doubt from the enchantment inherent to this universe), this frozen, childlike world is found to have been conceived and realized by a man who is himself now cryogenized: Walt Disney, who awaits his resurrection through an increase of 180 degrees centigrade.

Thus, everywhere in Disneyland the objective profile of America, down to the morphology of individuals and of the crowd, is drawn. All its values are exalted by the miniature and the comic strip. Embalmed and pacified. Whence the possibility of an ideological analysis of Disneyland (L. Marin did it very well in *Utopiques, jeux d'espace* [Utopias, play of space]): digest of the American way of life, panegyric of American values, idealized transposition of a contradictory reality. Certainly. But this masks something else and this "ideological" blanket functions as a cover for a *simulation of the third order*: Disneyland exists in order to hide that it is the "real" country, all of "real" America that *is* Disneyland (a bit like prisons are there to hide that it is the social in its entirety, in its banal omnipresence, that is carceral). Disneyland is presented as imaginary in order to make us believe that the rest is real, whereas all of Los Angeles and the America that surrounds it are no longer real, but belong to the hyperreal order and to the order of simulation. It is no longer a question of a false representation of reality (ideology) but of concealing the fact that the real is no longer real, and thus of saving the reality principle.

The imaginary of Disneyland is neither true nor false, it is a deterrence machine set up in order to rejuvenate the fiction of the real in the opposite camp. Whence the debility of this imaginary, its infantile degeneration. This world wants to be childish in order to make us believe that the adults are elsewhere, in the "real" world, and to conceal the fact that true childishness is everywhere — that it is that of the adults themselves who come here to act the child in order to foster illusions as to their real childishness.

Disneyland is not the only one, however. Enchanted Village, Magic Mountain, Marine World: Los Angeles is surrounded by these imaginary stations that feed reality, the energy of the real to a city whose mystery is precisely that of no longer being anything but a network of incessant, unreal circulation — a city of incredible proportions but without space, without dimension. As much as electrical and atomic power stations, as much as cinema studios, this city, which is no longer anything but an immense scenario and a perpetual pan shot, needs this old imaginary like a sympathetic nervous system made up of childhood signals and faked phantasms.

Disneyland: a space of the regeneration of the imaginary as waste-treatment plants are elsewhere, and even here. Everywhere today one must recycle waste, and the dreams, the phantasms, the historical, fairylike, legendary imaginary of children and adults is a waste product, the first great toxic excrement of a hyperreal civilization. On a mental level, Disneyland is the prototype of this new function. But all the sexual, psychic, somatic recycling institutes, which proliferate in California, belong to the same order. People no longer look at each other, but there are institutes for that. They no longer touch each other, but there is contactotherapy. They no longer walk, but they go jogging, etc. Everywhere one recycles lost faculties, or lost bodies, or lost sociality, or the lost taste for food. One reinvents penury, asceticism, vanished savage naturalness: natural food, health food, yoga. Marshall Sahlins's idea that it is the economy of the market and not of nature at all, that secretes penury, is verified, but at a secondary level: here, in the sophisticated confines of a triumphal market economy is reinvented a penury/sign, a penury/simulacrum, a simulated behavior of the underdeveloped (including the adoption of Marxist tenets) that, in the guise of ecology, of energy crises and the critique of capital, adds a final esoteric aureole to the triumph of an esoteric culture. Nevertheless, maybe a mental catastrophe, a mental implosion and involution without precedent lies in wait for a system of this kind, whose visible signs would be those of this strange obesity, or the incredible coexistence of the most bizarre theories and practices, which correspond to the improbable coalition of luxury, heaven, and money, to the improbable luxurious materialization of life and to undiscoverable contradictions. . . .

The End of the Panopticon[3]

It is still to this ideology of lived experience — exhumation of the real in its fundamental banality, in its radical authenticity — that the American TV verité experiment attempted on the Loud family in 1971 refers: seven months of uninterrupted shooting, three hundred hours of nonstop broadcasting, without a script or a screenplay, the odyssey of a family, its dramas, its joys, its unexpected events, nonstop — in short, a "raw" historical document, and the "greatest television performance, comparable, on the scale of our day-to-day life, to the footage of our landing on the moon." It becomes more complicated because this family fell apart during the filming: A crisis erupted, the Louds separated, etc. Whence that insoluble controversy: Was TV itself responsible? What would have happened *if TV hadn't been there?*

_____

3. The idea of a "panopticon" was suggested by nineteenth-century English philosopher and legal reformer Jeremy Bentham, who proposed that prisons be designed so that prisoners could be seen at all times, but would not know at any given time whether they were being observed. [Ed.]

More interesting is the illusion of filming the Louds *as if TV weren't there*. The producer's triumph was to say: "They lived as if we were not there." An absurd, paradoxical formula — neither true nor false: utopian. The "as if *we* were not there" being equal to "as if *you* were there." It is this utopia, this paradox that fascinated the twenty million viewers, much more than did the "perverse" pleasure of violating someone's privacy. In the "verité" experience it is not a question of secrecy or perversion, but of a sort of frisson of the real, or of an aesthetics of the hyperreal, a frisson of vertiginous and phony exactitude, a frisson of simultaneous distancing and magnification, of distortion of scale, of an excessive transparency. The pleasure of an excess of meaning, when the bar of the sign falls below the usual waterline of meaning: The nonsignifier is exalted by the camera angle. There one sees what the real never was (but "as if you were there"), without the distance that gives us perspectival space and depth vision (but "more real than nature"). Pleasure in the microscopic simulation that allows the real to pass into the hyperreal. (This is also somewhat the case in porno, which is fascinating more on a metaphysical than on a sexual level.)

Besides, this family was already hyperreal by the very nature of its selection: a typical ideal American family, California home, three garages, five children, assured social and professional status, decorative housewife, upper-middle-class standing. In a way it is this statistical perfection that dooms it to death. Ideal heroine of the American way of life, it is, as in ancient sacrifices, chosen in order to be glorified and to die beneath the flames of the medium, a modern *fatum*. Because heavenly fire no longer falls on corrupted cities, it is the camera lens that, like a laser, comes to pierce lived reality in order to put it to death. "The Louds: simply a family who agreed to deliver themselves into the hands of television, and to die by it," the director will say. Thus it is a question of a sacrificial process, of a sacrificial spectacle offered to twenty million Americans. The liturgical drama of a mass society.

TV verité. A term admirable in its ambiguity, does it refer to the truth of this family or to the truth of TV? In fact, it is TV that is the truth of the Louds, it is TV that is true, it is TV that renders true. Truth that is no longer the reflexive truth of the mirror, nor the perspectival truth of the panoptic system and of the gaze, but the manipulative truth of the test that sounds out and interrogates, of the laser that touches and pierces, of computer cards that retain your preferred sequences, of the genetic code that controls your combinations, of cells that inform your sensory universe. It is to this truth that the Loud family was subjected by the medium of TV, and in this sense it amounts to a death sentence (but is it still a question of truth?).

End of the panoptic system. The eye of TV is no longer the source of an absolute gaze, and the ideal of control is no longer that of transparency. This still presupposes an objective space (that of the Renaissance) and the omnipotence of the despotic gaze. It is still, if not a system of confinement, at least a system of mapping. More subtly, but always externally, playing on the opposition of seeing and being seen, even if the panoptic focal point may be blind.

Something else in regard to the Louds. "You no longer watch TV, it is TV that watches you (live)," or again: "You are no longer listening to Don't Panic, it is Don't Panic that is listening to you" — a switch from the panoptic mechanism of surveillance (*Discipline and Punish* [Surveiller et punir])[4] to a system of deterrence, in which the distinction between the passive and the active is abolished. There is no longer any imperative of submission to the model, or to the gaze "YOU are the model!" "YOU are the majority!" Such is the watershed of a hyperreal sociality, in which the real is confused with the model, as in the statistical operation, or with the medium, as in the Louds' operation. Such is the last stage of the social relation, ours, which is no longer one of persuasion (the classical age of propaganda, of ideology, of publicity, etc.) but one of deterrence: "YOU are information, you are the social, you are the event, you are involved, you have the word, etc." An about-face through which it becomes impossible to locate one instance of the model, of power, of the gaze, of the medium itself, because *you* are always already on the other side. No more subject, no more focal point, no more center or periphery: pure flexion or circular inflexion. No more violence or surveillance: only "information," secret virulence, chain reaction, slow implosion, and simulacra of spaces in which the effect of the real again comes into play.

We are witnessing the end of perspectival and panoptic space (which remains a moral hypothesis bound up with all the classical analyses on the "objective" essence of power), and thus to the *very abolition of the spectacular*. Television, for example in the case of the Louds, is no longer a spectacular medium. We are no longer in the society of the spectacle, of which the situationists spoke, nor in the specific kinds of alienation and repression that it implied. The medium itself is no longer identifiable as such, and the confusion of the medium and the message (McLuhan)[5] is

---

4. Baudrillard refers to Michel Foucault's famous book *Discipline and Punish: The Birth of the Modern Prison* (*Surveiller et punir: Naissance de la Prison*, 1975), which analyzes the ideology behind different types of punishment, from torture and execution to incarceration in the modern prison. [Ed.]
5. The medium/message confusion is certainly a corollary of that between the sender and the receiver, thus sealing the disappearance of all dual, polar structures that formed the discursive organization of language, of all determined articulation of meaning reflecting Jakobson's famous grid of functions. That discourse "circulates" is to be taken literally: That is, it no longer goes from one point to another, but it traverses a cycle that *without distinction* includes the positions of transmitter and receiver, now unlocatable as such. Thus there is no instance of power, no instance of transmission — power is something that circulates and whose source can no longer be located, a cycle in which the positions of the dominator and the dominated are exchanged in an endless reversion that is also the end of power in its classical definition. The circularization of power, of knowledge, of discourse puts an end to any localization of instances and poles. In the psychoanalytic interpretation itself, the "power" of the interpreter does not come from any outside instance but from the interpreted himself. This changes everything, because one can always ask of the traditional holders of power where they get their power from. Who made you duke? The king. Who made you king? God. Only God no longer answers. But to the question: who made you a psychoanalyst? the analyst can well reply: You. Thus is expressed, by an inverse simulation, the passage from the "analyzed" to the "analysand," from passive to active, which simply describes the spiraling effect of the shifting of poles, the effect of circularity in which power is lost, is dissolved, is resolved in perfect manipulation (it is no longer of the order of directive power and of the gaze, but of the order of tactility and commutation). See also the state/family circularity assured by the fluctuation and metastatic regulation of the images of the social and the private (J. Donzelot, *La police des familles* [The policing of families]).

the first great formula of this new era. There is no longer a medium in the literal sense: it is now intangible, diffused, and diffracted in the real, and one can no longer even say that the medium is altered by it.

Such a blending, such a viral, endemic, chronic, alarming presence of the medium, without the possibility of isolating the effects — spectralized, like these advertising laser sculptures in the empty space of the event filtered by the medium — dissolution of TV in life, dissolution of life in TV — indiscernible chemical solution: We are all Louds doomed not to invasion, to pressure, to violence and blackmail by the media and the models, but to their induction, to their infiltration, to their illegible violence.

But one must watch out for the negative turn that discourse imposes: It is a question neither of disease nor of a viral infection. One must think instead of the media as if they were, in outer orbit, a kind of genetic code that directs the mutation of the real into the hyperreal, just as the other micromolecular code controls the passage from a representative sphere of meaning to the genetic one of the programmed signal.

It is the whole traditional world of causality that is in question: the perspectival, determinist mode, the "active," critical mode, the analytic mode — the distinction between cause and effect, between active and passive, between subject and object, between the end and the means. It is in this sense that one can say: TV is watching us, TV alienates us, TV manipulates us, TV informs us. . . . In all this, one remains dependent on the analytical conception of the media, on an external active and effective agent, on "perspectival" information with the horizon of the real and of meaning as the vanishing point.

Now, one must conceive of TV along the lines of DNA as an effect in which the opposing poles of determination vanish, according to a nuclear contraction, retraction, of the old polar schema that always maintained a

---

Impossible now to pose the famous question: "From what position do you speak?" — "How do you know?" "From where do you get your power?" without hearing the immediate response: "But it is *of* you (from you) that I speak" — meaning, it is you who are speaking, you who know, you who are the power. Gigantic circumvolution, circumlocution of the spoken word, which is equal to a blackmail with no end, to a deterrence that cannot be appealed of the subject presumed to speak, leaving him without a reply, because to the question that he poses one ineluctably replies: but *you are* the answer, or: your question is already an answer, etc. — the whole strangulatory sophistication of intercepting speech, of the forced confession in the guise of freedom of expression, of trapping the subject in his own interrogation, of the precession of the reply to the question (all the violence of interpretation lies there, as well as that of the conscious or unconscious management of the "spoken word" [*parole*]).

This simulacrum of the inversion or the involution of poles, this clever subterfuge, which is the secret of the whole discourse of manipulation and thus, today, in every domain, the secret of any new power in the erasure of the scene of power, in the assumption of all words from which has resulted this fantastic silent majority characteristic of our time — all of this started without a doubt in the political sphere with the democratic simulacrum, which today is the substitution for the power of God with the power of the people as the source of power, and of power as *emanation* with power as *representation*. Anti-Copernican revolution: no transcendental instance either of the sun or of the luminous sources of power and knowledge — everything comes from the people and everything returns to them. It is with this magnificent recycling that the universal simulacrum of manipulation, from the scenario of mass suffrage to the present-day phantoms of opinion polls, begins to be put in place.

minimal distance between cause and effect, between subject and object: precisely the distance of meaning, the gap, the difference, the smallest possible gap (PPEP!),[6] irreducible under pain of reabsorption into an aleatory and indeterminate process whose discourse can no longer account for it, because it is itself a determined order.

It is this gap that vanishes in the process of genetic coding, in which indeterminacy is not so much a question of molecular randomness as of the abolition, pure and simple, of the *relation*. In the process of molecular control, which "goes" from the DNA nucleus to the "substance" that it "informs," there is no longer the traversal of an effect, of an energy, of a determination, of a message. "Order, signal, impulse, message": All of these attempt to render the thing intelligible to us, but by analogy, retranscribing in terms of inscription, of a vector, of decoding, a dimension of which we know nothing — it is no longer even a "dimension," or perhaps it is the fourth (which is defined, however, in Einsteinian relativity by the absorption of the distinct poles of space and time). In fact, this whole process can only be understood in its negative form: Nothing separates one pole from another anymore, the beginning from the end; there is a kind of contraction of one over the other, a fantastic telescoping, a collapse of the two traditional poles into each other: *implosion* — an absorption of the radiating mode of causality, of the differential mode of determination, with its positive and negative charge — an implosion of meaning. *That is where simulation begins.*

Everywhere, in no matter what domain — political, biological, psychological, mediatized — in which the distinction between these two poles can no longer be maintained, one enters into simulation, and thus into absolute manipulation — not into passivity, but into *the indifferentiation of the active and the passive*. DNA realizes this aleatory reduction at the level of living matter. Television, in the case of the Louds, also reaches this *indefinite* limit in which, vis-à-vis TV, they are neither more nor less active or passive than a living substance is vis-à-vis its molecular code. Here and there, a single nebula whose simple elements are indecipherable, whose truth is indecipherable.

Donna J. Haraway
A Cyborg Manifesto
(1985; 1991)

Literary theorist Donna Haraway (b. 1944) belongs to a school of thought known as post-structuralism, a philosophical and literary theory dating from

6. PPEP is an acronym for smallest gap, or "plus petit écart possible." [Trans.]

the late 1960s. Post-structuralists see traditional Western rationalist philosophy as a flawed system based on dichotomies — paired sets of opposite concepts such as White/Black, male/female, and human/machine — that are presented as natural truths but that are in fact fictional oppositions that serve to heighten the status of one term over the other. Post-structuralist theory seeks to undermine oppressive power relations by showing how these dichotomies are false and always break down under close examination. In this influential essay, Haraway proposes the idea of the cyborg — an amalgam of human and machine, biological and mechanical — as the model for a new form of consciousness and political activism. The cyborg for Haraway represents a hybrid, or mixed, state of being — a more complex, ambiguous, and fluid identity that can free us from the tyranny of binary oppositions in our political and personal relationships. Like many post-structuralist critics, Haraway uses a dense and challenging prose style that may seem daunting at first, but readers who are willing to suspend disbelief will soon begin to enjoy the audacity and evocative force of her metaphors and will discover, as her key terms gradually gain resonance and power over the course of the text, that she is a poet as much as a philosopher.

The interplay of textual references is an essential element of Haraway's writing, but can be daunting for the general reader. Accordingly, some of Haraway's footnotes have been edited for this edition, with the intent of keeping the focus on Haraway's own argument while still conveying a sense of the rich counterpoint these references provide.

AN IRONIC DREAM OF A COMMON LANGUAGE FOR WOMEN IN THE INTEGRATED CIRCUIT

This chapter is an effort to build an ironic political myth faithful to feminism, socialism, and materialism. Perhaps more faithful as blasphemy is faithful, than as reverent worship and identification. Blasphemy has always seemed to require taking things very seriously. I know no better stance to adopt from within the secular-religious, evangelical traditions of United States politics, including the politics of socialist feminism. Blasphemy protects one from the moral majority within, while still insisting on the need for community. Blasphemy is not apostasy. Irony is about contradictions that do not resolve into larger wholes, even dialectically, about the tension of holding incompatible things together because both or all are necessary and true. Irony is about humor and serious play. It is also a rhetorical strategy and a political method, one I would like to see more honored within socialist-feminism. At the center of my ironic faith, my blasphemy, is the image of the cyborg.

A cyborg is a cybernetic organism, a hybrid of machine and organism, a creature of social reality as well as a creature of fiction. Social reality is lived social relations, our most important political construction, a world-changing fiction. The international women's movements have constructed "women's experience," as well as uncovered or discovered this crucial collective object. This experience is a fiction and fact of the most crucial, political kind. Liberation rests on the construction of the consciousness, the imaginative apprehension, of oppression, and so of possibility. The cyborg is a matter of fiction and lived experience that changes what counts as women's experience in the late twentieth century. This is a struggle over life and death, but the boundary between science fiction and social reality is an optical illusion.

Contemporary science fiction is full of cyborgs — creatures simultaneously animal and machine, who populate worlds ambiguously natural and crafted. Modern medicine is also full of cyborgs, of couplings between organism and machine, each conceived as coded devices, in an intimacy and with a power that was not generated in the history of sexuality. Cyborg "sex" restores some of the lovely replicative baroque of ferns and invertebrates (such nice organic prophylactics against heterosexism). Cyborg replication is uncoupled from organic reproduction. Modern production seems like a dream of cyborg colonization work, a dream that makes the nightmare of Taylorism seem idyllic. And modern war is a cyborg orgy, coded by C^3I, command-control-communication-intelligence, an $84 billion item in 1984's U.S. defense budget. I am making an argument for the cyborg as a fiction mapping our social and bodily reality and as an imaginative resource suggesting some very fruitful couplings. Michael Foucault's biopolitics is a flaccid premonition of cyborg politics, a very open field.

By the late twentieth century, our time, a mythic time, we are all chimeras, theorized and fabricated hybrids of machine and organism; in short, we are cyborgs. The cyborg is our ontology; it gives us our politics. The cyborg is a condensed image of both imagination and material reality, the two joined centers structuring any possibility of historical transformation. In the traditions of "Western" science and politics — the tradition of racist, male-dominant capitalism; the tradition of progress; the tradition of the appropriation of nature as resource for the productions of culture; the tradition of reproduction of the self from the reflections of the other — the relation between organism and machine has been a border war. The stakes in the border war have been the territories of production, reproduction, and imagination. This chapter is an argument for *pleasure* in the confusion of boundaries and for *responsibility* in their construction. It is also an effort to contribute to socialist-feminist culture and theory in a postmodernist, non-naturalist mode and in the utopian tradition of imagining a world without gender, which is perhaps a world without genesis, but maybe also a world without end. The cyborg incarnation is outside salvation history. Nor does it mark time on an oedipal calendar, attempting to heal the terrible cleavages of gender in an oral symbiotic utopia or post-oedipal apocalypse. As Zoe Sofoulis argues in her unpublished manuscript on Jacques Lacan, Melanie Klein, and nuclear culture, *Lacklein*, the most terrible and perhaps the most promising monsters in cyborg worlds are embodied in non-oedipal narratives with a different logic of repression, which we need to understand for our survival.

The cyborg is a creature in a post-gender world; it has no truck with bisexuality, pre-oedipal symbiosis, unalienated labor, or other seductions to organic wholeness through a final appropriation of all the powers of the parts into a higher unity. In a sense, the cyborg has no origin story in the Western sense — a "final" irony since the cyborg is also the awful apocalyptic *telos* of the "West's" escalating dominations of abstract individuation, an ultimate self untied at last from all dependency, a man in space. An origin story in the "Western," humanist sense depends on the myth of original unity, fullness, bliss, and terror, represented by the phallic mother from whom all humans must separate, the task of individual development and of history, the twin potent myths inscribed most powerfully for us in psychoanalysis and Marxism. Hilary Klein has argued that both Marxism and psychoanalysis, in their concepts of labor and of individuation and gender formation, depend on the plot of original unity out of which difference must be produced and enlisted in a drama of escalating domination of woman/nature. The cyborg skips the step of original unity, of identification with nature in the Western sense. This is its illegitimate promise that might lead to subversion of its teleology as Star Wars.

The cyborg is resolutely committed to partiality, irony, intimacy, and perversity. It is oppositional, utopian, and completely without innocence. No longer structured by the polarity of public and private, the cyborg defines a technological polis based partly on a revolution of social relations in the *oikos*, the household. Nature and culture are reworked; the one can no longer be the resource for appropriation or incorporation by the other. The relationships for forming wholes from parts, including those of polarity and hierarchical domination, are at issue in the cyborg world. Unlike the hopes of Frankenstein's monster, the cyborg does not expect its father to save it through a restoration of the garden; that is, through the fabrication of a heterosexual mate, through its completion in a finished whole, a city and cosmos. The cyborg does not dream of community on the model of the organic family, this time without the oedipal project. The cyborg would not recognize the Garden of Eden; it is not made of mud and cannot dream of returning to dust. Perhaps that is why I want to see if cyborgs can subvert the apocalypse of returning to nuclear dust in the manic compulsion to name the Enemy. Cyborgs are not reverent; they do not remember the cosmos. They are wary of holism, but needy for connection — they seem to have a natural feel for united front politics, but without the vanguard party. The main trouble with cyborgs, of course, is that they are the illegitimate offspring of militarism and patriarchal capitalism, not to mention state socialism. But illegitimate offspring are often exceedingly unfaithful to their origins. Their fathers, after all, are inessential.

I will return to the science fiction of cyborgs at the end of this chapter, but now I want to signal three crucial boundary breakdowns that make the following political-fictional (political-scientific) analysis possible. By the late twentieth century in United States scientific culture, the boundary between human and animal is thoroughly breached. The last beachheads of uniqueness have been polluted if not turned into amusement parks — language, tool use, social behavior, mental events, nothing really convincingly settles the separation of human and animal. And many people no longer feel the need for such a separation; indeed, many branches of feminist culture affirm the pleasure of connection of human and other living creatures. Movements for animal rights are not irrational denials of human uniqueness; they are a clear-sighted recognition of connection across the discredited breach of nature and culture. Biology and evolutionary theory over the last two centuries have simultaneously produced modern organisms as objects of knowledge and reduced the line between humans and animals to a faint trace re-etched in ideological struggle or professional disputes between life and social science. Within this framework, teaching modern Christian creationism should be fought as a form of child abuse.

Biological-determinist ideology is only one position opened up in scientific culture for arguing the meanings of human animality. There is much room for radical political people to contest the meanings of the breached boundary.[1] The cyborg appears in myth precisely where the boundary between human and animal is transgressed. Far from signalling a walling off of people from other living beings, cyborgs signal disturbingly and pleasurably tight coupling. Bestiality has a new status in this cycle of marriage exchange.

The second leaky distinction is between animal-human (organism) and machine. Pre-cybernetic machines could be haunted; there was always the spectre of the ghost in the machine. This dualism structured the dialogue between materialism and idealism that was settled by a dialectical progeny, called spirit or history, according to taste. But basically machines were not self-moving, self-designing, autonomous. They could not achieve man's dream, only mock it. They were not man, an author to himself, but only a

1. Research was funded by an Academic Senate Faculty Research Grant from the University of California, Santa Cruz. An earlier version of the paper on genetic engineering appeared as "Lieber Kyborg als Göttin: für eine sozialistisch-feministische Unterwanderung der Gentechnologie," in Bernd-Peter Lange and Anna Marie Stuby eds, Berlin: Argument-Sonderband 105, 1984, pp 66–84. The cyborg manifesto grew from my "New machines, new bodies, new communities: political dilemmas of a cyborg feminist" "The Scholar and the Feminist X: The Question of Technology," Conference, Barnard College, April 1983.

The people associated with the History of Consciousness Board of UCSC have had an enormous influence on this paper, so that it feels collectively authored more than most, although those I cite may not recognize their ideas. In particular, members of graduate and undergraduate feminist theory, science, and politics, and theory and methods courses contributed to the cyborg manifesto. Particular debts here are due Hilary Klein, Paul Edwards, Lisa Lowe, and James Clifford.

Parts of the paper were my contribution to a collectively developed session, "Poetic Tools and Political Bodies: Feminist Approaches to High Technology Culture," 1984 California American Studies Association, with History of Consciousness graduate students Zoe Sofoulis, "Jupiter space"; Katie King, "The pleasures of repetition and the limits of identification in feminist science fiction: reimaginations of the body after the cyborg"; and Chela Sandoval, "The construction of subjectivity and oppositional consciousness in feminist film and video."

Barbara Epstein, Jeff Escoffier, Rusten Hogness, and Jaye Miler gave extensive discussion and editorial help. Members of the Silicon Valley Research Project of UCSC and participants in SVRP conferences and workshops were very important, especially Rick Gordon, Linda Kimball, Nancy Snyder, Langdon Winner, Judith Stacey, Linda Lim, Patricia Fernandez-Kelly, and Judith Gregory. Finally, I want to thank Nancy Hartsock for years of friendship and discussion on feminist theory and feminist science fiction. I also thank Elizabeth Bird for my favorite political button: 'Cyborgs for Earthly Survival.'

caricature of that masculinist reproductive dream. To think they were otherwise was paranoid. Now we are not so sure. Late twentieth-century machines have made thoroughly ambiguous the difference between natural and artificial, mind and body, self-developing and externally designed, and many other distinctions that used to apply to organisms and machines. Our machines are disturbingly lively, and we ourselves frighteningly inert.

Technological determination is only one ideological space opened up by the reconceptions of machine and organism as coded texts through which we engage in the play of writing and reading the world. "Textualization" of everything in poststructuralist, postmodernist theory has been damned by Marxists and socialist feminists for its utopian disregard for the lived relations of domination that ground the "play" of arbitrary reading.[2] It is certainly true that postmodernist strategies, like my cyborg myth, subvert myriad organic wholes (for example, the poem, the primitive culture, the biological organism). In short, the certainty of what counts as nature — a source of insight and promise of innocence — is undermined, probably fatally. The transcendent authorization of interpretation is lost, and with it the ontology grounding "Western" epistemology. But the alternative is not cynicism or faithlessness, that is, some version of abstract existence, like the accounts of technological determinism destroying "man" by the "machine" or "meaningful political action" by the "text." Who cyborgs will be is a radical question; the answers are a matter of survival. Both chimpanzees and artefacts have politics, so why shouldn't we (de Waal, 1982; Winner, 1980)?[3]

---

2. A provocative, comprehensive argument about the politics and theories of "postmodernism" is made by Fredric Jameson (1984), ["Post-modernism, or the Cultural Logic of Late Capitalism." *New Left Review* 146: 53–92.] who argues that postmodernism is not an option, a style among others, but a cultural dominant requiring radical reinvention of left politics from within; there is no longer any place from without that gives meaning to the comforting fiction of critical distance. Jameson also makes clear why one cannot be for or against postmodernism, an essentially moralist move. My position is that feminists (and others) need continuous cultural reinvention, postmodernist critique, and historical materialism; only a cyborg would have a chance. The old dominations of white capitalist patriarchy seem nostalgically innocent now: They normalized heterogeneity, into man and woman, white and black, for example. "Advanced capitalism" and postmodernism release heterogeneity without a norm, and we are flattened, without subjectivity, which requires depth, even unfriendly and drowning depths. It is time to write *The Death of the Clinic*. The clinic's methods required bodies and works; we have texts and surfaces. Our dominations don't work by medicalization and normalization any more; they work by networking, communications redesign, stress management. Normalization gives way to automation, utter redundancy. Michel Foucault's *Birth of the Clinic* (1963) [New York: Vintage], *History of Sexuality* (1976) [New York: Pantheon], and *Discipline and Punish* (1975) [New York: Vintage] name a form of power at its moment of implosion. The discourse of biopolitics gives way to technobabble, the language of the spliced substantive; no noun is left whole by the multinationals. These are their names, listed from one issue of *Science*: Tech-Knowledge, Genentech, Allergen, Hybritech, Compupro, Genen-cor, Syntex, Allelix, Agrigenetics Corp., Syntro, Codon, Repligen, MicroAngelo from Scion Corp., Percom Data, Inter Systems, Cyborg Corp., Statcom Corp., Intertec. If we are imprisoned by language, then escape from that prison-house requires language poets, a kind of cultural restriction enzyme to cut the code; cyborg heteroglossia is one form of radical cultural politics.

3. de Waal, Frans (1982). *Chimpanzee Politics: Power and Sex Among the Apes*. New York: Harper & Row; Winner, Langdon (1980). "Do Artifacts Have Politics?" *Daedalus* 109 (1): 121–36. [Ed.]

The third distinction is a subset of the second: The boundary between physical and non-physical is very imprecise for us. Pop physics books on the consequences of quantum theory and the indeterminacy principle are a kind of popular scientific equivalent to Harlequin romances as a marker of radical change in American white heterosexuality: They get it wrong, but they are on the right subject. Modern machines are quintessentially microelectronic devices: They are everywhere and they are invisible. Modern machinery is an irreverent upstart god, mocking the Father's ubiquity and spirituality. The silicon chip is a surface for writing; it is etched in molecular scales disturbed only by atomic noise, the ultimate interference for nuclear scores. Writing, power, and technology are old partners in Western stories of the origin of civilization, but miniaturization has changed our experience of mechanism. Miniaturization has turned out to be about power; small is not so much beautiful as pre-eminently dangerous, as in cruise missiles. Contrast the TV sets of the 1950s or the news cameras of the 1970s with the TV wrist bands or hand-sized video cameras now advertised. Our best machines are made of sunshine; they are all light and clean because they are nothing but signals, electromagnetic waves, a section of a spectrum, and these machines are eminently portable, mobile — a matter of immense human pain in Detroit and Singapore. People are nowhere near so fluid, being both material and opaque. Cyborgs are ether, quintessence.

The ubiquity and invisibility of cyborgs is precisely why these sunshine-belt machines are so deadly. They are as hard to see politically as materially. They are about consciousness — or its simulation. They are floating signifiers moving in pickup trucks across Europe, blocked more effectively by the witch-weavings of the displaced and so unnatural Greenham women, who read the cyborg webs of power so very well, than by the militant labor of older masculinist politics, whose natural constituency needs defense jobs. Ultimately the "hardest" science is about the realm of greatest boundary confusion, the realm of pure number, pure spirit, C^3I, cryptography, and the preservation of potent secrets. The new machines are so clean and light. Their engineers are sun-worshippers mediating a new scientific revolution associated with the night dream of post-industrial society. The diseases evoked by these clean machines are "no more" than the minuscule coding changes of an antigen in the immune system, "no more" than the experience of stress. The nimble fingers of "Oriental" women, the old fascination of little Anglo-Saxon Victorian girls with doll's houses, women's enforced attention to the small take on quite new dimensions in this world. There might be a cyborg Alice taking account of these new dimensions. Ironically, it might be the unnatural cyborg women making chips in Asia and spiral dancing in Santa Rita jail[4] whose constructed unities will guide effective oppositional strategies.

So my cyborg myth is about transgressed boundaries, potent fusions, and dangerous possibilities which progressive people might explore as one

4. A practice at once both spiritual and political that linked guards and arrested antinuclear demonstrators in the Alameda County jail in California in the early 1980s.

part of needed political work. One of my premises is that most American socialists and feminists see deepened dualisms of mind and body, animal and machine, idealism and materialism in the social practices, symbolic formulations, and physical artefacts associated with "high technology" and scientific culture. From *One-Dimensional Man* (Marcuse, 1964) to *The Death of Nature* (Merchant, 1980),[5] the analytic resources developed by progressives have insisted on the necessary domination of technics and recalled us to an imagined organic body to integrate our resistance. Another of my premises is that the need for unity of people trying to resist world-wide intensification of domination has never been more acute. But a slightly perverse shift of perspective might better enable us to contest for meanings, as well as for other forms of power and pleasure in technologically mediated societies.

From one perspective, a cyborg world is about the final imposition of a grid of control on the planet, about the final abstraction embodied in a Star Wars apocalypse waged in the name of defense, about the final appropriation of women's bodies in a masculinist orgy of war (Sofia, 1984).[6] From another perspective, a cyborg world might be about lived social and bodily realities in which people are not afraid of their joint kinship with animals and machines, not afraid of permanently partial identities and contradictory standpoints. The political struggle is to see from both perspectives at once because each reveals both dominations and possibilities unimaginable from the other vantage point. Single vision produces worse illusions than double vision or many-headed monsters. Cyborg unities are monstrous and illegitimate; in our present political circumstances, we could hardly hope for more potent myths for resistance and recoupling. I like to imagine LAG, the Livermore Action Group, as a kind of cyborg society, dedicated to realistically converting the laboratories that most fiercely embody and spew out the tools of technological apocalypse, and committed to building a political form that actually manages to hold together witches, engineers, elders, perverts, Christians, mothers, and Leninists long enough to disarm the state. Fission Impossible is the name of the affinity group in my town. (Affinity: related not by blood but by choice, the appeal of one chemical nuclear group for another, avidity.)[7] . . .

---

5. Marcuse, Herbert (1964). *One-Dimensional Man: Studies in the Ideology of Advanced Industrial Society.* Boston: Beacon; Merchant, Carolyn (1980). *The Death of Nature: Women, Ecology, and the Scientific Revolution.* New York: Harper & Row. [Ed.]
6. Sofia, Zoe (1984). "Jupiter Space." Paper delivered at the American Studies Association, Pomona, CA. [Ed.]
7. Without explicit irony, adopting the spaceship earth/whole earth logo of the planet photographed from space, set off by the slogan "Love Your Mother," the May 1987 Mothers and Others Day action at the nuclear weapons testing facility in Nevada none the less took account of the tragic contradictions of views of the earth. Demonstrators applied for official permits to be on the land from officers of the Western Shoshone tribe, whose territory was invaded by the U.S. government when it built the nuclear weapons test ground in the 1950s. Arrested for trespassing, the demonstrators argued that the police and weapons facility personnel, without authorization from the proper officials, were the trespassers. One affinity group at the women's action called themselves the Surrogate Others; and in solidarity with the creatures forced to tunnel in the same ground with the bomb, they enacted a cyborgian emergence from the constructed body of a large, non-heterosexual desert worm.

THE INFORMATICS OF DOMINATION

In this attempt at an epistemological and political position, I would like to sketch a picture of possible unity, a picture indebted to socialist and feminist principles of design. The frame for my sketch is set by the extent and importance of rearrangements in world-wide social relations tied to science and technology. I argue for a politics rooted in claims about fundamental changes in the nature of class, race, and gender in an emerging system of world order analogous in its novelty and scope to that created by industrial capitalism; we are living through a movement from an organic, industrial society to a polymorphous, information system — from all work to all play, a deadly game. Simultaneously material and ideological, the dichotomies may be expressed in the following chart of transitions from the comfortable old hierarchical dominations to the scary new networks I have called the informatics of domination:

Representation	Simulation
Bourgeois novel, realism	Science fiction, postmodernism
Organism	Biotic component
Depth, integrity	Surface, boundary
Heat	Noise
Biology as clinical practice	Biology as inscription
Physiology	Communications engineering
Small group	Subsystem
Perfection	Optimization
Eugenics	Population Control
Decadence, *Magic Mountain*	Obsolescence, *Future Shock*
Hygiene	Stress Management
Microbiology, tuberculosis	Immunology, AIDS
Organic division of labor	Ergonomics/cybernetics of labor
Functional specialization	Modular construction
Reproduction	Replication
Organic sex role specialization	Optimal genetic strategies
Biological determinism	Evolutionary inertia, constraints
Community ecology	Ecosystem
Racial chain of being	Neo-imperialism, United Nations humanism
Scientific management in home/ factory	Global factory/Electronic cottage
Family/Market/Factory	Women in the Integrated Circuit
Family wage	Comparable worth
Public/Private	Cyborg citizenship
Nature/Culture	Fields of difference
Co-operation	Communications enhancement
Freud	Lacan
Sex	Genetic engineering
Labor	Robotics
Mind	Artificial Intelligence

Second World War	Star Wars
White Capitalist Patriarchy	Informatics of Domination

This list suggests several interesting things. First, the objects on the right-hand side cannot be coded as "natural," a realization that subverts naturalistic coding for the left-hand side as well. We cannot go back ideologically or materially. It's not just that "god" is dead; so is the "goddess." Or both are revivified in the worlds charged with microelectronic and biotechnological politics. In relation to objects like biotic components, one must think not in terms of essential properties, but in terms of design, boundary constraints, rates of flows, systems logics, costs of lowering constraints. Sexual reproduction is one kind of reproductive strategy among many, with costs and benefits as a function of the system environment. Ideologies of sexual reproduction can no longer reasonably call on notions of sex and sex role as organic aspects in natural objects like organisms and families. Such reasoning will be unmasked as irrational, and ironically corporate executives reading *Playboy* and anti-porn radical feminists will make strange bedfellows in jointly unmasking the irrationalism.

Likewise for race, ideologies about human diversity have to be formulated in terms of frequencies of parameters, like blood groups or intelligence scores. It is "irrational" to invoke concepts like primitive and civilized. For liberals and radicals, the search for integrated social systems gives way to a new practice called "experimental ethnography" in which an organic object dissipates in attention to the play of writing. At the level of ideology, we see translations of racism and colonialism into languages of development and under-development, rates and constraints of modernization. Any objects or persons can be reasonably thought of in terms of disassembly and reassembly; no "natural" architectures constrain system design. The financial districts in all the world's cities, as well as the export processing and free-trade zones, proclaim this elementary fact of "late capitalism." The entire universe of objects that can be known scientifically must be formulated as problems in communications engineering (for the managers) or theories of the text (for those who would resist). Both are cyborg semiologies.

One should expect control strategies to concentrate on boundary conditions and interfaces, on rates of flow across boundaries — and not on the integrity of natural objects. "Integrity" or "sincerity" of the Western self gives way to decision procedures and expert systems. For example, control strategies applied to women's capacities to give birth to new human beings will be developed in the languages of population control and maximization of goal achievement for individual decision-makers. Control strategies will be formulated in terms of rates, costs of constraints, degrees of freedom. Human beings, like any other component or subsystem, must be localized in a system architecture whose basic modes of operation are probabilistic, statistical. No objects, spaces, or bodies are sacred in themselves; any component can be interfaced with any other if the proper standard, the proper code, can be constructed for processing signals in a common language. Exchange in this world transcends the universal translation effected by capitalist markets that Marx analyzed so well. The privileged pathology affecting all kinds of components in this universe is stress — communications breakdown (Hogness, 1983).[8] The cyborg is not subject to Foucault's biopolitics; the cyborg simulates politics, a much more potent field of operations.

This kind of analysis of scientific and cultural objects of knowledge which have appeared historically since the Second World War prepares us to notice some important inadequacies in feminist analysis which has proceeded as if the organic, hierarchical dualisms ordering discourse in "the West" since Aristotle still ruled. They have been cannibalized, or as Zoe Sofia (Sofoulis) might put it, they have been "techno-digested." The dichotomies between mind and body, animal and human, organism and machine, public and private, nature and culture, men and women, primitive and civilized are all in question ideologically. The actual situation of women is their integration/exploitation into a world system of production/reproduction and communication called the informatics of domination. The home, workplace, market, public arena, the body itself — all can be dispersed and interfaced in nearly infinite, polymorphous ways, with large consequences for women and others — consequences that themselves are very different for different people and which make potent oppositional international movements difficult to imagine and essential for survival. One important route for reconstructing socialist-feminist politics is through theory and practice addressed to the social relations of science and technology, including crucially the systems of myth and meanings structuring our imaginations. The cyborg is a kind of disassembled and reassembled, postmodern collective and personal self. This is the self feminists must code.

Communications technologies and biotechnologies are the crucial tools recrafting our bodies. These tools embody and enforce new social relations for women world-wide. Technologies and scientific discourses can be partially understood as formalizations, i.e., as frozen moments, of the fluid social interactions constituting them, but they should also be viewed as instruments for enforcing meanings. The boundary is permeable between tool and myth, instrument and concept, historical systems of social relations and historical anatomies of possible bodies, including objects of knowledge. Indeed, myth and tool mutually constitute each other.

Furthermore, communications sciences and modern biologies are constructed by a common move — *the translation of the world into a problem of coding*, a search for a common language in which all resistance to instrumental control disappears and all heterogeneity can be submitted to disassembly, reassembly, investment, and exchange.

In communications sciences, the translation of the world into a problem in coding can be illustrated by looking at cybernetic (feedback-

---

8. Hogness, E. Rusten (1983). "Why Stress? A Look at the Making of Stress, 1936–56." Unpublished paper. [Ed.]

controlled) systems theories applied to telephone technology, computer design, weapons deployment, or database construction and maintenance. In each case, solution to the key questions rests on a theory of language and control; the key operation is determining the rates, directions, and probabilities of flow of a quantity called information. The world is subdivided by boundaries differentially permeable to information. Information is just that kind of quantifiable element (unit, basis of unity) which allows universal translation, and so unhindered instrumental power (called effective communication). The biggest threat to such power is interruption of communication. Any system breakdown is a function of stress. The fundamentals of this technology can be condensed into the metaphor C^3I, command-control-communication-intelligence, the military's symbol for its operations theory.

In modern biologies, the translation of the world into a problem in coding can be illustrated by molecular genetics, ecology, sociobiological evolutionary theory, and immunobiology. The organism has been translated into problems of genetic coding and read-out. Biotechnology, a writing technology, informs research broadly. In a sense, organisms have ceased to exist as objects of knowledge, giving way to biotic components, i.e., special kinds of information-processing devices. The analogous moves in ecology could be examined by probing the history and utility of the concept of the ecosystem. Immunobiology and associated medical practices are rich exemplars of the privilege of coding and recognition systems as objects of knowledge, as constructions of bodily reality for us. Biology here is a kind of cryptography. Research is necessarily a kind of intelligence activity. Ironies abound. A stressed system goes awry; its communication processes break down; it fails to recognize the difference between self and other. Human babies with baboon hearts evoke national ethical perplexity — for animal rights activists at least as much as for the guardians of human purity. In the United States gay men and intravenous drug users are the "privileged" victims of an awful immune system disease that marks (inscribes on the body) confusion of boundaries and moral pollution (Treichler, 1987).[9]

But these excursions into communications sciences and biology have been at a rarefied level; there is a mundane, largely economic reality to support my claim that these sciences and technologies indicate fundamental transformations in the structure of the world for us. Communications technologies depend on electronics. Modern states, multinational corporations, military power, welfare state apparatuses, satellite systems, political processes, fabrication of our imaginations, labor-control systems, medical constructions of our bodies, commercial pornography, the international division of labor, and religious evangelism depend intimately upon electronics. Microelectronics is the technical basis of simulacra; that is, of copies without originals.

9. Treichler, Paula (1987). "AIDS, Homophobia, and Biomedical Discourse: An Epidemic of Signification." *October* 43: 31–70.

Microelectronics mediates the translations of labor into robotics and word processing, sex into genetic engineering and reproductive technologies, and mind into artificial intelligence and decision procedures. The new biotechnologies concern more than human reproduction. Biology as a powerful engineering science for redesigning materials and processes has revolutionary implications for industry, perhaps most obvious today in areas of fermentation, agriculture, and energy. Communications sciences and biology are constructions of natural-technical objects of knowledge in which the difference between machine and organism is thoroughly blurred; mind, body, and tool are on very intimate terms. The "multinational" material organization of the production and reproduction of daily life and the symbolic organization of the production and reproduction of culture and imagination seem equally implicated. The boundary-maintaining images of base and superstructure, public and private, or material and ideal never seemed more feeble.

I have used Rachel Grossman's (1980) image of women in the integrated circuit to name the situation of women in a world so intimately restructured through the social relations of science and technology.[10] I used the odd circumlocution, "the social relations of science and technology," to indicate that we are not dealing with a technological determinism, but with a historical system depending upon structured relations among people. But the phrase should also indicate that science and technology provide fresh sources of power, that we need fresh sources of analysis and political action (Latour, 1984).[11] Some of the rearrangements of race, sex, and class rooted in high-tech-facilitated social relations can make socialist-feminism more relevant to effective progressive politics. . . .

CYBORGS: A MYTH OF POLITICAL IDENTITY

I want to conclude with a myth about identity and boundaries which might inform late twentieth-century political imaginations. I am indebted in this story to writers like Joanna Russ, Samuel R. Delany, John Varley, James Tiptree Jr., Octavia Butler, Monique Wittig, and Vonda McIntyre.[12] These are our story-tellers exploring what it means to be embodied in high-tech worlds. They are theorists for cyborgs. Exploring conceptions of bodily boundaries and social order, the anthropologist Mary Douglas (1966, 1970)[13] should be credited with helping us to consciousness about how

---

10. Grossman, Rachel (1980). "Women's Place in the Integrated Circuit." *Radical America* 14 (1): 29–50.

11. Latour, Bruno (1984). *Les Microbes, Guerre et Paix, Ruivi des Irréductions*. Paris: Métailié.

12. Monique Wittig is a French feminist, author of *The Lesbian Body* (1973, New York: Avon), as well as a feminist utopian novel, *Les Gouérillieres*. All others in this list are American science fiction writers. Haraway credits the following essay for bringing these writers to her attention: Katie King (1984), "The Pleasure of Repetition and the Limits of Identification in Feminist Science Fiction: Reimaginations of the Body After the Cyborg." Paper delivered at the American Studies Association, Pomona, CA. [Ed.]

13. Douglas, Mary (1966). *Purity and Danger*. London: Routledge (1970). *Natural Symbols*. London: Cresset. [Ed.]

fundamental body imagery is to world view, and so to political language. French feminists like Luce Irigaray and Monique Wittig, for all their differences, know how to write the body; how to weave eroticism, cosmology, and politics from imagery of embodiment, and especially for Wittig, from imagery of fragmentation and reconstitution of bodies.[14]

American radical feminists like Susan Griffin, Audre Lorde, and Adrienne Rich have profoundly affected our political imaginations — and perhaps restricted too much what we allow as a friendly body and political language.[15] They insist on the organic, opposing it to the technological. But their symbolic systems and the related positions of ecofeminism and feminist paganism, replete with organicisms, can only be understood in Sandoval's terms as oppositional ideologies fitting the late twentieth century. They would simply bewilder anyone not preoccupied with the machines and consciousness of late capitalism. In that sense they are part of the cyborg world. But there are also great riches for feminists in explicitly embracing the possibilities inherent in the breakdown of clean distinctions between organism and machine and similar distinctions structuring the Western self. It is the simultaneity of breakdowns that cracks the matrices of domination and opens geometric possibilities. What might be learned from personal and political "technological" pollution? I look briefly at two overlapping groups of texts for their insight into the construction of a potentially helpful cyborg myth: constructions of women of color and monstrous selves in feminist science fiction.

Earlier I suggested that "women of color" might be understood as a cyborg identity, a potent subjectivity synthesized from fusions of outsider identities and in the complex political-historical layerings of her biomythography. . . . There are material and cultural grids mapping this potential. Audre Lorde (1984) captures the tone in the title of her *Sister Outsider*. In my political myth, Sister Outsider is the offshore woman, whom U.S. workers, female and feminized, are supposed to regard as the enemy preventing their solidarity, threatening their security. Onshore, inside the boundary of the United States, Sister Outsider is a potential amidst the races and ethnic identities of women manipulated for division, competition, and exploitation in the same industries. "Women of color" are the preferred labor force for the science-based industries, the real women for whom the world-wide sexual market, labor market, and politics of reproduction kaleidoscope into daily life. Young Korean women hired in the sex industry and in electronics assembly are recruited from high schools, educated for the integrated circuit. Literacy, especially in English, distinguishes the "cheap" female labor so attractive to the multinationals.

14. Wittig, Monique (1973). *The Lesbian Body*. New York: Avon; Irigaray, Luce (1977). *Ce Sexe Qui N'en est pas Un*. Paris: Minuit. [Ed.]

15. But all these poets are very complex, not least in their treatment of themes of lying and erotic, decentred collective and personal identities. Griffin, Susan (1978). *Women and Nature: The Roaring Inside Her*. New York: Harper & Row; Lorde, Audre (1984). *Sister Outsider*. Trumansberg, NY: Crossing; Rich, Adrienne (1978). *The Dream of a Common Language*. New York: Norton.

Contrary to orientalist stereotypes of the "oral primitive," literacy is a special mark of women of color, acquired by U.S. black women as well as men through a history of risking death to learn and to teach reading and writing. Writing has a special significance for all colonized groups. Writing has been crucial to the Western myth of the distinction between oral and written cultures, primitive and civilized mentalities, and more recently to the erosion of that distinction in "postmodernist" theories attacking the phallogocentrism of the West, with its worship of the monotheistic, phallic, authoritative, and singular work, the unique and perfect name. Contests for the meanings of writing are a major form of contemporary political struggle. Releasing the play of writing is deadly serious. The poetry and stories of U.S. women of color are repeatedly about writing, about access to the power to signify; but this time that power must be neither phallic nor innocent. Cyborg writing must not be about the Fall, the imagination of a once-upon-a-time wholeness before language, before writing, before Man. Cyborg writing is about the power to survive, not on the basis of original innocence, but on the basis of seizing the tools to mark the world that marked them as other.

The tools are often stories, retold stories, versions that reverse and displace the hierarchical dualisms of naturalized identities. In retelling origin stories, cyborg authors subvert the central myths of origin of Western culture. We have all been colonized by those origin myths, with their longing for fulfillment in apocalypse. The phallogocentric origin stories most crucial for feminist cyborgs are built into the literal technologies — technologies that write the world, biotechnology and microelectronics — that have recently textualized our bodies as code problems on the grid of C^3I. Feminist cyborg stories have the task of recoding communication and intelligence to subvert command and control.

Figuratively and literally, language politics pervade the struggles of women of color; and stories about language have a special power in the rich contemporary writing by U.S. women of color. For example, retellings of the story of the indigenous woman Malinche, mother of the mestizo "bastard" race of the new world, master of languages, and mistress of Cortés, carry special meaning for Chicana constructions of identity. Cherríe Moraga (1983) in *Loving in the War Years* explores the themes of identity when one never possessed the original language, never told the original story, never resided in the harmony of legitimate heterosexuality in the garden of culture, and so cannot base identity on a myth or a fall from innocence and right to natural names, mother's or father's.[16] Moraga's writing, her superb literacy, is presented in her poetry as the same kind of violation as Malinche's mastery of the conqueror's language — a violation, an illegitimate production, that allows survival. Moraga's language is not "whole," it is self-consciously spliced, a chimera of English and Spanish, both conqueror's languages. But it is this chimeric monster, without claim to an original

16. Moraga, Cherríe (1983). *Loving in the War Years: Lo que Nunca Pasó por Sus Labios*. Boston: South End. [Ed.]

language before violation, that crafts the erotic, competent, potent identities of women of color. Sister Outsider hints at the possibility of world survival not because of her innocence, but because of her ability to live on the boundaries, to write without the founding myth of original wholeness, with its inescapable apocalypse of final return to a deathly oneness that Man has imagined to be the innocent and all-powerful Mother, freed at the End from another spiral of appropriation by her son. Writing marks Moraga's body, affirms it as the body of a woman of color, against the possibility of passing into the unmarked category of the Anglo father or into the orientalist myth of "original illiteracy" of a mother that never was. Malinche was mother here, not Eve before eating the forbidden fruit. Writing affirms Sister Outsider, not the Woman-before-the-Fall-into-Writing needed by the phallogocentric Family of Man.

Writing is pre-eminently the technology of cyborgs, etched surfaces of the late twentieth century. Cyborg politics is the struggle for language and the struggle against perfect communication, against the one code that translates all meaning perfectly, the central dogma of phallogocentrism. That is why cyborg politics insist on noise and advocate pollution, rejoicing in the illegitimate fusions of animal and machine. These are the couplings which make Man and Woman so problematic, subverting the structure of desire, the force imagined to generate language and gender, and so subverting the structure and modes of reproduction of "Western" identity, of nature and culture, of mirror and eye, slave and master, body and mind. "We" did not originally choose to be cyborgs, but choice grounds a liberal politics and epistemology that imagines the reproduction of individuals before the wider replications of "texts."

From the perspective of cyborgs, freed of the need to ground politics in "our" privileged position of the oppression that incorporates all other dominations, the innocence of the merely violated, the ground of those closer to nature, we can see powerful possibilities. Feminisms and Marxisms have run aground on Western epistemological imperatives to construct a revolutionary subject from the perspective of a hierarchy of oppressions and/or a latent position of moral superiority, innocence, and greater closeness to nature. With no available original dream of a common language or original symbiosis promising protection from hostile "masculine" separation, but written into the play of a text that has no finally privileged reading or salvation history, to recognize "oneself" as fully implicated in the world, frees us of the need to root politics in identification, vanguard parties, purity, and mothering. Stripped of identity, the bastard race teaches about the power of the margins and the importance of a mother like Malinche. Women of color have transformed her from the evil mother of masculinist fear into the originally literate mother who teaches survival.

This is not just literary deconstruction, but liminal transformation. Every story that begins with original innocence and privileges the return to wholeness imagines the drama of life to be individuation, separation, the birth of the self, the tragedy of autonomy, the fall into writing, alienation;

that is, war, tempered by imaginary respite in the bosom of the Other. These plots are ruled by a reproductive politics — rebirth without flaw, perfection, abstraction. In this plot women are imagined either better or worse off, but all agree they have less selfhood, weaker individuation, more fusion to the oral, to Mother, less at stake in masculine autonomy. But there is another route to having less at stake in masculine autonomy, a route that does not pass through Woman, Primitive, Zero, the Mirror Stage and its imaginary. It passes through women and other present-tense, illegitimate cyborgs, not of Woman born, who refuse the ideological resources of victimization so as to have a real life. These cyborgs are the people who refuse to disappear on cue, no matter how many times a "Western" commentator remarks on the sad passing of another primitive, another organic group done in by "Western" technology, by writing.[17] These real-life cyborgs (for example, the Southeast Asian village women workers in Japanese and U.S. electronics firms described by Aihwa Ong)[18] are actively rewriting the texts of their bodies and societies. Survival is the stakes in this play of readings.

To recapitulate, certain dualisms have been persistent in Western traditions; they have all been systemic to the logics and practices of domination of women, people of color, nature, workers, animals — in short, domination of all constituted as others, whose task is to mirror the self. Chief among these troubling dualisms are self/other, mind/body, culture/nature, male/female, civilized/primitive, reality/appearance, whole/part, agent/resource, maker/made, active/passive, right/wrong, truth/illusion, total/partial, God/man. The self is the One who is not dominated, who knows that by the service of the other, the other is the one who holds the future, who knows that by the experience of domination, which gives the lie to the autonomy of the self. To be One is to be autonomous, to be powerful, to be God; but to be One is to be an illusion, and so to be involved in a dialectic of apocalypse with the other. Yet to be other is to be multiple, without clear boundary, frayed, insubstantial. One is too few, but two are too many.

High-tech culture challenges these dualisms in intriguing ways. It is not clear who makes and who is made in the relation between human and machine. It is not clear what is mind and what body in machines that resolve into coding practices. Insofar as we know ourselves in both formal discourse (for example, biology) and in daily practice (for example, the homework economy in the integrated circuit), we find ourselves to be cyborgs, hybrids, mosaics, chimeras. Biological organisms have become

17. The convention of ideologically taming militarized high technology by publicizing its applications to speech and motion problems of the disabled/differently abled takes on a special irony in monotheistic, patriarchal, and frequently anti-semitic culture when computer-generated speech allows a boy with no voice to chant the Haftorah at his bar mitzvah. See Sussman, Vic (1986). ["Personal Tech: Technology Lends a Hand." *The Washington Post Magazine*. 9 November, pp. 45–56.] Making the always context-relative social definitions of "ableness" particularly clear, military high-tech has a way of making human beings disabled by definition, a perverse aspect of much automated battlefield and Star Wars R&D. See Welford [Welford, John Noble (1 July 1986). "Pilot's Helmet Helps Interpret High Speed World." *New York Times*, pp. 21, 24.]
18. Ong, Aihwa (1987). *Spirits of Resistance and Capitalist Discipline: Factory Workers in Malaysia*. Albany: SUNY P. [Ed.]

biotic systems, communications devices like others. There is no fundamental, ontological separation in our formal knowledge of machine and
organism, of technical and organic. The replicant Rachel in the Ridley
Scott film *Blade Runner* stands as the image of a cyborg culture's fear, love,
and confusion.

One consequence is that our sense of connection to our tools is heightened. The trance state experienced by many computer users has become a
staple of science-fiction film and cultural jokes. Perhaps paraplegics and
other severely handicapped people can (and sometimes do) have the most
intense experiences of complex hybridization with other communication
devices. Anne McCaffrey's pre-feminist *The Ship Who Sang* (1969) explored
the consciousness of a cyborg, hybrid of girl's brain and complex machinery,
formed after the birth of a severely handicapped child. Gender, sexuality,
embodiment, skill: All were reconstituted in the story. Why should our bodies end at the skin, or include at best other beings encapsulated by skin?
From the seventeenth century till now, machines could be animated —
given ghostly souls to make them speak or move or to account for their orderly
development and mental capacities. Or organisms could be mechanized —
reduced to body understood as resource of mind. These machine/organism
relationships are obsolete, unnecessary. For us, in imagination and in other
practice, machines can be prosthetic devices, intimate components, friendly selves. We don't need organic holism to give impermeable wholeness, the
total woman and her feminist variants (mutants?). Let me conclude this
point by a very partial reading of the logic of the cyborg monsters of my second group of texts, feminist science fiction.

The cyborgs populating feminist science fiction make very problematic
the statuses of man or woman, human, artefact, member of a race, individual entity, or body. Katie King clarifies how pleasure in reading these fictions
is not largely based on identification. Students facing Joanna Russ for the
first time, students who have learned to take modernist writers like James
Joyce or Virginia Woolf without flinching, do not know what to make of *The
Adventures of Alyx* or *The Female Man*, where characters refuse the reader's
search for innocent wholeness while granting the wish for heroic quests,
exuberant eroticism, and serious politics. *The Female Man* is the story of
four versions of one genotype, all of whom meet, but even taken together
do not make a whole, resolve the dilemmas of violent moral action, or
remove the growing scandal of gender. The feminist science fiction of
Samuel R. Delany, especially *Tales of Nevèrÿon*, mocks stories of origin by
redoing the neolithic revolution, replaying the founding moves of Western
civilization to subvert their plausibility. James Tiptree Jr., an author whose
fiction was regarded as particularly manly until her "true" gender was
revealed, tells tales of reproduction based on non-mammalian technologies
like alternation of generations of male brood pouches and male nurturing.
John Varley constructs a supreme cyborg in his arch-feminist exploration of
Gaea, a mad goddess-planet-trickster-old woman-technological device on
whose surface an extraordinary array of post-cyborg symbioses are spawned.
Octavia Butler writes of an African sorceress pitting her powers of transfor-

mation against the genetic manipulations of her rival (*Wild Seed*), of time warps that bring a modern U.S. black woman into slavery where her actions in relation to her white master-ancestor determine the possibility of her own birth (*Kindred*), and of the illegitimate insights into identity and community of an adopted cross-species child who came to know the enemy as self (*Survivor*). In *Dawn* (1987), the first installment of a series called *Xenogenesis*, Butler tells the story of Lilith Iyapo, whose personal name recalls Adam's first and repudiated wife and whose family name marks her status as the widow of the son of Nigerian immigrants to the United States. A black woman and a mother whose child is dead, Lilith mediates the transformation of humanity through genetic exchange with extra-terrestrial lovers/rescuers/destroyers/genetic engineers, who reform earth's habitats after the nuclear holocaust and coerce surviving humans into intimate fusion with them. It is a novel that interrogates reproductive, linguistic, and nuclear politics in a mythic field structured by late twentieth-century race and gender.

Because it is particularly rich in boundary transgressions, Vonda McIntyre's *Superluminal* can close this truncated catalogue of promising and dangerous monsters who help redefine the pleasures and politics of embodiment and feminist writing. In a fiction where no character is "simply" human, human status is highly problematic. Orca, a genetically altered diver, can speak with killer whales and survive deep ocean conditions, but she longs to explore space as a pilot, necessitating bionic implants jeopardizing her kinship with the divers and cetaceans. Transformations are effected by virus vectors carrying a new developmental code, by transplant surgery, by implants of microelectronic devices, by analogue doubles, and other means. Laenea becomes a pilot by accepting a heart implant and a host of other alterations allowing survival in transit at speeds exceeding that of light. Radu Dracul survives a virus-caused plague in his outerworld planet to find himself with a time sense that changes the boundaries of spatial perception for the whole species. All the characters explore the limits of language; the dream of communicating experience; and the necessity of limitation, partiality, and intimacy even in this world of protean transformation and connection. *Superluminal* stands also for the defining contradictions of a cyborg world in another sense; it embodies textually the intersection of feminist theory and colonial discourse in the science fiction I have alluded to in this chapter. This is a conjunction with a long history that many "First World" feminists have tried to repress, including myself in my readings of *Superluminal* before being called to account by Zoe Sofoulis, whose different location in the world system's informatics of domination made her acutely alert to the imperialist moment of all science fiction cultures, including women's science fiction. From an Australian feminist sensibility, Sofoulis remembered more readily McIntyre's role as writer of the adventures of Captain Kirk and Spock in TV's *Star Trek* series than her rewriting the romance in *Superluminal*.

Monsters have always defined the limits of community in Western imaginations. The Centaurs and Amazons of ancient Greece established the limits of the centered polis of the Greek male human by their disruption of marriage and boundary pollutions of the warrior with animality and woman. Unseparated twins and hermaphrodites were the confused human material in early modern France who grounded discourse on the natural and supernatural, medical and legal, portents and diseases — all crucial to establishing modern identity. The evolutionary and behavioral sciences of monkeys and apes have marked the multiple boundaries of late twentieth-century industrial identities. Cyborg monsters in feminist science fiction define quite different political possibilities and limits from those proposed by the mundane fiction of Man and Woman.

There are several consequences to taking seriously the imagery of cyborgs as other than our enemies. Our bodies, ourselves; bodies are maps of power and identity. Cyborgs are no exception. A cyborg body is not innocent; it was not born in a garden; it does not seek unitary identity and so generate antagonistic dualisms without end (or until the world ends); it takes irony for granted. One is too few, and two is only one possibility. Intense pleasure in skill, machine skill, ceases to be a sin, but an aspect of embodiment. The machine is not an *it* to be animated, worshipped, and dominated. The machine is us, our processes, an aspect of our embodiment. We can be responsible for machines; *they* do not dominate or threaten us. We are responsible for boundaries; we are they. Up till now (once upon a time), female embodiment seemed to be given, organic, necessary; and female embodiment seemed to mean skill in mothering and its metaphoric extensions. Only by being out of place could we take intense pleasure in machines, and then with excuses that this was organic activity after all, appropriate to females. Cyborgs might consider more seriously the partial, fluid, sometimes aspect of sex and sexual embodiment. Gender might not be global identity after all, even if it has profound historical breadth and depth.

The ideologically charged question of what counts as daily activity, as experience, can be approached by exploiting the cyborg image. Feminists have recently claimed that women are given to dailiness, that women more than men somehow sustain daily life, and so have a privileged epistemological position potentially. There is a compelling aspect to this claim, one that makes visible unvalued female activity and names it as the ground of life. But *the* ground of life? What about all the ignorance of women, all the exclusions and failures of knowledge and skill? What about men's access to daily competence, to knowing how to build things, to take them apart, to play? What about other embodiments? Cyborg gender is a local possibility taking a global vengeance. Race, gender, and capital require a cyborg theory of wholes and parts. There is no drive in cyborgs to produce total theory, but there is an intimate experience of boundaries, their construction and deconstruction. There is a myth system waiting to become a political language to ground one way of looking at science and technology and challenging the informatics of domination — in order to act potently.

One last image: organisms and organismic, holistic politics depend on metaphors of rebirth and invariably call on the resources of reproductive sex. I would suggest that cyborgs have more to do with regeneration and are suspicious of the reproductive matrix and of most birthing. For salamanders, regeneration after injury, such as the loss of a limb, involves regrowth of structure and restoration of function with the constant possibility of twinning or other odd topographical productions at the site of former injury. The regrown limb can be monstrous, duplicated, potent. We have all been injured, profoundly. We require regeneration, not rebirth, and the possibilities for our reconstitution include the utopian dream of the hope for a monstrous world without gender.

Cyborg imagery can help express two crucial arguments in this essay: First, the production of universal, totalizing theory is a major mistake that misses most of reality, probably always, but certainly now; and second, taking responsibility for the social relations of science and technology means refusing an anti-science metaphysics, a demonology of technology, and so means embracing the skillful task of reconstructing the boundaries of daily life, in partial connection with others, in communication with all of our parts. It is not just that science and technology are possible means of great human satisfaction, as well as a matrix of complex dominations. Cyborg imagery can suggest a way out of the maze of dualisms in which we have explained our bodies and our tools to ourselves. This is a dream not of a common language, but of a powerful infidel heteroglossia. It is an imagination of a feminist speaking in tongues to strike fear into the circuits of the supersavers of the new right. It means both building and destroying machines, identities, categories, relationships, space stories. Though both are bound in the spiral dance, I would rather be a cyborg than a goddess.

Time

Epics are traditionally located in the mythic past; the early modern novel made a radical break with this tradition by situating its narratives squarely in the present. Science fiction introduced a new and equally radical temporal setting: the future. Futuristic settings are synonymous with science fiction in many people's minds, and many stories not explicitly "about" the future are implicitly set in the future. Given the early development of the genre during the Industrial Revolution, this new interest in the future as the realm of speculation can be seen as a response to the accelerated rate of technological and social change, lending urgency to the need to imagine the larger consequences of human innovation, and, at the same time, providing a radically new conceptual perspective for imagining alternatives.

With this idea of the future expanding its time-landscape, perhaps it is not surprising that time itself, and especially time travel, would become such a familiar theme in sf. The narrative device of a more or less scientific-sounding "time machine" — a term coined by H. G. Wells in his 1895 novel of that name — has become part of the common currency of the genre. And the preoccupation with time takes many other forms. Some writers set their stories in the future or in a distinctly altered past, inviting us to see ourselves from different vantage points, often with the goal of satirizing current society or issuing prophetic warnings about where we may be heading. Other writers focus on the idea of time itself, from a scientific or philosophical perspective — Wells's *Time Machine*, in addition to creating the time-travel plot, specifically described time as a "fourth dimension," a decade before Einstein's work would take up that same locution to explain special relativity.

Although in some ways the treatment of time in science fiction is distinctively modern, like many sf themes it has roots in older forms of speculative fiction. Fantasy and folklore often play with the traditional notion of time, whether by having characters awaken from enchanted sleep many years into the future or by having time in fairyland pass more slowly. In fact, time is one of the oldest preoccupations of humankind. Contemplating the nature of time raises existential questions about origins, identity, causation, and destiny: Who are we? Where did we come from? Where are we going? These are the kinds of fundamental questions that sf writers find especially intriguing.

Time is at the center of our identity as human beings and at the center of our understanding of the world. A particular conception of time — as linear or cyclical, stable or malleable, progressive or random — is at the heart of every thought system — religious, philosophical, historical, or scientific — that attempts to explain the nature of the world and our place within it. So far as we know, humans are the only animals who dwell in the past and the future. We seem to be innately narrative animals, viewing our lives as an unfolding of events across the years of our lifetimes — events that are not merely a random sequence but rather make up a meaningful and cohesive story. We spend much of our lives planning the future course of our lives, years into the future. We contemplate the inevitability of our own death, and we mourn the loss of the past. While other animals certainly have a capacity for memory and some understanding of consequences, it seems unlikely that they spend much time worrying what kind of world their grandchildren will live in. Science fiction gives plausible, concrete form to our concerns about the future and, through its incorporation of modern scientific ideas, offers new ways of thinking about time itself.

The stories in this chapter explore ideas about time in a variety of ways. Jules Verne's tale of a clockmaker's self-destructive hubris is — despite its Gothic-flavored setting — a very modern take on timekeeping as a form of control and a challenge to divine authority in the natural order. Miles J. Breuer and Robert Silverberg use time shifts of different kinds to satirize the authors' own societies. C. L. Moore and Robert Heinlein offer more conventional time-travel stories, though they too have broader implications — Moore uses hers to critique human nature, while Heinlein creates an outrageous and mind-boggling send-up of the conventions of the genre. Kim Stanley Robinson's story, which explores how things might have turned out differently if a few key variables of the past were changed, is a classic of the *alternate history* subgenre. Connie Willis makes time itself the subject of her story, taking readers on a romp through quantum physics. Meanwhile Ted Chiang and Benjamin Rosenbaum explore the personal dimension of time as an element of lived life while touching on larger social and philosophical questions. Each story offers us an opportunity to think about the essential human preoccupation with time in new ways.

The Critical Contexts provide three models for thinking about human beings' understanding of — and relationship to — time, drawing on the disciplines of philosophy, history, and physics. Jean-Paul Sartre examines the individual's relationship to his or her past, while E. H. Carr focuses on the historian's role in constructing the narrative of a shared past through which we understand the present. Michio Kaku offers an accessible overview of the scientific understanding of time and provides a window onto the relationship between science and science fiction.

Jules Verne

Master Zacharius

(1854; trans. 1874)

French writer Jules Verne (1828–1905) is rightly considered one of the
founders of sf, although he saw himself as part of the main literary tradition,
not as working in a new genre. His best-known works — *Journey to the
Center of the Earth* (1864; English translation 1872) and *Twenty Thousand
Leagues Under the Sea* (1870; English translation 1872) — combine a lively,
pragmatic interest in science and technology with a swashbuckling sensibility,
creating a new kind of adventure story, one where science itself is a primary
character. While countrymen like Camille Flammarion had used novels as vehicles for the didactic explication of scientific theories, Verne's novels celebrate
science as a means to an end, an ally in exploration of new worlds.

Verne grew up in the port city of Nantes, where his father was a lawyer.
He was expected to follow in his father's footsteps, and was sent to Paris to
study law. Verne had a rebellious streak, however (as a boy he had tried to
run away to sea), and he neglected his legal studies in favor of his passion
for the theater, soon becoming a moderately successful playwright. This
career generated little income, however, and, after marrying a widow with
two children, Verne was obliged to work as a stockbroker to support his
new family. Nonetheless, he continued to write, turning next to short fiction.
Verne admired Edgar Allan Poe, and the influence of stories like "A Descent
into the Maelstrom" (1841) can be seen in Verne's speculative adventure
stories or "Extraordinary Voyages," beginning with "A Voyage in a
Balloon" in 1851. After a slow start, Verne achieved extraordinary success
as a novelist, his works widely translated and his influence profound.

As the optimistic spokesperson of science and progress, Verne is often
contrasted with the moody and pessimistic H. G. Wells, and the two are sometimes seen as the founders of two different strands of sf: "hard" sf with an
emphasis on science and "soft" sf with an emphasis on society. Of course,
most sf stories have both "hard" and "soft" elements, and few writers can be
so easily pigeonholed. Wells was not at all ignorant of science, despite sometimes treating it cavalierly, and Verne's work has a darker, more pessimistic
strand, especially characteristic of his later work but also evident in early stories
such as the posthumously published *Paris in the Twentieth Century* (rejected by
Verne's publisher as too gloomy) as well as the story that follows.

"Master Zacharius" is an early story that has the feel of a gothic romance
in the tradition of Mary Shelley, Nathaniel Hawthorne, and especially E. T. A.
Hoffmann ("The Sandman"). A cautionary tale of scientific hubris, it is set in
the past and colored by the supernatural, but its skepticism about technology
and the desire to control natural processes reflects concerns typical of the
Industrial Revolution. This is not a story about time travel or a scientific exploration of the concept of time but rather a kind of parable about the mechanical regulation of time as a hallmark of the modern era.

Chapter 1: A Winter Night

The city of Geneva lies at the west end of the lake of the same name. The Rhône, which passes through the town at the outlet of the lake, divides it into two sections, and is itself divided in the center of the city by an island placed in mid-stream. A topographical feature like this is often found in the great depôts of commerce and industry. No doubt the first inhabitants were influenced by the easy means of transport which the swift currents of the rivers offered them — those "roads which walk along of their own accord," as Pascal puts it. In the case of the Rhône, it would be the road that ran along.

Both new and regular buildings were constructed on this island, which was enclosed like a Dutch galley in the middle of the river, the curious mass of houses, piled one on the other, presented a delightfully confused *coup-d'œil*. The small area of the island had compelled some of the buildings to be perched, as it were, on the piles, which were entangled in the rough currents of the river. The huge beams, blackened by time, and worn by the water, seemed like the claws of an enormous crab, and presented a fantastic appearance. The little yellow streams, which were like cobwebs stretched amid this ancient foundation, quivered in the darkness, as if they had been the leaves of some old oak forest, while the river engulfed in this forest of piles, foamed and roared most mournfully.

One of the houses of the island was striking for its curiously aged appearance. It was the dwelling of the old clockmaker, Master Zacharius, whose household consisted of his daughter Gerande, Aubert Thun, his apprentice, and his old servant Scholastique.

There was no man in Geneva to compare in interest with this Zacharius. His age was past finding out. Not the oldest inhabitant of the town could tell for how long his thin, pointed head had shaken above his shoulders, nor the day when, for the first time, he had walked through the streets, with his long white locks floating in the wind. The man did not live; he vibrated like the pendulum of his clocks. His spare and cadaverous figure was always clothed in dark colors. Like the pictures of Leonardo di Vinci, he was sketched in black.

Gerande had the pleasantest room in the whole house, whence, through a narrow window, she had the inspiring view of the snowy peaks of Jura; but the bedroom and workshop of the old man were a kind of cavern close on to the water, the floor of which rested on the piles.

From time immemorial Master Zacharius had never come out except at meal times, and when he went to regulate the different clocks of the town. He passed the rest of his time at his bench, which was covered with numerous clockwork instruments, most of which he had invented himself. For he was a clever man; his works were valued in all France and Germany. The best workers in Geneva readily recognized his superiority, and showed that he was an honor to the town, by saying, "To him belongs the glory of having invented the escapement." In fact, the birth of true clock-work dates from the invention which the talents of Zacharius had discovered not many years before.

After he had worked hard for a long time, Zacharius would slowly put his tools away, cover up the delicate pieces that he had been adjusting with glasses, and stop the active wheel of his lathe; then he would raise a trap-door constructed in the floor of his workshop, and, stooping down, used to inhale for hours together the thick vapors of the Rhône, as it dashed along under his eyes.

One winter's night the old servant Scholastique served the supper, which, according to old custom, she and the young mechanic shared with their master. Master Zacharius did not eat, though the food carefully prepared for him was offered him in a handsome blue and white dish. He scarcely answered the sweet words of Gerande, who evidently noticed her father's silence, and even the clatter of Scholastique herself no more struck his ear than the roar of the river, to which he paid no attention.

After the silent meal, the old clockmaker left the table without embracing his daughter, or saying his usual "Good-night" to all. He left by the narrow door leading to his den, and the staircase groaned under his heavy footsteps as he went down.

Gerande, Aubert, and Scholastique sat for some minutes without speaking. On this evening the weather was dull; the clouds dragged heavily on the Alps, and threatened rain; the severe climate of Switzerland made one feel sad, while the south wind swept round the house, and whistled ominously.

"My dear young lady," said Scholastique, at last, "do you know that our master has been out of sorts for several days? Holy Virgin! I know he has had no appetite, because his words stick in his inside, and it would take a very clever devil to drag even one out of him."

"My father has some secret cause of trouble, that I cannot even guess," replied Gerande, as a sad anxiety spread over her face.

"Mademoiselle, don't let such sadness fill your heart. You know the strange habits of Master Zacharius: Who can read his secret thoughts in his face? No doubt some fatigue has overcome him, but to-morrow he will have forgotten it, and be very sorry to have given his daughter pain."

It was Aubert who spoke thus, looking into Gerande's lovely eyes. Aubert was the first apprentice whom Master Zacharius had ever admitted to the intimacy of his labors, for he appreciated his intelligence, discretion, and goodness of heart; and this young man had attached himself to Gerande with the earnest devotion natural to a noble nature.

Gerande was eighteen years of age. Her oval face recalled that of the artless Madonnas whom veneration still displays at the street corners of the antique towns of Brittany. Her eyes betrayed an infinite simplicity. One would love her as the sweetest realization of a poet's dream. Her apparel was of modest colors, and the white linen which was folded about her shoulders had the tint and perfume peculiar to the linen of the church. She led a mystical existence in Geneva, which had not as yet been delivered over to the dryness of Calvinism.

While, night and morning, she read her Latin prayers in her iron-clasped missal, Gerande has also discovered a hidden sentiment in Aubert Thun's heart, and comprehended what a profound devotion the young workman had for her. Indeed, the whole world in his eyes was condensed into this old clockmaker's house, and he passed all his time near the young girl, when he left her father's workshop, after his work was over.

Old Scholastique saw all this, but said nothing. Her loquacity exhausted itself in preference on the evils of the times, and the little worries of the household. Nobody tried to stop its course. It was with her as with the musical snuff-boxes which they made at Geneva; once wound up, you must break them before you will prevent their playing all their airs through.

Finding Gerande absorbed in a melancholy silence, Scholastique left her old wooden chair, fixed a taper on the end of a candlestick, lit it, and placed it near a small waxen Virgin, sheltered in her niche of stone. It was the family custom to kneel before this protecting Madonna of the domestic hearth, and to beg her kindly watchfulness during the coming night; but on this evening Gerande remained silent in her seat.

"Well, well, dear demoiselle," said the astonished Scholastique, "supper is over, and it is time to go to bed. Why do you tire your eyes by sitting up late? Ah, Holy Virgin! It's much better to sleep, and to get a little comfort from happy dreams! In these detestable times in which we live, who can promise herself a fortunate day?"

"Ought we not to send for a doctor for my father?" asked Gerande.

"A doctor!" cried the old domestic. "Has Master Zacharius ever listened to their fancies and pompous sayings? He might accept medicines for the watches, but not for the body!"

"What shall we do?" murmured Gerande. "Has he gone to work, or to rest?"

"Gerande," answered Aubert softly, "some mental trouble annoys your father, that is all."

"Do you know what it is, Aubert?"

"Perhaps, Gerande."

"Tell us, then," cried Scholastique eagerly, economically extinguishing her taper.

"For several days, Gerande," said the young apprentice, "something absolutely incomprehensible has been going on. All the watches which your father has made and sold for some years have suddenly stopped. Very many of them have been brought back to him. He has carefully taken them to pieces; the springs were in good condition, and the wheels well set. He has put them together yet more carefully; but, despite his skill, they will not go."

"The devil's in it!" cried Scholastique.

"Why say you so?" asked Gerande. "It seems very natural to me. Nothing lasts for ever in this world. The infinite cannot be fashioned by the hands of men."

"It is none the less true," returned Aubert, "that there is in this something very mysterious and extraordinary. I have myself been helping Master Zacharius to search for the cause of this derangement of his watches; but I have not been able to find it, and more than once I have let my tools fall from my hands in despair."

"But why undertake so vain a task?" resumed Scholastique. "Is it natural that a little copper instrument should go of itself, and mark the hours? We ought to have kept to the sun-dial!"

"You will not talk thus, Scholastique," said Aubert, "when you learn that the sun-dial was invented by Cain."

"Good heavens! What are you telling me?"

"Do you think," asked Gerande simply, "that we might pray to God to give life to my father's watches?"

"Without doubt," replied Aubert.

"Good! They will be useless prayers," muttered the old servant, "but Heaven will pardon them for their good intent."

The taper was relighted. Scholastique, Gerande, and Aubert knelt down together upon the tiles of the room. The young girl prayed for her mother's soul, for a blessing for the night, for travellers and prisoners, for the good and the wicked, and more earnestly than all for the unknown misfortunes of her father.

Then the three devout souls rose with some confidence in their hearts, because they had laid their sorrow on the bosom of God.

Aubert repaired to his own room; Gerande sat pensively by the window, whilst the last lights were disappearing from the city streets; and Scholastique, having poured a little water on the flickering embers, and shut the two enormous bolts on the door, threw herself upon her bed, where she was soon dreaming that she was dying of fright.

Meanwhile the terrors of this winter's night had increased. Sometimes, with the whirlpools of the river, the wind engulfed itself among the piles, and the whole house shivered and shook; but the young girl, absorbed in her sadness, thought only of her father. After hearing what Aubert told her, the malady of Master Zacharius took fantastic proportions in her mind; and it seemed to her as if his existence, so dear to her, having become purely mechanical, no longer moved on its worn-out pivots without effort.

Suddenly the pent-house shutter, shaken by the squall, struck against the window of the room. Gerande shuddered and started up without understanding the cause of the noise which thus disturbed her reverie. When she became a little calmer she opened the sash. The clouds had burst, and a torrent-like rain pattered on the surrounding roofs. The young girl leaned out of the window to draw to the shutter shaken by the wind, but she feared to do so. It seemed to her that the rain and the river, confounding their tumultuous waters, were submerging the frail house, the planks of which creaked in every direction. She would have flown from her chamber, but she saw below the flickering of a light which appeared to come from Master Zacharius's retreat, and in one of those momentary calms during which the elements keep a sudden silence, her ear caught plaintive sounds. She tried to shut her window, but could not. The wind violently repelled her, like a thief who was breaking into a dwelling.

Gerande thought she would go mad with terror. What was her father doing? She opened the door, and it escaped from her hands, and slammed loudly with the force of the tempest. Gerande then found herself in the dark supper-room, succeeded in gaining, on tiptoe, the staircase which led to her father's shop, and pale and fainting, glided down.

The old watchmaker was upright in the middle of the room, which resounded with the roaring of the river. His bristling hair gave him a sinister aspect. He was talking and gesticulating, without seeing or hearing anything. Gerande stood still on the threshold.

"It is death!" said Master Zacharius, in a hollow voice; "it is death! Why should I live longer, now that I have dispersed my existence over the earth? For I, Master Zacharius, am really the creator of all the watches that I have fashioned! It is a part of my very soul that I have shut up in each of these cases of iron, silver, or gold! Every time that one of these accursed watches stops, I feel my heart cease beating, for I have regulated them with its pulsations!"

As he spoke in this strange way, the old man cast his eyes on his bench. There lay all the pieces of a watch that he had carefully taken apart. He took up a sort of hollow cylinder, called a barrel, in which the spring is enclosed, and removed the steel spiral, but instead of relaxing itself, according to the laws of its elasticity, it remained coiled on itself like a sleeping viper. It seemed knotted, like impotent old men whose blood has long been congealed. Master Zacharius vainly essayed to uncoil it with his thin fingers, the outlines of which were exaggerated on the wall; but he tried in vain, and soon, with a terrible cry of anguish and rage, he threw it through the trap-door into the boiling Rhône.

Gerande, her feet riveted to the floor, stood breathless and motionless. She wished to approach her father, but could not. Giddy hallucinations took possession of her. Suddenly she heard, in the shade, a voice murmur in her ears, —

"Gerande, dear Gerande! grief still keeps you awake. Go in again, I beg of you; the night is cold."

"Aubert!" whispered the young girl, "You?"

These soft words sent the blood back into the young girl's heart. She leaned on Aubert's arm, and said to him, —

"My father is very ill, Aubert! You alone can cure him, for this disorder of the mind would not yield to his daughter's consolings. His mind is attacked by a very natural delusion, and in working with him, repairing the watches, you will bring him back to reason. Aubert," she continued, "it is not true, is it, that his life is mixed up with that of his watches?"

Aubert did not reply.

"But is my father's trade condemned by God?" asked Gerande, trembling.

"I know not," returned the apprentice, warming the cold hands of the girl with his own. "But go back to your room, my poor Gerande, and with sleep recover hope!"

Gerande slowly returned to her chamber, and remained there till daylight, without sleep closing her eyelids. Meanwhile, Master Zacharius, always mute and motionless, gazed at the river as it rolled turbulently at his feet.

Chapter 2: The Pride of Science

The severity of the Geneva merchant in business matters has become prover-bial. He is rigidly honorable, and excessively just. What must, then, have been the shame of Master Zacharius, when he saw these watches, which he had so carefully constructed, returning to him from every direction?

It was certain that these watches had suddenly stopped, and without any apparent reason. The wheels were in a good condition and firmly fixed, but the springs had lost all elasticity. Vainly did the watchmaker try to replace them; the wheels remained motionless. These unaccountable derangements were greatly to the old man's discredit. His noble inventions had many times brought upon him suspicions of sorcery, which now seemed confirmed. These rumors reached Gerande, and she often trem-bled for her father, when she saw malicious glances directed towards him.

Yet on the morning after this night of anguish, Master Zacharius seemed to resume work with some confidence. The morning sun inspired him with some courage. Aubert hastened to join him in the shop, and received an affable "Good-day."

"I am better," said the old man. "I don't know what strange pains in the head attacked me yesterday, but the sun has quite chased them away, with the clouds of the night."

"In faith, master," returned Aubert, "I don't like the night for either of us!"

"And thou art right, Aubert. If you ever become a great man, you will understand that day is as necessary to you as food. A great savant should be always ready to receive the homage of his fellow-men."

"Master, it seems to me that the pride of science has possessed you."

"Pride, Aubert! Destroy my past, annihilate my present, dissipate my future, and then it will be permitted to me to live in obscurity! Poor boy, who comprehends not the sublime things to which my art is wholly devoted! Art thou not but a tool in my hands?"

"Yet, Master Zacharius," resumed Aubert, "I have more than once mer-ited your praise for the manner in which I adjusted the most delicate parts of your watches and clocks."

"No doubt, Aubert; thou art a good workman, such as I love; but when thou workest, thou thinkest thou has in thy hands but copper, silver, gold; thou dost not perceive these metals, which my genius animates, palpitat-ing like living flesh! So that thou wilt not die, with the death of thy works!"

Master Zacharius remained silent after these words; but Aubert essayed to keep up the conversation.

"Indeed, master," said he, "I love to see you work so unceasingly! You will be ready for the festival of our corporation, for I see that the work on this crystal watch is going forward famously."

"No doubt, Aubert," cried the old watchmaker, "and it will be no slight honor for me to have been able to cut and shape the crystal to the durabili-ty of a diamond! Ah, Louis Berghem did well to perfect the art of diamond-cutting, which has enabled me to polish and pierce the hardest stones!"

Master Zacharius was holding several small watch pieces of cut crystal, and of exquisite workmanship. The wheels, pivots, and case of the watch were of the same material, and he had employed remarkable skill in this very difficult task.

"Would it not be fine," said he, his face flushing, "to see this watch palpitating beneath its transparent envelope, and to be able to count the beatings of its heart?"

"I will wager, sir," replied the young apprentice, "that it will not vary a second in a year."

"And you would wager on a certainty! Have I not imparted to it all that is purest of myself? And does my heart vary? My heart, I say?"

Aubert did not dare to lift his eyes to his master's face. "Tell me frankly," said the old man sadly. "Have you never taken me for a madman? Do you not think me sometimes subject to dangerous folly? Yes; is it not so? In my daughter's eyes and yours, I have often read my condemnation. Oh!" he cried, as if in pain, "to be misunderstood by those whom one most loves in the world! But I will prove victoriously to thee, Aubert, that I am right! Do not shake thy head, for thou wilt be astounded. The day on which thou understandest how to listen to and comprehend me, thou wilt see that I have discovered the secrets of existence, the secrets of the mysterious union of the soul with the body!"

As he spoke thus, Master Zacharius appeared superb in his vanity. His eyes glittered with a supernatural fire, and his pride illumined every feature. And truly, if ever vanity was excusable, it was that of Master Zacharius!

The watchmaking art, indeed, down to his time, had remained almost in its infancy. From the day when Plato, four centuries before the Christian era, invented the night watch, a sort of clepsydra which indicated the hours of the night by the sound and playing of a flute, the science had continued nearly stationary. The masters paid more attention to the arts than to mechanics, and it was the period of beautiful watches of iron, copper, wood, silver, which were richly engraved, like one of Cellini's ewers. They made a masterpiece of chasing, which measured time imperfectly, but was still a masterpiece. When the artist's imagination was not directed to the perfection of modelling, it set to work to create clocks with moving figures and melodious sounds, whose appearance took all attention. Besides, who troubled himself, in those days, with regulating the advance of time? The delays of the law were not as yet invented; the physical and astronomical sciences had not as yet established their calculations on scrupulously exact measurements; there were neither establishments which were shut at a given hour, nor trains which departed at a precise moment. In the evening the curfew bell sounded; and at night the hours were cried amid the universal silence. Certainly people did not live so long, if existence is measured by the amount of business done; but they lived better. The mind was enriched with the noble sentiments born of the contemplation of chefs-d'-œuvré. They built a church in two centuries, a painter painted but few pictures in the course of his life, a poet only composed one great work; but these were so many masterpieces for after-ages to appreciate.

When the exact sciences began at last to make some progress, watch and clock making followed in their path, though it was always arrested by an insurmountable difficulty — the regular and continuous measurement of time.

It was in the midst of this stagnation that Master Zacharius invented the escapement, which enabled him to obtain a mathematical regularity by submitting the movement of the pendulum to a sustained force. This invention had turned the old man's head. Pride, swelling in his heart, like mercury in the thermometer, had attained the height of transcendent folly. By analogy he had allowed himself to be drawn to materialistic conclusions, and as he constructed his watches, he fancied that he had discovered the secrets of the union of the soul with the body.

Thus, on this day, perceiving that Aubert listened to him attentively, he said to him in a tone of simple conviction, —

"Dost thou know what life is, my child? Hast thou comprehended the action of those springs which produce existence? Hast thou examined thyself? No. And yet, with the eyes of science, thou mightest have seen the intimate relation which exists between God's work and my own; for it is from his creature that I have copied the combinations of the wheels of my clocks."

"Master," replied Aubert eagerly, "can you compare a copper or steel machine with that breath of God which is called the soul, which animates our bodies as the breeze stirs the flowers? What mechanism could be so adjusted as to inspire us with thought?"

"That is not the question" responded Master Zacharius gently, but with all the obstinacy of a blind man walking towards an abyss. "In order to understand me, thou must recall the purpose of the escapement which I have invented. When I saw the irregular working of clocks, I understood that the movements shut up in them did not suffice, and that it was necessary to submit them to the regularity of some independent force. I then thought that the balance-wheel might accomplish this, and I succeeded in regulating the movement! Now, was it not a sublime idea that came to me, to return to it its lost force by the action of the clock itself, which it was charged with regulating?"

Aubert made a sign of assent.

"Now, Aubert," continued the old man, growing animated, "cast thine eyes upon thyself! Dost thou not understand that there are two distinct forces in us, that of the soul and that of the body — that is, a movement and a regulator? The soul is the principle of life; that is, then, the movement. Whether it is produced by a weight, by a spring, or by an immaterial influence, it is none the less in the heart. But without the body this movement would be unequal, irregular, impossible! Thus the body regulates the soul, and, like the balance-wheel, it is submitted to regular oscillations. And this is so true, that one falls ill when one's drink, food, sleep — in a word, the functions of the body — are not properly regulated; just as in my watches the soul renders to the body the force lost by its oscillations. Well, what produces this intimate union between soul and body, if not a marvellous escapement, by which the wheels of the one work into the wheels of the other?

This is what I have discovered and applied; and there are no longer any secrets for me in this life, which is, after all, only an ingenious mechanism!"

Master Zacharius looked sublime in this hallucination, which carried him to the ultimate mysteries of the Infinite. But his daughter Gerande, standing on the threshold of the door, had heard all. She rushed into her father's arms, and he pressed her convulsively to his breast.

"What is the matter with thee, my daughter?" he asked.

"If I had only a spring here," said she, putting her hand on her heart, "I would not love you as I do, father."

Master Zacharius looked intently at Gerande, and did not reply. Suddenly he uttered a cry, carried his hand eagerly to his heart, and fell fainting on his old leathern chair.

"Father, what is the matter?"

"Help!" cried Aubert. "Scholastique!"

But Scholastique did not come at once. Some one was knocking at the front door; she had gone to open it, and when she returned to the shop, before she could open her mouth, the old watchmaker, having recovered his senses, spoke: —

"I divine, my old Scholastique, that you bring me still another of those accursed watches which have stopped."

"Lord, it is true enough!" replied Scholastique, handing a watch to Aubert.

"My heart could not be mistaken!" said the old man, with a sigh.

Meanwhile Aubert carefully wound up the watch, but it would not go.

Chapter 3: A Strange Visit

Poor Gerande would have lost her life with that of her father, had it not been for the thought of Aubert, who still attached her to the world.

The old watchmaker was, little by little, passing away. His faculties evidently grew more feeble, as he concentrated them on a single thought. By a sad association of ideas, he referred everything to his monomania, and a human existence seemed to have departed from him, to give place to the extra-natural existence of the intermediate powers. Moreover, certain malicious rivals revived the sinister rumors which had spread concerning his labours.

The news of the strange derangements which his watches betrayed had a prodigious effect upon the master clockmakers of Geneva. What signified this sudden paralysis of their wheels, and why these strange relations which they seemed to have with the old man's life? These were the kind of mysteries which people never contemplate without a secret terror. In the various classes of the town, from the apprentice to the great lord who used the watches of the old horologist, there was no one who could not himself judge of the singularity of the fact. The citizens wished, but in vain, to get to see Master Zacharius. He fell very ill; and this enabled his daughter to withdraw him from those incessant visits which had degenerated into reproaches and recriminations.

Medicines and physicians were powerless in the presence of this organic wasting away, the cause of which could not be discovered. It sometimes seemed as if the old man's heart had ceased to beat; then the pulsations were resumed with an alarming irregularity.

A custom existed in those days of publicly exhibiting the works of the masters. The heads of the various corporations sought to distinguish themselves by the novelty or the perfection of their productions; and it was among these that the condition of Master Zacharius excited the most lively, because most interested, commiseration. His rivals pitied him the more willingly because they feared him the less. They never forgot the old man's success, when he exhibited his magnificent clocks with moving figures, his repeaters, which provoked general admiration, and commanded such high prices in the cities of France, Switzerland, and Germany.

Meanwhile, thanks to the constant and tender care of Gerande and Aubert, his strength seemed to return a little; and in the tranquility in which his convalescence left him, he succeeded in detaching himself from the thoughts which had absorbed him. As soon as he could walk, his daughter lured him away from the house, which was still besieged with dissatisfied customers. Aubert remained in the shop, vainly adjusting and readjusting the rebel watches; and the poor boy, completely mystified, sometimes covered his face with his hands, fearful that he, like his master, might go mad.

Gerande led her father towards the more pleasant promenades of the town. With his arm resting on hers, she conducted him sometimes through the quarter of Saint Antoine, the view from which extends towards the Cologny hill, and over the lake; on fine mornings they caught sight of the gigantic peaks of Mount Buet against the horizon. Gerande pointed out these spots to her father, who had well-nigh forgotten even their names. His memory wandered; and he took a childish interest in learning anew what had passed from his mind. Master Zacharius leaned upon his daughter; and the two heads, one white as snow and the other covered with rich golden tresses, met in the same ray of sunlight.

So it came about that the old watchmaker at last perceived that he was not alone in the world. As he looked upon his young and lovely daughter, and on himself old and broken, he reflected that after his death she would be left alone without support. Many of the young mechanics of Geneva had already sought to win Gerande's love; but none of them had succeeded in gaining access to the impenetrable retreat of the watchmaker's household. It was natural, then, that during this lucid interval, the old man's choice should fall on Aubert Thun. Once struck with this thought, he remarked to himself that this young couple had been brought up with the same ideas and the same beliefs; and the oscillations of their hearts seemed to him, as he said one day to Scholastique, "isochronous."

The old servant, literally delighted with the word, though she did not understand it, swore by her holy patron saint that the whole town should hear it within a quarter of an hour. Master Zacharius found it difficult to calm her; but made her promise to keep on this subject a silence which she never was known to observe.

So, though Gerande and Aubert were ignorant of it, all Geneva was soon talking of their speedy union. But it happened also that, while the worthy folk were gossiping, a strange chuckle was often heard, and a voice saying, "Gerande will not wed Aubert."

If the talkers turned round, they found themselves facing a little old man who was quite a stranger to them.

How old was this singular being? No one could have told. People conjectured that he must have existed for several centuries, and that was all. His big flat head rested upon shoulders the width of which was equal to the height of his body; this was not above three feet. This personage would have made a good figure to support a pendulum, for the dial would have naturally been placed on his face, and the balance-wheel would have oscillated at its ease in his chest. His nose might readily have been taken for the style of a sun-dial, for it was narrow and sharp; his teeth, far apart, resembled the cogs of a wheel, and ground themselves between his lips; his voice had the metallic sound of a bell, and you could hear his heart beat like the tick of a clock. This little man, whose arms moved like the hands on a dial, walked with jerks, without ever turning round. If any one followed him, it was found that he walked a league an hour, and that his course was nearly circular.

This strange being had not long been seen wandering, or rather circulating, around the town; but it had already been observed that, every day, at the moment when the sun passed the meridian, he stopped before the Cathedral of Saint Pierre, and resumed his course after the twelve strokes of noon had sounded. Excepting at this precise moment, he seemed to become a part of all the conversations in which the old watchmaker was talked of; and people asked each other, in terror, what relation could exist between him and Master Zacharius. It was remarked, too, that he never lost sight of the old man and his daughter while they were taking their promenades.

One day Gerande perceived this monster looking at her with a hideous smile. She clung to her father with a frightened motion.

"What is the matter, my Gerande?" asked Master Zacharius.

"I do not know," replied the young girl.

"But thou art changed, my child. Art thou going to fall ill in thy turn? Ah, well," he added, with a sad smile, "then I must take care of thee, and I will do it tenderly."

"O father, it will be nothing. I am cold, and I imagine that it is — "

"What, Gerande?"

"The presence of that man, who always follows us," she replied in a low tone.

Master Zacharius turned towards the little old man.

"Faith, he goes well," said he, with a satisfied air, "for it is just four o'clock. Fear nothing, my child; it is not a man, it is a clock!"

Gerande looked at her father in terror. How could Master Zacharius read the hour on this strange creature's visage?

"By-the-bye," continued the old watchmaker, paying no further attention to the matter, "I have not seen Aubert for several days."

"He has not left us, however, father," said Gerande, whose thoughts turned into a gentler channel.

"What is he doing then?"

"He is working."

"Ah!" cried the old man. "He is at work repairing my watches, is he not? But he will never succeed; for it is not repair they need, but a resurrection!"

Gerande remained silent.

"I must know," added the old man, "if they have brought back any more of those accursed watches upon which the Devil has sent this epidemic!"

After these words Master Zacharius fell into complete silence, till he knocked at the door of his house, and for the first time since his convalescence descended to his shop, while Gerande sadly repaired to her chamber.

Just as Master Zacharius crossed the threshold of his shop, one of the many clocks suspended on the wall struck five o'clock. Usually the bells of these clocks — admirably regulated as they were — struck simultaneously, and this rejoiced the old man's heart; but on this day the bells struck one after another, so that for a quarter of an hour the ear was deafened by the successive noises. Master Zacharius suffered acutely; he could not remain still, but went from one clock to the other, and beat the time to them, like a conductor who no longer has control over his musicians.

When the last had ceased striking, the door of the shop opened, and Master Zacharius shuddered from head to foot to see before him the little old man, who looked fixedly at him and said, —

"Master, may I not speak with you a few moments?"

"Who are you?" asked the watchmaker abruptly.

"A colleague. It is my business to regulate the sun."

"Ah, you regulate the sun?" replied Master Zacharius eagerly, without wincing. "I can scarcely compliment you upon it. Your sun goes badly, and in order to make ourselves agree with it, we have to keep putting our clocks forward so much or back so much."

"And by the cloven foot," cried this weird personage, "you are right, my master! My sun does not always mark noon at the same moment as your clocks; but some day it will be known that this is because of the inequality of the earth's transfer, and a mean noon will be invented which will regulate this irregularity!"

"Shall I live till then?" asked the old man, with glistening eyes.

"Without doubt," replied the little old man, laughing. "Can you believe that you will ever die?"

"Alas! I am very ill now."

"Ah, let us talk of that. By Beelzebub! that will lead to just what I wish to speak to you about."

Saying this, the strange being leaped upon the old leather chair, and carried his legs one under the other, after the fashion of the bones which the painters of funeral hangings cross beneath death's heads. Then he resumed, in an ironical tone, —

"Let us see, Master Zacharius, what is going on in this good town of Geneva? They say that your health is failing, that your watches have need of a doctor!"

"Ah, do you believe that there is an intimate relation between their existence and mine?" cried Master Zacharius.

"Why, I imagine that these watches have faults, even vices. If these wantons do not preserve a regular conduct, it is right that they should bear the consequences of their irregularity. It seems to me that they have need of reforming a little!"

"What do you call faults?" asked Master Zacharius, reddening at the sarcastic tone in which these words were uttered. "Have they not a right to be proud of their origin?"

"Not too proud, not too proud," replied the little old man. "They bear a celebrated name, and an illustrious signature is graven on their cases, it is true, and theirs is the exclusive privilege of being introduced among the noblest families; but for some time they have got out of order, and you can do nothing in the matter, Master Zacharius; and the stupidest apprentice in Geneva could prove it to you!"

"To me, to me, — Master Zacharius!" cried the old man, with a flush of outraged pride.

"To you, Master Zacharius, — you, who cannot restore life to your watches!"

"But it is because I have a fever, and so have they also!" replied the old man, as a cold sweat broke out upon him.

"Very well, they will die with you, since you cannot impart a little elasticity to their springs."

"Die! No, for you yourself have said it! I cannot die, — I, the first watchmaker in the world; I, who, by means of these pieces and diverse wheels, have been able to regulate the movement with absolute precision! Have I not subjected time to exact laws, and can I not dispose of it like a despot? Before a sublime genius had arranged these wandering hours regularly, in what vast uncertainty was human destiny plunged? At what certain moment could the acts of life be connected with each other? But you, man or devil, whatever you may be, have never considered the magnificence of my art, which calls every science to its aid! No, no! I, Master Zacharius, cannot die, for, as I have regulated time, time would end with me! It would return to the infinite, whence my genius has rescued it, and it would lose itself irreparably in the abyss of nothingness! No, I can no more die than the Creator of this universe, that submitted to His laws! I have become His equal, and I have partaken of His power! If God has created eternity, Master Zacharius has created time!"

The old watchmaker now resembled the fallen angel, defiant in the presence of the Creator. The little old man gazed at him, and even seemed to breathe into him this impious transport.

"Well said, master," he replied. "Beelzebub had less right than you to compare himself with God! Your glory must not perish! So your servant here desires to give you the method of controlling these rebellious watches."

"What is it? what is it?" cried Master Zacharius.

"You shall know on the day after that on which you have given me your daughter's hand."

"My Gerande?"

"Herself!"

"My daughter's heart is not free," replied Master Zacharius, who seemed neither astonished nor shocked at the strange demand.

"Bah! She is not the least beautiful of watches; but she will end by stopping also — "

"My daughter, — my Gerande! No!"

"Well, return to your watches, Master Zacharius. Adjust and readjust them. Get ready the marriage of your daughter and your apprentice. Temper your springs with your best steel. Bless Aubert and the pretty Gerande. But remember, your watches will never go, and Gerande will not wed Aubert!"

Thereupon the little old man disappeared, but not so quickly that Master Zacharius could not hear six o'clock strike in his breast.

Chapter 4: The Church of Saint Pierre

Meanwhile Master Zacharius became more feeble in mind and body every day. An unusual excitement, indeed, impelled him to continue his work more eagerly than ever, nor could his daughter entice him from it.

His pride was still more aroused after the crises to which his strange visitor had hurried him so treacherously, and he resolved to overcome, by the force of genius, the malign influence which weighed upon his work and himself. He first repaired to the various clocks of the town which were confided to his care. He made sure, by a scrupulous examination, that the wheels were in good condition, the pivots firm, the weights exactly balanced. Every part, even to the bells, was examined with the minute attention of a physician studying the breast of a patient. Nothing indicated that these clocks were on the point of being affected by inactivity.

Gerande and Aubert often accompanied the old man on these visits. He would no doubt have been pleased to see them eager to go with him, and certainly he would not have been so much absorbed in his approaching end, had he thought that his existence was to be prolonged by that of these cherished ones, and had he understood that something of the life of a father always remains in his children.

The old watchmaker, on returning home, resumed his labors with feverish zeal. Though persuaded that he would not succeed, it yet seemed to him impossible that this could be so, and he unceasingly took to pieces the watches which were brought to his shop, and put them together again.

Aubert tortured his mind in vain to discover the causes of the evil.

"Master," said he, "this can only come from the wear of the pivots and gearing."

"Do you want, then, to kill me, little by little?" replied Master Zacharius passionately. "Are these watches child's work? Was it lest I should hurt my fingers that I worked the surface of these copper pieces in the lathe? Have I not forged these pieces of copper myself, so as to obtain a greater strength? Are not these springs tempered to a rare perfection? Could anybody have used finer oils than mine? You must yourself agree that it is impossible, and you avow, in short, that the devil is in it!"

From morning till night discontented purchasers besieged the house, and they got access to the old watchmaker himself, who knew not which of them to listen to.

"This watch loses, and I cannot succeed in regulating it," said one.

"This," said another, "is absolutely obstinate, and stands still, as did Joshua's sun."

"If it is true," said most of them, "that your health has an influence on that of your watches, Master Zacharius, get well as soon as possible."

The old man gazed at these people with haggard eyes, and only replied by shaking his head, or by a few sad words, —

"Wait till the first fine weather, my friends. The season is coming which revives existence in wearied bodies. We want the sun to warm us all!"

"A fine thing, if my watches are to be ill through the winter!" said one of the most angry. "Do you know, Master Zacharius, that your name is inscribed in full on their faces? By the Virgin, you do little honor to your signature!"

It happened at last that the old man, abashed by these reproaches, took some pieces of gold from his old trunk, and began to buy back the damaged watches. At news of this, the customers came in a crowd, and the poor watchmaker's money fast melted away; but his honesty remained intact. Gerande warmly praised his delicacy, which was leading him straight towards ruin; and Aubert soon offered his own savings to his master. "What will become of my daughter?" said Master Zacharius, clinging now and then in the shipwreck to his paternal love.

Aubert dared not answer that he was full of hope for the future, and of deep devotion to Gerande. Master Zacharius would have that day called him his son-in-law, and thus refuted the sad prophecy, which still buzzed in his ears, —

"Gerande will not wed Aubert."

By this plan the watchmaker at last succeeded in entirely despoiling himself. His antique vases passed into the hands of strangers; he deprived himself of the richly-carved panels which adorned the walls of his house; some primitive pictures of the early Flemish painters soon ceased to please his daughter's eyes, and everything, even the precious tools that his genius had invented, were sold to indemnify the clamorous customers.

Scholastique alone refused to listen to reason on the subject; but her efforts failed to prevent the unwelcome visitors from reaching her master, and from soon departing with some valuable object. Then her shattering was heard in all the streets of the neighborhood, where she had long been known. She eagerly denied the rumors of sorcery and magic on the part of Master Zacharius, which gained currency; but as at bottom she was persuaded of their truth, she said her prayers over and over again to redeem her pious falsehoods.

It had been noticed that for some time the old watchmaker had neglected his religious duties. Time was, when he had accompanied Gerande to church, and had seemed to find in prayer the intellectual charm which it imparts to thoughtful minds, since it is the most sublime exercise of the imagination. This voluntary neglect of holy practices, added to the secret habits of his life, had in some sort confirmed the accusations levelled against his labours. So, with the double purpose of drawing her father back to God, and to the world, Gerande resolved to call religion to her aid. She thought that it might give some vitality to his dying soul; but the dogmas of faith and humility had to combat, in the soul of Master Zacharius, an insurmountable pride, and come into collision with that vanity of science which connects everything with itself, without rising to the infinite source whence first principles flow.

It was under these circumstances that the young girl undertook her father's conversion; and her influence was so effective that the old watchmaker promised to attend high mass at the cathedral on the following Sunday. Gerande was in an ecstasy, as if heaven had opened to her view. Old Scholastique could not contain her joy, and at last found irrefutable arguments against the gossiping tongues which accused her master of impiety. She spoke of it to her neighbours, her friends, her enemies, to those whom she knew.

"In faith, we scarcely believe what you tell us, dame Scholastique," they replied; "Master Zacharius has always acted in concert with the devil!"

"You haven't counted, then," replied the old servant, "the fine bells which strike for my master's clocks? How many times they have struck the hours of prayer and the mass!"

"No doubt," they would reply. "But has he not invented machines which go all by themselves, and which actually do the work of a real man?"

"Could a child of the devil," exclaimed dame Scholastique wrathfully, "have executed the fine iron clock of the château of Andernatt, which the town of Geneva was not rich enough to buy? A pious motto appeared at each hour, and a Christian who obeyed them, would have gone straight to Paradise! Is that the work of the devil?"

This masterpiece, made twenty years before, had carried Master Zacharius's fame to its acme; but even then there had been accusations of sorcery against him. But at least the old man's visit to the Cathedral ought to reduce malicious tongues to silence.

Master Zacharius, having doubtless forgotten the promise made to his daughter, had returned to his shop. After being convinced of his powerlessness to give life to his watches, he resolved to try if he could not make some new ones. He abandoned all those useless works, and devoted himself to the completion of the crystal watch, which he intended to be his masterpiece, but in vain did he use his most perfect tools, and employ rubies and diamonds for resisting friction. The watch fell from his hands the first time that he attempted to wind it up!

The old man concealed this circumstance from every one, even from his daughter; but from that time his health rapidly declined. There were only the last oscillations of a pendulum, which goes slower when nothing restores its original force. It seemed as if the laws of gravity, acting directly upon him, were dragging him irresistibly down to the grave.

The Sunday so ardently anticipated by Gerande at last arrived. The weather was fine, and the temperature inspiriting. The people of Geneva were passing quietly through the streets, gaily chatting about the return of spring. Gerande, tenderly taking the old man's arm, directed her steps towards the cathedral, while Scholastique followed behind with the prayer-books. People looked curiously at them as they passed. The old watchmaker permitted himself to be led like a child, or rather like a blind man. The faithful of Saint Pierre were almost frightened when they saw him cross the threshold, and shrank back at his approach.

The chants of high mass were already resounding through the church. Gerande went to her accustomed bench, and kneeled with profound and simple reverence. Master Zacharius remained standing upright beside her.

The ceremonies continued with the majestic solemnity of that faithful age, but the old man had no faith. He did not implore the pity of Heaven with cries of anguish of the "Kyrie"; he did not, with the "Gloria in Excelsis," sing the splendors of the heavenly heights; the reading of the Testament did not draw him from his materialistic reverie, and he forgot to join in the homage of the "Credo." This proud old man remained motionless, as insensible and silent as a stone statue; and even at the solemn moment when the bell announced the miracle of transubstantiation, he did not bow his head, but gazed directly at the sacred host which the priest raised above the heads of the faithful. Gerande looked at her father, and a flood of tears moistened her missal. At this moment the clock of Saint Pierre struck half-past eleven. Master Zacharius turned quickly towards this ancient clock which still spoke. It seemed to him as if its face was gazing steadily at him; the figures of the hours shone as if they had been engraved in lines of fire, and the hands shot forth electric sparks from their sharp points.

The mass ended. It was customary for the "Angelus" to be said at noon, and the priests, before leaving the altar, waited for the clock to strike the hour of twelve. In a few moments this prayer would ascend to the feet of the Virgin.

But suddenly a harsh noise was heard. Master Zacharius uttered a piercing cry.

The large hand of the clock, having reached twelve, had abruptly stopped, and the clock did not strike the hour.

Gerande hastened to her father's aid. He had fallen down motionless, and they carried him outside the church.

"It is the death-blow!" murmured Gerande, sobbing.

When he had been borne home, Master Zacharius lay upon his bed utterly crushed. Life seemed only to still exist on the surface of his body, like the last whiffs of smoke about a lamp just extinguished.

When he came to his senses, Aubert and Gerande were leaning over him. In these last moments the future took in his eyes the shape of the present. He saw his daughter alone, without a protector.

"My son," said he to Aubert, "I give my daughter to thee."

So saying, he stretched out his hands towards his two children, who were thus united at his death-bed.

But soon Master Zacharius lifted himself up in a paroxysm of rage. The words of the little old man recurred to his mind.

"I do not wish to die!" he cried; "I cannot die! I, Master Zacharius, ought not to die! My books — my accounts! — "

With these words he sprang from his bed towards a book in which the names of his customers and the articles which had been sold to them were inscribed. He seized it and rapidly turned over its leaves, and his emaciated finger fixed itself on one of the pages.

"There!" he cried, "there! this old iron clock, sold to Pittonaccio! It is the only one that has not been returned to me! It still exists — it goes — it lives! Ah, I wish for it! — I must find it! I will take such care of it that death will no longer seek me!"

And he fainted away.

Aubert and Gerande knelt by the old man's bed-side and prayed together.

Chapter 5: The Hour of Death

Several days passed, and Master Zacharius, though almost dead, rose from his bed and returned to active life under a supernatural excitement. He lived by pride. But Gerande did not deceive herself; her father's body and soul were for ever lost.

The old man got together his last remaining resources, without thought of those who were dependent upon him. He betrayed an incredible energy, walking, ferreting about, and mumbling strange, incomprehensible words.

One morning Gerande went down to his shop. Master Zacharius was not there. She waited for him all day. Master Zacharius did not return.

Gerande wept bitterly, but her father did not reappear.

Aubert searched everywhere through the town, and soon came to the sad conviction that the old man had left it.

"Let us find my father!" cried Gerande, when the young apprentice told her this sad news.

"Where can he be?" Aubert asked himself.

An inspiration suddenly came to his mind. He remembered the last words which Master Zacharius had spoken. The old man only lived now in the old iron clock that had not been returned! Master Zacharius must have gone in search of it.

Aubert spoke of this to Gerande.

"Let us look at my father's book," she replied.

They descended to the shop. The book was open on the bench. All the watches or clocks made by the old man, and which had been returned to him because they were out of order, were stricken out excepting one: —

> *"Sold to M. Pittonaccio,*
> *an iron clock, with bell and moving figures;*
> *sent to his château at Andernatt."*

It was this "moral" clock of which Scholastique had spoken with so much enthusiasm.

"My father is there!" cried Gerande.

"Let us hasten thither," replied Aubert. "We may still save him!"

"Not for this life," murmured Gerande, "but at least for the other."

"By the mercy of God, Gerande! The château of Andernatt stands in the gorge of the 'Dents-du-Midi,' twenty hours from Geneva. Let us go!"

That very evening Aubert and Gerande, followed by the old servant, set out on foot by the road which skirts Lake Leman. They accomplished five leagues during the night, stopping neither at Bessinge nor at Ermance, where rises the famous château of the Mayors. They with difficulty forded the torrent of the Dranse, and everywhere they went they inquired for Master Zacharius, and were soon convinced that they were on his track.

The next morning, at daybreak, having passed Thonon, they reached Evian, whence the Swiss territory may be seen extended over twelve leagues. But the two betrothed did not even perceive the enchanting prospect. They went straight forward, urged on by a supernatural force. Aubert, leaning on a knotty stick, offered his arm alternately to Gerande and to Scholastique, and he made the greatest efforts to sustain his companions. All three talked of their sorrow, of their hopes, and thus passed along the beautiful road by the water-side, and across the narrow plateau which unites the borders of the lake with the heights of the Chalais. They soon reached Bouveret, where the Rhône enters the Lake of Geneva.

On leaving this town they diverged from the lake, and their weariness increased amid these mountain districts. Vionnaz, Chesset, Collombay, half-lost villages, were soon left behind. Meanwhile their knees shook, their feet were lacerated by the sharp points which covered the ground like a brushwood of granite; — but no trace of Master Zacharius!

He must be found, however, and the two young people did not seek repose either in the isolated hamlets or at the château of Monthay, which, with its dependencies, formed the appanage of Margaret of Savoy. At last, late in the day, and half dead with fatigue, they reached the hermitage of Notre-Dame-du-Sex, which is situated at the base of the Dents-du-Midi, six hundred feet above the Rhône.

The hermit received the three wanderers as night was falling. They could not have gone another step, and here they must needs rest.

The hermit could give them no news of Master Zacharius. They could scarcely hope to find him still living amid these sad solitudes. The night was dark, the wind howled amid the mountains, and the avalanches roared down from the summits of the broken crags.

Aubert and Gerande, crouching before the hermit's hearth, told him their melancholy tale. Their mantles, covered with snow, were drying in a corner; and without, the hermit's dog barked lugubriously, and mingled his voice with that of the tempest.

"Pride," said the hermit to his guests, "has destroyed an angel created for good. It is the stumbling-block against which the destinies of man strike. You cannot reason with pride, the principal of all the vices, since, by its very nature, the proud man refuses to listen to it. It only remains, then, to pray for your father!"

All four knelt down, when the barking of the dog redoubled, and some one knocked at the door of the hermitage.

"Open, in the devil's name!"

The door yielded under the blows, and a dishevelled, haggard, ill-clothed man appeared.

"My father!" cried Gerande.

It was Master Zacharius.

"Where am I?" said he. "In eternity! Time is ended — the hours no longer strike — the hands have stopped!"

"Father!" returned Gerande, with so piteous an emotion that the old man seemed to return to the world of the living.

"Thou here, Gerande?" he cried; "and thou, Aubert? Ah, my dear betrothed ones, you are going to be married in our old church!"

"Father," said Gerande, seizing him by the arm, "come home to Geneva — come with us!"

The old man tore away from his daughter's embrace and hurried towards the door, on the threshold of which the snow was falling in large flakes.

"Do not abandon your children!" cried Aubert.

"Why return," replied the old man sadly, "to those places which my life has already quitted, and where a part of myself is for ever buried?"

"Your soul is not dead," said the hermit solemnly.

"My soul? O no, — its wheels are good! I perceive it beating regularly — "

Your soul is immaterial, — your soul is immortal!" replied the hermit sternly.

"Yes — like my glory! But it is shut up in the château of Andernatt, and I wish to see it again!"

The hermit crossed himself; Scholastique became almost inanimate. Aubert held Gerande in his arms.

"The château of Andernatt is inhabited by one who is lost," said the hermit, "one who does not salute the cross of my hermitage."

"My father, go not thither!"

"I want my soul! My soul is mine — "

"Hold him! Hold my father!" cried Gerande.

But the old man had leaped across the threshold, and plunged into the night, crying, "Mine, mine, my soul!"

Gerande, Aubert, and Scholastique hastened after him. They went by difficult paths, across which Master Zacharius sped like a tempest, urged by an irresistible force. The snow raged around them, and mingled its white flakes with the froth of the swollen torrents.

As they passed the chapel erected in memory of the massacre of the Theban legion, they hurriedly crossed themselves. Master Zacharius was not to be seen.

At last the village of Evionnaz appeared in the midst of this sterile region. The hardest heart would have been moved to see this hamlet, lost among these horrible solitudes. The old man sped on, and plunged into the deepest gorge of the Dents-du-Midi, which pierce the sky with their sharp peaks.

Soon a ruin, old and gloomy as the rocks at its base, rose before him.

"It is there — there!" he cried, hastening his pace still more frantically.

The château of Andernatt was a ruin even then. A thick, crumbling tower rose above it, and seemed to menace with its downfall the old gables which reared themselves below. The vast piles of jagged stones were gloomy to look on. Several dark halls appeared amid the debris, with caved-in ceilings, now become the abode of vipers.

A low and narrow postern opening upon a ditch choked with rubbish, gave access to the château. Who had dwelt there none knew. No doubt some margrave, half lord, half brigand, had sojourned in it; to the margrave had succeeded bandits or counterfeit coiners, who had been hanged on the scene of their crime. The legend went that, on winter nights, Satan came to lead his diabolical dances on the slope of the deep gorges in which the shadow of these ruins was engulfed.

But Master Zacharius was not dismayed by their sinister aspect. He reached the postern. No one forbade him to pass. A spacious and gloomy court presented itself to his eyes; no one forbade him to cross it. He passed along the kind of inclined plane which conducted to one of the long corridors, whose arches seemed to banish daylight from beneath their heavy springings. His advance was unresisted. Gerande, Aubert, and Scholastique closely followed him.

Master Zacharius, as if guided by an irresistible hand, seemed sure of his way, and strode along with rapid step. He reached an old worm-eaten door, which fell before his blows, whilst the bats described oblique circles around his head.

An immense hall, better preserved than the rest, was soon reached. High sculptured panels, on which serpents, ghouls, and other strange figures seemed to disport themselves confusedly, covered its walls. Several long and narrow windows, like loopholes, shivered beneath the bursts of the tempest.

Master Zacharius, on reaching the middle of this hall, uttered a cry of joy.

On an iron support, fastened to the wall, stood the clock in which now resided his entire life. This unequalled masterpiece represented an ancient Roman church, with buttresses of wrought iron, with its heavy bell-tower, where there was a complete chime for the anthem of the day, the "Angelus," the mass, vespers, compline, and the benediction. Above the church door, which opened at the hour of the services, was placed a "rose," in the center of which two hands moved, and the archivault of which reproduced the twelve hours of the face sculptured in relief. Between the door and the rose, just as Scholastique had said, a maxim, relative to the employment of every moment of the day, appeared on a copper plate. Master Zacharius had once regulated this succession of devices with a really Christian solicitude; the hours of prayer, of work, of repast, of recreation, and of repose, followed each other according to the religious discipline, and were to infallibly insure salvation to him who scrupulously observed their commands.

Master Zacharius, intoxicated with joy, went forward to take possession of the clock, when a frightful roar of laughter resounded behind him.

He turned, and by the light of a smoky lamp recognized the little old man of Geneva.

"You are here?" cried he.

Gerande was afraid. She drew closer to Aubert.

"Good-day, Master Zacharius," said the monster.

"Who are you?"

"Signor Pittonaccio, at your service! You have come to give me your daughter! You have remembered my words, 'Gerande will not wed Aubert.'"

The young apprentice rushed upon Pittonaccio, who escaped from him like a shadow.

"Stop, Aubert!" cried Master Zacharius.

"Good-night," said Pittonaccio, and he disappeared.

"My father, let us fly from this hateful place!" cried Gerande. "My father!"

Master Zacharius was no longer there. He was pursuing the phantom of Pittonaccio across the rickety corridors. Scholastique, Gerande, and Aubert remained, speechless and fainting, in the large gloomy hall. The young girl had fallen upon a stone seat; the old servant knelt beside her, and prayed; Aubert remained erect, watching his betrothed. Pale lights wandered in the darkness, and the silence was only broken by the movements of the little animals which live in old wood, and the noise of which marks the hours of "death watch."

When daylight came, they ventured upon the endless staircase which wound beneath these ruined masses; for two hours they wandered thus without meeting a living soul, and hearing only a far-off echo responding to their cries. Sometimes they found themselves buried a hundred feet below the ground, and sometimes they reached places whence they could overlook the wild mountains.

Chance brought them at last back again to the vast hall, which had sheltered them during this night of anguish. It was no longer empty. Master Zacharius and Pittonaccio were talking there together, the one upright and rigid as a corpse, the other crouching over a marble table.

Master Zacharius, when he perceived Gerande, went forward and took her by the hand, and led her towards Pittonaccio, saying, "Behold your lord and master, my daughter. Gerande, behold your husband!"

Gerande shuddered from head to foot.

"Never!" cried Aubert, "for she is my betrothed."

"Never!" responded Gerande, like a plaintive echo.

Pittonaccio began to laugh.

"You wish me to die, then!" exclaimed the old man. "There, in that clock, the last which goes of all which have gone from my hands, my life is shut up; and this man tells me, 'When I have thy daughter, this clock shall belong to thee.' And this man will not rewind it. He can break it, and plunge me into chaos. Ah, my daughter, you no longer love me!"

"My father!" murmured Gerande, recovering consciousness.

"If you knew what I have suffered, far away from this principle of my existence!" resumed the old man. "Perhaps no one looked after this time-piece. Perhaps its springs were left to wear out, its wheels to get clogged. But now, in my own hands, I can nourish this health so dear, for I must not die, — I, the great watchmaker of Geneva. Look, my daughter, how these hands advance with certain step. See, five o'clock is about to strike. Listen well, and look at the maxim which is about to be revealed."

Five o'clock struck with a noise which resounded sadly in Gerande's soul, and these words appeared in red letters:

YOU MUST EAT OF THE FRUITS OF THE TREE OF SCIENCE.

Aubert and Gerande looked at each other stupefied. These were no longer the pious sayings of the Catholic watchmaker. The breath of Satan must have passed over it. But Zacharius paid no attention to this, and resumed —

"Dost thou hear, my Gerande? I live, I still live! Listen to my breathing, — see the blood circulating in my veins! No, thou wouldst not kill the father, and thou wilt accept this man for thy husband, so that I may become immortal, and at last attain the power of God!"

At these blasphemous words old Scholastique crossed herself, and Pittonaccio laughed aloud with joy.

"And then, Gerande, thou wilt be happy with him. See this man, — he is Time! Thy existence will be regulated with absolute precision. Gerande, since I gave thee life, give life to thy father!"

"Gerande," murmured Aubert, "I am thy betrothed."

"He is my father!" replied Gerande, fainting.

"She is thine!" said Master Zacharius. "Pittonaccio, thou wilt keep thy promise!"

"Here is the key of the clock," replied the horrible man.

Master Zacharius seized the long key, which resembled an uncoiled snake, and ran to the clock, which he hastened to wind up with fantastic rapidity. The creaking of the spring jarred upon the nerves. The old watchmaker wound and wound the key, without stopping a moment, and it seemed as if the movement were beyond his control. He wound more and more quickly, with strange contortions, until he fell from sheer weariness.

"There, it is wound up for a century!" he cried.

Aubert rushed from the hall is if he were mad. After long wandering, he found the outlet of the hateful château, and hastened into the open air.

He returned to the hermitage of Notre-Dame-du-Sex, and talked so despairingly to the holy recluse, that the latter consented to return with him to the château of Andernatt.

If, during these hours of anguish, Gerande had not wept, it was because her tears were exhausted.

Master Zacharius had not left the hall. He ran every moment to listen to the regular beating of the old clock.

Meanwhile the clock had struck, and to Scholastique's great terror, these words had appeared on the silver face: —

MAN OUGHT TO BECOME THE EQUAL OF GOD.

The old man had not only not been shocked by these impious maxims, but read them deliriously, and flattered himself with thoughts of pride, whilst Pittonaccio kept close by him.

The marriage-contract was to be signed at midnight. Gerande, almost unconscious, saw or heard nothing. The silence was only broken by the old man's words, and the chuckling of Pittonaccio.

Eleven o'clock struck. Master Zacharius shuddered, and read in a loud voice: —

MAN SHOULD BE THE SLAVE OF SCIENCE AND
SACRIFICE TO IT RELATIVES AND FAMILY.

"Yes!" he cried, "there is nothing but science in this world!"

The hands slipped over the face of the clock with the hiss of a serpent, and the pendulum beat with accelerated strokes.

Master Zacharius no longer spoke. He had fallen to the floor, his throat rattled, and from his oppressed bosom came only these half-broken words: "Life — science!"

The scene had now two new witnesses, the hermit and Aubert. Master Zacharius lay upon the floor; Gerande was praying beside him, more dead than alive.

Of a sudden a dry, hard noise was heard, which preceded the strike.

Master Zacharius sprang up.

"Midnight!" he cried.

The hermit stretched out his hands towards the old clock, — and midnight did not sound.

Master Zacharius uttered a terrible cry, which must have been heard in hell, when these words appeared: —

WHO EVER SHALL ATTEMPT TO MAKE HIMSELF THE
EQUAL OF GOD, SHALL BE FOR EVER DAMNED!

The old clock burst with a noise like thunder, and the spring, escaping, leaped across the hall with a thousand fantastic contortions; the old man rose, ran after it, trying in vain to seize it, and exclaiming, "My soul, — my soul!"

The spring bounded before him, first on one side, then on the other, and he could not reach it.

At last Pittonaccio seized it, and uttering a horrible blasphemy, ingulfed himself in the earth.

Master Zacharius fell backwards. He was dead.

The old watchmaker was buried in the midst of the peaks of Andernatt.

Then Aubert and Gerande returned to Geneva, and during the long life which God accorded to them, they made it a duty to redeem by prayer the soul of the castaway of science.

Miles J. Breuer

The Gostak and the Doshes
(1930)

Miles J. Breuer (1889–1947) was a medical doctor who wrote primarily short fiction in popular magazines, where he was an influential figure. Such "pulp" fiction is often characterized as crude and superficial, but the memorable and provocative story that follows shows a depth and delicacy that belies the stereotype. In "The Gostak and the Doshes," the narrator enters an alternate dimension after hearing a colleague's reflections on Einstein's theory of relativity. Once there, he finds himself on a university campus in a world very much like his own. Soon, however, this ordinary world takes a bizarre turn, and what had seemed a rather lighthearted science-adventure story quickly becomes dystopic. It seems as if the narrator has gone through the looking glass, entering a topsy-turvy world where up is down and people kill over nonsense. But is this really an alternate universe, or simply a distorted reflection of our own?

One does not have to look hard to see the satirical analogy. When Breuer published this story, Benito Mussolini's Fascist party was already well-established and the Nazis were making gains in Germany. The allegory, while broad, is arresting, and the story is both poignant in its historical foresight and enduring in its relevance.

> *Let the reader suppose that somebody states:* "The gostak distims the doshes." *You do not know what this means, nor do I. But if we assume that it is English, we know that the* doshes *are* distimmed *by the* gostak. *We know that one* distimmer *of the* doshes *is a* gostak. *If, moreover,* doshes *are* galloons, *we know that some* galloons *are distimmed by the* gostak. *And so we may go on, and so we often do go on.*
> — Unknown writer quoted by Ogden and Richards, in *The Meaning of Meanings*, Harcourt Brace & Co., 1923; also by Walter N. Polakov in *Man and His Affairs*, Williams & Wilkins, 1925.

W hy! That is lifting yourself by your own bootstraps!" I exclaimed in amazed incredulity. "It's absurd."

Woleshensky smiled indulgently. He towered in his chair as though in the infinite kindness of his vast mind there were room to understand and overlook all the foolish little foibles of all the weak little beings that called themselves men. A mathematical physicist lives in vast spaces where a light-year is a footstep, where universes are being born and blotted out, where space unrolls along a fourth dimension on a surface distended from a fifth. To him, human beings and their affairs do not loom very important.

"Relativity," he explained. In his voice there was a patient forbearance for my slowness of comprehension. "Merely relativity. It doesn't take much physical effort to make the moon move through the treetops, does it? Just enough to walk down the garden path."

I stared at him, and he continued: "If you had been born and raised on a moving train, no one could convince you that the landscape was not in rapid motion. Well, our conception of the universe is quite as relative as that. Sir Isaac Newton tried in his mathematics to express a universe as though beheld by an infinitely removed and perfectly fixed observer. Mathematicians since his time, realizing the futility of such an effort, have taken into consideration that what things 'are' depends upon the person who is looking at them. They have tried to express common knowledge, such as the law of gravitation, in terms that would hold good for all observers. Yet their leader and culminating genius, Einstein, has been unable to express knowledge in terms of pure relativity; he has had to accept the velocity of light as an arbitrarily fixed constant. Why should the velocity of light be any more fixed and constant than any other quantity in the universe?"

"But what's that got to do with going into the fourth dimension?" I broke in impatiently.

He continued as though I hadn't spoken.

"The thing that interests us now, and that mystifies modern mathematicians, is the question of movement, or, more accurately, translation. Is there such a thing as *absolute translation*? Can there be movement — translation — except in *relation* to something else than the thing that moves? All movement we know of is movement in relation to other objects, whether it be a walk down the street or the movement of the earth in its orbit around the sun. A change of *relative* position. But the mere translation of an isolated object existing alone in space is mathematically inconceivable, for there is no such thing as space in that sense."

"I thought you said something about going into another universe — " I interrupted again.

You can't argue with Woleshensky. His train of thought went on without a break.

"By translation we understand getting from one place to another. 'Going somewhere' originally meant a movement of our bodies. Yet, as a matter of fact, when we drive in an automobile we 'go somewhere' without moving our bodies at all. The scene is changed around us; we are somewhere else; and yet we haven't *moved* at all.

"Or suppose you could cast off gravitational attraction for a moment and let the earth rotate under you; you would be going somewhere and yet not moving — "

"But that is theory; you can't tinker with gravitation — "

"Every day you tinker with gravitation. When you start upward in an elevator your pressure, not your weight, against the floor of it is increased; apparent gravitation between you and the floor of the elevator is greater than before — and that like gravitation is anyway: inertia and acceleration. But we are talking about translation. The position of everything in the universe must be referred to some sort of coordinates. Suppose we change the angle or direction of the coordinates: then you have 'gone somewhere' and yet you haven't moved, nor has anything else moved."

I looked at him, holding my head in my hands.

"I couldn't swear that I understood that," I said slowly. "And I repeat looks like lifting yourself by your own bootstraps."

The homely simile did not dismay him. He pointed a finger at me as he spoke. "You've seen a chip of wood bobbing on the ripples of a pond. Now you think the chip is moving, now the water. Yet neither is moving; the only motion is of an abstract thing called a wave.

"You've seen those 'illusion' diagrams — for instance, this one of a group of cubes. Make up your mind that you are looking down upon their upper surfaces, and indeed they seem below you. Now change your mind and imagine that you are down below, looking up. Behold, you see their lower surfaces; you are indeed below them. You have 'gone somewhere,' yet there has been no translation of anything. You have merely changed coordinates."

"Which do you think will drive me insane more quickly — if you *show* me what you mean, or if you keep on talking without showing me?"

"I'll try to show you. There are some types of mind, you know, that cannot grasp the idea of relativity. It isn't the mathematics involved that matters; it's just the inability of some types of mental organizations to grasp the fact that the mind of the observer endows his environment with certain properties which have no absolute existence. Thus, when you walk through the garden at night the moon floats from one treetop to another. Is your mind good enough to invert this: make the moon stand still and let the trees move backward? Can you do that? If so, you can 'go somewhere' into another dimension."

Woleshensky rose and walked to the window. His office was an appropriate setting for such a modern discussion as ours — situated in a new, ultramodern building on the university campus, the varnish glossy, the walls clean, the books neatly arranged behind clean glass, the desk in most orderly array; the office was just as precise and modern and wonderful as the mind of its occupant.

"When do you want to go?" he asked.

"Now!"

"Then I have two more things to explain to you. The fourth dimension is just as much *here* as anywhere else. Right here around you and me things exist and go forward in the fourth dimension; but we do not see them and are not conscious of them because we are confined to our own three. Secondly: if we name the four coordinates as Einstein does, x, y, z, and t, then we exist in x, y, and z and move freely about in them, but are powerless to move in t. Why? Because t is the time dimension; and the time dimension is a difficult one for biological structures that depend on irreversible chemical reactions for their existence. But biochemical reactions can take place along any of the other dimensions as well as along t.

Therefore, let us transform coordinates. Rotate the property of chemical irreversibility from t to z. Since we are organically able to exist (or at least to perceive) in only three dimensions at once, our new time dimension will be z. We shall be unconscious of z and cannot travel in it. Our activities and consciousness will take place along x, y, and t.

According to fiction writers, to switch into the t dimension, some sort of apparatus with an electrical field ought to be necessary. It is not. You need nothing more to rotate into the t dimension than you do to stop the moon and make the trees move as you ride down the road; or than you do to turn the cubes upside down. It is a matter of *relativity*."

I had ceased trying to wonder or to understand.

"Show me!" was all I could gasp.

"The success of this experiment in changing from the z to the t coordinate has depended largely upon my lucky discovery of a favorable location. It is just as, when you want the moon to ride the treetops successfully, there have to be favorable features in the topography or it won't work. The edge of this building and that little walk between the two rows of Norway poplars seems to be an angle between planes in the z and t dimensions. It seems to slope downward, does it not? — Now walk from here to the end and imagine yourself going upward. That is all. Instead of feeling this building behind and *above* you, conceive it as behind and *below*. Just as on your ride by moonlight, you must tell yourself that the moon is not moving while the trees ride by. — Can you do that? Go ahead, then." He spoke in a confident tone, as though he knew exactly what would happen.

Half credulous, half wondering, I walked slowly out of the door. I noticed that Woleshensky settled himself down to the table with a pad and a pencil to some kind of study, and forgot me before I had finished turning around. I looked curiously at the familiar wall of the building and the still more familiar poplar walk, expecting to see some strange scenery, some unknown view from another world. But there were the same old bricks and trees that I had known so long, though my disturbed and wondering frame of mind endowed them with a sudden strangeness and unwontedness. Things I had known for some years, they were, yet so powerfully had Woleshensky's arguments impressed me that I already fancied myself in a different universe. According to the conception of relativity, objects of the x, y, z universe *ought* to look different when viewed from the x, y, t universe.

Strange to say, I had no difficulty at all in imagining myself as going *upward* on my stroll along the slope. I told myself that the building was behind and below me, and indeed it seemed real that it was that way. I walked some distance along the little avenue of poplars, which seemed familiar enough in all its details, though after a few minutes it struck me that the avenue seemed rather long. In fact, it was much longer than I had ever known it to be before.

With a queer Alice-in-Wonderland feeling I noted it stretching way on ahead of me. Then I looked back.

I gasped in astonishment. The building was indeed *below* me. I looked down upon it from the top of an elevation. The astonishment of that realization had barely broken over me when I admitted that there was a building down there; but what building? Not the new Morton Hall, at any rate. It was a long, three-story brick building, quite resembling Morton Hall, but it was not the same. And on beyond there were trees with buildings among them; but it was not the campus that I knew.

I paused in a kind of panic. What was I to do now? Here I was in a strange place. How I had gotten there I had no idea. What ought I to do about it? Where should I go? How was I to get back? Odd that I had neglected the precaution of how to get back. I surmised that I must be on the *t* dimension. Stupid blunder on my part, neglecting to find out how to get back.

I walked rapidly down the slope toward the building. Any hopes that I might have had about its being Morton Hall were thoroughly dispelled in a moment. It was a totally strange building, old, and old-fashioned looking. I had never seen it before in my life. Yet it looked perfectly ordinary and natural and was obviously a university classroom building.

I cannot tell whether it was an hour or a dozen that I spent walking frantically this way and that, trying to decide to go into this building or another, and at the last moment backing out in a sweat of hesitation. It seemed like a year but was probably only a few minutes. Then I noticed the people. They were mostly young people, of both sexes. Students, of course. Obviously I was on a university campus. Perfectly natural, normal young people, they were. If I were really on the *t* dimension, it certainly resembled the *z* dimension very closely.

Finally I came to a decision. I could stand this no longer. I selected a solitary, quiet-looking man and stopped him.

"Where am I?" I demanded.

He looked at me in astonishment. I waited for a reply, and he continued to gaze at me speechlessly. Finally it occurred to me that he didn't understand English.

"Do you speak English?" I asked hopelessly.

"Of course!" he said vehemently. "What's wrong with you?"

"Something's wrong with something," I exclaimed. "I haven't any idea where I am or how I got here."

"Synthetic wine?" he asked sympathetically.

"Oh, hell! Think I'm a fool? Say, do you have a good man in mathematical physics on the faculty? Take me to him."

"Psychology, I should think," he said, studying me. "Or psychiatry. But I'm a law student and know nothing of either."

"Then make it mathematical physics, and I'll be grateful to you."

So I was conducted to the mathematical physicist. The student led me into the very building that corresponded to Morton Hall, and into an office the position of which quite corresponded to that of Woleshensky's office. However, the office was older and dustier; it had a Victorian look about it and was not as modern as Woleshensky's room. Professor Vibens was a rather small, bald-headed man with a keen-looking face. As I thanked the law student and started on my story, he looked rather bored, as though wondering why I had picked on him with my tale of wonder. Before I had gotten very far he straightened up a little; and farther along he pricked up another notch; and before many minutes he was tense in his chair as he listened to me. When I finished, his comment was terse, like that of a man accustomed to thinking accurately and to the point.

"Obviously you come into this world from another set of coordinates. As we are on the z dimension, you must have come to us from the t dimension — "

He disregarded my attempts to protest at this point.

"Your man Woleshensky has evidently developed the conception of relativity further than we have, although Monpeters's theory comes close enough to it. Since I have no idea how to get you back, you must be my guest. I shall enjoy hearing about your world."

"That is very kind of you," I said gratefully. "I'm accepting because I can't see what else to do. At least until the time when I can find myself a place in your world or get back to my own. Fortunately," I added as an afterthought, "no one will miss me there, unless it be a few classes of students who will welcome the little vacation that must elapse before my successor is found."

Breathlessly eager to find out what sort of world I had gotten into, I walked with him to his home. And I may state at the outset that if I had found everything upside down and outlandishly bizarre, I should have been far less amazed and astonished than I was. For, from the walk that first evening from Professor Vibens's office along several blocks of residence street to his solid and respectable home, through all of my goings about the town and country during the years that I remained in the t-dimensional world, I found people and things thoroughly ordinary and familiar. They looked and acted as we do, and their homes and goods looked like ours. I cannot possibly imagine a world and a people that could be more similar to ours without actually being the same. It was months before I got over the idea that I had merely wandered into an unfamiliar part of my own city. Only the actual experience of wide travel and much sightseeing, and the knowledge that there was no such extensive English-speaking country in the world that I knew, convinced me that I must be on some other world, doubtless in the t dimension.

"A gentleman who has found his way here from another universe," the professor introduced me to a strapping young fellow who was mowing the lawn.

The professor's son was named John! Could anything be more commonplace?

"I'll have to take you around and show you things tomorrow," John said cordially, accepting the account of my arrival without surprise.

A redheaded servant girl, roast pork and rhubarb sauce for dinner, and checkers afterward, a hot bath at bedtime, the ringing of a telephone somewhere else in the house — is it any wonder that it was months before I would believe that I had actually come into a different universe? What slight differences there were in the people and the world merely served to emphasize the similarity. For instance, I think they were just a little more hospitable and "old-fashioned" than we are. Making due allowances for the fact that I was a rather remarkable phenomenon, I think I was welcomed more heartily in this home and in others later; people spared me more of their time and interest from their daily business than would have happened under similar circumstances in a correspondingly busy city in America.

Again, John found a lot of time to take me about the city and show me banks and stores and offices. He drove a little squat car with tall wheels, run by a spluttering gasoline motor. (The car was not as perfect as our modern cars, and horses were quite numerous in the streets. Yet John was a busy businessman, the district superintendent of a life-insurance agency.) Think of it! Life insurance in Einstein's t-dimension.

"You're young to be holding such an important position," I suggested.

"Got started early," John replied. "Dad is disappointed because I didn't see fit to waste time in college. Disgrace to the family, I am."

What in particular shall I say about the city? It might have been any one of a couple of hundred American cities. Only it wasn't. The electric streetcars, except for their bright green color, were perfect; they might have been brought over bodily from Oshkosh or Tulsa. The ten-cent stores with gold letters on their signs; drugstores with soft drinks; a mad, scrambling stock exchange; the blaring sign of an advertising dentist; brilliant entrances to motion-picture theaters were all there. The beauty shops did wonders to the women's heads, excelling our own by a good deal, if I am any judge; and at that time I had nothing more important on my mind than to speculate on that question. Newsboys bawled the *Evening Sun* and the *Morning Gale*, in whose curious, flat type I could read accounts of legislative doings, murders, and divorces quite as fluently as I could in my own *Tribune* at home. Strangeness and unfamiliarity had bothered me a good deal on a trip to Quebec a couple of years before; but they were not noticeable here in the t-dimension.

For three or four weeks the novelty of going around, looking at things, meeting people, visiting concerts, theaters, and department stores was sufficient to absorb my interest. Professor Vibens's hospitality was so sincerely extended that I did not hesitate to accept, though I assured him that I would repay it as soon as I got established in this world. In a few days I was thoroughly convinced that there was no way back home. Here I must stay, at least until I learned as much as Woleshensky knew about crossing dimensions. Professor Vibens eventually secured for me a position at the university.

It was shortly after I had accepted the position as instructor in experimental physics and had begun to get broken into my work that I noticed a strange commotion among the people of the city. I have always been a studious recluse, observing people as phenomena rather than participating in their activities. So for some time I noted only in a subconscious way the excited gathering in groups, the gesticulations and blazing eyes, the wild sale of extra editions of papers, the general air of disturbance. I even failed to take an active interest in these things when I made a railroad journey of three hundred miles and spent a week in another city; so thoroughly at home did I feel in this world that when the advisability arose of my studying laboratory methods in another university, I made the trip alone. So absorbed was I in my laboratory problems that I only noted with half an eye the commotion and excitement everywhere, and merely recollected it later. One night it suddenly popped into my head that the country was aroused over something.

That night I was with the Vibens family in their living room. John tuned in the radio. I wasn't listening to the thing very much; I had troubles of my own. $F = \dfrac{gm_1 m_2}{r^2}$ was familiar enough to me. It meant the same and held as rigidly here as in my old world. But what was the name of the bird who had formulated that law? Back home it was Newton. Tomorrow in class I would have to be thoroughly familiar with his name. Pasvieux, that's what it was. What messy surnames. It struck me that it was lucky that they expressed the laws of physics in the same form and even in the same algebraic letters, or I might have had a time getting them confused — when all of a sudden the radio blatantly bawled: "THE GOSTAK DISTIMS THE DOSHES!"

John jumped to his feet.

"Damn right!" he shouted, slamming the table with his fist.

Both his father and mother annihilated him with withering glances, and he slunk from the room. I gazed stupefied. My stupefaction continued while the professor shut off the radio and both of them excused themselves from my presence. Then suddenly I was alert.

I grabbed a bunch of newspapers, having seen none for several days. Great sprawling headlines covered the front pages:

"THE GOSTAK DISTIMS THE DOSHES."

For a moment I stopped, trying to recollect where I had heard those words before. They recalled something to me. Ah, yes! That very afternoon there had been a commotion beneath my window on the university campus. I had been busy checking over an experiment so that I might be sure of its success at tomorrow's class, and looked out rather absently to see what was going on. A group of young men from a dismissed class was passing and had stopped for a moment.

"I say, the gostak distims the doshes!" said a fine-looking young fellow. His face was pale and strained.

The young man facing him sneered derisively, "Aw, your grandmother! Don't be a feeble — "

He never finished. The first fellow's fist caught him in the cheek. Several books dropped to the ground. In a moment the two had clinched and were rolling on the ground, fists flying up and down, smears of blood appearing here and there. The others surrounded them and for a moment appeared to enjoy the spectacle, but suddenly recollected that it looked rather disgraceful on a university campus, and after a lively tussle separated the combatants. Twenty of them, pulling in two directions, tugged them apart.

The first boy strained in the grasp of his captors; his white face was flecked with blood and he panted for breath.

"Insult!" he shouted, giving another mighty heave to get free. He looked contemptuously around. "The whole bunch of you ought to learn to stand up for your honor. The gostak distims the doshes!"

That was the astonishing incident that these words called to my mind. I turned back to my newspapers.

"Slogan Sweeps the Country," proclaimed the subheads. "Ringing Expression of National Spirit! Enthusiasm Spreads Like Wildfire! The new patriotic slogan is gaining ground rapidly," the leading article went on. "The fact that it has covered the country almost instantaneously seems to indicate that it fills a deep and long felt want in the hearts of the people. It was first uttered during a speech in Walkingdon by that majestic figure in modern statesmanship, Senator Harob. The beautiful sentiment, the wonderful emotion of this sublime thought, are epoch-making. It is a great conception, doing credit to a great man, and worthy of being the guiding light of a great people — "

That was the gist of everything I could find in the papers. I fell asleep still puzzled about the thing. I was puzzled because — as I see now and didn't see then — I was trained in the analytical methods of physical science and knew little or nothing about the ways and emotions of the masses of the people.

In the morning the senseless expression popped into my head as soon as I awoke. I determined to waylay the first member of the Vibens family who showed up, and demand the meaning of the thing. It happened to be John.

"John, what's a gostak?"

John's face lighted up with pleasure. He threw out his chest and a look of pride replaced the pleasure. His eyes blazed, and with a consuming enthusiasm he shook hands with me, as deacons shake hands with a new convert — a sort of glad welcome

"The gostak!" he exclaimed. "Hurray for the gostak!"

"But what is a gostak?"

"Not a gostak! The gostak. The gostak is — the distimmer of the doshes — see! He distims 'em, see?"

"Yes, yes. But what is distimming? How do you distim?"

"No, no! Only the gostak can distim. The gostak distims the doshes. See?"

"Ah, I see!" I exclaimed. Indeed, I pride myself on my quick wit. "What are doshes? Why, they are the stuff distimmed by the gostak. Very simple!"

"Good for you!" John slapped my back in huge enthusiasm. "I think it wonderful for you to understand us so well after being here only a short time. You are very patriotic."

I gritted my teeth tightly to keep myself from speaking.

"Professor Vibens, what's a gostak?" I asked in the solitude of his office an hour later.

He looked pained.

He leaned back in his chair and looked me over elaborately, and waited some time before answering.

"Hush!" he finally whispered. "A scientific man may think what he pleases, but if he says too much, people in general may misjudge him. As a matter of fact, a good many scientific men are taking this so-called patriotism seriously. But a mathematician cannot use words loosely; it has become second nature with him to inquire closely into the meaning of every term he uses."

"Well, doesn't that jargon mean anything at all?" I was beginning to be puzzled in earnest.

"To me it does not. But it seems to mean a great deal to the public in general. It's making people do things, is it not?"

I stood a while in stupefied silence. That an entire great nation should become fired up over a meaningless piece of nonsense! Yet the astonishing thing was that I had to admit there was plenty of precedent for it in the history of my own z-dimensional world. A nation exterminating itself in civil wars to decide which of two profligate royal families should be privileged to waste the people's substance from the throne; a hundred thousand crusaders marching to death for an idea that to me means nothing; a meaningless, untrue advertising slogan that sells millions of dollars' worth of cigarettes to a nation, to the latter's own detriment — haven't we seen it over and over again?

"There's a public lecture on this stuff tonight at the First Church of the Salvation," Professor Vibens suggested.

"I'll be there," I said. "I want to look into the thing."

That afternoon there was another flurry of "extras" over the street; people gathered in knots and gesticulated with open newspapers.

"War! Let 'em have it!" I heard men shout.

"Is our national honor a rag to be muddied and trampled on?" the editorials asked.

As far as I could gather from reading the papers, there was a group of nations across an ocean that was not taking the gostak seriously. A ship whose pennant bore the slogan had been refused entrance to an Engtalian harbor because it flew the national ensign. The Executive had dispatched a diplomatic note. An evangelist who had attempted to preach the gospel of the distimmed doshes at a public gathering in Itland had been ridden on a rail and otherwise abused. The Executive was dispatching a diplomatic note.

Public indignation waxed high. Derogatory remarks about "wops" were flung about. Shouts of "Holy war!" were heard. I could feel the tension in the atmosphere as I took my seat in the crowded church in the evening. I had been assured that the message of the gostak and the doshes would be thoroughly expounded so that even the most simple-minded and uneducated people could understand it fully. Although I had my hands full at the university, I was so puzzled and amazed at the course events were taking that I determined to give the evening to finding out what the slogan meant.

There was a good deal of singing before the lecture began. Mimeographed copies of the words were passed about, but I neglected to preserve them and do not remember them. I know there was one solemn hymn that reverberated harmoniously through the great church, a chanting repetition of "The Gostak Distims the Doshes." There was another stirring martial air that began, "Oh, the Gostak! Oh, the Gostak!" — and ended with a swift cadence on "The Gostak Distims the Doshes!" The speaker had a rich, eloquent voice and a commanding figure. He stepped out and bowed solemnly.

"The gostak distims the doshes," he pronounced impressively. "Is it not comforting to know that there is a gostak; do we not glow with pride because the doshes are distimmed? In the entire universe there is no more profoundly significant fact: the gostak distims the doshes. Could anything be more complete yet more tersely emphatic! The gostak distims the doshes!" Applause. "This thrilling truth affects our innermost lives. What would we do if the gostak did not distim the doshes? Without the gostak, without doshes, what would we do? What would we think? How would we feel?" Applause again.

At first I thought this was some kind of introduction. I was inexperienced in listening to popular speeches, lectures, and sermons. I had spent most of my life in the study of physics and its accessory sciences. I could not help trying to figure out the meaning of whatever I heard. When I found none, I began to get impatient. I waited some more, thinking that soon he would begin on the real explanation. After thirty minutes of the same sort of stuff as I have just quoted, I gave up trying to listen. I just sat and hoped he would soon be through. The people applauded and grew more excited. After an hour I stirred restlessly; I slouched down in my seat and sat up by turns. After two hours I grew desperate; I got up and walked out. Most of the people were too excited to notice me. Only a few of them cast hostile glances at my retreat.

The next day the mad nightmare began for me. First there was a snowstorm of extras over the city, announcing the sinking of a merchantman by an Engtalian cruiser. A dispute had arisen between the officers of the merchantman and the port officials, because the latter had jeered disrespectfully at the gostak. The merchantman picked up and started out without having fulfilled all the customs requirements. A cruiser followed it and ordered it to return. The captain of the merchantman told them that the gostak distims the doshes, whereupon the cruiser fired twice and sank the merchantman. In the afternoon came the extras announcing the Executive's declaration of war.

Recruiting offices opened; the university was depleted of its young men; uniformed troops marched through the city, and railway trains full of them went in and out. Campaigns for raising war loans; home-guards, women's auxiliaries, ladies' aid societies making bandages, young women enlisting as ambulance drivers — it was indeed war; all of it to the constantly repeated slogan: "The gostak distims the doshes."

I could hardly believe that it was really true. There seemed to be no adequate cause for a war. The huge and powerful nation had dreamed a silly slogan and flung it in the world's face. A group of nations across the water had united into an alliance, claiming they had to defend themselves against having forced upon them a principle they did not desire. The whole thing at the bottom had no meaning. It did not seem possible that there would actually be a war; it seemed more like going through a lot of elaborate play-acting.

Only when the news came of a vast naval battle of doubtful issue, in which ships had been sunk and thousands of lives lost, did it come to me that they meant business. Black bands of mourning appeared on sleeves and in windows. One of the allied countries was invaded and a front line set up. Reports of a division wiped out by an airplane attack; of forty thousand dead in a five-day battle; of more men and more money needed, began to make things look real. Haggard men with bandaged heads and arms in slings appeared on the streets, a church and an auditorium were converted into hospitals, and trainloads of wounded were brought in. To convince myself that this thing was so, I visited these wards and saw with my own eyes the rows of cots, the surgeons working on ghastly wounds, the men with a leg missing or with a hideously disfigured face.

Food became restricted; there was no white bread, and sugar was rationed. Clothing was of poor quality; coal and oil were obtainable only on government permit. Businesses were shut down. John was gone; his parents received news that he was missing in action.

Real it was; there could be no more doubt of it. The thing that made it seem most real was the picture of a mangled, hopeless wreck of humanity sent back from the guns, a living protest against the horror of war. Suddenly someone would say, "The gostak distims the doshes!" and the poor wounded fragment would straighten up and put out his chest with pride, and an unquenchable fire would blaze in his eyes. He did not regret having given his all for that. How could I understand it?

And real it was when the draft was announced. More men were needed; volunteers were insufficient. Along with the rest, I complied with the order to register, doing so in a mechanical fashion, thinking little of it. Suddenly the coldest realization of the reality of it was flung at me when I was informed that my name had been drawn and that I would have to go!

All this time I had looked upon this mess as something outside of me, something belonging to a different world, of which I was not a part. Now here was a card summoning me to training camp. With all this death and mangled humanity in the background, I wasn't even interested in this world. I didn't belong here. To be called upon to undergo all the horrors of military life, the risk of a horrible death, for no reason at all! For a silly jumble of meaningless sounds.

I spent a sleepless night in maddened shock from the thing. In the morning a wild and haggard caricature of myself looked back at me from the mirror. But I had revolted. I intended to refuse service. If the words "conscientious objector" ever meant anything, I certainly was one. Even if they shot me for treason at once, that would be a fate less hard to bear than going out and giving my strength and my life for — for nothing at all.

My apprehensions were quite correct. With my usual success at self-control over a seething interior, I coolly walked to the draft office and informed them that I did not believe in their cause and could not see my way to fight for it. Evidently they had suspected something of the sort already, for they had the irons on my wrists before I had hardly done with my speech.

"Period of emergency," said a beefy tyrant at the desk. "No time for stringing out a civil trial. Court-martial!"

He said it to me vindictively, and the guards jostled me roughly down the corridor; even they resented my attitude. The court-martial was already waiting for me. From the time I walked out of the lecture at the church I had been under secret surveillance, and they knew my attitude thoroughly. That is the first thing the president of the court informed me.

My trial was short. I was informed that I had no valid reason for objecting. Objectors because of religion, because of nationality and similar reasons, were readily understood; a jail sentence to the end of the war was their usual fate. But I admitted that I had no intrinsic objection to fighting; I merely jeered at their holy cause. That was treason unpardonable.

"Sentenced to be shot at sunrise!" the president of the court announced.

The world spun around with me. But only for a second. My self-control came to my aid. With the curious detachment that comes to us in such emergencies, I noted that the court-martial was being held in Professor Vibens's office — that dingy little Victorian room where I had first told my story of traveling by relativity and had first realized that I had come to the t-dimensional world. Apparently it was also to be the last room I was to see in this same world. I had no false hopes that the execution would help me back to my own world, as such things sometimes do in stories. When life is gone, it is gone, whether in one dimension or another I would be just as dead in the z dimension as in the t dimension.

"Now, Einstein, or never!" I thought. "Come to my aid, O Riemann! O Lobachevsky! If anything will save me it will have to be a tensor or a geodesic."

I said it to myself rather ironically. Relativity had brought me here. Could it get me out of this?

Well! Why not?

If the form of a natural law, yea, if a natural object varies with the observer who expresses it, might not the truth and the meaning of the gostak slogan also be a matter of relativity? It was like making the moon ride the treetops again. If I could be a better relativist and put myself in these people's places, perhaps I could understand the gostak. Perhaps I would even be willing to fight for him or it.

The idea struck me suddenly. I must have straightened up and some bright change must have passed over my features, for the guards who led me looked at me curiously and took a firmer grip on me. We had descended the steps of the building and had started down the walk.

Making the moon ride the treetops! That was what I needed now. And that sounded as silly to me as the gostak. And the gostak did not seem so silly. I drew a deep breath and felt very much encouraged. The viewpoint of *relativity* was somehow coming back to me. Necessity manages much. I could understand how one might fight for the idea of a gostak distimming the doshes. I felt almost like telling these men. Relativity is a wonderful thing. They led me up the slope, between the rows of poplars.

Then it all suddenly popped into my head: how I had gotten here by changing my coordinates, insisting to myself that I was going *upward*. Just like making the moon stop and making the trees ride when you are out riding at night. Now I was going upward. In my own world, in the z dimension, this same poplar was *down* the slope.

"It's downward!" I insisted to myself. I shut my eyes and imagined the building behind and *above* me. With my eyes shut, it did seem downward. I walked for a long time before opening them. Then I opened them and looked around.

I was at the end of the avenue of poplars. I was surprised. The avenue seemed short. Somehow it had become shortened; I had not expected to reach the end so soon. And where were the guards in olive uniforms? There were none.

I turned around and looked back. The slope extended on backward above me. I had indeed walked downward. There were no guards, and the fresh, new building was on the hill behind me.

Woleshensky stood on the steps.

"Now what do you think of a *t* dimension?" he called out to me.

Woleshensky!

And a *new* building, modern! Vibens's office was in an old Victorian building. What was there in common between Vibens and Woleshensky? I drew a deep breath. The comforting realization spread gratefully over me that I was back in my native dimension. The gostak and the war were somewhere else. Here were peace and Woleshensky.

I hastened to pour out the story to him.

"What does it all mean?" I asked when I was through. "Somehow — vaguely — it seems that it ought to mean something."

"Perhaps," he said in his kind, sage way, "we really exist in four dimensions. A part of us and our world that we cannot see and are not conscious of projects on into another dimension, just like the front edges of the books in the bookcase, turned away from us. You know that the section of a conic cut by the *y* plane looks different from the section of the same conic cut by the *z* plane? Perhaps what you saw was our own world and our own selves intersected by a different set of coordinates. *Relativity*, as I told you in the beginning."

C. L. Moore

Vintage Season

(1946)

One of the first women to gain widespread recognition in the field of sf, Catherine Lucille Moore (1911–1987) wrote both on her own and in collaboration with her husband, fellow sf writer Henry Kuttner, using a variety of pseudonyms. The collaboration was a close one, and it is not always possible to separate their contributions, but it is generally agreed that works published under the name "Lewis Padgett" (like "Mimsy Were the Borogoves" elsewhere in this volume) were authored primarily by Kuttner, while Moore was the primary author of those signed "Laurence O'Donnell," as "Vintage Season" was.

Moore's work includes fine examples of full-blown space opera and Lovecraftian horror, but she is perhaps at her best when most restrained, as in the proto-feminist "No Woman Born" or the chilly time-travel story that follows.

In "Vintage Season," a man seeking to rent his house finds himself caught in a bidding war between two groups of mysterious "foreigners" remarkable for their elegance, their odd mannerisms, and their air of aloof condescension. We eventually learn that they value the house for its location in time, not space. Beneath the surface of their sophistication and beauty there is an even more disturbing coldness.

Time-travel stories are often concerned with whether the past can be changed. Here, however, the question is whether we would choose to change it if to do so threatened our own comfortable lot. This indifference to the suffering of others in the interest of the status quo is uncomfortably similar to real world analogs of slumming and third-world tourism.

Three people came up the walk to the old mansion just at dawn on a perfect May morning. Oliver Wilson in his pajamas watched them from an upper window through a haze of conflicting emotions, resentment predominant. He didn't want them there.

They were foreigners. He knew only that much about them. They had the curious name of Sancisco, and their first names, scrawled in loops on the lease, appeared to be Omerie, Kleph, and Klia, though it was impossible as he looked down upon them now to sort them out by signature. He hadn't even been sure whether they would be men or women, and he had expected something a little less cosmopolitan.

Oliver's heart sank a little as he watched them follow the taxi driver up the walk. He had hoped for less self-assurance in his unwelcome tenants, because he meant to force them out of the house if he could. It didn't look very promising from here.

The man went first. He was tall and dark, and he wore his clothes and carried his body with that peculiar arrogant assurance that comes from

517

perfect confidence in every phase of one's being. The two women were laughing as they followed him. Their voices were light and sweet, and their faces were beautiful, each in its own exotic way, but the first thing Oliver thought of when he looked at them was, Expensive!

It was not only that patina of perfection that seemed to dwell in every line of their incredibly flawless garments. There are degrees of wealth beyond which wealth itself ceases to have significance. Oliver had seen before, on rare occasions, something like this assurance that the earth turning beneath their well-shod feet turned only to their whim.

It puzzled him a little in this case, because he had the feeling as the three came up the walk that the beautiful clothing they wore so confidently was not clothing they were accustomed to. There was a curious air of condescension in the way they moved. Like women in costume. They minced a little on their delicate high heels, held out an arm to stare at the cut of the sleeve, twisted now and then inside their garments as if the clothing sat strangely on them, as if they were accustomed to something entirely different.

And there was an elegance about the way the garments fitted them which even to Oliver looked strikingly unusual. Only an actress on the screen, who can stop time and the film to adjust every disarrayed fold so that she looks perpetually perfect, might appear thus elegantly clad. But let these women move as they liked, and each fold of their clothing followed perfectly with the movement and fell perfectly into place again. One might almost suspect the garments were not cut of ordinary cloth, or that they were cut according to some unknown, subtle scheme, with many artful hidden seams placed by a tailor incredibly skilled at his trade.

They seemed excited. They talked in high, clear, very sweet voices, looking up at the perfect blue and transparent sky in which dawn was still frankly pink. They looked at the trees on the lawn, the leaves translucently green with an under color of golden newness, the edges crimped from constriction in the recent bud.

Happily and with excitement in their voices they called to the man, and when he answered his own voice blended so perfectly in cadence with theirs that it sounded like three people singing together. Their voices, like their clothing, seemed to have an elegance far beyond the ordinary, to be under a control such as Oliver Wilson had never dreamed of before this morning.

The taxi driver brought up the luggage, which was of a beautiful pale stuff that did not look quite like leather, and had curves in it so subtle it seemed square until you saw how two or three pieces of it fitted together when carried, into a perfectly balanced block. It was scuffed, as if from much use. And though there was a great deal of it, the taxi man did not seem to find his burden heavy. Oliver saw him look down at it now and then and heft the weight incredulously.

One of the women had very black hair and skin like cream, and smoke-blue eyes heavy-lidded with the weight of her lashes. It was the other woman Oliver's gaze followed as she came up the walk. Her hair was a clear, pale red, and her face had a softness that he thought would be like velvet to touch. She was tanned to a warm amber darker than her hair.

Just as they reached the porch steps the fair woman lifted her head and looked up. She gazed straight into Oliver's eyes and he saw that hers were very blue, and just a little amused, as if she had known he was there all along. Also they were frankly admiring.

Feeling a bit dizzy, Oliver hurried back to his room to dress.

"We are here on a vacation," the dark man said, accepting the keys. "We will not wish to be disturbed, as I made clear in our correspondence. You have engaged a cook and housemaid for us, I understand? We will expect you to move your own belongings out of the house, then, and — "

"Wait," Oliver said uncomfortably. "Something's come up. I — " He hesitated, not sure just how to present it. These were such increasingly odd people. Even their speech was odd. They spoke so distinctly, not slurring any of the words into contractions. English seemed as familiar to them as a native tongue, but they all spoke as trained singers sing, with perfect breath control and voice placement.

And there was a coldness in the man's voice, as if some gulf lay between him and Oliver, so deep no feeling of human contact could bridge it.

"I wonder," Oliver said, "if I could find you better living quarters somewhere else in town. There's a place across the street that — "

The dark woman said, "Oh, no!" in a lightly horrified voice, and all three of them laughed. It was cool, distant laughter that did not include Oliver.

The dark man said, "We chose this house carefully, Mr. Wilson. We would not be interested in living anywhere else."

Oliver said desperately, "I don't see why. It isn't even a modern house. I have two others in much better condition. Even across the street you'd have a fine view of the city. Here there isn't anything. The other houses cut off the view, and — "

"We engaged rooms here, Mr. Wilson," the man said with finality. "We expect to use them. Now will you make arrangements to leave as soon as possible?"

Oliver said, "No," and looked stubborn. "That isn't in the lease. You can live here until next month, since you paid for it, but you can't put me out. I'm staying."

The man opened his mouth to say something. He looked coldly at Oliver and closed it again. The feeling of aloofness was chill between them. There was a moment's silence. Then the man said, "Very well. Be kind enough to stay out of our way."

It was a little odd that he didn't inquire into Oliver's motives. Oliver was not yet sure enough of the man to explain. He couldn't very well say, "Since the lease was signed, I've been offered three times what the house is worth if I'll sell it before the end of May." He couldn't say, "I want the money, and I'm going to use my own nuisance-value to annoy you until you're willing to move out." After all, there seemed no reason why they shouldn't. After seeing them, there seemed doubly no reason, for it was clear they must be accustomed to surroundings infinitely better than this timeworn old house.

It was very strange, the value this house had so suddenly acquired. There was no reason at all why two groups of semi-anonymous people should be so eager to possess it for the month of May.

In silence Oliver showed his tenants upstairs to the three big bedrooms across the front of the house. He was intensely conscious of the red-haired woman and the way she watched him with a sort of obviously covert interest, quite warmly, and with a curious undertone to her interest that he could not quite place. It was familiar, but elusive. He thought how pleasant it would be to talk to her alone, if only to try to capture that elusive attitude and put a name to it.

Afterward he went down to the telephone and called his fiancée.

Sue's voice squeaked a little with excitement over the wire.

"Oliver, so early? Why, it's hardly six yet. Did you tell them what I said? Are they going to go?"

"Can't tell yet. I doubt it. After all, Sue, I did take their money, you know."

"Oliver, they've got to go! You've got to do something!"

"I'm trying, Sue. But I don't like it."

"Well, there isn't any reason why they shouldn't stay somewhere else. And we're going to need that money. You'll just have to think of something, Oliver."

Oliver met his own worried eyes in the mirror above the telephone and scowled at himself. His straw-colored hair was tangled and there was a shining stubble on his pleasant, tanned face. He was sorry the red-haired woman had first seen him in his untidy condition. Then his conscience smote him at the sound of Sue's determined voice and he said:

"I'll try, darling. I'll try. But I did take their money."

They had, in fact, paid a great deal of money, considerably more than the rooms were worth even in that year of high prices and high wages. The country was just moving into one of those fabulous eras which are later referred to as the Gay Forties or the Golden Sixties — a pleasant period of national euphoria. It was a stimulating time to be alive — while it lasted.

"All right," Oliver said resignedly. "I'll do my best."

But he was conscious, as the next few days went by, that he was not doing his best. There were several reasons for that. From the beginning the idea of making himself a nuisance to his tenants had been Sue's, not Oliver's. And if Oliver had been a little less determined the whole project would never have got under way. Reason was on Sue's side, but —

For one thing, the tenants were so fascinating. All they said and did had a queer sort of inversion to it, as if a mirror had been held up to ordinary living and in the reflection showed strange variations from the norm. Their minds worked on a different basic premise, Oliver thought, from his own. They seemed to derive covert amusement from the most unamusing things; they patronized, they were aloof with a quality of cold detachment which did not prevent them from laughing inexplicably far too often for Oliver's comfort.

He saw them occasionally, on their way to and from their rooms. They were polite and distant, not, he suspected, from anger at his presence but from sheer indifference.

Most of the day they spent out of the house. The perfect May weather held unbroken and they seemed to give themselves up wholeheartedly to admiration of it, entirely confident that the warm, pale-gold sunshine and the scented air would not be interrupted by rain or cold. They were so sure of it that Oliver felt uneasy.

They took only one meal a day in the house, a late dinner. And their reactions to the meal were unpredictable. Laughter greeted some of the dishes, and a sort of delicate disgust others. No one would touch the salad, for instance. And the fish seemed to cause a wave of queer embarrassment around the table.

They dressed elaborately for each dinner. The man — his name was Omerie — looked extremely handsome in his dinner clothes, but he seemed a little sulky and Oliver twice heard the women laughing because he had to wear black. Oliver entertained a sudden vision, for no reason, of the man in garments as bright and as subtly cut as the women's, and it seemed somehow very right for him. He wore even the dark clothing with a certain flamboyance, as if cloth-of-gold would be more normal for him.

When they were in the house at other mealtimes, they ate in their rooms. They must have brought a great deal of food with them, from whatever mysterious place they had come. Oliver wondered with increasing curiosity where it might be. Delicious odors drifted into the hall sometimes, at odd hours, from their closed doors. Oliver could not identify them, but almost always they smelled irresistible. A few times the food smell was rather shockingly unpleasant, almost nauseating. It takes a connoisseur, Oliver reflected, to appreciate the decadent. And these people, most certainly, were connoisseurs.

Why they lived so contentedly in this huge ramshackle old house was a question that disturbed his dreams at night. Or why they refused to move. He caught some fascinating glimpses into their rooms, which appeared to have been changed almost completely by additions he could not have defined very clearly from the brief sights he had of them. The feeling of luxury which his first glance at them had evoked was confirmed by the richness of the hangings they had apparently brought with them, the half-glimpsed ornaments, the pictures on the walls, even the whiffs of exotic perfume that floated from half-open doors.

He saw the women go by him in the halls, moving softly through the brown dimness in their gowns so uncannily perfect in fit, so lushly rich, so glowingly colored they seemed unreal. That poise born of confidence in the subservience of the world gave them an imperious aloofness, but more than once Oliver, meeting the blue gaze of the woman with the red hair and the soft, tanned skin, thought he saw quickened interest there. She smiled at him in the dimness and went by in a haze of fragrance and a halo of incredible richness, and the warmth of the smile lingered after she had gone.

He knew she did not mean this aloofness to last between them. From the very first he was sure of that. When the time came she would make the opportunity to be alone with him. The thought was confusing and tremendously exciting. There was nothing he could do but wait, knowing she would see him when it suited her.

On the third day he lunched with Sue in a little downtown restaurant overlooking the great sweep of the metropolis across the river far below. Sue had shining brown curls and brown eyes, and her chin was a bit more prominent than is strictly accordant with beauty. From childhood Sue had known what she wanted and how to get it, and it seemed to Oliver just now that she had never wanted anything quite so much as the sale of this house.

"It's such a marvelous offer for the old mausoleum," she said, breaking into a roll with a gesture of violence. "We'll never have a chance like that again, and prices are so high we'll need the money to start housekeeping. Surely you can do *something*, Oliver!"

"I'm trying," Oliver assured her uncomfortably.

"Have you heard anything more from that madwoman who wants to buy it?"

Oliver shook his head. "Her attorney phoned again yesterday. Nothing new. I wonder who she is."

"I don't think even the attorney knows. All this mystery — I don't like it, Oliver. Even those Sancisco people — What did they do today?"

Oliver laughed. "They spent about an hour this morning telephoning movie theaters in the city, checking up on a lot of third-rate films they want to see parts of."

"Parts of? But why?"

"I don't know. I think . . . oh, nothing. More coffee?"

The trouble was, he thought he did know. It was too unlikely a guess to tell Sue about, and without familiarity with the Sancisco oddities she would only think Oliver was losing his mind. But he had from their talk, a definite impression that there was an actor in bit parts in all these films whose performances they mentioned with something very near to awe. They referred to him as Golconda, which didn't appear to be his name, so that Oliver had no way of guessing which obscure bit-player it was they admired so deeply. Golconda might have been the name of a character he had once played — and with superlative skill, judging by the comments of the Sanciscos — but to Oliver he meant nothing at all.

"They do funny things," he said, stirring his coffee reflectively. "Yesterday Omerie — that's the man — came in with a book of poems published about five years ago, and all of them handled it like a first edition of Shakespeare. I never even heard of the author, but he seems to be a tin god in their country, wherever that is."

"You still don't know? Haven't they even dropped any hints?"

"We don't do much talking," Oliver reminded her with some irony.

"I know, but — Oh, well, I guess it doesn't matter. Go on, what else do they do?"

"Well, this morning they were going to spend studying 'Golconda' and his great art, and this afternoon I think they're taking a trip up the river to some sort of shrine I never heard of. It isn't very far, wherever it is, because I know they're coming back for dinner. Some great man's birthplace, I think — they promised to take home souvenirs of the place if they could get any. They're typical tourists, all right — if I could only figure out what's behind the whole thing. It doesn't make sense."

"Nothing about that house makes sense any more. I do wish — "

She went on in a petulant voice, but Oliver ceased suddenly to hear her, because just outside the door, walking with imperial elegance on her high heels, a familiar figure passed. He did not see her face, but he thought he would know that poise, that richness of line and motion, anywhere on earth.

"Excuse me a minute," he muttered to Sue, and was out of his chair before she could speak. He made the door in half a dozen long strides, and the beautifully elegant passerby was only a few steps away when he got there. Then, with the words he had meant to speak already half-uttered, he fell silent and stood there staring.

It was not the red-haired woman. It was not her dark companion. It was a stranger. He watched, speechless, while the lovely, imperious creature moved on through the crowd and vanished, moving with familiar poise and assurance and an equally familiar strangeness as if the beautiful and exquisitely fitted garments she wore were an exotic costume to her, as they had always seemed to the Sancisco women. Every other woman on the street looked untidy and ill at ease beside her. Walking like a queen, she melted into the crowd and was gone.

She came from *their* country, Oliver told himself dizzily. So someone else nearby had mysterious tenants in this month of perfect May weather. Someone else was puzzling in vain today over the strangeness of the people from the nameless land.

In silence he went back to Sue.

The door stood invitingly ajar in the brown dimness of the upper hall. Oliver's steps slowed as he drew near it, and his heart began to quicken correspondingly. It was the red-haired woman's room, and he thought the door was not open by accident. Her name, he knew now, was Kleph.

The door creaked a little on its hinges and from within a very sweet voice said lazily, "Won't you come in?"

The room looked very different indeed. The big bed had been pushed back against the wall and a cover thrown over it that brushed the floor all around looked like soft-haired fur except that it was a pale blue-green and sparkled as if every hair were tipped with invisible crystals. Three books lay open on the fur, and a very curious-looking magazine with faintly luminous printing and a page of pictures that at first glance appeared three-dimensional. Also a tiny porcelain pipe encrusted with porcelain flowers, and a thin wisp of smoke floating from the bowl.

Above the bed a broad picture hung, framing a square of blue water so real Oliver had to look twice to be sure it was not rippling gently from left to right. From the ceiling swung a crystal globe on a glass cord. It turned gently, the light from the windows making curved rectangles in its sides.

Under the center window a sort of chaise longue stood which Oliver had not seen before. He could only assume it was at least partly pneumatic and had been brought in the luggage. There was a very rich-looking quilted cloth covering and hiding it, embossed all over in shining metallic patterns.

Kleph moved slowly from the door and sank upon the chaise longue with a little sigh of content. The couch accommodated itself to her body with what looked like delightful comfort. Kleph wriggled a little and then smiled up at Oliver.

"Do come on in. Sit over there, where you can see out the window. I love your beautiful spring weather. You know, there never was a May like it in civilized times." She said that quite seriously, her blue eyes on Oliver's, and there was a hint of patronage in her voice, as if the weather had been arranged especially for her.

Oliver started across the room and then paused and looked down in amazement at the floor, which felt unstable. He had not noticed before that the carpet was pure white, unspotted, and sank about an inch under the pressure of the feet. He saw then that Kleph's feet were bare, or almost bare. She wore something like gossamer buskins of filmy net, fitting her feet exactly. The bare soles were pink as if they had been rouged, and the nails had a liquid gleam like tiny mirrors. He moved closer, and was not as surprised as he should have been to see that they really were tiny mirrors, painted with some lacquer that gave them reflecting surfaces.

"Do sit down," Kleph said again, waving a white-sleeved arm toward a chair by the window. She wore a garment that looked like short, soft down, loosely cut but following perfectly every motion she made. And there was something curiously different about her very shape today. When Oliver saw her in street clothes, she had the square-shouldered, slim-flanked figure that all women strove for, but here in her lounging robe she looked — well, different. There was an almost swanlike slope to her shoulders today, a roundness and softness to her body that looked unfamiliar and very appealing.

"Will you have some tea?" Kleph asked, and smiled charmingly.

A low table beside her held a tray and several small covered cups, lovely things with an inner glow like rose quartz, the color shining deeply as if from within layer upon layer of translucence. She took up one of the cups — there were no saucers — and offered it to Oliver.

It felt fragile and thin as paper in his hand. He could not see the contents because of the cup's cover, which seemed to be one with the cup itself and left only a thin open crescent at the rim. Steam rose from the opening.

Kleph took up a cup of her own and tilted it to her lips, smiling at Oliver over the rim. She was very beautiful. The pale red hair lay in shining loops against her head and the corona of curls like a halo above her forehead might have been pressed down like a wreath. Every hair kept order as perfectly as if it had been painted on, though the breeze from the window stirred now and then among the softly shining strands.

Oliver tried the tea. Its flavor was exquisite, very hot, and the taste that lingered upon his tongue was like the scent of flowers. It was an extremely feminine drink. He sipped again, surprised to find how much he liked it.

The scent of flowers seemed to increase as he drank, swirling through his head like smoke. After the third sip there was a faint buzzing in his ears. The bees among the flowers, perhaps, he thought incoherently — and sipped again.

Kleph watched him, smiling.

"The others will be out all afternoon," she told Oliver comfortably. "I thought it would give us a pleasant time to be acquainted."

Oliver was rather horrified to hear himself saying, "What makes you talk like that?" He had had no idea of asking the question; something seemed to have loosened his control over his own tongue.

Kleph's smile deepened. She tipped the cup to her lips and there was indulgence in her voice when she said, "What do you mean 'like that'?"

He waved his hand vaguely, noting with some surprise that at a glance it seemed to have six or seven fingers as it moved past his face.

"I don't know — precision, I guess. Why don't you say 'don't,' for instance?"

"In our country we are trained to speak with precision," Kleph explained. "Just as we are trained to move and dress and think with precision. Any slovenliness is trained out of us in childhood. With you, of course — " She was polite. "With you, this does not happen to be a national fetish. With us, we have time for the amenities. We like them."

Her voice had grown sweeter and sweeter as she spoke, until by now it was almost indistinguishable from the sweetness of the flower-scent in Oliver's head, and the delicate flavor of the tea.

"What country do you come from?" he asked, and tilted the cup again to drink, mildly surprised to notice that it seemed inexhaustible.

Kleph's smile was definitely patronizing this time. It didn't irritate him. Nothing could irritate him just now. The whole room swam in a beautiful rosy glow as fragrant as the flowers.

"We must not speak of that, Mr. Wilson."

"But — " Oliver paused. After all, it was, of course, none of his business. "This is a vacation?" he asked vaguely.

"Call it a pilgrimage, perhaps."

"Pilgrimage?" Oliver was so interested that for an instant his mind came back into sharp focus. "To — what?"

"I should not have said that, Mr. Wilson. Please forget it. Do you like the tea?"

"Very much."

"You will have guessed by now that it is not only tea, but an euphoriac."

Oliver stared. "Euphoriac?"

Kleph made a descriptive circle in the air with one graceful hand, and laughed. "You do not feel the effects yet? Surely you do?"

"I feel," Oliver said, "the way I'd feel after four whiskeys."

Kleph shuddered delicately. "We get our euphoria less painfully. And without the aftereffects your barbarous alcohols used to have." She bit her lip. "Sorry. I must be euphoric myself to speak so freely. Please forgive me. Shall we have some music?"

Kleph leaned backward on the chaise longue and reached toward the wall beside her. The sleeve, falling away from her round tanned arm, left bare the inside of the wrist, and Oliver was startled to see there a long, rosy streak of fading scar. His inhibitions had dissolved in the fumes of the fragrant tea; he caught his breath and leaned forward to stare.

Kleph shook the sleeve back over the scar with a quick gesture. Color came into her face beneath the softly tinted tan and she would not meet Oliver's eyes. A queer shame seemed to have fallen upon her.

Oliver said tactlessly, "What is it? What's the matter?"

Still she would not look at him. Much later he understood that shame and knew she had reason for it. Now he listened blankly as she said:

"Nothing . . . nothing at all. A . . . an inoculation. All of us . . . oh, never mind. Listen to the music."

This time she reached out with the other arm. She touched nothing, but when she had held her hand near the wall a sound breathed through the room. It was the sound of water, the sighing of waves receding upon long, sloped beaches. Oliver followed Kleph's gaze toward the picture of the blue water above the bed.

The waves there were moving. More than that, the point of vision moved. Slowly the seascape drifted past, moving with the waves, following them toward shore. Oliver watched, half-hypnotized by a motion that seemed at the time quite acceptable and not in the least surprising.

The waves lifted and broke in creaming foam and ran seething up a sandy beach. Then through the sound of the water music began to breathe, and through the water itself a man's face dawned in the frame, smiling intimately into the room. He held an oddly archaic musical instrument, lute-shaped, its body striped light and dark like a melon and its long neck bent back over his shoulder. He was singing, and Oliver felt mildly astonished at the song. It was very familiar and very odd indeed. He groped through the unfamiliar rhythms and found at least a thread to catch the tune by — it was "Make-Believe," from "Showboat," but certainly a showboat that had never steamed up the Mississippi.

"What's he doing to it?" he demanded after a few moments of outraged listening. "I never heard anything like it!"

Kleph laughed and stretched out her arm again. Enigmatically she said, "We call it kyling. Never mind. How do you like this?"

It was a comedian, a man in semi-clown make-up, his eyes exaggerated so that they seemed to cover half his face. He stood by a broad glass pillar before a dark curtain and sang a gay, staccato song interspersed with patter that sounded impromptu, and all the while his left hand did an intricate, musical tattoo of the nailtips on the glass of the column. He strolled around and around it as he sang. The rhythms of his fingernails blended with the song and swung widely away into patterns of their own, and blended again without a break.

It was confusing to follow. The song made even less sense than the monologue, which had something to do with a lost slipper and was full of allusions which made Kleph smile, but were utterly unintelligible to Oliver. The man had a dry, brittle style that was not very amusing, though Kleph seemed fascinated. Oliver was interested to see in him an extension and a variation of that extreme smooth confidence which marked all three of the Sanciscos. Clearly a racial trait, he thought.

Other performances followed, some of them fragmentary as if lifted out of a completer version. One he knew. The obvious, stirring melody struck his recognition before the figures — marching men against a haze, a great banner rolling backward above them in the smoke, foreground figures striding gigantically and shouting in rhythm, "Forward, forward the lily banners go!"

The music was tinny, the images blurred and poorly colored, but there was a gusto about the performance that caught at Oliver's imagination. He stared, remembering the old film from long ago. Dennis King and a ragged chorus, singing "The Song of the Vagabonds" from — was it "Vagabond King"?

"A very old one," Kleph said apologetically. "But I like it."

The steam of the intoxicating tea swirled between Oliver and the picture. Music swelled and sank through the room and the fragrant fumes and his own euphoric brain. Nothing seemed strange. He had discovered how to drink the tea. Like nitrous oxide, the effect was not cumulative. When you reached a peak of euphoria, you could not increase the peak. It was best to wait for a slight dip in the effect of the stimulant before taking more.

Otherwise it had most of the effects of alcohol — everything after awhile dissolved into a delightful fog through which all he saw was uniformly enchanting and partook of the qualities of a dream. He questioned nothing. Afterward he was not certain how much of it he really had dreamed.

There was the dancing doll, for instance. He remembered it quite clearly, in sharp focus — a tiny, slender woman with a long-nosed, dark-eyed face and a pointed chin. She moved delicately across the white rug — knee-high, exquisite. Her features were as mobile as her body, and she danced lightly, with resounding strokes of her toes, each echoing like a bell. It was a formalized sort of dance, and she sang breathlessly in accompaniment, making amusing little grimaces. Certainly it was a portrait-doll, animated to mimic the original perfectly in voice and motion. Afterward, Oliver knew he must have dreamed it.

What else happened he was quite unable to remember later. He knew Kleph had said some curious things, but they all made sense at the time, and afterward he couldn't remember a word. He knew he had been offered little glittering candies in a transparent dish, and that some of them had been delicious and one or two so bitter his tongue still curled the next day when he recalled them, and one — Kleph sucked luxuriantly on the same kind — of a taste that was actively nauseating.

As for Kleph herself — he was frantically uncertain the next day what had really happened. He thought he could remember the softness of her white-downed arms clasped at the back of his neck, while she laughed up at him and exhaled into his face the flowery fragrance of the tea. But beyond that he was totally unable to recall anything, for a while.

There was a brief interlude later, before the oblivion of sleep. He was almost sure he remembered a moment when the other two Sanciscos stood looking down at him, the man scowling, the smoky-eyed woman smiling a derisive smile.

The man said, from a vast distance, "Kleph, you know this is against every rule — " His voice began in a thin hum and soared in fantastic flight beyond the range of hearing. Oliver thought he remembered the dark woman's laughter, thin and distant too, and the hum of her voice like bees in flight.

"Kleph, Kleph, you silly little fool, can we never trust you out of our sight?"

Kleph's voice then said something that seemed to make no sense. "What does it matter, *here*?"

The man answered in that buzzing, faraway hum. "The matter of giving your bond before you leave, not to interfere. You know you signed the rules — "

Kleph's voice, nearer and more intelligible: "But here the difference is . . . it does not matter *here*! You both know that. How could it matter?"

Oliver felt the downy brush of her sleeve against his cheek, but he saw nothing except the slow, smokelike ebb and flow of darkness past his eyes. He heard the voices wrangle musically from far away, and he heard them cease.

When he woke the next morning, alone in his own room, he woke with the memory of Kleph's eyes upon him very sorrowfully, her lovely tanned face looking down on him with the red hair falling fragrantly on each side of it and sadness and compassion in her eyes. He thought he had probably dreamed that. There was no reason why anyone should look at him with such sadness.

Sue telephoned that day.

"Oliver, the people who want to buy the house are here. That madwoman and her husband. Shall I bring them over?"

Oliver's mind all day had been hazy with the vague, bewildering memories of yesterday. Kleph's face kept floating before him, blotting out the room. He said, "What? I . . . oh, well, bring them if you want to. I don't see what good it'll do."

"Oliver, what's wrong with you? We agreed we needed the money, didn't we? I don't see how you can think of passing up such a wonderful bargain without even a struggle. We could get married and buy our own house right away, and you know we'll never get such an offer again for that old trashheap. Wake up, Oliver!"

Oliver made an effort. "I know, Sue — I know. But — "

"Oliver, you've got to think of something!" Her voice was imperious.

He knew she was right. Kleph or no Kleph, the bargain shouldn't be ignored if there was any way at all of getting the tenants out. He wondered again what made the place so suddenly priceless to so many people. And what the last week in May had to do with the value of the house.

A sudden sharp curiosity pierced even the vagueness of his mind today. May's last week was so important that the whole sale of the house stood or fell upon occupancy by then. Why? *Why?*

"What's going to happen next week?" he asked rhetorically of the telephone. "Why can't they wait till these people leave? I'd knock a couple of thousand off the price if they'd — "

"You would not, Oliver Wilson! I can buy all our refrigeration units with that extra money. You'll just have to work out some way to give possession by next week, and that's that. You hear me?"

"Keep your shirt on," Oliver said practically. "I'm only human, but I'll try."

"I'm bringing the people over right away," Sue told him. "While the Sanciscos are still out. Now you put your mind to work and think of something, Oliver." She paused, and her voice was reflective when she spoke again. "They're . . . awfully odd people, darling."

"Odd?"

"You'll see."

It was an elderly woman and a very young man who trailed Sue up the walk. Oliver knew immediately what had struck Sue about them. He was somehow not at all surprised to see that both wore their clothing with the familiar air of elegant self-consciousness he had come to know so well. They, too, looked around them at the beautiful, sunny afternoon with conscious enjoyment and an air of faint condescension. He knew before he heard them speak how musical their voices would be and how meticulously they would pronounce each word.

There was no doubt about it. The people of Kleph's mysterious country were arriving here in force — for something. For the last week of May? He shrugged mentally; there was no way of guessing — yet. One thing only was sure: all of them must come from that nameless land where people controlled their voices like singers and their garments like actors who could stop the reel of time itself to adjust every disordered fold.

The elderly woman took full charge of the conversation from the start. They stood together on the rickety, unpainted porch, and Sue had no chance even for introductions.

"Young man, I am Madame Hollia. This is my husband." Her voice had an underrunning current of harshness, which was perhaps age. And her face looked almost corsetted, the loose flesh coerced into something like firmness by some invisible method Oliver could not guess at. The make-up was so skillful he could not be certain it was make-up at all, but he had a definite feeling that she was much older than she looked. It would have taken a lifetime of command to put so much authority into the harsh, deep, musically controlled voice.

The young man said nothing. He was very handsome. His type, apparently, was one that does not change much no matter in what culture or country it may occur. He wore beautifully tailored garments and carried in one gloved hand a box of red leather, about the size and shape of a book.

Madame Hollia went on. "I understand your problem about the house. You wish to sell to me, but are legally bound by your lease with Omerie and his friends. Is that right?"

Oliver nodded. "But — "

"Let me finish. If Omerie can be forced to vacate before next week, you will accept our offer. Right? Very well. Hara!" She nodded to the young man beside her. He jumped to instant attention, bowed slightly, said, "Yes, Hollia," and slipped a gloved hand into his coat.

Madame Hollia took the little object offered on his palm, her gesture as she reached for it almost imperial, as if royal robes swept from her out-stretched arm.

"Here," she said, "is something that may help us. My dear — " She held it out to Sue — "if you can hide this somewhere about the house, I believe your unwelcome tenants will not trouble you much longer."

Sue took the thing curiously. It looked like a tiny silver box, no more than an inch square, indented at the top and with no line to show it could be opened.

"Wait a minute," Oliver broke in uneasily. "What is it?"

"Nothing that will harm anyone, I assure you."

"Then what — "

Madame Hollia's imperious gesture at one sweep silenced him and commanded Sue forward. "Go on, my dear. Hurry, before Omerie comes back. I can assure you there is no danger to anyone."

Oliver broke in determinedly. "Madame Hollia, I'll have to know what your plans are. I — "

"Oh, Oliver, please!" Sue's fingers closed over the silver cube. "Don't worry about it. I'm sure Madame Hollia knows best. Don't you *want* to get those people out?"

"Of course I do. But I don't want the house blown up or — "

Madame Hollia's deep laughter was indulgent. "Nothing so crude, I promise you, Mr. Wilson. Remember, we want the house! Hurry, my dear."

Sue nodded and slipped hastily past Oliver into the hall. Outnumbered, he subsided uneasily. The young man, Hara, tapped a negligent foot and admired the sunlight as they waited. It was an afternoon as perfect as all of May had been, translucent gold, balmy with an edge of chill lingering in the air to point up a perfect contrast with the summer to come. Hara looked around him confidently, like a man paying just tribute to a stage-set provided wholly for himself. He even glanced up at a drone from above and followed the course of a big transcontinental plane half dissolved in golden haze high in the sun. "Quaint," he murmured in a gratified voice.

Sue came back and slipped her hand through Oliver's arm, squeezing excitedly. "There," she said. "How long will it take, Madame Hollia?"

"That will depend, my dear. Not very long. Now, Mr. Wilson, one word with you. You live here also, I understand? For your own comfort, take my advice and — "

Somewhere within the house a door slammed and a clear high voice rang wordlessly up a rippling scale. Then there was the sound of feet on the stairs, and a single line of song. "*Come hider, love, to me* — "

Hara started, almost dropping the red leather box he held.

"Kleph!" he said in a whisper. "Or Klia. I know they both just came on from Canterbury. But I thought — "

"Hush." Madame Hollia's features composed themselves into an imperious blank. She breathed triumphantly through her nose, drew back upon herself and turned an imposing façade to the door.

Kleph wore the same softly downy robe Oliver had seen before, except that today it was not white, but a pale, clear blue that gave her tan an apricot flush. She was smiling.

"Why, Hollia!" Her tone was at its most musical. "I thought I recognized voices from home. How nice to see you. No one knew you were coming to the — " She broke off and glanced at Oliver and then away again. "Hara, too," she said. "What a pleasant surprise."

Sue said flatly, "When did *you* get back?"

Kleph smiled at her. "You must be the little Miss Johnson. Why, I did not go out at all. I was tired of sightseeing. I have been napping in my room."

Sue drew in her breath in something that just escaped being a disbelieving sniff. A look flashed between the two women, and for an instant held — and that instant was timeless. It was an extraordinary pause in which a great deal of wordless interplay took place in the space of a second.

Oliver saw the quality of Kleph's smile at Sue, that same look of quiet confidence he had noticed so often about all of these strange people. He saw Sue's quick inventory of the other woman, and he saw how Sue squared her shoulders and stood up straight, smoothing down her summer frock over her flat hips so that for an instant she stood posed consciously, looking down on Kleph. It was deliberate. Bewildered, he glanced again at Kleph.

Kleph's shoulders sloped softly, her robe was belted to a tiny waist and hung in deep folds over frankly rounded hips. Sue's was the fashionable figure — but Sue was the first to surrender.

Kleph's smile did not falter. But in the silence there was an abrupt reversal of values, based on no more than the measureless quality of Kleph's confidence in herself, the quiet, assured smile. It was suddenly made very clear that fashion is not a constant. Kleph's curious, out-of-mode curves without warning became the norm, and Sue was a queer, angular, half-masculine creature beside her.

Oliver had no idea how it was done. Somehow the authority passed in a breath from one woman to the other. Beauty is almost wholly a matter of fashion; what is beautiful today would have been grotesque a couple of generations ago and will be grotesque a hundred years ahead. It will be worse than grotesque; it will be outmoded and therefore faintly ridiculous.

Sue was that. Kleph had only to exert her authority to make it clear to everyone on the porch. Kleph was a beauty, suddenly and very convincingly, beautiful in the accepted mode, and Sue was amusingly old-fashioned, an anachronism in her lithe, square-shouldered slimness. She did not belong. She was grotesque among these strangely immaculate people.

Sue's collapse was complete. But pride sustained her, and bewilderment. Probably she never did grasp entirely what was wrong. She gave Kleph one glance of burning resentment and when her eyes came back to Oliver there was suspicion in them, and mistrust.

Looking backward later, Oliver thought that in that moment, for the first time clearly, he began to suspect the truth. But he had no time to ponder it, for after the brief instant of enmity the three people from — elsewhere — began to speak all at once, as if in a belated attempt to cover something they did not want noticed.

Kleph said, "This beautiful weather — " and Madame Hollia said, "So fortunate to have this house — " and Hara, holding up the red leather box, said loudest of all, "Cenbe sent you this, Kleph. His latest."

Kleph put out both hands for it eagerly, the eiderdown sleeves falling back from her rounded arms. Oliver had a quick glimpse of that mysterious scar before the sleeve fell back, and it seemed to him that there was the faintest trace of a similar scar vanishing into Hara's cuff as he let his own arm drop.

"Cenbe!" Kleph cried, her voice high and sweet and delighted. "How wonderful! What period?"

"From November 1664," Hara said. "London, of course, though I think there may be some counterpoint from the 1347 November. He hasn't finished — of course." He glanced almost nervously at Oliver and Sue. "A wonderful example," he said quickly. "Marvelous. If you have the taste for it, of course."

Madame Hollia shuddered with ponderous delicacy.

"That man!" she said. "Fascinating, of course — a great man. But — so advanced!"

"It takes a connoisseur to appreciate Cenbe's work fully," Kleph said in a slightly tart voice. "We all admit that."

"Oh yes, we all bow to Cenbe," Hollia conceded. "I confess the man terrifies me a little, my dear. Do we expect him to join us?"

"I suppose so," Kleph said. "If his — work — is not yet finished, then of course. You know Cenbe's tastes."

Hollia and Hara laughed together. "I know when to look for him, then," Hollia said. She glanced at the staring Oliver and the subdued but angry Sue, and with a commanding effort brought the subject back into line.

"So fortunate, my dear Kleph, to have this house," she declared heavily. "I saw a tridimensional of it — afterward — and it was still quite perfect. Such a fortunate coincidence. Would you consider parting with your lease, for a consideration? Say, a coronation seat at — "

"Nothing could buy us, Hollia," Kleph told her gaily, clasping the red box to her bosom.

Hollia gave her a cool stare. "You may change your mind, my dear Kleph," she said pontifically. "There is still time. You can always reach us through Mr. Wilson here. We have rooms up the street in the Montgomery House — nothing like yours, of course, but they will do. For us, they will do."

Oliver blinked. The Montgomery House was the most expensive hotel in town. Compared to this collapsing old ruin, it was a palace. There was no understanding these people. Their values seemed to have suffered a complete reversal.

Madame Hollia moved majestically toward the steps.

"Very pleasant to see you, my dear," she said over one well-padded shoulder. "Enjoy your stay. My regards to Omerie and Klia. Mr. Wilson — " she nodded toward the walk. "A word with you."

Oliver followed her down toward the street. Madame Hollia paused halfway there and touched his arm.

"One word of advice," she said huskily. "You say you sleep here? Move out, young man. Move out before tonight."

Oliver was searching in a half-desultory fashion for the hiding place Sue had found for the mysterious silver cube, when the first sounds from above began to drift down the stairwell toward him. Kleph had closed her door, but the house was old, and strange qualities in the noise overhead seemed to seep through the woodwork like an almost visible stain.

It was music, in a way. But much more than music. And it was a terrible sound, the sounds of calamity and of all human reaction to calamity, everything from hysteria to heartbreak, from irrational joy to rationalized acceptance.

The calamity was — single. The music did not attempt to correlate all human sorrows; it focused sharply upon one and followed the ramifications out and out. Oliver recognized these basics to the sounds in a very brief moment. They were essentials, and they seemed to beat into his brain with the first strains of the music which was so much more than music.

But when he lifted his head to listen he lost all grasp upon the meaning of the noise and it was sheer medley and confusion. To think of it was to blur it hopelessly in the mind, and he could not recapture that first instant of unreasoning acceptance.

He went upstairs almost in a daze, hardly knowing what he was doing. He pushed Kleph's door open. He looked inside —

What he saw there he could not afterward remember except in a blurring as vague as the blurred ideas the music roused in his brain. Half the room had vanished behind a mist, and the mist was a three-dimensional screen upon which were projected — He had no words for them. He was not even sure if the projections were visual. The mist was spinning with motion and sound, but essentially it was neither sound nor motion that Oliver saw.

This was a work of art. Oliver knew no name for it. It transcended all art-forms he knew, blended them, and out of the blend produced subtleties his mind could not begin to grasp. Basically, this was the attempt of a master composer to correlate every essential aspect of a vast human experience into something that could be conveyed in a few moments to every sense at once.

The shifting visions on the screen were not pictures in themselves, but hints of pictures, subtly selected outlines that plucked at the mind and with one deft touch set whole chords ringing through the memory. Perhaps each beholder reacted differently, since it was in the eye and the mind of the beholder that the truth of the picture lay. No two would be aware of the same symphonic panorama, but each would see essentially the same terrible story unfold.

Every sense was touched by that deft and merciless genius. Color and shape and motion flickered in the screen, hinting much, evoking unbearable memories deep in the mind; odors floated from the screen and touched the heart of the beholder more poignantly than anything visual could do. The skin crawled sometimes as if to a tangible cold hand laid upon it. The tongue curled with remembered bitterness and remembered sweet.

It was outrageous. It violated the innermost privacies of a man's mind, called up secret things long ago walled off behind mental scar tissue, forced its terrible message upon the beholder relentlessly though the mind might threaten to crack beneath the stress of it.

And yet, in spite of all this vivid awareness, Oliver did not know what calamity the screen portrayed. That it was real, vast, overwhelmingly dreadful he could not doubt. That it had once happened was unmistakable. He caught flashing glimpses of human faces distorted with grief and disease and death — real faces, faces that had once lived and were seen now in the instant of dying. He saw men and women in rich clothing superimposed in panorama upon reeling thousands of ragged folk, great throngs of them swept past the sight in an instant, and he saw that death made no distinction among them.

He saw lovely women laugh and shake their curls, and the laughter shriek into hysteria and the hysteria into music. He saw one man's face, over and over — a long, dark, saturnine face, deeply lined, sorrowful, the face of a powerful man wise in worldliness, urbane — and helpless. That face was for a while a recurring motif, always more tortured, more helpless than before.

The music broke off in the midst of a rising glide. The mist vanished and the room reappeared before him. The anguished dark face for an instant seemed to Oliver printed everywhere he looked, like after-vision on the eyelids. He knew that face. He had seen it before, not often, but he should know its name —

"Oliver, Oliver — " Kleph's sweet voice came out of a fog at him. He was leaning dizzily against the doorpost looking down into her eyes. She, too, had that dazed blankness he must show on his own face. The power of the dreadful symphony still held them both. But even in this confused moment Oliver saw that Kleph had been enjoying the experience.

He felt sickened to the depths of his mind, dizzy with sickness and revulsion because of the superimposing of human miseries he had just beheld. But Kleph — only appreciation showed upon her face. To her it had been magnificence, and magnificence only.

Irrelevantly Oliver remembered the nauseating candies she had enjoyed, the nauseating odors of strange food that drifted sometimes through the hall from her room.

What was it she had said downstairs a little while ago? Connoisseur, that was it. Only a connoisseur could appreciate work as — as *advanced* — as the work of someone called Cenbe.

A whiff of intoxicating sweetness curled past Oliver's face. Something cool and smooth was pressed into his hand.

"Oh, Oliver, I am so sorry," Kleph's voice murmured contritely. "Here, drink the euphoriac and you will feel better. Please drink!"

The familiar fragrance of the hot sweet tea was on his tongue before he knew he had complied. Its relaxing fumes floated up through his brain and in a moment or two the world felt stable around him again. The room was as it had always been. And Kleph —

Her eyes were very bright. Sympathy showed in them for him, but for herself she was still brimmed with the high elation of what she had just been experiencing.

"Come and sit down," she said gently, tugging at his arm. "I am so sorry — I should not have played that over, where you could hear it. I have no excuse, really. It was only that I forgot what the effect might be on one who had never heard Cenbe's symphonies before. I was so impatient to see what he had done with . . . with his new subject. I am so very sorry, Oliver!"

"What was it?" His voice sounded steadier than he had expected. The tea was responsible for that. He sipped again, glad of the consoling euphoria its fragrance brought.

"A . . . a composite interpretation of . . . oh, Oliver, you know I must not answer questions!"

"But — "

"No — drink your tea and forget what it was you saw. Think of other things. Here, we will have music — another kind of music, something gay — "

She reached for the wall beside the window, and as before, Oliver saw the broad framed picture of blue water above the bed ripple and grow pale. Through it another scene began to dawn like shapes rising beneath the surface of the sea.

He had a glimpse of a dark-curtained stage upon which a man in a tight dark tunic and hose moved with a restless, sidelong pace, his hands and face startlingly pale against the black about him. He limped; he had a crooked back and he spoke familiar lines. Oliver had seen John Barrymore once as the crook-backed Richard, and it seemed vaguely outrageous to him that any other actor should essay that difficult part. This one he had never seen before, but the man had a fascinatingly smooth manner and his interpretation of the Plantagenet king was quite new and something Shakespeare probably never dreamed of.

"No," Kleph said, "not this. Nothing gloomy." And she put out her hand again. The nameless new Richard faded and there was a swirl of changing pictures and changing voices, all blurred together, before the scene steadied upon a stageful of dancers in pastel ballet skirts, drifting effortlessly through some complicated pattern of motion. The music that went with it was light and effortless too. The room filled up with the clear, floating melody.

Oliver set down his cup. He felt much surer of himself now, and he thought the euphoriac had done all it could for him. He didn't want to blur again mentally. There were things he meant to learn about. Now. He considered how to begin.

Kleph was watching him. "That Hollia," she said suddenly. "She wants to buy the house?"

Oliver nodded. "She's offering a lot of money. Sue's going to be awfully disappointed if — " He hesitated. Perhaps, after all, Sue would not be disappointed. He remembered the little silver cube with the enigmatic function and he wondered if he should mention it to Kleph. But the euphoriac had not reached that level of his brain, and he remembered his duty to Sue and was silent.

Kleph shook her head, her eyes upon his warm with — was it sympathy?

"Believe me," she said, "you will not find that — important — after all. I promise you, Oliver."

He stared at her. "I wish you'd explain."

Kleph laughed on a note more sorrowful than amused. But it occurred to Oliver suddenly that there was no longer condescension in her voice. Imperceptibly that air of delicate amusement had vanished from her manner toward him. The cool detachment that still marked Omerie's attitude, and Klia's, was not in Kleph's any more. It was a subtlety he did not think she could assume. It had to come spontaneously or not at all. And for no reason he was willing to examine, it became suddenly very important to Oliver that Kleph should not condescend to him, that she should feel toward him as he felt toward her. He would not think of it.

He looked down at his cup, rose-quartz, exhaling a thin plume of steam from its crescent-slit opening. This time, he thought, maybe he could make the tea work for him. For he remembered how it loosened the tongue, and there was a great deal he needed to know. The idea that had come to him on the porch in the instant of silent rivalry between Kleph and Sue seemed now too fantastic to entertain. But some answer there must be.

Kleph herself gave him the opening.

"I must not take too much euphoriac this afternoon," she said, smiling at him over her pink cup. "It will make me drowsy, and we are going out this evening with friends."

"More friends?" Oliver asked. "From your country?"

Kleph nodded. "Very dear friends we have expected all this week."

"I wish you'd tell me," Oliver said bluntly, "where it is you come from. It isn't from here. Your culture is too different from ours — even your names — " He broke off as Kleph shook her head.

"I wish I could tell you. But that is against all the rules. It is even against the rules for me to be here talking to you now."

"What rules?"

She made a helpless gesture. "You must not ask me, Oliver." She leaned back on the chaise longue, which adjusted itself luxuriously to the motion, and smiled very sweetly at him. "We must not talk about things like that. Forget it, listen to the music, enjoy yourself if you can — " She closed her eyes and laid her head back against the cushions. Oliver saw the round tanned throat swell as she began to hum a tune. Eyes still closed, she sang again the words she had sung upon the stairs. "*Come hider, love, to me — *"

A memory clicked over suddenly in Oliver's mind. He had never heard the queer, lagging tune before, but he thought he knew the words. He remembered what Hollia's husband had said when he heard that line of song, and he leaned forward. She would not answer a direct question, but perhaps —

"Was the weather this warm in Canterbury?" he asked, and held his breath. Kleph hummed another line of the song and shook her head, eyes still closed.

"It was autumn there," she said. "But bright, wonderfully bright. Even their clothing, you know . . . everyone was singing that new song, and I can't get it out of my head." She sang another line, and the words were almost unintelligible — English, yet not an English Oliver could understand.

He stood up. "Wait," he said. "I want to find something. Back in a minute."

She opened her eyes and smiled mistily at him, still humming. He went downstairs as fast as he could — the stairway swayed a little, though his head was nearly clear now — and into the library. The book he wanted was old and battered, interlined with the penciled notes of his college days. He did not remember very clearly where the passage he wanted was, but he thumbed fast through the columns and by sheer luck found it within a few minutes. Then he went back upstairs, feeling a strange emptiness in his stomach because of what he almost believed now.

"Kleph," he said firmly, "I know that song. I know the year it was new."

Her lids rose slowly; she looked at him through a mist of euphoriac. He was not sure she had understood. For a long moment she held him with her gaze. Then she put out one downy-sleeved arm and spread her tanned fingers toward him. She laughed deep in her throat.

"*Come hider, love, to me*," she said.

He crossed the room slowly, took her hand. The fingers closed warmly about his. She pulled him down so that he had to kneel beside her. Her other arm lifted. Again she laughed, very softly, and closed her eyes, lifting her face to his.

The kiss was warm and long. He caught something of her own euphoria from the fragrance of the tea breathed into his face. And he was startled at the end of the kiss, when the clasp of her arms loosened about his neck, to feel the sudden rush of her breath against his cheek. There were tears on her face, and the sound she made was a sob.

He held her off and looked down in amazement. She sobbed once more, caught a deep breath, and said, "Oh, Oliver, Oliver — " Then she shook her head and pulled free, turning away to hide her face. "I . . . I am sorry," she said unevenly. "Please forgive me. It does not matter . . . I *know* it does not matter . . . but — "

"What's wrong? What doesn't matter?"

"Nothing. Nothing . . . please forget it. Nothing at all." She got a handkerchief from the table and blew her nose, smiling at him with an effect of radiance through the tears.

Suddenly he was very angry. He had heard enough evasions and mystifying half-truths. He said roughly, "Do you think I'm crazy? I know enough now to — "

"Oliver, please!" She held up her own cup, steaming fragrantly. "Please, no more questions. Here, euphoria is what you need, Oliver. Euphoria, not answers."

"What year was it when you heard that song in Canterbury?" he demanded, pushing the cup aside.

She blinked at him, tears bright on her lashes. "Why . . . what year do you think?"

"I know," Oliver told her grimly. "I know the year that song was popular. I know you just came from Canterbury — Hollia's husband said so. It's May now, but it was autumn in Canterbury, and you just came from there, so lately the song you heard is still running through your head. Chaucer's Pardoner sang that song some time around the end of the fourteenth century. Did you see Chaucer, Kleph? What was it like in England that long ago?"

Kleph's eyes fixed his for a silent moment. Then her shoulders drooped and her whole body went limp with resignation beneath the soft blue robe. "I am a fool," she said gently. "It must have been easy to trap me. You really believe — what you say?"

Oliver nodded.

She said in a low voice. "Few people do believe it. That is one of our maxims, when we travel. We are safe from much suspicion because people before The Travel began will not believe."

The emptiness in Oliver's stomach suddenly doubled in volume. For an instant the bottom dropped out of time itself and the universe was unsteady about him. He felt sick. He felt naked and helpless. There was a buzzing in his ears and the room dimmed before him.

He had not really believed — not until this instant. He had expected some rational explanation from her that would tidy all his wild half-thoughts and suspicions into something a man could accept as believable. Not this.

Kleph dabbed at her eyes with the pale-blue handkerchief and smiled tremulously.

"I know," she said. "It must be a terrible thing to accept. To have all your concepts turned upside down — We know it from childhood, of course, but for you . . . here, Oliver. The euphoriac will make it easier."

He took the cup, the faint stain of her lip rouge still on the crescent opening. He drank, feeling the dizzy sweetness spiral through his head, and his brain turned a little in his skull as the volatile fragrance took effect. With that turning, focus shifted and all his values with it.

He began to feel better. The flesh settled on his bones again, and the warm clothing of temporal assurance settled upon his flesh, and he was no longer naked and in the vortex of unstable time.

"The story is very simple, really," Kleph said. "We — travel. Our own time is not terribly far ahead of yours. No. I must not say how far. But we still remember your songs and poets and some of your great actors. We are a people of much leisure, and we cultivate the art of enjoying ourselves.

"This is a tour we are making — a tour of a year's seasons. Vintage seasons. That autumn in Canterbury was the most magnificent autumn our researchers could discover anywhere. We rode in a pilgrimage to the shrine — it was a wonderful experience, though the clothing was a little hard to manage.

"Now this month of May is almost over — the loveliest May in recorded times. A perfect May in a wonderful period. You have no way of knowing what a good, gay period you live in, Oliver. The very feeling in the air of the cities — that wonderful national confidence and happiness — everything going as smoothly as a dream. There were other Mays with fine weather, but each of them had a war or a famine, or something else wrong." She hesitated, grimaced and went on rapidly. "In a few days we are to meet at a coronation in Rome," she said. "I think the year will be 800 — Christmastime. We — "

"But why," Oliver interrupted, "did you insist on this house? Why do the others want to get it away from you?"

Kleph stared at him. He saw the tears rising again in small bright crescents that gathered above her lower lids. He saw the look of obstinacy that came upon her soft, tanned face. She shook her head.

"You must not ask me that." She held out the steaming cup. "Here, drink and forget what I have said. I can tell you no more. No more at all."

When he woke, for a little while he had no idea where he was. He did not remember leaving Kleph or coming to his own room. He didn't care, just then. For he woke to a sense of overwhelming terror.

The dark was full of it. His brain rocked on waves of fear and pain. He lay motionless, too frightened to stir, some atavistic memory warning him to lie quiet until he knew from which direction the danger threatened. Reasonless panic broke over him in a tidal flow; his head ached with its violence and the dark throbbed to the same rhythms.

A knock sounded at the door. Omerie's deep voice said, "Wilson! Wilson, are you awake?"

Oliver tried twice before he had breath to answer. "Y-yes — what is it?"

The knob rattled. Omerie's dim figure groped for the light switch and the room sprang into visibility. Omerie's face was drawn with strain, and he held one hand to his head as if it ached in rhythm with Oliver's.

It was in that moment, before Omerie spoke again, that Oliver remembered Hollia's warning. "Move out, young man — move out before tonight." Wildly he wondered what threatened them all in this dark house that throbbed with the rhythms of pure terror.

Omerie in an angry voice answered the unspoken question.

"Someone has planted a subsonic in the house, Wilson. Kleph thinks you may know where it is."

"S-subsonic?"

"Call it a gadget," Omerie interpreted impatiently. "Probably a small metal box that — "

Oliver said, "Oh," in a tone that must have told Omerie everything.

"Where is it?" he demanded. "Quick. Let's get this over."

"I don't know." With an effort Oliver controlled the chattering of his teeth. "Y-you mean all this — all this is just from the little box?"

"Of course. Now tell me how to find it before we all go crazy."

Oliver got shakily out of bed, groping for his robe with nerveless hands. "I s-suppose she hid it somewhere downstairs," he said. "S-she wasn't gone long."

Omerie got the story out of him in a few brief questions. He clicked his teeth in exasperation when Oliver had finished it.

"That stupid Hollia — "

"Omerie!" Kleph's plaintive voice wailed from the hall. "Please hurry, Omerie! This is too much to stand! Oh, Omerie, please!"

Oliver stood up abruptly. Then a redoubled wave of the inexplicable pain seemed to explode in his skull at the motion, and he clutched the bedpost and reeled.

"Go find the thing yourself," he heard himself saying dizzily. "I can't even walk — "

Omerie's own temper was drawn wire-tight by the pressure in the room. He seized Oliver's shoulder and shook him, saying in a tight voice, "You let it in — now help us get it out, or — "

"It's a gadget out of your world, not mine!" Oliver said furiously.

And then it seemed to him there was a sudden coldness and silence in the room. Even the pain and the senseless terror paused for a moment. Omerie's pale, cold eyes fixed upon Oliver a stare so chill he could almost feel the ice in it.

"What do you know about our — world?" Omerie demanded.

Oliver did not speak a word. He did not need to; his face must have betrayed what he knew. He was beyond concealment in the stress of this nighttime terror he still could not understand.

Omerie bared his white teeth and said three perfectly unintelligible words. Then he stepped to the door and snapped, "Kleph!"

Oliver could see the two women huddled together in the hall, shaking violently with involuntary waves of that strange, synthetic terror. Klia, in a luminous green gown, was rigid with control, but Kleph made no effort whatever at repression. Her downy robe had turned soft gold tonight; she shivered in it and the tears ran down her face unchecked.

"Kleph," Omerie said in a dangerous voice, "you were euphoric again yesterday?"

Kleph darted a scared glance at Oliver and nodded guiltily.

"You talked too much." It was a complete indictment in one sentence. "You know the rules, Kleph. You will not be allowed to travel again if anyone reports this to the authorities."

Kleph's lovely creamy face creased suddenly into impenitent dimples.

"I know it was wrong. I am very sorry — but you will not stop me if Cenbe says no."

Klia flung out her arms in a gesture of helpless anger. Omerie shrugged. "In this case, as it happens, no great harm is done," he said, giving Oliver an unfathomable glance. "But it might have been serious. Next time perhaps it will be. I must have a talk with Cenbe."

"We must find the subsonic first of all," Klia reminded them, shivering. "If Kleph is afraid to help, she can go out for a while. I confess I am very sick of Kleph's company just now."

"We could give up the house!" Kleph cried wildly. "Let Hollia have it! How can you stand this long enough to hunt — "

"Give up the house?" Klia echoed. "You must be mad! With all our invitations out?"

"There will be no need for that," Omerie said. "We can find it if we all hunt. You feel able to help?" He looked at Oliver.

With an effort Oliver controlled his own senseless panic as the waves of it swept through the room. "Yes," he said. "But what about me? What are you going to do?"

"That should be obvious," Omerie said, his pale eyes in the dark face regarding Oliver impassively. "Keep you in the house until we go. We can certainly do no less. You understand that. And there is no reason for us to do more, as it happens. Silence is all we promised when we signed our travel papers."

"But — " Oliver groped for the fallacy in that reasoning. It was no use. He could not think clearly. Panic surged insanely through his mind from the very air around him. "All right," he said. "Lets hunt."

It was dawn before they found the box, tucked inside the ripped seam of a sofa cushion. Omerie took it upstairs without a word. Five minutes later the pressure in the air abruptly dropped and peace fell blissfully upon the house.

"They will try again," Omerie said to Oliver at the door of the back bedroom. "We must watch for that. As for you, I must see that you remain in the house until Friday. For your own comfort, I advise you to let me know if Hollia offers any further tricks. I confess I am not quite sure how to enforce your staying indoors. I could use methods that would make you very uncomfortable. I would prefer to accept your word on it."

Oliver hesitated. The relaxing of pressure upon his brain had left him exhausted and stupid, and he was not at all sure what to say.

Omerie went on after a moment. "It was partly our fault for not insuring that we had the house to ourselves," he said. "Living here with us, you could scarcely help suspecting. Shall we say that in return for your promise, I reimburse you in part for losing the sale price on this house?"

Oliver thought that over. It would pacify Sue a little. And it meant only two days indoors. Besides, what good would escaping do? What could he say to outsiders that would not lead him straight to a padded cell?

"All right," he said wearily. "I promise."

By Friday morning there was still no sign from Hollia. Sue telephoned at noon. Oliver knew the crackle of her voice over the wire when Kleph took the call. Even the crackle sounded hysterical; Sue saw her bargain slipping hopelessly through her grasping little fingers.

Kleph's voice was soothing. "I am sorry," she said many times, in the intervals when the voice paused. "I am truly sorry. Believe me, you will find it does not matter. I know . . . I am sorry — "

She turned from the phone at last. "The girl says Hollia has given up," she told the others.

"Not Hollia," Klia said firmly.

Omerie shrugged. "We have very little time left. If she intends anything more, it will be tonight. We must watch for it."

"Oh, not tonight!" Kleph's voice was horrified. "Not even Hollia would do that!"

"Hollia, my dear, in her own way is quite as unscrupulous as you are," Omerie told her with a smile.

"But — would she spoil things for us just because she can't be here?"

"What do you think?" Klia demanded.

Oliver ceased to listen. There was no making sense out of their talk, but he knew that by tonight whatever the secret was must surely come into the open at last. He was willing to wait and see.

For two days excitement had been building up in the house and the three who shared it with him. Even the servants felt it and were nervous and unsure of themselves. Oliver had given up asking questions — it only embarrassed his tenants — and watched.

All the chairs in the house were collected in the three front bedrooms. The furniture was rearranged to make room for them, and dozens of covered cups had been set out on trays. Oliver recognized Kleph's rose-quartz set among the rest. No steam rose from the thin crescent-openings, but the cups were full. Oliver lifted one and felt a heavy liquid move within it, like something half-solid, sluggishly.

Guests were obviously expected, but the regular dinner hour of nine came and went, and no one had yet arrived. Dinner was finished; the servants went home. The Sanciscos went to their rooms to dress, amid a feeling of mounting tension.

Oliver stepped out on the porch after dinner, trying in vain to guess what it was that had wrought such a pitch of expectancy in the house. There was a quarter moon swimming in haze on the horizon, but the stars which had made every night of May thus far a dazzling translucency, were very dim tonight. Clouds had begun to gather at sundown, and the undimmed weather of the whole month seemed ready to break at last.

Behind Oliver the door opened a little, and closed. He caught Kleph's fragrance before he turned, and a faint whiff of the fragrance of the euphoriac she was much too fond of drinking. She came to his side and slipped a hand into his, looking up into his face in the darkness.

"Oliver," she said very softly. "Promise me one thing. Promise me not to leave the house tonight."

"I've already promised that," he said a little irritably.

"I know. But tonight — I have a very particular reason for wanting you indoors tonight." She leaned her head against his shoulder for a moment, and despite himself his irritation softened. He had not seen Kleph alone since that last night of her revelations; he supposed he never would be alone with her again for more than a few minutes at a time. But he knew he would not forget those two bewildering evenings. He knew too, now, that she was very weak and foolish — but she was still Kleph and he had held her in his arms, and was not likely ever to forget it.

"You might be — hurt — if you went out tonight," she was saying in a muffled voice. "I know it will not matter, in the end, but — remember you promised, Oliver."

She was gone again, and the door had closed behind her, before he could voice the futile questions in his mind.

The guests began to arrive just before midnight. From the head of the stairs Oliver saw them coming in by twos and threes, and was astonished at how many of these people from the future must have gathered here in the past weeks. He could see quite clearly now how they differed from the norm of his own period. Their physical elegance was what one noticed first — perfect grooming, meticulous manners, meticulously controlled voices. But because they were all idle, all, in a way, sensation-hunters, there was a certain shrillness underlying their voices, especially when heard all together. Petulance and self-indulgence showed beneath the good manners. And tonight, an all-pervasive excitement.

By one o'clock everyone had gathered in the front rooms. The teacups had begun to steam, apparently of themselves, around midnight, and the house was full of the faint, thin fragrance that induced a sort of euphoria all through the rooms, breathed in with the perfume of the tea.

It made Oliver feel light and drowsy. He was determined to sit up as long as the others did, but he must have dozed off in his own room, by the window, an unopened book in his lap.

For when it happened he was not sure for a few minutes whether or not it was a dream.

The vast, incredible crash was louder than sound. He felt the whole house shake under him, felt rather than heard the timbers grind upon one another like broken bones, while he was still in the borderland of sleep. When he woke fully he was on the floor among the shattered fragments of the window.

How long or short a time he had lain there he did not know. The world was still stunned with that tremendous noise, or his ears still deaf from it, for there was no sound anywhere.

He was halfway down the hall toward the front rooms when sound began to return from outside. It was a low, indescribable rumble at first, prickled with countless tiny distant screams. Oliver's eardrums ached from the terrible impact of the vast unheard noise, but the numbness was wearing off and he heard before he saw it the first voices of the stricken city.

The door to Kleph's room resisted him for a moment. The house had settled a little from the violence of the — the explosion? — and the frame was out of line. When he got the door open he could only stand blinking stupidly into the darkness within. All the lights were out, but there was a breathless sort of whispering going on in many voices.

The chairs were drawn around the broad front windows so that everyone could see out; the air swam with the fragrance of euphoria. There was light enough here from outside for Oliver to see that a few onlookers still had their hands to their ears, but all were craning eagerly forward to see.

Through a dreamlike haze Oliver saw the city spread out with impossible distinctness below the window. He knew quite well that a row of houses across the street blocked the view — yet he was looking over the city now, and he could see it in a limitless panorama from here to the horizon. The houses between had vanished.

On the far skyline fire was already a solid mass, painting the low clouds crimson. That sulphurous light reflecting back from the sky upon the city made clear the rows upon rows of flattened houses with flame beginning to lick up among them, and farther out the formless rubble of what had been houses a few minutes ago and was now nothing at all.

The city had begun to be vocal. The noise of the flames rose loudest, but you could hear a rumble of human voices like the beat of surf a long way off, and staccato noises of screaming made a sort of pattern that came and went continuously through the web of sound. Threading it in undulating waves the shrieks of sirens knit the web together into a terrible symphony that had, in its way, a strange, inhuman beauty.

Briefly through Oliver's stunned incredulity went the memory of that other symphony Kleph had played there one day, another catastrophe retold in terms of music and moving shapes.

He said hoarsely, "Kleph — "

The tableau by the window broke. Every head turned, and Oliver saw the faces of strangers staring at him, some few in embarrassment avoiding his eyes, but most seeking them out with that avid, inhuman curiosity which is common to a type in all crowds at accident scenes. But these people were here by design, audience at a vast disaster timed almost for their coming.

Kleph got up unsteadily, her velvet dinner gown tripping her as she rose. She set down a cup and swayed a little as she came toward the door, saying, "Oliver . . . Oliver — " in a sweet, uncertain voice. She was drunk, he saw, and wrought up by the catastrophe to a pitch of stimulation in which she was not very sure what she was doing.

Oliver heard himself saying in a thin voice not his own, "W-what was it, Kleph? What happened? What — " But *happened* seemed so inadequate a word for the incredible panorama below that he had to choke back hysterical laughter upon the struggling questions, and broke off entirely; trying to control the shaking that had seized his body.

Kleph made an unsteady stoop and seized a steaming cup. She came to him, swaying, holding it out — her panacea for all ills.

"Here, drink it, Oliver — we are all quite safe here, quite safe." She thrust the cup to his lips and he gulped automatically, grateful for the fumes that began their slow, coiling surcease in his brain with the first swallow.

"It was a meteor," Kleph was saying. "Quite a small meteor, really. We are perfectly safe here. This house was never touched."

Out of some cell of the unconscious Oliver heard himself saying incoherently, "Sue? Is Sue — " he could not finish.

Kleph thrust the cup at him again. "I think she may be safe — for awhile. Please, Oliver — forget about all that and drink."

"But you *knew*!" Realization of that came belatedly to his stunned brain. "You could have given warning, or — "

"How could we change the past?" Kleph asked. "We knew — but could we stop the meteor? Or warn the city? Before we come we must give our word never to interfere — "

Their voices had risen imperceptibly to be audible above the rising volume of sound from below. The city was roaring now, with flames and cries and the crash of falling buildings. Light in the room turned lurid and pulsed upon the walls and ceiling in red light and redder dark.

Downstairs a door slammed. Someone laughed. It was high, hoarse, angry laughter. Then from the crowd in the room someone gasped and there was a chorus of dismayed cries. Oliver tried to focus upon the window and the terrible panorama beyond, and found he could not.

It took several seconds of determined blinking to prove that more than his own vision was at fault. Kleph whimpered softly and moved against him. His arms closed about her automatically, and he was grateful for the warm, solid flesh against him. This much at least he could touch and be sure of, though everything else that was happening might be a dream. Her perfume and the heady perfume of the tea rose together in his head, and for an instant, holding her in this embrace that must certainly be the last time he ever held her, he did not care that something had gone terribly wrong with the very air of the room.

It was blindness — not continuous, but a series of swift, widening ripples between which he could catch glimpses of the other faces in the room, strained and astonished in the flickering light from the city.

The ripples came faster. There was only a blink of sight between them now, and the blinks grew briefer and briefer, the intervals of darkness more broad.

From downstairs the laughter rose again up the stairwell. Oliver thought he knew the voice. He opened his mouth to speak, but a door nearby slammed open before he could find his tongue, and Omerie shouted down the stairs.

"Hollia?" he roared above the roaring of the city. "Hollia, is that you?"

She laughed again, triumphantly. "I warned you!" her hoarse, harsh voice called. "Now come out in the street with the rest of us if you want to see any more!"

"Hollia!" Omerie shouted desperately. "Stop this or — "

The laughter was derisive. "What will you do, Omerie? This time I hid it too well — come down in the street if you want to watch the rest."

There was angry silence in the house. Oliver could feel Kleph's quick, excited breathing light upon his cheek, feel the soft motions of her body in his arms. He tried consciously to make the moment last, stretch it out to infinity. Everything had happened too swiftly to impress very clearly on his mind anything except what he could touch and hold. He held her in an embrace made consciously light, though he wanted to clasp her in a tight, despairing grip, because he was sure this was the last embrace they would ever share.

The eye-straining blinks of light and blindness went on. From far away below the roar of the burning city rolled on, threaded together by the long, looped cadences of the sirens that linked all sounds into one.

Then in the bewildering dark another voice sounded from the hall downstairs. A man's voice, very deep, very melodious, saying:

"What is this? What are you doing here? Hollia — is that you?"

Oliver felt Kleph stiffen in his arms. She caught her breath, but she said nothing in the instant while heavy feet began to mount the stairs, coming up with a solid, confident tread that shook the old house to each step.

Then Kleph thrust herself hard out of Oliver's arms. He heard her high, sweet, excited voice crying, "Cenbe! Cenbe!" and she ran to meet the newcomer through the waves of dark and light that swept the shaken house.

Oliver staggered a little and felt a chair seat catching the back of his legs. He sank into it and lifted to his lips the cup he still held. Its steam was warm and moist in his face, though he could scarcely make out the shape of the rim.

He lifted it with both hands and drank.

When he opened his eyes it was quite dark in the room. Also it was silent except for a thin, melodious humming almost below the threshold of sound. Oliver struggled with the memory of a monstrous nightmare. He put it resolutely out of his mind and sat up, feeling an unfamiliar bed creak and sway under him.

This was Kleph's room. But no — Kleph's no longer. Her shining hangings were gone from the walls, her white resilient rug, her pictures. The room looked as it had looked before she came, except for one thing.

In the far corner was a table — a block of translucent stuff — out of which light poured softly. A man sat on a low stool before it, leaning forward, his heavy shoulders outlined against the glow. He wore earphones and he was making quick, erratic notes upon a pad on his knee, swaying a little as if to the tune of unheard music.

The curtains were drawn, but from beyond them came a distant, muffled roaring that Oliver remembered from his nightmare. He put a hand to his face, aware of a feverish warmth and a dipping of the room before his eyes. His head ached, and there was a deep malaise in every limb and nerve.

As the bed creaked, the man in the corner turned, sliding the earphones down like a collar. He had a strong, sensitive face above a dark beard, trimmed short. Oliver had never seen him before, but he had that air Oliver knew so well by now, of remoteness which was the knowledge of time itself lying like a gulf between them.

When he spoke his deep voice was impersonally kind.

"You had too much euphoriac, Wilson," he said, aloofly sympathetic. You slept a long while."

"How long?" Oliver's throat felt sticky when he spoke.

The man did not answer. Oliver shook his head experimentally. He said, "I thought Kleph said you don't get hangovers from — " Then another thought interrupted the first, and he said quickly, "Where is Kleph?" He looked confusedly toward the door.

"They should be in Rome by now. Watching Charlemagne's coronation at St. Peter's on Christmas Day a thousand years from here."

That was not a thought Oliver could grasp clearly. His aching brain sheered away from it; he found thinking at all was strangely difficult. Staring at the man, he traced an idea painfully to its conclusion.

"So they've gone on — but you stayed behind? Why? You . . . you're Cenbe? I heard your — symphonia, Kleph called it."

"You heard part of it. I have not finished yet. I needed — this." Cenbe inclined his head toward the curtains beyond which the subdued roaring still went on.

"You needed — the meteor?" The knowledge worked painfully through his dulled brain until it seemed to strike some area still untouched by the aching, an area still alive to implication. "The *meteor*? But — "

There was a power implicit in Cenbe's raised hand that seemed to push Oliver down upon the bed again. Cenbe said patiently, "The worst of it is past now, for a while. Forget if you can. That was days ago. I said you were asleep for some time. I let you rest. I knew this house would be safe — from the fire at least."

"Then — something more's to come?" Oliver only mumbled his question. He was not sure he wanted an answer. He had been curious so long, and now that knowledge lay almost within reach, something about his brain seemed to refuse to listen. Perhaps this weariness, this feverish, dizzy feeling would pass as the effect of the euphoriac wore off.

Cenbe's voice ran on smoothly, soothingly, almost as if Cenbe, too, did not want him to think. It was easiest to lie here and listen.

"I am a composer," Cenbe was saying. "I happen to be interested in interpreting certain forms of disaster into my own terms. That is why I stayed on. The others were dilettantes. They came for the May weather and the spectacle. The aftermath — well why should they wait for that? As for myself — I suppose I am a connoisseur. I find the aftermath rather fascinating. And I need it. I need to study it at first hand, for my own purposes."

His eyes dwelt upon Oliver for an instant very keenly, like a physician's eyes, impersonal and observing. Absently he reached for his stylus and the note pad. And as he moved, Oliver saw a familiar mark on the underside of the thick, tanned wrist.

"Kleph had that scar, too," he heard himself whisper. "And the others."

Cenbe nodded. "Inoculation. It was necessary, under the circumstances. We did not want disease to spread in our own time-world."

"Disease?"

Cenbe shrugged. "You would not recognize the name."

"But, if you can inoculate against disease — " Oliver thrust himself up on an aching arm. He had a half-grasp upon a thought now which he did not want to let go. Effort seemed to make the ideas come more clearly through his mounting confusion. With enormous effort he went on.

"I'm getting it now," he said. "Wait. I've been trying to work this out. You can change history? You can! I know you can. Kleph said she had to promise not to interfere. You all had to promise. Does that mean you really could change your own past — our time?"

Cenbe laid down his pad again. He looked at Oliver thoughtfully, a dark, intent look under heavy brows. "Yes," he said. "Yes, the past can be changed, but not easily. And it changes the future, too, necessarily. The lines of probability are switched into new patterns — but it is extremely difficult, and it has never been allowed. The physio-temporal course tends to slide back to its norm, always. That is why it is so hard to force any alteration." He shrugged. "A theoretical science. We do not change history, Wilson. If we changed our past, our present would be altered, too. And our time-world is entirely to our liking. There may be a few malcontents there, but they are not allowed the privilege of temporal travel."

Oliver spoke louder against the roaring from beyond the windows. "But you've got the power! You could alter history, if you wanted to — wipe out all the pain and suffering and tragedy — "

"All of that passed away long ago," Cenbe said.

"Not — *now*! Not — *this*!"

Cenbe looked at him enigmatically for a while. Then — "This, too," he said.

And suddenly Oliver realized from across what distances Cenbe was watching him. A vast distance, as time is measured. Cenbe was a composer and a genius, and necessarily strongly empathic, but his psychic locus was very far away in time. The dying city outside, the whole world of *now* was not quite real to Cenbe, falling short of reality because of that basic variance in time. It was merely one of the building blocks that had gone to support the edifice on which Cenbe's culture stood in a misty, unknown, terrible future.

It seemed terrible to Oliver now. Even Kleph — all of them had been touched with a pettiness, the faculty that had enabled Hollia to concentrate on her malicious, small schemes to acquire a ringside seat while the meteor thundered in toward Earth's atmosphere. They were all dilettantes, Kleph and Omerie and the other. They toured time, but only as onlookers. Were they bored — sated — with their normal existence?

Not sated enough to wish change, basically. Their own time-world was a fulfilled womb, a perfection made manifest for their needs. They dared not change the past — they could not risk flawing their own present.

Revulsion shook him. Remembering the touch of Kleph's lips, he felt a sour sickness on his tongue. Alluring she had been; he knew that too well. But the aftermath —

There was something about this race from the future. He had felt it dimly at first, before Kleph's nearness had drowned caution and buffered his sensibilities. Time traveling purely as an escape mechanism seemed almost blasphemous. A race with such power —

Kleph — leaving him for the barbaric, splendid coronation at Rome a thousand years ago — *how had she seen him?* Not as a living, breathing man. He knew that, very certainly. Kleph's race were spectators.

But he read more than casual interest in Cenbe's eyes now. There was an avidity there, a bright, fascinated probing. The man had replaced his earphones — he was different from the others. He was a connoisseur. After the vintage season came the aftermath — and Cenbe.

Cenbe watched and waited, light flickering softly in the translucent block before him, his fingers poised over the note pad. The ultimate connoisseur waited to savor the rarities that no non-gourmet could appreciate.

Those thin, distant rhythms of sound that was almost music began to be audible again above the noises of the distant fire. Listening, remembering, Oliver could very nearly catch the pattern of the symphonia as he had heard it, all intermingled with the flash of changing faces and the rank upon rank of the dying —

He lay back on the bed letting the room swirl away into the darkness behind his closed and aching lids. The ache was implicit in every cell of his body, almost a second ego taking possession and driving him out of himself, a strong, sure ego taking over as he himself let go.

Why, he wondered dully, should Kleph have lied? She had said there was no aftermath to the drink she had given him. No aftermath — and yet this painful possession was strong enough to edge him out of his own body.

Kleph had not lied. It was no aftermath to drink. He knew that — but the knowledge no longer touched his brain or his body. He lay still, giving them up to the power of the illness which was aftermath to something far stronger than the strongest drink. The illness that had no name — yet.

Cenbe's new symphonia was a crowning triumph. It had its premiere from Antares Hall, and the applause was an ovation. History itself, of course, was the artist — opening with the meteor that forecast the great plagues of the fourteenth century and closing with the climax Cenbe had caught on the threshold of modern times. But only Cenbe could have interpreted it with such subtle power.

Critics spoke of the masterly way in which he had chosen the face of the Stuart king as a recurrent motif against the montage of emotion and sound and movement. But there were other faces, fading through the great sweep of the composition, which helped to build up to the tremendous climax. One face in particular, one moment that the audience absorbed greedily. A moment in which one man's face loomed huge in the screen, every feature clear. Cenbe had never caught an emotional crisis so effectively, the critics agreed. You could almost read the man's eyes.

After Cenbe had left, he lay motionless for a long while. He was thinking feverishly —

I've got to find some way to tell people. If I'd known in advance, maybe something could have been done. We'd have forced them to tell us how to change the probabilities. We could have evacuated the city.

If I could leave a message —

Maybe not for today's people. But later. They visit all through time. If they could be recognized and caught somewhere, sometime, and made to change destiny —

It wasn't easy to stand up. The room kept tilting. But he managed it. He found pencil and paper and through the swaying of the shadows he wrote down what he could. Enough. Enough to warn, enough to save.

He put the sheets on the table, in plain sight, and weighted them down before he stumbled back to bed through closing darkness.

The house was dynamited six days later, part of the futile attempt to halt the relentless spread of the Blue Death.

Robert A. Heinlein

"All You Zombies — "
(1959)

Robert A. Heinlein (1907–1988) is one of the most widely recognized names in
sf. The star of the second generation of writers in John W. Campbell Jr.'s stable, Heinlein became the defining voice of American sf throughout the 1940s
and 1950s; he left a lasting mark on the genre, and his influence continues to
be felt today. With his colorful characters and his confident, breezy style,
Heinlein evoked a future that seemed both plausible and exciting.

Before becoming a science fiction writer, Heinlein served as a naval officer and studied physics, and the influence of both his military and his scientific backgrounds can be seen in his work. Heinlein believed in moral imperatives, gifted leaders, and the idea of progress. Often described as a social
conservative and an advocate for "hard" (science-oriented) sf, in fact Heinlein
is more complicated. It is true that he followed developments in science and
enjoyed extrapolating new technologies — he was one of the first to write
about the dangers of radioactivity, and one of his fictional inventions, the
waldo, gave its name to an actual device still used today. It is also true that
he can be didactic and militaristic at times, particularly in his later fiction. Yet
neither the conservative nor the hard sf label is a perfect fit. His most popular
novel, *Stranger in a Strange Land*, with its emphasis on mysticism and free
love, became a cult novel for the counterculture of the 1960s and 1970s.
Similarly, there are often sexist elements in his work, yet he also created bold
and accomplished female characters who broke from the stereotypical roles
of the genre. And, although he was fond of gadgets and prided himself on
his predictive abilities, it was always the social effects of new technologies
that most interested him. The seeming contradictions in Heinlein's political
philosophy can be reconciled by realizing that he was above all an individualist, a libertarian who believed in radical personal liberty with minimum interference by the state. As to the hard versus soft sf dichotomy, however useful
it may be as shorthand, it has never been adequate for describing the work
of the genre's great writers.

With his broad interests and inventive imagination, Heinlein left his mark
on many classic sf themes. The story that follows is one of the most famous
treatments of the time-paradox idea. Anyone who gives serious thought to the
idea of time travel will quickly realize the problems of causality that might arise
were such a thing possible. Among the most famous of such problems is the
so-called grandfather paradox: What if you went back in time and killed your
grandfather? Would you ever exist? And, if not, how could you have gone
back and killed him? Here, in Heinlein's hands, the already confusing question
of causality and identity inherent in the grandfather paradox becomes even
more complicated.

2217 Time Zone V (EST) 7 Nov. 1970 — NYC –"Pop's Place": I was polishing a brandy snifter when the Unmarried Mother came in. I noted the time — 10:17 p.m., zone five, or eastern time, November 7th, 1970. Temporal agents always notice time and date; we must.

The Unmarried Mother was a man twenty-five years old, no taller than I am, childish features and a touchy temper. I didn't like his looks — I never had — but he was a lad I was here to recruit, he was my boy. I gave him my best barkeep's smile.

Maybe I'm too critical. He wasn't swish; his nickname came from what he always said when some nosy type asked him his line: "I'm an unmarried mother." If he felt less than murderous he would add: "at four cents a word. I write confession stories."

If he felt nasty, he would wait for somebody to make something of it. He had a lethal style of infighting, like a female cop — one reason I wanted him. Not the only one.

He had a load on and his face showed that he despised people more than usual. Silently I poured a double shot of Old Underwear and left the bottle. He drank it, poured another.

I wiped the bar top. "How's the 'Unmarried Mother' racket?"

His fingers tightened on the glass and he seemed about to throw it at me; I felt for the sap under the bar. In temporal manipulation you try to figure everything, but there are so many factors that you never take needless risks.

I saw him relax that tiny amount they teach you to watch for in the Bureau's training school. "Sorry," I said. "Just asking, 'How's business?' Make it 'How's the weather?' "

He looked sour. "Business is okay. I write 'em, they print 'em, I eat."

I poured myself one, leaned toward him. "Matter of fact," I said, "you write a nice stick — I've sampled a few. You have an amazingly sure touch with the woman's angle."

It was a slip I had to risk; he never admitted what pen-names he used. But he was boiled enough to pick up only the last: " 'Woman's angle!' " he repeated with a snort. "Yeah, I know the woman's angle. I should."

"So?" I said doubtfully. "Sisters?"

"No. You wouldn't believe me if I told you."

"Now, now," I answered mildly, "bartenders and psychiatrists learn that nothing is stranger than truth. Why, son, if you heard the stories I do — well, you'd make yourself rich. Incredible."

"You don't know what 'incredible' means!"

"So? Nothing astonishes me. I've always heard worse."

He snorted again. "Want to bet the rest of the bottle?"

"I'll bet a full bottle." I placed one on the bar.

"Well — " I signaled my other bartender to handle the trade. We were at the far end, a single-stool space that I kept private by loading the bar top by it with jars of pickled eggs and other clutter. A few were at the other end watching the fights and somebody was playing the juke box — private as a bed where we were.

"Okay," he began, "to start with, I'm a bastard."

"No distinction around here," I said.

"I mean it," he snapped. "My parents weren't married."

"Still no distinction," I insisted. "Neither were mine."

"When — " He stopped, gave me the first warm look I ever saw on him. "You mean that?"

"I do. A one-hundred-percent bastard. In fact," I added, "no one in my family ever marries. All bastards."

"Oh, that." I showed it to him. "It just looks like a wedding ring; I wear it to keep women off." It is an antique I bought in 1985 from a fellow operative — he had fetched it from pre-Christian Crete. "The Worm Ouroboros . . . the World Snake that eats its own tail, forever without end. A symbol of the Great Paradox."

He barely glanced at it. "If you're really a bastard, you know how it feels. When I was a little girl — "

"Wups!" I said. "Did I hear you correctly?"

"Who's telling this story? When I was a little girl — Look, ever hear of Christine Jorgensen? Or Roberta Cowell?"

"Uh, sex-change cases? You're trying to tell me — "

"Don't interrupt or swelp me, I won't talk. I was a foundling, left at an orphanage in Cleveland in 1945 when I was a month old. When I was a little girl, I envied kids with parents. Then, when I learned about sex — and, believe me, Pop, you learn fast in an orphanage — "

"I know."

" — I made a solemn vow that any kid of mine would have both a pop and a mom. It kept me 'pure,' quite a feat in that vicinity — I had to learn to fight to manage it. Then I got older and realized I stood darn little chance of getting married — for the same reason I hadn't been adopted." He scowled. "I was horse-faced and buck-toothed, flat-chested and straight-haired."

"You don't look any worse than I do."

"Who cares how a barkeep looks? Or a writer? But people wanting to adopt pick little blue-eyed golden-haired morons. Later on, the boys want bulging breasts, a cute face, and an Oh-you-wonderful-male manner." He shrugged. "I couldn't compete. So I decided to join the W.E.N.C.H.E.S."

"Eh?"

"Women's Emergency National Corps, Hospitality & Entertainment Section, what they now call 'Space Angels' — Auxiliary Nursing Group, Extraterrestrial Legions."

I knew both terms, once I had them chronized. We use still a third name, it's that elite military service corps: Women's Hospitality Order Refortifying & Encouraging Spacemen. Vocabulary shift is the worst hurdle in time-jumps — did you know that "service station" once meant a dispensary for petroleum fractions? Once on an assignment in the Churchill Era, a woman said to me, "Meet me at the service station next door" — which is not what it sounds; a "service station" (then) wouldn't have a bed in it.

He went on: "It was when they first admitted you can't send men into space for months and years and not relieve the tension. You remember how the wowsers screamed? — that improved my chance, since volunteers were scarce. A gal had to be respectable, preferably virgin (they liked to train them from scratch), above average mentally, and stable emotionally. But most volunteers were old hookers, or neurotics who would crack up ten days off Earth. So I didn't need looks; if they accepted me, they would fix my buck teeth, put a wave in my hair, teach me to walk and dance and how to listen to a man pleasingly, and everything else — plus training for the prime duties. They would even use plastic surgery if it would help — nothing too good for Our Boys.

"Best yet, they made sure you didn't get pregnant during your enlistment — and you were almost certain to marry at the end of your hitch. Same way today, A.N.G.E.L.S. marry spacers — they talk the language.

"When I was eighteen I was placed as a 'mother's helper.' This family simply wanted a cheap servant but I didn't mind as I couldn't enlist till I was twenty-one. I did housework and went to night school — pretending to continue my high school typing and shorthand but going to a charm class instead to better my chances for enlistment.

"Then I met this city slicker with his hundred-dollar bills." He scowled. "The no-good actually did have a wad of hundred-dollar bills. He showed me one night, told me to help myself.

"But I didn't. I liked him. He was the first man I ever met who was nice to me without trying games with me. I quit night school to see him oftener. It was the happiest time of my life.

"Then one night in the park the games began."

He stopped. I said, "And then?"

"And then *nothing*! I never saw him again. He walked me home and told me he loved me — and kissed me good-night and never came back." He looked grim. "If I could find him, I'd kill him!"

"Well," I sympathized, "I know how you feel. But killing him — just for doing what comes naturally — hmm . . . Did you struggle?"

"Huh? What's that got to do with it?"

"Quite a bit. Maybe he deserves a couple of broken arms for running out on you, but — "

"He deserves worse than that! Wait till you hear. Somehow I kept anyone from suspecting and decided it was all for the best. I hadn't really loved him and probably would never love anybody — and I was more eager to join the W.E.N.C.H.E.S. than ever. I wasn't disqualified, they didn't insist on virgins. I cheered up.

"It wasn't until my skirts got tight that I realized."

"Pregnant?"

"He had me higher 'n a kite! Those skinflints I lived with ignored it as long as I could work — then kicked me out and the orphanage wouldn't take me back. I landed in a charity ward surrounded by other big bellies and trotted bedpans until my time came.

"One night I found myself on an operating table, with a nurse saying, 'Relax. Now breathe deeply.'

"I woke up in bed, numb from the chest down. My surgeon came in. 'How do you feel?' he says cheerfully.

" 'Like a mummy.'

" 'Naturally. You're wrapped like one and full of dope to keep you numb. You'll get well — but a Caesarean isn't a hangnail.'

"'Caesarean,' I said. 'Doc — *did I lose the baby?*'

"'Oh, no. Your baby's fine.'

"'Oh, boy or girl?'

"'A healthy little girl. Five pounds, three ounces.'

"I relaxed. It's something, to have made a baby. I told myself I would go somewhere and tack 'Mrs.' on my name and let the kid think her papa was dead — no orphanage for *my* kid!

"But the surgeon was talking. 'Tell me, uh — ' He avoided my name. ' — did you ever think your glandular setup was odd?'

"I said, 'Huh? Of course not. What are you driving at?'

"He hesitated. I'll give you this in one dose, then a hypo to let you sleep off your jitters. You'll have 'em.'

" 'Why?' I demanded.

" 'Ever hear of that Scottish physician who was female until she was thirty-five? — then had surgery and became legally and medically a man? Got married. All okay.'

" 'What's that got to do with me?'

"'That's what I'm saying. You're a man.'

"I tried to sit up. '*What?*'

"'Take it easy. When I opened you, I found a mess. I sent for the Chief of Surgery while I got the baby out, then we held a consultation with you on the table — and worked for hours to salvage what we could. You had two full sets of organs, both immature, but with the female set well enough developed for you to have a baby. They could never be any use to you again, so we took them out and rearranged things so that you can develop properly as a man.' He put a hand on me. 'Don't worry. You're young, your bones will readjust, we'll watch your glandular balance — and make a fine young man out of you.'

"I started to cry. 'What about my *baby?*'

" 'Well, you can't nurse her, you haven't milk enough for a kitten. If I were you, I wouldn't see her — put her up for adoption.'

"'No!'

"He shrugged. 'The choice is yours; you're her mother — well, her parent. But don't worry now; we'll get you well first.'

"Next day they let me see the kid and I saw her daily — trying to get used to her. I had never seen a brand-new baby and had no idea how awful they look — my daughter looked like an orange monkey. My feelings changed to cold determination to do right by her. But four weeks later that didn't mean anything."

"Eh?"

"She was snatched."

"Snatched?"

The Unmarried Mother almost knocked over the bottle we had bet. "Kidnapped — stolen from the hospital nursery!" He breathed hard. "How's that for taking the last a man's got to live for?"

"A bad deal," I agreed. "Let's pour you another. No clues?"

"Nothing the police could trace. Somebody came to see her, claimed to be her uncle. While the nurse had her back turned, he walked out with her."

"Description?"

"Just a man, with a face-shaped face, like yours or mine." He frowned. "I think it was the baby's father. The nurse swore it was an older man but he probably used makeup. Who else would swipe my baby? Childless women pull such stunts — but whoever heard of a man doing it?"

"What happened to you then?"

"Eleven more months of that grim place and three operations. In four months I started to grow a beard; before I was out I was shaving regularly . . . and no longer doubted that I was male." He grinned wryly. "I was staring down nurses' necklines."

"Well," I said, "seems to me you came through okay. Here you are, a normal man, making good money, no real troubles. And the life of a female is not an easy one."

He glared at me. "A lot you know about it!"

"So?"

"Ever hear the expression 'a ruined woman'?"

"Mmm, years ago. Doesn't mean much today."

"I was as ruined as a woman can be; that bum *really* ruined me — I was no longer a woman . . . and I didn't know *how* to be a man."

"Takes getting used to, I suppose."

"You have no idea. I don't mean learning how to dress, or not walking into the wrong rest room; I learned those in the hospital. But how could I *live*? What job could I get? Hell, I couldn't even drive a car, I didn't know a trade; I couldn't do manual labor — too much scar tissue, too tender.

"I hated him for having ruined me for the W.E.N.C.H.E.S., too, but I didn't know how much until I tried to join the Space Corps instead. One look at my belly and I was marked unfit for military service. The medical officer spent time on me just from curiosity; he had read about my case.

"So I changed my name and came to New York. I got by as a fry cook, then rented a typewriter and set myself up as a public stenographer — what a laugh! In four months I typed four letters and one manuscript. The manuscript was for *Real Life Tales* and a waste of paper, but the goof who wrote it sold it. Which gave me an idea; I bought a stack of confession magazines and studied them." He looked cynical. "Now you know how I get the authentic woman's angle on an unmarried-mother story . . . through the only version I haven't sold — the true one. Do I win the bottle?"

I pushed it toward him. I was upset myself, but there was work to do. I said, "Son, you still want to lay hands on that so-and-so?"

His eyes lighted up — a feral gleam.

"Hold it!" I said. "You wouldn't kill him?"

He chuckled nastily. "Try me."

"Take it easy. I know more about it than you think I do. I can help you. I know where he is."

He reached across the bar. "*Where is he?*"

I said softly, "Let go my shirt, sonny — or you'll land in the alley and we'll tell the cops you fainted." I showed him the sap.

He let go. "Sorry. But where is he?" He looked at me. "And how do you know so much?"

"All in good time. There are records — hospital records, orphanage records, medical records. The matron of your orphanage was Mrs. Fetherage — right? She was followed by Mrs. Gruenstein — right? Your name, as a girl, was 'Jane' — right? And you didn't tell me any of this — right?"

I had him baffled and a bit scared. "What's this? You trying to make trouble for me?"

"No indeed. I've your welfare at heart. I can put this character in your lap. You do to him as you see fit — and I guarantee that you'll get away with it. But I don't think you'll kill him. You'd be nuts to — and you aren't nuts. Not quite."

He brushed it aside. "Cut the noise. *Where is he?*"

I poured him a short one; he was drunk but anger was offsetting it. "Not so fast. I do something for you — you do something for me."

"Uh . . . what?"

"You don't like your work. What would you say to high pay, steady work, unlimited expense account, your own boss on the job, and lots of variety and adventure?"

He stared. "I'd say, 'Get those goddam reindeer off my roof!' Shove it, Pop — there's no such job."

"Okay, put it this way: I hand him to you, you settle with him, then try my job. If it's not all I claim — well, I can't hold you."

He was wavering; the last drink did it. "When d'yuh d'liver 'im?" he said thickly.

He shoved out his hand. "It's a deal!"

"If it's a deal — *right now!*"

I nodded to my assistant to watch both ends, noted the time — 2300 — started to duck through the gate under the bar — when the juke box blared out: "I'm My Own Grandpaw!" The service man had orders to load it with Americana and classics because I couldn't stomach the "music" of 1970, but I hadn't known that tape was in it. I called out, "Shut that off! Give the customer his money back." I added, "Storeroom, back in a moment," and headed there with my Unmarried Mother following.

It was down the passage across from the johns, a steel door to which no one but my day manager and myself had a key; inside was a door to an inner room to which only I had a key. We went there.

He looked blearily around at windowless walls. "Where is 'e?"

"Right away." I opened a case, the only thing in the room; it was a U.S.F.F. Co-ordinates Transformer Field Kit, series 1992, Mod. II — a beauty, no moving parts, weight twenty-three kilos fully charged, and shaped to pass as a suitcase. I had adjusted it precisely earlier that day; all I had to do was to shake out the metal net which limits the transformation field.

Which I did. "What's that?" he demanded.

"Time machine," I said and tossed the net over us.

"Hey!" he yelled and stepped back. There is a technique to this; the net has to be thrown so that the subject will instinctively step back *onto* the metal mesh, then you close the net with both of you inside completely — else you might leave shoe soles behind or a piece of foot, or scoop up a slice of floor. But that's all the skill it takes. Some agents con a subject into the net; I tell the truth and use that instant of utter astonishment to flip the switch. Which I did.

1030-VI-3 April 1963 — Cleveland, Ohio–Apex Bldg.: "Hey!" he repeated. "Take this damn thing off!"

"Sorry," I apologized and did so, stuffed the net into the case, closed it. "You said you wanted to find him."

"But — you said that was a time machine!"

I pointed out a window. "Does that look like November? Or New York?" While he was gawking at new buds and spring weather, I reopened the case, took out a packet of hundred-dollar bills, checked that the numbers and signatures were compatible with 1963. The Temporal Bureau doesn't care how much you spend (it costs nothing) but they don't like unnecessary anachronisms. Too many mistakes, and a general court-martial will exile you for a year in a nasty period, say 1974 with its strict rationing and forced labor. I never make such mistakes, the money was okay.

He turned around and said, "What happened?"

"He's here. Go outside and take him. Here's expense money." I shoved it at him and added, "Settle him, then I'll pick you up."

Hundred-dollar bills have a hypnotic effect on a person not used to them. He was thumbing them unbelievingly as I eased him into the hall, locked him out. The next jump was easy, a small shift in era.

7100-VI-10 March 1964 — Cleveland–Apex Bldg.: There was a notice under the door saying that my lease expired next week; otherwise the room looked as it had a moment before. Outside, trees were bare and snow threatened; I hurried, stopping only for contemporary money and a coat, hat, and topcoat I had left there when I leased the room. I hired a car, went to the hospital. It took twenty minutes to bore the nursery attendant to the point where I could swipe the baby without being noticed. We went back to the Apex Building. This dial setting was more involved, as the building did not yet exist in 1945. But I had precalculated it.

0100-VI-20 Sept. 1945 — Cleveland–Skyview Motel: Field kit, baby, and I arrived in a motel outside town. Earlier I had registered as "Gregory Johnson, Warren, Ohio," so we arrived in a room with curtains closed, windows locked, and doors bolted, and the floor cleared to allow for waver as the machine hunts. You can get a nasty bruise from a chair where it shouldn't be — not the chair, of course, but backlash from the field.

No trouble. Jane was sleeping soundly; I carried her out, put her in a grocery box on the seat of a car I had provided earlier, drove to the orphanage, put her on the steps, drove two blocks to a "service station" (the petroleum-products sort) and phoned the orphanage, drove back in time to see them taking the box inside, kept going and abandoned the car near the motel — walked to it and jumped forward to the Apex Building in 1963.

2200-VI-24 April 1963 — Cleveland–Apex Bldg.: I had cut the time rather fine — temporal accuracy depends on span, except on return to zero. If I had it right, Jane was discovering, out in the park this balmy spring night, that she wasn't quite as "nice" a girl as she had thought. I grabbed a taxi to the home of those skinflints, had the hackie wait around a corner while I lurked in shadows.

Presently I spotted them down the street, arms around each other. He took her up on the porch and made a long job of kissing her good-night — longer than I thought. Then she went in and he came down the walk, turned away. I slid into step and hooked an arm in his. "That's all, son," I announced quietly. "I'm back to pick you up."

"*You!*" He gasped and caught his breath.

"Me. Now you know who *he* is — and after you think it over you'll know who you are . . . and if you think hard enough, you'll figure out who the baby is . . . and who *I* am."

He didn't answer, he was badly shaken. It's a shock to have it proved to you that you can't resist seducing yourself. I took him to the Apex Building and we jumped again.

2300-VIII-1 Aug. 1985 — Sub Rockies Base: I woke the duty sergeant, showed my I.D., told the sergeant to bed my companion down with a happy pill and recruit him in the morning. The sergeant looked sour, but rank is rank, regardless of era; he did what I said — thinking, no doubt, that the next time we met he might be the colonel and I the sergeant. Which can happen in our corps. "What name?" he asked.

I wrote it out. He raised his eyebrows. "Like so, eh? *Hmm* — "

"You just do your job, Sergeant." I turned to my companion.

"Son, your troubles are over. You're about to start the best job a man ever held — and you'll do well. *I know.*"

"That you will!" agreed the sergeant. "Look at me — born in 1917 — still around, still young, still enjoying life." I went back to the jump room, set everything on preselected zero.

2301-V-7 Nov. 1970 — NYC–"Pop's Place": I came out of the storeroom carrying a fifth of Drambuie to account for the minute I had been gone. My assistant was arguing with the customer who had been playing "I'm My Own Grandpaw!" I said, "Oh, let him play it, then unplug it." I was very tired.

It's rough, but somebody must do it and it's very hard to recruit anyone in the later years, since the Mistake of '72. Can you think of a better source than to pick people all fouled up where they are and give them well-paid, interesting (even though dangerous) work in a necessary cause? Everybody knows now why the Fizzle War of 1963 fizzled. The bomb with New York's number on it didn't go off, a hundred other things didn't go as planned — all arranged by the likes of me.

But not the Mistake of '72; that one is not our fault — and can't be undone; there's no paradox to resolve. A thing either is, or it isn't, now and forever amen. But there won't be another like it; an order dated "1992" takes precedence any year.

I closed five minutes early, leaving a letter in the cash register telling my day manager that I was accepting his offer to buy me out, so see my lawyer as I was leaving on a long vacation. The Bureau might or might not pick up his payments, but they want things left tidy. I went to the room back of the storeroom and forward to 1993.

2200-VII-12 Jan. 1993 — Sub Rockies Annex–HQ Temporal DOL: I checked in with the duty officer and went to my quarters, intending to sleep for a week. I had fetched the bottle we bet (after all, I won it) and took a drink before I wrote my report. It tasted foul and I wondered why I had ever liked Old Underwear. But it was better than nothing; I don't like to be cold sober, I think too much. But I don't really hit the bottle either; other people have snakes — I have people.

I dictated my report; forty recruitments all okayed by the Psych Bureau — counting my own, which I knew would be okayed. I was here, wasn't I? Then I taped a request for assignment to operations; I was sick of recruiting. I dropped both in the slot and headed for bed.

My eye fell on "The By-Laws of Time," over my bed:

> *Never Do Yesterday What Should Be Done Tomorrow.*
> *If at Last You Do Succeed, Never Try Again.*
> *A Stitch in Time Saves Nine Billion.*
> *A Paradox May be Paradoctored.*
> *It Is Earlier When You Think.*
> *Ancestors Are Just People.*
> *Even Jove Nods.*

They didn't inspire me the way they had when I was a recruit; thirty subjective-years of time-jumping wears you down. I undressed and when I got down to the hide I looked at my belly. A Caesarean leaves a big scar but I'm so hairy now that I don't notice it unless I look for it.

Then I glanced at the ring on my finger.

The Snake That Eats Its Own Tail, Forever and Ever . . . I *know* where *I came* from — but *where did all you zombies come from?*

I felt a headache coming on, but a headache powder is one thing I do not take. I did once — and you all went away.

So I crawled into bed and whistled out the light.

You aren't really there at all. There isn't anybody but me — Jane here alone in the dark.

I miss you dreadfully!

Robert Silverberg

When We Went to See the End of the World
(1972)

A prolific writer with a long and varied career, Robert Silverberg (b. 1935) has won major sf awards in every decade from the 1950s to the 1990s, including five Nebulas and four Hugos. He is also important for his work as an editor. Silverberg has often been drawn to explorations of time, either through the cyclical notion of death and rebirth, or in more traditional — but always original — time-travel stories. He is particularly accomplished in the shorter forms, as "When We Went to See the End of the World" amply demonstrates. In this mordant satire, jaded socialites at a fashionable dinner party share their experiences with the latest novelty, a time-travel machine that takes affluent customers into the future to witness the end of the world. As they recount their stories, it becomes clear that everyone has seen something entirely different. At first it seems that this intriguing discrepancy will be central to the plot resolution, but the reader's attention is gradually shifted from foreground to background. The outside world begins to intrude on the dinner party, forming an ominous counterpoint to the guests' self-indulgent voyeurism and providing another answer to how the world might end, one to which the partygoers seem oblivious.

Written in the early 1970s, a millennialist era during which many felt that social and environmental collapse was imminent, Silverberg's story functions both as an apocalyptic warning and a dry critique of status-seeking consumerism and the preference for escapist thrills over direct confrontation with truly frightening realities.

Nick and Jane were glad that they had gone to see the end of the world, because it gave them something special to talk about at Mike and Ruby's party. One always likes to come to a party armed with a little conversation. Mike and Ruby give marvelous parties. Their home is superb, one of the finest in the neighborhood. It is truly a home for all seasons, all moods. Their very special corner of the world. With more space indoors and out . . . more wide-open freedom. The living room with its exposed ceiling beams is a natural focal point for entertaining. Custom-finished, with a conversation pit and fireplace. There's also a family room with beamed ceiling and wood paneling . . . plus a study. And a magnificent master suite with twelve-foot dressing room and private bath. Solidly impressive exterior design. Sheltered courtyard. Beautifully wooded $^1/_3$-acre grounds. Their parties are highlights of any month. Nick and Jane waited until they thought enough people had arrived. Then Jane nudged Nick and Nick said gaily, "You know what we did last week? Hey, we went to see the end of the world!"

"The end of the world?" Henry asked.

"You went to see it?" said Henry's wife Cynthia.

"How did you manage that?" Paula wanted to know.

"It's been available since March," Stan told her. "I think a division of American Express runs it."

Nick was put out to discover that Stan already knew. Quickly, before Stan could say anything more, Nick said, "Yes, it's just started. Our travel agent found out for us. What they do is they put you in this machine, it looks like a tiny teeny submarine, you know, with dials and levers up front behind a plastic wall to keep you from touching anything, and they send you into the future. You can charge it with any of the regular credit cards."

"It must be very expensive," Marcia said.

"They're bringing the costs down rapidly," Jane said. "Last year only millionaires could afford it. Really, haven't you heard about it before?"

"What did you see?" Henry asked.

"For a while, just grayness outside the porthole," said Nick. "And a kind of flickering effect." Everybody was looking at him. He enjoyed the attention. Jane wore a rapt, loving expression. "Then the haze cleared and a voice said over a loudspeaker that we had now reached the very end of time, when life had become impossible on Earth. Of course we were sealed into the submarine thing. Only looking out. On this beach, this empty beach. The water a funny gray color with a pink sheen. And then the sun came up. It was red like it sometimes is at sunrise, only it stayed red as it got to the middle of the sky, and it looked lumpy and sagging at the edges. Like a few of us, hah hah. Lumpy and sagging at the edges. A cold wind blowing across the beach."

"If you were sealed in the submarine, how did you know there was a cold wind?" Cynthia asked.

Jane glared at her. Nick said, "We could see the sand blowing around. And it *looked* cold. The gray ocean. Like in winter."

"Tell them about the crab," said Jane.

"Yes, and the crab. The last life-form on Earth. It wasn't really a crab, of course, it was something about two feet wide and a foot high, with thick shiny green armor and maybe a dozen legs and some curving horns coming up, and it moved slowly from right to left in front of us. It took all day to cross the beach. And toward nightfall it died. Its horns went limp and it stopped moving. The tide came in and carried it away. The sun went down. There wasn't any moon. The stars didn't seem to be in the right places. The loudspeaker told us we had just seen the death of Earth's last living thing."

"How *eerie!*" cried Paula.

"Were you gone very long?" Ruby asked.

"Three hours," Jane said. "You can spend weeks or days at the end of the world, if you want to pay extra, but they always bring you back to a point three hours after you went. To hold down the babysitter expenses."

Mike offered Nick some pot. "That's really something," he said. "To have gone to the end of the world. Hey, Ruby, maybe we'll talk to the travel agent about it."

Nick took a deep drag and passed the joint to Jane. He felt pleased with himself about the way he had told the story. They had all been very impressed. That swollen red sun, that scuttling crab. The trip had cost more than a month in Japan, but it had been a good investment. He and Jane were the first in the neighborhood who had gone. That was important. Paula was staring at him in awe. Nick knew that she regarded him in a completely different light now. Possibly she would meet him at a motel on Tuesday at lunchtime. Last month she had turned him down but now he had an extra attractiveness for her. Nick winked at her. Cynthia was holding hands with Stan. Henry and Mike both were crouched at Jane's feet. Mike and Ruby's twelve-year-old son came into the room and stood at the edge of the conversation pit. He said, "There just was a bulletin on the news. Mutated amoebas escaped from a government research station and got into Lake Michigan. They're carrying a tissue-dissolving virus and everybody in seven states is supposed to boil their water until further notice." Mike scowled at the boy and said, "It's after your bedtime, Timmy." The boy went out. The doorbell rang. Ruby answered it and returned with Eddie and Fran.

Paula said, "Nick and Jane went to see to end of the world. They've just been telling us all about it."

"Gee," said Eddie, "we did that too, on Wednesday night."

Nick was crestfallen. Jane bit her lip and asked Cynthia quietly why Fran always wore such flashy dresses. Ruby said, "You saw the whole works, eh? The crab and everything?"

"The crab?" Eddie said. "What crab? We didn't see the crab."

"It must have died the time before," Paula said. "When Nick and Jane were there."

Mike said, "A fresh shipment of Cuernavaca Lightning is in. Here, have a toke."

"How long ago did you do it?" Eddie said to Nick.

"Sunday afternoon. I guess we were about the first."

"Great trip, isn't it?" Eddie said. "A little somber, though. When the last hill crumbles into the sea."

"That's not what we saw," said Jane. "And you didn't see the crab? Maybe we were on different trips."

Mike said, "What was it like for you, Eddie?"

Eddie put his arms around Cynthia from behind. He said. "They put us into this little capsule, with a porthole, you know, and a lot of instruments and — "

"We heard that part," said Paula. "What did you *see*?"

"The end of the world," Eddie said. "When water covers everything. The sun and the moon were in the sky at the same time — "

"We didn't see the moon at all," Jane remarked. "It just wasn't there."

"It was on one side and the sun was on the other," Eddie went on. "The moon was closer than it should have been. And a funny color, almost like bronze. And the ocean creeping up. We went halfway around the world and all we saw was ocean. Except in one place, there was this chunk of land sticking up, this hill, and the guide told us it was the top of Mount Everest." He waved to Fran. "That was groovy, huh, floating in our tin boat next to the top of Mount Everest. Maybe ten feet of it sticking up. And the water rising all the time. Up, up, up. Up and over the top. Glub. No land left. I have to admit it was a little disappointing, except of course the *idea* of the thing. That human ingenuity can design a machine that can send people billions of years forward in time and bring them back, wow! But there was just this ocean."

"How strange," said Jane. "We saw an ocean too, but there was a beach, a kind of nasty beach, and the crab-thing walking along it, and the sun — it was all red, was the sun red when you saw it?"

"A kind of pale green," Fred said.

"Are you people talking about the end of the world?" Tom asked. He and Harriet were standing by the door taking off their coats. Mike's son must have let them in. Tom gave his coat to Ruby and said, "Man, what a spectacle!"

"So you did it too?" Jane asked, a little hollowly.

"Two weeks ago," said Tom. "The travel agent called and said, Guess what we're offering now, the end of the goddamned world! With all the extras it didn't really cost so much. So we went right down there to the office, Saturday, I think — was it a Friday? — the day of the big riot, anyway, when they burned St. Louis — "

"That was a Saturday," Cynthia said. "I remember I was coming back from the shopping center when the radio said they were using nuclears — "

"Saturday, yes," Tom said. "And we told them we were ready to go, and off they sent us."

"Did you see a beach with crabs," Stan demanded, "or was it a world full of water?"

"Neither one. It was like a big ice age. Glaciers covered everything. No oceans showing, no mountains. We flew clear around the world and it was all a huge snowball. They had floodlights on the vehicle because the sun had gone out."

"I was sure I could see the sun still hanging up there," Harriet put in. "Like a ball of cinders in the sky. But the guide said no, nobody could see it."

"How come everybody gets to visit a different kind of end of the world?" Henry asked. "You'd think there'd be only one kind of end of the world. I mean, it ends, and this is how it ends, and there can't be more than one way."

"Could it be a fake?" Stan asked. Everybody turned around and looked at him. Nick's face got very red. Fran looked so mean that Eddie let go of Cynthia and started to rub Fran's shoulders. Stan shrugged. "I'm not suggesting it is," he said defensively. "I was just wondering."

"Seemed pretty real to me," said Tom. "The sun burned out. A big ball of ice. The atmosphere, you know, frozen. The end of the goddamned world."

The telephone rang. Ruby went to answer it. Nick asked Paula about lunch on Tuesday. She said yes. "Let's meet at the motel," he said, and she grinned. Eddie was making out with Cynthia again. Henry looked very stoned and was having trouble staying awake. Phil and Isabel arrived. They heard Tom and Fran talking about their trips to the end of the world and Isabel said she and Phil had gone only the day before yesterday. "Goddamn," Tom said, "everybody's doing it! What was your trip like?"

Ruby came back into the room. "That was my sister calling from Fresno to say she's safe. Fresno wasn't hit by the earthquake at all."

"Earthquake?" Paula said.

"In California," Mike told her. "This afternoon. You didn't know? Wiped out most of Los Angeles and ran right up the coast practically to Monterey. They think it was on account of the underground bomb test in the Mohave Desert."

"California's always having such awful disasters," Marcia said.

"Good thing those amoebas got loose back east," said Nick. "Imagine how complicated it would be if they had them in L.A. now too."

"They will," Tom said. "Two to one they reproduce by airborne spores."

"Like the typhoid germs last November," Jane said.

"That was typhus," Nick corrected.

"Anyway," Phil said, "I was telling Tom and Fran about what we saw at the end of the world. It was the sun going nova. They showed it very cleverly, too. I mean, you can't actually sit around and *experience* it, on account of the heat and the hard radiation and all. But they give it to you in a peripheral way, very elegant in the McLuhanesque[1] sense of the word. First they take you to a point about two hours before the blowup, right? It's I don't know how many jillion years from now, but a long way, anyhow, because the trees are all different, they've got blue scales and ropy branches, and the animals are like things with one leg that jump on pogo sticks — "

"Oh, I don't *believe* that," Cynthia drawled.

Phil ignored her gracefully. "And we didn't see any sign of human beings, not a house, not a telephone pole, nothing, so I suppose we must have been extinct a long time before. Anyway, they let us look at that for a

---

1. Marshall McLuhan (1911–1980) was a scholar, media critic, and communication theorist whose analysis of the way electronic media transformed culture was enormously influential in the 1960s and 1970s. He is famous for coining the phrases "the Global Village" and "the medium is the message." [Ed.]

while. Not getting out of our time machine, naturally, because they said the atmosphere was wrong. Gradually the sun started to puff up. We were nervous — weren't we, Iz? — I mean, suppose they miscalculated things? This whole trip is a very new concept and things might go wrong. The sun was getting bigger and bigger, and then this thing like an arm seemed to pop out of its left side, a big fiery arm reaching out across space, getting closer and closer. We saw it through smoked glass, like you do an eclipse. They gave us about two minutes of the explosion, and we could feel it getting hot already. Then we jumped a couple of years forward in time. The sun was back to its regular shape, only it was smaller, sort of like a little white sun instead of a big yellow one. And on Earth everything was ashes."

"Ashes," Isabel said, with emphasis.

"It looked like Detroit after the union nuked Ford," Phil said. "Only much, much worse. Whole mountains were melted. The oceans were dried up. Everything was ashes." He shuddered and took a joint from Mike. "Isabel was crying."

"The things with one leg," Isabel said. "I mean, they must have all been wiped *out*." She began to sob. Stan comforted her. "I wonder why it's a different way for everyone who goes," he said. "Freezing. Or the oceans. Or the sun blowing up. Or the thing Nick and Jane saw."

"I'm convinced that each of us had a genuine experience in the far future," said Nick. He felt he had to regain control of the group somehow. It had been so good when he was telling his story, before those others had come. "That is to say, the world suffers a variety of natural calamities, it doesn't just have *one* end of the world, and they keep mixing things up and sending people to different catastrophes. But never for a moment did I doubt that I was seeing an authentic event."

"We have to do it," Ruby said to Mike. "It's only three hours. What about calling them first thing Monday and making an appointment for Thursday night?"

"Monday's the President's funeral," Tom pointed out. "The travel agency will be closed."

"Have they caught the assassin yet?" Fran asked.

"They didn't mention it on the four o'clock news," said Stan. "I guess he'll get away like the last one."

"Beats me why anybody wants to be President," Phil said.

Mike put on some music. Nick danced with Paula. Eddie danced with Cynthia. Henry was asleep. Dave, Paula's husband, was on crutches because of his mugging, and he asked Isabel to sit and talk with him. Tom danced with Harriet even though he was married to her. She hadn't been out of the hospital more than a few months since the transplant and he treated her extremely tenderly. Mike danced with Fran. Phil danced with Jane. Stan danced with Marcia. Ruby cut in on Eddie and Cynthia. Afterward Tom danced with Jane and Phil danced with Paula. Mike and Ruby's little girl woke up and came out to say hello. Mike sent her back to bed. Far away there was the sound of an explosion. Nick danced with Paula again, but he didn't want her to get bored with him before Tuesday, so he excused himself and went to talk with Dave. Dave handled most of Nick's investments. Ruby said to Mike, "The day after the funeral, will you call the travel agent?" Mike said he would, but Tom said somebody would probably shoot the new President too and there'd be another funeral. These funerals were demolishing the gross national product, Stan observed, on account of how everything had to close all the time. Nick saw Cynthia wake Henry up and ask him sharply if he would take her on the end-of-the-world trip. Henry looked embarrassed. His factory had been blown up at Christmas in a peace demonstration and everybody knew he was in bad shape financially. "You can *charge* it," Cynthia said, her fierce voice carrying above the chitchat. "And it's so *beautiful*, Henry. The ice. Or the sun exploding. I want to go."

"Lou and Janet were going to be here tonight too," Ruby said to Paula. "But their younger boy came back from Texas with that new kind of cholera and they had to cancel."

Phil said, "I understand that one couple saw the moon come apart. It got too close to the Earth and split into chunks and the chunks fell like meteors. Smashing everything up, you know. One big piece nearly hit their time machine."

"I wouldn't have liked that at all," Marcia said.

"Our trip was very lovely," said Jane. "No violent things at all. Just the big red sun and the tide and that crab creeping along the beach. We were both deeply moved."

"It's amazing what science can accomplish nowadays," Fran said.

Mike and Ruby agreed they would try to arrange a trip to the end of the world as soon as the funeral was over. Cynthia drank too much and got sick. Phil, Tom, and Dave discussed the stock market. Harriet told Nick about her operation. Isabel flirted with Mike, tugging her neckline lower. At midnight someone turned on the news. They had some shots of the earthquake and a warning about boiling your water if you lived in the affected states. The President's widow was shown visiting the last President's widow to get some pointers for the funeral. Then there was an interview with an executive of the time-trip company. "Business is phenomenal," he said. "Time-tripping will be the nation's number one growth industry next year." The reporter asked him if his company would soon be offering something besides the end-of-the-world trip. "Later on, we hope to," the executive said. "We plan to apply for Congressional approval soon. But meanwhile the demand for our present offering is running very high. You can't imagine. Of course, you have to expect apocalyptic stuff to attain immense popularity in times like these." The reporter said, "What do you mean, times like these?" but as the time-trip man started to reply, he was interrupted by the commercial. Mike shut off the set. Nick discovered that he was extremely depressed. He decided that it was because so many of his friends had made the journey, and he had thought he and Jane were the only ones who had. He found himself standing next to Marcia and tried to describe the way the crab had moved, but Marcia only shrugged. No one was talking about time-trips now. The party had moved beyond that point. Nick and Jane left quite early and went right to sleep, without making love. The next morning the Sunday paper wasn't delivered because of the Bridge Authority strike, and the radio said that the mutant amoebas were proving harder to eradicate than originally anticipated. They were spreading into Lake Superior and everyone in the region would have to boil all drinking water. Nick and Jane discussed where they would go for their next vacation. "What about going to see the end of the world all over again?" Jane suggested, and Nick laughed quite a good deal.

Kim Stanley Robinson

The Lucky Strike

(1984)

Kim Stanley Robinson (b. 1952) emerged as an important writer in the mid-1980s, when his meticulously detailed and realistic meditations on future scenarios were contrasted with the flashier and more impressionistic work of his cyberpunk contemporaries. Robinson began publishing sf in 1975, and earned a doctorate in English at the University of California in San Diego in 1982 with a critical study of Philip K. Dick. He came to prominence with the publication of his first novel, *The Wild Shore*, in 1984. This book was the first installment in a loosely connected series known as the Three Californias trilogy that explores three different possible futures, utopian and dystopian. This work was followed by an acclaimed trilogy about the colonization of Mars, beginning with the Nebula award–winning *Red Mars* in 1992. Both sequels, *Green Mars* (1993) and *Blue Mars* (1996), won Hugos. Robinson's work tends to focus on utopian and environmental themes and is marked by a thoughtful, philosophical writerly voice.

"The Lucky Strike" is an alternate history set in the last days of World War II, as U.S. fighter pilots on a secluded Pacific island train for a secret mission. Into this historically accurate and highly realistic account, Robinson introduces a seemingly minor deviation from history that culminates in an alternate outcome of vast consequence.

Robinson — who is, after all, best known for a completely persuasive account of terraforming Mars — has a gift for crafting painstakingly credible solutions to intractable problems. In "The Lucky Strike," his deceptively low-key and matter-of-fact narration provides a texture of realism that makes this alternate history seem completely plausible. There are no flashy special effects, unlikely coincidences, or startling plot twists; instead, Robinson takes a quiet, incremental approach to character, plot, and setting, and the story unfolds with a stately inevitability.

Alternate histories are not time-travel stories; rather, they are visions of a past that might have been and that might have created a different present than the one in which we now live. This story is also a psychological study, a consideration of how experience and personality can affect our decisions. It poses questions about moral choice and the individual conscience, and it leads us to wonder whether one person really can change the world.

War breeds strange pastimes. In July of 1945 on Tinian Island in the North Pacific, Captain Frank January had taken to piling pebble cairns on the crown of Mount Lasso — one pebble for each B-29 takeoff, one cairn for each mission. The largest cairn had four hundred stones in it. It was a mindless pastime, but so was poker. The men of the 509th had played a million hands of poker, sitting in the shade of a palm around an upturned crate sweating in their skivvies, swearing and betting all their pay and cigarettes, playing hand after hand after hand, until the cards got so soft and dog-eared you could have used them for toilet paper. Captain January had gotten sick of it, and after he lit out for the hilltop a few times some of his crewmates started trailing him. When their pilot Jim Fitch joined them it became an official pastime, like throwing flares into the compound or going hunting for stray Japs. What Captain January thought of the development he didn't say. The others grouped near Captain Fitch, who passed around his battered flask. "Hey, January," Fitch called. "Come have a shot."

January wandered over and took the flask. Fitch laughed at his pebble. "Practising your bombing up here, eh, Professor?"

"Yah," January said sullenly. Anyone who read more than the funnies was Professor to Fitch. Thirstily January knocked back some rum. He could drink it any way he pleased up here, out from under the eye of the group psychiatrist. He passed the flask on to Lieutenant Matthews, their navigator.

"That's why he's the best," Matthews joked. "Always practising."

Fitch laughed. "He's best because I make him be best, right, Professor?"

January frowned. Fitch was a bulky youth, thick-featured, pig-eyed — a thug, in January's opinion. The rest of the crew were all in their mid-twenties like Fitch, and they liked the captain's bossy roughhouse style. January, who was thirty-seven, didn't go for it. He wandered away, back to the cairn he had been building. From Mount Lasso they had an overview of the whole island, from the harbor at Wall Street to the north field in Harlem. January had observed hundreds of B-29s roar off the four parallel runways of the north field and head for Japan. The last quartet of this particular mission buzzed across the width of the island, and January dropped four more pebbles, aiming for crevices in the pile. One of them stuck nicely.

"There they are!" said Matthews. "They're on the taxiing strip."

January located the 509th's first plane. Today, the first of August, there was something more interesting to watch than the usual Superfortress parade. Word was out that General Le May wanted to take the 509th's mission away from it. Their commander Colonel Tibbets had gone and bitched to Le May in person, and the general had agreed the mission was theirs, but on one condition: one of the general's men was to make a test flight with the 509th, to make sure they were fit for combat over Japan. The general's man had arrived, and now he was down there in the strike plane, with Tibbets and the whole first team. January sidled back to his mates to view the takeoff with them.

"Why don't the strike plane have a name, though?" Haddock was saying.

Fitch said, "Lewis won't give it a name because it's not his plane, and he knows it." The others laughed. Lewis and his crew were naturally unpopular, being Tibbets's favorites.

"What do you think he'll do to the general's man?" Matthews asked.

The others laughed at the very idea. "He'll kill an engine at takeoff, I bet you anything," Fitch said. He pointed at the wrecked B-29s that marked the end of every runway, planes whose engines had given out on takeoff. "He'll want to show that he wouldn't go down if it happened to him."

"Course he wouldn't!" Matthews said.

"You hope," January said under his breath.

"They let those Wright engines out too soon," Haddock said seriously. "They keep busting under the takeoff load."

"Won't matter to the old bull," Matthews said. Then they all started in about Tibbets's flying ability, even Fitch. They all thought Tibbets was the greatest. January, on the other hand, liked Tibbets even less than he liked Fitch. That had started right after he was assigned to the 509th. He had been told he was part of the most important group in the war, and then given a leave. In Vicksburg a couple of fliers just back from England had bought him a lot of whiskies, and since January had spent several months stationed near London they had talked for a good long time and gotten pretty drunk. The two were really curious about what January was up to now, but he had stayed vague on it and kept returning the talk to the blitz. He had been seeing an English nurse, for instance, whose flat had been bombed, family and neighbors killed. . . . But they had really wanted to know. So he had told them he was onto something special, and they had flipped out their badges and told him they were Army Intelligence, and that if he ever broke security like that again he'd be transferred to Alaska. It was a dirty trick. January had gone back to Wendover and told Tibbets so to his face, and Tibbets had turned red and threatened him some more. January despised him for that. The upshot was that January was effectively out of the war, because Tibbets really played his favorites. January wasn't sure he really minded, but during their year's training he had bombed better than ever, as a way of showing the old bull he was wrong to write January off. Every time their eyes had met it was clear what was going on. But Tibbets never backed off no matter how precise January's bombing got. Just thinking about it was enough to cause January to line up a pebble over an ant and drop it.

"Will you cut that out?" Fitch complained. "I swear you must hang from the ceiling when you take a shit so you can practice aiming for the toilet." The men laughed.

"Don't I bunk over you?" January asked. Then he pointed. "They're going."

Tibbets's plane had taxied to runway Baker. Fitch passed the flask around again. The tropical sun beat on them, and the ocean surrounding the island blazed white. January put up a sweaty hand to aid the bill of his baseball cap.

The four props cut in hard, and the sleek Superfortress quickly trundled up to speed and roared down Baker. Three-quarters of the way down the strip the outside right prop feathered.

"Yow!" Fitch crowed. "I told you he'd do it!"

The plane nosed off the ground and slewed right, then pulled back on course to cheers from the four young men around January. January pointed again. "He's cut number three, too."

The inside right prop feathered, and now the plane was pulled up by the left wing only, while the two right props windmilled uselessly. "Holy smoke!" Haddock cried. "Ain't the old bull something?"

They whooped to see the plane's power, and Tibbets's nervy arrogance.

"By God, Le May's man will remember this flight," Fitch hooted. "Why, look at that! He's banking!"

Apparently taking off on two engines wasn't enough for Tibbets; he banked the plane right until it was standing on its dead wing, and it curved back toward Tinian.

Then the inside left engine feathered.

War tears at the imagination. For three years Frank January had kept his imagination trapped, refusing to give it any play whatsoever. The dangers threatening him, the effects of the bombs, the fate of the other participants in the war, he had refused to think about any of it. But the war tore at his control. That English nurse's flat. The missions over the Ruhr. The bomber just below him blown apart by flak. And then there had been a year in Utah, and the vise-like grip that he had once kept on his imagination had slipped away.

So when he saw the number two prop feather, his heart gave a little jump against his sternum and helplessly he was up there with Ferebee, the first team bombardier. He would be looking over the pilots' shoulders. . . .

"Only one engine?" Fitch said.

"That one's for real," January said harshly. Despite himself he *saw* the panic in the cockpit, the frantic rush to power the two right engines. The plane was dropping fast and Tibbets leveled it off, leaving them on a course back toward the island. The two right props spun, blurred to a shimmer. January held his breath. They needed more lift; Tibbets was trying to pull it over the island. Maybe he was trying for the short runway on the south half of the island.

But Tinian was too tall, the plane too heavy. It roared right into the jungle above the beach, where 42nd Street met their East River. It exploded in a bloom of fire. By the time the sound of the explosion struck them they knew no one in the plane had survived.

Black smoke towered into white sky. In the shocked silence on Mount Lasso insects buzzed and creaked. The air left January's lungs with a gulp. He had been with Ferebee there at the end, he had heard the desperate shouts, seen the last green rush, been stunned by the dentist-drill-all-over pain of the impact.

"Oh my God," Fitch was saying. "Oh my God." Matthews was sitting. January picked up the flask, tossed it at Fitch.

"C-come on," he stuttered. He hadn't stuttered since he was sixteen. He led the others in a rush down the hill. When they got to Broadway a jeep careened toward them and skidded to a halt. It was Colonel Scholes, the old bull's exec. "What happened?"

Fitch told him.

"Those damned Wrights," Scholes said as the men piled in. This time one had failed at just the wrong moment; some welder stateside had kept flame to metal a second less than usual — or something equally minor, equally trivial — and that had made all the difference.

They left the jeep at 42nd and Broadway and hiked east over a narrow track to the shore. A fairly large circle of trees was burning. The fire trucks were already there.

Scholes stood beside January, his expression bleak. "That was the whole first team," he said.

"I know," said January. He was still in shock, in imagination crushed, incinerated, destroyed. Once as a kid he had tied sheets to his arms and waist, jumped off the roof and landed right on his chest; this felt like that had. He had no way of knowing what would come of this crash, but he had a suspicion that he had indeed smacked into something hard.

Scholes shook his head. A half-hour had passed, the fire was nearly out. January's four mates were over chattering with the Seabees. "He was going to name the plane after his mother," Scholes said to the ground. "He told me that just this morning. He was going to call it *Enola Gay*."

At night the jungle breathed, and its hot wet breath washed over the 509th's compound. January stood in the doorway of his Quonset barracks hoping for a real breeze. No poker tonight. Voices were hushed, faces solemn. Some of the men had helped box up the dead crew's gear. Now most lay on their bunks. January gave up on the breeze, climbed onto his top bunk to stare at the ceiling.

He observed the corrugated arch over him. Cricketsong sawed through his thoughts. Below him a rapid conversation was being carried on in guilty undertones, Fitch at its center. "January is the best bombardier left," he said. "And I'm as good as Lewis was."

"But so is Sweeney," Matthews said. "And he's in with Scholes."

They were figuring out who would take over the strike. January scowled. Tibbets and the rest were less than twelve hours dead, and they were squabbling over who would replace them.

January grabbed a shirt, rolled off his bunk, put the shirt on.

"Hey, Professor," Fitch said. "Where you going?"

"Out."

Though midnight was near it was still sweltering. Crickets shut up as he walked by, started again behind him. He lit a cigarette. In the dark the

MPs patrolling their fenced-in compound were like pairs of walking arm-bands. The 509th, prisoners in their own army. Fliers from other groups had taken to throwing rocks over the fence. Forcefully January expelled smoke, as if he could expel his disgust with it. They were only kids, he told himself. Their minds had been shaped in the war, by the war, and for the war. They knew you couldn't mourn the dead for long; carry around a load like that and your own engines might fail. That was all right with January. It was an attitude that Tibbets had helped to form, so it was what he deserved. Tibbets would *want* to be forgotten in favor of the mission, all he had lived for was to drop the gimmick on the Japs, he was oblivious to any-thing else, men, wife, family, anything.

So it wasn't the lack of feeling in his mates that bothered January. And it was natural of them to want to fly the strike they had been training a year for. Natural, that is, if you were a kid with a mind shaped by fanatics like Tibbets, shaped to take orders and never imagine consequences. But January was not a kid, and he wasn't going to let men like Tibbets do a thing to his mind. And the gimmick . . . the gimmick was not natural. A chemical bomb of some sort, he guessed. Against the Geneva Convention. He stubbed his cigarette against the sole of his sneaker, tossed the butt over the fence. The tropical night breathed over him. He had a headache.

For months now he had been sure he would never fly a strike. The dis-like Tibbets and he had exchanged in their looks (January was acutely aware of looks) had been real and strong. Tibbets had understood that January's record of pinpoint accuracy in the runs over the Salton Sea had been a way of showing contempt, a way of saying *you can't get rid of me even though you hate me and I hate you.* The record had forced Tibbets to keep January on one of the four second-string teams, but with the fuss they were making over the gimmick January had figured that would be far enough down the ladder to keep him out of things.

Now he wasn't so sure. Tibbets was dead. He lit another cigarette, found his hand shaking. The Camel tasted bitter. He threw it over the fence at a receding armband, and regretted it instantly. A waste. He went back inside.

Before climbing onto his bunk he got a paperback out of his footlocker. "Hey, Professor, what you reading now?" Fitch said, grinning.

January showed him the blue cover. *Winter's Tales,* by an Isak Dinesen. Fitch examined the little wartime edition. "Pretty racy, eh?"

"You bet," January said heavily, "This guy puts sex on every page." He climbed onto his bunk, opened the book. The stories were strange, hard to follow. The voices below bothered him. He concentrated harder.

As a boy on the farm in Arkansas, January had read everything he could lay his hands on. On Saturday afternoons he would race his father down the muddy lane to the mailbox (his father was a reader too), grab the *Saturday Evening Post* and run off to devour every word of it. That meant he had another week with nothing new to read, but he couldn't help it. His favorites were the Hornblower stories, but anything would do. It was a way off the farm, a way into the world. He had become a man who could slip between the covers of a book whenever he chose.

But not on this night.

The next day the chaplain gave a memorial service, and on the morning after that Colonel Scholes looked in the door of their hut right after mess. "Briefing at eleven," he announced. His face was haggard. "Be there early," He looked at Fitch with bloodshot eyes, crooked a finger. "Fitch, January, Matthews — come with me."

January put on his shoes. The rest of the men sat on their bunks and watched them wordlessly. January followed Fitch and Matthews out of the hut.

"I've spent most of the night on the radio with General Le May," Scholes said. He looked them each in the eye. "We've decided you're to be the first crew to make a strike."

Fitch was nodding, as if he had expected it.

"Think you can do it?" Scholes said.

"Of course," Fitch replied. Watching him January understood why they had chosen him to replace Tibbets: Fitch was like the old bull, he had that same ruthlessness. The young bull.

"Yes, sir," Matthews said.

Scholes was looking at him. "Sure," January said, not wanting to think about it. "Sure." His heart was pounding directly on his sternum. But Fitch and Matthews looked serious as owls, so he wasn't going to stick out by looking odd. It was big news, after all; anyone would be taken aback by it. Nevertheless, January made an effort to nod.

"Okay," Scholes said. "McDonald will be flying with you as co-pilot." Fitch frowned. "I've got to go tell those British officers that Le May doesn't want them on the strike with you. See you at the briefing."

"Yes, sir."

As soon as Scholes was around the corner Fitch swung a fist at the sky. "Yow!" Matthews cried. He and Fitch shook hands. "We did it!" Matthews took January's hand and wrung it, his face plastered with a goofy grin. "We did it!"

"Somebody did it, anyway," January said.

"Ah, Frank," Matthews said. "Show some spunk, You're always so cool."

"Old Professor Stoneface," Fitch said, glancing at January with a trace of amused contempt. "Come on, let's get to the briefing."

The briefing hut, one of the longer Quonsets, was completely surrounded by MPs holding carbines. "Gosh," Matthews said, subdued by the sight. Inside it was already smoky. The walls were covered by the usual maps of Japan. Two blackboards at the front were draped with sheets. Captain Shepard, the naval officer who worked with the scientists on the gimmick, was in back with his assistant Lieutenant Stone, winding a reel of film onto a projector. Dr. Nelson, the group psychiatrist, was already seated on a front bench near the wall. Tibbets had recently sicced the psychiatrist on the group — another one of his great ideas, like the spies in the bar. The man's questions had struck January as stupid. He hadn't even been able to figure out that Easterly was a flake, something that was clear to anybody who flew with him, or even played him in a single round of poker. January slid onto a bench beside his mates.

The two Brits entered, looking furious in their stiff-upper-lip way. They sat on the bench behind January. Sweeney's and Easterly's crew filed in; followed by the other men, and soon the room was full. Fitch and the rest pulled out Lucky Strikes and lit up; since they had named the plane only January had stuck with Camels.

Scholes came in with several men January didn't recognize, and went to the front. The chatter died, and all the smoke plumes ribboned steadily into the air.

Scholes nodded, and two intelligence officers took the sheets off the blackboards, revealing aerial reconnaissance photos.

"Men," Scholes said, "these are the target cities."

Someone cleared his throat.

"In order of priority they are Hiroshima, Kokura, and Nagasaki. There will be three weather scouts: *Straight Flush* to Hiroshima, *Strange Cargo* to Kokura, and *Full House* to Nagasaki. *The Great Artiste* and *Number 91* will be accompanying the mission to take photos. And *Lucky Strike* will fly the bomb."

There were rustles, coughs. Men turned to look at January and his mates, and they all sat up straight. Sweeney stretched back to shake Fitch's hand, and there were some quick laughs. Fitch grinned.

"Now listen up," Scholes went on. "The weapon we are going to deliver was successfully tested stateside a couple of weeks ago. And now we've got orders to drop it on the enemy." He paused to let that sink in. "I'll let Captain Shepard tell you more."

Shepard walked to the blackboard slowly, savoring his entrance. His forehead was shiny with sweat, and January realized he was excited or nervous. He wondered what the shrink would make of that.

"I'm going to come right to the point," Shepard said. "The bomb you are going to drop is something new in history. We think it will knock out everything within four miles."

Now the room was completely still. January noticed that he could see a great deal of his nose, eyebrows, and cheeks; it was as if he were receding back into his body, like a fox into its hole. He kept his gaze rigidly on Shepard, steadfastly ignoring the feeling. Shepard pulled a sheet back over a blackboard while someone else turned down the lights.

"This is a film of the only test we have made," Shepard said. The film started, caught, started again. A wavery cone of bright cigarette smoke speared the length of the room, and on the sheet sprang a dead gray landscape: a lot of sky, a smooth desert floor, hills in the distance. The projector went *click-click-click-click, click-click-click-click.* "The bomb is on top of the tower," Shepard said, and January focused on the pin-like object sticking out of the desert floor, off against the hills. It was between eight and ten miles from the camera, he judged; he had gotten good at calculating distances. He was still distracted by his face.

Click-click-click-click, click — then the screen went white for a second, filling even their room with light. When the picture returned the desert floor was filled with a white bloom of fire. The fireball coalesced and then quite suddenly it leaped off the earth all the way into the *stratosphere*, by God, like a tracer bullet leaving a machine-gun, trailing a whitish pillar of smoke behind it. The pillar gushed up and a growing ball of smoke billowed outward, capping the pillar. January calculated the size of the cloud, but was sure he got it wrong. There it stood. The picture flickered, and then the screen went white again, as if the camera had melted or that part of the world had come apart. But the flapping from the projector told them it was the end of the film.

January felt the air suck in and out of his open mouth. The lights came on in the smoky room and for a second he panicked, he struggled to shove his features into an accepted pattern, the shrink would be looking around at them all — and then he glanced around and realized he needn't have worried, that he wasn't alone. Faces were bloodless, eyes were blinky or bug-eyed with shock, mouths hung open or were clamped whitely shut. For a few moments they all had to acknowledge what they were doing. January, scaring himself, felt an urge to say, "Play it again, will you?" Fitch was pulling his curled black hair off his thug's forehead uneasily. Beyond him January saw that one of the Limeys had already reconsidered how mad he was about missing the flight. Now he looked sick. Someone let out a long *whew*, another whistled. January looked to the front again, where the shrink watched them, undisturbed.

Shepard said, "It's big, all right. And no one knows what will happen when it's dropped from the air. But the mushroom cloud you saw will go to at least thirty thousand feet, probably sixty. And the flash you saw at the beginning was hotter than the sun."

Hotter than the sun. More licked lips, hard swallows, readjusted baseball caps. One of the intelligence officers passed out tinted goggles like welder's glasses. January took his and twiddled the opacity dial.

Scholes said, "You're the hottest thing in the armed forces, now. So no talking, even among yourselves." He took a deep breath. "Let's do it the way Colonel Tibbets would have wanted us to. He picked every one of you because you were the best, and now's the time to show he was right. So — so let's make the old man proud."

The briefing was over. Men filed out into the sudden sunlight. Into the heat and glare. Captain Shepard approached Fitch. "Stone and I will be flying with you to take care of the bomb," he said.

Fitch nodded. "Do you know how many strikes we'll fly?"

"As many as it takes to make them quit." Shepard stared hard at all of them. "But it will only take one."

War breeds strange dreams. That night January writhed over his sheets in the hot wet vegetable darkness, in that frightening half-sleep when you sometimes know you are dreaming but can do nothing about it, and he dreamed he was walking . . .

. . . walking through the streets when suddenly the sun swoops down, the sun touches down and everything is instantly darkness and smoke and silence, a deaf roaring. Walls of fire. His head hurts and in the middle of his vision is a bluewhite blur as if God's camera went off in his face. Ah — the sun fell, he thinks. His arm is burned. Blinking is painful. People stumbling by, mouths open, horribly burned —

He is a priest, he can feel the clerical collar, and the wounded ask him for help. He points to his ears, tries to touch them but can't. Pall of black smoke over everything, the city has fallen into the streets. Ah, it's the end of the world. In a park he finds shade and cleared ground. People crouch under bushes like frightened animals. Where the park meets the river red and black figures crowd into steaming water. A figure gestures from a copse of bamboo. He enters it, finds five or six faceless soldiers huddling. Their eyes have melted, their mouths are holes. Deafness spares him their words. The sighted soldier mimes drinking. The soldiers are thirsty. He nods and goes to the river in search of a container. Bodies float downstream.

Hours pass as he hunts fruitlessly for a bucket. He pulls people from the rubble. He hears a bird screeching and he realizes that his deafness is the roar of the city burning, a roar like the blood in his ears but he is not deaf, he only thought he was deaf because there are no human cries. The people are suffering in silence. Through the dusky night he stumbles back to the river, pain crashing through his head. In a field men are pulling potatoes out of the ground that have been baked well enough to eat. He shares one with them. At the river everyone is dead —

— and he struggled out of the nightmare drenched in rank sweat, the taste of dirt in his mouth, his stomach knotted with horror. He sat up and the wet rough sheet clung to his skin. His heart felt crushed between lungs desperate for air. The flowery rotting jungle smell filled him and images from the dream flashed before him so vividly that in the dim hut he saw nothing else. He grabbed his cigarettes and jumped off the bunk, hurried out into the compound. Trembling he lit up, started pacing around. For a moment he worried that the idiot psychiatrist might see him, but then he dismissed the idea. Nelson would be asleep. They were all asleep. He shook his head, looked down at his right arm and almost dropped his cigarette — but it was just his stove scar, an old scar, he'd had it most of his life, since the day he'd pulled the frypan off the stove and onto his arm, burning it with oil. He could still remember the round O of fear that his mother's mouth had made as she rushed in to see what was wrong. Just an old burn scar, he thought, let's not go overboard here. He pulled his sleeve down.

For the rest of the night he tried to walk it off, cigarette after cigarette. The dome of the sky lightened until all the compound and the jungle beyond it was visible. He was forced by the light of day to walk back into his hut and lie down as if nothing had happened.

Two days later Scholes ordered them to take one of Le May's men over Rota for a test run. This new lieutenant colonel ordered Fitch not to play with the engines on takeoff. They flew a perfect run. January put the dummy gimmick right on the aiming point just as he had so often in the Salton Sea, and Fitch powered the plane down into the violent bank that started their 150-degree turn and flight for safety. Back on Tinian the lieutenant colonel congratulated them and shook each of their hands. January smiled with the rest, palms cool, heart steady. It was as if his body were a shell, something he could manipulate from without, like a bombsight. He ate well, he chatted as much as he ever had, and when the psychiatrist ran him to earth for some questions he was friendly and seemed open.

"Hello, doc."

"How do you feel about all this, Frank?"

"Just like I always have, sir. Fine."

"Eating well?"

"Better than ever."

"Sleeping well?"

"As well as I can in this humidity. I got used to Utah, I'm afraid." Dr. Nelson laughed. Actually January had hardly slept since his dream. He was afraid of sleep. Couldn't the man see that?

"And how do you feel about being part of the crew chosen to make the first strike?"

"Well, it was the right choice, I reckon. We're the b — the best crew left."

"Do you feel sorry about Tibbets's crew's accident?"

"Yes, sir, I do." You better believe it.

After the jokes and firm handshakes that ended the interview January walked out into the blaze of the tropical noon and lit a cigarette. He allowed himself to feel how much he despised the psychiatrist and his blind profession at the same time he was waving good-bye to the man. Ounce brain. Why couldn't he have seen? Whatever happened it would be his fault. . . . With a rush of smoke out of him January realized how painfully easy it was to fool someone if you wanted to. All action was no more than a mask that could be perfectly manipulated from somewhere else. And all the while in that somewhere else January lived in a *click-click-click* of film, in the silent roaring of a dream, struggling against images he couldn't dispel. The heat of the tropical sun — ninety-three million miles away, wasn't it? — pulsed painfully on the back of his neck.

As he watched the psychiatrist collar their tail-gunner Kochenski, he thought of walking up to the man and saying *I quit. I don't want to do this.* In imagination he saw the look that would form in the man's eye, in Fitch's eye, in Tibbets's eye, and his mind recoiled from the idea. He felt too much contempt for them. He wouldn't for anything give them a means to despise him, a reason to call him coward. Stubbornly he banished the whole complex of thought. Easier to go along with it.

And so a couple of disjointed days later, just after midnight of August 9th, he found himself preparing for the strike. Around him Fitch and Matthews and Haddock were doing the same. How odd were the everyday motions of getting dressed when you were off to demolish a city, to end a hundred thousand lives! January found himself examining his hands, his boots, the cracks in the linoleum. He put on his survival vest, checked the pockets abstractedly for fish-hooks, water kit, first aid package, emergency rations. Then the parachute harness, and his coveralls over it all. Tying his bootlaces took minutes; he couldn't do it when watching his fingers so closely.

"Come on, Professor!" Fitch's voice was tight. "The big day is here."

He followed the others into the night. A cool wind was blowing. The chaplain said a prayer for them. They took jeeps down Broadway to runway Able. *Lucky Strike* stood in a circle of spotlights and men, half of them with cameras, the rest with reporter's pads. They surrounded the crew; it reminded January of a Hollywood premiere. Eventually he escaped up the hatch and into the plane. Others followed. Half an hour passed before Fitch joined them, grinning like a movie star. They started the engines, and January was thankful for their vibrating, thought-smothering roar. They taxied away from the Hollywood scene and January felt relief for a moment, until he remembered where they were going. On runway Able the engines pitched up to their twenty-three hundred rpm whine, and looking out the clear windscreen he saw the runway paintmarks move by ever faster. Fitch kept them on the runway till Tinian had run out from under them, then quickly pulled up. They were on their way.

When they got to altitude January climbed past Fitch and McDonald to the bombardier's seat and placed his parachute on it. He leaned back. The roar of the four engines packed around him like cotton batting. He was on the flight, nothing to be done about it now. The heavy vibration was a comfort, he liked the feel of it there in the nose of the plane. A drowsy, sad acceptance hummed through him.

Against his closed eyelids flashed a black eyeless face and he jerked awake, heart racing. He was on the flight, no way out. Now he realized how easy it would have been to get out of it. He could have just said he didn't want to. The simplicity of it appalled him. Who gave a damn what the psychiatrist or Tibbets or anyone else thought, compared to this? Now there was no way out. It was a comfort, in a way. Now he could stop worrying, stop thinking he had any choice.

Sitting there with his knees bracketing the bombsight January dozed, and as he dozed he daydreamed his way out. He could climb the step to Fitch and McDonald and declare he had been secretly promoted to Major and ordered to re-direct the mission. They were to go to Tokyo and drop the bomb in the bay. The Jap war cabinet had been told to watch this demonstration of the new weapon, and when they saw that fireball boil the bay and bounce into heaven they'd run and sign surrender papers as fast as they could write, kamikazes or not. They weren't crazy, after all. No need to murder a whole city. It was such a good plan that the generals back home were no doubt changing the mission at this very minute, desperately radioing their instructions to Tinian, only to find out it was too late . . . so that when they returned to Tinian January would become a hero for guessing what the generals really wanted, and for risking all to do it. It would be like one of the Hornblower stories in the *Saturday Evening Post*.

Once again January jerked awake. The drowsy pleasure of the fantasy was replaced with desperate scorn. There wasn't a chance in hell that he could convince Fitch and the rest that he had secret orders superseding theirs. And he couldn't go up there and wave his pistol around and *order* them to drop the bomb in Tokyo Bay, because he was the one who had to actually drop it, and he couldn't be down in front dropping the bomb and up ordering the others around at the same time. Pipe dreams.

Time swept on, slow as a second hand. January's thoughts, however, matched the spin of the props; desperately they cast about, now this way now that, like an animal caught by the leg in a trap. The crew was silent. The clouds below were a white scree on the black ocean. January's knee vibrated against the squat stand of the bombsight. He was the one who had to drop the bomb. No matter where his thoughts lunged they were brought up short by that. He was the one, not Fitch or the crew, not Le May, not the generals and scientists back home, not Truman and his advisors. Truman — suddenly January hated him. Roosevelt would have done it differently. If only Roosevelt had lived! The grief that had filled January when he learned of Roosevelt's death reverberated through him again, more strongly than ever. It was unfair to have worked so hard and then not see the war's end. And FDR would have ended it differently. Back at the start of it all he had declared that civilian centers were never to be bombed, and if he had lived, if, if, if. But he hadn't. And now it was smiling bastard Harry Truman, ordering *him*, Frank January, to drop the sun on two hundred thousand women and children. Once his father had taken him to see the Browns play before twenty thousand, a giant crowd — "I never voted for you," January whispered viciously, and jerked to realize he had spoken aloud. Luckily his microphone was off. And Roosevelt would have done it differently, he *would have*.

The bombsight rose before him, spearing the black sky and blocking some of the hundreds of little cruciform stars. *Lucky Strike* ground on toward Iwo Jima, minute by minute flying four miles closer to their target. January leaned forward and put his face in the cool headrest of the bombsight, hoping that its grasp might hold his thoughts as well as his forehead. It worked surprisingly well.

His earphones crackled and he sat up. "Captain January." It was Shepard. "We're going to arm the bomb now, want to watch?"

"Sure thing." He shook his head, surprised at his own duplicity. Stepping up between the pilots, he moved stiffly to the roomy cabin behind the cockpit. Matthews was at his desk taking a navigational fix on the radio signals from Iwo Jima and Okinawa, and Haddock stood beside him. At the back of the compartment was a small circular hatch, below the larger tunnel leading to the rear of the plane. January opened it, sat down and swung himself feet first through the hole.

The bomb bay was unheated, and the cold air felt good. He stood facing the bomb. Stone was sitting on the floor of the bay; Shepard was laid out under the bomb, reaching into it. On a rubber pad next to Stone were tools, plates, several cylindrical blocks. Shepard pulled back, sat up, sucked a scraped knuckle. He shook his head ruefully: "I don't dare wear gloves with this one."

"I'd be just as happy myself if you didn't let something slip," January joked nervously. The two men laughed.

"Nothing can blow till I change those green wires to the red ones," Stone said.

"Give me the wrench," Shepard said. Stone handed it to him, and he stretched under the bomb again. After some awkward wrenching inside it he lifted out a cylindrical plug. "Breech plug," he said, and set it on the mat.

January found his skin goose-pimpling in the cold air. Stone handed Shepard one of the blocks. Shepard extended under the bomb again. "Red ends toward the breech." "I know." Watching them January was reminded of auto mechanics on the oily floor of a garage, working under a car. He had spent a few years doing that himself, after his family moved to Vicksburg. Hiroshima was a river town. One time a flat-bed truck carrying bags of cement powder down Fourth Street hill had lost its brakes and careened into the intersection with River Road, where despite the driver's efforts to turn it smashed into a passing car. Frank had been out in the yard playing, had heard the crash and saw the cement dust rising. He had been one of the first there. The woman and child in the passenger seat of the Model T had been killed. The woman driving was okay. They were from Chicago. A group of folks subdued the driver of the truck, who kept trying to help at the Model T, though he had a bad cut on his head and was covered with white dust.

"Okay, let's tighten the breech plug." Stone gave Shepard the wrench. "Sixteen turns exactly," Shepard said. He was sweating even in the bay's chill, and he paused to wipe his forehead. "Let's hope we don't get hit by lightning." He put the wrench down and shifted onto his knees, picked up a circular plate. Hubcap, January thought. Stone connected wires, then helped Shepard install two more plates. Good old American know-how, January thought, goose-pimples rippling across his skin like cat's-paws over water. There was Shepard, a scientist, putting together a bomb like he was an auto mechanic changing oil and plugs. January felt a tight rush of rage at the scientists who had designed the bomb. They had worked on it for over a year down there in New Mexico, had none of them in all that time ever stopped to think what they were doing?

But none of them had to drop it. January turned to hide his face from Shepard, stepped down the bay. The bomb looked like a big long trashcan, with fins at one end and little antennae at the other. Just a bomb, he thought, damn it, it's just another bomb.

Shepard stood and patted the bomb gently. "We've got a live one now." Never a thought about what it would do. January hurried by the man, afraid that hatred would crack his shell and give him away. The pistol strapped to his belt caught on the hatchway and he imagined shooting Shepard — shooting Fitch and McDonald and plunging the controls forward so that *Lucky Strike* tilted and spun down into the sea like a spent tracer bullet, like a plane broken by flak, following the arc of all human ambition. Nobody would ever know what had happened to them, and their trashcan would be dumped at the bottom of the Pacific where it belonged. He could even shoot everyone and parachute out, and perhaps be rescued by one of the Superdumbos following them. . . .

The thought passed and remembering it January squinted with disgust. But another part of him agreed that it was a possibility. It could be done. It would solve his problem. His fingers explored his holster snap.

"Want some coffee?" Matthews asked.

"Sure," January said, and took his hand from the gun to reach for the cup. He sipped: hot. He watched Matthews and Benton tune the loran equipment. As the beeps came in Matthews took a straightedge and drew lines from Okinawa and Iwo Jima on his map table. He tapped a finger on the intersection. "They've taken the art out of navigation," he said to January. "They might as well stop making the navigator's dome," thumbing up at the little bubble over them.

"Good old American know-how," January said.

Matthews nodded. With two fingers he measured the distance between their position and Iwo Jima. Benton measured with a ruler.

"Rendezvous at five thirty-five, eh?" Matthews said. They were to rendezvous with the two trailing planes over Iwo.

Benton disagreed: "I'd say five-fifty."

"What? Check again, guy, we're not in no tugboat here."

"The wind — "

"Yah, the wind. Frank, you want to add a bet to the pool?"

"Five thirty-six," January said promptly.

They laughed. "See, he's got more confidence in me," Matthews said with a dopey grin.

January recalled his plan to shoot the crew and tip the plane into the sea, and he pursed his lips, repelled. Not for anything would he be able to shoot these men, who, if not friends, were at least companions. They passed for friends. They meant no harm.

Shepard and Stone climbed into the cabin. Matthews offered them coffee. "The gimmick's ready to kick their ass, eh?" Shepard nodded and drank.

January moved forward, past Haddock's console. Another plan that wouldn't work. What to do? All the flight engineer's dials and gauges showed conditions were normal. Maybe he could sabotage something? Cut a line somewhere?

Fitch looked back at him and said, "When are we due over Iwo?"

"Five forty, Matthews says."

"He better be right."

A thug. In peacetime Fitch would be hanging around a pool table giving the cops trouble. He was perfect for war. Tibbets had chosen his men well — most of them, anyway. Moving back past Haddock January stopped to stare at the group of men in the navigation cabin. They joked, drank coffee. They were all a bit like Fitch: young toughs, capable and thoughtless.

They were having a good time, an adventure. That was January's dominant impression of his companions in the 509th; despite all the bitching and the occasional moments of overmastering fear, they were having a good time. His mind spun forward and he saw what these young men would grow up to be like as clearly as if they stood before him in businessmen's suits, prosperous and balding. They would be tough and capable and thoughtless, and as the years passed and the great war receded in time they would look back on it with ever-increasing nostalgia, for they would be the survivors and not the dead. Every year of this war would feel like ten in their memories, so that the war would always remain the central experience of their lives — time when history lay palpable in their hands, when each of their daily acts affected it, when moral issues were simple, and others told them what to do — so that as more years passed and the survivors aged, bodies falling apart, lives in one rut or another, they would unconsciously push harder and harder to thrust the world into war again, thinking somewhere inside themselves that if they could only return to world war then they would magically be again as they were in the last one — young, and free, and happy. And by that time they would hold the positions of power, they would be capable of doing it.

So there would be more wars, January saw. He heard it in Matthews's laughter, saw it in their excited eyes. "There's Iwo, and it's five thirty-one. Pay up! I win!" And in future wars they'd have more bombs like the gimmick, hundreds of them no doubt. He saw more planes, more young crews like this one, flying to Moscow no doubt or to wherever, fireballs in every capital, why not? And to what end? To what end? So that the old men could hope to become magically young again. Nothing more sane than that.

They were over Iwo Jima. Three more hours to Japan. Voices from *The Great Artiste* and *Number 91* crackled on the radio. Rendezvous accomplished, the three planes flew northwest, toward Shikoku, the first Japanese island in their path. January went aft to use the toilet. "You okay, Frank?" Matthews asked. "Sure. Terrible coffee, though." "Ain't it always," January tugged at his baseball cap and hurried away. Kochenski and the other gunners were playing poker. When he was done he returned forward. Matthews sat on the stool before his maps, readying his equipment for the constant monitoring of drift that would now be required. Haddock and Benton were also busy at their stations. January maneuvered between the pilots down into the nose. "Good shooting," Matthews called after him.

Forward it seemed quieter. January got settled, put his headphones on and leaned forward to look out the ribbed Plexiglas.

Dawn had turned the whole vault of the sky pink. Slowly the radiant shade shifted through lavender to blue, pulse by pulse a different color. The ocean below was a glittering blue plane, marbled by a pattern of puffy pink cloud. The sky above was a vast dome, darker above than on the horizon. January had always thought that dawn was the time when you could see most clearly how big the earth was, and how high above it they flew. It seemed they flew at the very upper edge of the atmosphere, and January saw how thin it was, how it was just a skin of air really, so that even if you flew up to its top the earth still extended away infinitely in every direction. The coffee had warmed January, he was sweating. Sunlight blinked off the Plexiglas. His watch said six. Plane and hemisphere of blue were split down the middle by the bombsight. His earphones crackled and he listened in to the reports from the lead planes flying over the target cities. Kokura, Nagasaki, Hiroshima, all of them had six-tenths cloud cover. Maybe they would have to cancel the whole mission because of weather. "We'll look at Hiroshima first," Fitch said. January peered down at the fields of miniature clouds with renewed interest. His parachute slipped under him. Readjusting it he imagined putting it on, sneaking back to the central escape hatch under the navigator's cabin, opening the hatch . . . he could be out of the plane and gone before anyone noticed. Leave it up to them. They could bomb or not but it wouldn't be January's doing. He could float down onto the world like a puff of dandelion, feel cool air rush around him, watch the silk canopy dome hang over him like a miniature sky, a private world.

An eyeless black face. January shuddered; it was as though the nightmare could return any time. If he jumped nothing would change, the bomb would still fall — would he feel any better, floating on his Inland Sea? Sure, one part of him shouted; maybe, another conceded; the rest of him saw that face. . . .

Earphones crackled. Shepard said, "Lieutenant Stone has now armed the bomb, and I can tell you all what we are carrying. Aboard with us is the world's first atomic bomb."

Not exactly, January thought. Whistles squeaked in his earphones. The first one went off in New Mexico. Splitting atoms: January had heard the term before. Tremendous energy in every atom, Einstein had said. Break one, and — he had seen the result on film. Shepard was talking about radiation, which brought back more to January. Energy released in the form of X-rays. Killed by X-rays! It would be against the Geneva Convention if they had thought of it.

Fitch cut in. "When the bomb is dropped Lieutenant Benton will record our reaction to what we see. This recording is being made for history, so watch your language." Watch your language! January choked back a laugh. Don't curse or blaspheme God at the sight of the first atomic bomb incinerating a city and all its inhabitants with X-rays!

Six twenty. January found his hands clenched together on the headrest of the bombsight. He felt as if he had a fever. In the harsh wash of morning light the skin on the backs of his hands appeared slightly translucent. The whorls in the skin looked like the delicate patterning of waves on the sea's surface. His hands were made of atoms. Atoms were the smallest building block of matter, it took billions of them to make those tense, trembling hands. Split one atom and you had the fireball. That meant that the energy contained in even one hand . . . he turned up a palm to look at the lines and the mottled flesh under the transparent skin. A person was a bomb that could blow up the world. January felt that latent power stir in him, pulsing with every hard heart-knock. What beings they were, and in what a blue expanse of a world! — And here they spun on to drop a bomb and kill a hundred thousand of these astonishing beings.

When a fox or raccoon is caught by the leg in a trap, it lunges until the leg is frayed, twisted, perhaps broken, and only then does the animal's pain and exhaustion force it to quit. Now in the same way January wanted to quit. His mind hurt. His plans to escape were so much crap — stupid, useless. Better to quit. He tried to stop thinking, but it was hopeless. How could he stop? As long as he was conscious he would be thinking. The mind struggles longer in its traps than any fox.

Lucky Strike tilted up and began the long climb to bombing altitude. On the horizon the clouds lay over a green island. Japan. Surely it had gotten hotter, the heater must be broken, he thought. Don't think. Every few minutes Matthews gave Fitch small course adjustments. "Two seventy-five, now. That's it." To escape the moment January recalled his childhood. Following a mule and plow. Moving to Vicksburg (rivers). For a while there in Vicksburg, since his stutter made it hard to gain friends, he had played a game with himself. He had passed the time by imagining that everything he did was vitally important and determined the fate of the world. If he crossed a road in front of a certain car, for instance, then the car wouldn't make it through the next intersection before a truck hit it, and so the man driving would be killed and wouldn't be able to invent the flying boat that would save President Wilson from kidnappers — so he had to wait for that car because everything afterward depended on it. Oh damn it, he thought, damn it, think of something *different*. The last Hornblower story he had read — how would *he* get out of this? The round O of his mother's face as she ran in and saw his arm — The Mississippi, mud-brown behind its levees — Abruptly he shook his head, face twisted in frustration and despair, aware at last that no possible avenue of memory would serve as an escape for him now, for now there was no part of his life that did not apply to the situation he was in, and no matter where he cast his mind it was going to shore up against the hour facing him.

Less than an hour. They were at thirty thousand feet, bombing altitude. Fitch gave him altimeter readings to dial into the bombsight. Matthews gave him windspeeds. Sweat got in his eye and he blinked furiously. The sun rose behind them like an atomic bomb, glinting off every corner and edge of the Plexiglas, illuminating his bubble compartment with a fierce blare. Broken plans jumbled together in his mind, his breath was short, his throat dry. Uselessly and repeatedly he damned the scientists, damned Truman. Damned the Japanese for causing the whole mess in the first place, damned yellow killers, they had brought this on themselves. Remember Pearl. American men had died under bombs when no war had been declared; they had started it and now it was coming back to them with a vengeance. And they deserved it. And an invasion of Japan would take years, cost millions of lives — end it now, end it, they deserved it, they deserved it steaming river full of charcoal people silently dying damned stubborn race of maniacs!

"There's Honshu," Fitch said, and January returned to the world of the plane. They were over the Inland Sea. Soon they would pass the secondary target Kokura, a bit to the south. Seven thirty. The island was draped more heavily than the sea by clouds, and again January's heart leaped with the idea that weather would cancel the mission. But they did deserve it. It was a mission like any other mission. He had dropped bombs on Africa, Sicily, Italy, all Germany. . . . He leaned forward to take a look through the sight. Under the X of the crosshairs was the sea, but at the lead edge of the sight was land. Honshu. At two hundred and thirty miles an hour that gave them about a half hour to Hiroshima. Maybe less. He wondered if his heart could beat so hard for that long.

Fitch said, "Matthews, I'm giving over guidance to you. Just tell us what to do."

"Bear south two degrees," was all Matthews said. At last their voices had taken on a touch of awareness, even fear.

"January, are you ready?" Fitch asked,

"I'm just waiting," January said. He sat up, so Fitch could see the back of his head. The bombsight stood between his legs. A switch on its side would start the bombing sequence; the bomb would not leave the plane immediately upon the flick of the switch, but would drop after a fifteen-second radio tone warned the following planes. The sight was adjusted accordingly.

"Adjust to a heading of two sixty-five," Matthews said. "We're coming in directly upwind." This was to make any side-drift adjustments for the bomb unnecessary. "January, dial it down to two hundred and thirty-one miles per hour."

"Two thirty-one."

Fitch said, "Everyone but January and Matthews, get your goggles on."

January took the darkened goggles from the floor. One needed to protect one's eyes or they might melt. He put them on, put his forehead on the headrest. They were in the way. He took them off. When he looked through the sight again there was land under the crosshairs. He checked his watch. Eight o'clock. Up and reading the papers, drinking tea.

"Ten minutes to AP," Matthews said. The aiming point was Aioi Bridge, a T-shaped bridge in the middle of the delta-straddling city. Easy to recognize.

"There's a lot of cloud down there," Fitch noted. "Are you going to be able to see?"

"I won't be sure until we try it," January said.

"We can make another pass and use radar if we need to," Matthews said.

Fitch said, "Don't drop it unless you're sure, January."

"Yes, sir."

Through the sight a grouping of rooftops and gray roads was just visible between broken clouds. Around it green forest. "All right," Matthews exclaimed, "here we go! Keep it right on this heading, Captain! January, we'll stay at two thirty-one."

"And same heading," Fitch said. "January, she's all yours. Everyone make sure your goggles are on. And be ready for the turn."

January's world contracted to the view through the bombsight. A stippled field of cloud and forest. Over a small range of hills and into Hiroshima's watershed. The broad river was mud-brown, the land pale hazy green, the growing network of roads flat gray. Now the tiny rectangular shapes of buildings covered almost all the land, and swimming into the sight came the city proper, narrow islands thrusting into a dark blue bay. Under the crosshairs the city moved island by island, cloud by cloud. January had stopped breathing, his fingers were rigid as stone on the switch. And there was Aioi Bridge. It slid right under the crosshairs, a tiny T right in a gap in the clouds. January's fingers crushed the switch. Deliberately he took a breath, held it. Clouds swam under the crosshairs, then the next island. "Almost there," he said calmly into his microphone. "Steady." Now that he was committed his heart was humming like the Wrights'. He counted to ten. Now flowing under the crosshairs were clouds alternating with green forest, leaden roads. "I've turned the switch, but I'm not getting a tone!" he croaked into the mike. His right hand held the switch firmly in place. Fitch was shouting something — Matthews' voice cracked across it — "Flipping it b-back and forth," January shouted, shielding the bombsight with his body from the eyes of the pilots, "But *still* — wait a second —"

He pushed the switch down. A low hum filled his ears. "That's it! It started!"

"But where will it land?" Matthews cried.

"Hold steady!" January shouted.

Lucky Strike shuddered and lofted up ten or twenty feet. January twisted to look down and there was the bomb, flying just below the plane. Then with a wobble it fell away.

The plane banked right and dove so hard that the centrifugal force threw January against the Plexiglas. Several thousand feet lower Fitch leveled it out and they hurtled north.

"Do you see anything?" Fitch cried.

From the tailgun Kochenski gasped "Nothing." January struggled upright. He reached for the welder's goggles, but they were no longer on his head. He couldn't find them. "How long has it been?" he said.

"Thirty seconds," Matthews replied.

January clamped his eyes shut.

The blood in his eyelids lit up red, then white.

On the earphones a clutter of voices: "Oh my God. Oh my God." The plane bounced and tumbled, metallically shrieking. January pressed himself off the Plexiglas, "Nother shockwave!" Kochenski yelled. The plane rocked again, bounced out of control, this is it, January thought, end of the world, I guess that solves my problem.

He opened his eyes and found he could still see. The engines still roared, the props spun. "Those were the shockwaves from the bomb," Fitch called. "We're okay now. Look at that! Will you look at that son-ofabitch go!"

January looked. The cloud layer below had burst apart, and a black column of smoke billowed up from a core of red fire. Already the top of the column was at their height. Exclamations of shock clattered painfully in January's ears. He stared at the fiery base of the cloud, at the scores of fires feeding into it. Suddenly he could see past the cloud, and his fingernails cut into his palms. Through a gap in the clouds he saw it clearly, the delta, the six rivers, there off to the left of the tower of smoke; the city of Hiroshima, untouched.

"We missed!" Kochenski yelled. "We missed it!"

January turned to hide his face from the pilots; on it was a grin like a rictus. He sat back in his seat and let the relief fill him.

Then it was back to it. "God damn it!" Fitch shouted down at him. McDonald was trying to restrain him. "January, get up here!"

"Yes, sir." Now there was a new set of problems.

January stood and turned, legs weak. His right fingertips throbbed painfully. The men were crowded forward to look out the Plexiglas. January looked with them.

The mushroom cloud was forming. It roiled out as if it might continue to extend forever, fed by the inferno and the black stalk below it. It looked about two miles wide, and half a mile tall, and it extended well above the height they flew at, dwarfing their plane entirely. "Do you think we'll all be sterile?" Matthews said.

"I can taste the radiation," McDonald declared. "Can you? It tastes like lead."

Bursts of flame shot up into the cloud from below, giving a purplish tint to the stalk. There it stood: lifelike, malignant, sixty thousand feet tall. One bomb. January shoved past the pilots into the navigation cabin, overwhelmed.

"Should I start recording everyone's reactions, Captain?" asked Benton.

"To hell with that," Fitch said, following January back. But Shepard got there first, descending quickly from the navigation dome. He rushed across the cabin, caught January on the shoulder. "You bastard!" he screamed as January stumbled back. "You lost your nerve, coward!"

January went for Shepard, happy to have a target at last, but Fitch cut in and grabbed him by the collar, pulled him around until they were face to face —

"Is that right?" Fitch cried, as angry as Shepard. "Did you screw up on purpose?"

"No," January grunted, and knocked Fitch's hands away from his neck. He swung and smacked Fitch on the mouth, caught him solid. Fitch staggered back, recovered, and no doubt would have beaten January up, but Matthews and Benton and Stone leaped in and held him back, shouting for order. "Shut up! Shut up!" McDonald screamed from the cockpit, and for a moment it was bedlam, but Fitch let himself be restrained, and soon only McDonald's shouts for quiet were heard. January retreated to between the pilot seats, right hand on his pistol holster.

"The city was in the crosshairs when I flipped the switch," he said, "But the first couple of times I flipped it nothing happened — "

"That's a lie!" Shepard shouted, "There was nothing wrong with the switch, I checked it myself. Besides, the bomb exploded *miles* beyond Hiroshima, look for yourself! That's *minutes*." He wiped spit from his chin and pointed at January. "You did it."

"You don't know that," January said. But he could see the men had been convinced by Shepard, and he took a step back. "You just get me to a board of inquiry, quick. And leave me alone till then. If you touch me again," glaring venomously at Fitch and then Shepard, "I'll shoot you." He turned and hopped down to his seat, feeling exposed and vulnerable, like a treed raccoon.

"They'll shoot *you* for this," Shepard screamed after him. "Disobeying orders — treason — " Matthews and Stone were shutting him up.

"Let's get out of here," he heard McDonald say. "I can taste the lead, can't you?"

January looked out the Plexiglas. The giant cloud still burned and roiled. One atom. . . . Well, they had really done it to that forest. He almost laughed but stopped himself, afraid of hysteria. Through a break in the clouds he got a clear view of Hiroshima for the first time. It lay spread over its islands like a map, unharmed. Well, that was that. The inferno at the base of the mushroom cloud was eight or ten miles around the shore of the bay, and a mile or two inland. A certain patch of forest would be gone, destroyed — utterly blasted from the face of the earth. The Japs would be able to go out and investigate the damage. And if they were told it was a demonstration, a warning — and if they acted fast — well, they had their chance. Maybe it would work.

The release of tension made January feel sick. Then he recalled Shepard's words and he knew that whether his plan worked or not he was still in trouble. In trouble! It was worse than that. Bitterly he cursed the Japanese, he even wished for a moment that he *had* dropped it on them. Wearily he let his despair empty him.

A long while later he sat up straight. Once again he was a trapped animal. He began lunging for escape, casting about for plans. One alternative after another. All during the long grim flight home he considered it, mind spinning at the speed of the props and beyond. And when they came down on Tinian he had a plan. It was a long shot, he reckoned, but it was the best he could do.

The briefing hut was surrounded by MPs again. January stumbled from the truck with the rest and walked inside. He was more than ever aware of the looks given him, and they were hard, accusatory. He was too tired to care. He hadn't slept in more than thirty-six hours, and had slept very little since the last time he had been in the hut, a week before. Now the room quivered with the lack of engine vibration to stabilize it, and the silence roared. It was all he could do to hold on to the bare essentials of his plan. The glares of Fitch and Shepard, the hurt incomprehension of Matthews, they had to be thrust out of his focus. Thankfully, he lit a cigarette.

In a clamor of question and argument the others described the strike. Then the haggard Scholes and an intelligence officer led them through the bombing run. January's plan made it necessary to hold to his story: ". . . and when the AP was under the crosshairs I pushed down the switch, but got no signal. I flipped it up and down repeatedly until the tone kicked in. At that point there was still fifteen seconds to the release."

"Was there anything that may have caused the tone to start when it did?"

"Not that I noticed immediately, but — "

"It's impossible," Shepard interrupted, face red. "I checked the switch before we flew and there was nothing wrong with it. Besides, the drop occurred over a minute — "

"Captain Shepard," Scholes said. "We'll hear from you presently."

"But he's obviously lying — "

"Captain Shepard! It's not at all obvious. Don't speak unless questioned."

"Anyway," January said, hoping to shift the questions away from the issue of the long delay, "I noticed something about the bomb when it was falling that could explain why it stuck. I need to discuss it with one of the scientists familiar with the bomb's design."

"What was that?" Scholes asked suspiciously.

January hesitated. "There's going to be an inquiry, right?"

Scholes frowned. "This is the inquiry, Captain January. Tell us what you saw."

"But there will be some proceeding beyond this one?"

"It looks like there's going to be a court-martial, yes, Captain."

"That's what I thought. I don't want to talk to anyone but my counsel, and some scientist familiar with the bomb."

"*I'm* a scientist familiar with the bomb," Shepard burst out. "You could tell me if you really had anything, you — "

"I said I need a scientist!" January exclaimed, rising to face the scarlet Shepard across the table. "Not a G-God damned mechanic." Shepard started to shout, others joined in and the room rang with argument. While Scholes restored order January sat down, and he refused to be drawn out again.

"I'll see you're assigned counsel, and initiate the court-martial," Scholes said, clearly at a loss. "Meanwhile you are under arrest, on suspicion of disobeying orders in combat." January nodded, and Scholes gave him over to MPs.

"One last thing," January said, fighting exhaustion. "Tell General Le May that if the Japs are told this drop was a warning, it might have the same effect as — "

"I told you!" Shepard shouted. "I told you he did it on purpose!"

Men around Shepard restrained him. But he had convinced most of them, and even Matthews stared at him with surprised anger.

January shook his head wearily. He had the dull feeling that his plan, while it had succeeded so far, was ultimately not a good one. "Just trying to make the best of it." It took all of his remaining will to force his legs to carry him in a dignified manner out of the hut.

His cell was an empty NCO's office. MPs brought his meals. For the first couple of days he did little but sleep. On the third day he glanced out the office's barred window, and saw a tractor pulling a tarpaulin-draped trolley out of the compound, followed by jeeps filled with MPs. It looked like a military funeral. January rushed to the door and banged on it until one of the young MPs came.

"What's that they're doing out there?" January demanded.

Eyes cold and mouth twisted, the MP said, "They're making another strike. They're going to do it right this time."

"No!" January cried. "No!" He rushed the MP, who knocked him back and locked the door. "No!" He beat the door until his hands hurt, cursing wildly. "You don't *need* to do it, it isn't *necessary*." Shell shattered at last, he collapsed on the bed and wept. Now everything he had done would be rendered meaningless. He had sacrificed himself for nothing.

A day or two after that the MPs led in a colonel, an iron-haired man who stood stiffly and crushed January's hand when he shook it. His eyes were a pale, icy blue.

"I am Colonel Dray," he said. "I have been ordered to defend you in court-martial." January could feel the dislike pouring from the man. "To do that I'm going to need every fact you have, so let's get started."

"I'm not talking to anybody until I've seen an atomic scientist."

"I am your *defense* counsel — "

"I don't care who you are," January said. "Your defense of me depends on you getting one of the scientists *here*. The higher up he is, the better. And I want to speak to him alone."

"I will have to be present."

So he would do it. But now January's counsel, too, was an enemy.

"Naturally," January said. "You're my counsel. But no one else. Our atomic secrecy may depend on it."

"You saw evidence of sabotage?"

"Not one word more until that scientist is here."

Angrily the colonel nodded and left.

Late the next day the colonel returned with another man. "This is Dr. Forest."

"I helped develop the bomb," Forest said. He had a crew-cut and dressed in fatigues, and to January he looked more Army than the colonel. Suspiciously he stared back and forth at the two men.

"You'll vouch for this man's identity on your word as an officer?" he asked Dray.

"Of course," the colonel said stiffly, offended.

"So," Dr. Forest said. "You had some trouble getting it off when you wanted to. Tell me what you saw."

"I saw nothing," January said harshly. He took a deep breath; it was time to commit himself. "I want you to take a message back to the scientists. You folks have been working on this thing for years, and you must have had time to consider how the bomb should have been used. You know we could have convinced the Japs to surrender by showing them a demonstration — "

"Wait a minute," Forest said. "You're saying you didn't see anything? There wasn't a malfunction?"

"That's right," January said, and cleared his throat. "It wasn't *necessary*, do you understand?"

Forest was looking at Colonel Dray. Dray gave him a disgusted shrug. "He told he saw evidence of sabotage."

"I want you to go back and ask the scientists to intercede for me," January said, raising his voice to get the man's attention. "I haven't got a chance in that court-martial. But if the scientists defend me then maybe they'll let me live, see? I don't want to get shot for doing something every one of you scientists would have done."

Dr. Forest had backed away. Color rising, he said, "What makes you think that's what we would have done? Don't you think we considered it? Don't you think men better qualified than you made the decision?" He waved a hand — "God damn it — what made you think you were competent to decide something as important as that!"

January was appalled at the man's reaction; in his plan it had gone differently. Angrily he jabbed a finger at Forest. "Because *I* was the man doing it, *Doctor* Forest. You take even one step back from that and suddenly you can pretend it's not your doing. Fine for you, but I *was there*."

At every word the man's color was rising. It looked like he might pop a vein in his neck. January tried once more. "Have you ever tried to imagine what one of your bombs would do to a city full of people?"

"I've had enough!" the man exploded. He turned to Dray. "I'm under no obligation to keep what I've heard here confidential. You can be sure it will be used as evidence in Captain January's court-martial." He turned and gave January a look of such blazing hatred that January understood it. For these men to admit he was right would mean admitting that they were wrong — that every one of them was responsible for his part in the construction of the weapon January had refused to use. Understanding that, January knew he was doomed.

The bang of Dr. Forest's departure still shook the little office. January sat on his cot, got out a smoke. Under Colonel Dray's cold gaze he lit one shakily, took a drag. He looked up at the colonel, shrugged. "It was my best chance," he explained. That did something — for the first and only time the cold disdain in the colonel's eyes shifted to a little, hard, lawyerly gleam of respect.

The court-martial lasted two days. The verdict was guilty of disobeying orders in combat, and of giving aid and comfort to the enemy. The sentence was death by firing squad.

For most of his remaining days January rarely spoke, drawing ever further behind the mask that had hidden him for so long. A clergyman came to see him, but it was the 509th's chaplain, the one who had said the prayer blessing the *Lucky Strike*'s mission before they took off. Angrily January sent him packing.

Later, however, a young Catholic priest dropped by. His name was Patrick Getty. He was a little pudgy man, bespectacled and, it seemed, somewhat afraid of January. January let the man talk to him. When he returned the next day January talked back a bit, and on the day after that he talked some more. It became a habit.

Usually January talked about his childhood. He talked of plowing mucky black bottom land behind a mule. Of running down the lane to the mailbox. Of reading books by the light of the moon after he had been ordered to sleep, and of being beaten by his mother for it with a high-heeled shoe. He told the priest the story of the time his arm had been burnt, and about the car crash at the bottom of Fourth Street. "It's the truck driver's face I remember, do you see, Father?"

"Yes," the young priest said. "Yes."

And he told him about the game he had played in which every action he took tipped the balance of world affairs. "When I remembered that game I thought it was dumb. Step on a sidewalk crack and cause an earthquake — you know, it's stupid. Kids are like that." The priest nodded. "But now I've been thinking that if everybody were to live their whole lives like that, thinking that every move they made really was important, then . . . it might make a difference." He waved a hand vaguely, expelled cigarette smoke. "You're accountable for what you do."

"Yes," the priest said. "Yes, you are."

"And if you're given orders to do something wrong, you're still accountable, right? The orders don't change it."

"That's right."

"Hmph." January smoked a while. "So they say, anyway. But look what happens." He waved at the office. "I'm like the guy in a story I read — he thought everything in books was true, and after reading a bunch of westerns he tried to rob a train. They tossed him in jail." He laughed shortly. "Books are full of crap."

"Not all of them," the priest said. "Besides, you weren't trying to rob a train."

They laughed at the notion. "Did you read that story?"

"No."

"It was the strangest book — there were two stories in it, and they alternated chapter by chapter, but they didn't have a thing to do with each other! I didn't get it."

". . . Maybe the writer was trying to say that everything connects to everything else."

"Maybe. But it's a funny way to say it."

"I like it."

And so they passed the time, talking.

So it was the priest who was the one to come by and tell January that his request for a Presidential pardon had been refused. Getty said awkwardly, "It seems the President approves the sentence."

"That bastard," January said weakly. He sat on his cot.

Time passed. It was another hot, humid day.

"Well," the priest said. "Let me give you some better news. Given your situation I don't think telling you matters, though I've been told not to. The second mission — you know there was a second strike?"

"Yes."

"Well, they missed too."

"What?" January cried, and bounced to his feet. "You're kidding!"

"No. They flew to Kokura, but found it covered by clouds. It was the same over Nagasaki and Hiroshima, so they flew back to Kokura and tried to drop the bomb using radar to guide it, but apparently there was a — a genuine equipment failure this time, and the bomb fell on an island."

January was hopping up and down, mouth hanging open. "So we n-never — "

"We never dropped an atom bomb on a Japanese city. That's right." Getty grinned. "And get this — I heard this from my superior — they sent a message to the Japanese government telling them that the two explosions were warnings, and that if they didn't surrender by September first we would drop bombs on Kyoto and Tokyo, and then wherever else we had to. Word is that the Emperor went to Hiroshima to survey the damage, and when he saw it he ordered the Cabinet to surrender. So. . . ."

"So it worked," January said. He hopped around, "It worked, it worked!"

"Yes."

"Just like I said it would!" he cried, and hopping before the priest he laughed.

Getty was jumping around a little too, and the sight of the priest bouncing was too much for January. He sat on his cot and laughed till the tears ran down his cheeks.

"So — " he sobered quickly. "So Truman's going to shoot me anyway, eh?"

"Yes," the priest said unhappily. "I guess that's right."

This time January's laugh was bitter. "He's a bastard, all right. And proud of being a bastard, which makes it worse." He shook his head. "If Roosevelt had lived. . . ."

"It would have been different," Getty finished. "Yes. Maybe so. But he didn't." He sat beside January. "Cigarette?" He held out a pack, and January noticed the white wartime wrapper. He frowned.

"You haven't got a Camel?"

"Oh. Sorry."

"Oh well. That's all right." January took one of the Lucky Strikes, lit up. "That's awfully good news." He breathed out. "I never believed Truman would pardon me anyway, so mostly you've brought good news. Ha. They *missed*. You have no idea how much better that makes me feel."

"I think I do."

January smoked the cigarette.

". . . So I'm a good American after all. I *am* a good American," he insisted, "no matter what Truman says."

"Yes," Getty replied, and coughed. "You're better than Truman any day."

"Better watch what you say, Father." He looked into the eyes behind the glasses, and the expression he saw there gave him pause. Since the drop every look directed at him had been filled with contempt. He'd seen it so often during the court-martial that he'd learned to stop looking; and now he had to teach himself to see again. The priest looked at him as if he were . . . as if he were some kind of hero. That wasn't exactly right. But seeing it. . . .

January would not live to see the years that followed, so he would never know what came of his action. He had given up casting his mind forward and imagining possibilities, because there was no point to it. His planning was ended. In any case he would not have been able to imagine the course of the post-war years. That the world would quickly become an armed camp pitched on the edge of atomic war, he might have predicted. But he never would have guessed that so many people would join a January Society. He would never know of the effect the Society had on Dewey during the Korean crisis, never know of the Society's successful campaign for the test ban treaty, and never learn that thanks in part to the Society and its allies, a treaty would be signed by the great powers that would reduce the number of atomic bombs year by year, until there were none left.

Frank January would never know any of that. But in that moment on his cot looking into the eyes of young Patrick Getty, he guessed an inkling of it — he felt, just for an instant, the impact on history.

And with that he relaxed. In his last week everyone who met him carried away the same impression, that of a calm, quiet man, angry at Truman and others, but in a withdrawn, matter-of-fact way. Patrick Getty, a strong force in the January Society ever after, said January was talkative for some time after he learned of the missed attack on Kokura. Then he became quieter and quieter, as the day approached. On the morning that they woke him at dawn to march him out to a hastily constructed execution shed, his MPs shook his hand. The priest was with him as he smoked a final cigarette, and they prepared to put the hood over his head. January looked at him calmly. "They load one of the guns with a blank cartridge, right?"

"Yes," Getty said.

"So each man in the squad can imagine he may not have shot me?"

"Yes. That's right."

A tight, unhumorous smile was January's last expression. He threw down the cigarette, ground it out, poked the priest in the arm. "But I *know*." Then the mask slipped back into place for good, making the hood redundant, and with a firm step January went to the wall. One might have said he was at peace.

Connie Willis

At the Rialto

(1989)

Connie Willis (b. 1945) began publishing in 1971 but was not widely known until a period of heightened productivity in the 1980s led to a series of acclaimed time-travel stories, culminating in the 1992 Nebula award–winning novel *Doomsday Book*. She has won more Hugos and Nebulas than any other writer to date and is unusual in being equally adept in comic and sober modes and in blending genres in innovative ways. In "At the Rialto," she combines elements of academic farce, romance, and philosophical tale. Set at a chaotic physics conference convened at a Hollywood hotel, the story takes readers on a comic romp through quantum physics.

The protagonist, Dr. Ruth Baringer, arrives at the conference with an earnest desire to improve her knowledge of some of the thornier theoretical questions of her field, but, as the keynote speaker quoted at the beginning of the story suggests, "seriousness of mind" may not be the best way to apprehend the strangeness that is quantum theory. As the same speaker suggests elsewhere in the story, we need a new paradigm or metaphor to help us conceptualize it, which is what Willis brilliantly provides. The key concept in this story is *entanglement*, a recent finding that under certain circumstances, subatomic particles continue to influence each other's behaviors even when separated in space, suggesting an instantaneous mode of communication that would violate the theory of special relativity, which holds that nothing can exceed the speed of light.

> *"Seriousness of mind was a prerequisite for understanding Newtonian physics. I am not convinced it is not a handicap in understanding quantum theory."*
> — Excerpt from Dr. Gedanken's keynote address to the 1989 International Congress of Quantum Physicists Annual Meeting, Hollywood, California

I got to Hollywood around one-thirty and started trying to check into the Rialto.

"Sorry, we don't have any rooms," the girl behind the desk said. "We're all booked up with some science thing."

"I'm with the science thing," I said. "Dr. Ruth Baringer. I reserved a double."

"There are a bunch of Republicans here, too, and a tour group from Finland. They told me when I started work here that they got all these movie people, but the only one so far was that guy who played the friend of that other guy in that one movie. You're not a movie person, are you?"

"No," I said. "I'm with the science thing. Dr. Ruth Baringer."

"My name's Tiffany," she said. "I'm not actually a hotel clerk at all. I'm just working here to pay for my transcendental posture lessons. I'm really a model/actress."

"I'm a quantum physicist," I said, trying to get things back on track. "The name is Ruth Baringer."

She messed with the computer for a minute. "I don't show a reservation for you."

"Maybe it's in Dr. Mendoza's name. I'm sharing a room with her."

She messed with the computer some more. "I don't show a reservation for her either. Are you sure you don't want the Disneyland Hotel? A lot of people get the two confused."

"I want the Rialto," I said, rummaging through my bag for my notebook. "I have a confirmation number. W37420."

She typed it in. "Are you Dr. Gedanken?" she asked.

"Excuse me," an elderly man said.

"I'll be right with you," Tiffany told him. "How long do you plan to stay with us, Dr. Gedanken?" she asked me.

"*Excuse* me," the man said, sounding desperate. He had bushy white hair and a dazed expression, as if he had just been through a horrific experience or had been trying to check into the Rialto.

He wasn't wearing any socks. I wondered if *he* was Dr. Gedanken. Dr. Gedanken was the main reason I'd decided to come to the meeting. I had missed his lecture on wave/particle duality last year, but I had read the text of it in the *ICQP Journal*, and it had actually seemed to make sense, which is more than you can say for most of quantum theory. He was giving the keynote address this year, and I was determined to hear it.

It wasn't Dr. Gedanken. "My name is Dr. Whedbee," the elderly man said. "You gave me the wrong room."

"All our rooms are pretty much the same," Tiffany said. "Except for how many beds they have in them and stuff."

"My room has a *person* in it!" he said. "Dr. Sleeth. From the University of Texas at Austin. She was changing her clothes." His hair seemed to get wilder as he spoke. "She thought I was a serial killer."

"And your name is Dr. Whedbee?" Tiffany asked, fooling with the computer again. "I don't show a reservation for you."

Dr. Whedbee began to cry. Tiffany got out a paper towel, wiped off the counter, and turned back to me. "May I help you?" she said.

> Thursday, 7:30–9 p.m. *Opening Ceremonies.* Dr. Halvard Onofrio,
> University of Maryland at College Park, will speak on the topic,
> "Doubts Surrounding the Heisenberg Uncertainty Principle."
> Ballroom.

I finally got my room at five after Tiffany went off duty. Till then I sat around the lobby with Dr. Whedbee, listening to Abey Fields complain about Hollywood.

"What's wrong with Racine?" he said. "Why do we always have to go to these exotic places, like Hollywood? And St. Louis last year wasn't much better. The Institut Henri Poincaré people kept going off to see the arch and Busch Stadium."

"Speaking of St. Louis," Dr. Takumi said, "have you seen David yet?"

"No," I said.

"Oh, really?" she said. "Last year at the annual meeting you two were practically inseparable. Moonlight riverboat rides and all."

"What's on the programming tonight?" I said to Abey.

"David was just here," Dr. Takumi said. "He said to tell you he was going out to look at the stars in the sidewalk."

"That's exactly what I'm talking about," Abey said. "Riverboat rides and movie stars. What do those things have to do with quantum theory? Racine would have been an appropriate setting for a group of physicists. Not like this . . . this . . . do you realize we're practically across the street from Grauman's Chinese Theatre? And Hollywood Boulevard's where all those gangs hang out. If they catch you wearing red or blue, they'll — "

He stopped. "Is that Dr. Gedanken?" he asked, staring at the front desk.

I turned and looked. A short roundish man with a mustache was trying to check in. "No," I said. "That's Dr. Onofrio."

"Oh, yes," Abey said, consulting his program book. "He's speaking tonight at the opening ceremonies. On the Heisenberg uncertainty principle. Are you going?"

"I'm not sure," I said, which was supposed to be a joke, but Abey didn't laugh.

"I must meet Dr. Gedanken. He's just gotten funding for a new project."

I wondered what Dr. Gedanken's new project was — I would have loved to work with him.

"I'm hoping he'll come to my workshop on the wonderful world of quantum physics," Abey said, still watching the desk. Amazingly enough, Dr. Onofrio seemed to have gotten a key and was heading for the elevators. "I think his project has something to do with understanding quantum theory."

Well, that let me out. I didn't understand quantum theory at all. I sometimes had a sneaking suspicion nobody else did either, including Abey Fields, and that they just weren't willing to admit it.

I mean, an electron is a particle except it acts like a wave. In fact, a neutron acts like two waves and interferes with itself (or each other), and you can't really measure any of this stuff properly because of the Heisenberg uncertainty principle, and that isn't the worst of it. When you set up a Josephson junction to figure out what rules the electrons obey, they sneak past the barrier to the other side, and they don't seem to care much about the limits of the speed of light either, and Schrödinger's cat is neither alive nor dead till you open the box, and it all makes about as much sense as Tiffany's calling me Dr. Gedanken.

Which reminded me, I had promised to call Darlene and give her our room number. I didn't have a room number, but if I waited much longer, she'd have left. She was flying to Denver to speak at C.U. and then coming on to Hollywood sometime tomorrow morning. I interrupted Abey in the middle of his telling me how beautiful Racine was in the winter and went to call her.

"I don't have a room yet," I said when she answered. "Should I leave a message on your answering machine or do you want to give me your number in Denver?"

"Never mind all that," Darlene said. "Have you seen David yet?"

> *"To illustrate the problems of the concept of wave function,*
> *Dr. Schrödinger imagines a cat being put into a box with a*
> *piece of uranium, a bottle of poison gas, and a Geiger*
> *counter. If a uranium nucleus disintegrates while the cat is*
> *in the box, it will release radiation which will set off the*
> *Geiger counter and break the bottle of poison gas. Since it*
> *is impossible in quantum theory to predict whether a ura-*
> *nium nucleus will disintegrate while the cat is in the box,*
> *and only possible to calculate uranium's probable half-life,*
> *the cat is neither alive nor dead until we open the box."*
> — From "The Wonderful World of Quantum Physics," a seminar
> presented at the ICQP Annual Meeting by A. Fields, Ph.D.,
> University of Nebraska at Wahoo

I completely forgot to warn Darlene about Tiffany, the model-slash-actress.

"What do you mean you're trying to avoid David?" she had asked me at least three times. "Why would you do a stupid thing like that?"

Because in St. Louis I ended up on a riverboat in the moonlight and didn't make it back until the conference was over.

"Because I want to attend the programming," I said the third time around, "not a wax museum. I am a middle-aged woman."

"And David is a middle-aged man who, I might add, is absolutely charming. In fact, he may be the last charming man left in the universe."

→ "Charm is for quarks," I said and hung up, feeling smug until I remembered I hadn't told her about Tiffany. I went back to the front desk, thinking maybe Dr. Onofrio's success signaled a change. Tiffany asked, "May I help you?" and left me standing there.

After a while I gave up and went back to the red-and-gold sofas.

"David was here again," Dr. Takumi said. "He said to tell you he was going to the wax museum."

"There *are* no wax museums in Racine," Abey said.

"What's the programming for tonight?" I said, taking Abey's program away from him.

"There's a mixer at six-thirty and the opening ceremonies in the ballroom and then some seminars." I read the descriptions of the seminars. There was one on the Josephson junction. Electrons were able to somehow tunnel through an insulated barrier even though they didn't have the required energy. Maybe I could somehow get a room without checking in.

"If we were in Racine," Abey said, looking at his watch, "we'd already be checked in and on our way to dinner."

Dr. Onofrio emerged from the elevator, still carrying his bags. He came over and sank down on the sofa next to Abey.

"Did they give you a room with a semi-naked woman in it?" Dr. Whedbee asked.

"I don't know," Dr. Onofrio said. "I couldn't find it." He looked sadly at the key. "They gave me 1282, but the room numbers only go up to seventy-five."

"I think I'll attend the seminar on chaos," I said.

> "The most serious difficulty quantum theory faces today
> is not the inherent limitation of measurement capability
> or the EPR paradox. It is the lack of a paradigm.
> Quantum theory has no working model, no metaphor
> that properly defines it."
> — Excerpt from Dr. Gedanken's keynote address

I got to my room at six, after a brief skirmish with the bellboy-slash-actor who couldn't remember where he'd stored my suitcase, and unpacked. My clothes, which had been permanent press all the way from MIT, underwent a complete wave function collapse the moment I opened my suitcase, and came out looking like Schrödinger's almost-dead cat.

By the time I had called housekeeping for an iron, taken a bath, given up on the iron, and steamed a dress in the shower, I had missed the "Mixer with Munchies" and was half an hour late for Dr. Onofrio's opening remarks.

I opened the door to the ballroom as quietly as I could and slid inside. I had hoped they would be late getting started, but a man I didn't recognize was already introducing the speaker. " — and an inspiration to all of us in the field."

I dived for the nearest chair and sat down.

"Hi," David said. "I've been looking all over for you. Where were you?"

"Not at the wax museum," I whispered.

"You should have been," he whispered back. "It was great. They had John Wayne, Elvis, and Tiffany the model-slash-actress with the brain of a pea-slash-amoeba."

"Shh," I said.

" — the person we've all been waiting to hear, Dr. Ringgit Dinari."

"What happened to Dr. Onofrio?" I asked.

"Shhh," David said.

Dr. Dinari looked a lot like Dr. Onofrio. She was short, roundish, and mustached, and was wearing a rainbow-striped caftan. "I will be your guide this evening into a strange new world," she said, "a world where all that you thought you knew, all common sense, all accepted wisdom, must be discarded. A world where all the rules have changed and it sometimes seems there are no rules at all."

She sounded just like Dr. Onofrio, too. He had given this same speech two years ago in Cincinnati. I wondered if he had undergone some strange transformation during his search for Room 1282 and was now a woman.

"Before I go any farther," Dr. Dinari said, "how many of you have already channeled?"

> *"Newtonian physics had as its model the machine. The metaphor of the machine, with its interrelated parts, its gears and wheels, its causes and effects, was what made it possible to think about Newtonian physics."*
> — Excerpt from Dr. Gedanken's keynote address

"You *knew* we were in the wrong place," I hissed at David when we got out to the lobby.

When we stood up to leave, Dr. Dinari had extended her pudgy hand in its rainbow-striped sleeve and called out in a voice a lot like Charlton Heston's, "O Unbelievers! Leave not, for here only is reality!"

"Actually, channeling would explain a lot," David said, grinning.

"If the opening remarks aren't in the ballroom, where are they?"

"Beats me," he said. "Want to go see the Capitol Records Building? It's shaped like a stack of records."

"I want to go to the opening remarks."

"The beacon on top blinks out Hollywood in Morse code."

I went over to the front desk.

"Can I help you?" the clerk behind the desk said. "My name is Natalie, and I'm an — "

"Where is the ICQP meeting this evening?" I said.

"They're in the ballroom."

"I'll bet you didn't have any dinner," David said. "I'll buy you an ice-cream cone. There's this great place that has the ice-cream cone Ryan O'Neal bought for Tatum in *Paper Moon*."

"A channeler's in the ballroom," I told Natalie. "I'm looking for the ICQP."

She fiddled with the computer. "I'm sorry. I don't show a reservation for them."

"How about Grauman's Chinese?" David said. "You want reality? You want Charlton Heston? You want to see quantum theory in action?" He grabbed my hands. "Come with me," he said seriously.

In St. Louis I had suffered a wave function collapse a lot like what had happened to my clothes when I opened the suitcase. I had ended up on a riverboat halfway to New Orleans that time. It happened again, and the next thing I knew I was walking around the courtyard of Grauman's Chinese Theatre, eating an ice-cream cone and trying to fit my feet in Myrna Loy's footprints.

She must have been a midget or had her feet bound as a child. So, apparently, had Debbie Reynolds, Dorothy Lamour, and Wallace Beery. The only footprints I came close to fitting were Donald Duck's.

"I see this as a map of the microcosm," David said, sweeping his hand over the slightly irregular pavement of printed and signed cement squares. "See, there are all these tracks. We know something's been here, and the prints are pretty much the same, only every once in a while you've got this," he knelt down and pointed at the print of John Wayne's clenched fist, "and over here," he walked toward the box office and pointed to the print of Betty Grable's leg, "and we can figure out the signatures, but what is this reference to 'Sid' on all these squares? And what does this mean?"

He pointed at Red Skelton's square. It said, "Thanks Sid We Dood It."

"You keep thinking you've found a pattern," David said, crossing over to the other side, "but Van Johnson's square is kind of sandwiched in here at an angle between Esther Williams and Cantinflas, and who the hell is May Robson? And why are all these squares over here empty?"

He had managed to maneuver me over behind the display of Academy Award winners. It was an accordionlike wrought-iron screen. I was in the fold between 1944 and 1945.

"And as if that isn't enough, you suddenly realize you're standing in the courtyard. You're not even in the theater."

"And that's what you think is happening in quantum theory?" I said weakly. I was backed up into Bing Crosby, who had won for Best Actor in *Going My Way*. "You think we're not in the theater yet?"

"I think we know as much about quantum theory as we can figure out about May Robson from her footprints," he said, putting his hand up to Ingrid Bergman's cheek (Best Actress, *Gaslight*) and blocking my escape. "I don't think we understand anything *about* quantum theory, not tunneling, not complementarity." He leaned toward me. "Not passion."

The best movie of 1945 was *Lost Weekend*. "Dr. Gedanken understands it," I said, disentangling myself from the Academy Award winners and David. "Did you know he's putting together a new research team for a big project on understanding quantum theory?"

"Yes," David said. "Want to see a movie?"

"There's a seminar on chaos at nine," I said, stepping over the Marx Brothers. "I have to get back."

"If it's chaos you want, you should stay right here," he said, stopping to look at Irene Dunne's handprints. "We could see the movie and then go have dinner. There's this place near Hollywood and Vine that has the mashed potatoes Richard Dreyfus made into Devil's Tower in *Close Encounters*."

"I want to meet Dr. Gedanken," I said, making it safely to the sidewalk. I looked back at David. He had gone back to the other side of the courtyard and was looking at Roy Rogers's signature.

"Are you kidding? He doesn't understand it any better than we do."

"Well, at least he's trying."

"So am I. The problem is, how can one neutron interfere with itself, and why are there only two of Trigger's hoofprints here?"

"It's eight fifty-five," I said. "I am going to the chaos seminar."

"If you can find it," he said, getting down on one knee to look at the signature.

"I'll find it," I said grimly.

He stood up and grinned at me, his hands in his pockets, "It's a great movie," he said.

It was happening again. I turned and practically ran across the street.

"*Benji Nine* is showing," he shouted after me. "He accidentally exchanges bodies with a Siamese cat."

> Thursday, 9–10 p.m. "The Science of Chaos." I. Durcheinander,
> University of Leipzig. A seminar on the structure of chaos.
> Principles of chaos will be discussed, including the Butterfly
> Effect, fractals, and insolid billowing. Clara Bow Room.

I couldn't find the chaos seminar. The Clara Bow Room, where it was supposed to be, was empty. A meeting of vegetarians was next door in the Fatty Arbuckle Room, and all the other conference rooms were locked. The channeler was still in the ballroom. "Come!" she commanded when I opened the door. "Understanding awaits!" I went upstairs to bed.

I had forgotten to call Darlene. She would have left for Denver already, but I called her answering machine and told it the room number in case she picked up her messages. In the morning I would have to tell the front desk to give her a key. I went to bed.

I didn't sleep well. The air conditioner went off during the night, which meant I didn't have to steam my suit when I got up the next morning. I got dressed and went downstairs. The programming started at nine o'clock with Abey Fields's Wonderful World workshop in the Mary Pickford Room, a breakfast buffet in the ballroom, and a slide presentation on "Delayed Choice Experiments" in Cecil B. DeMille A on the mezzanine level.

The breakfast buffet sounded wonderful, even though it always turns out to be urn coffee and donuts. I hadn't had anything but an ice-cream cone since noon the day before, but if David were around, he would be somewhere close to the food, and I wanted to steer clear of him. Last night it had been Grauman's Chinese. Today I was likely to end up at Knott's Berry Farm. I wasn't going to let that happen, even if he was charming.

It was pitch-dark inside Cecil B. DeMille A. Even the slide on the screen up front appeared to be black. "As you can see," Dr. Lvov said, "the laser pulse is already in motion before the experimenter sets up the wave or particle detector." He clicked to the next slide, which was dark gray. "We used a Mach-Zender interferometer with two mirrors and a particle detector. For the first series of tries we allowed the experimenter to decide which apparatus he would use by whatever method he wished. For the second series, we used that most primitive of randomizers — "

He clicked again, to a white slide with black polka dots that gave off enough light for me to be able to spot an empty chair on the aisle ten rows up. I hurried to get to it before the slide changed, and sat down.

" — a pair of dice. Alley's experiments had shown us that when the particle detector was in place, the light was detected as a particle, and when the wave detector was in place, the light showed wavelike behavior, no matter when the choice of apparatus was made."

"Hi," David said. "You've missed five black slides, two gray ones, and a white with black polka dots."

"Shh," I said.

"In our two series, we hoped to ascertain whether the consciousness of the decision affected the outcome." Dr. Lvov clicked to another black slide. "As you can see, the graph shows no effective difference between the tries in which the experimenter chose the detection apparatus and those in which the apparatus was randomly chosen."

"You want to go get some breakfast?" David whispered.

"I already ate," I whispered back, and waited for my stomach to growl and give me away. It did.

"There's a great place down near Hollywood and Vine that has the waffles Katharine Hepburn made for Spencer Tracy in *Woman of the Year*."

"Shh," I said.

"And after breakfast, we could go to Frederick's of Hollywood and see the bra museum."

"Will you please be quiet? I can't hear."

"Or see," he said, but he subsided more or less for the remaining ninety-two black, gray, and polka-dotted slides.

Dr. Lvov turned on the lights and blinked smilingly at the audience. "Consciousness had no discernible effect on the results of the experiment. As one of my lab assistants put it, 'The little devil knows what you're going to do before you know it yourself.' "

This was apparently supposed to be a joke, but I didn't think it was very funny. I opened my program and tried to find something to go to that David wouldn't be caught dead at.

"Are you two going to breakfast?" Dr. Thibodeaux asked.

"Yes," David said.

"No," I said.

"Dr. Hotard and I wished to eat somewhere that is *vraiment* Hollywood."

"David knows just the place," I said. "He's been telling me about this great place where they have the grapefruit James Cagney shoved in Mae Clark's face in *Public Enemy*."

Dr. Hotard hurried up, carrying a camera and four guidebooks. "And then perhaps you would show us Grauman's Chinese Theatre," he asked David.

"Of course he will," I said, "I'm sorry I can't go with you, but I promised Dr. Verikovsky I'd be at his lecture on Boolean logic. And after Grauman's Chinese, David can take you to the bra museum at Frederick's of Hollywood."

"And the Brown Derby?" Thibodeaux asked. "I have heard it is shaped like a *chapeau*."

They dragged him off. I watched till they were safely out of the lobby and then ducked upstairs and into Dr. Whedbee's lecture on information theory. Dr. Whedbee wasn't there.

"He went to find an overhead projector," Dr. Takumi said. She had half a donut on a paper plate in one hand and a Styrofoam cup in the other.

"Did you get that at the breakfast buffet?" I asked.

"Yes. It was the last one. And they ran out of coffee right after I got there. You weren't in Abey Fields's thing, were you?" She set the coffee cup down and took a bite of the donut.

"No," I said, wondering if I should try to take her by surprise or just wrestle the donut away from her.

"You didn't miss anything. He raved the whole time about how we should have had the meeting in Racine." She popped the last piece of donut in her mouth. "Have you seen David yet?"

Friday, 9–10 p.m. "The Eureka Experiment: A Slide Presentation." J. Lvov, Eureka College. Descriptions, results, and conclusions of Lvov's delayed conscious/randomed choice experiments. Cecil B. DeMille A.

Dr. Whedbee eventually came in carrying an overhead projector, the cord trailing behind him. He plugged it in. The light didn't go on.

"Here," Dr. Takumi said, handing me her plate and cup. "I have one of these at Caltech. It needs its fractal basin boundaries adjusted." She whacked the side of the projector.

There weren't even any crumbs left of the donut. There was about a millimeter of coffee in the bottom of the cup. I was about to stoop to new depths when she hit the projector again. The light came on. "I learned that in the chaos seminar last night," she said, grabbing the cup away from me and draining it. "You should have been there. The Clara Bow Room was packed."

"I believe I'm ready to begin," Dr. Whedbee said. Dr. Takumi and I sat down. "Information is the transmission of meaning," Dr. Whedbee said. He wrote "meaning" or possibly "information" on the screen with a green Magic Marker. "When information is randomized, meaning cannot be transmitted, and we have a state of entropy." He wrote it under "meaning" with a red Magic Marker. His handwriting appeared to be completely illegible.

"States of entropy vary from low entropy, such as the mild static on your car radio, to high entropy, a state of complete disorder, of randomness and confusion, in which no information at all is being communicated."

Oh, my God, I thought. I forgot to tell the hotel about Darlene. The next time Dr. Whedbee bent over to inscribe hieroglyphics on the screen, I sneaked out and went down to the desk, hoping Tiffany hadn't come on duty yet. She had.

"May I help you?" she asked.

"I'm in Room 663," I said. "I'm sharing a room with Dr. Darlene Mendoza. She's coming in this morning, and she'll be needing a key."

"For what?" Tiffany said.

"To get into the room. I may be in one of the lectures when she gets 155 here."

"Why doesn't she have a key?"

"Because she isn't here yet."

"I thought you said she was sharing a room with you."

"She *will* be sharing a room with me. Room 663. Her name is Darlene Mendoza."

"And your name?" she asked, hands poised over the computer.

"Ruth Baringer."

"We don't show a reservation for you."

> *"We have made impressive advances in quantum physics in the ninety years since Planck's constant, but they have by and large been advances in technology, not theory. We can only make advances in theory when we have a model we can visualize."*
> — Excerpt from Dr. Gedanken's keynote address

I high-entropied with Tiffany for a while on the subjects of my not having a reservation and the air conditioning and then switched back suddenly to the problem of Darlene's key, in the hope of catching her off guard. It worked about as well as Alley's delayed choice experiments.

In the middle of my attempting to explain that Darlene was not the air-conditioning repairman, Abey Fields came up.

"Have you seen Dr. Gedanken?"

I shook my head.

"I was sure he'd come to my Wonderful World workshop, but he didn't, and the hotel says they can't find his reservation," he said, scanning the lobby. "I found out what his new project is, incidentally, and I'd be perfect for it. He's going to find a paradigm for quantum theory. Is that him?" he said, pointing at an elderly man getting in the elevator.

"I think that's Dr. Whedbee," I said, but he had already sprinted across the lobby to the elevator.

He nearly made it. The elevator slid to a close just as he got there. He pushed the elevator button several times to make the door open again, and when that didn't work, tried to readjust its fractal basin boundaries. I turned back to the desk.

"May I help you?" Tiffany said.

"You may," I said. "My roommate, Darlene Mendoza, will be arriving sometime this morning. She's a producer. She's here to cast the female lead in a new movie starring Robert Redford and Harrison Ford. When she gets here, give her her key. And fix the air-conditioning."

"Yes, ma'am," she said.

"The Josephson junction is designed so that electrons must obtain additional energy to surmount the energy barrier. It has been found, however, that some electrons simply tunnel, as Heinz Pagels put it, 'right through the wall.' "
— From " The Wonderful World of Quantum Physics,"
A. Fields, UNW

Abey had stopped banging on the elevator button and was trying to pry the elevator doors apart. I went out the side door and up to Hollywood Boulevard. David's restaurant was near Hollywood and Vine. I turned the other direction, toward Grauman's Chinese, and ducked into the first restaurant I saw.

"I'm Stephanie," the waitress said. "How many are there in your party?"

There was no one remotely in my vicinity. "Are you an actress-slash-model?" I asked her.

"Yes," she said. "I'm working here part-time to pay for my holistic hair-styling lessons."

"There's one of me," I said, holding up my forefinger to make it perfectly clear. "I want a table away from the window."

She led me to a table in front of the window, handed me a menu the size of the macrocosm, and put another one down across from me. "Our breakfast specials today are papaya stuffed with salmon-berries and nasturtium/radicchio salad with a balsamic vinaigrette. I'll take your order when your other party arrives."

I stood the extra menu up so it hid me from the window, opened the other one, and read the breakfast entrees. They all seemed to have cilantro or lemongrass in their names. I wondered if radicchio could possibly be Californian for donut.

"Hi," David said, grabbing the standing-up menu and sitting down. "The sea urchin pâté looks good."

I was actually glad to see him. "How did you get here?" I asked.

"Tunneling," he said. "What exactly is extra-virgin olive oil?"

"I wanted a donut," I said pitifully.

He took my menu away from me, laid it on the table, and stood up. "There's a great place next door that's got the donut Clark Gable taught Claudette Colbert how to dunk in *It Happened One Night*."

The great place was probably out in Long Beach someplace, but I was too weak with hunger to resist him. I stood up. Stephanie hurried over.

"Will there be anything else?" she asked.

"We're leaving," David said.

"Okay, then," she said, tearing a check off her pad and slapping it down on the table. "I hope you enjoyed your breakfast."

"Finding such a paradigm is difficult, if not impossible. Due to Planck's constant the world we see is largely

*dominated by Newtonian mechanics. Particles are par-
ticles, waves are waves, and objects do not suddenly
vanish through walls and reappear on the other side.
It is only on the subatomic level that quantum
effects dominate."*
— Excerpt from Dr. Gedanken's keynote address

The restaurant was next door to Grauman's Chinese, which made me a little nervous, but it had eggs and bacon and toast and orange juice and coffee. And donuts.

"I thought you were having breakfast with Dr. Thibodeaux and Dr.
Hotard," I said, dunking one in my coffee. "What happened to them?"

"They went to Forest Lawn. Dr. Hotard wanted to see the church
where Ronald Reagan got married."

"He got married at Forest Lawn?"

He took a bite of my donut. "In the Wee Kirk of the Heather. Did you
know Forest Lawn's got the World's Largest Oil Painting Incorporating a
Religious Theme?"

"So why didn't you go with them?"

"And miss the movie?" He grabbed both my hands across the table.
"There's a matinee at two o'clock. Come with me."

I could feel things starting to collapse. "I have to get back," I said, trying
to disentangle my hands. "There's a panel on the EPR paradox at two o'clock."

"There's another showing at five. And one at eight."

"Dr. Gedanken's giving the keynote address at eight."

"You know what the problem is?" he said, still holding on to my hands.
"The problem is, it isn't really Grauman's Chinese Theatre, it's Mann's, so
Sid isn't even around to ask. Like, why do some pairs like Joanne Woodward
and Paul Newman share the same square and other pairs don't? Like Ginger
Rogers and Fred Astaire?"

"You know what the problem is?" I said, wrenching my hands free.
"The problem is you don't take anything seriously. This is a conference, but
you don't care anything about the programming or hearing Dr. Gedanken
speak or trying to understand quantum theory!" I fumbled in my purse for
some money for the check.

"I thought that was what we were talking about," David said, sounding
surprised. "The problem is, where do those lion statues that guard the door
fit in? And what about all those empty spaces?"

Friday, 2–3 p.m. *Panel Discussion on the EPR Paradox.* I. Takumi, moderator, R. Iverson, L. S. Ping. A discussion of the latest research in
singlet-state correlations including nonlocal influences, the Calcutta
proposal, and passion. Keystone Kops Room.

I went up to my room as soon as I got back to the Rialto to see if Darlene
was there yet. She wasn't, and when I tried to call the desk, the phone wouldn't
work. I went back down to the registration desk. There was no one there. I
waited fifteen minutes and then went into the panel on the EPR paradox.

"The Einstein-Podolsky-Rosen paradox cannot be reconciled with quantum theory," Dr. Takumi was saying. "I don't care what the experiments seem to indicate. Two electrons at opposite ends of the universe can't affect each other simultaneously without destroying the entire theory of the space-time continuum."

She was right. Even if it were possible to find a model of quantum theory, what about the EPR paradox? If an experimenter measured one of a pair of electrons that had originally collided, it changed the cross-correlation of the other instantaneously, even if the electrons were light-years apart. It was as if they were eternally linked by that one collision, sharing the same square forever, even if they were on opposite sides of the universe.

"If the electrons *communicated* instantaneously, I'd agree with you," Dr. Iverson said, "but they don't, they simply influence each other. Dr. Shimony defined this influence in his paper on passion, and my experiment clearly — "

I thought of David leaning over me between the best pictures of 1944 and 1945, saying, "I think we know as much about quantum theory as we do about May Robson from her footprints."

"You can't explain it away by inventing new terms," Dr. Takumi said.

"I completely disagree," Dr. Ping said. "Passion at a distance is not just an invented term. It's a demonstrated phenomenon."

It certainly is, I thought, thinking about David taking the macrocosmic menu out of the window and saying, "The sea urchin pâté looks good." It didn't matter where the electron went after the collision. Even if it went in the opposite direction from Hollywood and Vine, even if it stood a menu in the window to hide it, the other electron would still come and rescue it from the radicchio and buy it a donut.

"A demonstrated phenomenon!" Dr. Takumi said. "Ha!" She banged her moderator's gavel for emphasis.

"Are you saying passion doesn't exist?" Dr. Ping said, getting very red in the face.

"I'm saying one measly experiment is hardly a demonstrated phenomenon."

"One measly experiment! I spent five years on this project!" Dr. Iverson said, shaking his fist at her. "I'll show you passion at a distance!"

"Try it, and I'll adjust your fractal basin boundaries!" Dr. Takumi said, and hit him over the head with the gavel.

> "Yet finding a paradigm is not impossible. Newtonian
> physics is not a machine. It simply shares some of the
> attributes of a machine. We must find a model some-
> where in the visible world that shares the often bizarre
> attributes of quantum physics. Such a model, unlikely
> as it sounds, surely exists somewhere, and it is up
> to us to find it."
> — Excerpt from Dr. Gedanken's keynote address

I went up to my room before the police came. Darlene still wasn't there, and the phone and air-conditioning still weren't working. I was really beginning to get worried. I walked up to Grauman's Chinese to find David, but he wasn't there. Dr. Whedbee and Dr. Sleeth were behind the Academy Award Winners folding screen.

"You haven't seen David, have you?" I asked.

Dr. Whedbee removed his hand from Norma Shearer's cheek.

"He left," Dr. Sleeth said, disentangling herself from the Best Movie of 1929–30.

"He said he was going out to Forest Lawn," Dr. Whedbee said, trying to smooth down his bushy white hair.

"Have you seen Dr. Mendoza? She was supposed to get in this morning."

They hadn't seen her, and neither had Drs. Hotard and Thibodeaux, who stopped me in the lobby and showed me a postcard of Aimee Semple McPherson's tomb. Tiffany had gone off duty. Natalie couldn't find my reservation. I went back up to the room to wait, thinking Darlene might call.

The air-conditioning still wasn't fixed. I fanned myself with a Hollywood brochure and then opened it up and read it. There was a map of the courtyard of Grauman's Chinese on the back cover. Deborah Kerr and Yul Brynner didn't have a square together either, and Katharine Hepburn and Spencer Tracy weren't even on the map. She had made him waffles in *Woman of the Year,* and they hadn't even given them a square. I wondered if Tiffany the model-slash-actress had been in charge of assigning the cement. I could see her looking blankly at Spencer Tracy and saying, "I don't show a reservation for you."

What exactly was a model-slash-actress? Did it mean she was a model *or* an actress or a model *and* an actress? She certainly wasn't a hotel clerk. Maybe electrons were the Tiffanys of the microcosm, and that explained their wave-slash-particle duality. Maybe they weren't really electrons at all. Maybe they were just working part-time at being electrons to pay for their singlet-state lessons.

Darlene still hadn't called by seven o'clock. I stopped fanning myself and tried to open a window. It wouldn't budge. The problem was, nobody knew anything about quantum theory. All we had to go on were a few colliding electrons that nobody could see and that couldn't be measured properly because of the Heisenberg uncertainty principle. And there was chaos to consider, and entropy, and all those empty spaces. We didn't even know who May Robson was.

At seven-thirty the phone rang. It was Darlene.

"What happened?" I said. "Where are you?"

"At the Beverly Wilshire."

"In Beverly Hills?"

"Yes. It's a long story. When I got to the Rialto, the hotel clerk, I think her name was Tiffany, told me you weren't there. She said they were booked solid with some science thing and had had to send the overflow to other hotels. She said you were at the Beverly Wilshire in Room 1027. How's David?"

"Impossible," I said. "He's spent the whole conference looking at Deanna Durbin's footprints at Grauman's Chinese Theatre and trying to talk me into going to the movies."

"And are you going?"

"I can't. Dr. Gedanken's giving the keynote address in half an hour."

"He is?" Darlene said, sounding surprised. "Just a minute." There was a silence, and then she came back on and said, "I think you should go to the movies. David's one of the last two charming men in the universe."

"But he doesn't take quantum theory seriously. Dr. Gedanken is hiring a research team to design a paradigm, and David keeps talking about the beacon on top of the Capitol Records Building."

"You know, he may be on to something there. I mean, seriousness was all right for Newtonian physics, but maybe quantum theory needs a different approach. Sid says — "

"Sid?"

"This guy who's taking me to the movies tonight. It's a long story. Tiffany gave me the wrong room number, and I walked in on this guy in his underwear. He's a quantum physicist. He was supposed to be staying at the Rialto, but Tiffany couldn't find his reservation."

> "The major implication of wave/particle duality is that
> an electron has no precise location. It exists in a super-
> position of probable locations. Only when the
> experimenter observes the electron does it 'collapse'
> into a location."
> — "The Wonderful World of Quantum Physics,"
> A. Fields, UNW

Forest Lawn had closed at five o'clock. I looked it up in the Hollywood brochure after Darlene hung up. There was no telling where he might have gone: the Brown Derby or the La Brea Tar Pits or some great place near Hollywood and Vine that had the alfalfa sprouts John Hurt ate right before his chest exploded in *Alien*.

At least I knew where Dr. Gedanken was. I changed my clothes and got in the elevator, thinking about wave/particle duality and fractals and high entropy states and delayed choice experiments. The problem was, where could you find a paradigm that would make it possible to visualize quantum theory when you had to include Josephson junctions and passion and all those empty spaces? It wasn't possible. You had to have more to work with than a few footprints and the impression of Betty Grable's leg.

The elevator door opened, and Abey Fields pounced on me. "I've been looking all over for you," he said. "You haven't seen Dr. Gedanken, have you?"

"Isn't he in the ballroom?"

"No," he said. "He's already fifteen minutes late, and nobody's seen him. You have to sign this," he said, shoving a clipboard at me.

"What is it?"

"It's a petition," He grabbed it back from me. " 'We the undersigned demand that annual meetings of the International Congress of Quantum Physicists henceforth be held in appropriate locations.' Like Racine," he added, shoving the clipboard at me again. "*Unlike* Hollywood."

Hollywood.

"Are you aware it took the average ICQP delegate two hours and thirty-six minutes to check in? They even sent some of the delegates to a hotel in Glendale."

"And Beverly Hills," I said absently. Hollywood. Bra museums and the Marx Brothers and gangs that would kill you if you wore red or blue and Tiffany/Stephanie and the World's Largest Oil Painting Incorporating a Religious Theme.

"Beverly Hills," Abey muttered, pulling an automatic pencil out of his pocket protector and writing a note to himself. "I'm presenting the petition during Dr. Gedanken's speech. Well, go on, sign it," he said, handing me the pencil. "Unless you want the annual meeting to be here at the Rialto next year."

I handed the clipboard back to him. "I think from now on the annual meeting might be here every year," I said, and took off running for Grauman's Chinese.

> "When we have that paradigm, one that embraces both
> the logical and the nonsensical aspects of quantum
> theory, we will be able to look past the colliding elec-
> trons and the mathematics and see the microcosm in
> all its astonishing beauty."
> — Excerpt from Dr. Gedanken's keynote address

"I want a ticket to *Benji Nine*," I told the girl at the box office. Her name tag said, "Welcome to Hollywood. My name is Kimberly."

"Which theater?" she said.

"Grauman's Chinese," I said, thinking, This is no time for a high entropy state.

"Which theater?"

I looked up at the marquee. *Benji IX* was showing in all three theaters, the huge main theater and the two smaller ones on either side. "They're doing audience reaction surveys," Kimberly said, "Each theater has a different ending."

"Which one's in the main theater?"

"I don't know. I just work here part-time to pay for my organic breathing lessons."

"Do you have any dice?" I asked, and then realized I was going about this all wrong. This was quantum physics, not Newtonian. It didn't matter which theater I chose or which seat I sat down in. This was a delayed choice experiment and David was already in flight.

"The one with the happy ending," I said.

"Center theater," she said,

I walked past the stone lions and into the lobby. Rhonda Fleming and some Chinese wax figures were sitting inside a glass case next to the door to the rest rooms. There was a huge painted screen behind the concessions stand. I bought a box of Raisinets, a tub of popcorn, and a box of jujubes and went inside the theater.

It was bigger than I had imagined. Rows and rows of empty red chairs curved between the huge pillars and up to the red curtains where the screen must be. The walls were covered with intricate drawings. I stood there, holding my jujubes and Raisinets and popcorn, staring at the chandelier overhead. It was an elaborate gold sunburst surrounded by silver dragons. I had never imagined it was anything like this.

The lights went down, and the red curtains opened, revealing an inner curtain like a veil across the screen. I went down the dark aisle and sat down in one of the seats. "Hi," I said, and handed the Raisinets to David.

"Where have you been?" he said. "The movie's about to start."

"I know," I said. I leaned across him and handed Darlene her popcorn and Dr. Gedanken his jujubes. "I was working on the paradigm for quantum theory."

"And?" Dr. Gedanken said, opening his jujubes.

"And you're both wrong," I said. "It isn't Grauman's Chinese. It isn't movies either, Dr. Gedanken."

"Sid," Dr. Gedanken said. "If we're all going to be on the same research team, I think we should use first names."

"If it isn't Grauman's Chinese or the movies, what is it?" Darlene asked, eating popcorn.

"It's Hollywood."

"Hollywood," Dr. Gedanken said thoughtfully.

"Hollywood," I said. "Stars in the sidewalk and buildings that look like stacks of records and hats, and radicchio and audience surveys and bra museums. And the movies. And Grauman's Chinese."

"And the Rialto," David said.

"Especially the Rialto."

"And the ICQP," Dr. Gedanken said.

I thought about Dr. Lvov's black and gray slides and the disappearing chaos seminar and Dr. Whedbee writing "meaning" or possibly "information" on the overhead projector. "And the ICQP," I said.

"Did Dr. Takumi really hit Dr. Iverson over the head with a gavel?" Darlene asked.

"Shh," David said. "I think the movie's starting." He took hold of my hand. Darlene settled back with her popcorn, and Dr. Gedanken put his feet up on the chair in front of him. The inner curtain opened, and the screen lit up.

Ted Chiang

Story of Your Life

(1998)

Ted Chiang (b. 1967) made a stunning debut in 1990, winning a Nebula with his very first published story, "Tower of Babylon." In "Story of Your Life," another Nebula award winner, Chiang approaches the question of time from a philosophical perspective, exploring the nature of narrative consciousness and the simultaneous rather than sequential apprehension of the passage of time. This is a story about the nature of language and thought, causality and choice. The narrator is a linguist who finds her perception of time changing as it adapts to an alien cognitive system. The story resonates with perennial questions about foreknowledge, predestination, and free will. If you knew the future but could not change it, would you do anything differently? What meaning and value would you find in a life where your actions were predetermined, the outcome already known?

To recreate the protagonist's altered sense of time, Chiang creates a unique narrative voice that moves freely among past, present, and future tenses, a stylistic device that might have seemed mannered in the hands of a lesser writer, but here simply heightens the lyrical quality of this achingly sad story.

Although the plot is premised on an unusual event that is pure sf, in a sense this story is about the common tragedy of the human condition. We all already know the ending to the story of our lives. Out of the narrator's confrontation with, and acceptance of, the mortal and finite nature of all human life, Chiang conjures something redemptive. Love is still love, and life is no less precious for its fragility.

Your father is about to ask me the question. This is the most important moment in our lives, and I want to pay attention, note every detail. Your dad and I have just come back from an evening out, dinner and a show; it's after midnight. We came out onto the patio to look at the full moon; then I told your dad I wanted to dance, so he humors me and now we're slow-dancing, a pair of thirtysomethings swaying back and forth in the moonlight like kids. I don't feel the night chill at all. And then your dad says, "Do you want to make a baby?"

Right now your dad and I have been married for about two years, living on Ellis Avenue; when we move out you'll still be too young to remember the house, but we'll show you pictures of it, tell you stories about it. I'd love to tell you the story of this evening, the night you're conceived, but the right time to do that would be when you're ready to have children of your own, and we'll never get that chance.

Telling it to you any earlier wouldn't do any good; for most of your life you won't sit still to hear such a romantic — you'd say sappy — story. I remember the scenario of your origin you'll suggest when you're twelve.

"The only reason you had me was so you could get a maid you wouldn't have to pay," you'll say bitterly, dragging the vacuum cleaner out of the closet.

"That's right," I'll say. "Thirteen years ago I knew the carpets would need vacuuming around now, and having a baby seemed to be the cheapest and easiest way to get the job done. Now kindly get on with it."

"If you weren't my mother, this would be illegal," you'll say, seething as you unwind the power cord and plug it into the wall outlet.

That will be in the house on Belmont Street. I'll live to see strangers occupy both houses: the one you're conceived in and the one you grow up in. Your dad and I will sell the first a couple years after your arrival. I'll sell the second shortly after your departure. By then Nelson and I will have moved into our farmhouse, and your dad will be living with what's-her-name.

I know how this story ends; I think about it a lot. I also think a lot about how it began, just a few years ago, when ships appeared in orbit and artifacts appeared in meadows. The government said next to nothing about them, while the tabloids said every possible thing.

And then I got a phone call, a request for a meeting.

I spotted them waiting in the hallway, outside my office. They made an odd couple; one wore a military uniform and a crewcut, and carried an aluminum briefcase. He seemed to be assessing his surroundings with a critical eye. The other one was easily identifiable as an academic: full beard and mustache, wearing corduroy. He was browsing through the overlapping sheets stapled to a bulletin board nearby.

"Colonel Weber, I presume?" I shook hands with the soldier. "Louise Banks."

"Dr. Banks. Thank you for taking the time to speak with us," he said.

"Not at all; any excuse to avoid the faculty meeting."

Colonel Weber indicated his companion. "This is Dr. Gary Donnelly, the physicist I mentioned when we spoke on the phone."

"Call me Gary," he said as we shook hands. "I'm anxious to hear what you have to say."

We entered my office. I moved a couple of stacks of books off the second guest chair, and we all sat down. You said you wanted me to listen to a recording. I presume this has something to do with the aliens?"

"All I can offer is the recording," said Colonel Weber.

"Okay, let's hear it."

Colonel Weber took a tape machine out of his briefcase and pressed PLAY. The recording sounded vaguely like that of a wet dog shaking the water out of its fur.

"What do you make of that?" he asked.

I withheld my comparison to a wet dog. "What was the context in which this recording was made?"

"I'm not at liberty to say."

"It would help me interpret those sounds. Could you see the alien while it was speaking? Was it doing anything at the time?"

"The recording is all I can offer."

"You won't be giving anything away if you tell me that you've seen the aliens; the public's assumed you have."

Colonel Weber wasn't budging. "Do you have any opinion about its linguistic properties?" he asked.

"Well, it's clear that their vocal tract is substantially different from a human vocal tract. I assume that these aliens don't look like humans?"

The colonel was about to say something noncommittal when Gary Donnelly asked, "Can you make any guesses based on the tape?"

"Not really. It doesn't sound like they're using a larynx to make those sounds, but that doesn't tell me what they look like."

"Anything — is there anything else you can tell us?" asked Colonel Weber.

I could see he wasn't accustomed to consulting a civilian. "Only that establishing communications is going to be really difficult because of the difference in anatomy. They're almost certainly using sounds that the human vocal tract can't reproduce, and maybe sounds that the human ear can't distinguish."

"You mean infra- or ultrasonic frequencies?" asked Gary Donnelly.

"Not specifically. I just mean that the human auditory system isn't an absolute acoustic instrument; it's optimized to recognize the sounds that a human larynx makes. With an alien vocal system, all bets are off." I shrugged. "*Maybe* we'll be able to hear the difference between alien phonemes, given enough practice, but it's possible our ears simply can't recognize the distinctions they consider meaningful. In that case we'd need a sound spectrograph to know what an alien is saying."

Colonel Weber asked, "Suppose I gave you an hour's worth of recordings; how long would it take you to determine if we need this sound spectrograph or not?"

"I couldn't determine that with just a recording no matter how much time I had. I'd need to talk with the aliens directly."

The colonel shook his head. "Not possible."

I tried to break it to him gently. "That's your call, of course. But the only way to learn an unknown language is to interact with a native speaker, and by that I mean asking questions, holding a conversation, that sort of thing. Without that, it's simply not possible. So if you want to learn the aliens' language, someone with training in field linguistics — whether it's me or someone else — will have to talk with an alien. Recordings alone aren't sufficient."

Colonel Weber frowned. "You seem to be implying that no alien could have learned human languages by monitoring our broadcasts."

"I doubt it. They'd need instructional material specifically designed to teach human languages to nonhumans. Either that, or interaction with a human. If they had either of those, they could learn a lot from TV, but otherwise, they wouldn't have a starting point."

The colonel clearly found this interesting; evidently his philosophy was, the less the aliens knew, the better. Gary Donnelly read the colonel's expression too and rolled his eyes. I suppressed a smile.

Then Colonel Weber asked, "Suppose you were learning a new language by talking to its speakers; could you do it without teaching them English?"

"That would depend on how cooperative the native speakers were. They'd almost certainly pick up bits and pieces while I'm learning their language, but it wouldn't have to be much if they're willing to teach. On the other hand, if they'd rather learn English than teach us their language, that would make things far more difficult."

The colonel nodded. "I'll get back to you on this matter."

The request for that meeting was perhaps the second most momentous phone call in my life. The first, of course, will be the one from Mountain Rescue. At that point your dad and I will be speaking to each other maybe once a year, tops. After I get that phone call, though, the first thing I'll do will be to call your father.

He and I will drive out together to perform the identification, a long silent car ride. I remember the morgue, all tile and stainless steel, the hum of refrigeration and smell of antiseptic. An orderly will pull the sheet back to reveal your face. Your face will look wrong somehow, but I'll know it's you.

"Yes, that's her," I'll say. "She's mine."

You'll be twenty-five then.

The MP checked my badge, made a notation on his clipboard, and opened the gate; I drove the off-road vehicle into the encampment, a small village of tents pitched by the Army in a farmer's sun-scorched pasture. At the center of the encampment was one of the alien devices, nicknamed "looking glasses."

According to the briefings I'd attended, there were nine of these in the United States, one hundred and twelve in the world. The looking glasses acted as two-way communication devices, presumably with the ships in orbit. No one knew why the aliens wouldn't talk to us in person; fear of cooties, maybe. A team of scientists, including a physicist and a linguist, was assigned to each looking glass; Gary Donnelly and I were on this one.

Gary was waiting for me in the parking area. We navigated a circular maze of concrete barricades until we reached the large tent that covered the looking glass itself. In front of the tent was an equipment cart loaded with goodies borrowed from the school's phonology lab; I had sent it ahead for inspection by the Army.

Also outside the tent were three tripod-mounted video cameras whose lenses peered, through windows in the fabric wall, into the main room. Everything Gary and I did would be reviewed by countless others, including military intelligence. In addition we would each send daily reports, of which mine had to include estimates on how much English I thought the aliens could understand.

Gary held open the tent flap and gestured for me to enter. "Step right up," he said, circus-barker-style. "Marvel at creatures the likes of which have never been seen on God's green earth."

"And all for one slim dime," I murmured, walking through the door. At the moment the looking glass was inactive, resembling a semicircular mirror over ten feet high and twenty feet across. On the brown grass in front of the looking glass, an arc of white spray paint outlined the activation area. Currently the area contained only a table, two folding chairs, and a power strip with a cord leading to a generator outside. The buzz of fluorescent lamps, hung from poles along the edge of the room, commingled with the buzz of flies in the sweltering heat.

Gary and I looked at each other, and then began pushing the cart of equipment up to the table. As we crossed the paint line, the looking glass appeared to grow transparent; it was as if someone was slowly raising the illumination behind tinted glass. The illusion of depth was uncanny; I felt I could walk right into it. Once the looking glass was fully lit it resembled a life-sized diorama of a semicircular room. The room contained a few large objects that might have been furniture, but no aliens. There was a door in the curved rear wall.

We busied ourselves connecting everything together: microphone, sound spectrograph, portable computer, and speaker. As we worked, I frequently glanced at the looking glass, anticipating the aliens' arrival. Even so I jumped when one of them entered.

It looked like a barrel suspended at the intersection of seven limbs. It was radially symmetric, and any of its limbs could serve as an arm or a leg. The one in front of me was walking around on four legs, three nonadjacent arms curled up at its sides. Gary called them "heptapods."

I'd been shown videotapes, but I still gawked. Its limbs had no distinct joints; anatomists guessed they might be supported by vertebral columns. Whatever their underlying structure, the heptapod's limbs conspired to move it in a disconcertingly fluid manner. Its "torso" rode atop the rippling limbs as smoothly as a hovercraft.

Seven lidless eyes ringed the top of the heptapod's body. It walked back to the doorway from which it entered, made a brief sputtering sound, and returned to the center of the room followed by another heptapod; at no point did it ever turn around. Eerie, but logical; with eyes on all sides, any direction might as well be "forward."

Gary had been watching my reaction. "Ready?" he asked.

I took a deep breath. "Ready enough." I'd done plenty of fieldwork before, in the Amazon, but it had always been a bilingual procedure: either my informants knew some Portuguese, which I could use, or I'd previously gotten an introduction to their language from the local missionaries. This would be my first attempt at conducting a true monolingual discovery procedure. It was straightforward enough in theory, though.

I walked up to the looking glass and a heptapod on the other side did the same. The image was so real that my skin crawled. I could see the texture of its gray skin, like corduroy ridges arranged in whorls and loops. There was no smell at all from the looking glass, which somehow made the situation stranger.

I pointed to myself and said slowly, "Human." Then I pointed to Gary. "Human." Then I pointed at each heptapod and said, "What are you?"

No reaction. I tried again, and then again.

One of the heptapods pointed to itself with one limb, the four terminal digits pressed together. That was lucky. In some cultures a person pointed with his chin; if the heptapod hadn't used one of its limbs, I wouldn't have known what gesture to look for. I heard a brief fluttering sound, and saw a puckered orifice at the top of its body vibrate; it was talking. Then it pointed to its companion and fluttered again.

I went back to my computer; on its screen were two virtually identical spectrographs representing the fluttering sounds. I marked a sample for playback. I pointed to myself and said "Human" again, and did the same with Gary. Then I pointed to the heptapod, and played back the flutter on the speaker.

The heptapod fluttered some more. The second half of the spectrograph for this utterance looked like a repetition: call the previous utterances [flutter1], then this one was [flutter2flutter1].

I pointed at something that might have been a heptapod chair. "What is that?"

The heptapod paused, and then pointed at the "chair" and talked some more. The spectrograph for this differed distinctly from that of the earlier sounds: [flutter3]. Once again, I pointed to the "chair" while playing back [flutter3].

The heptapod replied; judging by the spectrograph, it looked like [flutter3flutter2]. Optimistic interpretation: the heptapod was confirming my utterances as correct, which implied compatibility between heptapod and human patterns of discourse. Pessimistic interpretation: it had a nagging cough.

At my computer I delimited certain sections of the spectrograph and typed in a tentative gloss for each: "heptapod" for [flutter1], "yes" for [flutter2], and "chair" for [flutter3]. Then I typed "Language: Heptapod A" as a heading for all the utterances.

Gary watched what I was typing. "What's the 'A' for?"

"It just distinguishes this language from any other ones the heptapods might use," I said. He nodded.

"Now let's try something, just for laughs." I pointed at each heptapod and tried to mimic the sound of [flutter1]: "heptapod." After a long pause, the first heptapod said something and then the second one said something else, neither of whose spectrographs resembled anything said before. I couldn't tell if they were speaking to each other or to me since they had no faces to turn. I tried pronouncing [flutter1] again, but there was no reaction.

"Not even close," I grumbled.

"I'm impressed you can make sounds like that at all," said Gary.

"You should hear my moose call. Sends them running."

I tried again a few more times, but neither heptapod responded with anything I could recognize. Only when I replayed the recording of the heptapod's pronunciation did I get a confirmation; the heptapod replied with [flutter2], "yes."

"So we're stuck with using recordings?" asked Gary.

I nodded. "At least temporarily."

"So now what?"

"Now we make sure it hasn't actually been saying 'aren't they cute' or 'look what they're doing now.' Then we see if we can identify any of these words when that other heptapod pronounces them." I gestured for him to have a seat. "Get comfortable; this'll take a while."

In 1770, Captain Cook's ship *Endeavour* ran aground on the coast of Queensland, Australia. While some of his men made repairs, Cook led an exploration party and met the aboriginal people. One of the sailors pointed to the animals that hopped around with their young riding in pouches, and asked an aborigine what they were called. The aborigine replied, "Kanguru." From then on Cook and his sailors referred to the animals by this word. It wasn't until later that they learned it meant "What did you say?"

I tell that story in my introductory course every year. It's almost certainly untrue, and I explain that afterwards, but it's a classic anecdote. Of course, the anecdotes my undergraduates will really want to hear are ones featuring the heptapods; for the rest of my teaching career, that'll be the reason many of them sign up for my courses. So I'll show them the old videotapes of my sessions at the looking glass, and the sessions that the other linguists conducted; the tapes are instructive, and they'll be useful if we're ever visited by aliens again, but they don't generate many good anecdotes.

When it comes to language-learning anecdotes, my favorite source is child language acquisition. I remember one afternoon when you are five years old, after you have come home from kindergarten. You'll be coloring with your crayons while I grade papers.

"Mom," you'll say, using the carefully casual tone reserved for requesting a favor, "can I ask you something?"

"Sure, sweetie. Go ahead."

"Can I be, um, honored?"

I'll look up from the paper I'm grading. "What do you mean?"

"At school Sharon said she got to be honored."

"Really? Did she tell you what for?"

"It was when her big sister got married. She said only one person could be, um, honored, and she was it."

"Ah, I see. You mean Sharon was maid of honor?"

"Yeah, that's it. Can I be made of honor?"

Gary and I entered the prefab building containing the center of operations for the looking glass site. Inside it looked like they were planning an invasion, or perhaps an evacuation: crewcut soldiers worked around a large map of the area, or sat in front of burly electronic gear while speaking into headsets. We were shown into Colonel Weber's office, a room in the back that was cool from air conditioning.

We briefed the colonel on our first day's results. "Doesn't sound like you got very far," he said.

"I have an idea as to how we can make faster progress," I said. "But you'll have to approve the use of more equipment."

"What more do you need?"

"A digital camera, and a big video screen." I showed him a drawing of the setup I imagined. "I want to try conducting the discovery procedure using writing; I'd display words on the screen, and use the camera to record the words they write. I'm hoping the heptapods will do the same."

Weber looked at the drawing dubiously. "What would be the advantage of that?"

"So far I've been proceeding the way I would with speakers of an unwritten language. Then it occurred to me that the heptapods must have writing, too."

"So?"

"If the heptapods have a mechanical way of producing writing, then their writing ought to be very regular, very consistent. That would make it easier for us to identify graphemes instead of phonemes. It's like picking out the letters in a printed sentence instead of trying to hear them when the sentence is spoken aloud."

"I take your point," he admitted. "And how would you respond to them? Show them the words they displayed to you?"

"Basically. And if they put spaces between words, any sentences we write would be a lot more intelligible than any spoken sentence we might splice together from recordings."

He leaned back in his chair. "You know we want to show as little of our technology as possible."

"I understand, but we're using machines as intermediaries already. If we can get them to use writing, I believe progress will go much faster than if we're restricted to the sound spectrographs."

The colonel turned to Gary. "Your opinion?"

"It sounds like a good idea to me. I'm curious whether the heptapods might have difficulty reading our monitors. Their looking glasses are based on a completely different technology than our video screens. As far as we can tell, they don't use pixels or scan lines, and they don't refresh on a frame-by-frame basis."

"You think the scan lines on our video screens might render them unreadable to the heptapods?"

"It's possible," said Gary. "We'll just have to try it and see."

Weber considered it. For me it wasn't even a question, but from his point of view it was a difficult one; like a soldier, though, he made it quickly. "Request granted. Talk to the sergeant outside about bringing in what you need. Have it ready for tomorrow."

I remember one day during the summer when you're sixteen. For once, the person waiting for her date to arrive is me. Of course, you'll be waiting around, too, curious to see what he looks like. You'll have a friend of yours, a blond girl with the unlikely name of Roxie, hanging out with you, giggling.

"You may feel the urge to make comments about him," I'll say, checking myself in the hallway mirror. "Just restrain yourselves until we leave."

"Don't worry, Mom," you'll say. "We'll do it so that he won't know. Roxie, you ask me what I think the weather will be like tonight. Then I'll say what I think of Mom's date."

"Right," Roxie will say.

"No, you most definitely will not," I'll say.

"Relax, Mom. He'll never know; we do this all the time."

"What a comfort that is."

A little later on, Nelson will arrive to pick me up. I'll do the introductions, and we'll all engage in a little small talk on the front porch. Nelson is ruggedly handsome, to your evident approval. Just as we're about to leave, Roxie will say to you casually, "So what do you think the weather will be like tonight?"

"I think it's going to be really hot," you'll answer.

Roxie will nod in agreement. Nelson will say, "Really? I thought they said it was going to be cool."

"I have a sixth sense about these things," you'll say. Your face will give nothing away. "I get the feeling it's going to be a scorcher. Good thing you're dressed for it, Mom."

I'll glare at you, and say good night.

As I lead Nelson toward his car, he'll ask me, amused, "I'm missing something here, aren't I?"

"A private joke," I'll mutter. "Don't ask me to explain it."

At our next session at the looking glass, we repeated the procedure we had performed before, this time displaying a printed word on our computer screen at the same time we spoke: showing HUMAN while saying "Human," and so forth. Eventually, the heptapods understood what we wanted, and set up a flat circular screen mounted on a small pedestal. One heptapod spoke, and then inserted a limb into a large socket in the pedestal; a doodle of script, vaguely cursive, popped onto the screen.

We soon settled into a routine, and I compiled two parallel corpora: one of spoken utterances, one of writing samples. Based on first impressions, their writing appeared to be logographic, which was disappointing; I'd been hoping for an alphabetic script to help us learn their speech. Their logograms might include some phonetic information, but finding it would be a lot harder than with an alphabetic script.

By getting up close to the looking glass, I was able to point to various heptapod body parts, such as limbs, digits, and eyes, and elicit terms for each. It turned out that they had an orifice on the underside of their body, lined with articulated bony ridges: probably used for eating, while the one at the top was for respiration and speech. There were no other conspicuous orifices; perhaps their mouth was their anus, too. Those sorts of questions would have to wait.

I also tried asking our two informants for terms for addressing each individually; personal names, if they had such things. Their answers were of course unpronounceable, so for Gary's and my purposes, I dubbed them Flapper and Raspberry. I hoped I'd be able to tell them apart.

The next day I conferred with Gary before we entered the looking-glass tent. "I'll need your help with this session," I told him.

"Sure. What do you want me to do?"

"We need to elicit some verbs, and it's easiest with third-person forms. Would you act out a few verbs while I type the written form on the computer? If we're lucky, the heptapods will figure out what we're doing and do the same. I've brought a bunch of props for you to use."

"No problem," said Gary, cracking his knuckles. "Ready when you are."

We began with some simple intransitive verbs: walking, jumping, speaking, writing. Gary demonstrated each one with a charming lack of self-consciousness; the presence of the video cameras didn't inhibit him at all. For the first few actions he performed, I asked the heptapods, "What do you call that?" Before long, the heptapods caught on to what we were trying to do; Raspberry began mimicking Gary, or at least performing the equivalent heptapod action, while Flapper worked their computer, displaying a written description and pronouncing it aloud.

In the spectrographs of their spoken utterances, I could recognize their word I had glossed as "heptapod." The rest of each utterance was presumably the verb phrase; it looked like they had analogs of nouns and verbs, thank goodness.

In their writing, however, things weren't as clear-cut. For each action, they had displayed a single logogram instead of two separate ones. At first I thought they had written something like "walks," with the subject implied. But why would Flapper say "the heptapod walks" while writing "walks," instead of maintaining parallelism? Then I noticed that some of the logograms looked like the logogram for "heptapod" with some extra strokes added to one side or another. Perhaps their verbs could be written as affixes to a noun. If so, why was Flapper writing the noun in some instances but not in others?

I decided to try a transitive verb; substituting object words might clarify things. Among the props I'd brought were an apple and a slice of bread. "Okay," I said to Gary, "show them the food, and then eat some. First the apple, then the bread."

Gary pointed at the Golden Delicious and then he took a bite out of it, while I displayed the "what do you call that?" expression. Then we repeated it with the slice of whole wheat.

Raspberry left the room and returned with some kind of giant nut or gourd and a gelatinous ellipsoid. Raspberry pointed at the gourd while Flapper said a word and displayed a logogram. Then Raspberry brought the gourd down between its legs, a crunching sound resulted, and the gourd reemerged minus a bite; there were cornlike kernels beneath the shell. Flapper talked and displayed a large logogram on their screen. The sound spectrograph for "gourd" changed when it was used in the sentence; possibly a case marker. The logogram was odd: after some study, I could identify graphic elements that resembled the individual logograms for "heptapod" and "gourd." They looked as if they had been melted together, with several extra strokes in the mix that presumably meant "eat." Was it a multiword ligature?

Next we got spoken and written names for the gelatin egg, and descriptions of the act of eating it. The sound spectrograph for "heptapod eats gelatin egg" was analyzable; "gelatin egg" bore a case marker, as expected, though the sentence's word order differed from last time. The written form, another large logogram, was another matter. This time it took much longer for me to recognize anything in it; not only were the individual logograms melted together again, it looked as if the one for "heptapod" was laid on its back, while on top of it the logogram for "gelatin egg" was standing on its head.

"Uh-oh." I took another look at the writing for the simple noun-verb examples, the ones that had seemed inconsistent before. Now I realized all of them actually did contain the logogram for "heptapod"; some were rotated and distorted by being combined with the various verbs, so I hadn't recognized them at first. "You guys have got to be kidding," I muttered.

"What's wrong?" asked Gary.

"Their script isn't word-divided; a sentence is written by joining the logograms for the constituent words. They join the logograms by rotating and modifying them. Take a look." I showed him how the logograms were rotated.

"So they can read a word with equal ease no matter how it's rotated," Gary said. He turned to look at the heptapods, impressed. "I wonder if it's a consequence of their bodies' radial symmetry: their bodies have no 'forward' direction, so maybe their writing doesn't either. Highly neat."

I couldn't believe it; I was working with someone who modified the word "neat" with "highly." "It certainly is interesting," I said, "but it also means there's no easy way for us to write our own sentences in their language. We can't simply cut their sentences into individual words and recombine them; we'll have to learn the rules of their script before we can write anything legible. It's the same continuity problem we'd have had splicing together speech fragments, except applied to writing."

I looked at Flapper and Raspberry in the looking glass, who were waiting for us to continue, and sighed. "You aren't going to make this easy for us, are you?"

To be fair, the heptapods were completely cooperative. In the days that followed, they readily taught us their language without requiring us to teach them any more English. Colonel Weber and his cohorts pondered the implications of that, while I and the linguists at the other looking glasses met via video conferencing to share what we had learned about the heptapod language. The videoconferencing made for an incongruous working environment: our video screens were primitive compared to the heptapods' looking glasses, so that my colleagues seemed more remote than the aliens. The familiar was far away, while the bizarre was close at hand.

It would be a while before we'd be ready to ask the heptapods why they had come, or to discuss physics well enough to ask them about their technology. For the time being, we worked on the basics: phonemics/graphemics, vocabulary, syntax. The heptapods at every looking glass were using the same language, so we were able to pool our data and coordinate our efforts.

Our biggest source of confusion was the heptapods' "writing." It didn't appear to be writing at all; it looked more like a bunch of intricate graphic designs. The logograms weren't arranged in rows, or a spiral, or any linear fashion. Instead, Flapper or Raspberry would write a sentence by sticking together as many logograms as needed into a giant conglomeration.

This form of writing was reminiscent of primitive sign systems, which required a reader to know a message's context in order to understand it. Such systems were considered too limited for systematic recording of information. Yet it was unlikely that the heptapods developed their level of technology with only an oral tradition. That implied one of three possibilities: the first was that the heptapods had a true writing system, but they didn't want to use it in front of us; Colonel Weber would identify with that one. The second was that the heptapods hadn't originated the technology they were using; they were illiterates using someone else's technology. The third, and most interesting to me, was that the heptapods were using a nonlinear system of orthography that qualified as true writing.

I remember a conversation we'll have when you're in your junior year of high school. It'll be Sunday morning, and I'll be scrambling some eggs while you set the table for brunch. You'll laugh as you tell me about the party you went to last night.

"Oh man," you'll say, "they're not kidding when they say that body weight makes a difference. I didn't drink any more than the guys did, but I got so much *drunker*."

I'll try to maintain a neutral, pleasant expression. I'll really try. Then you'll say, "Oh, come on, Mom."

"What?"

"You know you did the exact same things when you were my age."

I did nothing of the sort, but I know that if I were to admit that, you'd lose respect for me completely. "You know never to drive, or get into a car if — "

"God, of course I know that. Do you think I'm an idiot?"

"No, of course not."

What I'll think is that you are clearly, maddeningly not me. It will remind me, again, that you won't be a clone of me; you can be wonderful, a daily delight, but you won't be someone I could have created by myself.

The military had set up a trailer containing our offices at the looking-glass site. I saw Gary walking toward the trailer, and ran to catch up with him. "It's a semasiographic writing system," I said when I reached him.

"Excuse me?" said Gary.

"Here, let me show you." I directed Gary into my office. Once we were inside, I went to the chalkboard and drew a circle with a diagonal line bisecting it. "What does this mean?"

" 'Not allowed'?"

"Right." Next I printed the words NOT ALLOWED on the chalkboard. "And so does this. But only one is a representation of speech."

Gary nodded. "Okay."

"Linguists describe writing like this — " I indicated the printed words " — as 'glottographic,' because it represents speech. Every human written language is in this category. However, this symbol — " I indicated the circle and diagonal line " — is 'semasiographic' writing, because it conveys meaning without reference to speech. There's no correspondence between its components and any particular sounds."

"And you think all of heptapod writing is like this?"

"From what I've seen so far, yes. It's not picture writing, it's far more complex. It has its own system of rules for constructing sentences, like a visual syntax that's unrelated to the syntax for their spoken language."

"A visual syntax? Can you show me an example?"

"Coming right up." I sat down at my desk and, using the computer, pulled up a frame from the recording of yesterday's conversation with Raspberry. I turned the monitor so he could see it. "In their spoken language, a noun has a case marker indicating whether it's a subject or object. In their written language, however, a noun is identified as subject or object based on the orientation of its logogram relative to that of the verb. Here, take a look." I pointed at one of the figures. "For instance, when 'heptapod' is integrated with 'hears' this way, with these strokes parallel, it means that the heptapod is doing the hearing." I showed him a different one. "When they're combined this way, with the strokes perpendicular, it means that the heptapod is being heard. This morphology applies to several verbs.

"Another example is the inflection system." I called up another frame from the recording. "In their written language, this logogram means roughly 'hear easily' or 'hear clearly.' See the elements it has in common with the logogram for 'hear'? You can still combine it with 'heptapod' in the same ways as before, to indicate that the heptapod can hear something clearly or that the heptapod is clearly heard. But what's really interesting is that the modulation of 'hear' into 'hear clearly' isn't a special case; you see the transformation they applied?"

Gary nodded, pointing. "It's like they express the idea of 'clearly' by changing the curve of those strokes in the middle."

"Right. That modulation is applicable to lots of verbs. The logogram for 'see' can be modulated in the same way to form 'see clearly,' and so can the logogram for 'read' and others. And changing the curve of those strokes has no parallel in their speech; with the spoken version of these verbs, they add a prefix to the verb to express ease of manner, and the prefixes for 'see' and 'hear' are different.

"There are other examples, but you get the idea. It's essentially a grammar in two dimensions."

He began pacing thoughtfully. "Is there anything like this in human writing systems?"

"Mathematical equations, notations for music and dance. But those are all very specialized; we couldn't record this conversation using them. But I suspect, if we knew it well enough, we could record this conversation in the heptapod writing system. I think it's a full-fledged, general-purpose graphical language."

Gary frowned. "So their writing constitutes a completely separate language from their speech, right?"

"Right. In fact, it'd be more accurate to refer to the writing system as 'Heptapod B,' and use 'Heptapod A' strictly for referring to the spoken language."

"Hold on a second. Why use two languages when one would suffice? That seems unnecessarily hard to learn."

"Like English spelling?" I said. "Ease of learning isn't the primary force in language evolution. For the heptapods, writing and speech may play such different cultural or cognitive roles that using separate languages makes more sense than using different forms of the same one."

He considered it. "I see what you mean. Maybe they think our form of writing is redundant, like we're wasting a second communications channel."

"That's entirely possible. Finding out why they use a second language for writing will tell us a lot about them."

"So I take it this means we won't be able to use their writing to help us learn their spoken language."

I sighed. "Yeah, that's the most immediate implication. But I don't think we should ignore either Heptapod A or B; we need a two-pronged approach." I pointed at the screen. "I'll bet you that learning their two-dimensional grammar will help you when it comes time to learn their mathematical notation."

"You've got a point there. So are we ready to start asking about their mathematics?"

"Not yet. We need a better grasp on this writing system before we begin anything else," I said, and then smiled when he mimed frustration. "Patience, good sir. Patience is a virtue."

You'll be six when your father has a conference to attend in Hawaii, and we'll accompany him. You'll be so excited that you'll make preparations for weeks beforehand. You'll ask me about coconuts and volcanoes and surfing, and practice hula dancing in the mirror. You'll pack a suitcase with the clothes and toys you want to bring, and you'll drag it around the house to see how long you can carry it. You'll ask me if I can carry your Etch-a-Sketch in my bag, since there won't be any more room for it in yours and you simply can't leave without it.

"You won't need all of these," I'll say. "There'll be so many fun things to do there, you won't have time to play with so many toys."

You'll consider that; dimples will appear above your eyebrows when you think hard. Eventually you'll agree to pack fewer toys, but your expectations will, if anything, increase.

"I wanna be in Hawaii now," you'll whine.

"Sometimes it's good to wait," I'll say. "The anticipation makes it more fun when you get there."

You'll just pout.

In the next report I submitted, I suggested that the term "logogram" was a misnomer because it implied that each graph represented a spoken word, when in fact the graphs didn't correspond to our notion of spoken words at all. I didn't want to use the term "ideogram" either because of how it had been used in the past; I suggested the term "semagram" instead.

It appeared that a semagram corresponded roughly to a written word in human languages: it was meaningful on its own, and in combination with other semagrams could form endless statements. We couldn't define it precisely, but then no one had ever satisfactorily defined "word" for human languages either. When it came to sentences in Heptapod B, though, things became much more confusing. The language had no written punctuation: its syntax was indicated in the way the semagrams were combined, and there was no need to indicate the cadence of speech. There was certainly no way to slice out subject-predicate pairings neatly to make sentences. A "sentence" seemed to be whatever number of semagrams a heptapod wanted to join together; the only difference between a sentence and a paragraph, or a page, was size.

When a Heptapod B sentence grew fairly sizable, its visual impact was remarkable. If I wasn't trying to decipher it, the writing looked like fanciful praying mantids drawn in a cursive style, all clinging to each other to form an Escheresque lattice, each slightly different in its stance. And the biggest sentences had an effect similar to that of psychedelic posters: sometimes eye-watering, sometimes hypnotic.

I remember a picture of you taken at your college graduation. In the photo you're striking a pose for the camera, mortarboard stylishly tilted on your head, one hand touching your sunglasses, the other hand on your hip, holding open your gown to reveal the tank top and shorts you're wearing underneath.

I remember your graduation. There will be the distraction of having Nelson and your father and what's-her-name there all at the same time, but that will be minor. That entire weekend, while you're introducing me to your classmates and hugging everyone incessantly, I'll be all but mute with amazement. I can't believe that you, a grown woman taller than me and beautiful enough to make my heart ache, will be the same girl I used to lift off the ground so you could reach the drinking fountain, the same girl who used to trundle out of my bedroom draped in a dress and hat and four scarves from my closet.

And after graduation, you'll be heading for a job as a financial analyst. I won't understand what you do there, I won't even understand your fascination with money, the preeminence you gave to salary when negotiating job offers. I would prefer it if you'd pursue something without regard for its monetary rewards, but I'll have no complaints. My own mother could never understand why I couldn't just be a high school English teacher. You'll do what makes you happy, and that'll be all I ask for.

As time went on, the teams at each looking glass began working in earnest on learning heptapod terminology for elementary mathematics and physics. We worked together on presentations, with the linguists focusing on procedure and the physicists focusing on subject matter. The physicists showed us previously devised systems for communicating with aliens, based on mathematics, but those were intended for use over a radio telescope. We reworked them for face-to-face communication.

Our teams were successful with basic arithmetic, but we hit a road block with geometry and algebra. We tried using a spherical coordinate system instead of a rectangular one, thinking it might be more natural to the heptapods given their anatomy, but that approach wasn't any more fruitful. The heptapods didn't seem to understand what we were getting at.

Likewise, the physics discussions went poorly. Only with the most concrete terms, like the names of the elements, did we have any success; after several attempts at representing the periodic table, the heptapods got the idea. For anything remotely abstract, we might as well have been gibbering. We tried to demonstrate basic physical attributes like mass and acceleration so we could elicit their terms for them, but the heptapods simply responded with requests for clarification. To avoid perceptual problems that might be associated with any particular medium, we tried physical demonstrations as well as line drawings, photos, and animations; none were effective. Days with no progress became weeks, and the physicists were becoming disillusioned.

By contrast, the linguists were having much more success. We made steady progress decoding the grammar of the spoken language, Heptapod A. It didn't follow the pattern of human languages, as expected, but it was comprehensible so far: free word order, even to the extent that there was no preferred order for the clauses in a conditional statement, in defiance of a human language "universal." It also appeared that the heptapods had no objection to many levels of center-embedding of clauses, something that quickly defeated humans. Peculiar, but not impenetrable.

Much more interesting were the newly discovered morphological and grammatical processes in Heptapod B that were uniquely two-dimensional. Depending on a semagram's declension, inflections could be indicated by varying a certain stroke's curvature, or its thickness, or its manner of undulation; or by varying the relative sizes of two radicals, or their relative distance to another radical, or their orientations; or various other means. These were nonsegmental graphemes; they couldn't be isolated from the rest of a semagram. And despite how such traits behaved in human writing, these had nothing to do with calligraphic style; their meanings were defined according to a consistent and unambiguous grammar.

We regularly asked the heptapods why they had come. Each time, they answered "to see," or "to observe." Indeed, sometimes they preferred to watch us silently rather than answer our questions. Perhaps they were scientists, perhaps they were tourists. The State Department instructed us to reveal as little as possible about humanity, in case that information could be used as a bargaining chip in subsequent negotiations. We obliged, though it didn't require much effort: the heptapods never asked questions about anything. Whether scientists or tourists, they were an awfully incurious bunch.

I remember once when we'll be driving to the mall to buy some new clothes for you. You'll be thirteen. One moment you'll be sprawled in your seat, completely unselfconscious, all child; the next, you'll toss your hair with a practiced casualness, like a fashion model in training.

You'll give me some instructions as I'm parking the car. "Okay, Mom, give me one of the credit cards, and we can meet back at the entrance here in two hours."

I'll laugh. "Not a chance. All the credit cards stay with me."

"You're kidding." You'll become the embodiment of exasperation. We'll get out of the car and I will start walking to the mall entrance. After seeing that I won't budge on the matter, you'll quickly reformulate your plans.

"Okay Mom, okay. You can come with me, just walk a little ways behind me, so it doesn't look like we're together. If I see any friends of mine, I'm gonna stop and talk to them, but you just keep walking, okay? I'll come find you later."

I'll stop in my tracks. "Excuse me? I am not the hired help, nor am I some mutant relative for you to be ashamed of."

"But Mom, I can't let anyone see you with me."

"What are you talking about? I've already met your friends; they've been to the house."

"That was different," you'll say, incredulous that you have to explain it. "This is shopping."

"Too bad."

Then the explosion: "You won't do the least thing to make me happy! You don't care about me at all!"

It won't have been that long since you enjoyed going shopping with me; it will forever astonish me how quickly you grow out of one phase and enter another. Living with you will be like aiming for a moving target; you'll always be further along than I expect.

I looked at the sentence in Heptapod B that I had just written, using simple pen and paper. Like all the sentences I generated myself, this one looked misshapen, like a heptapod-written sentence that had been smashed with a hammer and then inexpertly taped back together. I had sheets of such inelegant semagrams covering my desk, fluttering occasionally when the oscillating fan swung past.

It was strange trying to learn a language that had no spoken form. Instead of practicing my pronunciation, I had taken to squeezing my eyes shut and trying to paint semagrams on the insides of my eyelids.

There was a knock at the door and before I could answer Gary came in looking jubilant. "Illinois got a repetition in physics."

"Really? That's great; when did it happen?"

"It happened a few hours ago; we just had the videoconference. Let me show you what it is." He started erasing my blackboard.

"Don't worry, I didn't need any of that."

"Good." He picked up a nub of chalk and drew a diagram:

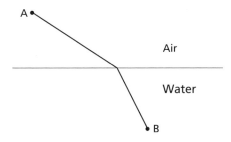

"Okay, here's the path a ray of light takes when crossing from air to water. The light ray travels in a straight line until it hits the water; the water has a different index of refraction, so the light changes direction. You've heard of this before, right?"

I nodded. "Sure."

"Now here's an interesting property about the path the light takes. The path is the fastest possible route between these two points."

"Come again?"

"Imagine, just for grins, that the ray of light traveled along this path." He added a dotted line to his diagram:

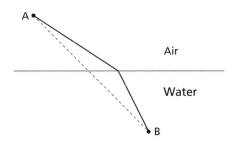

"This hypothetical path is shorter than the path the light actually takes. But light travels more slowly in water than it does in air, and a greater percentage of this path is underwater. So it would take longer for light to travel along this path than it does along the real path."

"Okay, I get it."

"Now imagine if light were to travel along this other path." He drew a second dotted path:

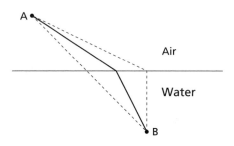

"This path reduces the percentage that's underwater, but the total length is larger. It would also take longer for light to travel along this path than along the actual one."

Gary put down the chalk and gestured at the diagram on the chalkboard with white-tipped fingers. "Any hypothetical path would require more time to traverse than the one actually taken. In other words, the route that the light ray takes is always the fastest possible one. That's Fermat's Principle of Least Time."

"Hmm, interesting. And this is what the heptapods responded to?"

"Exactly. Moorehead gave an animated presentation of Fermat's Principle at the Illinois looking glass, and the heptapods repeated it back. Now he's trying to get a symbolic description." He grinned. "Now is that highly neat, or what?"

"It's neat all right, but how come I haven't heard of Fermat's Principle before?" I picked up a binder and waved it at him; it was a primer on the physics topics suggested for use in communication with the heptapods. "This thing goes on forever about Planck masses and the spin-flip of atomic hydrogen, and not a word about the refraction of light."

"We guessed wrong about what'd be most useful for you to know," Gary said without embarrassment. "In fact, it's curious that Fermat's Principle was the first breakthrough; even though it's easy to explain, you need calculus to describe it mathematically. And not ordinary calculus; you need the calculus of variations. We thought that some simple theorem of geometry or algebra would be the breakthrough."

"Curious indeed. You think the heptapods' idea of what's simple doesn't match ours?"

"Exactly, which is why I'm *dying* to see what their mathematical description of Fermat's Principle looks like." He paced as he talked. "If their version of the calculus of variations is simpler to them than their equivalent of algebra, that might explain why we've had so much trouble talking about physics; their entire system of mathematics may be topsy-turvy compared to ours." He pointed to the physics primer. "You can be sure that we're going to revise that."

"So can you build from Fermat's Principle to other areas of physics?"

"Probably. There are lots of physical principles just like Fermat's."

"What, like Louise's principle of least closet space? When did physics become so minimalist?"

"Well, the word 'least' is misleading. You see, Fermat's Principle of Least Time is incomplete; in certain situations light follows a path that takes *more* time than any of the other possibilities. It's more accurate to say that light always follows an *extreme* path, either one that minimizes the time taken or one that maximizes it. A minimum and a maximum share certain mathematical properties, so both situations can be described with one equation. So to be precise, Fermat's Principle isn't a minimal principle; instead it's what's known as a 'variational' principle."

"And there are more of these variational principles?"

He nodded. "In all branches of physics. Almost every physical law can be restated as a variational principle. The only difference between these principles is in which attribute is minimized or maximized." He gestured as if the different branches of physics were arrayed before him on a table. "In optics, where Fermat's Principle applies, time is the attribute that has to be an extreme. In mechanics, it's a different attribute. In electromagnetism, it's something else again. But all these principles are similar mathematically."

"So once you get their mathematical description of Fermat's Principle, you should be able to decode the other ones."

"God, I hope so. I think this is the wedge that we've been looking for, the one that cracks open their formulation of physics. This calls for a celebration." He stopped his pacing and turned to me. "Hey, Louise, want to go out for dinner? My treat."

I was mildly surprised. "Sure," I said.

It'll be when you first learn to walk that I get daily demonstrations of the asymmetry in our relationship. You'll be incessantly running off somewhere, and each time you walk into a door frame or scrape your knee, the pain feels like it's my own. It'll be like growing an errant limb, an extension of myself whose sensory nerves report pain just fine, but whose motor nerves don't convey my commands at all. It's so unfair: I'm going to give birth to an animated voodoo doll of myself. I didn't see this in the contract when I signed up. Was this part of the deal?

And then there will be the times when I see you laughing. Like the time you'll be playing with the neighbor's puppy, poking your hands through the chain-link fence separating our back yards, and you'll be laughing so hard you'll start hiccupping. The puppy will run inside the neighbor's house, and your laughter will gradually subside, letting you catch your breath. Then the puppy will come back to the fence to lick your fingers again, and you'll shriek and start laughing again. It will be the most wonderful sound I could ever imagine, a sound that makes me feel like a fountain, or a wellspring.

Now if only I can remember that sound the next time your blithe disregard for self-preservation gives me a heart attack.

After the breakthrough with Fermat's Principle, discussions of scientific concepts became more fruitful. It wasn't as if all of heptapod physics was suddenly rendered transparent, but progress was steady. According to Gary, the heptapods' formulation of physics was indeed topsy-turvy relative to ours. Physical attributes that humans defined using integral calculus were seen as fundamental by the heptapods. As an example, Gary described an attribute that, in physics jargon, bore the deceptively simple name "action," which represented "the difference between kinetic and potential energy, integrated over time," whatever that meant. Calculus for us; elementary to them.

Conversely, to define attributes that humans thought of as fundamental, like velocity, the heptapods employed mathematics that were, Gary assured me, "highly weird." The physicists were ultimately able to prove the equivalence of heptapod mathematics and human mathematics; even though their approaches were almost the reverse of one another, both were systems of describing the same physical universe.

I tried following some of the equations that the physicists were coming up with, but it was no use. I couldn't really grasp the significance of physical attributes like "action"; I couldn't, with any confidence, ponder the significance of treating such an attribute as fundamental. Still, I tried to ponder questions formulated in terms more familiar to me: what kind of worldview did the heptapods have, that they would consider Fermat's Principle the simplest explanation of light refraction? What kind of perception made a minimum or maximum readily apparent to them?

Your eyes will be blue like your dad's, not mud brown like mine. Boys will stare into those eyes the way I did, and do, into your dad's, surprised and enchanted, as I was and am, to find them in combination with black hair. You will have many suitors.

I remember when you are fifteen, coming home after a weekend at your dad's, incredulous over the interrogation he'll have put you through regarding the boy you're currently dating. You'll sprawl on the sofa, recounting your dad's latest breach of common sense: "You know what he said? He said, 'I know what teenage boys are like.'" Roll of the eyes. "Like I don't?"

"Don't hold it against him," I'll say. "He's a father; he can't help it." Having seen you interact with your friends, I won't worry much about a boy taking advantage of you; if anything, the opposite will be more likely. I'll worry about that.

"He wishes I were still a kid. He hasn't known how to act toward me since I grew breasts."

"Well, that development was a shock for him. Give him time to recover."

"It's been *years*, Mom. How long is it gonna take?"

"I'll let you know when my father has come to terms with mine."

During one of the videoconferences for the linguists, Cisneros from the Massachusetts looking glass had raised an interesting question: was there a particular order in which semagrams were written in a Heptapod B sentence? It was clear that word order meant next to nothing when speaking in Heptapod A; when asked to repeat what it had just said, a heptapod would likely as not use a different word order unless we specifically asked them not to. Was word order similarly unimportant when writing in Heptapod B?

Previously, we had only focused our attention on how a sentence in Heptapod B looked once it was complete. As far as anyone could tell, there was no preferred order when reading the semagrams in a sentence; you could start almost anywhere in the nest, then follow the branching clauses until you'd read the whole thing. But that was reading; was the same true about writing?

During my most recent session with Flapper and Raspberry I had asked them if, instead of displaying a semagram only after it was completed, they could show it to us while it was being written. They had agreed. I inserted the videotape of the session into the VCR, and on my computer I consulted the session transcript.

I picked one of the longer utterances from the conversation. What Flapper had said was that the heptapods' planet had two moons, one significantly larger than the other; the three primary constituents of the planet's atmosphere were nitrogen, argon, and oxygen; and fifteen twenty-eighths of the planet's surface was covered by water. The first words of the spoken utterance translated literally as "inequality-of-size rocky-orbiter rocky-orbiters related-as-primary-to-secondary."

Then I rewound the videotape until the time signature matched the one in the transcription. I started playing the tape, and watched the web of semagrams being spun out of inky spider's silk. I rewound it and played it several times. Finally I froze the video right after the first stroke was completed and before the second one was begun; all that was visible onscreen was a single sinuous line.

Comparing that initial stroke with the completed sentence, I realized that the stroke participated in several different clauses of the message. It began in the semagram for 'oxygen,' as the determinant that distinguished it from certain other elements; then it slid down to become the morpheme of comparison in the description of the two moons' sizes; and lastly it flared out as the arched backbone of the semagram for 'ocean.' Yet this stroke was a single continuous line, and it was the first one that Flapper wrote. That meant the heptapod had to know how the entire sentence would be laid out before it could write the very first stroke.

The other strokes in the sentence also traversed several clauses, making them so interconnected that none could be removed without redesigning the entire sentence. The heptapods didn't write a sentence one semagram at a time; they built it out of strokes irrespective of individual semagrams. I had seen a similarly high degree of integration before in calligraphic designs, particularly those employing the Arabic alphabet. But those designs had required careful planning by expert calligraphers. No one could lay out such an intricate design at the speed needed for holding a conversation. At least, no human could.

There's a joke that I once heard a comedienne tell. It goes like this: "I'm not sure if I'm ready to have children. I asked a friend of mine who has children, 'Suppose I do have kids. What if when they grow up, they blame me for everything that's wrong with their lives?' She laughed and said, What do you mean, if?'"

That's my favorite joke.

Gary and I were at a little Chinese restaurant, one of the local places we had taken to patronizing to get away from the encampment. We sat eating the appetizers: potstickers, redolent of pork and sesame oil. My favorite.

I dipped one in soy sauce and vinegar. "So how are you doing with your Heptapod B practice?" I asked.

Gary looked obliquely at the ceiling. I tried to meet his gaze, but he kept shifting it.

"You've given up, haven't you?" I said. "You're not even trying any more."

He did a wonderful hangdog expression. "I'm just no good at languages," he confessed. "I thought learning Heptapod B might be more like learning mathematics than trying to speak another language, but it's not. It's too foreign for me."

"It would help you discuss physics with them."

"Probably, but since we had our breakthrough, I can get by with just a few phrases."

I sighed. "I suppose that's fair; I have to admit, I've given up on trying to learn the mathematics."

"So we're even?"

"We're even." I sipped my tea. "Though I did want to ask you about Fermat's Principle. Something about it feels odd to me, but I can't put my finger on it. It just doesn't sound like a law of physics."

A twinkle appeared in Gary's eyes. "I'll bet I know what you're talking about." He snipped a potsticker in half with his chopsticks. "You're used to thinking of refraction in terms of cause and effect: reaching the water's surface is the cause, and the change in direction is the effect. But Fermat's Principle sounds weird because it describes light's behavior in goal-oriented terms. It sounds like a commandment to a light beam: 'Thou shalt minimize or maximize the time taken to reach thy destination.'"

I considered it. "Go on."

"It's an old question in the philosophy of physics. People have been talking about it since Fermat first formulated it in the 1600s; Planck wrote volumes about it. The thing is, while the common formulation of physical laws is causal, a variational principle like Fermat's is purposive, almost teleological."

"Hmm, that's an interesting way to put it. Let me think about that for a minute." I pulled out a felt-tip pen and, on my paper napkin, drew a copy of the diagram that Gary had drawn on my blackboard. "Okay," I said, thinking aloud, "so let's say the goal of a ray of light is to take the fastest path. How does the light go about doing that?"

"Well, if I can speak anthropomorphic-projectionally, the light has to examine the possible paths and compute how long each one would take." He plucked the last potsticker from the serving dish.

"And to do that," I continued, "the ray of light has to know just where its destination is. If the destination were somewhere else, the fastest path would be different."

Gary nodded again. "That's right; the notion of a 'fastest path' is meaningless unless there's a destination specified. And computing how long a given path takes also requires information about what lies along that path, like where the water's surface is."

I kept staring at the diagram on the napkin. "And the light ray has to know all that ahead of time, before it starts moving, right?"

"So to speak," said Gary. "The light can't start traveling in any old direction and make course corrections later on, because the path resulting from such behavior wouldn't be the fastest possible one. The light has to do all its computations at the very beginning."

I thought to myself, *the ray of light has to know where it will ultimately end up before it can choose the direction to begin moving in.* I knew what that reminded me of. I looked up at Gary. "That's what was bugging me."

I remember when you're fourteen. You'll come out of your bedroom, a graffiti-covered notebook computer in hand, working on a report for school.

"Mom, what do you call it when both sides can win?"

I'll look up from my computer and the paper I'll be writing. "What, you mean a win-win situation?"

"There's some technical name for it, some math word. Remember that time Dad was here, and he was talking about the stock market? He used it then."

"Hmm, that sounds familiar, but I can't remember what he called it."

"I need to know. I want to use that phrase in my social studies report. I can't even search for information on it unless I know what it's called."

"I'm sorry, I don't know it either. Why don't you call your dad?"

Judging from your expression, that will be more effort than you want to make. At this point, you and your father won't be getting along well. "Can you call Dad and ask him? But don't tell him it's for me."

"I think you can call him yourself."

You'll fume, "Jesus, Mom, I can never get help with my homework since you and Dad split up."

It's amazing the diverse situations in which you can bring up the divorce. "I've helped you with your homework."

"Like a million years ago, Mom."

I'll let that pass. "I'd help you with this if I could, but I don't remember what it's called."

You'll head back to your bedroom in a huff.

I practiced Heptapod B at every opportunity, both with the other linguists and by myself. The novelty of reading a semasiographic language made it compelling in a way that Heptapod A wasn't, and my improvement in writing it excited me. Over time, the sentences I wrote grew shapelier, more cohesive. I had reached the point where it worked better when I didn't think about it too much. Instead of carefully trying to design a sentence before writing, I could simply begin putting down strokes immediately; my initial strokes almost always turned out to be compatible with an elegant rendition of what I was trying to say. I was developing a faculty like that of the heptapods.

More interesting was the fact that Heptapod B was changing the way I thought. For me, thinking typically meant speaking in an internal voice; as we say in the trade, my thoughts were phonologically coded. My internal voice normally spoke in English, but that wasn't a requirement. The summer after my senior year in high school, I attended a total immersion program for learning Russian; by the end of the summer, I was thinking and even dreaming in Russian. But it was always *spoken* Russian. Different language, same mode: a voice speaking silently aloud.

The idea of thinking in a linguistic yet nonphonological mode always intrigued me. I had a friend born of deaf parents; he grew up using American Sign Language, and he told me that he often thought in ASL instead of English. I used to wonder what it was like to have one's thoughts be manually coded, to reason using an inner pair of hands instead of an inner voice.

With Heptapod B, I was experiencing something just as foreign: my thoughts were becoming graphically coded. There were trancelike moments during the day when my thoughts weren't expressed with my internal voice; instead, I saw semagrams with my mind's eye, sprouting like frost on a windowpane.

As I grew more fluent, semagraphic designs would appear fully formed, articulating even complex ideas all at once. My thought processes weren't moving any faster as a result, though. Instead of racing forward, my mind hung balanced on the symmetry underlying the semagrams. The semagrams seemed to be something more than language; they were almost like mandalas. I found myself in a meditative state, contemplating the way in which premises and conclusions were interchangeable. There was no direction inherent in the way propositions were connected, no "train of thought" moving along a particular route; all the components in an act of reasoning were equally powerful, all having identical precedence.

A representative from the State Department named Hossner had the job of briefing the U.S. scientists on our agenda with the heptapods. We sat in the videoconference room, listening to him lecture. Our microphone was turned off, so Gary and I could exchange comments without interrupting Hossner. As we listened, I worried that Gary might harm his vision, rolling his eyes so often.

"They must have had some reason for coming all this way," said the diplomat, his voice tinny through the speakers. "It does not look like their reason was conquest, thank God. But if that's not the reason, what is? Are they prospectors? Anthropologists? Missionaries? Whatever their motives, there must be something we can offer them. Maybe it's mineral rights to our solar system. Maybe it's information about ourselves. Maybe it's the right to deliver sermons to our populations. But we can be sure that there's something.

"My point is this: their motive might not be to trade, but that doesn't mean that we cannot conduct trade. We simply need to know why they're here, and what we have that they want. Once we have that information, we can begin trade negotiations.

"I should emphasize that our relationship with the heptapods need not be adversarial. This is not a situation where every gain on their part is a loss on ours, or vice versa. If we handle ourselves correctly, both we and the heptapods can come out winners."

"You mean it's a non-zero-sum game?" Gary said in mock incredulity. "Oh my gosh."

"A non-zero-sum game."

"What?" You'll reverse course, heading back from your bedroom.

"When both sides can win: I just remembered, it's called a non-zero-sum game."

"That's it!" you'll say, writing it down on your notebook. "Thanks, Mom!"

"I guess I knew it after all," I'll say. "All those years with your father, some of it must have rubbed off."

"I knew you'd know it," you'll say. You'll give me a sudden, brief hug, and your hair will smell of apples. "You're the best."

"Louise?"

"Hmm? Sorry, I was distracted. What did you say?"

"I said, what do you think about our Mr. Hossner here?"

"I prefer not to."

"I've tried that myself: ignoring the government, seeing if it would go away. It hasn't."

As evidence of Gary's assertion, Hossner kept blathering: "Your immediate task is to think back on what you've learned. Look for anything that might help us. Has there been any indication of what the heptapods want? Of what they value?"

"Gee, it never occurred to us to look for things like that," I said. "We'll get right on it, sir."

"The sad thing is, that's just what we'll have to do," said Gary.

"Are there any questions?" asked Hossner.

Burghart, the linguist at the Fort Worth looking glass, spoke up. "We've been through this with the heptapods many times. They maintain that they're here to observe, and they maintain that information is not tradable."

"So they would have us believe," said Hossner. "But consider: how could that be true? I know that the heptapods have occasionally stopped talking to us for brief periods. That may be a tactical maneuver on their part. If we were to stop talking to them tomorrow — "

"Wake me up if he says something interesting," said Gary.

"I was just going to ask you to do the same for me."

That day when Gary first explained Fermat's Principle to me, he had mentioned that almost every physical law could be stated as a variational principle. Yet when humans thought about physical laws, they preferred to work with them in their causal formulation. I could understand that: the physical attributes that humans found intuitive, like kinetic energy or acceleration, were all properties of an object at a given moment in time. And these were conducive to a chronological, causal interpretation of events: one moment growing out of another, causes and effects created a chain reaction that grew from past to future.

In contrast, the physical attributes that the heptapods found intuitive, like "action" or those other things defined by integrals, were meaningful only over a period of time. And these were conducive to a teleological interpretation of events: by viewing events over a period of time, one recognized that there was a requirement that had to be satisfied, a goal of minimizing or maximizing. And one had to know the initial and final states to meet that goal; one needed knowledge of the effects before the causes could be initiated.

I was growing to understand that, too.

"Why?" you'll ask again. You'll be three.

"Because it's your bedtime," I'll say again. We'll have gotten as far as getting you bathed and into your jammies, but no further than that.

"But I'm not sleepy," you'll whine. You'll be standing at the bookshelf, pulling down a video to watch: your latest diversionary tactic to keep away from your bedroom.

"It doesn't matter: you still have to go to bed."

"But why?"

"Because I'm the mom and I said so."

I'm actually going to say that, aren't I? God, somebody please shoot me.

I'll pick you up and carry you under my arm to your bed, you wailing piteously all the while, but my sole concern will be my own distress. All those vows made in childhood that I would give reasonable answers when I became a parent, that I would treat my own child as an intelligent, thinking individual, all for naught: I'm going to turn into my mother. I can fight it as much as I want, but there'll be no stopping my slide down that long, dreadful slope.

Was it actually possible to know the future? Not simply to guess at it; was it possible to *know* what was going to happen, with absolute certainty and in specific detail? Gary once told me that the fundamental laws of physics were time-symmetric, that there was no physical difference between past and future. Given that, some might say, "yes, theoretically." But speaking more concretely, most would answer "no," because of free will.

I liked to imagine the objection as a Borgesian fabulation: consider a person standing before the *Book of Ages*, the chronicle that records every event, past and future. Even though the text has been photoreduced from the full-sized edition, the volume is enormous. With magnifier in hand, she flips through the tissue-thin leaves until she locates the story of her life. She finds the passage that describes her flipping through the *Book of Ages*, and she skips to the next column, where it details what she'll be doing later in the day: acting on information she's read in the *Book*, she'll bet one hundred dollars on the racehorse Devil May Care and win twenty times that much.

The thought of doing just that had crossed her mind, but being a contrary sort, she now resolves to refrain from betting on the ponies altogether.

There's the rub. The *Book of Ages* cannot be wrong; this scenario is based on the premise that a person is given knowledge of the actual future, not of some possible future. If this were Greek myth, circumstances would conspire to make her enact her fate despite her best efforts, but prophecies in myth are notoriously vague; the *Book of Ages* is quite specific, and there's no way she can be forced to bet on a racehorse in the manner specified. The result is a contradiction: the *Book of Ages* must be right, by definition; yet no matter what the *Book* says she'll do, she can choose to do otherwise. How can these two facts be reconciled?

They can't be, was the common answer. A volume like the *Book of Ages* is a logical impossibility, for the precise reason that its existence would result in the above contradiction. Or, to be generous, some might say that the *Book of Ages* could exist, as long as it wasn't accessible to readers: that volume is housed in a special collection, and no one has viewing privileges.

The existence of free will meant that we couldn't know the future. And we knew free will existed because we had direct experience of it. Volition was an intrinsic part of consciousness.

Or was it? What if the experience of knowing the future changed a person? What if it evoked a sense of urgency, a sense of obligation to act precisely as she knew she would?

. . . .

I stopped by Gary's office before leaving for the day. "I'm calling it quits. Did you want to grab something to eat?"

"Sure, just wait a second," he said. He shut down his computer and gathered some papers together. Then he looked up at me. "Hey, want to come to my place for dinner tonight? I'll cook."

I looked at him dubiously. "You can cook?"

"Just one dish," he admitted. "But it's a good one."

"Sure," I said. "I'm game."

"Great. We just need to go shopping for the ingredients."

"Don't go to any trouble — "

"There's a market on the way to my house. It won't take a minute."

We took separate cars, me following him. I almost lost him when he abruptly turned in to a parking lot. It was a gourmet market, not large, but fancy; tall glass jars stuffed with imported foods sat next to specialty utensils on the store's stainless-steel shelves.

I accompanied Gary as he collected fresh basil, tomatoes, garlic, linguini. "There's a fish market next door; we can get fresh clams there," he said.

"Sounds good." We walked past the section of kitchen utensils. My gaze wandered over the shelves — peppermills, garlic presses, salad tongs — and stopped on a wooden salad bowl.

When you are three, you'll pull a dishtowel off the kitchen counter and bring that salad bowl down on top of you. I'll make a grab for it, but I'll miss. The edge of the bowl will leave you with a cut, on the upper edge of your forehead, that will require a single stitch. Your father and I will hold you, sobbing and stained with Caesar salad dressing, as we wait in the emergency room for hours.

I reached out and took the bowl from the shelf. The motion didn't feel like something I was forced to do. Instead it seemed just as urgent as my rushing to catch the bowl when it falls on you: an instinct that I felt right in following.

"I could use a salad bowl like this."

Gary looked at the bowl and nodded approvingly. "See, wasn't it a good thing that I had to stop at the market?"

"Yes it was." We got in line to pay for our purchases.

Consider the sentence "The rabbit is ready to eat." Interpret "rabbit" to be the object of "eat," and the sentence was an announcement that dinner would be served shortly. Interpret "rabbit" to be the subject of "eat," and it was a hint, such as a young girl might give her mother so she'll open a bag of Purina Bunny Chow. Two very different utterances; in fact, they were probably mutually exclusive within a single household. Yet either was a valid interpretation; only context could determine what the sentence meant.

Consider the phenomenon of light hitting water at one angle, and traveling through it at a different angle. Explain it by saying that a difference in the index of refraction caused the light to change direction, and one saw the world as humans saw it. Explain it by saying that light minimized the time needed to travel to its destination, and one saw the world as the heptapods saw it. Two very different interpretations.

The physical universe was a language with a perfectly ambiguous grammar. Every physical event was an utterance that could be parsed in two entirely different ways, one causal and the other teleological, both valid, neither one disqualifiable no matter how much context was available.

When the ancestors of humans and heptapods first acquired the spark of consciousness, they both perceived the same physical world, but they parsed their perceptions differently; the worldviews that ultimately arose were the end result of that divergence. Humans had developed a sequential mode of awareness, while heptapods had developed a simultaneous mode of awareness. We experienced events in an order, and perceived their relationship as cause and effect. They experienced all events at once, and perceived a purpose underlying them all. A minimizing, maximizing purpose.

I have a recurring dream about your death. In the dream, I'm the one who's rock climbing — me, can you imagine it? — and you're three years old, riding in some kind of backpack I'm wearing. We're just a few feet below a ledge where we can rest, and you won't wait until I've climbed up to it. You start pulling yourself out of the pack; I order you to stop, but of course you ignore me. I feel your weight alternating from one side of the pack to the other as you climb out; then I feel your left foot on my shoulder, and then your right. I'm screaming at you, but I can't get a hand free to grab you. I can see the wavy design on the soles of your sneakers as you climb, and then I see a flake of stone give way beneath one of them. You slide right past me, and I can't move a muscle. I look down and see you shrink into the distance below me.

Then, all of a sudden, I'm at the morgue. An orderly lifts the sheet from your face, and I see that you're twenty-five.

"You okay?"

I was sitting upright in bed; I'd woken Gary with my movements. "I'm fine. I was just startled; I didn't recognize where I was for a moment."

Sleepily, he said, "We can stay at your place next time."

I kissed him. "Don't worry; your place is fine." We curled up, my back against his chest, and went back to sleep.

When you're three and we're climbing a steep, spiral flight of stairs, I'll hold your hand extra tightly. You'll pull your hand away from me. "I can do it by myself," you'll insist, and then move away from me to prove it, and I'll remember that dream. We'll repeat that scene countless times during your childhood. I can almost believe that, given your contrary nature, my attempts to protect you will be what create your love of climbing: first the jungle gym at the playground, then trees out in the green belt around our neighborhood, the rock walls at the climbing club, and ultimately cliff faces in national parks.

. . . .

I finished the last radical in the sentence, put down the chalk, and sat down in my desk chair. I leaned back and surveyed the giant Heptapod B sentence I'd written that covered the entire blackboard in my office. It included several complex clauses, and I had managed to integrate all of them rather nicely.

Looking at a sentence like this one, I understood why the heptapods had evolved a semasiographic writing system like Heptapod B; it was better suited for a species with a simultaneous mode of consciousness. For them, speech was a bottleneck because it required that one word follow another sequentially. With writing, on the other hand, every mark on a page was visible simultaneously. Why constrain writing with a glottographic straitjacket, demanding that it be just as sequential as speech? It would never occur to them. Semasiographic writing naturally took advantage of the page's two-dimensionality; instead of doling out morphemes one at a time, it offered an entire page full of them all at once.

And now that Heptapod B had introduced me to a simultaneous mode of consciousness, I understood the rationale behind Heptapod A's grammar: what my sequential mind had perceived as unnecessarily convoluted, I now recognized as an attempt to provide flexibility within the confines of sequential speech. I could use Heptapod A more easily as a result, though it was still a poor substitute for Heptapod B.

There was a knock at the door and then Gary poked his head in. "Colonel Weber'll be here any minute."

I grimaced. "Right." Weber was coming to participate in a session with Flapper and Raspberry; I was to act as translator, a job I wasn't trained for and that I detested.

Gary stepped inside and closed the door. He pulled me out of my chair and kissed me.

I smiled. "You trying to cheer me up before he gets here?"

"No, I'm trying to cheer me up."

"You weren't interested in talking to the heptapods at all, were you? You worked on this project just to get me into bed."

"Ah, you see right through me."

I looked into his eyes. "You better believe it," I said.

I remember when you'll be a month old, and I'll stumble out of bed to give you your 2:00 a.m. feeding. Your nursery will have that "baby smell" of diaper rash cream and talcum powder, with a faint ammoniac whiff coming from the diaper pail in the corner. I'll lean over your crib, lift your squalling form out, and sit in the rocking chair to nurse you.

The word "infant" is derived from the Latin word for "unable to speak," but you'll be perfectly capable of saying one thing: "I suffer," and you'll do it tirelessly and without hesitation. I have to admire your utter commitment to that statement; when you cry, you'll become outrage incarnate, every fiber of your body employed in expressing that emotion. It's funny: when you're tranquil, you will seem to radiate light, and if someone were to paint a portrait of you like that, I'd insist that they include the halo. But when you're unhappy, you will become a klaxon, built for radiating sound; a portrait of you then could simply be a fire alarm bell.

At that stage of your life, there'll be no past or future for you; until I give you my breast, you'll have no memory of contentment in the past nor expectation of relief in the future. Once you begin nursing, everything will reverse, and all will be right with the world. NOW is the only moment you'll perceive; you'll live in the present tense. In many ways, it's an enviable state.

The heptapods are neither free nor bound as we understand those concepts; they don't act according to their will, nor are they helpless automatons. What distinguishes the heptapods' mode of awareness is not just that their actions coincide with history's events; it is also that their motives coincide with history's purposes. They act to create the future, to enact chronology.

Freedom isn't an illusion; it's perfectly real in the context of sequential consciousness. Within the context of simultaneous consciousness, freedom is not meaningful, but neither is coercion; it's simply a different context, no more or less valid than the other. It's like that famous optical illusion, the drawing of either an elegant young woman, face turned away from the viewer, or a wart-nosed crone, chin tucked down on her chest. There's no "correct" interpretation; both are equally valid. But you can't see both at the same time.

Similarly, knowledge of the future was incompatible with free will. What made it possible for me to exercise freedom of choice also made it impossible for me to know the future. Conversely, now that I know the future, I would never act contrary to that future, including telling others what I know: those who know the future don't talk about it. Those who've read the *Book of Ages* never admit to it.

I turned on the VCR and slotted a cassette of a session from the Fort Worth looking glass. A diplomatic negotiator was having a discussion with the heptapods there, with Burghart acting as translator.

The negotiator was describing humans' moral beliefs, trying to lay some groundwork for the concept of altruism. I knew the heptapods were familiar with the conversation's eventual outcome, but they still participated enthusiastically.

If I could have described this to someone who didn't already know, she might ask, if the heptapods already knew everything that they would ever say or hear, what was the point of their using language at all? A reasonable question. But language wasn't only for communication: it was also a form of action. According to speech act theory, statements like "You're under arrest," "I christen this vessel," or "I promise" were all performative: a speaker could perform the action only by uttering the words. For such acts, knowing what would be said didn't change anything. Everyone at a wedding anticipated the words "I now pronounce you husband and wife," but until the minister actually said them, the ceremony didn't count. With performative language, saying equaled doing.

For the heptapods, all language was performative. Instead of using language to inform, they used language to actualize. Sure, heptapods already knew what would be said in any conversation; but in order for their knowledge to be true, the conversation would have to take place.

"First Goldilocks tried the papa bear's bowl of porridge, but it was full of brussels sprouts, which she hated."

You'll laugh. "No, that's wrong!" We'll be sitting side by side on the sofa, the skinny, overpriced hardcover spread open on our laps.

I'll keep reading. "Then Goldilocks tried the mama bear's bowl of porridge, but it was full of spinach, which she also hated."

You'll put your hand on the page of the book to stop me. "You have to read it the right way!"

"I'm reading just what it says here," I'll say, all innocence.

"No you're not. That's not how the story goes."

"Well if you already know how the story goes, why do you need me to read it to you?"

"Cause I wanna hear it!"

The air conditioning in Weber's office almost compensated for having to talk to the man.

"They're willing to engage in a type of exchange," I explained, "but it's not trade. We simply give them something, and they give us something in return. Neither party tells the other what they're giving beforehand."

Colonel Weber's brow furrowed just slightly. "You mean they're willing to exchange gifts?"

I knew what I had to say. "We shouldn't think of it as 'gift-giving.' We don't know if this transaction has the same associations for the heptapods that gift-giving has for us."

"Can we — " he searched for the right wording " — drop hints about the kind of gift we want?"

"They don't do that themselves for this type of transaction. I asked them if we could make a request, and they said we could, but it won't make them tell us what they're giving." I suddenly remembered that a morphological relative of "performative" was "performance," which could describe the sensation of conversing when you knew what would be said: it was like performing in a play.

"But would it make them more likely to give us what we asked for?" Colonel Weber asked. He was perfectly oblivious of the script, yet his responses matched his assigned lines exactly.

"No way of knowing," I said. "I doubt it, given that it's not a custom they engage in."

"If we give our gift first, will the value of our gift influence the value of theirs?" He was improvising, while I had carefully rehearsed for this one and only show.

"No," I said. "As far as we can tell, the value of the exchanged items is irrelevant."

"If only my relatives felt that way," murmured Gary wryly.

I watched Colonel Weber turn to Gary. "Have you discovered anything new in the physics discussions?" he asked, right on cue.

"If you mean, any information new to mankind, no," said Gary. "The heptapods haven't varied from the routine. If we demonstrate something to them, they'll show us their formulation of it, but they won't volunteer anything and they won't answer our questions about what they know."

An utterance that was spontaneous and communicative in the context of human discourse became a ritual recitation when viewed by the light of Heptapod B.

Weber scowled. "All right then, we'll see how the State Department feels about this. Maybe we can arrange some kind of gift-giving ceremony."

Like physical events, with their casual and teleological interpretations, every linguistic event had two possible interpretations: as a transmission of information and as the realization of a plan.

"I think that's a good idea, Colonel," I said.

It was an ambiguity invisible to most. A private joke; don't ask me to explain it.

Even though I'm proficient with Heptapod B, I know I don't experience reality the way a heptapod does. My mind was cast in the mold of human, sequential languages, and no amount of immersion in an alien language can completely reshape it. My worldview is an amalgam of human and heptapod.

Before I learned how to think in Heptapod B, my memories grew like a column of cigarette ash, laid down by the infinitesimal sliver of combustion that was my consciousness, marking the sequential present. After I learned Heptapod B, new memories fell into place like gigantic blocks, each one measuring years in duration, and though they didn't arrive in order or land contiguously, they soon composed a period of five decades. It is the period during which I know Heptapod B well enough to think in it, starting during my interviews with Flapper and Raspberry and ending with my death.

Usually, Heptapod B affects just my memory: my consciousness crawls along as it did before, a glowing sliver crawling forward in time, the difference being that the ash of memory lies ahead as well as behind: there is no real combustion. But occasionally I have glimpses when Heptapod B truly reigns, and I experience past and future all at once; my consciousness becomes a half-century-long ember burning outside time. I perceive — during those glimpses — that entire epoch as a simultaneity. It's a period encompassing the rest of my life, and the entirety of yours.

I wrote out the semagrams for "process create-endpoint inclusive-we," meaning "let's start." Raspberry replied in the affirmative, and the slide shows began. The second display screen that the heptapods had provided began presenting a series of images, composed of semagrams and equations, while one of our video screens did the same.

This was the second "gift exchange" I had been present for, the eighth one overall, and I knew it would be the last. The looking-glass tent was crowded with people; Burghart from Fort Worth was here, as were Gary and a nuclear physicist, assorted biologists, anthropologists, military brass, and diplomats. Thankfully they had set up an air conditioner to cool the place off. We would review the tapes of the images later to figure out just what the heptapods' "gift" was. Our own "gift" was a presentation on the Lascaux cave paintings.

We all crowded around the heptapods' second screen, trying to glean some idea of the images' content as they went by. "Preliminary assessments?" asked Colonel Weber.

"It's not a return," said Burghart. In a previous exchange, the heptapods had given us information about ourselves that we had previously told them. This had infuriated the State Department, but we had no reason to think of it as an insult: it probably indicated that trade value really didn't play a role in these exchanges. It didn't exclude the possibility that the heptapods might yet offer us a space drive, or cold fusion, or some other wish-fulfilling miracle.

"That looks like inorganic chemistry," said the nuclear physicist, pointing at an equation before the image was replaced.

Gary nodded. "It could be materials technology," he said.

"Maybe we're finally getting somewhere," said Colonel Weber.

"I wanna see more animal pictures," I whispered, quietly so that only Gary could hear me, and pouted like a child. He smiled and poked me. Truthfully, I wished the heptapods had given another xenobiology lecture, as they had on two previous exchanges; judging from those, humans were more similar to the heptapods than any other species they'd ever encountered. Or another lecture on heptapod history; those had been filled with apparent non-sequiturs, but were interesting nonetheless. I didn't want the heptapods to give us new technology, because I didn't want to see what our government might do with it.

I watched Raspberry while the information was being exchanged, looking for any anomalous behavior. It stood barely moving as usual; I saw no indications of what would happen shortly.

After a minute, the heptapod's screen went blank, and a minute after that, ours did, too. Gary and most of the other scientists clustered around a tiny video screen that was replaying the heptapods' presentation. I could hear them talk about the need to call in a solid-state physicist.

Colonel Weber turned. "You two," he said, pointing to me and then to Burghart, "schedule the time and location for the next exchange." Then he followed the others to the playback screen.

"Coming right up," I said. To Burghart, I asked, "Would you care to do the honors, or shall I?"

I knew Burghart had gained a proficiency in Heptapod B similar to mine. "It's your looking glass," he said. "You drive."

I sat down again at the transmitting computer. "Bet you never figured you'd wind up working as a Army translator back when you were a grad student."

"That's for goddamn sure," he said. "Even now I can hardly believe it." Everything we said to each other felt like the carefully bland exchanges of spies who meet in public, but never break cover.

I wrote out the semagrams for "locus exchange-transaction converse inclusive-we" with the projective aspect modulation.

Raspberry wrote its reply. That was my cue to frown, and for Burghart to ask, "What does it mean by that?" His delivery was perfect.

I wrote a request for clarification; Raspberry's reply was the same as before. Then I watched it glide out of the room. The curtain was about to fall on this act of our performance.

Colonel Weber stepped forward. "What's going on? Where did it go?"

"It said that the heptapods are leaving now," I said. "Not just itself; all of them."

"Call it back here now. Ask it what it means."

"Um, I don't think Raspberry's wearing a pager," I said.

The image of the room in the looking glass disappeared so abruptly that it took a moment for my eyes to register what I was seeing instead: it was the other side of the looking-glass tent. The looking glass had become completely transparent. The conversation around the playback screen fell silent.

"What the hell is going on here?" said Colonel Weber.

Gary walked up to the looking glass, and then around it to the other side. He touched the rear surface with one hand; I could see the pale ovals where his fingertips made contact with the looking glass. "I think," he said, "we just saw a demonstration of transmutation at a distance."

I heard the sounds of heavy footfalls on dry grass. A soldier came in through the tent door, short of breath from sprinting, holding an oversize walkie-talkie. "Colonel, message from — "

Weber grabbed the walkie-talkie from him.

I remember what it'll be like watching you when you are a day old. Your father will have gone for a quick visit to the hospital cafeteria, and you'll be lying in your bassinet, and I'll be leaning over you.

So soon after the delivery, I will still be feeling like a wrung-out towel. You will seem incongruously tiny, given how enormous I felt during the pregnancy; I could swear there was room for someone much larger and more robust than you in there. Your hands and feet will be long and thin, not chubby yet. Your face will still be all red and pinched, puffy eyelids squeezed shut, the gnomelike phase that precedes the cherubic.

I'll run a finger over your belly, marveling at the uncanny softness of your skin, wondering if silk would abrade your body like burlap. Then you'll writhe, twisting your body while poking out your legs one at a time, and I'll recognize the gesture as one I had felt you do inside me, many times. So *that's* what it looks like.

I'll feel elated at this evidence of a unique mother-child bond, this certitude that you're the one I carried. Even if I had never laid eyes on you before, I'd be able to pick you out from a sea of babies: Not that one. No, not her either. Wait, that one over there.

Yes, that's her. She's mine.

That final "gift exchange" was the last we ever saw of the heptapods. All at once, all over the world, their looking glasses became transparent and their ships left orbit. Subsequent analysis of the looking glasses revealed them to be nothing more than sheets of fused silica, completely inert. The information from the final exchange session described a new class of superconducting materials, but it later proved to duplicate the results of research just completed in Japan: nothing that humans didn't already know.

We never did learn why the heptapods left, any more than we learned what brought them here, or why they acted the way they did. My own new awareness didn't provide that type of knowledge; the heptapods' behavior was presumably explicable from a sequential point of view, but we never found that explanation.

I would have liked to experience more of the heptapods' worldview, to feel the way they feel. Then, perhaps I could immerse myself fully in the necessity of events, as they must, instead of merely wading in its surf for the rest of my life. But that will never come to pass. I will continue to practice the heptapod languages, as will the other linguists on the looking-glass teams, but none of us will ever progress any further than we did when the heptapods were here.

Working with the heptapods changed my life. I met your father and learned Heptapod B, both of which make it possible for me to know you now, here on the patio in the moonlight. Eventually, many years from now, I'll be without your father, and without you. All I will have left from this moment is the heptapod language. So I pay close attention, and note every detail.

From the beginning I knew my destination, and I chose my route accordingly. But am I working toward an extreme of joy, or of pain? Will I achieve a minimum, or a maximum?

These questions are in my mind when your father asks me, "Do you want to make a baby?" And I smile and answer, "Yes," and I unwrap his arms from around me, and we hold hands as we walk inside to make love, to make you.

Benjamin Rosenbaum

Start the Clock

(2004)

Benjamin Rosenbaum (b. 1969) is a relatively new voice in sf, having published his first story in 2001. Since then, however, he has been prolific. His full-length stories have been collected in *The Ant King: And Other Stories* (2008), following a collection of short-shorts in 2003 (*Other Cities*). Rosenbaum has been nominated for several major awards, including the Hugo, the Nebula, and the Sturgeon, for which "Start the Clock" made the short list. Rosenbaum majored in computer science and religious studies at Brown University, and worked for many years as a computer programmer. He has traveled extensively and lived abroad in Italy, Switzerland, and Israel. Rosenbaum is associated with a genre-transcending literary trend that became prominent in the 1990s variously labeled as slipstream, postmodern fabulism, or the New Weird. These terms describe a type of fiction that incorporates fantastic elements in an otherwise realistic story without explanation. Often ironic and self-referential, slipstream is sometimes linked to the Latin American tradition exemplified by Jorge Luis Borges and to mainstream postmodernists like Donald Barthelme as well as to New Wave science fiction of the 1960s and 1970s. In keeping with slipstream's crossover appeal, Rosenbaum's stories have been published in cutting-edge mainstream periodicals like *McSweeney's* as well as more traditional sf magazines. The story that follows, however, is solidly located in the tradition of science fiction.

"Start the Clock" begins as a playfully nostalgic fantasy about eternal childhood, but it is ultimately a story about accepting change — not on a social or technological level so much as on a personal level. If we could freeze our personalities in time, would we? What would be the costs? Rosenbaum's insights into childhood are amusing, startling, and instantly recognizable as true. Yet to be fully human, Rosenbaum implies, means embracing all the stages of life and accepting the losses along with the gains. The tone of the story, both humorous and poignant, is perfectly maintained from beginning to end.

The real estate agent for Pirateland was old. Nasty old. It's harder to tell with Geezers, but she looked to be somewhere in her Thirties. They don't have our suppleness of skin, but with the right oils and powders they can avoid most of the wrinkles. This one hadn't taken much care. There were furrows around her eyes and eyebrows.

She had that Mommystyle thing going on: blue housedress, frilly apron, Betty Crocker white gloves. If you're going to be running around this part of Montana sporting those gigantic, wobbly breasts and hips, I guess it's a necessary form of obeisance.

She said something to someone in the back of her van, then hurried up the walk toward us. "It's a lovely place," she called. "And a very nice area."

"Look, Suze, it's your mom," Tommy whispered in my ear. His breath tickled, I pushed him.

651

It was deluxe, I'll give her that. We were standing under the fifty-foot prow of the galleon we'd come to see. All around us a flotilla of men-of-war, sloops, frigates, and cutters rode the manicured lawns and steel-gray streets. Most of the properties were closed up, the lawns pristine. Only a few looked inhabited — lawns strewn with gadgets, excavations begun with small bulldozers and abandoned, Pack or Swarm or Family flags flying from the mainmasts. Water cannons menacing passersby.

I put my hands in my pants pockets and picked at the lint. "So this is pretty much all Nines?"

The Thirtysomething Lady frowned. "Ma'am, I'm afraid the Anti-Redlining Act of 2035 — "

"Uh-huh, race, gender, aetial age, chronological age, stimulative preference, or national origin — I know the law. But who else wants to live in Pirateland, right?"

Thirtysomething Lady opened her mouth and didn't say anything.

"Or can afford it," Shiri called. She had gone straight for the rope ladder and was halfway up. Her cherry-red sneakers felt over the side for the gunnel running around the house. Thirtysomething Lady's hands twitched in a kind of helpless half-grasping motion. Geezers always do that when we climb.

"Are you poor?" Tommy asked. "Is that why you dress like that?"

"Quit taunting the Lady," Max growled. Max is our token Eight, and he takes aetial discrimination more seriously than the rest of us. Plus, he's just nicer than we are. He's also Pumped Up: he's only four feet tall, but he has bioengineered muscles like grapefruit. He has to eat a pound or two of medicated soysteak a day just to keep his bulk on.

Thirtysomething Lady put her hand up to her eyes and blinked ferociously, as if she were going to cry. Now that would be something! They almost never cry. We'd hardly been mean to her at all. I felt sorry for her, so I walked over and put my hand in hers. She flinched and pulled her hand away. So much for cross-aetial understanding and forgiveness.

"Let's just look at the house," I said, putting my hands in my pockets.

"Galleon," she said tightly.

"Galleon then."

Her fingers twitched out a passkey mudra and the galleon lowered a boarding plank. Nice touch.

Frankly, we were excited. This move was what our Pack needed — the four of us, at least, were sure of it. We were all tired of living in the ghetto — we were in three twentieth-century townhouses in Billings, in an "age-mixed" area full of marauding Thirteens and Fourteens and Fifteens. Talk about a people damned by CDAS — when the virus hit them, it had stuck their pituitaries and thyroids like throttles jammed open. It wasn't just the giantism and health problems caused by a thirty-year overdose on growth hormones, testosterone, estrogen, and androgen. They suffered more from their social problems — criminality, violence, orgies, jealousy — and their endless self-pity.

Okay, Max liked them. And most of the rest of us had been at least entertained by living in the ghetto. At birthday parties, we could always shock the other Packs with our address. But that was when all eight of us were there, before Katrina and Ogbu went south. With eight of us, we'd felt like a full Pack — invincible, strong enough to laugh at anyone.

I followed the others into the galleon's foyer. Video game consoles on the walls, swimming pool under a retractable transparent superceramic floor. The ceiling — or upper deck, I guess — was thirty feet up, accessible by rope ladders and swing ropes. A parrot fluttered onto a roost — it looked real, but probably wasn't. I walked through a couple of bulk-heads. Lots of sleeping nooks; lockers, shelves; workstations, both flatscreen and retinal-projection. I logged onto one as guest. Plenty of bandwidth. That's good for me. I may dress like a male twentieth-century stockbroker, double-breasted suit and suspenders, but I'm actually a found footage editor. (Not a lot of Nines are artists — our obsessive problem solving and intense competitiveness make us good market speculators, gamblers, programmers, and biotechs. That's where we've made our money and our reputation. Not many of us have the patience or interest for art.)

I logged out. Max had stripped and dived into the pool — or maybe it was meant as a giant bathtub. Tommy and Shiri were bouncing on the trampoline, making smart-aleck remarks. The real estate agent had given up on getting anyone to listen to her pitch. She was sitting in a floppy gel chair, massaging the sole of one foot with her hands. I walked into the kitchen. Huge table, lots of chairs and sitballs, enormous programmable foodcenter.

I walked out, back to the Lady, "No stove."

"Stove?" she said, blinking.

I ran one hand down a suspender. "I cook," I said.

"You cook?"

I felt my jaw and shoulders tense — I'm sick of being told Nines don't cook — but then I saw her eyes. They were sparkling with delight. Indulgent delight. It reminded me of my own mother, oohing and aahing over brick-hard cookies I'd baked her one winter morning in the slums of Maryland, back when my aetial age was still tied to Nature's clock. My mother holding up the wedding dress she'd planned to give me away in, its lacy waist brushing my chin. One evening in college, when I'd looked up at the dinner table, halfway through a sentence — I'd been telling her about *The Hat on the Cat*, my distributed documentary (a firebrand polemic for Under-Five Emancipation; how cybernetics would liberate the Toddlers from lives of dependence) — and saw in her eyes how long ago she'd stopped listening. Saw that I wasn't Nine to her, but nine. Saw that she wasn't looking at me, but through me, a long way off — toward another now, another me: a Woman. Big globes of fatty breasts dangling from that other-me's chest; tall as a doorway, man-crazy, marriageable; a great sexualized monster like herself, a walking womb, a proto-Mommy. She was waiting for that Susan, Woman-Susan, who would never show up.

"I cook," I said, looking away from the Lady's eyes, putting my hands in my pants pockets. I could have used a hug, but Max was underwater and

Tommy and Shiri were trying to knock each other off the trampoline. I went outside.

"We could bring in a stove module," the Lady called.

Outside, a pigeon was poking through the lawn. It was mangy and nervous enough to be real. I stood for a while watching it, then my earring buzzed. I made the Accept mudra.

"Suze?" Travis said.

"Why are you asking, Travis? Who do you think is wearing my earring?"

"Suze, Abby's gone."

"What do you mean, gone?"

"She's not picking up. Her locator's off. I can't find her anywhere." When Travis was nervous, his voice squeaked. Now he sounded like a mouse caught in a trap.

I looked at the active tattoo readout on my left palm. Travis was home. I made the mudra for Abby. No location listed. "Stay there, Travis. We're on our way."

I ran up the plank. Max was dressed again, rubbing his dreadlocks with a towel from the poolside toweltree. Tommy and Shiri were sitting at a table with the Real Estate Lady, looking over paperwork in the tabletop display.

"We've got to go. A personal emergency has come up," I said. Max was at my side instantly.

"Listen, we want this place," Shiri said.

"Shiri, we all have to talk about it," I said.

"What's to talk about?" Tommy said. "It's *awesome*."

"This is the first place we've looked at," I said.

"So?"

The Real Estate Lady was watching us with a guarded expression. I didn't want to say that Abby was missing. Not in front of her. Not in front of that can-you-really-be-trusted-to-look-after-yourselves-all-on-your-own-without-any-grownups attitude that came off her like a stink. I took my hands out of my pockets and balled them into fists. "You're being totally stupid!" I said.

"What's the emergency?" Max said quietly.

"I know what Travis and Abby would say," Tommy said. "They totally want a place like this. Let's just get it and we'll have the rest of the day free."

"We can go windgliding," Shiri said.

"Travis and Abby didn't even agree to getting a house yet, never mind this house," I said. I felt Max's hand on my shoulder.

"That's because they haven't seen it," Tommy said.

"What's the emergency?" Max said.

"There's probably been a train wreck and Suze has to make sure she's the first ghoul at her flatscreen," Shiri said.

"Screw you," I said and walked out of the house. I was shaking a little with adrenaline. I got in our clowncar and clicked on the engine. Max hurried out the door behind me. I slid over to the passenger seat and he got in to drive.

"We can pick them up later," he said. "Or they can take a cab. What's up?"

I made the Abby mudra and showed him my palm. "Abby's missing. Travis hasn't seen her, and she's not picking up."

Max pulled out into the street. "She left the house this morning early, with that old black-and-white camera you got her. She was going to shoot some pictures."

I flipped open the flatscreen in the passenger-side dash and logged in. "That's no reason for her to turn off her locator. I hope she didn't stay near the house — a Nine walking around alone in the ghetto, taking photographs — imagine how that looks."

We hummed and whooshed out of Pirateland, up a ramp onto I-90. "Abby wouldn't be that dumb," Max said. But he didn't sound too sure. Abby's impetuous, and she'd been melancholy lately. "Police?" he asked, after a moment.

I shot him a sharp look. The police are Geezers — height requirements keep Under Twelves out of their ranks, and the Teens are mostly too uneducated and unruly. I didn't have any strings to pull with them, and neither did Max. "We wait until we have more data," I said. "Now shut up and let me work. Head home."

Most people have the notion that the public footage is this permanent, universal, easily searchable archive of everything that ever happens, clearly shot, from any angle. It's the job of people in my profession to help perpetuate that illusion. Actually, the networks are surprisingly spotty. There are millions of swarmcams wandering around in any major urban area, but they have a high failure and bug rate, and their pictures are grainy and indistinct — only a lot of imaginative algorithmic reconstruction makes them viewable. There are plenty of larger cameras linked to the net, but often hidden in a byzantine maze of permissions and protocols. And there are billions of motion sensors, audio pickups, locator tags, and data traffic monitors added to the mix, but they're not well correlated with each other. In a few hours on a Sunday morning, one square mile of downtown Billings generates enough data to fill all the computers of the twentieth century, plus all the paper libraries of the centuries before. It's hell to search.

But I'm good. I had enough footage of Abby on file to construct a good bloodhound, and then I spawned a dozen of them and seeded them well. Pretty soon the hits started coming back. Abby had crossed the street in front of our house at 09:06, and turned her locator tag off — on purpose, I imagined, since there was no error log. She'd stopped for bagels and udon in a deli on Avenue C at 09:22; shot pictures in the park until 09:56. She'd talked to a couple of Fifteens there and taken something from them. I couldn't see what, in the grainy gray swarmcam pictures, but it made the hair on the back of my neck rise.

From 10:03 I lost her; she'd gone up an elevator in a bank and disappeared. There's a network of private walkways and an aerial tram in that part of Billings that are poorly monitored. I had a cold feeling in my gut; that was a great way to lose me, if you were trying to.

I searched all the exits to those walkways and the tramway for Abby, buying a bunch of extra processing power on the exchange to run it faster. Nothing.

Max had entered among the spires and alleys of Billings. Dappled shadows of metal and translucent plastics and ceramics rippled over the clowncar. I looked out at the people walking through the corridors around us, all ages and sizes and colors. An old woman was walking slowly on a slidewalk just above us — she must have been an aetial Ninety, which made her a hundred and twenty or so. Walking, slowly, under her own steam. You don't see that every day.

I went back to some old footage I had of a birthday party and grabbed a sequence of Abby walking. I built an ergodynamic profile of her and fed that to my bloodhounds.

Bingo. At 10:42, Abby had left the aerial tramway in disguise. Platform shoes, trenchcoat, false breasts and hips and shoulders — she was impersonating a Fourteen or so. It looked ridiculous, like Halloween. She'd consulted a piece of paper from her pocket.

By 10:54 she was in a bad area. "Head for 30th and Locust," I told Max.

"Shit," he said. "No police?"

"I don't have anything yet that would warrant their attention. Nothing that proves she was coerced."

"So we need other backup," Max said grimly.

"Yeah." I looked up. "Can you get it?"

"I think so," he said. He made some Call mudras with one hand and started talking. "Hey, Dave, how you doing? Listen, man — " I tuned him out as he made his calls.

My last shot of Abby was at 11:06. She was being hustled into a doorway by a gargantuan Fifteen. His hand was on her elbow. Biodynamic readouts from a few stray hospital swarmcams confirmed that her pulse was elevated. Should I send this to the police? Would it prove Abby was coerced? But what was she doing with the weird disguise and the sneaking around? Just slumming? Or would I get her in trouble?

Was Abby buying drugs?

"Parkhill and 32nd," I said to Max. My fingers were still and I was just looking at that last picture, Abby and the giant, him pulling her into darkness.

"Can you meet us at Parkhill and 32nd?" Max was saying. "Damn, I know, man — that's why we need you."

When we got there, five of Max's friends were waiting. Four were clearly from his gym. Two of them were probably Nines or Tens (one swarthy, one red-haired and freckled) and they were even musclier than Max, their heads perched like small walnuts on their blockbuster bodies. The other two were Pumped Up Teens — maybe Fifteen or Sixteen. Their blond, Slavic-boned faces sat on bodies like overstuffed family room sofas or industrial refrigerators: fingers the size of my forearm, thighs the size of my entire body. I wasn't sure how we were going to get them in the building.

And then there was the fifth — an Augmented Three. She stood a little apart from the others, her tiny arms at her sides. They were clearly afraid of her. One soft brown eye scanned the clouds, and she had a beatific smile on her face. Her other eye was the glistening jewel of a laserlight connector, and there were other plugs and ports glistening in her brown scalp among her cornrows.

Max stopped the car.

"Who's the Three?" I asked.

Max turned to me. He looked nervous, like he thought I was going to make fun of him. "That's my sister, Carla."

"Cool," I said quickly. He got out before I could say anything yet stupider, like, "How nice that you've stayed close."

I opened my door and froze — Carla was running toward us. "Max!" she warbled, and flung her arms around his waist, burying her face in his stomach.

"Hi, honey-girl," he said, hugging her back.

I glanced at my palm readout. It had gone blank. So had the flatscreen in the car. It was a safe bet nothing near Carla would be recorded. You could sometimes tell where Augmented Threes and Twos were in the public footage by tracking the blank areas, the little blobs of inexplicable malfunction that followed them around. I once did an experimental documentary on Under-Five Augmentation using that blanked-out footage. It was called *Be Careful What You Wish For* — kind of a rueful, years-later followup to *The Hat on the Cat*.

"Carry me!" Carla said, and Max dutifully swung her tiny body onto his shoulders.

"Carla, this is Suze," Max said.

"I don't like her," Carla announced. Max's face went slack with fear, and my heart lurched. I grabbed the car door so hard my fingernails sank into the frame.

Carla exploded in giggles, then started to hiccup. "Just — *kidding!*" she choked out between hiccups. "You guys are so *silly!*"

I tried to smile. Max turned, slowly, toward the door. It was a formidable steel monstrosity, the kind with a biodynamic access plate governing its security system. Those things are supposed to be off-net, more or less invulnerable to cybernetic hacking. Carla waved at it and it popped open. The four muscleboys crowded their way inside — eager to get to Abby, and away from Carla — and the three of us brought up the rear, Carla still perched on Max's shoulders.

The stairway was dark and rank — it smelled like Teenagers, all their glands and excretions, smeared and sour. Most of the wallglow was dead, and one malfunctioning patch at the top of the stairs was flashing green and red, so that the bodies of the muscleboys ascended the stairs in strobed staccato.

The freckled gymrat was first to the doorway at the top. As he reached for the doorknob, we heard a long moan, and then a series of grunts. Almost snarls. And then, softer, a whimper — a high, female whimper — like the sound of someone tortured, someone in despair.

Carla started to cry. "I don't like it!"

"What is it, honey-baby?" Max said, his voice afraid, *"What's behind that door?"*

"Don't ask her that!" I barked. "Distract her, you idiot!"

"Max, should I make it go away?" Carla wailed. "Should I make them stop, Max?"

"No!" Max and I shouted at the same time.

"Max," I said as pleasantly as I could manage, "why don't you and Carla go play a nice game in the car?"

"But maybe I should — " Max said, looking at me from between Carla's tiny, shaking knees.

"Now!" I barked, and pushed past them.

Panting came from under the door, panting and groans. The muscleboys looked at me nervously. I heard Max's shoes clumping down the stairs behind me, and he started singing "The Itsy-Bitsy Spider."

"In!" I hissed, pointing at the door. The two overmuscled Nines threw their shoulders against it. It strained and buckled, but held. From inside the door came a strangled scream. The two Pumped-Up Teens braced themselves against the wall and each other, bent their knees, and crouched down with their shoulders under the Nines' butts. "Ready — now!" called the biggest, and all four of them pushed. The door shot open, and the muscleboys tumbled and collapsed through it. I sprinted over their bodies, springing from a buttock to a shoulder to a back to another shoulder, and I was through.

On a tiger-skin throwrug in the midst of a pile of trash, two huge naked Fifteens looked up. The male's skin was a mass of pimples and grease; shaggy hair fell over his shoulders and muscles. The female was pinned under him, her gigantic breasts flopping to either side of her thin ribcage, her knees pinioned around his hips. Between the wiry forests of their pubic hair, a portion of the male's penis ran like a swollen purple bridge.

"Ewww!" I shouted, as they flopped down, pulling the tigerskin over themselves. "Where's Abby??"

"Hi, Suze," said Abby dryly from an overstuffed chair to my left. She was wearing a white jumpsuit, and holding a pen and a paper notebook.

"What the hell are you doing?" I shouted.

"I might ask you the same." She motioned to the pile of muscleboys, who were struggling to their feet with dazed expressions.

"Abby! You disappeared!" I was waving my arms around like a Macromuppet. "Locator — bad area — disguise — scary — aargh!"

"Are you going to follow me around with a small army every time I turn off my locator?"

"Yes!!"

She sighed and put down her pencil and paper. "I'm really sorry," she called to the Fifteens. "My time was almost up anyway. Um, do you mind if we talk in here for a few minutes?"

"Yes!" gurgled the female.

"Abby, come on," I said. "They can't just stop in the middle. They have to, you know, finish what they were — doing. Until it's finished their brains won't work properly."

"Okay," Abby said. "All right, ah — thanks."

In the stairway, I said, "You couldn't just watch a porn channel?"

"It's not the same," she said. "That's all packaged and commercial. I wanted to interview them before and after. I have to know — what it's like."

"Why?"

She paused on the stairs, and I stopped too. The muscleboys, muttering, went out onto the street, and we were alone in the flashing green and red light.

"Suze, I'm going to start the clock."

Like she'd poured a bucket of ice water down my spine. "You're what?"

"I'm going to take the treatments." She spoke quickly, as if afraid I'd interrupt her. "They've gotten much better in the past couple of years; there are basically no side effects. They're even making headway with infants. In five years, it looks like most babies won't have any arrestation effects at all, and — "

Tears had sprung to my eyes. "What are you talking about?" I cried. "Why are you talking like *them*? Why are you talking like being like us is something to be *cured*?" I punched the wall, which hurt my hand. I sat down on the step and cried.

"Suze," Abby said. She sat down next to me and put her hand on my shoulder. "I love being like us — but I want — "

"That?" I shouted, pointing up to the top of the stairs, where they were grunting again. "That's what you want? You'd rather have that than us?"

"I want everything, Suze. I want every stage of life — "

"Oh, every stupid *stage*, as designed by stupid God, who also gave us death and cancer, and — "

She grabbed my shoulders. "Suze, listen. I want to know what *that* up there is like. Maybe I won't like it, and then I won't do it. But Suze, I want to have babies."

"Babies? Abby, your eggs are forty years old — "

"Exactly! Exactly, my eggs are only forty years old, and most of them are still good. Who do you want to have the babies, Suze? The Geezers? The world is starting again, Suze, and I — "

"The world was fine!" I pulled away from her. "The world was just fine!" Snot and tears were running down my nose into my mouth, salty and gooey. I wiped my face on the sleeve of my stockbroker's suit, leaving a slick trail like a slug. "We were fine — "

"This isn't about us — "

"Oh baloney!!" I lurched to my feet, grabbing the railing for balance. "As if you're going to live with us in a galleon and fire water cannons and go to birthday parties! You're just not, Abby, don't kid yourself! You're going to be *that*!" I pointed up the stairs. "Sexual jealousy and sexual exchange economy and cheating and mutual-exploitation-and-ownership and serial monogamy and divorce and the whole stupid crazy boring . . ."

"Suze — " she said in a small voice.

"Just don't!" I said. "Don't drag it out! If you want to do it, do it, but then leave us alone! Okay? You're not welcome." I turned and headed down the stairs, "Get the hell out."

Max was standing at the bottom of the stairs. I didn't like the way he was looking at me. I brushed past.

The boys from the gym were in the car, eating yard-long submarine sandwiches with great gusto. Carla sat on the front steps, talking to a rag doll. She looked up, and her red jewel of an eye flashed — for a moment it was as bright as looking into the Sun at noon. Then she looked past me, into the sky.

"What are you afraid of?" she asked.

I leaned against the doorframe and said nothing. A wind came down the street and crumpled sheets of paper danced along it.

"I'm afraid of cows," she volunteered. "And Millie" — she held up the rag doll — "is afraid of, um, um, you know the thing where if you take all the money people spend and the way they looked at each other that day and you put it inside what the weather's going to do and then you can sing to cats and stuff? She's afraid of that."

I wiped my eyes on my sleeve. "Can you see the future, Carla?"

She giggled, and then she looked serious. "You guys are all wrong about that. It's just a game you made up. There isn't any future."

"Do you like being Augmented?" I asked.

"I like it but Millie doesn't like it. Millie thinks it's scary but she's just silly. Millie wishes we were like people and trees and we didn't have to make things okay all the time. But then we couldn't play with bolshoiye-gemeinschaft-episteme-mekhashvei-ibura."

"Okay," I said.

"Max is coming out with Abby four thousand five hundred and sixty-two milliseconds after I finish talking right now and projected group cohesion rises by thirty-six percent if you don't have a fight now so you should take the clowncar and I'll give them a ride and I'd love to live with you but I know I'm too scary but it's okay but can I visit on Max's birthday?"

"Yes," I said. "You can visit on my birthday too."

"I can? I can?" She jumped up and hugged me, flinging her arms around my waist, pressing her cheek into my chest. "Wow, I didn't even know you'd say that!" She pulled away, beaming at me, then pointed to the car. "Okay, quick, go! Bye!"

I got in the car and clicked on the engine. Carla waved and she held Millie's arm and waved it too. The door behind her opened, I saw Max's shoe, and I drove off.

A quarter mile away from Carla, the flatscreen blinked on again, and my earring started buzzing like crazy. I told it to let Travis through.

"Abby's fine," I said. "She's with Max. They'll be coming home."

"Cool," Travis said. "Whew! That's a relief!"

"Yeah."

"So Tommy and Shiri sent me video of the house. It looks *awesome*. Do you love it too?"

"Yeah, I love it." I was on I-90 now. Beyond the spires and aerial trams of Billings, I could see the funhouse suburbs spreading out before me — windmills, castles, ships, domes, faerie forests.

"Cool, because I think they signed some papers or something."

"What? Travis, we all have to agree!" As I said it, it occurred to me that the only one who hadn't seen the place was Abby. I gripped the wheel and burst out crying.

"What? What?" Travis said.

"Travis!" I wailed. "Abby wants to start the clock!"

"I know," Travis muttered.

"What? You *know*?"

"She told me this morning."

"Why didn't you say anything?"

"She made me promise not to."

"Travis!"

"I was hoping you'd talk her out of it."

I took the exit for Pirateland, swooshing through an orange plastic tunnel festooned with animated skeletons climbing out of Davy Jones's lockers. "You can't talk Abby out of anything."

"But we've got to, Suze, we've got to. C'mon, we can't just fall apart like this. Katrina and Ogbu — " he was doing his panic-stricken ratsqueak again, and suddenly I was very sick of it.

"Just shut up and stop whining, Travis!" I shouted. "Either she'll change her mind or she won't, but she won't, so you'll just have to deal with it."

Travis didn't say anything. I told my earring to drop the connection and block all calls.

I pulled up outside the galleon and got out. I found a handkerchief in the glove compartment and cleaned my face thoroughly. My suit, like the quality piece of work it was, had already eaten and digested all the snot I'd smeared on it — the protein would probably do it good. I checked myself in the mirror — I didn't want the Real Estate Lady to see me weepy. Then I got out and stood looking at the house. If I knew Tommy and Shiri, they were still inside, having discovered a roller-skating rink or rodeo room.

Parked at the side of the house was the Real Estate Lady's old-fashioned van — a real classic, probably gasoline-burning. I walked over to it. The side door was slid open. I looked in.

Inside, reading a book, was a Nine. She was tricked out in total Kidgear — pony tails, barrettes, t-shirt with a horse on it, socks with flashy dangly things. Together with the Lady's Mommystyle getup, it made perfect, if twisted, sense. Personally I find that particular game of Let's-Pretend sort of depressing and pitiful, but to each her own kink.

"Hey," I said. She looked up.

"Um, hi," she said.

"You live around here?"

She wrinkled her nose. "My mom, um, kinda doesn't really want me to tell that to strangers."

I rolled my eyes. "Give the role-playing a rest, would you? I just asked a simple question."

She glared at me. "You shouldn't make so many assumptions about people," she said, and pointedly lifted her book up in front of her face.

The clop-clop of the Lady's shoes came down the drive. My scalp was prickling. Something was not altogether kosher in this sausage.

"Oh, hello," the Lady said brightly, if awkwardly. "I see you've met my daughter."

"Is that your actual daughter, or can the two of you just not get out of character?"

The Lady crossed her arms and fixed me with her green-eyed stare. "Corintha contracted Communicative Developmental Arrestation Syndrome when she was two years old. She started the treatments seven years ago."

I realized my mouth was hanging open. "She's a clock-started Two? She spent twenty-five years as an unaugmented two-year-old?"

The Lady leaned past me into the van. "You okay in here, honey?"

"Great," said Corintha from behind her book. "Other than the occasional ignoramus making assumptions."

"Corintha, please don't be rude," the Lady said.

"Sorry," she said.

The Lady turned to me. I think my eyes must have been bugging out of my head. She laughed. "I've seen your documentaries, you know."

"You *have*?"

"Yes." She leaned up against the van. "They're technically very well done, and I think some of what you have to say is very compelling. That one with all the blanked-out footage — that gave me a real feeling for what it's like for those children who are wired up into the Internet."

An odd and wrongheaded way of putting it, but I limited myself to saying, "Uh — thanks."

"But I think you're very unfair to those of us who didn't Augment our children. To watch your work, you'd think every parent who didn't Augment succumbed to Parenting Fatigue and sent their toddlers off to the government daycare farms, visiting only at Christmas. Or that they lived some kind of barbaric, abusive, incestuous existence." She looked over at her daughter. "Corintha has been a joy to me every day of her life — "

"Oh, Mom!" Corintha said from behind her book.

" — but I never wanted to stand in the way of her growing up. I just didn't think Augmentation was the answer. Not for her."

"And you thought you had the right to decide," I said.

"Yes." She nodded vigorously. "I thought I had the obligation to decide."

The Suze everyone who knows me knows would have made some sharp rejoinder. None came. I watched Corintha peek out from behind her book.

There was silence for a while. Corintha went back to reading.

"My friends still inside?" I asked.

"Yes," the Lady said. "They want the place. I think it fits six very comfortably, and — "

"Five," I said huskily. "I think it's going to be five."

"Oh," the Lady looked nonplussed. "I'm — sorry to hear that."

Corintha put her book down. "How come?"

The Lady and I looked at her.

"Oh, is that a rude question?" Corintha said.

"It's a bit prying, dear," the Lady said.

"Ah — " I said. I looked at Corintha. "One of us wants to — start the clock. Start the conventional biological aging process."

"So?" Corintha said.

"Honey," said the Lady. "Sometimes if people — change — they don't want to live together anymore."

"That's really dumb," said Corintha. "If you didn't even have a fight or anything. If it's just that somebody wants to grow up. I would never get rid of my friends over that."

"Corintha!"

"Would you let her talk? I'm trying to respect your archaic ideas of parent-child relationships here, Lady, but you're not making it easy."

The Lady cleared her throat. "Sorry," she said after a moment.

I looked out at the mainmast and the cannons of our galleon. The rolling lawn. This place had everything. The trampolines and the pools, the swingropes and the games. I could just imagine the birthday parties we'd have here, singing and cake and presents and dares, everyone getting wet, foamguns and crazy mixed-up artificial animals. We could hire clowns and acrobats, storytellers and magicians. At night we'd sleep in hammocks on deck or on blankets on the lawn, under the stars, or all together in a pile, in the big pillowspace in the bow.

And I couldn't see Abby here. Not a growing-upward Abby, getting taller, sprouting breasts, wanting sex with some huge apes of men or women or both. Wanting privacy, wanting to bring her clock-started friends over to whisper and laugh about menstruation and courtship rituals. Abby with a mate. Abby with children.

"There's a place over by Rimrock Road," the Lady said slowly. "It's an old historic mansion. It's not quite as deluxe or as — thematic as this. But the main building has been fitted out for recreation-centered group living. And there are two outbuildings that allow some privacy and — different styles of life."

I stood up. I brushed off my pants. I put my hands in my pockets.

"I want us to go see that one," I said.

Critical Contexts for Time

Jean-Paul Sartre

From Being and Nothingness
(1943)

French writer and existential philosopher Jean-Paul Sartre (1905–1980) was one of the leading intellectual figures of the twentieth century. Sartre completed his *agregation* (the French equivalent of a Ph.D.) in philosophy in 1929; while a student, he met Simone de Beauvoir, who became his lifelong partner in an unconventional "open" relationship. Sartre held several teaching posts after taking his degree, but he preferred the life of a public intellectual to that of a traditional academic and eventually became a full-time writer. Among his most famous works are the plays *The Flies* (1943) and *No Exit* (1947), which he used to communicate his philosophical views to a popular audience. Sartre served in the French Army during World War II and later worked for the French Resistance, though the extent of his involvement with the Resistance movement is disputed. He was a vocal supporter of controversial political causes throughout his life, most notably Algeria's struggle for independence from France. He was an early supporter of Communist Russia, though he later became disillusioned by the Soviet regime. Sartre was awarded a Nobel Prize in literature in 1964, but he declined to accept it because he felt uneasy about the institutionalization of fame that it implied.

The selection that follows is taken from *Being and Nothingness: An Essay in Phenomenological Ontology*, an examination of the nature of existence that is Sartre's most important philosophical work. In this selection, Sartre explains the relationship we have to our past. Although the facts of the past cannot be changed — for an individual or a nation — the meaning of the past is determined by the choices we make in the present. Sartre is committed to personal responsibility and opposed to any form of determinism. We are not compelled by past actions to follow any course of action in the present. In this sense, only the present moment is truly meaningful; through the choices we make in the present we create both our past and our future, and every subsequent choice we make will again alter or confirm the narrative of self and the world that we have constructed. Radical free will is one of the chief tenets of Sartre's existentialism. People often see themselves as being constrained by circumstances or external events or even by their own past actions. But from the point of view

Translated by Hazel Barnes.

of existentialism, we are always free to alter these circumstances by making new and different choices. This freedom, which arises from our uniqueness as conscious beings whose self-awareness gives meaning to the universe, is as much a burden as a gift because of the heavy weight of responsibility it loads us with. No matter how dire our circumstances, we alone are answerable for our actions and can never shift the blame or appeal to a higher power to guide us in our choices.

Sartre's concept of the connection among past, present, and future in the narrative of becoming is of obvious relevance for stories about time travel and particularly for alternate history, where the reworking of the past reflects an impulse to understand the nature of our choices and who we are in the present. More broadly, Sartre's view of the interrelationship of being, consciousness, and objective phenomena is suggestive for considering the metaphysical dimension of our relationship to time, particularly in stories like Ted Chiang's "Story of Your Life."

We have a past. Of course we have been able to establish that this past does not determine our acts as a prior phenomenon determines a consequent phenomenon; we have shown that the past is without force to constitute the present and to sketch out the future. Nevertheless the fact remains that the freedom which escapes toward the future can not give itself any past it likes according to its fancy; there are even more compelling reasons for the fact that it can not produce itself without a past. It has to be its own past, and this past is irremediable. It even seems at first glance that freedom can not modify its past in any way; the past is that which is out of reach and which haunts us at a distance without our even being able to turn back to face it in order to consider it. If the past does not determine our actions, at least it is such that we can not take a new decision except *in terms of it*. If I have been trained at a naval academy, and if I have become an officer in the Navy, at each moment that I assume myself and consider myself, I am engaged; at the very instant when I apprehend myself, I am on watch on the bridge of the ship of which I am second in command. I can suddenly revolt against this fact, hand in my resignation, decide on suicide. These extreme measures are taken in connection with the past which is mine; if they aim at destroying it, this is because my past exists, and my most radical decisions can succeed only in taking a negative position with respect to my past. But basically this is to recognize the past's immense importance as a backdrop and a point of view. Every action designed to wrench me away from my past must first be conceived in terms of my particular past; that is, the action must before all recognize that it is born out of the particular past which it wishes to destroy. Our acts, says the proverb, follow after us. The past is present and melts insensibly into the present; it is the suit of clothes which I selected six months ago, the house which I have had built, the book which I began last winter, my wife, the promises which I have made to her, my children; all which I *am* I have to be in the mode of having-been. Thus the importance of the past can not be exaggerated since for me "Wesen ist was gewesen ist," essence is what has been. But we find here the paradox pointed out previously: I can not conceive of myself without a past; better yet, I can no longer *think* anything about myself since I think about what I *am* and since I am in the past; but on the other hand I am the being through whom the past comes to myself and to the world.

Let us examine this paradox more closely. Since freedom is choice, it is change. It is defined by the end which it projects; that is, by the future which it has to be. But precisely because the future is *the not-yet-existing-state of what is*, it can be conceived only within a narrow connection with what is. It is not possible that what is should illuminate what is not yet, for what is is a *lack* and consequently can be known as such only in terms of that which it lacks. The end illuminates what is. But to go looking for the end to-come in order by means of it to make known that-which-is, requires being already beyond what-is in a nihilating withdrawal which makes what-is appear clearly in the state of an isolated-system. What-is, therefore, takes on its meaning only when it is *surpassed* toward the future. Therefore what-is is the past. We see how the past as "that which is to be changed" is indispensable to the choice of the future and how consequently no free surpassing can be effected except in terms of a past, but we can see too how the very *nature* of the past comes to the past from the original choice of a future. In particular the irremediable quality of the past comes from my actual choice of the future; if the past is that in terms of which I conceive and project a new state of things in the future, then the past itself is that which is *left in place*, that which consequently is itself outside all perspective of change. Thus in order for the future to be realizable, it is necessary that the past be irremediable.

It is possible for me not to exist; but if I exist, I can not lack having a past. Such is the form which is assumed here by the "necessity of my contingency." But on the other hand, as we have seen, two existential characteristics in particular qualify the For-itself:

1. Nothing is in consciousness which is not consciousness of being.

2. In my being, my being is in question. This means that nothing comes to me which *is not chosen*.

We have seen, indeed, that a Past which was only Past would collapse in an honorary existence in which it would have lost all connection with the present. In order for us to "have" a past, it is necessary that we maintain it in existence by our very project towards the future; we do not receive our past, but the necessity of our contingency implies that we are not able not to choose it. This is what it means "to have to be one's own past." We see that this necessity, considered here from a purely temporal point of view, is not basically distinct from the primary structure of freedom, which must be the nihilation of the being which it is and which, by this very nihilation, brings it about that *there is* a being which it is.

But while freedom is the choice of an end in terms of the past, conversely the past is what it is only in relation to the end chosen. There is an unchangeable element in the past, (*e.g.*, I had whooping cough when I was five years old) and an element which is eminently variable (the meaning of the brute fact in relation to the totality of my being). But since, on the other hand, the meaning of the past fact penetrates it through and through (I can not "recall" my childhood whooping cough outside of a precise project which defines its meaning), it is finally impossible for me to distinguish the unchangeable brute existence from the variable meaning which it includes. To say, "I had whooping cough when I was four years old"[1] supposes a thousand projects, in particular the adoption of the calendar as a system of reference for my individual existence (hence the adoption of an original position with regard to the social order) and a confident belief in the accounts which third persons give of my childhood, a belief which certainly goes along with a respect or an affection for my parents, a respect which shapes its meaning for me, etc. That brute fact itself *is*, but apart from the witness of others, its date, the technical name of the illness (an ensemble of meanings which depend on my projects) what can it *be*? Thus this brute existence, *although necessarily existent and unchangeable* stands as the ideal end — beyond reach — of a systematic specification of all the meanings included in a memory. There is, of course, a "pure matter" of memory in the sense in which Bergson speaks of pure memory; but when it shows itself, it is always in and through a project which includes the appearance of this matter in its purity.

Now the meaning of the past is strictly dependent on my present project. This certainly does not mean that I can make the meaning of my previous acts vary in any way I please; quite the contrary, it means that the fundamental project which I am decides absolutely the meaning which the past which I have to be can have for me and for others. I alone in fact can decide at each moment the *bearing* of the past. I do not decide it by debating it, by deliberating over it, and in each instance evaluating the importance of this or that prior event; but by projecting myself toward my ends, I preserve the past with me, and by action I *decide* its meaning. Who shall decide whether that mystic crisis in my fifteenth year "was" a pure accident of puberty or, on the contrary, the first sign of a future conversion? I myself, according to whether I shall decide — at twenty years of age, at thirty years — to be converted. The project of conversion by a single stroke confers on an adolescent crisis the value of a premonition which I had not taken seriously. Who shall decide whether the period which I spent in prison after a theft was fruitful or deplorable? I — according to whether I give up stealing or become hardened. Who can decide the educational value of a trip, the sincerity of a profession of love, the purity of a past intention, etc.? It is I, always I, according to the ends by which I illuminate these past events.

Thus all my past is there pressing, urgent, imperious, but its meanings and the orders which it gives me I choose by the very project of my end.

---

1. Sartre's uncertainty as to just when he had whooping cough seems to imply even more shiftiness on the part of the past than his philosophy justifies! [Trans.]

Of course the engagements which I have undertaken weigh upon me. Of course the marriage I made earlier, the house I bought and furnished last year limit my possibilities and dictate my conduct; but precisely because my projects are such I reassume the marriage contract. In other words, precisely because I do not make of it a "marriage contract which is past, surpassed, dead" and because, on the contrary, my projects imply fidelity to the engagements undertaken or the decision to have an "honorable life" as a husband and a father, etc., these projects necessarily come to illuminate the past marriage vow and to confer on it its always actual value. Thus the urgency of the past comes from the future.

Suppose that in the manner of Schlumberger's hero[2] I radically modify my fundamental project, that I seek, for example, to free myself from a continued state of happiness, and my earlier engagements will lose all their urgency. They will no longer be here except as the towers and ramparts of the Middle Ages are here, structures which one can not deny but which have no other meaning than that of recalling a stage previously traversed, a civilization and a period of political and economic existence which today are surpassed and perfectly dead. It is the future which decides whether the past is living or dead. The past, in fact, is originally a project, as the actual upsurge of my being. And to the same extent that it is a project, it is an anticipation; its meaning comes to it from the future which it sketches in outline. When the past slips wholly into the past, its absolute value depends on the validation or invalidation of the anticipations which it was. But it depends on my actual freedom to confirm the meaning of these anticipations by again accepting responsibility for them — i.e., by anticipating the future which they anticipated — or to invalidate them by simply anticipating another future. In this case the past falls back as a disarmed and duped expectation; it is "without force." This is because the only force of the past comes to it from the future; no matter how I live or evaluate my past, I can do so only in the light of a project of myself toward the future.

Thus the order of my choices of the future is going to determine an order of my past, and this order will contain nothing of the chronological. There will be first the *always living* past which is always confirmed: my promise of love, certain business contracts, a certain picture of myself to which I am faithful. Then there is the ambiguous past which has ceased to please me and to which I still hold indirectly: for example, this suit which I am wearing, and which I bought at a certain period when I had the desire to be fashionable, displeases me extremely at present; hence the past in which I "chose" the suit is truly dead. But on the other hand, my actual project of economy is such that I must continue to wear this suit rather than get another. Hence it belongs to a past which is both dead and living like those social institutions which having been created for a determined end, have now outlived the regime which established them and

---

2. Sartre refers to a novel by Jean Schlumberger, *Un Homme heureux* (*A Happy Man*) (1920). [Ed.]

have been made to serve altogether different ends, sometimes even opposed ends. A living past, a half-dead past, survivals, ambiguities, discrepancies: the ensemble of these layers of pastness is organized by the unity of my project. It is by means of this project that there is installed the complex system of references which causes any fragment of my past to enter into an hierarchical, plurivalent organization in which, as in a work of art, each partial structure indicates in different ways, various other partial structures and the total structure.

Furthermore this decision with respect to the value, the order, and the nature of our past is simply the *historical choice* in general. If human societies are historical, this does not stem simply from the fact that they have a past but from the fact that they reassume the past by making it a *memorial*. When American capitalism decides to enter the European war of 1914–1918 because it sees there the opportunity for profitable transactions, it is not *historical*; it is only utilitarian. But when in the light of its utilitarian projects, it recovers the previous relations of the United States with France and gives to them the *meaning* of the paying of a debt of honor by Americans to France, then it becomes historical. In particular it makes itself historical by the famous sentence: "Lafayette, we are here!" It goes without saying that if a different view of her real interests had led the United States to place itself on the side of Germany, she would not have lacked past elements to recover on the memorial level. One can imagine, for example, propaganda based on "blood kinship," which chiefly would have taken into account the proportion of Germans in the emigration to America in the nineteenth century. It would be in vain to try to view these references to the past as purely publicity enterprises; actually the essential fact is that they are *necessary* in order to gain the adherence of the masses and that therefore the masses demand a political project which illuminates and justifies their past. Moreover, it is evident that the past is thus *created*. *There has been* in this way the construction of a common French-American past which, on the one hand, *signified* the great economic interests of the Americans and, on the other hand, the *actual* affinities of two democratic capitalisms. Similarly about 1938 we saw how a new generation, concerned with the international events which were in preparation, now suddenly illuminated the period of 1918–1938 with a new light by calling it "the period between the wars" even before war actually had burst forth in 1939. Suddenly the period under consideration (1918–1938) was constituted in a form which was limited, surpassed, and repudiated whereas those who had lived through it by projecting themselves toward a future in continuity with their present and their immediate past had experienced it as the start of a continuous and unlimited progress. The actual project therefore decides whether a defined period of the past is in continuity with the present or whether it is a discontinuous fragment from which one is emerging and which is put at a distance.

Thus human history would have to be *finished* before a particular event, for example the taking of the Bastille, could receive a definitive *meaning*. Nobody denies, of course, that the Bastille was taken in 1789;

there is the immutable fact. But are we to see in this event a revolt with-out consequence, a popular outburst against a half dismantled fortress, an event which the Convention, anxious to create a famous past for itself, was able to transform into a glorious deed? Or should we consider it as the first manifestation of popular strength by which the populace asserted itself, gave itself confidence, and put itself in a position to effect the march on Versailles in those "Last Days of October"? He who would like to decide the question today forgets that the historian is himself *historical*; that is, that he historicizes himself by illuminating "history" in the light of his proj-ects and of those of his society. Thus it is necessary to say that the mean-ing of the social past is perpetually "in suspense."

Now exactly like societies, the human person has a *memorial* past *in suspense*. It is this perpetual putting into question of the past which the sages realized very early and which the Greek tragedians expressed, for example, by that proverb which appears in all their plays: "No man can be called happy before his death." The perpetual historization of the For-itself is the perpetual affirmation of its freedom.[3]

Once this fact is established, it is not necessary to hold that the past's character as "in suspense" appears to the For-itself in the form of a vague or incomplete aspect of its prior history. On the contrary, quite as much as the choice of the For-itself, which in its own way it expresses, the Past is apprehended by the For-itself each moment as strictly defined. Similarly the Arch of Titus or the Column of Trajan, whatever may be the historical evolution of their meaning elsewhere, appear to the Roman or the tourist who considers them, as realities perfectly individualized. In the light of the project which illuminates it, the Past is revealed as perfectly compelling. The suspended character of the Past is in no way miraculous; it only serves to express — on the level of making-past and of the In-itself — the projec-tive and expectant aspect which human reality *had* before turning to the past. It is because this human-reality was a free project eaten away by an unpredictable freedom that it becomes "in the past" a tributary of the fur-ther projects of the For-itself. Human reality is condemned to make-itself-past and hence to wait forever for the confirmation which it expected from the future. Thus the past is indefinitely in suspense because human-reality "was" and "will be" perpetually expecting. Expectation and suspense only succeed in affirming still more plainly that freedom is their original con-stituent. To say that the past of the For-itself is in suspense, to say that its present is an expecting, to say that its future is a free project, or that it can be nothing without having to be it, or that it is a totality-detotalized — all these are one and the same thing. But this does not imply any indetermi-nation in my past as it is revealed to me at present; it means simply that the right of my actual revelation of my past to be definitive is put into ques-

---

3. Sartre distinguishes between two types of being, "For-itself" (*pour-soi*) and "In-itself" (*en-soi*). Being In-itself refers to the state of simply existing and can be applied to objects as well as human beings, while being for-itself is distinguished by human consciousness.

tion. But just as my present is an expectation of a confirmation or of an invalidation which nothing allows it to foresee, so the past, which is involved in this expectation is precise to the same extent that the expectation is precise. But the meaning of the past, although strictly individualized, is totally dependent on this expectation which itself depends on an absolute nothingness; that is, on a free project which does not yet exist. My past therefore is a concrete and precise proposition which *as such* awaits ratification. This is certainly one of the meanings which Kafka's *The Trial* tries to bring to light, the characteristic in human reality of being perpetually *in court*. To be free is to *have one's freedom perpetually on trial*. The result is that the past while confined within my actual free choice is — once this choice has determined it — an integral and necessary condition of my project.

An example may make this point clearer. The past of a retired soldier under the Restoration is to have been a hero of the retreat from Russia. And what we have explained just now enables us to understand that this past itself is a free choice of the future. It is by choosing not to join in with the government of Louis XVIII and the new customs, by choosing until the end to hope for the triumphal return of the Emperor, by choosing even to conspire to hasten this return and to prefer to be a retired soldier rather than an active solider that the old solider of Napoleon chooses for himself a past as a hero of Beresina. Another soldier who had formed the project of going over to the new government would certainly not have chosen the same past. But conversely, if we are considering only one retired solider, if he lives in almost indecent poverty, if he is embittered, and if he longs for the Emperor's return, this is because he was a hero of the retreat from Russia. We must be sure to understand this: the past does not act before any constituting recovery, and it does not in any way act deterministically; but once the past "soldier of the Empire" has been *chosen*, then the conduct of the For-itself *realizes* this past. There is even no difference between the soldier's choosing this past and his realizing it by his behavior. Thus the For-itself by endeavoring to make of its past glory an intersubjective reality, constitutes it in the eyes of others as being an objectivity-for-others (the reactions of the officials, for example, to the danger represented by these old soldiers). Treated as such by others, the soldier acts henceforth in such a way as to render himself worthy of a past which he has chosen in order to compensate for his present misery and failure. He shows himself intransigent, he loses every chance of a pension; this is because he "can not" be unworthy of his past.

Thus we choose our past in the light of a certain end, but from then on it imposes itself upon us and devours us. This is not because this past has an existence *by itself* different from that which we have to be but simply because: (1) it is the actually revealed materialization of the end which we are; (2) it appears in the midst of the world for us and for others, is never alone but sinks into the universal past and thereby offers itself to the evaluation of others. Just as the geometrician is free to create a particular figure which pleases him but can not conceive of one which does not immediately enter into an infinity of relations with the infinity of other possible figures, so our free choice of ourselves by causing the upsurge of a certain evaluative order of our past, causes the appearance in the world of an infinity of relations of this past to the world and to the Other. And this infinity of relations is presented to us as an *infinity of conducts to be adopted* since it is in the future that we evaluate our past. We are *compelled* to adopt these conducts in so far as our past appears within the compass of our essential project. To will this project, in fact, is to will the past; and to will this past is to will to realize it by a thousand secondary behaviors. Logically the requirements of the past are hypothetical imperatives: "If you wish to have such and such a past, act in such and such a way." But as the first term is a concrete and categorical choice, the imperative also is transformed into a categorical imperative.

But since the force of compulsion in my past is borrowed from my free, reflecting choice and from the very power which this choice has given itself, it is impossible to determine *a priori* the compelling power of a past. It is not only its content and the order of this content which my free choice decides; it is also the adherence of my past to my actuality. If within a fundamental perspective which we do not yet have to determine, one of my principal projects is to *progress* — i.e., to be always at any cost a little further advanced along a certain path than I was yesterday or an hour earlier, this progressive project involves in relation to my past a series of "uprootings." The past — which now from the height of my progress I regard with a slightly scornful pity — is that which is strictly a *passive object* for moral evaluation and judgment. "How stupid I was then!" or "How wicked I was!" It exists only because I can dissociate myself from it. I no longer enter into it, nor do I any longer wish to enter into it. This is not, of course, because it ceases to exist, but it exists only as *that self which I no longer am* — i.e., that being which I have to *be as the self which I am no longer*. Its function is to be what I have chosen of myself in order to oppose myself to it, that which enables me to measure myself. Such a For-itself chooses itself therefore without solidarity with itself, which means not that it abolishes its past but that it posits its past so as not to be associated with it, exactly so as to affirm its total freedom (that which is past is a certain kind of engagement with respect to the past and a certain kind of tradition). On the other hand, there are other For-itselfs whose project implies the rejection of time and a narrow solidarity with the past. In their desire to find a solid ground these latter have, by contrast, chosen the past as that which they *are*, everything else being only an indefinite and unworthy flight from tradition. They have chosen *at the start* the refusal of flight; that is, *the refusal to refuse*. The past consequently has the function of requiring of them a fidelity. Thus we shall see that the former persons admit scornfully and easily to a mistake which they have made whereas the very admission will be impossible for the others without their deliberately changing their fundamental project; the latter will then employ all the bad faith in the world and all the subterfuges which they can invent in order to avoid breaking that faith in "what is" which constitutes an essential structure of their project.

Thus like place, the past is integrated with the situation when the For-itself by its choice of the future confers on its past facticity a value, an hierarchical order, and an urgency in terms of which this facticity *motivates* the act and conduct of the For-itself.

E. H. Carr
The Historian and His Facts
(1961)

Edward Hallett Carr (1892–1982) was a British historian and diplomat who specialized in international relations. After taking his degree in classics from Cambridge University, he served as a diplomat from 1916 to 1936 and helped draft the Treaty of Versailles, the controversial peace treaty that ended World War I. Carr was a professor at the University of Wales, Cambridge University, and Oxford University and also served as an editor for *The Times* of London for five years. His books include the classic analysis of the period between the wars, *The Twenty Years Crisis* (1939) and a ten-volume history of the Soviet Union. He is considered one of the founders of what is called the Classical Realism school of international relations theory, a pragmatic approach that works from existing conditions rather than utopian ideals and that emphasizes power relations as the necessary foundation for all international relations. In fact, however, Carr was neither wholly realist nor wholly idealist but rather favored a balance between the two. This measured approach is characteristic of all his works, including *What Is History?*, which is still widely used as an introductory textbook in the study of history.

What Is History? explores the theoretical foundations of history as a discipline. For a long time, historians viewed their work as an objective science based simply on the transcription of factual data. At the time of Carr's writing, however, historians had become increasingly aware that facts could be interpreted in different ways, leading some to suggest that the "truth" of history could never be known. In his introductory chapter, "The Historian and His Facts," Carr advocates a middle path between the naïve view of history as a collection of objective, freestanding facts and an extreme relativism that views everything as subjective and truth as unknowable. Concrete facts do exist, Carr argues, and are the necessary basis of any historical investigation. At the same time, we must be aware that the interpretation of facts is always guided by the historian's individual beliefs and by the perspective of the current historical moment in which he or she lives. The very language we use to organize the past betrays a particular historical perspective — for instance, only someone looking back on an era and judging it relatively unimportant could invent the term "the Middle Ages." Even the selection of specific facts from the mass of historical data involves subjective judgment. There was a time, for instance, when historians were only concerned with wars and politics — the actions of famous men. Now, however, they focus increasingly on the everyday lives of common people. History is a narrative that is not static and frozen in the past but rather constantly changing based on our shifting values and understanding of the contemporary world. The stories we tell about the past help us to make meaning of who we are today.

Science fiction stories featuring alternate history and time travel reflect a similar fascination with the past as a means of understanding the present, and their writers share with historians a curiosity about causes and effects, about what counts as important, and about how things might have gone differently. In this context, Carr's views on the nature of historical inquiry as speculative and provisional provide a useful perspective.

What is history? Lest anyone think the question meaningless or superfluous, I will take as my text two passages relating respectively to the first and second incarnations of *The Cambridge Modern History*. Here is Acton in his report of October 1896 to the Syndics of the Cambridge University Press on the work which he had undertaken to edit:

> It is a unique opportunity of recording, in the way most useful to the greatest number, the fullness of the knowledge which the nineteenth century is about to bequeath. . . . By the judicious division of labor we should be able to do it, and to bring home to every man the last document, and the ripest conclusions of international research.
>
> Ultimate history we cannot have in this generation; but we can dispose of conventional history, and show the point we have reached on the road from one to the other, now that all information is within reach, and every problem has become capable of solution.[1]

And almost exactly sixty years later Professor Sir George Clark, in his general introduction to the second *Cambridge Modern History*, commented on this belief of Acton and his collaborators that it would one day be possible to produce "ultimate history," and went on:

> Historians of a later generation do not look forward to any such prospect. They expect their work to be superseded again and again.

---

1. *The Cambridge Modern History: Its Origin, Authorship, and Production* (Cambridge University Press, 1907): 10–12. [The quotation is taken from John Dalberg-Acton (1834–1902), commonly known as Lord Acton. Acton was an important historian who was the founding editor of *The Cambridge Modern History*. In this selection, Carr refers to the methods and approaches of many historians of various nationalities, as well as quoting fictional characters such as Mr. Gradgrind (a character from Charles Dickens's *Hard Times*). [Ed.]

They consider that knowledge of the past has come down through one or more human minds, has been "processed" by them, and therefore cannot consist of elemental and impersonal atoms which nothing can alter. . . . The exploration seems to be endless, and some impatient scholars take refuge in scepticism, or at least in the doctrine that, since all historical judgments involve persons and points of view, one is as good as another and there is no "objective" historical truth.[2]

Where the pundits contradict each other so flagrantly the field is open to enquiry. I hope that I am sufficiently up-to-date to recognize that anything written in the 1890s must be nonsense. But I am not yet advanced enough to be committed to the view that anything written in the 1950s necessarily makes sense. Indeed, it may already have occurred to you that this enquiry is liable to stray into something even broader than the nature of history. The clash between Acton and Sir George Clark is a reflection of the change in our total outlook on society over the interval between these two pronouncements. Acton speaks out of the positive belief, the clear-eyed self-confidence of the later Victorian age; Sir George Clark echoes the bewilderment and distracted scepticism of the beat generation. When we attempt to answer the question, What is history?, our answer, consciously or unconsciously, reflects our own position in time, and forms part of our answer to the broader question, what view we take of the society in which we live. I have no fear that my subject may, on closer inspection, seem trivial. I am afraid only that I may seem presumptuous to have broached a question so vast and so important.

The nineteenth century was a great age for facts. "What I want," said Mr. Gradgrind in *Hard Times*, "is Facts. . . . Facts alone are wanted in life." Nineteenth-century historians on the whole agreed with him. When Ranke in the 1830s, in legitimate protest against moralizing history, remarked that the task of the historian was "simply to show how it really was (*wie es eigentlich gewesen*)" this not very profound aphorism had an astonishing success. Three generations of German, British, and even French historians marched into battle intoning the magic words, "*Wie es eigentlich gewesen*" like an incantation — designed, like most incantations, to save them from the tiresome obligation to think for themselves. The positivists, anxious to stake out their claim for history as a science, contributed the weight of their influence to this cult of facts. First ascertain the facts, said the positivists, then draw your conclusions from them. In Great Britain, this view of history fitted in perfectly with the empiricist tradition which was the dominant strain in British philosophy from Locke to Bertrand Russell. The empirical theory of knowledge presupposes a complete separation between subject and object. Facts, like sense-impressions, impinge on the observer from outside, and are independent of his consciousness. The process of reception is passive: having received the data, he then acts on them. *The*

2. *The New Cambridge Modern History*, I (Cambridge University Press, 1957), pp. xxiv–xxv.

Shorter Oxford English Dictionary, a useful but tendentious work of the empirical school, clearly marks the separateness of the two processes by defining a fact as "a datum of experience as distinct from conclusions." This is what may be called the common-sense view of history. History consists of a corpus of ascertained facts. The facts are available to the historian in documents, inscriptions, and so on, like fish on the fishmonger's slab. The historian collects them, takes them home, and cooks and serves them in whatever style appeals to him. Acton, whose culinary tastes were austere, wanted them served plain. In his letter of instructions to contributors to the first *Cambridge Modern History* he announced the requirement "that our Waterloo must be one that satisfies French and English, German and Dutch alike; that nobody can tell, without examining the list of authors, where the Bishop of Oxford laid down the pen, and whether Fairbairn or Gasquet, Liebermann or Harrison took it up."[3] Even Sir George Clark, critical as he was of Acton's attitude, himself contrasted the "hard core of facts" in history with the "surrounding pulp of disputable interpretation"[4] — forgetting perhaps that the pulpy part of the fruit is more rewarding than the hard core. First get your facts straight, then plunge at your peril into the shifting sands of interpretation — that is the ultimate wisdom of the empirical, common-sense school of history. It recalls the favorite dictum of the great liberal journalist C. P. Scott: "Facts are sacred, opinion is free."

Now this clearly will not do. I shall not embark on a philosophical discussion of the nature of our knowledge of the past. Let us assume for present purposes that the fact that Caesar crossed the Rubicon and the fact that there is a table in the middle of the room are facts of the same or of a comparable order, that both these facts enter our consciousness in the same or in a comparable manner, and that both have the same objective character in relation to the person who knows them. But, even on this bold and not very plausible assumption, our argument at once runs into the difficulty that not all facts about the past are historical facts, or are treated as such by the historian. What is the criterion which distinguishes the facts of history from other facts about the past?

What is a historical fact? This is a crucial question into which we must look a little more closely. According to the common-sense view, there are certain basic facts which are the same for all historians and which form, so to speak, the backbone of history — the fact, for example, that the Battle of Hastings was fought in 1066. But this view calls for two observations. In the first place, it is not with facts like these that the historian is primarily concerned. It is no doubt important to know that the great battle was fought in 1066 and not in 1065 or 1067, and that it was fought at Hastings and not at Eastbourne or Brighton. The historian must not get these things wrong. But when points of this kind are raised, I am reminded of Housman's

---

3. Acton, *Lectures on Modern History* (London: Macmillan & Co., 1906), p. 318.
4. Quoted in *The Listener* (June 19, 1952), p. 992.

remark that "accuracy is a duty, not a virtue."[5] To praise a historian for his accuracy is like praising an architect for using well-seasoned timber or properly mixed concrete in his building. It is a necessary condition of his work, but not his essential function. It is precisely for matters of this kind that the historian is entitled to rely on what have been called the "auxiliary sciences" of history — archaeology, epigraphy, numismatics, chronology, and so forth. The historian is not required to have the special skills which enable the expert to determine the origin and period of a fragment of pottery or marble, to decipher an obscure inscription, or to make the elaborate astronomical calculations necessary to establish a precise date. These so-called basic facts which are the same for all historians commonly belong to the category of the raw materials of the historian rather than of history itself. The second observation is that the necessity to establish these basic facts rests not on any quality in the facts themselves, but on an *a priori* decision of the historian. In spite of C. P. Scott's motto, every journalist knows today that the most effective way to influence opinion is by the selection and arrangement of the appropriate facts. It used to be said that facts speak for themselves. This is, of course, untrue. The facts speak only when the historian calls on them: it is he who decides to which facts to give the floor, and in what order or context. It was, I think, one of Pirandello's characters who said that a fact is like a sack — it won't stand up till you've put something in it. The only reason why we are interested to know that the battle was fought at Hastings in 1066 is that historians regard it as a major historical event. It is the historian who has decided for his own reasons that Caesar's crossing of that petty stream, the Rubicon, is a fact of history, whereas the crossing of the Rubicon by millions of other people before or since interests nobody at all. The fact that you arrived in this building half an hour ago on foot, or on a bicycle, or in a car, is just as much a fact about the past as the fact that Caesar crossed the Rubicon. But it will probably be ignored by historians. Professor Talcott Parsons once called science "a selective system of cognitive orientations to reality."[6] It might perhaps have been put more simply. But history is, among other things, that. The historian is necessarily selective. The belief in a hard core of historical facts existing objectively and independently of the interpretation of the historian is a preposterous fallacy, but one which it is very hard to eradicate.

Let us take a look at the process by which a mere fact about the past is transformed into a fact of history. At Stalybridge Wakes in 1850, a vendor of gingerbread, as the result of some petty dispute, was deliberately kicked to death by an angry mob. Is this a fact of history? A year ago I should unhesitatingly have said "no." It was recorded by an eyewitness in

---

5. M. Manilius, *Astronomicon: Liber Primus*, 2nd ed. (Cambridge University Press, 1937), p. 87.
6. Talcott Parsons and Edward A, Shils, *Toward a General Theory of Action*, 3rd ed. (Cambridge, Mass.: Harvard University Press, 1954), p. 167.

some little-known memoirs;[7] but I had never seen it judged worthy of mention by any historian. A year ago Dr. Kitson Clark cited it in his Ford lectures in Oxford.[8] Does this make it into a historical fact? Not, I think, yet. Its present status, I suggest, is that it has been proposed for membership of the select club of historical facts. It now awaits a seconder and sponsors. It may be that in the course of the next few years we shall see this fact appearing first in footnotes, then in the text, of articles and books about nineteenth-century England, and that in twenty or thirty years' time it may be a well established historical fact. Alternatively, nobody may take it up, in which case it will relapse into the limbo of unhistorical facts about the past from which Dr. Kitson Clark has gallantly attempted to rescue it. What will decide which of these two things will happen? It will depend, I think, on whether the thesis or interpretation in support of which Dr. Kitson Clark cited this incident is accepted by other historians as valid and significant. Its status as a historical fact will turn on a question of interpretation. This element of interpretation enters into every fact of history.

May I be allowed a personal reminiscence? When I studied ancient history in this university many years ago, I had as a special subject "Greece in the period of the Persian Wars." I collected fifteen or twenty volumes on my shelves and took it for granted that there, recorded in these volumes, I had all the facts relating to my subject. Let us assume — it was very nearly true — that those volumes contained all the facts about it that were then known, or could be known. It never occurred to me to enquire by what accident or process of attrition that minute selection of facts, out of all the myriad facts that must have once been known to somebody, had survived to become *the* facts of history. I suspect that even today one of the fascinations of ancient and mediaeval history is that it gives us the illusion of having all the facts at our disposal within a manageable compass: the nagging distinction between the facts of history and other facts about the past vanishes because the few known facts are all facts of history. As Bury, who had worked in both periods, said, "the records of ancient and mediaeval history are starred with lacunae."[9] History has been called an enormous jig-saw with a lot of missing parts. But the main trouble does not consist of the lacunae. Our picture of Greece in the fifth century B.C. is defective not primarily because so many of the bits have been accidentally lost, but because it is, by and large, the picture formed by a tiny group of people in the city of Athens. We know a lot about what fifth-century Greece looked like to an Athenian citizen; but hardly anything about what it looked like to a Spartan, a Corinthian, or a Theban — not to mention a Persian, or a slave or other non-citizen resident in Athens. Our picture has been preselected and predetermined for us, not so much by accident as by people who were consciously or unconsciously imbued with a particular view and thought the facts which supported that view worth preserving. In the same

7. Lord George Sanger, *Seventy Years a Showman* (London: J. M. Dent & Sons, 1926), pp. 188–89.
8. These will shortly be published under the title *The Making of Victorian England*.
9. John Bagnell Bury, *Selected Essays* (Cambridge University Press, 1930), p. 52.

way, when I read in a modern history of the Middle Ages that the people of the Middle Ages were deeply concerned with religion, I wonder how we know this, and whether it is true. What we know as the facts of mediaeval history have almost all been selected for us by generations of chroniclers who were professionally occupied in the theory and practice of religion, and who therefore thought it supremely important, and recorded everything relating to it, and not much else. The picture of the Russian peasant as devoutly religious was destroyed by the revolution of 1917. The picture of mediaeval man as devoutly religious, whether true or not, is indestructible, because nearly all the known facts about him were pre-selected for us by people who believed it, and wanted others to believe it, and a mass of other facts, in which we might possibly have found evidence to the contrary, has been lost beyond recall. The dead hand of vanished generations of historians, scribes, and chroniclers has determined beyond the possibility of appeal the pattern of the past. "The history we read," writes Professor Barraclough, himself trained as a mediaevalist, "though based on facts, is, strictly speaking, not factual at all, but a series of accepted judgments."[10]. . .

But I want to carry the story one step further. Let us . . . be thankful that we can, if we choose, consult the authentic papers of a leading participant in some important events of recent European history. What do the papers tell us? Among other things they contain records of some hundreds of Stresemann's conversations with the Soviet ambassador in Berlin and of a score or so with Chicherin. These records have one feature in common. They depict Stresemann as having the lion's share of the conversations and reveal his arguments as invariably well put and cogent, while those of his partner are for the most part scanty, confused, and unconvincing. This is a familiar characteristic of all records of diplomatic conversations. The documents do not tell us what happened, but only what Stresemann thought had happened, or what he wanted others to think, or perhaps what he wanted himself to think, had happened. It was not Sutton or Bernhardt, but Stresemann himself, who started the process of selection. And, if we had, say, Chicherin's records of these same conversations, we should still learn from them only what Chicherin thought, and what really happened would still have to be reconstructed in the mind of the historian. Of course, facts and documents are essential to the historian. But do not make a fetish of them. They do not by themselves constitute history; they provide in themselves no ready-made answer to this tiresome question: What is history?

At this point I should like to say a few words on the question of why nineteenth-century historians were generally indifferent to the philosophy of history. The term was invented by Voltaire, and has since been used in different senses; but I shall take it to mean, if I use it at all, our answer to the question: What is history? The nineteenth century was, for the intellectuals of Western Europe, a comfortable period exuding confidence and optimism. The facts were on the whole satisfactory; and the inclination to ask and

---

10. Geoffrey Barraclough, *History in a Changing World* (London: Basil Blackwell & Mott, 1955), p. 14.

answer awkward questions about them was correspondingly weak. Ranke piously believed that divine providence would take care of the meaning of history if he took care of the facts; and Burckhardt with a more modern touch of cynicism observed that "we are not initiated into the purposes of the eternal wisdom." Professor Butterfield as late as 1931 noted with apparent satisfaction that "historians have reflected little upon the nature of things and even the nature of their own subject."[11] But my predecessor in these lectures, Dr. A. L. Rowse, more justly critical, wrote of Sir Winston Churchill's *The World Crisis* — his book about the First World War — that, while it matched Trotsky's *History of the Russian Revolution* in personality, vividness, and vitality, it was inferior in one respect: it had "no philosophy of history behind it."[12] British historians refused to be drawn, not because they believed that history had no meaning, but because they believed that its meaning was implicit and self-evident. The liberal nineteenth-century view of history had a close affinity with the economic doctrine of *laissez-faire* — also the product of a serene and self-confident outlook on the world. Let everyone get on with his particular job, and the hidden hand would take care of the universal harmony. The facts of history were themselves a demonstration of the supreme fact of a beneficent and apparently infinite progress towards higher things. This was the age of innocence, and historians walked in the Garden of Eden, without a scrap of philosophy to cover them, naked and unashamed before the god of history. Since then, we have known Sin and experienced a Fall; and those historians who today pretend to dispense with a philosophy of history are merely trying, vainly and self-consciously, like members of a nudist colony, to recreate the Garden of Eden in their garden suburb. Today the awkward question can no longer be evaded. . . .

In the first place, the facts of history never come to us "pure," since they do not and cannot exist in a pure form: they are always refracted through the mind of the recorder. It follows that when we take up a work of history, our first concern should be not with the facts which it contains but with the historian who wrote it. . . .

The second point is the more familiar one of the historian's need of imaginative understanding for the minds of the people with whom he is dealing, for the thought behind their acts: I say "imaginative understanding," not "sympathy," lest sympathy should be supposed to imply agreement. The nineteenth century was weak in mediaeval history, because it was too much repelled by the superstitious beliefs of the Middle Ages and by the barbarities which they inspired, to have any imaginative understanding of mediaeval people. Or take Burckhardt's censorious remark about the Thirty Years' War: "It is scandalous for a creed, no matter whether it is Catholic or Protestant, to place its salvation above the integrity of the nation."[13] It was extremely difficult for a nineteenth-century liberal histo-

---

11. Herbert Butterfield, *The Whig Interpretation of History* (London: George Bell & Sons, 1931), p. 67.
12. Alfred L. Rowse, *The End of an Epoch* (London: Macmillan & Co., 1947), pp. 282–83.
13. Jacob Burckhardt, *Judgments on History and Historians* (London: S. J. Reginald Saunders & Company, 1958), p. 179.

rian, brought up to believe that it is right and praiseworthy to kill in defense of one's country, but wicked and wrong-headed to kill in defence of one's religion, to enter into the state of mind of those who fought the Thirty Years' War. This difficulty is particularly acute in the field in which I am now working. Much of what has been written in English-speaking countries in the last ten years about the Soviet Union, and in the Soviet Union about the English-speaking countries, has been vitiated by this inability to achieve even the most elementary measure of imaginative understanding of what goes on in the mind of the other party, so that the words and actions of the other are always made to appear malign, senseless, or hypocritical. History cannot be written unless the historian can achieve some kind of contact with the mind of those about whom he is writing.

The third point is that we can view the past, and achieve our understanding of the past, only through the eyes of the present. The historian is of his own age, and is bound to it by the conditions of human existence. The very words which he uses — words like democracy, empire, war, revolution — have current connotations from which he cannot divorce them. Ancient historians have taken to using words like *polis* and *plebs* in the original, just in order to show that they have not fallen into this trap. This does not help them. They, too, live in the present, and cannot cheat themselves into the past by using unfamiliar or obsolete words, any more than they would become better Greek or Roman historians if they delivered their lectures in a *chlamys* or a *toga*. The names by which successive French historians have described the Parisian crowds which played so prominent a role in the French revolution — *les sans-culottes, le peuple, la canaile, les bras-nus* — are all, for those who know the rules of the game, manifestos of a political affiliation and of a particular interpretation. Yet the historian is obliged to choose: the use of language forbids him to be neutral. Nor is it a matter of words alone. Over the past hundred years the changed balance of power in Europe has reversed the attitude of British historians to Frederick the Great. The changed balance of power within the Christian churches between Catholicism and Protestantism has profoundly altered their attitude to such figures as Loyola, Luther, and Cromwell. It requires only a superficial knowledge of the work of French historians of the last forty years on the French revolution to recognize how deeply it has been affected by the Russian revolution of 1917. The historian belongs not to the past but to the present. Professor Trevor-Roper tells us that the historian "ought to love the past."[14] This is a dubious injunction. To love the past may easily be an expression of the nostalgic romanticism of old men and old societies, a symptom of loss of faith and interest in the present or future.[15] *Cliché* for *cliché*, I should prefer the one about freeing oneself

14. Introduction to Burckhardt, *Judgments on History and Historians*, p. 17.
15. Compare Nietzsche's view of history: "To old age belongs the old man's business of looking back and casting up his accounts, of seeking consolation in the memories of the past, in historical culture" (*Thoughts Out of Season* [London: Macmillan & Co., 1909], II, pp. 65–66).

from "the dead hand of the past." The function of the historian is neither to love the past nor to emancipate himself from the past, but to master and understand it as the key to the understanding of the present.

If, however, these are some of the insights of what I may call the Collingwood view of history, it is time to consider some of the dangers. The emphasis on the role of the historian in the making of history tends, if pressed to its logical conclusion, to rule out any objective history at all: history is what the historian makes. Collingwood seems indeed, at one moment, in an unpublished note quoted by his editor, to have reached this conclusion:

> St. Augustine looked at history from the point of view of the early Christian; Tillemont, from that of a seventeenth-century Frenchman; Gibbon, from that of an eighteenth-century Englishman; Mommsen, from that of a nineteenth-century German. There is no point in asking which was the right point of view. Each was the only one possible for the man who adopted it.[16]

This amounts to total scepticism, like Froude's remark that history is "a child's box of letters with which we can spell any word we please."[17] Collingwood, in his reaction against "scissors-and-paste history," against the view of history as a mere compilation of facts, comes perilously near to treating history as something spun out of the human brain, and leads back to the conclusion referred to by Sir George Clark in the passage which I quoted earlier, that "there is no 'objective' historical truth." In place of the theory that history has no meaning, we are offered here the theory of an infinity of meanings, none any more right than any other — which comes to much the same thing. The second theory is surely as untenable as the first. It does not follow that, because a mountain appears to take on different shapes from different angles of vision, it has objectively either no shape at all or an infinity of shapes. It does not follow that, because interpretation plays a necessary part in establishing the facts of history, and because no existing interpretation is wholly objective, one interpretation is as good as another, and the facts of history are in principle not amenable to objective interpretation. I shall have to consider at a later stage what exactly is meant by objectivity in history.

But a still greater danger lurks in the Collingwood hypothesis. If the historian necessarily looks at his period of history through the eyes of his own time, and studies the problems of the past as a key to those of the present, will he not fall into a purely pragmatic view of the facts, and maintain that the criterion of a right interpretation is its suitability to some present purpose? On this hypothesis, the facts of history are nothing, interpretation is everything. Nietzsche had already enunciated the principle: "The

---

16. Robin G. Collingwood, *The Idea of History* (London: Oxford University Press, 1946), p. xii.
17. James Anthony Froude, *Short Studies on Great Subjects* (1894), I, p. 21.

falseness of an opinion is not for us any objection to it. . . . The question is how far it is life-furthering, life-preserving, species-preserving, perhaps species-creating."[18] The American pragmatists moved, less explicitly and less wholeheartedly, along the same line. Knowledge is knowledge for some purpose. The validity of the knowledge depends on the validity of the purpose. But, even where no such theory has been professed, the practice has often been no less disquieting. In my own field of study I have seen too many examples of extravagant interpretation riding roughshod over facts, not to be impressed with the reality of this danger. It is not surprising that perusal of some of the more extreme products of Soviet and anti-Soviet schools of historiography should sometimes breed a certain nostalgia for that illusory nineteenth-century haven of purely factual history.

How then, in the middle of the twentieth century, are we to define the obligation of the historian to his facts? I trust that I have spent a sufficient number of hours in recent years chasing and perusing documents, and stuffing my historical narrative with properly footnoted facts, to escape the imputation of treating facts and documents too cavalierly. The duty of the historian to respect his facts is not exhausted by the obligation to see that his facts are accurate. He must seek to bring into the picture all known or knowable facts relevant, in one sense or another, to the theme on which he is engaged and to the interpretation proposed. If he seeks to depict the Victorian Englishman as a moral and rational being, he must not forget what happened at Stalybridge Wakes in 1850. But this, in turn, does not mean that he can eliminate interpretation, which is the life-blood of history. Laymen — that is to say, non-academic friends or friends from other academic disciplines — sometimes ask me how the historian goes to work when he writes history. The commonest assumption appears to be that the historian divides his work into two sharply distinguishable phases or periods. First, he spends a long preliminary period reading his sources and filling his notebooks with facts: then, when this is over, he puts away his sources, takes out his notebooks, and writes his book from beginning to end. This is to me an unconvincing and unplausible picture. For myself, as soon as I have got going on a few of what I take to be the capital sources, the itch becomes too strong and I begin to write — not necessarily at the beginning, but somewhere, anywhere. Thereafter, reading and writing go on simultaneously. The writing is added to, subtracted from, re-shaped, cancelled, as I go on reading. The reading is guided and directed and made fruitful by the writing: the more I write, the more I know what I am looking for, the better I understand the significance and relevance of what I find. Some historians probably do all this preliminary writing in their head without using pen, paper, or typewriter, just as some people play chess in their heads without recourse to board and chess-men: this is a talent which I envy, but cannot emulate. But I am convinced that, for any historian worth the name, the two processes of what economists call "input" and

---

18. Froude, *Beyond Good and Evil,* Ch. i.

"output" go on simultaneously and are, in practice, parts of a single process. If you try to separate them, or to give one priority over the other, you fall into one of two heresies. Either you write scissors-and-paste history without meaning or significance; or you write propaganda or historical fiction, and merely use facts of the past to embroider a kind of writing which has nothing to do with history.

Our examination of the relation of the historian to the facts of history finds us, therefore, in an apparently precarious situation, navigating delicately between the Scylla of an untenable theory of history as an objective compilation of facts, of the unqualified primacy of fact over interpretation, and the Charybdis of an equally untenable theory of history as the subjective product of the mind of the historian who establishes the facts of history and masters them through the process of interpretation, between a view of history having the center of gravity in the past and the view having the center of gravity in the present. But our situation is less precarious than it seems. We shall encounter the same dichotomy of fact and interpretation again in these lectures in other guises — the particular and the general, the empirical and the theoretical, the objective and the subjective. The predicament of the historian is a reflection of the nature of man. Man, except perhaps in earliest infancy and in extreme old age, is not totally involved in his environment and unconditionally subject to it. On the other hand, he is never totally independent of it and its unconditional master. The relation of man to his environment is the relation of the historian to his theme. The historian is neither the humble slave, nor the tyrannical master, of his facts. The relation between the historian and his facts is one of equality, of give-and-take. As any working historian knows, if he stops to reflect what he is doing as he thinks and writes, the historian is engaged on a continuous process of moulding his facts to his interpretation and his interpretation to his facts. It is impossible to assign primacy to one over the other.

The historian starts with a provisional selection of facts and a provisional interpretation in the light of which that selection has been made — by others as well as by himself. As he works, both the interpretation and the selection and ordering of facts undergo subtle and perhaps partly unconscious changes through the reciprocal action of one or the other. And this reciprocal action also involves reciprocity between present and past, since the historian is part of the present and the facts belong to the past. The historian and the facts of history are necessary to one another. The historian without his facts is rootless and futile; the facts without their historian are dead and meaningless. My first answer therefore to the question, What is history?, is that it is a continuous process of interaction between the historian and his facts, an unending dialogue between the present and the past.

Michio Kaku

To Build a Time Machine
(1994)

Michio Kaku (b. 1947) is a professor of theoretical physics at the City College
of New York and is also one of the foremost explicators of science in the mass
media. He is the host of a syndicated radio show, *Science Fantastic*, and has
been featured on popular TV shows like *Larry King Live*, *Nightline*, and *Good
Morning America*; he has also contributed to science documentaries for PBS
and the BBC. *Hyperspace: A Scientific Odyssey Through Parallel Universes,
Time Warps, and the Tenth Dimension*, from which this selection is taken, is
one of Kaku's best-selling popular science books. In the introduction, Kaku
describes how, as a boy growing up in San Francisco, a visit to the Japanese
Tea Garden sparked his interest in the nature of the universe. Watching carp
swimming in a pond, he was struck by how differently they would perceive the
world from their underwater perspective, and wondered if it were possible that
humans, too, were limited in their perspective.

Kaku is one of the leading theorists of string theory, a model of physics
that attempts to explain the structure of the universe and to unite the theories
of the four fundamental forces of nature into one grand "theory of everything." String theory seeks to account for inconsistencies in the behavior of
subatomic particles by conceptualizing them not as isolated points but as
effects of vibrational patterns situated on long, string-like structures that compose the universe. String theory relies on the notion of *hyperspace*, the idea
that there are multiple dimensions beyond the four we know — the three
familiar dimensions of space and the fourth dimension of time. According to
this theory, the cosmos was originally ten dimensional but split into two separate universes — the one we know and a tiny contracted one nested within
ours. The conjecture of hyperspace allows for the possibility of many strange
phenomena, including time travel.

Those who have not followed recent developments in theoretical physics
may be surprised to learn that time travel is a subject of serious debate among
physicists. In fact, since Einstein introduced his theory of relativity, the idea has
come to seem more plausible. Einstein's insight that time is variable rather than
constant produced a radical shift in our understanding of the cosmos. Though
Einstein himself did not believe in time travel, his assertion that time was not
absolute but rather could be stretched or warped was a radical breakthrough
in our understanding of the basic laws of the universe; it led many to contemplate the possibility that time could be manipulated, perhaps even allowing
people to move backward or forward within it rather than experiencing it as a
steady forward sequence. Today, some physicists, like distinguished Caltech
professor Kip Thorne, believe that time travel is theoretically possible, while
even those who have serious doubts about its possibility, like Stephen
Hawking, treat the idea seriously.

Science fiction writers often have scientific training and follow new developments eagerly, incorporating the latest scientific ideas into their speculations. However, the influence goes both ways; scientists are often science fiction fans who are inspired by the literature to undertake new thought experiments. Kaku, who mentions Isaac Asimov as an early influence on his thinking, is clearly an enthusiast of the genre, and in the chapter that follows he uses science fiction, most notably Robert A. Heinlein's paradoxical "All You Zombies — " (included earlier in this chapter) to illustrate some of the problems posed by time travel. In this selection, Kaku provides a good introduction to some of the leading theories and debates about the possibility of time travel. His lively writing style and willingness to speculate also convey the restless curiosity and "sense of wonder" that scientists share with science fiction writers.

> *People like us, who believe in physics, know that the distinction between past, present, and future is only a stubbornly persistent illusion.*[1]
>
> — Albert Einstein

Time Travel

Can we go backward in time?

Like the protagonist in H. G. Wells's *The Time Machine*, can we spin the dial of a machine and leap hundreds of thousands of years to the year 802,701? Or, like Michael J. Fox, can we hop into our plutonium-fired cars and go back to the future?

The possibility of time travel opens up a vast world of interesting possibilities. Like Kathleen Turner in *Peggy Sue Got Married*, everyone harbors a secret wish somehow to relive the past and correct some small but vital mistake in one's life. In Robert Frost's poem "The Road Not Taken," we wonder what might have happened, at key junctures in our lives, if we had made different choices and taken another path. With time travel, we could go back to our youth and erase embarrassing events from our past, choose a different mate, or enter different careers; or we could even change the outcome of key historical events and alter the fate of humanity.

For example, in the climax of *Superman*, our hero is emotionally devastated when an earthquake ravages most of California and crushes his lover under hundreds of tons of rock and debris. Mourning her horrible death, he is so overcome by anguish that he rockets into space and violates his oath not to tamper with the course of human history. He increases his velocity until he shatters the light barrier, disrupting the fabric of space and time. By traveling at the speed of light, he forces time to slow down,

---

1. Quoted in Anthony Zee, *Fearful Symmetry* (New York: Macmillan, 1986), 68.

then to stop, and finally to go backward, to a time before Lois Lane was crushed to death.

This trick, however, is clearly not possible. Although time does slow down when you increase your velocity, you cannot go faster than the speed of light (and hence make time go backward) because special relativity states that your mass would become infinite in the process. Thus the faster-than-light travel method preferred by most science-fiction writers contradicts the special theory of relativity.

Einstein himself was well aware of this impossibility, as was A. H. R. Buller when he published the following limerick in *Punch*:

> There was a young lady girl named Bright,
> Whose speed was far faster than light,
> She traveled one day,
> In a relative way,
> And returned on the previous night.

Most scientists, who have not seriously studied Einstein's equations, dismiss time travel as poppycock, with as much validity as lurid accounts of kidnappings by space aliens. However, the situation is actually quite complex.

To resolve the question, we must leave the simpler theory of special relativity, which forbids time travel, and embrace the full power of the *general* theory of relativity, which may permit it. General relativity has much wider validity than special relativity. While special relativity describes only objects moving at constant velocity far away from any stars, the general theory of relativity is much more powerful, capable of describing rockets accelerating near supermassive stars and black holes. The general theory therefore supplants some of the simpler conclusions of the special theory. For any physicist who has seriously analyzed the mathematics of time travel within Einstein's general theory of relativity, the final conclusion is, surprisingly enough, far from clear.

Proponents of time travel point out that Einstein's equations for general relativity do allow some forms of time travel. They acknowledge, however, that the energies necessary to twist time into a circle are so great that Einstein's equations break down. In the physically interesting region where time travel becomes a serious possibility, quantum theory takes over from general relativity.

Einstein's equations, we recall, state that the curvature or bending of space and time is determined by the matter–energy content of the universe. It is, in fact, possible to find configurations of matter–energy powerful enough to force the bending of time and allow for time travel. However, the concentrations of matter–energy necessary to bend time backward are so vast that general relativity breaks down and quantum corrections begin to dominate over relativity. Thus the final verdict on time travel cannot be answered within the framework of Einstein's equations, which break down in extremely large gravitational fields, where we expect quantum theory to become dominant.

This is where the hyperspace theory can settle the question. Because both quantum theory and Einstein's theory of gravity are united in ten-dimensional space, we expect that the question of time travel will be settled decisively by the hyperspace theory. As in the case of wormholes and dimensional windows, the final chapter will be written when we incorporate the full power of the hyperspace theory.

Let us now describe the controversy surrounding time travel and the delicious paradoxes that inevitably arise.

Collapse of Causality

Science-fiction writers have often wondered what might happen if a single individual went back in time. Many of these stories, on the surface, appear plausible. But imagine the chaos that would arise if time machines were as common as automobiles, with tens of millions of them commercially available. Havoc would soon break loose, tearing at the fabric of our universe. Millions of people would go back in time to meddle with their own past and the past of others, rewriting history in the process. A few might even go back in time armed with guns to shoot down the parents of their enemies before they were born. It would thus be impossible to take a simple census to see how many people there were at any given time.

If time travel is possible, then the laws of causality crumble. In fact, all of history as we know it might collapse as well. Imagine the chaos caused by thousands of people going back in time to alter key events that changed the course of history. All of a sudden, the audience at Ford's Theater would be crammed with people from the future bickering among themselves to see who would have the honor of preventing Lincoln's assassination. The landing at Normandy would be botched as thousands of thrill seekers with cameras arrived to take pictures.

The key battlefields of history would be changed beyond recognition. Consider Alexander the Great's decisive victory over the Persians, led by Darius III, in 331 B.C. at the Battle of Gaugamela. This battle led to the collapse of the Persian forces and ended their rivalry with the West, which helped allow the flourishing of Western civilization and culture over the world for the next 1,000 years. But consider what would happen if a small band of armed mercenaries equipped with small rockets and modern artillery were to enter the battle. The slightest display of modern firepower would rout Alexander's terrified soldiers. This meddling in the past would cripple the expansion of Western influence in the world.

Time travel would mean that any historical event could never be completely resolved. History books could never be written. Some die-hard would always be trying to assassinate General Ulysses S. Grant or give the secret of the atomic bomb to the Germans in the 1930s.

What would happen if history could be rewritten as casually as erasing a blackboard? Our past would be like the shifting sands at the seashore, constantly blown this way or that by the slightest breeze. History would be constantly changing every time someone spun the dial of a time machine and blundered his or her way into the past. History, as we know it, would be impossible. It would cease to exist.

Most scientists obviously do not relish this unpleasant possibility. Not only would it be impossible for historians to make any sense out of "history," but genuine paradoxes immediately arise whenever we enter the past or future. Cosmologist Stephen Hawking, in fact, has used this situation to provide "experimental" evidence that time travel is not possible. He believes that time travel is not possible by "the fact that we have not been invaded by hordes of tourists from the future."

Time Paradoxes

To understand the problems with time travel, it is first necessary to classify the various paradoxes. In general, most can be broken down into one of two principal types:

1. Meeting your parents before you are born
2. The man with no past

The first type of time travel does the most damage to the fabric of space–time because it alters previously recorded events. For example, remember that in *Back to the Future*, our young hero goes back in time and meets his mother as a young girl, just before she falls in love with his father. To his shock and dismay, he finds that he has inadvertently prevented the fateful encounter between his parents. To make matters worse, his young mother has now become amorously attracted to him! If he unwittingly prevents his mother and father from falling in love and is unable to divert his mother's misplaced affections, he will disappear because his birth will never happen.

The second paradox involves events without any beginning. For example, let's say that an impoverished, struggling inventor is trying to construct the world's first time machine in his cluttered basement. Out of nowhere, a wealthy, elderly gentleman appears and offers him ample funds and the complex equations and circuitry to make a time machine. The inventor subsequently enriches himself with the knowledge of time travel, knowing beforehand exactly when stock-market booms and busts will occur before they happen. He makes a fortune betting on the stock market, horse races, and other events. Decades later, as a wealthy, aging man, he goes back in time to fulfill his destiny. He meets himself as a young man working in his basement, and gives his younger self the secret of time travel and the money to exploit it. The question is: Where did the idea of time travel come from?

Perhaps the craziest of these time travel paradoxes of the second type was cooked up by Robert Heinlein in his classic short story "All You Zombies — ."

A baby girl is mysteriously dropped off at an orphanage in Cleveland in 1945. "Jane" grows up lonely and dejected, not knowing who her parents are, until one day in 1963 she is strangely attracted to a drifter. She falls in love with him. But just when things are finally looking up for Jane, a series of disasters strike. First, she becomes pregnant by the drifter, who then disappears. Second, during the complicated delivery, doctors find that Jane has both sets of sex organs, and to save her life, they are forced to surgically convert "her" to a "him." Finally, a mysterious stranger kidnaps her baby from the delivery room.

Reeling from these disasters, rejected by society, scorned by fate, "he" becomes a drunkard and drifter. Not only has Jane lost her parents and her lover, but he has lost his only child as well. Years later, in 1970, he stumbles into a lonely bar, called Pop's Place, and spills out his pathetic story to an elderly bartender. The sympathetic bartender offers the drifter the chance to avenge the stranger who left her pregnant and abandoned, on the condition that he join the "time travelers corps." Both of them enter a time machine, and the bartender drops off the drifter in 1963. The drifter is strangely attracted to a young orphan woman, who subsequently becomes pregnant.

The bartender then goes forward 9 months, kidnaps the baby girl from the hospital, and drops off the baby in an orphanage back in 1945. Then the bartender drops off the thoroughly confused drifter in 1985, to enlist in the time travelers corps. The drifter eventually gets his life together, becomes a respected and elderly member of the time travelers corps, and then disguises himself as a bartender and has his most difficult mission: a date with destiny, meeting a certain drifter at Pop's Place in 1970.

The question is: Who is Jane's mother, father, grandfather, grandmother, son, daughter, granddaughter, and grandson? The girl, the drifter, and the bartender, of course, are all the same person. These paradoxes can make your head spin, especially if you try to untangle Jane's twisted parentage. If we draw Jane's family tree, we find that all the branches are curled inward back on themselves, as in a circle. We come to the astonishing conclusion that she is her own mother and father! She is an entire family tree unto herself.

World Lines

Relativity gives us a simple method to sort through the thorniest of these paradoxes. We will make use of the "world line" method, pioneered by Einstein.

For example, say our alarm clock wakes us up one day at 8:00 a.m., and we decide to spend the morning in bed instead of going to work. Although it appears that we are doing nothing by loafing in bed, we are actually tracing out a "world line."

Take a sheet of graph paper, and on the horizontal scale put "distance" and on the vertical scale put "time." If we simply lie in bed from 8:00 to 12:00, our world line is a straight vertical line. We went 4 hours into the future, but traveled no distance. Even engaging in our favorite pastime, doing nothing, creates a world line. (If someone ever criticizes us for loafing, we can truthfully claim that, according to Einstein's theory of relativity, we are tracing out a world line in four-dimensional space–time.)

Now let's say that we finally get out of bed at noon and arrive at work at 1:00 p.m. Our world line becomes slanted because we are moving in space as well as time. In the lower left corner is our home, and on the upper right is our office (Figure 1). If we take the car to work, though, we arrive at the office earlier, at 12:30. This means that the faster we travel, the more our world line deviates from the vertical. (Notice that there is also a "forbidden region" in the diagram that our world line can't enter because we would have to be going faster than the speed of light.)

One conclusion is immediate. Our world line never really begins or ends. Even when we die, the world lines of the molecules in our bodies keep going. These molecules may disperse into the air or soil, but they will trace out their own never-ending world lines. Similarly, when we are born, the world lines of the molecules coming from our mother coalesce into a baby. At no point do world lines break off or appear from nothing.

To see how this all fits together, take the simple example of our own personal world line. In 1950, say, our mother and father met, fell in love, and produced a baby (us). Thus the world lines of our mother and father collided and produced a third world line (ours). Eventually, when someone dies, the world lines forming the person disperse into billions of world lines of our molecules. From this point of view, a human being can be defined as a temporary collection of world lines of molecules. These world lines were scattered before we were born, came together to form our bodies, and will rescatter after we die. The Bible says, "from dust to dust." In this relativistic picture, we might say, "from world lines to world lines."

Our world line thus contains the entire body of information concerning our history. Everything that ever happened to us — from our first bicycle, to our first date, to our first job — is recorded in our world line. In fact, the great Russian cosmologist George Gamow, who was famous for approaching Einstein's work with wit and whimsy, aptly titled his autobiography *My World Line*.

With the aid of the world line, we can now picture what happens when we go back in time. Let's say we enter a time machine and meet our mother before we are born. Unfortunately, she falls in love with us and jilts our father. Do we really disappear, as depicted in *Back to the Future*? On a world line, we now see why this is impossible. When we disappear, our world line disappears. However, according to Einstein, world lines cannot be cut. Thus altering the past is not possible in relativity.

The second paradox, involving re-creating the past, poses interesting problems, however. For example, by going back in time, we are fulfilling the past, not destroying it. Thus the world line of the inventor of time travel is a closed loop. His world line *fulfills*, rather than changes, the past.

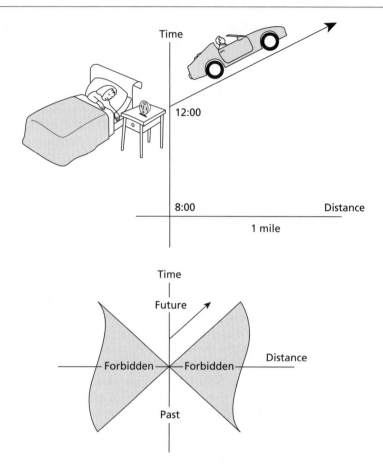

Figure 1. Our world line summarizes our entire history, from birth to death. For example, if we lie in bed from 8:00 a.m. to 12:00 p.m., our world line is a vertical line. If we travel by car to work, then our world becomes a slanted line. The faster we move, the more slanted our world line becomes. The fastest we can travel, however, is the speed of light. Thus part of this space–time diagram is "forbidden"; that is, we would have to go faster than the speed of light to enter into this forbidden zone.

Much more complicated is the world line of "Jane," the woman who is her own mother and father and son and daughter.

Notice, once again, that we cannot alter the past. When our world line goes back in time, it simply fulfills what is already known. In such a universe, therefore, it is possible to meet yourself in the past. If we live through one cycle, then sooner or later we meet a young man or woman who happens to be ourselves when we were younger. We tell this young person that he or she looks suspiciously familiar. Then, thinking a bit, we remember that when we were young, we met a curious, older person who claimed that we looked familiar.

Thus perhaps we can fulfill the past, but never alter it. World lines, as we have stressed, cannot be cut and cannot end. They can perhaps perform loops in time, but never alter it.

These light cone diagrams, however, have been presented only in the framework of special relativity, which can describe what happens if we enter the past, but is too primitive to settle the question of whether time travel makes any sense. To answer this larger question, we must turn to the general theory of relativity, where the situation becomes much more delicate.

With the full power of general relativity, we see that these twisted world lines might be physically allowed. These closed loops go by the scientific name *closed timelike curves* (CTCs). The debate in scientific circles is whether CTCs are allowed by general relativity and quantum theory.

Spoiler of Arithmetic and General Relativity

In 1949, Einstein was concerned about a discovery by one of his close colleagues and friends, the Viennese mathematician Kurt Gödel, also at the Institute for Advanced Study at Princeton, where Einstein worked. Gödel found a disturbing solution to Einstein's equations that allowed for violations of the basic tenets of common sense: His solution allowed for certain forms of time travel. For the first time in history, time travel was given a mathematical foundation.

In some quarters, Gödel was known as a spoiler. In 1931, he became famous (or, actually, infamous) when he proved, contrary to every expectation, that you cannot prove the self-consistency of arithmetic. In the process, he ruined a 2,000-year-old dream, dating back to Euclid and the Greeks, which was to have been the crowning achievement of mathematics: to reduce all of mathematics to a small, self-consistent set of axioms from which everything could be derived.

In a mathematical tour de force, Gödel showed that there will always be theorems in arithmetic whose correctness or incorrectness can never be demonstrated from the axioms of arithmetic; that is, arithmetic will always be incomplete. Gödel's result was the most startling, unexpected development in mathematical logic in perhaps a thousand years.

Mathematics, once thought to be the purest of all sciences because it was precise and certain, untarnished by the unpleasant crudeness of our material world, now became uncertain. After Gödel, the fundamental basis for mathematics seemed to be left adrift. (Crudely speaking, Gödel's remarkable proof began by showing that there are curious paradoxes in logic. For example, consider the statement "This sentence is false." If the sentence is true, then it follows that it is false. If the sentence is false, then the sentence is true. Or consider the statement "I am a liar." Then I am a liar only if I tell the truth. Gödel then formulated the statement "This sentence cannot be proved true." If the sentence is correct, then it cannot be proved to be correct. By carefully building a complex web of such paradoxes,

Gödel showed that there are true statements that cannot be proved using arithmetic.)

After demolishing one of the most cherished dreams of all of mathematics, Gödel next shattered the conventional wisdom surrounding Einstein's equations. He showed that Einstein's theory contains some surprising pathologies, including time travel.

He first assumed that the universe was filled with gas or dust that was slowly rotating. This seemed reasonable, since the far reaches of the universe do seem to be filled with gas and dust. However, Gödel's solution caused great concern for two reasons.

First, his solution violated Mach's principle. He showed that *two* solutions of Einstein's equations were possible with the same distribution of dust and gas. (This meant that Mach's principle was somehow incomplete, that hidden assumptions were present.)

More important, he showed that certain forms of time travel were permitted. If one followed the path of a particle in a Gödel universe, eventually it would come back and meet itself in the past. He wrote, "By making a round trip on a rocket ship in a sufficiently wide curve, it is possible in these worlds to travel into any region of the past, present, and future, and back again."[2] Thus Gödel found the first CTC in general relativity.

Previously, Newton considered time to be moving like a straight arrow, which unerringly flies forward toward its target. Nothing could deflect or change the course of this arrow once it was shot. Einstein, however, showed that time was more like a mighty river, moving forward but often meandering through twisting valleys and plains. The presence of matter or energy might momentarily shift the direction of the river, but overall the river's course was smooth: It never abruptly ended or jerked backward. However, Gödel showed that the river of time could be smoothly bent backward into a circle. Rivers, after all, have eddy currents and whirlpools. In the main, a river may flow forward, but at the edges there are always side pools where water flows in a circular motion.

Gödel's solution could not be dismissed as the work of a crackpot because Gödel had used Einstein's own field equations to find strange solutions in which time bent into a circle. Because Gödel had played by the rules and discovered a legitimate solution to his equations, Einstein was forced to take the evasive route and dismiss it because it did not fit the experimental data.

The weak spot in Gödel's universe was the assumption that the gas and dust in the universe were slowly rotating. Experimentally, we do not see any rotation of the cosmic dust and gas in space. Our instruments have verified that the universe is expanding, but it does not appear to be rotating. Thus the Gödel universe can be safely ruled out. (This leaves us with the rather disturbing, although plausible, possibility that if our universe did rotate, as Gödel speculated, then CTCs and time travel would be physically possible.)

2. K. Gödel, "An Example of a New Type of Cosmological Solution of Einstein's Field Equations of Gravitation," *Reviews of Modern Physics* 21 (1949): 447.

Einstein died in 1955, content that disturbing solutions to his equations could be swept under the rug for experimental reasons and that people could not meet their parents before they were born.

Living in the Twilight Zone

Then, in 1963, Ezra Newman, Theodore Unti, and Louis Tamburino discovered a new solution to Einstein's equations that was even crazier than Gödel's. Unlike the Gödel universe, their solution was not based on a rotating dust-filled universe. On the surface, it resembled a typical black hole.

As in the Gödel solution, their universe allowed for CTCs and time travel. Moreover, when going 360 degrees around the black hole, you would not wind up where you originally started. Instead, like living on a universe with a Riemann cut, you would wind up on another sheet of the universe. The topology of a Newman–Unti–Tamburino universe might be compared to living on a spiral staircase. If we move 360 degrees around the staircase, we do not arrive at the same point at which we started, but on another landing of the staircase. Living in such a universe would surpass our worst nightmare, with common sense being completely thrown out the window. In fact, this bizarre universe was so pathological that it was quickly coined the NUT universe, after the initials of its creators.

At first, relativists dismissed the NUT solution in the same way they had dismissed the Gödel solution; that is, our universe didn't seem to evolve in the way predicted by these solutions, so they were arbitrarily discarded for experimental reasons. However, as the decades went by, there was a flood of such bizarre solutions to Einstein's equations that allowed for time travel. In the early 1970s, Frank J. Tipler at Tulane University in New Orleans reanalyzed an old solution to Einstein's equations found by W. J. van Stockum in 1936, even before Gödel's solution. This solution assumed the existence of an infinitely long, rotating cylinder. Surprisingly enough, Tipler was able to show that this solution also violated causality.

Even the Kerr solution (which represents the most physically realistic description of black holes in outer space) was shown to allow for time travel. Rocket ships that pass through the center of the Kerr black hole (assuming they are not crushed in the process) could violate causality.

Soon, physicists found that NUT-type singularities could be inserted into any black hole or expanding universe. In fact, it now became possible to cook up an infinite number of pathological solutions to Einstein's equations. For example, every wormhole solution to Einstein's equations could be shown to allow some form of time travel.

According to relativist Frank Tipler, "solutions to the field equations can be found which exhibit virtually any type of bizarre behavior."[3] Thus an explosion of pathological solutions to Einstein's equations was discovered that certainly would have horrified Einstein had he still been alive.

---

3. F. Tipler, "Causality Violation in Asymptotically Flat Space-Times," *Physical Review Letters* 37 (1976): 979.

Einstein's equations, in some sense, were like a Trojan horse. On the surface, the horse looks like a perfectly acceptable gift, giving us the observed bending of starlight under gravity and a compelling explanation of the origin of the universe. However, inside lurk all sorts of strange demons and goblins, which allow for the possibility of interstellar travel through wormholes and time travel. The price we had to pay for peering into the darkest secrets of the universe was the potential downfall of some of our most commonly held beliefs about our world — that its space is simply connected and its history is unalterable.

But the question still remained: Could these CTCs be dismissed on purely experimental grounds, as Einstein did, or could someone show that they were theoretically possible and then actually build a time machine?

To Build a Time Machine

In June 1988, three physicists (Kip Thorne and Michael Morris at the California Institute of Technology and Ulvi Yurtsever at the University of Michigan) made the first serious proposal for a time machine. They convinced the editors of *Physical Review Letters*, one of the most distinguished publications in the world, that their work merited serious consideration. (Over the decades, scores of crackpot proposals for time travel have been submitted to mainstream physics journals, but all have been rejected because they were not based on sound physical principles or Einstein's equations.) Like experienced scientists, they presented their arguments in accepted field theoretical language and then carefully explained where their weakest assumptions were.

To overcome the skepticism of the scientific community, Thorne and his colleagues realized that they would have to overcome the standard objections to using wormholes as time machines. First, as mentioned earlier, Einstein himself realized that the gravitational forces at the center of a black hole would be so enormous that any spacecraft would be torn apart. Although wormholes were mathematically possible, they were, in practice, useless.

Second, wormholes might be unstable. One could show that small disturbances in wormholes would cause the Einstein–Rosen bridge to collapse. Thus a spaceship's presence inside a black hole would be sufficient to cause a disturbance that would close the entrance to the wormhole.

Third, one would have to go faster than the speed of light actually to penetrate the wormhole to the other side.

Fourth, quantum effects would be so large that the wormhole might close by itself. For example, the intense radiation emitted by the entrance to the black hole not only would kill anyone who tried to enter the black hole, but also might close the entrance.

Fifth, time slows down in a wormhole and comes to a complete stop at the center. Thus wormholes have the undesirable feature that as seen by someone on the earth, a space traveler appears to slow down and come to a total halt at the center of the black hole. The space traveler looks like he or she is frozen in time. In other words, it takes an infinite amount of time for a space traveler to go through a wormhole. Assuming, for the moment, that one could somehow go through the center of the wormhole and return to earth, the distortion of time would still be so great that millions or even billions of years may have passed on the earth.

For all these reasons, the wormhole solutions were never taken seriously.

Thorne is a serious cosmologist, one who might normally view time machines with extreme skepticism or even derision. However, Thorne was gradually drawn into this quest in the most curious way. In the summer of 1985, Carl Sagan sent to Thorne the prepublication draft of his next book, a novel called *Contact*, which seriously explores the scientific and political questions surrounding an epoch-making event: making contact with the first extraterrestrial life in outer space. Every scientist pondering the question of life in outer space must confront the question of how to break the light barrier. Since Einstein's special theory of relativity explicitly forbids travel faster than the speed of light, traveling to the distant stars in a conventional spaceship may take thousands of years, thereby making interstellar travel impractical. Since Sagan wanted to make his book as scientifically accurate as possible, he wrote to Thorne asking whether there was any scientifically acceptable way of evading the light barrier.

Sagan's request piqued Thorne's intellectual curiosity. Here was an honest, scientifically relevant request made by one scientist to another that demanded a serious reply. Fortunately, because of the unorthodox nature of the request, Thorne and his colleagues approached the question in a most unusual way: They worked *backward*. Normally, physicists start with a certain known astronomical object (a neutron star, a black hole, the Big Bang) and then solve Einstein's equations to find the curvature of the surrounding space. The essence of Einstein's equations, we recall, is that the matter and energy content of an object determines the amount of curvature in the surrounding space and time. Proceeding in this way, we are guaranteed to find solutions to Einstein's equations for astronomically relevant objects that we expect to find in outer space.

However, because of Sagan's strange request, Thorne and his colleagues approached the question backward. They started with a rough idea of what they wanted to find. They wanted a solution to Einstein's equations in which a space traveler would not be torn apart by the tidal effects of the intense gravitational field. They wanted a wormhole that would be stable and not suddenly close up in the middle of the trip. They wanted a wormhole in which the time it takes for a round trip would be measured in days, not millions or billions of earth years, and so on. In fact, their guiding principle was that they wanted a time traveler to have a reasonably comfortable ride back through time after entering the wormhole. Once they decided what their wormhole would look like, then, and only then, did they begin to calculate the amount of energy necessary to create such a wormhole.

From their unorthodox point of view, they did not particularly care if the energy requirements were well beyond twentieth-century science. To them, it was an engineering problem for some future civilization actually to construct the time machine. They wanted to prove that it was scientifically feasible, not that it was economical or within the bounds of present-day earth science:

> Normally, theoretical physicists ask, "What are the laws of physics?" and/or "What do those laws predict about the Universe?" In this Letter, we ask, instead, "What constraints do the laws of physics place on the activities of an arbitrarily advanced civilization?" This will lead to some intriguing queries about the laws themselves. We begin by asking whether the laws of physics permit an arbitrarily advanced civilization to construct and maintain wormholes for interstellar travel.[4]

The key phrase, of course, is "arbitrarily advanced civilization." The laws of physics tell us what is possible, not what is practical. The laws of physics are independent of what it might cost to test them. Thus what is theoretically possible may exceed the gross national product of the planet earth. Thorne and his colleagues were careful to state that this mythical civilization that can harness the power of wormholes must be "arbitrarily advanced" — that is, capable of performing all experiments that are possible (even if they are not practical for earthlings).

Much to their delight, with remarkable ease they soon found a surprisingly simple solution that satisfied all their rigid constraints. It was *not* a typical black hole solution at all, so they didn't have to worry about all the problems of being ripped apart by a collapsed star. They christened their solution the "transversible wormhole," to distinguish it from the other wormhole solutions that are not transversible by spaceship. They were so excited by their solution that they wrote back to Sagan, who then incorporated some of their ideas in his novel. In fact, they were so surprised by the simplicity of their solution that they were convinced that a beginning graduate student in physics would be able to understand their solution. In the autumn of 1985, on the final exam in a course on general relativity given at Caltech, Thorne gave the wormhole solution to the students without telling them what it was, and they were asked to deduce its physical properties. (Most students gave detailed mathematical analyses of the solution, but they failed to grasp that they were looking at a solution that permitted time travel.)

If the students had been a bit more observant on that final exam, they would have been able to deduce some rather astonishing properties of the wormhole. In fact, they would have found that a trip through this transversible wormhole would be as comfortable as a trip on an airplane. The maximum gravitational forces experienced by the travelers would not exceed 1 g. In other words, their apparent weight would not exceed their weight on the earth. Furthermore, the travelers would never have to worry about the entrance of the wormhole closing up during the journey. Thorne's

4. M. S. Morris , K. S. Thorne, and U. Yurtsever, "Wormholes, Time Machines and the Weak Energy Condition," *Physical Review Letters* 61 (1988): 1446.

wormhole is, in fact, permanently open. Instead of taking a million or a billion years, a trip through the transversible wormhole would be manageable. Morris and Thorne write that "the trip will be fully comfortable and will require a total of about 200 days," or less.[5]

So far, Thorne notes that the time paradoxes that one usually encounters in the movies are not to be found: "From exposure to science fiction scenarios (for example, those in which one goes back in time and kills oneself) one might expect CTCs to give rise to initial trajectories with zero multiplicities" (that is, trajectories that are impossible).[6] However, he has shown that the CTCs that appear in his wormhole seem to *fulfill* the past, rather than change it or initiate time paradoxes.

Finally, in presenting these surprising results to the scientific community, Thorne wrote, "A new class of solutions of the Einstein field equations is presented, which describe wormholes that, in principle, could be traversed by human beings."

There is, of course, a catch to all this, which is one reason why we do not have time machines today. The last step in Thorne's calculation was to deduce the precise nature of the matter and energy necessary to create this marvelous transversible wormhole. Thorne and his colleagues found that at the center of the wormhole, there must be an "exotic" form of matter that has unusual properties. Thorne is quick to point out that this "exotic" form of matter, although unusual, does not seem to violate any of the known laws of physics. He cautions that, at some future point, scientists may prove that exotic matter does not exist. However, at present, exotic matter seems to be a perfectly acceptable form of matter *if* one has access to sufficiently advanced technology. Thorne writes confidently that "from a single wormhole an arbitrarily advanced civilization can construct a machine for backward time travel."

Blueprint for a Time Machine

Anyone who has read H. G. Wells's *The Time Machine*, however, may be disappointed with Thorne's blueprint for a time machine. You do not sit in a chair in your living room, turn a few dials, see blinking lights, and witness the vast panorama of history, including destructive world wars, the rise and fall of great civilizations, or the fruits of futuristic scientific marvels.

One version of Thorne's time machine consists of two chambers, each containing two parallel metal plates. The intense electric fields created between each pair of plates (larger than anything possible with today's technology) rips the fabric of space–time, creating a hole in space that links the two chambers. One chamber is then placed in a rocket ship and is accelerated to near-light velocities, while the other chamber stays on the

---

5. M. S. Morris and K. S. Thorne, "Wormholes in Spacetime and Their Use for Interstellar Travel: A Tool for Teaching General Relativity," *American Journal of Physics* 56 (1988): 411.

6. Fernando Echeverria, Gunnar Klinkhammer, and Kip S. Thorne, "Billiard Balls in Wormhole Spacetimes with Closed Timelike Curves: Classical Theory," *Physical Review D* 44 (1991): 1079.

earth. Since a wormhole can connect two regions of space with different times, a clock in the first chamber ticks slower than a clock in the second chamber. Because time would pass at different rates at the two ends of the wormhole, anyone falling into one end of the wormhole would be instantly hurled into the past or the future.

Another time machine might look like the following. If exotic matter can be found and shaped like metal, then presumably the ideal shape would be a cylinder. A human stands in the center of the cylinder. The exotic matter then warps the space and time surrounding it, creating a wormhole that connects to a distant part of the universe in a different time. At the center of the vortex is the human, who then experiences no more than 1 g of gravitational stress as he or she is then sucked into the wormhole and finds himself or herself on the other end of the universe.

On the surface, Thorne's mathematical reasoning is impeccable. Einstein's equations indeed show that wormhole solutions allow for time to pass at different rates on either side of the wormhole, so that time travel, in principle, is possible. The trick, of course, is to create the wormhole in the first place. As Thorne and his collaborators are quick to point out, the main problem is how to harness enough energy to create and maintain a wormhole with exotic matter.

Normally, one of the basic tenets of elementary physics is that all objects have positive energy. Vibrating molecules, moving cars, flying birds, and soaring rockets all have positive energy. (By definition, the empty vacuum of space has zero energy.) However, if we can produce objects with "negative energies" (that is, something that has an energy content less than the vacuum), then we might be able to generate exotic configurations of space and time in which time is bent into a circle.

This rather simple concept goes by a complicated-sounding title: the *averaged weak energy condition* (AWEC). As Thorne is careful to point out, the AWEC must be violated; energy must become temporarily *negative* for time travel to be successful. However, negative energy has historically been anathema to relativists, who realize that negative energy would make possible antigravity and a host of other phenomena that have never been seen experimentally.

But Thorne is quick to point out that there is a way to obtain negative energy, and this is through quantum theory. In 1948, the Dutch physicist Henrik Casimir demonstrated that quantum theory can create negative energy: Just take two large, uncharged parallel metal plates. Ordinarily, common sense tells us that these two plates, because they are electrically neutral, have no force between them. But Casimir proved that the vacuum separating these two plates, because of the Heisenberg Uncertainty Principle, is actually teeming with activity, with trillions of particles and antiparticles constantly appearing and disappearing. They appear out of nowhere and disappear back into the vacuum. Because they are so fleeting, they are, for the most part, unobservable, and they do not violate any of the laws of physics. These "virtual particles" create a net attractive force between these two plates that Casimir predicted was measurable.

When Casimir first published his paper, it met with extreme skepticism. After all, how can two electrically neutral objects attract each other, thereby violating the usual laws of classical electricity? This was unheard of. However, in 1958 physicist M. J. Sparnaay observed this effect in the laboratory, exactly as Casimir had predicted. Since then, it has been christened the *Casimir effect*.

One way of harnessing the Casimir effect is to place two large conducting parallel plates at the entrance of each wormhole, thereby creating negative energy at each end. As Thorne and his colleagues conclude, "It may turn out that the average weak energy condition can never be violated, in which case there could be no such things as transversible wormholes, time travel, or a failure of causality. It's premature to try to cross a bridge before you come to it."[7]

At present, the jury is still out on Thorne's time machine. The decisive factor, all agree, is to have a fully quantized theory of gravity settle the matter once and for all. For example, Stephen Hawking has pointed out that the radiation emitted at the wormhole entrance will be quite large and will contribute back into the matter–energy content of Einstein's equations. This feedback into Einstein's equations will distort the entrance to the wormhole, perhaps even closing it forever. Thorne, however, disagrees that the radiation will be sufficient to close the entrance.

This is where superstring theory comes in. Because superstring theory is a fully quantum-mechanical theory that includes Einstein's theory of general relativity as a subset, it can be used to calculate corrections to the original wormhole theory. In principle, it will allow us to determine whether the AWEC condition is physically realizable, and whether the wormhole entrance stays open for time travelers to enjoy a trip to the past.

Hawking has expressed reservations about Thorne's wormholes. However, this is ironic because Hawking himself has proposed a new theory of wormholes that is even more fantastic. Instead of connecting the present with the past, Hawking proposes to use wormholes to connect our universe with an infinite number of parallel universes!

---

7. Morris, Thorne, and Yurtsever, "Wormholes," 1447.

Utopias and Dystopias

Utopian literature has been one of the most powerful influences on the development of sf, and indeed the two genres seem so inextricably linked that some critics have suggested that utopian literature is really a subcategory of sf. Utopias are, after all, speculative fictions by their very nature, and nearly all the influential literary utopias of the twentieth century, including George Orwell's *1984*, Aldous Huxley's *Brave New World*, and Margaret Atwood's *The Handmaid's Tale*, can certainly be classified as sf.

As commonly used, the word *utopia* refers to an ideal society, a harmonious community that reflects a set of values about how people should live and what it takes to be truly happy. Attractive though these visions may be, such a state of perfection is probably by its nature unattainable, and thus "utopian" has also gained the derogatory connotation of something absurdly impractical. Thomas More was well aware of this paradox when he coined the word in his wistful yet ironic depiction of the ideal state in 1516, using the title to pun on eutopia (good place) and utopia (no place).

More's influential book gave the literary genre of utopia its name, but More was hardly the first to imaginatively explore the idea of a perfect society. Visions of earthly or celestial paradises are common in all cultures, but utopias are distinct in terms of being human-engineered societies rather than naturally endowed lands of abundance or divinely ordained states of grace. A utopia is a way of organizing human culture and government. In the West, one of the earliest and most influential of these visions is Plato's *Republic*, which envisioned an enlightened society ruled by a philosopher king. The *Republic*, and particularly the famous Allegory of the Cave contained in that book, are frequently referenced by sf writers, as is More's *Utopia* — as can be seen from the stories in this chapter.

Writers of utopian stories are often fascinated by working out pragmatic details of how their imaginary communities will function, such as the allocation of resources, division of labor, manner of education, and role of the family. Underpinning their solutions to even the most mundane of these challenges, however, is always a deeper set of beliefs about human nature and moral values — a belief in the primacy of communalism over individualism, for example, or of the spiritual over the sensual. In this sense, utopias, though they sometimes read like instruction manuals, are really philosophical thought experiments, radical and profound explorations of alternatives to our present social arrangements.

Historically, many attempts have been made actually to create utopian or "intentional communities," although they seldom last or are fully successful. To maintain the rigorously consistent values such communities generally require, some sacrifice of individual freedom is necessary, resulting in what often comes to be seen as an intolerable level of social control. From revolutionary France to the former Soviet Union, states planned on utopian ideals have a tendency to become repressive and corrupt. Smaller social experiments (kibbutzes, hippie communes, Shakers, and others) are often more successful in realizing their values, but they lose steam as the fully committed founders age and the youthful generation rebels against the restrictions such communities necessitate.

Even imaginary utopias are often deeply flawed. Both More's and Plato's societies have communal and egalitarian features, for instance; yet, Plato's republic has rigid class divisions, and the leisure time so essential for the intellectual and artistic pursuits of citizens in More's *Utopia* is underwritten in part by slave labor. The simple reason for these inconsistencies is that we have not yet discovered the solution to perennial human problems — if we had, presumably, we would already be living in utopia and would not need to imagine it. Nonetheless, utopian thinking is immensely valuable because it frees us to explore new possibilities and to contemplate how human life might be organized to better reflect our values. While utopia may never be realized in its pure form, the radical alternatives that utopian thinking provides can help us to reconsider our values and shape our societies toward our ideals.

The flip side of a utopia is what is sometimes known as a *dystopia*, or bad place. Indeed, this has been the dominant form in twentieth-century literature. Some reject the division because, since utopias themselves are so often ambiguous, it can be argued that every utopia — when viewed from another angle — is also a dystopia. If utopias are attempts to radically reimagine human relations, dystopias place more emphasis on satirizing existing societies and warning us about where we may be heading. While some works emphasize the negative and others the positive, however, it is fair to say that each type contains both critique and idealism.

Many sf stories have utopian or dystopian elements implicit in their settings, even when their focus is not directly on utopian world-building. In those works where the utopian project is central, the focus is often on a particular element with transformative potential, most commonly class, gender, government, technology, or ecology. (To date, surprisingly few utopias have focused primarily on race — it is an element in works like Ursula K. Le Guin's *Lathe of Heaven* or Nalo Hopkinson's story in this chapter, but not the focus.) And, although sf in general is a self-referential genre, in utopian literature there is an unusual degree of intertextuality; the entire body of utopian literature may be seen as an ongoing dialogue. In the most obvious example, both Samuel Butler's *Erewhon* and William Morris's *News from Nowhere* play on the title of More's *Utopia*. H. G. Wells's foundational novella, "In the Country of the Blind" is clearly a pessimistic reading of Plato's Allegory of the Cave, in which the inhabitants prefer to remain in their benighted state. In turn, Damon Knight's "The

Country of the Kind" and John Varley's "The Persistence of Vision" — both included in this chapter — are direct responses to Wells's story as well as exchanges in the larger debate of the utopian tradition. Joanna Russ's exploration of gender in "When It Changed" engages with earlier texts like Charlotte Perkins Gilman's *Herland* and, in turn, has become a reference point for all the feminist utopias that have followed.

The most influential political dystopia of the twentieth century is no doubt Yevgeny Zamyatin's depiction of a totalitarian state in *We*. Though not published in Zamyatin's native Russia until 1988 (fifty-one years after his death) the English translation was the inspiration for George Orwell's celebrated *1984* and thus, directly or indirectly, for every political utopia or dystopia written since. Zamyatin's and Orwell's most obvious target is Soviet-style communism, but both books also contain important critiques of the techno-bureaucracies and mindless conformism of Western capitalism.

Recognizing these kinds of references and rejoinders and tracing the web of interconnections that links these stories is one of the pleasures of reading in the utopian tradition, and it deepens our understanding of the complexity of the issues involved. At the same time, each story in this chapter stands on its own artistically, and each provides a unique jolt of realization as it startles us into new ways of thinking.

In the Critical Contexts section, Hannah Arendt and William H. Whyte Jr. provide perspectives on two very different forms of dystopia that have been influential in the twentieth century — the nightmare of totalitarianism and the anesthetized cocoon of corporate capitalism. Fredric Jameson focuses on the paradoxes inherent in the form of the literary utopia itself, with an emphasis on modern science fiction.

Yevgeny Zamyatin

From We

(1921; trans. 1972)

Yevgeny Zamyatin (1884–1937) was born to dissent. The son of an Orthodox Russian priest, Zamyatin became a Bolshevik as a young man and embarked on a life of conflict with authority. Repeatedly jailed and exiled, his works banned first by czarist and then by communist regimes, Zamyatin was both an outspoken critic of governmental abuse and a patriot, an idealist who believed that human society could achieve a more utopian organization without sacrificing individual expression and freedom of speech. *We* was a major influence on both George Orwell's *1984* and Aldous Huxley's *Brave New World*, and through them on every major literary utopia since.

Translated by Mirra Ginsburg.

Zamyatin wrote *We* in 1921, just four years after the Russian Revolution, in which he had participated directly and enthusiastically. A scathing satire of state control and dehumanization, *We* presented a prescient vision of the worst abuses that would soon follow in Stalinist Russia. It is a testament to the novel's power that it proved impossible to publish in Russia until 1988, shortly before the collapse of the Soviet Union and fifty-one years after Zamyatin's own death. It was, however, circulated in manuscript form and published abroad. Although *We* is clearly a warning about the direction Russia was heading, Zamyatin was neither an anticommunist nor an anti-utopian. He remained an ardent and outspoken socialist throughout his life and never gave up his revolutionary dreams for a better society. He was able to maintain his faith partly because he didn't believe in progress as a movement toward some final goal of static perfection but rather as a continual process.

We is written as a series of diary entries by a man who is, as Zamyatin was, an engineer and a builder of ships. It takes place in an enclosed city, completely separated from nature, its citizens assigned numbers rather than names. All aspects of life are mechanically regulated and every minute of the day accounted for. This is a world purged of the irrational, of emotion, of individuality, and of creativity, except in service of the single-minded aggrandizement of the One State. Or so it seems. From the very beginning, the narrator has a distinctive, frenetic voice and a degree of self-regard in his role as scientific creator that marks him as a unique individual. Soon he meets a mysterious woman who introduces him to new ways of thinking and disrupts his accustomed modes of thought.

Zamyatin's achievement also extends beyond the importance of his message; *We* is experimental in form, too, its chapters structured as much by ideas and images as by plot, its language poetic, the world it constructs both completely absurd and uncomfortably believable. This mirroring of ideas and form is not unique to science fiction, but when it works best — as in *We* — the altered world of the novel comes even more eerily alive. And for a novel with such serious purposes, the humor in *We* is very important — there's a black humor to the depiction of daily life, and yet also there's a certain exuberant joy in the telling that makes you feel Zamyatin is anything but despairing. It is likely these same qualities that allowed Zamyatin to keep believing in the eventual success of the revolution even when it took such disturbing directions and even when its excesses curtailed his own life and artistic freedom.

First Entry

TOPICS: *A Proclamation*
            The Wisest of Lines
            A Poem

I shall simply copy, word for word, the proclamation that appeared today in the *One State Gazette*:

The building of the *Integral* will be completed in one hundred and twenty days. The great historic hour when the first *Integral* will soar into cosmic space is drawing near. One thousand years ago your heroic ancestors subdued the entire terrestrial globe to the power of the One State. Yours will be a still more glorious feat: you will integrate the infinite equation of the universe with the aid of the fire-breathing, electric, glass *Integral*. You will subjugate the unknown beings on other planets, who may still be living in the primitive condition of freedom, to the beneficent yoke of reason. If they fail to understand that we bring them mathematically infallible happiness, it will be our duty to compel them to be happy. But before resorting to arms, we shall try the power of words.

In the name of the Benefactor, therefore, we proclaim to all the numbers of the One State:

Everyone who feels capable of doing so must compose tracts, odes, manifestoes, poems, or other works extolling the beauty and the grandeur of the One State.

This will be the first cargo to be carried by the *Integral*.

Long live the One State, long live the numbers, long live the Benefactor!

I write this, and I feel: my cheeks are burning. Yes, to integrate the grandiose cosmic equation. Yes, to unbend the wild, primitive curve and straighten it to a tangent — an asymptote — a straight line. For the line of the One State is the straight line. The great, divine, exact, wise straight line — the wisest of all lines.

I, D-503, Builder of the *Integral*, am only one of the mathematicians of the One State. My pen, accustomed to figures, does not know how to create the music of assonances and rhymes. I shall merely attempt to record what I see and think, or, to be more exact, what we think (precisely so — we, and let this *We* be the title of my record). But since this record will be a derivative of our life, of the mathematically perfect life of the One State, will it not be, of itself, and regardless of my will or skill, a poem? It will. I believe, I know it.

I write this, and my cheeks are burning. This must be similar to what a woman feels when she first senses within herself the pulse of a new, still tiny, still blind little human being. It is I, and at the same time, not I. And for many long months it will be necessary to nourish it with my own life, my own blood, then tear it painfully from myself and lay it at the feet of the One State.

But I am ready, like every one, or almost every one, of us. I am ready.

Second Entry

TOPICS: *Ballet*

              Square Harmony

              X

Spring. From beyond the Green Wall, from the wild, invisible plains, the wind brings yellow honey pollen of some unknown flowers. The sweet pollen dries your lips, and every minute you pass your tongue over them. The lips of all the women you see must be sweet (of the men, too, of course). This interferes to some extent with the flow of logical thought.

But the sky! Blue, unblemished by a single cloud. (How wild the tastes of the ancients, whose poets could be inspired by those absurd, disorderly, stupidly tumbling piles of vapor!) I love — I am certain I can safely say, we love — only such a sterile, immaculate sky. On days like this the whole world is cast of the same impregnable, eternal glass as the Green Wall, as all our buildings. On days like this you see the bluest depth of things, their hitherto unknown, astonishing equations — you see them even in the most familiar everyday objects.

Take, for instance, this. In the morning I was at the dock where the *Integral* is being built, and suddenly I *saw*: the lathes; the regulator spheres rotating with closed eyes, utterly oblivious of all; the cranks flashing, swinging left and right; the balance beam proudly swaying its shoulders; the bit of the slotting machine dancing up and down in time to unheard music. Suddenly I saw the whole beauty of this grandiose mechanical ballet, flooded with pale blue sunlight.

And then, to myself: Why is this beautiful? Why is dance beautiful? Answer: because it is *unfree* motion, because the whole profound meaning of dance lies precisely in absolute, esthetic subordination, in ideal unfreedom. And if it is true that our forebears abandoned themselves to dance at the most exalted moments of their lives (religious mysteries, military parades), it means only one thing: the instinct of unfreedom is organically inherent in man from time immemorial, and we, in our present life, are only consciously. . . .

I will have to finish later: the annunciator clicked. I looked up: O-90, of course. In half a minute she'll be here, for our daily walk.

Dear O! It always seems to me that she looks exactly like her name: about ten centimeters shorter than the Maternal Norm, and therefore carved in the round, all of her, with that pink O, her mouth, open to meet every word I say. And also, that round, plump fold on her wrist, like a baby's.

When she came in, the flywheel of logic was still humming at full swing within me, and I began, by sheer force of inertia, to speak to her about the formula I had just established, which encompassed everything — dance, machines, and all of us.

"Marvelous, isn't it?" I asked.

"Yes, marvelous." O-90 smiled rosily at me. "It's spring."

Well, wouldn't you know: spring . . . She talks about spring. Women . . . I fell silent.

Downstairs, the avenue was full. In such weather, the afternoon personal hour is used for an additional walk. As always, the Music Plant played the "March of the One State" with all its trumpets. The numbers walked in even ranks, four abreast, ecstatically stepping in time to the music — hundreds, thousands of numbers, in pale blue unifs,[1] with golden

1. Derived apparently from the ancient "uniform."

badges on their breasts, bearing the State Number of each man and woman. And I — the four of us — but one of the innumerable waves in this mighty stream. On my left, O-90 (if this were being written by one of my hairy ancestors a thousand years ago, he probably would have described her by that funny word "mine"); on my right, two numbers I did not know, male and female.

Blessedly blue sky, tiny baby suns in every badge, faces unshadowed by the insanity of thoughts . . . Rays. Do you understand that? Everything made of some single, radiant, smiling substance. And the brass rhythms: "Ta-ta-ta-tam! Ta-ta-ta-tam!" Like brass stairs gleaming in the sun, and every step taking you higher and higher, into the dizzying blue. . . .

And again, as this morning at the dock, I saw everything as though for the first time in my life: the straight, immutable streets, the glittering glass of the pavements, the divine parallelepipeds of the transparent houses, the square harmony of the gray-blue ranks. And I felt: it was not the generations before me, but I — yes, I — who had conquered the old God and the old life. It was I who had created all this. And I was like a tower, I dared not move an elbow lest walls, cupolas, machines tumble in fragments about me.

Then — a leap across the centuries, from + to −. I remembered (evidently an association by contrast) — I suddenly remembered a picture I had seen in a museum: one of their avenues, out of the twentieth century, dazzlingly motley, a teeming crush of people, wheels, animals, posters, trees, colors, birds. . . . And they say this had really existed — could exist. It seemed so incredible, so preposterous that I could not contain myself and burst out laughing.

And immediately, there was an echo — laughter — on my right. I turned: a flash of white — extraordinarily white and sharp teeth, an unfamiliar female face.

"Forgive me," she said, "but you looked at everything around you with such an inspired air, like some mythical god on the seventh day of creation. It seems to me you are sure that even I was created by you, and by no one else. I am very flattered. . . ."

All this — without a smile; I would even say, with a certain deference (perhaps she knew that I am the Builder of the *Integral*). But in the eyes, or in the eyebrows — I could not tell — there was a certain strange, irritating X, which I could not capture, could not define in figures.

For some odd reason, I felt embarrassed and tried, in a rather stumbling manner, to explain my laughter to her logically. It was entirely clear, I said, that this contrast, this impassable abyss between the present and the past . . .

"But why impassable?" (What white teeth!) "A bridge can be thrown across an abyss. Just think: drums, battalions, ranks — all this has also existed in the past; and, consequently . . ."

"But of course!" I cried. (What an astonishing coincidence of ideas: she spoke almost my own words, the words I had written down before our walk.) "You understand, even ideas. And this is because nobody is 'one,' but 'one of.' We are so alike. . . ."

She: "Are you sure?"

I saw her eyebrows raised to her temples at a sharp angle, like the pointed horns of an X, and again I was confused. I glanced right, left, and . . .

On my right — she, slender, sharp, stubbornly pliant, like a whip, I-330 (I could see her number now); on my left — O, altogether different, all curves, with that childish fold on her wrist; and at the other end of our row, a male number I did not know — strange, doubly bent somehow, like the letter S. All of us so different . . .

That one on the right, I-330, seemed to have intercepted my flustered glance, and with a sigh she said, "Yes. . . . Alas!"

Actually, this "alas" was entirely appropriate. But again there was that something in her face, or in her voice. . . . And with a sharpness unusual for me, I said, "No reason for 'Alas.' Science progresses, and it is obvious that, if not now, then in fifty or a hundred years . . ."

"Even everyone's noses . . ."

"Yes," I almost shouted, "noses. If there is any ground for envy, no matter what it is . . . If I have a button-nose and another . . ."

"Oh, your nose is 'classical,' as they used to say in olden times. But your hands . . . No, let us see, let us see your hands!"

I detest to have anyone look at my hands: all hairy, shaggy — a stupid atavism. I held out my hand and said, as indifferently as I could, "An ape's hands."

She glanced at my hands, then at my face. "A most interesting conjunction." She weighed me with her eyes as on a scale, and the horns flicked again at the corners of her eyebrows.

"He is registered with me." O-90's lips opened rosily, with eager joy.

I wished she had kept silent — this was altogether out of place. Generally, this dear O . . . how shall I put it . . . her tongue is wrongly timed; the speed of the tongue should always be some seconds behind the speed of thought, but certainly not the other way around.

At the end of the avenue, the bell on the Accumulator Tower was loudly striking seventeen. The personal hour was over. I-330 was leaving with the S-shaped male number. His face somehow inspired respect, and now it seemed familiar. I must have met him somewhere, but where?

In parting, I-330 said with another of her X-smiles, "Come to auditorium 112 the day after tomorrow."

I shrugged. "If I am assigned to that auditorium . . ."

And she, with an odd certainty, "You will be."

The woman affected me as unpleasantly as an irresolvable irrational member that has somehow slipped into an equation. And I was glad to remain for at least a few moments alone with dear O.

Hand in hand, we crossed four lines of avenues. At the corner she had to turn right, and I, left.

"I'd like so much to come to you today and let down the blinds. Today, right now . . ." O timidly raised her round, blue-crystal eyes to me.

How funny she is. What could I say to her? She had come to me only the day before, and she knew as well as I did that our next sexual day was the day after tomorrow. It was simply a case of her usual "words ahead of thought" — like the occasional (and sometimes damaging) premature supply of a spark to a motor.

Before we parted, I kissed her lovely blue eyes, unshadowed by a single cloud, two — no, let me be precise — three times.

Third Entry

TOPICS: *Coat*
                Wall
                Tables

I have just looked over what I had written yesterday, and I see that I did not express myself clearly enough. Of course, it is all entirely clear to any of us. But perhaps you, the unknown readers to whom the *Integral* will bring my notes, have reached only that page in the great book of civilization that our ancestors read some nine hundred years ago. Perhaps you do not know even about such elementary things as the Table of Hours, the Personal Hour, the Maternity Norm, the Green Wall, and the Benefactor. It seems to me ridiculous yet very difficult to speak about all this. It is as if a writer of, say, the twentieth century had to explain in his novel the meaning of "coat," or "apartment," or "wife." Yet, if his novel were to be translated for savages, how could he avoid explaining what a "coat" meant?

I am certain that a savage would look at the "coat" and wonder, "What is it for? It's only a hindrance." It seems to me that your response may be exactly the same when I tell you that none of us has been beyond the Green Wall since the Two Hundred Years' War.

But, my dear readers, a man must think, at least a little. It helps. After all, it is clear that the entire history of mankind, insofar as we know it, is the history of transition from nomadic to increasingly settled forms of existence. And does it not follow that the most settled form (ours) is at the same time the most perfect (ours)? People rushed about from one end of the earth to the other only in prehistoric times, when there were nations, wars, commerce, discoveries of all sorts of Americas. But who needs that now? What for?

I admit, the habit of such settled existence was not achieved easily, or all at once. During the Two Hundred Years' War, when all the roads fell into ruin and were overgrown with grass, it must at first have seemed extremely inconvenient to live in cities cut off from one another by green jungles. But what of it? After man's tail dropped off, it must have been quite difficult for him at first to learn to drive off flies without its aid. In the beginning he undoubtedly missed his tail. But now — can you imagine yourself with a tail? Or can you imagine yourself in the street naked, without a coat? (For you may still be trotting about in "coats.") And so it is with me: I cannot imagine a city that is not clad in a Green Wall; I cannot imagine a life that is not regulated by the figures of our Table.

The Table . . . At this very moment, from the wall in my room, its purple figures on a field of gold stare tenderly and sternly into my eyes. Involuntarily, my mind turns to what the ancients called an "icon," and I long to compose poems or prayers (which are the same thing). Oh, why am I not a poet, to render fitting praise to the Table, the heart and pulse of the One State!

As schoolchildren we all read (perhaps you have, too) that greatest literary monument to have come down to us from ancient days — "The Railway Guide." But set it side by side with our Table, and it will be as graphite next to a diamond: both consist of the same element — carbon — yet how eternal, how transparent is the diamond, how it gleams! Whose breath will fail to quicken as he rushes clattering along the pages of "The Railway Guide"? But our Table of Hours! Why, it transforms each one of us into a figure of steel, a six-wheeled hero of a mighty epic poem. Every morning, with six-wheeled precision, at the same hour and the same moment, we — millions of us — get up as one. At the same hour, in million-headed unison, we start work; and in million-headed unison we end it. And, fused into a single million-handed body, at the same second, designated by the Table, we lift our spoons to our mouths. At the same second, we come out for our walk, go to the auditorium, go to the hall for Taylor exercises, fall asleep. . . .

I shall be entirely frank: even we have not yet found an absolute, precise solution to the problem of happiness. Twice a day, from sixteen to seventeen, and from twenty-one to twenty-two, the single mighty organism breaks up into separate cells; these are the Personal Hours designated by the Table. In these hours you will see modestly lowered shades in the rooms of some; others will walk with measured tread along the avenue, as though climbing the brass stairs of the March; still others, like myself now, are at their desks. But I am confident — and you may call me an idealist and dreamer — I am confident that sooner or later we shall fit these Personal Hours as well into the general formula. Some day these 86,400 seconds will also be entered in the Table of Hours.

I have read and heard many incredible things about those times when people still lived in a free, i.e., unorganized, savage condition. But most incredible of all, it seems to me, is that the state authority of that time — no matter how rudimentary — could allow men to live without anything like our Table, without obligatory walks, without exact regulation of mealtimes, getting up and going to bed whenever they felt like it. Some historians even say that in those times the street lights burned all night, and people walked and drove around in the streets at all hours of the night.

Try as I may, I cannot understand it. After all, no matter how limited their intelligence, they should have understood that such a way of life was truly mass murder — even if slow murder. The state (humaneness) forbade the killing of a single individual, but not the partial killing of millions day by day. To kill one individual, that is, to diminish the total sum of human lives by fifty years, was criminal. But to diminish the sum of human lives by fifty million years was not considered criminal. Isn't that absurd? Today, any ten-year-old will solve this mathematical-moral problem in half a minute. They, with all their Kants taken together, could not solve it (because it never occurred to any of the Kants to build a system of scientific ethics, i.e., ethics based on subtraction, addition, division, and multiplication).

And wasn't it absurd that the state (it dared to call itself a state!) could leave sexual life without any semblance of control? As often and as much as anyone might wish. . . . Totally unscientific, like animals. And blindly, like animals, they bore their young. Isn't it ridiculous: to know agriculture, poultry-breeding, fish-breeding (we have exact information that they knew all this), yet fail to go on to the ultimate step of this logical ladder — child-breeding; fail to establish such a thing as our Maternal and Paternal Norms.

It is so absurd, so unbelievable, that I am afraid, as I write this, that you, my unknown readers, will think me a malicious joker. I am afraid you may decide that I am merely trying to mock you, telling you utter nonsense with a straight face.

But, to begin with, I am incapable of jokes, for every joke contains a lie as an implicit function. Secondly, our One State Science asserts that this was how the ancients lived, and our State Science never errs. Besides, where would state logic have come from at a time when men were living in the condition of freedom — the condition of animals, apes, the herd? What could be expected of them, when even in our time the wild, apelike echo still occasionally rises from somewhere below, from some shaggy depth?

Fortunately, only on rare occasions. Fortunately, they are only breakdowns of minor parts which can easily be repaired without halting the eternal, grandiose movement of the entire Machine. And to expel the warped bolt, we have the skilled, heavy hand of the Benefactor and the experienced eyes of the Guardians.

And, by the way, I've just remembered. That number I saw yesterday, bent like an S — I think I've seen him coming out of the Office of the Guardians. Now I understand that instinctive feeling of respect I had for him, and the sense of awkwardness when the strange I-330 spoke before him. . . . I must confess that this I-330 . . .

The bell for bedtime: it is past twenty-two. Until tomorrow. . . .

Sixteenth Entry

TOPICS: *Yellow*

            Two-Dimensional Shadow

            Incurable Soul

I have not written anything for several days, I don't know how many. All the days are one day. All the days are one color — yellow, like parched, fiery sand. And there is not a spot of shadow, not a drop of water. . . .

On and on endlessly over the yellow sand. I cannot live without her, yet since she vanished so incomprehensibly that day in the Ancient House, she . . .

I have seen her only once since that day, during the daily walk. Two, three, four days ago — I do not know; all the days are one. She flashed by, filling for a second the yellow, empty world. And, hand in hand with her, up to her shoulder, the double-bent S and the paper-thin doctor. And there was a fourth one — I remember nothing but his fingers: they would fly out of the sleeves of his unif like clusters of rays, incredibly thin, white, long. I-330 raised her hand and waved to me. Over her neighbor's head she bent toward the one with the raylike fingers. I caught the word *Integral*. All four glanced back at me. Then they were lost in the gray-blue sky, and again — the yellow, dessicated road.

That evening she had a pink coupon to visit me. I stood before the annunciator and implored it, with tenderness, with hatred, to click, to register in the white slot: I-330. Doors slammed; pale, tall, rosy, swarthy numbers came out of the elevator, shades were pulled down on all sides. She was not there. She did not come.

And possibly, just at this very moment, exactly at twenty-two, as I am writing this, she stands with closed eyes, leaning against someone with her shoulder, saying to someone, "Do you love?" To whom? Who is he? The one with the raylike fingers, or the thick-lipped, sputtering R? Or S?

S . . . Why am I constantly hearing his flat steps all these days, splashing as through puddles? Why is he following me all these days like a shadow? Before me, beside me, behind — a gray-blue, two-dimensional shadow. Others pass through it, step on it, but it is invariably here, bound to me as by some invisible umbilical cord. Perhaps this cord is she — I-330? I don't know. Or perhaps they, the Guardians, already know that I . . .

Suppose you were told: Your shadow sees you, sees you all the time. Do you understand me? And suddenly you have the strangest feeling: your hands are not your own, they interfere with you. And I catch myself constantly swinging my arms absurdly, out of time with my steps. Or suddenly I feel that I must glance back, but it's impossible, no matter how I try, my neck is rigid, locked. And I run, I run faster and faster, and feel with my back — my shadow runs faster behind me, and there is no escape, no escape anywhere. . . .

Alone, at last, in my room. But here there is something else — the telephone. I pick up the receiver. "Yes, I-330, please." And again I hear a rustle in the receiver, someone's steps in the hall, past her room — and silence. . . . I throw down the receiver — I can't, I can't endure it any longer. I must run there, to her.

This happened yesterday. I hurried there, and wandered for an hour, from sixteen to seventeen, near the house where she lives. Numbers marched past me, row after row. Thousands of feet stepped rhythmically, a million-footed monster floated, swaying, by. And only I was alone, cast out by a storm upon a desert island, seeking, seeking with my eyes among the gray-blue waves.

A moment, and I shall see the sharply mocking angle of the eyebrows lifted to the temples, the dark windows of the eyes, and there, within them, the burning fireplace, the stirring shadows. And I will step inside directly, I will say, "You know I cannot live without you. Why, then . . ." I will use the warm, familiar "thou" — only "thou."

But she is silent. Suddenly I hear the silence, I do not hear the Music Plant, and I realize it is past seventeen, everybody else is gone, I am alone, I am late. Around me — a glass desert, flooded by the yellow sun. In the smooth glass of the pavement, as in water, I see the gleaming walls suspended upside down, and myself, hung mockingly head down, feet up.

I must hurry, this very second, to the Medical Office to get a certificate of illness, otherwise they'll take me and . . . But perhaps that would be best? To stay here and calmly wait until they see me and take me to the Operational Section — and so put an end to everything, atone for everything at once.

A faint rustle, and a doubly bent shadow before me. Without looking, I felt two steel-gray gimlets drill into me. With a last effort, I smiled and said — I had to say something — "I . . . I must go to the Medical Office."

"What's the problem, then? Why do you stand here?"

Absurdly upside down, hung by the feet, I was silent, burning up with shame.

"Come with me," S said harshly.

I followed obediently, swinging my unnecessary, alien arms. It was impossible to raise my eyes; I walked all the way through a crazy, upside-down world: some strange machines, their bases up; people glued antipodally to the ceiling; and, lower still, beneath it all, the sky locked into the thick glass of the pavement. I remember: what I resented most of all was that, for this last time in my life, I was seeing everything in this absurdly upside-down, unreal state. But it was impossible to raise my eyes.

We stopped. A staircase rose before me. Another step, and I would see the figures in white medical smocks, the huge, mute Bell. . . .

With an enormous effort, I finally tore my eyes away from the glass underfoot, and suddenly the golden letters of MEDICAL OFFICE burst into my face. At that moment it had not even occurred to me to wonder why he had spared me, why he had brought me here instead of to the Operational Section. At a single bound I swung across the steps, slammed the door firmly behind me, and took a deep breath. I felt: I had not breathed since morning, my heart had not been beating — and it was only now that I had taken my first breath, only now that the sluices in my breast had opened. . . .

There were two of them: one short, with tubby legs, weighing the patients with his eyes as though lifting them on horns; the other paper-thin, with gleaming scissor-lips, his nose a finest blade. . . . The same one.

I rushed to him as to someone near and dear, mumbling about insomnia, dreams, shadows, a yellow world. The scissor-lips gleamed, smiled.

"You're in a bad way! Apparently, you have developed a soul."

A soul? That strange, ancient, long-forgotten word. We sometimes use the words "soul-stirring," "soulless," but "soul" . . . ?

"Is it . . . very dangerous?" I muttered.

"Incurable," the scissors snapped.

"But . . . what, essentially, does it mean? I somehow don't . . . don't understand it."

"Well, you see . . . How can I explain it to you? . . . You are a mathematician, aren't you?"

"Yes."

"Well, then — take a plane, a surface — this mirror, say. And on this surface are you and I, you see? We squint against the sun. And here, the blue electric spark inside that tube, and there — the passing shadow of an aero. All of it only on the surface, only momentary. But imagine this impermeable substance softened by some fire; and nothing slides across it any more, everything enters into it, into this mirror world that we examined with such curiosity when we were children. Children are not so foolish, I assure you. The plane has acquired volume, it has become a body, a world, and everything is now inside the mirror — inside you: the sun, the blast of the whirling propeller, your trembling lips, and someone else's. Do you understand? The cold mirror reflects, throws back, but this one absorbs, and everything leaves its trace — forever. A moment, a faint line on someone's face — and it remains in you forever. Once you heard a drop fall in the silence, and you hear it now. . . ."

"Yes, yes, exactly. . . ." I seized his hand. I heard it now — drops falling slowly from the washstand faucet. And I knew: this was forever. "But why, why suddenly a soul? I've never had one, and suddenly . . . Why . . . No one else has it, and I . . . ?"

I clung even more violently to the thin hand; I was terrified of losing the lifeline.

"Why? Why don't you have feathers, or wings — only shoulder blades, the base for wings? Because wings are no longer necessary, we have the aero, wings would only interfere. Wings are for flying, and we have nowhere else to fly: we have arrived, we have found what we had been searching for. Isn't that so?"

I nodded in confusion. He looked at me with a scalpel-sharp laugh. The other heard it, pattered in from his office on his tubby feet, lifted my paper-thin doctor, lifted me on his horn-eyes.

"What's the trouble? A soul? A soul, you say? What the devil! We'll soon return to cholera if you go on that way. I told you" (raising the paper-thin one on his horns) " — I told you, we must cut out imagination. In everyone. . . . Extirpate imagination. Nothing but surgery, nothing but surgery will do. . . ."

He saddled his nose with huge X-ray glasses, circled around and around me for a long time, peered through the bones of my skull, examining the brain, and writing something in his book.

"Curious, most curious! Listen, would you consent to . . . to being preserved in alcohol? It would be extremely useful to the One State. . . . It would help us prevent an epidemic. . . . Of course, unless you have some special reasons to . . ."

"Well, you see," said the thin one, "Number D-503 is the Builder of the *Integral*, and I am sure it would interfere with . . ."

"U-um." The other grunted and pattered back to his office.

We remained alone. The paper-thin hand fell lightly, gently on my hand, the profile face bent close to mine. He whispered, "I'll tell you in confidence — you are not the only one. It was not for nothing that my colleague spoke about an epidemic. Try to remember — haven't you noticed anything like it, very much like it, very similar in anyone else?" He peered at me closely. What was he hinting at? Whom did he mean? Could it be . . . ?

"Listen." I jumped up from the chair.

But he was already speaking loudly about other things. "As far as your insomnia and your dreams, I can suggest one thing — do more walking. Start tomorrow morning, go out and take a walk . . . well, let's say to the Ancient House."

He pierced me with his eyes again, smiling his thinnest smile. And it seemed to me — I saw quite clearly a word, a letter, a name, the only name, wrapped in the finest tissue of that smile. . . . Or was this only my imagination again?

I could barely wait until he wrote out a certificate of illness for that day and the next. Silently I pressed his hand once more, and ran out.

My heart, fast and light as an aero, swept me up and up. I knew — some joy awaited me tomorrow. What was it?

A. E. van Vogt

The Weapon Shop
(1942)

Canadian-born A[lfred] E[lton] van Vogt (1912–2000) was a prominent member of the Golden Age circle centered on John W. Campbell Jr. and *Astounding Science-Fiction* in the 1930s and 1940s. Van Vogt's fiction tends to be inventive and fast-paced in the best pulp style, and his stories, populated by seemingly ordinary people who discover superhuman abilities or join secret organizations, were perfectly calibrated to fulfill the fantasies of the frustrated adolescents who formed sf's core audience at the time. Convention-goers identified with the misunderstood and secretly superior hero of his novel *Slan*, wearing t-shirts that proclaimed "Fans are Slans!" Although van Vogt's style —full of strange leaps in logic, startling plot complications, and sometimes frenetic pacing — is worlds apart from the meticulous realism and minimalist plots favored by sf writers today, his work retains its emotional power and exhilarating sense of possibility.

One of van Vogt's finest achievements is *The Weapon Shop* series, originally published as short stories and later assembled into book-length sagas. These stories, which feature an antiauthoritarian opposition to repressive government, are strongly libertarian in flavor.

The story that follows is set in a wholesome-seeming community of traditional, small-town values and features a strikingly complacent protagonist whose blind faith in the status quo is undermined as he finds himself a victim of larger forces. Neither the government he reveres nor the Weapon Shop are quite what they seem, and he learns to see his family's involvement in society more complexly.

Many people today will be troubled by the story's enthusiasm for guns and its blithe acceptance of violence as a means of resolving problems. One may also wonder how the bureaucratic machinery of the Weapon Shop fits with the story's advocacy of individual rights. These elements, however, are also part of what makes the story provocative and intriguing.

The village at night made a curiously timeless picture. Fara walked contentedly beside his wife along the street. The air was like wine; and he was thinking dimly of the artist who had come up from Imperial City, and made what the telestats called — he remembered the phrase vividly — "a symbolic painting reminiscent of a scene in the electrical age of seven thousand years ago."

Fara believed that utterly. The street before him with its weedless, automatically tended gardens, its shops set well back among the flowers, its perpetual hard, grassy sidewalks, and its street lamps that glowed from every pore of their structure — this was a restful paradise where time had stood still.

And it was like being a part of life that the great artist's picture of this quiet, peaceful scene before him was now in the collection of the empress herself. She had praised it, and naturally the thrice-blest artist had immediately and humbly begged her to accept it.

What a joy it must be to be able to offer personal homage to the glorious, the divine, the serenely gracious and lovely Innelda Isher, one thousand one hundred eightieth of her line.

As they walked, Fara half turned to his wife. In the dim light of the nearest street lamp, her kindly, still youthful face was almost lost in shadow. He murmured softly, instinctively muting his voice to harmonize with the pastel shades of night:

"She said — our empress said — that our little village of Glay seemed to her to have in it all the wholesomeness, the gentleness, that constitutes the finest qualities of her people. Wasn't that a wonderful thought, Creel? She must be a marvelously understanding woman. I — "

He stopped. They had come to a side street, and there was something about a hundred and fifty feet along it that —

"Look!" Fara said hoarsely.

He pointed with rigid arm and finger at a sign that glowed in the night, a sign that read:

FINE WEAPONS
THE RIGHT TO BUY WEAPONS IS THE RIGHT
TO BE FREE

Fara had a strange, empty feeling as he stared at the blazing sign. He saw that other villagers were gathering. He said finally, huskily:

"I've heard of these shops. They're places of infamy, against which the government of the empress will act one of these days. They're built in hidden factories, and then transported whole to towns like ours and set up in gross defiance of property rights. That one wasn't there an hour ago."

Fara's face hardened. His voice had a harsh edge in it, as he said: "Creel, go home."

Fara was surprised when Creel did not move off at once. All their married life, she had had a pleasing habit of obedience that had made cohabitation a wonderful thing. He saw that she was looking at him wide-eyed, and that it was a timid alarm that held her there. She said:

"Fara, what do you intend to do? You're not thinking of — "

"Go home!" Her fear brought out all the grim determination in his nature. "We're not going to let such a monstrous thing desecrate our village. Think of it" — his voice shivered before the appalling thought — "this fine, old-fashioned community, which we had resolved always to keep exactly as the empress has it in her picture gallery, debauched now, ruined by this . . . this thing — But we won't have it; that's all there is to it."

Creel's voice came softly out of the half-darkness of the street corner, the timidity gone from it: "Don't do anything rash, Fara. Remember it is not the first new building to come into Glay — since the picture was painted."

Fara was silent. This was a quality of his wife of which he did not approve, this reminding him unnecessarily of unpleasant facts. He knew exactly what she meant. The gigantic, multitentacled corporation, Automatic Atomic Motor Repair Shops, Inc., had come in under the laws of the State with their flashy building, against the wishes of the village council — and had already taken half of Fara's repair business.

"That's different!" Fara growled finally. "In the first place people will discover in good time that these new automatic repairers do a poor job. In the second place it's fair competition. But this weapon shop is a defiance of all the decencies that make life under the House of Isher such a joy. Look at the hypocritical sign: 'The right to buy weapons — ' Aaaaahh!"

He broke off with: "Go home, Creel. We'll see to it that they sell no weapons in this town."

He watched the slender woman-shape move off into the shadows. She was halfway across the street when a thought occurred to Fara. He called:

"And if you see that son of ours hanging around some street corner, take him home. He's got to learn to stop staying out so late at night."

The shadowed figure of his wife did not turn; and after watching her for a moment moving along against the dim background of softly glowing street lights, Fara twisted on his heel, and walked swiftly toward the shop. The crowd was growing larger every minute, and the night pulsed with excited voices.

Beyond doubt, here was the biggest thing that had ever happened to the village of Glay.

The sign of the weapon shop was, he saw, a normal-illusion affair. No matter what his angle of view, he was always looking straight at it. When he paused finally in front of the great display window, the words had pressed back against the store front, and were staring unwinkingly down at him.

Fara sniffed once more at the meaning of the slogan, then forgot the simple thing. There was another sign in the window, which read:

THE FINEST ENERGY WEAPONS IN THE KNOWN UNIVERSE

A spark of interest struck fire inside Fara. He gazed at that brilliant display of guns, fascinated in spite of himself. The weapons were of every size, ranging from tiny little finger pistols to express rifles. They were made of every one of the light, hard, ornamental substances: glittering glassein, the colorful but opaque Ordine plastic, viridescent magnesitic beryllium. And others.

It was the very deadly extent of the destructive display that brought a chill to Fara. So many weapons for the little village of Glay, where not more than two people to his knowledge had guns, and those only for hunting. Why, the thing was absurd, fantastically mischievous, utterly threatening.

Somewhere behind Fara, a man said: "It's right on Lan Harris's lot. Good joke on that old scoundrel. Will he raise a row!"

There was a faint titter from several men that made an odd patch of sound on the warm, fresh air. And Fara saw that the man had spoken the truth. The weapon shop had a forty-foot frontage. And it occupied the very center of the green, gardenlike lot of tight-fisted old Harris.

Fara frowned. The clever devils, the weapon-shop people, selecting the property of the most disliked man in town, coolly taking it over and giving everybody an agreeable titillation. But the very cunning of it made it vital that the trick shouldn't succeed.

He was still scowling anxiously when he saw the plump figure of Mel Dale, the mayor. Fara edged toward him hurriedly, touched his hat respectfully, and said:

"Where's Jor?"

"Here." The village constable elbowed his way through a little bundle of men. "Any plans?" he said.

"There's only one plan," said Fara boldly. "Go in and arrest them."

To Fara's amazement, the two men looked at each other, then at the ground. It was the big constable who answered shortly:

"Door's locked. And nobody answers our pounding. I was just going to suggest we let the matter ride until morning."

"Nonsense!" His very astonishment made Fara impatient. "Get an ax and we'll break the door down. Delay will only encourage such riffraff to resist. We don't want their kind in our village for so much as a single night. Isn't that so?"

There was a hasty nod of agreement from everybody in his immediate vicinity. Too hasty. Fara looked around puzzled at eyes that lowered before his level gaze. He thought: "They are all scared. And unwilling." Before he could speak, Constable Jor said:

"I guess you haven't heard about those doors or these shops. From all accounts, you can't break into them."

It struck Fara with a sudden pang that it was he who would have to act here. He said, "I'll get my atomic cutting machine from my shop. That'll fix them. Have I your permission to do that, Mr. Mayor?"

In the glow of the weapon-shop window, the plump man was sweating visibly. He pulled out a handkerchief, and wiped his forehead. He said:

"Maybe I'd better call the commander of the Imperial garrison at Ferd, and ask them."

"No!" Fara recognized evasion when he saw it. He felt himself steel; the conviction came that all the strength in this village was in him. "We must act ourselves. Other communities have let these people get in because they took no decisive action. We've got to resist to the limit. Beginning now. This minute. Well?"

The mayor's "All right!" was scarcely more than a sigh of sound. But it was all Fara needed.

He called out his intention to the crowd; and then, as he pushed his way out of the mob, he saw his son standing with some other young men staring at the window display.

Fara called: "Cayle, come and help me with the machine."

Cayle did not even turn; and Fara hurried on, seething. That wretched boy! One of these days he, Fara, would have to take firm action there. Or he'd have a no-good on his hands.

The energy was soundless — and smooth. There was no sputter, no fireworks. It glowed with a soft, pure white light, almost caressing the metal panels of the door — but not even beginning to sear them.

Minute after minute, the dogged Fara refused to believe the incredible failure, and played the boundlessly potent energy on that resisting wall. When he finally shut off his machine, he was perspiring freely.

"I don't understand it," he gasped. "Why — no metal is supposed to stand up against a steady flood of atomic force. Even the hard metal plates used inside the blast chamber of a motor take the explosions in what is called infinite series, so that each one has unlimited rest. That's the theory, but actually steady running crystallizes the whole plate after a few months."

"It's as Jor told you," said the mayor. "These weapon shops are — big. They spread right through the empire, *and they don't recognize the empress.*"

Fara shifted his feet on the hard grass, disturbed. He didn't like this kind of talk. It sounded — sacrilegious. And besides it was nonsense. It must be. Before he could speak, a man said somewhere behind him:

"I've heard it said that that door will open only to those who cannot harm the people inside."

The words shocked Fara out of his daze. With a start, and for the first time, he saw that his failure had had a bad psychological effect. He said sharply:

"That's ridiculous! If there were doors like that, we'd all have them. We — "

The thought that stopped his words was the sudden realization that *he* had not seen anybody try to open the door; and with all this reluctance around him it was quite possible that —

He stepped forward, grasped at the doorknob, and pulled. The door opened with an unnatural weightlessness that gave him the fleeting impression that the knob had come loose into his hand. With a gasp, Fara jerked the door wide open.

"Jor!" he yelled. "Get in!"

The constable made a distorted movement — distorted by what must have been a will to caution, followed by the instant realization that he could not hold back before so many. He leaped awkwardly toward the open door — and it closed in his face.

Fara stared stupidly at his hand, which was still clenched. And then, slowly, a hideous thrill coursed along his nerves. The knob had — withdrawn. It had twisted, become viscous, and slipped amorphously from his straining fingers. Even the memory of that brief sensation gave him a feeling of unnormal things.

He grew aware that the crowd was watching with a silent intentness. Fara reached again for the knob, not quite so eagerly this time; and it was only a sudden realization of his reluctance that made him angry when the handle neither turned nor yielded in any way.

Determination returned in full force, and with it came a thought. He motioned to the constable. "Go back, Jor, while I pull."

The man retreated, but it did no good. And tugging did not help. The door would not open. Somewhere in the crowd, a man said darkly:

"It decided to let you in, then it changed its mind."

"What foolishness are you talking!" Fara spoke violently. "*It* changed its mind. Are you crazy? A door has no sense."

But a surge of fear put a half-quaver into his voice. It was the sudden alarm that made him bold beyond all his normal caution. With a jerk of his body, Fara faced the shop.

The building loomed there under the night sky, in itself bright as day, huge in width and length, and alien, menacing, no longer easily conquerable. The dim queasy wonder came as to what the soldiers of the empress would do if they were invited to act. And suddenly — a bare, flashing glimpse of a grim possibility — the feeling grew that even they would be able to do nothing.

Abruptly, Fara was conscious of horror that such an idea could enter his mind. He shut his brain tight, said wildly:

"The door opened for me once. It will open again."

It did. Quite simply it did. Gently, without resistance, with that same sensation of weightlessness, the strange, sensitive door followed the tug of his fingers. Beyond the threshold was dimness, a wide, darkened alcove. He heard the voice of Mel Dale behind him, the mayor saying:

"Fara, don't be a fool. What will you do inside?"

Fara was vaguely amazed to realize that he had stepped across the threshold. He turned, startled, and stared at the blur of faces. "Why — " he began blankly; then he brightened; he said, "Why, I'll buy a gun, of course."

The brilliance of his reply, the cunning implicit in it, dazzled Fara for a half a minute longer. The mood yielded slowly, as he found himself in the dimly lighted interior of the weapon shop.

It was preternaturally quiet inside. Not a sound penetrated from the night from which he had come; and the startled thought came that the people of the shop might actually be unaware that there was a crowd outside.

Fara walked forward gingerly on a rugged floor that muffled his footsteps utterly. After a moment, his eyes accustomed themselves to the soft lighting, which came like a reflection from the walls and ceilings. In a vague way, he had expected ultranormalness; and the ordinariness of the atomic lighting acted like a tonic to his tensed nerves.

He shook himself angrily. Why should there be anything really superior? He was getting as bad as those credulous idiots out in the street.

He glanced around with gathering confidence. The place looked quite common. It was a shop, almost scantily furnished. There were showcases on the walls and on the floor, glitteringly lovely things, but nothing unusual, and not many of them — a few dozens. There was in addition a double, ornate door leading to a back room —

Fara tried to keep one eye on that door, as he examined several showcases, each with three or four weapons either mounted or arranged in boxes or holsters.

Abruptly, the weapons began to excite him. He forgot to watch the door, as the wild thought struck that he ought to grab one of those guns from a case, and then the moment someone came, force him outside where Jor would perform the arrest and —

Behind him, a man said quietly: "You wish to buy a gun?"

Fara turned with a jump. Brief rage flooded him at the way his plan had been wrecked by the arrival of the clerk.

The anger died as he saw that the intruder was a fine-looking, silver-haired man, older than himself. That was immeasurably disconcerting. Fara had an immense and almost automatic respect for age, and for a long second he could only stand there gaping. He said at last, lamely:

"Yes, yes, a gun."

"For what purpose?" said the man in his quiet voice.

Fara could only look at him blankly. It was too fast. He wanted to get mad. He wanted to tell these people what he thought of them. But the age of this representative locked his tongue, tangled his emotions. He managed speech only by an effort of will:

"For hunting." The plausible word stiffened his mind. "Yes, definitely for hunting. There is a lake to the north of here," he went on more fulsomely, glibly, "and —"

He stopped, scowling, startled at the extent of his dishonesty. He was not prepared to go so deeply into prevarication. He said curtly:

"For hunting."

Fara was himself again. Abruptly, he hated the man for having put him so completely at a disadvantage. With smoldering eyes he watched the old fellow click open a showcase, and take out a green-shining rifle.

As the man faced him, weapon in hand, Fara was thinking grimly, "Pretty clever, having an old man as a front." It was the same kind of cunning that had made them choose the property of Miser Harris. Icily furious, taut with his purpose, Fara reached for the gun; but the man held it out of his reach, saying:

"Before I can even let you test this, I am compelled by the by-laws of the weapon shops to inform you under what circumstances you may purchase a gun."

So they had private regulations. What a system of psychology tricks to impress gullible fools! Well, let the old scoundrel talk. As soon as he, Fara, got hold of the rifle, he'd put an end to hypocrisy.

"We weapons makers," the clerk was saying mildly, "have evolved guns that can, in their particular ranges, destroy any machine or object made of what is called matter. Thus whoever possesses one of our weapons is the equal and more of any soldier of the empress. I say more because each gun is the center of a field of force which acts as a perfect screen against immaterial destructive forces. That screen offers no resistance to clubs or spears or bullets, or other material substances, but it would require a small atomic cannon to penetrate the superb barrier it creates around its owner.

"You will readily comprehend," the man went on, "that such a potent weapon could not be allowed to fall, unmodified, into irresponsible hands. Accordingly, no gun purchased from us may be used for aggression or murder. In the case of the hunting rifle, only such specified game birds and animals as we may from time to time list in our display windows may be shot. Finally, no weapon can be resold without our approval. Is that clear?"

Fara nodded dumbly. For the moment, speech was impossible to him. The incredible, fantastically stupid words were still going round and around in his head. He wondered if he ought to laugh out loud, or curse the man for daring to insult his intelligence so tremendously.

So the gun mustn't be used for murder or robbery. So only certain birds and animals could be shot. And as for reselling it, suppose — suppose he bought this thing, took a trip of a thousand miles, and offered it to some wealthy stranger for two credits — who would ever know?

Or suppose he held up the stranger. Or shot him. How would the weapon shop ever find out? The thing was so ridiculous that —

He grew aware that the gun was being held out to him stock first. He took it eagerly, and had to fight the impulse to turn the muzzle directly on the old man. Mustn't rush this, he thought tautly. He said:

"How does it work?"

"You simply aim it, and pull the trigger. Perhaps you would like to try it on a target we have."

Fara swung the gun up. "Yes," he said triumphantly, "and you're it. Now, just get over there to the front door, and then outside."

He raised his voice: "And if anybody's thinking of coming through the back door, I've got that covered, too."

He motioned jerkily at the clerk. "Quick now, move! I'll shoot! I swear I will."

The man was cool, unflustered. "I have no doubt you would. When we decided to attune the door so that you could enter despite your hostility, we assumed the capacity for homicide. However, this is our party. You had better adjust yourself accordingly, and look behind you —"

There was silence. Finger on trigger, Fara stood moveless. Dim thoughts came of all the *half-things* he had heard in his days about the weapon shops: that they had secret supporters in every district, that they had a private and ruthless hidden government, and that once you got into their clutches, the only way out was death and —

But what finally came clear was a mind picture of himself, Fara Clark, family man, faithful subject of the empress, standing here in this dimly lighted store, deliberately fighting an organization so vast and menacing that — He must have been mad.

Only — here he was. He forced courage into his sagging muscles. He said:

"You can't fool me with pretending there's someone behind me. Now, get to that door. And *fast!*"

The firm eyes of the old man were looking past him. The man said quietly: "Well, Rad, have you all the data?"

"Enough for a primary," said a young man's baritone voice behind Fara. "Type A-7 conservative. Good average intelligence, but a Monaric development peculiar to small towns. One-sided outlook fostered by the Imperial schools present in exaggerated form. Extremely honest. Reason would be useless. Emotional approach would require extended treatment. I see no reason why we should bother. Let him live his life as it suits him."

"If you think," Fara said shakily, "that that trick voice is going to make me turn, you're crazy. That's the left wall of the building. I know there's no one there."

"I'm all in favor, Rad," said the old man, "of letting him live his life. But he was the prime mover of the crowd outside. I think he should be discouraged."

"We'll advertise his presence," said Rad. "He'll spend the rest of his life denying the charge."

Fara's confidence in the gun had faded so far that, as he listened in puzzled uneasiness to the incomprehensible conversation, he forgot it completely. He parted his lips, but before he could speak, the old man cut in, persistently:

"I think a little emotion might have a long-run effect. Show him the palace."

Palace! The startling word tore Fara out of his brief paralysis. "See here," he began, "I can see now that you lied to me. This gun isn't loaded at all. It's — "

His voice failed him. Every muscle in his body went rigid. He stared like a madman. *There was no gun in his hands.*

"Why, you — " he began wildly. And stopped again. His mind heaved with imbalance. With a terrible effort he fought off the spinning sensation, thought finally, tremblingly: Somebody must have sneaked the gun from him. That meant — there was someone behind him. The voice was no mechanical thing. Somehow, they had —

He started to turn — and couldn't. What in the name of — He struggled, pushing with his muscles. And couldn't move, couldn't budge, couldn't even —

The room was growing curiously dark. He had difficulty seeing the old man and — He would have shrieked then if he could. Because the weapon shop was gone. He was —

He was standing in the sky above an immense city.

In the sky, and nothing beneath him, nothing around him but air, and blue summer heaven, and the city a mile, two miles below.

Nothing, nothing — He would have shrieked, but his breath seemed solidly embedded in his lungs. Sanity came back as the remote awareness impinged upon his terrified mind that he was actually standing on a hard floor, and that the city must be a picture somehow focused directly into his eyes.

For the first time, with a start, Fara recognized the metropolis below. It was the city of dreams, Imperial City, capital of the glorious Empress Isher — From his great height, he could see the gardens, the gorgeous grounds of the silver palace, the official Imperial residence itself —

The last tendrils of his fear were fading now before a gathering fascination and wonder; they vanished utterly as he recognized with a ghastly thrill of uncertain expectancy that the palace was drawing nearer at great speed.

"Show him the palace," they had said. Did that mean, could it mean —

That spray of tense thoughts splattered into nonexistence, as the glittering roof flashed straight at his face. He gulped, as the solid metal of it passed through him, and then other walls and ceilings.

His first sense of imminent and mind-shaking desecration came as the picture paused in a great room where a score of men sat around a table at the head of which sat — a young woman.

The inexorable, sacrilegious, limitlessly powered cameras that were taking the picture swung across the table, and caught the woman full face.

It was a handsome face, but there was passion and fury twisting it now, and a very blaze of fire in her eyes, as she leaned forward, and said in a voice at once familiar — how often Fara had heard its calm, measured tones on the telestats — and distorted. Utterly distorted by anger and an insolent certainty of command. That caricature of a beloved voice slashed across the silence as clearly as if he, Fara, was there in that room:

"I want that skunk killed, do you understand? I don't care how you do it, but I want to hear by tomorrow night that he's dead."

The picture snapped off and instantly — it was as swift as that — Fara was back in the weapon shop. He stood for a moment, swaying, fighting to accustom his eyes to the dimness; and then —

His first emotion was contempt at the simpleness of the trickery — a motion picture. What kind of a fool did they think he was, to swallow something as transparently unreal as that? He'd —

Abruptly, the appalling lechery of the scheme, the indescribable wickedness of what was being attempted here brought red rage.

"Why, you scum!" he flared. "So you've got somebody to act the part of the empress, trying to pretend that — Why, you — "

"That will do," said the voice of Rad; and Fara shook as a big young man walked into his line of vision. The alarmed thought came that people who would besmirch so vilely the character of her imperial majesty would not hesitate to do physical damage to Fara Clark. The young man went on in a steely tone:

"We do not pretend that what you saw was taking place this instant in the palace. That would be too much of a coincidence. But it was taken two weeks ago; the woman *is* the empress. The man whose death she ordered is one of her many former lovers. He was found murdered two weeks ago; his name, if you care to look it up in the news files, is Banton McCreddie. However, let that pass. We're finished with you now and — "

"But I'm not finished," Fara said in a thick voice. "I've never heard or seen so much infamy in all my life. If you think this town is through with you, you're crazy. We'll have a guard on this place day and night, and nobody will get in or out. We'll — "

"That will do." It was the silver-haired man; and Fara stopped out of respect for age, before he thought. The old man went on: "The examination has been most interesting. As an honest man, you may call on us if you are ever in trouble. That is all. Leave through the side door."

It *was* all. Impalpable forces grabbed him, and he was shoved at a door that appeared miraculously in the wall, where seconds before the palace had been.

He found himself standing dazedly in a flower bed, and there was a swarm of men to his left. He recognized his fellow townsmen and that he was — outside.

The incredible nightmare was over.

"Where's the gun?" said Creel, as he entered the house half an hour later.

"The gun?" Fara stared at his wife.

"It said over the radio a few minutes ago that you were the first customer of the new weapon shop. I thought it was queer, but — "

He was eerily conscious of her voice going on for several words longer, but it was the purest jumble. The shock was so great that he had the horrible sensation of being on the edge of an abyss.

So that was what the young man had meant: "Advertise! We'll advertise his presence and — "

Fara thought: His reputation! Not that his was a great name, but he had long believed with a quiet pride that Fara Clark's motor repair shop was widely known in the community and countryside.

First, his private humiliation inside the shop. And now this — lying — to people who didn't know why he had gone into the store. Diabolical.

His paralysis ended, as a frantic determination to rectify the base charge drove him to the telestat. After a moment, the plump, sleepy face of Mayor Mel Dale appeared on the plate. Fara's voice made a barrage of sound, but his hopes dashed, as the man said:

"I'm sorry, Fara. I don't see how you can have free time on the telestat. You'll have to pay for it. They did."

"They did!" Fara wondered vaguely if he sounded as empty as he felt.

"And they've just paid Lan Harris for his lot. The old man asked top price, and got it. He just phoned me to transfer the title."

"Oh!" The world was shattering. "You mean nobody's going to do anything. What about the Imperial garrison at Ferd?"

Dimly, Fara was aware of the mayor mumbling something about the empress's soldiers refusing to interfere in civilian matters.

"Civilian matters!" Fara exploded. "You mean these people are just going to be allowed to come here whether we want them or not, illegally forcing the sale of lots by first taking possession of them?"

A sudden thought struck him breathless. "Look, you haven't changed your mind about having Jor keep guard in front of the shop?"

With a start, he saw that the plump face in the telestat plate had grown impatient. "Now, see here, Fara," came the pompous words, "let the constituted authorities handle this matter."

"But you're going to keep Jor there," Fara said doggedly.

The mayor looked annoyed, said finally peevishly: "I promised, didn't I? So he'll be there. And now — do you want to buy time on the telestat? It's fifteen credits for one minute. Mind you, as a friend, I think you're wasting your money. No one has ever caught up with a false statement."

Fara said grimly: "Put two on, one in the morning, one in the evening."

"All right. We'll deny it completely. Good night."

The telestat went blank; and Fara sat there. A new thought hardened his face. "That boy of ours — there's going to be a showdown. He either works in my shop, or he gets no more allowance."

Creel said: "You've handled him wrong. He's twenty-three, and you treat him like a child. Remember, at twenty-three, you were a married man."

"That was different," said Fara. "I had a sense of responsibility. Do you know what he did tonight?"

He didn't quite catch her answer. For the moment, he thought she said: "No; in what way did you humiliate him first?"

Fara felt too impatient to verify the impossible words. He rushed on: "He refused in front of the whole village to give me help. He's a bad one, all bad."

"Yes," said Creel in a bitter tone, "he is all bad. I'm sure you don't realize how bad. He's as cold as steel, but without steel's strength or integrity. He took a long time, but he hates even me now, because I stood up for your side so long, knowing you were wrong."

"What's that?" said Fara, startled; then gruffly: "Come, come, my dear, we're both upset. Let's go to bed."

He slept poorly.

There were days then when the conviction that this was a personal fight between himself and the weapon shop lay heavily on Fara. Grimly, though it was out of his way, he made a point of walking past the weapon shop, always pausing to speak to Constable Jor and —

On the fourth day, the policeman wasn't there.

Fara waited patiently at first, then angrily; then he walked hastily to his shop, and called Jor's house. No, Jor wasn't home. He was guarding the weapon store.

Fara hesitated. His own shop was piled with work, and he had a guilty sense of having neglected his customers for the first time in his life. It would be simple to call up the mayor and report Jor's dereliction. And yet —

He didn't want to get the man into trouble —

Out in the street, he saw that a large crowd was gathering in front of the weapon shop. Fara hurried. A man he knew greeted him excitedly:

"Jor's been murdered, Fara!"

"Murdered!" Fara stood stock-still, and at first he was not clearly conscious of the grisly thought that was in his mind: Satisfaction! A flaming satisfaction. Now, he thought, even the soldiers would have to act. They —

With a gasp, he realized the ghastly tenor of his thoughts. He shivered, but finally pushed the sense of shame out of his mind. He said slowly:

"Where's the body?"

"Inside."

"You mean, those . . . scum — " In spite of himself, he hesitated over the epithet; even now, it was difficult to think of the fine-faced, silver-haired old man in such terms. Abruptly, his mind hardened; he flared: "You mean those scum actually killed him, then pulled his body inside?"

"Nobody saw the killing," said a second man beside Fara, "but he's gone, hasn't been seen for three hours. The mayor got the weapon shop on the telestat, but they claim they don't know anything. They've done away with him, that's what, and now they're pretending innocence. Well, they won't get out of it as easily as that. Mayor's gone to phone the soldiers at Ferd to bring up some big guns and — "

Something of the intense excitement that was in the crowd surged through Fara, the feeling of big things brewing. It was the most delicious sensation that had ever tingled along his nerves, and it was all mixed with a strange pride that he had been so right about this, that he at least had never doubted that here was evil.

He did not recognize the emotion as the full-flowering joy that comes to a member of a mob. But his voice shook, as he said:

"Guns? Yes, that will be the answer, and the soldiers will have to come, of course."

Fara nodded to himself in the immensity of his certainty that the Imperial soldiers would now have no excuse for not acting. He started to say something dark about what the empress would do if she found out that a man had lost his life because the soldiers had shirked their duty, but the words were drowned in a shout:

"Here comes the mayor! Hey, Mr. Mayor, when are the atomic cannons due?"

There was more of the same general meaning, as the mayor's sleek, all-purpose car landed lightly. Some of the questions must have reached his honor, for he stood up in the open two-seater, and held up his hand for silence.

To Fara's astonishment, the plump-faced man looked at him with accusing eyes. The thing seemed so impossible that, quite instinctively, Fara looked behind him. But he was almost alone; everybody else had crowded forward.

Fara shook his head, puzzled by that glare; and then, astoundingly, Mayor Dale pointed a finger at him, and said in a voice that trembled:

"There's the man who's responsible for the trouble that's come upon us. Stand forward, Fara Clark, and show yourself. You've cost this town seven hundred credits that we could ill afford to spend."

Fara couldn't have moved or spoken to save his life. He just stood there in a maze of dumb bewilderment. Before he could even think, the mayor went on, and there was quivering self-pity in his tone:

"We've all known that it wasn't wise to interfere with these weapon shops. So long as the Imperial government leaves them alone, what right have we to set up guards, or act against them? That's what I've thought from the beginning, but this man . . . this . . . this Fara Clark kept after all of us, forcing us to move against our wills, and so now we've got a seven-hundred-credit bill to meet and — "

He broke off with: "I might as well make it brief. When I called the garrison, the commander just laughed and said that Jor would turn up. And I had barely disconnected when there was a money call from Jor. He's on Mars."

He waited for the shouts of amazement to die down. "It'll take three weeks for him to come back by ship, and we've got to pay for it, and Fara Clark is responsible. He — "

The shock was over. Fara stood cold, his mind hard. He said finally scathingly: "So you're giving up, and trying to blame me all in one breath. I say you're all fools."

As he turned away, he heard Mayor Dale saying something about the situation not being completely lost, as he had learned that the weapon shop had been set up in Glay because the village was equidistant from four cities, and that it was the city business the shop was after. This would mean tourists, and accessory trade for the village stores and —

Fara heard no more. Head high, he walked back toward his shop. There were one or two catcalls from the mob, but he ignored them.

He had no sense of approaching disaster, simply a gathering fury against the weapon shop, which had brought him to this miserable status among his neighbors.

The worst of it, as the days passed, was the realization that the people of the weapon shop had no personal interest in him. They were remote, superior, undefeatable. That unconquerableness was a dim, suppressed awareness inside Fara.

When he thought of it, he felt a vague fear at the way they had transferred Jor to Mars in a period of less than three hours, when all the world knew that the trip by fastest spaceship required nearly three weeks.

Fara did not go to the express station to see Jor arrive home. He had heard that the council had decided to charge Jor with half of the expense of the trip, on the threat of losing his job if he made a fuss.

On the second night after Jor's return, Fara slipped down to the constable's house, and handed the officer one hundred seventy-five credits. It wasn't that he was responsible, he told Jor, but —

The man was only too eager to grant the disclaimer, provided the money went with it. Fara returned home with a clearer conscience.

It was on the third day after that that the door of his shop banged open and a man came in. Fara frowned as he saw who it was: Castler, a village hanger-on. The man was grinning:

"Thought you might be interested, Fara. Somebody came out of the weapon shop today."

Fara strained deliberately at the connecting bolt of a hard plate of the atomic motor he was fixing. He waited with a gathering annoyance that the man did not volunteer further information. Asking questions would be a form of recognition of the worthless fellow. A developing curiosity made him say finally, grudgingly:

"I suppose the constable promptly picked him up."

He supposed nothing of the kind, but it was an opening.

"It wasn't a man. It was a girl."

Fara knitted his brows. He didn't like the idea of making trouble for women. But — the cunning devils! Using a girl, just as they had used an old man as a clerk. It was a trick that deserved to fail, the girl probably a tough one who needed rough treatment. Fara said harshly:

"Well, what's happened?"

"She's still out, bold as you please. Pretty thing, too."

The bolt off, Fara took the hard plate over to the polisher, and began patiently the long, careful task of smoothing away the crystals that heat had seared on the once shining metal. The soft throb of the polisher made the background to his next words:

"Has anything been done?"

"Nope. The constable's been told, but he says he doesn't fancy being away from his family for another three weeks, and paying the cost into the bargain."

Fara contemplated that darkly for a minute, as the polisher throbbed on. His voice shook with suppressed fury, when he said finally:

"So they're letting them get away with it. It's all been as clever as hell. Can't they see that they musn't give an inch before these . . . these transgressors. It's like giving countenance to sin."

From the corner of his eye, he noticed that there was a curious grin on the face of the other. It struck Fara suddenly that the man was enjoying his anger. And there was something else in that grin; something — a secret knowledge.

Fara pulled the engine plate away from the polisher. He faced the ne'er-do-well, scathed at him:

"Naturally, that sin part wouldn't worry you much."

"Oh," said the man nonchalantly, "the hard knocks of life make people tolerant. For instance, after you know the girl better, you yourself will probably come to realize that there's good in all of us."

It was not so much the words, as the curious I've-got-secret-information tone that made Fara snap:

"What do you mean — if I get to know the girl better! I won't even speak to the brazen creature."

"One can't always choose," the other said with enormous casualness. "Suppose he brings her home."

"Suppose who brings who home?" Fara spoke irritably. "Castler, you — "

He stopped; a dead weight of dismay plumped into his stomach; his whole being sagged. "You mean — " he said.

"I mean," replied Castler with a triumphant leer, "that the boys aren't letting a beauty like her be lonesome. And, naturally, your son was the first to speak to her."

He finished: "They're walkin' together now on Second Avenue, comin' this way, so — "

"Get out of here!" Fara roared. "And stay away from me with your gloating. Get out!"

The man hadn't expected such an ignominious ending. He flushed scarlet, then went out, slamming the door.

Fara stood for a moment, every muscle stiff; then, with an abrupt, jerky movement, he shut off his power, and went out into the street.

The time to put a stop to that kind of thing was — now!

He had no clear plan, just that violent determination to put an immediate end to an impossible situation. And it was all mixed up with his anger against Cayle. How could he have had such a worthless son, he who paid his debts and worked hard, and tried to be decent and to live up to the highest standards of the empress?

A brief, dark thought came to Fara that maybe there was some bad blood on Creel's side. Not from her mother, of course — Fara added the mental thought hastily. *There* was a fine, hard-working woman, who hung on to her money, and who would leave Creel a tidy sum one of these days.

But Creel's father had disappeared when Creel was only a child, and there had been some vague scandal about his having taken up with a tele-stat actress.

And now Cayle with this weapon-shop girl. A girl who had let herself be picked up —

He saw them, as he turned the corner onto Second Avenue. They were walking a hundred feet distant, and heading away from Fara. The girl was tall and slender, almost as big as Cayle, and, as Fara came up, she was saying:

"You have the wrong idea about us. A person like you can't get a job in our organization. You belong in the Imperial Service, where they can use young men of good education, good appearance and no scruples. I — "

Fara grasped only dimly that Cayle must have been trying to get a job with these people. It was not clear; and his own mind was too intent on his purpose for it to mean anything at the moment. He said harshly:

"Cayle!"

The couple turned, Cayle with the measured unhurriedness of a young man who has gone a long way on the road to steellike nerves; the girl was quicker, but withal dignified.

Fara had a vague, terrified feeling that his anger was too great, self-destroying, but the very violence of his emotions ended that thought even as it came. He said thickly:

"Cayle, get home — at once."

Fara was aware of the girl looking at him curiously from strange, gray-green eyes. No shame, he thought, and his rage mounted several degrees, driving away the alarm that came at the sight of the flush that crept into Cayle's cheeks.

The flush faded into a pale, tight-lipped anger; Cayle half-turned to the girl, said:

"This is the childish old fool I've got to put up with. Fortunately, we seldom see each other; we don't even eat together. What do you think of him?"

The girl smiled impersonally: "Oh, we know Fara Clark; he's the backbone of the empress in Glay."

"Yes," the boy sneered. "You ought to hear him. He thinks we're living in heaven; and the empress is the divine power. The worst part of it is that there's no chance of his ever getting that stuffy look wiped off his face."

They walked off; and Fara stood there. The very extent of what had happened had drained anger from him as if it had never been. There was the realization that he had made a mistake so great that —

He couldn't grasp it. For long, long now, since Cayle had refused to work in his shop, he had felt this building up to a climax. Suddenly, his own uncontrollable ferocity stood revealed as a partial product of that — deeper — problem.

Only, now that the smash was here, he didn't want to face it —

All through the day in his shop, he kept pushing it out of his mind; kept thinking:

Would this go on now, as before, Cayle and he living in the same house, not even looking at each other when they met, going to bed at different times, getting up, Fara at 6:30, Cayle at noon? Would *that* go on through all the days and years to come?

When he arrived home, Creel was waiting for him. She said:

"Fara, he wants you to loan him five hundred credits, so that he can go to Imperial City."

Fara nodded wordlessly. He brought the money back to the house the next morning, and gave it to Creel, who took it into the bedroom.

She came out a minute later. "He says to tell you good-by."

When Fara came home that evening, Cayle was gone. He wondered whether he ought to feel relieved or — what?

The days passed. Fara worked. He had nothing else to do, and the gray thought was often in his mind that now he would be doing it till the day he died. Except —

Fool that he was — he told himself a thousand times how big a fool — he kept hoping that Cayle would walk into the shop and say:

"Father, I've learned my lesson. If you can ever forgive me, teach me the business, and then you retire to a well-earned rest."

It was exactly a month to a day after Cayle's departure that the telestat clicked on just after Fara had finished lunch. "Money call," it sighed, "money call."

Fara and Creel looked at each other. "Eh," said Fara finally, "money call for us."

He could see from the gray look in Creel's face the thought that was in her mind. He said under his breath: "Damn that boy!"

But he felt relieved. Amazingly, relieved! Cayle was beginning to appreciate the value of parents and —

He switched on the viewer. "Come and collect," he said.

The face that came on the screen was heavy-jowled, beetle-browed — and strange. The man said:

"This is Clerk Pearton of the Fifth Bank of Ferd. We have received a sight draft on you for ten thousand credits. With carrying charges and government tax, the sum required will be twelve thousand one hundred credits. Will you pay it now or will you come in this afternoon and pay it?"

"B-but . . . b-but — " said Fara. "W-who — "

He stopped, conscious of the stupidity of the question, dimly conscious of the heavy-faced man saying something about the money having been paid out to one Cayle Clark, that morning, in Imperial City. At last, Fara found his voice:

"But the bank had no right," he expostulated, "to pay out the money without my authority. I — "

The voice cut him off coldly: "Are we then to inform our central that the money was obtained under false pretenses? Naturally, an order will be issued immediately for the arrest of your son."

"Wait . . . wait — " Fara spoke blindly. He was aware of Creel beside him, shaking her head at him. She was as white as a sheet, and her voice was a sick, stricken thing, as she said:

"Fara, let him go. He's through with us. We must be as hard — let him go."

The words rang senselessly in Fara's ears. They didn't fit into any normal pattern. He was saying:

"I . . . I haven't got — How about my paying . . . installments? I — "

"If you wish a loan," said Clerk Pearton, "naturally we will be happy to go into the matter. I might say that when the draft arrived, we checked up on your status, and we are prepared to loan you eleven thousand credits on indefinite call with your shop as security. I have the form here, and if you are agreeable, we will switch this call through the registered circuit, and you can sign at once."

"Fara, no."

The clerk went on: "The other eleven hundred credits will have to be paid in cash. Is that agreeable?"

"Yes, yes, of course, I've got twenty-five hund — " He stopped his chattering tongue with a gulp; then: "Yes, that's satisfactory."

The deal completed, Fara whirled on his wife. Out of the depths of his hurt and bewilderment, he raged:

"What do you mean, standing there and talking about not paying it? You said several times that I was responsible for his being what he is. Besides, we don't know why he needed the money. He — "

Creel said in a low, dead tone: "In one hour, he's stripped us of our life work. He did it deliberately, thinking of us as two old fools, who wouldn't know any better than to pay it."

Before he could speak, she went on: "Oh, I know I blamed you, but in the final issue, I knew it was he. He was always cold and calculating, but I was weak, and I was sure that if you handled him in a different . . . and besides I didn't want to see his faults for a long time. He — "

"All I see," Fara interrupted doggedly, "is that I have saved our name from disgrace."

His high sense of duty rightly done lasted until midafternoon, when the bailiff from Ferd came to take over the shop.

"But what — " Fara began.

The bailiff said: "The Automatic Atomic Repair Shops, Limited, took over your loan from the bank, and are foreclosing. Have you anything to say?"

"It's unfair," said Fara. "I'll take it to court. I'll — "

He was thinking dazedly: "If the empress ever learned of this, she'd . . . she'd — "

The courthouse was a big, gray building; and Fara felt emptier and colder every second, as he walked along the gray corridors. In Glay, his decision not to give himself into the hands of a bloodsucker of a lawyer had seemed a wise act. Here, in these enormous halls and palatial rooms, it seemed the sheerest folly.

He managed, nevertheless, to give an articulate account of the criminal act of the bank in first giving Cayle the money, then turning over the note to his chief competitor, apparently within minutes of his signing it. He finished with:

"I'm sure, sir, the empress would not approve of such goings-on against honest citizens. I — "

"How dare you," said the cold-voiced creature on the bench, "use the name of her holy majesty in support of your own gross self-interest?"

Fara shivered. The sense of being intimately a member of the empress's great human family yielded to a sudden chill and a vast mind-picture of the ten million icy courts like this, and the myriad malevolent and heartless men — *like this* — who stood between the empress and her loyal subject, Fara.

He thought passionately: If the empress knew what was happening here, how unjustly he was being treated, she would —

Or would she?

He pushed the crowding, terrible doubt out of his mind — came out of his hard reverie with a start, to hear the Cadi saying:

"Plaintiff's appeal dismissed, with costs assessed at seven hundred credits, to be divided between the court and the defense solicitor in the ratio of five to two. See to it that the appellant does not leave till the costs are paid. Next case — "

Fara went alone the next day to see Creel's mother. He called first at "Farmer's Restaurant" at the outskirts of the village. The place was, he noted with satisfaction in the thought of the steady stream of money flowing in, half full, though it was only midmorning. But madame wasn't there. Try the feed store.

He found her in the back of the feed store, overseeing the weighing out of grain into cloth measures. The hard-faced old woman heard his story without a word. She said finally, curtly:

"Nothing doing, Fara. I'm one who has to make loans often from the bank to swing deals. If I tried to set you up in business, I'd find the Automatic Atomic Repair people getting after me. Besides, I'd be a fool to turn money over to a man who lets a bad son squeeze a fortune out of him. Such a man has no sense about worldly things.

"And I won't give you a job because I don't hire relatives in my business." She finished: "Tell Creel to come and live at my house. I won't support a man, though. That's all."

He watched her disconsolately for a while, as she went on calmly superintending the clerks who were manipulating the old, no longer accurate measuring machines. Twice her voice echoed through the dust-filled interior, each time with a sharp: "That's overweight, a gram at least. Watch your machine."

Though her back was turned, Fara knew by her posture that she was still aware of his presence. She turned at last with an abrupt movement, and said:

"Why don't you go to the weapon shop? You haven't anything to lose, and you can't go on like this."

Fara went out, then, a little blindly. At first the suggestion that he buy a gun and commit suicide had no real personal application. But he felt immeasurably hurt that his mother-in-law should have made it.

Kill himself? Why, it was ridiculous. He was still only a young man, going on fifty. Given the proper chance, with his skilled hands, he could wrest a good living even in a world where automatic machines were encroaching everywhere. There was always room for a man who did a good job. His whole life had been based on that credo.

Kill himself —

He went home to find Creel packing. "It's the common sense thing to do," she said. "We'll rent the house and move into rooms."

He told her about her mother's offer to take her in, watching her face as he spoke. Creel shrugged.

"I told her 'No' yesterday," she said thoughtfully. "I wonder why she mentioned it to you."

Fara walked swiftly over to the great front window overlooking the garden, with its flowers, its pool, its rockery. He tried to think of Creel away from this garden of hers, this home of two thirds a life-time, Creel living in rooms — and knew what her mother had meant. There was one more hope —

He waited till Creel went upstairs, then called Mel Dale on the telestat. The mayor's plump face took on an uneasy expression as he saw who it was.

But he listened pontifically, said finally: "Sorry, the council does not loan money; and I might as well tell you, Fara — I have nothing to do with this, mind you — but you can't get a license for a shop any more."

"W-what?"

"I'm sorry!" The mayor lowered his voice. "Listen, Fara, take my advice and go to the weapon shop. These places have their uses."

There was a click, and Fara sat staring at the blank face of the viewing screen.

So it was to be — death!

He waited until the street was empty of human beings, then slipped across the boulevard, past a design of flower gardens, and so to the door of the shop. The brief fear came that the door wouldn't open, but it did, effortlessly.

As he emerged from the dimness of the alcove into the shop proper, he saw the silver-haired old man sitting in a corner chair, reading under a softly bright light. The old man looked up, put aside his book, then rose to his feet.

"It's Mr. Clark," he said quietly. "What can we do for you?"

A faint flush crept into Fara's cheeks. In a dim fashion, he had hoped that he would not suffer the humiliation of being recognized; but now that his fear was realized, he stood his ground stubbornly. The important thing about killing himself was that there be no body for Creel to bury at great expense. Neither knife nor poison would satisfy that basic requirement.

"I want a gun," said Fara, "that can be adjusted to disintegrate a body six feet in diameter in a single shot. Have you that kind?"

Without a word, the old man turned to a showcase, and brought forth a sturdy gem of a revolver that glinted with all the soft colors of the inimitable Ordine plastic. The man said in a precise voice:

"Notice the flanges on this barrel are little more than bulges. This makes the model ideal for carrying in a shoulder holster under the coat; it can be drawn very swiftly because, when properly attuned, it will leap toward the reaching hand of its owner. At the moment it is attuned to me. Watch while I replace it in its holster and — "

The speed of the draw was absolutely amazing. The old man's fingers moved; and the gun, four feet away, was in them. There was no blur of movement. It was like the door the night that it had slipped from Fara's grasp, and slammed noiselessly in Constable Jor's face. *Instantaneous!*

Fara, who had parted his lips as the old man was explaining, to protest the utter needlessness of illustrating any quality of the weapon except what he had asked for, closed them again. He stared in a brief, dazed fascination; and something of the wonder that was here held his mind and his body.

He had seen and handled the guns of soldiers, and they were simply ordinary metal or plastic things that one used clumsily like any other material substance, not like this at all, not possessed of a dazzling life of their own, leaping with an intimate eagerness to assist with all their superb power the will of their master. They —

With a start, Fara remembered his purpose. He smiled wryly, and said:

"All this is very interesting. But what about the beam that can fan out?"

The old man said calmly: "At pencil thickness, this beam will pierce any body except certain alloys of lead up to four hundred yards. With proper adjustment of the firing nozzle, you can disintegrate a six-foot object at fifty yards or less. This screw is the adjustor."

He indicated a tiny device in the muzzle itself. "Turn it to the left to spread the beam, to the right to close it."

Fara said: "I'll take the gun. How much is it?"

He saw that the old man was looking at him thoughtfully; the oldster said finally, slowly: "I have previously explained our regulations to you, Mr. Clark. You recall them, of course?"

"Eh!" said Fara, and stopped, wide-eyed. It wasn't that he didn't remember them. It was simply —

"You mean," he gasped, "those things actually apply. They're not — "

With a terrible effort, he caught his spinning brain and blurring voice. Tense and cold, he said:

"All I want is a gun that will shoot in self-defense, but which I can turn on myself if I have to or — want to."

"Oh, suicide!" said the old man. He looked as if a great understanding had suddenly dawned on him. "My dear sir, we have no objection to your killing yourself at any time. That is your personal privilege in a world where privileges grow scanter every year. As for the price of this revolver, it's four credits."

"Four cre . . . only four credits!" said Fara.

He stood, absolutely astounded, his whole mind snatched from its dark purpose. Why, the plastic alone was — and the whole gun with its fine, intricate workmanship — twenty-five credits would have been dirt cheap.

He felt a brief thrill of utter interest; the mystery of the weapon shops suddenly loomed as vast and important as his own black destiny. But the old man was speaking again:

"And now, if you will remove your coat, we can put on the holster — "

Quite automatically, Fara complied. It was vaguely startling to realize that, in a few seconds, he would be walking out of here, equipped for self-murder, and that there was now not a single obstacle to his death.

Curiously, he was disappointed. He couldn't explain it, but somehow there had been in the back of his mind a hope that these shops might just might — what?

What indeed? Fara sighed wearily — and grew aware again of the old man's voice, saying:

"Perhaps you would prefer to step out of our side door. It is less conspicuous than the front."

There was no resistance in Fara. He was dimly conscious of the man's fingers on his arm, half guiding him; and then the old man pressed one of several buttons on the wall — so that's how it was done — and there was the door.

He could see flowers beyond the opening; without a word he walked toward them. He was outside almost before he realized it.

Fara stood for a moment in the neat little pathway, striving to grasp the finality of his situation. But nothing would come except a curious awareness of many men around him; for a long second, his brain was like a log drifting along a stream at night.

Through that darkness grew a consciousness of something wrong; the wrongness was there in the back of his mind, as he turned leftward to go to the front of the weapon store.

Vagueness transformed to a shocked, startled sound. For — he was not in Glay, and the weapon shop *wasn't* where it had been. In its place —

A dozen men brushed past Fara to join a long line of men farther along. But Fara was immune to their presence, their strangeness. His whole mind, his whole vision, his very being was concentrating on the section of machine that stood where the weapon shop had been.

A machine, oh, a machine —

His brain lifted up, up in his effort to grasp the tremendousness of the dull-metaled immensity of what was spread here under a summer sun beneath a sky as blue as a remote southern sea.

The machine towered into the heavens, five great tiers of metal, each a hundred feet high; and the superbly streamlined five hundred feet ended in a peak of light, a gorgeous spire that tilted straight up a sheer two hundred feet farther, and matched the very sun for brightness.

And it *was* a machine, not a building, because the whole lower tier was alive with shimmering lights, mostly green, but sprinkled colorfully with red and occasionally a blue and yellow. Twice, as Fara watched, green lights directly in front of him flashed unscintillatingly into red.

The second tier was alive with white and red lights, although there were only a fraction as many lights as on the lowest tier. The third section had on its dull-metal surface only blue and yellow lights; they twinkled softly here and there over the vast area.

The fourth tier was a series of signs that brought the beginning of comprehension. The whole sign was:

WHITE	—	BIRTHS
RED	—	DEATHS
GREEN	—	LIVING
BLUE	—	IMMIGRATION TO EARTH
YELLOW	—	EMIGRATION

The fifth tier was also all sign, finally explaining:

POPULATIONS

SOLAR SYSTEM	19,174,463,747
EARTH	11,193,247,361
MARS	1,097,298,604
VENUS	5,141,053,811
MOONS	1,742,863,971

The numbers changed, even as he looked at them, leaping up and down, shifting below and above what they had first been. People were dying, being born, moving to Mars, to Venus, to the moons of Jupiter, to Earth's moon, and others coming back again, landing minute by minute in the thousands of spaceports. Life went on in its gigantic fashion — and here was the stupendous record. Here was —

"Better get in line," said a friendly voice beside Fara. "It takes quite a while to put through an individual case, I understand."

Fara stared at the man. He had the distinct impression of having had senseless words flung at him. "In line?" he started — and stopped himself with a jerk that hurt his throat.

He was moving forward, blindly, ahead of the younger man, thinking a curious jumble about that this must have been how Constable Jor was transported to Mars — when another of the man's words penetrated.

"Case?" said Fara violently. "Individual case!"

The man, a heavy-faced, blue-eyed young chap of around thirty-five, looked at him curiously: "You must know why you're here," he said. "Surely, you wouldn't have been sent through here unless you had a problem of some kind that the weapons shop courts will solve for you; there's no other reason for coming to Information Center."

Fara walked on because he was in the line now, a fast-moving line that curved him inexorably around the machine; and seemed to be heading him toward a door that led into the interior of the great metal structure.

So it was a building as well as a machine.

A problem, he was thinking, why, of course, he had a problem, a hopeless, insoluble, completely tangled problem so deeply rooted in the basic structure of Imperial civilization that the whole world would have to be overturned to make it right.

With a start, he saw that he was at the entrance. And the awed thought came: In seconds he would be committed irrevocably to — what?

Inside was a long, shining corridor, with scores of completely transparent hallways leading off the main corridor. Behind Fara, the young man's voice said:

"There's one, practically empty. Let's go."

Fara walked ahead; and suddenly he was trembling. He had already noticed that at the end of each side hallway were some dozen young women sitting at desks, interviewing men and . . . and, good heavens, was it possible that all this meant —

He grew aware that he had stopped in front of one of the girls.

She was older than she had looked from a distance, over thirty, but good-looking, alert. She smiled pleasantly, but impersonally, and said:

"Your name, please?"

He gave it before he thought and added a mumble about being from the village of Glay. The woman said:

"Thank you. It will take a few minutes to get your file. Won't you sit down?"

He hadn't noticed the chair. He sank into it; and his heart was beating so wildly that he felt choked. The strange thing was that there was scarcely a thought in his head, nor a real hope; only an intense, almost mind-wrecking excitement.

With a jerk, he realized that the girl was speaking again, but only snatches of her voice came through that screen of tension in his mind:

" — Information Center is . . . in effect . . . a bureau of statistics. Every person born . . . registered here . . . their education, change of address . . . occupation . . . and the highlights of their life. The whole is maintained by . . . combination of . . . unauthorized and unsuspected liaison with . . . Imperial Chamber of Statistics and . . . through medium of agents . . . in every community — "

It seemed to Fara that he was missing vital information, and that if he could only force his attention and hear more — He strained, but it was no use; his nerves were jumping madly and —

Before he could speak, there was a click, and a thin, dark plate slid onto the woman's desk. She took it up, and examined it. After a moment, she said something into a mouthpiece, and in a short time two more plates precipitated out of the empty air onto her desk. She studied them impassively, looked up finally.

"You will be interested to know," she said, "that your son, Cayle, bribed himself into a commission in the Imperial army with five thousand credits."

"Eh?" said Fara. He half rose from his chair, but before he could say anything, the young woman was speaking again, firmly:

"I must inform you that the weapon shops take no action against individuals. Your son can have his job, the money he stole; we are not concerned with moral correction. That must come naturally from the individual, and from the people as a whole — and now if you will give me a brief account of your problem for the record and the court."

Sweating, Fara sank back into his seat; his mind was heaving; most desperately, he wanted more information about Cayle. He began:

"But . . . but what . . . how — " He caught himself; and in a low voice described what had happened. When he finished, the girl said:

"You will proceed now to the Name Room; watch for your name, and when it appears go straight to Room 474. Remember, 474 — and now, the line is waiting, if you please — "

She smiled politely, and Fara was moving off almost before he realized it. He half turned to ask another question, but an old man was sinking into his chair. Fara hurried on, along a great corridor, conscious of curious blasts of sound coming from ahead.

Eagerly, he opened the door; and the sound crashed at him with all the impact of a sledge-hammer blow.

It was such a colossal, incredible sound that he stopped short, just inside the door, shrinking back. He stood then trying to blink sense into a visual confusion that rivaled in magnitude that incredible tornado of noise.

Men, men, men everywhere; men by the thousands in a long, broad, auditorium, packed into rows of seats, pacing with an abandon of restlessness up and down aisles, and all of them staring with a frantic interest at a long board marked off into squares, each square lettered from the alphabet, from A, B, C and so on to Z. The tremendous board with its lists of names ran the full length of the immense room.

The Name Room, Fara was thinking shakily, as he sank into a seat — and his name would come up in the C's, and then —

It was like sitting in at a no-limit poker game, watching the jewel-precious cards turn up. It was like playing the exchange with all the world at stake during a stock crash. It was nerve-racking, dazzling, exhausting, fascinating, terrible, mind-destroying, stupendous. It was —

It was like nothing else on the face of the earth.

New names kept flashing on to the twenty-six squares; and men would shout like insane beings and some fainted, and the uproar was absolutely shattering; the pandemonium raged on, one continuous, unbelievable sound.

And every few minutes a great sign would flash along the board, telling everyone:

"WATCH YOUR OWN INITIALS."

Fara watched, trembling in every limb. Each second it seemed to him that he couldn't stand it an instant longer. He wanted to scream at the room to be silent; he wanted to jump up to pace the floor, but others who did that were yelled at hysterically, threatened wildly, hated with a mad, murderous ferocity.

Abruptly, the blind savagery of it scared Fara. He thought unsteadily: "I'm not going to make a fool of myself. I — "

"Clark, Fara — " winked the board. "Clark, Fara — "

With a shout that nearly tore off the top of his head, Fara leaped to his feet. "That's me!" he shrieked, "Me!"

No one turned; no one paid the slightest attention. Shamed, he slunk across the room where an endless line of men kept crowding into a corridor beyond.

The silence in the long corridor was almost as shattering as the mind-destroying noise it replaced. It was hard to concentrate on the idea of a number — 474.

It was completely impossible to imagine what could lie beyond — .

The room was small. It was furnished with a small, business-type table and two chairs. On the table were seven neat piles of folders, each pile of different color. The piles were arranged in a row in front of a large, milky-white globe, that began to glow with a soft light. Out of its depths, a man's baritone voice said:

"Fara Clark?"

"Yes," said Fara.

"Before the verdict is rendered in your case," the voice went on quietly, "I want you to take a folder from the blue pile. The list will show the Fifth Interplanetary Bank in its proper relation to yourself and the world, and it will be explained to you in due course."

The list, Fara saw, was simply that, a list of the names of companies. The names ran from A to Z, and there were about five hundred of them.

The folder carried no explanation; and Fara slipped it automatically into his side pocket, as the voice came again from the shining globe:

"It has been established," the words came precisely, "that the Fifth Interplanetary Bank perpetrated upon you a gross swindle, and that it is further guilty of practicing scavengery, deception, blackmail and was accessory in a criminal conspiracy.

"The bank made contact with your son, Cayle, through what is quite properly known as a scavenger, that is, an employee who exists by finding young men and women who are normally capable of drawing drafts on their parents or other victims. The scavenger obtains for this service a commission of eight percent, which is always paid by the person making the loan, in this case your son.

"The bank practiced deception in that its authorized agents deceived you in the most culpable fashion by pretending that it had already paid out the ten thousand credits to your son, whereas the money was not paid over until your signature had been obtained.

"The blackmail guilt arises out of a threat to have your son arrested for falsely obtaining a loan, a threat made at a time when no money had exchanged hands. The conspiracy consists of the action whereby your note was promptly turned over to your competitor.

"The bank is accordingly triple-fined, thirty-six thousand three hundred credits. It is not in our interest, Fara Clark, for you to know how this money is obtained. Suffice to know that the bank pays it, and that of the fine the weapon shops allocate to their own treasury a total of one half. The other half — "

There was a *plop*; a neatly packaged pile of bills fell onto the table. "For you," said the voice; and Fara, with trembling fingers, slipped the package into his coat pocket. It required the purest mental and physical effort for him to concentrate on the next words that came:

"You must not assume that your troubles are over. The re-establishment of your motor repair shop in Glay will require force and courage. Be discreet, brave, and determined, and you cannot fail. Do not hesitate to use the gun you have purchased in defense of your rights. The plan will be explained to you. And now, proceed through the door facing you — "

Fara braced himself with an effort, opened the door and walked through.

It was a dim, familiar room that he stepped into, and there was a silver-haired, fine-faced man who rose from a reading chair, and came forward in the dimness, smiling gravely.

The stupendous, fantastic, exhilarating adventure was over; and he was back in the weapon shop of Glay.

He couldn't get over the wonder of it — this great and fascinating organization established here in the very heart of a ruthless civilization, a civilization that had in a few brief weeks stripped him of everything he possessed.

With a deliberate will, he stopped that glowing flow of thought. A dark frown wrinkled his solidly built face; he said:

"The . . . judge — " Fara hesitated over the name, frowned again, annoyed at himself, then went on: "The judge said that, to re-establish myself I would have to — "

"Before we go into that," said the old man quietly, "I want you to examine the blue folder you brought with you."

"Folder?" Fara echoed blankly. It took a long moment to remember that he had picked up a folder from the table in Room 474.

He studied the list of company names with a gathering puzzlement, noting that the name of Automatic Atomic Motor Repair Shops was well down among the A's, and the Fifth Interplanetary Bank only one of several great banks included. Fara looked up finally:

"I don't understand," he said; "are these the companies you have had to act against?"

The silver-haired man smiled grimly, shook his head. "That is not what I mean. These firms constitute only a fraction of the eight hundred thousand companies that are constantly in our books."

He smiled again, humorlessly: "These companies all know that, because of us, their profits on paper bear no relation to their assets. What they don't know is how great the difference really is; and, as we want a general improvement in business morals, not merely more skillful scheming to outwit us, we prefer them to remain in ignorance."

He paused, and this time he gave Fara a searching glance, and said at last: "The unique feature of the companies on this particular list is that they are every one wholly owned by Empress Isher."

He finished swiftly: "In view of your past opinions on that subject, I do not expect you to believe me."

Fara stood as still as death, for — he did believe with unquestioning conviction, completely, finally. The amazing, the unforgivable thing was that all his life he had watched the march of ruined men into the oblivion of poverty and disgrace — and blamed *them*.

Fara groaned. "I've been like a madman," he said. "Everything the empress and her officials did was right. No friendship, no personal relationship could survive with me that did not include belief in things as they were. I suppose if I started to talk against the empress I would receive equally short shrift."

"Under no circumstances," said the old man grimly, "must you say anything against her majesty. The weapon shops will not countenance any such words, and will give no further aid to anyone who is so indiscreet. The reason is that, for the moment, we have reached an uneasy state of peace with the Imperial government. We wish to keep it that way; beyond that I will not enlarge on our policy.

"I am permitted to say that the last great attempt to destroy the weapon shops was made seven years ago, when the glorious Innelda Isher was twenty-five years old. That was a secret attempt, based on a new invention; and failed by purest accident because of our sacrifice of a man from seven thousand years in the past. That may sound mysterious to you, but I will not explain.

"The worst period was reached some forty years ago when every person who was discovered receiving aid from us was murdered in some fashion. You may be surprised to know that your father-in-law was among those assassinated at that time."

"Creel's father!" Fara gasped. "But — "

He stopped. His brain was reeling; there was such a rush of blood to his head that for an instant he could hardly see.

"But," he managed at last, "it was reported that he ran away with another woman."

"They always spread a vicious story of some kind," the old man said; and Fara was silent, stunned.

The other went on: "We finally put a stop to their murders by killing the three men from the top down, *excluding* the royal family, who gave the order for the particular execution involved. But we do not again want that kind of bloody murder.

"Nor are we interested in any criticism of our toleration of so much that is evil. It is important to understand that *we do not interfere in the main stream of human existence*. We right wrongs; we act as a barrier between the people and their more ruthless exploiters. Generally speaking, we help only honest men; that is not to say that we do not give assistance to the less scrupulous, but only to the extent of selling them guns — which is a very great aid indeed, and which is one of the reasons why the government is relying almost exclusively for its power on an economic chicanery.

"In the four thousand years since the brilliant genius Walter S. DeLany invented the vibration process that made the weapon shops possible, and laid down the first principles of weapon shop political philosophy, we have watched the tide of government swing backward and forward between democracy under a limited monarchy to complete tyranny. And we have discovered one thing:

"*People always have the kind of government they want.* When they want change, they must change it. As always we shall remain an incorruptible core — and I mean that literally; we have a psychological machine that never lies about a man's character — I repeat, an incorruptible core of human idealism, devoted to relieving the ills that arise inevitably under any form of government.

"But now — your problem. It is very simple, really. You must fight, as all men have fought since the beginning of time for what they valued, for their just rights. As you know, the Automatic Repair people removed all your machinery and tools within an hour of foreclosing on your shop. This material was taken to Ferd, and then shipped to a great warehouse on the coast.

"We recovered it, and with our special means of transportation have now replaced the machines in your shop. You will accordingly go there and — "

Fara listened with a gathering grimness to the instructions, nodded finally, his jaw clamped tight.

"You can count on me," he said curtly. "I've been a stubborn man in my time; and though I've changed sides, I haven't changed *that*."

Going outside was like returning from life to — death; from hope to — reality.

Fara walked along the quiet streets of Glay at darkest night. For the first time it struck him that the weapon shop Information Center must be halfway around the world, for it had been day, brilliant day.

The picture vanished as if it had never existed, and he grew aware again, preternaturally aware of the village of Glay asleep all around him. Silent, peaceful — yet ugly, he thought, ugly with the ugliness of evil enthroned.

He thought: The right to buy weapons — and his heart swelled into his throat; the tears came to his eyes.

He wiped his vision clear with the back of his hand, thought of Creel's long dead father, and strode on, without shame. Tears were good for an angry man.

The shop was the same, but the hard metal padlock yielded before the tiny, blazing, supernal power of the revolver. One flick of fire; the metal dissolved — and he was inside.

It was dark, too dark to see, but Fara did not turn on the lights immediately. He fumbled across to the window control, turned the windows to darkness vibration, and then clicked on the lights.

He gulped with awful relief. For the machines, his precious tools that he had seen carted away within hours after the bailiff's arrival, were here again, ready for use.

Shaky from the pressure of his emotion, Fara called Creel on the telestat. It took a little while for her to appear; and she was in her dressing robe. When she saw who it was she turned a dead white.

"Fara, oh, Fara, I thought — "

He cut her off grimly: "Creel, I've been to the weapon shop. I want you to do this: go straight to your mother. I'm here at my shop. I'm going to stay here day and night until it's settled that I *stay*. . . . I shall go home later for some food and clothing, but I want you to be gone by then. Is that clear?"

Color was coming back into her lean, handsome face. She said: "Don't you bother coming home, Fara. I'll do everything necessary. I'll pack all that's needed into the carplane, including a folding bed. We'll sleep in the back room of the shop."

Morning came palely, but it was ten o'clock before a shadow darkened the open door; and Constable Jor came in. He looked shame-faced:

"I've got an order here for your arrest," he said.

"Tell those who sent you," Fara replied deliberately, "that I resisted arrest — with a gun."

The deed followed the words with such rapidity that Jor blinked. He stood like that for a moment, a big, sleepy-looking man, staring at that gleaming, magical revolver; then:

"I have a summons here ordering you to appear at the great court of Ferd this afternoon. Will you accept it?"

"Certainly."

"Then you will be there?"

"I'll send my lawyer," said Fara. "Just drop the summons on the floor there. Tell them I took it."

The weapon shop man had said: "Do not ridicule by word any legal measure of the Imperial authorities. Simply disobey them."

Jor went out, and seemed relieved. It took an hour before Mayor Mel Dale came pompously through the door.

"See here, Fara Clark," he bellowed from the doorway. "You can't get away with this. This is defiance of the law."

Fara was silent as His Honor waddled farther into the building. It was puzzling, almost amazing, that Mayor Dale would risk his plump, treasured body. Puzzlement ended as the mayor said in a low voice:

"Good work, Fara; I knew you had it in you. There's dozens of us in Glay behind you, so stick it out. I had to yell at you just now, because there's a crowd outside. Yell back at me, will you? Let's have a real name calling. But, first, a word of warning: the manager of the Automatic Repair Shop is on his way here with his bodyguards, two of them — "

Shakily, Fara watched the mayor go out. The crisis was at hand. He braced himself, thought: "Let them come, let them — "

It was easier than he had thought — for the men who entered the shop turned pale when they saw the holstered revolver. There was a violence of blustering, nevertheless, that narrowed finally down to:

"Look here," the man said, "we've got your note for twelve thousand one hundred credits. You're not going to deny you owe that money."

"I'll buy it back," said Fara in a stony voice, "for exactly half, not a cent more."

The strong-jawed young man looked at him for a long time. "We'll take it," he said finally, curtly

Fara said: "I've got the agreement here — "

His first customer was old man Miser Lan Harris. Fara stared at the long-faced oldster with a vast surmise, and his first, amazed comprehension came of how the weapon shop must have settled on Harris' lot — by arrangement.

It was an hour after Harris had gone that Creel's mother stamped into the shop. She closed the door.

"Well," she said, "you did it, eh? Good work. I'm sorry if I seemed rough with you when you came to my place, but we weapon-shop supporters can't afford to take risks for those who are not on our side.

"But never mind that. I've come to take Creel home. The important thing is to return everything to normal as quickly as possible."

It was over; incredibly it was over. Twice, as he walked home that might, Fara stopped in midstride, and wondered if it had not all been a dream. The air was like wine. The little world of Glay spread before him, green and gracious, a peaceful paradise where time had stood still.

Damon Knight

The Country of the Kind

(1955)

Damon Knight (1922–2002) was a true sf insider — not only an important writer and editor but also an early fan, a member of the "Futurians" group that included many notable sf writers of the 1940s, and a founder of both the renowned Clarion Science Fiction Writers' Workshop (where he taught with his wife, Kate Wilhelm, for many years) and the Science Fiction Writers of America, the professional association that awards the Nebula. Knight was one of the first serious sf critics; his collected reviews, published in *In Search of Wonder*, earned a Hugo in 1956.

As a writer, Knight is most famous for short stories marked by irony and dark humor. Among the best known of his stories is the ambiguously titled "To Serve Man" (1950), which was made into a memorable episode of the popular 1960s TV show *The Twilight Zone*. "The Country of the Kind" is a fine example of this style of writing, with an emphasis on social commentary. The country in question is portrayed obliquely but seems, at least superficially, quite utopian — a land of material comfort and gentle manners, its people unaccustomed to violence or conflict. But this cozy existence comes at a price. While the narrator is not a very sympathetic character, we can't help but identify with his loneliness and isolation, and his very existence makes us feel uneasy about this country and its "kindness."

The attendant at the car lot was daydreaming when I pulled up — a big, lazy-looking man in black satin chequered down the front. I was wearing scarlet, myself; it suited my mood. I got out, almost on his toes.

"Park or storage?" he asked automatically, turning around. Then he realized who I was, and ducked his head away.

"Neither," I told him.

There was a hand torch on a shelf in the repair shed right behind him. I got it and came back. I knelt down to where I could reach behind the front wheel, and ignited the torch. I turned it on the axle and suspension. They glowed cherry red, then white, and fused together. Then I got up and turned the flame on both tires until the rubberoid stank and sizzled and melted down to the pavement. The attendant didn't say anything.

I left him there, looking at the mess on his nice clean concrete.

It had been a nice car, too; but I could get another any time. And I felt like walking. I went down the winding road, sleepy in the afternoon sunlight, dappled with shade and smelling of cool leaves. You couldn't see the houses; they were all sunken or hidden by shrubbery, or a little of both. That was the fad I'd heard about; it was what I'd come here to see. Not that anything the dulls did would be worth looking at.

I turned off at random and crossed a rolling lawn, went through a second hedge of hawthorn in blossom, and came out next to a big sunken games court.

The tennis net was up, and two couples were going at it, just working up a little sweat — young, about half my age, all four of them. Three dark-haired, one blonde. They were evenly matched, and both couples played well together; they were enjoying themselves.

I watched for a minute. But by then the nearest two were beginning to sense I was there, anyhow. I walked down onto the court, just as the blonde was about to serve. She looked at me frozen across the net, poised on tiptoe. The others stood.

"Off," I told them. "Game's over."

I watched the blonde. She was not especially pretty, as they go, but compactly and gracefully put together. She came down slowly, flat-footed without awkwardness, and tucked the racket under her arm; then the surprise was over and she was trotting off the court after the other three.

I followed their voices around the curve of the path, between towering masses of lilacs, inhaling the sweetness, until I came to what looked like a little sunning spot. There was a sundial, and a birdbath, and towels lying around on the grass. One couple, the dark-haired pair, was still in sight farther down the path, heads bobbing along. The other couple had disappeared.

I found the handle in the grass without any trouble. The mechanism responded, and an oblong section of turf rose up. It was the stair I had, not the elevator, but that was all right. I ran down the steps and into the first door I saw, and was in the top-floor lounge, an oval room lit with diffused simulated sunlight from above. The furniture was all comfortably bloated, sprawling and ugly; the carpet was deep, and there was a fresh flower scent in the air.

The blonde was over at the near end with her back to me, studying the autochef keyboard. She was half out of her playsuit. She pushed it the rest of the way down and stepped out of it, then turned and saw me.

She was surprised again; she hadn't thought I might follow her down.

I got up close before it occurred to her to move; then it was too late. She knew she couldn't get away from me; she closed her eyes and leaned back against the paneling, turning a little pale. Her lips and her golden brows went up in the middle.

I looked her over and told her a few uncomplimentary things about herself. She trembled, but didn't answer. On an impulse, I leaned over and dialed the autochef to hot cheese sauce. I cut the safety out of circuit and put the quantity dial all the way up. I dialed *soup tureen* and then *punch bowl*.

The stuff began to come out in about a minute, steaming hot. I took the tureens and splashed them up and down the wall on either side of her. Then when the first punch bowl came out I used the empty bowls as scoops. I clotted the carpet with the stuff; I made streamers of it all along the walls, and dumped puddles into what furniture I could reach. Where it cooled it would harden, and where it hardened it would cling.

I wanted to splash it across her body, but it would've hurt, and we couldn't have that. The punch bowls of hot sauce were still coming out of the autochef, crowding each other around the vent. I punched *cancel*, and then *sauterne (swt., Calif.)*.

It came out well chilled in open bottles. I took the first one and had my arm back just about to throw a nice line of the stuff right across her midriff, when a voice said behind me:

"Watch out for cold wine."

My arm twitched and a little stream of the wine splashed across her thighs. She was ready for it; her eyes had opened at the voice, and she barely jumped.

I whirled around, fighting mad. The man was standing there where he had come out of the stair well. He was thinner in the face than most, bronzed, wide-chested, with alert blue eyes. If it hadn't been for him, I knew it would have worked — the blonde would have mistaken the chill splash for a scalding one.

I could hear the scream in my mind, and I wanted it.

I took a step toward him, and my foot slipped. I went down clumsily, wrenching one knee. I got up shaking and tight all over. I wasn't in control of myself. I screamed, "You — you — " I turned and got one of the punch bowls and lifted it in both hands, heedless of how the hot sauce was slopping over onto my wrists, and I had it almost in the air toward him when the sickness took me — that damned buzzing in my head, louder, louder, drowning everything out.

When I came to, they were both gone. I got up off the floor, weak as death, and staggered over to the nearest chair. My clothes were slimed and sticky. I wanted to die. I wanted to drop into that dark furry hole that was yawning for me and never come up; but I made myself stay awake and get out of the chair.

Going down in the elevator, I almost blacked out again. The blonde and the thin man weren't in any of the second-floor bedrooms. I made sure of that, and then I emptied the closets and bureau drawers onto the floor, dragged the whole mess into one of the bathrooms and stuffed the tub with it, then turned on the water.

I tried the third floor: maintenance and storage. It was empty. I turned the furnace on and set the thermostat up as high as it would go. I disconnected all the safety circuits and alarms. I opened the freezer doors and dialed them to defrost. I propped the stair well door open and went back up in the elevator.

On the second floor I stopped long enough to open the stairway door there — the water was halfway toward it, creeping across the floor — and then searched the top floor. No one was there. I opened book reels and threw them unwinding across the room; I would have done more, but I could hardly stand. I got up to the surface and collapsed on the lawn: that furry pit swallowed me up, dead and drowned.

While I slept, water poured down the open stair well and filled the third level. Thawing food packages floated out into the rooms. Water seeped into wall panels and machine housings; circuits shorted and fuses blew. The air conditioning stopped, but the pile kept heating. The water rose.

Spoiled food, floating supplies, grimy water surged up the stair well. The second and first levels were bigger and would take longer to fill, but they'd fill. Rugs, furnishings, clothing, all the things in the house would be water-logged and ruined. Probably the weight of so much water would shift the house, rupture water pipes and other fluid intakes. It would take a repair crew more than a day just to clean up the mess. The house itself was done for, not repairable. The blonde and the thin man would never live in it again.

Serve them right.

The dulls could build another house; they built like beavers. There was only one of me in the world.

The earliest memory I have is of some woman, probably the cresh-mother, staring at me with an expression of shock and horror. Just that. I've tried to remember what happened directly before or after, but I can't. Before, there's nothing but the dark formless shaft of no-memory that runs back to birth. Afterward, the big calm.

From my fifth year, it must have been, to my fifteenth, everything I can remember floats in a pleasant dim sea. Nothing was terribly important. I was languid and soft; I drifted. Waking merged into sleep.

In my fifteenth year it was the fashion in love-play for the young people to pair off for months or longer. "Loving steady," we called it. I remember how the older people protested that it was unhealthy; but we were all normal juniors, and nearly as free as adults under the law.

All but me.

The first steady girl I had was named Elen. She had blonde hair, almost white, worn long; her lashes were dark and her eyes pale green. Startling eyes: they didn't look as if they were looking at you. They looked blind.

Several times she gave me strange startled glances, something between fright and anger. Once it was because I held her too tightly, and hurt her; other times, it seemed to be for nothing at all.

In our group, a pairing that broke up sooner than four weeks was a lit-tle suspect — there must be something wrong with one partner or both, or the pairing would have lasted longer.

Four weeks and a day after Elen and I made our pairing, she told me she was breaking it.

I'd thought I was ready. But I felt the room spin half around me till the wall came against my palm and stopped.

The room had been in use as a hobby chamber; there was a rack of plasticraft knives under my hand. I took one without thinking, and when I saw it I thought, *I'll frighten her.*

And I saw the startled, half-angry look in her pale eyes as I went toward her; but this is curious: she wasn't looking at the knife. She was looking at my face.

The elders found me later with the blood on me, and put me into a locked room. Then it was my turn to be frightened, because I realized for the first time that it was possible for a human being to do what I had done.

And if I could do it to Elen, I thought, surely they could do it to me.

But they couldn't. They set me free: they had to.

And it was then I understood that I was the king of the world. . . .

The sky was turning clear violet when I woke up, and shadow was spilling out from the hedges. I went down the hill until I saw the ghostly blue of photon tubes glowing in a big oblong, just outside the commerce area. I went that way, by habit.

Other people were lining up at the entrance to show their books and be admitted. I brushed by them, seeing the shocked faces and feeling their bodies flinch away, and went on into the robing chamber.

Straps, aqualungs, masks and flippers were all for the taking. I stripped, dropping the clothes where I stood, and put the underwater equipment on. I strode out to the poolside, monstrous, like a being from another world. I adjusted the lung and the flippers, and slipped into the water.

Underneath, it was all crystal blue, with the forms of swimmers sliding through it like pale angels. Schools of small fish scattered as I went down. My heart was beating with a painful joy.

Down, far down, I saw a girl slowly undulating through the motions of sinuous underwater dance, writhing around and around a ribbed column of imitation coral. She had a suction-tipped fish lance in her hand, but she was not using it; she was only dancing, all by herself, down at the bottom of the water.

I swam after her. She was young and delicately made, and when she saw the deliberately clumsy motions I made in imitation of hers, her eyes glinted with amusement behind her mask. She bowed to me in mockery, and slowly glided off with simple, exaggerated movements, like a child's ballet.

I followed. Around her and around I swam, stiff-legged, first more child-like and awkward than she, then subtly parodying her motions; then improving on them until I was dancing an intricate, mocking dance around her.

I saw her eyes widen. She matched her rhythm to mine, then, and together, apart, together again we coiled the wake of our dancing. At last, exhausted, we clung together where a bridge of plastic coral arched over us. Her cool body was in the bend of my arm; behind two thicknesses of vitrin — a world away! — her eyes were friendly and kind.

There was a moment when, two strangers yet one flesh, we felt our souls speak to one another across that abyss of matter. It was a truncated embrace — we could not kiss, we could not speak — but her hands lay confidingly on my shoulders, and her eyes looked into mine.

That moment had to end. She gestured toward the surface, and left me. I followed her up. I was feeling drowsy and almost at peace, after my sickness. I thought . . . I don't know what I thought.

We rose together at the side of the pool. She turned to me, removing her mask: and her smile stopped, and melted away. She stared at me with a horrified disgust, wrinkling her nose.

"*Pyah!*" she said, and turned, awkward in her flippers. Watching her, I saw her fall into the arms of a white-haired man, and heard her hysterical voice tumbling over itself.

"But don't you remember?" the man's voice rumbled. "You should know it by heart." He turned. "Hal, is there a copy of it in the clubhouse?"

A murmur answered him, and in a few moments a young man came out holding a slender brown pamphlet.

I knew that pamphlet. I could even have told you what page the white-haired man opened it to; what sentences the girl was reading as I watched.

I waited. I don't know why.

I heard her voice rising: "To think that I let him *touch* me!" And the white-haired man reassured her, the words rumbling, too low to hear. I saw her back straighten. She looked across at me . . . only a few yards in that scented, blue-lit air; a world away . . . and folded up the pamphlet into a hard wad, threw it, and turned on her heel.

The pamphlet landed almost at my feet. I touched it with my toe, and it opened to the page I had been thinking of:

. . . sedation until his fifteenth year, when for sexual reasons it became no longer practicable. While the advisors and medical staff hesitated, he killed a girl of the group by violence.

And farther down:

The solution finally adopted was three-fold.
1. *A sanction* — the only sanction possible to our humane, permissive society. Excommunication: not to speak to him, touch him willingly, or acknowledge his existence.
2. *A precaution*. Taking advantage of a mild predisposition to epilepsy, a variant of the so-called Kusko analog technique was employed, to prevent by an epileptic seizure any future act of violence.
3. *A warning*. A careful alternation of his body chemistry was affected to make his exhaled and exuded wastes emit a strongly pungent and offensive odor. In mercy, he himself was rendered unable to detect this smell.

Fortunately, the genetic and environmental accidents which combined to produce this atavism have been fully explained and can never again . . .

The words stopped meaning anything, as they always did at that point. I didn't want to read any farther; it was all nonsense, anyway. I was the king of the world.

I got up and went away, out into the night, blind to the dulls who thronged the rooms I passed.

Two squares away was the commerce area. I found a clothing outlet and went in. All the free clothes in the display cases were drab: those were for worthless floaters, not for me. I went past them to the specials, and found a combination I could stand — silver and blue, with a severe black piping down the tunic. A dull would have said it was "nice." I punched for it. The automatic looked me over with its dull glassy eye, and croaked, "Your contribution book, please."

I could have had a contribution book, for the trouble of stepping out into the street and taking it away from the first passer-by; but I didn't have the patience. I picked up the one-legged table from the refreshing nook, hefted it, and swung it at the cabinet door. The metal shrieked and dented, opposite the catch. I swung once more to the same place, and the door sprang open. I pulled out clothing in handfuls till I got a set that would fit me.

I bathed and changed, and then went prowling in the big multi-outlet down the avenue. All those places are arranged pretty much alike, no matter what the local managers do to them. I went straight to the knives, and picked out three in graduated sizes, down to the size of my fingernail. Then I had to take my chances. I tried the furniture department, where I had had good luck once in a while, but this year all they were using was metal. I had to have seasoned wood.

I knew where there was a big cache of cherry wood, in good-sized blocks, in a forgotten warehouse up north at a place called Kootenay. I could have carried some around with me — enough for years — but what for, when the world belonged to me?

It didn't take me long. Down in the workshop section, of all places, I found some antiques — tables and benches, all with wooden tops. While the dulls collected down at the other end of the room, pretending not to notice, I sawed off a good oblong chunk of the smallest bench, and made a base for it out of another.

As long as I was there, it was a good place to work, and I could eat and sleep upstairs, so I stayed.

I knew what I wanted to do. It was going to be a man, sitting, with legs crossed and his forearms resting down along his calves. His head was going to be tilted back, and his eyes closed, as if he were turning his face up to the sun.

In three days it was finished. The trunk and limbs had a shape that was not man and not wood, but something in between: something that hadn't existed before I made it.

Beauty. That was the old word.

I had carved one of the figure's hands hanging loosely, and the other one curled shut. There had to be a time to stop and say it was finished. I took the smallest knife, the one I had been using to scrape the wood smooth, and cut away the handle and ground down what was left of the shaft to a thin spike. Then I drilled a hole into the wood of the figurine's hand, in the hollow between thumb and curled finger. I fitted the knife blade in there; in the small hand it was a sword.

I cemented it in place. Then I took the sharp blade and stabbed my thumb, and smeared the blade.

I hunted most of that day, and finally found the right place — a niche in an outcropping of striated brown rock, in a little triangular half-wild patch that had been left where two roads forked. Nothing was permanent, of course, in a community like this one that might change its houses every five years or so, to follow the fashion; but this spot had been left to itself a long time. It was the best I could do.

I had the paper ready: it was one of a batch I had printed up a year ago. The paper was treated, and I knew it would stay legible a long time. I hid a little photo capsule in the back of the niche, and ran the control wire to a staple in the base of the figurine. I put the figurine down on top of the paper, and anchored it lightly to the rock with two spots of all-cement. I had done it so often that it came naturally; I knew just how much cement would hold the figurine steady against a casual hand, but yield to one that really wanted to pull it down.

Then I stepped back to look: and the power and the pity of it made my breath come short, and tears start to my eyes.

Reflected light gleamed fitfully on the dark-stained blade that hung from his hand. He was sitting alone in that niche that closed him in like a coffin. His eyes were shut, and his head tilted back, as if he were turning his face up to the sun.

But only rock was over his head. There was no sun for him.

Hunched on the cool bare ground under a pepper tree, I was looking down across the road at the shadowed niche where my figurine sat.

I was all finished here. There was nothing more to keep me, and yet I couldn't leave.

People walked past now and then — not often. The community seemed half deserted, as if most of the people had flocked off to a surf party somewhere, or a contribution meeting, or to watch a new house being dug to replace the one I had wrecked. . . . There was a little wind blowing toward me, cool and lonesome in the leaves.

Up the other side of the hollow there was a terrace, and on that terrace half an hour ago, I had seen a brief flash of color — a boy's head, with a red cap on it, moving past and out of sight.

That was why I had to stay. I was thinking how that boy might come down from his terrace and into my road, and passing the little wild triangle of land, see my figurine. I was thinking he might not pass by indifferently but stop: and go closer to look: and pick up the wooden man: and read what was written on the paper underneath.

I believed that sometime it had to happen. I wanted it so hard that I ached.

My carvings were all over the world, wherever I had wandered. There was one in Congo City, carved of ebony, dusty-black; one on Cyprus, of bone; one in New Bombay, of shell; one in Chang-teh, of jade.

They were like signs printed in red and green, in a color-blind world. Only the one I was looking for would ever pick one of them up, and read the message I knew by heart.

TO YOU WHO CAN SEE, the first sentence said, I OFFER YOU A WORLD. . . .

There was a flash of color up on the terrace. I stiffened. A minute later, here it came again, from a different direction: it was the boy clambering down the slope, brilliant against the green, with his red sharp-billed cap like a woodpecker's head.

I held my breath.

He came toward me through the fluttering leaves, ticked off by pencils of sunlight as he passed. He was a brown boy, I could see at this distance, with a serious thin face. His ears stuck out, flickering pink with the sun behind them, and his elbow and knee pads made him look knobby.

He reached the fork in the road, and chose the path on my side. I huddled into myself as he came nearer. *Let him see it, let him not see me*, I thought fiercely.

My fingers closed around a stone.

He was nearer, walking jerkily with his hands in his pockets, watching his feet mostly.

When he was almost opposite me, I threw the stone.

It rustled through the leaves below the niche in the rock. The boy's head turned. He stopped, staring. I think he saw the figurine then. I'm sure he saw it.

He took one step.

"Risha!" came floating down from the terrace.

And he looked up. "Here," he piped.

I saw the woman's head, tiny at the top of the terrace. She called something I didn't hear; I was standing up, tight with anger.

Then the wind shifted. It blew from me to the boy. He whirled around, his eyes big, and clapped a hand to his nose.

"Oh, what a stench!" he said.

He turned to shout, "Coming!" and then he was gone, hurrying back up the road, into the unstable blur of green.

My own chance, ruined. He would have been the image, I knew, if it hadn't been for that damned woman, and the wind shifting. . . . They were all against me, people, wind and all.

And the figurine still sat, blind eyes turned up to the rocky sky.

There was something inside me that told me to take my disappointment and go away from there, and not come back.

I knew I would be sorry. I did it anyway: took the image out of the niche, and the paper with it, and climbed the slope. At the top I heard his clear voice laughing.

There was a thing that might have been an ornamental mound, or the camouflaged top of a buried house. I went around it, tripping over my own feet, and came upon the boy kneeling on the turf. He was playing with a brown and white puppy.

He looked up with the laughter going out of his face. There was no wind, and he could smell me. I knew it was bad. No wind, and the puppy to distract him — everything about it was wrong. But I went to him blindly anyhow, and fell on one knee, and shoved the figurine at his face.

"Look — " I said.

He went over backwards in his hurry: he couldn't even have seen the image, except as a brown blur coming at him. He scrambled up, with the puppy whining and yapping around his heels, and ran for the mound.

I was up after him, clawing up moist earth and grass as I rose. In the other hand I still had the image clutched, and the paper with it.

A door popped open and swallowed him and popped shut again in my face. With the flat of my hand I beat the vines around it until I hit the door-plate by accident and the door opened. I dived in, shouting, "Wait," and was in a spiral passage, lit pearl-gray, winding downward. Down I went headlong, and came out at the wrong door — an underground conservatory, humid and hot under the yellow lights, with dripping rank leaves in long rows. I went down the aisle raging, overturning the tanks, until I came to a vestibule and an elevator.

Down I went again to the third level and a labyrinth of guest rooms, all echoing, all empty. At last I found a ramp leading upward, past the conservatory, and at the end of it voices.

The door was clear vitrin, and I paused on the near side of it looking and listening. There was the boy, and a woman old enough to be his mother, just — sister or cousin, more likely — and an elderly woman in a hard chair holding the puppy. The room was comfortable and tasteless, like other rooms.

I saw the shock grow on their faces as I burst in: it was always the same, they knew I would like to kill them, but they never expected that I would come uninvited into a house. It was not done.

There was that boy, so close I could touch him, but the shock of all of them was quivering in the air, smothering, like a blanket that would deaden my voice. I felt I had to shout.

"Everything they tell you is lies!" I said. "See here — here, this is the truth!" I had the figurine in front of his eyes, but he didn't see.

"Risha, go below," said the young woman quietly. He turned to obey quick as a ferret. I got in front of him again. "Stay," I said, breathing hard. "Look — "

"Remember, Risha, don't speak," said the woman.

I couldn't stand any more. Where the boy went I don't know; I ceased to see him. With the image in one hand and the paper with it, I leaped at the woman. I was almost quick enough; I almost reached her; but the buzzing took me in the middle of a step, louder, louder, like the end of the world.

It was the second time that week. When I came to, I was sick and too faint to move for a long time.

The house was silent. They had gone, of course . . . the house had been defiled, having me in it. They wouldn't live here again, but would build elsewhere.

My eyes blurred. After a while I stood up and looked around at the room. The walls were hung with a gray close-woven cloth that looked as if it would tear, and I thought of ripping it down in strips, breaking furniture, stuffing carpets and bedding into the oubliette. . . . But I didn't have the heart for it. I was too tired. Thirty years. . . . They had given me all the kingdoms of the world, and the glory thereof, thirty years ago. It was more than one man alone could bear, for thirty years.

At last I stooped and picked up the figurine, and the paper that was supposed to go under it — crumpled now, with the forlorn look of a message that someone has thrown away unread.

I sighed bitterly.

I smoothed it out and read the last part.

YOU CAN SHARE THE WORLD WITH ME. THEY CAN'T STOP YOU. STRIKE NOW — PICK UP A SHARP THING AND STAB, OR A HEAVY THING AND CRUSH. THAT'S ALL. THAT WILL MAKE YOU FREE. ANYONE CAN DO IT.

Anyone. Someone. Anyone.

Harlan Ellison

"Repent, Harlequin!" Said the Ticktockman
(1965)

Harlan Ellison (b. 1934) is one of sf's great short-story writers and editors, even though he rejects the "science fiction writer" label, preferring broader terms like "fabulist" or "surrealist." An iconoclast and a rebel who believed that in order to write one should also live fully, Ellison had a colorful youth that reputedly included time spent working on tuna boats, in logging camps, and at carnivals, as well as riding the railroad with hobos and going undercover as a gang member in Brooklyn, an adventure that provided material for his first novel. A prolific writer, he is the winner of three Nebulas and eight Hugos, as well as numerous awards for horror, mystery, journalism, and film. He is an accomplished screenwriter whose credits include the famous *Star Trek* episode "City on the Edge of Forever," and he has served as a consultant on *The New Twilight Zone* and *Babylon 5*.

Ellison is closely associated with the New Wave, both through his own fiction and through his work as editor of the groundbreaking *Dangerous Visions* anthologies, which expanded the notion of what topics and styles were acceptable in sf. In his own fiction, Ellison is noted for his unflinching examinations of the darker side of human nature, and his stories have a disturbing, emotional rawness that is seldom matched.

"'Repent, Harlequin!' Said the Ticktockman," which won both the Hugo and the Nebula in 1966, is a countercultural fable perfectly suited for its times. Featuring a trickster figure who Ellison acknowledges has an autobiographical basis, this story is a protest against utilitarianism and a declaration of the value of spontaneity and playful self-expression. Like many of Ellison's stories, it is a strange mixture of exuberance and despair.

There are always those who ask, what is it all about? For those who need to ask, for those who need points sharply made, who need to know "where it's at," this:

> The mass of men serve the state thus, not as men mainly, but as machines, with their bodies. They are the standing army, and the militia, jailors, constables, posse comitatus, etc. In most cases there is no free exercise whatever of the judgment or of the moral sense; but they put themselves on a level with wood and earth and stones; and wooden men can perhaps be manufactured that will serve the purpose as well. Such command no more respect than men of straw or a lump of dirt. They have the same sort of worth only as horses and dogs. Yet such as these even are commonly esteemed good citizens. Others — as most legislators, politicians, lawyers, ministers, and officeholders — serve the state chiefly with their heads; and, as they rarely make any moral distinctions, they are as likely to serve the Devil, without intending it, as God. A very few, as heroes, patriots, martyrs, reformers in the great sense, and *men*, serve the state with their consciences also, and so necessarily resist it for the most part; and they are commonly treated as enemies by it.
>
> —Henry David Thoreau,
> *Civil Disobedience*

That is the heart of it. Now begin in the middle, and later learn the beginning; the end will take care of itself.

But because it was the very world it was, the very world they had allowed it to *become*, for months his activities did not come to the alarmed attention of The Ones Who Kept The Machine Functioning Smoothly, the ones who poured the very best butter over the cams and mainsprings of the culture. Not until it had become obvious that somehow, someway, he had become a notoriety, a celebrity, perhaps even a hero for (what Officialdom inescapably tagged) "an emotionally disturbed segment of the populace," did they turn it over to the Ticktockman and his legal machinery. But by then, because it was the very world it was, and they had no way to predict he would happen — possibly a strain of disease long-defunct, now, suddenly; reborn in a system where immunity had been forgotten, had lapsed — he had been allowed to become too real. Now he had form and substance.

He had become a *personality*, something they had filtered out of the system many decades before. But there it was, and there *he* was, a very definitely imposing personality. In certain circles — middle-class circles — it was thought disgusting. Vulgar ostentation. Anarchistic. Shameful. In others, there was only sniggering: those strata where thought is subjugated to form and ritual, niceties, proprieties. But down below, ah, down below, where the people always needed their saints and sinners, their bread and circuses, their heroes and villains, he was considered a Bolivar; a Napoleon; a Robin Hood; a Dick Bong (Ace of Aces); a Jesus; a Jomo Kenyatta.

And at the top — where, like socially-attuned Shipwreck Kellys, every tremor and vibration threatens to dislodge the wealthy, powerful, and titled from their flagpoles — he was considered a menace; a heretic; a rebel; a disgrace; a peril. He was known down the line, to the very heart-meat core, but the important reactions were high above and far below. At the very top, at the very bottom.

So his file was turned over, along with his time-card and his cardio-plate, to the office of Ticktockman.

The Ticktockman: very much over six feet tall, often silent, a soft purring man when things went timewise. The Ticktockman.

Even in the cubicles of the hierarchy, where fear was generated, seldom suffered, he was called the Ticktockman. But no one called him that to his mask.

You don't call a man a hated name, not when that man, behind his mask, is capable of revoking the minutes, the hours, the days and nights, the years of your life. He was called the Master Timekeeper to his mask. It was safer that way.

"This is *what* he is," said the Ticktockman with genuine softness, but not *who* he is. This time-card I'm holding in my left hand has a name on it, but it is the name of *what* he is, not *who* he is. The cardioplate here in my right hand is also named, but not *whom* named, merely *what* named. Before I can exercise proper revocation, I have to know *who* this *what* is."

To his staff, all the ferrets, all the loggers, all the finks, all the commex, even the mineez, he said, "Who is this Harlequin?"

He was not purring smoothly. Timewise, it was jangle.

However, it *was* the longest speech they had ever heard him utter at one time, the staff, the ferrets, the loggers, the finks, the commex, but not the mineez, who usually weren't around to know, in any case. But even they scurried to find out.

Who is the Harlequin?

High above the third level of the city, he crouched on the humming aluminum-frame platform of the air-boat (foof! air-boat, indeed! swizzleskid is what it was, with a tow-rack jerry-rigged) and he stared down at the neat Mondrian arrangement of the buildings.

Somewhere nearby, he could hear the metronomic left-right-left of the 2:47 p.m. shift, entering the Timkin roller-bearing plant in their sneakers. A minute later, precisely, he heard the softer right-left-right of the 5:00 a.m. formation, going home.

An elfin grin spread across his tanned features, and his dimples appeared for a moment. Then, scratching at his thatch of auburn hair, he shrugged within his motley, as though girding himself for what came next, and threw the joystick forward, and bent into the wind as the airboat dropped. He skimmed over a slidewalk, purposely dropping a few feet to crease the tassels of the ladies of fashion, and — inserting thumbs in large ears — he stuck out his tongue, rolled his eyes and went wugga-wugga-wugga. It was a minor diversion. One pedestrian skittered and tumbled, sending parcels everywhichway, another wet herself, a third keeled slant-wise and the walk was stopped automatically by the servitors till she could be resuscitated. It was a minor diversion.

Then he swirled away on a vagrant breeze, and was gone. Hi-ho.

As he rounded the cornice of the Time-Motion Study Building, he saw the shift, just boarding the slidewalk. With practiced motion and an absolute conservation of movement, they side-stepped up onto the slow-strip and (in a chorus line reminiscent of a Busby Berkeley film of the ante-diluvian 1930s) advanced across the strips ostrich-walking till they were lined upon the expresstrip.

Once more, in anticipation, the elfin grin spread, and there was a tooth missing back there on the left side. He dipped, skimmed, and swooped over them; and then, scrunching about on the air-boat, he released the holding pins that fastened shut the ends of the homemade pouring troughs that kept his cargo from dumping prematurely. And as he pulled the trough-pins, the air-boat slid over the factory workers and one hundred and fifty thousand dollars worth of jelly beans cascaded down on the expresstrip.

Jelly beans! Millions and billions of purples and yellows and greens and licorice and grape and raspberry and mint and round and smooth and crunchy outside and soft mealy inside and sugary and bouncing jouncing tumbling clittering clattering skittering fell on the heads and shoulders and hardhats and carapaces of the Timkin workers, tinkling on the slidewalk and bouncing away and rolling about underfoot and filling the sky on their way down with all the colors of joy and childhood and holidays, coming down in a steady rain, a solid wash, a torrent of color and sweetness out of the sky from above, and entering a universe of sanity and metronomic order with quite-mad coocoo newness. Jelly beans!

The shift workers howled and laughed and were pelted, and broke ranks, and the jelly beans managed to work their way into the mechanism of the slidewalks after which there was a hideous scraping as the sound of a million fingernails rasped down a quarter of a million blackboards, fol-lowed by a coughing and a sputtering, and then the slidewalks all stopped and everyone was dumped thisawayandthataway in a jackstraw tumble, still laughing and popping little jelly bean eggs of childish color into their mouths. It was a holiday, and a jollity, an absolute insanity, a giggle. But . . .

The shift was delayed seven minutes.

They did not get home for seven minutes.

The master schedule was thrown off by seven minutes.

Quotas were delayed by inoperative slidewalks for seven minutes.

He had tapped the first domino in the line, and one after another, like chik chik chik, the others had fallen.

The System had been seven minutes worth of disrupted. It was a tiny matter, one hardly worthy of note, but in a society where the single driving force was order and unity and equality and promptness and clocklike precision and attention to the clock, reverence of the gods of the passage of time, it was a disaster of major importance.

So he was ordered to appear before the Ticktockman. It was broadcast across every channel of the communications web. He was ordered to be *there* at 7:00 dammit on time. And they waited, and they waited, but he didn't show up till almost ten-thirty, at which time he merely sang a little song about moonlight in a place no one had ever heard of, called Vermont, and vanished again. But they had all been waiting since seven, and it wrecked *hell* with their schedules. So the question remained: Who is the Harlequin?

But the *unasked* question (more important of the two) was: how did we get *into* this position, where a laughing, irresponsible japer of jabberwocky and jive could disrupt our entire economic and cultural life with a hundred and fifty thousand dollars worth of jelly beans . . .

Jelly for God's sake *beans*! This is madness! Where did he get the money to buy a hundred and fifty thousand dollars worth of jelly beans? (They knew it would have cost that much, because they had a team of Situation Analysts pulled off another assignment, and rushed to the slide-walk scene to sweep up and count the candies, and produce findings, which disrupted *their* schedules and threw their entire branch at least a day behind.) Jelly beans! Jelly . . . *beans*? Now wait a second — a second accounted for — no one has manufactured jelly beans for over a hundred years. Where did he get jelly beans?

That's another good question. More than likely it will never be answered to your complete satisfaction. But then, how many questions ever are?

The middle you know. Here is the beginning. How it starts:

A desk pad. Day for day, and turn each day. 9:00 — open the mail. 9:45 — appointment with planning commission board. 10:30 — discuss installation progress charts with J.L. 11:45 — pray for rain. 12:00 — lunch. *And so it goes.*

"I'm sorry, Miss Grant, but the time for interviews was set at 2:30, and it's almost five now. I'm sorry you're late, but those are the rules. You'll have to wait till next year to submit application for this college again." *And so it goes.*

The 10:10 local stops at Cresthaven, Galesville, Tonawanda Junction, Selby, and Farnhurst, but not at Indiana City, Lucasville, and Colton, except on Sunday. The 10:35 express stops at Galesville, Selby, and Indiana City, except on Sundays & Holidays, at which time it stops at . . . *and so it goes.*

"I couldn't wait, Fred. I had to be at Pierre Cartain's by 3:00, and you said you'd meet me under the clock in the terminal at 2:45, and you weren't there, so I had to go on. You're always late, Fred. If you'd been there, we could have sewed it up together, but as it was, well, I took the order alone . . ." *And so it goes.*

Dear Mr. and Mrs. Atterley: in reference to your son Gerold's constant tardiness, I am afraid we will have to suspend him from school unless some more reliable method can be instituted guaranteeing he will arrive at his classes on time. Granted he is an exemplary student, and his marks are high, his constant flouting of the schedules of this school makes it impractical to maintain him in a system where the other children seem capable of getting where they are supposed to be on time *and so it goes.*

YOU CANNOT VOTE UNLESS YOU APPEAR AT 8:45 A.M.

"I don't care if the script is *good,* I need it Thursday!"

CHECK-OUT TIME IS 2:00 P.M.

"You got here late. The job's taken. Sorry."

YOUR SALARY HAS BEEN DOCKED FOR TWENTY MINUTES TIME LOST.

"God, what time is it, I've gotta run!"

And so it goes. And so it goes. And so it goes. And so it goes goes goes goes goes tick tock tick tock tick tock and one day we no longer let time serve us, we serve time and we are slaves of the schedule, worshippers of the sun's passing; bound into a life predicated on restrictions because the system will not function if we don't keep the schedule tight.

Until it becomes more than a minor inconvenience to be late. It becomes a sin. Then a crime. Then a crime punishable by this:

EFFECTIVE 15 JULY 2389 12:00:00 midnight, the office of the Master Timekeeper will require all citizens to submit their timecards and cardioplates for processing. In accordance with Statute 555-7-SGH 999 governing the revocation of time per capita, all cardioplates will be keyed to the individual holder and —

What they had done, was to devise a method of curtailing the amount of life a person could have. If he was ten minutes late, he lost ten minutes of his life. An hour was proportionately worth more revocation. If someone was consistently tardy, he might find himself, on a Sunday night, receiving a communique from the Master Timekeeper that his time had run out, and he would be "turned off" at high noon on Monday, please straighten your affairs, sir, madame or bisex.

And so, by this simple scientific expedient (utilizing a scientific process held dearly secret by the Ticktockman's office) the System was maintained. It was the only expedient thing to do. It was, after all, patriotic. The schedules had to be met. After all, there *was* a war on!

But, wasn't there always?

"Now that is really disgusting," the Harlequin said, when Pretty Alice showed him the wanted poster. "Disgusting and *highly* improbable. After all, this isn't the days of desperadoes. A *wanted* poster!"

"You know," Pretty Alice noted, "you speak with a great deal of inflection."

"I'm sorry," said the Harlequin, humbly.

"No need to be sorry. You're always saying 'I'm sorry.' You have such massive guilt, Everett, it's really very sad."

"I'm sorry," he repeated, then pursed his lips so the dimples appeared momentarily. He hadn't wanted to say that at all. "I have to go out again. I have to *do* something."

Pretty Alice slammed her coffee-bulb down on the counter. "Oh for God's *sake*, Everett, can't you stay home just *one* night! Must you always be out in that ghastly clown suit, running around an*noy*ing people?"

"I'm — " He stopped, and clapped the jester's hat onto his auburn thatch with a tiny tingling of bells. He rose, rinsed out his coffee-bulb at the spray, and put it into the drier for a moment. "I have to go."

She didn't answer. The faxbox was purring, and she pulled a sheet out, read it, threw it toward him on the counter, "It's about you. Of course. You're ridiculous."

He read it quickly. It said the Ticktockman was trying to locate him. He didn't care, he was going out to be late again. At the door, dredging for an exit line, he hurled back petulantly, "Well, *you* speak with inflection, *too!*"

Pretty Alice rolled her pretty eyes heavenward. "You're ridiculous." The Harlequin stalked out, slamming the door, which sighed shut softly, and locked itself.

There was a gentle knock, and Pretty Alice got up with an exhalation of exasperated breath, and opened the door. He stood there. "I'll be back about ten-thirty, okay?"

She pulled a rueful face. "Why do you tell me that? Why? You *know* you'll be late! You *know it!* You're *always* late, so why do you tell me these dumb things?" She closed the door.

On the other side, the Harlequin nodded to himself. *She's right. She's always right. I'll be late. I'm always late. Why do I tell her these dumb things?*

He shrugged again, and went off to be late once more.

He had fired off the firecracker rockets that said: I will attend the 115th annual International Medical Association Invocation at 8:00 p.m. precisely. I do hope you will all be able to join me.

The words had burned in the sky, and of course the authorities were there, lying in wait for him. They assumed, naturally, that he would be late. He arrived twenty minutes early, while they were setting up the spiderwebs to trap and hold him. Blowing a large bullhorn, he frightened and unnerved them so, their own moisturized encirclement webs sucked closed, and they were hauled up, kicking and shrieking, high above the amphitheater's floor. The Harlequin laughed and laughed, and apologized profusely. The physicians, gathered in solemn conclave, roared with laughter, and accepted the Harlequin's apologies with exaggerated bowing and posturing, and a merry time was had by all, who thought the Harlequin was a regular foofaraw in fancy pants; all, that is, but the authorities, who had been sent out by the office of the Ticktockman; they hung there like so much dockside cargo, hauled up above the floor of the amphitheater in a most unseemly fashion.

(In another part of the same city where the Harlequin carried on his "activities," totally unrelated in every way to what concerns us here, save that it illustrates the Ticktockman's power and import, a man named Marshall Delahanty received his turn-off notice from the Ticktockman's office. His wife received the notification from the gray-suited minee who delivered it, with the traditional "look of sorrow" plastered hideously across his face. She knew what it was, even without unsealing it. It was a billet-doux of immediate recognition to everyone these days. She gasped, and held it as though it were a glass slide tinged with botulism, and prayed it was not for her. Let it be for Marsh, she thought, brutally, realistically, or one of the kids, but not for me, please dear God, not for me. And then she opened it, and it *was* for Marsh, and she was at one and the same time horrified and relieved. The next trooper in the line had caught the bullet. "Marshall," she screamed, "Marshall! Termination, Marshall! OhmiGod, Marshall, whattl we do, whattl we do, Marshall omigodmarshall . . ." and in their home that night was the sound of tearing paper and fear, and the stink of madness went up the flue and there was nothing, absolutely nothing they could do about it.

(But Marshall Delahanty tried to run. And early the next day, when turn-off time came, he was deep in the Canadian forest two hundred miles away, and the office of the Ticktockman blanked his cardioplate, and Marshall Delahanty keeled over, running, and his heart stopped, and the blood dried up on its way to his brain, and he was dead that's all. One light went out on the sector map in the office of the Master Timekeeper, while notification was entered for fax reproduction, and Georgette Delahanty's name was entered on the dole roles till she could remarry. Which is the end of the footnote, and all the point that need be made, except don't laugh, because that is what would happen to the Harlequin if ever the Ticktockman found out his real name. It isn't funny.)

The shopping level of the city was thronged with the Thursday-colors of the buyers. Women in canary yellow chitons and men in pseudo-Tyrolean outfits that were jade and leather and fit very tightly, save for the balloon pants.

When the Harlequin appeared on the still-being-constructed shell of the new Efficiency Shopping Center, his bullhorn to his elfishly-laughing lips, everyone pointed and stared, and he berated them:

"Why let them order you about? Why let them tell you to hurry and scurry like ants or maggots? Take your time! Saunter a while! Enjoy the sunshine, enjoy the breeze, let life carry you at your own pace! Don't be slaves of time, it's a helluva way to die, slowly, by degrees . . . down with the Ticktockman!"

Who's the nut? Most of the shoppers wanted to know. Who's the nut oh wow I'm gonna be late I gotta run. . . .

And the construction gang on the Shopping Center received an urgent order from the office of the Master Timekeeper that the dangerous criminal known as the Harlequin was atop their spire, and their aid was urgently needed in apprehending him. The work crew said no, they would lose time on their construction schedule, but the Ticktockman managed to pull the proper threads of governmental webbing, and they were told to cease work and catch that nitwit up there on the spire; up there with the bullhorn. So a dozen and more burly workers began climbing into their construction platforms, releasing the a-gray plates, and rising toward the Harlequin.

After the debacle (in which, through the Harlequin's attention to personal safety, no one was seriously injured), the workers tried to reassemble, and assault him again, but it was too late. He had vanished. It had attracted quite a crowd, however, and the shopping cycle was thrown off by hours, simply hours. The purchasing needs of the System were therefore falling behind, and so measures were taken to accelerate the cycle for the rest of the day, but it got bogged down and speeded up and they sold too many float-valves and not nearly enough wegglers, which meant that the popli ratio was off, which made it necessary to rush cases and cases of spoiling Smash-O to stores that usually needed a case only every three or four hours. The shipments were bollixed, the transshipments were misrouted, and in the end, even the swizzleskid industries felt it.

"Don't come back till you have him!" the Ticktockman said, very quietly, very sincerely, extremely dangerously.

They used dogs. They used probes. They used cardioplate crossoffs. They used teepers. They used bribery. They used stiktytes. They used intimidation. They used torment. They used torture. They used finks. They used cops. They used search&seizure. They used fallaron. They used betterment incentive. They used fingerprints. They used the Bertillon system. They used cunning. They used guile. They used treachery. They used Raoul Mitgong, but he didn't help much. They used applied physics. They used techniques of criminology.

And what the hell: they caught him.

After all, his name was Everett C. Marm, and he wasn't much to begin with, except a man who had no sense of time.

"Repent, Harlequin!" said the Ticktockman.

"Get stuffed!" the Harlequin replied, sneering.

"You've been late a total of sixty-three years, five months, three weeks, two days, twelve hours, forty-one minutes, fifty-nine seconds, point oh three six one one one microseconds. You've used up everything you can, and more. I'm going to turn you off."

"Scare someone else. I'd rather be dead than live in a dumb world with a bogeyman like you."

"It's my job."

"You're full of it. You're a tyrant. You have no right to order people around and kill them if they show up late."

"You can't adjust. You can't fit in."

"Unstrap me, and I'll fit my fist into your mouth."

"You're a non-conformist."

"That didn't used to be a felony."

"It is now. Live in the world around you."

"I hate it. It's a terrible world."

"Not everyone thinks so. Most people enjoy order."

"I don't, and most of the people I know don't."

"That's not true. How do you think we caught you?"

"I'm not interested."

"A girl named Pretty Alice told us who you were."

"That's a lie."

"It's true. You unnerve her. She wants to belong, she wants to conform, I'm going to turn you off."

"Then do it already, and stop arguing with me."

"I'm not going to turn you off."

"You're an idiot!"

"Repent, Harlequin!" said the Ticktockman.

"Get stuffed."

So they sent him to Coventry. And in Coventry they worked him over. It was just like what they did to Winston Smith in *1984*, which was a book none of them knew about, but the techniques are really quite ancient, and so they did it to Everett C. Marm, and one day quite a long time later, the Harlequin appeared on the communications web, appearing elfin and dimpled and bright-eyed, and not at all brainwashed, and he said he had been wrong, that it was a good, a very good thing indeed, to belong, to be right on time hip-ho and away we go, and everyone stared up at him on the public screens that covered an entire city block, and they said to themselves, well, you see, he was just a nut after all, and if that's the way the system is run, then let's do it that way, because it doesn't pay to fight city hall, or in this case, the Ticktockman. So Everett C. Marm was destroyed, which was a loss, because of what Thoreau said earlier, but you can't make an omelet without breaking a few eggs, and in every revolution a few die who shouldn't, but they have to, because that's the way it happens, and if you make only a little change, then it seems to be worthwhile. Or, to make the point lucidly:

"Uh, excuse me, sir, I, uh, don't know how to uh, to uh, tell you this, but you were three minutes late. The schedule is a little, uh, bit off."

He grinned sheepishly.

"That's ridiculous!" murmured the Ticktockman behind his mask. "Check your watch." And then he went into his office, going mrmee, mrmee, mrmee, mrmee.

Joanna Russ

When It Changed

(1972)

Joanna Russ (b. 1937) began publishing sf in 1959, but it was during the 1970s — as her work became increasingly explicit in its feminism — that she emerged as one of the foremost writers of the era and left her mark on the genre. Russ is famous both for her fiction and for provocative essays like "What Can a Heroine Do? Or Why Women Can't Write," which critiques writers' surrender to stereotypical narratives and calls for new work that will radically reimagine women's roles and break away from the restrictions and assumptions of the past.

Russ's novel, *The Female Man* (1975), was a groundbreaking work in this respect and remains one of sf's most ambitious and successful experiments in form. *The Female Man* examines women's roles in different social systems — variously oppressive or liberated — by following the interwoven narratives of four women who may in fact be the same character as shaped by four alternative realities. Whether these are possible futures or allegorical elements equally present in our own timeline is ambiguous.

"When It Changed" (which won a Nebula in 1973) is the short story that became the basis for *The Female Man*. It is set on the planet Whileaway, an exclusively female utopia that we see on the brink of transformation. The story is notable for its deceptive simplicity and its casual realism, which startle us into awareness of our own assumptions.

Katy drives like a maniac; we must have been doing over 120 kilometers per hour on those turns. She's good, though, extremely good, and I've seen her take the whole car apart and put it together again in a day. My birthplace on Whileaway was largely given to farm machinery and I refuse to wrestle with a five-gear shift at unholy speeds, not having been brought up to it, but even on those turns in the middle of the night, on a country road as bad as only our district can make them, Katy's driving didn't scare me. The funny thing about my wife, though: she will not handle guns. She has even gone hiking in the forests above the forty-eighth parallel without firearms, for days at a time. And that *does* scare me.

Katy and I have three children between us, one of hers and two of mine. Yuriko, my eldest, was asleep in the back seat, dreaming twelve-year-old dreams of love and war: running away to sea, hunting in the North, dreams of strangely beautiful people in strangely beautiful places, all the wonderful guff you think up when you're turning twelve and the glands start going. Some day soon, like all of them, she will disappear for weeks on end to come back grimy and proud, having knifed her first cougar or shot her first bear, dragging some abominably dangerous dead beastie behind her, which I will never forgive for what it might have done to my daughter. Yuriko says Katy's driving puts her to sleep.

For someone who has fought three duels, I am afraid of far, far too much. I'm getting old. I told this to my wife.

"You're thirty-four," she said. Laconic to the point of silence, that one. She flipped the lights on, on the dash — three kilometers to go and the road getting worse all the time. Far out in the country. Electric-green trees rushed into our headlights and around the car. I reached down next to me where we bolt the carrier panel to the door and eased my rifle into my lap. Yuriko stirred in the back. My height but Katy's eyes, Katy's face. The car engine is so quiet, Katy says, that you can hear breathing in the back seat. Yuki had been alone in the car when the message came, enthusiastically decoding her dot-dashes (silly to mount a wide-frequency transceiver near an I. C. engine, but most of Whileaway is on steam). She had thrown herself out of the car, my gangly and gaudy offspring, shouting at the top of her lungs, so of course she had had to come along. We've been intellectually prepared for this ever since the Colony was founded, ever since it was abandoned, but this is different. This is awful.

"Men!" Yuki had screamed, leaping over the car door. "They've come back! Real Earth men!"

We met them in the kitchen of the farmhouse near the place where they had landed; the windows were open, the night air very mild. We had passed all sorts of transportation when we parked outside — steam tractors, trucks, an I. C. flatbed, even a bicycle. Lydia, the district biologist, had come out of her Northern taciturnity long enough to take blood and urine samples and was sitting in a corner of the kitchen shaking her head in astonishment over the results; she even forced herself (very big, very fair, very shy, always painfully blushing) to dig up the old language manuals — though I can talk the old tongues in my sleep. And do. Lydia is uneasy with us; we're Southerners and too flamboyant. I counted twenty people in that kitchen, all the brains of North Continent. Phyllis Spet, I think, had come in by glider. Yuki was the only child there.

Then I saw the four of them.

They are bigger than we are. They are bigger and broader. Two were taller than I, and I am extremely tall, one meter eighty centimeters in my bare feet. They are obviously of our species but *off*, indescribably off, and as my eyes could not and still cannot quite comprehend the lines of those alien bodies, I could not, then, bring myself to touch them, though the one who spoke Russian — what voices they have — wanted to "shake hands," a custom from the past, I imagine. I can only say they were apes with human faces. He seemed to mean well, but I found myself shuddering back almost the length of the kitchen — and then I laughed apologetically — and then to set a good example (*interstellar amity*, I thought) did "shake hands" finally. A hard, hard hand. They are heavy as draft horses. Blurred, deep voices. Yuriko had sneaked in between the adults and was gazing at *the men* with her mouth open.

He turned *his* head — those words have not been in our language for six hundred years — and said, in bad Russian:

"Who's that?"

"My daughter," I said, and added (with that irrational attention to good manners we sometimes employ in moments of insanity), "My daughter, Yuriko Janetson. We use the patronymic. You would say matronymic."

He laughed, involuntarily. Yuki exclaimed, "I thought they would be *good-looking!*" greatly disappointed at this reception of herself. Phyllis Helgason Spet, whom someday I shall kill, gave me across the room a cold, level, venomous look, as if to say: *Watch what you say. You know what I can do.* It's true that I have little formal status, but Madam President will get herself in serious trouble with both me and her own staff if she continues to consider industrial espionage good clean fun. Wars and rumors of wars, as it says in one of our ancestors' books. I translated Yuki's words into the *man's* dog-Russian, once our *lingua franca*, and *the man* laughed again.

"Where are all your people?" he said conversationally.

I translated again and watched the faces around the room; Lydia embarrassed (as usual), Spet narrowing her eyes with some damned scheme, Katy very pale.

"This is Whileaway," I said.

He continued to look unenlightened.

"Whileaway," I said. "Do you remember? Do you have records? There was a plague on Whileaway."

He looked moderately interested. Heads turned in the back of the room, and I caught a glimpse of the local professions-parliament delegate; by morning every town meeting, every district caucus, would be in full session.

"Plague?" he said. "That's most unfortunate."

"Yes," I said. "Most unfortunate. We lost half our population in one generation."

He looked properly impressed.

"Whileaway was lucky," I said. "We had a big initial gene pool, we had been chosen for extreme intelligence, we had a high technology and a large remaining population in which every adult was two-or-three experts in one. The soil is good. The climate is blessedly easy. There are thirty millions of us now. Things are beginning to snowball in industry — do you understand? — give us seventy years and we'll have more than one real city, more than a few industrial centers, full-time professions, full-time radio operators, full-time machinists, give us seventy years and not everyone will have to spend three-quarters of a lifetime on the farm." And I tried to explain how hard it is when artists can practice full-time only in old age, when there are so few, so very few who can be free, like Katy and myself. I tried also to outline our government, the two houses, the one by professions and the geographic one; I told him the district caucuses handled problems too big for the individual towns. And that population control was not a political issue, not yet, though give us time and it would be. This was a delicate point in our history; give us time. There was no need to sacrifice the quality of life for an insane rush into industrialization. Let us go our own pace. Give us time.

"Where are all the people?" said that monomaniac.

I realized then that he did not mean people, he meant *men*, and he was giving the word the meaning it had not had on Whileaway for six centuries.

"They died," I said. "Thirty generations ago."

I thought we had poleaxed him. He caught his breath. He made as if to get out of the chair he was sitting in; he put his hand to his chest; he looked around at us with the strangest blend of awe and sentimental tenderness. Then he said, solemnly and earnestly:

"A great tragedy."

I waited, not quite understanding.

"Yes," he said, catching his breath again with the queer smile, that adult-to-child smile that tells you something is being hidden and will be presently produced with cries of encouragement and joy, "a great tragedy. But it's over." And again he looked around at all of us with the strangest deference. As if we were invalids.

"You've adapted amazingly," he said.

"To what?" I said. He looked embarrassed. He looked inane. Finally he said, "Where I come from, the women don't dress so plainly."

"Like you?" I said. "Like a bride?" for the men were wearing silver from head to foot. I had never seen anything so gaudy. He made as if to answer and then apparently thought better of it; he laughed at me again. With an odd exhilaration — as if we were something childish and something wonderful, as if he were doing us an enormous favor — he took one shaky breath and said, "Well, we're here."

I looked at Spet, Spet looked at Lydia, Lydia looked at Amalia, who is the head of the local town meeting, Amalia looked at I don't know whom. My throat was raw. I cannot stand local beer, which the farmers swill as if their stomachs had iridium linings, but I took it anyway, from Amalia (it was her bicycle we had seen outside as we parked), and swallowed it all. This was going to take a long time. I said, "Yes, here you are," and smiled (feeling like a fool), and wondered seriously if male-Earth-people's minds worked so very differently from female-Earth-people's minds, but that couldn't be so or the race would have died out long ago. The radio network had got the news around planet by now and we had another Russian speaker, flown in from Varna; I decided to cut out when *the man* passed around pictures of his wife, who looked like the priestess of some arcane cult. He proposed to question Yuki, so I barreled her into a back room in spite of her furious protests, and went out on the front porch. As I left, Lydia was explaining the difference between parthenogenesis (which is so easy that anyone can practice it) and what we do, which is the merging of ova. That is why Katy's baby looks like me. Lydia went on to the Ansky Process and Katy Ansky, our one full-polymath genius and the great-great I don't know how many times great-grandmother of my own Katharina.

A dot-dash transmitter in one of the outbuildings chattered faintly to itself: operators flirting and passing jokes down the line.

There was a man on the porch. The other tall man. I watched him for a few minutes — I can move very quietly when I want to and when I allowed him to see me, he stopped talking into the little machine hung around his neck. Then he said calmly, in excellent Russian, "Did you know that sexual equality has been reestablished on Earth?"

"You're the real one," I said, "aren't you? The other one's for show." It was a great relief to get things cleared up. He nodded affably.

"As a people, we are not very bright," he said. "There's been too much genetic damage in the last few centuries. Radiation. Drugs. We can use Whileaway's genes, Janet." Strangers do not call strangers by the first name.

"You can have cells enough to drown in," I said. "Breed your own."

He smiled. "That's not the way we want to do it." Behind him I saw Katy come into the square of light that was the screened-in door. He went on, low and urbane, not mocking me, I think, but with the self-confidence of someone who has always had money and strength to spare, who doesn't know what it is to be second-class or provincial. Which is very odd, because the day before, I would have said that was an exact description of me.

"I'm talking to you, Janet," he said, "because I suspect you have more popular influence than anyone else here. You know as well as I do that parthenogenetic culture has all sorts of inherent defects, and we do not — if we can help it — mean to use you for anything of the sort. Pardon me; I should not have said 'use.' But surely you can see that this kind of society is unnatural."

"Humanity is unnatural," said Katy. She had my rifle under her left arm. The top of that silky head does not quite come up to my collarbone, but she is as tough as steel; he began to move, again with that queer smiling deference (which his fellow had showed to me but he had not), and the gun slid into Katy's grip as if she had shot with it all her life.

"I agree," said the man. "Humanity is unnatural. I should know. I have metal in my teeth and metal pins here." He touched his shoulder. "Seals are harem animals," he added, "and so are men; apes are promiscuous and so are men; doves are monogamous and so are men; there are even celibate men and homosexual men. There are homosexual cows, I believe. But Whileaway is still missing something." He gave a dry chuckle. I will give him the credit of believing that it had something to do with nerves.

"I miss nothing," said Katy, "except that life isn't endless."

"You are — ?" said the man, nodding from me to her.

"Wives," said Katy. "We're married." Again the dry chuckle.

"A good economic arrangement," he said, "for working and taking care of the children. And as good an arrangement as any for randomizing heredity, if your reproduction is made to follow the same pattern. But think, Katharina Michaelason, if there isn't something better that you might secure for your daughters. I believe in instincts, even in Man, and I can't think that the two of you — a machinist, are you? and I gather you are some sort of chief of police — don't feel somehow what even you must miss. You know it intellectually, of course. There is only half a species here. Men must come back to Whileaway."

Katy said nothing.

"I should think, Katharina Michaelason," said the man gently, "that you, of all people, would benefit most from such a change," and he walked past Katy's rifle into the square of light coming from the door. I think it was then that he noticed my scar, which really does not show unless the light is from the side: a fine line that runs from temple to chin. Most people don't even know about it.

"Where did you get that?" he said, and I answered with an involuntary grin. "In my last duel." We stood there bristling at each other for several seconds (this is absurd but true) until he went inside and shut the screen door behind him. Katy said in a brittle voice, "You damned fool, don't you know when we've been insulted?" and swung up the rifle to shoot him through the screen, but I got to her before she could fire and knocked the rifle out of aim; it burned a hole through the porch floor. Katy was shaking. She kept whispering over and over, "That's why I never touched it, because I knew I'd kill someone. I knew I'd kill someone." The first man — the one I'd spoken with first — was still talking inside the house, something about the grand movement to recolonize and rediscover all the Earth had lost. He stressed the advantages to Whileaway: trade, exchange of ideas, education. He, too, said that sexual equality had been reestablished on Earth.

Katy was right, of course; we should have burned them down where they stood. Men are coming to Whileaway. When one culture has the big guns and the other has none, there is a certain predictability about the outcome. Maybe men would have come eventually in any case. I like to think that a hundred years from now my great-grandchildren could have stood them off or fought them to a standstill, but even that's no odds; I will remember all my life those four people I first met who were muscled like bulls and who made me — if only for a moment — feel small. A neurotic reaction, Katy says. I remember everything that happened that night; I remember Yuki's excitement in the car, I remember Katy's sobbing when we got home as if her heart would break, I remember her lovemaking, a little peremptory as always, but wonderfully soothing and comforting. I remember prowling restlessly around the house after Katy fell asleep with one bare arm hung into a patch of light from the hall. The muscles of her forearms are like metal bars from all that driving and testing of her machines. Sometimes I dream about Katy's arms. I remember wandering into the nursery and picking up my wife's baby, dozing for a while with the poignant, amazing warmth of an infant in my lap, and finally returning to the kitchen to find Yuriko fixing herself a late snack. My daughter eats like a Great Dane.

"Yuki," I said, "do you think you could fall in love with a man?" and she whooped derisively. "With a ten-foot toad!" said my tactful child.

But men are coming to Whileaway. Lately I sit up nights and worry about the men who will come to this planet, about my two daughters and Betta Katharinason, about what will happen to Katy, to me, to my life. Our ancestors' journals are one long cry of pain and I suppose I ought to be glad now, but one can't throw away six centuries, or even (as I have lately discovered) thirty-four years. Sometimes I laugh at the question those four men hedged about all evening and never quite dared to ask, looking at the lot of us, hicks in overalls, farmers in canvas pants and plain shirts: *Which of you plays the role of the man?* As if we had to produce a carbon copy of their mistakes! I doubt very much that sexual equality has been reestablished on Earth. I do not like to think of myself mocked, of Katy deferred to as if she were weak, of Yuki made to feel unimportant or silly, of my other children cheated of their full humanity or turned into strangers. And I'm afraid that my own achievements will dwindle from what they were — or what I thought they were — to the not-very-interesting curiosa of the *human* race, the oddities you read about in the back of the book, things to laugh at sometimes because they are so exotic, quaint but not impressive, charming but not useful. I find this more painful than I can say. You will agree that for a woman who has fought three duels, all of them kills, indulging in such fears is ludicrous. But what's around the corner now is a duel so big that I don't think I have the guts for it; in Faust's words: *Verweile doch, du bist so schoen!* Keep it as it is. Don't change.

Sometimes at night I remember the original name of this planet, changed by the first generation of our ancestors, those curious women for whom, I suppose, the real name was too painful a reminder after the men died. I find it amusing, in a grim way, to see it all so completely turned around. This, too, shall pass. All good things must come to an end.

Take my life but don't take away the meaning of my life.

For-A-While.

John Varley
The Persistence of Vision
(1978)

John [Herbert] Varley (b. 1947) made his name in the late 1970s, largely on the basis of short stories that were smart, idiosyncratic, and informed by popular culture. If the New Wave writers of the 1960s were self-consciously outrageous hipsters, Varley belonged to the generation that naturalized the countercultural values of the times with their matter-of-fact treatment of unconventional lifestyles and sexuality.

"The Persistence of Vision," which won both the Hugo and the Nebula in 1979, is one of Varley's finest stories and a good example of the best work of the period. The narrator is a seeker, capable of functioning in the mainstream world but vaguely dissatisfied with the emptiness and lack of direction in his life. He wanders through New Mexico, sampling the alternative lifestyles available in the communes there. It is only when he discovers the remarkable community known as Keller that he awakens to a greater sense of meaning.

"Persistence of vision" is a technical term for the phenomenon whereby an image imprinted on the retina continues to be seen after the stimulus has been removed. The most familiar example is the afterimage created by a bright flash of light from a camera. This phenomenon was once thought to explain our perception of motion when watching movies. In Varley's story, the term functions as a complex metaphor with many shades of meaning.

Though grounded in a familiar world very like our own, the story has fantasy elements as well; the unique nature of Keller and its inhabitants are never fully explained as they might be in a more traditional science fiction story. For this reason, it is best classified under the broader term of *speculative fiction*.

The story's treatment of both sexuality and mysticism has a certain earnest naïveté that may discomfort some readers today, but the frightening and beautiful ending is evidence that Varley is well aware of this utopia's moral ambiguity and the complex issues it raises.

It was the year of the fourth non-depression. I had recently joined the ranks of the unemployed. The President had told me that I had nothing to fear but fear itself. I took him at his word, for once, and set out to backpack to California.

I was not the only one. The world's economy had been writhing like a snake on a hot griddle for the last twenty years, since the early seventies. We were in a boom-and-bust cycle that seemed to have no end. It had wiped out the sense of security the nation had so painfully won in the golden years after the thirties. People were accustomed to the fact that they could be rich one year and on the breadlines the next. I was on the breadlines in '81, and again in '88. This time I decided to use my freedom from the time clock to see the world. I had ideas of stowing away to Japan. I was forty-seven years old and might not get another chance to be irresponsible.

This was in late summer of the year. Sticking out my thumb along the interstate, I could easily forget that there were food riots back in Chicago. I slept at night on top of my bedroll and saw stars and listened to crickets.

I must have walked most of the way from Chicago to Des Moines. My feet toughened up after a few days of awful blisters. The rides were scarce, partly competition from other hitchhikers and partly the times we were living in. The locals were none too anxious to give rides to city people, who they had heard were mostly a bunch of hunger-crazed potential mass murderers. I got roughed up once and told never to return to Sheffield, Illinois.

But I gradually learned the knack of living on the road. I had started with a small supply of canned goods from the welfare and by the time they ran out, I had found that it was possible to work for a meal at many of the farmhouses along the way.

Some of it was hard work, some of it was only a token from people with a deeply ingrained sense that nothing should come for free. A few meals were gratis, at the family table, with grandchildren sitting around while grandpa or grandma told oft-repeated tales of what it had been like in the Big One back in '29, when people had not been afraid to help a fellow out when he was down on his luck. I found that the older the person, the more likely I was to get a sympathetic ear. One of the many tricks you learn. And most older people will give you anything if you'll only sit and listen to them. I got very good at it.

The rides began to pick up west of Des Moines, then got bad again as I neared the refugee camps bordering the China Strip. This was only five years after the disaster, remember, when the Omaha nuclear reactor melted down and a hot mass of uranium and plutonium began eating its way into the earth, headed for China, spreading a band of radioactivity six hundred kilometers downwind. Most of Kansas City, Missouri, was still living in plywood and sheet-metal shantytowns till the city was rendered habitable again.

The refugees were a tragic group. The initial solidarity people show after a great disaster had long since faded into the lethargy and disillusionment of the displaced person. Many of them would be in and out of hospitals for the rest of their lives. To make it worse, the local people hated them, feared them, would not associate with them. They were modern pariahs, unclean. Their children were shunned. Each camp had only a number to identify it, but the local populace called them all Geigertowns.

I made a long detour to Little Rock to avoid crossing the Strip, though it was safe now as long as you didn't linger. I was issued a pariah's badge by the National Guard — a dosimeter — and wandered from one Geigertown to the next. The people were pitifully friendly once I made the first move, and I always slept indoors. The food was free at the community messes.

Once at little Rock, I found that the aversion to picking up stranger — who might be tainted with "radiation disease" — dropped off, and I quickly moved across Arkansas, Oklahoma, and Texas. I worked a little here and there, but many of the rides were long. What I saw of Texas was through a car window.

I was a little tired of that by the time I reached New Mexico. I decided to do some more walking. By then I was less interested in California than in the trip itself.

I left the roads and went cross-country where there were no fences to stop me. I found that it wasn't easy, even in New Mexico, to get far from signs of civilization.

Taos was the center, back in the '60's of cultural experiments in alternative living. Many communes and cooperatives were set up in the surrounding hills during that time. Most of them fell apart in a few months or years, but a few survived. In later years, any group with a new theory of living and a yen to try it out seemed to gravitate to that part of New Mexico. As a result, the land was dotted with ramshackle windmills, solar heating panels, geodesic domes, group marriages, nudists, philosophers, theoreticians, messiahs, hermits, and more than a few just plain nuts.

Taos was great. I could drop into most of the communes and stay for a day or a week, eating organic rice and beans and drinking goat's milk. When I got tired of one, a few hours' walk in any direction would bring me to another. There, I might be offered a night of prayer and chanting or a ritualistic orgy. Some of the groups had spotless barns with automatic milkers for the herds of cows. Others didn't even have latrines; they just squatted. In some, the members dressed like nuns, or Quakers in early Pennsylvania. Elsewhere, they went nude and shaved all their body hair and painted themselves purple. There were all-male and all-female groups. I was urged to stay at most of the former; at the latter, the responses ranged from a bed for the night and good conversation to being met at a barbed-wire fence with a shotgun.

I tried not to make judgments. These people were doing something important, all of them. They were testing ways whereby people didn't have to live in Chicago. That was a wonder to me. I had thought Chicago was inevitable, like diarrhea.

This is not to say they were all successful. Some made Chicago look like Shangri-La. There was one group who seemed to feel that getting back to nature consisted of sleeping in pigshit and eating food a buzzard wouldn't touch. Many were obviously doomed. They would leave behind a group of empty hovels and the memory of cholera.

So the place wasn't paradise, not by a long way. But there were successes. One or two had been there since '63 or '64 and were raising their third generation. I was disappointed to see that most of these were the ones that departed least from established norms of behavior, though some of the differences could be startling. I suppose the most radical experiments are the least likely to bear fruit.

I stayed through the winter. No one was surprised to see me a second time. It seems that many people came to Taos and shopped around. I seldom stayed more than three weeks at any one place, and always pulled my weight. I made many friends and picked up skills that would serve me if I stayed off the roads. I toyed with the idea of staying at one of them forever. When I couldn't make up my mind, I was advised that there was no hurry. I could go to California and return. They seemed sure I would.

So when spring came I headed west over the hills. I stayed off the roads and slept in the open. Many nights I would stay at another commune, until they finally began to get farther apart, then tapered off entirely. The country was not as pretty as before.

Then, three days' leisurely walking from the last commune, I came to a wall.

In 1964, in the United States, there was an epidemic of German measles, or rubella. Rubella is one of the mildest of infectious diseases. The only time it's a problem is when a woman contracts it in the first four months of her pregnancy. It is passed to the fetus, which usually develops complications. These complications include deafness, blindness, and damage to the brain.

In 1964, in the old days before abortion became readily available, there was nothing to be done about it. Many pregnant women caught rubella and went to term. Five thousand deaf-blind children were born in one year. The normal yearly incidence of deaf-blind children in the United States is one hundred and forty.

In 1970 these five thousand potential Helen Kellers were all six years old. It was quickly seen that there was a shortage of Anne Sullivans. Previously, deaf-blind children could be sent to a small number of special institutions.

It was a problem. Not just anyone can cope with a blind-deaf child. You can't tell them to shut up when they moan; you can't reason with them, tell them that the moaning is driving you crazy. Some parents were driven to nervous breakdowns when they tried to keep their children at home.

Many of the five thousand were badly retarded and virtually impossible to reach, even if anyone had been trying. These ended up, for the most part, warehoused in the hundreds of anonymous nursing homes and institutes for "special" children. They were put into beds, cleaned up once a day by a few overworked nurses, and generally allowed the full blessings of liberty: they were allowed to rot freely in their own dark, quiet, private universes. Who can say if it was bad for them? None of them were heard to complain.

Many children with undamaged brains were shuffled in among the retarded because they were unable to tell anyone that they were in there behind the sightless eyes. They failed the batteries of tactile tests, unaware that their fates hung in the balance when they were asked to fit round pegs into round holes to the ticking of a clock they could not see or hear. As a result, they spent the rest of their lives in bed, and none of them complained, either. To protest, one must be aware of the possibility of something better. It helps to have a language, too.

Several hundred of the children were found to have IQs within the normal range. There were news stories about them as they approached puberty and it was revealed that there were not enough good people to properly handle them. Money was spent, teachers were trained. The education expenditures would go on for a specified period of time, until the children were grown, then things would go back to normal and everyone could congratulate themselves on having dealt successfully with a tough problem.

And indeed, it did work fairly well. There are ways to reach and teach such children. They involve patience, love, and dedication, and the teachers brought all that to their jobs. All the graduates of the special schools left knowing how to speak with their hands. Some could talk. A few could write. Most of them left the institutions to live with parents or relatives, or, if neither was possible, received counseling and help in fitting themselves into society. The options were limited, but people can live rewarding lives under the most severe handicaps. Not everyone, but most of the graduates, were as happy with their lot as could reasonably be expected. Some achieved the almost saintly peace of their role model, Helen Keller. Others became bitter and withdrawn. A few had to be put in asylums, where they became indistinguishable from the others of their group who had spent the last twenty years there. But for the most part, they did well.

But among the group, as in any group, were some misfits. They tended to be among the brightest, the top ten percent in the IQ scores. This was not a reliable rule. Some had unremarkable test scores and were still infected with the hunger to do something, to change things, to rock the boat. With a group of five thousand, there were certain to be a few geniuses, a few artists, a few dreamers, hell-raisers, individualists, movers and shapers: a few glorious maniacs.

There was one among them who might have been President but for the fact that she was blind, deaf, and a woman. She was smart, but not one of the geniuses. She was a dreamer, a creative force, an innovator. It was she who dreamed of freedom. But she was not a builder of fairy castles. Having dreamed it, she had to make it come true.

The wall was made of carefully fitted stone and was about five feet high. It was completely out of context with anything I had seen in New Mexico, though it was built of native rock. You just don't build that kind of wall out there. You use barbed wire if something needs fencing in, but many people still made use of the free range and brands. Somehow it seemed transplanted from New England.

It was substantial enough that I felt it would be unwise to crawl over it. I had crossed many wire fences in my travels and had not gotten in trouble for it yet, though I had some talks with some ranchers. Mostly they told me to keep moving, but didn't seem upset about it. This was different. I set out to walk around it. From the lay of the land, I couldn't tell how far it might reach, but I had time.

At the top of the next rise I saw that I didn't have far to go. The wall made a right-angle turn just ahead. I looked over it and could see some buildings. They were mostly domes, the ubiquitous structure thrown up by communes because of the combination of ease of construction and durability. There were sheep behind the wall, and a few cows. They grazed on grass so green I wanted to go over and roll in it. The wall enclosed a rectangle of green. Outside, where I stood, it was all scrub and sage. These people had access to Rio Grande irrigation water.

I rounded the corner and followed the wall west again.

I saw a man on horseback about the same time he spotted me. He was south of me, outside the wall, and he turned and rode in my direction.

He was a dark man with thick features, dressed in denim and boots with a gray battered stetson. Navaho, maybe. I don't know much about Indians, but I'd heard they were out here.

"Hello," I said when he'd stopped. He was looking me over. "Am I on your land?"

"Tribal land," he said. "Yeah, you're on it."

"I didn't see any signs."

He shrugged.

"It's okay, bud. You don't look like you out to rustle cattle." He grinned at me. His teeth were large and stained with tobacco. "You be camping out tonight?"

"Yes. How much farther does the, uh, tribal land go? Maybe I'll be out of it before tonight?"

He shook his head gravely. "Nah. You won't be off it tomorrow. 'S all right. You make a fire, you be careful, huh?" He grinned again and started to ride off.

"Hey, what is this place?" I gestured to the wall and he pulled his horse up and turned around again. It raised a lot of dust.

"Why you asking?" He looked a little suspicious.

"I dunno. Just curious. It doesn't look like the other places I've been to. This wall . . ."

He scowled. "Damn wall." Then he shrugged. I thought that was all he was going to say. Then he went on.

"These people, we look out for 'em, you hear? Maybe we don't go for what they're doin'. But they got it rough, you know?" He looked at me, expecting something. I never did get the knack of talking to these laconic Westerners. I always felt that I was making my sentences too long. They use a shorthand of grunts and shrugs and omitted parts of speech, and I always felt like a dude when I talked to them.

"Do they welcome guests?" I asked. "I thought I might see if I could spend the night."

He shrugged again, and it was a whole different gesture.

"Maybe. They all deaf and blind, you know?" And that was all the conversation he could take for the day. He made a clucking sound and galloped away.

I continued down the wall until I came to a dirt road that wound up the arroyo and entered the wall. There was a wooden gate, but it stood open, I wondered why they took all the trouble with the wall only to leave the gate like that. Then I noticed a circle of narrow-gauge train tracks that came out of the gate, looped around outside it, and rejoined itself. There was a small siding that ran along the outer wall for a few yards.

I stood there a few moments. I don't know what entered into my decision. I think I was a little tired of sleeping out, and I was hungry for a home-cooked meal. The sun was getting closer to the horizon. The land to the west looked like more of the same. If the highway had been visible, I might have headed that way and hitched a ride. But I turned the other way and went through the gate.

I walked down the middle of the tracks. There was a wooden fence on each side of the road, built of horizontal planks, like a corral. Sheep grazed on one side of me. There was a Shetland sheepdog with them, and she raised her ears and followed me with her eyes as I passed, but did not come when I whistled.

It was about half a mile to the cluster of buildings ahead. There were four or five domes made of something translucent, like greenhouses, and several conventional square buildings. There were two windmills turning lazily in the breeze. There were several banks of solar water heaters. These are flat constructions of glass and wood, held off the ground so they can tilt to follow the sun. They were almost vertical now, intercepting the oblique rays of sunset. There were a few trees, what might have been an orchard.

About halfway there I passed under a wooden footbridge. It arched over the road, giving access from the east pasture to the west pasture. I wondered, What was wrong with a simple gate?

Then I saw something coming down the road in my direction. It was traveling on the tracks and it was very quiet. I stopped and waited.

It was a sort of converted mining engine, the sort that pulls loads of coal up from the bottom of shafts. It was battery-powered, and it had gotten quite close before I heard it. A small man was driving it. He was pulling a car behind him and singing as loud as he could with absolutely no sense of pitch.

He got closer and closer, moving about five miles per hour, one hand held out as if he was signaling a left turn. Suddenly I realized what was happening, as he was bearing down on me. He wasn't going to stop. He was counting fenceposts with his hand. I scrambled up the fence just in time. There wasn't more than six inches of clearance between the train and the fence on either side. His palm touched my leg as I squeezed close to the fence, and he stopped abruptly.

He leaped from the car and grabbed me and I thought I was in trouble. But he looked concerned, not angry, and felt me all over, trying to discover if I was hurt. I was embarrassed. Not from the examination; because I had been foolish. The Indian had said they were all deaf and blind but I guess I hadn't quite believed him.

He was flooded with relief when I managed to convey to him that I was all right. With eloquent gestures he made me understand that I was not to stay on the road. He indicated that I should climb over the fence and continue through the fields. He repeated himself several times to be sure I understood, then held on to me as I climbed over to assure himself that I was out of the way. He reached over the fence and held my shoulders, smiling at me. He pointed to the road and shook his head, then pointed to the buildings and nodded. He touched my head and smiled when I nodded. He climbed back onto the engine and started up, all the time nodding and pointing where he wanted me to go. Then he was off again.

I debated what to do. Most of me said to turn around, go back to the wall by way of the pasture and head back into the hills. These people probably wouldn't want me around. I doubted that I'd be able to talk to them, and they might even resent me. On the other hand, I was fascinated, as who wouldn't be? I wanted to see how they managed it. I still didn't believe that they were *all* deaf and blind. It didn't seem possible.

The Sheltie was sniffing at my pants. I looked down at her and she backed away, then daintily approached me as I held out my open hand. She sniffed, then licked me. I patted her on the head, and she hustled back to her sheep.

I turned toward the buildings.

The first order of business was money.

None of the students knew much about it from experience, but the library was full of Braille books. They started reading.

One of the first things that became apparent was that when money was mentioned, lawyers were not far away. The students wrote letters. From the replies, they selected a lawyer and retained him.

They were in a school in Pennsylvania at the time. The original pupils of the special schools, five hundred in number, had been narrowed down to about seventy as people left to live with relatives or found other solutions to their special problems. Of those seventy, some had places to go but didn't want to go there; others had few alternatives. Their parents were either dead or not interested in living with them. So the seventy had been gathered from the schools around the country into this one, while ways to deal with them were worked out. The authorities had plans, but the students beat them to it

Each of them had been entitled to a guaranteed annual income since 1980. They had been under the care of the government, so they had not received it. They sent their lawyer to court. He came back with a ruling that they could not collect. They appealed, and won. The money was paid retroactively, with interest, and came to a healthy sum. They thanked their lawyer and retained a real estate agent. Meanwhile, they read.

They read about communes in New Mexico, and instructed their agent to look for something out there. He made a deal for a tract to be leased in perpetuity from the Navaho nation. They read about the land, found that it would need a lot of water to be productive in the way they wanted it to be.

They divided into groups to research what they would need to be self-sufficient.

Water could be obtained by tapping into the canals that carried it from the reservoirs on the Rio Grande into the reclaimed land in the south. Federal money was available for the project through a labyrinthine scheme involving HEW, the Agriculture Department, and the Bureau of Indian Affairs. They ended up paying little for their pipeline.

The land was arid. It would need fertilizer to be of use in raising sheep without resorting to open range techniques. The cost of fertilizer could be subsidized through the Rural Resettlement Program. After that, planting clover would enrich the soil with all the nitrates they could want.

There were techniques available to farm ecologically, without worrying about fertilizers or pesticides. Everything was recycled. Essentially, you put sunlight and water into one end and harvested wool, fish, vegetables, apples, honey, and eggs at the other end. You used nothing but the land, and replaced even that as you recycled your waste products back into the soil. They were not interested in agribusiness with huge combine harvesters and crop dusters. They didn't even want to turn a profit. They merely wanted sufficiency.

The details multiplied. Their leader, the one who had had the original idea and the drive to put it into action in the face of overwhelming obstacles, was a dynamo named Janet Reilly. Knowing nothing about the techniques generals and executives employ to achieve large objectives, she invented them herself and adapted them to the peculiar needs and limitations of her group. She assigned task forces to look into solutions of each aspect of their project: law, science, social planning, design, buying, logistics, construction. At any one time, she was the only person who knew everything about what was happening. She kept it all in her head, without notes of any kind.

It was in the area of social planning that she showed herself to be a visionary and not just a superb organizer. Her idea was not to make a place where they could lead a life that was a sightless, soundless imitation of their unafflicted peers. She wanted a whole new start, a way of living that was by and for the blind-deaf, a way of living that accepted no convention just because that was the way it had always been done. She examined every human cultural institution from marriage to indecent exposure to see how it related to her needs and the needs of her friends. She was aware of the peril of this approach, but was undeterred. Her Social Task Force read about every variant group that had ever tried to make it on its own anywhere, and brought her reports about how and why they had failed or succeeded. She filtered this information through her own experiences to see how it would work for her unusual group with its own set of needs and goals.

The details were endless. They hired an architect to put their ideas into Braille blueprints. Gradually the plans evolved. They spent more money. The construction began, supervised on the site by their architect, who by now was so fascinated by the scheme that she donated her services. It was an important break, for they needed someone there whom they could trust. There is only so much that can be accomplished at such a distance.

When things were ready for them to move, they ran into bureaucratic trouble. They had anticipated it, but it was a setback. Social agencies charged with overseeing their welfare doubted the wisdom of the project. When it became apparent that no amount of reasoning was going to stop it, wheels were set in motion that resulted in a restraining order, issued for their own protection, preventing them from leaving the school. They were twenty-one years old by then, all of them, but were judged mentally incompetent to manage their own affairs. A hearing was scheduled.

Luckily, they still had access to their lawyer. He also had become infected with the crazy vision, and put on a great battle for them. He succeeded in getting a ruling concerning the rights of institutionalized persons, later upheld by the Supreme Court, which eventually had severe repercussions in state and county hospitals. Realizing the trouble they were already in regarding the thousands of patients in inadequate facilities across the country, the agencies gave in.

By then, it was the spring of 1986, one year after their target date. Some of their fertilizer had washed away already for lack of erosion-preventing clover. It was getting late to start crops, and they were running short of money. Nevertheless, they moved to New Mexico and began the backbreaking job of getting everything started. There were fifty-five of them, with nine children aged three months to six years.

I don't know what I expected. I remember that everything was a surprise, either because it was so normal or because it was so different. None of my idiot surmises about what such a place might be like proved to be true. And of course I didn't know the history of the place; I learned that later, picked up in bits and pieces.

I was surprised to see lights in some of the buildings. The first thing I had assumed was that they would have no need of them. That's an example of something so normal that it surprised me.

As to the differences, the first thing that caught my attention was the fence around the rail line. I had a personal interest in it, having almost been injured by it. I struggled to understand, as I must if I was to stay even for a night.

The wood fences that enclosed the rails on their way to the gate continued up to a barn, where the rails looped back on themselves in the same way they did outside the wall. The entire line was enclosed by the fence. The only access was a loading platform by the barn, and the gate to the outside. It made sense. The only way a deaf-blind person could operate a conveyance like that would be with assurances that there was no one on the track. These people would *never* go on the tracks; there was no way they could be warned of an approaching train.

There were people moving around me in the twilight as I made my way into the group of buildings. They took no notice of me, as I had expected. They moved fast; some of them were actually running. I stood still, eyes searching all around me so no one would come crashing into me. I had to figure out how they kept from crashing into each other before I got bolder.

I bent to the ground and examined it. The light was getting bad, but I saw immediately that there were concrete sidewalks crisscrossing the area. Each of the walks was etched with a different sort of pattern in grooves that had been made before the stuff set — lines, waves, depressions, patches of rough and smooth. I quickly saw that the people who were in a hurry moved only on those walkways, and they were all barefoot. It was no trick to see that it was some sort of traffic pattern read with the feet. I stood up.

I didn't need to know how it worked. It was sufficient to know what it was and stay off the paths.

The people were unremarkable. Some of them were not dressed, but I was used to that by now. They came in all shapes and sizes, but all seemed to be about the same age except for the children. Except for the fact that they did not stop and talk or even wave as they approached each other, I would never have guessed they were blind. I watched them come to intersections in the pathway — I didn't know how they knew they were there, but could think of several ways — and slow down as they crossed. It was a marvelous system.

I began to think of approaching someone. I had been there for almost half an hour, an intruder. I guess I had a false sense of these people's vulnerability; I felt like a burglar.

I walked along beside a woman for a minute. She was very purposeful in her eyes-ahead stride, or seemed to be. She sensed something, maybe my footsteps. She slowed a little, and I touched her on the shoulder, not knowing what else to do. She stopped instantly and turned toward me. Her eyes were open but vacant. Her hands were all over me, lightly touching my face, my chest, my hands, fingering my clothing. There was no doubt in my mind that she knew me for a stranger, probably from the first tap on the shoulder. But she smiled warmly at me, and hugged me. Her hands were very delicate and warm. That's funny, because they were calloused from hard work. But they felt sensitive.

She made me to understand — by pointing to the building, making eating motions with an imaginary spoon, and touching a number on her watch — that supper was served in an hour, and that I was invited. I nodded and smiled beneath her hands; she kissed me on the cheek and hurried off.

Well. It hadn't been so bad. I had worried about my ability to communicate. Later I found out she learned a great deal more about me than I had told.

I put off going into the mess hall or whatever it was. I strolled around in the gathering darkness looking at their layout. I saw the little Sheltie bringing the sheep back to the fold for the night. She herded them expertly through the open gate without any instructions, and one of the residents closed it and locked them in. The man bent and scratched the dog on the head and got his hand licked. Her chores done for the night, the dog hurried over to me and sniffed my pant leg. She followed me around the rest of the evening.

Everyone seemed so busy that I was surprised to see one woman sitting on a rail fence, doing nothing. I went over to her.

Closer, I saw that she was younger than I had thought. She was thirteen, I learned later. She wasn't wearing any clothes. I touched her on the shoulder, and she jumped down from the fence and went through the same routine as the other woman had, touching me all over with no reserve. She took my hand and I felt her fingers moving rapidly in my palm. I couldn't understand it, but knew what it was. I shrugged, and tried out other gestures to indicate that I didn't speak hand talk. She nodded, still feeling my face with her hands.

She asked me if I was staying to dinner. I assured her that I was. She asked me if I was from a university. And if you think that's easy to ask with only body movements, try it. But she was so graceful and supple in her movements, so deft at getting her meaning across. It was beautiful to watch her. It was speech and ballet at the same time.

I told her I wasn't from a university, and launched into an attempt to tell her a little about what I was doing and how I got there. She listened to me with her hands, scratching her head graphically when I failed to make my meanings clear. All the time the smile on her face got broader and broader, and she would laugh silently at my antics. All this while standing very close to me, touching me. At last she put her hands on her hips.

"I guess you need the practice," she said, "but if it's all the same to you, could we talk mouthtalk for now? You're cracking me up."

I jumped as if stung by a bee. The touching, while something I could ignore for a deaf-blind girl, suddenly seemed out of place. I stepped back a little, but her hands returned to me. She looked puzzled, then read the problem with her hands.

"I'm sorry," she said. "You thought I was deaf and blind. If I'd known I would have told you right off."

"I thought everyone here was."

"Just the parents. I'm one of the children. We all hear and see quite well. Don't be so nervous. If you can't stand touching, you're not going to like it here. Relax, I won't hurt you." And she kept her hands moving over me, mostly my face. I didn't understand it at the time, but it didn't seem sexual. Turned out I was wrong, but it wasn't blatant.

"You'll need me to show you the ropes," she said, and started for the domes. She held my hand and walked close to me. Her other hand kept moving to my face every time I talked.

"Number one, stay off the concrete paths. That's where — "

"I already figured that out."

"You did? How long have you been here?" Her hands searched my face with renewed interest. It was quite dark.

"Less than an hour. I was almost run over by your train."

She laughed, then apologized and said she knew it wasn't funny to me.

I told her it *was* funny to me now, though it hadn't been at the time. She said there was a warning sign on the gate, but I had been unlucky enough to come when the gate was open — they opened it by remote control before a train started up — and I hadn't seen it.

"What's your name?" I asked her, as we neared the soft yellow lights coming from the dining room.

Her hand worked reflexively in mine, then stopped. "Oh, I don't know. I *have* one; several, in fact. But they're in bodytalk. I'm . . . Pink. It translates as Pink, I guess."

There was a story behind it. She had been the first child born to the school students. They knew that babies were described as being pink, so they called her that. She felt pink to them. As we entered the hall, I could see that her name was visually inaccurate. One of her parents had been black. She was dark, with blue eyes and curly hair lighter than her skin. She had a broad nose, but small lips.

She didn't ask my name, so I didn't offer it. No one asked my name, in speech, the entire time I was there. They called me many things in bodytalk, and when the children called me it was "Hey, you!" They weren't big on spoken words.

The dining hall was in a rectangular building made of brick. It connected to one of the large domes. It was dimly lighted. I later learned that the lights were for me alone. The children didn't need them for anything but reading. I held Pink's hand, glad to have a guide. I kept my eyes and ears open.

"We're informal," Pink said. Her voice was embarrassingly loud in the large room. No one else was talking at all; there were just the sounds of movement and breathing. Several of the children looked up. "I won't introduce you around now. Just feel like part of the family. People will feel you later, and you can talk to them. You can take your clothes off here at the door."

I had no trouble with that. Everyone else was nude, and I could easily adjust to household customs by that time. You take your shoes off in Japan, you take your clothes off in Taos. What's the difference?

Well, quite a bit, actually. There was all the touching that went on. Everybody touched everybody else, as routinely as glancing. Everyone touched my face first, then went on with what seemed like total innocence to touch me everywhere else. As usual, it was not quite what it seemed. It was *not* innocent, and it was not the usual treatment they gave others in their group. They touched each other's genitals a lot *more* than they touched mine. They were holding back with me so I wouldn't be frightened. They were very polite with strangers.

There was a long, low table, with everyone sitting on the floor around it. Pink led me to it.

"See the bare strips on the floor? Stay out of them. Don't leave anything in them. That's where people walk. Don't *ever* move anything. Furniture, I mean. That has to be decided at full meetings, so we'll all know where everything is. Small things, too. If you pick up something, put it back exactly where you found it."

"I understand."

People were bringing bowls and platters of food from the adjoining kitchen. They set them on the table, and the diners began feeling them. They ate with their fingers, without plates, and they did it slowly and lovingly. They smelled things for a long time before they took a bite. Eating was very sensual to these people.

They were *terrific* cooks. I have never, before or since, eaten as well as I did at Keller. (That's my name for it, in speech, though their bodytalk name was something very like that. When I called it Keller, everyone knew what I was talking about.) They started off with good, fresh produce, something that's hard enough to find in the cities, and went at the cooking with artistry and imagination. It wasn't like any national style I've eaten. They improvised, and seldom cooked the same thing the same way twice.

I sat between Pink and the fellow who had almost run me down earlier. I stuffed myself disgracefully. It was too far removed from beef jerky and the organic dry cardboard I had been eating for me to be able to resist. I lingered over it, but still finished long before anyone else. I watched them as I sat back carefully and wondered if I'd be sick. (I wasn't, thank God.) They fed themselves and each other, sometimes getting up and going clear around the table to offer a choice morsel to a friend on the other side. I was fed in this way by all too many of them, and nearly popped until I learned a pidgin phrase in handtalk, saying I was full to the brim. I learned from Pink that a friendlier way to refuse was to offer something myself.

Eventually I had nothing to do but feed Pink and look at the others. I began to be more observant. I had thought they were eating in solitude, but soon saw that lively conversation was flowing around the table. Hands were busy, moving almost too fast to see. They were spelling into each other's palms, shoulders, legs, arms, bellies; any part of the body. I watched in amazement as a ripple of laughter spread like falling dominoes from one end of the table to the other as some witticism was passed along the line. It was *fast*. Looking carefully, I could see the thoughts moving, reaching one person, passed on while a reply went in the other direction and was in turn passed on, other replies originating all along the line and bouncing back and forth. They were a wave form, like water.

It was messy. Let's face it; eating with your fingers and talking with your hands is going to get you smeared with food. But no one minded. *I* certainly didn't. I was too busy feeling left out. Pink talked to me, but I knew I was finding out what it's like to be deaf. These people were friendly and seemed to like me, but could do nothing about it. We couldn't communicate.

Afterwards, we all trooped outside, except the cleanup crew, and took a shower beneath a set of faucets that gave out very cold water. I told Pink I'd like to help with the dishes, but she said I'd just be in the way. I couldn't do anything around Keller until I learned their very specific ways of doing things. She seemed to be assuming already that I'd be around that long.

Back into the building to dry off, which they did with their usual puppy dog friendliness, making a game and a gift of toweling each other, and then we went into the dome.

It was warm inside, warm and dark. Light entered from the passage to the dining room, but it wasn't enough to blot out the stars through the lattice of triangular panes overhead. It was almost like being out in the open.

Pink quickly pointed out the positional etiquette within the dome. It wasn't hard to follow, but I still tended to keep my arms and legs pulled in close so I wouldn't trip someone by sprawling into a walk space.

My misconceptions got me again. There was no sound but the soft whisper of flesh against flesh, so I thought I was in the middle of an orgy.

I had been at them before, in other communes, and they looked pretty much like this. I quickly saw that I was wrong, and only later found out I had been right. In a sense.

What threw my evaluations out of whack was the simple fact that group conversation among these people *had* to look like an orgy. The much subtler observation that I made later was that with a hundred naked bodies sliding, rubbing, kissing, caressing, all at the same time, what was the point in making a distinction? There was no distinction.

I have to say that I use the noun "orgy" only to get across a general idea of many people in close contact. I don't like the word, it is too ripe with connotations. But I had these connotations myself at the time, so I was relieved to see that it was not an orgy. The ones I had been to had been tedious and impersonal, and I had hoped for better from these people.

Many wormed their way through the crush to get to me and meet me. Never more than one at a time; they were constantly aware of what was going on and were waiting their turn to talk to me. Naturally, I didn't know it then. Pink sat with me to interpret the hard thoughts. I eventually used her words less and less, getting into the spirit of tactile seeing and understanding. No one felt they really knew me until they had touched every part of my body, so there were hands on me all the time. I timidly did the same.

What with all the touching, I quickly got an erection, which embarrassed me quite a bit. I was berating myself for being unable to keep sexual responses out of it, for not being able to operate on the same intellectual plane I thought they were on, when I realized with some shock that the couple next to me was making love. They had been doing it for the last ten minutes, actually, and it had seemed such a natural part of what was happening that I had known it and not known it at the same time.

No sooner had I realized it than I suddenly wondered if I was right. *Were they?* It was very slow and the light was bad. But her legs were up, and he was on top of her, that much I was sure of. It was foolish of me, but I really had to know. I had to find out *what the hell I was in.* How could I give the proper social responses if I didn't know the situation?

I was very sensitive to polite behavior after my months at the various communes. I had become adept at saying prayers before supper in one place, chanting Hare Krishna at another, and going happily nudist at still another. It's called "when in Rome," and if you can't adapt to it you shouldn't go visiting. I would kneel to Mecca, burp after my meals, toast anything that was proposed, eat organic rice, and compliment the cook; but to do it right, you have to know the customs. I had thought I knew them, but had changed my mind three times in as many minutes.

They *were* making love, in the sense that he was penetrating her. They were also deeply involved with each other. Their hands fluttered like butterflies all over each other, filled with meanings I couldn't see or feel. But they were being touched by and were touching many other people around them. They were talking to all these people, even if the message was as simple as a pat on the forehead or arm.

Pink noticed where my attention was. She was sort of wound around me, without really doing anything I would have thought of as provocative. I just couldn't *decide*. It seemed so innocent, and yet it wasn't.

"That's (—) and (—)," she said, the parentheses indicating a series of hand motions against my palm. I never learned a sound word as a name for any of them but Pink, and I can't reproduce the bodytalk names they had. Pink reached over, touched the woman with her foot, and did some complicated business with her toes. The woman smiled and grabbed Pink's foot, her fingers moving.

"(—) would like to talk with you later," Pink told me. "Right after she's through talking to (—). You met her earlier, remember? She says she likes your hands."

Now this is going to sound crazy, I know. It sounded pretty crazy to me when I thought of it. It dawned on me with a sort of revelation that her word for talk and mine were miles apart. Talk, to her, meant a complex interchange involving all parts of the body. She could read words or emotions in every twitch of my muscles, like a lie detector. Sound, to her, was only a minor part of communication. It was something she used to speak to outsiders. Pink talked with her whole being.

I didn't have the half of it, even then, but it was enough to turn my head entirely around in relation to these people. They talked with their bodies. It wasn't all hands, as I'd thought. Any part of the body in contact with any other was communication, sometimes a very simple and basic sort — think of McLuhan's light bulb as the basic medium of information — perhaps saying no more than "I am here." But talk was talk, and if conversation evolved to the point where you needed to talk to another with your genitals, it was still a part of the conversation. What I wanted to know was *what were they saying?* I knew, even at that dim moment of realization, that it was much more than I could grasp. Sure, you're saying. You know about talking to your lover with your body as you make love. That's not such a new idea. Of course it isn't, but think how wonderful that talk is even when you're not primarily tactile-oriented. Can you carry the thought from there, or are you doomed to be an earthworm thinking about sunsets?

While this was happening to me, there was a woman getting acquainted with my body. Her hands were on me, in my lap, when I felt myself ejaculating. It was a big surprise to me, but to no one else. I had been telling everyone around me for many minutes, through signs they could feel with their hands, that it was going to happen. Instantly, hands were all over my body. I could almost understand them as they spelled tender thoughts to me. I got the gist, anyway, if not the words. I was terribly embarrassed for only a moment, then it passed away in the face of the easy acceptance. It was very intense. For a long time I couldn't get my breath.

The woman who had been the cause of it touched my lips with her fingers. She moved them slowly, but meaningfully I was sure. Then she melted back into the group.

"What did she say?" I asked Pink.

She smiled at me. "You know, of course. If you'd only cut loose from your verbalizing. But, generally, she meant 'How nice for you.' It also translates as 'How nice for me.' And 'me,' in this sense, means all of us. The organism."

I knew I had to stay and learn to speak.

The commune had its ups and downs. They had expected them, in general, but had not known what shape they might take.

Winter killed many of their fruit trees. They replaced them with hybrid strains. They lost more fertilizer and soil in windstorms because the clover had not had time to anchor it down. Their schedule had been thrown off by the court actions, and they didn't really get things settled in a groove for more than a year.

Their fish all died. They used the bodies for fertilizer and looked into what might have gone wrong. They were using a three-stage ecology of the type pioneered by the New Alchemists in the '70's. It consisted of three domed ponds: one containing fish, another with crushed shells and bacteria in one section and algae in another, and a third full of daphnids. The water containing fish waste from the first pond was pumped through the shells and bacteria, which detoxified it and converted the ammonia it contained into fertilizer for the algae. The algae water was pumped into the second pond to feed the daphnids. Then daphnids and algae were pumped to the fish pond as food and the enriched water was used to fertilize greenhouse plants in all of the domes.

They tested the water and the soil and found that chemicals were being leached from impurities in the shells and concentrated down the food chain. After a thorough cleanup, they restarted and all went well. But they had lost their first cash crop.

They never went hungry. Nor were they cold; there was plenty of sunlight year-round to power the pumps and the food cycle and to heat their living quarters. They had built their buildings half-buried with an eye to the heating and cooling powers of convective currents. But they had to spend some of their capital. The first year they showed a loss.

One of their buildings caught fire during the first winter. Two men and a small girl were killed when a sprinkler system malfunctioned. This was a shock to them. They had thought things would operate as advertised. None of them knew much about the building trades, about estimates as opposed to realities. They found that several of their installations were not up to specifications, and instituted a program of periodic checks on everything. They learned to strip down and repair anything on the farm. If something contained electronics too complex for them to cope with, they tore it out and installed something simpler.

Socially, their progress had been much more encouraging. Janet had wisely decided that there would be only two hard and fast objectives in the realm of their relationships. The first was that she refused to be their president, chairwoman, chief, or supreme commander. She had seen from the start that a driving personality was needed to get the planning done and the land bought and a sense of purpose fostered from their formless desire for an alternative. But once at the promised land, she abdicated. From that point they would operate as a democratic communism. If that failed, they would adopt a new approach. Anything but a dictatorship with her at the head. She wanted no part of that.

The second principle was to accept nothing. There had never been a blind-deaf community operating on its own. They had no expectations to satisfy, they did not need to live as the sighted did. They were alone. There was no one to tell them not to do something simply because it was not done.

They had no clearer idea of what their society would be than anyone else. They had been forced into a mold that was not relevant to their needs, but beyond that they didn't know. They would search out the behavior that made sense, the moral things for blind-deaf people to do. They understood the basic principles of morals: that nothing is moral always, and anything is moral under the right circumstances. It all had to do with social context. They were starting from a blank slate, with no models to follow.

By the end of the second year they had their context. They continually modified it, but the basic pattern was set. They knew themselves and what they were as they had never been able to do at the school. They defined themselves in their own terms.

I spent my first day at Keller in school. It was the obvious and necessary step. I had to learn handtalk.

Pink was kind and very patient. I learned the basic alphabet and practiced hard at it. By the afternoon she was refusing to talk to me, forcing me to speak with my hands. She would speak only when pressed hard, and eventually not at all. I scarcely spoke a single word after the third day.

This is not to say that I was suddenly fluent. Not at all. At the end of the first day I knew the alphabet and could laboriously make myself understood. I was not so good at reading words spelled into my own palm. For a long time I had to look at the hand to see what was spelled. But like any language, eventually you think in it. I speak fluent French, and I can recall my amazement when I finally reached the point where I wasn't translating my thoughts before I spoke. I reached it at Keller in about two weeks.

I remember one of the last things I asked Pink in speech. It was something that was worrying me.

"Pink, am I welcome here?"

"You've been here three days. Do you feel rejected?"

"No, it's not that. I guess I just need to hear your policy about outsiders. How *long* am I welcome?"

She wrinkled her brow. It was evidently a new question.

"Well, practically speaking, until a majority of us decide we want you to go. But that's never happened. No one's stayed here much longer than a few days. We've never had to evolve a policy about what to do, for instance, if someone who sees and hears wants to join us. No one has, so far, but I guess it could happen. My guess is that they wouldn't accept it.

They're very independent and jealous of their freedom, though you might not have noticed it. I don't think you could ever be one of them. But as long as you're willing to think of yourself as a guest, you could probably stay for twenty years."

"You said 'they.' Don't you include yourself in the group?"

For the first time she looked a little uneasy. I wish I had been better at reading body language at the time. I think my hands could have told me volumes about what she was thinking.

"Sure," she said, "The children are part of the group. We like it. I sure wouldn't want to be anywhere else, from what I know of the outside."

"I don't blame you." There were things left unsaid here, but I didn't know enough to ask the right questions. "But it's never a problem, being able to see when none of your parents can? They don't . . . resent you in any way?"

This time she laughed. "Oh, no. Never that. They're much too independent for that. You've seen it. They don't *need* us for anything they can't do themselves. We're part of the family. We do exactly the same things they do. And it really doesn't matter. Sight, I mean. Hearing, either. Just look around you. Do I have any special advantages because I can see where I'm going?"

I had to admit that she didn't. But there was still the hint of something she wasn't saying to me.

"I know what's bothering you. About staying here." She had to draw me back to my original question; I had been wandering.

"What's that?"

"You don't feel a part of the daily life. You're not doing your share of the chores. You're very conscientious and you want to do your part. I can tell."

She read me right, as usual, and I admitted it.

"And you won't be able to until you can talk to everybody. So let's get back to your lessons. Your fingers are still very sloppy."

There was a lot of work to be done. The first thing I had to learn was to slow down. They were slow and methodical workers, made few mistakes, and didn't care if a job took all day so long as it was done well. When I was working by myself I didn't have to worry about it: sweeping, picking apples, weeding in the gardens. But when I was on a job that required teamwork I had to learn a whole new pace. Eyesight enables a person to do many aspects of a job at once with a few quick glances. A blind person will take each aspect of the job in turn if the job is spread out. Everything has to be verified by touch. At a bench job, though, they could be much faster than I. They could make me feel as though I was working with my toes instead of fingers.

I never suggested that I could make anything quicker by virtue of my sight or hearing. They quite rightly would have told me to mind my own business. Accepting sighted help was the first step to dependence, and after all, they would still be here with the same jobs to do after I was gone.

And that got me to thinking about the children again. I began to be positive that there was an undercurrent of resentment, maybe unconscious, between the parents and children. It was obvious that there was a great deal of love between them, but how could the children fail to resent the rejection of their talent? So my reasoning went, anyway.

I quickly fit myself into the routine. I was treated no better or worse than anyone else, which gratified me. Though I would never become part of the group, even if I should desire it, there was absolutely no indication that I was anything but a full member. That's just how they treated guests: as they would one of their own number.

Life was fulfilling out there in a way it has never been in the cities. It wasn't unique to Keller, this pastoral peace, but the people there had it in generous helpings. The earth beneath your bare feet is something you can never feel in a city park.

Daily life was busy and satisfying. There were chickens and hogs to feed, bees and sheep to care for, fish to harvest, and cows to milk. Everybody worked: men, women, and children. It all seemed to fit together without any apparent effort. Everybody seemed to know what to do when it needed doing. You could think of it as a well-oiled machine, but I never liked that metaphor, especially for people. I thought of it as an organism. Any social group is, but this one *worked*. Most of the other communes I'd visited had glaring flaws. Things would not get done because everyone was too stoned or couldn't be bothered or didn't see the necessity of doing it in the first place. That sort of ignorance leads to typhus and soil erosion and people freezing to death and invasions of social workers who take your children away. I'd seen it happen.

Not here. They had a good picture of the world as it is, not the rosy misconceptions so many other utopians labor under. They did the jobs that needed doing.

I could never detail all the nuts and bolts (there's that machine metaphor again) of how the place worked. The fish-cycle ponds alone were complicated enough to overawe me. I killed a spider in one of the greenhouses, then found out it had been put there to eat a specific set of plant predators. Same for the frogs. There were insects in the water to kill other insects; it got to a point where I was afraid to swat a mayfly without prior okay.

As the days went by I was told some of the history of the place. Mistakes had been made, though surprisingly few. One had been in the area of defense. They had made no provision for it at first, not knowing much about the brutality and random violence that reaches even to the out-of-the-way corners. Guns were the logical and preferred choice out here, but were beyond their capabilities.

One night a carload of men who had had too much to drink showed up. They had heard of the place in town. They stayed for two days, cutting the phone lines and raping many of the women.

The people discussed all the options after the invasion was over, and settled on the organic one. They bought five German shepherds. Not the psychotic wretches that are marketed under the description of "attack dogs," but specially trained ones from a firm recommended by the

Albuquerque police. They were trained as both Seeing-Eye and police dogs. They were perfectly harmless until an outsider showed overt aggression; then they were trained, not to disarm, but to go for the throat.

It worked, like most of their solutions. The second invasion resulted in two dead and three badly injured, all on the other side. As a backup in case of a concerted attack, they hired an ex-marine to teach them the fundamentals of close-in dirty fighting. These were not dewy-eyed flower children.

There were three superb meals a day. And there was leisure time, too. It was not all work. There was time to take a friend out and sit in the grass under a tree, usually around sunset, just before the big dinner. There was time for someone to stop working for a few minutes, to share some special treasure. I remember being taken by the hand by one woman — whom I must call Tall-one-with-the-green-eyes — to a spot where mushrooms were growing in the cool crawl space beneath the barn. We wriggled under until our faces were buried in the patch, picked a few, and smelled them. She showed me how to smell. I would have thought a few weeks before that we had ruined their beauty, but after all it was only visual. I was already beginning to discount that sense, which is so removed from the essence of an object. She showed me that they were still beautiful to touch and smell after we had apparently destroyed them. Then she was off to the kitchen with the pick of the bunch in her apron. They tasted all the better that night.

And a man — I will call him Baldy — who brought me a plank he and one of the women had been planing in the woodshop. I touched its smoothness and smelled it and agreed with him how good it was.

And after the evening meal, the Together.

During my third week there I had an indication of my status with the group. It was the first real test of whether I meant anything to them. Anything special, I mean. I wanted to see them as my friends, and I suppose I was a little upset to think that just anyone who wandered in here would be treated the way I was. It was childish and unfair to them, and I wasn't even aware of the discontent until later.

I had been hauling water in a bucket into the field where a seedling tree was being planted. There was a hose for that purpose, but it was in use on the other side of the village. This tree was not in reach of the automatic sprinklers and it was drying out. I had been carrying water to it until another solution was found.

It was hot, around noon. I got the water from a standing spigot near the forge. I set the bucket down on the ground behind me and leaned my head into the flow of water. I was wearing a shirt made of cotton, unbuttoned in the front. The water felt good running through my hair and soaking into the shirt. I let it go on for almost a minute.

There was a crash behind me and I bumped my head when I raised it up too quickly under the faucet. I turned and saw a woman sprawled on her face in the dust. She was turning over slowly, holding her knee. I realized with a sinking feeling that she had tripped over the bucket I had carelessly left on the concrete express lane. Think of it: ambling along on ground that you trust to be free of all obstruction, suddenly you're sitting on the ground. Their system would only work with trust, and it had to be total; everybody had to be responsible all the time. I had been accepted into that trust and I had blown it. I felt sick.

She had a nasty scrape on her left knee that was oozing blood. She felt it with her hands, sitting there on the ground, and she began to howl. It was weird, painful. Tears came from her eyes, then she pounded her fists on the ground, going "Hunnnh, hunnnh, *hunnnh!*" with each blow. She was angry, and she had every right to be.

She found the pail as I hesitantly reached out for her. She grabbed my hand and followed it up to my face. She felt my face, crying all the time, then wiped her nose and got up. She started off for one of the buildings. She limped slightly.

I sat down and felt miserable. I didn't know what to do.

One of the men came out to get me. It was Big Man. I called him that because he was the tallest person at Keller. He wasn't any sort of policeman, I found out later; he was just the first one the injured woman had met. He took my hand and felt my face. I saw tears start when he felt the emotions there. He asked me to come inside with him.

An impromptu panel had been convened. Call it a jury. It was made up of anyone who was handy, including a few children. There were ten or twelve of them. Everyone looked very sad. The woman I had hurt was there, being consoled by three or four people. I'll call her Scar, for the prominent mark on her upper arm.

Everybody kept telling me — in handtalk, you understand — how sorry they were for me. They petted and stroked me, trying to draw some of the misery away.

Pink came racing in. She had been sent for to act as a translator if needed. Since this was a formal proceeding it was necessary that they be sure I understood everything that happened. She went to Scar and cried with her for a bit, then came to me and embraced me fiercely, telling me with her hands how sorry she was that this had happened. I was already figuratively packing my bags. Nothing seemed to be left but the formality of expelling me.

Then we all sat together on the floor. We were close, touching on all sides. The hearing began.

Most of it was in handtalk, with Pink throwing in a few words here and there. I seldom knew who said what, but that was appropriate. It was the group speaking as one. No statement reached me without already having become a consensus.

"You are accused of having violated the rules," said the group, "and of having been the cause of an injury to (the one I called Scar). Do you dispute this? Is there any fact that we should know?"

"No," I told them. "I was responsible. It was my carelessness."

"We understand. We sympathize with you in your remorse, which is evident to all of us. But carelessness is a violation. Do you understand this?

This is the offense for which you are (——)." It was a set of signals in shorthand.

"What was that?" I asked Pink.

"Uh . . . 'brought before us'? 'Standing trial'?" She shrugged, not happy with either interpretation.

"Yes. I understand."

"The facts not being in question, it is agreed that you are guilty." (" 'Responsible,' " Pink whispered in my ear.) "Withdraw from us a moment while we come to a decision."

I got up and stood by the wall, not wanting to look at them as the debate went back and forth through the joined hands. There was a burning lump in my throat that I could not swallow. Then I was asked to rejoin the circle.

"The penalty for your offense is set by custom. If it were not so, we would wish we could rule otherwise. You now have the choice of accepting the punishment designated and having the offense wiped away, or of refusing our jurisdiction and withdrawing your body from our land. What is your choice?"

I had Pink repeat this to me, because it was so important that I know what was being offered. When I was sure I had read it right, I accepted their punishment without hesitation. I was very grateful to have been given an alternative.

"Very well. You have elected to be treated as we would treat one of our own who had done the same act. Come to us."

Everyone drew in closer. I was not told what was going to happen. I was drawn in and nudged gently from all directions.

Scar was sitting with her legs crossed more or less in the center of the group. She was crying again, and so was I, I think. It's hard to remember. I ended up face down across her lap. She spanked me.

I never once thought of it as improbable or strange. It flowed naturally out of the situation. Everyone was holding on to me and caressing me, spelling assurances into my palms and legs and neck and cheeks. We were all crying. It was a difficult thing that had to be faced by the whole group. Others drifted in and joined us. I understood that this punishment came from everyone there, but only the offended person, Scar, did the actual spanking. That was one of the ways I had wronged her, beyond the fact of giving her a scraped knee. I had laid on her the obligation of disciplining me and that was why she had sobbed so loudly, not from the pain of her injury, but from the pain of knowing she would have to hurt me.

Pink later told me that Scar had been the staunchest advocate of giving me the option to stay. Some had wanted to expel me outright, but she paid me the compliment of thinking I was a good enough person to be worth putting herself and me through the ordeal. If you can't understand that, you haven't grasped the feeling of community I felt among these people.

It went on for a long time. It was very painful, but not cruel. Nor was it primarily humiliating. There was some of that, of course. But it was essentially a practical lesson taught in the most direct terms. Each of them had undergone it during the first months, but none recently. You *learned* from it, believe me.

I did a lot of thinking about it afterward. I tried to think of what else they might have done. Spanking grown people is really unheard of, you know, though that didn't occur to me until long after it had happened. It seemed so natural when it was going on that the thought couldn't even enter my mind that this was a weird situation to be in.

They did something like this with the children, but not as long or as hard. Responsibility was lighter for the younger ones. The adults were willing to put up with an occasional bruise or scraped knee while the children learned.

But when you reached what they thought of as adulthood — which was whenever a majority of the adults thought you had or when you assumed the privilege yourself — that's when the spanking really got serious.

They had a harsher punishment, reserved for repeated or malicious offenses. They had not had to invoke it often. It consisted of being sent to Coventry. No one would touch you for a specified period of time. By the time I heard of it, it sounded like a very tough penalty. I didn't need it explained to me.

I don't know how to explain it, but the spanking was administered in such a loving way that I didn't feel violated. *This hurts me as much as it hurts you. I'm doing this for your own good. I love you, that's why I'm spanking you.* They made me understand those old clichés by their actions.

When it was over, we all cried together. But it soon turned to happiness. I embraced Scar and we told each other how sorry we were that it had happened. We talked to each other — made love if you like — and I kissed her knee and helped her dress it.

We spent the rest of the day together, easing the pain.

As I became more fluent in handtalk, "the scales fell from my eyes." Daily, I would discover a new layer of meaning that had eluded me before; it was like peeling the skin of an onion to find a new skin beneath it. Each time I thought I was at the core, only to find that there was another layer I could not yet see.

I had thought that learning handtalk was the key to communication with them. Not so. Handtalk was baby talk. For a long time I was a baby who could not even say goo-goo clearly. Imagine my surprise when, having learned to say it, I found that there were syntax, conjunctions, parts of speech, nouns, verbs, tense, agreement, and the subjunctive mood. I was wading in a tide pool at the edge of the Pacific Ocean.

By handtalk I mean the International Manual Alphabet. Anyone can learn it in a few hours or days. But when you talk to someone in speech, do you spell each word? Do you read each letter as you read this? No, you grasp words as entities, hear groups of sounds and see groups of letters as a gestalt full of meaning.

Everyone at Keller had an absorbing interest in language. They each knew several languages — spoken languages — and could read and spell them fluently.

While still children they had understood the fact that handtalk was a way for blind-deaf people to talk to *outsiders*. Among themselves it was much too cumbersome. It was like Morse Code: useful when you're limited to on-off modes of information transmission, but not the preferred mode. Their ways of speaking to each other were much closer to our type of written or verbal communication, and — dare I say it? — better.

I discovered this slowly, first by seeing that though I could spell rapidly with my hands, it took *much* longer for me to say something than it took anyone else. It could not be explained by differences in dexterity. So I asked to be taught their shorthand speech. I plunged in, this time taught by everyone, not just Pink.

It was hard. They could say any word in any language with no more than two moving hand positions. I knew this was a project for years, not days. You learn the alphabet and you have all the tools you need to spell any word that exists. That's the great advantage in having your written and spoken speech based on the same set of symbols. Shorthand was not like that at all. It partook of none of the linearity or commonality of handtalk; it was not code for English or any other language; it did not share construction or vocabulary with any other language. It was wholly constructed by the Kellerites according to their needs. Each word was something I had to learn and memorize separately from the handtalk spelling.

For months I sat in the Togethers after dinner saying things like "Me love Scar much much well," while waves of conversation ebbed and flowed and circled around me, touching me only at the edges. But I kept at it, and the children were endlessly patient with me. I improved gradually. Understand that the rest of the conversations I will relate took place in either handtalk or shorthand, limited to various degrees by my fluency. I did not speak nor was I spoken to orally from the day of my punishment.

I was having a lesson in bodytalk from Pink. Yes, we were making love. It had taken me a few weeks to see that she was a sexual being, that her caresses, which I had persisted in seeing as innocent — as I had defined it at the time — both were and weren't innocent. She understood it as perfectly natural that the result of her talking to my penis with her hands might be another sort of conversation. Though still in the middle flush of puberty, she was regarded by all as an adult and I accepted her as such. It was cultural conditioning that had blinded me to what she was saying.

So we talked a lot. With her, I understood the words and music of the body better than with anyone else. She sang a very uninhibited song with her hips and hands, free of guilt, open and fresh with discovery in every note she touched.

"You haven't told me much about yourself," she said. "What did you do on the outside?" I don't want to give the impression that this speech was in sentences, as I have presented it. We were bodytalking, sweating and smelling each other. The message came through from hands, feet, mouth.

I got as far as the sign for pronoun, first person singular, and was stopped.

How could I tell her of my life in Chicago? Should I speak of my early ambition to be a writer, and how that didn't work out? And why hadn't it? Lack of talent, or lack of drive? I could tell her about my profession, which was meaningless shuffling of papers when you got down to it, useless to anything but the Gross National Product. I could talk of the economic ups and downs that had brought me to Keller when nothing else could dislodge me from my easy sliding through life. Or the loneliness of being forty-seven years old and never having found someone worth loving, never having been loved in return. Of being a permanently displaced person in a stainless-steel society. One-night stands, drinking binges, nine-to-five, Chicago Transit Authority, dark movie houses, football games on television, sleeping pills, the John Hancock Tower where the windows won't open so you can't breathe the smog or jump out. That was me, wasn't it?

"I see," she said.

"I travel around," I said, and suddenly realized that it was the truth.

"I see," she repeated. It was a different sign for the same thing. Context was everything. She had heard and understood both parts of me, knew one to be what I had been, the other to be what I hoped I was.

She lay on top of me, one hand lightly on my face to catch the quick interplay of emotions as I thought about my life for the first time in years. And she laughed and nipped my ear playfully when my face told her that for the first time I could remember, I was happy about it. Not just telling myself I was happy, but truly happy. You cannot lie in bodytalk any more than your sweat glands can lie to a polygraph.

I noticed that the room was unusually empty. Asking around in my fumbling way, I learned that only the children were there.

"Where is everybody?" I asked.

"They are all out *** ," she said. It was like that: three sharp slaps on the chest with the fingers spread. Along with the finger configuration for "verb form, gerund," it meant that they were all out *** ing. Needless to say, it didn't tell me much.

What did tell me something was her bodytalk as she said it. I read her better than I ever had. She was upset and sad. Her body said something like "Why can't I join them? Why can't I (smell-taste-touch-hear-see) *sense* with them?" That is exactly what she said. Again, I didn't trust my understanding enough to accept that interpretation. I was still trying to force my conceptions on the things I experienced there. I was determined that she and the other children be resentful of their parents in some way, because I was sure they had to be. They *must* feel superior in some way, they *must* feel held back.

I found the adults, after a short search of the area, out in the north pasture. All the parents, none of the children. They were standing in a group with no apparent pattern. It wasn't a circle, but it was almost round. If there was any organization, it was in the fact that everybody was about the same distance from everybody else.

The German shepherds and the Sheltie were out there, sitting on the cool grass facing the group of people. Their ears were perked up, but they were not moving.

I started to go up to the people. I stopped when I became aware of the concentration. They were touching, but their hands were not moving. The silence of seeing all those permanently moving people standing that still was deafening to me.

I watched them for at least an hour. I sat with the dogs and scratched them behind the ears. They did that chop-licking thing that dogs do when they appreciate it, but their full attention was on the group.

It gradually dawned on me that the group was moving. It was very slow, just a step here and another there, over many minutes. It was expanding in such a way that the distance between any of the individuals was the same. Like the expanding universe, where all galaxies move away from all others. Their arms were extended now; they were touching only with fingertips, in a crystal lattice arrangement.

Finally they were not touching at all. I saw their fingers straining to cover distances that were too far to bridge. And still they expanded equilaterally. One of the shepherds began to whimper a little. I felt the hair on the back of my neck stand up. Chilly out here, I thought.

I closed my eyes, suddenly sleepy.

I opened them, shocked. Then I forced them shut. Crickets were chirping in the grass around me.

There was something in the darkness behind my eyeballs. I felt that if I could turn my eyes around I would see it easily, but it eluded me in a way that made peripheral vision seem like reading headlines. If there was ever anything impossible to pin down, much less describe, that was it. It tickled at me for a while as the dogs whimpered louder, but I could make nothing of it. The best analogy I could think of was the sensation a blind person might feel from the sun on a cloudy day.

I opened my eyes again.

Pink was standing there beside me. Her eyes were screwed shut, and she was covering her ears with her hands. Her mouth was open and working silently. Behind her were several of the older children. They were all doing the same thing.

Some quality of the night changed. The people in the group were about a foot away from each other now, and suddenly the pattern broke. They all swayed for a moment, then laughed in that eerie, unself-conscious noise deaf people use for laughter. They fell in the grass and held their bellies, rolled over and over and roared.

Pink was laughing, too. To my surprise, so was I. I laughed until my face and sides were hurting, like I remembered doing sometimes when I'd smoked grass.

And that was *** ing.

. . .

I can see that I've only given a surface view of Keller. And there are some things I should deal with, lest I foster an erroneous view.

Clothing, for instance. Most of them wore something most of the time. Pink was the only one who seemed temperamentally opposed to clothes. She never wore anything.

No one ever wore anything I'd call a pair of pants. Clothes were loose: robes, shirts, dresses, scarves and such. Lots of men wore things that would be called women's clothes. They were simply more comfortable.

Much of it was ragged. It tended to be made of silk or velvet or something else that felt good. The stereotyped Kellerite would be wearing a Japanese silk robe, hand-embroidered with dragons, with many gaping holes and loose threads and tea and tomato stains all over it while she sloshed through the pigpen with a bucket of slop. Wash it at the end of the day and don't worry about the colors running.

I also don't seem to have mentioned homosexuality. You can mark it down to my early conditioning that my two deepest relationships at Keller were with women: Pink and Scar. I haven't said anything about it simply because I don't know how to present it. I talked to men and women equally, on the same terms. I had surprisingly little trouble being affectionate with the men.

I could not think of the Kellerites as bisexual, though clinically they were. It was much deeper than that. They could not even recognize a concept as poisonous as a homosexuality taboo. It was one of the first things they learned. If you distinguish homosexuality from heterosexuality you are cutting yourself off from communication — *full* communication — with half the human race. They were pansexual; they could not separate sex from the rest of their lives. They didn't even have a word in shorthand that could translate directly into English as sex. They had words for male and female in infinite variation, and words for degrees and varieties of physical experience that would be impossible to express in English, but all those words included other parts of the world of experience also; none of them walled off what we call *sex* into its own discrete cubbyhole.

There's another question I haven't answered. It needs answering, because I wondered about it myself when I first arrived. It concerns the necessity for the commune in the first place. Did it really have to be like this? Would they have been better off adjusting themselves to our ways of living?

All was not a peaceful idyll. I've already spoken of the invasion and rape. It could happen again, especially if the roving gangs that operate around the cities start to really rove. A touring group of motorcyclists could wipe them out in a night.

There were also continuing legal hassles. About once a year the social workers descended on Keller and tried to take their children away. They had been accused of everything possible, from child abuse to contributing to delinquency. It hadn't worked so far, but it might someday.

And after all, there are sophisticated devices on the market that allow a blind and deaf person to see and hear a little. They might have been helped by some of those.

I met a blind-deaf woman living in Berkeley once. I'll vote for Keller.

As to those machines . . .

In the library at Keller there is a seeing machine. It uses a television camera and a computer to vibrate a closely set series of metal pins. Using it, you can feel a moving picture of whatever the camera is pointed at. It's small and light, made to be carried with the pin-pricker touching your back. It cost about thirty-five thousand dollars.

I found it in the corner of the library. I ran my finger over it and left a gleaming streak behind as the thick dust came away.

Other people came and went, and I stayed on.

Keller didn't get as many visitors as the other places I had been. It was out of the way.

One man showed up at noon, looked around, and left without a word.

Two girls, sixteen-year-old runaways from California, showed up one night. They undressed for dinner and were shocked when they found out I could see. Pink scared the hell out of them. Those poor kids had a lot of living to do before they approached Pink's level of sophistication. But then Pink might have been uneasy in California. They left the next day, unsure if they had been to an orgy or not. All that touching and no getting down to business, very strange.

There was a nice couple from Santa Fe who acted as a sort of liaison between Keller and their lawyer. They had a nine-year-old boy who chattered endlessly in handtalk to the other kids. They came up about every other week and stayed a few days, soaking up sunshine and participating in the Together every night. They spoke halting shorthand and did me the courtesy of not speaking to me in speech.

Some of the Indians came around at odd intervals. Their behavior was almost aggressively chauvinistic. They stayed dressed at all times in their Levis and boots. But it was evident that they had a respect for the people, though they thought them strange. They had business dealings with the commune. It was the Navahos who trucked away the produce that was taken to the gate every day, sold it, and took a percentage. They would sit and powwow in sign language spelled into hands. Pink said they were scrupulously honest in their dealings.

And about once a week all the parents went out in the field and *** ed.

I got better and better at shorthand and bodytalk. I had been breezing along for about five months and winter was in the offing. I had not examined my desires as yet, not really thought about what it was I wanted to do with the rest of my life. I guess the habit of letting myself drift was too ingrained. I was there, and constitutionally unable to decide whether to go or to face up to the problem if I wanted to stay for a long, long time.

Then I got a push.

For a long time I thought it had something to do with the economic situation outside. They were aware of the outside world at Keller. They knew that isolation and ignoring problems that could easily be dismissed as not relevant to them was a dangerous course, so they subscribed to the Braille *New York Times* and most of them read it. They had a television set that got plugged in about once a month. The kids would watch it and translate for their parents.

So I was aware that the non-depression was moving slowly into a more normal inflationary spiral. Jobs were opening up, money was flowing again. When I found myself on the outside again shortly afterward, I thought that was the reason.

The real reason was more complex. It had to do with peeling off the onion layer of shorthand and discovering another layer beneath it.

I had learned handtalk in a few easy lessons. Then I became aware of shorthand and bodytalk, and of how much harder they would be to learn. Through five months of constant immersion, which is the only way to learn a language, I had attained the equivalent level of a five- or six-year-old in shorthand. I knew I could master it, given time. Bodytalk was another matter. You couldn't measure progress as easily in bodytalk. It was a variable and highly interpersonal language that evolved according to the person, the time, the mood. But I was learning.

Then I became aware of Touch. That's the best I can describe it in a single, unforced English noun. What *they* called this fourth-stage language varied from day to day, as I will try to explain.

I first became aware of it when I tried to meet Janet Reilly. I now knew the history of Keller, and she figured very prominently in all the stories. I knew everyone at Keller, and I could find her nowhere. I knew everyone by names like Scar, and She-with-the-missing-front-tooth, and Man-with-wiry-hair. These were shorthand names that I had given them myself, and they all accepted them without question. They had abolished their outside names within the commune. They meant nothing to them; they told nothing and described nothing.

At first I assumed that it was my imperfect command of shorthand that made me unable to clearly ask the right question about Janet Reilly. Then I saw that they were not telling me on purpose. I saw why, and I approved, and thought no more about it. The name Janet Reilly described what she had been *on the outside*, and one of her conditions for pushing the whole thing through in the first place had been that she be no one special on the inside. She melted into the group and disappeared. She didn't want to be found. All right.

But in the course of pursuing the question I became aware that each of the members of the commune had no specific name at all. That is, Pink, for instance, had no less than one hundred and fifteen names, one from each of the commune members. Each was a contextual name that told the story of Pink's relationship to a particular person. My simple names, based on physical descriptions, were accepted as the names a child would apply to people. The children had not yet learned to go beneath the outer layers and use names that told of themselves, their lives, and their relationships to others.

What is even more confusing, the names evolved from day to day. It was my first glimpse of Touch, and it frightened me. It was a question of permutations. Just the first simple expansion of the problem meant there were no less than thirteen thousand names in use, and they wouldn't stay still so I could memorize them. If Pink spoke to me of Baldy, for instance, she would use her Touch name for him, modified by the fact that she was speaking to me and not Short-chubby-man.

Then the depths of what I had been missing opened beneath me and I was suddenly breathless with fear of heights.

Touch was what they spoke to each other. It was an incredible blend of all three other modes I had learned, and the essence of it was that it never stayed the same. I could listen to them speak to me in shorthand, which was the real basis for Touch, and be aware of the currents of Touch flowing just beneath the surface.

It was a language of inventing languages. Everyone spoke their own dialect because everyone spoke with a different instrument: a different body and set of life experiences. It was modified by everything. *It would not stand still.*

They would sit at the Together and invent an entire body of Touch responses in a night; idiomatic, personal, totally naked in its honesty. And they used it only as a building block for the next night's language.

I didn't know if I wanted to be that naked. I had looked into myself a little recently and had not been satisfied with what I found. The realization that every one of them knew more about it than I, because my honest body had told what my frightened mind had not wanted to reveal, was shattering. I was naked under a spotlight in Carnegie Hall, and all the no-pants nightmares I had ever had came out to haunt me. The fact that they all loved me with all my warts was suddenly not enough. I wanted to curl up in a dark closet with my ingrown ego and let it fester.

I might have come through this fear. Pink was certainly trying to help me. She told me that it would only hurt for a while, that I would quickly adjust to living my life with my darkest emotions written in fire across my forehead. She said Touch was not as hard as it looked at first, either. Once I learned shorthand and bodytalk, Touch would flow naturally from it like sap rising in a tree. It would be unavoidable, something that would happen to me without much effort at all.

I almost believed her. But she betrayed herself. No, no, no. Not that, but the things in her concerning *** ing convinced me that if I went through this I would only bang my head hard against the next step up the ladder.

***

I had a little better definition now. Not one that I can easily translate into English, and even that attempt will only convey my hazy concept of what it was.

"It is the mode of touching without touching," Pink said, her body going like crazy in an attempt to reach me with her own imperfect concept of what it was, handicapped by my illiteracy. Her body denied the truth of her shorthand definition, and at the same time admitted to me that she did not know what it was herself.

"It is the gift whereby one can expand oneself from the eternal quiet and dark into something else." And again her body denied it. She beat on the floor in exasperation.

"It is an attribute of being in the quiet and dark all the time, touching others. All I know for sure is that vision and hearing preclude it or obscure it. I can make it as quiet and dark as I possibly can and be aware of the edges of it, but the visual orientation of the mind persists. That door is closed to me, and to all the children."

Her verb "to touch" in the first part of that was a Touch amalgam, one that reached back into her memories of me and what I had told her of my experiences. It implied and called up the smell and feel of broken mushrooms in soft earth under the barn with Tall-one-with-green-eyes, she who taught me to feel the essence of an object. It also contained references to our bodytalking while I was penetrating into the dark and wet of her, and her running account to me of what it was like to receive me into herself. This was all one word.

I brooded on that for a long time. What was the point of suffering through the nakedness of Touch, only to reach the level of frustrated blindness enjoyed by Pink?

What was it that kept pushing me away from the one place in my life where I had been happiest?

One thing was the realization, quite late in coming, that can be summed up as "What the hell am I *doing* here?" The question that should have answered that question was "What the hell would I do if I *left*?"

I was the only visitor, the only one in *seven years* to stay at Keller for longer than a few days. I brooded on that. I was not strong enough or confident enough in my opinion of myself to see it as anything but a flaw in *me*, not in those others. I was obviously too easily satisfied, too complacent to see the flaws that those others had seen.

It didn't have to be flaws in the people of Keller, or in their system. No, I loved and respected them too much to think that. What they had going certainly came as near as anyone ever has in this imperfect world to a sane, rational way for people to exist without warfare and with a minimum of politics. In the end, those two old dinosaurs are the only ways humans have yet discovered to be social animals. Yes, I do see war as a way of living with another; by imposing your will on another in terms so unmistakable that the opponent has to either knuckle under to you, die, or beat your brains out. And if that's a solution to anything, I'd rather live without solutions. Politics is not much better. The only thing going for it is that it occasionally succeeds in substituting talk for fists.

Keller *was* an organism. It was a new way of relating, and it seemed to work. I'm not pushing it as a solution for the world's problems. It's possible that it could only work for a group with a common self-interest as binding and rare as deafness and blindness. I can't think of another group whose needs are so interdependent.

The cells of the organism cooperated beautifully. The organism was strong, flourishing, and possessed of all the attributes I've ever heard used in defining life except the ability to reproduce. That might have been its fatal flaw, if any. I certainly saw the seeds of something developing in the children.

The strength of the organism was communication. There's no way around it. Without the elaborate and impossible-to-falsify mechanisms for communication built into Keller, it would have eaten itself in pettiness, jealousy, possessiveness, and any dozen other "innate" human defects.

The nightly Together was the basis of the organism. Here, from after dinner till it was time to fall asleep, everyone talked in a language that was incapable of falsehood. If there was a problem brewing, it presented itself and was solved almost automatically. Jealousy? Resentment? Some little festering wrong that you're nursing? You couldn't conceal it at the Together, and soon everyone was clustered around you and loving the sickness away. It acted like white corpuscles, clustering around a sick cell, not to destroy it, but to heal it. There seemed to be no problem that couldn't be solved if it was attacked early enough, and with Touch, your neighbors knew about it before you did and were already laboring to correct the wrong, heal the wound, to make you feel better so you could laugh about it. There was a lot of laughter at the Togethers.

I thought for a while that I was feeling possessive about Pink. I know I had done so a little at first. Pink was my special friend, the one who had helped me out from the first, who for several days was the only one I could talk to. It was her hands that had taught me handtalk. I know I felt stirrings of territoriality the first time she lay in my lap while another man made love to her. But if there was any signal the Kellerites were adept at reading, it was that one. It went off like an alarm bell in Pink, the man, and the women and men around me. They soothed me, coddled me, told me in every language that it was all right, not to feel ashamed. Then the man in question began loving *me*. Not Pink, but the man. An observational anthropologist would have had subject matter for a whole thesis. Have you seen the films of baboons' social behavior? Dogs do it, too. Many male mammals do it. When males get into dominance battles, the weaker can defuse the aggression by submitting, by turning tail and surrendering. I have never felt so defused as when that man surrendered the object of our clash of wills — Pink — and turned his attention to me. What could I do? What I did was laugh, and he laughed, and soon we were all laughing, and that was the end of territoriality.

That's the essence of how they solved most "human nature" problems at Keller. Sort of like an oriental martial art; you yield, roll with the blow so that your attacker takes a pratfall with the force of the aggression. You do that until the attacker sees that the initial push wasn't worth the effort, that it was a pretty silly thing to do when no one was resisting you. Pretty soon he's not Tarzan of the Apes, but Charlie Chaplin. And he's laughing.

So it wasn't Pink and her lovely body and my realization that she could never be all mine to lock away in my cave and defend with a gnawed-off

808 • Utopias and Dystopias

thighbone. If I'd persisted in that frame of mind she would have found me about as attractive as an Amazonian leech, and that was a great incentive to confound the behaviorists and overcome it.

So I was back to those people who had visited and left, and what did they see that I didn't see?

Well, there was something pretty glaring. I was not part of the organism, no matter how nice the organism was to me. I had no hopes of ever becoming a part, either. Pink had said it in the first week. She felt it herself, to a lesser degree. She could not * * *, though that fact was not going to drive her away from Keller. She had told me that many times in shorthand and confirmed it in bodytalk. If I left, it would be without her.

Trying to stand outside and look at it, I felt pretty miserable. What was I trying to *do*, anyway? Was my goal in life *really* to become a part of a blind-deaf commune? I was feeling so low by that time that I actually thought of that as denigrating, in the face of all the evidence to the contrary. I should be out in the real world where the real people lived, not these freakish cripples.

I backed off from that thought very quickly. I was not totally out of my mind, just on the lunatic edges. These people were the best friends I'd ever had, maybe the only ones. That I was confused enough to think that of them even for a second worried me more than anything else. It's possible that it's what pushed me finally into a decision. I saw a future of growing disillusion and unfulfilled hopes. Unless I was willing to put out my eyes and ears, I would always be on the outside. *I* would be the blind and deaf one. I would be the freak. I didn't want to be a freak.

They knew I had decided to leave before I did. My last few days turned into a long goodbye, with a loving farewell implicit in every word touched to me. I was not really sad, and neither were they. It was nice, like everything they did. They said goodbye with just the right mix of wistfulness and life-must-go-on, and hope-to-touch-you-again.

Awareness of Touch scratched on the edges of my mind. It was not bad, just as Pink had said. In a year or two I could have mastered it.

But I was set now. I was back in the life groove that I had followed for so long. Why is it that once having decided what I must do, I'm afraid to reexamine my decision? Maybe because the original decision cost me so much that I didn't want to go through it again.

I left quietly in the night for the highway and California. They were out in the fields, standing in that circle again. Their fingertips were farther apart than ever before. The dogs and children hung around the edges like beggars at a banquet. It was hard to tell which looked more hungry and puzzled.

The experiences at Keller did not fail to leave their mark on me. I was unable to live as I had before. For a while I thought I could not live at all, but I did. I was too used to living to take the decisive step of ending my life. I would wait. Life had brought one pleasant thing to me; maybe it would bring another.

I became a writer. I found I now had a better gift for communicating than I had before. Or maybe I had it now for the first time. At any rate, my writing came together and I sold. I wrote what I wanted to write, and was not afraid of going hungry. I took things as they came.

I weathered the non-depression of '97, when unemployment reached twenty percent and the government once more ignored it as a temporary downturn. It eventually upturned, leaving the jobless rate slightly higher than it had been the time before, and the time before that. Another million useless persons had been created with nothing better to do than shamble through the streets looking for beatings in progress, car smashups, heart attacks, murders, shootings, arson, bombings, and riots: the endlessly inventive street theater. It never got dull.

I didn't become rich, but I was usually comfortable. That is a social disease, the symptoms of which are the ability to ignore the fact that your society is developing weeping pustules and having its brains eaten out by radioactive maggots. I had a nice apartment in Marin County, out of sight of the machine-gun turrets. I had a car, at a time when they were beginning to be luxuries.

I had concluded that my life was not destined to be all I would like it to be. We all make some sort of compromise, I reasoned, and if you set your expectations too high you are doomed to disappointment. It did occur to me that I was settling for something far from "high," but I didn't know what to do about it. I carried on with a mixture of cynicism and optimism that seemed about the right mix for me. It kept my motor running, anyway.

I even made it to Japan, as I had intended in the first place.

I didn't find someone to share my life. There was only Pink for that, Pink and all her family, and we were separated by a gulf I didn't dare cross. I didn't even dare think about her too much. It would have been very dangerous to my equilibrium. I lived with it, and told myself that it was the way I was. Lonely.

The years rolled on like a caterpillar tractor at Dachau, up to the penultimate day of the millennium.

San Francisco was having a big bash to celebrate the year 2000. Who gives a shit that the city is slowly falling apart, that civilization is disintegrating into hysteria? Let's have a party!

I stood on the Golden Gate Dam on the last day of 1999. The sun was setting in the Pacific, on Japan, which had turned out to be more of the same but squared and cubed with neo-samurai. Behind me the first bombshells of a firework celebration of holocaust tricked up to look like festivity competed with the flare of burning buildings as the social and economic basket cases celebrated the occasion in their own way. The city quivered under the weight of misery, anxious to slide off along the fracture lines of some subcortical San Andreas Fault. Orbiting atomic bombs twinkled in my mind, up there somewhere, ready to plant mushrooms when we'd exhausted all the other possibilities.

I thought of Pink.

I found myself speeding through the Nevada desert, sweating, gripping the steering wheel. I was crying aloud but without sound, as I had learned to do at Keller.

Can you go back?

I slammed the citicar over the potholes in the dirt road. The car was falling apart. It was not built for this kind of travel. The sky was getting light in the east. It was the dawn of a new millennium. I stepped harder on the gas pedal and the car bucked savagely. I didn't care. I was not driving back down that road, not ever. One way or another, I was here to stay.

I reached the wall and sobbed my relief. The last hundred miles had been a nightmare of wondering if it had been a dream. I touched the cold reality of the wall and it calmed me. Light snow had drifted over everything, gray in the early dawn.

I saw them in the distance. All of them, out in the field where I had left them. No, I was wrong. It was only the children. Why had it seemed like so many at first?

Pink was there. I knew her immediately, though I had never seen her in winter clothes. She was taller, filled out. She would be nineteen years old. There was a small child playing in the snow at her feet, and she cradled an infant in her arms. I went to her and talked to her hand.

She turned to me, her face radiant with welcome, her eyes staring in a way I had never seen. Her hands flitted over me and her eyes did not move.

"I touch you, I welcome you," her hands said. "I wish you could have been here just a few minutes ago. Why did you go away darling? Why did you stay away so long?" Her eyes were stones in her head. She was blind. She was deaf.

All the children were. No, Pink's child sitting at my feet looked up at me with a smile.

"Where is everybody?" I asked when I got my breath. "Scar? Baldy? Green-eyes? And what's happened? What's happened to you?" I was tottering on the edge of a heart attack or nervous collapse or something. My reality felt in danger of dissolving.

"They've gone," she said. The word eluded me, but the context put it with the *Mary Celeste* and Roanoke, Virginia. It was complex, the way she used the word *gone*. It was like something she had said before: unattainable, a source of frustration like the one that had sent me running from Keller. But now her word told of something that was not hers yet, but was within her grasp. There was no sadness in it.

"Gone?"

"Yes. I don't know where. They're happy. They *** ed. It was glorious. We could only touch a part of it."

I felt my heart hammering to the sound of the last train pulling away from the station. My feet were pounding along the ties as it faded into the fog. Where are the Brigadoons of yesterday? I've never yet heard of a fairy tale where you can go back to the land of enchantment. You wake up, you find that your chance is gone. You threw it away. *Fool!* You only get one chance; that's the moral, isn't it?

Pink's hands laughed along my face.

"Hold this part-of-me-who-speaks-mouth-to-nipple," she said, and handed me her infant daughter. "I will give you a gift."

She reached up and lightly touched my ears with her cold fingers. The sound of the wind was shut out, and when her hands came away it never came back. She touched my eyes, shut out all the light, and I saw no more.

We live in the lovely quiet and dark.

Mike Resnick

Kirinyaga

(1988)

Mike Resnick (b. 1942) began his writing career in the 1960s with space opera and works in other popular genres, but he gained prominence as a sophisticated and an innovative sf writer in the 1980s. Resnick, who has won five Hugos and one Nebula, is best known for a series of stories set in *Kirinyaga*, an orbital utopian community modeled on the traditional culture of the Kikuyu people of Kenya.

The use of an African cultural setting by a white writer was controversial to some and made more so by several troubling comments Resnick made about the alien quality of Africa. Although some readers have criticized him for cultural imperialism, however, others have welcomed his extension of the imaginative resources available to sf, which has tended to draw materials primarily from European traditions.

Resnick is a provocative and original writer who is drawn to complex ethical dilemmas. Stories like "Kirinyaga" (which won a Hugo in 1989) are powerful and unsettling not only because the material is racially charged but also because Resnick insists on confronting directly the dual nature inherent in any utopia or planned community: the conflict between society and individual, dedication to principle and openness to change. The narrator, Koriba, has an uncompromising commitment to tradition that makes him, depending on one's point of view, either a visionary leader or a dangerous autocrat — or both. Any planned community founded on strong principles must face choices between individual rights and adaptation to new conditions that may threaten the purity of its initial vision, perhaps even its very existence.

In the beginning, Ngai lived alone atop the mountain called Kirinyaga. In the fullness of time, he created three sons, who became fathers of the Maasai, the Kamba, and the Kikuyu races; and to each son he offered a spear, a bow, and a digging stick. The Maasai chose the spear, and was told to tend herds on the vast savannah. The Kamba chose the bow, and was sent to the dense forests to hunt for game. But Gikuyu, the first Kikuyu, knew that Ngai loved the earth and the seasons, and chose the digging stick. To reward him for this, Ngai not only taught him the secrets of the seed and the harvest, but gave him Kirinyaga, with its holy fig tree and rich lands.

The sons and daughters of Gikuyu remained on Kirinyaga until the white man came and took their lands away; and even when the white man had been banished, they did not return, but chose to remain in the cities, wearing Western clothes and using Western machines and living Western lives. Even I, who am a *mundumugu* — a witch doctor — was born in the city. I have never seen the lion or the elephant or the rhinoceros, for all of them were extinct before my birth; nor have I seen Kirinyaga as Ngai meant it to be seen, for a bustling, overcrowded city of 3 million inhabitants covers its slopes, every year approaching closer and closer to Ngai's throne at the summit. Even the Kikuyu have forgotten its true name, and now know it only as Mount Kenya.

To be thrown out of Paradise, as were the Christian Adam and Eve, is a terrible fate, but to live beside a debased Paradise is infinitely worse. I think about them frequently, the descendants of Gikuyu who have forgotten their origin and their traditions and are now merely Kenyans, and I wonder why more of them did not join with us when we created the Eutopian world of Kirinyaga.

True, it is a harsh life, for Ngai never meant life to be easy; but it is also a satisfying life. We live in harmony with our environment; we offer sacrifices when Ngai's tears of compassion fall upon our fields and give sustenance to our crops; we slaughter a goat to thank Him for the harvest.

Our pleasures are simple: a gourd of *pombe* to drink, the warmth of a *boma* when the sun has gone down, the wail of a newborn son or daughter, the footraces and spear throwing and other contests, the nightly singing and dancing.

Maintenance watches Kirinyaga discreetly, making minor orbital adjustments when necessary, assuring that our tropical climate remains constant. From time to time they have subtly suggested that we might wish to draw upon their medical expertise, or perhaps allow our children to make use of their educational facilities, but they have taken our refusal with good grace, and have never shown any desire to interfere in our affairs.

Until I strangled the baby.

It was less than an hour later that Koinnage, our paramount chief, sought me out.

"That was an unwise thing to do, Koriba," he said grimly.

"It was not a matter of choice," I replied. "You know that."

"Of course you had a choice," he responded. "You could have let the infant live." He paused, trying to control his anger and his fear. "Maintenance has never set foot on Kirinyaga before, but now they will come."

"Let them," I said with a shrug. "No law has been broken."

"We have killed a baby," he replied. "They will come, and they will revoke our charter!"

I shook my head. "No one will revoke our charter."

"Do not be too certain of that, Koriba," he warned me. "You can bury a goat alive, and they will monitor us and shake their heads and speak contemptuously among themselves about our religion. You can leave the aged and the infirm out for the hyenas to eat, and they will look upon us with disgust and call us godless heathens. But I tell you that killing a newborn infant is another matter. They will not sit idly by; they will come."

"If they do, I shall explain why I killed it," I replied calmly.

"They will not accept your answers," said Koinnage. "They will not understand."

"They will have no choice but to accept my answers," I said. "This is Kirinyaga, and they are not permitted to interfere."

"They will find a way," he said with an air of certainty. "We must apologize and tell them that it will not happen again."

"We will not apologize," I said sternly. "Nor can we promise that it will not happen again."

"Then, as paramount chief, *I* will apologize."

I stared at him for a long moment, then shrugged. "Do what you must do," I said.

Suddenly I could see the terror in his eyes.

"What will you do to me?" he asked fearfully.

"I? Nothing at all," I said "Are you not my chief ?" As he relaxed, I added: "But if I were you, I would beware of insects."

"Insects?" he repeated. "Why?"

"Because the next insect that bites you, be it spider or mosquito or fly, will surely kill you," I said. "Your blood will boil within your body, and your bones will melt. You will want to scream out your agony, yet you will be unable to utter a sound." I paused. "It is not a death I would wish on a friend," I added seriously.

"Are we not friends, Koriba?" he said, his ebon face turning an ash gray.

"I thought we were," I said. "But my friends honor our traditions. They do not apologize for them to the white man."

"I will not apologize!" he promised fervently. He spat on both his hands as a gesture of his sincerity.

I opened one of the pouches I kept around my waist and withdrew a small polished stone, from the shore of our nearby river. "Wear this around your neck," I said, handing it to him, "and it shall protect you from the bites of insects."

"Thank you, Koriba!" he said with sincere gratitude, and another crisis had been averted.

We spoke about the affairs of the village for a few more minutes, and finally he left me. I sent for Wambu, the infant's mother, and led her through the ritual of purification, so that she might conceive again. I also gave her an ointment to relieve the pain in her breasts, since they were heavy with milk. Then I sat down by the fire within my *boma* and made myself available to my people, settling disputes over the ownership of chickens and goats, and supplying charms against demons, and instructing my people in the ancient ways.

By the time of the evening meal, no one had a thought for the dead baby. I ate alone in my *boma*, as befitted my status, for the *mundumugu* always lives and eats apart from his people. When I had finished, I wrapped a blanket around my body to protect me from the cold and walked down the dirt path to where all the other *bomas* were clustered. The cattle and goats and chickens were penned up for the night, and my people, who had slaughtered and eaten a cow, were now singing and dancing and drinking great quantities of *pombe*. As they made way for me, I walked over to the caldron and took a drink of *pombe*, and then, at Kanjara's request, I slit open a goat and read its entrails and saw that his youngest wife would soon conceive, which was cause for more celebration. Finally the children urged me to tell them a story.

"But not a story of Earth," complained one of the taller boys. "We hear those all the time. This must be a story about Kirinyaga."

"All right," I said. "If you will all gather around, I will tell you a story of Kirinyaga." The youngsters all moved closer. "This," I said, "is the story of the Lion and the Hare." I paused until I was sure that I had everyone's attention, especially that of the adults. "A hare was chosen by his people to be sacrificed to a lion, so that the lion would not bring disaster to their village. The hare might have run away, but he knew that sooner or later the lion would catch him, so instead he sought out the lion and walked right up to him, and as the lion opened his mouth to swallow him, the hare said, 'I apologize, Great Lion.'

" 'For what?' asked the lion curiously.

" 'Because I am such a small meal,' answered the hare. 'For that reason, I brought honey for you as well.'

" 'I see no honey,' said the lion.

" 'That is why I apologized,' answered the hare. 'Another lion stole it from me. He is a ferocious creature, and says that he is not afraid of you.'

"The lion rose to his feet. 'Where is this other lion?' he roared.

"The hare pointed to a hole in the earth. 'Down there,' he said, 'but he will not give you back your honey.'

" 'We shall see about that!' growled the lion.

"He jumped into the hole, roaring furiously, and was never seen again, for the hare had chosen a very deep hole indeed. Then the hare went home to his people and told them that the lion would never bother them again."

Most of the children laughed and clapped their hands in delight, but the same young boy voiced his objection.

"That is not a story of Kirinyaga," he said scornfully. "We have no lions here."

"It *is* a story of Kirinyaga," I replied. "What is important about the story is not that it concerned a lion and a hare, but that it shows that the weaker can defeat the stronger if he uses his intelligence."

"What has that to do with Kirinyaga?" asked the boy.

"What if we pretend that the men of Maintenance, who have ships and weapons, are the lion, and the Kikuyu are the hares?" I suggested. "What shall the hares do if the lion demands a sacrifice?"

The boy suddenly grinned. "Now I understand! We shall throw the lion down a hole!"

"But we have no holes here," I pointed out.

"Then what shall we do?"

"The hare did not know that he would find the lion near a hole," I replied. "Had he found him by a deep lake, he would have said that a large fish took the honey."

"We have no deep lakes."

"But we do have intelligence," I said. "And if Maintenance ever interferes with us, we will use our intelligence to destroy the lion of Maintenance, just as the hare used his intelligence to destroy the lion of the fable."

"Let us think how to destroy Maintenance right now!" cried the boy. He picked up a stick and brandished it at an imaginary lion as if it were a spear and he a great hunter.

I shook my head. "The hare does not hunt the lion, and the Kikuyu do not make war. The hare merely protects himself, and the Kikuyu do the same."

"Why would Maintenance interfere with us?" asked another boy, pushing his way to the front of the group. "They are our friends."

"Perhaps they will not," I answered reassuringly. "But you must always remember that the Kikuyu have no true friends except themselves."

"Tell us another story, Koriba!" cried a young girl.

"I am an old man," I said. "The night has turned cold, and I must sleep."

"Tomorrow?" she asked. "Will you tell us another tomorrow?"

I smiled. "Ask me tomorrow, after all the fields are planted and the cattle and goats are in their enclosures and the food has been made and the fabrics have been woven."

"But girls do not herd the cattle and goats," she protested. "What if my brothers do not bring all their animals to the enclosure?"

"Then I will tell a story just to the girls," I said.

"It must be a long story," she insisted seriously, "for we work much harder than the boys."

"I will watch you in particular, little one," I replied, "and the story will be as long or as short as your work merits."

The adults all laughed, and suddenly she looked very uncomfortable, but then I chuckled and hugged her and patted her head, for it was necessary that the children learn to love their *mundumugu* as well as hold him in awe, and finally she ran off to play and dance with the other girls, while I retired to my *boma*.

Once inside, I activated my computer and discovered that a message was waiting for me from Maintenance, informing me that one of their number would be visiting me the following morning. I made a very brief reply — "Article II, Paragraph 5," which is the ordinance forbidding intervention — and lay down on my sleeping blanket, letting the rhythmic chanting of the singers carry me off to sleep.

I awoke with the sun the next morning and instructed my computer to let me know when the Maintenance ship had landed. Then I inspected my cattle and my goats — I, alone of my people, planted no crops, for the Kikuyu feed their *mundumugu*, just as they tend his herds and weave his blankets and keep his *boma* clean — and stopped by Simani's *boma* to deliver a balm to fight the disease that was afflicting his joints. Then, as the sun began warming the earth, I returned to my own *boma*, skirting the pastures where the young men were tending their animals. When I arrived, I knew the ship had landed, for I found the droppings of a hyena on the ground near my hut, and that is the surest sign of a curse.

I learned what I could from the computer, then walked outside and scanned the horizon while two naked children took turns chasing a small dog and running away from it. When they began frightening my chickens, I gently sent them back to their own *boma*, and then seated myself beside my fire. At last I saw my visitor from Maintenance, coming up the path from Haven. She was obviously uncomfortable in the heat, and she slapped futilely at the flies that circled her head. Her blonde hair was starting to turn gray, and I could tell by the ungainly way she negotiated the steep, rocky path that she was unused to such terrain. She almost lost her balance a number of times, and it was obvious that her proximity to so many animals frightened her, but she never slowed her pace, and within another ten minutes she stood before me.

"Good morning," she said.

"*Jambo, Memsaab*," I replied.

"You are Koriba, are you not?"

I briefly studied the face of my enemy; middle-aged and weary, it did not appear formidable. "I am Koriba," I replied.

"Good," she said. "My name is — "

"I know who you are," I said, for it is best, if conflict cannot be avoided, to take the offensive.

"You do?"

I pulled the bones out of my pouch and cast them on the dirt. "You are Barbara Eaton, born of Earth," I intoned, studying her reactions as I picked up the bones and cast them again. "You are married to Robert Eaton, and you have worked for Maintenance for nine years." A final cast of the bones. "You are forty-one years old, and you are barren."

"How did you know all that?" she asked with an expression of surprise.

"Am I not the *mundumugu*?"

She stared at me for a long minute. "You read my biography on your computer," she concluded at last.

"As long as the facts are correct, what difference does it make whether I read them from the bones or the computer?" I responded, refusing to confirm her statement. "Please sit down, *Memsaab* Eaton."

She lowered herself awkwardly to the ground, wrinkling her face as she raised a cloud of dust.

"It's very hot," she noted uncomfortably.

"It is very hot in Kenya," I replied.

"You could have created any climate you desired," she pointed out.

"We *did* create the climate we desired," I answered.

"Are there predators out there?" she asked, looking out over the savannah.

"A few," I replied.

"What kind?"

"Hyenas."

"Nothing larger?" she asked.

"There *is* nothing larger anymore," I said.

"I wonder why they didn't attack me?"

"Perhaps because you are an intruder," I suggested.

"Will they leave me alone on my way back to Haven?" she asked nervously, ignoring my comment.

"I will give you a charm to keep them away."

"I'd prefer an escort."

"Very well," I said.

"They're such ugly animals," she said with a shudder. "I saw them once when we were monitoring your world."

"They are very useful animals," I answered, "for they bring many omens, both good and bad."

"Really?"

I nodded. "A hyena left me an evil omen this morning."

"And?" she asked curiously.

"And here you are," I said.

She laughed. "They told me you were a sharp old man."

"They are mistaken," I replied. "I am a feeble old man who sits in front of his *boma* and watches younger men tend his cattle and goats."

"You are a feeble old man who graduated with honors from Cambridge and then acquired two postgraduate degrees from Yale," she replied.

"Who told you that?"

She smiled. "You're not the only one who reads biographies."

I shrugged. "My degrees did not help me become a better *mundumugu*," I said. "The time was wasted."

"You keep using that word. What, exactly, is a *mundumugu*?"

"You would call him a witch doctor," I answered. "But in truth the *mundumugu*, while he occasionally casts spells and interprets omens, is more a repository of the collected wisdom and traditions of his race."

"It sounds like an interesting occupation," she said.

"It is not without its compensations."

"And *such* compensations!" she said with false enthusiasm as a goat bleated in the distance and a young man yelled at it in Swahili. "Imagine having the power of life and death over an entire Eutopian world!"

So now it comes, I thought. Aloud I said: "It is not a matter of exercising power, *Memsaab* Eaton, but of maintaining traditions."

"I rather doubt that," she said bluntly.

"Why should you doubt what I say?" I asked.

"Because if it were traditional to kill newborn infants, the Kikuyu would have died out after a single generation."

"If the slaying of the infant arouses your disapproval," I said calmly, "I am surprised Maintenance has not previously asked about our custom of leaving the old and the feeble out for the hyenas."

"We know that the elderly and the infirm have consented to your treatment of them, much as we may disapprove of it," she replied. "We also know that a newborn infant could not possibly consent to its own death." She paused, staring at me. "May I ask why this particular baby was killed?"

"That *is* why you have come here, is it not?"

"I have been sent here to evaluate the situation," she replied, brushing an insect from her cheek and shifting her position on the ground. "A newborn child was killed. We would like to know why."

I shrugged. "It was killed because it was born with a terrible *thahu* upon it."

She frowned. "A *thahu*? What is that?"

"A curse."

"Do you mean that it was deformed?" she asked.

"It was not deformed."

"Then what was this curse that you refer to?"

"It was born feet-first," I said.

"That's it?" she asked, surprised. "That's the curse?"

"Yes."

"It was murdered simply because it came out feet-first?"

"It is not murder to put a demon to death," I explained patiently. "Our tradition tells us that a child born in this manner is actually a demon."

"You are an educated man, Koriba," she said. "How can you kill a perfectly healthy infant and blame it on some primitive tradition?"

"You must never underestimate the power of tradition, *Memsaab* Eaton," I said. "The Kikuyu turned their backs on their traditions once; the result is a mechanized, impoverished, overcrowded country that is no longer populated by Kikuyu, or Maasai, or Luo, or Wakamba, but by a new, artificial tribe known only as Kenyans. We here on Kirinyaga are true Kikuyu, and we will not make that mistake again. If the rains are late, a ram must be sacrificed. If a man's veracity is questioned, he must undergo the ordeal of the *githani* trial. If an infant is born with a *thahu* upon it, it must be put to death."

"Then you intend to continue killing any children that are born feet-first?" she asked.

"That is correct," I responded.

A drop of sweat rolled down her face as she looked directly at me and said: "I don't know what Maintenance's reaction will be."

"According to our charter, Maintenance is not permitted to interfere with us," I reminded her.

"It's not that simple, Koriba," she said. "According to your charter, any member of your community who wishes to leave your world is allowed free passage to Haven from which he or she can board a ship to Earth." She paused. "Was that baby you killed given such a choice?"

"I did not kill a baby, but a demon," I replied, turning my head slightly as a hot breeze stirred up the dust around us.

She waited until the breeze died down, then coughed before speaking. "You do understand that not everyone in Maintenance may share that opinion?"

"What Maintenance thinks is of no concern to us," I said.

"When innocent children are murdered, what Maintenance thinks is of supreme importance to you," she responded. "I am sure you do not want to defend your practices in the Eutopian Court."

"Are you here to evaluate the situation, as you said, or to threaten us?" I asked calmly.

"To evaluate the situation," she replied. "But there seems to be only one conclusion that I can draw from the facts that you have presented to me."

"Then you have not been listening to me," I said, briefly closing my eyes as another, stronger, breeze swept past us.

"Koriba, I know that Kirinyaga was created so that you could emulate the ways of your forefathers — but surely you must see the difference between the torture of animals as a religious ritual and the murder of a human baby."

I shook my head. "They are one and the same," I replied. "We cannot change our way of life because it makes you uncomfortable. We did that once before, and within a mere handful of years, your culture had corrupted our society. With every factory we built, with every job we created, with every bit of Western technology we accepted, with every Kikuyu who converted to Christianity, we became something we were not meant to be." I stared directly into her eyes. "I am the *mundumugu*, entrusted with preserving all that makes us Kikuyu, and I will not allow that to happen again."

"There are alternatives," she said.

"Not for the Kikuyu," I replied adamantly.

"There *are*," she insisted, so intent upon what she had to say that she paid no attention to a black-and-gold centipede that crawled over her boot. "For example, years spent in space can cause certain physiological and hormonal changes in humans. You noted when I arrived that I am forty-one years old and childless. That is true. In fact, many of the women in Maintenance are childless. If you will turn the babies over to us, I am sure we can find families for them. This would effectively remove them from your society without the necessity of killing them. I could speak to my superiors about it; I think that there is an excellent chance that they would approve."

"That is a thoughtful and innovative suggestion, *Memsaab* Eaton," I said truthfully. "I am sorry that I must reject it."

"But why?" she demanded.

"Because the first time we betray our traditions, this world will cease to be Kirinyaga, and will become merely another Kenya, a nation of men awkwardly pretending to be something they are not."

"I could speak to Koinnage and the other chiefs about it," she suggested meaningfully.

"They will not disobey my instructions," I replied confidently.

"You hold that much power?"

"I hold that much respect," I answered. "A chief may enforce the law, but it is the *mundumugu* who interprets it."

"Then let us consider other alternatives."

"No."

"I am trying to avoid a conflict between Maintenance and your people," she said, her voice heavy with frustration. "It seems to me that you could at least make the effort to meet me halfway."

"I do not question your motives, *Memsaab* Eaton," I replied, "but you are an intruder representing an organization that has no legal right to interfere with our culture. We do not impose our religion or our morality upon Maintenance, and Maintenance may not impose its religion or morality upon us."

"It is not that simple."

"It is precisely that simple," I said.

"That is your last word on the subject?" she asked.

"Yes."

She stood up. "Then I think it is time for me to leave and make my report."

I stood up as well, and a shift in the wind brought the odors of the village: the scent of bananas, the smell of a fresh caldron of *pombe*, even the pungent odor of a bull that had been slaughtered that morning.

"As you wish, *Memsaab* Eaton," I said. "I will arrange for your escort." I signaled to a small boy who was tending three goats and instructed him to go to the village and send back two young men.

"Thank you," she said. "I know it's an inconvenience, but I just don't feel safe with hyenas roaming loose out there."

"You are welcome," I said. "Perhaps, while we are waiting for the men who will accompany you, you would like to hear a story about the hyena."

She shuddered involuntarily. "They are such ugly beasts!" she said distastefully. "Their hind legs seem almost deformed." She shook her head. "No, I don't think I'd be interested in hearing a story about a hyena."

"You will be interested in *this* story," I told her.

She stared at me curiously and shrugged. "All right," she said. "Go ahead."

"It is true that hyenas are deformed, ugly animals," I began, "but once, a long time ago, they were as lovely and graceful as the impala. Then one day a Kikuyu chief gave a hyena a young goat to take as a gift to Ngai, who lived atop the holy mountain Kirinyaga. The hyena took the goat between his powerful jaws and headed toward the distant mountain — but on the way he passed a settlement filled with Europeans and Arabs. It abounded in guns and machines and other wonders he had never seen before, and he stopped to look, fascinated. Finally an Arab noticed him staring intently, and asked if he, too, would like to become a civilized man — and as he opened his mouth to say that he would, the goat fell to the ground and ran away. As the goat raced out of sight, the Arab laughed and explained that he was only joking, that of course no hyena could become a man." I paused for a moment, and then continued. "So the hyena proceeded to Kirinyaga, and when he reached the summit, Ngai asked him what had become of the goat. When the hyena told him, Ngai hurled him off the mountaintop for having the audacity to believe he could become a man. He did not die from the fall, but his rear legs were crippled, and Ngai declared that from that day forward, all hyenas would appear thus — and to remind them of the foolishness of trying to become something that they were not, he also gave them a fool's laugh." I paused again, and stared at her. "*Memsaab* Eaton, you do not hear the Kikuyu laugh like fools, and I will not let them become crippled like the hyena. Do you understand what I am saying?"

She considered my statement for a moment, then looked into my eyes. "I think we understand each other perfectly, Koriba," she said.

The two young men I had sent for arrived just then, and I instructed them to accompany her to Haven. A moment later they set off across the dry savannah, and I returned to my duties.

I began by walking through the fields, blessing the scarecrows. Since a number of the smaller children followed me, I rested beneath the trees more often than was necessary, and always, whenever we paused, they begged me to tell them more stories. I told them the tale of the Elephant and the Buffalo, and how the Maasai *elmoran* cut the rainbow with his spear so that it never again came to rest upon the earth, and why the nine Kikuyu tribes are named after Gikuyu's nine daughters, and when the sun became too hot, I led them back to the village.

Then, in the afternoon, I gathered the older boys about me and explained once more how they must paint their faces and bodies for their forthcoming circumcision ceremony. Ndemi, the boy who had insisted upon a story about Kirinyaga the night before, sought me out privately to complain that he had been unable to slay a small gazelle with his spear, and asked for a charm to make its flight more accurate. I explained to him that there would come a day when he faced a buffalo or a hyena with no charm, and that he must practice more before he came to me again. He was one to watch, this little Ndemi, for he was impetuous and totally without fear; in the old days, he would have made a great warrior, but on Kirinyaga we had no warriors. If we remained fruitful and fecund, however, we would someday need more chiefs and even another *mundumugu*, and I made up my mind to observe him closely.

In the evening, after I ate my solitary meal, I returned to the village, for Njogu, one of our young men, was to marry Kamiri, a girl from the next village. The bride price had been decided upon, and the two families were waiting for me to preside at the ceremony.

Njogu, his face streaked with paint, wore an ostrich-feather headdress, and looked very uneasy as he and his betrothed stood before me. I slit the throat of a fat ram that Kamiri's father had brought for the occasion, and then I turned to Njogu.

"What have you to say?" I asked.

He took a step forward. "I want Kamiri to come and till the fields of my *shamba*," he said, his voice cracking with nervousness as he spoke the prescribed words, "for I am a man, and I need a woman to tend to my *shamba* and dig deep around the roots of my plantings, that they may grow well and bring prosperity to my house."

He spit on both his hands to show his sincerity, and then, exhaling deeply with relief, he stepped back.

I turned to Kamiri.

"Do you consent to till the *shamba* of Njogu, son of Muchiri?" I asked her.

"Yes," she said softly, bowing her head. "I consent."

I held out my right hand, and the bride's mother placed a gourd of *pombe* in it.

"If this man does not please you," I said to Kamiri, "I will spill the *pombe* upon the ground."

"Do not spill it," she replied.

"Then drink," I said, handing the gourd to her.

She lifted it to her lips and took a swallow, then handed it to Njogu, who did the same.

When the gourd was empty, the parents of Njogu and Kamiri stuffed it with grass, signifying the friendship between the two clans.

Then a cheer rose from the onlookers, the ram was carried off to be roasted, more *pombe* appeared as if by magic, and while the groom took the bride off to his *boma*, the remainder of the people celebrated far into the night. They stopped only when the bleating of the goats told them that some hyenas were nearby, and then the women and children went off to their *bomas* while men took their spears and went into the fields to frighten the hyenas away.

Koinnage came up to me as I was about to leave.

"Did you speak to the woman from Maintenance?" he asked.

"I did," I replied.

"What did she say?"

"She said that they do not approve of killing babies who are born feet-first."

"And what did *you* say?" he asked nervously.

"I told her that we did not need the approval of Maintenance to practice our religion," I replied.

"Will Maintenance listen?"

"They have no choice," I said. "And *we* have no choice, either," I added. "Let them dictate one thing that we must or must not do, and soon they will dictate *all* things. Give them their way, and Njogu and Kamiri would have recited wedding vows from the Bible or the Koran. It happened to us in Kenya; we cannot permit it to happen on Kirinyaga."

"But they will not punish us?" he persisted.

"They will not punish us," I replied.

Satisfied, he walked off to his *boma* while I took the narrow, winding path to my own. I stopped by the enclosure where my animals were kept and saw that there were two new goats there, gifts from the bride's and groom's families in gratitude for my services. A few minutes later I was asleep within the walls of my own *boma*.

The computer woke me a few minutes before sunrise. I stood up, splashed my face with water from the gourd I keep by my sleeping blanket, and walked over to the terminal.

There was a message for me from Barbara Eaton, brief and to the point:

> It is the preliminary finding of Maintenance that infanticide, for any reason, is a direct violation of Kirinyaga's charter. No action will be taken for past offenses.
>
> We are also evaluating your practice of euthanasia, and may require further testimony from you at some point in the future.
>
> Barbara Eaton

A runner from Koinnage arrived a moment later, asking me to attend a meeting of the Council of Elders, and I knew that he had received the same message.

I wrapped my blanket around my shoulders and began walking to Koinnage's *shamba*, which consisted of his *boma* as well as those of his three sons and their wives. When I arrived, I found not only the local elders waiting for me, but also two chiefs from neighboring villages.

"Did you receive the message from Maintenance?" demanded Koinnage, as I seated myself opposite him.

"I did."

"I warned you that this would happen!" he said. "What will we do now?"

"We will do what we have always done," I answered calmly.

"We cannot," said one of the neighboring chiefs. "They have forbidden it."

"They have no right to forbid it," I replied.

"There is a woman in my village whose time is near," continued the chief, "and all of the signs and omens point to the birth of twins. We have been taught that the firstborn must be killed, for one mother cannot produce two souls — but now Maintenance has forbidden it. What are we to do?"

"We must kill the firstborn," I said, "for it will be a demon."

"And then Maintenance will make us leave Kirinyaga!" said Koinnage bitterly.

"Perhaps we could let the child live," said the chief. "That might satisfy them, and then they might leave us alone."

I shook my head, "They will not leave you alone. Already they speak about the way we leave the old and feeble out for the hyenas, as if this were some enormous sin against their God. If you give in on the one, the day will come when you must give in on the other."

"Would that be so terrible?" persisted the chief. "They have medicines that we do not possess; perhaps they could make the old young again."

"You do not understand," I said, rising to my feet. "Our society is not a collection of separate people and customs and traditions. No, it is a complex system, with all the pieces as dependent upon each other as the animals and vegetation of the Savannah. If you burn the grass, you will not only kill the impala who feeds upon it, but the predator who feeds upon the impala, and the ticks and flies who live upon the predator, and the vultures and maribou storks who feed upon his remains when he dies. You cannot destroy the part without destroying the whole."

I paused to let them consider what I had said, and then continued speaking: "Kirinyaga is like the savannah. If we do not leave the old and feeble out for the hyenas, the hyenas will starve. If the hyenas starve, the grass eaters will become so numerous that there is no land left for our cattle and goats to graze. If the old and feeble do not die when Ngai decrees it, then soon we will not have enough food to go around."

I picked up a stick and balanced it precariously on my forefinger.

"This stick," I said, "is the Kikuyu people, and my finger is Kirinyaga. They are in perfect balance." I stared at the neighboring chief. "But what will happen if I alter the balance and put my finger *here*?" I asked, gesturing to the end of the stick.

"The stick will fall to the ground."

"And here?" I asked, pointing to a spot an inch away from the center.

"It will fall."

"Thus is it with us," I explained. "Whether we yield on one point or all points, the result will be the same: the Kikuyu will fall as surely as the stick will fall. Have we learned nothing from our past? We *must* adhere to our traditions; they are all that we have!"

"But Maintenance will not allow us to do so!" protested Koinnage.

"They are not warriors, but civilized men," I said, allowing a touch of contempt to creep into my voice. "Their chiefs and their *mundumugus* will not send them to Kirinyaga with guns and spears. They will issue warnings and findings and declarations, and finally, when that fails, they will go to the Eutopian Court and plead their case, and the trial will be postponed many times and reheard many more times." I could see them finally relaxing, and I smiled confidently at them. "Each of you will have died from the burden of your years before Maintenance does anything other than talk. I am your *mundumugu*; I have lived among civilized men, and I tell you that this is the truth."

The neighboring chief stood up and faced me. "I will send for you when the twins are born," he pledged.

"I will come," I promised him.

We spoke further, and then the meeting ended and the old men began wandering off to their *bomas*, while I looked to the future, which I could see more clearly than Koinnage or the elders.

I walked through the village until I found the bold young Ndemi, brandishing his spear and hurling it at a buffalo he had constructed out of dried grasses.

"*Jambo*, Koriba!" he greeted me.

"*Jambo*, my brave young warrior," I replied.

"I have been practicing, as you ordered."

"I thought you wanted to hunt the gazelle," I noted.

"Gazelles are for children," he answered. "I will slay *mbogo*, the buffalo."

"*Mbogo* may feel differently about it," I said.

"So much the better," he said confidently. "I have no wish to kill an animal as it runs away from me."

"And when will you go out to slay the fierce *mbogo*?"

He shrugged. "When I am more accurate." He smiled up at me. "Perhaps tomorrow."

I stared at him thoughtfully for a moment, and then spoke: "Tomorrow is a long time away. We have business tonight."

"What business?" he asked.

"You must find ten friends, none of them yet of circumcision age, and tell them to come to the pond within the forest to the south. They must come after the sun has set, and you must tell them that Koriba the *mundumugu* commands that they tell no one, not even their parents, that they are coming." I paused. "Do you understand, Ndemi?"

"I understand."

"Then go," I said. "Take my message to them."

He retrieved his spear from the straw buffalo and set off at a trot, young and tall and strong and fearless.

You are the future, I thought, as I watched him run toward the village. *Not Koinnage, not myself, not even the young bridegroom Njogu, for their time will have come and gone before the battle is joined. It is you, Ndemi, upon whom Kirinyaga must depend if it is to survive.*

Once before, the Kikuyu had to fight for their freedom. Under the leadership of Jomo Kenyatta, whose name has been forgotten by most of your parents, we took the terrible oath of Mau Mau, and we maimed and we killed and we committed such atrocities that finally we achieved Uhuru, for against such butchery civilized men have no defense but to depart.

And tonight, young Ndemi, while your parents are asleep, you and your companions will meet me deep in the woods, and you in your turn and they in theirs will learn one last tradition of the Kikuyu, for I will invoke not only the strength of Ngai but also the indomitable spirit of Jomo Kenyatta. I will administer a hideous oath and force you to do unspeakable things to prove your fealty, and I will teach each of you, in turn, how to administer the oath to those who come after you.

There is a season for all things: for birth, for growth, for death. There is unquestionably a season for Utopia, but it will have to wait.

For the season of Uhuru is upon us.

Geoff Ryman

Dead Space for the Unexpected
(1994)

Canadian-born Geoff Ryman (b. 1951) currently lives in England and teaches at the University of Manchester. Ryman published his first sf short story in 1976, and while his output has been relatively slow, the quality of his writing more than makes up for quantity. *The Unconquered Country* (1984) won both the British Science Fiction Association Award and the World Fantasy Award, and *The Child Garden* (1989) won the Arthur C. Clarke Award and the John W. Campbell Memorial Award. More recently, his critically acclaimed novel *Air* won the British Science Fiction Award, the Arthur C. Clarke Award, and the James Tiptree, Jr. Award. Ryman's short fiction has been nominated for several Nebulas and appears regularly in annual best-of collections.

Ryman's work is socially conscious, reflecting a liberal, humanistic viewpoint often expressed through the exploration of near-future dystopias. "Dead Space for the Unexpected" is one of his shorter and more straightforward stories, but the length and focus lend themselves to a heightened, realistic intensity. The ruthlessly competitive world of corporate ladder-climbing portrayed in this story is so close to reality that, apart from a few technological innovations, it is scarcely sf. Like any good satire, it is not so much a warning about the future as a critique of the present.

Jonathan was going to have to fire Simon. It was a big moment in Jonathan's day, a solid achievement from the point of view of the company. Jonathan knew that his handling of the whole procedure had been model — so far. He had warned Simon a month ago that termination was a possibility and that plans should be made. Jonathan knew that he had felt all the appropriate feelings — sympathy, regret, and an echoing in himself of the sick, sad panic of redundancy.

Well, if you have sincere emotion, hang onto it. Use it. Hell, there even been a sting of tears around the bottom of his eyes as he told Simon. Jonathan's score for that session had been 9.839 out of 10, a personal best for a counselling episode.

Now he had to be even better. The entire Team's average had nosedived. So had Jonathan's own scores. He, the Team, needed a good score. Next month's printouts were at stake.

So Jonathan waited in the meeting room with a sign up on the door that said IN USE. On his eyes were contact lenses that were marked for accurate measurement, and which flickered and swerved as his eyes moved. There was a bright pattern of stripes and squares and circles on his shirt, to highlight breathing patterns. Galvanic skin resistance was monitored by his watch strap. It was, of course, a voluntary program, designed to give managers and staff alike feedback on their performance.

There was a knock on the door and Simon came in, handsome, neat, running a bit to fat, 52 years old.

It would be the benches for Simon, the park benches in summer with the civic chess board with the missing pieces. Then the leaves and seasonal chill in autumn. Winter would be the packed and steamy public library with the unwashed bodies, and the waiting for a chance to read the job ads, check the terminals, scan the benefits information. It would be bye-bye to clean shirts, ties without food stains, a desk, the odd bottle of wine, pride. For just a moment, Jonathan saw it all clearly in his mind.

Either you were a performer or you weren't.

"Hi, Simon, have a good weekend?"

"Yes, thank you," said Simon, as he sat down, his face impassive, his movements contained and neat.

Jonathan sighed. "I wanted to give you this now, before I sent it to anyone else. I wanted you to be the first to know I'm very sorry."

Jonathan held out a sealed, white, blank envelope. Simon, primed for a month, simply nodded.

"I hope you know there's nothing personal in this. I've tried to explain why it's necessary, but just to be clear, there has been a severe drop in our performance and we simply must up our averages, and be seen to be taking some positive action. In terms of more staff training, that sort of thing."

Already this was not going well. The opening line about the weekend could not be less appropriate, and nobody was going to think that being fired was a positive step or care two hoots about the training other people were going to get. Inwardly, Jonathan winced. "Anyway," he shrugged with regret, still holding out the envelope that Simon had not taken. Jonathan tossed it across the table and it spun on a cushion of air across the wood-patterned surface.

Simon made no move to pick it up. "We all get old," he said. "You will, too."

"And when my scores slip," said Jonathan, trying to generate some fellow feeling, "I expect the same thing will happen to me."

"I hope so," said Simon.

Right, counselling mode. Jonathan remembered his training. Unfortunately, so did Simon — they had been on the same courses.

"Are you angry, would you like to talk?" said Jonathan, remembering: keep steady eye contact, or rather contact with the forehead or bridge of the nose, which is less threatening. Lean backwards so less aggression, but echo body language.

Simon smiled slightly and started to pick his nose, very messily, and look at the result. He held the result up towards Jonathan as if to say echo this.

Jonathan nodded as if in agreement. "It's only natural that you should feel some resentment, but it might be more constructive if you expressed it verbally. You know, say what you feel, blow off some steam. If not to me, then to someone, the Welfare Officer perhaps."

"I don't need to blow off steam," said Simon and stood up and walked to the door.

Procedures were not being followed; discipline was important.

"Simon, you haven't taken your letter."

Simon stood at the door for a moment. "It's not my letter. It's not written for me, it's addressed to Personnel so they can stop paying me."

Boy, thought Jonathan, if you were still being marked, you'd be in trouble, buddy.

"You forget," said Simon his blue eyes gray and flinty, "I used to work in Accounts." He picked up the letter, paused, and wiped his finger on it. Then he left the room.

Jonathan sat at the table, trembling with rage. Fuck counselling, he wanted to haul off and slug the guy. He took a deep breath, just like in the handling stress course, then stood up and left the meeting room, remembering to change the sign on the door. VACANT it said.

Back in his own office, he checked his score. It was bad form to check your scores too often; it showed insecurity, but Jonathan couldn't help himself. He verballed to the computer.

"Performance feedback, Dayplan Item One."

His mark was higher than he had thought it would be: 7.2, well over a five and edging towards a 7.5 for a pretty tough situation. But it was not the high score the Team needed.

It was 8:42. Three minutes ahead of schedule.

"Dayplan complete," he verballed, and his day was laid out before him on the screen.

```
8:30    Simon Hasley (actioned)
8:45    Dayplan confirmed and in tray
8:50    Sally meeting prep
9:00    Sally meeting
9:30    Sales meeting William
10:00   Dead space for the unexpected . . .
```

It was important that work was seen to be prioritized, that nothing stayed on the desk, or queued up on the machine. It all had to be handled in the right order. The computer worked that out for you from the priority rating you gave each item, gave you optimum work times and the corporate cost, and if you did not object, those were your targets for the first half of the day.

Right. In-tray. There was a management report on purchasing. Jonathan did not purchase, but he needed to know the new procedures his Finance Officer was supposed to follow. So make that a priority eight, book in a reading for it next week, and ask for the machine to prepare a precis. Next was a memo with spreadsheet from Admin. Admin acted as a kind of prophylactic against Accounts, giving early warning of what would strike

Accounts as below par performance. Jonathan's heart sank. Late invoices. Holy shit, not again, an average of 12 days?

Thanks a lot, George, thanks a fucking lot. Shit, piss, fuck, I'll cut off that god-damned asshole's head and stick it up his own greased asshole.

Ho-boy, Jonathan, that's anger. Channel it, use it. Right, we got ourselves a priority one here, schedule it in Dead Space. Jonathan slammed his way into George's network terminal. Which at 8:47 in the morning was not switched on.

PRIORITY 1
George, we have a serious issue to discuss. Can you come to my office at 10:00 am today, Thursday 17th. Please come with figures on speed of invoicing.
J Rosson, III 723, nc 11723JR.

There goes our cash flow down the fucking tube. And interest payments to the Center. Great.

There was a fretful knocking at his door. Jonathan could guess who it was. Two minutes was all the time he had.

In came Harriet, gray hair flying. What you might call an individual. Jonathan swivelled, knowing his body language showed no surprise or alarm. His greeting was warm, friendly, in control. So far, so good.

"Hello, Harriet, good to see you, but I'm afraid I'm up against it this morning. I expect you've heard about Simon."

"Yes, I have actually," said Harriet, eyes bright, smile wide. She was preparing to sit down.

No, my door is not always open. Don't mess with my time management, lady. "I'd love to talk to you about it when I can give you some time. How about 10:10 this morning?"

"This will only take a minute." Harriet was still smiling. A tough old bird.

"I doubt that very much. It's an important issue, and I'd like to talk to you about it properly." With a flourish, he keyed her into his Dayplan. "There we go. 10:10. See you then?"

Harriet accepted defeat with good grace. "Lovely," she said. "I'll look forward to that." She even gave him a sweet little wave as she left.

Poor old cow is scared, thought Jonathan. Well, there are no plans to get rid of her, so that should be a fairly easy session.

Next. Up came a report on a new initiative in timekeeping, a hobby horse of Jonathan's. Was a priority one justified just because he was interested in it? He decided to downgrade it, show he was keeping a sense of proportion, that he was a team player. He gave it a two and booked it in for Friday.

He was behind schedule. Thanks, Harriet. Next was a note of praise for a job well done from that crawler Jason. The guy even writes memos to apologize for not writing memos. Jonathan wastebinned it with a grin. Next was a welfare report on the Team's resident schizophrenic. Jonathan was sure the poor guy had been hired just to give them a bit of an obstacle to show jump. The Welfare Officer was asking him to counsel the man to reduce his smoking in the office. But. He was to remember that the stress of giving up smoking could trigger another schizophrenic episode.

Oh come on, this really must be a monitoring exercise. Jonathan thought a moment. He should therefore show that he knew it was an exercise and not take it too seriously. So, he delegated. He dumped the whole report off his own screen and into the Dayplan of his Supporting Officer.

And so, 8:55. Five minutes to prep for Sally. Jeez, thought Jonathan. I hope I'm not showing. Not showing fear. Which meant, of course, that he was.

Simply, Sally was one of the big boys. She was the same grade as Jonathan, a 1.1 on a level D, but she was younger, whiplash quick, utterly charming, and she always won. Jonathan knew her scores were infinitely better than his own.

Sally had been naughty. Her Division and his Team had to cooperate on projects that were both above and below the line. Without telling him, she had called a meeting on his own grade 2s, flattered them no end, and then got the poor lambs to agree, just as a point of procedure, that all joint projects would be registered with her Division. This would cost his Team about three hundred thousand a year in turnover.

Jonathan had countered with a report on procedures, reminding all concerned that such decisions needed to be made at Divisional level, and suggesting a more thorough procedural review. Sally had countered with enthusiastic agreement, deadly, but said a joint presentation on procedures might eliminate misunderstanding. The difference between discussion and presentation was the difference between procedures up for grabs, and procedures already set and agreed.

When Jonathan pointed this out at a Divisional Liaison, Sally had said "Awwww!" as if he were a hurt, suspicious child. She had even started to counsel him — in front of management! Jonathan had never felt so angry, so outmaneuvered. Now his Team had noticed pieces of artwork they should have controlled going elsewhere and wanted him to do something about it. Too late, guys. Bloody Harry, his boss, was too dim to see what had happened, or too feeble to fight. Harry had agreed to the presentation.

So, he told himself. The posture has to be teamwork, cooperation between different parts of the same organization, steer like hell to get back what he could. And keep smiling.

He put his phone and mail through to Support and went downstairs.

Sally's office was neater than his own, and had tiny white furniture. It was like sitting on porcelain teacups. He was sure she chose the furniture deliberately to make large men feel clumsy. Sally offered him coffee. Christ, what was his caffeine count already? Too many stimulants, you lost points. Was she trying to jangle him, get him shaky?

"Oh, great, thanks," he said. "White with one sugar."

"Help yourself," she said. Her smile was warm and friendly. What she meant was: help yourself, I'm not your mother.

"Real cream," acknowledged Jonathan as he poured.

"Nothing but the best is good enough for us," said Sally. She was luxuriantly made up, frosted with sheen. She sat down opposite him. Her hair was in different streaks of honey, beige and blonde, and she was slim under her sharp and padded suit. Her entire mien was sociable and open, inviting trust.

"Thanks for the report," she said. "It was very useful, and I really want to thank you for organizing the presentation for us."

Jonathan had fought it every step of the way. "My pleasure," he said. "We really need to get the two teams together to talk. I just want to be clear that what we're aiming to do is work towards a set of procedures for shared work, which keeps everything going to the right people."

Sally nodded. But she didn't speak.

Jonathan double-checked. "Am I right?"

Her smile broadened just a stretch. "Uh-huh. We do have a set of procedures that your own staff agreed on."

"Not all my staff, and not the Quality Action Units who should have been involved. The idea is to empower everyone in the organization."

"Well, I'm sure we can iron out any points of difference. Refer them to the Quasi. OK?"

Jonathan played back the same trick, an uncommitted shrug. But it was one up to him.

A peace offering? Sally kept on. "I also thought that we should present to you first. Most of my staff are familiar with what you do, but our CD ROM work is new, and we need to go over it with your team."

Can I let her get away with that? The clock was ticking, his heart was racing. Caffeine and three hundred thousand smackers. Basically, her staff would NOT be there, say just three of them. They would have the floor and the agenda, but his people would outnumber them, and it would be very easy to take pot shots from the audience. On balance, yes, he could go along with that.

So he agreed. They set dates and agreed how to split the cost of wine and food. Sally gave him a warm and enveloping smile as he left.

Climbing back up the stairs, he reckoned he had scored a five. She still had the initiative, she'd gone no distance towards giving up registration of his jobs, but then, it could be argued that Harry had given them away. I got some points across, but anyone could see I was tense. Jeez. Why do I do it to myself?

Right, now it was Billy, then Dead Space, then the brief on the Commission tender, then lunch.

Lunch with Harry, his boss. Harry was shy and hated schmoozing, which was endearing in a boss, if only he didn't wring his hands for hours at a time and utterly fail to make decisions. Jonathan braced himself for an hour of whining. Jonathan used to work out at lunchtime, till he realized that he scored a full .03 higher if he social-grazed instead. He was climbing the stairs now, to keep fit, though he was not too sure if anyone was noticing. For some reason, he was feeling mean when William arrived for the Sales Meeting.

"Template?" Jonathan snapped at him. William's eyes glittered. Look at those lenses dive for cover. William was in his early twenties, uncomely, gay, nervous. He was supposed to have the agreed agenda and a place for agreed action notes. "Ah. It's just here." When William found his sheet, the agenda section was left blank.

Jonathan tapped the white space, and chuckled, and shook his head, like an indulgent father. "Billy, Billy, what am I going to do with you? Couldn't you remember to print it out? Here, use mine and photocopy it to me after the meeting. Did we get the form letters out?"

Billy had. Well, what do you know?

"All sixty? Great. Thanks very much. Now. The new fax number. We sent all our customers the new fax number, right? Fine. Then why did the Commission fax us a copy of a tender brief on the old number?"

Billy's face fell.

"They sent us a tender, Billy, and it went to our old number, which is with Interactive Media now, who are not necessarily our greatest chums, where it sat for a full afternoon. So now we have four days instead of a working week to develop a full tender with designs. Do you see the problem here?"

Billy's face went white and distressed.

The real problem, Jonathan cursed to himself, is that management expects me to make sales without any funding, so I have to use poor Billy from Support who is as sweet as a lamb, but Jeez! Jonathan watched as William scrambled through his shaggy files. OK.

Jonathan decided to try a new management technique. He tried to make himself fancy Billy sexually. LLA, Low Level Attraction, could generate good Team bonding. In fact, people with low to middle bisexuality scores had a favoured Starting-Gun Profile.

So Jonathan looked at Billy and tried, but Billy had chalk white skin and lank black hair, and spots, the thick, clotted, dumb kind of spot that never comes to a head.

I hate this guy, this puny, nervy little idiot; I just can't resist trying to break him.

"Um," said Billy, miserable, balancing his spread-eagled file on his lap. "Yeah, well, I, uh, didn't fax the Commission because it was among my problems to be resolved."

"You mean you didn't know the Commission was one of your clients?" Jonathan managed to say it more in sorrow than in anger.

"I think it was that I didn't know who were our contact names there."

Neither, now that he thought about it, did Jonathan. "OK," he sighed. "Look. Talk to Clara, she'll know them, and then just send the notification you've got. Don't apologize or let them know that we didn't tell them in time. If they ask, the number has just changed. I don't want them to know we had this little hiccup. OK?"

"OK," Billy murmured.

"And, Billy, please. Don't try to keep all your correspondence in one file? You'll find it easier if you keep things separate."

Billy thanked him for the advice. Then he suggested that Jonathan might like to come around to his place for drinks.

I don't believe this. This kid was making a pass at him, he was so desperate. OK, we're both playing the same LLA game. How can we both win? Don't be judgmental, turn the attraction, if that was what you could call it, into friendliness, team bonding.

"That's a great idea, Billy. But I've been feeling bad about not inviting you to my place. I think you've met my wife, but you've never even seen my daughter. Are you free next week?"

Billy looked relieved. Jonathan was relieved too, and thanked him for the job he was doing, and in the general thanking and summing up the invitations were forgotten.

Billy left and Jonathan sat back and sighed. He was feeling tired a lot these days. He saw Sally's face, pink glossy lips parted, as she gave a tiny cry. He sat still for a moment, his eyes closed.

It was 9:57. Jonathan couldn't help himself. He checked his scores again. He really must stop doing this. It was like when he got hooked on the I Ching, and had to have Chaos Therapy to kick it. But all he wanted was a breakdown, a fuller breakdown of this morning's score with Simon.

Verbal content 4.79.

OK, I knew I was bad, but that bad?

Body Language 4.5.

What? Oh, come on. What was I supposed to do, pick my nose? Jonathan actioned a more in-depth analysis. Artificiality, his machine told him, a lack of visible sincerity.

Christ! You can't move around this place. If I'd been sincere, I would have said, you fucked up that own-account job 18 months ago, and you've been a liability ever since and you've done nothing any better, so we're ditching you like we should have done even earlier. I was just trying to be fucking kind. What should I have done, told him to fuck off?

So what got me my good score? This breakdown is terrible.

10:00 Dead Space.

And the computer flipped itself out into a proactive intervention.

Suddenly, it started to play him the tape of the morning's session with Simon.

There he was, fat, stone-faced, saying, "It's not written for me. It's written for Personnel."

A full analysis scrolled up on the screen. Flesh tones, oxygen use, body language, uncharacteristic verbals, atypical eye use.

Behavior typical of industrial sabotage. Rage mixed with satisfaction.

In other words, Simon had become dangerous. Not a little bit dangerous, very dangerous. Determined, apparently, to get revenge.

In-house sabotage is one of the greatest problems now facing both manufacturing and service industries.

Yeah, yeah, yeah, I've been on the course. Jonathan glanced up at the door to make sure it was closed. He could verbal and no one would hear. George was supposed to be seeing him, but George, thank heaven, was late as usual.

"First." Jonathan asked the computer. "Why didn't you warn me before?"

Programmed to hold all proactive interventions until Dead Space

"Alright, reprogram. If you get a priority like this again, you are to intervene immediately. Please confirm."

Confirmed

"What are the possible actions taken by Simon Hasley?"

Action taken

"Fine. What is it?"

There was no response at all. It was almost as though the machine had crashed, right in the middle of proactive intervention. It simply went back to what it had been doing before.

The machine had been analyzing Jonathan's performance.

This time he noticed the total score in the upper right hand corner. His total score was 5.2. It had been 7.2. If Jonathan knew anything, he knew his own scores.

Simon was changing them.

"CV, please, full CV on Simon Hasley."

Not available.
File cancelled due to termination of employment

"Simon Hasley is here until 31st August. His files are not cancelled."

Not available.
File cancelled due to termination of employment

"Then open the ex-employee file."

??????????????????

"Action. Restore scores for Dayplan Item One to 7.2."

ACTION NOT AUTHORIZED.

Jonathan slammed the top of his desk.

George walked in. To talk about late invoicing. And the bloody machine flipped back to its proactive intervention.

"It's not my letter," Simon was saying. Jeez, how embarrassing, right in front of other staff.

"Stop intervention," Jonathan ordered. "Sit down, George."

Then Jonathan remembered. What had Simon said? Something about Accounts, that he'd worked in Accounts. Accounts with their big system who did all the monitoring. The really big boys. Simon would have swept up after them, wiped their asses, what does he know about the system?

George was talking to him, and Jonathan realized he had not heard a word. He was losing this, he was not handling it.

". . . it's the same story. We have to wait for extra-contractuals before we know what the job costs, and so we can't bill." George was smiling his noncommissioned, sleeves-up, man-on-the-shop-floor smile.

"That's not what the people upstairs think."

"Well, with the best will in the world, they're not down here doing the work are they?"

"They don't have to. George, I'm sorry to pull the rug from under you, but I want to change the agenda for this meeting."

George sucked his teeth, scoring points, tut, bad meeting management.

"You know I would never do this normally, but I've just had an intervention on Simon as you came in. How is he taking it?"

The shop-floor smile was still there. "Like a prince. He's calm, in fact, you could say he looks quite happy about it, like he has a card up his sleeve. You give him a good severance deal or something?"

"We can't afford severance deals. This is in confidence. Simon is changing people's performance scores. He's got access to Accounts somehow. The machine can't change them back."

"You're joking," said George, his pink face going slack. Then he began to chuckle. "No wonder he looks so pleased. He's changing people's scores. Well, well, I didn't know he had it in him."

Managers must never lose their sense of humour. Jonathan managed to find an answering smile. "It's one way of getting your own back." There was sweat on his forehead.

"Changing yours, is he?" George's red moustache seemed to glow redder.

"Screwed both of us. You're in charge of monitoring." Jonathan's own smile was a bit harder. "So. How could he have done it? How can we stop him?"

"Beats me. Unless he got hold of the password when he was in Accounts."

"You mean the access code."

"No. This is different, it really lays open the whole network. I think only the Chairman has it, maybe Head of Accounts. You get hold of that you can change any information you like and then ice it, so it can never be changed. Change it invisibly I mean."

"Great for when the Auditors call."

"I expect so."

"Can you change it on verbal? By mail?"

"By camel, I imagine. It's only a rumor but I've heard a few funny things."

"From Simon?"

George grinned back at him.

And then in waltzed Harriet. It was 10:10 after all, and here he was, still in his previous meeting, so his time management score would be fucked, and Harriet would know that, and wouldn't she just love that?

Harriet loved something. She had gone doo-lally with pleasure. She started to do a dance around Jonathan's desk. "Ring around the rosy, a pocketful of posy, husha, husha, they all fall down." Harriet roared her hearty, Hooray Henry laugh that Jonathan had not heard in so long. "Did you know that that is a song about the plague?"

"Someone's caught a cold," said George and his and Harriet's eyes seemed to harpoon each other, and both of them grinned.

Bad behavior from staff depressed their own scores, but insubordination knocked the stuffing out of their manager's profile. They knew it. They were enjoying this.

I am fed up with this crap, I am fed up trying to keep people happy. I am not responsible for keeping people happy.

"Harriet. The stress has gotten to you," Jonathan said. "Come back when you're more in control."

"When you are more in control, you mean." Harriet was beaming, and about to chuckle again. "Come on, George, let's leave him to it."

"George. Please. We're not finished. We still have to talk about invoicing."

"Oh Jesus," and both he and Harriet cracked up.

"I want a breakdown of every invoice on this printout and why it's late. Friday will do. And please remember that you are responsible for ensuring we hold to financial targets. If you don't, you aren't meeting the minimum requirements of your job. I'll give you a box four marking. And if it doesn't improve, I'll write one of those hilarious little warning letters. Oh, and Harriet, your anti-blood pressure medicine. I know about it. It does have strange side effects, doesn't it. I can recommend Medical Leave. I will be recommending a check-up."

In other words, baby, you may just have lost your job. Harriet's smile slipped.

He verballed it. "Action. Store session. Copy. H. Pednorowska's behavior to the Medical Department."

All this counselling shit to one side, the thing he knew he was really good at was being a bit of a bastard.

"Harriet. George. Thanks for coming to see me. Harriet, I'm sorry you're unwell. George, I'm sure you'll be able to cope with your invoicing problem. Please ask Simon to come in and see me."

Their smiles had not quite faded.

"Meeting over, Team."

Gloves off. Simon had slow reaction times. He needed time to think about things. Well, he had had a whole month to work through this, thanks to Jonathan being so nice. It had probably taken him all month, but he had done it. And he's got me by the balls. He can change my scores, and leave no trace, unless the Chairman is prepared to admit the existence of the password. The computer's got me and George on record and knows our suspicions but that's not proof. I have to wrong foot him. I could say that he'd been monitored telling Harriet what he'd done. But what if he hadn't, or asked "How could they read the note, it was in code?" Jonathan would just have to wing it.

Simon came back in. He looked as calm and unperturbed as this morning.

"An impressive display, Simon."

Simon was saying nothing.

"It wasn't age, you idiot," said Jonathan. "It wasn't slowed-down reaction times. Don't you know when you're being let off? They knew, Simon! That's why you were fired. You didn't think you could use the Chairman's password without all the right protocols did you? They were letting you go without any noise. Then you had to go and tamper with my scores this morning, you stupid, dumb, poor, idiot little lamb, and I don't know if I can stop it this time, Simon. I think they're going to send you to jail."

Simon sat unmoving, in silence. But silence was not a denial, or shocked surprise. Would that be enough?

"I mean, as if I didn't signal it, as if I didn't near as dammit tell you, in those private little sessions, you've got a month, keep your nose clean. I don't want to see you go to jail!"

Jonathan raised his hands and let them fall. "I really thought you were smarter than that."

Simon had not moved, not an involuntary flicker of the eyeballs, not a heave of the prison-patterned shirt. Except, he was weeping. He sat very still and a thick, heavy tear that seemed to be made of glucose crept down his cheek.

"They always have one up on you, don't they?" he said.

In the corner of Jonathan's screen, a tiny white square was flashing on and off, in complete silence. A security alert.

"You work your butt off, they keep you dancing for twenty years, and they make a fortune out of you."

This was going to be very sweet indeed, thought Jonathan. Talk about two birds with one stone. Fancy Accounts letting something like the password out. They'd all be for the high jump. Bloody Accounts, who were always breathing down Jonathan's neck about invoices, or performance scores or project costs or unit cost reduction. They would all have their necks wrung like chickens. What a wonderful world this could be.

"It was a dumb thing to do," Simon admitted, laying each word with a kind of finality, like bricks.

"Well. I reckon you'll have revenge. At least on Accounts," said Jonathan.

The door burst open, and Custody came in like it was a drug bust and they were Supercops. In their dumb blue little uniforms.

"What the fuck kept you?" Jonathan demanded.

"By the way, Simon," he added. "We didn't know for sure, until a second ago. Thanks."

Simon didn't move a muscle. When Jonathan checked later, he found he'd scored a ten. Hot damn, it felt good to be so creative.

He got home after fitting in his evening workout. Got up to one hundred on the bench press. Shows what a little adrenaline could do. He got home, to the ethnic wallpaper and the books and the CDs, and he knew he was not a bad man. Life was tough, but that was business. Home was different.

His wife was a painter, and she wore a smock covered in fresh pistachio, magenta, cobalt. He had to lean forward to kiss her lest the smock print paint on his suit. "We should hang that coat of yours in a gallery," he said. It would be nice to live like this too, in a quiet home, but then someone had to bring home the bacon.

"Daddy, Daddy," called Christine from the bedroom. She wouldn't go to sleep until she had seen him, no matter how long she had to wait, and she was not even his child. He went to her room and sat on the bed and kissed her. She smelled of orange juice and children's shampoo. "Play a game with me," she said, and out came the little screen. Mickey had to shoot the basketball through the hoop to escape the aliens. The score was on the screen. "Daddy, I got an eight!" she cried. He chuckled, but a part of his mind said in a slow, dark voice: get them young.

That night he dreamed he had old hands, and they mumbled through job ads. He couldn't feel anything with them. His fingers were dead.

Nalo Hopkinson

Something to Hitch Meat To
(2001)

Nalo Hopkinson (b. 1960) belongs to the latest generation of writers to extend the boundaries of sf, both in terms of style and subject matter. Her work crosses genre boundaries by combining elements of fantasy and horror with science fiction, and she often draws on Caribbean folklore, a welcome infusion of fresh cultural materials in a genre dominated by European traditions. Hopkinson did not begin publishing professionally until 1997, but she quickly rose to prominence. After the publication of her debut novel, *Brown Girl in the Ring*, in 1998, she won both the Locus Award for Best First Novel and the John W. Campbell Award for Best New Author, and various works have been nominated for the Hugo, Nebula, Philip K. Dick, and James Tiptree Jr. awards. The collection *Skin Folk*, from which "Something to Hitch Meat To" is taken, won the World Fantasy Award in 2002. Hopkinson has also edited several important anthologies, including *So Long Been Dreaming: Postcolonial Science Fiction and Fantasy.*

Hopkinson has an avowed interest in hybrid forms with mixed origins, whether in terms of genre or thematically and linguistically. Her work ranges freely over the speculative fiction spectrum, bringing together realism and the fantastic, technology and the supernatural, and tradition and innovation, in ways that always seem fresh and surprising. She writes in conscious dialogue with various traditions, experimenting with new fusions and intersections, whether by reworking traditional materials from fairy tales and literary classics or by importing traditional folklore into modern urban settings. Many of her stories weave together Caribbean creole and standard English in a style she refers to as *code sliding*. And of course the Caribbean materials she draws on are themselves a rich amalgam of European and African traditions.

In keeping with her interest in hybrids and the ways intermingling can result in new and sometimes surprising forms, many of Hopkinson's stories focus on transformations that are both disturbing and liberating. A superb stylist, she draws much of her power from the contrast between the delicacy and control of her writing and the rawness of her materials. Her stories are humorous and startling, peopled by emotionally complex and vividly portrayed characters.

"Something to Hitch Meat To" is one such story of transformation. It is a story about the gap between superficial appearance and reality and the way we allow false perceptions to shape the reality of what we see. From the beginning of the story, we see the protagonist as a man whose identity is misjudged by onlookers, and his job involves the digital manipulation of images that are inauthentic in more ways than one. Through the mysterious intervention of an African trickster deity, he discovers a way of revealing the truth beneath the deception of artificial surfaces. "Something to Hitch Meat To" is not a utopian story in the sense of imagining an ideal society but rather a parable about discovering the tools to transform the world we live in. Rather than focusing on the external conditions and structures that might lead to utopia, Hopkinson works from the belief that utopia is already potentially present if we can only shift our gaze and harness the transformative potential of perception.

Artho picked up a bone lying in the street. No reason, just one of those irrational things you do when your brain is busy with something else, like whether you remembered to buy avocados or not. The alligator-tail chain of a day care snaked past him, each toddler hanging on dutifully to one of the knots in the rope by which they were being led. One of the young, gum-popping nannies said:

"So then little Zukie draws herself up real tall, and she says, 'No, silly. The purpose of the skeleton is something to hitch meat to.' Really! I swear, I nearly died laughing, she sounded so serious."

The woman eyed him as she walked past, smiled a little, glanced down. She played with her long hair and stage-whispered to her co-worker, "God, Latino men are just so hot, don't you think?" They giggled and moved on, trailing children.

The gears of Artho's brain kicked back into realtime. He was standing at the southwest corner of King and Bay, holding a chicken thighbone. Fleshless and parched, it felt dusty between his fingers. He dropped it and wiped his hand off on his jeans. Latino? What the hell?

Streetcar coming. Artho got on, elbowing himself some rush hour standing room between an old man with a bound live chicken that lay gasping in his market basket and three loud, hormonal young women, all politics and piercings. Artho reached for a steady strap. Traffic was grid-locked. He stared blankly out the window as the streetcar inched its way past a woman struggling with two huge dogs on leashes. Bergers des Pyrenées, they were; giant, woolly animals bred for rescuing skiers trapped under alpine avalanches. They were so furry that Artho could barely make out their legs. They lumbered along in a smooth, four-on-the-floor gait. The dogs' handler tugged futilely at their leashes, barely able to keep up. The beasts could probably cover miles in effortless minutes, snowshoeing on their woolly feet. Artho fancied that they would move even faster, smoother, if you changed them to have six legs, or eight. They would glide along like enormous tarantulas. Artho looked at their handler's legs and had the oddest feeling, like when an old film skips a frame, and for an instant, you can see the hole-punched edges of the film strip, black and chitinous on the screen, and then it jerks back into place, but now you're looking at a different scene than you were before. It was like that, Artho looking at this woman walking on ordinary woman legs, then reality skipped frames, and he was seeing instead a being whose natural four-legged stance had been twisted and warped so that all it could manage was this ungainly two-legged jerking from foot to foot. Made into something it wasn't.

Alarmed, Artho blinked. He made himself relax. Tired. Too many hours at work in front of a computer screen, staring at all that skin. He leaned his head against the streetcar window and dozed, thinking hungrily of the stewed chicken and rice he would have for dinner, with avocado — his dad always called them alligator pears — on the side. He could see the fleshy avocado in his mind's eye: slit free of its bumpy rind; pegged and sitting on a plate; beads of salt melting on the sweating, creamy skin. He imagined biting into a slice, his teeth meeting in its spineless centre. His mouth watered.

It wasn't until he reached his stop that he realized he really had forgotten to buy the damned avocados. He found some tired, wrinkly ones in the corner store near his apartment. The man behind the counter, who served Artho at least twice a week when he came in for cigarettes or munchies, grumbled at the fifty dollar bill that Artho gave him, and made a big show over holding it up to the light to see if it was counterfeit. Artho had seen the same man cheerfully make change from bills that large for old women or guys in suits. He handed Artho a couple of twenties and some coins, scowling. Artho held each twenty up to the light before putting it into his pocket. "Thank you," he said sweetly to the guy, who glared. Artho took his avocados and went home. When he sliced into them, one of them was hard and black inside. He threw it out.

"So," Artho's brother said, "I'm out with the guys the other night, and . . ."

"Huh? What'd you say?" Artho asked. Something was obscuring Aziman's voice on the phone, making rubbing and clicking sounds over and around his speech. "What's that noise?" Artho asked the receiver. "Like dice rolling together or something."

"One dice, two die. Or is it the other way around? Anyway, so I'm . . ."

"What're you eating? I can't make out what you're saying."

"Hold on." Silence. Then Aziman came on again. "This any better?"

"Yeah. What was that?"

"This hard candy the kids brought home. Got me hooked on it. These little round white thingies, y'know? I had a mouthful of them."

"Did you spit them out?"

"Well, not round exactly. Kinda egg-shaped, but squarer than that. Is 'squarer' a word?"

"Did you spit them out?" Artho was just being pissy, and he knew it. He could tell that Aziman had gotten rid of the candies somehow. His voice was coming through clearly now.

"Yeah, Artho. Can I tell my story now?"

"Where'd you spit them?"

"What's up with you today? Down the kitchen sink."

And Aziman started in with his story again, but Artho was distracted, thinking on the tiny white candies disappearing into the drain, perhaps washed down with water.

". . . so this man walks up to us, a kid really, y'know? Smart-ass yuppie cornfed kid with naturally blond hair and a polo shirt on. Probably an MBA. And he says to me, ''s up, man?' only he says it 'mon.' I mean, I guess he's decided I'm from Jamaica or something, you know?"

"Yeah," said Artho. "I know."

"He gives me this weird handshake; grabs my thumb and then makes a fist and I'm supposed to touch my fist to his, I think, I dunno if I did it right. But he says, ''s up' again, and I realize I didn't answer him, so I just say, 'Uh, nothing much,' which I guess isn't the lingo, right? But I dunno what I'm supposed to say; I mean, you and me, we're freaking north Toronto niggers, right? And this white guy's got Toronto suburbs written all over him, too. Probably never been any farther than Buffalo. So what's he trying to pull with that fake ghetto street shit anyway, you know? And he leans in close, kinda chummy like, and whispers, 'Think you could sell me some shit, man?' And I'm thinking, *Like the kind you're trying to sell me on right now?* I mean, he's asking me for dope, or something."

Artho laughed. "Yeah, happens to me, too. It's always the same lame-ass question, never changes. I just point out the meanest-looking, blackest motherfucker in the joint and say, 'Not me, man, but I bet that guy'll be able to help you out.' "

"Shit. I'll try that next time."

"Though I guess it isn't fair, you know, my doing that. It's like I'm picking on guys just 'cause they're blacker than me."

"Heh. I guess, if you want to look at things that way. You going to Mom's for Easter?"

"Is Aunt Dee going to be there?"

But Aziman's only reply was a rustling, shucking type of noise. Then, "Shit!"

"What?"

"I stuck my hand into the bag for more candy, y'know? Just figured out what these things are."

"What?"

"Skulls. Little sugar skulls, f'chrissake."

Dead people bits. That's what the candy was. It was all in the way you looked at it.

"No," said Artho. "It'll be just like last year. I'm not going to Mom's for Easter."

A few days later it happened again, a weird unfamiliarity when Artho looked at human bodies. He was in the mall food court on his lunch hour. When he went back to work, it would be to spend the rest of the day updating the Tit for Twat site: *Horny Vixens in Heat! No Holes Barred!*

The food court was crowded. People in business suits wolfed down Jolly Meals, barked on cell phones. The buzz of conversation was a formless noise, almost soothing.

Not many empty spaces. Artho had to share a table for two with a thirtyish man in fine beige wool, engrossed in the financial pages of the *Globe & Mail* newspaper. The man had shaved his head completely. Artho liked it. There was something sensuous about the baldness, like the domed heads of penises. Cute. Artho was thinking of something to say to him, some kind of opener, when the man's ears caught his gaze. They jutted out from the side of his head like knurls of deformed cartilage. There really was nothing odd about the guy's ears — that's just how ears were — but they still gave Artho a queasy feeling. With one hand, he worried at his own ear. He looked around at other people in the food court. All their ears seemed like twisted carbuncles of flesh sprouting from the sides of their heads, odd excrescenses. Nausea and doubt squirmed like larvae in Artho's chest. His fingers twitched, the ones that he would use a few minutes from now to point, click, and drag his mouse as he smoothed out the cellulite and firmed up the pecs of the perfect naked models on the screen, making them even more perfect. He closed his eyes to block out the sight of all those ugly ears.

Someone was singing. A child's voice, tuneless and repetitive, threaded its whiny way through the rumble of lunchtime chatter:

"Tain't no sin,
Take off your skin,
And dance around in your bones.
Tain't no sin . . ."[1]

Artho opened his eyes. Wriggly as only seven-year-olds can be, a little girl slouched beside her father at a table for four, sitting on her spine so she could kick at the center pole supporting the table welded to its four seats. Her wiry black hair was braided into thousands of dark medusa

1. "Tain't No Sin (To Dance Around in Your Bones)," words by Edgar Leslie, music by Walter Donaldson, 1929.

strands. The brown bumps of her knees were ashy with dry skin. The lumpy edge of a brightly colored Spider Man knapsack jutted out from behind her back.

"Tain't no sin . . ." She kicked and kicked at the pole. An old man who'd been forced to share the table with them looked up from his chow mein and gave her a strained nice-little-girl smile.

"Quit it, Nancy." Not even glancing at his daughter — was she his daughter? — her father reached out with one hand and stilled the thin, kicking legs. With his other hand he hurriedly stuffed a burger into his mouth. Green relish oozed between his fingers.

The little girl stopped kicking, but all that energy had to have some outlet. She immediately started swaying her upper body from side to side, jerking her knapsack about so that something thumped around inside it. She bobbed her head in time to her little song. Her braids flowed like cilia. She looked around her. Her gaze connected with Artho's. "Daddy," she said loudly to the man beside her, "can you see me?" She wore glasses with jam-jar-thick lenses, which refracted and multiplied her eyes. She didn't look up at her father.

And he didn't look down at her, just kept gnawing on his burger. "Can't see you at all, little girl," he mumbled. "I only think I can. You're nowhere to be seen."

She smiled at that. "I'm everywhere, though, Daddy."

Must be some kind of weird game they had between the two of them. Then she started singing again. Artho found himself swaying slightly from side to side in time with her song. He looked away. He'd always hated Spider Man. As a kid, the comic book character had frightened him. His costume made him look like a skeleton, a clattery skin-and-bone man that someone had painted red as blood.

" . . . dance around in your bones!" the little girl shouted, glaring at him from the depths of her specs.

Artho leapt to his feet and dumped the remainder of his lunch in the garbage, fled the girl's irritating ditty. His table partner still had his nose buried in his paper.

As Artho walked the last few feet to the elevator of his office building, he suddenly became aware of the movement of his legs: push off with left leg, bending toes for leverage; contract right knee to extend right leg, heel first; shift weight; step onto right foot; bend right knee; repeat on the other side. For a ludicrous moment, he nearly tripped over his own feet. It was like some kind of weird jig. He stumbled into the elevator, smiled I'm-fine-really at a plump young woman in a business suit who was gazing at him curiously. She looked away. Then he did. They stared politely at the opaque white numbers, knobbled as vertebrae, that indicated each floor. The numbers clicked over, lighting up one at a time: 10 . . . 11 . . . 12 . . . *Roll the bones*, thought Artho.

"Um . . . do you know what time it is?" the woman asked him.

He checked his watch, smiled at her. "Almost ten to one." The deep rust of the suit made her flawless cinnamon skin glow, hinted at the buxom swell of breast, belly, hip, and thigh. Yum. Artho's mouse fingers stopped twitching.

She smiled back nervously. The smile quirked friendly lines at the corners of her mouth. "Thanks. Guess I'm on time after all, then."

"Job interview?"

"Uh-huh. Marketing. Up at Joint Productions."

"The design place? Cool. They've done some great stuff."

She looked even more interested, leaned forward a little. "Oh, you work there?"

Shit. "Uh, no."

"In the building, then?"

"Yeah. Web design. For, um, Tri-Ex Media."

She frowned a little, took a bit of a step back. "Another design place?"

"Yeah, sort of. We . . ."

The elevator stopped and the door slid noiselessly open.

"Oh, my stop," she said. "Nice talking to you."

"Yeah. Bye." If she got the job, that'd be the last civil conversation he had with her. The people at Joint acted like Tri-Ex Media was the very source and center of evil in the universe. She'd probably get bitten by the same bug. Artho got out at 17.

Cold air prickled his forearms into goose bumps when he opened the door to Tri-Ex Media. The office was air-conditioned year-round to protect the expensive computer equipment. The not-so-pricey staff just wore sweaters. "Close the fucking door!" growled Charlie, his boss. Artho uncurled his spine to stand tall. He stitched a smile across his face and stepped inside, gently pulling the door shut behind him. "Miss me?" he cooed at Charlie.

People just look really weird, Artho thought. He contemplated the image up on his screen: a buff, tattooed man in a shoulder stand who'd curled himself tight as a fiddlehead fern so as to suck his own cock. Well, actually, he hadn't quite been able to reach it. His searching tongue was just a few inches away. Probably would have helped if he'd been interested enough in the procedure to have a hard-on. That was where Artho came in. He giggled, began the process of stiffening and elongating the man's dick. "Virtual fluffer, that's me," he said, aiming the comment at the general air.

Only Glenn looked up, scowling over the top of his terminal and flicking a lank lick of Popsicle pink hair out of his eyes. "Yeah? Just keep it in your pants, Mouse Boy." He grinned a little to take the sting of the comment out.

That uncomfortable little grin. Taboo subject at work, sex. Staring all day at pictures of spread, penetrated flesh — flesh more shapely than any of them in the office had: plump, perky breasts, impossibly slim waists; muscled thighs and ever-ready cocks — but talk about any of it?

"Hey, Artho?" Tamara called quietly from across the room.

"Yeah?" Today her thick wool sweater had a picture on it of that guy from the Fabulous Four comics, the one who turned into fire? *Flame on.* Johnny, his name was? Where in hell did Tamara find the stuff she wore?

Tamara pulled the sleeves of her sweater down over her hands, trapped them against her palm with three fingers on each hand, kept typing with the free forefingers and thumbs. "You doing anything for Easter?"

Easter again. Long-distance phone call from Vancouver Island from his father. "I long to see you and your brother," he'd say. But it never happened. And if Artho visited his mother with her stiff, dead, pressed hair and the pale pink lipstick blanching her full brown lips, she'd ask if he was still working at *that place* and whisper prayers under her breath when he said yes. Aunt Dee would be there too, with her look of fearful hunger and her Doberman's knack of going for the soft underbelly of all their relatives: *Uncle James starting to lose his hair; Cousin Melba have neither chick nor child to look after; and eh-eh, look at old Uncle Cecil, taking up with a twenty-year-old chick in his dotage.* Aziman would be sitting in the basement with the basketball game turned up loud. Holidays always made him morose about his own divorce. He'd get steadily drunker on Wincarnis Tonic Wine (sugar code 17) while his boy and girl screamed and romped and fought around him. "No," Artho told Tamara. "Gonna stay home, where it's quiet."

There. The autofellatio man looked like he was sucking his own dick now. It was moderately convincing. It'd do.

Easter meant that Aziman, after fueling himself with enough of the sugary wine, would flare, shouting insults at the players on the TV, yelling at his kids to quiet down, brown face flushing burgundy with the barely contained heat. Their mother would make him and the children spend the night at her place. "You can drive tomorrow, when you cool down," she'd say. Artho hoped that one day the fire inside Aziman would come busting out, fry away the polite surface he always presented.

How did that Johnny guy's flame really work? Artho wondered. Was he always flame on the inside?

On his screen, Artho checked out the autofellatio man's skin and hair; this one was going on the "Banjee Boys" page, whatever a banjee was, and Charlie thought a light brown black man just didn't fit the image. Good thing the position the man was in now obscured that aquiline nose, those thin lips. Smiling to himself, Artho painted another tattoo on the man's beefy shoulder; "nkyin kyin," the West African Adinkra symbol for "always changing oneself." He bet Charlie'd never recognize it in a million years.

Charlie came huffing by, glanced at the screen. "Artho, you still working on that fucking thing? Time is money here, y'know. I want Tit for Twat uploaded before you leave tonight. And no whining at me about overtime, either."

Artho sighed. "It'll be done before five." As if. But so long as it was up and running when Charlie came in on Monday, he'd never notice.

"Better be. And make that guy blacker. Looks like a dago." Charlie turned away. Stopped. Turned back and peered at the screen. Guffawed, "Jesus, Arth! He's darker than you! Well, whaddya know 'bout that? Betcha his dick's no match for yours, though. Eh? Eh?" Charlie cackled and elbowed Artho in the ribs, then shaking his head and chuckling at his own wit, stumped his way out of the office. He slammed the door behind him. Everyone jumped at the thump. People avoided Artho's eyes.

Artho sighed and got to work again with his mouse, sticking cocoa-colored pigment to the man like tar on the Tar Baby. He ignored the feeling of his ears burning. It went away eventually.

He finished blackening the man up, then opened up the working files Tit for Twat. He imported the new images, new inane text (*"When Daddy's not home, see these blond sisters work each other up!"*). The "blond" was bleach, the "sisters" Tania and Raven no relation at all, and they were doing their best straight guy's lesbian fantasy. As soon as they got out of the studio, they shucked the whole act like corn trash from corn and hugged each other good-bye before going their separate ways. Raven was a CGA student, blissfully married to a quiet, balding guy with a paunch, wore high-top sneakers everywhere, showed around pictures of her kids every chance she got. And Tania, as she walked out the door, would be peeling off her false two-inch nails, muttering that her girlfriends would never let her near them with knives on the tips of her fingers.

" . . . good weekend, Artho."

"Huh? Oh, yeah. Bye, Glenn," he said as Glenn let himself out.

Artho looked around for the first time in hours. It was well past five. He straightened up, groaning; he could feel each of his vertebrae popping as he uncurled from the computer screen. And he was freezing. Charlie was long gone. He and Tamara were the only ones left.

"Lost in the land of skin?" she chuckled at him.

"Yeah. Be done soon now, though." He set the files to render, moved to the next computer over — Rahim worked at that one, but he was gone too — and called up Tomb Raider. Artho'd gotten pretty good at the game. Masquerading as the impossibly firm-breasted Lara Croft, he hunted in a nightmare landscape of demons. He was just killing a ghoul in a spray of blood and bone when the door to the office whispered open. A tiny face poked round it.

"Hey, Artho?" Tamara said, waving sweater-covered fingers at him. "Relative of yours? This isn't exactly the place for a kid, you know."

It was the little girl, the one from the food court.

"What're you doing here?" Artho blurted out. "Where's your dad?"

"Daddy's always busy making stuff," came the scratchy response from the tiny face hanging in the doorway. "We do his work for him instead."

"Huh?" was all that Artho managed in response.

"Yeah. Each one of us has different jobs. Mine is that I get to go wherever I want, keep an eye on stuff." The little girl stalked on spindly legs into the room. Her knees were still ashy, the lenses of her specs still woozily thick. The wormy mass of her long, messy braids seemed to be wriggling out from their ribbons as Artho watched.

"That's ridiculous! It's" — Artho glanced at the clock on his screen — "almost seven-thirty in the evening! You can't be more than seven years old! Who're your parents? Why are you alone?"

"So you don't know her, then?" asked Tamara. She got up, went and knelt by the child. "What's your name, little girl?" she asked sweetly.

"Didn't come for you. Came for him." And the child stomped right past an astonished Tamara. "Whatcha doin?" On the screen, Lara Croft waited to be activated by a mouse click. "Oh," said the little girl. "Do you like that?"

Artho shrugged. "It's something to do."

She turned to the other screen with its bodies frozen in mid-writhe.

"Don't look at those!" Artho said.

"Just skins sewed together," she replied, grinning. "Do you like those, then?"

"Artho, do you know this kid or not?"

Artho found himself answering the child instead of Tamara: "No, I don't like them so much. I like people to look more real."

"Well, why do you make them look not real, then?"

From the mouths of babes and sucklings. "That's why they pay me the big bucks," he said ruefully, thinking of how far his paycheck wouldn't stretch this month.

"Do you like people making *you* be not real?"

Artho thought how he'd been late for work that morning because six taxis in a row had refused to stop for him. Thought of the guy in the corner store inspecting his money. Of Charlie elbowing him in the ribs a few hours ago. He felt a burn of rage beginning. "No, dammit!"

The ugly child just stood and stared at him from the depths of her ugly glasses.

"But it's not like I can do anything about it!" Artho said.

"Do you wanna?" She was shrugging out of her Spider Man knapsack.

He turned so he could scowl at her face straight on. "Shit, girl, what d'you think? Yes!"

Tamara giggled. Fuck, why was he talking to a kid this way? He started slamming pens and pencils around on the desk.

"Well, change things, then!" the child squealed. She lunged at Artho and swung her Spider Man knapsack right at his forehead.

It was like slo-mo; Artho could see the oddly muscular bulge of her lats powering the swing, almost had time to wonder how a seven-year-old could be that built, then he had barely focused on the red and black image of Spidey coming for him, reaching for him, when *bang*, the knapsack connected and something exploded inside Artho's skull.

Tamara yelled. Artho shouted, tried to reach for the kid through the stars flaring behind his eyes. Jesus, felt like a bag of bones the damned child had in there. "Shit, shit, shit," Artho moaned, holding his aching head. He dimly saw the child slither out of Tamara's grasp and run, no, glide out of the room on those skin-and-boneless legs. She had a big butt, too, that child; as she ran, it worked under her little plaid skirt like that of someone three times her size.

"Artho, you okay? I'm calling security."

He paid Tamara no mind. He was dizzy. He put his head down between his knees. It was wet, his forehead was *wet* where he was holding it. He was bleeding! Damned girl. He took his hand away, raised his head enough to inspect it.

"Yeah, Muhammed? Can you come up to Tri-Ex Media on 17? We got a little girl loose on this floor. No, don't know where she came from. Look, she just *hit* Artho, okay? I think he's hurt. Yes, a kid did it, she's little, maybe six, seven. Little black girl, school uniform, thick glasses. Says her parents aren't with her. Okay. Okay." She hung up. "He's coming."

There was no blood. At least, the stuff leaking out of him didn't look like blood. The liquid on his hand seemed to glow one minute and go milky the next, like a smear of syrup. "What is this shit?"

"Here, let me see." Tamara crouched down by him like she had by the little girl Nancy. That's what her dad had called her. What kind of dad let his young kid roam around loose like that?

Tamara frowned. "Yeah, you're cut, but there's this weird . . . stuff coming out. Oh. Never mind, it's stopped now. How d'you feel, Artho?"

"What the hell was in that knapsack? Where'd she go?"

"I'll go see." Tamara jumped up, left the office.

Artho's head was clearing. It didn't hurt so much now. He touched where the cut was, couldn't feel one. The goop was still on his fingers, though. He rubbed the fingers together to smear the stuff away. His fingers kind of tingled.

But really, he felt a lot better now. He chuckled a little, thinking of the comic books he'd read as a kid. He'd been bitten by an overactive spider.

His computer pinged to tell him that it was done rendering. Shit. Had to get that stuff done tonight, or Charlie'd have his head. He moved back to his terminal to upload Tit for Twat. He reached for the mouse. He clicked on it, and the click felt like it traveled all the way through his arm. No, like it had come *from* his arm, down through his hand, to the mouse. Weird.

Tamara came back. "Found a little girl with her dad in the elevator. Could have been her. Looked a little bit like her, I guess. I mean, I can't tell, you know, they all look . . . I mean . . ." She stopped, blushing.

They all look alike. The superintendent of Artho's apartment building always mixed him up with Patrice who lived on the 27th floor, never mind that Patrice was dark café cru to Artho's caramel, was balding, had arms like thighs, and spoke with a strong French accent. Tamara had always been nice to Artho, though. And she knew what a bonehead she'd just been, he could tell. Right? Right. He swallowed, didn't say anything. Let Tamara believe he hadn't guessed what she'd almost said.

"Anyway," Tamara continued, "she's gone now. Muhammed's gone back to his desk. You feeling any better?"

"Yeah, thanks."

"Well." She stood there, still looking sheepish and uncomfortable. "Um, I'm going home now."

"See ya." He watched her put on her coat. He waved good-bye to her. Then he uploaded the site, ignoring the odd clicking feeling in his mouse arm. God, it made him feel clumsy. He'd have to get that checked out.

Probably some kind of overuse thing. He clicked the file closed. Behind it was the autofellatio man. Hadn't he uploaded that one too? He went to do it, but the hand with the mouse slipped, and he ended up instead selecting the "changing oneself always" symbol he'd put on the man's arm as a joke. Yeah, better take that off. Just in case Charlie did figure out he'd done it. Didn't want to get his ass in trouble. He dragged the nkyin kyin symbol off the guy's arm, and what the fuck, it came all the way *off* the screen, skidded right across the keyboard, and came to rest on his thigh. Alarmed, he released the mouse. The symbol melted through the cloth into the meat of his leg. "Shit!" It tingled for a second, then faded.

Ah, fuck. Bloody weird day. He reached for the mouse again. When he clicked on it this time, something subtle changed about the autofellatio man. Artho stared hard at the image on the screen to try to see what was different. Yes, the nkyin kyin was back on the man's shoulder. And he was a little pudgier. And were those crow's-feet around his eyes? A hint of a smile around his wide-stretched mouth?

Whatever. Artho shrugged and uploaded the damned thing, ignoring the weird feeling in his arm every time he clicked the mouse.

Enough. Time to go home. Artho grabbed his coat, locked up, and left.

By the time the elevator had made it to the first floor, Artho was feeling really odd. Not sick, really, just faintly unreal, like when he smoked a joint too fast, or took sinus meds. He sighed, hoping he wasn't going to spend the weekend with the flu. At least it'd give him an excuse to skip going to his mum's. He put his hand on the door of the building to let himself out. *Click.* When he took the hand away, the nkyin kyin symbol was on it. He peered at the handle. Had it always been ornate worked brass? In the form of some kind of bug? No, now it looked like . . . a skeleton? Artho touched the handle again, double-clicked. And the handle was a plain aluminum strip once more.

Artho's skin began to prickle. Not with fear, not with fever. With hope. He rushed outside the building, put his palm against its dull brick exterior. Clicked. The walls flushed red, then purple. Fluted columns started to sprout beside the doors, which were quickly changing from sliding glass and steel to intricately joined oak. With big knockers. Artho giggled. Pretty damned tarty. He wondered if that had been the builder's original dream for the building. He double-clicked. The building reverted to its usual form.

"You're getting it."

When he turned towards the voice, Artho wasn't at all surprised to see the little girl. She was crouched down beside the steps, jam-jar glasses winking at him. Her hair knotted and unknotted itself.

"Can I change everything?" Artho asked.

"Course not, silly! Changing things isn't *your* job. You're not changing things; that'll happen anyway. You're just helping them peel off the fake skins."

"How's that work?"

"You'll just have to try it and see." She stuck her tongue out at him too. It was too pointy, and more lavender than pink. She leapt, stuck to the side of the building, started climbing smoothly up it, with two legs, with four. No wonder her behind had looked so, well, well-endowed. Must have had the other pair of legs hitched up under her skirt. The little girl was far above Artho now. He could just make out white panties with her legs sticking out of four leg holes. She climbed with two arms, with four. Ah. That well-muscled back. Artho smiled. He watched her until she disappeared into the darkness. He'd figured out who, what she was. Appeared as a skeleton sometimes, in a top hat. Watcher at the boundaries, at the crossroads. Sometimes man, sometimes woman. Always trickster. He couldn't really tell in the dark, but she seemed furrier now, or more bristly, or something. Sometimes spider? He wondered if this was the kind of thing her dad had really meant her to do.

Ah, well; she was notoriously capricious. She might decide to take her gift away again, so he'd better use it while he could. He set off for the streetcar stop, almost bouncing, dancing along in his excitement, thinking where he'd like to implant the Adinkra symbol next. On Charlie? Maybe Charlie really was the way he appeared to be. Oog. His Aunt Dee? What would Dee be like if she could peel away all that unhappiness?

How about on Aziman? All these choices. "Good evening," Artho said to the tired people waiting at the stop. One white woman clutched her purse tighter when she saw him. Hmm. Maybe he should work that nkyin kyin thing on himself; it was in him, after all. He wondered what she would see then.

Critical Contexts for Utopias and Dystopias

Hannah Arendt

Ideology and Terror: A Novel Form of Government

(1951)

Political theorist Hannah Arendt (1906–1975) was born in Germany and completed her doctoral thesis in philosophy at Heidelberg University. As a Jew and a vocal opponent of Nazism, however, she was forced to flee to France when Hitler came to power in 1933. In Paris, she worked on behalf of Jewish refugees for several years, before being forced to flee once again when Germany invaded. Arendt became a naturalized American citizen in 1950 and held positions at a series of prominent universities, including Princeton — where, in 1959, she became the first woman to be granted a full professorship —

before taking a permanent position at the New School for Social Research in New York City. Her works include *The Human Condition* (1958), a philosophical treatise, and *Eichmann in Jerusalem* (1963), a report on the war-crimes trial of Nazi leader Adolf Eichmann for his role in the Holocaust. It was in the latter work, which was originally written for the *New Yorker* magazine, that Arendt coined the memorable phrase "the banality of evil."

The *Origins of Totalitarianism*, from which this excerpt is taken, was Arendt's first major book, a groundbreaking study that quickly became a classic and continues to be influential today. *Totalitarianism* refers to a form of government in which the state controls all forms of human behavior. The term was popularized by Mussolini, dictator of Italy from 1922 to 1943, and is often used as a synonym for Fascism. Arendt, however, prefers a narrower definition, reserving the term for only the most extreme forms of state domination, specifically those practiced in Nazi Germany and Stalinist Russia. In Arendt's judgment, what distinguishes totalitarianism from other autocratic political systems is its radical commitment to deconstructing human nature. Through the use of terror, totalitarian regimes systematically dehumanize both victims and executioners and destroy all capacity for individual action.

This selection, taken from the closing chapter of the book, is particularly relevant for understanding Yevgeny Zamyatin's *We*, which was written in the historical context of Stalinism. But Arendt's ideas have broader implications as well — implications for any utopian project that seeks to radically transform human nature.

In the preceding chapters we emphasized repeatedly that the means of total domination are not only more drastic but that totalitarianism differs essentially from other forms of political oppression known to us such as despotism, tyranny and dictatorship. Wherever it rose to power, it developed entirely new political institutions and destroyed all social, legal, and political traditions of the country. No matter what the specifically national tradition or the particular spiritual source of its ideology, totalitarian government always transformed classes into masses, supplanted the party system, not by one-party dictatorships, but by a mass movement, shifted the center of power from the army to the police, and established a foreign policy openly directed toward world domination. Present totalitarian governments have developed from one-party systems; whenever these became truly totalitarian, they started to operate according to a system of values so radically different from all others, that none of our traditional legal, moral, or common sense utilitarian categories could any longer help us to come to terms with, or judge, or predict their course of action.

If it is true that the elements of totalitarianism can be found by retracing the history and analyzing the political implications of what we usually call the crisis of our century, then the conclusion is unavoidable that this crisis is no mere threat from the outside, no mere result of some aggressive foreign policy of either Germany or Russia, and that it will no more disappear with the death of Stalin than it disappeared with the fall of Nazi

Germany. It may even be that the true predicaments of our time will assume their authentic form — though not necessarily the cruelest — only when totalitarianism has become a thing of the past.

It is in the line of such reflections to raise the question whether totalitarian government, born of this crisis and at the same time its clearest and only unequivocal symptom, is merely a makeshift arrangement, which borrows its methods of intimidation, its means of organization and its instruments of violence from the well-known political arsenal of tyranny, despotism and dictatorships, and owes its existence only to the deplorable, but perhaps accidental failure of the traditional political forces — liberal or conservative, national or socialist, republican or monarchist, authoritarian or democratic. Or whether, on the contrary, there is such a thing as the *nature* of totalitarian government, whether it has its own essence and can be compared with and defined like other forms of government such as Western thought has known and recognized since the times of ancient philosophy. If this is true, then the entirely new and unprecedented forms of totalitarian organization and course of action must rest on one of the few basic experiences which men can have whenever they live together, and are concerned with public affairs. If there is a basic experience which finds its political expression in totalitarian domination, then, in view of the novelty of the totalitarian form of government, this must be an experience which, for whatever reason, has never before served as the foundation of a body politic and whose general mood — although it may be familiar in every other respect — never before has pervaded, and directed the handling of, public affairs.

If we consider this in terms of the history of ideas, it seems extremely unlikely. For the forms of government under which men live have been very few; they were discovered early, classified by the Greeks, and have proved extraordinarily long-lived. If we apply these findings, whose fundamental idea, despite many variations, did not change in the two and a half thousand years that separate Plato from Kant, we are tempted at once to interpret totalitarianism as some modern form of tyranny, that is a lawless government where power is wielded by one man. Arbitrary power, unrestricted by law, wielded in the interest of the ruler and hostile to the interests of the governed, on one hand, fear as the principle of action, namely fear of the people by the ruler and fear of the ruler by the people, on the other — these have been the hallmarks of tyranny throughout our tradition.

Instead of saying that totalitarian government is unprecedented, we could also say that it has exploded the very alternative on which all definitions of the essence of governments have been based in political philosophy, that is the alternative between lawful and lawless government, between arbitrary and legitimate power. That lawful government and legitimate power, on one side, lawlessness and arbitrary power on the other, belonged together and were inseparable has never been questioned. Yet, totalitarian rule confronts us with a totally different kind of government. It defies, it is true, all positive laws, even to the extreme of defying those which it has itself established (as in the case of the Soviet Constitution of 1936, to quote only the most outstanding example) or which it did not care to abolish (as in the case of the Weimar Constitution which the Nazi government never revoked). But it operates neither without guidance of law nor is it arbitrary, for it claims to obey strictly and unequivocally those laws of Nature or of History from which all positive laws always have been supposed to spring.

It is the monstrous, yet seemingly unanswerable claim of totalitarian rule that, far from being "lawless," it goes to the sources of authority from which positive laws received their ultimate legitimation, that far from being arbitrary it is more obedient to these suprahuman forces than any government ever was before, and that far from wielding its power in the interest of one man, it is quite prepared to sacrifice everybody's vital immediate interests to the execution of what it assumes to be the law of History or the law of Nature. Its defiance of positive laws claims to be a higher form of legitimacy which, since it is inspired by the sources themselves, can do away with petty legality. Totalitarian lawfulness pretends to have found a way to establish the rule of justice on earth — something which the legality of positive law admittedly could never attain. The discrepancy between legality and justice could never be bridged because the standards of right and wrong into which positive law translates its own source of authority — "natural law" governing the whole universe, or divine law revealed in human history, or customs and traditions expressing the law common to the sentiments of all men — are necessarily general and must be valid for a countless and unpredictable number of cases, so that each concrete individual case with its unrepeatable set of circumstances somehow escapes it.

Totalitarian lawfulness, defying legality and pretending to establish the direct reign of justice on earth, executes the law of History or of Nature without translating it into standards of right and wrong for individual behavior. It applies the law directly to mankind without bothering with the behavior of men. The law of Nature or the law of History, if properly executed, is expected to produce mankind as its end product; and this expectation lies behind the claim to global rule of all totalitarian governments. Totalitarian policy claims to transform the human species into an active unfailing carrier of a law to which human beings otherwise would only passively and reluctantly be subjected. If it is true that the link between totalitarian countries and the civilized world was broken through the monstrous crimes of totalitarian regimes, it is also true that this criminality was not due to simple aggressiveness, ruthlessness, warfare, and treachery, but to a conscious break of that *consensus iuris*,[1] which, according to Cicero, constitutes a "people," and which, as international law, in modern times has constituted the civilized world insofar as it remains the foundation-stone of international relations even under the conditions of war. Both moral judgment and legal punishment presuppose this basic consent; the criminal can be

---

1. Roman statesman Marcus Tullius Cicero argued that part of what makes a people into a State is *consensus iuris* — a shared agreement about law that binds them together as a political community. [Ed.]

judged justly only because he takes part in the *consensus iuris*, and even the revealed law of God can function among men only when they listen and consent to it.

At this point the fundamental difference between the totalitarian and all other concepts of law comes to light. Totalitarian policy does not replace one set of laws with another, does not establish its own *consensus iuris*, does not create, by one revolution, a new form of legality. Its defiance of all, even its own positive laws implies that it believes it can do without any *consensus iuris* whatever, and still not resign itself to the tyrannical state of lawlessness, arbitrariness and fear. It can do without the *consensus iuris* because it promises to release the fulfillment of law from all action and will of man; and it promises justice on earth because it claims to make mankind itself the embodiment of the law. . . .

In the interpretation of totalitarianism, all laws have become laws of movement. When the Nazis talked about the law of nature or when the Bolsheviks talk about the law of history, neither nature nor history is any longer the stabilizing source of authority for the actions of mortal men; they are movements in themselves. Underlying the Nazis' belief in race laws as the expression of the law of nature in man, is Darwin's idea of man as the product of a natural development which does not necessarily stop with the present species of human beings, just as under the Bolsheviks' belief in class-struggle as the expression of the law of history lies Marx's notion of society as the product of a gigantic historical movement which races according to its own law of motion to the end of historical times when it will abolish itself. . . .

The tremendous intellectual change which took place in the middle of the last century consisted in the refusal to view or accept anything "as it is" and in the consistent interpretation of everything as being only a stage of some further development. Whether the driving force of this development was called nature or history is relatively secondary. In these ideologies, the term "law" itself changed its meaning: from expressing the framework of stability within which human actions and motions can take place, it became the expression of the motion itself.

Totalitarian politics which proceeded to follow the recipes of ideologies has unmasked the true nature of these movements insofar as it clearly showed that there could be no end to this process. If it is the law of nature to eliminate everything that is harmful and unfit to live, it would mean the end of nature itself if new categories of the harmful and unfit-to-live could not be found; if it is the law of history that in a class struggle certain classes "wither away," it would mean the end of human history itself if rudimentary new classes did not form, so that they in turn could "wither away" under the hands of totalitarian rulers. In other words, the law of killing by which totalitarian movements seize and exercise power would remain a law of the movement even if they ever succeeded in making all of humanity subject to their rule.

By lawful government we understand a body politic in which positive laws are needed to translate and realize the immutable *ius naturale* or the eternal commandments of God into standards of right and wrong. Only in these standards, in the body of positive laws of each country, do the *ius naturale* or the Commandments of God achieve their political reality. In the body politic of totalitarian government, this place of positive laws is taken by total terror, which is designed to translate into reality the law of movement of history or nature. Just as positive laws, though they define transgressions, are independent of them — the absence of crimes in any society does not render laws superfluous but, on the contrary, signifies their most perfect rule — so terror in totalitarian government has ceased to be a mere means for the suppression of opposition, though it is also used for such purposes. Terror becomes total when it becomes independent of all opposition; it rules supreme when nobody any longer stands in its way. If lawfulness is the essence of non-tyrannical government and lawlessness is the essence of tyranny, then terror is the essence of totalitarian domination.

Terror is the realization of the law of movement; its chief aim is to make it possible for the force of nature or of history to race freely through mankind, unhindered by any spontaneous human action. As such, terror seeks to "stabilize" men in order to liberate the forces of nature or history. It is this movement which singles out the foes of mankind against whom terror is let loose, and no free action of either opposition or sympathy can be permitted to interfere with the elimination of the "objective enemy" of History or Nature, of the class or the race. Guilt and innocence become senseless notions; "guilty" is he who stands in the way of the natural or historical process which has passed judgment over "inferior races," over individuals "unfit to live," over "dying classes and decadent peoples." Terror executes these judgments, and before its court, all concerned are subjectively innocent: the murdered because they did nothing against the system, and the murderers because they do not really murder but execute a death sentence pronounced by some higher tribunal. The rulers themselves do not claim to be just or wise, but only to execute historical or natural laws; they do not apply laws, but execute a movement in accordance with its inherent law. Terror is lawfulness, if law is the law of the movement of some suprahuman force, Nature or History.

Terror as the execution of a law of movement whose ultimate goal is not the welfare of men or the interest of one man but the fabrication of mankind, eliminates individuals for the sake of the species, sacrifices the "parts" for the sake of the "whole." The suprahuman force of Nature or History has its own beginning and its own end, so that it can be hindered only by the new beginning and the individual end which the life of each man actually is.

Positive laws in constitutional government are designed to erect boundaries and establish channels of communication between men whose community is continually endangered by the new men born into it. With each new birth, a new beginning is born into the world, a new world has potentially come into being. The stability of the laws corresponds to the constant motion of all human affairs, a motion which can never end as long as men are born and die. The laws hedge in each new beginning and at the same time assure its freedom of movement, the potentiality of something entirely new and unpredictable; the boundaries of positive laws are for the political existence of man what memory is for his historical existence: they guarantee the pre-existence of a common world, the reality of some continuity which transcends the individual life span of each generation, absorbs all new origins and is nourished by them.

Total terror is so easily mistaken for a symptom of tyrannical government because totalitarian government in its initial stages must behave like a tyranny and raze the boundaries of man-made law. But total terror leaves no arbitrary lawlessness behind it and does not rage for the sake of some arbitrary will or for the sake of despotic power of one man against all, least of all for the sake of a war of all against all. It substitutes for the boundaries and channels of communication between individual men a band of iron which holds them so tightly together that it is as though their plurality had disappeared into One Man of gigantic dimensions. To abolish the fences of laws men — as tyranny does — means to take away man's liberties and destroy freedom as a living political reality; for the space between men as it is hedged in by laws, is the living space of freedom. Total terror uses this old instrument of tyranny but destroys at the same time also the lawless, fenceless wilderness of fear and suspicion which tyranny leaves behind. This desert, to be sure, is no longer a living space of freedom, but it still provides some room for the fear-guided movements and suspicion-ridden actions of its inhabitants.

By pressing men against each other, total terror destroys the space between them; compared to the condition within its iron band, even the desert of tyranny, insofar as it is still some kind of space, appears like a guarantee of freedom. Totalitarian government does not just curtail liberties or abolish essential freedoms; nor does it, at least to our limited knowledge, succeed in eradicating the love for freedom from the hearts of man. It destroys the one essential prerequisite of all freedom which is simply the capacity of motion which cannot exist without space.

Total terror, the essence of totalitarian government, exists neither for nor against men. It is supposed to provide the forces of nature or history with an incomparable instrument to accelerate their movement. This movement, proceeding according to its own law, cannot in the long run be hindered; eventually its force will always prove more powerful than the most powerful forces engendered by the actions and the will of men. But it can be slowed down and is slowed down almost inevitably by the freedom of man, which even totalitarian rulers cannot deny, for this freedom — irrelevant and arbitrary as they may deem it — is identical with the fact that men are being born and that therefore each of them *is* a new beginning, begins, in a sense, the world anew. From the totalitarian point of view, the fact that men are born and die can be only regarded as an annoying interference with higher forces. Terror, therefore, as the obedient servant of natural or historical movement has to eliminate from the process not only freedom in any specific sense, but the very source of freedom which is given with the fact of the birth of man and resides in his capacity to make a new beginning. In the iron band of terror, which destroys the plurality of men and makes out of many the One who unfailingly will act as though he himself were part of the course of history or nature, a device has been found not only to liberate the historical and natural forces, but to accelerate them to a speed they never would reach if left to themselves. Practically speaking, this means that terror executes on the spot the death sentences which Nature is supposed to have pronounced on races or individuals who are "unfit to live," or History on "dying classes," without waiting for the slower and less efficient processes of nature or history themselves. . . .

While under present conditions totalitarian domination still shares with other forms of government the need for a guide for the behavior of its citizens in public affairs, it does not need and could not even use a principle of action strictly speaking, since it will eliminate precisely the capacity of man to act. Under conditions of total terror not even fear can any longer serve as an advisor of how to behave, because terror chooses its victims without reference to individual actions or thoughts, exclusively in accordance with the objective necessity of the natural or historical process. Under totalitarian conditions, fear probably is more widespread than ever before; but fear has lost its practical usefulness when actions guided by it can no longer help to avoid the dangers man fears. The same is true for sympathy or support of the regime; for total terror not only selects its victims according to objective standards; it chooses its executioners with as complete a disregard as possible for the candidate's conviction and sympathies. The consistent elimination of conviction as a motive for action has become a matter of record since the great purges in Soviet Russia and the satellite countries. The aim of totalitarian education has never been to instill convictions but to destroy the capacity to form any. The introduction of purely objective criteria into the selective system of the SS troops was Himmler's great organizational invention; he selected the candidates from photographs according to purely racial criteria. Nature itself decided, not only who was to be eliminated, but also who was to be trained as an executioner.

No guiding principle of behavior, taken itself from the realm of human action, such as virtue, honor, fear, is necessary or can be useful to set into motion a body politic which no longer uses terror as a means of intimidation, but whose essence *is* terror. In its stead, it has introduced an entirely new principle into public affairs that dispenses with human will to action altogether and appeals to the craving need for some insight into the law of movement according to which the terror functions and upon which, therefore, all private destinies depend.

The inhabitants of a totalitarian country are thrown into and caught in the process of nature or history for the sake of accelerating its movement; as such, they can only be executioners or victims of its inherent law. The process may decide that those who today eliminate races and individuals or the members of dying classes and decadent peoples are tomorrow those who must be sacrificed. What totalitarian rule needs to guide the behavior of its subjects is a preparation to fit each of them equally well for the role of executioner and the role of victim. This two-sided preparation, the substitute for a principle of action, is the ideology.

Ideologies — isms which to the satisfaction of their adherents can explain everything and every occurrence by deducing it from a single premise — are a very recent phenomenon and, for many decades, played a negligible role in political life. Only with the wisdom of hindsight can we discover in them certain elements which have made them so disturbingly useful for totalitarian rule. Not before Hitler and Stalin were the great political potentialities of the ideologies discovered.

Ideologies are known for their scientific character: they combine the scientific approach with results of philosophical relevance and pretend to be scientific philosophy. The word "ideology" seems to imply that an idea can become the subject matter of a science just as animals are the subject matter of zoology, and that the suffix -logy in ideology, as in zoology, indicates nothing but the logoi, the scientific statements made on it. If this were true, an ideology would indeed be a pseudo-science and a pseudo-philosophy, transgressing at the same time the limitations of science and the limitations of philosophy. Deism, for example, would then be the ideology which treats the idea of God, with which philosophy is concerned, in the scientific manner of theology for which God is a revealed reality. (A theology which is not based on revelation as a given reality but treats God as an idea would be as mad as a zoology which is no longer sure of the physical, tangible existence of animals.) Yet we know that this is only part of the truth. Deism, though it denies divine revelation, does not simply make "scientific" statements on a God which is only an "idea," but uses the idea of God in order to explain the course of the world. The "ideas" of isms — race in racism, God in deism, etc. — never form the subject matter of the ideologies and the suffix -logy never indicates simply a body of "scientific" statements.

An ideology is quite literally what its name indicates: it is the logic of an idea. Its subject matter is history, to which the "idea" is applied; the result of this application is not a body of statements about something that is, but the unfolding of a process which is in constant change. The ideology treats the course of events as though it followed the same "law" as the logical exposition of its "idea." Ideologies pretend to know the mysteries of the whole historical process — the secrets of the past, the intricacies of the present, the uncertainties of the future — because of the logic inherent in their respective ideas.

Ideologies are never interested in the miracle of being. They are historical, concerned with becoming and perishing, with the rise and fall of cultures, even if they try to explain history by some "law of nature." The word "race" in racism does not signify any genuine curiosity about the human races as a field for scientific exploration, but is the "idea" by which the movement of history is explained as one consistent process. . . .

The device both totalitarian rulers used to transform their respective ideologies into weapons with which each of their subjects could force himself into step with the terror movement was deceptively simple and incon-spicuous: they took them dead seriously, took pride in the one in his supreme gift for "ice cold reasoning" (Hitler) and the other in the "mercilessness of his dialectics," and proceeded to drive ideological implications into extremes of logical consistency which, to the onlooker, looked preposter-ously "primitive" and absurd: a "dying class" consisted of people con-demned to death; races that are "unfit to live" were to be exterminated. Whoever agreed that there are such things as "dying classes" and did not draw the consequence of killing their members, or that the right to live had something to do with race and did not draw the consequence of killing "unfit races," was plainly either stupid or a coward. This stringent logicality as a guide to action permeates the whole structure of totalitarian move-ments and governments. It is exclusively the work of Hitler and Stalin who, although they did not add a single new thought to the ideas and propaganda slogans of their movements, for this reason alone must be considered ide-ologists of the greatest importance.

What distinguished these new totalitarian ideologists from their prede-cessors was that it was no longer primarily the "idea" of the ideology — the struggle of classes and the exploitation of the workers or the struggle of races and the care for Germanic peoples — which appealed to them, but the logical process which could be developed from it. According to Stalin, neither the idea nor the oratory but "the irresistible force of logic thoroughly overpowered [Lenin's] audience." The power, which Marx thought was born when the idea seized the masses, was discovered to reside, not in the idea itself, but in its logical process which "like a mighty tentacle seizes you on all sides as in a vise and from whose grip you are powerless to tear yourself away; you must either surrender or make up your mind to utter defeat."[2] Only when the realization of the ideological aims, the classless society or the master race, was at stake, could this force show itself. In the process of realization, the original substance upon which the ideologies based them-selves as long as they had to appeal to the masses — the exploitation of the workers or the national aspirations of Germany — is gradually lost, devoured as it were by the process itself: in perfect accordance with "ice cold reasoning" and the "irresistible force of logic," the workers lost under Bolshevik rule even those rights they had been granted under Tsarist oppression and the German people suffered a kind of warfare which did not pay the slightest regard to the minimum requirements for survival of the German nation. It is in the nature of ideological politics — and is not sim-ply a betrayal committed for the sake of self-interest or lust for power — that the real content of the ideology (the working class or the Germanic peo-ples), which originally had brought about the "idea" (the struggle of classes as the law of history or the struggle of races as the law of nature), is devoured by the logic with which the "idea" is carried out. . . .

---

2. Stalin's speech of January 28, 1924; quoted from Lenin, *Selected Works*, Vol. I, p. 33, Moscow, 1947. — It is interesting to note that Stalin's "logic" is among the few qualities that Khrushchev praises in his devastating speech at the Twentieth Party Congress.

The compulsion of total terror on one side, which, with its iron band, presses masses of isolated men together *and* supports them in a world which has become a wilderness for them, and the self-coercive force of logical deduction on the other, which prepares each individual in his lonely isolation against all others, correspond to each other and need each other in order to set the terror-ruled movement into motion and keep it moving. Just as terror, even in its pre-total, merely tyrannical form ruins all relationships between men, so the self-compulsion of ideological thinking ruins all relationships with reality. The preparation has succeeded when people have lost contact with their fellow men as well as the reality around them; for together with these contacts, men lose the capacity of both experience and thought. The ideal subject of totalitarian rule is not the convinced Nazi or the convinced Communist, but people for whom the distinction between fact and fiction (i.e., the reality of experience) and the distinction between true and false (i.e., the standards of thought) no longer exist.

The question we raised at the start of these considerations and to which we now return is what kind of basic experience in the living-together of men permeates a form of government whose essence is terror and whose principle of action is the logicality of ideological thinking. That such a combination was never used before in the varied forms of political domination is obvious. Still, the basic experience on which it rests must be human and known to men, insofar as even this most "original" of all political bodies has been devised by, and is somehow answering the needs of, men.

It has frequently been observed that terror can rule absolutely only over men who are isolated against each other and that, therefore, one of the primary concerns of all tyrannical government is to bring this isolation about. Isolation may be the beginning of terror; it certainly is its most fertile ground; it always is its result. This isolation is, as it were, pretotalitarian; its hallmark is impotence insofar as power always comes from men acting together, "acting in concert" (Burke); isolated men are powerless by definition.

Isolation and impotence, that is the fundamental inability to act at all, have always been characteristic of tyrannies. Political contacts between men are severed in tyrannical government and the human capacities for action and power are frustrated. But not all contacts between men are broken and not all human capacities destroyed. The whole sphere of private life with the capacities for experience, fabrication, and thought are left intact. We know that the iron band of total terror leaves no space for such private life and that the self-coercion of totalitarian logic destroys man's capacity for experience and thought just as certainly as his capacity for action.

What we call isolation in the political sphere, is called loneliness in the sphere of social intercourse. Isolation and loneliness are not the same. I can be isolated — that is in a situation in which I cannot act, because there is nobody who will act with me — without being lonely; and I can be lonely — that is in a situation in which I as a person feel myself deserted by all human companionship — without being isolated. Isolation is that impasse into which men are driven when the political sphere of their lives, where they act together in the pursuit of a common concern, is destroyed. Yet isolation, though destructive of power and the capacity for action, not only leaves intact but is required for all so-called productive activities of men. . . . In isolation, man remains in contact with the world as the human artifice; only when the most elementary form of human creativity, which is the capacity to add something of one's own to the common world, is destroyed, isolation becomes altogether unbearable. This can happen in a world whose chief values are dictated by labor, that is where all human activities have been transformed into laboring. Under such conditions, only the sheer effort of labor which is the effort to keep alive is left and the relationship with the world as a human artifice is broken. . . . Isolation then becomes loneliness. Tyranny based on isolation generally leaves the productive capacities of man intact; a tyranny over "laborers," however, as for instance the rule over slaves in antiquity, would automatically be a rule over lonely, not only isolated, men and tend to be totalitarian.

While isolation concerns only the political realm of life, loneliness concerns human life as a whole. Totalitarian government, like all tyrannies, certainly could not exist without destroying the public realm of life, that is, without destroying, by isolating men, their political capacities. But totalitarian domination as a form of government is new in that it is not content with this isolation and destroys private life as well. It bases itself on loneliness, on the experience of not belonging to the world at all, which is among the most radical and desperate experiences of man.

Loneliness, the common ground for terror, the essence of totalitarian government, and for ideology or logicality, the preparation of its executioners and victims, is closely connected with uprootedness and superfluousness which have been the curse of modern masses since the beginning of the industrial revolution and have become acute with the rise of imperialism at the end of the last century and the break-down of political institutions and social traditions in our own time. To be uprooted means to have no place in the world, recognized and guaranteed by others; to be superfluous means not to belong to the world at all. Uprootedness can be the preliminary condition for superfluousness, just as isolation can (but must not) be the preliminary condition for loneliness. Taken in itself, without consideration of its recent historical causes and its new role in politics, loneliness is at the same time contrary to the basic requirements of the human condition *and* one of the fundamental experiences of every human life. Even the experience of the materially and sensually given world depends upon my being in contact with other men, upon our *common* sense which regulates and controls all other senses and without which each of us would be enclosed in his own particularity of sense data which in themselves are unreliable and treacherous. Only because we have common sense, that is only because not one man, but men in the plural inhabit the earth can we trust our immediate sensual experience. Yet, we have only to remind ourselves that one day we shall have to leave this common world which will go on as before and for whose continuity we are superfluous in order to realize loneliness, the experience of being abandoned by everything and everybody.

Loneliness is not solitude. Solitude requires being alone, whereas loneliness shows itself most sharply in company with others. . . . In solitude, in other words, I am "by myself," together with my self, and therefore two-in-one, whereas in loneliness I am actually one, deserted by all others. All thinking, strictly speaking, is done in solitude and is a dialogue between me and myself; but this dialogue of the two-in-one does not lose contact with the world of my fellow-men because they are represented in the self with whom I lead the dialogue of thought. The problem of solitude is that this two-in-one needs the others in order to become one again: one unchangeable individual whose identity can never be mistaken for that of any other. For the confirmation of my identity I depend entirely upon other people; and it is the great saving grace of companionship for solitary men that it makes them "whole" again, saves them from the dialogue of thought in which one remains always equivocal, restores the identity which makes them speak with the single voice of one unexchangeable person.

Solitude can become loneliness; this happens when all by myself I am deserted by my own self. Solitary men have always been in danger of loneliness, when they can no longer find the redeeming grace of companionship to save them from duality and equivocality and doubt. Historically, it seems as though this danger became sufficiently great to be noticed by others and recorded by history only in the nineteenth century. . . .

What makes loneliness so unbearable is the loss of one's own self which can be realized in solitude, but confirmed in its identity only by the trusting and trustworthy company of my equals. In this situation, man loses trust in himself as the partner of his thoughts and that elementary confidence in the world which is necessary to make experiences at all. Self and world, capacity for thought and experience are lost at the same time. . . .

A lonely man, says, Luther, "always deduces one thing from the other and thinks everything to the worst."[3] The famous extremism of totalitarian movements, far from having anything to do with true radicalism, consists indeed in this "thinking everything to the worst," in this deducing process which always arrives at the worst possible conclusions.

What prepares men for totalitarian domination in the non-totalitarian world is the fact that loneliness, once a borderline experience usually suffered in certain marginal social conditions like old age, has become an everyday experience of the evergrowing masses of our century. The merciless process into which totalitarianism drives and organizes the masses looks like a suicidal escape from this reality. The "ice-cold reasoning" and

---

3. "*Ein solcher (sc. einsamer) Mensch folgert immer eins aus dem andern und denkt alles zum Argsten.*" In *Erbauliche Schriften*, "Warum die Einsamkeit zu fliehen?" [Martin Luther (1483–1546) was a German priest and theologian whose questioning of the Catholic Church sparked the Protestant Reformation. — Ed.]

the "mighty tentacle" of dialectics which "seizes you as in a vise" appears like a last support in a world where nobody is reliable and nothing can be relied upon. It is the inner coercion whose only content is the strict avoidance of contradictions that seems to confirm a man's identity outside all relationships with others. It fits him into the iron band of terror even when he is alone, and totalitarian domination tries never to leave him alone except in the extreme situation of solitary confinement. By destroying all space between men and pressing men against each other, even the productive potentialities of isolation are annihilated; by teaching and glorifying the logical reasoning of loneliness where man knows that he will be utterly lost if ever he lets go of the first premise from which the whole process is being started, even the slim chances that loneliness may be transformed into solitude and logic into thought are obliterated. If this practice is compared with that of tyranny, it seems as if a way had been found to set the desert itself in motion, to let loose a sand storm that could cover all parts of the inhabited earth.

The conditions under which we exist today in the field of politics are indeed threatened by these devastating sand storms. Their danger is not that they might establish a permanent world. Totalitarian domination, like tyranny, bears the germs of its own destruction. Just as fear and the impotence from which fear springs are antipolitical principles and throw men into a situation contrary to political action, so loneliness and the logical-ideological deducing the worst that comes from it represent an antisocial situation and harbor a principle destructive for all human living-together. Nevertheless, organized loneliness is considerably more dangerous than the unorganized impotence of all those who are ruled by the tyrannical and arbitrary will of a single man. Its danger is that it threatens to ravage the world as we know it — a world which everywhere seems to have come to an end — before a new beginning rising from this end has had time to assert itself.

Apart from such considerations — which as predictions are of little avail and less consolation — there remains the fact that the crisis of our time and its central experience have brought forth an entirely new form of government which as a potentiality and an ever-present danger is only too likely to stay with us from now on, just as other forms of government which came about at different historical moments and rested on different fundamental experiences have stayed with mankind regardless of temporary defeats — monarchies, and republics, tyrannies, dictatorships, and despotism.

But there remains also the truth that every end in history necessarily contains a new beginning; this beginning is the promise, the only "message" which the end can ever produce. Beginning, before it becomes a historical event, is the supreme capacity of man; politically, it is identical with man's freedom. *Initium ut esset homo creatus est* — "that a beginning be made man was created" said Augustine.[4] This beginning is guaranteed by each new birth; it is indeed every man.

---

4. *De Civitate Dei*, Book 12, chapter 20.

William H. Whyte Jr.

From The Organization Man

(1956)

William Hollingsworth ("Holly") Whyte (1917–1999) graduated from Princeton University and served in the Marines during World War II before joining the business magazine *Fortune* in 1946. Although best remembered for his controversial bestseller *The Organization Man*, Whyte was also an influential figure in the development of modern city planning. While working for the New York City Planning Commission in the 1970s, he applied the anthropological approach of firsthand observation to assess how people actually used public space, commencing a decades-long project on urban land use and social behavior. His complete findings were eventually published as *City: Rediscovering the Center* in 1988. Whyte was also a professor at Hunter College of the City University of New York.

The Organization Man, Whyte's landmark sociological study of American corporate life, was based on a series of interviews with chief executive officers that he undertook while working at *Fortune*. He wrote the book at a time when large corporations and other bureaucracies were just beginning to dominate American life, and the practice of business — particularly in the area of management — was coming to be viewed as a specialized science. Through an examination of corporate culture, Whyte argues that the dominant American ideology, the Protestant ethic (which emphasizes individual effort, hard work, and thrift as the keys to success) was being replaced by a new belief system he calls "the Social Ethic." The Social Ethic emphasized the group over the individual and enforced unquestioned loyalty and conformity in its employees, particularly the mid-level managers who were becoming an influential group in society.

Whyte's emphasis on lifelong allegiance to a group identity may seem dated today, when the corporate workforce is increasingly mobile and indeed expendable. But his observations on the professionalization of business — and on the coercive use of social sciences like psychology to ensure passive obedience — remain relevant.

Whyte's work provides a historical context for understanding the attitudes toward conformity displayed by sf authors like Damon Knight and Harlan Ellison, but it is equally applicable to more recent stories like Geoff Ryman's "Dead Space for the Unexpected." While Hannah Arendt's piece deals with fanatical utopian systems like that of the Soviet Union, Whyte sheds light on the subtler but more pervasive influence of modern capitalism.

Chapter 1: Introduction

This book is about the organization man. If the term is vague, it is because I can think of no other way to describe the people I am talking about. They are not the workers, nor are they the white-collar people in the usual, clerk sense of the word. These people only work for The Organization. The ones I am talking about *belong* to it as well. They are the ones of our middle class who have left home, spiritually as well as physically, to take the vows of organization life, and it is they who are the mind and soul of our great self-perpetuating institutions. Only a few are top managers or ever will be. In a system that makes such hazy terminology as "junior executive" psychologically necessary, they are of the staff as much as the line, and most are destined to live poised in a middle area that still awaits a satisfactory euphemism. But they are the dominant members of our society nonetheless. They have not joined together into a recognizable elite — our country does not stand still long enough for that — but it is from their ranks that are coming most of the first and second echelons of our leadership, and it is their values which will set the American temper.

The corporation man is the most conspicuous example, but he is only one, for the collectivization so visible in the corporation has affected almost every field of work. Blood brother to the business trainee off to join Du Pont is the seminary student who will end up in the church hierarchy, the doctor headed for the corporate clinic, the physics Ph.D. in a government laboratory, the intellectual on the foundation-sponsored team project, the engineering graduate in the huge drafting room at Lockheed, the young apprentice in a Wall Street law factory.

They are all, as they so often put it, in the same boat. Listen to them talk to each other over the front lawns of their suburbia and you cannot help but be struck by how well they grasp the common denominators which bind them. Whatever the differences in their organization ties, it is the common problems of collective work that dominate their attentions, and when the Du Pont man talks to the research chemist or the chemist to the army man, it is these problems that are uppermost. The word *collective* most of them can't bring themselves to use — except to describe foreign countries or organizations they don't work for — but they are keenly aware of how much more deeply beholden they are to organization than were their elders. They are wry about it, to be sure; they talk of the "treadmill," the "rat race," of the inability to control one's direction. But they have no great sense of plight; between themselves and organization they believe they see an ultimate harmony and, more than most elders recognize, they are building an ideology that will vouchsafe this trust.

It is the growth of this ideology, and its practical effects, that is the thread I wish to follow in this book. America has paid much attention to the economic and political consequences of big organization — the concentration of power in large corporations, for example, the political power of the civil-service bureaucracies, the possible emergence of a managerial hierarchy that might dominate the rest of us. These are proper concerns, but no less important is the personal impact that organization life has had on the individuals within it. A collision has been taking place — indeed, hundreds of thousands of them, and in the aggregate they have been producing what I believe is a major shift in American ideology.

Officially, we are a people who hold to the Protestant Ethic. Because of the denominational implications of the term many would deny its relevance to them, but let them eulogize the American Dream, however, and they virtually define the Protestant Ethic. Whatever the embroidery, there is almost always the thought that pursuit of individual salvation through hard work, thrift, and competitive struggle is the heart of the American achievement.

But the harsh facts of organization life simply do not jibe with these precepts. This conflict is certainly not a peculiarly American development. In their own countries such Europeans as Max Weber and [Emile] Durkheim many years ago foretold the change, and though Europeans now like to see their troubles as an American export, the problems they speak of stem from a bureaucratization of society that has affected every Western country.

It is in America, however, that the contrast between the old ethic and current reality has been most apparent — and most poignant. Of all peoples it is we who have led in the public worship of individualism. One hundred years ago [Alexis] De Tocqueville was noting that though our special genius — and failing — lay in co-operative action, we talked more than others of personal independence and freedom. We kept on, and as late as the twenties, when big organization was long since a fact, affirmed the old faith as if nothing had really changed at all.

Today many still try, and it is the members of the kind of organization most responsible for the change, the corporation, who try the hardest. It is the corporation man whose institutional ads protest so much that Americans speak up in town meeting, that Americans are the best inventors because Americans don't care that other people scoff, that Americans are the best soldiers because they have so much initiative and native ingenuity, that the boy selling papers on the street corner is the prototype of our business society. Collectivism? He abhors it, and when he makes his ritualistic attack on Welfare Statism, it is in terms of a Protestant Ethic undefiled by change — the sacredness of property, the enervating effect of security, the virtues of thrift, of hard work and independence. Thanks be, he says, that there are some people left — e.g., businessmen — to defend the American Dream.

He is not being hypocritical, only compulsive. He honestly wants to believe he follows the tenets he extols, and if he extols them so frequently it is, perhaps, to shut out a nagging suspicion that he, too, the last defender of the faith, is no longer pure. Only by using the language of individualism to describe the collective can he stave off the thought that he himself is in a collective as pervading as any ever dreamed of by the reformers, the intellectuals, and the utopian visionaries he so regularly warns against.

The older generation may still convince themselves; the younger generation does not. When a young man says that to make a living these days you must do what somebody else wants you to do, he states it not only as a fact of life that must be accepted but as an inherently good proposition. If the American Dream deprecates this for him, it is the American Dream that is going to have to give, whatever its more elderly guardians may think. People grow restive with a mythology that is too distant from the way things actually are and as more lives have been encompassed by the organization way of life, the pressures for an accompanying ideological shift have been mounting. The pressures of the group, the frustrations of individual creativity, the anonymity of achievement: are these defects to struggle against — or are they virtues in disguise? The organization man seeks a redefinition of his place on earth — a faith that will satisfy him that what he must endure has a deeper meaning than appears on the surface. He needs, in short, something that will do for him what the Protestant Ethic did once. And slowly, almost imperceptibly, a body of thought has been coalescing that does that.

I am going to call it a Social Ethic. With reason it could be called an organization ethic, or a bureaucratic ethic; more than anything else it rationalizes the organization's demands for fealty and gives those who offer it wholeheartedly a sense of dedication in doing so — *in extremis*, you might say, it converts what would seem in other times a bill of no rights into a restatement of individualism.

But there is a real moral imperative behind it, and whether one inclines to its beliefs or not he must acknowledge that this moral basis, not mere expediency, is the source of its power. Nor is it simply an opiate for those who must work in big organizations. The search for a secular faith that it represents can be found throughout our society — and among those who swear they would never set foot in a corporation or a government bureau. Though it has its greatest applicability to the organization man, its ideological underpinnings have been provided not by the organization man but by intellectuals he knows little of and toward whom, indeed, he tends to be rather suspicious.

Any groove of abstraction, [Alfred North] Whitehead, once remarked, is bound to be an inadequate way of describing reality, and so with the concept of the Social Ethic. It is an attempt to illustrate an underlying consistency in what in actuality is by no means an orderly system of thought. No one says, "I believe in the social ethic," and though many would subscribe wholeheartedly to the separate ideas that make it up, these ideas have yet to be put together in the final, harmonious synthesis. But the unity is there.

In looking at what might seem dissimilar aspects of organization society, it is this unity I wish to underscore. The "professionalization" of the manager, for example, and the drive for a more practical education are parts of the same phenomenon; just as the student now feels technique more vital than content, so the trainee believes managing an end in itself, an *expertise* relatively independent of the content of what is being managed. And the reasons are the same. So too in other sectors of our society; for all the differences in particulars, dominant is a growing accommodation to the needs of society — and a growing urge to justify it. . . .

. . .

It is possible that I am attaching too much weight to what, after all, is something of a mythology. Those more sanguine than I have argued that this faith is betrayed by reality in some key respects and that because it cannot long hide from organization man that life is still essentially competitive the faith must fall of its own weight. They also maintain that the Social Ethic is only one trend in a society which is a prolific breeder of counter-trends. The farther the pendulum swings, they believe, the more it must eventually swing back.

I am not persuaded. We are indeed a flexible people, but society is not a clock and to stake so much on counter-trends is to put a rather heavy burden on providence. Let me get ahead of my story a bit with two examples of trend vs. counter-trend. One is the long-term swing to the highly vocational business-administration courses. Each year for seven years I have collected all the speeches by businessmen, educators, and others on the subject, and invariably each year the gist of them is that this particular pendulum has swung much too far and that there will shortly be a reversal. Similarly sanguine, many academic people have been announcing that they discern the beginnings of a popular swing back to the humanities. Another index is the growth of personality testing. Regularly year after year many social scientists have assured me that this bowdlerization of psychology is a contemporary aberration soon to be laughed out of court.

Meanwhile, the organization world grinds on. Each year the number of business-administration majors has increased over the last year — until, in 1954, they together made up the largest single field of undergraduate instruction outside of the field of education itself. Personality testing? Again, each year the number of people subjected to it has grown, and the criticism has served mainly to make organizations more adept in sugarcoating their purpose. No one can say whether these trends will continue to outpace the counter-trends, but neither can we trust that an equilibrium-minded providence will see to it that excesses will cancel each other out. Counter-trends there are. There always have been, and in the sweep of ideas ineffectual many have proved to be.

It is also true that the Social Ethic is something of a mythology, and there is a great difference between mythology and practice. An individualism as stringent, as selfish as that often preached in the name of the Protestant Ethic would never have been tolerated, and in reality our predecessors co-operated with one another far more skillfully than nineteenth-century oratory would suggest. Something of the obverse is true of the Social Ethic; so complete a denial of individual will won't work either, and even the most willing believers in the group harbor some secret misgivings, some latent antagonism toward the pressures they seek to deify.

But the Social Ethic is no less powerful for that, and though it can never produce the peace of mind it seems to offer, it will help shape the nature of the quest in the years to come. The old dogma of individualism betrayed reality too, yet few would argue, I dare say, that it was not an immensely powerful influence in the time of its dominance. So I argue of the Social Ethic; call it mythology, if you will, but it is becoming the dominant one. . . .

. . .

While the burden of this book is reportorial, I take a position and, in fairness to the reader, I would like to make plain the assumptions on which I base it. To that end, let me first say what I am *not* talking about.

This book is not a plea for nonconformity. Such pleas have an occasional therapeutic value, but as an abstraction, nonconformity is an empty goal, and rebellion against prevailing opinion merely because it is prevailing should no more be praised than acquiescence to it. Indeed, it is often a mask for cowardice, and few are more pathetic than those who flaunt outer differences to expiate their inner surrender.

I am not, accordingly, addressing myself to the surface uniformities of U.S. life. There will be no strictures in this book against "Mass Man" — a person the author has never met — nor will there be any strictures against ranch wagons, or television sets, or gray flannel suits. They are irrelevant to the main problem, and, furthermore, there's no harm in them. I would not wish to go to the other extreme and suggest that these uniformities per se are good, but the spectacle of people following current custom for lack of will or imagination to do anything else is hardly a new failing, and I am not convinced that there has been any significant change in this respect except in the nature of the things we conform to. Unless one believes poverty ennobling, it is difficult to see the three-button suit as more of a strait jacket than overalls, or the ranch-type house than old law tenements.

And how important, really, are these uniformities to the central issue of individualism? We must not let the outward forms deceive us. If individualism involves following one's destiny as one's own conscience directs, it must for most of us be a realizable destiny, and a sensible awareness of the rules of the game can be a condition of individualism as well as a constraint upon it. The man who drives a Buick Special and lives in a ranch-type house just like hundreds of other ranch-type houses can assert himself as effectively and courageously against his particular society as the bohemian against his particular society. He usually does not, it is true, but if he does, the surface uniformities can serve quite well as protective coloration. The organization people who are best able to control their environment rather than be controlled by it are well aware that they are not too easily distinguishable from the others in the outward obeisances paid to the good opinions of others. And that is one of the reasons they do control. They disarm society.

I do not equate the Social Ethic with conformity, nor do I believe those who urge it wish it to be, for most of them believe deeply that their work will help, rather than harm, the individual. I think their ideas are out of joint with the needs of the times they invoke, but it is their ideas, and not their good will, I wish to question. As for the lackeys of organization and the charlatans, they are not worth talking about.

Neither do I intend this book as a censure of the fact of organization society. We have quite enough problems today without muddying the issue with misplaced nostalgia, and in contrasting the old ideology with the new I mean no contrast of paradise with paradise lost, an idyllic eighteenth century with a dehumanized twentieth. Whether or not our own era is worse than former ones in the climate of freedom is a matter that can be left to later historians, but for the purposes of this book I write with the optimistic premise that individualism is as possible in our times as in others.

I speak of individualism *within* organization life. This is not the only kind, and someday it may be that the mystics and philosophers more distant from it may prove the crucial figures. But they are affected too by the center of society, and they can be of no help unless they grasp the nature of the main stream. Intellectual scoldings based on an impossibly lofty ideal may be of some service in upbraiding organization man with his failures, but they can give him no guidance. The organization man may agree that industrialism has destroyed the moral fabric of society and that we need to return to the agrarian virtues, or that business needs to be broken up into a series of smaller organizations, or that it's government that needs to be broken up, and so on. But he will go his way with his own dilemmas left untouched.

I am going to argue that he should fight the organization. But not self-destructively. He may tell the boss to go to hell, but he is going to have another boss, and, unlike the heroes of popular fiction, he cannot find surcease by leaving the arena to be a husbandman. If he chafes at the pressures of his particular organization, either he must succumb, resist them, try to change them, or move to yet another organization.

Every decision he faces on the problem of the individual versus authority is something of a dilemma. It is not a case of whether he should fight against black tyranny or blaze a new trail against patent stupidity. That would be easy — intellectually, at least. The real issue is far more subtle. For it is not the evils of organization life that puzzle him, *but its very beneficence*. He is imprisoned in brotherhood. Because his area of maneuver seems so small and because the trapping so mundane, his fight lacks the heroic cast, but it is for all this as tough a fight as ever his predecessors had to fight.

Thus to my thesis. I believe the emphasis of the Social Ethic is wrong for him. People do have to work with others, yes; the well-functioning team is a whole greater than the sum of its parts, yes — all this is indeed true. But is it the truth that now needs belaboring? Precisely because it *is* an age of organization, it is the other side of the coin that needs emphasis. We do need to know how to co-operate with The Organization but, more than ever, so do we need to know how to resist it. Out of context this would be an irresponsible statement. Time and place are critical, and history has taught us that a philosophical individualism can venerate conflict too much and co-operation too little. But what is the context today? The tide has swung far enough the other way, I submit, that we need not worry that a counteremphasis will stimulate people to an excess of individualism.

The energies Americans have devoted to the co-operative, to the social, are not to be demeaned; we would not, after all, have such a problem to discuss unless we had learned to adapt ourselves to an increasingly collective society as well as we have. An ideal of individualism which denies the obligations of man to others is manifestly impossible in a society such as ours, and it is a credit to our wisdom that while we preached it, we never fully practiced it.

But in searching for that elusive middle of the road, we have gone very far afield, and in our attention to making organization work we have come close to deifying it. We are describing its defects as virtues and denying that there is — or should be — a conflict between the individual and organization. This denial is bad for the organization. It is worse for the individual. What it does, in soothing him, is to rob him of the intellectual armor he so badly needs. For the more power organization has over him, the more he needs to recognize the area where he must assert himself against it. And this, almost because we have made organization life so equable, has become excruciatingly difficult.

To say that we must recognize the dilemmas of organization society is not to be inconsistent with the hopeful premise that organization society can be as compatible for the individual as any previous society. We are not hapless beings caught in the grip of forces we can do little about, and wholesale damnations of our society only lend a further mystique to organization. Organization has been made by man; it can be changed by man. It has not been the immutable course of history that has produced such constrictions on the individual as personality tests. It is organization man who has brought them to pass and it is he who can stop them.

The fault is not in organization, in short; it is in our worship of it. It is in our vain quest for a utopian equilibrium, which would be horrible if it ever did come to pass; it is in the soft-minded denial that there is a conflict between the individual and society. There must always be, and it is the price of being an individual that he must face these conflicts. He cannot evade them, and in seeking an ethic that offers a spurious peace of mind, thus does he tyrannize himself.

There are only a few times in organization life when he can wrench his destiny into his own hands — and if he does not fight then, he will make a surrender that will later mock him. But when is that time? Will he know the time when he sees it? By what standards is he to judge? He does feel an obligation to the group; he does sense moral constraints on his free will. If he goes against the group, is he being courageous — or just stubborn? Helpful — or selfish? Is he, as he so often wonders, right after all? It is in the resolution of a multitude of such dilemmas, I submit, that the real issue of individualism lies today. . . .

Chapter 4: Belongingness

What kind of society is to be engineered? Some critics of social engineering are sure that what is being cooked up for us is a socialistic paradise, a radically new, if not brave, world, alien to every tradition of man. This is wrong. Lump together the social engineers' prescriptions for the new society and you find they are anything but radical. Boiled down, what they ask for is an environment in which everyone is tightly knit into a belongingness with one another; one in which there is no restless wandering but rather the deep emotional security that comes from total integration with the group. Radical? It is like nothing so much as the Middle Ages.

And what, some have been asking, was so wrong with the Middle Ages anyway? They had excellent human relations. They didn't have the self-consciousness about their society to make them rationalize it or the scientific approach with which to do it. But belongingness they had. They knew where they stood — peasant and noble alike. They saw the fruit of their labor, and the tiny world about them protected as well as demanded. Psychologically, they had a home.

Not that we should go back to all this, mind you. The job, to paraphrase, is to *re-create* the belongingness of the Middle Ages. What with the Enlightenment, the Industrial Revolution, and other calamities, the job is immensely more difficult than it was in those simpler days. But with new scientific techniques we can solve the problem. What we must do is to learn consciously to achieve what once came naturally. We must form an elite of skilled leaders who will guide men back, benevolently, to group belongingness.

An unfair paraphrase? The young men who enthuse so unqualifiedly about human relations as the last best hope would be shocked to be accused of holding so reactionary a view. The people who have been the intellectual founders of the human-relations gospel, however, have not been so muddy-minded. They were not the cheery optimists their latter-day followers seem to be; they were rather pessimistic about the capacities of man, and the society they prescribed was by no means a utopia which would be all things to all men. A man would have to make sacrifices to enjoy it, and the prophets of belongingness stated this with admirable toughness of mind.

The father of the human-relations school is Elton Mayo. Mayo, professor of industrial research at the Harvard Business School, was concerned with the anomie, or rootlessness, of the industrial worker. Ever since he first started studying industry in Australia in 1903 he had been looking for a way to reconcile the worker's need for belongingness with the conflicting allegiances of the complex world he now finds himself in.

For Mayo, and his colleagues, the great turning point came as the result of what started to be a very modest experiment. In 1927 some of Mayo's colleagues began the now celebrated study at the Hawthorne, Illinois, plant of Western Electric.[1] The company had a challenging problem for them. For several years it had been trying to measure how much more telephone equipment the workers would produce as lighting was improved in the rooms they worked in. The researchers chose three rooms

---

1. For a full account of this experiment, see *Management and the Worker*, by F. S. Roethlisberger and William J. Dickson (Cambridge, Massachusetts: Harvard University Press, 1939). A good summary is to be found in Stuart Chase's *The Proper Study of Mankind* (New York: Harper and Brothers, 1948).

and progressively increased the illumination in each, at the same time keeping a careful record of the work output. To their surprise, there seemed no clear relation between production and better illumination. They tried a more careful experiment: this time they would use only two rooms, one a "control" group where conditions would be left the same and the experimental room where the changes would be introduced. Again, mixed results: output went up in the experimental room — but so did it go up in the control room.

At this point the Harvard group entered the picture and collaborated with the company on a more elaborate experiment: in a "relay assembly" test room they isolated a group of women operators from others doing the same work and one by one introduced changes — not only lighting, but changes in rest periods, hours, and economic incentives. According to the commonly accepted "scientific management principles" earlier advanced by Frederick Taylor, these changes in physical conditions and, most particularly, incentives would make the test group more productive than the other. But they didn't. As experiment followed experiment (the research was to continue until 1932) it became abundantly clear that physical changes were not the key. As in the earlier experiments, output did shoot ahead where conditions were changed, but so did output shoot ahead where no changes had been made.

How come? The researchers came to the conclusion that output shot up in both groups because in both groups the workers' participation had been solicited and this involvement, clearly, was more important than physical perquisites. The workers were a social system; the system was informal but it was what really determined the worker's attitude toward his job. This social system could work against management, but if the managers troubled themselves to understand the system and its functions for the worker, the system could work for management.

In the literature of human relations the Hawthorne experiment is customarily regarded as a discovery. In large part it was; more than any other event, it dramatized the inadequacy of the purely economic view of man. The conclusions that flowed from the experiment, however, were a good bit more than a statement of objective fact, for Mayo and his group were evangelists as well as researchers. He had come to quite similar conclusions many years before, and for him the Hawthorne experiment did not reveal so much as confirm.

The two slim books Mayo published since Hawthorne have proved to be an immensely powerful manifesto. Mayo never pretended that he was free from values and he frankly presents an argument as well as a diagnosis. In *The Social Problems of an Industrial Civilization*, he opens his case by picturing man's happiness in more primitive times. "Historically and traditionally our fathers worked for social co-operation — and achieved it. This is true also of any primitive society. But we, for at least a century of the most amazing scientific and material progress, have abandoned the effort — by inadvertence, it is true — and we are now reaping the consequences."

In the Middle Ages people had been disciplined by social codes into working well together. The Industrial Revolution, as Mayo described the consequences, had split society into a whole host of conflicting groups. Part of a man belonged to one group, part to another, and he was bewildered; no longer was there *one* group in which he could sublimate himself. The liberal philosophers, who were quite happy to see an end to feudal belongingness, interpreted this release from the group as freedom. Mayo does not see it this way. To him, the dominant urge of mankind is to belong: "Man's desire to be continuously associated in work with his fellows," he states, "is a strong, if not the strongest, human characteristic."

Whether the urge to co-operate is in fact man's most dominant drive, it does not follow that the co-operation is necessarily good. What is he going to co-operate *about*? What ends is the group working toward? But these questions do not greatly interest Mayo, and he seems to feel that the sheer fact of "spontaneous" co-operation carries its own ethic. "For *all* of us," Mayo states, "the feeling of security and certainty derives *always* from assured membership of a group." (Italics mine.)

Suppose there is a conflict between the individual and the group? Mayo sees conflict primarily as a breakdown in communication. If a man is unhappy or dissatisfied in his work, it is not that there is a conflict to be resolved so much as a misunderstanding to be cleared up. The worker might not see it this way, and most certainly the unions do not, but we have already been told that the individual is a nonlogical animal incapable of rationally solving his own problems or, in fact, of recognizing what the problem is.

At this point the human relations doctrine comes perilously close to demanding that the individual sacrifice his own beliefs that he may belong. The only way to escape this trap would be through the notion that by the process of equilibrium, a clarification of which never seems to detain anyone very long, what's good for the group is good for the individual. In speaking of the primitive group Mayo writes, "The situation is not simply that the society exercises a forceful compulsion on the individual; on the contrary, the social code and the desire of the individual are, for all practical purposes, identical. Every member of the group participates in all social activities because it is his chief desire to do so."

How to get back to this idyllic state? Mayo does not recommend a return to the Middle Ages. Too much water — and damn muddy water too, if you ask Mayo — has flowed under the bridge for that. The goal must be "an *adaptive* society" — a society in which we can once again enjoy the belongingness of primitive times but without the disadvantages of them.

This won't come about naturally. What with the mischief caused by the philosophers of individualism, most contemporary leaders are untrained in the necessary social skill to bring the adaptive society to pass. What is needed is an administrative elite, people trained to recognize that what man really wants most is group solidarity even if he does not realize it himself. They won't push him around; they won't even argue with him — unfettered as they will be of "prejudice and emotion," they won't have any philosophy, other than co-operation, to argue about. They will adjust him. Through the scientific application of human relations, these neutralist technicians will guide him into satisfying solidarity with the group so skillfully and unobtrusively that he will scarcely realize how the benefaction has been accomplished.

When Mayo got down to cases he was entirely consistent with his philosophy. His advocacy of "nondirective counseling" is a good case in point. In the course of their interviewing at Hawthorne, Mayo and his colleagues became impressed with the therapeutic effects the interviews had on the workers and went on to make the interview a management tool. The idea was to have a group of counselors who would be paid by management but who would not report to management what the workers said to them when they spilled their troubles. Since the workers knew this they could feel free to talk out their problems.

Implicit in this technique is the assumption that the worker's problems can indeed be *talked out*. He is to adjust to the group rather than vice versa; and the alternative of actually changing reality is hardly considered. If a worker is sore at his foreman the chances are good that he is not really sore at the foreman because of some rational gripe but is merely venting on the foreman certain repressed feelings. By listening patiently, like a psychiatrist, the counselor helps such persons understand that what they are really sore about flows from inner, subjective conflict. Characteristically, Mayo cites a woman worker who "discovered for herself during an interview that her dislike of a certain supervisor was based upon a fancied resemblance to a detested stepfather."

In similar cases it is possible the worker might not be maladjusted at all. The foreman might have been dividing up the workload problem badly, and maybe he had a few syndromes himself. The nondirective counseling idea, however, pooh-poohs the possibility: if there is a conflict of values that can't be talked out the interview has no provision in it for action to be taken — the setup itself, in short, is a value judgment that adjustment, rather than change, is the desideratum.

For a number of reasons, one being the hostility of the unions to it, the nondirective counseling system as such has never taken hold of the American industry. But the basic idea has. As I hope to demonstrate in later chapters, many of the more popular techniques — such as psychological "personality" testing, conference techniques — are all manifestations of the same principle. The rock is the group and maladjustment is disharmony with it.

Ironically, the primary target of this adjustment has become the managers themselves. While Mayo intended human relations to apply to the workers and managers both, the managers first seized on it as an excellent tool for manipulating the workers into a chronic contentment that would turn them away from the unions. But manipulation is a two-edged weapon; having learned how illogical workers were, managerial pioneers of human relations soon began to ponder the fact that their colleagues weren't so logical either. They needed to belong too — and even more than the worker, for more of their life was involved in the organization. Looking at the neuroses about him, many a progressive young organization man resolved that here, not on the shop floor, was the place that needed human relations most.

The use of psychological tests, if I may get a bit ahead of my story, is symptomatic. Originally, they were introduced by the managers as a tool for weeding out unqualified workers. As time went on, and personality tests were added to aptitude tests, the managers began using them on other managers, present and prospective, and today most personality testing is directed not at the worker, but at the organization man. If he is being hoist, it is by his own philosophy.

Fredric Jameson

Progress versus Utopia; or, Can We Imagine the Future?

(1982)

Fredric Jameson (b. 1934) is one of America's foremost Marxist literary critics. He received his Ph.D. from Yale University in 1959 and since then has held teaching positions at several prominent universities, most recently at Duke, where he is a professor of comparative literature and romance studies. His most famous books include *The Prison-House of Language* (1972), and *Postmodernism; or, the Cultural Logic of Late Capitalism* (1991). Over the years he has grown increasingly interested in science fiction, and one of his most recent books is *Archaeologies of the Future: The Desire Called Utopia and Other Science Fictions* (2005).

In various forms, Marxism has influenced literary criticism for more than one hundred years. Like other historical approaches, it encourages readers to think about how texts reflect, reinforce, or challenge prevailing social conditions and beliefs. An alternative to this kind of criticism is called *formalism*, an approach that tries to evaluate the impact of a text's structure, language, and imagery with minimal reference to external factors. Both approaches have strengths and weaknesses; historical criticism can be reductive and formalist criticism naïve. Jameson's balanced method makes use of both approaches, practicing a historically situated cultural analysis that is grounded in Marxist theory but sensitive to the formal properties and genre history of the literature he studies. His approach was influenced by the famous scholar of literary representation, Erich Auerbach — who directed Jameson's dissertation — as well as by European critics (sometimes referred to as "Western Marxists") such as Walter Benjamin, Theodor Adorno, and Louis Althusser.

In "Progress versus Utopia," originally published in *Science-Fiction Studies* in 1982, Jameson suggests that literary works are manifestations of the "political unconscious," borrowing the idea of the unconscious from Freud and applying it to societies rather than individuals. In Jameson's view, literature is an arena where cultural fears and desires are played out, often in subtle and contradictory ways. Noting that capitalist production altered traditional ways of organizing and experiencing time, Jameson points to the fact that futuristic sf emerged as a genre shortly after the historical novel did. These forms, he suggests, are not really about the past or the future but rather are attempts to understand our own present world by situating it within a larger narrative. For instance, if we envision a future of paranoid totalitarianism, our current surveillance culture becomes the inevitable beginning of that future. However, if we imagine a libertarian future where individual freedom is the only law, our current society's preoccupation with surveillance is a bizarre anomaly, a temporary state of affairs against which we will soon rebel. In either case, the way we envision the future is a reflection of our beliefs about the present.

Jameson is particularly interested in utopian sf novels that push the boundaries of what we can imagine from our current perspective in history. He sees these novels as self-referential works that are really about the impossibility of depicting utopia. Paradoxically, such works acknowledge the futility of imagining a radically different world, while at the same time providing a tantalizing glimpse of the possibility that other ways of being may exist.

> It will then turn out that the world has long dreamt of that of which it had only to have a clear idea to possess it really.
> — Karl Marx to Arnold Ruge (1843)

> A storm is blowing from Paradise; it has got caught in his wings with such violence that the angel can no longer close them. The storm irresistibly propels him into the future to which his back is turned, while the pile of debris before him grows skyward. This storm is what we call progress.
> — Walter Benjamin, *Theses on the Philosophy of History* (1939)

What if the "idea" of progress were not an idea at all but rather the symptom of something else? This is the perspective suggested, not merely by the interrogation of cultural texts, such as SF, but by the contemporary discovery of the Symbolic in general. Indeed, following the emergence of psychoanalysis, of structuralism in linguistics and anthropology, of semiotics together with its new field of "narratology," of communications theory, and even of such events as the emergence of a politics of "surplus consciousness" (Rudolf Bahro) in the 1960s, we have come to feel that abstract ideas and concepts are not necessarily intelligible entities in their own right. This was of course already the thrust of Marx's discovery of the dynamics of ideology; but while the older terms in which that discovery was traditionally formulated — "false consciousness" versus "science" — remain generally true, the Marxian approach to ideology, itself fed by all the discoveries enumerated above, has also become a far more sophisticated and non-reductive form of analysis than the classical opposition tends to suggest.

From the older standpoint of a traditional "history of ideas," however, ideology was essentially grasped as so many *opinions* vehiculated by a narrative text such as an SF novel, from which, as Lionel Trilling once put it, like so many raisins and currants they are picked out and exhibited in isolation. Thus [Jules] Verne is thought to have "believed" in progress,[1] while the originality of [H. G.] Wells was to have entertained an ambivalent and agonizing love-hate relationship with this "value," now affirmed and now denounced in the course of his complex artistic trajectory.[2]

The discovery of the Symbolic, however, suggests that for the individual subject as well as for groups, collectivities, and social classes, abstract opinion is, but a symptom or an index of some vaster *pensée sauvage*[3] about history itself, whether personal or collective. This thinking, in which a particular conceptual enunciation such as the "idea" of progress finds its structural intelligibility, may be said to be of a more properly *narrative* kind, analogous in that respect to the constitutive role played by master-fantasies in the Freudian model to the Unconscious. Nevertheless, the analogy is misleading to the degree to which it may awaken older attitudes about objective truth and subjective or psychological "projection," which are explicitly overcome and transcended by the notion of the Symbolic itself. In other words, we must resist the reflex which concludes that the narrative fantasies which a collectivity entertains about its past and its future are "merely" mythical, archetypal, and projective, as opposed to "concepts" like progress or cyclical return, which can somehow be tested for their objective or even scientific validity. This reflex is itself the last symptom of that dissociation of the private and the public, the subject and the object, the personal and the political, which has characterized the social life of capitalism. A theory of some narrative *pensée sauvage* — what I have elsewhere termed the political unconscious[4] — will, on the contrary, want to affirm the epistemological priority of such "fantasy" in theory and praxis alike.

1. See, on Verne, Pierre Macherey's stimulating chapter in *Pour une théorie de la production littéraire* (Paris, 1966).
2. The literature on Wells is enormous: see, for an introduction and select bibliography, Darko Suvin, *Metamorphoses of Science Fiction* (New Haven, 1979). This work is a pioneering theoretical and structural analysis of the genre to which I owe a great deal.
3. French anthropologist Claude Levi-Strauss used the term *la pensée sauvage* (the savage mind, or primitive thought) to characterize a way of thinking that begins with the concrete rather than the abstract. — Ed.
4. See *The Political Unconscious* (Ithaca, NY: 1981).

The task of such analysis would then be to detect and to reveal — behind such written *traces* of the political unconscious as the narrative texts of high or mass culture, but also behind those other symptoms or traces which are opinion, ideology, and even philosophical systems — the outlines of some deeper and vaster narrative movement in which the groups of a given collectivity at a certain historical conjuncture anxiously interrogate their fate, and explore it with hope or dread. Yet the nature of this vaster collective sub-text, with its specific structural limits and permutations, will be registered above all in terms of properly narrative categories: closure, recontainment, the production of episodes, and the like. Once again, a crude analogy with the dynamics of the individual unconscious may be useful. Proust's restriction to the windless cork-lined room, for instance, the emblematic eclipse of his own possible relationships to any concrete personal or historical future, determines the formal innovations and wondrous structural subterfuges of his now exclusively retrospective narrative production. Yet such narrative categories are themselves fraught with contradiction: in order for narrative to project some sense of a totality of experience in space and time, it must surely know some closure (a narrative must have an ending, even if it is ingeniously organized around the structural repression of endings as such). At the same time, however, closure or the narrative ending is the mark of that boundary or limit beyond which thought cannot go. The merit of SF is to dramatize this contradiction on the level of plot itself, since the vision of future history cannot know any punctual ending of this kind, at the same time that its novelistic expression demands some such ending. Thus [Isaac] Asimov has consistently refused to complete or terminate his *Foundation* series; while the most obvious ways in which an SF novel can wrap its story up — as in an atomic explosion that destroys the universe, or the static image of some future totalitarian world-state — are also clearly the places in which our own ideological limits are the most surely inscribed.

It will, I trust, already have become clear that this ultimate "text" or object of study — the master-narratives of the political unconscious — is a *construct*: it exists nowhere in "empirical" form, and therefore must be re-constructed on the basis of empirical "texts" of all sorts, in much the same way that the master-fantasies of the individual unconscious are reconstructed through the fragmentary and symptomatic "texts" of dreams, values, behavior, verbal free-association, and the like. This is to say that we must necessarily make a place for the formal and textual *mediations* through which such deeper narratives find a partial articulation. No serious literary critic today would suggest that content — whether social or psychoanalytic — inscribes itself immediately and transparently on the works of "high" literature: instead, the latter find themselves inserted in a complex and semi-autonomous dynamic of their own — the history of forms — which has its own logic and whose relationship to content per se is necessarily mediated, complex, and indirect (and takes very different structural paths at different moments of formal as well as social development). It is perhaps less widely accepted that the forms and texts of mass culture are fully as mediated as this: and that here too, collective and political fantasies do not find some simple transparent expression in this or that film or TV show. It would in my opinion be a mistake to make the "apologia" for SF in terms of specifically "high" literary values — to try, in other words, to recuperate this or that major text as exceptional, in much the same way as some literary critics have tried to recuperate Hammett or Chandler for the lineage of Dostoyevsky, say, or Faulkner.[5] SF is a sub-genre with a complex and interesting formal history of its own, and with its own dynamic, which is not that of high culture, but which stands in a complementary and dialectical relationship to high culture or modernism as such. We must therefore first make a detour through the dynamics of this specific form, with a view to grasping its emergence as a formal and historical event.

1. Whatever its illustrious precursors, it is a commonplace of the history of SF that it emerged, virtually full-blown, with Jules Verne and H. G. Wells, during the second half of the nineteenth century, a period also characterized by the production of a host of utopias of a more classical type. It would seem appropriate to register this generic emergence as the symptom of a mutation in our relationship to historical time itself: but this is a more complex proposition than it may seem, and demands to be argued in a more theoretical way.

I will suggest that the model for this kind of analysis, which grasps an entire genre as a symptom and reflex of historical change, may be found in Georg Lukács' classical study, *The Historical Novel* (1936). Lukács began with an observation that should not have been particularly surprising: it was no accident, he said, that the period which knew the emergence of historical thinking, of historicism in its peculiarly modern sense — the late eighteenth and early nineteenth century — should also have witnessed, in the work of Sir Walter Scott, the emergence of a narrative form peculiarly restructured to express that new consciousness. Just as modern historical consciousness was preceded by other, for us now archaic, forms of historiography — the chronicle or the annals — so the historical novel in its modern sense was certainly preceded by literary works which evoked the past and recreated historical settings of one kind or another: the history plays of Shakespeare or Corneille, *La Princesse de Clèves*, even Arthurian romance; yet all these works in their various ways affirm the past as being essentially the same as the present, and do not yet confront the great discovery of the modern historical sensibility, that the past, the various pasts, are culturally original, and radically distinct from our own experience of the object-world of the present. That discovery may now be seen as part of what may in the largest sense be called the *bourgeois cultural revolution*, the process whereby the definitive establishment of a properly capitalist mode of production as it were reprograms and utterly restructures the values, life rhythms, cultural

---

5. Dashiell Hammett (1894–1961) and Raymond Chandler (1888–1959) were famous writers of detective novels. — Ed.

habits, and temporal sense of its subjects. Capitalism demands in this sense a different experience of temporality from that which was appropriate to a feudal or tribal system, to the polis or to the forbidden city of the sacred despot: it demands a *memory* of qualitative social change, a concrete vision of the past which we may expect to find completed by that far more abstract and empty conception of some future terminus which we sometimes call "progress." Sir Walter Scott can in retrospect be seen to have been uniquely positioned for the creative opening of literary and narrative form to this new experience: on the very meeting place between two modes of production, the commercial activity of the Lowlands and the archaic, virtually tribal system of the surviving Highlanders, he is able to take a distanced and marginal view of the emergent dynamics of capitalism in the neighboring nation-state from the vantage point of a national experience — that of Scotland — which was the last arrival to capitalism and the first semi-peripheral zone of a foreign capitalism all at once.[6]

What is original about Lukács' book is not merely this sense of the historical meaning of the emergence of this new genre, but also and above all a more difficult perception: namely, of the profound historicity of the genre itself, its increasing incapacity to register its content, the way in which, with Flaubert's *Salammbô* in the mid-nineteenth century, it becomes emptied of its vitality and survives as a dead form, a museum piece, as "archeological" as its own raw materials, yet resplendent with technical virtuosity. A contemporary example may dramatize this curious destiny: Stanley Kubrick's *Barry Lyndon*, with its remarkable reconstruction of a whole vanished eighteenth-century past. The paradox, the historical mystery of the devitalization of form, will be felt by those for whom this film, with its brilliant images and extraordinary acting, is somehow profoundly *gratuitous*, an object floating in the void which could just as easily not have existed, its technical intensities far too great for any merely formal exercise, yet somehow profoundly and disturbingly unmotivated. This is to say something rather different from impugning the content of the Kubrick film: it would be easy to imagine any number of discussions of the vivid picture of eighteenth-century war, for example, or of the grisly instrumentality of human relationships, which might establish the relevance and the claims of this narrative on us today. It is rather the relationship to the past which is at issue, and the feeling that any other moment of the past would have done just as well. The sense that this determinate moment of history is, of organic necessity, precursor to the present has vanished into the pluralism of the Imaginary Museum, the wealth and endless variety of culturally or temporally distinct forms, all of which are now rigorously equivalent. Flaubert's Carthage and Kubrick's eighteenth century, but also the industrial turn of the century or the nostalgic 1930s or '50s of the American experience, find themselves emptied of their

6. An important discussion of Scotland's unique place in the development of capitalism can be found in Tom Nairn, *The Break-Up of Britain* (London: New Left Books, 1977).

necessity, and reduced to pretexts for so many glossy images. In its (post-) contemporary form, this replacement of the historical by the nostalgic, this volatilization of what was once a *national* past, in the moment of emergence of the nation-states and of nationalism itself, is of course at one with the disappearance of historicity from consumer society today, with its rapid media exhaustion of yesterday's events and of the day-before-yesterday's star players (who was Hitler anyway? who was Kennedy? who, finally, was Nixon?).

The moment of Flaubert, which Lukács saw as the beginning of this process, and the moment in which the historical novel as a genre ceases to be functional, is also the moment of the emergence of SF, with the first novels of Jules Verne. We are therefore entitled to complete Lukács' account of the historical novel with the counter-panel of its opposite number, the emergence of the new genre of SF as a form which now registers some nascent sense of the future, and does so in the space on which a sense of the past had once been inscribed. It is time to examine more closely the seemingly transparent ways in which SF registers fantasies about the future.

2. The common-sense position on the anticipatory nature of SF as a genre is what we would today call a *representational* one. These narratives are evidently for the most part not modernizing, not reflexive and self-undermining and deconstructing affairs. They go about their business with the full baggage and paraphernalia of a conventional realism, with this one difference: that the full "presence" — the settings and actions to be "rendered" — are the merely possible and conceivable ones of a near or far future. Whence the canonical defense of the genre: in a moment in which technological change has reached a dizzying tempo, in which so-called "future shock" is a daily experience, such narratives have the social function of accustoming their readers to rapid innovation, of preparing our consciousness and our habits for the otherwise demoralizing impact of change itself. They train our organisms to expect the unexpected and thereby insulate us, in much the same way that, for Walter Benjamin, the big city modernism of Baudelaire provided an elaborate shock-absorbing mechanism for the otherwise bewildered visitor to the new world of the great nineteenth-century industrial city.

If I cannot accept this account of SF, it is at least in part because it seems to me that, for all kinds of reasons, we no longer entertain such visions of wonder-working, properly "S-F" futures of technological automation. These visions are themselves now historical and dated — streamlined cities of the future on peeling murals — while our lived experience of our greatest metropolises is one of urban decay and blight. That particular Utopian future has in other words turned out to have been merely the future of one moment of what is now our own past. Yet, even if this is the case, it might at best signal a transformation in the historical function of present-day SF.

In reality, the relationship of this form of representation, this specific narrative apparatus, to its ostensible content — the future — has always been more complex than this. For the apparent realism, or representationality, of SF has concealed another, far more complex temporal structure: not to give us "images" of the future — whatever such images might mean for a reader who will necessarily predecease their "materialization" — but rather to defamiliarize and restructure our experience of our own *present*, and to do so in specific ways distinct from all other forms of defamiliarization. From the great intergalactic empires of an Asimov, or the devastated and sterile Earth of the post-catastrophe novels of a John Wyndham, all the way back in time to the nearer future of the organ banks and space miners of a Larry Niven, or the conapts, autofabs, or psycho-suitcases of the universe of Philip K. Dick, all such apparently full representations function in a process of distraction and displacement, repression and lateral perceptual renewal, which has its analogies in other forms of contemporary culture. Proust was only the most monumental "high" literary expression of this discovery: that the present — in this society, and in the physical and psychic dissociation of the human subjects who inhabit it — is inaccessible directly, is numb, habituated, empty of affect. Elaborate strategies of indirection are therefore necessary if we are somehow to break through our monadic insulation and to "experience," for some first and real time, this "present," which is after all all we have. In Proust, the retrospective fiction of memory and rewriting after the fact is mobilized in order for the intensity of a now merely remembered present to be experienced in some time-released and utterly unexpected posthumous actuality.

Elsewhere, with reference to another sub-genre or mass-cultural form, the detective story, I have tried to show that at its most original, in writers like Raymond Chandler, the ostensible plots of this peculiar form have an analogous function.[7] What interested Chandler was the here-and-now of the daily experience of the now historical Los Angeles: the stucco dwellings, cracked sidewalks, tarnished sunlight, and roadsters in which the curiously isolated yet typical specimens of an unimaginable Southern Californian social flora and fauna ride in the monadic half-light of their dashboards. Chandler's problem was that his readers — ourselves — desperately needed not to see that reality: humankind, as T. S. Eliot's magical bird sang, is able to bear very little of the unmediated, unfiltered experience of the daily life of capitalism. So, by a dialectical sleight-of-hand, Chandler formally mobilized an "entertainment" genre to distract us in a very special sense: not from the real life of private and public worries in general, but very precisely from our own defense mechanisms against that reality. The excitement of the mystery story plot is, then, a blind, fixing our attention on its own ostensible but in reality quite trivial puzzles and suspense in such a way that the intolerable space of Southern California can enter the eye laterally, with its intensity undiminished.

It is an analogous strategy of indirection that SF now brings to bear on the ultimate object and ground of all human life, History itself. How to fix

7. Fredric Jameson, "On Raymond Chandler," *Southern Review*, 6 (Summer 1970): 624–50.

this intolerable present of history with the naked eye? We have seen that in the moment of the emergence of capitalism the present could be intensified, and prepared for individual perception, by the construction of a historical past from which as a process it could be felt to issue slowly forth, like the growth of an organism. But today the past is dead, transformed into a packet of well-worn and thumbed glossy images. As for the future, which may still be alive in some small heroic collectivities on the Earth's surface, it is for us either irrelevant or unthinkable. Let the Wagnerian and Spenglerian world-dissolutions of J. G. Ballard stand as exemplary illustrations of the ways in which the imagination of a dying class — in this case the cancelled future of a vanished colonial and imperial destiny — seeks to intoxicate itself with images of death that range from the destruction of the world by fire, water, and ice to lengthening sleep or the berserk orgies of high-rise buildings or superhighways reverting to barbarism.

Ballard's work — so rich and corrupt — testifies powerfully to the contradictions of a properly representational attempt to grasp the future directly. I would argue, however, that the most characteristic SF does not seriously attempt to imagine the "real" future of our social system. Rather, its multiple mock futures serve the quite different function of transforming our own present into the determinate past of something yet to come. It is this present moment — unavailable to us for contemplation in its own right because the sheer quantitative immensity of objects and individual lives it comprises is untotalizable and hence unimaginable, and also because it is occluded by the density of our private fantasies as well as of the proliferating stereotypes of a media culture that penetrates every remote zone of our existence — that upon our return from the imaginary constructs of SF is offered to us in the form of some future world's remote past, as if posthumous and as though collectively remembered. Nor is this only an exercise in historical melancholy: there is, indeed, something also at least vaguely comforting and reassuring in the renewed sense that the great supermarkets and shopping centers, the garish fast-food stores and ever more swiftly remodelled shops and store-front businesses of the near future of Chandler's now historic Los Angeles, the burnt-out-center cities of small mid-Western towns, nay even the Pentagon itself and the vast underground networks of rocket-launching pads in the picture-post-card isolation of once characteristic North American "natural" splendor, along with the already cracked and crumbling futuristic architecture of newly built atomic power plants — that all these things are not seized, immobile forever, in some "end of history," but move steadily in time towards some unimaginable yet inevitable "real" future. SF thus enacts and enables a structurally unique "method" for apprehending the present as history, and this is so irrespective of the "pessimism" or "optimism" of the imaginary future world which is the pretext for that defamiliarization. The present is in fact no less a past if its destination proves to be the technological marvels of Verne or, on the contrary, the shabby and maimed automata of P. K. Dick's near future.

We must therefore now return to the relationship of SF and future history and reverse the stereotypical description of this genre: what is indeed authentic about it, as a mode of narrative and a form of knowledge, is not at all its capacity to keep the future alive, even in imagination. On the contrary, its deepest vocation is over and over again to demonstrate and to dramatize our incapacity to imagine the future, to body forth, through apparently full representations which prove on closer inspection to be structurally and constitutively impoverished, the atrophy in our time of what [Herbert] Marcuse has called the *utopian imagination*, the imagination of otherness and radical difference; to succeed by failure, and to serve as unwitting and even unwilling vehicles for a meditation, which, setting forth for the unknown, finds itself irrevocably mired in the all-too-familiar, and thereby becomes unexpectedly transformed into a contemplation of our own absolute limits.

This is indeed, since I have pronounced the word, the unexpected rediscovery of the nature of utopia as a genre in our own time.[8] The overt utopian text or discourse has been seen as a sub-variety of SF in general. What is paradoxical is that at the very moment in which utopias were supposed to have come to an end, and in which that asphyxiation of the utopian impulse alluded to above is everywhere more and more tangible, SF has in recent years rediscovered its own utopian vocation, and given rise to a whole series of powerful new works — utopian and SF all at once — of which Ursula Le Guin's *The Dispossessed*, Joanna Russ' *The Female Man*, Marge Piercy's *Woman on the Edge of Time*, and Samuel Delany's *Triton* are only the most remarkable monuments. A few final remarks are necessary, therefore, on the proper use of these texts, and the ways in which their relationship to social history is to be interrogated and decoded.

3. After what has been said about SF in general, the related proposition on the nature and the political function of the utopian genre will come as no particular surprise: namely, that its deepest vocation is to bring home, in local and determinate ways, and with a fullness of concrete detail, our constitutional inability to imagine Utopia itself, and this, not owing to any individual failure of imagination but as the result of the systemic, cultural, and ideological closure of which we are all in one way or another prisoners. This proposition, however, now needs to be demonstrated in a more concrete analytical way, with reference to the texts themselves.

It is fitting that such a demonstration should take as its occasion not American SF, whose affinities with the dystopia rather than the utopia, with fantasies of cyclical regression or totalitarian empires of the future, have until recently been marked (for all the obvious political reasons); but

8. A fuller discussion of these propositions and some closer analyses of More's *Utopia* in particular, will be found in my review-article of Louis Marin's *Utopiques* (which also see!), "Of Islands and Trenches," *Diacritics*, 7 (June 1977):2–21. See also the related discussion in "World Reduction in Le Guin: The Emergence of Utopian Narrative," *SFS*, 2 (1975):221–30.

rather Soviet SF, whose dignity as a "high" literary genre and whose social functionality within a socialist system have been, in contrast, equally predictable and no less ideological. The renewal of the twin Soviet traditions of Utopia and SF may very precisely be dated from the publication of Efremov's *Andromeda* (1958), and from the ensuing public debate over a work which surely, for all its naïveté, is one of the most single-minded and extreme attempts to produce a full representation of a future, classless, harmonious, world-wide utopian society. We may measure our own resistance to the utopian impulse by means of the boredom the sophisticated American reader instinctively feels for Efremov's culturally alien "libidinal apparatus":

> "We began," continued the beautiful historian, "with the complete redistribution of Earth's surface into dwelling and industrial zones.
>
> "The brown stripes running between thirty and forty degrees of North and South latitude represent an unbroken chain of urban settlements built on the shores of warm seas with a mild climate and no winters. Mankind no longer spends huge quantities of energy warming houses in winter and making himself clumsy clothing. The greatest concentration of people is around the cradle of human civilization, the Mediterranean Sea. The subtropical belt was doubled in breadth after the ice on the polar caps had melted. To the north of the zone of habitation lie prairies and meadows where countless herds of domestic animals graze. . . .
>
> "One of man's greatest pleasures is travel, an urge to move from place to place that we have inherited from our distant forefathers, the wandering hunters and gatherers of scanty food. Today the entire planet is encircled by the Spiral Way whose gigantic bridges link all the continents. . . . Electric trains move along the Spiral Way all the time and hundreds of thousands of people can leave the inhabited zone very speedily for the prairies, open fields, mountains or forests."[9]

The question one must address to such a work — the analytical way into the utopian text in general from Thomas More all the way down to this historically significant Soviet novel — turns on the status of the *negative* in what is given as an effort to imagine a world without negativity. The repression of the negative, the place of that repression, will then allow us to formulate the essential contradiction of such texts, which we have expressed in a more abstract fashion above, as the dialectical reversal of intent, the inversion of representation, the "ruse of history" whereby the effort to imagine utopia ends up betraying the impossibility of doing so. The content of such repressed "semes" of negativity will then serve as an indicator of the ways in which a narrative's contradiction or antinomy is to be formulated and reconstructed.

---

9. Ivan Efremov, *Andromeda* (Moscow: Foreign Language Publishing House, 1959), pp. 54–55.

Efremov's novel is predictably enough organized around the most obvious dilemma the negative poses for a utopian vision: namely, the irreducible fact of death. But equally characteristically, the anxiety of individual death is here "recontained" as a collective destiny, the loss of the starship *Parvus*, easily assimilable to a whole rhetoric of collective sacrifice in the service of mankind. I would suggest that this facile *topos* functions to displace two other, more acute and disturbing, forms of negativity. One is the emotional fatigue and deep psychic depression of the administrator Darr Veter, "cured" by a period of physical labor in the isolation of an ocean laboratory; the other is the *hubris* and crime of his successor, Mven Mass, whose personal involvement with an ambitious new energy program results in a catastrophic accident and loss of life. Mven Mass is "rehabilitated" after a stay on "the island of oblivion," a kind of idyllic Ceylonese Gulag on which deviants and anti-socials are released to work out their own salvation in any way they choose. We will say that these two episodes are the nodal points or symptoms at which the deeper contradictions of the *psychiatric* and the *penal*, respectively, interrupt the narrative functioning of the Soviet Utopian Imagination. Nor is it any accident that these narrative symptoms take spatial and geographical form. Already in Thomas More, the imagining of Utopia is constitutively related to the possibility of establishing some spatial *closure* (the digging of the great trench which turns "Utopia" into a self-contained island).[10] The lonely oceanographic station and the penal island thus mark the return of devices of spatial closure and separation which, formally required for the establishment of some "pure" and positive utopian space, thus always tend to betray the ultimate contradictions in the production of utopian figures and narratives.

Other people's ideologies always being more "self-evident" than our own, it is not hard to grasp the ideological function of this kind of non-conflictual utopia in a Soviet Union in which, according to Stalin's canonical formula, class struggle was at the moment of "socialism" supposed to have come to an end. Is it necessary to add that no intelligent Marxist today can believe such a thing, and that the process of class struggle is if anything exacerbated precisely in the moment of socialist construction, with its "primacy of the political"? I will nevertheless complicate this diagnosis with the suggestion that what is ideological for the Soviet reader may well be Utopian for us. We may indeed want to take into account the possibility that alongside the obvious qualitative differences between our own First World culture (with its dialectic of modernism and mass culture) and that of the Third World, we may want to make a place for a specific and original culture of the Second World, whose artifacts (generally in the form of Soviet and East European novels and films) have generally produced the unformulated and disquieting impression on the Western reader or spectator of a simplicity indistinguishable from naïve sentimentalism. Such a

---

10. Compare "Of Islands and Trenches" (see note 8).

renewed confrontation with Second World culture would have to take into account something it is hard for us to remember within the ahistorical closure of our own *"société de consommation"*: the radical strangeness and freshness of human existence and of its object world in a non-commodity atmosphere, in a space from which that prodigious saturation of messages, advertisements, and packaged libidinal fantasies of all kinds, which characterizes our own daily experience, is suddenly and unexpectedly stilled. We receive this culture with all the perplexed exasperation of the city dweller condemned to insomnia by the oppressive silence of the countryside at night; for us, then, it can serve the defamiliarizing function of those wondrous words which William Morris inscribed under the title of his own great Utopia, "an epoch of rest."

All of this can be said in another way by showing that, if Soviet images of Utopia are ideological, our own characteristically Western images of *dystopia* are no less so, and fraught with equally virulent contradictions.[11] George Orwell's classical and virtually inaugural work in this sub-genre, *1984*, can serve as a text-book exhibit for this proposition, even if we leave aside its more obviously pathological features. Orwell's novel, indeed, set out explicitly to dramatize the tyrannical omnipotence of a bureaucratic elite, with its perfected and omnipresent technological control. Yet the narrative, seeking to reinforce this already oppressive closure, subsequently overstates its case in a manner which specifically undermines its first ideological proposition. For, drawing on another topos of counterrevolutionary ideology, Orwell then sets out to show how, without freedom of thought, no science or scientific progress is possible, a thesis vividly reinforced by images of squalor and decaying buildings. The contradiction lies of course in the logical impossibility of reconciling these two propositions: if science and technological mastery are now hampered by the lack of freedom, the absolute technological power of the dystopian bureaucracy vanishes along with it and "totalitarianism" ceases to be a dystopia in Orwell's sense. Or the reverse: if these Stalinist masters dispose of some perfected scientific and technological power, then genuine freedom of inquiry must exist *somewhere* within this state, which was precisely what was not to have been demonstrated.

4. The thesis concerning the structural impossibility of utopian representation outlined above now suggests some unexpected consequences in the aesthetic realm. It is by now, I hope, a commonplace that the very thrust of literary modernism — with its *public introuvable* and the breakdown of traditional cultural institutions, in particular the social "contract" between writer and reader — has had as one significant structural consequence the transformation of the cultural text into an *auto-referential* discourse, whose content is a perpetual interrogation of its own conditions of

---

11. In other words, to adapt Claudel's favorite proverb, "le pire n'est pas toujours sûr, non plus!" [it's not always clear which is the worse].

possibility.[12] We may now show that this is no less the case with the utopian text. Indeed, in the light of everything that has been said, it will not be surprising to discover that as the true vocation of the utopian narrative begins to rise to the surface — to confront us with our incapacity to imagine Utopia — the center of gravity of such narratives shifts towards an auto-referentiality of a specific, but far more concrete type: such texts then explicitly or implicitly, and as it were against their own will, find their deepest "subjects" in the possibility of their own production, in the interrogation of the dilemmas involved in their own emergence as utopian texts.

Ursula Le Guin's only "contemporary" SF novel, the underrated *Lathe of Heaven* (1971), may serve as documentation for this more general proposition. In this novel, which establishes Le Guin's home city of Portland, Oregon, alongside Berkeley and Los Angeles, as one of the legendary spaces of contemporary SF, a hapless young man finds himself tormented by the unwanted power to dream "effective dreams," those which in other words change external reality itself, and reconstruct the latter's historical past in such a way that the previous "reality" disappears without a trace. He places himself in the hands of an ambitious psychiatrist, who then sets out to use his enormous proxy power to change the world for the benefit of mankind. But reality is a seamless web: change one detail and unexpected, sometimes monstrous transformations occur in other apparently unrelated zones of life, as in the classical time-travel stories where one contemporary artifact, left behind by accident in a trip to the Jurassic age, transforms human history like a thunderclap. The other archetypal reference is the dialectic of "wishes" in fairy tales, where one gratification is accompanied with a most unwanted secondary effect, which must then be wished away in its turn (its removal bringing yet another undesirable consequence, and so forth).

The ideological content of Le Guin's novel is clear, although its political resonance is ambiguous: from the central position of her mystical Taoism, the effort to "reform" and to ameliorate, to transform society in a liberal or revolutionary way is seen, after the fashion of Edmund Burke, as a dangerous expression of individual *hubris* and a destructive tampering with the rhythms of "nature." Politically, of course, this ideological message may be read either as the liberal's anxiety in the face of a genuinely revolutionary transformation of society or as the expression of more conservative misgivings about the New-Deal type reformism and do-goodism of the welfare state.[13]

On the aesthetic level, however — which is what concerns us here — the deeper subject of this fascinating work can only be the dangers of

12. See my *The Prison-House of Language* (Princeton, 1972), pp. 203–5.
13. That the author of *The Dispossessed* is also capable of indulging in a classical Dostoyevskian and counterrevolutionary anti-utopianism may be documented by her nasty little fable, "The Ones Who Walk Away from Omelas," in *The Wind's Twelve Quarters* (New York: Harper & Row, 1975), pp. 275–84.

imagining Utopia and more specifically of writing the utopian text itself. More transparently than much other SF, this book is "about" its own process of production, which is recognized as impossible: George Orr cannot dream utopia; yet in the very process of exploring the contradictions of that production, the narrative gets written, and "Utopia" is "produced" in the very movement by which we are shown that an "achieved" Utopia — a full representation — is a contradiction in terms. We may thus apply to *The Lathe of Heaven* those prophetic words of Roland Barthes about the dynamics of modernism generally, that the latter's monuments "linger as long as possible, in a sort of miraculous suspension, on the threshold of Literature itself [read, in this context: Utopia], in this anticipatory situation in which the density of life is given and developed without yet being destroyed through its consecration as an [institutionalized] sign system."[14]

It is, however, more fitting to close this discussion with another SF-Utopian text from the Second World today, one of the most glorious of all contemporary Utopias, the Strugatsky Brothers' astonishing *Roadside Picnic* (1977; first serialized in 1972).[15] This text moves in a space beyond the facile and obligatory references to the two rival social systems; and it cannot be coherently decoded as yet another *samizdat*[16] message or expression of liberal political protest by Soviet dissidents.[17] Nor, although its figural material is accessible and rewritable in a way familiar to readers who live within the rather different constraints of either of the two industrial and bureaucratic systems, is it an affirmation or demonstration of what is today called "convergence" theory. Finally, while the narrative turns on the mixed blessings of wonder-working technology, this novel does not seem to me to be programmed by the category of "technological determinism" in either the Western or the Eastern style: that is, it is locked neither into a Western notion of infinite industrial progress of a non-political type, nor into the Stalinist notion of socialism as the "development of the forces of production."

On the contrary, the "zone" — a geographical space in which, as the result of some inexplicable alien contact, artifacts can be found whose powers transcend the explanatory capacities of human science — is at one and the same time the object of the most vicious bootlegging and military-industrial Greed, and of the purest religious — I would like to say Utopian — Hope. The "quest for narrative," to use Todorov's expression,[18] is here very specifically the quest for the Grail; and the Strugatskys' deviant

---

14. Roland Barthes, *Writing Degree Zero*, trans. Annette Lavers and Colin Smith (London, 1967), p. 39.

15. Arkady and Boris Strugatsky, *Roadside Picnic*, trans. A. W. Bouis (New York: Macmillan, 1977).

16. Because of censorship of the press in the former Soviet Union and other communist countries, controversial literary and political works were often disseminated clandestinely as *samizdat* — handmade or photocopied duplicates that were passed from hand to hand. — Ed.

17. This is not to say that the Strugatskys have not had their share of personal and publishing problems.

18. Tzvetan Todorov, *Poétique de la prose* (Paris, 1971).

hero — marginal, and as "antisocial" as one likes; the Soviet equivalent of the ghetto or countercultural anti-heroes of our own tradition — is perhaps a more sympathetic and human figure for us than Le Guin's passive-contemplative and mystical innocent. No less than *The Lathe of Heaven*, then, *Roadside Picnic* is self-referential, its narrative production determined by the structural impossibility of producing that Utopian text which it nonetheless miraculously becomes. Yet what we must cherish in this text — a formally ingenious collage of documents, an enigmatic cross-cutting between unrelated characters in social and temporal space, a desolate reconfirmation of the inextricable relationship of the utopian quest to crime and suffering, with its climax in the simultaneous revenge-murder of an idealistic and guiltless youth and the apparition of the Grail itself — is the unexpected emergence, as it were, beyond "the nightmare of History" and from out of the most archaic longings of the human race, of the impossible and inexpressible Utopian impulse here nonetheless briefly glimpsed: "Happiness for everybody! . . . Free! . . . As much as you want! . . . Everybody come here! . . . HAPPINESS FOR EVERYBODY, FREE, AND NO ONE WILL GO AWAY UNSATISFIED!"

Chapter

5

Disasters and Apocalypses

The specter of worldwide disaster has always haunted the human imagination and has been a common theme in sf — from early works like Mary Shelley's 1826 plague story *The Last Man* to the popular films of today. The word *disaster* means "bad star" and derives from the traditional fear of comets, those once inexplicable glowing objects that appear periodically in our skies and have often been taken as portents of evil. It seems fitting, then, that science fiction, with its characteristic interest in the extraterrestrial regions of space, has often focused on the theme of disaster. Indeed, sf writers from Camille Flammarion, with whom this section begins, to more recent writers like Arthur C. Clarke have written disaster scenarios in which Earth is threatened by comets or other near-Earth objects. Ironically, although the fear of comets was once dismissed as superstition, both Flammarion and Clarke were scientists as well as writers of fiction, and science has once again begun to take the threat of near-Earth objects like meteors seriously, particularly with large-scale acceptance of the Alvarez theory that the extinction of dinosaurs was caused by a meteor strike. Science fiction depictions of disaster have not been limited to astronomical themes, however. Writers have shown us a variety of disasters, large and small, resulting from natural, supernatural, or human-made phenomena. They have also explored the political and psychological causes of disaster and the effects of its aftermath. Indeed, disaster is such a common theme in sf that it has spawned a number of recognizable motifs, including the end-of-the-world, nuclear holocaust, Adam and Eve, the lone survivor, and the postapocalyptic nightmare.

Speculation about the end of the world of course predates science fiction; stories of destruction are as central to mythic narratives as are stories of creation. Western audiences are most familiar with the biblical accounts of Noah's flood or the prophecy of end-times in Revelations, but cataclysmic disasters of one sort or another are featured in ancient religious traditions from Sumeria to India to the Americas. Apocalyptic imagery has often been used in mythologizing historical events as well, most obviously in the rhetoric of the French and Russian revolutions. Significantly, these stories are rarely exclusively negative and are often as much about new beginnings as about endings. Apocalyptic narratives, whether religious or political, are often tied to a utopian vision: the Earth must be washed clean of sin and corruption so that a fresh start can be made and a new order established. The word *apocalypse* itself — commonly used to signify a cataclysmic or world-ending disaster — actually means "to uncover" and was originally used to emphasize divine revelation rather than the tragedy of disaster.

Speculation about the world's end is perhaps natural for a species aware of its own finite nature and can be seen as the horror of personal death writ large. Myths about cataclysmic disasters can be seen as an attempt to explain the inexplicable, to make sense of what can't be controlled. Early human populations were vulnerable to all sorts of natural disasters — floods, fires, plagues, earthquakes, volcanic eruptions, tidal waves. Even today we are not immune to such natural forces, and now more than ever we also have to worry about the catastrophic effects of our own actions, from nuclear war to global warming.

There is an undeniably lurid element in our fascination with destruction, which has been exploited in modern culture since the cheap thrills of 1950s monster movies. But sf writers often have serious intentions in exploring the theme of disaster. Often such stories function as allegories or satire, serving as early warnings about the outcomes of our actions if we do not change them.

The stories in this section approach the idea of disaster in different ways. Some, like C. J. Cherryh's "Cassandra" and J. G. Ballard's "The Terminal Beach," focus on the personal and psychological dimensions of disaster, while others, like Alfred Bester's "Adam and No Eve" and Sakyo Komatsu's "Take Your Choice," put more emphasis on social or historical conditions and serve in part as cautionary tales. The stories may be as surreal and fantastic as Arthur C. Clarke's "The Nine Billion Names of God," or Stanislaw Lem's technology parable "How the World Was Saved" — or they may be as quietly realistic as William Sanders's "When This World Is All on Fire." Many partake of more than one of these elements, and often they are ambiguous or disquieting in ways that go beyond the simple horror of disaster itself, probing the part of human nature that is attracted to destruction and complicit in realizing apocalyptic visions.

Likewise, the Critical Contexts provide a variety of ways of thinking about disaster, from Susan Sontag's cultural analysis of disaster movies and Mircea Eliade's examination of cyclical and linear religious narratives to Paul Boyer's historical snapshot of a moment when the apocalypse seemed imminent. In all of these pieces, the emphasis is not so much on disaster itself but on human nature and the choices we make in the face of disaster.

Camille Flammarion

From Omega: The Last Days of the World
(1893)

French astronomer and writer Nicolas Camille Flammarion (1842–1925) was a prominent scientist who was dedicated to sharing his knowledge with a wider audience; his *Popular Astronomy* was the leading introductory text of the period. Flammarion also communicated his enthusiasm for the field by writing pioneering works of science fiction that incorporated the latest astronomical findings. Like his countryman and contemporary Jules Verne, Flammarion relished descriptive exposition and accurate scientific detail, but he also had a lyrical and even mystical side that exerted an influence on later writers like Olaf Stapledon. Flammarion delighted in speculation, and he fully exploited the imaginative possibilities of the genre. He was intrigued by the prospect of life on other planets, and fascinated by the long-term prospects of human physical, cultural, and spiritual evolution.

Set in twenty-fifth-century Paris, *Omega* opens with the Earth threatened by annihilation as a vast comet approaches. Moving out from this dramatic frame, Flammarion uses the occasion to speculate about all the possible ways the Earth may end, eventually predicting the fate of the Earth, humankind, and the cosmos in a visionary scenario that reaches millions of years into the future. In the selection that follows, we see the first news of the impending disaster spread and hear some of the scientific consultations that result as human beings across the globe contemplate their fate. One of the earliest stories to depict a catastrophic comet strike, *Omega* influenced many later works, from H. G. Wells's famous story "The Star" (1897) to many speculations about asteroid strikes by modern writers like Arthur C. Clarke, as well as numerous disaster films.

CHAPTER I

The magnificent marble bridge which unites the Rue de Rennes with the Rue de Louvre, and which, lined with the statues of celebrated scientists and philosophers, emphasizes the monumental avenue leading to the new portico of the Institute, was absolutely black with people. A heaving crowd surged, rather than walked, along the quays, flowing out from every street and pressing forward toward the portico, long before invaded by a tumultuous throng. Never, in that barbarous age preceding the constitution of the United States of Europe, when might was greater than right, when military despotism ruled the world and foolish humanity quivered in the relentless grasp of war — never before in the stormy period of a great revolution, or in those feverish days which accompanied a declaration of war, had the approaches of the house of the people's representatives, or the Place de la Concorde presented such a spectacle. It was no longer the case of a band of fanatics rallied about a flag, marching to some conquest of the sword, and followed by a throng of the curious and the idle, eager to see what would happen; but of the entire population, anxious, agitated, terrified, composed of every class of society without distinction, hanging upon the decision of an oracle, waiting feverishly the result of the calculations which a celebrated astronomer was to announce that very Monday, at three o'clock, in the session of the Academy of Sciences. Amid the flux of politics and society the Institute survived, maintaining still in Europe its supremacy in science, literature, and art. The center of civilization, however, had moved westward, and the focus of progress shone on the shores of Lake Michigan, in North America.

This new palace of the Institute, with its lofty domes and terraces, had been erected upon the ruins remaining after the great social revolution of the international anarchists who, in 1950, had blown up the greater portion of the metropolis as from the vent of a crater.

On the Sunday evening before, one might have seen from the car of a balloon all Paris abroad upon the boulevards and public squares, circulating slowly and as if in despair, without interest in anything. The gay aerial ships no longer cleaved the air; aeroplanes and aviators had all ceased to circulate. The aerial stations upon the summits of the towers and buildings were empty and deserted. The course of human life seemed arrested, and anxiety was depicted upon every face. Strangers addressed each other without hesitation; and but one question fell from pale and trembling lips: "Is it then true?" The most deadly pestilence would have carried far less terror to the heart than the astronomical prediction on every tongue; it would have made fewer victims, for already, from some unknown cause, the death-rate was increasing. At every instant one felt the electric shock of a terrible fear.

A few, less dismayed, wished to appear more confident, and sounded now and then a note of doubt, even of hope, as: "It may prove a mistake"; or, "It will pass on one side"; or, again: "It will amount to nothing; we shall get off with a fright," and other like assurances.

But expectation and uncertainty are often more terrible than the catastrophe itself. A brutal blow knocks us down once for all, prostrating us more or less completely. We come to our senses, we make the best of it, we recover, and take up life again. But this was the unknown, the expectation of something inevitable but mysterious, terrible, coming from without the range of experience. One was to die, without doubt, but how? By the sudden shock of collision, crushed to death? By fire, the conflagration of a world? By suffocation, the poisoning of the atmosphere? What torture awaited humanity? Apprehension was perhaps more frightful than the reality itself. The mind cannot suffer beyond a certain limit. To suffer by inches, to ask every evening what the morning may bring, is to suffer a thousand deaths. Terror, that terror which congeals the blood in the veins, which annihilates the courage, haunted the shuddering soul like an invisible spectre.

For more than a month the business of the world had been suspended; a fortnight before the committee of administrators (formerly the chamber and senate) had adjourned, every other question having sunk into insignificance. For a week the exchanges of Paris, London, New York, and Peking, had closed their doors. What was the use of occupying oneself with business affairs, with questions of internal or foreign policy, of revenue or of reform, if the end of the world was at hand? Politics, indeed! Did one even remember to have ever taken any interest in them? The courts themselves had no cases; one does not murder when one expects the end of the world. Humanity no longer attached importance to anything; its heart beat furiously, as if about to stop forever. Every face was emaciated, every countenance discomposed, and haggard with sleeplessness. Feminine coquetry alone held out, but in a superficial, hesitating, furtive manner, without thought of the morrow.

The situation was indeed serious, almost desperate, even in the eyes of the most stoical. Never, in the whole course of history had the race of Adam found itself face to face with such a peril. The portents of the sky confronted it unceasingly with a question of life and death.

But, let us go back to the beginning.

Three months before the day of which we speak, the director of the observatory of Mount Gaurisankar had sent the following telephonic message to the principal observatories of the globe, and especially to that of Paris:[1]

"A telescopic comet discovered tonight, in 290°, 15' right ascension, and 21°, 54' south declination. Slight diurnal motion. Is of greenish hue."

Not a month passed without the discovery of telescopic comets, and their announcement to the various observatories, especially since the installation of intrepid astronomers in Asia on the lofty peaks of Gaurisankar, Dapsang, and Kanchinjinga; in South America, on Aconcagua, Illampon, and Chimborazo, as also in Africa on Kilimanjaro, and in Europe on Elburz and Mont Blanc. This announcement, therefore, had not excited more comment among astronomers than any other of a like nature which they were constantly receiving. A large number of observers had sought the comet in the position indicated, and had carefully followed its motion. Their observations had been published in the Neuastronomischenachrichten, and a German mathematician had calculated a provisional orbit and ephemeris. . . .

While the astronomers of Europe were discussing the orbit of the new comet and establishing the precision of the computations which foretold its convergence upon the earth and the collision of the two bodies in space, a new phonographic message was sent out from the Himalayan observatory:

"The comet will soon become visible to the naked eye. Still of greenish hue. Its course is earthward."

---

1. For about 300 years the observatory of Paris had ceased to be an observing station, and had been perpetuated only as the central administrative bureau of French astronomy. Astronomical observations were made under far more satisfactory conditions upon mountain summits in a pure atmosphere, free from disturbing influences. Observers were in direct and constant communication by telephone with the central office, whose instruments were used only to verify certain discoveries or to satisfy the curiosity of savants detained in Paris by their sedentary occupation.

The complete agreement between the astronomical data, whether from European, American, or Asiatic sources, could leave no further doubt of their exactness. The daily papers sowed broadcast this alarming news, embellished with sinister comments and numberless interviews in which the most astonishing statements were attributed to scientists. Their only concern was to outdo the ascertained facts, and to exaggerate their bearing by more or less fanciful additions. As for that matter, the journals of the world had long since become purely business enterprises. The sole preoccupation of each was to sell every day the greatest possible number of copies. They invented false news, travestied the truth, dishonored men and women, spread scandal, lied without shame, explained the devices of thieves and murderers, published the formulæ of recently invented explosives, imperilled their own readers, and betrayed every class of society, for the sole purpose of exciting to the highest pitch the curiosity of the public and of "selling copies."

Everything had become a pure matter of business. For science, art, literature, philosophy, study, and research, the press cared nothing. An acrobat, a runner, or a jockey, an air-ship or water-velocipede, attained more celebrity in a day than the most eminent scientist, or the most ingenious inventor — for these two classes made no return to the stockholders. Everything was adroitly decked out with the rhetoric of patriotism, a sentiment which still exercised some empire over the minds of men. In short, from every point of view, the pecuniary interests of the publication dominated all considerations of public interest and general progress. Of all this the public had been for a long time the dupe; but, at the time of which we are now speaking, it had surrendered to the situation, so that there was no longer any newspaper, properly speaking, but only sheets of notices and advertisements of a commercial nature. Neither the first announcement of the press, that a comet was approaching with a high velocity and would collide with the earth at a date already determined; nor the second, that the wandering star might bring about a general catastrophe by rendering the atmosphere irrespirable, had produced the slightest impression; this two-fold prophecy, if noticed at all by the heedless reader, had been received with profound incredulity, attracting no more attention than the simultaneous announcement of the discovery of the fountain of perpetual youth in the cellars of the Palais des Fées on Montmartre (erected on the ruins of the cathedral of the Sacré-Cœur).

Moreover, astronomers themselves had not, at first, evinced any anxiety about the collision, so far as it affected the fate of humanity, and the astronomical journals (which alone retained any semblance of authority) had as yet referred to the subject simply as a computation to be verified. Scientists had treated the problem as one of pure mathematics, regarding it only as an interesting case of celestial mechanics. In the interviews to which they had been subjected they had contented themselves with saying that a collision was possible, even probable, but of no interest to the public.

Meanwhile, a new message was received by telephone, this time from Mount Hamilton in California, which produced a sensation among the chemists and physiologists:

"Spectroscopic observation establishes the fact that the comet is a body of considerable density, composed of several gases the chief of which is carbonic-oxide."

Matters were becoming serious. That a collision with the earth would occur was certain. If astronomers were not especially preoccupied by this fact, accustomed as they were for centuries to consider these celestial conjunctions as harmless: if the most celebrated even of their number had, at last, coldly shown the door to the many beardless reporters constantly importuning them, declaring that this prediction was of no interest to the people at large and was a strictly astronomical question which did not concern them, physicians, on the other hand, had begun to agitate the subject and to discuss gravely, among each other, the possibilities of asphyxia, or poisoning. Less indifferent to public opinion, so far from turning a cold shoulder to the journalists, they had welcomed them, and in a few days the subject suddenly entered upon a new phase. From the domain of astronomy it had passed into that of philosophy, and the name of every well-known or famous physician appeared in large letters on the title-pages of the daily papers; their portraits were reproduced in the illustrated journals, and the formula, "Interviews on the Comet," was to be seen on every hand. Already, even, the variety and diversity of conflicting opinions had created hostile camps, which hurled at each other the most grotesque abuse, and asserted that all physicians were "charlatans eager for notoriety." . . .

The spectroscope indicated especially the presence of carbonic-oxide in the chemical constitution of the comet. The chief point under discussion in the scientific reviews was whether the mixture of this noxious gas with the atmosphere would poison the entire population of the globe, human and animal, as the president of the academy of medicine affirmed would be the case.

Carbonic-oxide! Nothing else was talked of. The spectroscope could not be in error. Its methods were too sure, its processes too precise. Everybody knew that the smallest admixture of this gas with the air we breathe meant a speedy death. Now, a later despatch from the observatory of Gaurisankar had more than confirmed that received from Mount Hamilton. This despatch read:

"The earth will be completely submerged in the nucleus of the comet, whose diameter is already thirty times that of the globe and is daily increasing."

Thirty times the diameter of the earth! Even then, though the comet should pass between the earth and the moon, it would touch them both, since a bridge of thirty earths would span the distance between our world and the moon.

Then, too, during the three months whose history we have recapitulated, the comet had emerged from regions accessible only to the telescope and had become visible to the naked eye. In full view of the earth it hovered now like a threat from heaven among the army of stars. Terror itself, advancing slowly but inexorably, was suspended like a mighty sword above every head. A last effort was made, not indeed to turn the comet from its path — an idea conceived by that class of visionaries who recoil before nothing, and who had even imagined that an electric storm of vast magnitude might be produced by batteries suitably distributed over that face of the globe which was to receive the shock — but to examine once more the great problem under every aspect, and perhaps to reassure the public mind and rekindle hope by the discovery of some error in the conclusions which had been drawn, some forgotten fact in the observations or computations. This collision might not after all prove so fatal as the pessimists had foretold. A general presentation of the case from every point of view was announced for this very Monday at the Institute, just four days before the prophesied moment of collision, which would take place on Friday, July 13th. The most celebrated astronomer of France, at that time director of the Paris observatory; the president of the academy of medicine, an eminent physiologist and chemist; the president of the astronomical society, a skillful mathematician, and other orators also, among them a woman distinguished for her discoveries in the physical sciences, were among the speakers announced. The last word had not yet been spoken. Let us enter the venerable dome and listen to the discussion.

But before doing so, let us ourselves consider this famous comet which for the time being absorbed every thought.

CHAPTER II

The stranger had emerged slowly from the depths of space. Instead of appearing suddenly, as more than once the great comets have been observed to do, — either because coming into view immediately after their perihelion passage, or after a long series of storms or moonlight nights has prevented the search of the sky by the comet-seekers — this floating star-mist had at first remained in regions visible only to the telescope, and had been watched only by astronomers. For several days after its discovery, none but the most powerful equatorials of the observatories could detect its presence. But the well-informed were not slow to examine it for themselves. Every modern house was crowded with a terrace, partly for the purpose of facilitating aerial embarkations. Many of them were provided with revolving domes. Few well-to-do families were without a telescope, and no home was complete without a library, well furnished with scientific books.

The comet had been observed by everybody, so to speak, from the instant it became visible to instruments of moderate power. As for the laboring classes, whose leisure moments were always provided for, the telescopes set up in the public squares had been surrounded by impatient crowds from the first moment of visibility, and every evening the receipts of these astronomers of the open air had been incredible and without precedent. Many workmen, too, had their own instruments, especially in the provinces, and justice, as well as truth, compels us to acknowledge that the first discoverer of the comet (outside of the professional observers) had not been a man of the world, a person of importance, or an academician, but a plain workman of the town of Soissons, who passed the greater portion of his nights under the stars, and who had succeeded in purchasing out of his laboriously accumulated savings an excellent little telescope with which he was in the habit of studying the wonders of the sky. And it is a notable fact that prior to the twenty-fourth century, nearly all the inhabitants of the earth had lived without knowing where they were, without even feeling the curiosity to ask, like blind men, with no other preoccupation than the satisfaction of their appetites; but within a hundred years the human race had begun to observe and reason upon the universe about them.

The comet was now visible to the naked eye. On the night of the new moon, the atmosphere being perfectly clear, it had been detected by a few keen eyes without the aid of a glass, not far from the zenith near the edge of the milky way to the south of the star Omicron in the constellation of Andromeda, as a pale nebula, like a puff of very light smoke, quite small, almost round, slightly elongated in a direction opposed to that of the sun — a gaseous elongation, outlining a rudimentary tail. This, indeed, had been its appearance since its first discovery by the telescope. From its inoffensive aspect no one could have suspected the tragic role which this new star was to play in the history of humanity. Analysis alone indicated its march toward the earth.

But the mysterious star approached rapidly. The very next day the half of those who searched for it had detected it, and the following day only the near-sighted, with eye-glasses of insufficient power, had failed to make it out. In less than a week every one had seen it. In all the public squares, in every city, in every village, groups were to be seen watching it, or showing it to others.

Day by day it increased in size. The telescope began to distinguish distinctly a luminous nucleus. The excitement increased at the same time, invading every mind. When, after the first quarter and during the full moon, it appeared to remain stationary and even to lose something of its brilliancy, as it had been expected to grow rapidly larger, it was hoped that some error had crept into the computations, and a period of tranquillity and relief followed. After the full moon the barometer fell rapidly. A violent storm-center, coming from the Atlantic, passed north of the British Isles. For twelve days the sky was entirely obscured over nearly the whole of Europe.

Once more the sun shone in purified atmosphere, the clouds dissolved and the blue sky reappeared pure and unobscured; it was not without emotion that men waited for the setting of the sun — especially as several aerial expeditions had succeeded in rising above the cloud-belts, and aeronauts had asserted that the comet was visibly larger. Telephone messages sent out from the mountains of Asia and America announced also its rapid approach. But great was the surprise when at nightfall every eye was turned heavenward to seek the flaming star. It was no longer a comet, a classic comet such as one had seen before, but an aurora borealis of a new kind, a gigantic celestial fan, with seven branches, shooting into space seven greenish streamers, which appeared to issue from a point hidden below the horizon. . . .

It was in the midst of this state of general anxiety that the session of the Institute, whose utterance was awaited as the last word of an oracle, was opened.

The director of the observatory of Paris was naturally to be the first speaker; but what seemed to excite the greatest interest in the public was the opinion of the president of the academy of medicine on the probable effects of carbonic-oxide. The president of the geological society of France was also to make an address, and the general object of the session was to pass in review all the possible ways in which our earth might come to an end. Evidently, however, the discussion of its collision with the comet would hold the first place.

. . . the threatening star hung above every head; everybody could see it; it was growing larger day by day; it was approaching with an increasing velocity; it was known to be at a distance of only 17,992,000 kilometers, and that this distance would be passed over in five days. Every hour brought this menacing hand, ready to strike, 149,000 kilometers nearer. In six days anxious humanity would breathe freely — or not at all.

. . .

Chapter 3 and the beginning of Chapter 4 describe a lengthy discussion, in which scientists debate the seriousness of the threat posed by the comet and speculate about various ways that earth may be destroyed, whether by this or other natural causes. At the end of the discussion the director of the Paris observatory summarizes the various opinions and reflects on the fragility of life on our planet.

CHAPTER IV

. . .

"Thus our planet pursues its way along its heavenly path, with a speed of more than 100,000 kilometers per hour, and, at the same time, the sun hurries it on, with all the planets, toward the constellation of Hercules. Recapitulating what has just been said, and allowing for what may have been omitted: it may meet a comet ten or twenty times larger than itself, composed of deleterious gases which would render the atmosphere irrespirable; it may encounter a swarm of uranolites, which would have upon it the effect of a charge of shot upon a meadow lark; it may meet in its path an invisible sun, much larger than itself, whose shock would reduce it to vapor; it may encounter a sun which would consume it in the twinkling of an eye, as a furnace would consume an apple thrown into it; it may be caught in a system of electric forces, which would act like a brake upon its eleven motions, and which would either melt it, or set it afire, like a platinum wire in a strong current; it may lose the oxygen which supports life; it may be blown up like the crust over a crater; it may collapse in some great earthquake; its dry land may disappear, in a second deluge, more universal than the first; it may, on the contrary, lose all its water, an element essential to its organic life; under the attraction of some passing body, it may be detached from the sun and carried away into the cold of stellar space; it may part, not only with the last vestige of its internal heat, which long since has ceased to have any influence upon its surface, but also with the protecting envelope which maintains the temperature necessary to life; one of these days, when the sun has grown dark and cold, it may be neither lighted, nor warmed, nor fertilized; on the other hand, it may be suddenly scorched by an outburst of heat, analogous to what has been observed in temporary stars; not to speak of many other sources of accidents and mortal peril, whose easy enumeration we leave to the geologists, paleontologists, meteorologists, physicists, chemists, biologists, physicians, botanists, and even to the veterinary surgeons, inasmuch as the arrival of an army of invisible microbes, if they be but deadly enough, or a well-established epidemic, would suffice to destroy the human race and the principal animal and vegetable species, without working the least harm to the planet itself, from a strictly astronomical point of view."

Just as the speaker was uttering these last words, a voice, which seemed to come from a distance, fell, as it were, from the ceiling overhead. But a few words of explanation may here perhaps be desirable.

As we have said, the observatories established on the higher mountains of the globe were connected by telephone, with the observatory of Paris, and the sender of the message could be heard at a distance from the receiver, without being obliged to apply any apparatus directly to the ear. The reader doubtless recollects that, at the close of the preceding session, a phonogram from Mt. Gaurisankar stated that a photophonic message, which would be at once deciphered, had been received from the inhabitants of Mars. As the translation of this cipher had not arrived at the opening of the evening session, the bureau of communications had connected the Institute with the observatory by suspending a telephonoscope from the dome of the amphitheater.

The voice from above said:

"The astronomers of the equatorial city of Mars warn the inhabitants of the earth that the comet is moving directly toward the earth with a velocity nearly double that of the orbital velocity of Mars. Mechanical motion to be transformed into heat, and heat into electrical energy. Terrible magnetic storms. Move away from Italy."

The voice ceased amid general silence and consternation. There were, however, a few skeptics left, one of whom, editor of La Libre Critique, raising his monocle to his right eye, had risen from the reporter's desk and had exclaimed in a penetrating voice:

"I am afraid that the venerable doctors of the Institute are the victims of a huge joke. No one can ever persuade me that the inhabitants of Mars — admitting that there are any and they have really sent us a warning — know Italy by name. I doubt very much if one of them ever heard of the Commentaries of Cæsar or the History of the Popes, especially as" —

The orator, who was launching into an interesting dithyrambus, was at this point suddenly squelched by the turning off of the electric lights. With the exception of the illuminated square in the ceiling, the room was plunged in darkness and the voice added these six words: "This is the despatch from Mars;" and thereupon the following symbols appeared on the plate of the telephonoscope:

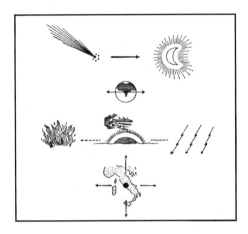

As this picture could only be seen by holding the head in a very fatiguing position, the president touched a bell and an assistant appeared, who by means of a projector and mirror transferred these hieroglyphics to a screen on the wall behind the desk, so that every one could readily see and analyze them at their leisure. Their interpretation was easy; nothing indeed could be more simple. The figure representing the comet needed no explanation. The arrow indicates the motion of the comet towards a heavenly body, which as seen from Mars presents phases, and sparkles like a star; this means the earth, naturally so delineated by the Martians, for their eyes, developed in a medium less luminous than ours, are somewhat more sensitive and distinguish the phases of the earth, and this the more readily because their atmosphere is rarer and more transparent. (For us the phases of Venus are just on the limit of visibility.) The double globe represents Mars looking at the Kaiser sea, the most characteristic feature of Martian geography, and indicates a velocity for the comet double the orbital velocity, or a little less, for the line does not quite reach the edge. The flames indicate the transformation of motion into heat; the aurora borealis and the lightning which follow, the transformation into electric and magnetic force. Finally, we recognize the boot of Italy, visible from Mars, and the black spot marks the locality threatened, according to their calculation, by one of the most dangerous fragments of the head of the comet; while the four arrows radiating in the direction of the four cardinal points of the compass seem to counsel removal from the point menaced.

The photophonic message from the Martians was much longer and far more complicated. The astronomers on Mt. Gaurisankar had previously received several such, and had discovered that they were sent from a very important, intellectual, and scientific center situated in the equatorial zone not far from Meridian bay. The last message, whose general meaning is given above, was the most important. The remainder of it had not been transmitted, as it was obscure and it was not certain that its exact meaning had been made out.

The president rang his bell for order. He was about to sum up what had been said, before adjourning the meeting.

"Gentlemen," he began, "although it is after midnight, it will be of interest, before we separate, to summarize what has been told us in these two solemn sessions.

"The last despatch from Gaurisankar may well impress you. It seems clear that the inhabitants of Mars are farther advanced in science than ourselves, and this is not surprising, for they are a far older race and have had centuries innumerable in which to achieve this progress. Moreover, they may be much more highly organized than we are, they may possess better eyes, instruments of greater perfection, and intellectual faculties of a higher order. We observe, too, that their calculations, while in accord with ours as to the collision, are more precise, for they designate the very point which is to receive the greatest shock. The advice to flee from Italy should therefore be followed, and I shall at once telephone the Pope, who at this very moment is assembling the prelates of entire Christendom.

"So the comet will collide with the earth, and no one can yet foresee the consequences. But in all probability the disturbance will be local and the world will not be destroyed. The carbonic-oxide is not likely to penetrate the respirable portions of the atmosphere, but there will be an enormous development of heat.

"As to the veritable end of the world, of all the hypotheses which today permit us to forecast that event the most probable is the last — that explained to us by the learned chancellor of the Columbian academy: the life of the planet depends upon the sun; so long as the sun shines humanity is safe, unless indeed the diminution of the atmosphere and aqueous vapor should usher in before that time the reign of cold. In the former case we have yet before us twenty million years of life; in the latter only ten.

"Let us then await the night of July 13–14 without despair. I advise those who can to pass these fête days in Chicago, or better still in San Francisco, Honolulu, or Noumea. The trans-Atlantic electric air-ships are so numerous and well managed that millions of travellers may make the journey before Saturday night."

Alfred Bester

Adam and No Eve

(1941)

The career of Alfred Bester (1913–1987) spanned more than four decades, from 1939 to the early 1980s, though most of his work dates from the 1940s and 1950s, when he began publishing stories in Golden Age magazines like *Astounding*. During this period, he also wrote for comic books and radio, working on such memorable series as *Superman, Batman,* and *The Shadow*. Beginning in the late 1950s, Bester worked primarily as a mainstream magazine writer and editor, although he continued writing sf periodically throughout his life.

Two of Bester's novels have been especially influential: *The Stars My Destination,* an obsessive tale of vengeance that was first published in 1956 as *Tyger! Tyger!,* and *The Demolished Man,* a stylish future detective novel that won the first Hugo in 1953. Bester's notable short stories include "Fondly Fahrenheit" (1954) and "The Men Who Murdered Mohammed" (1959). His work has often been cited in Locus Polls, and he was awarded the Nebula Grand Master Award in 1988.

Bester is known for fast-paced stories marked by dark, ironic humor; for stories featuring vivid future societies; and for his psychological exploration of morally ambiguous characters. These characteristics, along with a tone reminiscent of the crime stories of the 1940s and 1950s film noir period, make him an important influence in the development of New Wave and, later, cyberpunk writers.

In "Adam and No Eve," the psychological immersion in the narrator's fevered imaginings is typical of Bester, as is the initial withholding of information — the significance of events slowly unfolding through flashbacks. This is a classic story about the consequences of scientific overreaching. It is an early example of the kind of apocalyptic narrative that would become prominent in post–World War II American sf.

K rane knew this must be the seacoast. Instinct told him; but more than instinct, the few shreds of knowledge that clung to his torn brain told him; the stars that had shown at night through the rare breaks in the clouds, and his compass that still pointed a trembling finger north. That was strangest of all, Krane thought. The rubbled Earth still retained its polarity.

It was no longer a coast; there was no longer any sea. Only the faint line of what had been a cliff stretched north and south for endless miles. It was a line of gray ash; the same gray ash and cinders that lay behind him and stretched before him. . . . Fine silt, knee-deep, that swirled up at every motion and choked him; cinders that scudded in dense night clouds when the mad winds blew; black dust that was churned to mud when the frequent rains fell.

The sky was jet overhead. The heavy clouds rode high and were pierced with shafts of sunlight that marched swiftly over the Earth. Where the light struck a cinder storm, it was filled with gusts of dancing, gleaming particles. Where it played through rain it brought the arches of rainbows into being. Rain fell; cinder-storms blew; light thrust down — together, alternately and continually in a jigsaw of black and white violence. So it had been for months. So it was over every mile of the broad Earth.

Krane passed the edge of the ashen cliffs and began crawling down the even slope that had once been the ocean bed. He had been traveling so long that pain had become part of him. He braced elbows and dragged his body forward. Then he brought his right knee under him and reached forward with elbows again. Elbows, knee, elbows, knee — He had forgotten what it was to walk.

Life, he thought dazedly, is miraculous. It adapts itself to anything. If it must crawl, it crawls. Callus forms on the elbows and knees. The neck and shoulders toughen. The nostrils learn to snort away the ashes before they breathe. The bad leg swells and festers. It numbs, and presently it will rot and fall off.

"I beg pardon?" Krane said, "I didn't quite get that — "

He peered up at the tall figure before him and tried to understand the words. It was Hallmyer. He wore his stained lab coat and his gray hair was awry. Hallmyer stood delicately on top of the ashes and Krane wondered why he could see the scudding cinder clouds through his body.

"How do you like your world, Steven?" Hallmyer asked.

Krane shook his head miserably.

"Not very pretty, eh?" said Hallmyer. "Look around you. Dust, that's all; dust and ashes. Crawl, Steven, crawl. You'll find nothing but dust and ashes — "

Hallmyer produced a goblet of water from nowhere. It was clear and cold. Krane could see the fine mist of dew on its surface and his mouth was suddenly coated with grit.

"Hallmyer!" he cried. He tried to get to his feet and reach for the water, but the jolt of pain in his right leg warned him. He crouched back. Hallmyer sipped and then spat in his face. The water felt warm.

"Keep crawling," said Hallmyer bitterly. "Crawl round and round the face of the Earth. You'll find nothing but dust and ashes — " He emptied the goblet on the ground before Krane. "Keep crawling. How many miles? Figure it out for yourself. Pi-times D. The diameter is eight thousand or so — "

He was gone, coat and goblet. Krane realized that rain was falling again. He pressed his face into the warm cinder mud, opened his mouth and tried to suck the moisture. Presently he began crawling again.

There was an instinct that drove him on. He had to get somewhere. It was associated, he knew, with the sea — with the edge of the sea. At the shore of the sea something waited for him. Something that would help him understand all this. He had to get to the sea — that is, if there was a sea any more.

The thundering rain beat his back like heavy planks. Krane paused and yanked the knapsack around to his side where he probed in it with one hand. It contained exactly three things. A gun, a bar of chocolate, and a can of peaches. All that was left of two months' supplies. The chocolate was pulpy and spoiled. Krane knew he had best eat it before all the value rotted away. But in another day he would lack the strength to open the can. He pulled it out and attacked it with the opener. By the time he had pierced and pried away a flap of tin, the rain had passed.

As he munched the fruit and sipped the juice, he watched the wall of rain marching before him down the slope of the ocean bed. Torrents of water were gushing through the mud. Small channels had already been cut — channels that would be new rivers some day; a day he would never see; a day that no living thing would ever see. As he flipped the empty can aside, Krane thought: The last living thing on Earth eats its last meal. Metabolism begins the last act.

Wind would follow the rain. In the endless weeks that he had been crawling, he had learned that. Wind would come in a few minutes and flog him with its clouds of cinders and ashes. He crawled forward, bleary eyes searching the flat gray miles for cover.

Evelyn tapped his shoulder.

Krane knew it was she before he turned his head. She stood alongside, fresh and gay in her bright dress, but her lovely face was puckered with alarm.

"Steven," she said, "you've got to hurry!"

He could only admire the way her smooth hair waved to her shoulders.

"Oh, darling!" she said, "you've been hurt!" Her quick gentle hands touched his legs and back. Krane nodded.

"Got it landing," he said. "I wasn't used to a parachute. I always thought you came down gently — like plumping onto a bed. But the earth came up at me like a fist — And Umber was fighting around in my arms. I couldn't let him drop, could I?"

"Of course not, dear," Evelyn said.

"So I just held on to him and tried to get my legs under me," Krane said. "And then something smashed my legs and side — "

He hesitated, wondering how much she knew of what really had happened. He didn't want to frighten her.

"Evelyn, darling — " he said, trying to reach up his arms.

"No dear," she said. She looked back in fright. "You've got to hurry. You've got to watch out behind!"

"The cinder storms?" He grimaced. "I've been through them before."

"Not the storms!" Evelyn cried. "Something else. Oh, Steven — "

Then she was gone, but Krane knew she had spoken the truth. There was something behind — something that had been following him. In the back of his mind he had sensed the menace. It was closing in on him like a shroud. He shook his head. Somehow that was impossible. He was the last living thing on Earth. How could there be a menace?

The wind roared behind him, and an instant later came the heavy clouds of cinders and ashes. They lashed over him, biting his skin. With dimming eyes, he saw the way they coated the mud and covered it with a fine dry carpet. Krane drew his knees under him and covered his head with his arms. With the knapsack as a pillow, he prepared to wait out the storm. It would pass as quickly as the rain.

The storm whipped up a great bewilderment in his sick head. Like a child he pushed at the pieces of his memory, trying to fit them together. Why was Hallmyer so bitter toward him? It couldn't have been that argument, could it?

What argument?

Why, that one before all this happened.

Oh, that!

Abruptly, the pieces locked together.

Krane stood alongside the sleek lines of his ship and admired it tremendously. The roof of the shed had been removed and the nose of the ship hoisted so that it rested on a cradle pointed toward the sky. A workman was carefully burnishing the inner surfaces of the rocket jets.

The muffled sounds of swearing came from within the ship and then a heavy clanking. Krane ran up the short iron ladder to the port and thrust his head inside. A few feet beneath him, two men were clamping the long tanks of ferrous solution into place.

"Easy there," Krane called. "Want to knock the ship apart?"

One looked up and grinned. Krane knew what he was thinking. That the ship would tear itself apart. Everyone said that. Everyone except Evelyn. She had faith in him. Hallmyer never said it either, but Hallmyer thought he was crazy in another way. As he descended the ladder, Krane saw Hallmyer come into the shed, lab coat flying.

"Speak of the devil!" Krane muttered.

Hallmyer began shouting as soon as he saw Krane. "Now listen — "

"Not all over again," Krane said.

Hallmyer dug a sheaf of papers out of his pocket and waved it under Krane's nose.

"I've been up half the night," he said, "working it through again. I tell you I'm right. I'm absolutely right — "

Krane looked at the tight-written equations and then at Hallmyer's bloodshot eyes. The man was half mad with fear.

"For the last time," Hallmyer went on. "You're using your new catalyst on iron solution. All right. I grant that it's a miraculous discovery. I give you credit for that."

Miraculous was hardly the word for it. Krane knew that without conceit, for he realized he'd only stumbled on it. You had to stumble on a catalyst that would induce atomic disintegration of iron and give 10×10^{10} foot-pounds of energy for every gram of fuel. No man was smart enough to think all that up by himself.

"You don't think I'll make it?" Krane asked.

"To the Moon? Around the Moon? Maybe. You've got a fifty-fifty chance." Hallmyer ran fingers through his lank hair. "But for God's sake, Steven, I'm not worried about you. If you want to kill yourself, that's your own affair. It's the Earth I'm worried about — "

"Nonsense. Go home and sleep it off."

"Look — " Hallmyer pointed to the sheets of paper with a shaky hand — "No matter how you work the feed and mixing system you can't get 100 per cent efficiency in the mixing and discharge."

"That's what makes it a fifty-fifty chance," Krane said. "So what's bothering you?"

"The catalyst that will escape through the rocket tubes. Do you realize what it'll do if a drop hits the Earth? It'll start a chain of disintegration that'll envelop the globe. It'll reach out to every iron atom — and there's iron everywhere. There won't be any Earth left for you to return to — "

"Listen," Krane said wearily, "we've been through all this before."

He took Hallmyer to the base of the rocket cradle. Beneath the iron framework was a two-hundred-foot pit, fifty feet wide and lined with fire-brick.

"That's for the initial discharge flames. If any of the catalyst goes through, it'll be trapped in this pit and taken care of by the secondary reactions. Satisfied now?"

"But while you're in flight," Hallmyer persisted, "you'll be endangering the Earth until you're beyond Roche's limit. Every drop of non-activated catalyst will eventually sink back to the ground and — "

"For the very last time," Krane said grimly, "the flame of the rocket discharge takes care of that. It will envelop any escaped particles and destroy them. Now get out. I've got work to do."

As Krane pushed him to the door, Hallmyer screamed and waved his arms. "I won't let you do it!" he repeated over and over. "I won't let you risk it — "

Work? No, it was sheer intoxication to labor over the ship. It had the fine beauty of a well-made thing. The beauty of polished armor, of a balanced swept-hilt rapier, of a pair of matched guns. There was no thought of danger and death in Krane's mind as he wiped his hands with waste after the last touches were finished.

She lay in the cradle ready to pierce the skies. Fifty feet of slender steel, the rivet heads gleaming like jewels. Thirty feet were given over to fuel and catalyst. Most of the forward compartment contained the spring hammock Krane had devised to absorb the acceleration strain. The ship's nose was a porthole of natural crystal that stared upward like a cyclopian eye.

Krane thought: She'll die after this trip. She'll return to the Earth and smash in a blaze of fire and thunder, for there's no way yet of devising a safe landing for a rocket ship. But it's worth it. She'll have had her one great flight, and that's all any of us should want. One great beautiful flight into the unknown —

As he locked the workshop door, Krane heard Hallmyer shouting from the cottage across the fields. Through the evening gloom he could see him waving urgently. He trotted through the crisp stubble, breathing the sharp air deeply, grateful to be alive.

"It's Evelyn on the phone," Hallmyer said.

Krane stared at him. Hallmyer refused to meet his eyes.

"What's the idea?" Krane asked. "I thought we agreed that she wasn't to call — wasn't to get in touch with me until I was ready to start? You been putting ideas into her head? Is this the way you're going to stop me?"

Hallmyer said: "No — " and studiously examined the darkening horizon.

Krane went into his study and picked up the phone.

"Now listen, darling," he said without preamble, "there's no sense getting alarmed now. I explained everything very carefully. Just before the ship crashes, I take to a parachute. I love you very much and I'll see you Wednesday when I start. So long — "

"Good-bye, sweetheart," Evelyn's clear voice said, "and is that what you called me for?"

"Called you!"

A brown hulk disengaged itself from the hearth rug and lifted itself to strong legs. Umber, Krane's mastiff, sniffed and cocked an ear. Then he whined.

"Did you say I called you?" Krane repeated.

Umber's throat suddenly poured forth a bellow. He reached Krane in a single bound, looked up into his face and whined and roared all at once.

"Shut up, you monster!" Krane said. He pushed Umber away with his foot.

"Give Umber a kick for me," Evelyn laughed. "Yes, dear. Someone called and said you wanted to speak to me."

"They did, eh? Look, honey, I'll call you back — "

Krane hung up. He arose doubtfully and watched Umber's uneasy actions. Through the windows, the late evening glow sent flickering shadows of orange light. Umber gazed at the light, sniffed and bellowed again. Suddenly struck, Krane leaped to the window.

Across the fields a mass of flame thrust high into the air, and within it was the crumbling walls of the workshop. Silhouetted against the blaze, the figures of half a dozen men darted and ran.

Krane shot out of the cottage and with Umber hard at his heels, sprinted toward the shed. As he ran he could see the graceful nose of the spaceship within the fire, still looking cool and untouched. If only he could reach it before the flames softened its metal and started the rivets.

The workmen trotted up to him, grimy and panting. Krane gaped at them in a mixture of fury and bewilderment.

"Hallmyer!" he shouted. "Hallmyer!"

Hallmyer pushed through the crowd. His eyes gleamed with triumph.

"Too bad," he said. "I'm sorry, Steven — "

"You bastard!" Krane shouted. He grasped Hallmyer by the lapels and shook him once. Then he dropped him and started into the shed.

Hallmyer snapped orders to the workmen and an instant later a body hurtled against Krane's calves and spilled him to the ground. He lurched to his feet, fists swinging. Umber was alongside, growling over the roar of the flames. Krane battered a man in the face, and saw him stagger back against a second. He lifted a knee in a vicious drive that sent the last workman crumpling to the ground. Then he ducked his head and plunged into the shop.

The scorch felt cool at first, but when he reached the ladder and began mounting to the port, he screamed with the agony of his burns. Umber was howling at the foot of the ladder, and Krane realized that the dog could never escape from the rocket blasts. He reached down and hauled Umber into the ship.

Krane was reeling as he closed and locked the port. He retained consciousness barely long enough to settle himself in the spring hammock. Then instinct alone prompted his hands to reach out toward the control board; instinct and the frenzied refusal to let his beautiful ship waste itself in the flames. He would fail — yes. But he would fail trying.

His fingers tripped the switches. The ship shuddered and roared. And blackness descended over him.

How long was he unconscious? There was no telling. Krane awoke with cold pressing against his face and body, and the sound of frightened yelps in his ears. Krane looked up and saw Umber tangled in the springs and straps of the hammock. His first impulse was to laugh, then suddenly he realized; he had looked *up*! He had looked up at the hammock.

He was lying curled in the cup of the crystal nose. The ship had risen high — perhaps almost to Roche's zone, to the limit of the Earth's gravitational attraction, but then without guiding hands at the controls to continue its flight, had turned and was dropping back toward Earth. Krane peered through the crystal and gasped.

Below him was the ball of the Earth. It looked three times the size of the Moon. And it was no longer his Earth. It was a globe of fire mottled with black clouds. At the northernmost pole there was a tiny patch of white, and even as Krane watched, it was suddenly blotted over with hazy tones of red, scarlet, and crimson. Hallmyer had been right.

Krane lay frozen in the cup of the nose as the ship descended, watching the flames gradually fade away to leave nothing but the dense blanket of black around the Earth. He lay numb with horror, unable to understand — unable to reckon up a people snuffed out, a green fair planet reduced to ashes and cinders. Everything that was once dear and close to him — gone. He could not think of Evelyn.

Air, whistling outside, awoke some instinct in him. The few shreds of reason left told him to go down with his ship and forget everything in the thunder and destruction, but the instinct of life forced him to action. He climbed up to the store chest and prepared for the landing. Parachute, a small oxygen tank — a knapsack of supplies. Only half aware of what he was doing he dressed for the descent, buckled on the 'chute and opened the port. Umber whined pathetically, and he took the heavy dog in his arms and stepped out into space.

But space hadn't been so clogged, the way it was now. Then it had been difficult to breathe. But that was because the air had been rare — not filled with clogging grit like now.

Every breath was a lungful of ground glass — or ashes — or cinders — he had returned to a suffocating black present that hugged him with soft weight and made him fight for breath. Krane struggled in panic, and then relaxed.

It had happened before. A long time past he'd been buried deep under ashes when he'd stopped to remember. Weeks ago — or days — or months. Krane clawed with his hands, inching out of the mound of cinders that the wind had thrown over him. Presently he emerged into the light again. The wind had died away. It was time to begin his crawl to the sea once more.

The vivid pictures of his memory scattered again before the grim vista that stretched out ahead. Krane scowled. He remembered too much, and too often. He had the vague hope that if he remembered hard enough, he might change one of the things he had done — just a very little thing — and then all this would become untrue. He thought: It might help if every-one remembered and wished at the same time — but there isn't any every-one. I'm the only one. I'm the last memory on Earth. I'm the last life.

He crawled. Elbows, knee, elbows, knee — And then Hallmyer was crawling alongside and making a great game of it. He chortled and plunged in the cinders like a happy sea lion.

Krane said: "But why do we have to get to the sea?"

Hallmyer blew a spume of ashes.

"Ask her," he said, pointing to Krane's other side.

Evelyn was there, crawling seriously, intently, mimicking Krane's small-est action.

"It's because of our house," she said. "You remember our house, dar-ling? High on the cliff. We were going to live there forever and ever. I was there when you left. Now you're coming back to the house at the edge of the sea. Your beautiful flight is over, dear, and you're coming back to me. We'll live together, just we two, like Adam and Eve — "

Krane said: "That's nice."

Then Evelyn turned her head and screamed: "Oh, Steven! Watch out!" and Krane felt the menace closing in on him again. Still crawling, he stared back at the vast gray plains of ash, and saw nothing. When he looked at Evelyn again he saw only his shadow, sharp and black. Presently, it, too, faded away as the marching shaft of sunlight passed.

But the dread remained. Evelyn had warned him twice, and she was always right. Krane stopped and turned, and settled himself to watch. If he was really being followed, he would see whatever it was, coming along his tracks.

There was a painful moment of lucidity. It cleaved through his fever and bewilderment, bringing with it the sharpness and strength of a knife.

I'm mad, he thought. The corruption in my leg has spread to my brain. There is no Evelyn, no Hallmyer, no menace. In all this land there is no life but mine — and even ghosts and spirits of the underworld must have perished in the inferno that girdled the planet. No — there is nothing but me and my sickness. I'm dying — and when I perish, everything will per-ish. Only a mass of lifeless cinders will go on.

But there was a movement.

Instinct again — Krane dropped his head and lay still. Through slitted eyes he watched the ashen plains, wondering if death was playing tricks with his eyes. Another façade of rain was beating down toward him, and he hoped he could make sure before all vision was obliterated.

Yes. There.

A quarter mile back, a gray-brown shape was flitting along the gray surface. Despite the drone of the distant rain, Krane could hear the whisper of trodden cinders and see the little clouds kicking up. Stealthily he groped for the revolver in the knapsack as his mind reached feebly for explanations and recoiled from fear.

The thing approached, and suddenly Krane squinted and understood. He recalled Umber kicking with fear and springing away from him when the 'chute landed them on the ashen face of the Earth.

"Why, it's Umber," he murmured. He raised himself. The dog halted. "Here, boy!" Krane croaked gaily. "Here, boy!"

He was overcome with joy. He realized that loneliness had hung over him, a horrible sensation of oneness in emptiness. Now his was not the only life. There was another. A friendly life that could offer love and companionship. Hope kindled again.

"Here, boy!" he repeated. "Come on, boy — "

After a while he stopped trying to snap his fingers. The Mastiff hung back, showing fangs and a lolling tongue. The dog was emaciated and its eyes gleamed red in the dusk. As Krane called once more, the dog snarled. Puffs of ash leaped beneath its nostrils.

He's hungry, Krane thought, that's all. He reached into the knapsack and at the gesture the dog snarled again. Krane withdrew the chocolate bar and laboriously peeled off the paper and silver foil. Weakly he tossed it toward Umber. It fell far short. After a minute of savage uncertainty, the dog advanced slowly and snapped up the food. Ashes powered its muzzle. It licked its chops ceaselessly and continued to advance on Krane.

Panic jerked within him. A voice persisted: This is no friend. He has no love or companionship for you. Love and companionship have vanished from the land along with life. Now there is nothing left but hunger.

"No — " Krane whispered. "That isn't right that we should tear at each other and seek to devour — "

But Umber was advancing with a slinking sidle, and his teeth showed sharp and white. And even as Krane stared at him, the dog snarled and lunged.

Krane thrust up an arm under the dog's muzzle, but the weight of the charge carried him backward. He cried out in agony as his broken, swollen leg was struck by the weight of the dog. With his free hand he struck weakly, again and again, scarcely feeling the grind of teeth on his left arm. Then something metallic was pressed under him and he realized he was lying on the revolver he had let fall.

He groped for it and prayed the cinders had not clogged it. As Umber let go his arm and tore at his throat, Krane brought the gun up and jabbed the muzzle blindly against the dog's body. He pulled and pulled the trigger until the roars died away and only empty clicks sounded. Umber shuddered in the ashes before him, his body nearly shot in two. Thick scarlet stained the gray.

Evelyn and Hallmyer looked down sadly at the broken animal. Evelyn was crying, and Hallmyer reached nervous fingers through his hair in the same old gesture.

"This is the finish, Steven," he said. "You've killed part of yourself. Oh — you'll go on living, but not all of you. You'd best bury that body, Steven. It's the corpse of your soul."

"I can't," Krane said. "The wind will blow the cinders away."

"Then burn it," Hallmyer ordered with dream-logic.

It seemed that they helped him thrust the dead dog into his knapsack. They helped him take off his clothes and packed them underneath. They cupped their hands around the matches until the cloth caught fire, and blew on the weak flame until it sputtered and burned limply. Krane crouched by the fire and nursed it. Then he turned and once again began crawling down the ocean bed. He was naked now. There was nothing left of what-had-been but his flickering little life.

He was too heavy with sorrow to notice the furious rain that slammed and buffeted him, or the searing pains that were searing through his blackened leg and up his hip. He crawled. Elbows, knee, elbows, knee — Woodenly, mechanically, apathetic to everything . . . to the latticed skies, the dreary ashen plains and even the dull glint of water that lay far ahead.

He knew it was the sea — what was left of the old, or a new one in the making. But it would be an empty, lifeless sea that some day would lap against a dry, lifeless shore. This would be a planet of stone and dust, of metal and snow and ice and water, but that would be all. No more life. He, alone, was useless. He was Adam, but there was no Eve.

Evelyn waved gaily to him from the shore. She was standing alongside the white cottage with the wind snapping her dress to show the slender lines of her figure. And when he came a little closer, she ran out to him and helped him. She said nothing — only placed her hands under his shoulders and helped him lift the weight of his heavy pain-ridden body. And so at last he reached the sea.

It was real. He understood that. For even after Evelyn and the cottage had vanished, he felt the cool waters bathe his face.

Here's the sea, Krane thought, and here am I. Adam and no Eve. It's hopeless.

He rolled a little farther into the waters. They laved his torn body. He lay with his face to the sky, peering at the high menacing heavens, and the bitterness within him welled up.

"It's not right!" he cried. "It's not right that all this should pass away. Life is too beautiful to perish at the mad act of one mad creature — "

Quietly the waters laved him. Quietly . . . Calmly . . .

The sea rocked him gently, and even the death that was reaching up toward his heart was no more than a gloved hand. Suddenly the skies split apart — for the first time in all those months — and Krane stared up at the stars.

Then he knew. This was not the end of life. There could never be an end of life. Within his body, within the rotting tissues rocking gently in the sea was the source of ten million-million lives. Cells — tissues — bacteria — amoeba — Countless infinities of life that would take new root in the waters and live long after he was gone.

They would live on his rotting remains. They would feed on each other. They would adapt themselves to the new environment and feed on the minerals and sediments washed into this new sea. They would grow, burgeon, evolve. Life would reach out to the lands once more. It would begin again the same old repeated cycle that had begun perhaps with the rotting corpse of some last survivor of interstellar travel. It would happen over and over in the future ages.

And then he knew what had brought him back to the sea. There need be no Adam — no Eve. Only the sea, the great mother of life was needed. The sea had called him back to her depths that presently life might emerge once more, and he was content.

Quietly the waters comforted him. Quietly . . . Calmly . . . The mother of life rocked the last-born of the old cycle who would become the first-born of the new. And with glazing eyes Steven Krane smiled up at the stars, stars that were sprinkled evenly across the sky. Stars that had not yet formed into the familiar constellations, and would not for another hundred million centuries.

Arthur C. Clarke

The Nine Billion Names of God

(1953)

Sometimes grouped with Isaac Asimov and Robert Heinlein as one of the "Big Three," British writer Arthur C[harles] Clarke (1917–2008) is among the most well-known and popular figures in sf. Clarke won numerous awards in both the United States and the United Kingdom, including the Nebula Grand Master Award for lifetime achievement in 1986. In addition, a prestigious British sf award is named after him. A serious science writer and editor as well as a writer of fiction, Clarke is credited with proposing the outline for modern satellite communications. Indeed, he is a model of the hard sf ideal of uniting scientific expertise with literary achievement. A prominent advocate for space programs, Clarke was also recognized with a Special Achievement Award from the Association of Space Explorers. He was knighted in 1998.

A prolific writer, Clarke published more than sixty books and upwards of one hundred short stories. His most famous work is *2001: A Space Odyssey* — both the script for the acclaimed film, which he collaborated on with Stanley Kubrick, and the novel, which Clarke wrote concurrently (both based on Clarke's 1951 story "The Sentinel"). Other important works include *Childhood's End* (1953), and the multiple award–winning *Rendezvous with Rama* (1972). Many of Clarke's works describe human encounters with alien intelligence.

"The Nine Billion Names of God" is one of Clarke's most celebrated short stories and one of the most original disaster stories of all time. Like many magazine stories of its era, it is a tight, cleverly written conceptual piece with a surprise twist. It is much more than a gag story, however. Clarke was interested in metaphysics as well as science, and much of the story's unique savor comes from its seemingly dissonant marriage of religious and technological viewpoints.

"This is a slightly unusual request," said Dr. Wagner, with what he hoped was commendable restraint. "As far as I know, it's the first time anyone's been asked to supply a Tibetan monastery with an Automatic Sequence Computer. I don't wish to be inquisitive, but I should hardly have thought that your — ah — establishment had much use for such a machine. Could you explain just what you intend to do with it?"

"Gladly," replied the lama, readjusting his silk robes and carefully putting away the slide rule he had been using for currency conversions. "Your Mark V Computer can carry out any routine mathematical operation involving up to ten digits. However, for our work we are interested in *letters*, not numbers. As we wish you to modify the output circuits, the machine will be printing words, not columns of figures."

"I don't quite understand. . . ."

"This is a project on which we have been working for the last three centuries — since the lamasery was founded, in fact. It is somewhat alien to your way of thought, so I hope you will listen with an open mind while I explain it."

"Naturally."

"It is really quite simple. We have been compiling a list which shall contain all the possible names of God."

"I beg your pardon?"

"We have reason to believe," continued the lama imperturbably, "that all such names can be written with not more than nine letters in an alphabet we have devised."

"And you have been doing this for three centuries?"

"Yes: we expected it would take us about fifteen thousand years to complete the task."

"Oh," Dr. Wagner looked a little dazed. "Now I see why you wanted to hire one of our machines. But exactly what is the *purpose* of this project?"

The lama hesitated for a fraction of a second, and Wagner wondered if he had offended him. If so, there was no trace of annoyance in the reply.

"Call it ritual, if you like, but it's a fundamental part of our belief. All the many names of the Supreme Being — God, Jehovah, Allah, and so on — they are only man-made labels. There is a philosophical problem of some difficulty here, which I do not propose to discuss, but somewhere among all the possible combinations of letters that can occur are what one may call the *real* names of God. By systematic permutation of letters, we have been trying to list them all."

"I see. You've been starting at AAAAAAA . . . and working up to ZZZZZZZ. . . ."

"Exactly — though we use a special alphabet of our own. Modifying the electromatic typewriters to deal with this is, of course, trivial. A rather more interesting problem is that of devising suitable circuits to eliminate ridiculous combinations. For example, no letter must occur more than three times in succession."

"Three? Surely you mean two."

"Three is correct: I am afraid it would take too long to explain why, even if you understood our language."

"I'm sure it would," said Wagner hastily. "Go on."

"Luckily, it will be a simple matter to adapt your Automatic Sequence Computer for this work, since once it has been programed properly it will permute each letter in turn and print the result. What would have taken us fifteen thousand years it will be able to do in a hundred days."

Dr. Wagner was scarcely conscious of the faint sounds from the Manhattan streets far below. He was in a different world, a world of natural, not man-made, mountains. High up in their remote aeries these monks had been patiently at work, generation after generation, compiling their lists of meaningless words. Was there any limit to the follies of mankind? Still, he must give no hint of his inner thoughts. The customer was always right. . . .

"There's no doubt," replied the doctor, "that we can modify the Mark V to print lists of this nature. I'm much more worried about the problem of installation and maintenance. Getting out to Tibet, in these days, is not going to be easy."

"We can arrange that. The components are small enough to travel by air — that is one reason why we chose your machine. If you can get them to India, we will provide transport from there."

"And you want to hire two of our engineers?"

"Yes, for the three months that the project should occupy."

"I've no doubt that Personnel can manage that." Dr. Wagner scribbled a note on his desk pad. "There are just two other points — "

Before he could finish the sentence the lama had produced a small slip of paper.

"This is my certified credit balance at the Asiatic Bank."

"Thank you. It appears to be — ah — adequate. The second matter is so trivial that I hesitate to mention it — but it's surprising how often the obvious gets overlooked. What source of electrical energy have you?"

"A diesel generator providing fifty kilowatts at a hundred and ten volts. It was installed about five years ago and is quite reliable. It's made life at the lamasery much more comfortable, but of course it was really installed to provide power for the motors driving the prayer wheels."

"Of course," echoed Dr. Wagner. "I should have thought of that."

. . .

The view from the parapet was vertiginous, but in time one gets used to anything. After three months, George Hanley was not impressed by the two-thousand-foot swoop into the abyss or the remote checkerboard of fields in the valley below. He was leaning against the wind-smoothed stones and staring morosely at the distant mountains whose names he had never bothered to discover.

This, thought George, was the craziest thing that had ever happened to him. "Project Shangri-La," some wit back at the labs had christened it. For weeks now the Mark V had been churning out acres of sheets covered with gibberish. Patiently, inexorably, the computer had been rearranging letters in all their possible combinations, exhausting each class before going on to the next. As the sheets had emerged from the electromatic typewriters, the monks had carefully cut them up and pasted them into enormous books. In another week, heaven be praised, they would have finished. Just what obscure calculations had convinced the monks that they needn't bother to go on to words of ten, twenty, or a hundred letters, George didn't know. One of his recurring nightmares was that there would be some change of plan, and that the high lama (whom they'd naturally called Sam Jaffe, though he didn't look a bit like him) would suddenly announce that the project would be extended to approximately A.D. 2060. They were quite capable of it.

George heard the heavy wooden door slam in the wind as Chuck came out onto the parapet beside him. As usual, Chuck was smoking one of the cigars that made him so popular with the monks — who, it seemed, were quite willing to embrace all the minor and most of the major pleasures of life. That was one thing in their favor: they might be crazy, but they weren't bluenoses. Those frequent trips they took down to the village, for instance . . .

"Listen, George," said Chuck urgently. "I've learned something that means trouble."

"What's wrong? Isn't the machine behaving?" That was the worst contingency George could imagine. It might delay his return, and nothing could be more horrible. The way he felt now, even the sight of a TV commercial would seem like manna from heaven. At least it would be some link with home.

"No — it's nothing like that." Chuck settled himself on the parapet, which was unusual because normally he was scared of the drop. "I've just found what all this is about."

"What d'ya mean? I thought we knew."

"Sure — we know what the monks are trying to do. But we didn't know why. It's the craziest thing — "

"Tell me something new," growled George.

" — but old Sam's just come clean with me. You know the way he drops in every afternoon to watch the sheets roll out. Well, this time he seemed rather excited, or at least as near as he'll ever get to it. When I told him that we were on the last cycle he asked me, in that cute English accent of his, if I'd ever wondered what they were trying to do. I said, 'Sure' — and he told me."

"Go on: I'll buy it."

"Well, they believe that when they have listed all His names — and they reckon that there are about nine billion of them — God's purpose will be achieved. The human race will have finished what it was created to do, and there won't be any point in carrying on. Indeed, the very idea is something like blasphemy."

"Then what do they expect us to do? Commit suicide?"

"There's no need for that. When the list's completed, God steps in and simply winds things up . . . bingo!"

"Oh, I get it. When we finish our job, it will be the end of the world." Chuck gave a nervous little laugh.

"That's just what I said to Sam. And do you know what happened? He looked at me in a very queer way, like I'd been stupid in class, and said, 'It's nothing as trivial as *that*.'"

George thought this over for a moment.

"That's what I call taking the Wide View," he said presently. "But what d'you suppose we should do about it? I don't see that it makes the slightest difference to us. After all, we already knew that they were crazy."

"Yes — but don't you see what may happen? When the list's complete and the Last Trump doesn't blow — or whatever it is they expect — *we* may get the blame. It's our machine they've been using. I don't like the situation one little bit."

"I see," said George slowly. "You've got a point there. But this sort of thing's happened before, you know. When I was a kid down in Louisiana we had a crackpot preacher who once said the world was going to end next Sunday. Hundreds of people believed him — even sold their homes. Yet when nothing happened, they didn't turn nasty, as you'd expect. They just decided that he'd made a mistake in his calculations and went right on believing. I guess some of them still do."

"Well, this isn't Louisiana, in case you hadn't noticed. There are just two of us and hundreds of these monks. I like them, and I'll be sorry for old Sam when his lifework backfires on him. But all the same, I wish I was somewhere else."

"I've been wishing that for weeks. But there's nothing we can do until the contract's finished and the transport arrives to fly us out."

"Of course," said Chuck thoughtfully, "we could always try a bit of sabotage."

"Like hell we could! That would make things worse."

"Not the way I meant. Look at it like this. The machine will finish its run four days from now, on the present twenty-hours-a-day basis. The transport calls in a week. O.K. — then all we need to do is to find something that needs replacing during one of the overhaul periods — something that will hold up the works for a couple of days. We'll fix it of course, but not too quickly. If we time matters properly, we can be down at the airfield when the last name pops out of the register. They won't be able to catch us then."

"I don't like it," said George. "It will be the first time I ever walked out on a job. Besides, it would make them suspicious. No, I'll sit tight and take what comes."

. . .

"I *still* don't like it," he said, seven days later, as the tough little mountain ponies carried them down the winding road. "And don't you think I'm running away because I'm afraid. I'm just sorry for those poor old guys up there, and I don't want to be around when they find what suckers they've been. Wonder how Sam will take it?"

"It's funny," replied Chuck, "but when I said good-by I got the idea he knew we were walking out on him — and that he didn't care because he knew the machine was running smoothly and that the job would soon be finished. After that — well, of course, for him there just isn't any After That. . . ."

George turned in his saddle and stared back up the mountain road. This was the last place from which one could get a clear view of the lamasery. The squat, angular buildings were silhouetted against the afterglow of the sunset: here and there, lights gleamed like portholes in the side of an ocean liner. Electric lights, of course, sharing the same circuit as the Mark V. How much longer would they share it? wondered George. Would the monks smash up the computer in their rage and disappointment? Or would they just sit down quietly and begin their calculations all over again?

He knew exactly what was happening up on the mountain at this very moment. The high lama and his assistants would be sitting in their silk robes, inspecting the sheets as the junior monks carried them away from the typewriters and pasted them into the great volumes. No one would be saying anything. The only sound would be the incessant patter, the never-ending rainstorm of the keys hitting the paper, for the Mark V itself was utterly silent as it flashed through its thousands of calculations a second. Three months of this, thought George, was enough to start anyone climbing up the wall.

"There she is!" called Chuck, pointing down into the valley. "Ain't she beautiful!"

She certainly was, thought George. The battered old DC3 lay at the end of the runway like a tiny silver cross. In two hours she would be bearing them away to freedom and sanity. It was a thought worth savoring like a fine liqueur. George let it roll round his mind as the pony trudged patiently down the slope.

The swift night of the high Himalayas was now almost upon them. Fortunately, the road was very good, as roads went in that region, and they were both carrying torches. There was not the slightest danger, only a certain discomfort from the bitter cold. The sky overhead was perfectly clear, and ablaze with the familiar, friendly stars. At least there would be no risk, thought George, of the pilot being unable to take off because of weather conditions. That had been his only remaining worry.

He began to sing, but gave it up after a while. This vast arena of mountains, gleaming like whitely hooded ghosts on every side, did not encourage such ebullience. Presently George glanced at his watch.

"Should be there in an hour," he called back over his shoulder to Chuck. Then he added, in an afterthought: "Wonder if the computer's finished its run. It was due about now."

Chuck didn't reply, so George swung round in his saddle. He could just see Chuck's face, a white oval turned toward the sky.

"Look," whispered Chuck, and George lifted his eyes to heaven. (There is always a last time for everything.)

Overhead, without any fuss, the stars were going out.

J. G. Ballard

The Terminal Beach

(1964)

Iconoclastic British writer J[ames] G[raham] Ballard (b. 1930) was a leading figure in the New Wave of the 1960s, a movement that strove to infuse sf with the experimental techniques of modernist fiction and to counter the technophilia and sometimes naïve optimism that had come to mark 1950s sf, particularly in the United States. Much of Ballard's early work focused on mysterious natural disasters, as can be inferred from the titles of novels like *The Drowned World* (1962), *The Burning World* (1964), and *The Crystal World* (1966), each of which explored a different apocalyptic scenario. His later sf, such as the stories collected in *The Atrocity Exhibition* (1970), while equally nihilistic, focused more on media and politics and was increasingly experimental in form. These works, which he described as "condensed novels," present surreal mélanges of pop culture that result in disturbing social critiques. In recent years, Ballard has moved away from sf in works like the autobiographical novel *Empire of the Sun* (1984), which is based on his childhood experience of living in a Japanese prison camp during World War II and was made into a film by Steven Spielberg in 1987. Another novel, *Crash* (1973), was the basis for a controversial film directed by David Cronenberg in 1996 (not to be confused with the 2005 film of the same name).

One of Ballard's great strengths is his atmospheric description of symbolic landscapes, as can be seen in the story that follows. Like many of his stories, "The Terminal Beach" portrays a desolate, haunted landscape whose features seem to embody the darker and more destructive elements of the human unconscious. "The Terminal Beach" is a dense and sometimes difficult story, but it rewards careful reading and rereading. The story is divided by suggestive headings more typical of poetry than prose, and it incorporates a variety of forms, including lists and dramatic dialogue. To best appreciate its power, it is helpful to relinquish expectations for traditional narrative and realize that the story is meant to reproduce in the reader the experience of the narrator, who wanders through a symbolic landscape, groping for meaning.

"The Terminal Beach" is not a typical disaster story, but rather an exploration of the correspondence between the internal and the external, spiritual and physical sites of destruction. Eniwetok, where this story is set, is a Pacific atoll where the United States tested the first hydrogen bomb in 1952.

At night, as he lay asleep on the floor of the ruined bunker, Traven heard the waves breaking along the shore of the lagoon, reminding him of the deep Atlantic rollers on the beach at Dakar, where he had been born, and of waiting in the evenings for his parents to drive home along the corniche road from the airport. Overcome by this long-forgotten memory, he woke uncertainly from the bed of old magazines on which he slept and ran toward the dunes that screened the lagoon.

Through the cold night air he could see the abandoned superfortresses lying among the palms, beyond the perimeter of the emergency landing field three hundred yards away. Traven walked through the dark sand, already forgetting where the shore lay, although the atoll was only half a mile in width. Above him, along the crests of the dunes, the tall palms leaned into the dim air like the symbols of some cryptic alphabet. The landscape of the island was covered by strange ciphers.

Giving up the attempt to find the beach, Traven stumbled into a set of tracks left years earlier by a large Caterpillar vehicle. The heat released by one of the weapons tests had fused the sand, and the double line of fossil imprints, uncovered by the evening air, wound its serpentine way among the hollows like the footfalls of an ancient saurian.

Too weak to walk any further, Traven sat down between the tracks. With one hand he began to excavate the wedge-shaped grooves from a drift into which they disappeared, hoping that they might lead him toward the sea. He returned to the bunker shortly before dawn, and slept through the hot silences of the following noon.

The Blocks

As usual on these enervating afternoons, when not even the faintest breath of offshore breeze disturbed the dust, Traven sat in the shadow of one of the blocks, lost somewhere within the center of the maze. His back resting against the rough concrete surface, he gazed with a phlegmatic eye down the surrounding aisles and at the line of doors facing him. Each afternoon he left his cell in the abandoned camera bunker and walked down into the blocks. For the first half an hour he restricted himself to the perimeter aisle, now and then trying one of the doors with the rusty key in his pocket — he had found it among the litter of smashed bottles in the isthmus of sand separating the testing ground from the airstrip — and then, inevitably, with a sort of drugged stride, he set off into the center of the blocks, breaking into a run and darting in and out of the corridors, as if trying to flush some invisible opponent from his hiding place. Soon he would be completely lost. Whatever his efforts to return to the perimeter, he found himself once more in the center.

Eventually he would abandon the task, and sit down in the dust, watching the shadows emerge from their crevices at the foot of the blocks. For some reason he always arranged to be trapped when the sun was at zenith — on Eniwetok, a thermonuclear noon.

. . .

One question in particular intrigued him: "What sort of people would inhabit this minimal concrete city?"

The Synthetic Landscape

"This island is a state of mind," Osborne, one of the biologists working in the old submarine pens, was later to remark to Traven. The truth of this became obvious to Traven within two or three weeks of his arrival. Despite the sand and the few anemic palms, the entire landscape of the island was synthetic, a manmade artifact with all the associations of a vast system of derelict concrete motorways. Since the moratorium on atomic tests, the island had been abandoned by the Atomic Energy Commission, and the wilderness of weapons aisles, towers, and blockhouses ruled out any attempt to return it to its natural state. (There were also stronger unconscious motives, Traven recognized, for leaving it as it was: if primitive man felt the need to assimilate events in the external world to his own psyche, twentieth century man had reversed this process — by this Cartesian yardstick, the island at least *existed*, in a sense true of few other places.)

But apart from a few scientific workers, no one yet felt any wish to visit the former testing ground, and the naval patrol boat anchored in the lagoon had been withdrawn five years before Traven's arrival. Its ruined appearance and the associations of the island with the period of the Cold War — what Traven had christened the "Pre-Third" — were profoundly depressing, an Auschwitz of the soul whose mausoleums contained the mass graves of the still undead. With the Russo-American détente this nightmarish chapter of history had been gladly forgotten.

The Pre-Third

"The actual and potential destructiveness of the atomic bomb plays straight into the hands of the Unconscious. The most cursory study of the dream-life and fantasies of the insane shows that ideas of world-destruction are latent in the unconscious mind. Nagasaki destroyed by the magic of science is the nearest man had yet approached to the realization of dreams that even during the safe immobility of sleep are accustomed to develop into nightmares of anxiety."
— Glover, *War, Sadism, and Pacifism*

The Pre-Third: the period had been characterized in Traven's mind above all by its moral and psychological inversions, by its sense of the whole of history, and in particular of the immediate future — the two decades, 1945–1965 — suspended from the quivering volcano's lip of World War III. Even the death of his wife and six-year-old son in a motor accident seemed only part of this immense synthesis of the historical and psychic zero, the frantic highways where each morning they met their deaths, the advance causeways to the global Armageddon.

Third Beach

He had come ashore at midnight, after a hazardous search for an opening in the reef. The small motorboat he had hired from an Australian pearldiver at Charlotte Island subsided into the shallows, its hull torn by the sharp coral. Exhausted, Traven walked through the darkness among the dunes, where the dim outlines of bunkers and concrete towers loomed between the palms.

He woke the next morning into bright sunlight, lying halfway down the slope of a wide concrete beach. This ringed what appeared to be an empty reservoir or target basin, some two hundred feet in diameter, part of a system of artificial lakes built down the center of the atoll. Leaves and dust choked the waste grills, and a pool of warm water two feet deep lay in the center, reflecting a distant line of palms.

Traven sat up and took stock of himself. This brief inventory, which merely confirmed his physical identity, was limited to little more than his thin body in its frayed cotton garments. In the context of the surrounding terrain, however, even this collection of tatters seemed to possess a unique vitality. The emptiness of the island, and the absence of any local fauna, were emphasized by the huge sculptural forms of the target basins let into its surface. Separated from each other by narrow isthmuses, the lakes stretched away along the curve of the atoll. On either side, sometimes shaded by the few palms that had gained a precarious purchase in the cracked cement, were roadways, camera towers, and isolated blockhouses, together forming a continuous concrete cap upon the island, a functional megalithic architecture as gray and minatory (and apparently as ancient, in its projection into, and from, time future) as any of Assyria and Babylon.

The series of weapons tests had fused the sand in layers, and the pseudogeological strata condensed the brief epochs, microseconds in duration, of the thermonuclear age. "The key to the past lies in the present." Typically the island inverted this geologist's maxim. Here the key to the present lay in the future. The island was a fossil of time future, its bunkers and blockhouses illustrating the principle that the fossil record of life is one of armor and the exoskeleton.

Traven knelt in the warm pool and splashed his shirt and trousers. The reflection revealed the watery image of a thinly bearded face and gaunt shoulders. He had come to the island with no supplies other than a small bar of chocolate, expecting that in some way the island would provide its own sustenance. Perhaps, too, he had identified the need for food with a forward motion in time, and that with his return to the past, or at most into a zone of nontime, this need would be obviated. The privations of the previous six months, during his journey across the Pacific, had reduced his always thin body to that of a migrant beggar, held together by little more than the preoccupied gaze in his eye. Yet this emaciation, by stripping away the superfluities of the flesh, seemed to reveal an inner sinewy toughness, and economy and directness of movement.

For several hours he wandered about, inspecting one bunker after another for a convenient place to sleep. He crossed the remains of a small landing strip, next to a dump where a dozen B-29s lay across one another like dead reptile birds.

The Corpses

Once he entered a small street of metal shacks, containing a cafeteria, recreation rooms, and shower stalls. A wrecked jukebox lay half-buried in the sand behind the cafeteria, its selection of records still in their rack.

Further along, flung into a small target basin fifty yards from the shacks, were the bodies of what at first he thought were the inhabitants of this ghost town — a dozen life-size plastic models. Their half-melted faces, contorted into bleary grimaces, gazed up at him from the jumble of legs and torsos.

On either side of him, muffled by the dunes, came the sounds of waves, the great rollers on the seaward side breaking over the reefs, and onto the beaches within the lagoon. However, he avoided the sea, hesitating before any rise that might take him within its sight. Everywhere the camera towers offered him a convenient aerial view of the confused topography of the island, but he avoided their rusting ladders.

He soon realized that however confused and random the blockhouses and camera towers might seem, their common focus dominated the landscape and gave to it a unique perspective. As Traven noticed when he sat down to rest in the window slit of one of the blockhouses, all these observation posts occupied positions on a series of concentric perimeters, moving in tightening arcs toward the inmost sanctuary. This ultimate circle, below ground zero, remained hidden beyond a line of dunes a quarter of a mile to the west.

The Terminal Bunker

After sleeping for a few nights in the open, Traven returned to the concrete beach where he had woken on his first morning on the island, and made his home — if the term could be applied to that damp crumbling hovel — in a camera bunker fifty yards from the target lakes. The dark chamber between the thick canted walls, tomblike though it might seem, gave him a sense of physical reassurance. Outside, the sand drifted against the sides, half burying the narrow doorway, as if crystallizing the immense epoch of time that had elapsed since the bunker's construction. The narrow rectangles of the five camera slits, their shapes and positions determined by the instruments, studded the east wall like cryptic ideograms. Variations of these ciphers decorated the walls of the other bunkers. In the morning, if Traven was awake, he would always find the sun divided into five emblematic beacons.

Most of the time the chamber was filled only by a damp gloomy light. In the control tower at the landing field Traven found a collection of discarded magazines, and used these to make a bed. One day, lying in the bunker shortly after the first attack of beriberi, he pulled out a magazine pressing into his back and found inside it a full-page photograph of a six-year-old girl. This blond-haired child, with her composed expression and self-immersed eyes, filled him with a thousand painful memories of his son. He pinned the page to the wall and for days gazed at it through his reveries.

For the first few weeks Traven made little attempt to leave the bunker, and postponed any further exploration of the island. The symbolic journey through its inner circles set its own times of arrival and departure. He evolved no routine for himself. All sense of time soon vanished; his life became completely existential, an absolute break separating one moment from the next like two quantal events. Too weak to forage for food, he lived on the old ration packs he found in the wrecked superfortresses. Without any implements, it took him all day to open the cans. His physical decline continued, but he watched his spindling arms and legs with indifference.

By now he had forgotten the existence of the sea and vaguely assumed the atoll to be part of some continuous continental table. A hundred yards away to the north and south of the bunker a line of dunes, topped by the palisade of enigmatic palms, screened the lagoon and sea, and the faint muffled drumming of the waves at night had fused with his memories of war and childhood. To the east was the emergency landing field and the abandoned aircraft. In the afternoon light their shifting rectangular shadows would appear to writhe and pivot. In front of the bunker, where he sat, was the system of target lakes, the shallow basins extending across the center of the atoll. Above him the five apertures looked out upon this scene like the tutelary deities of some futuristic myth.

The Lakes and the Specters

The lakes had been designed originally to reveal any radiobiological changes in a selected range of flora and fauna, but the specimens had long since bloomed into grotesque parodies of themselves and been destroyed.

Sometimes in the evenings, when a sepulchral light lay over the concrete bunkers and causeways, and the basins seemed like ornamental lakes in a city of deserted mausoleums, abandoned even by the dead, he would see the specters of his wife and son standing on the opposite bank. Their solitary figures appeared to have been watching him for hours. Although they never moved, Traven was sure they were beckoning to him. Roused from his reverie, he would stumble across the dark sand to the edge of the lake and wade through the water, shouting at the two figures as they moved away hand in hand among the lakes and disappeared across the distant causeways.

Shivering with cold, Traven would return to the bunker and lie on the bed of old magazines, waiting for their return. The image of their faces, the pale lantern of his wife's cheeks, floated on the river of his memory.

The Blocks (II)

It was not until he discovered the blocks that Traven realized he would never leave the island.

At this stage, some two months after his arrival, Traven had exhausted the small cache of food, and the symptoms of beriberi had become more acute. The numbness in his hands and feet, and the gradual loss of strength, continued. Only by an immense effort, and the knowledge that the inner sanctum of the island still lay unexplored, did he manage to leave the paliasse of magazines and make his way from the bunker.

As he sat in the drift of sand by the doorway that evening, he noticed a light shining through the palms far into the distance around the atoll. Confusing this with the image of his wife and son, and visualizing them waiting for him at some warm hearth among the dunes, Traven set off toward the light. Within fifty yards he lost his sense of direction. He blundered about for several hours on the edges of the landing strip, and succeeded only in cutting his foot on a broken Coca-Cola bottle in the sand.

After postponing his search for the night, he set out again in earnest the next morning. As he moved past the towers and blockhouses the heat lay over the island in an unbroken mantle. He had entered a zone devoid of time. Only the narrowing perimeters of the bunkers warned him that he was crossing the inner field of the firetable.

He climbed the ridge which marked the furthest point in his previous exploration of the island. The plain beyond was covered with target aisles and explosion breaks. On the gray walls of the recording towers, which rose into the air like obelisks, were the faint outlines of human forms in stylized postures, the flash-shadows of the target community burned into the cement. Here and there, where the concrete apron had cracked, a line of palms hung precariously in the motionless air. The target lakes were smaller, filled with the broken bodies of plastic dummies. Most of them still lay in the inoffensive domestic postures into which they had been placed before the tests.

Beyond the furthest line of dunes, where the camera towers began to turn and face him, were the tops of what seemed to be a herd of square-backed elephants. They were drawn up in precise ranks in a hollow that formed a shallow coral.

Traven advanced toward them, limping on his cut foot. On either side of him the loosening sand had excavated the dunes, and several of the blockhouses tilted on their sides. This plain of bunkers stretched for some quarter of a mile. To one side the half-submerged hulks of a group of concrete shelters, bombed out onto the surface in some earlier test, lay like the husk of the abandoned wombs that had given birth to this herd of megaliths.

The Blocks (III)

To grasp something of the vast number and oppressive size of the blocks, and their impact upon Traven, one must try to visualize sitting in the shade of one of these concrete monsters, or walking about in the center of this enormous labyrinth which extended across the central table of the island. There were some two thousand of them, each a perfect cube fifteen feet in height, regularly spaced at ten-yard intervals. They were arranged in a series of tracts, each composed of two hundred blocks, inclined to one another and to the direction of the blast. They had weathered only slightly in the years since they were first built, and their gaunt profiles were like the cutting faces of an enormous die-plate, designed to stamp out huge rectilinear volumes of air. Three of the sides were smooth and unbroken, but the fourth, facing away from the direction of the blast, contained a narrow inspection door.

It was this feature of the blocks that Traven found particularly disturbing. Despite the considerable number of doors, by some freak of perspective only those in a single aisle were visible at any point within the maze, the rest obscured by the intervening blocks. As he walked from the perimeter into the center of the massif, line upon line of the small metal doors appeared and receded, a world of closed exits concealed behind endless corners.

Approximately twenty of the blocks, those immediately below ground zero, were solid, the walls of the remainder of varying thicknesses. From the outside they appeared to be of uniform solidity.

As he entered the first of the long aisles, Traven felt his step lighten; the sense of fatigue that had dogged him for so many months begin to lift. With their geometric regularity and finish, the blocks seemed to occupy more than their own volume of space, imposing on him a mood of absolute calm and order. He walked on into the center of the maze, eager to shut out the rest of the island. After a few random turns to left and right, he found himself alone, the vistas to the sea, lagoon, and island closed.

Here he sat down with his back against one of the blocks, the quest for his wife and son forgotten. For the first time since his arrival at the island the sense of dissociation prompted by its fragmenting landscape began to recede.

One development he did not expect. With dusk, and the need to leave blocks and find food, he realized that he had lost himself. However he retraced his steps, struck out left or right at an oblique course, oriented himself around the sun and pressed on resolutely north or south, he found himself back at his starting point. Despite his best efforts, he was unable to make his way out of the maze. That he was aware of his motives gave him little help. Only when hunger overcame the need to remain did he manage to escape.

Abandoning his former home near the aircraft dump, Traven collected together what canned food he could find in the waist turret and cockpit lockers of the superfortresses and pulled them across the island on a crude sledge. Fifty yards from the perimeter of the blocks he took over a tilting bunker, and pinned the fading photograph of the blond-haired child to the wall beside the door. The page was falling to pieces, like his fragmenting image of himself. Each evening when he woke he would eat uneagerly and then go out into the blocks. Sometimes he took a canteen of water with him and remained there for two or three days.

Traven: In Parenthesis

Elements in a quantal world:

> The terminal beach.
> The terminal bunker.
> The blocks.

The landscape is coded.

Entry points into the future=levels in a spinal landscape=zones of significant time.

The Submarine Pens

This precarious existence continued for the following weeks. As he walked out to the blocks one evening, he again saw his wife and son, standing among the dunes below a solitary tower, their faces watching him calmly. He realized that they had followed him across the island from their former haunt among the dried-up lakes. Once again he saw the beckoning light, and he decided to continue his exploration of the island.

Half a mile further along the atoll he found a group of four submarine pens, built over an inlet, now drained, which wound through the dunes from the sea. The pens still contained several feet of water, filled with strange luminescent fish and plants. A warning light winked at intervals from a metal tower. The remains of a substantial camp, only recently vacated, stood on the concrete pier outside. Greedily Traven heaped his sledge with the provisions stacked inside one of the metal shacks. With this change of diet the beriberi receded, and during the next days he returned to the camp. It appeared to be the site of a biological expedition. In a field office he came across a series of large charts of mutated chromosomes. He rolled them up and took them back to his bunker. The abstract patterns were meaningless, but during his recovery he amused himself by devising suitable titles for them. (Later, passing the aircraft dump on one of his forays, he found the half-buried jukebox, and tore the list of records from the selection panel, realizing that these were the most appropriate captions for the charts. Thus embroidered, they took on many layers of cryptic associations.)

Traven Lost Among the Blocks

> *August 5. Found the man Traven. A strange derelict figure, hiding in a bunker in the deserted interior of the island. He is suffering from severe exposure and malnutrition, but is unaware of this, or, for that matter, of any other events in the world around him. . . .*
>
> *He maintains that he came to the island to carry out some scientific project — unstated — but I suspect that he understands his real motives and the unique role of the island. . . . In some way its landscape seems to be involved with certain unconscious notions of time, and in particular with those that may be a repressed premonition of our own deaths. The attractions and dangers of such an architecture, as the past has shown, need no stressing.*

*August 6. He has the eyes of the possessed. I would
guess that he is neither the first, nor the last, to visit
the island.*
— from Dr. C. Osborne, "Eniwetok Diary"

With the exhaustion of his supplies, Traven remained within the perimeter of the blocks almost continuously, conserving what strength remained to him to walk slowly down their empty corridors. The infection in his right foot made it difficult for him to replenish his supplies from the stores left by the biologists, and as his strength ebbed he found progressively less incentive to make his way out of the blocks. The system of megaliths now provided a complete substitute for those functions of his mind which gave to it its sense of the sustained rational order of time and space, his awareness kindled from levels above those of his present nervous system (if the autonomic system is dominated by the past, the cerebro-spinal reaches toward the future). Without the blocks, his sense of reality shrank to little more than the few square inches of sand beneath his feet.

On one of his last ventures into the maze, he spent all night and much of the following morning in a futile attempt to escape. Dragging himself from one rectangle of shadow to another, his leg as heavy as a club and apparently inflamed to the knee, he realized that he must soon find an equivalent for the blocks or he would end his life within them, trapped within this self-constructed mausoleum as surely as the retinue of Pharaoh.

He was sitting exhausted somewhere within the center of the system, the faceless lines of the tomb-booths receding from him, when the sky was slowly divided by the drone of a light aircraft. This passed overhead, and then, five minutes later, returned. Seizing his opportunity, Traven struggled to his feet and made his exit from the blocks, his head raised to follow the glistening exhaust trail.

As he lay down in the bunker he dimly heard the aircraft return and carry out an inspection of the site.

A Belated Rescue

"Who are you?" A small sandy-haired man was peering down at him with a severe expression, then put away a syringe in his valise. "Do you realize you're on your last legs?"

"Traven . . . I've had some sort of accident. I'm glad you flew over."

"I'm sure you are. Why didn't you use our emergency radio? Anyway, we'll call the Navy and have you picked up."

"No . . ." Traven sat up on one elbow and felt weakly in his hip pocket. "I have a pass somewhere. I'm carrying out research."

"Into what?" The question assumed a complete understanding of Traven's motives. Traven lay in the shade beside the bunker, and drank weakly from a canteen as Dr. Osborne dressed his foot. "You've also been stealing our stores."

Traven shook his head. Fifty yards away the blue and white Cessna stood on the concrete apron like a large dragon-fly. "I didn't realize you were coming back."

"You must be in a trance."

The young woman at the controls of the aircraft climbed from the cockpit and walked over to them, glancing at the gray bunkers and blocks. She seemed unaware of or uninterested in the decrepit figure of Traven. Osborne spoke to her over his shoulder, and after a downward glance at Traven she went back to the aircraft. As she turned Traven rose involuntarily, recognizing the child in the photograph he had pinned to the wall. Then he remembered that the magazine could not have been more than four or five years old.

The engine of the aircraft started. It turned onto one of the roadways and took off into the wind.

The young woman drove over by jeep that afternoon with a small camp bed and a canvas awning. During the intervening hours Traven had slept, and woke refreshed when Osborne returned from his scrutiny of the surrounding dunes.

"What are you doing here?" the young woman asked as she secured one of the guy-ropes to the bunker.

"I'm searching for my wife and son," Traven said.

"They're on this island?" Surprised, but taking the reply at face value, she looked around her. "Here?"

"In a manner of speaking."

After inspecting the bunker, Osborne joined them. "The child in the photograph. Is she your daughter?"

"No." Traven tried to explain. "She's adopted *me*."

Unable to make sense of his replies, but accepting his assurances that he would leave the island, Osborne and the young woman returned to their camp. Each day Osborne returned to change the dressing, driven by the young woman, who seemed to grasp the role cast for her by Traven in his private mythology. Osborne, when he learned of Traven's previous career as a military pilot, assumed that he was a latter-day martyr left high and dry by the moratorium on thermonuclear tests.

"A guilt complex isn't an indiscriminate supply of moral sanctions. I think you may be overstretching yours."

When he mentioned the name Eatherly, Traven shook his head.

Undeterred, Osborne pressed: "Are you sure you're not making similar use of the image of Eniwetok waiting for your pentecostal wind?"

"Believe me, Doctor, no," Traven replied firmly. "For me the H-Bomb is a symbol of absolute freedom. Unlike Eatherly, I feel it's given me the right — the obligation, even — to do anything I choose."

"That seems strange logic," Osborne commented. "Aren't we at least responsible for our physical selves?"

Traven shrugged. "Not now, I think. After all, aren't we in effect men raised from the dead?"

Often, however, he thought of Eatherly: the prototypal Pre-Third Man, dating the Pre-Third from August 6, 1945, carrying a full load of cosmic guilt.

Shortly after Traven was strong enough to walk again he had to be rescued from the blocks for a second time. Osborne became less conciliatory.

"Our work is almost complete," he warned Traven. "You'll die here. Traven, what are you looking for?"

To himself Traven said: the tomb of the unknown civilian. *Homo Hydrogenensis*, Eniwetok Man. To Osborne he said: "Doctor, your laboratory is at the wrong end of this island."

"I'm aware of that, Traven. There are rarer fish swimming in your head that in any submarine pen."

On the day before they left Traven and the young woman drove over to the lakes where he had first arrived. As a final present from Osborne, an ironic gesture unexpected from the elderly biologist, she had brought the correct list of legends for the chromosome charts. They stopped by the derelict jukebox and she pasted them on to the selection panel.

They wandered among the supine wrecks of the superfortresses. Traven lost sight of her, and for the next ten minutes searched in and out of the dunes. He found her standing in a small amphitheater formed by the sloping mirrors of a solar energy device, built by one of the visiting expeditions. She smiled to him as he stepped through the scaffolding. A dozen fragmented images of herself were reflected in the broken panes. In some she was sans head, in others multiples of her raised arms circled her like those of a Hindu goddess. Exhausted, Traven turned away and walked back to the jeep.

As they drove away he described his glimpses of his wife and son. "Their faces are always calm. My son's particularly, although he was never really like that. The only time his face was grave was when be was being born — then he seemed millions of years old."

The young woman nodded. "I hope you find them." As an afterthought she added: "Dr. Osborne is going to tell the Navy you're here. Hide somewhere."

Traven thanked her. When she flew away from the island for the last time he waved to her from his seat beside the blocks.

The Naval Party

When the search party came for him Traven hid in the only logical place. Fortunately the search was perfunctory, and was called off after a few hours. The sailors had brought a supply of beer with them, and the search soon turned into a drunken ramble. On the walls of the recording towers Traven later found balloons of obscene dialogue chalked into the mouths of the shadow figures, giving their postures the priapic gaiety of the dancers in cave drawings.

The climax of the party was the ignition of a store of gasoline in an underground tank near the airstrip. As he listened, first to the megaphones shouting his name, the echoes receding among the dunes like the forlorn calls of dying birds, then to the boom of the explosion and the laughter as the landing craft left, Traven felt a premonition that these were the last sounds he would hear.

He had hidden in one of the target basins, lying down among the bodies of the plastic dummies. In the hot sunlight their deformed faces gaped at him sightlessly from the tangle of limbs, their blurred smiles like those of the soundlessly laughing dead. Their faces filled his mind as he climbed over the bodies and returned to the bunker.

As he walked toward the blocks he saw the figures of his wife and son standing in his path. They were less than ten yards from him, their white faces watching him with a look of almost overwhelming expectancy. Never had Traven seen them so close to the blocks. His wife's pale features seemed illuminated from within, her lips parted as if in greeting, one hand raised to take his own. His son's grave face, with its curiously fixed expression, regarded him with the same enigmatic smile of the girl in the photograph.

"Judith! David!" Startled, Traven ran forward to them. Then, in a sudden movement of light, their clothes turned into shrouds, and he saw the wounds that disfigured their necks and chests. Appalled, he cried out to them. As they vanished he fled into the safety and sanity of the blocks.

The Catechism of Goodbye

This time he found himself, as Osborne had predicted, unable to leave the blocks.

Somewhere in the shifting center of the maze, he sat with his back against one of the concrete flanks, his eyes raised to the sun. Around him the lines of cubes formed the horizons of his world. At times they would appear to advance toward him, looming over him like cliffs, the intervals between them narrowing so that they were little more than an arm's length apart, a labyrinth of narrow corridors running between them. Then they would recede from him, separating from each other like points in an expanding universe, until the nearest line formed an intermittent palisade along the horizon.

Time had become quantal. For hours it would be noon, the shadows contained within the motionless bulk of the blocks, the heat reverberating off the concrete floor. Abruptly he would find it was early afternoon or evening, the shadows everywhere like pointing fingers.

"Good-bye, Eniwetok," he murmured.

Somewhere there was a flicker of light, as if one of the blocks, like a counter on an abacus, had been plucked away.

"Good-bye, Los Alamos." Again a block seemed to vanish. The corridors around him remained intact, but somewhere, Traven was convinced, in the matrix superimposed on his mind, a small interval of neutral space had been punched.

Good-bye, Hiroshima.
Good-bye, Alamagordo.
Good-bye, Moscow, London, Paris, New York. . . .

Shuttles flickered, a ripple of integers. Traven stopped, accepting the futility of this megathlon farewell. Such a leave-taking required him to fix his signature on every one of the particles in the universe.

Total Noon: Eniwetok

The blocks now occupied positions on an endlessly revolving circus wheel. They carried him upward, to heights from which he could see the whole island and the sea, and then down again through the opaque disc of the floor. From here he looked up at the undersurface of the concrete cap, an inverted landscape of rectilinear hollows, the dome-shaped mounds of the lake-system, the thousands of empty cubic pits of the blocks.

"Good-bye, Traven"

To his disappointment he found that this ultimate act of rejection gained him nothing.

In an interval of lucidity, he looked down at his emaciated arms and legs propped loosely in front of him, the brittle wrists and hands covered with a lacework of ulcers. To his right was a trail of disturbed dust, the marks of slack heels.

In front of him lay a long corridor between the blocks, joining an oblique series a hundred yards away. Among these, where a narrow interval revealed the open space beyond, was a crescent-shaped shadow, poised in the air.

During the next half-hour it moved slowly, turning as the sun swung.

The outline of a dune.

Seizing on this cipher, which hung before him like a symbol on a shield, Traven pushed himself through the dust. He climbed precariously to his feet, and covered his eyes from all sight of the blocks.

Ten minutes later he emerged from the western perimeter. The dune whose shadow had guided him lay fifty yards away. Beyond it, bearing the shadow like a screen, was a ridge of limestone, which ran away among the hillocks of a wasteland. The remains of old bulldozers, bales of barbed wire, and fifty-gallon drums lay half-buried in the sand.

Traven approached the dune, reluctant to leave this anonymous swell of sand. He shuffled around its edges, and then sat down in the shade by a narrow crevice in the ridge.

Ten minutes later he noticed that someone was watching him.

The Marooned Japanese

This corpse, whose eyes stared up at Traven, lay to his left at the bottom of the crevice. That of a man of middle age and powerful build, it lay on its side with its head on a pillow of stone, as if surveying the window of the sky. The fabric of the clothes had rotted to a gray tattered vestment, but in the absence of any small animal predators on the island the skin and musculature had been preserved. Here and there, at the angle of knee or wrist, a bony point shone through the leathery integument of the yellow skin, but the facial mask was still intact, and revealed a male Japanese of the professional classes. Looking down at the strong nose, high forehead, and broad mouth, Traven guessed that the Japanese had been a doctor or lawyer.

Puzzled as to how the corpse had found itself here, Traven slid a few feet down the slope. There were no radiation burns on the skin, which indicated that the Japanese had been there for less than five years. Nor did he appear to be wearing a uniform, so had not been a member of a military or scientific mission.

To the left of the corpse, within reach of his hand, was a frayed leather case, the remains of a map wallet. To the right was the bleached husk of a haversack, open to reveal a canteen of water and a small jerrican.

Greedily, the reflex of starvation making him for the moment ignore this discovery that the Japanese had deliberately chosen to die in the crevice, Traven slid down the slope until his feet touched the splitting soles of the corpse's shoes. He reached forward and seized the canteen. A cupful of flat water swilled around the rusting bottom. Traven gulped down the water, the dissolved metal salts cloaking his lips and tongue with a bitter film. He pried the lid off the jerrican, which was empty but for a tacky coating of condensed syrup. He scraped at this with the lid and chewed at the tarry flakes. They filled his mouth with an almost intoxicating sweetness. After a few moments he felt light-headed and sat back beside the corpse. Its sightless eyes regarded him with unmoving compassion.

The Fly

(*A small fly, which Traven presumes has followed him into the crevice, now buzzes about the corpse's face. Traven leans forward to kill it, then reflects that perhaps this minuscule sentry had been the corpse's faithful companion, in return fed on the rich liqueurs and distillation of its pores. Carefully, to avoid injuring the fly, he encourages it to alight on his wrist.*)

DR. YASUDA: Thank you, Traven. (*The voice is rough, as if unused to conversation.*) In my position, you understand.

TRAVEN: Of course, doctor. I'm sorry I tried to kill it. These ingrained habits, you know, they're not easy to shrug off. Your sister's children in Osaka in '44, the exigencies of war, I hate to plead them, most known motives are so despicable one searches the unknown in the hope that. . . .

YASUDA: Please, Traven, do not be embarrassed. The fly is lucky to retain its identity for so long. That son you mourn, not to mention my own two nieces and nephew, did they not die each day? Every parent in the world mourns the lost sons and daughters of their past childhoods.

TRAVEN: You're very tolerant, doctor. I wouldn't dare —

YASUDA: Not at all, Traven. I make no apologies for you. After all, each of us is little more than the meager residue of the infinite unrealized possibilities of our lives. But your son and my nieces are fixed in our minds forever, their identities as certain as the stars.

TRAVEN: (*not entirely convinced*) That may be so, doctor, but it leads to a dangerous conclusion in the case of this island. For instance, the blocks. . . .

YASUDA: They are precisely what I refer. Here among the blocks, Traven, you at last find the image of yourself free of time and space. This island is an ontological Garden of Eden; why try to expel yourself into a quantal world?

TRAVEN: Excuse me. (*The fly has flown back to the corpse's faces and sits in one of the orbits, giving the good doctor an expression of quizzical beadiness. Reaching forward, Traven entices it onto his palm.*) Well, yes, these bunkers may be ontological objects, but whether this is the ontological fly seems doubtful. It's true that on this island it's the only fly, which is the next best thing.

YASUDA: You can't accept the plurality of the universe, Traven. Ask yourself, why? Why should this obsess you. It seems to me that you are hunting for the white leviathan, zero. The beach is a dangerous zone; avoid it. Have a proper humility; pursue a philosophy of acceptance.

TRAVEN: Then may I ask why you came here, doctor?

YASUDA: To feed this fly. "What greater love — ?"

TRAVEN: (*still puzzling*) It doesn't really solve my problem. The blocks, you see. . . .

YASUDA: Very well, if you must have it that way . . .

TRAVEN: But, Doctor —

YASUDA: (*peremptorily*) Kill that fly!

TRAVEN: That's not an end, or a beginning. (*Hopelessly he kills the fly. Exhausted, he falls asleep beside the corpse.*)

The Terminal Beach

Searching for a piece of rope in the refuse dump behind the dunes, Traven found a bale of rusty wire. He unwound it, then secured a harness around the corpse's chest, and dragged it from the crevice. The lid of a wooden crate served as a sledge. Traven fastened the corpse into a sitting position, and set off along the perimeter of the blocks. Around him the island was silent. The lines of palms hung in the sunlight, only his own motion varying the shifting ciphers of their crisscrossing trunks. The square turrets of the camera towers jutted from the dunes like forgotten obelisks.

An hour later, when Traven reached his bunker, he untied the wire cord he had fastened around his waist. He took the chair left for him by Dr. Osborne and carried it to a point midway between the bunker and the blocks. Then he tied the body of the Japanese to the chair, arranging the hands so that they rested on the wooden arms, giving the moribund figure a posture of calm repose.

This done to his satisfaction, Traven returned to the bunker and squatted under the awning.

As the next days passed into weeks, the dignified figure of the Japanese sat in his chair fifty yards from him, guarding Traven from the blocks. Their magic still filled Traven's reveries, but he now had sufficient strength to rouse himself and forage for food. In the hot sunlight the skin of the Japanese became more and more bleached, and sometimes Traven would wake at night to find the white sepulchral figure sitting there, arms resting at its sides, in the shadows that crossed the concrete floor. At these moments he would often see his wife and son watching him from the dunes. As time passed they came closer, and he would sometimes turn to find them only a few yards behind him.

Patiently Traven waited for them to speak to him, thinking of the great blocks whose entrance was guarded by the seated figure of the dead archangel, as the waves broke on the distant shore and the burning bombers fell through his dreams.

Stanislaw Lem

How the World Was Saved

(1967)

Polish writer Stanislaw Lem (1921–2006) was one of the most important figures in world sf; his groundbreaking and influential works have been translated into forty languages. Lem trained as a medical doctor, but his studies were interrupted by World War II; Lem, who was of Jewish ancestry, survived the Nazi occupation by forging identity papers and working as a mechanic, reputedly doing his own small part for the Resistance by subtly sabotaging the German vehicles he repaired. Lem completed his medical studies after the war but did not take his exams in order to avoid being drafted into the military. Instead of practicing medicine, Lem worked as a scientific researcher while pursuing his literary interests, before turning to writing as a full-time career. His novels include *His Master's Voice* (1968) and *Solaris* (1961), which was twice adapted for film, first by Russian director Andrei Tarkovsky in 1971, then by American Steven Soderbergh in 2002.

Lem, a European intellectual with high literary standards, wrote provocative and important criticism of sf. He was intolerant of mediocrity and critical both of the banality of some American sf and the jingoism that often marked the Soviet variety. He was granted an honorary membership in the Science Fiction Writers of America (SFWA) association in 1973, but his membership was revoked in 1976 following a controversy over his criticism of American sf.

Translated by Michael Kandel.

The story that follows is taken from *The Cyberiad* (first published in Polish in 1967), a collection of short stories about the exploits of Trurl and Klapaucius, two talented but comical and trouble-prone inventors who happen to be robots. The full title of the book, *The Cyberiad: Fables for the Cybernetic Age*, suggests that the book is both an epic and a collection of fanciful tales with a serious moral intent. To say that this book provides fables for the cybernetic age implies that these stories, however playful, are intended as philosophical lessons on technology in the modern world.

"How the World Was Saved" begins with the seemingly absurd premise of a machine that can create anything beginning with the letter *n*. The title of this story is both appropriate and ironic. Like all the stories in *The Cyberiad*, "How the World Was Saved" is full of verbal puns and linguistic, philosophical, and scientific jokes. While maintaining the comic tone, however, the story takes a darker turn, becoming a kind of inverted creation story. It is a parable about the dangers of invention and about being careful what you wish for.

One day Trurl the constructor put together a machine that could create anything starting with *n*. When it was ready, he tried it out, ordering it to make needles, then nankeens and negligees, which it did, then nail the lot to narghiles filled with nepenthe and numerous other narcotics. The machine carried out his instructions to the letter. Still not completely sure of its ability, he had it produce, one after the other, nimbuses, noodles, nuclei, neutrons, naphtha, noses, nymphs, naiads, and *natrium*. This last it could not do, and Trurl, considerably irritated, demanded an explanation.

"Never heard of it," said the machine.

"What? But it's only sodium. You know, the metal, the element . . ."

"Sodium starts with an *s*, and I work only in *n*."

"But in Latin it's *natrium*."

"Look, old boy," said the machine, "if I could do everything starting with *n* in every possible language, I'd be a Machine That Could Do Everything in the Whole Alphabet, since any item you care to mention undoubtedly starts with *n* in one foreign language or another. It's not that easy. I can't go beyond what you programmed. So no sodium."

"Very well," said Trurl and ordered it to make Night, which it made at once — small perhaps, but perfectly nocturnal. Only then did Trurl invite over his friend Klapaucius the constructor, and introduced him to the machine, praising its extraordinary skill at such length, that Klapaucius grew annoyed and inquired whether he too might not test the machine.

"Be my guest," said Trurl. "But it has to start with *n*."

"N?" said Klapaucius. "All right, let it make Nature."

The machine whined, and in a trice Trurl's front yard was packed with naturalists. They argued, each publishing heavy volumes, which the others tore to pieces; in the distance one could see flaming pyres, on which martyrs to Nature were sizzling; there was thunder, and strange mushroom-shaped columns of smoke rose up; everyone talked at once, no one listened, and there were all sorts of memoranda, appeals, subpoenas, and other documents, while off to the side sat a few old men, feverishly scribbling on scraps of paper.

"Not bad, eh?" said Trurl with pride. "Nature to a T, admit it!"

But Klapaucius wasn't satisfied.

"What, that mob? Surely you're not going to tell me that's Nature?"

"Then give the machine something else," snapped Trurl. "Whatever you like." For a moment Klapaucius was at a loss for what to ask. But after a little thought he declared that he would put two more tasks to the machine; if it could fulfill them, he would admit that it was all Trurl said it was. Trurl agreed to this, whereupon Klapaucius requested Negative.

"Negative?!" cried Trurl. "What on earth is Negative?"

"The opposite of positive, of course," Klapaucius coolly replied. "Negative attitudes, the negative of a picture, for example. Now don't try to pretend you never heard of Negative. All right, machine, get to work!"

The machine, however, had already begun. First it manufactured antiprotons, then antielectrons, antineutrons, antineutrinos, and labored on, until from out of all this antimatter an antiworld took shape, glowing like a ghostly cloud above their heads.

"H'm," muttered Klapaucius, displeased. "That's supposed to be Negative? Well . . . let's say it is, for the sake of peace. . . . But now here's the third command: Machine, do Nothing!"

The machine sat still. Klapaucius rubbed his hands in triumph, but Trurl said:

"Well, what did you expect? You asked it to do nothing, and it's doing nothing."

"Correction: I asked it to do Nothing, but it's doing nothing."

"Nothing is nothing!"

"Come, come. It was supposed to do Nothing, but it hasn't done anything, and therefore I've won. For Nothing, my dear and clever colleague, is not your run-of-the-mill nothing, the result of idleness and inactivity, but dynamic, aggressive Nothingness, that is to say, perfect, unique, ubiquitous, in other words Nonexistence, ultimate and supreme, in its very own nonperson!"

"You're confusing the machine!" cried Trurl. But suddenly its metallic voice rang out:

"Really, how can you two bicker at a time like this? Oh yes, I know what Nothing is, and Nothingness, Nonexistence, Nonentity, Negation, Nullity, and Nihility, since all these come under the heading of n, n as in Nil. Look then upon your world for the last time, gentlemen! Soon it shall no longer be . . ."

The constructors froze, forgetting their quarrel, for the machine was in actual fact doing Nothing, and it did it in this fashion: one by one, various things were removed from the world, and the things, thus removed, ceased to exist, as if they had never been. The machine had already disposed of nolars, nightzcbs, nocs, necs, nallyrakers, neotremes and nonmalrigers. At moments, though, it seemed that instead of reducing, diminishing, and subtracting, the machine was increasing, enhancing, and adding, since it liquidated, in turn: nonconformists, nonentities, nonsense, nonsupport, nearsightedness, narrowmindedness, naughtiness, neglect, nausea, necrophilia, and nepotism. But after a while the world very definitely began to thin out around Trurl and Klapaucius.

"Omigosh!" said Trurl. "If only nothing bad comes out of all this . . ."

"Don't worry," said Klapaucius. "You can see it's not producing Universal Nothingness, but only causing the absence of whatever starts with n. Which is really nothing in the way of nothing, and nothing is what your machine, dear Trurl, is worth!"

"Do not be deceived," replied the machine. "I've begun, it's true, with everything in n, but only out of familiarity. To create however is one thing, to destroy, another thing entirely. I can blot out the world for the simple reason that I'm able to do anything and everything — and everything means everything — in n, and consequently Nothingness is child's play for me. In less than a minute now you will cease to have existence, along with everything else, so tell me now, Klapaucius, and quickly, that I am really and truly everything I was programmed to be, before it is too late."

"But — " Klapaucius was about to protest, but noticed, just then, that a number of things were indeed disappearing, and not merely those that started with n. The constructors were no longer surrounded by the gruncheons, the targalisks, the shupops, the calinatifacts, the thists, worches, and pritons.

"Stop! I take it all back! Desist! Whoa! Don't do Nothing!!" screamed Klapaucius. But before the machine could come to a full stop, all the brashations, plusters, laries, and zits had vanished away. Now the machine stood motionless. The world was a dreadful sight. The sky had particularly suffered: there were only a few, isolated points of light in the heavens — no trace of the glorious worches and zits that had, till now, graced the horizon!

"Great Gauss!" cried Klapaucius. "And where are the gruncheons? Where my dear, favorite pritons? Where now the gentle zits?!"

"They no longer are, nor ever will exist again," the machine said calmly. "I executed, or rather only began to execute, your order . . ."

"I tell you to do Nothing, and you . . . you . . ."

"Klapaucius, don't pretend to be a greater idiot than you are," said the machine. "Had I made Nothing outright, in one fell swoop, everything would have ceased to exist, and that includes Trurl, the sky, the Universe, and you — and even myself. In which case who could say and to whom could it be said that the order was carried out and I am an efficient and capable machine? And if no one could say it to no one, in what way then could I, who also would not be, be vindicated?"

"Yes, fine, let's drop the subject," said Klapaucius. "I have nothing more to ask of you, only please, dear machine, please return the zits, for without them life loses all its charm . . ."

"But I can't, they're in z," said the machine. "Of course, I can restore nonsense, narrowmindedness, nausea, necrophilia, neuralgia, nefariousness, and noxiousness. As for the other letters, however, I can't help you."

"I want my zits!" bellowed Klapaucius.

"Sorry, no zits," said the machine. "Take a good look at this world, how riddled it is with huge, gaping holes, how full of Nothingness, the Nothingness that fills the bottomless void between the stars, how everything about us has become lined with it, how it darkly lurks behind each shred of matter. This is your work, envious one! And I hardly think the future generations will bless you for it . . ."

"Perhaps . . . they won't find out, perhaps they won't notice," groaned the pale Klapaucius, gazing up incredulously at the black emptiness of space and not daring to look his colleague, Trurl, in the eye. Leaving him beside the machine that could do everything in *n*, Klapaucius skulked home — and to this day the world has remained honeycombed with nothingness, exactly as it was when halted in the course of its liquidation. And as all subsequent attempts to build a machine on any other letter met with failure, it is to be feared that never again will we have such marvelous phenomena as the worches and the zits — no, never again.

C. J. Cherryh

Cassandra

(1978)

C. J. Cherryh (Carolyn Janice Cherry, b. 1942) is a prolific and highly respected writer of both fantasy and science fiction, with over forty novels to her name. A former teacher with a master's degree in Classics, Cherryh's many interests include ancient history and archaeology. Cherryh has received six major sf awards, including the John W. Campbell Award for Best New Writer (1976) and Hugos for *Downbelow Station* (1982) and *Cyteen* (1989), which also won the Locus Award. "Cassandra," which won the Hugo in 1979, was also nominated for the Nebula. As a writer, Cherryh is noted for her creation of elaborate worlds with diverse cultures and for her sophisticated handling of moral ambiguity, particularly in novels like the three-volume "future history" *Cyteen.* Although her world-building talents are best suited to a novelist, the story that follows demonstrates how much emotional depth Cherryh can convey in a terse and relatively simple narrative.

"Cassandra" is a haunting apocalyptic tale that focuses on the trauma of a narrator who sees things others do not — a mysterious ability that serves only to intensify her isolation. In Homer's *Iliad*, Cassandra was a Trojan princess cursed with the ability to see the future without being able to change it or to persuade others to heed her warnings.

*F*ires.
They grew unbearable here.

Alis felt for the door of the flat and knew that it would be solid. She could feel the cool metal of the knob amid the flames . . . saw the shadow-stairs through the roiling smoke outside clearly enough to feel her way down them, convincing her senses that they would bear her weight.

Crazy Alis. She made no haste. The fires burned steadily. She passed through them, descended the insubstantial steps to the solid ground — she could not abide the elevator, that closed space with the shadow-floor, that plummeted down and down; she made the ground floor, averted her eyes from the red, heatless flames.

A ghost said good morning to her . . . old man Willis, thin and transparent against the leaping flames. She blinked, bade it good morning in return — did not miss old Willis's shake of the head as she opened the door and left. Noon traffic passed, heedless of the flames, the hulks that blazed in the street, the tumbling brick.

The apartment caved in — black bricks falling into the inferno, Hell amid the green, ghostly trees. Old Willis fled, burning, fell — turned to jerking, blackened flesh — died, daily. Alis no longer cried, hardly flinched. She ignored the horror spilling about her, forced her way through crumbling brick that held no substance, past busy ghosts that could not be troubled in their haste.

Kingsley's Café stood, whole, more so than the rest. It was refuge for the afternoon, a feeling of safety. She pushed open the door, heard the tinkle of a lost bell. Shadowy patrons looked, whispered.

Crazy Alis.

The whispers troubled her. She avoided their eyes and their presence, settled in a booth in the corner that bore only traces of the fire.

WAR, the headline in the vendor said in heavy type. She shivered, looked up into Sam Kingsley's wraithlike face.

"Coffee," she said. "Ham sandwich." It was constantly the same. She varied not even the order. Mad Alis. Her affliction supported her. A check came each month, since the hospital had turned her out. Weekly she returned to the clinic, to doctors who now faded like the others. The building burned about them. Smoke rolled down the blue, antiseptic halls. Last week a patient ran — burning —

A rattle of china. Sam set the coffee on the table, came back shortly and brought the sandwich. She bent her head and ate, transparent food on half-broken china, a cracked, fire-smudged cup with a transparent handle. She ate, hungry enough to overcome the horror that had become ordinary. A hundred times seen, the most terrible sights lost their power over her: she no longer cried at shadows. She talked to ghosts and touched them, ate the food that somehow stilled the ache in her belly, wore the same too-large black sweater and worn blue shirt and gray slacks because they were all she had that seemed solid. Nightly she washed them and dried them and put them on the next day, letting others hang in the closet. They were the only solid ones.

She did not tell the doctors these things. A lifetime in and out of hospitals had made her wary of confidences. She knew what to say. Her half-vision let her smile at ghost-faces, cannily manipulate their charts and cards, sitting in the ruins that had begun to smolder by late afternoon. A blackened corpse lay in the hall. She did not flinch when she smiled good-naturedly at the doctor.

They gave her medicines. The medicines stopped the dreams, the siren screams, the running steps in the night past her apartment. They let her sleep in the ghostly bed, high above ruin, with the flames crackling and the voices screaming. She did not speak of these things. Years in hospitals had taught her. She complained only of nightmares, and restlessness, and they let her have more of the red pills.

WAR, the headline blazoned.

The cup rattled and trembled against the saucer as she picked it up. She swallowed the last bit of bread and washed it down with coffee, tried not to look beyond the broken front window, where twisted metal hulks smoked on the street. She stayed, as she did each day, and Sam grudgingly refilled her cup, which she would nurse as far as she could and then she would order another one. She lifted it, savoring the feeling of it, stopping the trembling of her hands.

The bell jingled faintly. A man closed the door, settled at the counter.

Whole, clear in her eyes. She stared at him, startled, heart pounding. He ordered coffee, moved to buy a paper from the vendor, settled again, and let the coffee grow cold while he read the news. She had a view only of his back while he read — scuffed brown leather coat, brown hair a little over his collar. At last he drank the cooled coffee all at one draught, shoved money onto the counter, and left the paper lying, headlines turned face down.

A young face, flesh and bone among the ghosts. He ignored them all and went for the door.

Alis thrust herself from her booth.

"Hey!" Sam called at her.

She rummaged in her purse as the bell jingled, flung a bill onto the counter, heedless that it was a five. Fear was coppery in her mouth; he was gone. She fled the café, edged round debris without thinking of it, saw his back disappearing among the ghosts.

She ran, shouldering them, braving the flames — cried out as debris showered painlessly on her, and kept running.

Ghosts turned and stared, shocked — *he* did likewise, and she ran to him, stunned to see the same shock on his face, regarding her.

"What is it?" he asked.

She blinked, dazed to realize he saw her no differently than the others. She could not answer. In irritation he started walking again, and she followed. Tears slid down her face, her breath hard in her throat. People stared. He noticed her presence and walked faster, through debris, through fires. A wall began to fall, and she cried out despite herself.

He jerked about. The dust and the soot rose up as a cloud behind him. His face was distraught and angry. He stared at her as the others did. Mothers drew children away from the scene. A band of youths stared, cold-eyed and laughing.

"Wait," she said. He opened his mouth as if he would curse her; she flinched, and the tears were cold in the heatless wind of the fires. His face twisted in an embarrassed pity. He thrust a hand into his pocket and began to pull out money, hastily, tried to give it to her. She shook her head furiously, trying to stop the tears — stared upward, flinching, as another building fell into flames.

"What's wrong?" he asked her. "What's wrong with you?"

"Please," she said. He looked about at the staring ghosts, then began to walk slowly. She walked with him, nerving herself not to cry out at the ruin, the pale moving figures that wandered through burned shells of buildings, the twisted corpses in the street, where traffic moved.

"What's your name?" he asked. She told him. He gazed at her from time to time as they walked, a frown creasing his brow. He had a face well-worn for youth, a tiny scar beside the mouth. He looked older than she. She felt uncomfortable in the way his eyes traveled over her: she decided to accept it — to bear with anything that gave her this one solid presence. Against every inclination she reached her hand into the bend of his arm, tightened her fingers on the worn leather. He accepted it.

And after a time he slid his arm behind her and about her waist, and they walked like lovers.

WAR, the headline at the newsstand cried.

He started to turn into a street by Tenn's Hardware. She balked at what she saw there. He paused when he felt it, faced her with his back to the fires of that burning.

"Don't go," she said.

"Where do you want to go?"

She shrugged helplessly, indicated the main street, the other direction.

He talked to her then, as he might talk to a child, humoring her fear. It was pity. Some treated her that way. She recognized it, and took even that.

His name was Jim. He had come into the city yesterday, hitched rides. He was looking for work. He knew no one in the city. She listened to his rambling awkwardness, reading through it. When he was done, she stared at him still, and saw his face contract in dismay at her.

"I'm not crazy," she told him, which was a lie that everyone in Sudbury would have known, only *he* would not, knowing no one. His face was true and solid, and the tiny scar by the mouth made it hard when he was thinking; at another time she would have been terrified of him. Now she was terrified of losing him amid the ghosts.

"It's the war," he said.

She nodded, trying to look at him and not at the fires. His fingers touched her arm, gently. "It's the war," he said again. "It's all crazy. Everyone's crazy."

And then he put his hand on her shoulder and turned her back the other way, toward the park, where green leaves waved over black, skeletal limbs. They walked along the lake, and for the first time in a long time she drew breath and felt a whole, sane presence beside her.

They bought corn and sat on the grass by the lake and flung it to the spectral swans. Wraiths of passersby were few, only enough to keep a feeling of occupancy about the place — old people, mostly, tottering about the deliberate tranquility of their routine despite the headlines.

"Do you see them," she ventured to ask him finally, "all thin and gray?"

He did not understand, did not take her literally, only shrugged. Warily, she abandoned that questioning at once. She rose to her feet and stared at the horizon, where the smoke bannered on the wind.

"Buy you supper?" he asked.

She turned, prepared for this, and managed a shy, desperate smile. "Yes," she said, knowing what else he reckoned to buy with that — willing, and hating herself, and desperately afraid that he would walk away, tonight, tomorrow. She did not know men. She had no idea what she could say or do to prevent his leaving, only that he would when someday he recognized her madness.

Even her parents had not been able to bear with that — visited her only at first in the hospitals, and then only on holidays, and then not at all. She did not know where they were.

There was a neighbor boy who drowned. She had said he would. She had cried for it. All the town said it was she who pushed him.

Crazy Alis.

Fantasizes, the doctors said. Not dangerous.

They let her out. There were special schools, state schools.

And from time to time — hospitals.

Tranquilizers.

She had left the red pills at home. The realization brought sweat to her palms. They gave sleep. They stopped the dreams. She clamped her lips against the panic and made up her mind that she would not need them — not while she was not alone. She slipped her hand into his arm and walked with him, secure and strange, up the steps from the park to the streets.

And stopped.

The fires were out.

Ghost-buildings rose above their jagged and windowless shells. Wraiths moved through masses of debris, almost obscured at times. He tugged her on, but her step faltered, made him look at her strangely and put his arm about her.

"You're shivering," he said. "Cold?"

She shook her head, tried to smile. The fires were out. She tried to take it for a good omen. The nightmare was over. She looked up into his solid, concerned face, and her smile almost became a wild laugh.

"I'm hungry," she said.

They lingered over a dinner in Graben's — he in his battered jacket, she in her sweater that hung at the tails and elbows: the spectral patrons were in far better clothes and stared at them, and they were set in a corner nearest the door, where they would be less visible. There was cracked crystal and broken china on insubstantial tables, and the stars winked coldly in gaping ruin above the wan glittering of the broken chandeliers.

Ruins, cold, peaceful ruin.

Alis looked about her calmly. One could live in ruins, only so the fires were gone.

And there was Jim, who smiled at her without any touch of pity, only a wild, fey desperation that she understood — who spent more than he could afford in Graben's, the inside of which she had never hoped to see — and told her — predictably — that she was beautiful. Others had said it. Vaguely she resented such triteness from him, from him whom she had decided to trust. She smiled sadly when he said it; and gave it up for a frown; and, fearful of offending him with her melancholies, made it a smile again.

Crazy Alis. He would learn and leave tonight if she were not careful. She tried to put on gaiety, tried to laugh.

And then the music stopped in the restaurant, and the noise of the other diners went dead, and the speaker was giving an inane announcement.

Shelters . . . shelters . . . shelters.

Screams broke out. Chairs overturned.

Alis went limp in her chair, felt Jim's cold, solid hand tugging at hers, saw his frightened face mouthing her name as he took her up into his arms, pulled her with him, started running.

The cold air outside hit her, shocked her into sight of the ruins again, wraith figures pelting toward that chaos where the fires had been worst.

And she knew.

"No!" she cried, pulling at his arm. "No!" she insisted, and bodies half-seen buffeted them in a rush to destruction. He yielded to her sudden certainty, gripped her hand, and fled with her against the crowds as the sirens wailed madness through the night — fled with her as she ran her sighted way through the ruin.

And into Kingsley's, where café tables stood abandoned with food still on them, doors ajar, chairs overturned. Back they went into the kitchens and down and down into the cellar, the dark, the cold safety from the flames.

No others found them there. At last the earth shook, too deep for sound. The sirens ceased and did not come on again.

They lay in the dark and clutched each other and shivered, and above them for hours raged the sound of fire, smoke sometimes drifting in to sting their eyes and noses. There was the distant crash of brick, rumblings that shook the ground, that came near, but never touched their refuge.

And in the morning, with the scent of fire still in the air, they crept up into the murky daylight.

The ruins were still and hushed. The ghost-buildings were solid now, mere shells. The wraiths were gone. It was the fires themselves that were strange, some true, some not, playing above dark, cold brick, and most were fading.

Jim swore softly, over and over again, and wept.

When she looked at him she was dry-eyed, for she had done her crying already.

And she listened as he began to talk about food, about leaving the city, the two of them. "All right," she said.

Then clamped her lips, shut her eyes against what she saw in his face. When she opened them it was still true, the sudden transparency, the wash of blood. She trembled, and he shook at her, his ghost-face distraught.

"What's wrong?" he asked. "What's wrong?"

She could not tell him, would not. She remembered the boy who had drowned, remembered the other ghosts. Of a sudden she tore from his hands and ran, dodging the maze of debris that, this morning, was solid.

"Alis!" he cried and came after her.

"No!" she cried suddenly, turning, seeing the unstable wall, the cascading brick. She started back and stopped, unable to force herself. She held out her hands to warn him back, saw them solid.

The brick rumbled, fell. Dust came up, thick for a moment, obscuring everything.

She stood still, hands at her sides, then wiped her sooty face and turned and started walking, keeping to the center of the dead streets.

Overhead, clouds gathered, heavy with rain.

She wandered at peace now, seeing the rain spot the pavement, not yet feeling it.

In time the rain did fall, and the ruins became chill and cold. She visited the dead lake and the burned trees, the ruin of Graben's, out of which she gathered a string of crystal to wear.

She smiled when, a day later, a looter drove her from her food supply. He had a wraith's look, and she laughed from a place he did not dare to climb and told him so.

And recovered her cache later when it came true, and settled among the ruined shells that held no further threat, no other nightmares, with her crystal necklace and tomorrows that were the same as today.

One could live in ruins, only so the fires were gone.

And the ghosts were all in the past, invisible.

Sakyo Komatsu

Take Your Choice

(1967; trans. 1987)

Sakyo Komatsu (b. 1931) is among the foremost sf writers in Japan. He is the recipient of numerous honors and an active figure in the international science fiction community, and his books have been the basis of several major films. His most famous novel is *Nippon Chinbotsu* (1973), which was translated into English as *Japan Sinks* (1976). A film version of *Nippon Chinbotsu* was directed by Toho Eiga in 1973 and released in a freely adapted version by Richard Corman as *Tidal Wave* in 1974.

Japanese sf is best known internationally through its films and graphic novels, but Japan has also produced a great deal of high-quality literary sf,

Translated by Shiro Tamura and Grania Davis.

including work by genre authors and by high-profile mainstream writers like Kobo Abe. Although sf has been written in Japan since the late nineteenth century, the genre experienced a surge in popularity after World War II. Not surprisingly, given Japan's history as the only country thus far to have suffered a nuclear strike, much of its postwar fiction focuses on apocalyptic themes. Although this continues to be an interest for many Japanese writers, more recent Japanese sf is marked by a surreal, dreamlike quality that incorporates traditional mythology and mysticism along with stylistic experimentation.

Like many Japanese sf writers, Komatsu has focused on disaster scenarios in many of his stories. "Take Your Choice," however, is a disaster story with a difference, a provocative thought experiment with an unsettling twist — several twists, actually, by turns comic and grim. The title is a fittingly ironic reminder that we are all responsible for the consequences of our choices.

A t first he thought he'd been following the streets as he'd been directed, but he seemed to have missed the landmark somewhere along the way, as he wandered here and there among the intricate alleyways and back streets. Now he was unable to find his way.

Since he could think of no other way out, he decided to leave the squalid tangle of back streets and go back to the main street, where he could start again from the very beginning. But no sooner had he started walking than the landmark appeared.

But the appearance of the shop before him was quite different from what he'd been told. The man who described the shop said that it was for underwater swimming equipment. This shop was apparently a secondhand shop packed with old fashioned robots and two-dimensional TV sets now considered almost antique.

However, he decided to speak to the elderly man in the shop who seemed to be the proprietor.

"Can I take a choice?"

The elderly man with too shiny hair, which was doubtless a wig, turned his lusterless eyes from the three-dimensional TV set that he'd been watching. One of his eyes was an ash-colored electron-glass eye which was oddly distorted sideways.

"Have some kind of introduction from someone?" asked the elderly proprietor unamiably.

He produced from his pocket a piece of paper with a strange sign on it, which he got from his acquaintance as a token of introduction, and a five credit bill.

The elderly proprietor looked at the sign on the paper, then he put it under a machine that resembled a check examiner — then he put the five credit bill into his pocket and stood up to open the door at the end of the room.

"Please . . ." The elderly proprietor showed him the way, thrusting out his chin.

"Are you remodeling the shop?" he asked. "I heard that it was shop for underwater swimming equipment."

"Oh *that*! There's another entrance facing the other side of the block," explained the elderly proprietor. "It's just opposite the next block of buildings — so you came back here by mistake. But it's all the same once you're inside the shop."

Behind the door were steep stairs going downward. Pointing his forefinger toward the door at the foot of the stairs, the elderly proprietor said, "It's inside that door. It's pretty dark down there, but you keep on walking straight as there will be only one corridor — mind your step."

It was quite understandable that he gave such a warning, for if you looked carefully, the stairs were made of prefabricated feather-weight framing structures used for scaffolding at building sites. It appeared so fragile that if your fingernail should accidentally catch any part sticking out of the structure, it would likely fall into pieces, he thought.

The walls weren't illuminated, but there was an outdated fluorescent lamp hanging from the ceiling. At his every step and movement, the stairs trembled and made loud creaking noises. The stairs were on wheels and the entrance had recently been installed, so he concluded that the whole structure could be removed at a moment's notice if necessary.

As soon as he opened the odd looking hatch-like iron door at the bottom of the stairs, he smelled unpleasantly damp air surrounding him. He guessed that there must be a hidden ion air-cleaning device working somewhere, but even so the place didn't deceive him for he sensed a sewerish atmosphere, even though it was furnished with a red carpet and the walls in a subtle color were attractive enough. Judging from the feel of the floor, he was sure this corridor was a prefabricated structure.

It smells rotten, he thought — but if it is really . . . Again there was another door at the end of the corridor. When he knocked on the door, he thought he heard the clicking sound of a camera-eye blink, then the door opened solemnly — this door seemed unnaturally dignified.

Inside the door was an oblong waiting room, as if it were still a continuation of the corridor. It looked rather like the inside of a lounge-type, old fashioned railroad car. The floor was furnished with a dark green carpet which looked luxurious at first sight, but the furniture was of very poor taste, and a flashy three-dimensional TV set was mounted on the wall. It still looked like a special private coach compartment, despite all that. If he had visited a red light district a long time ago, it would have reminded him of a brothel waiting parlor. He sniffed and frowned a bit as he eyed the furniture — he hesitated for a moment deciding whether to sit on a grimy looking chair and didn't dare to do it. While he was still standing beside the chair, the door of the next room was opened by a little man with dull eyes asking him to come in. "This way, please."

Wondering how many doors he must go through, he followed the man into the next room. At first sight, he thought he'd come to the dead end of the passage he'd been through, but then he noticed that there again were three doors on the wall beyond a big desk in front of him. Observing carefully, he noticed that the upper part of the doors appeared to be a screen of some kind.

"Please sit down." The little man with the absent-minded expression spoke to him with the same vague voice as before.

As he sat on the chair facing the desk, he expected to see an office manager appear from one of these doors, but none of them opened. Instead the little man with the vacant look who'd admitted him walked around the desk and comfortably seated himself on the chair.

"Has anyone given you an introduction . . . ?" asked the small man with the vacant face — this was partly because his grey-white eyes were unmistakably crossed.

When he mentioned the token name of the stranger he'd met at a bar where he learned about this place, the little man languidly nodded.

"I see — it seems all right. Yes, he's one of my trusted friends," said the little man. "By the way . . . are you prepared to pay the full fee here?"

"Yes, I've brought the money with me," he said. "Two million five hundred thousand credits, isn't it?"

"By check or in cash?"

"Credits in cash — in small units."

"Good." The little man nodded but stopped him from taking his wallet from his pocket. "No, that's not necessary for the moment. You can pay later. It's such a large sum of money, you should pay the fee when you actually do it."

He thought this was merely a gesture on the part of this shabby-looking man — but of course there's no point hurrying to pay, so he removed his hand from his pocket.

"Well . . ." The little man with his chin in his palms gave him a sharp look. "How much do you know about this thing?"

"I heard that one can choose his future or something like that."

"Is that all?"

"Y-yes . . ."

The little man stood up and rubbed his head with one hand, chewing a fingernail at the same time. "That would be a bit difficult," he said. "I don't know exactly what you have in mind — but it won't be as fantastic as you imagine. It will only have a subtle effect on your immediate future life. It really isn't such an exciting discovery or anything, since it came about rather by pure chance."

"Whatever it is, explain it to me will you . . . ?" he said eagerly. In fact his curiosity was aroused by the little man's reluctant attitude — though that also might be a trick.

"Then I'll tell you the truth. I — and my partner, too — aren't people of this present world."

"Then you are . . . ?" He had to swallow hard before he could say it. "By any chance you are . . . ?"

"Yes, we are. We're from the future, so to speak. We've time traveled as sort of escapees or violators of the time traveler control laws in our world."

He wondered if what he'd just heard was at all true, as he gazed intently at the little man. In his appearance there was nothing remarkably different from us, except his vagueness and a slipshod manner in his behavior.

"Then?" he urged the man.

"So then by producing in this world a more powerful time travel mechanism with prolonged mobility, we could fly into a time and place which would be beyond the control of our Time Authorities. We would simply fade somewhere into the intricate network of time."

"Wait a moment!" he interrupted. "Why are you in trouble with . . . ?"

"You couldn't understand the strictness of the time travel regulations, no matter how hard I try to explain it." The little man shook his head sadly. "In order to get a permit, we must go through all sorts of red-tape procedures, and a most demanding inspection is required. Above all, we must always be with an official guide of the Time Travel Control Department. An individual time-traveling alone is an act of first class crime in our society."

"Well, that's adequate," he nodded. "I can't understand the ways of your society. Those who lived in a car-less era would never be able to comprehend the offense of excessive speeding on the highways. But choosing one's future — by using your time mechanism?"

"Well, no, not exactly. Strictly speaking, it's done through the use of certain functions of the mechanism — only the time-space channel selector and time-scope are needed."

"I don't think I follow you."

"If you aren't aware of the fundamentals of time travel, it's very difficult to explain it to you. Anyway, we can't use the drive energy of the mechanism too readily. In short, we can't afford to put you in the machine and send you into the future or past worlds. If we did that, the wave impact of the mechanism in motion would attract the attention of the Time Patrol."

"I see. Then . . . ?"

"Then we can use the time-space channel. That is, we merely have to make a whole of part of a multi-dimensional area — so it's really nothing difficult."

"Do you think you could explain that more simply?" he said, feeling slightly irritated. "Why on earth will that lead to a choice in my future?"

"It's something to do with why one can time-travel," said the little man with a sympathetic smile. "Any explanation would be incomprehensible for you, I'm afraid, so I'll make it more symbolic. Did you know that our world and our history aren't the only possibilities? There are infinite possibilities into the past or into the future existing side by side."

"No . . . I didn't," he answered vaguely. "But I think I've heard something like that before, and it isn't impossible to conceive of an idea like that — to a certain extent."

"You see, it's similar to the theory in non-Euclidian geometry that you can draw unlimited numbers of lines parallel to a line passing a point — which aren't on the line. Because of that, in the early age of time travel, there were many incidents in which travelers didn't return to the time-space point of departure after their trip to the future or the past. For instance, suppose you are starting from the point P to a certain point A in the future. This future isn't the only possibility of A extended from point P, there are also A_2, A_3, A_4 . . . an infinite number of possibilities into the future. Anyway, you go to a point A in one future among the others, but when you try to return to the starting point by descending the time ladder to the past, you often find yourself unable to do so. Because the course from point A to the past is also divided into unlimited numbers of $P_2, P_3 \ldots P_n$."

"I see." He gave a disgusted look of faked comprehension. "So?"

"To avoid such a labyrinth effect, the time-space channel selector was invented, which uses a kind of resonance phenomenon. By making use of the time-space resonance between point A and point P and driving the time mechanism along the resonance channel, you can travel from P to A, and then return from A to P without going astray. But with this method you can't go into future or past worlds which are variably spread as unlimited numbers of branches — you have access only to several channels at the resonance juncture, depending on the efficiency of the oscillator. The more powerful an oscillator is, the more channels you will have. *Our* time mechanism has only three channels."

At last he began to understand a little. "Therefore," he said, "I can choose my future. Am I right?"

"Well, yes, in a manner of speaking," nodded the little man. "This channel selector will give you a direction from this very room in this world at this moment towards three possible directions into the future. But this only gives you a certain direction, so your choice of a future world won't immediately materialize. You can take your choice among the future worlds we offer, and we send you into the channel of your choice. Then from that point on, among all the possible future worlds to which we have access, you, your surroundings, and the history of the entire world will move in a certain direction."

"In other words . . ." The words stuck in his throat. "There are three different passages into the future from this room, aren't there?"

"Exactly." The little man pointed a finger behind him. "An oscillator is installed behind those three doors, and once you go through one of the channel doors there will be a time-space world with a distinct direction toward its future."

"What are these three future worlds? Will I learn about them in advance?" He leaned forward as he felt his voice begin to tremble with excitement.

"One moment, please . . ." The little man reached his hand under the desk. "I'll show you a bit of the future by operating the time scope along the channels."

The room suddenly became dark. The upper panels of the three doors began to shine with pale light. "From the right-hand corner these are numbers one, two, and three history courses," said the little man. "Starting number one, then . . ." The door panel on the right-hand side shone brighter than before. "The upper part of the panel is the time scope . . ."

There was something moving in the light, then it slowly took shape — it resembled a three-dimensional color TV set, he thought.

The scene appearing on the screen was that of a future city being built vigorously, at incredible speed. Covered by a bubble-dome, there were buildings of various shapes; a circular cone, a honeycomb pattern, a cylinder and ball — which themselves were cities, joined by pipeways spreading among them like the meshes of a spider's web.

Without any visible device, people themselves were flying in the air — perhaps by using a gravity control device — and a huge rocket, also a city, was heading for a planet or star. Factories, buildings, and artificial land were spreading over the surface of the earth, now orbited by a large number of man-made satellite cities.

"Seen enough?" asked the little man.

"All right," he murmured. "Second course, please . . ."

The second door panel began to glitter. It was a kind of Restoration scene. The city was far more simple in its designs than in the first scene, and buildings weren't soaring into the sky, but were distributed harmoniously among the scenic beauties of nature. Roads bordered with beautiful flowers and trees were spaciously etched on the land. Gracefully designed cars were moving slowly on the wide roads, while producing no exhaust fumes, noise, or dust.

People's clothes were also simple, but the men were handsome as Adonis, and all the women had a nymph-like appearance. The sun, shimmering and golden, seemed to be artificial, and the climate seemed to be under human control. But the machines and all devices seemed harmoniously designed, though most of them were hidden behind the classical façade of the city. Its appearance showed the most beautiful moment of the history it had reached.

Athletic meetings were being held in stadiums and pools, while music played continuously at outdoor concert halls. Recitations of poetry were taking place in public salons where any passerby could drop in freely. Among the white clouds in the sky there was a swan-shaped aircraft with a gravity control device, floating like a waterbird on a lake . . .

"Classical esthetic harmony . . ." he murmured. "They must have made some daring artificial changes."

"Next — may I?" the little man asked.

"Please . . ." he answered.

The screen of the third door panel didn't brighten for a while — but there was a sense of something busily moving behind the dim light. Soon there appeared a city and its people walking in confusion this way and that. It seemed to him that the appearance of this city wasn't much different from the present world. Dust, smog, bustling streets, dingy-looking tall buildings, decaying apartment buildings that had become slums . . .

But somewhere above the city there was a sense of uneasiness. People's faces were tense with inexplicable anticipation mixed with anxiety, impatience, and resignation. Suddenly at the corner of the street someone shouted as he looked up at the sky. The tensed faces of the fearful people turned at once in the same direction.

Immediately after that, a blinding flash beamed on the screen and he had to turn his face from it. The light was so strong that it left some red and green hazy images in his eyes for a while, and he could see nothing else.

"Is that all?" he asked.

"No, not yet; there's a bit more to it," the little man's voice was heard from the darkness near him. "Here comes the scene."

At first he couldn't make out what it was. Something like a big black stain. It took some time for him to realize that it was actually a gigantic hole that covered the entire city. Around the burnt-out hole there were ruins — looking like mere masses of melted glass which spread for several miles, and even the mountains in the far distance were turned into masses of molten rock. Within several hundred miles of the crater no grass or trees or perhaps even bacteria survived, not to mention birds and animals. Every sign of life in the area was gone. High in the sky there hung the reddish-brown colored clouds of radioactive dust being blown by the wind.

Tidal waves struck everywhere and typhoons were born by the thousands. There was no sign of surviving human beings, as if they'd never existed at all. It seemed that they'd turned into a heap of carbon or light ashes, and most of them must now be floating in the air as a mass of lethal radioactivity.

The light was turned on and the image on the screen faded.

"Well," said the little man in his usual indifferent, monotonous voice. "These are the three possible futures that our time-space channel selector can contact. Whichever you fancy — take your choice, please."

"I have a question," he said, his voice a little husky. "What's the distance in time to the era just seen on the screen of what you call a time scope?"

"These three are almost the same distance from the present time. They aren't really very distant futures. The distance in time covered by this time scope isn't always the same, but it's more or less between several years ahead to a little more than a decade into the future — perhaps twenty years ahead of us at maximum."

"One more thing," he said. "Can I come back here at all?"

"I'm afraid you can't do that. To return to this world you'd need a time mechanism." The little man yawned slightly as he spoke. "Well now, take your choice, please . . ."

He thought for a moment or two then said, "Number two seems like a good choice."

"Then we'd like to charge you the fixed fee," said the little man. "You might think it's a very large sum, but you may consider it as some sort of donation to the liberalists from the future world — to help their escape."

He took out his bulging wallet and paid the little man the amount of money charged.

"I'm going to open the door of channel two now. . . ." The little man put the money into a drawer and stood up. "And there are things we want you to be aware of after you've selected your future."

He felt his forehead sweating unreasonably hard. Wiping it with the back of his hand, he looked again at the three doors in turn, comparing them carefully.

"As I told you many times, this will only give you a certain direction towards your future, but you're not going to be sent immediately into the future world that you've just seen on the screen. You see, we must make sure that you don't misunderstand that point. For this reason, the world beyond this door won't be any different from this present world you're now in. Your everyday life, the city, family and friends, all of those will be exactly the same as in this world. But of course there will be some changes taking place in the future, and as time passes it will become different from all the other worlds, and will definitely move towards the future you've just seen. And . . ."

"Excuse me . . ." he said hesitatingly, in a quiet voice.

"And you must promise us one thing. We'd like you to keep your mouth shut in the world of the other side, about the fact that you've come from this side and met us here. It wouldn't do you any harm, nor would it give you any advantage if you told the whole story, but we're bound to get in trouble if any of the Time Patrolmen secretly mingle among the people of that era and learn about this operation here. Please promise me not to say a word about this, will you? Now . . ."

"Just a moment . . ." he said. "Can I still change my choice?"

"Well, I suppose you could, but . . ."

"Let me see the three future worlds once more, will you?"

The little man switched on the machine again. Watching the scenes simultaneously appear on the three door panels, he swallowed hard.

"All right," he said in a painful voice. "I've made up my mind. It'll be number three."

"Did you say *number three*?" the little man replied with some amazement. "That's an odd choice to make. As you see, this is just . . ."

"I know," he answered, wiping the cold sweat off his face. "The other two futures are so predictable that they will be realized sooner or later even if I don't try to create them by paying a large sum of money."

"The third one might well be the same, don't you think?"

"No . . ." Painfully clearing his throat he continued, "Rather than living in an uncertain world where a holocaust is always present as a possibility, I think I can be at ease in a world where the holocaust is sure to take place. What's more, I feel that this future isn't so easily obtainable by other means. A world that will *certainly see its holocaust while I'm alive* — such a world . . ."

"As you like . . ." The little man shrugged. "There are many customers who've said the same thing. Then please come to the front of the number three door."

Feeling his mouth drying, he advanced towards the third door.

The thought that he was taking such an irrevocable step made his whole body tense. *Get back!* an inner voice shouted. *What a foolish choice you're making! It's not too late yet. Get back!*

His entire body — every living cell, all resisted with their total strength against the choice that would bring him certain death. Even so, he was still standing in front of the third door as he nervously rubbed his hands. He was now drenched with sweat.

"Now please . . ." said the little man in a disinterested voice. "Beyond this door is a passage. You may feel some discomfort when you enter the time-space channel, but it won't be unbearable, I assure you. Go straight. At the end of the passage there will be another door, and on the other side is a room exactly the same as this one. Its appearance is the same — but it won't be on this side any longer. You won't have any trouble over there. You'll be able to live the same life that you've been leading in this world. That is . . . for the time being. Now, good luck."

With a faint creaking noise, the door opened. Shivering as if suffering from a fever, he walked towards the darkness that now opened in front of him — as though he were pulled by some unseen string.

Get back! Such words still echoed somewhere inside his body, but he kept on walking. He didn't notice when he'd passed the entrance, but suddenly he heard the door slam shut behind him, and he was now in total darkness. Frantically he groped in the darkness and looked back at the door he'd just entered.

But he was surrounded by utter blackness, and he couldn't even tell how wide the place was. He began to move very slowly, step by step. The passage was a gentle slope going downward. As he walked, the floor of the passage abruptly became soft like jelly. It was so sudden that he lost his balance and crashed into a wall. He felt peculiar vibrations all around him, and he couldn't help feeling sick with a painful headache and giddiness.

He felt as if the darkness itself began to revolve around him, but he kept on walking with gritted teeth, though he often lost his balance and crashed here and there as he tried to advance.

When he finally recovered, he was leaning against something cold. He touched it with his hand; it seemed to be an iron door. He had finally reached the end of the passage.

He knocked on the door as many times as he was told, and the door opened without a sound. For a while he couldn't see anything because of the blinding brightness that filled the room, so he stood there with unsteady feet. Beyond the door was just as the little man had told him; a room which appeared exactly the same as the last one.

At first he was under the false impression that he had returned to the original room. But soon he noticed that the room was one that belonged to the world of the other side because there was only one door in this room, though there had been three in the previous room from which he'd just exited.

"Welcome to this world . . ." said a little man — actually not the same little man, but a little man belonging to this world — but with the same dull voice as before. "This is the way out, please."

"Before I leave, I'd like to ask you one thing," he finally said with some difficulty. "I've just come from the world of the other side. If that is the case, what will happen to the relation between the other 'I', who was originally in this world, and myself? Won't we clash in some way?"

"Oh, that's OK, don't worry . . ." the little man told him in a tired manner. "It would be a long story if I had to explain it, but anyway we've sent another 'you' belonging to this world into the world you were living in before, through a certain method — so there's no problem."

"But how did you . . . ?"

"This is the way out, please," said the little man. "Goodbye."

He sensed there was no more chance for him to get further explanations, so he left the room without argument. The same corridor, the same stairs and second-hand shop — he walked through all these and came out to the same dingy back streets where he'd walked before.

The place looked exactly the same as the one he'd just been through. Every detail of the scene was the same, even the scribbling on a fence and the thickness of the clouds in the sky.

But — he knew. This world was destined to be cut off from its future at some point by an inevitable holocaust. That was a fact known only to him — and to those others who had chosen door number three from those three doors. This secret was the sort of thing that most of the populace would never have dreamed of.

I am the only one, he said to himself as he looked up at the polluted sky of the city. *No one except me definitely knows the fate of this world. Several years, or perhaps a decade from now — I will see that blinding flash of light above this city, and everything will come to an end. What absolute certainty!*

Unlike those other two worlds beyond the doors, this world has no future after that. There will be no tedious, prolonged years that will be recorded as an infinite repetition of daily life. When seen in that light, every aspect of the city — scattered litter, a snotty urchin, wandering stray dogs, and even flashing sign-boards, everything was framed in pathetic outline. It seemed to him as though they were delineated by the vivid and sharp lines of death and destruction. And for the first time in ten years he felt clarity, liveliness, and tragic satisfaction filling his heart.

With a steady gait he began to walk towards an area of the city that knew nothing — but was moving poignantly towards the inevitable holocaust of the future . . . his future.

"We're making a fortune, my friend, said the little man as he took out a cash credit ledger from the desk. "It's nearly a billion now. Are we going to continue doing this?"

"Of course," said the other man, the friend. "Our boss is also happy with the results. Anyway, there's no other scam as profitable as this, right? Time machine and time channel . . . well, aren't we clever to make up such a story! We use a pipe from a sewer and if we get into trouble by any chance, we'll simply disappear. But I'm sure it's going to be OK for quite a while."

"That's right," said the little man with his vague voice. "Going to be more customers day after day, and if we stick to this method no one will suspect us. Since each one believes that he's in another world, no one opens his mouth. Above all, they're afraid of being looked at as complete nuts if they try to tell a story like that."

"Time-space channel . . ." said his pal with a chuckle. "Using only ordinary doors of no special value and shopworn sf films — don't you think that's pretty good? Ask them to step in the door with an air of importance. Make them faint once in the next small room with an anesthetic gas and a vibrating device, and when they come out through the very same door, we make sure they think they're in another world. You know, people are so funny. When they enter the next room, we show them three doors and when they come out we hide the two other doors with curtains, and that's all they need to make them believe they've come into a different room. Nobody suspects or tries to check the room."

"But, my friend," the little man said in a subdued voice, "there's one thing bothering me a bit . . ."

"Our boss says he's going to set up more branches throughout the world," the friend said in a lordly manner. "As long as we've got customers, we're going to make money. There are already 400 'shops' in the world, and there'll be more to come. So what's bothering you?"

"The other day at headquarters I had a look at the statistical data," said the little man, frowning. "One after another, most of the customers choose door number three. Why is that? It's the same here — nearly every one of them chooses number three after a moment of hesitation."

"That shows, contrary to one's expectations, that people have a strong desire for destruction," the friend chuckled. "Though they may speak of peace and humanism when they open their mouths, in their minds — consciously or otherwise — they all want to witness the end of the world — the final dramatic holocaust, rather than a tedious thriving, if they can vanish with the others without suffering. People are, in one way or another, very lewd. Can't help having a wish to peep. To satisfy this secret lustful desire for peeping, they don't care if the world is blown up. So that's what they are — but it's going to be OK. It'll be a long time before they finally realize that they've been deceived. Probably not for a decade, right?"

"But my friend," said the little man with a hollow voice, "already, just at our store alone, more than several thousand people have all gone through door number three. In the coming years, if those people increase at this rate, what's going to happen to the world? If the people who believe that this world will definitely be finished in little more than a decade are going to increase in large numbers all over the world . . . ? You know, among our customers there were many officials, officers, politicians . . ."

Ian McDonald

Recording Angel

(1996)

One of the United Kingdom's most important contemporary sf writers, Ian McDonald has won a number of awards, including the Philip K. Dick, the Sturgeon, and the Locus best first novel award. Among his three British Science Fiction Association awards are one for his critically acclaimed 2004 novel *River of Gods* and one for "The Djinn's Wife" — which also won the

Hugo — in 2007. Many of McDonald's works — like the story that follows — are set in developing countries and explore postcolonial issues — perhaps not surprising for someone who has lived most of his life in Northern Ireland.

"Recording Angel" (which is an outtake from the highly regarded novel *Evolution's Shore*, published in the United Kingdom in 1995 as *Chaga*), is a strange kind of alien-invasion story, a story of identity, destiny, and transformation set in near-future Kenya, where a young reporter is sent to cover a celebrity-studded end-of-the-world party at a famous tourist hotel.

"Recording Angel" strongly echoes Ballard's *Crystal World*, although McDonald denies any influence; the echoes may come via Joseph Conrad's *Heart of Darkness*, which was an influence on Ballard as well. In "Recording Angel," the reader may be discomfited by references to a primordial "dark Africa" and a romanticized "Great White Hunter," but the story wears its clichés, as the characters do their khaki safari clothes, with — as McDonald puts it — a certain air of "twenty-first-century *knowing*."

For the last ten miles she drove past refugees from the xenoforming. Some were in their own vehicles. Many rode town buses that had been commandeered to take the people south, or the grubby white trucks of the UNHCR. Most walked, pushing the things they had saved from the advancing Chaga on handcarts or barrows, or laden on the heads and backs of women and children. That has always been the way of it, the woman thought as she drove past the unbroken file of people. The world ends, the women and children must carry it, and the United Nations sends its soldiers to make sure they do not drop it. And the news corporations send their journalists to make sure that the world sees without being unduly disturbed. After all, they are only Africans. A continent is being devoured by some thing from the stars, and I am sent to write the obituary of a hotel.

"I don't do gossip," she had told T. P. Costello, SkyNet's Nairobi station chief when he told her of the international celebrities who were coming to the death-party of the famous Treehouse Hotel. "I didn't come to this country to cream myself over who's wearing which designer dress or who's having an affair with or getting from whom."

"I know, I know," T. P. Costello had said. "You came to Kenya to be a player in Earth's first contact with the alien. Everyone did. That's why I'm sending you. Who cares what Brad Pitt thinks about the Gas Cloud theory versus the Little Gray Men theory? Angles are what I want. You can get angles, Gaby. What can you get?"

"Angles, T. P.," she had replied, wearily, to her editor's now-familiar litany.

"That's correct. And you'll be up there with it, right on terminum. That's what you want, isn't it?"

That's correct, T. P., she thought. Three months in Kenya and all she had seen of the Chaga had been a distant line of color, like surf on a far reef, under the clouded shadow of Kilimanjaro, advancing imperceptibly but inexorably across the Amboseli plain. The spectator's view. Up there, on the highlands around Kirinyaga where the latest biological package had come down, she would be within touching distance of it. The player's view.

There was a checkpoint up at Nanyuki. The South African soldiers in blue UN helmets at first did not know how to treat her, thinking that with her green eyes and long mahogany hair she might be another movie star or television celebrity. When her papers identified her as Gaby McAslan, on-line multimedia journalist with SkyNet East Africa, they stopped being respectful. A woman they could flirt with, a journalist they could touch for bribes. Gaby endured their flirtations and gave their commanding officer three of the dwindling stock of duty-free Swatches she had bought expressly for the purpose of petty corruption. In return she was given a map of the approved route to the hotel. If she stayed on it she would be safe. The bush patrols had orders to shoot suspected looters or loiterers.

Beyond the checkpoint there were no more refugees. The only vehicles were carrying celebrities to the party at the end of the world, and the news corporations following them. The Kikuyu *shambas* on either side of the road had been long abandoned. Wild Africa was reclaiming them. For a while, then something else would reclaim them from wild Africa. Reverse terraforming, she thought. Instead of making an alien world into Earth, Earth is made into an alien world. In her open-top SkyNet 4x4, Gaby could sense the Chaga behind the screen of heavy high-country timber, and edgy presence of the alien, and electric tingle of anticipation. She had never been this close before.

When the first biological package came down on the summit of Kilimanjaro, she had known, in SkyNet Multimedia News's U.K. office among the towers of London's Docklands, that this fallen star had her name written on it. The stuff that had come out of it, that looked a little like rain forest and a little like drained coral reef but mostly like nothing anyone had ever seen before, that disassembled terrestrial vegetation into its component molecules and incorporated them into its own matrix at an unstoppable fifty meters every day, confirmed her holy business. The others that came down in the Bismarck Archipelago, the Ruwenzori, in Ecuador and Papua New Guinea and the Maldives, these were only memos from the star gods. It's here, it's waiting for you. Hurry up now.

Now, the Nyandarua package, drawing its trail of plasma over Lake Victoria and the Rift Valley, would bring her at last face-to-face with life from the stars.

She came across a conga-line of massive tracked transporters, each the size of a large house, wedged into the narrow red-dirt road. Prefabricated accommodation cabins were piled up on top of the transporters. Branches bent and snapped as the behemoths ground past at walking pace. Gaby had heard that UNECTA, the United Nations agency that coordinated research into the Chagas, had dismantled its Ol Tukai base, one of four positioned around Kilimanjaro, all moving backward in synchrony with the advance of the southern Chaga, and sent it north. UNECTA's pockets were not deep enough, it seemed, to buy a new mobile base, especially now that the multinationals had cut their contributions in the absence of any exploitable technologies coming out of the Chaga.

UNECTA staff on the tops of the mobile towers waved as she drove carefully past in the red muddy verges. They can probably see the snows of Kirinyaga from that height, she thought. Between the white mountains. We run from the south, we run from the north but the expanding circles of vegetation are closing on us and we cannot escape. Why do we run? We will all have to face it in the end, when it takes everything we know and changes it beyond recognition. We have always imagined that because it comes down in the tropics it is confined here. Why should climate stop it? Nothing else has. Maybe it will only stop when it closes around the poles. Xenoforming complete.

The hotel was one of those buildings that are like animals in zoos, that by their stillness and coloration can hide from you even when you are right in front of them, and you only know they are there because of the sign on the cage. Two Kenyan soldiers far too young for the size of their weapons met her from the car park full of tour buses and news-company 4x4s. They escorted her along a dirt path between skinny, gray-trunked trees. She could still not see the hotel. She commented on the small wooden shelters that stood every few meters along the path.

"In case of charging animals," the slightly older soldier said. "But this is better." He stroked his weapon as if it were a breast. "Thirty heavy-caliber rounds per second. That will stop more than any wooden shelter."

"Since the Chaga has come there are many more animals around," the younger soldier said. He had taken the laces out of his boots, in the comfortable, country way.

"Running away," Gaby said. "Like any sane thing should."

"No," the young, laceless soldier said. "Running into."

There was a black-painted metal fire escape at the end of the track. As Gaby squinted at the incongruity, the hotel resolved out of the greenery before her. Many of the slim, silver tree trunks were wooden piles, the mass of leaves and creepers concealed the superstructure bulking over her.

The steward met her at the top of the stairs, checked her name against the guest list, and showed her her room, a tiny wooden cabin with a view of leaves. Gaby thought it must be like this on one of the UNECTA mobile bases; minimal, monastic. She did something to her face and went up to the party on the roof. It had been running for three days. It would only end when the hotel did. The party at the edge of the end of the world. In one glance she saw thirty newsworthy faces and peeked into her bag to check the charge level on her disc recorder. She talked to it as she moved between the faces to the bar. The *Out of Africa* look was the thing among the newsworthy this year: riding breeches, leather, with the necessary twist of twenty-first-century *knowing* with the addition of animal-skin prints.

Gaby ordered a piña colada from the Kenyan barman and wondered as he shook it what incentive the management had offered him — all the staff — to stay. Family relocation to other hotels, on the Coast, down in

Zanzibar, she reckoned. And where do they go when they run out of hotels to relocate to? Interesting, but not the angle, she decided as the barman poured out the thick, semeny proof of his ability.

"Bugger all here, T. P.," she said to the little black machine in her shirt pocket. Then cocktail-party dynamics parted the people in front of her and there it was, one hundred feet away beyond the gray wooden railing, at the edge of the artificial water hole they dredged with bulldozers in the off-season. One hundred feet. Fifteen seconds walk. Eighteen hours crawl. If you kept very still and concentrated you would be able to see it moving, as you could see the slow sweep of the minute hand of your watch. This was the Chaga not on the geographical scale, devouring whole landscapes, but on the molecular.

Gaby walked through the gap in the bright and the beautiful. She walked past Brad Pitt. She walked past Antonio Banderas, with his new supermodel girlfriend. She walked past Julia Roberts so close she could see the wrinkles and sags that the editing computers digitally smoothed. They were only celebrities. They could not change the world, or suffer to have their world changed, even by alien intervention. Gaby rested her hands on the rail and looked over the Chaga.

"It's like being on the sundeck of a great, archaic, ocean-liner, cruising close to the shore of an alien archipelago," she told the recorder. The contrast between the place she was and the place out there was as great as between land and sea, the border between the two as shifting and inexact. There was no line where earth became un-earth; rather a gradual infection of the highland forest with the colored hexagons of alien ground cover that pushed up fingers and feelers and strange blooms between the tree trunks into the disturbing pseudocoral forms of the low Chaga. With distance the alien reef grew denser and the trees fewer; only the tallest and strongest withstood the attack of the molecular processors, lifted high like the masts of beached ships. A kilometer beyond the tide line a wall of red pillars rose a sheer three hundred meters from the rumbled land reefs before opening into a canopy of interlinked hexagonal leaf plates.

"The Great Wall," Gaby said, describing the scene before her to the disc. The Chaga beyond offered only glimpses of itself as it rose toward cloud-shrouded Kirinyaga: a gleam of the open white palm of a distant hand-tree, the sway of moss-covered balloons, the glitter of light from crystals. What kind of small craft might put forth from such a shore to meet this ship of vanities? she wondered.

"Seven minutes. Thirteen centimeters. That's longer than most."

Until he spoke, Gaby had not noticed the white man standing beside her at the rail. She could not remember whether he had been there before her, or arrived later. He was small, balding, running to late-40s, early-50s belly. His skin was weathered brown, his teeth were not good, and he spoke with a White African accent. He could not be Beautiful, nor even Press. He must be Staff. He was dressed in buffs and khakis and a vest of pockets, without the least necessary touch of twenty-first-century *knowing*. He looked like the last of the Great White Hunters.

He was.

He was called Prenderleith. He had impeccable manners.

"Pardon me for interrupting your contemplation, but if people see me talking to someone they won't come and ask me about things I've killed."

"Isn't that your job?"

"Killing, or telling?"

"Whichever."

"Whichever, it doesn't include being patronized by movie stars, piss-artists, and bloody journalists."

"I am a bloody journalist."

"But the first thing you did was come over to the rail and look at that bloody thing out there. For seven minutes."

"And that makes this journalist worth talking to."

"Yes," he said, simply.

And it makes you worth talking to, Gaby thought, because maybe you are my angle on this thing. The Last White Hunter. But you are as wary as the creatures you hunt, and if I tell you this it will scare you away, so I must be as stealthy as you. Gaby surreptitiously turned up the recording level on her little black machine. Enhancement software back at Tom M'boya Street would edit the chatter and fluff.

"So what do you think it is?" Gaby asked. Across the terrace a dissension between Bret Easton Ellis and Damien Hirst was escalating into an argument. Guests flocked in, anticipating a fistfight. Cameras whirred. Prenderleith rested his arms on the rail and looked out across the Chaga.

"I don't know about all this aliens-from-another-world stuff."

"Latest theory is that it wasn't built by little gray men, but originated in gas clouds in Rho Ophiuchi, eight hundred light-years away. They've found signatures of the same complex fullerenes that are present in the Chaga. An entire civilization, growing up in space. They estimate it's at least a hundred thousand years old."

" 'They,' " Prenderleith said.

"UNECTA," Gaby said.

"They're probably right. They know more about this than I do, so if they say it's gas, then it's gas. Gas clouds, little gray men, I don't know about either of them; it's just not part of my world. See, they brought me up with just enough education to be able to manage, to do things well; not to think. Kenya wasn't the kind of country that needed thinking, we thought. You did things, not thought. Riding, farming, hunting, driving, flying. Doing things. The country decided what you needed to think. None of us could see the changes happening under our feet. I was brought up obsolete, no bloody use in the new Kenya, that thought, at all. All I could do was find a job in something as obsolete and useless as myself. This bloody place has nothing to do with the real Kenya. Bloody theme park. Even the animals are fake; they bulldozed a water hole so Americans would have elephants to photograph. Irony is: Now the tourists are gone, there've never been so many bloody animals, all headed in. Counted forty-five elephant in one day; no one gives a stuff anymore. Tell me, how can it be alien if the animals are going in there?

How could gas know how to build something like that? Feels to me like it's something very old, that animals knew once and have never forgotten, that's come out of Africa itself. Everything starts here, in East Africa; the land is very old, and has a long memory. And strong: Maybe Africa has had enough of what people are doing to it — enough thinking — and has decided to claim itself back. That's why the animals aren't afraid. It's giving it back to them."

"But taking yours away," Gaby said.

"Not my Africa." Prenderleith glanced around at the famous and beautiful people. The fight had evaporated into sulks and looks. Leaf Phoenix was passing round cigarettes, to the thrilled horror of the other guests. Chimes filled the air. Heads turned. A waiter in an untwenty-first-century-*knowing* leopard-print jacket moved across the roof terrace, playing a set of handheld chime bars.

"Dinner," Prenderleith announced.

The seating plan put Gaby at the far end of the long table, between a hack she knew from BBC on-line and a Hollywood film god who talked of working on fifteen musicals simultaneously and little else. Prenderleith had been placed at the far end of the table, in the champion's seat, hemmed in by the famous. Gaby watched him telling his much-told tales of stalkings and killings. He would glance up from time to time and she would catch his eye, and it was like a little conspiracy. I should tell him that he is an angle, Gaby thought. I should admit to the recorder.

The famous claimed Prenderleith for the remainder of the evening, a small court surrounding his seat by the picture window with its floodlit view of the Chaga approaching molecule by molecule. Gaby sat at the bar and watched him telling his stories of that other Africa. There was a light in his eye. Gaby could not decide if it was nostalgia or anticipation of when it would all fall and come apart.

Out in the dark beyond the floodlights, trees fell, brought down by the Chaga, dissolver of illusions. The wooden piers of the hotel creaked and clicked. The celebrities glanced at each other, afraid.

The knock came at 1:27 according to the luminous hands of the bedside clock. Gaby had not long gone to sleep after dictating commentary. Noise from the upper decks; the party would gradually wind down with the hour until the soldiers came with the morning to clear everyone out. One of the guests, high and hopeful? A second polite knock. The politeness told her.

She could see from the way Prenderleith stood in the corridor that he was a little drunk and that, had he not been, he would not have done this. He was carrying his gun, like an adored child.

"Something you should see," he said.

"Why me?" Gaby asked, pulling on clothes and boots.

"Because no one else could understand. Because of those seven minutes you stared at that bloody thing out there and nothing else existed. You know the truth: Nothing does exist, apart from that. Make sure you bring whatever you've been recording on with you."

"You guessed."

"I noticed."

"Hunter's senses. Sorry, I should have told you, I suppose."

"No matter to me."

"You're the only one here has a story worth telling, who will actually lose something when this comes down."

"You think so?"

The light was poor in the wooden corridor. Gaby could not read his expression right. Prenderleith led her to a service staircase down to ground level. Stepping onto the dark surface between the piers, Gaby imagined setting first foot on an alien planet. Close to the truth there, she thought. Prenderleith unslung his rifle and led her out from under the hotel into the shadows along the edge of the floodlights. The night felt huge and close around Gaby, full of breathings and tiny movements. Her breath steamed, it was cold upon the shoulder lands of Kirinyaga. She inhaled the perfume of the Chaga. It was a smell you imagined you knew, because it evoked so many memories, as smell does more powerfully than any other sense. But you could not know it, and when you realized that, all the parts that reminded you of other things collapsed together and the spicy, musky, chemically scent of it was nothing you could remember for no one had ever known anything like this before. It pushed you forward, not back.

Prenderleith led her toward terminum. It was not very far. The Chaga grew taller and more complex as the floodlight waned. Looming, like the waking memory of a nightmare. Gaby could hear the groan and smash of trees falling in the darkness. Prenderleith stopped her half a meter from the edge. Half a meter, fifteen minutes, Gaby thought. She curled her toes inside her boots, feeling infected. Prenderleith squatted on his heels, rested his weight on his gun, like a staff, hunting.

"Wind's right," he said.

Gaby squatted beside him. She switched on the recorder, listened to the silence, and watched the Chaga approach her, out of the shadows. Terminum was a grid of small hexagons of a mosslike substance. The hexagons were of all colors; Gaby knew intuitively that no color was ever next to itself. The corners of the foremost hexagons were sending dark lines creeping out into the undergrowth. Blades of grass, plant stems, fell before the molecule machines and were reduced to their components. Every few centimeters the crawling lines would bifurcate; a few centimeters more they would divide again to build hexagons. Once enclosed, the terrestrial vegetation would wilt and melt and blister into pinpoint stars of colored pseudomoss.

On a sudden urge, Gaby pressed her hand down on the black lines. It did not touch flesh. It had never touched flesh. Yet she flinched as she felt Chaga beneath her bare skin. Oh she of little faith. She felt the molecule-by-molecule advance as a subtle tickle, like the march of small, slow insects across the palm of her hand.

She started as Prenderleith touched her gently on the shoulder.

"It's here," he whispered.

She did not have the hunter's skill, so for long seconds she saw it only as a deeper darkness moving in the shadows. Then it emerged into the twilight between the still-standing trees and the tall fingers of pseudocoral and Gaby gasped.

It was an elephant; an old bull with a broken tusk. Prenderleith rose to his feet. There was not ten meters between them. Elephant and human regarded each other. The elephant took a step forward, out of the shadows into the full light. As it raised its trunk to taste the air, Gaby saw a mass of red, veiny flesh clinging to its neck like a parasitic organ. Beneath the tusks it elongated into flexible limbs. Each terminated in something disturbingly like a human hand. Shocked, Gaby watched the red limbs move and the fingers open and shut. Then the elephant turned and with surprising silence retreated into the bush. The darkness of the Chaga closed behind it.

"Every night, same time," Prenderleith said after a long silence. "For the past six days. Right to the edge, no further. Little closer every day."

"Why?"

"It looks at me, I look at it. We understand each other."

"That thing, around its neck; those arms . . ." Gaby could not keep the disgust from her voice.

It changes things. Makes things more what they could be. Should be, maybe. Perhaps all elephants have ever needed have been hands, to become what they could be."

"Bootstrap evolution."

"If that's what you believe in."

"What do you believe in?"

"Remember how I answered when you told me the Chaga was taking my Africa away?"

"Not your Africa."

"Understand what I meant now?"

"The Africa it's taking away is the one you never understood, the one you weren't made for. The Africa it's giving is the one you never knew but that was bred into your bones; the great untamed, unexplored, dark Africa, the Africa without nations and governments and borders and economies; the Africa of action, not thought, of being, not becoming, where a single man can lose himself and find himself at the same time; return to a more simple, physical, animal level of existence."

"You say it very prettily. Suppose it's your job."

Gaby understood another thing. Prenderleith had asked her to speak for him because he had not been made able to say such things for himself, and wanted them said right for those who would read Gaby's story about him. He wanted a witness, a faithful recording angel. Understanding this, she knew a third thing about Prenderleith, which could never be spoken and preserved on disc.

"Let's go in again," Prenderleith said eventually. "Bloody freezing out here."

The soldiers came through the hotel at 6:30 in the morning, knocking at every bedroom door, though all the guests had either been up and ready long before, or had not slept at all. In view of the fame of the guests, the soldiers were very polite. They assembled everyone in the main lounge. Like a slow sinking, Gaby thought. A No Abandon–ship. The reef has reached us at last. She looked out of the window. Under darkness the hexagon moss had crossed the artificial water hole and was climbing the piles of the old hotel. The trees out of which the elephant had emerged in the night were festooned with orange spongy encrustations and webs of tubing.

The main lounge lurched. Glasses fell from the back bar and broke. People screamed a little. The male Hollywood stars tried to look brave, but this was no screenplay. This was the real end of the world. Prenderleith had gathered with the rest of the staff in the farthest corner from the door and was trying to sow calm. It is like the *Titanic*, Gaby thought. Crew last. She went to stand with them. Prenderleith gave her a puzzled frown.

"The punters have to know if the captain goes down with his ship," she said, patting the little black recorder in the breast pocket of her bush shirt. Prenderleith opened his mouth to speak and the hotel heaved again, more heavily. Beams snapped. The picture window shattered and fell outward. Gaby grabbed the edge of the bar and talked fast and panicky at her recorder. Alarmed, the soldiers hurried the celebrities out of the lounge and along the narrow wooden corridors toward the main staircase. The lounge sagged, the floor tilted, tables and chairs slid toward the empty window.

"Go!" Prenderleith shouted.

They were already going. Jammed into the wooden corridor, she tried not to think of bottomless coffins as she tried to shout through the other shouting voices into the microphone. Behind her the lounge collapsed and fell. She fought her way through the press of bodies into the sunlight, touched the solidity of the staircase. Crawling. She snatched her fingers away. The creeping, branching lines of Chaga-stuff were moving down the stairs, through the paintwork.

"It's on the stairs," she whispered breathlessly into the mike. The wooden wall behind her was a mosaic of hexagons. She clutched the recorder on her breast. A single spore would be enough to dissolve it and her story. She plunged down the quivering stairs.

Heedless of dangerous animals, the soldiers hurried the guests toward the vehicles on the main road. The news people paused to shoot their final commentaries on the fall of the Treehouse.

"It's coming apart," she said as a section of roof tilted up like the stern of a sinking liner and slid through the bubbling superstructure to the ground. The front of the hotel was a smash of wood and the swelling, bulbous encrustations of Chaga-stuff. The snapped piles were fingers of yellow sponge and pseudocoral. Gaby described it all. Soldiers formed a cordon between the spectators and the Chaga. Gaby found Prenderleith beside her.

"You'll need to know how the story ends," he said. "Keep this for me." He handed Gaby his rifle. She shook her head.

"I don't do good on guns."

He laid it at her.

"I know," she said.

"Then you'll help me."

"Do you hate this that much?"

"Yes," he said. There was a detonation of breaking wood and a gasp from soldiers and civilians alike. The hotel had snapped in the middle and folded up like two wings. They slowly collapsed into piles of voraciously feeding Chaga life.

He made the move while everyone's attention but Gaby's was distracted by the end of the old hotel. She had known he would do it. He ran fast for a tired old white hunter, running to fat.

"He's halfway there," she said to her recorder. "I admire his courage; going gladly into this new dark continent. Or is it the courage to make the choice that eventually the Chaga may make for all of us on this planet formerly known as Earth?"

She broke off. The soldier in front of her had seen Prenderleith. He lifted his Kalashnikov and took aim.

"Prenderleith!" Gaby yelled. He ran on. He seemed more intent on doing something with his shirt buttons. He was across the edge now, spores flying up from his feet as he crushed the hexagon moss.

"No!" Gaby shouted, but the soldier was under orders, and both he and the men who gave the orders feared the Chaga above all else. She saw the muscles tighten in his neck, the muzzle of the gun weave a little this way, a little that way. She looked for something to stop him. Prenderleith's rifle. No. That would get her shot too.

The little black disc recorder hit the soldier, hard, on the shoulder. She had thrown it, hard. The shot skyed. Birds went screeching up from their roosts. Otherwise, utter silence from soldiers and staff and celebrities. The soldier whirled on her, weapon raised. Gaby danced back, hands held high. The soldier snapped his teeth at her and brought the butt of the gun down on the disc recorder. While he smashed it to shards of plastic and circuitry, Gaby saw the figure of Prenderleith disappear into the pseudocoral fungus of the alien landscape. He had lost his shirt.

The last vestiges of the tourist hotel — half a room balanced atop a pillar; the iron staircase, flowering sulphur-yellow buds, leading nowhere, a tangle of plumbing, washbasins, and toilets held out like begging bowls — tumbled and fell. Gaby watched mutely. She had nothing to say, and nothing to say it to. The Chaga advanced onward, twenty-five centimeters every minute. The people dispersed. There was nothing more to see than the millimetric creep of another world.

The soldiers checked Gaby's press accreditations with five different sources before they would let her take the SkyNet car. They were pissed at her but they could not touch her. They smiled a lot, though, because they had smashed her story and she would be in trouble with her editor.

You're wrong, she thought as she drove away down the safe road in the long convoy of news-company vehicles and tour buses. Story is in the heart. Story is never broken. Story is never lost.

That night, as she dreamed among the doomed towers of Nairobi, the elephant came to her again. It stood on the border between worlds and raised its trunk and its alien hands and spoke to her. It told her that only fools feared the change that would make things what they could be, and should be; that change was the special gift of whatever had made the Chaga. She knew in her dream that the elephant was speaking with the voice of Prenderleith, but she could not see him, except as a silent shadow moving in the greater dark beyond humanity's floodlights: Adam again, hunting in the Africa of his heart.

William Sanders

When This World Is All on Fire

(2001)

The author of numerous books, both fiction and nonfiction, William Sanders (b. 1942) is best known for his short stories, particularly those sf works dealing with Native American themes. His other works include mysteries and thrillers, as well as books on history and outdoor sports. Sanders, like many sf writers, prefers the more inclusive term "speculative fiction" to "science fiction" in describing his work. Several of his stories have been nominated for Hugo, Nebula, and Sturgeon awards. Two of his short stories have won Sidewise Awards for Alternate History: "The Undiscovered" in 1998 and "Empire" in 2003. Sanders, who has held an intriguing variety of jobs and includes pictures of his gun collection on his homepage, has constructed a crotchety, hard-bitten persona for himself that seems much like a character from one of his stories, which are often Western-themed and dryly humorous. He is disenchanted with the publishing industry and describes himself as semiretired, but he continues to write and to edit an online sf magazine, Helix.

"When This World Is All on Fire" is set in a near-future America on the brink of ecological collapse, but it is the psychological complexity of its characters that gives it depth. This is a somber, haunting story that feels all too plausible, and the ironic twist of renewed battles over Native American land gives it an added bite.

"Squatters," Jimmy Lonekiller said as he swung the jeep off the narrow old blacktop onto the narrower and older gravel side road. "I can't believe we got squatters again."

Sitting beside him, bracing himself against the bumping and bouncing, Sergeant Davis Blackbear said, "Better get used to it. We kick this bunch out, there'll be more."

Jimmy Lonekiller nodded. "Guess that's right," he said. "They're not gonna give up, are they?"

He was a husky, dark-skinned young man, and tall for a Cherokee; among the women of the reservation, he was generally considered something of a hunk. His khaki uniform was neat and crisply pressed, despite the oppressive heat. Davis Blackbear, feeling his own shirt wilting and sticking to his skin, wondered how he did it. Maybe fullbloods didn't sweat as much. Or maybe it was something to do with being young.

Davis said, "Would you? Give up, I mean, if you were in their shoes?"

Jimmy didn't reply for a moment, being busy fighting the wheel as the jeep slammed over a series of potholes. They were on a really bad stretch now, the road narrowed to a single-lane dirt snaketrack; the overhanging trees on either side, heavy with dust-greyed festoons of kudzu vine, shut out the sun without doing anything much about the heat. This was an out-of-the-way part of the reservation; Davis had had to check the map at the tribal police headquarters to make sure he knew how to get here.

The road began to climb now, up the side of a steep hill. The jeep slowed to not much better than walking speed; the locally distilled alcohol might burn cooler and cleaner than gasoline but it had no power at all. Jimmy Lonekiller spoke then: "Don't guess I would, you put it that way. Got to go somewhere, poor bastards."

They were speaking English; Davis was Oklahoma Cherokee, having moved to the North Carolina reservation only a dozen years ago, when he married a Qualla Band woman. He could understand the Eastern dialect fairly well by now, enough for cop purposes anyway, but he still wasn't up to a real conversation.

"Still," Jimmy went on, "you got to admit it's a hell of a thing. Twenty-first century, better than five hundred years after Columbus, and here we are again with white people trying to settle on our land. What little bit we've got left," he said, glancing around at the dusty woods. "There's gotta be somewhere else they can go."

"Except," Davis said, "somebody's already there too."

"Probably so," Jimmy admitted. "Seems like they're running out of places for people to be."

He steered the jeep around a rutted hairpin bend, while Davis turned the last phrase over in his mind, enjoying the simple precision of it: running out of places for people to be, that was the exact and very well-put truth. Half of Louisiana and more than half of Florida under water now, the rest of the coastline inundated, Miami and Mobile and Savannah and most of Houston, and, despite great and expensive efforts, New Orleans too.

And lots more land, farther inland, that might as well be submerged for all the good it did anybody: all that once-rich farm country in southern Georgia and Alabama and Mississippi, too hot and dry now to grow anything, harrowed tornadoes and dust storms, while raging fires destroyed the last remnants of the pine forests and the cypress groves of the dried-up swamplands. Not to mention the quake, last year, shattering Memphis and eastern Arkansas, demolishing the levees and turning the Mississippi loose on what was left of the Delta country. Seemed everybody either had way too much water or not enough.

He'd heard a black preacher, on the radio, declare that it was all God's judgment on the South because of slavery and racism. But that was bullshit; plenty of other parts of the country were getting it just as bad. Like Manhattan, or San Francisco — and he didn't even want to think about what it must be like in places like Arizona. And Africa, oh, Jesus. Nobody in the world wanted to think about Africa now.

The road leveled out at the top of the hill and he pointed. "Pull over there. I want to do a quick scout before we drive up."

Jimmy stopped the jeep and Davis climbed out and stood in the middle of the dirt road. "Well," Jimmy said, getting out too, "I wish somebody else would get the job of running them off now and then." He gave Davis a mocking look. "It's what I get, letting myself get partnered with an old 'breed. Everybody knows why Ridge always puts you in charge of the evictions."

Davis didn't rise to the bait; he knew what Jimmy was getting at. It was something of a standing joke among the reservation police that Davis always got any jobs that involved dealing with white people. Captain Ridge claimed it was because of his years of experience on the Tulsa PD, but Jimmy and others claimed it was really because he was quarter-blood and didn't look all that Indian and therefore might make whites less nervous.

In his own estimation, he didn't look particularly Indian or white or anything else, just an average-size man with a big bony face and too many wrinkles and dark brown hair that was now getting heavily streaked with gray. He doubted that his appearance inspired much confidence in people of any race.

The dust cloud was beginning to settle over the road behind them. A black-and-white van appeared, moving slowly, and pulled to a stop behind the jeep. Corporal Roy Smoke stuck his head out the window and said, "Here?"

"For now," Davis told him. "I'm going to go have a look, scope out the scene before we move in. You guys wait here." He turned. "Jimmy, you come with me."

The heat was brutal as they walked down the road, even in the shady patches. At the bottom of the hill, though, Davis led the way off the road and up a dry creek bed, and back in the woods it was a little cooler. Away from the road, there wasn't enough sunlight for the kudzu vines to take over, and beneath the trees the light was pleasantly soft and green. Still too damn dry, Davis thought, feeling leaves and twigs crunching under his boot soles. Another good reason to get this eviction done quickly; squatters tended to be careless with fire. The last bad woods fire on the reservation, a couple of months ago, had been started by a squatter family trying to cook a stolen hog.

They left the creek bed and walked through the woods, heading roughly eastward. "Hell," Jimmy murmured, "I know where this is now. They're on the old Birdshooter place, huh? Shit, nobody's lived there for years. Too rocky to grow anything, no water since the creek went dry."

Davis motioned for silence. Moving more slowly now, trying to step quietly though it wasn't easy in the dry underbrush, they worked their way to the crest of a low ridge. Through the trees, Davis could see a cleared area beyond. Motioning to Jimmy to wait, he moved up to the edge of the woods and paused in the shadow of a half-grown oak, and that was when he heard the singing.

At first he didn't even recognize it as singing; the sound was so high and clear and true that he took it for some sort of instrument. But after a second he realized it was a human voice, though a voice like none he'd ever heard. He couldn't make out the words, but the sound alone was enough to make the hair stand up on his arms and neck, and the air suddenly felt cooler under the trees.

It took Davis a moment to get unstuck; he blinked rapidly and took a deep breath. Then, very cautiously, he peered around the trunk of the oak.

The clearing wasn't very big; wasn't very clear, either, any more, having been taken over by brush and weeds. In the middle stood the ruins of a small frame house, its windows smashed and its roof fallen in.

Near the wrecked house sat a green pickup truck, its bed covered with a boxy, homemade-looking camper shell — plywood, it looked like from where Davis stood, and painted a dull uneven gray. The truck's own finish was badly faded and scabbed with rust; the near front fender was crumpled. Davis couldn't see any license plates.

A kind of lean-to had been erected at the rear of the truck, a sagging blue plastic tarp with guy-ropes tied to trees and bushes. As Davis watched, a lean, long-faced man in bib overalls and a red baseball cap came out from under the tarp and stood looking about.

Then the red-haired girl came around the front of the truck, still singing, the words clear now:

> *"Oh, when this world is all on fire*
> *Where you gonna go?*
> *Where you gonna go?"*

She was, Davis guessed, maybe twelve or thirteen, though he couldn't really tell at this distance. Not much of her, anyway; he didn't figure she'd go over eighty pounds or so. Her light blue dress was short and sleeveless, revealing thin pale arms and legs. All in all, it didn't seem possible for all that sound to be coming from such a wispy little girl; and yet there was no doubt about it, he could see her mouth moving:

> *"Oh, when this world is all on fire*
> *Where you gonna go?"*

The tune was a simple one, an old-fashioned modal-sounding melody line, slow and without a pronounced rhythm. It didn't matter; nothing mattered but that voice. It soared through the still mountain air like a whippoorwill calling beside a running stream. Davis felt his throat go very tight.

> *"Run to the mountains to hide your face*
> *Never find no hiding place*

> *Oh, when this world is all on fire*
> *Where you gonna go?"*

The man in the baseball cap put his hands on his hips. "Eva May!" he shouted.

The girl stopped singing and turned. Her red hair hung down her back almost to her waist. "Yes, Daddy?" she called.

"Quit the damn fooling around," the man yelled. His voice was rough, with the practiced anger of the permanently angry man. "Go help your brother with the fire."

Fire? Davis spotted it then, a thin trace of bluish-white smoke rising from somewhere on the far side of the parked truck. "Shit!" he said soundlessly, and turned and began picking his way back down the brushy slope.

"What's happening?" Jimmy Lonekiller said as Davis reappeared. "What was that music? Sounded like — "

"Quiet," Davis said, "Come on. We need to hurry."

"Go," Davis said to Jimmy as they turned off the road and up the brush-choked track through the trees. "No use trying to sneak up. They've heard us coming by now."

Sure enough, the squatters were already standing in the middle of the clearing, watching, as the jeep bumped to a stop in front of them. The man in the red baseball cap stood in the middle, his face dark with anger. Beside him stood a washed-out-looking blond woman in a faded flower-print dress, and, next to her, a tall teenage boy wearing ragged jeans and no shirt. The boy's hair had been cropped down almost flush with his scalp.

The woman was holding a small baby to her chest. Great, Davis thought with a flash of anger, just what a bunch of homeless drifters needed. Running out of places for people to be, but not out of people, hell, no. . . .

The red-haired girl was standing off to one side, arms folded. Close up, Davis revised his estimate of her age; she had to be in her middle to late teens at least. There didn't appear to be much of a body under that thin blue dress, but it was definitely not that of a child. Her face, as she watched the two men get out of the jeep, was calm and without expression.

The van came rocking and swaying up the trail and stopped behind the jeep. Davis waited while Roy Smoke and the other four men got out — quite a force to evict one raggedy-ass family, but Captain Ridge believed in being careful — and then he walked over to the waiting squatters and said, "Morning. Where you folks from?"

The man in the red baseball cap spat on the ground, not taking his eyes off Davis. "Go to hell, Indian."

Oh oh. Going to be like that, was it? Davis said formally, "Sir, you're on Cherokee reservation land. Camping isn't allowed except by permit and in designated areas. I'll have to ask you to move out."

The woman said, "Oh, why can't you leave us alone? We're not hurting anybody. You people have all this land, why won't you share it?"

We tried that, lady, Davis thought, and look where it got us. Aloud he said, "Ma'am, the laws are made by the government of the Cherokee nation. I just enforce them."

"Nation!" The man snorted. "Bunch of woods niggers, hogging good land while white people starve. You got no right."

"I'm not here to argue about it," Davis said. "I'm just here to tell you you've got to move on."

The boy spoke up suddenly. "You planning to make us?"

Davis looked at him. Seventeen or eighteen, he guessed, punk-mean around the eyes and that Johnny Pissoff stance that they seemed to develop at that age; ropy muscles showing under bare white skin, forearms rippling visibly as he clenched both fists.

"Yes," Davis told him. "If necessary, we'll move you."

To the father — he assumed — he added, "I'm hoping you won't make it necessary. If you like, we'll give you a hand — "

He didn't get to finish. That was when the boy came at him, fists up, head hunched down between his shoulders, screaming as he charged: "*Redskin motherfu* — "

Davis shifted his weight, caught the wild swing in a cross-arm block, grasped the kid's wrist and elbow and pivoted, all in one smooth motion. The boy yelped in pain as he hit the ground, and then grunted as Jimmy Lonekiller landed on top of him, handcuffs ready.

The man in the red cap had taken a step forward, but he stopped as Roy Smoke moved in front of him and tapped him gently on the chest with his nightstick. "No," Roy said, "you don't want to do that. Stand still, now."

Davis said, "Wait up, Jimmy," and then to the man in the red cap, "all right, there's two ways we can do this. We can take this boy to Cherokee town and charge him with assaulting an officer, and he can spend the next couple of months helping us fix the roads. Probably do him a world of good."

"No," the woman cried. The baby in her arms was wailing now, a thin weak piping against her chest, but she made no move to quiet it. "Please, no."

"Or," Davis went on, "you can move out of here, right now, without any more trouble, and I'll let you take him with you."

The girl, he noticed, hadn't moved the whole time, just stood there watching with no particular expression on her face, except that there might be a tiny trace of a smile on her lips as she looked at the boy on the ground.

"No," the woman said again. "Vernon, no, you can't let them take Ricky — "

"All right," the man said, "We'll go, Indian. Let him up. He won't give you no more trouble. Ricky, behave yourself or I'll whup your ass."

Davis nodded to Jimmy Lonekiller, who released the kid. "Understand this," Davis said, "we don't give second warnings. If you're found on Cherokee land again, you'll be arrested, your vehicle will be impounded, and you might do a little time."

The boy was getting to his feet, rubbing his arm. The woman started to move toward him but the man said, "He's all right, damn it. Get busy packing up." He turned his head and scowled at the girl. "You too, Eva May."

Davis watched as the squatters began taking down the tarp. The girl's long red hair fairly glowed in the midday sun; he felt a crazy impulse to go over and touch it. He wished she'd sing some more, but he didn't imagine she felt like singing now.

He said, "Roy, have somebody kill that fire. Make sure it's dead and buried. This place is a woods fire waiting to happen."

Davis lived in a not very big trailer on the outskirts of Cherokee town. Once he had had a regular house, but after his wife had taken off, a few years ago, with that white lawyer from Gatlinburg, he'd moved out and let a young married couple have the place.

The trailer's air conditioning was just about shot, worn out from the constant unequal battle with the heat, but after the sun went down it wasn't too bad except on the hottest summer nights. Davis took off his uniform and hung it up and stretched out on the bed while darkness fell outside and the owls began calling in the trees. Sweating, waiting for the temperature to drop, he closed his eyes and heard again in his mind, over the rattle of the laboring air conditioner:

> "Oh, when this world is all on fire
> Where you gonna go?
> Where you gonna go?"

It was the following week when he saw the girl again.

He was driving through Waynesville, taking one of the force's antique computers for repairs, when he saw her crossing the street up ahead. Even at half a block's distance, he was sure it was the same girl; there couldn't be another head of hair like that in these mountains. She was even wearing what looked like the same blue dress.

But he was caught in slow traffic, and she disappeared around the corner before he could get any closer. Sighing, making a face at himself for acting like a fool, he drove on. By the time he got to the computer shop, he had convinced himself it had all been his imagination.

He dropped off the computer and headed back through town, taking it easy and keeping a wary eye on the traffic, wondering as always how so many people still managed to drive, despite fuel shortages and sky-high prices; and all the new restrictions, not that anybody paid them any mind, the government having all it could do just keeping the country more or less together.

An ancient minivan, a mattress roped to its roof, made a sudden left turn from the opposite lane. Davis hit the brakes, cursing — a fenderbender in a tribal patrol car, that would really make the day — and that was when he saw the red-haired girl coming up the sidewalk on the other side of the street.

Some asshole behind him was honking; Davis put the car in motion again, going slow, looking for a parking place. There was a spot up near the next corner and he turned into it and got out and locked up the cruiser, all without stopping to think what he thought he was doing or why he was doing it.

He crossed the street and looked along the sidewalk, but he couldn't see the girl anywhere. He began walking back the way she'd been going, looking this way and that. The street was mostly lined with an assortment of small stores — leftovers, probably, from the days when Waynesville had been a busy tourist resort, before tourism became a meaningless concept — and he peered in through a few shop windows, without any luck.

He walked a couple of blocks that way and then decided she couldn't have gotten any farther in that little time. He turned and went back, and stopped at the corner and looked up and down the cross street, wondering if she could have gone that way. Fine Indian you are, he thought, one skinny little white girl with hair like a brush fire and you keep losing her.

Standing there, he became aware of a growing small commotion across the street, noises coming from the open door of the shop on the corner: voices raised, a sound of scuffling. A woman shouted, "No you don't — "

He ran across the street, dodging an oncoming BMW, and into the shop. It was an automatic cop reaction, unconnected to his search; but then immediately he saw the girl, struggling in the grip of a large steely-haired woman in a long black dress. "Stop fighting me," the woman was saying in a high strident voice. "Give me that, young lady. I'm calling the police — "

Davis said, "What's going on here?"

The woman looked around. "Oh," she said, looking pleased, not letting go the girl's arm. "I'm glad to see you, officer. I've got a little shoplifter for you."

The girl was looking at Davis too. If she recognized him she gave no sign. Her face was flushed, no doubt from the struggle, but still as expressionless as ever.

"What did she take?" Davis asked.

"This." The woman reached up and pried the girl's right hand open, revealing something shiny. "See, she's still holding it!"

Davis stepped forward and took the object from the girl's hand: a cheap-looking little pendant, silver or more likely silver-plated, in the shape of a running dog, with a flimsy neck chain attached.

"I want her arrested," the woman said. "I'll be glad to press charges. I'm tired of these people, coming around here ruining this town, stealing everyone blind."

Davis said, "I'm sorry, ma'am, I don't have any jurisdiction here. You'll need to call the local police."

She blinked, doing a kind of ladylike double-take, looking at Davis's uniform. "Oh. Excuse me, I thought — " She managed to stop before actually saying, "I thought you were a real policeman." It was there on her face, though.

Davis looked again at the pendant, turning it over in his hand, finding the little white price tag stuck on the back of the running dog: $34.95. A ripoff even in the present wildly inflated money; but after a moment he reached for his wallet an said, "Ma'am, how about if I just pay you for it?"

The woman started to speak and then stopped, her eyes locking on the wallet in his hand. Not doing much business these days, he guessed; who had money to waste on junk like this?

While she hesitated, Davis pulled out two twenties and laid them on the nearby counter top. "With a little extra to pay for your trouble," he added.

That did it. She let go the girl's arm and scooped up the money with the speed of a professional gambler. "All right," she said, "but get her out of here!"

The girl stood still, staring at Davis. The woman said, "I mean it! Right now!"

Davis tilted his head in the direction of the door. The girl nodded and started to move, not particularly fast. Davis followed her, hearing the woman's voice behind him: "And if you ever come back — "

Out on the sidewalk, Davis said, "I'm parked down this way."

She looked at him. "You arresting me?"

Her speaking voice — he realized suddenly that this was the first time he'd heard it — was surprisingly ordinary; soft and high, rather pleasant, but nothing to suggest what it could do in song. There was no fear in it, or in her face; she might have been asking what time it was.

Davis shook his head. "Like I told that woman, I don't have any authority here."

"So you can't make me go with you."

"No," he said. "But I'd say you need to get clear of this area pretty fast. She's liable to change her mind and call the law after all."

"Guess that's right. Okay." She fell in beside him, sticking her hands in the pockets of the blue dress. He noticed her feet were barely covered by a pair of old tennis shoes, so ragged they were practically sandals. "Never rode in a police car before."

As they came up to the parked cruiser he stopped and held out his hand. "Here. You might as well have this."

She took the pendant and held it up in front of her face, looking at it, swinging it from side to side. After a moment she slipped the chain over her head and tucked the pendant down the front of her dress. "Better hide it," she said. "Ricky sees it, he'll steal it for sure."

He said, "Not much of a thing to get arrested for."

She shrugged. "I like dogs. We had a dog, back home in Georgia, before we had to move. Daddy wouldn't let me take him along."

"Still," he said, "you could have gone to jail."

She shrugged, a slight movement of her small shoulders. "So? Wouldn't be no worse than how I got to live now."

"Yes it would," he told her. "You've got no idea what it's like in those forced labor camps. How old are you?"

"Seventeen," she said. "Well, next month."

"Then you're an adult, as far's the law's concerned. Better watch it from now on." He opened the right door. "Get in."

She climbed into the car and he closed the door and went around. As he slid in under the wheel, she said, "Okay, I know what comes next. Where do you want to go?"

"What?" Davis looked at her, momentarily baffled. "Well, I was just going to take you home. Wherever your family — "

"Oh, come on." Her voice held an edge of scorn now. "You didn't get me out of there for nothing. You want something, just like everybody always does, and I know what it is because there ain't nothing else I got. Well, all right," she said. "I don't guess I mind. So where do you want to go to do it?"

For a moment, Davis was literally speechless. The idea simply hadn't occurred to him; he hadn't thought of her in that way at all. It surprised him, now he considered it. After all, she was a pretty young girl — you could have said beautiful, in a way — and he had been living alone for a long time. Yet so it was; he felt no stirrings of that kind toward this girl, not even now with her close up and practically offering herself.

When he could speak he said, "No, no. Not that. Believe me."

"Really?" She looked very skeptical. "Then what do you want?"

"Right now," he said, "I want to buy you a pair of shoes."

An hour or so later, coming out of the discount shoe store out by the highway, she said, "I know what this is all about. You feel bad because you run us off, back last week."

"No." Davis's voice held maybe a little bit more certainty than he felt, but he added, "Just doing my job. Anyway, you couldn't have stayed there. No water, nothing to eat, how would you live?"

"You still didn't have no right to run us off."

"Sure I did. It's our land," he said. "All we've got left."

She opened her mouth and he said, "Look, we're not going to talk about it, all right?"

They walked in silence the rest of the way across the parking lot. She kept looking down at her feet, admiring the new shoes. They weren't much, really, just basic white no-name sport shoes, but he supposed they looked pretty fine to her. At that they hadn't been all that cheap. In fact between the shoes and the pendant he'd managed to go through a couple days' pay. Not that he was likely to get paid any time soon; the tribe had been broke for a long time.

As he started the car, she said, "You sure you don't want to, you know, do it?"

He looked at her and she turned sidewise in the seat, moving her thin pale legs slightly apart, shifting her narrow hips. "Hey," she said, "somebody's gotta be the first. Might as well be you."

Her mouth quirked. "If it ain't you it'll prob'ly be Ricky. He sure keeps trying."

With some difficulty Davis said, "Turn around, please, and do up your safety belt."

"All right." She giggled softly. "Just don't know what it is you want from me, that's all."

He didn't respond until they were out of the parking lot and rolling down the road, back into Waynesville. Then he said, "Would you sing for me?"

"What?" Her voice registered real surprise. "Sing? You mean right now, right here in the car?"

"Yes," Davis said. "Please."

"Well, I be damn." She brushed back her hair and studied him for a minute. "You mean it, don't you? All right . . . what you want me to sing? If I know it."

"That song you were singing that morning up on the reservation," he said. "Just before we arrived."

She thought about it. "Oh," she said. "You mean — "

She tilted her head back and out it came, like a flood of clear spring water.

> "Oh, when this world is all on fire
> Where you gonna go?"

"Yes," Davis said very softly. "That's it. Sing it. Please."

Her family was staying in a refugee camp on the other side of town; a great hideous sprawl of cars and trucks and buses and campers and trailers of all makes and ages and states of repair, bright nylon tents and crude plastic-tarp shelters and pathetic, soggy arrangements of cardboard boxes, spread out over a once-beautiful valley.

"You better just drop me off here," the girl said as he turned off the road.

"That's okay," Davis said. "Which way do I go?"

At her reluctant direction, he steered slowly down a narrow muddy lane between parked vehicles and outlandish shelters, stopping now and then as children darted across in front of the car. People came out and stared as the big police cruiser rolled past. Somebody threw something unidentifiable, that bounced off the windshield leaving a yellowish smear. By now Davis was pretty sure this hadn't been a good idea.

But the girl said, "Up there," and there it was, the old truck with the homemade camper bed and the blue plastic awning rigged out behind, just like before. He stopped the car and got out and went around to open the passenger door.

The air was thick with wood smoke and the exhausts of worn-out engines, and the pervasive reek of human waste. The ground underfoot was soggy with mud and spilled motor oil and God knew what else. Davis looked around at the squalid scene, remembering what this area used to look like, only a few years ago. Now, it looked like the sort of thing they used to show on the news, in countries you'd never heard of. The refugee camps in Kosovo, during his long-ago army days, hadn't been this bad.

Beyond, up on the mountainsides, sunlight glinted on the windows of expensive houses. A lot of locals had thought it was wonderful, back when the rich people first started buying up land and building homes up in the mountain country, getting away from the heat and the flooding. They hadn't been as happy about the second invasion, a year or so later, by people bringing nothing but their desperation. . . .

Davis shook his head and opened the door. Even the depressing scene couldn't really get him down, right now. It had been an amazing experience, almost religious, driving along with that voice filling the dusty interior of the old cruiser; he felt light and loose, as if coming off a marijuana high. He found himself smiling —

A voice behind him said, "What the hell?" and then, "Eva May!"

He turned and saw the man standing there beside the truck, still wearing the red cap and the angry face. "Hello," he said, trying to look friendly or at least inoffensive. "Just giving your daughter a lift from town. Don't worry, she's not in any trouble — "

"Hell she's not," the man said, looking past Davis. "Eva May, git your ass out of that thing! What you doing riding around with this God-damn woods nigger?"

The girl swung her feet out of the car. Davis started to give her a hand but decided that might be a bad move right now. She got out and stepped past Davis. "It's all right, Daddy," she said. "He didn't do nothing bad. Look, he bought me some new shoes!"

"No shit." The man looked down at her feet, at the new shoes standing out white and clean against the muddy ground. "New shoes, huh? Git 'em off."

She stopped. "But Daddy — "

His hand came up fast; it made an audible crack against the side of her face. As she stumbled backward against the side of the truck he said, "God damn it, I *said* take them shoes off."

He spun about to face Davis. "You don't like that, Indian? Maybe you wanta do something about it?"

Davis did, in fact, want very much to beat this worthless *yoneg* within half an inch of his life. But he forced himself to stand still and keep his hands down at his sides. Start a punch-out in here, and almost certainly he'd wind up taking on half the men in the camp. Or using the gun on his belt, which would bring down a whole new kind of disaster.

Even then he might have gone for it, but he knew that anything he did to the man would later be taken out on Eva May. It was a pattern all too familiar to any cop.

She had one shoe off now and was jerking at the other, standing on one foot, leaning against the trailer, sobbing. She got it off and the man jerked it out of her hand. "Here." He half-turned and threw the shoe, hard, off somewhere beyond the old school bus that was parked across the lane. He bent down and picked up the other shoe and hurled it in the opposite direction.

"Ain't no damn Indian buying *nothing* for my kid," he said, "Or going anywhere *near* her. You understand that, Chief?"

From inside the camper came the sound of a baby crying. A woman's voice said, "Vernon? What's going on, Vernon?"

"Now," the man said, "you get out of here, woods nigger."

The blood was singing in Davis's ears and there was a taste in his mouth like old pennies. Still he managed to check himself, and to keep his voice steady as he said, "Sir, whatever you think of me, your daughter has a great gift. She should have the opportunity — "

"Listen close, Indian." The man's voice was low, now, and very intense. "You shut your mouth and you git back in that car and you drive outta here, right damn *now*, or else I'm gon' find out if you got the guts to use that gun. Plenty white men around here, be glad to help stomp your dirty red ass."

Davis glanced at Eva May, who was still leaning against the truck, weeping and holding the side of her face. Her bare white feet were already spotted with mud.

And then, because there was nothing else to do, he got back in the car and drove away. He didn't look back. There was nothing there he wanted to see; nothing he wouldn't already be seeing for a long time to come.

"Blackbear," Captain Ridge said, next morning. "I don't believe this."

He was seated at his desk in his office, looking up at Davis. His big dark face was not that of a happy man.

"I got a call just now," he said, "from the sheriff's office over in Waynesville. Seems a reservation officer, man about your size and wearing sergeant's stripes picked up a teenage girl on the street. Made her get into a patrol car, tried to get her to have sex, even bought her presents to entice her. When she refused he took her back to the refugee camp and made threats against her family."

Davis said, "Captain — "

"No," Captain Ridge said, and slapped a hand down on his desk top. "No, Blackbear, I don't want to hear it. See, you're about to tell me it's a lot of bullshit, and I *know* it's a lot of bullshit, and it doesn't make a damn bit of difference. You listen to me, Blackbear. Whoever those people are, you stay away from them. You stay out of Waynesville, till I tell you different. On duty or off, I don't care."

He leaned back in his chair. "Because if you show up there again, you're going to be arrested — the sheriff just warned me — and there won't be a thing I can do about it. And you know what kind of chance you'll have in court over there. They like us even less than they do the squatters."

Davis said, "All right. I wasn't planning on it anyway."

But of course he went back. Later, he thought that the only surprising thing was that he waited as long as he did.

He went on Sunday morning. It was an off-duty day and he drove his own car; that, plus the nondescript civilian clothes he wore, ought to cut down the chances of his being recognized. He stopped at an all-hours one-stop in Maggie Valley and bought a pair of cheap sunglasses and a butt-ugly blue mesh-back cap with an emblem of a jumping fish on the front. Pulling the cap down low, checking himself out in the old Dodge's mirror, he decided he looked like a damn fool, but as camouflage it ought to help.

But when he got to the refugee camp he found it had all been for nothing. The truck was gone and so was Eva May's family; an elderly couple in a Buick were already setting up camp in the spot. No, they said, they didn't know anything; the place had been empty when they got here, just a little while ago.

Davis made a few cautious inquiries, without finding out much more. The woman in the school bus across the lane said she'd heard them leaving a little before daylight. She had no idea where they'd gone and doubted if anyone else did.

"People come and go," she said. "There's no keeping track. And they weren't what you'd call friendly neighbors."

Well, Davis thought as he drove back to the reservation, so much for that. He felt sad and empty inside, and disgusted with himself for feeling that way. Good thing the bars and liquor stores weren't open on Sunday; he could easily go on a serious drunk right now.

He was coming over the mountains east of Cherokee when he saw the smoke.

It was the worst fire of the decade. And could have been much worse; if the wind had shifted just right, it might have taken out the whole reservation. As it was, it was three days before the fire front crossed the reservation border and became somebody else's problem.

For Davis Blackbear it was a very long three days. Afterward, he estimated that he might have gotten three or four hours of sleep the whole time. None of the tribal police got any real time off, the whole time; it was one job after another, evacuating people from the fire's path, setting up roadblocks, keeping traffic unsnarled, and, in the rare times there was nothing else to do, joining the brutally overworked firefighting crews. By now almost every able-bodied man in the tribe was helping fight the blaze; or else already out of action, being treated for burns or smoke inhalation or heat stroke.

At last the fire ate its way over the reservation boundary and into the national parkland beyond; and a few hours later, as Wednesday's sun slid down over the mountains, Davis Blackbear returned to his trailer and fell across the bed, without bothering to remove his sweaty uniform or even to kick off his ruined shoes. And lay like a dead man through the rest of the day and all through the night, until the next morning's light came in the trailer's windows; and then he got up and undressed and went back to bed and slept some more.

A little before noon he woke again, and knew before he opened his eyes what he was going to do.

Captain Ridge had told him to take the day off and rest up; but Ridge wasn't around when Davis came by the station, and nobody paid any attention when Davis left his car and drove off in one of the jeeps. Or stopped him when he drove past the roadblocks that were still in place around the fire zone; everybody was too exhausted to ask unnecessary questions.

It was a little disorienting, driving across the still-smoking land; the destruction had been so complete that nothing was recognizable. He almost missed a couple of turns before he found the place he was looking for.

A big green pickup truck was parked beside the road, bearing the insignia of the U.S. Forest Service. A big stocky white man in a green uniform stood beside it, watching as Davis drove up and parked the jeep and got out. "Afternoon," he said.

He stuck out a hand as Davis walked across the road. "Bob Lindblad," he said as Davis shook his hand. "Fire inspector. They sent me down to have a look, seeing as it's on federal land now."

He looked around and shook his head. "Hell of a thing," he said, and wiped his forehead with the back of his hand.

It certainly was a strange-looking scene. On the northeast side of the road, there was nothing but ruin, an ash-covered desolation studded with charred tree stumps, stretching up the hillside and over the ridge and out of sight. The other side of the road, however, appeared untouched; except for a thin coating of powdery ash on the bushes and the kudzu vines, it looked exactly as it had when Davis came this way a couple of weeks ago.

The Forest Service man said, "Anybody live around here?"

"Not close, no. Used to be a family named Birdshooter, lived up that way, but they moved out a long time ago."

Lindblad nodded. "I saw some house foundations."

Davis said, "This was where it started?"

"Where it *was* started," Lindblad said. "Yes."

"Somebody set it?"

"No question about it," Lindblad waved a big hand. "Signs all over the place. They set it at half a dozen points along this road. The wind was at their backs, out of the southwest — that's why the other side of the road didn't take — so they weren't in any danger. Bastards," he added.

Davis said, "Find anything to show who did it?"

Lindblad shook his head. "Been too much traffic up and down this road, last few days, to make any sense of the tracks. I'm still looking, though."

"All right if I look around too?" Davis asked.

"Sure. Just holler," Lindblad said, "if you find anything. I'll be somewhere close by."

He walked off up the hill, his shoes kicking up little white puffs of ash. Davis watched him a minute and then started to walk along the road, looking at the chewed-up surface. The Forest Service guy was right, he thought, no way in hell could anybody sort out all these tracks and ruts. Over on the unburned downhill side, somebody had almost gone into the ditch —

Davis almost missed it. A single step left or right, or the sun at a different angle, and he'd never have seen the tiny shininess at the bottom of the brush-choked ditch. He bent down and groped, pushing aside a clod of roadway dirt, and felt something tangle around his fingers. He tugged gently and it came free. He straightened up and held up his hand in front of his face.

The sun glinted off the little silver dog as it swung from side to side at the end of the broken chain.

Up on the hillside, Lindblad called, "Find anything?"

Davis turned and looked. Lindblad was poking around near the ruins of the old house, nearly hidden by a couple of black tree stubs. His back was to the road.

"No," Davis yelled back, walking across the road. "Not a thing."

He drew back his arm and hurled the pendant high out over the black-and-gray waste. It flashed for an instant against the sky before vanishing, falling somewhere on the burned earth.

Critical Contexts for Disasters and Apocalypses

Mircea Eliade

From The Myth of the Eternal Return
(1949; trans. 1954)

Mircea Eliade's work analyzing the structure of the world's religions was part of an intellectual movement that revolutionized modern religious studies. Born and educated in Romania, Eliade (1907–1986) lived in Paris after World War II before moving to the United States, where he served on the faculty of the University of Chicago for thirty years. His studies of yoga and shamanism are still widely read in the field, but he is perhaps best known for his contributions to comparative religion. Eliade takes an anthropological and philosophical approach to the study of religion, with an emphasis on structural analysis and on the relationship between myth and ritual. One of the cornerstones of his thought is the distinction between *sacred time* — a realm of transcendent experience that is always accessible but exists outside of historical, chronological time — and *profane time*, which is the ordinary experience of modern life. According to Eliade, early cultures that depended on nature's seasonal cycles viewed time as a circular repetition of death and rebirth. The Judeo-Christian tradition, in contrast, constructed a linear, historical narrative with a definite endpoint.

Eliade explores this distinction in the selection that follows, focusing on Judaism and Christianity. The Hebrew Bible recounts divine intervention in a historical narrative, and the messianic tradition in both Judaism and, especially, Christianity, constructs an apocalyptic narrative in which the end of days is welcomed — not merely as a temporary stage in an ongoing process but as a cul-

Translated by Willard R. Trask.

minating event that will put an end to history and life as we know it. While contrasting the cyclical and historical notions of time, Eliade also acknowledges overlapping patterns: holidays like Passover and Christmas echo the cycles of nature, and Christianity was influenced by earlier traditions of a dying and rising god as a seasonal deity.

Eliade is sometimes criticized for inconsistencies, and his reputation has suffered from the disclosure of fascist sympathies during World War II. Nonetheless, he provided a paradigm for religious studies that remains powerful. Rather than focus on specific religious practices, Eliade perceived that a wide range of rituals shared the purpose of allowing celebrants to transcend ordinary time. It is participation in ritual that allows someone to enter into sacred time and thus participate directly in the enactment of mythic narratives. Like both Carl Jung and Joseph Campbell, Eliade saw myths as not simply stories but meaningful realms of symbolic enactment that transcend history. Because individual humans are finite and unique, they are perishable, but if they participate in a larger cycle of natural and cosmic renewal, they are in a sense eternal. This insight is especially relevant for thinking about images of apocalypse and disaster, where questions of the finite and the eternal are always at stake.

Normality of Suffering

With this chapter, we hope to approach human life and historical existence from a new point of view. Archaic man, as has been shown, tends to set himself in opposition, by every means in his power, to history, regarded as a succession of events that are irreversible, unforeseeable, possessed of autonomous value. He refuses to accept it and to grant it value as such, as *history* — without, however, always being able to exorcise it; for example, he is powerless against cosmic catastrophes, military disasters, social injustices bound up with the very structure of society, personal misfortunes, and so forth. Thus it would be interesting to learn how this "history" was tolerated by archaic man; that is, how he endured the calamities, the mishaps, and the "sufferings" that entered into the lot of each individual and each collectivity.

What does living mean for a man who belongs to a traditional culture? Above all, it means living in accordance with extrahuman models, in conformity with archetypes. Hence it means living at the heart of the *real* since . . . there is nothing truly real except the archetypes. Living in conformity with the archetypes amounted to respecting the "law," since the law was only a primordial hierophany, the revelation *in illo tempore*[1] of the norms of existence, a disclosure by a divinity or a mystical being. And if, through the repetition of paradigmatic gestures and by means of periodic ceremonies, archaic man succeeded, as we have seen, in annulling time, he nonetheless

---

1. Eliade uses the Latin phrase *in illo tempore* (in that time) to delineate a mythic time that exists outside of history but can be accessed through ritual. [Ed.]

lived in harmony with the cosmic rhythms; we could even say that he entered into these rhythms (we need only remember how "real" night and day are to him, and the seasons, the cycles of the moon, the solstices).

In the frame of such an existence, what could suffering and pain signify? Certainly not a meaningless experience that man can only "tolerate" insofar as it is inevitable, as, for example, he tolerates the rigors of climate. Whatever its nature and whatever its apparent cause, his suffering had a meaning; it corresponded, if not always to a prototype, at least to an order whose value was not contested. It has been said that one of the great superiorities of Christianity, compared with the old Mediterranean ethics, was that it gave value to suffering: transforming pain from a negative condition to an experience with a positive spiritual content. The assertion is valid insofar as it refers to a giving of value to suffering and even to a seeking out of pain for its salutary qualities. But if pre-Christian humanity did not seek out suffering and did not grant it value (with a few rare exceptions) as an instrument of purification and spiritual ascent, it was never regarded as meaningless. Of course, we here refer to suffering as an event, as a historical fact, to suffering brought on by a cosmic catastrophe (drought, flood, storm), by an invasion (incendiarism, slavery, humiliation), by social injustices, and so on.

If it was possible to tolerate such sufferings, it is precisely because they seemed neither gratuitous nor arbitrary. It would be superfluous to cite examples; they are to be found everywhere. The primitive who sees his field laid waste by drought, his cattle decimated by disease, his child ill, himself attacked by fever or too frequently unlucky as a hunter, knows that all these contingencies are not due to chance but to certain magical or demonic influences, against which the priest or sorcerer possesses weapons. Hence he does as the community does in the case of a catastrophe: he turns to the sorcerer to do away with the magical effect, or to the priest to make the gods favorable to him. If the intervention of priest or sorcerer produces no result, the interested parties recollect the existence of the Supreme Being, who is almost forgotten at other times, and pray to him by offering sacrifices. "Thou who art above, take not my child; he is too young," pray the nomadic Selk'nam of Tierra del Fuego. "O, Tsuni-Goam!" the Hottentots wail. "Thou alone knowest that I am not guilty!" During a storm, the Semang pygmies scratch their calves with bamboo knives and scatter drops of blood in all directions, crying: "Ta Pedn! I am not hardened, I pay for my fault! Accept my debt, I pay it!"[2] We must, in passing, emphasize a point which we developed in detail in our *Patterns in Comparative Religion*: in the cults of the so-called primitive peoples, the celestial Supreme Beings intervene only as the last resort, when every address to gods, demons, and sorcerers, to the end of banishing a suffering (drought, excessive rains, calamity, illness, etc.), has failed. On such an occasion, the Semang pygmies confess the faults of which

2. See also further examples in Ch. II of our *Patterns in Comparative Religion* (English trans., London and New York, 1958), pp. 46 ff.

they believe themselves guilty, a custom which we find sporadically among other peoples, always as an accompaniment to the last recourse to escape from suffering.

Meanwhile, every moment of the magico-religious treatment of suffering most clearly illustrates its meaning: suffering proceeds from the magical action of an enemy, from breaking a taboo, from entering a baneful zone, from the anger of a god, or — when all other hypotheses have proven insufficient — from the will or the wrath of the Supreme Being. The primitive — and not the primitive alone, as we shall see in a moment — cannot conceive of an unprovoked suffering;[3] it arises from a personal fault (if he is convinced that it is a religious fault) or from his neighbor's malevolence (in cases where the sorcerer discovers that magical action is involved); but there is always a fault at the bottom of it, or at the very least a cause, recognized in the will of the forgotten Supreme God, to whom man is finally forced to address himself. In each case, the suffering becomes intelligible and hence tolerable. Against this suffering, the primitive struggles with all the magico-religious means available to him — but he tolerates it morally because *it is not absurd.* The critical moment of the suffering lies in its appearance; suffering is perturbing only insofar as its cause remains undiscovered. As soon as the sorcerer or the priest discovers what is causing children or animals to die, drought to continue, rain to increase, game to disappear, the suffering begins to become tolerable; it has a meaning and a cause, hence it can be fitted into a system and explained.

What we have just said of the primitive applies in large measure to the man of the archaic cultures. Naturally, the motifs that yield a justification for suffering and pain vary from people to people, but the justification is found everywhere. In general, it may be said that suffering is regarded as the consequence of a deviation in respect to the "norm." That this norm differs from people to people, and from civilization to civilization, goes without saying. But the important point for us is that nowhere — within the frame of the archaic civilizations — are suffering and pain regarded as "blind" and without meaning.

Thus the Indians quite early elaborated a conception of universal causality, the karma concept, which accounts for the actual events and sufferings of the individual's life and at the same time explains the necessity for transmigrations. In the light of the law of karma, sufferings not only find a meaning but also acquire a positive value. The sufferings of one's present life are not only deserved — since they are in fact the fatal effect of crimes and faults committed in previous lives — they are also welcome, for it is only in this way that it is possible to absorb and liquidate part of the karmic debt that burdens the individual and determines the cycle of his future existences. According to the Indian conception, every man is born with a

---

3. We emphasize once again that, from the point of view of an historical peoples or classes, "suffering" is equivalent to "history." This equivalence can be observed even today in the peasant civilizations of Europe.

debt, but with freedom to contract new debts. His existence forms a long series of payments and borrowings, the account of which is not always obvious. A man not totally devoid of intelligence can serenely tolerate the sufferings, griefs, and blows that come to him, the injustices of which he is the object, because each of them solves a karmic equation that had remained unsolved in some previous existence. Naturally, Indian speculation very early sought and discovered means through which man can free himself from this endless chain of cause-effect-cause, and so on, determined by the law of karma. But such solutions do nothing to invalidate the meaning of suffering; on the contrary, they strengthen it. Like Yoga, Buddhism sets out from the principle that all existence is pain, and it offers the possibility of a concrete and final way of escape from this unbroken succession of sufferings to which, in the last analysis, every human life can be reduced. But Buddhism, like Yoga, and indeed like every other Indian method of winning liberation, never for a moment casts any doubt upon the "normality" of pain. As to Vedānta, for it suffering is "illusory" only insofar as the whole universe is illusory; neither the human experience of suffering nor the universe is a reality in the ontological sense of the word. With the exception constituted by the materialistic Lokāyata and Chārvāka schools — for which neither the "soul" nor "God" exists and which consider avoiding pain and seeking pleasure the only rational end that man can set himself — all India has accorded to sufferings, whatever their nature (cosmic, psychological, or historical), a clearly defined meaning and function. Karma ensures that everything happening in the world takes place in conformity with the immutable law of cause and effect.

If the archaic world nowhere presents us with a formula as explicit as that of karma to explain the normality of suffering, we do everywhere find in it an equal tendency to grant suffering and historical events a "normal meaning." To treat all the expressions of this tendency here is out of the question. Almost everywhere we come upon the archaic concept (predominant among primitives) according to which suffering is to be imputed to the divine will, whether as directly intervening to produce it or as permitting other forces, demonic or divine, to provoke it. The destruction of a harvest, drought, the sack of a city by an enemy, loss of freedom or life, any calamity (epidemic, earthquake, and so on) — there is nothing that does not, in one way or another, find its explanation and justification in the transcendent, in the divine economy. Whether the god of the conquered city was less powerful than the god of the victorious army; whether a ritual fault, on the part of the entire community or merely on that of a single family, was committed in respect to one divinity or another; whether spells, demons, negligences, curses are involved — an individual or a collective suffering always has its explanation. And, consequently, it is, it *can be*, tolerable.

Nor is this all. In the Mediterranean-Mesopotamian area, man's sufferings were early connected with those of a god. To do so was to endow them with an archetype that gave them both reality and normality. The very ancient myth of the suffering, death, and resurrection of Tammuz has replicas and imitations almost throughout the Paleo-Oriental world, and traces of its scenario were preserved even down to post-Christian gnosticism. This is not the place to enter into the cosmologico-agricultural origins and the eschatological structure of Tammuz. We shall confine ourselves to a reminder that the sufferings and resurrection of Tammuz also provided a model for the sufferings of other divinities (Marduk, for example) and doubtless were mimed (hence repeated) each year by the king. The popular lamentations and rejoicings that commemorated the sufferings, death, and resurrection of Tammuz, or of any other cosmico-agrarian divinity, produced, in the consciousness of the East, a repercussion whose extent has been badly underestimated. For it was not a question merely of a presentiment of the resurrection that will follow death, but also, and no less, of the consoling power of Tammuz's sufferings for each individual. Any suffering could be tolerated if the drama of Tammuz was remembered.

For this mythical drama reminded men that suffering is never final; that death is always followed by resurrection; that every defeat is annulled and transcended by the final victory. . . . What we wish to emphasize at this point is that Tammuz, or any other variant of the same archetype, justifies — in other words, renders tolerable — the sufferings of the "just." The god — as so often the "just," the "innocent" — suffered without being guilty. He was humiliated, flogged till the lash drew blood, imprisoned in a "pit," that is, in hell. Here it was that the Great Goddess (or, in the later, gnostic versions, a "messenger") visited him, encouraged him, and revived him. This consoling myth of the god's sufferings was long in fading from the consciousness of the peoples of the East. Professor Widengren, for instance, believes that it is among the Manichaean and Mandaean prototypes,[4] though of course with the inevitable changes and new valences that it acquired during the period of Greco-Oriental syncretism. In any case, one fact forces itself upon our attention: such mythological scenarios present an extremely archaic structure, which derives — if not "historically," at least morphologically — from lunar myths whose antiquity we have no reason to question. We have observed that lunar myths afforded an optimistic view of life in general; everything takes place cyclically, death is inevitably followed by resurrection, cataclysm by a new Creation. The paradigmatic myth of Tammuz (also extended to other Mesopotamian divinities) offers us a new ratification of this same optimism: it is not only the individual's death that is "saved"; the same is true of his sufferings. At least the gnostic, Mandaean, and Manichaean echoes of the Tammuz myth suggest this. For these sects, man as such must bear the lot that once fell to Tammuz; fallen into the pit, slave to the Prince of Darkness, man is awakened by a messenger who brings him the good tidings of his imminent salvation, of his "liberation." Lacking though we are in documents that would allow us to extend the same conclusions to Tammuz, we are nevertheless inclined to believe that his drama was not looked upon as foreign to the human drama. Hence the great popular success of rites connected with the so-called vegetation divinities.

---

4. Geo Widengren, *King and Saviour*, II (Uppsala, 1947).

History Regarded as Theophany

Among the Hebrews, every new historical calamity was regarded as a punishment inflicted by Yahweh, angered by the orgy of sin to which the chosen people had abandoned themselves. No military disaster seemed absurd, no suffering was vain, for, beyond the "event," it was always possible to perceive the will of Yahweh. Even more: these catastrophes were, we may say, necessary; they were foreseen by God so that the Jewish people should not contravene its true destiny by alienating the religious heritage left by Moses. Indeed, each time that history gave them the opportunity, each time that they enjoyed a period of comparative peace and economic prosperity, the Hebrews turned from Yahweh and to the Baals and Astartes of their neighbors. Only historical catastrophes brought them back to the right road by forcing them to look toward the true God. Then "they cried unto the Lord, and said, We have sinned, because we have forsaken the Lord, and have served Baalim and Ashtaroth: but now deliver us out of the hand of our enemies, and we will serve thee" (I Samuel 12:10). This return to the true God in the hour of disaster reminds us of the desperate gesture of the primitive, who, to rediscover the existence of the Supreme Being, requires the extreme of peril and the failure of all addresses to other divine forms (gods, ancestors, demons). Yet the Hebrews, from the moment the great military Assyro-Babylonian empires appeared on their historical horizon, lived constantly under the threat proclaimed by Yahweh: "But if ye will not obey the voice of the Lord, but rebel against the commandment of the Lord, then shall the hand of the Lord be against you, as it was against your fathers" (I Samuel 12:15).

Through their terrifying visions, the prophets but confirmed and amplified Yahweh's ineluctable chastisement upon His people who had not kept the faith. And it is only insofar as such prophecies were ratified by catastrophes (as, indeed, was the case from Elijah to Jeremiah) that historical events acquired religious significance; i.e., that they clearly appeared as punishments inflicted by the Lord in return for the impiousness of Israel. Because of the prophets, who interpreted contemporary events in the light of a strict faith, these events were transformed into "negative theophanies," into Yahweh's "wrath." Thus they not only acquired a meaning (because, as we have seen, for the entire Oriental world, every historical event had its own signification) but they also revealed their hidden coherence by proving to be the concrete expression of the same single divine will. Thus, for the first time, the prophets placed a value on history, succeeded in transcending the traditional vision of the cycle (the conception that ensures all things will be repeated forever), and discovered a one-way time. This discovery was not to be immediately and fully accepted by the consciousness of the entire Jewish people, and the ancient conceptions were still long to survive.

But, for the first time, we find affirmed, and increasingly accepted, the idea that historical events have a value in themselves, insofar as they are determined by the will of God. This God of the Jewish people is no longer an Oriental divinity, creator of archetypal gestures, but a personality who ceaselessly intervenes in history, who reveals his will through events (invasions, sieges, battles, and so on). Historical facts thus become "situations" of man in respect to God, and as such they acquire a religious value that nothing had previously been able to confer on them. It may, then, be said with truth that the Hebrews were the first to discover the meaning of history as the epiphany of God, and this conception, as we should expect, was taken up and amplified by Christianity.

We may even ask ourselves if monotheism, based upon the direct and personal revelation of the divinity, does not necessarily entail the "salvation" of time, its value within the frame of history. Doubtless the idea of revelation is found, in more or less perspicuous form, in all religions, we could even say in all cultures. In fact . . . , the archetypal gestures — finally reproduced in endless succession by man — were at the same time hierophanies or theophanies. The first dance, the first duel, the first fishing expedition, like the first marriage ceremony or the first ritual, became examples for humanity because they revealed a mode of existence of the divinity, of the primordial man, of the civilizing Hero. But these revelations occurred in *mythical time*, at the extratemporal instant of the beginning; thus, . . . everything in a certain sense coincided with the beginning of the world, with the cosmogony. Everything had taken place and had been revealed at that moment, *in illo tempore*: the creation of the world, and that of man, and man's establishment in the situation provided for him in the cosmos, down to the least details of that situation (physiology, sociology, culture, and so on).

The situation is altogether different in the case of the monotheistic revelation. This takes place in time, in historical duration: Moses receives the Law at a certain place and at a certain date. Of course, here too archetypes are involved, in the sense that these events, raised to the rank of examples, will be repeated; but they will not be repeated until the times are accomplished, that is, in a new *illud tempus*. For example, as Isaiah (11 :15–16) prophesies, the miraculous passages of the Red Sea and the Jordan will be repeated "in the day." Nevertheless, the moment of the revelation made to Moses by God remains a limited moment, definitely situated in time. And, since it also represents a theophany, it thus acquires a new dimension: it becomes precious inasmuch as it is no longer reversible, as it is historical event.

Yet Messianism hardly succeeds in accomplishing the eschatological valorization of time: the future will regenerate time; that is, will restore its original purity and integrity. Thus, *in illo tempore* is situated not only at the beginning of time but also at its end.[5] In these spacious Messianic visions it is also easy to discern the very old scenario of annual regeneration of the cosmos by repetition of the Creation and by the drama of the suffering king. The Messiah — on a higher plane, of course — assumes the eschatological role of the king as god, or as representing the divinity on earth, whose chief mission was the periodical regeneration of all nature. His sufferings recalled those of the king, but, as in the ancient scenarios, the victory was always

---

5. Cf. G. van der Leeuw, "Primordial Time and Final Time," in *Man and Time* (New York and London, 1957), pp. 324–50.

finally the king's. The only difference is that this victory over the forces of darkness and chaos no longer occurs regularly every year but is projected into a future and Messianic *illud tempus.*

Under the "pressure of history" and supported by the prophetic and Messianic experience, a new interpretation of historical events dawns among the children of Israel. Without finally renouncing the traditional concept of archetypes and repetitions, Israel attempts to "save" historical events by regarding them as active presences of Yahweh. Whereas, for example, among the Mesopotamian peoples individual or collective sufferings were tolerated insofar as they were caused by the conflict between divine and demonic forces, that is, formed a part of the cosmic drama (the Creation being, from time immemorial and *ad infinitum*, preceded by chaos and tending to be reabsorbed in it; a new birth implying, from time immemorial and *ad infinitum*, sufferings and passions, etc.), in the Israel of the Messianic prophets, historical events could be tolerated because, on the one hand, they were willed by Yahweh, and, on the other hand, because they were necessary to the final salvation of the chosen people. Rehandling the old scenarios (type: Tammuz) of the "passion" of a god, Messianism gives them a new value, especially by abolishing their possibility of repetition *ad infinitum*. When the Messiah comes, the world will be saved once and for all and history will cease to exist. In this sense we are justified in speaking not only of an eschatological granting of value to the future, to "that day," but also of the "salvation" of historical becoming. History no longer appears as a cycle that repeats itself *ad infinitum*, as the primitive peoples represented it (creation, exhaustion, destruction, annual re-creation of the cosmos), and as it was formulated — as we shall see immediately — in theories of Babylonian origin (creation, destruction, creation extending over considerable periods of time: millennia, Great Years, aeons). Directly ordered by the will of Yahweh, history appears as a series of theophanies, negative or positive, each of which has its intrinsic value. Certainly, all military defeats can be referred back to an archetype: Yahweh's wrath. But each of these defeats, though basically a repetition of the same archetype, nevertheless acquires a coefficient of irreversibility: Yahweh's personal intervention. The fall of Samaria, for example, though assimilable to that of Jerusalem, yet differs from it in the fact that it was provoked by a new gesture on the part of Yahweh, by a new intervention of the Lord in history.

But it must not be forgotten that these Messianic conceptions are the exclusive creation of a religious elite. For many centuries, this elite undertook the religious education of the people of Israel, without always being successful in eradicating the traditional Paleo-Oriental granting of value to life and history. The Hebrews' periodic returns to the Baals and Astartes are also largely to be explained by their refusal to allow a value to history, that is, to regard it as a theophany. For the popular strata, and especially for the agrarian communities, the old religious concept (that of the Baals and Astartes) was preferable; it kept them closer to "life" and helped them to tolerate history if not to ignore it. The Messianic prophets' steadfast will to look history in the face and to accept it as a terrifying dialogue with Yahweh, their will to make military defeats bear moral and religious fruit and to tolerate them because they were regarded as *necessary* to Yahweh's reconciliation with the people of Israel and its final salvation — their will, again, to regard any and every moment as a decisive moment and hence to give it worth religiously — demanded too great a religious tension, and the majority of the Israelites refused to submit to it,[6] just as the majority of Christians, and especially the popular elements, refuse to live the genuine life of Christianity. It was more consoling, and easier, in misfortunes and times of trial, to go on accusing an "accident" (e.g., a spell) or a "negligence" (e.g., a ritual fault) that could easily be made good by a sacrifice (even though it were the sacrifice of infants to Moloch).

In this respect, the classic example of Abraham's sacrifice admirably illustrates the difference between the traditional conception of the repetition of an archetypal gesture and the new dimension, *faith*, acquired through religious experience.[7] Morphologically considered, Abraham's sacrifice is nothing but the sacrifice of the first born, a frequent practice in this Paleo-Oriental world in which the Hebrews evolved down to the period of the prophets. The first child was often regarded as the child of a god; indeed, throughout the archaic East, unmarried girls customarily spent a night in the temple and thus conceived by the god (by his representative, the priest, or by his envoy, the "stranger"). The sacrifice of this first child restored to the divinity what belonged to him. Thus the young blood increased the exhausted energy of the god (for the so-called fertility gods exhausted their own substance in the effort expended in maintaining the world and ensuring it abundance; hence they themselves needed to be periodically regenerated). And, in a certain sense, Isaac was a son of God, since he had been given to Abraham and Sarah when Sarah had long passed the age of fertility. But Isaac was given them through their faith; he was the son of the promise and of faith. His sacrifice by Abraham, although in form it resembles all the sacrifices of newborn infants in the Paleo-Semitic world, differs from them fundamentally in content. Whereas, for the entire Paleo-Semitic world, such a sacrifice, despite its religious function, was only a custom, a rite whose meaning was perfectly intelligible, in

---

6. Without religious elites, and more especially without the prophets, Judaism would not have become anything very different from the religion of the Jewish colony in Elephantine, which preserved the popular Palestinian religious viewpoint down to the fifth century B.C.; cf. Albert Vincent, *La Religion des Judéo-Araméens d'Éléphantine* (Paris, 1937). History had allowed these Hebrews of the Diaspora to retain, side by side with Yahweh (Jaho), other divinities (Bethel, Harambethel, Ashumbethel), and even the goddess Anath, in a convenient syncretism. This is one more confirmation of the importance of history in the development of Judaic religious experience and its maintenance under high tensions. For, as we must not forget, the institutions of prophecy and Messianism were above all validated by the pressure of contemporary history.

7. It may be of some service to point out that what is called "faith" in the Judaeo-Christian sense differs, regarded structurally, from other archaic religious experiences. The authenticity and religious validity of these latter must not be doubted, because they are based upon a universally verified dialectic of the sacred. But the experience of faith is due to a new theophany, a new revelation, which, for the respective elites, annuls the validity of other hierophanies. On this subject, see our *Patterns in Comparative Religion*, Ch. I.

Abraham's case it is an act of faith. He does not understand why the sacrifice is demanded of him; nevertheless he performs it because it was the Lord who demanded it. By this act, which is apparently absurd, Abraham initiates a new religious experience, faith. All others (the whole Oriental world) continue to move in an economy of the sacred that will be transcended by Abraham and his successors. To employ Kierkegaard's terminology, their sacrifices belonged to the "general"; that is, they were based upon archaic theophanies that were concerned only with the circulation of sacred energy in the cosmos (from the divinity to man and nature, then from man — through sacrifice — back to the divinity, and so on). These were acts whose justification lay in themselves; they entered into a logical and coherent system: what had belonged to God must be returned to him. For Abraham, Isaac was a *gift* from the Lord and not the product of a direct and material conception. Between God and Abraham yawned an abyss; there was a fundamental break in continuity. Abraham's religious act inaugurates a new religious dimension: God reveals himself as personal, as a "totally distinct" existence that ordains, bestows, demands, without any rational (i.e., general and foreseeable) justification, and for which all is possible. This new religious dimension renders "faith" possible in the Judaeo-Christian sense.

We have cited this example in order to illuminate the novelty of the Jewish religion in comparison with the traditional structures. Just as Abraham's experience can be regarded as a new religious position of man in the cosmos, so, through the prophetic office and Messianism, historical events reveal themselves, in the consciousness of the Israelitic elites, as a dimension they had not previously known: the historical event becomes a theophany, in which are revealed not only Yahweh's will but also the personal relations between him and his people. The same conception, enriched through the elaboration of Christology, will serve as the basis for the philosophy of history that Christianity, from St. Augustine on, will labor to construct. But let us repeat: neither in Christianity nor in Judaism does the discovery of this new dimension in religious experience, faith, produce a basic modification of traditional conceptions. Faith is merely made possible for each individual Christian. The great majority of so-called Christian populations continue, down to our day, to preserve themselves from history by ignoring it and by tolerating it rather than by giving it the meaning of a negative or positive theophany.[8]

However, the acceptance and consecration of history by Judaic elites does not mean that the traditional attitude . . . is transcended. Messianic beliefs in a final regeneration of the world themselves also indicate an antihistoric attitude. Since he can no longer ignore or periodically abolish history, the Hebrew tolerates it in the hope that it will finally end, at some

---

8. This does not imply that these populations (which are for the most part agrarian in structure) are nonreligious; it implies only the "traditional" (archetypal) "revalorization" that they have given to Christian experience.

more or less distant future moment. The irreversibility of historical events and of time is compensated by the limitation of history to time. In the spiritual horizon of Messianism, resistance to history appears as still more determined than in the traditional horizon of archetypes and repetitions; if, here, history was refused, ignored, or abolished by the periodic repetition of the Creation and by the periodic regeneration of time, in the Messianic conception history must be tolerated because it has an eschatological function, but it can be tolerated only because it is known that, one day or another, it will cease. History is thus abolished, not through consciousness of living an eternal present (coincidence with the atemporal instant of the revelation of archetypes), nor by means of a periodically repeated ritual (for example, the rites for the beginning of the year) — it is abolished in the future. Periodic regeneration of the Creation is replaced by a single regeneration that will take place in an *in illo tempore* to come. But the will to put a final and definitive end to history is itself still an antihistorical attitude, exactly as are the other traditional conceptions.

Cosmic Cycles and History

. . .

We observed that the myth of eternal repetition, as reinterpreted by Greek speculation, has the meaning of a supreme attempt toward the "staticization" of becoming, toward annulling the irreversibility of time. If all moments and all situations of the cosmos are repeated *ad infinitum*, their evanescence is, in the last analysis, patent; *sub specie infinitatis*, all moments and all situations remain stationary and thus acquire the ontological order of the archetype. Hence, among all the forms of becoming, historical becoming too is saturated with being. From the point of view of eternal repetition, historical events are transformed into categories and thus regain the ontological order they possessed in the horizon of archaic spirituality. In a certain sense it can even be said that the Greek theory of eternal return is the final variant undergone by the myth of the repetition of an archetypal gesture, just as the Platonic doctrine of Ideas was the final version of the archetype concept, and the most fully elaborated. And it is worth noting that these two doctrines found their most perfect expression at the height of Greek philosophical thought.

But it was especially the myth of universal conflagration that achieved a marked success throughout the Greco-Oriental world. It appears more and more probable that the myth of an end of the world by fire, from which the good will escape unharmed, is of Iranian origin (c.f., for example, *Bundahišn*, XXX, 18), at least in the form known to the "western mages" who, as Cumont has shown,[9] disseminated it in the West. Stoicism, the *Sibylline Oracles* (for example II, 253), and Judaeo-Christian literature make this myth the foundation of their apocalypses and their eschatology. Strange as it may seem, the myth was consoling. In fact, fire renews the world; through it will come the

---

9. Op. cit., pp. 39 ff.

restoration of "a new world, free from old age, death, decomposition and corruption, living eternally, increasing eternally, when the dead shall rise, when
immortality shall come to the living, when the world shall be perfectly
renewed" (*Yašt*, XIX, 14, 89).[10] This, then, is an *apokatastasis* from which the
good have nothing to fear. The final catastrophe will put an end to history,
hence will restore man to eternity and beatitude. . . .

A series of calamities will announce the approach of the end of the
world; and the first of them will be the fall of Rome and the destruction of
the Roman Empire, a frequent anticipation in the Judaeo-Christian apocalypse, but also not unknown to the Iranians.[11] The apocalyptic syndrome is,
furthermore, common to all these traditions. Both Lactantius and the
Bahman-Yašt announce that "the year will be shortened, the month will
diminish, and the day will contract,"[12] a vision of cosmic and human deterioration that we have also found in India (where human life decreases from
80,000 to 100 years) and that astrological doctrines popularized in the Greco-
Oriental world. Then the mountains will crumble and the earth become
smooth, men will desire death and envy the dead, and but a tenth of them
will survive. "It will be a time," writes Lactantius, "when justice will be rejected and innocence odious, when the wicked will prey as enemies upon the
good, when neither law nor order nor military discipline will be observed,
when none will respect gray hairs, or do the offices of piety, nor take pity upon
women and children; all things will be confounded and mixed, against divine
and natural law. . . ."[13] But after this premonitory phase, the purifying fire will
come down to destroy the wicked and will be followed by the millennium of
bliss that the Christian chiliasts also expected and Isaiah and the *Sibylline
Oracles* had earlier foretold. Men will know a new golden age that will last
until the end of the seventh millennium; for after this last conflict, a universal *ekpyrosis* will absorb the whole universe in fire, thus permitting the birth
of a new world, an eternal world of justice and happiness, not subject to astral
influences and freed from the dominion of time.

The Hebrews likewise limited the duration of the world to seven millennia,[14] but the rabbinate never encouraged mathematical calculations to
determine the end of the world. They confined themselves to stating that
a series of cosmic and historical calamities (famines, droughts, wars, and
so forth) would announce the end of the world. The Messiah would come;
the dead would rise again (Isaiah 26:19); God would conquer death and
the renewal of the world would follow (Isaiah 65:17; Book of Jubilees I :29,
even speaks of a new Creation).[15]

Here again, as everywhere in the apocalyptic doctrines referred to
above, we find the traditional motif of extreme decadence, of the tri-

---

10. After James Darmesteter's trans. In *Le Zend-Avesta* (Paris, 1892).
11. Ibid., p. 72.
12. Texts in ibid., p. 78, note 1.
13. *Divinae Institutiones*, VII, 17, 9; Cumont, p. 81.
14. Cf., for example, *Testamentum Abrahami, Ethica Enochi*, etc.
15. On cosmic signs presaging the Messiah in rabbinical literature, see Raphael Patai, *Man and
Temple* (London, 1947), pp. 203 ff.

umph of evil and darkness, which precede the change of aeon and the renewal of the cosmos. A Babylonian text translated by A. Jeremias[16] thus foresees the apocalypse: "When such and such things happen in heaven, then will the clear become dull, the pure dirty, the lands will fall into confusion, prayers will not be heard, the signs of the prophets will become unfavorable. . . . Under his [i.e., a prince who does not obey the commands of the gods] rule the one will devour the other, the people will sell their children for gold, the husband will desert his wife, the wife her husband, the mother will bolt the door against her daughter." Another hymn foretells that, in those days, the sun will no longer rise, the moon no longer appear, and so on.

In the Babylonian conception, however, this crepuscular period is always followed by a new paradisal dawn. Frequently, as we should expect, the paradisal period opens with the enthronement of a new sovereign. Ashurbanipal regards himself as a regenerator of the cosmos, for "since the time the gods in their friendliness did set me on the throne of my fathers, Ramman has sent forth his rain . . . the harvest was plentiful, the corn was abundant . . . the cattle multiplied exceedingly." Nebuchadrezzar says of himself: "A reign of abundance, years of exuberance in my country I cause to be." In a Hittite text, Murshilish thus describes the reign of his father: ". . . under him the whole land of Katti prospered, and in his time people, cattle, sheep multiplied."[17] The conception is archaic and universal: we find it in Homer, in Hesiod, in the Old Testament, in China, and elsewhere.[18]

Simplifying, we might say that, among the Iranians as among the Jews and Christians, the "history" apportioned to the universe is limited, and that the end of the world coincides with the destruction of sinners, the resurrection of the dead, and the victory of eternity over time. But although this doctrine becomes increasingly popular during the first century B.C. and the early centuries of our era, it does not succeed in finally doing away with the traditional doctrine of periodic regeneration of the world through annual repetition of the Creation. We saw . . . that vestiges of this latter doctrine were preserved among the Iranians until far into the Middle Ages. Similarly dominant in pre-Messianic Judaism, it was never totally eliminated, for rabbinic circles hesitated to be precise as to the duration that God had fixed for the cosmos and confined themselves to declaring that the *illud tempus* would certainly arrive one day. In Christianity, on the other hand, the evangelical tradition itself implies that βασίλεια τοῦ θεοῦ is already present "among" (ἐντός) those who believe, and that hence the *illud tempus* is eternally of the present and accessible to anyone, at any moment, through *metanoia*.[19] Since what is involved is a

16. Hastings, I, p. 187.

17. Ivan Engnell, *Studies in Divine Kingship in the Ancient Near East* (Uppsala, 1943), pp. 43, 44, 68; Jeremias, *Handbuch*, pp. 32 ff.

18. *Odyssey*, XIX, 108 ff.; Hesiod, *Erga*, 225–27; our *Patterns in Comparative Religion*, pp. 255 ff.; Patai, p. 180 (rabbinical literature); Léon Wieger, *Histoire des croyances religieuses et des opinions philosophiques en Chine* (Hsien-hsien, 1922), p. 64.

19. Conversion; spiritual rebirth. [Ed.]

religious experience wholly different from the traditional experience, since what is involved is faith, Christianity translates the periodic regeneration of the world into a regeneration of the human individual. But for him who shares in this eternal *nunc* of the reign of God, history ceases as totally as it does for the man of the archaic cultures, who abolishes it periodically. Consequently, for the Christian too, history can be regenerated, by and through each individual believer, even before the Savior's second coming, when it will utterly cease for all Creation.

An adequate discussion of the revolution that Christianity introduced into the dialectic of the abolition of history, and of the escape from the ascendancy of time, would lead us too far beyond the limits of this essay. Let us simply note that even within the frame of the three great religions — Iranian, Judaic, and Christian — that have limited the duration of the cosmos to some specific number of millennia and affirm that history will finally cease *in illo tempore*, there still survive certain traces of the ancient doctrine of the periodic regeneration of history. In other words, history can be abolished, and consequently renewed, a number of times, before the final *eschaton* is realized. Indeed, the Christian liturgical year is based upon a periodic and real repetition of the Nativity, Passion, death, and Resurrection of Jesus, with all that this mystical drama implies for a Christian; that is, personal and cosmic regeneration through reactualization *in concreto* of the birth, death, and resurrection of the Savior.

Destiny and History

We have referred to all these Hellenistic-Oriental doctrines relative to cosmic cycles for only one purpose — that of discovering the answer to the question that we posed at the beginning of this chapter: How has man tolerated history? The answer is discernible in each individual system: His very place in the cosmic cycle — whether the cycle be capable of repetition or not — lays upon man a certain historical destiny. We must beware of seeing no more here than a fatalism, whatever meaning we ascribe to the term, that would account for the good and bad fortune of each individual taken separately. These doctrines answer the questions posed by the destiny of contemporary history in its entirety, not only those posed by the individual destiny. A certain quantity of suffering is in store for humanity (and by the word "humanity" each person means the mass of men known to himself) by the simple fact that humanity finds itself at a certain historical moment, that is, in a cosmic cycle that is in its descending phase or nearing its end. Individually, each is free to withdraw from this historical moment and to console himself for its baneful consequences, whether through philosophy or through mysticism. (The mere mention of the swarm of gnosticisms, sects, mysteries, and philosophies that overran the Mediterranean-Oriental world during the centuries of historical tension will suffice to give an idea of the vastly increasing proportion of those who attempted to withdraw from history.) The historical moment in its totality, however, could not avoid the destiny that was the inevitable consequence of its very position upon the descending trajectory of the cycle to which it belonged. Just as, in the Indian view, every man of the Kali Yuga is stimulated to seek his freedom and spiritual beatitude, yet at the same time cannot avoid the final dissolution of this crepuscular world in its entirety, so, in the view of the various systems to which we have referred, the historical moment, despite the possibilities of escape it offers contemporaries, can never, in its entirety, be anything but tragic, pathetic, unjust, chaotic, as any moment that heralds the final catastrophe must be.

In fact, a common characteristic relates all the cyclical systems scattered through the Hellenistic-Oriental world: in the view of each of them, the contemporary historical moment (whatever its chronological position) represents a decadence in relation to preceding historical moments. Not only is the contemporary aeon inferior to the other ages (gold, silver, and so on) but, even within the frame of the reigning age (that is, of the reigning cycle), the "instant" in which man lives grows worse as time passes. This tendency toward devaluation of the contemporary moment should not be regarded as a sign of pessimism. On the contrary, it reveals an excess of optimism, for, in the deterioration of the contemporary situation, at least a portion of mankind saw signs foretelling the regeneration that must necessarily follow. Since the days of Isaiah, a series of military defeats and political collapses had been anxiously awaited as an ineluctable syndrome of the Messianic *illud tempus* that was to regenerate the world.

However, different as were the possible positions of man, they displayed one common characteristic: history could be tolerated, not only because it had a meaning but also because it was, in the last analysis, necessary. For those who believed in a repetition of an entire cosmic cycle, as for those who believed only in a single cycle nearing its end, the drama of contemporary history was necessary and inevitable. Plato, even in his day, and despite his acceptance of some of the schemata of Chaldaean astrology, was profuse in his sarcasms against those who had fallen into astrological fatalism or who believed in an eternal repetition in the strict (Stoic) sense of the term (cf., for example, *Republic*, VIII, 546 ff.). As for the Christian philosophers, they fiercely combated the same astrological fatalism,[20] which had increased during the last centuries of the Roman Empire. As we shall see in a moment, Saint Augustine will defend the idea of a perennial Rome solely to escape from accepting *fatum* determined by cyclical theories. It is, nevertheless, true that astrological fatalism itself accounted for the course of historical events, and hence helped the contemporary to understand them and tolerate them, just as successfully as did the various Greco-Oriental gnosticisms, Neo-Stoicism and

20. Among many other liberations, Christianity effected liberation from astral destiny: "We are above Fate," Tatian writes (*Oratio ad Graecos*, 9), summing up Christian doctrine. "The sun and the moon were made for us; how am I to worship what are my servitors" (ibid., 4). Cf. also St. Augustine, *De civitate Dei*, XII, Ch. X–XIII; on the ideas of St. Basil, Origen, St. Gregory, and St. Augustine, and their opposition to cyclical theories, see Pierre Duhem, *Le Système du monde* (Paris, 1913–17), II, pp. 446 ff. See also Henri-Charles Puech, "Gnosis and Time," in *Man and Time*, pp. 38 ff.

Neo-Pythagoreanism. For example, whether history was governed by the movements of the heavenly bodies or purely and simply by the cosmic process, which necessarily demanded a disintegration inevitably linked to an original integration, whether, again, it was subject to the will of God, a will that the prophets had been able to glimpse, the result was the same: none of the catastrophes manifested in history was arbitrary. Empires rose and fell; wars caused innumerable sufferings; immorality, dissoluteness, social injustice, steadily increased — because all this was necessary, that is, was willed by the cosmic rhythm, by the demiurge, by the constellations, or by the will of God.

In this view, the history of Rome takes on a noble gravity. Several times in the course of their history, the Romans underwent the terror of an imminent end to their city, whose duration — as they believed — had been determined at the very moment of its foundation by Romulus. In *Les Grands Mythes de Rome*, Jean Hubaux has penetratingly analyzed the critical moments of the drama provoked by the uncertainties in calculations of the "life" of Rome, while Jérôme Carcopino has recorded the historical events and the spiritual tension that justified the hope for a noncatastrophic resurrection of the city.[21] At every historical crisis two crepuscular myths obsessed the Roman people: (1) the life of the city is ended, its duration being limited to a certain number of years (the "mystic number" revealed by the twelve eagles seen by Romulus); and (2) the Great Year will put an end to all history, hence to that of Rome, by a universal *ekpyrosis*. Roman history itself undertook to show the baselessness of these fears, down to a very late period. For at the end of 120 years after the foundation of Rome, it was realized that the twelve eagles seen by Romulus did not signify 120 years of historical life for the city, as many had feared. At the end of 365 years, it became apparent that there was no question of a Great Year, in which each year of the city would be equivalent to a day, and it was supposed that destiny had granted Rome another kind of Great Year, composed of twelve months of 100 years. As for the myth of regressive "ages" and eternal return, professed by the Sibyl and interpreted by the philosophers through their theories of cosmic cycles, it was more than once hoped that the transition from one age to the other could be effected without a universal *ekpyrosis*. But this hope was always mingled with anxiety. Each time historical events accentuated their catastrophic rhythm, the Romans believed that the Great Year was on the point of ending and that Rome was on the eve of her fall. When Caesar crossed the Rubicon, Nigidius Figulus foresaw the beginning of a cosmico-historical drama which would put an end to Rome and the human race.[22] But the same Nigidius Figulus believed[23] that an *ekpyrosis* was not inevitable, and that a renewal, the Neo-Pythagorean *metacosmesis*, was also possible without a cosmic catastrophe — an idea that Virgil was to take up and elaborate.

---

21. Jean Hubaux, *Les Grands Mythes de Rome* (Paris, 1945); Carcopino, op. cit.
22. Lucan, *Pharsalia*, 639, 642–45; Carcopino, p. 147.
23. Ibid., pp. 52 ff.

Horace, in his *Epode XVI*, had been unable to conceal his fear as to the future fate of Rome. The Stoics, the astrologers, and Oriental gnosticism saw in the wars and calamities of the time signs that the final catastrophe was imminent. Reasoning either from calculation of the life of Rome or from the doctrine of cosmico-historical cycles, the Romans knew that, whatever else might happen, the city was fated to disappear before the beginning of a new aeon. But the reign of Augustus, coming after a series of long and sanguinary civil wars, seemed to inaugurate a *pax aeterna*. The fears inspired by the two myths — the "age" of Rome and the theory of the Great Year — now proved groundless: "Augustus has founded Rome anew and we have nothing to fear as to its life," those who had been concerned over the mystery of Romulus's twelve eagles could assure themselves. "The transition from the age of iron to the age of gold has been accomplished without an *ekpyrosis*," those who had been obsessed by the theory of cycles could say. Thus Virgil, for the last *saeculum*, that of the sun, which was to bring about the combustion of the universe, could substitute the *saeculum* of Apollo, avoiding an *ekpyrosis* and assuming that the recent wars had themselves been the sign of the transition from the age of iron to the age of gold.[24] Later, when Augustus's reign seemed indeed to have inaugurated the age of gold, Virgil undertook to reassure the Romans as to the duration of the city. In the *Aeneid* (I, 255 ff.) Jupiter, addressing Venus, assures her that he will lay no bounds of space or time upon the Romans: "empire without end have I given them."[25] And it was not until after the publication of the *Aeneid* that Rome was called *urbs aeterna*, Augustus being proclaimed the second founder of the city. His birthday, September 23, was regarded "as the point of departure of the Universe, whose existence had been saved, and whose face had been changed, by Augustus."[26] Then arose the hope that Rome could regenerate itself periodically *ad infinitum*. Thus it was that, liberated from the myths of the twelve eagles and of the *ekpyrosis*, Rome could increase until, as Virgil foretells, it embraced even the regions "beyond the paths of the sun and the year" ("*extra anni solisque vias*").

In all this, as we see, there is a supreme effort to liberate history from astral destiny or from the law of cosmic cycles and to return, through the myth of the eternal renewal of Rome, to the archaic myth of the annual (and in particular the noncatastrophic!) regeneration of the cosmos through its eternal re-creation by the sovereign or the priest. It is above all an attempt to give value to history on the cosmic plane; that is, to regard historical events and catastrophes as genuine cosmic combustions or dissolutions that must periodically put an end to the universe in order to permit its regeneration. The wars, the destruction, the sufferings of history are no longer the premonitory signs of the transition from one age to another,

---

24. Cf. ibid., p. 45, etc.
25. "His ego nec metas rerum nec tempora pono: imperium sine fine dedi"; cf. Hubaux, pp. 128 ff.
26. Carcopino, p. 200.

but themselves constitute the transition. Thus in each period of peace, history renews itself and, consequently, a new world begins; in the last analysis (as we saw in the case of the myth built up around Augustus), the sovereign repeats the Creation of the cosmos.

We have adduced the example of Rome to show how historical events could be given value by the expedient of the myths examined in the present chapter. Adapted to a particular myth theory (age of Rome, Great Year), catastrophes could not only be tolerated by their contemporaries but also *positively* accorded a value immediately after their appearance. Of course, the age of gold inaugurated by Augustus has survived only through what it created in Latin culture. Augustus was no sooner dead than history undertook to belie the age of gold, and once again people began living in expectation of imminent disaster. When Rome was occupied by Alaric, it seemed that the sign of Romulus's twelve eagles had triumphed: the city was entering its twelfth and last century of existence. Only Saint Augustine attempted to show that no one could know the moment at which God would decide to put an end to history, and that in any case, although cities by their very nature have a limited duration, the only "eternal city" being that of God, no astral destiny can decide the life or death of a nation. Thus Christian thought tended to transcend, once and for all, the old themes of eternal repetition, just as it had undertaken to transcend all the other archaic viewpoints by revealing the importance of the religious experience of faith and that of the value of the human personality.

Susan Sontag

The Imagination of Disaster
(1965)

Literary and cultural critic Susan Sontag (1933–2004) was a public intellectual and member of the New York intelligentsia who also became an iconic figure and pop celebrity. Born in New York, the highly educated and cosmopolitan Sontag grew up in Arizona and California, graduated from the University of Chicago, earned master's degrees in literature and philosophy from Harvard University, spent a semester at Oxford University, and lived briefly in Paris before returning to New York, where she made her home. She moved in circles that included not only writers and journalists but also artists and filmmakers like Andy Warhol, Woody Allen, and her longtime partner, photographer Annie Leibovitz. A precocious student and voracious reader, Sontag's insatiable curiosity extended beyond literature and art to pop culture, politics, and the cultural understanding of disease. She often took controversial positions, as when she praised Nazi filmmaker Leni Riefenstahl on purely aesthetic grounds, but she was not afraid to rethink these positions in later critiques.

Sontag was a journalist, a political activist, and an occasional film director. Her works include novels, short stories, and plays. She is most famous, however, for her essays on literature, art, and contemporary life, in works like *On Photography* (1977), *AIDS and Its Metaphors* (1989), and *Regarding the Pain of Others* (2003). Her debut collection, *Against Interpretation* (1968), which includes the famous essay "On Camp" as well as the essay that follows, illustrates her characteristic interest in a broad range of phenomena, bringing a similarly intense attention to both "high" and "low" culture. Sontag received many awards and honors, including a National Book Circle Critics Award, a National Book Award, and a MacArthur Foundation "genius" grant.

In "The Imagination of Disaster," Sontag analyzes the narrative, imagery, and appeal of science fiction films of the 1950s and early 1960s. These films shared a number of narrative conventions, and Sontag examines how these motifs reflect cultural preoccupations with the memory of World War II, with the advance of technology represented by the atomic bomb, and even with the more general anxiety about the dehumanization of modern life. In addition to tracing elements of plot and character, Sontag highlights the sensuous and emotional appeal of the very images of disaster these movies project, seeing in them signs of a cultural unconscious formed from pride and fear, something of a modern mythology about how humans might adapt (or devolve) to the challenges of the nuclear age.

The typical science fiction film has a form as predictable as a Western, and is made up of elements which, to a practiced eye, are as classic as the saloon brawl, the blonde schoolteacher from the East, and the gun duel on the deserted main street.

One model scenario proceeds through five phases.

(1) The arrival of the thing. (Emergence of the monsters, landing of the alien spaceship, etc.) This is usually witnessed or suspected by just one person, a young scientist on a field trip. Nobody, neither his neighbors nor his colleagues, will believe him for some time. The hero is not married, but has a sympathetic though also incredulous girl friend.

(2) Confirmation of the hero's report by a host of witnesses to a great act of destruction. (If the invaders are beings from another planet, a fruitless attempt to parley with them and get them to leave peacefully.) The local police are summoned to deal with the situation and massacred.

(3) In the capital of the country, conferences between scientists and the military take place, with the hero lecturing before a chart, map, or blackboard. A national emergency is declared. Reports of further destruction. Authorities from other countries arrive in black limousines. All international tensions are suspended in view of the planetary emergency. This stage often includes a rapid montage of news broadcasts in various languages, a meeting at the UN, and more conferences between the military and the scientists. Plans are made for destroying the enemy.

(4) Further atrocities. At some point the hero's girl friend is in grave danger. Massive counter-attacks by international forces, with brilliant displays of rocketry, rays, and other advanced weapons, are all unsuccessful.

Enormous military casualties, usually by incineration. Cities are destroyed and/or evacuated. There is an obligatory scene here of panicked crowds stampeding along a highway or a big bridge, being waved on by numerous policemen who, if the film is Japanese, are immaculately white-gloved, preternaturally calm, and call out in dubbed English, "Keep moving. There is no need to be alarmed."

(5) More conferences, whose motif is: "They must be vulnerable to something." Throughout the hero has been working in his lab to this end. The final strategy, upon which all hopes depend, is drawn up; the ultimate weapon — often a super-powerful, as yet untested, nuclear device — is mounted. Countdown. Final repulse of the monster or invaders. Mutual congratulations, while the hero and girl friend embrace cheek to cheek and scan the skies sturdily. "But have we seen the last of them?"

The film I have just described should be in color and on a wide screen. Another typical scenario, which follows, is simpler and suited to black-and-white films with a lower budget. It has four phases.

(1) The hero (usually, but not always, a scientist) and his girl friend, or his wife and two children, are disporting themselves in some innocent ultra-normal middle-class surroundings — their house in a small town, or on vacation (camping, boating). Suddenly, someone starts behaving strangely; or some innocent form of vegetation becomes monstrously enlarged and ambulatory. If a character is pictured driving an automobile, something gruesome looms up in the middle of the road. If it is night, strange lights hurtle across the sky.

(2) After following the thing's tracks, or determining that It is radioactive, or poking around a huge crater — in short, conducting some sort of crude investigation — the hero tries to warn the local authorities, without effect; nobody believes anything is amiss. The hero knows better. If the thing is tangible, the house is elaborately barricaded. If the invading alien is an invisible parasite, a doctor or friend is called in, who is himself rather quickly killed or "taken possession of" by the thing.

(3) The advice of whoever further is consulted proves useless. Meanwhile, It continues to claim other victims in the town, which remains implausibly isolated from the rest of the world. General helplessness.

(4) One of two possibilities. Either the hero prepares to do battle alone, accidentally discovers the thing's one vulnerable point, and destroys it. Or, he somehow manages to get out of town and succeeds in laying his case before competent authorities. They, along the lines of the first script but abridged, deploy a complex technology which (after initial setbacks) finally prevails against the invaders.

Another version of the second script opens with the scientist-hero in his laboratory, which is located in the basement or on the grounds of his tasteful, prosperous house. Through his experiments, he unwittingly causes a frightful metamorphosis in some class of plants or animals which turn carnivorous and go on a rampage. Or else, his experiments have caused him to be injured (sometimes irrevocably) or "invaded" himself. Perhaps he has been experimenting with radiation, or has built a machine to communicate with beings from other planets or transport him to other places or times.

Another version of the first script involves the discovery of some fundamental alteration in the conditions of existence of our planet, brought about by nuclear testing, which will lead to the extinction in a few months of all human life. For example: the temperature of the earth is becoming too high or too low to support life, or the earth is cracking in two, or it is gradually being blanketed by lethal fallout.

A third script, somewhat but not altogether different from the first two, concerns a journey through space — to the moon, or some other planet. What the space-voyagers discover commonly is that the alien terrain is in a state of dire emergency, itself threatened by extra-planetary invaders or nearing extinction through the practice of nuclear warfare. The terminal dramas of the first and second scripts are played out there, to which is added the problem of getting away from the doomed and/or hostile planet and back to Earth.

I am aware, of course, that there are thousands of science fiction novels (their heyday was the late 1940s), not to mention the transcriptions of science fiction themes which, more and more, provide the principal subject-matter of comic books. But I propose to discuss science fiction films (the present period began in 1950 and continues, considerably abated, to this day) as an independent subgenre, without reference to other media — and, most particularly, without reference to the novels from which, in many cases, they were adapted. For, while novel and film may share the same plot, the fundamental difference between the resources of the novel and the film makes them quite dissimilar.

Certainly, compared with the science fiction novels, their film counterparts have unique strengths, one of which is the immediate representation of the extraordinary: physical deformity and mutation, missile and rocket combat, toppling skyscrapers. The movies are, naturally, weak just where the science fiction novels (some of them) are strong — on science. But in place of an intellectual workout, they can supply something the novels can never provide — sensuous elaboration. In the films it is by means of images and sounds, not words that have to be translated by the imagination, that one can participate in the fantasy of living through one's own death and more, the death of cities, the destruction of humanity itself.

Science fiction films are not about science. They are about disaster, which is one of the oldest subjects of art. In science fiction films disaster is rarely viewed intensively; it is always extensive. It is a matter of quantity and ingenuity. If you will, it is a question of scale. But the scale, particularly in the wide-screen color films (of which the ones by the Japanese director Inoshiro Honda and the American director George Pal are technically the most convincing and visually the most exciting), does raise the matter to another level.

Thus, the science fiction film (like that of a very different contemporary genre, the Happening) is concerned with the aesthetics of destruction, with the peculiar beauties to be found in wreaking havoc, making a mess. And it is in the imagery of destruction that the core of a good science fiction film lies. Hence, the disadvantage of the cheap film — in which the monster appears or the rocket lands in a small dull-looking town. (Hollywood budget needs usually dictate that the town be in the Arizona or California desert. In *The Thing From Another World* [1951] the rather sleazy and confined set is supposed to be an encampment near the North Pole.) Still, good black-and-white science fiction films have been made. But a bigger budget, which usually means color, allows a much greater play back and forth among several model environments. There is the populous city. There is the lavish but ascetic interior of the spaceship — either the invaders' or ours — replete with streamlined chromium fixtures and dials and machines whose complexity is indicated by the number of colored lights they flash and strange noises they emit. There is the laboratory crowded with formidable boxes and scientific apparatus. There is a comparatively old-fashioned-looking conference room, where the scientists unfurl charts to explain the desperate state of things to the military. And each of these standard locales or backgrounds is subject to two modalities — intact and destroyed. We may, if we are lucky, be treated to a panorama of melting tanks, flying bodies, crashing walls, awesome craters and fissures in the earth, plummeting spacecraft, colorful deadly rays; and to a symphony of screams, weird electronic signals, the noisiest military hardware going, and the leaden tones of the laconic denizens of alien planets and their subjugated earthlings.

Certain of the primitive gratifications of science fiction films — for instance, the depiction of urban disaster on a colossally magnified scale — are shared with other types of films. Visually there is little difference between mass havoc as represented in the old horror and monster films and what we find in science fiction films, except (again) scale. In the old monster films, the monster always headed for the great city, where he had to do a fair bit of rampaging, hurling busses off bridges, crumpling trains in his bare hands, toppling buildings, and so forth. The archetype is King Kong, in Schoedsack and Cooper's great film of 1933, running amok, first in the native village (trampling babies, a bit of footage excised from most prints), then in New York. This is really no different in spirit from the scene in Inoshiro Honda's *Rodan* (1957) in which two giant reptiles — with a wingspan of 500 feet and supersonic speed — by flapping their wings whip up a cyclone that blows most of Tokyo to smithereens. Or the destruction of half of Japan by the gigantic robot with the great incinerating ray that shoots forth from his eyes, at the beginning of Honda's *The Mysterians* (1959). Or, the devastation by the rays from a fleet of flying saucers of New York, Paris, and Tokyo, in *Battle in Outer Space* (1960). Or, the inundation of New York in *When Worlds Collide* (1951). Or, the end of London in 1966 depicted in George Pal's *The Time Machine* (1960). Neither do these sequences differ in aesthetic intention from the destruction scenes in the big sword, sandal, and orgy color spectaculars set in Biblical and Roman time — the end of Sodom in Aldrich's *Sodom and Gomorrah*, of Gaza in De Mille's *Samson and Delilah*, of Rhodes in *The Colossus of Rhodes*, and of Rome in a dozen Nero movies. Griffith began it with the Babylon sequence in *Intolerance*, and to this day there is nothing like the thrill of watching all those expensive sets come tumbling down.

In other respects as well, the science fiction films of the 1950s take up familiar themes. The famous 1930s movie serials and comics of the adventures of Flash Gordon and Buck Rogers, as well as the more recent spate of comic book superheroes with extraterrestrial origins (the most famous is Superman, a foundling from the planet Krypton, currently described as having been exploded by a nuclear blast), share motifs with more recent science fiction movies. But there is an important difference. The old science fiction films, and most of the comics, still have an essentially innocent relation to disaster. Mainly they offer new versions of the oldest romance of all — of the strong invulnerable hero with a mysterious lineage come to do battle on behalf of good and against evil. Recent science fiction films have a decided grimness, bolstered by their much greater degree of visual credibility, which contrasts strongly with the older films. Modern historical reality has greatly enlarged the imagination of disaster, and the protagonists — perhaps by the very nature of what is visited upon them — no longer seem wholly innocent.

The lure of such generalized disaster as a fantasy is that it releases one from normal obligations. The trump card of the end-of-the-world movies — like *The Day the Earth Caught Fire* (1962) — is that great scene with New York or London or Tokyo discovered empty, its entire population annihilated. Or, as in *The World, The Flesh, and The Devil* (1957), the whole movie can be devoted to the fantasy of occupying the deserted metropolis and starting all over again, a world Robinson Crusoe.

Another kind of satisfaction these films supply is extreme moral simplification — that is to say, a morally acceptable fantasy where one can give outlet to cruel or at least amoral feelings. In this respect, science fiction films partly overlap with horror films. This is the undeniable pleasure we derive from looking at freaks, beings excluded from the category of the human. The sense of superiority over the freak conjoined in varying proportions with the titillation of fear and aversion makes it possible for moral scruples to be lifted, for cruelty to be enjoyed. The same thing happens in science fiction films. In the figure of the monster from outer space, the freakish, the ugly, and the predatory all converge — and provide a fantasy target for righteous bellicosity to discharge itself, and for the aesthetic enjoyment of suffering and disaster. Science fiction films are one of the purest forms of spectacle; that is, we are rarely inside anyone's feelings. (An exception is Jack Arnold's *The Incredible Shrinking Man* [1957].) We are merely spectators; we watch.

But in science fiction films, unlike horror films, there is not much horror. Suspense, shocks, surprises are mostly abjured in favor of a steady, inexorable plot. Science fiction films invite a dispassionate, aesthetic view of destruction and violence — a *technological* view. Things, objects, machinery play a major role in these films. A greater range of ethical values is embodied in the décor of these films than in the people. Things, rather than the helpless humans, are the locus of values because we experience them, rather than people, as the sources of power. According to science fiction films, man is naked without his artifacts. *They* stand for different values, they are potent, they are what get destroyed, and they are the indispensable tools for the repulse of the alien invaders or the repair of the damaged environment.

The science fiction films are strongly moralistic. The standard message is the one about the proper, or humane, use of science, versus the mad, obsessional use of science. This message the science fiction films share in common with the classic horror films of the 1930s, like *Frankenstein, The Mummy, Island of Lost Souls, Dr. Jekyll and Mr. Hyde.* (Georges Franju's brilliant *Les Yeux Sans Visage* [1959], called here *The Horror Chamber of Doctor Faustus*, is a more recent example.) In the horror films, we have the mad or obsessed or misguided scientist who pursues his experiments against good advice to the contrary, creates a monster or monsters, and is himself destroyed — often recognizing his folly himself, and dying in the successful effort to destroy his own creation. One science fiction equivalent of this is the scientist, usually a member of a team, who defects to the planetary invaders because "their" science is more advanced than "ours."

This is the case in *The Mysterians*, and, true to form, the renegade sees his error in the end, and from within the Mysterian space ship destroys it and himself. In *This Island Earth* (1955), the inhabitants of the beleaguered planet Metaluna propose to conquer earth, but their project is foiled by a Metalunan scientist named Exeter who, having lived on earth a while and learned to love Mozart, cannot abide such viciousness. Exeter plunges his spaceship into the ocean after returning a glamorous pair (male and female) of American physicists to earth. Metaluna dies. In *The Fly* (1958), the hero, engrossed in his basement-laboratory experiments on a matter-transmitting machine, uses himself as a subject, exchanges head and one arm with a housefly which had accidentally gotten into the machine, becomes a monster, and with his last shred of human will destroys his laboratory and orders his wife to kill him. His discovery, for the good of mankind, is lost.

Being a clearly labeled species of intellectual, scientists in science fiction films are always liable to crack up or go off the deep end. In *Conquest of Space* (1955), the scientist-commander of an international expedition to Mars suddenly acquires scruples about the blasphemy involved in the undertaking, and begins reading the Bible mid-journey instead of attending to his duties. The commander's son, who is his junior officer and always addresses his father as "General," is forced to kill the old man when he tries to prevent the ship from landing on Mars. In this film, both sides of the ambivalence toward scientists are given voice. Generally, for a scientific enterprise to be treated entirely sympathetically in these films, it needs the certificate of utility. Science, viewed without ambivalence, means an efficacious response to danger. Disinterested intellectual curiosity rarely appears in any form other than caricature, as a maniacal dementia that cuts one off from normal human relations. But this suspicion is usually directed at the scientist rather than his work. The creative scientist may become a martyr to his own discovery, through an accident or by pushing things too far. But the implication remains that other men, less imaginative — in short, technicians — could have administered the same discovery better and more safely. The most ingrained contemporary mistrust of the intellect is visited, in these movies, upon the scientist-as-intellectual.

The message that the scientist is one who releases forces which, if not controlled for good, could destroy man himself seems innocuous enough. One of the oldest images of the scientist is Shakespeare's Prospero, the overdetached scholar forcibly retired from society to a desert island, only partly in control of the magic forces in which he dabbles. Equally classic is the figure of the scientist as satanist (*Doctor Faustus*, and stories of Poe and Hawthorne). Science is magic, and man has always known that there is black magic as well as white. But it is not enough to remark that contemporary attitudes — as reflected in science fiction films — remain ambivalent, that the scientist is treated as both satanist and savior. The proportions have changed, because of the new context in which the old admiration and fear of the scientist are located. For his sphere of influence is no longer local, himself or his immediate community. It is planetary, cosmic.

One gets the feeling, particularly in the Japanese films but not only there, that a mass trauma exists over the use of nuclear weapons and the possibility of future nuclear wars. Most of the science fiction films bear witness to this trauma, and, in a way, attempt to exorcise it.

The accidental awakening of the super-destructive monster who has slept in the earth since prehistory is, often, an obvious metaphor for the Bomb. But there are many explicit references as well. In *The Mysterians*, a probe ship from the planet Mysteroid has landed on earth, near Tokyo. Nuclear warfare having been practiced on Mysteroid for centuries (their civilization is "more advanced than ours"), ninety percent of those now born on the planet have to be destroyed at birth, because of defects caused by the huge amounts of Strontium 90 in their diet. The Mysterians have come to earth to marry earth women, and possibly to take over our relatively uncontaminated planet. . . . In *The Incredible Shrinking Man*, the John Doe hero is the victim of a gust of radiation which blows over the water, while he is out boating with his wife; the radiation causes him to grow smaller and smaller, until at the end of the movie he steps through the fine mesh of a window screen to become "the infinitely small." . . . In *Rodan*, a horde of monstrous carnivorous prehistoric insects, and finally a pair of giant flying reptiles (the prehistoric Archeopteryx), are hatched from dormant eggs in the depths of a mine shaft by the impact of nuclear test explosions, and go on to destroy a good part of the world before they are felled by the molten lava of a volcanic eruption. . . . In the English film, *The Day the Earth Caught Fire*, two simultaneous hydrogen bomb tests by the

United States and Russia change by 11 degrees the tilt of the earth on its axis and alter the earth's orbit so that it begins to approach the sun.

Radiation casualties — ultimately, the conception of the whole world as a casualty of nuclear testing and nuclear warfare — is the most ominous of all the notions with which science fiction films deal. Universes become expendable. Worlds become contaminated, burnt out, exhausted, obsolete. In *Rocketship X-M* (1950) explorers from the earth land on Mars, where they learn that atomic warfare has destroyed Martian civilization. In George Pal's *The War of the Worlds* (1953), reddish spindly alligator-skinned creatures from Mars invade the earth because their planet is becoming too cold to be inhabitable. In *This Island Earth*, also American, the planet Metaluna, whose population has long ago been driven underground by warfare, is dying under the missile attacks of an enemy planet. Stocks of uranium, which power the force field shielding Metaluna, have been used up; and an unsuccessful expedition is sent to earth to enlist earth scientists to devise new sources for nuclear power. In Joseph Losey's *The Damned* (1961), nine icy-cold radioactive children are being reared by a fanatical scientist in a dark cave on the English coast to be the only survivors of the inevitable nuclear Armageddon.

There is a vast amount of wishful thinking in science fiction films, some of it touching, some of it depressing. Again and again, one detects the hunger for a "good war," which poses no moral problems, admits of no moral qualifications. The imagery of science fiction films will satisfy the most bellicose addict of war films, for a lot of the satisfactions of war films pass, untransformed, into science fiction films. Examples: the dogfights between earth "fighter rockets" and alien spacecraft in the *Battle in Outer Space* (1960); the escalating firepower in the successive assaults upon the invaders in *The Mysterians*, which Dan Talbot correctly described as a nonstop holocaust; the spectacular bombardment of the underground fortress of Metaluna in *This Island Earth*.

Yet at the same time the bellicosity of science fiction films is neatly channeled into the yearning for peace, or for at least peaceful coexistence. Some scientist generally takes sententious note of the fact that it took the planetary invasion to make the warring nations of the earth come to their senses and suspend their own conflicts. One of the main themes of many science fiction films — the color ones usually, because they have the budget and resources to develop the military spectacle — is this UN fantasy, a fantasy of united warfare. (The same wishful UN theme cropped up in a recent spectacular which is not science fiction, *Fifty-Five Days in Peking* [1963]. There, topically enough, the Chinese, the Boxers, play the role of Martian invaders who unite the earthmen, in this case the United States, England, Russia, France, Germany, Italy, and Japan.) A great enough disaster cancels all enmities and calls upon the utmost concentration of earth resources.

Science — technology — is conceived of as the great unifier. Thus the science fiction films also project a Utopian fantasy. In the classic models of Utopian thinking — Plato's Republic, Campanella's City of the Sun, More's Utopia, Swift's land of the Houyhnhnms, Voltaire's Eldorado — society had worked out a perfect consensus. In these societies reasonableness had achieved an unbreakable supremacy over the emotions. Since no disagreement or social conflict was intellectually plausible, none was possible. As in Melville's *Typee*, "they all think the same." The universal rule of reason meant universal agreement. It is interesting, too, that societies in which reason was pictured as totally ascendant were also traditionally pictured as having an ascetic or materially frugal and economically simple mode of life. But in the Utopian world community projected by science fiction films, totally pacified and ruled by scientific consensus, the demand for simplicity of material existence would be absurd.

Yet, alongside the hopeful fantasy of moral simplification and international unity embodied in the science fiction films lurk the deepest anxieties about contemporary existence. I don't mean only the very real trauma of the Bomb — that it has been used, that there are enough now to kill everyone on earth many times over, that those new bombs may very well be used. Besides these new anxieties about physical disaster, the prospect of universal mutilation and even annihilation, the science fiction films reflect powerful anxieties about the condition of the individual psyche.

For science fiction films may also be described as a popular mythology for the contemporary *negative* imagination about the impersonal. The other-world creatures that seek to take "us" over are an "it," not a "they." The planetary invaders are usually zombie-like. Their movements are either cool, mechanical, or lumbering, blobby. But it amounts to the same thing. If they are non-human in form, they proceed with an absolutely regular, unalterable movement (unalterable save by destruction). If they are human in form — dressed in space suits, etc. — then they obey the most rigid military discipline, and display no personal characteristics whatsoever. And it is this regime of emotionlessness, of impersonality, of regimentation, which they will impose on the earth if they are successful. "No more love, no more beauty, no more pain," boasts a converted earthling in *The Invasion of the Body Snatchers* (1956). The half-earthling, half-alien children in *The Children of the Damned* (1960) are absolutely emotionless, move as a group and understand each others' thoughts, and are all prodigious intellects. They are the wave of the future, man in his next stage of development.

These alien invaders practice a crime which is worse than murder. They do not simply kill the person. They obliterate him. In *The War of the Worlds*, the ray which issues from the rocket ship disintegrates all persons and objects in its path, leaving no trace of them but a light ash. In Honda's *The H-Man* (1959), the creeping blob melts all flesh with which it comes in contact. If the blob, which looks like a huge hunk of red Jello and can crawl across floors and up and down walls, so much as touches your bare foot, all that is left of you is a heap of clothes on the floor. (A more articulated, size-multiplying blob is the villain in the English film *The Creeping*

Unknown [1956].) In another version of this fantasy, the body is preserved but the person is entirely reconstituted as the automatized servant or agent of the alien powers. This is, of course, the vampire fantasy in new dress. The person is really dead, but he doesn't know it. He is "undead," he has become an "unperson." It happens to a whole California town in *The Invasion of the Body Snatchers*, to several earth scientists in *This Island Earth*, and to assorted innocents in *It Came From Outer Space, Attack of the Puppet People* (1958), and *The Brain Eaters* (1958). As the victim always backs away from the vampire's horrifying embrace, so in science fiction films the person always fights being "taken over"; he wants to retain his humanity. But once the deed has been done, the victim is eminently satisfied with his condition. He has not been converted from human amiability to monstrous "animal" bloodlust (a metaphoric exaggeration of sexual desire), as in the old vampire fantasy. No, he has simply become far more efficient — the very model of the technocratic man, purged of emotions, volitionless, tranquil, obedient to all orders. (The dark secret behind human nature used to be the upsurge of the animal — as in *King Kong*. The threat to man, his availability to dehumanization, lay in his own animality. Now the danger is understood as residing in man's ability to be turned into a machine.

The rule, of course, is that this horrible and irremediable form of murder can strike anyone in the film except the hero. The hero and his family, while greatly threatened, always escape this fate and by the end of the film the invaders have been repulsed or destroyed. I know of only one exception, *The Day That Mars Invaded Earth* (1963), in which after all the standard struggles the scientist-hero, his wife, and their two children are "taken over" by the alien invaders — and that's that. (The last minutes of the film show them being incinerated by the Martians' rays and their ash silhouettes flushed down their empty swimming pool, while their simulacra drive off in the family car.) Another variant but upbeat switch on the rule occurs in *The Creation of the Humanoids* (1964), where the hero discovers at the end of the film that he, too, has been turned into a metal robot, complete with highly efficient and virtually indestructible mechanical insides, although he didn't know it and detected no difference in himself. He learns, however, that he will shortly be upgraded into a "humanoid" having all the properties of a real man.

Of all the standard motifs of science fiction films, this theme of dehumanization is perhaps the most fascinating. For, as I have indicated, it is scarcely a black-and-white situation, as in the old vampire films. The attitude of the science fiction films toward depersonalization is mixed. On the one hand, they deplore it as the ultimate horror. On the other hand, certain characteristics of the dehumanized invaders, modulated and disguised — such as the ascendancy of reason over feelings, the idealization of teamwork, and the consensus-treating activities of science, a marked degree of moral simplification — are precisely traits of the savior-scientist. It is interesting that when the scientist in these films is treated negatively, it is usually done through the portrayal of an individual scientist who holes up in his laboratory and neglects his fiancée or his loving wife and children, obsessed by his daring and dangerous experiments. The scientist as a loyal member of a team, and therefore considerably less individualized, is treated quite respectfully.

There is absolutely no social criticism, of even the most implicit kind, in science fiction films. No criticism, for example, of the conditions of our society which create the impersonality and dehumanization which science fiction fantasies displace onto the influence of an alien It. Also, the notion of science as a social activity, interlocking with social and political interests, is unacknowledged. Science is simply either adventure (for good or evil) or a technical response to danger. And, typically, when the fear of science is paramount — when science is conceived of as black magic rather than white — the evil has no attribution beyond that of the perverse will of an individual scientist. In science fiction films the antithesis of black magic and white is drawn as a split between technology, which is beneficent, and the errant individual will of a lone intellectual.

Thus, science fiction films can be looked at as thematically central allegory, replete with standard modern attitudes. The theme of depersonalization (being "taken over") which I have been talking about is a new allegory reflecting the age-old awareness of man that, sane, he is always perilously close to insanity and unreason. But there is something more here than just a recent, popular image which expresses man's perennial, but largely unconscious, anxiety about his sanity. The image derives most of its power from a supplementary and historical anxiety, also not experienced *consciously* by most people, about the depersonalizing conditions of modern urban life. Similarly, it is not enough to note that science fiction allegories are one of the new myths about — that is, one of the ways of accommodating to and negating — the perennial human anxiety about death. (Myths of heaven and hell, and of ghosts, had the same function.) For, again, there is a historically specifiable twist which intensifies the anxiety. I mean, the trauma suffered by everyone in the middle of the twentieth century when it became clear that, from now on to the end of human history, every person would spend his individual life under the threat not only of individual death, which is certain, but of something almost insupportable psychologically — collective incineration and extinction which could come at any time, virtually without warning.

From a psychological point of view, the imagination of disaster does not greatly differ from one period in history to another. But from a political and moral point of view, it does. The expectation of the apocalypse may be the occasion for a radical disaffiliation from society, as when thousands of Eastern European Jews in the seventeenth century, hearing that Sabbatai Zevi had been proclaimed the Messiah and that the end of the world was imminent, gave up their homes and businesses and began the trek to Palestine. But people take the news of their doom in diverse ways. It is reported that in 1945 the populace of Berlin received without great agitation the news that Hitler had decided to kill them all, before the Allies arrived, because they had not been worthy enough to win the war. We are, alas, more in the position of the Berliners of 1945 than of the Jews of seventeenth century Eastern Europe; and our response is closer to theirs, too. What I am suggesting is that the imagery of disaster in science fiction is above all the emblem of an *inadequate response*. I don't mean to bear down on the films for this. They themselves are only a sampling, stripped of sophistication, of the inadequacy of most people's response to the unassimilable terrors that infect their consciousness. The interest of the films, aside from their considerable amount of cinematic charm, consists in this intersection between a naïve and largely debased commercial art product and the most profound dilemmas of the contemporary situation.

Ours is indeed an age of extremity. For we live under continual threat of two equally fearful, but seemingly opposed, destinies: unremitting banality and inconceivable terror. It is fantasy, served out in large rations by the popular arts, which allows most people to cope with these twin specters. For one job that fantasy can do is to lift us out of the unbearably humdrum and to distract us from terrors — real or anticipated — by an escape into exotic, dangerous situations which have last-minute happy endings. But another of the things that fantasy can do is to normalize what is psychologically unbearable, thereby inuring us to it. In one case, fantasy beautifies the world. In the other, it neutralizes it.

The fantasy in science fiction films does both jobs. The films reflect world-wide anxieties, and they serve to allay them. They inculcate a strange apathy concerning the processes of radiation, contamination, and destruction which I for one find haunting and depressing. The naïve level of the films neatly tempers the sense of otherness, of alien-ness, with the grossly familiar. In particular, the dialogue of most science fiction films, which is of a monumental but often touching banality, makes them wonderfully, unintentionally funny. Lines like "Come quickly, there's a monster in my bathtub," "We must do something about this," "Wait, Professor. There's someone on the telephone," "But that's incredible," and the old American stand-by, "I hope it works!" are hilarious in the context of picturesque and deafening holocaust. Yet the films also contain something that is painful and in deadly earnest.

There is a sense in which all these movies are in complicity with the abhorrent. They neutralize it, as I have said. It is no more, perhaps, than the way all art draws its audience into a circle of complicity with the thing represented. But in these films we have to do with things which are (quite literally) unthinkable. Here, "thinking about the unthinkable" — not in the way of Herman Kahn, as a subject for calculation, but as a subject for fantasy — becomes, however inadvertently, itself a somewhat questionable act from a moral point of view. The films perpetuate clichés about identity, volition, power, knowledge, happiness, social consensus, guilt, responsibility, which are, to say the least, not serviceable in our present extremity. But collective nightmares cannot be banished by demonstrating that they are, intellectually and morally, fallacious. This nightmare — the one reflected, in various registers, in the science fiction film — is too close to our reality.

Paul Boyer

The Whole World Gasped

(1994)

A prominent scholar of American history, Paul S. Boyer (b. 1935) is professor emeritus at the University of Wisconsin–Madison. He is the editor-in-chief of *The Oxford Companion to American History* and has written and edited many other books and articles, including several about the impact of nuclear weapons on American culture. In *By the Bomb's Early Light: Thought and Culture at the Dawn of the Atomic Age*, from which this excerpt is taken, Boyer examines original sources to illuminate how nuclear weapons affected American cultural consciousness from the bombing of Hiroshima and Nagasaki through the early years of the Cold War. In this engaging and highly readable account, Boyer sifts through the statements of scientists, politicians, religious leaders, and psychologists, examining news sources, advertisements, government pamphlets, and literary works — including a section on the reaction of science fiction writers. In the excerpt that follows, Boyer focuses on reactions in print and broadcast media in the immediate aftermath of the bombing of Japan.

Apocalyptic scenarios — explicitly nuclear or otherwise — were especially common in the sf of the late 1940s and 1950s, and it is useful to understand the cultural climate in which these stories were written. While the threat of nuclear weapons certainly has not disappeared in recent times, Boyer helps recapture the horrible immediacy with which the bomb gripped people's imagination in that period and also shows something of the ambivalence with which people greeted the new state of human affairs — not only fear but also denial and even erotic desire.

> *Just as people recall the circumstances under which they first heard the news of the attack on Pearl Harbor, so they will remember how the atomic bomb first burst upon their consciousness.*
>
> — *Scientific Monthly*, September 1945

August 6, 1945. President Truman was aboard the U.S.S. Augusta, steaming across the Atlantic on his way home from the Potsdam conference, when he received the word: an American atomic bomb had been successfully detonated over Hiroshima, Japan. Excitedly Truman rushed to the officers' wardroom and told them the news. The navy men burst into cheers.

At the White House, it was a slow news day and only a few reporters were on duty. In mid-morning, assistant press secretary Eben Ayres strolled into the press room and told the reporters something might be coming later.

At 10:45 A.M., Eastern War Time, Ayres released the story. At first the reporters seemed to hesitate, then they rushed for the telephones. The first bulletin went out over the Associated Press wire at 11:03.

John Haynes Holmes, minister of the Community Church of New York City, was vacationing at his summer cottage in Kennebunk, Maine, that day. Soon after, he described his feelings on hearing the news: "Everything else seemed suddenly to become insignificant. I seemed to grow cold, as though I had been transported to the waste spaces of the moon. The summer beauty seemed to vanish, and the waves of the sea to be pounding upon the shores of an empty world. . . . For I knew that the final crisis in human history had come. What that atomic Bomb had done to Japan, it could do to us."[1]

How does a people react when the entire basis of its existence is fundamentally altered? Most such changes occur gradually; they are more discernible to historians than to the individuals living through them. The nuclear era was different. It burst upon the world with terrifying suddenness. From the earliest moments, the American people recognized that things would never be the same again.

Perhaps the best way to convey a sense of the earliest days of what almost immediately began to be called the "Atomic Age" is not to impose too much order or coherence on them retrospectively. Out of the initial confusion of emotions and welter of voices, certain cultural themes would quickly emerge. But first, the Event.

The first to hear the news that distant Monday were those who happened to be near a radio at midday — housewives, children, the elderly, war workers enjoying a vacation day at home:

This is Don Goddard with your news at noon. A little less than an hour ago, newsmen were called to the White House down in Washington, and there they were read a special announcement written by President Truman. . . . This was the story of a new bomb, so powerful that only the imagination of a trained scientist could dream of its existence. Without qualification, the President said that Allied scientists have now harnessed the basic power of the universe. They have harnessed the atom.[2]

As the sultry August afternoon wore on, the news spread by word of mouth. The evening papers reported it in screaming headlines:

1. *New York Times*, August 7, 1945, p. 2; *Editor and Publisher*, August 11, 1945, p. 7; John Haynes Holmes, "Editorial Comment," *Unity*, September 1945, p. 99: Stanley N. Katz to author, December 18, 1984.
2. *Atomic War/Atomic Peace: Life in the Nuclear Age* (Visual Education Corp., Princeton, N.J., 1975), Cassette 2, side 2.

ATOMIC BOMB LOOSED ON JAPAN
ONE EQUALS 20,000 TONS OF TNT
FIRST TARGET IS ARMY BASE OF HIROSHIMA
DUST AND SMOKE OBSCURE RESULT.

On his six o'clock newscast, Lowell Thomas of CBS radio, already assuming that everyone had heard the story, began in his folksy, avuncular voice:

That news about the atomic bomb overshadows everything else today; and the story of the dropping of the first one on Japan. The way the Japanese describe last night's raid on Hiroshima indicates that this one bomb was so destructive that the Japs thought they had been blasted by squadrons of B-29s.[3]

Meanwhile, over at NBC, the dean of radio news commentators, H. V. Kaltenborn, was preparing the script of his 7:45 P.M. broadcast. The first draft began by describing the atomic bomb as "one of the greatest scientific developments in the history of man." Hastily, Kaltenborn penciled in a punchier opening: "Anglo-Saxon science has developed a new explosive 2,000 times as destructive as any known before."[4]

Continuing in his stern, professorial voice, Kaltenborn struck a somber note: "For all we know, we have created a Frankenstein! We must assume that with the passage of only a little time, an improved form of the new weapon we use today can be turned against us."

Kaltenborn was far from alone in perceiving the nightmarish possibilities. Science may have "signed the mammalian world's death warrant," warned the St. Louis Post-Dispatch on August 7, "and deeded an earth in ruins to the ants." A Milwaukee Journal editorial on the same day speculated about "a self-perpetuating chain of atomic destruction" that, like "a forest fire sweeping before high winds," could obliterate the entire planet.

In a broadcast that evening, Don Goddard added a chilling concreteness to these ominous forebodings:

There is reason to believe tonight that our new atomic bomb destroyed the entire Japanese city of Hiroshima in a single blast. . . . It would be the same as Denver, Colorado, with a population of 350,000 persons being there one moment, and wiped out the next.[5]

Thus in the earliest moments of the nuclear era, the fear that would be the constant companion of Americans for the rest of their lives, and of millions not yet born in 1945, had already found urgent expression.

3. Lowell Thomas, History as You Heard It (Garden City, N.Y., 1957), p. 296; Milwaukee Journal, August 6, 1945.
4. H. V. Kaltenborn Papers, State Historical Society of Wisconsin, Madison Broadcast transcripts.
5. Atomic War/Atomic Peace, Cassette 2, side 2 (Goddard); "A Decision for Mankind," St. Louis Post-Dispatch, August 7, 1945; "The Beginning or the End?" Milwaukee Journal, August 7, 1945, p. 12.

1018 • Disasters and Apocalypses: Critical Contexts

The carefully orchestrated government press releases, illustrated with a set of officially approved photographs, only partially allayed the gathering fear and uncertainty. Hiroshima itself was enveloped in an eerie silence that the outside world only gradually penetrated. "As for the actual havoc wrought by that first atomic bomb," said Lowell Thomas on August 7, "one earlier report was that the photographic observation planes on the job shortly after the cataclysmic blast at Hiroshima had been unable to penetrate the cloud of smoke and dust that hung over that devastated area." An air force spokesman on Okinawa said Hiroshima "seemed to have been ground into dust by a giant foot."

At a hectic news conference on Guam, Col. Paul Tibbets, Jr., pilot of the *Enola Gay*, the atomic-bomb plane, compared the cloud over the city to "boiling dust." Navy captain William S. Parsons, the scientist responsible for the final bomb assembly aboard the plane, extended an open palm to represent Hiroshima and said that only the fingers — the docks jutting into Hiroshima Bay — had been visible after the blast. The news conference was continually interrupted by a cigar-chomping Gen. Curtis LeMay with a terse, "No, you better not say that."[6]

Speculation and "human interest" stories supplemented the tightly controlled official releases. Newsmen compared the atomic bomb to the 1917 explosion of a munitions ship in the harbor of Halifax, Nova Scotia, that had killed eighteen hundred people. They interviewed the wife of Gen. Leslie R. Groves, military chief of the Manhattan Project ("I didn't know anything about it until this morning, the same as everyone else"). They sought out Eleanor Roosevelt, who gave FDR's posthumous benediction to the atomic bomb: "The President would have been much relieved had he known we had it."

Journalists strove for a local angle: "DEADLIEST WEAPONS IN WORLD'S HISTORY MADE IN SANTA FE VICINITY" was the headline carried by the *Santa Fe New Mexican* over its story about tiny Los Alamos, nerve center of the Manhattan Project. Tennessee papers played up what the *New York Times* dramatically called the "secret empire" at Oak Ridge, where work on the atomic bomb had been conducted in a vast "labyrinthine concrete fortress." In Hanford, Washington, reporters found the local residents surprised to learn that the vast secret facility nearby had been making plutonium; they had assumed poison gas. The Albany newspapers noted that General Groves was the son of a Presbyterian minister who had once had a church in that city.[7]

---

6. "War Department Called *Times* Reporter to Explain Bomb's Intricacies to Public," *New York Times*, August 7, 1945, p. 5; *Atomic War/Atomic Peace*, Cassette 2, side 1, side 2; Donald Porter Geddes, ed., *The Atomic Age Opens* (New York, 1945), p. 31.

7. John Gunther, *Inside USA* (New York, 1947), p. 119; "Peace and Mrs. Roosevelt," *New Yorker*, August 25, 1945, pp. 16–17; "Key Man's Wife Not in on Secret," *New York Times*, August 7, 1945, p. 7; *Santa Fe New Mexican*, August 6, 1945, p. 1; "More Atom Plants Rise at Oak Ridge," *New York Times*, August 8, 1945, p. 6; "Gen. Groves, 48, Guided Job on Atomic Bomb," *New York Herald Tribune*, August 7, 1945, p. 6.

The secret atomic-bomb test conducted at Alamogordo, New Mexico, on July 16, 1945, was now revealed. Lowell Thomas quoted a railway engineer who had been in the cab of the *Santa Fe* over 100 miles away at the moment of the predawn test: "All at once, it seemed as if the sun suddenly appeared out of the darkness. . . . The glare lasted about three minutes, then all was dark again." Newspaper stories told of Georgia Green, a blind girl in Albuquerque, 120 miles from Alamogordo, who at the moment of detonation had cried out, "What was that?"[8]

On August 9, with Hiroshima still dominating the nation's consciousness, came a further shock: a second atomic bomb had been dropped on the Japanese city of Nagasaki. "It is an awful responsibility which has come to us," intoned President Truman on nationwide radio the next day. "We thank God that it has come to us instead of to our enemies; and we pray that He may guide us to use it in His ways and for His purposes."[9]

Amid the stupefying rush of events, people could only assure each other that something momentous, almost unfathomable, had occurred. "[One] forgets the effect on Japan. . . . ," said the *New York Herald Tribune*, "as one senses the foundations of one's own universe trembling." The papers were full of such observations. The bomb, commented *Christian Century* magazine, had "cast a spell of dark foreboding over the spirit of humanity." In the *New York Times's* first letter-to-the-editor about the atomic bomb (forerunner of thousands that would appear in the years to follow), A. Garcia Diaz of New York City spoke of the "creeping feeling of apprehension" pervading the nation. (With characteristic understatement, the *Times* captioned this letter: "Atomic Bomb Poses Problem.") In the *New York Sun*, correspondent Phelps Adams described the mood in Washington: "For forty-eight hours now, the new bomb has been virtually the only topic of conversation and discussion. . . . For two days it has been an unusual thing to see a smile among the throngs that crowd the streets. The entire city is pervaded by a kind of sense of oppression." Political cartoonist D. R. Fitzpatrick of the *St. Louis Post-Dispatch* pictured a tiny human figure desperately clinging to a pair of reins attached to an awesome lightning bolt streaking across the skies. The caption was: "Little Man, Where To?"[10]

On August 10, a day after the Nagasaki bombing, the Japanese offered to surrender if Emperor Hirohito could keep his throne. The Allies agreed, and on August 14, World War II ended. The nation's cities erupted in fren-

---

8. "Bomb's Fury Shown in Test," *Milwaukee Journal*, August 6, 1945; Edward Teller, *The Legacy of Hiroshima* (Garden City, N.Y., 1962), p. 5; *The Decades: The 1940s* (Visual Education Corp., Princeton, N.J., 1975), Cassette 3, side 1.

9. Geddes, *Atomic Age Opens*, p. 38.

10. Fitzpatrick cartoon reprinted in *The Rotarian*, October 1945, p. 9; "The Atomic Bomb," *New York Herald Tribune*, August 7, 1945, p. 22; "Man and the Atom," *Christian Century*, August 22, 1945, p. 951; Atomic Bomb Poses Problem," *New York Times*, August 9, 1945, p. 20; Adams quoted in "The Atom Bomb," *Catholic World*, September 1945, p. 452.

zied celebration, but the underlying mood remained sober and apprehensive. In Washington, the *New Republic* reported, the war's end did nothing to mitigate the post-Hiroshima gloom or the "curious new sense of insecurity, rather incongruous in the face of military victory." Thanks to the atomic bomb, wrote an official of the Rockefeller Foundation a few weeks later, the nation's mood at the moment of victory was bleaker than in December 1941 when much of the Pacific Fleet had lain in ruins at Pearl Harbor.[11] "Seldom, if ever," agreed CBS radio commentator Edward R. Murrow on August 12, "has a war ended leaving the victors with such a sense of uncertainty and fear, with such a realization that the future is obscure and that survival is not assured."[12]

On August 17, amid stories of the surrender ceremonies in Tokyo Bay, H. V. Kaltenborn reported a sobering assessment by Air Force General H. H. ("Hap") Arnold of what an atomic war would be like. "As we listen to the newscast tonight, as we read our newspapers tomorrow," said Kaltenborn, "let us think of the mass murder which will come with World War III." A few days later he added, "We are like children playing with a concentrated instrument of death whose destructive potential our little minds cannot grasp."

"The knowledge of victory was as charged with sorrow and doubt as with joy and gratitude," observed *Time* in its first postwar issue.

> In what they said and did, men are still, as in the aftershock of a great wound, bemused and only semi-articulate. . . . But in the dark depths of their minds and hearts, huge forms moved and silently arrayed themselves: Titans, arranging out of the chaos an age in which victory was already only the shout of a child in the streets.

The war itself had shrunk to "minor significance," *Time* added, and its outcome seemed the "most grimly Pyrrhic of victories."[13]

The best known of these early postwar editorials, Norman Cousins's "Modern Man Is Obsolete," which appeared in the *Saturday Review* four days after the Japanese surrender, exuded this spirit of apprehension. "Whatever elation there is in the world today," wrote Cousins,

> is severely tempered by . . . a primitive fear, the fear of the unknown, the fear of forces man can neither channel nor comprehend. This fear is not new; in its classical form it is the fear of irrational death. But overnight it has become intensified, magnified. It has burst out of the subconscious and into the conscious, filling the mind with primordial apprehensions.[14]

11. Joseph H. Willits, "Social Adjustment to Atomic Energy," Proceedings of the *American Philosophical Society* 90 (January 1946): 51 (address delivered November 16, 1945); "Atomic Anxieties," *New Republic*, August 20, 1945, p. 222.
12. *In Search of Light: The Broadcasts of Edward R. Murrow, 1938–1961* (New York, 1967), p. 102.
13. "The Bomb," *Time*, August 20, 1945, p. 19; "A Strange Place," ibid., p. 29; Kaltenborn broadcasts, August 17, September 6, 1945, Kaltenborn Papers.
14. [Norman Cousins], "Modern Man Is Obsolete," *Saturday Review of Literature*, August 18, 1945, p. 5.

Among book publishers, the post-Hiroshima race was won by Pocket Books, which on August 17 published *The Atomic Age Opens*, a 256-page paperback compendium of news stories, editorials, and pronouncements by world leaders intended to help those who were "grasping for solid ideas through the haze of the first excitement." The general tenor of these utterances is summed up in one chapter title: "The Whole World Gasped."[15]

Perhaps the most important print medium through which the American people formed their initial impressions of the atomic bomb was Henry Luce's photo magazine *Life*, with its five million-plus circulation. *Life* devoted much of its August 20, 1945, issue to the bomb; here, in full-page photographs of Hiroshima and Nagasaki, many Americans encountered for the first time the towering mushroom-shaped cloud that would become the quintessential visual symbol of the new era. Hiroshima, said *Life*, had literally been "blown . . . off the face of the earth." Nagasaki, it added, choosing its words carefully, had been "disemboweled."

Underscoring a point made frequently in this early postwar period, *Life* noted that the atomic bombings were simply an extension of the massive B-29 "fire-bomb missions" under General LeMay that had already "ripped the guts out of Japan's great cities." These raids, *Life* explained, relied on

> the newly developed "jelly" bombs, which were aimed at different spots in a city and calculated to merge into one huge conflagration. Airmen called them "burn jobs" and a good-sized "burn job" did almost as much damage to property as the atomic bomb did and it also killed almost as many people.

In a lengthy background feature, *Life* insisted that the most important story concerning the debut of atomic energy was the scientific one: "Even the appalling fact that some 100,000 Japanese had died seemed incidental to the fact — which touched the destiny of everyone alive — that a way had been found to release the forces which killed these 100,000." Through several pages of simplified text and drawings, *Life* introduced its readers to the mysteries of the atom, uranium, and nuclear fission.

But what did it all mean? In an editorial titled "The Atomic Age" and in an essay, "The Atom Bomb and Future War," by *New York Times* military analyst Hanson W. Baldwin, *Life* tried to place the devastating events in context. Baldwin minced no words. As soon as the long-range rockets developed by the Germans were fitted with atomic warheads capable of "destroy[ing] cities at one breath," he wrote, echoing H. V. Kaltenborn, mankind would have "unleashed a Frankenstein monster." If conventional infantrymen had any future role at all, Baldwin continued, it would be as "an army of moles, specially trained in underground fighting."

In its editorial, by contrast, *Life* strove for a hopeful note: Atomic fission was a major breakthrough in humankind's long struggle to understand and subdue nature, and the world should be grateful that "Prometheus, the

---

15. Geddes, *Atomic Age Opens*, pp. 38, 40.

subtle artificer and friend of man, is still an American citizen." The future would be different, certainly, but it need not terrify. Even Hanson Baldwin's grim predictions could be viewed in an optimistic light. After all, "consider the ant, whose social problems much resemble man's":

> Ants have lived on this planet for 50 times as many millions of years as man. In all that time they have not committed race suicide and they have not abolished warfare either. Their nations rise and fall and never wholly merge. Constructing beautiful urban palaces and galleries, many ants have long lived underground in entire satisfaction.

But whatever the long-range reassurance offered by entomology or Greek mythology, the compelling immediate fact was that atomic fission had just been used to vaporize two cities. To its credit, *Life* confronted this fact squarely. The increasing ferocity of strategic bombing since the late 1930s, it said, "led straight to Hiroshima, and Hiroshima was, and was intended to be, almost pure *Schrecklichkeit* [terror]." All the belligerents, the United States no less than Nazi Germany, had emerged from World War II "with, radically different practices and standards of permissible behavior toward others."

Despite these bleak reflections, the editorial concluded on a note of moral elevation. Above all else, the atomic bomb raised "the question of power. The atomic scientists had to learn new ways to control it; so now does political man":

> Power in society has never been controlled by anything but morality. . . . Our sole safeguard against the very real danger of a reversion to barbarism is the kind of morality which compels the individual conscience, be the group right or wrong. The individual conscience against the atomic bomb? Yes, there is no other way.
>
> No limits are set to our Promethean ingenuity, provided we remember that we are not Jove.[16]

Many readers responded with lavish praise. The editorial was a reminder, said one, that "the simplest language is the best vehicle for the profoundest thoughts."[17] But what was *Life* actually saying? Evidently this: the same individuals who had acquiesced in the degradation of warfare into *Schrecklichkeit* were now being exhorted to confront the atomic bomb with consciences finely tuned to moral considerations. The American Prometheus who had assumed Jove's mantle and obliterated two cities with his newly discovered atomic thunderbolts was now being sternly told that he must resist the temptation ever again to play god. . . .

---

16. "The Atomic Age," *Life*, August 20, 1945, p. 32; "The Atomic Bomb: Its First Explosion Opens a New Era," ibid., pp. 87B–93, quoted passage, p. 87B; Hanson W. Baldwin, "The Atom Bomb and Future War," ibid., pp. 19–20; ibid., pp. 27, 28, 29, 30, 31; John Kieran, ed., *Information Please Almanac, 1948* (Garden City, N.Y., 1948), p. 330 (magazine circulation statistics).
17. George E. Eustis, Aiken, S.C., Letter to the Editor, *Life*, September 10, 1945, p. 6.

But given the heavily racist wartime climate, post-Hiroshima vindictiveness proved surprisingly short-lived and was quickly overshadowed by a growing fear of what might lie ahead. The bomb might indeed force Japan to her knees, wrote Hanson W. Baldwin in the *New York Times* on August 7, but it would also bring incalculable new dangers. "We have," he concluded bleakly, "sowed the whirlwind."[18]

Nor did the promise of a peacetime atomic Utopia initially do much to diminish post-Hiroshima fear. Typically, the editor of a religious periodical noted in September 1945 that such speculations were being advanced, but confessed that "at the moment we can visualize only the unutterably shattering effect upon civilization and the wholesale destruction of millions of human beings."[19]

The darkening national mood was intensified by the reaction from abroad. While the news of Hiroshima and Nagasaki did not have as sharp and immediate an impact in Europe (itself devastated and prostrate) as it did in the United States, awareness of the bomb's ominous implications came quickly. In a statement that somehow gained force from its stilted, Latinate English, the Vatican newspaper *Osservatore Romano* declared on August 7: "The last twilight of the war is colored by mortal flames never before seen on the horizons of the universe, from its heavenly dawn to this infernal era. This war gives us a catastrophic conclusion that seems not to put an end to its apocalyptic surprises." In contrast to President Truman's gloating, Winston Churchill struck a somber note: "This revelation of the secrets of nature, long mercifully withheld from man," he declared, "should arouse the most solemn reflections in the mind and conscience of every human being capable of comprehension."[20]

Reinforced by such pronouncements from abroad, the "Great Fear" was open, palpable, and starkly literal in its expression. Newsman Don Goddard, as we have seen, quickly transmuted the devastation of Hiroshima into visions of American cities in smoldering ruins, and millions of Americans soon made the same imaginative leap. Physically untouched by the war, the United States at the moment of victory perceived itself as naked and vulnerable. Sole possessors and users of a devastating new instrument of mass destruction, Americans envisioned themselves not as a potential threat to other peoples, but as potential victims. "In that terrible flash 10,000 miles away, men here have seen not only the fate of Japan, but have glimpsed the future of America," wrote James Reston in the *New York Times*.

The *Milwaukee Journal* on August 8 published a large map of the city overlaid by concentric circles of destruction. And worse lay ahead. The primitive atomic bombs of 1945, observed the *New York Times* on August 12, were analogous to "the steam engine of James Watt, the telegraph of

---

18. Hanson W. Baldwin, "The Atomic Weapon," *New York Times*, August 7, 1945, p. 10.

19. Herbert E. Benton, "The Present Challenge," *Christian Leader*, September 15, 1945, p. 420.

20. J. D. Bernal, "Everybody's Atom," *Nation*, September 1, 1945, p. 201 (Churchill); "Vatican Deplores Use of Atom Bomb," *New York Times*, August 8, 1945, p. 6.

Morse, the flying machines of the Wrights." As soon as the atomic bomb was paired up with the guided missile, speculated the *Detroit News* on August 17, the threat to civilization would rise to "a new pitch of terror." In an interview with the *New Yorker*, John W. Campbell Jr., the editor of *Astounding Science Fiction*, offered a similar vision of World War III: "Every major city will be wiped out in thirty minutes. . . . New York will be a slag heap. . . . Radioactive energy . . . will leave the land uninhabitable for periods ranging from ten months to five hundred years, depending on the size of the bomb." Speaking on a New York radio station days after Hiroshima, the sociologist Harvey W. Zorbaugh (a member of the wartime Committee for National Morale) predicted "an armament race such as the world has never seen."[21] The life expectancy of the human species, said the *Washington Post* on August 26, had "dwindled immeasurably in the course of two brief weeks."

From our contemporary perspective, such fears seem so familiar as to be almost trite, but it is important to recognize how *quickly* Americans began to articulate them. Years before the world's nuclear arsenals made such a holocaust likely or even possible, the prospect of global annihilation already filled the national consciousness. This awareness and the bone-deep fear it engendered are the fundamental psychological realities underlying the broader intellectual and cultural responses of this period.

This primal fear of extinction cut across all political and ideological lines, from the staunchly conservative *Chicago Tribune*, which wrote bleakly of an atomic war that would leave Earth "a barren waste, in which the survivors of the race will hide in caves or live among ruins," to such liberal voices as the *New Republic*, which offered an almost identical vision of a conflict that would "obliterate all the great cities of the belligerents, [and] bring industry and technology to a grinding halt, . . . [leaving only] scattered remnants of humanity living on the periphery of civilization."[22]

This fear pervaded all society, from nuclear physicists and government leaders to persons who barely grasped what had happened, but who sensed that it was deeply threatening. Indeed, the more knowledgeable and highly placed the individual, it seemed, the greater the unease. The "strange disquiet" and "very great apprehension" the atomic bomb had left in its wake, wrote theologian Reinhold Niebuhr, was particularly intense among "the more sober and thoughtful sections of our nation." Eugene Rabinowitch, a Manhattan Project chemist at the University of Chicago, later recalled walking the streets of Chicago in the summer of 1945 haunted by visions of "the sky suddenly lit by a giant fireball, the steel skeletons of skyscrapers bend-

21. "Last Judgment," *Washington Post*, August 26, 1945, p. 4B; James Reston, "Dawn of the Atom Era Perplexes Washington," *New York Times*, August 12, 1945, "News of the Week in Review," p. 6; *Milwaukee Journal*, August 8, 1945, p. 12; "One Victory Not Yet Won," *New York Times*, August 12, 1945, p. 8; "Answer to Atomic Bomb," *Detroit News*, August 17, 1945; "1945 Cassandra" *New Yorker*, August 25, 1945, p. 16; Geddes, *Atomic Age Opens*, p. 174 (Zorbaugh); *Who Was Who in America* 4 (Chicago, 1968): 1047 (Zorbaugh).
22. "The Bomb and the Future," *New Republic*, August 20, 1945, p. 210; Arthur H. Compton, "Now That We've Burst the Atom," *Rotarian*, October 1945, p. 53 (*Chicago Tribune* quote).

ing into grotesque shapes and their masonry raining down into the streets below, until a great cloud of dust rose and settled over the crumbling city." As the members of the U.S. Strategic Bombing Survey probed the ruins of Hiroshima and Nagasaki in September 1945, an "insistent question" formed itself in their minds: "What if the target for the bomb had been an American city?"[23]

So palpable was the depression in Washington, D.C., wrote newsman Phelps Adams, that many were admitting "they would be happier if this $2,000,000,000 gamble had failed," or if the new knowledge could be "bundled up in a sack and lost in the river like an unwanted kitten." The malaise gripping the capital, agreed the *New Republic*, was not rooted in dismay over what the atomic bomb had already done, but in "thoughts of its future use elsewhere and specifically against ourselves or our children." Even if the secret remained secure for fifteen years, said radio commentator Elmer Davis on December 30, 1945, that was a short time "for people who are raising children."[24]

Children were on many minds in these unsettled weeks. *Life* flippantly suggested that a generation weaned on Flash Gordon would be unfazed by the atomic bomb; but within days of Hiroshima, the *New Yorker* reported this moment observed among children at play in Manhattan:

> For years the playground in Washington Square has resounded to the high-strung anh-anh-anh of machine guns and the long-drawn-out whine of high-velocity shells. Last Saturday morning a great advance was made. We watched a military man of seven or eight climb onto a seesaw, gather a number of his staff officers around him, and explain the changed situation. "Look," he said, "I'm an atomic bomb. I just go 'boom.' Once. Like this." He raised his arms, puffed out his cheeks, jumped down from the seesaw, and went "Boom!" Then he led his army away, leaving Manhattan in ruins behind him.

Some time later, another observer of juvenile life in New York City noted a change in the Broadway penny arcades: "Where during the war for a nickel you could try your luck shooting at a helpless parachutist as he drifted toward the ground, you can now try your luck at wiping out a whole city, with an atomic bomb — all for five cents."[25]

As the historian shifts focus to the level of individual experience, the evidence becomes tantalizingly fragmentary: the child who, in a prayer

---

23. United States Strategic Bombing Survey, *The Effects of Atomic Bombs on Hiroshima and Nagasaki* (Washington, D.C., 1946), p. 36; Reinhold Niebuhr, "Our Relations to Japan," *Christianity and Crisis*, September 17, 1945, p. 5; Eugene Rabinowitch, "Five Years After," *Bulletin of the Atomic Scientists*, January 1951, p. 3.

24. Elmer Davis, ABC radio newscast, December 30, 1945, Davis Papers, Library of Congress; Phelps Adams in the *New York Sun*, quoted in "The Atom Bomb," *Catholic World*, September 1945, p. 452; "The Bomb and the Future," *New Republic*, August 20, 1945, p. 212.

25. Foulkes, "The Atom: Death — or Life Abundant?" p. 345; "Adjustment," *New Yorker*, August 18, 1945, p. 17.

shortly after Hiroshima, asked God to let his family all die together; the little girl who, when asked what she wanted to be when she grew up, replied
"alive"; the young mother in Pelham Manor, New York, who had just given
birth to her second son when the Hiroshima news came and who three
days later recorded her feelings in a letter to H. V. Kaltenborn:

> Since then I have hardly been able to smile, the future seems so utterly
> grim for our two little boys. Most of the time I have been in tears or
> near-tears, and fleeting but torturing regrets that I have brought children
> into the world to face such a dreadful thing as this have shivered
> through me. It seems that it will be for them all their lives like living on
> a keg of dynamite which may go off at any moment, and which undoubt-
> edly will go off before their lives have progressed very far.[26]

Such scattered evidence gives us a glimpse into the consciousness and
culture of childhood, as well as the concerns of adults trying to fathom the
bomb's impact on the generation that would grow up in its shadow. It is
perhaps noteworthy that John Hersey chose to conclude his influential
1946 work *Hiroshima* with the recollections of a ten-year-old survivor. The
lad's account is terse and noncommittal, but Hersey does not assume that
the emotional effects of the experience were therefore negligible. "It would
be impossible to say," he observes, "what horrors were embedded in the
minds of the children who lived through the day of the bombing in
Hiroshima."[27] Comparable fears about American children contributed to
the larger uneasiness that seeped through the culture in the weeks after
August 6, 1945.

Rather than diminishing, this mood deepened as weeks stretched into
months. America was in the grip of a "fear psychosis," said anthropologist
Robert Redfield in November 1945; atomic anxiety had become "a nightmare in the minds of men." *The First One Hundred Days of the Atomic Age*,
a paperback published in late November, offered yet another potpourri of
statements still "pouring forth from all sides" and reflecting "ever widening
concern and alarm." Despite the passage of several months, wrote Hertha
Pauli in the December *Commentary*, the bomb seemed to "weigh more and
more heavily on the minds of more and more men." When *Time* named
Harry Truman "Man of the Year" on December 21, 1945, the president's
picture on the cover was dwarfed by a mushroom-shaped cloud and a hand
gripping a lightning bolt. All the year's great events, said *Time*, including
the deaths of FDR and Hitler and the surrender of Germany and Japan,
paled before the awesome reality of the bomb:

> What the world would best remember of 1945 was the deadly mush-
> room clouds over Hiroshima and Nagasaki. Here were the force, the

---

26. Patricia E. Munk, Pelham Manor, N.Y., to H. V. Kaltenborn, August 9, 1945, Kaltenborn Papers;
Kahler, "The Reality of Utopia," p. 179; Dwight Macdonald, "Note by Editor," *Politics*, May 1946, p.
150.
27. John Hersey, *Hiroshima* (New York, 1946), p. 118.

threat, the promise of the future. In their giant shadows . . . all men were pygmies. . . . Even Presidents, even Men of the Year, [were] mere foam flecks on the tide. . . . In such a world, who dared be optimistic?[28]

Nor did the new year bring relief. In January, a State Department official commented on the undiminished "hysteria" and "poisonous fog" of suspicion and fear still pervading the country. Talk of the bomb was continuing to "boom on unceasingly from radio, press, and platforms," wrote another observer. A mental-health writer who made a national lecture tour that spring found "general fear and confusion." Bob Hope joked about this fear. "Have you noticed the modern trend in verses this year?" he said on his radio show on Valentine's Day 1946. "No more of this 'Roses are red, violets are blue.' I picked up one and it showed an atom bomb exploding, and under it a verse that read: 'Will you be my little geranium, until we are both blown up by uranium?'" The strain in such humor was apparent. . . .

---

28. "The Bomb and the Man," *Time*, December 31, 1945, pp. 15, 16.

Evolutions

C harles Darwin's theory of evolution describes the gradual process by which life-forms adapt to changing environmental circumstances through natural selection. The power of this insight into the nature of biological change over time is such that it has often been applied outside the realm of science to describe broader, less concrete processes, such as social, spiritual, or artistic development; indeed, it has become the guiding metaphor of our time. Given the emergence of science fiction in the same historical period that the idea of evolution first gained currency and given the genre's orientation toward science, the future, and the new, it is no surprise that many science fiction stories directly or indirectly reference the idea of evolution. Evolution is, after all, change, and many critics, most notably James Gunn, have identified the idea of change as science fiction's central preoccupation and defining feature.

Historically, science fiction emerged as a genre at the beginning of the Industrial Revolution, a period when innovations in science and technology were transforming both human society and the natural environment, introducing change of all kinds at a pace never before experienced. In the social sphere, the Enlightenment had introduced the idea of progress and the perfectibility of human institutions, leading to new forms of education and government and helping to pave the way for the French and American revolutions. This was the context from which thinkers like Darwin and Karl Marx emerged in the mid-nineteenth century, changing the way we thought about development over time, whether biological or societal, moving us from an older, static worldview to one marked by a continual process of change.

Darwin published his groundbreaking work *On the Origin of Species* in 1859 and in doing so radically shifted our understanding of humans' place in the natural order. Darwin described evolution as a strictly biological mechanism that occurred over almost unimaginably gradual periods of time, where the organisms best adapted to their environment would reproduce most successfully. Contrary to popular notions, in scientific terms evolution does not necessarily mean progress but simply the gradual process of adaptation to changing conditions. Nature is not concerned with efficiency of design and is not directed toward any higher goal.

The stories in this section reflect evolution's focus on adaptation — specifically how new biological and cultural forms are shaped by function, by the demands of a changing environment — and raise questions about the role of human beings in altering nature. These stories describe transformations of various kinds, offering speculations about what the next developmental stage might be for humans or, more generally, for consciousness. The stories often approach the idea of evolution imaginatively rather than scientifically, describing profound and often sudden transformations, whether physical or spiritual, of individuals or species. In many cases, they are more concerned with changes wrought by the intervention of human science than with natural processes.

Two selections in this chapter lay out two contrasting visions that represent the dominant models for science fiction's treatment of evolution. Nathaniel Hawthorne's story is a cautionary tale about the immorality of meddling with nature, while Olaf Stapledon's much later but highly influential novel takes a more optimistic stance, celebrating the contributions of culture to a larger narrative of progress in the evolution of consciousness. The other selections reflect both of these viewpoints, but they are often more ambiguous. They include physical, cultural, and spiritual evolutions. Some of them describe sudden and mysterious transformations, as in Terry Bisson's "Bears Discover Fire" while others, like Greg Bear's "Blood Music," depict the outcome of deliberate experiments. Many of them are primarily concerned with speculation about where we are heading, as a species or a civilization, and about what will come after us.

The pieces included in Critical Contexts offer several different ways of thinking about these questions. Stephen Jay Gould provides a useful corrective to current misconceptions about evolution in the strictly biological sense. Marvin Minsky believes that the next stage of evolution will be technological, and he celebrates the possibility that human beings will soon have the capacity to shape their own biological destiny. Finally, Steven Johnson presents a developmental model drawn from new findings in computer science and human cognition that offers one explanation of how organisms move toward greater complexity.

Nathaniel Hawthorne

Rappaccini's Daughter
(1844)

Long recognized as one of the great American writers, Nathaniel Hawthorne (1804–1864) is also — along with his compatriots and contemporaries Herman Melville and Edgar Allan Poe — an important figure in the development of speculative fiction. Although quite different, all three incorporated nonrealistic or fantastic elements in their writing. Their fascination with imagination and the supernatural marks them as second-generation Romantic writers in the tradition of Mary Shelley and E. T. A. Hoffmann, whose fiction is featured in Chapter 2.

Hawthorne, who is most famous for his stories set in Puritan New England, was interested in the relationship between past and present, the nature of guilt and atonement, and the psychology of repression and obsession. Like all Romantics, he sided with nature and emotion over the artificial constraints of society, and in works like *The Scarlet Letter* (1850) he was particularly sensitive to the plight of women in a restrictive society. His work is marked by vivid imagery and is often heavily symbolic, even allegorical. Many of his most famous stories, such as "Young Goodman Brown," explore the ambiguous borderlands between psychological and supernatural phenomena.

"Rappaccini's Daughter" is one of several Hawthorne stories (including "The Birthmark") about men of science who allow their obsessions to overpower their natural feelings of human affection. In this gothic tale of generational conflict and thwarted love, Hawthorne depicts the scientist as a creator who violates the laws of nature with horrible consequences. The parallels to *Frankenstein* are obvious, but Rappaccini is a very different type of scientist from the tortured Victor — cooler, and perhaps more modern.

This story is dense with literary and religious allusions — to Dante's *Inferno*, Shakespeare's *The Tempest*, and, especially, *Genesis*; Dr. Rappaccini's garden is explicitly described as a kind of new and sinister Eden. "Rappaccini's Daughter" represents one of two common approaches to the idea of evolution in sf: a view of science as a cold and sinister force whose modifications of nature, however impressive, are ultimately grotesque and deadly.

Preface: From the Writings of Aubépine.

We do not remember to have seen any translated specimens of the productions of M. de l'Aubépine — a fact the less to be wondered at, as his very name is unknown to many of his own countrymen as well as to the student of foreign literature. As a writer, he seems to occupy an unfortunate position between the Transcendentalists (who, under one name or another, have their share in all the current literature of the world) and the great body of pen-and-ink men who address the intellect and sympathies of the multitude. If not too refined, at all events too remote, too shadowy, and unsubstantial in his modes of development to suit the taste of the latter class, and yet too popular to satisfy the spiritual or metaphysical requisitions of the former, he must necessarily find himself without an audience, except here and there an individual or possibly an isolated clique. His writings, to do them justice, are not altogether destitute of fancy and originality; they might have won him greater reputation but for an inveterate love of allegory, which is apt to invest his plots and characters with the aspect of scenery and people in the clouds, and to steal away the human warmth out of his conceptions. His fictions are sometimes historical, sometimes of the present day, and sometimes, so far as can be discovered, have little or no reference either to time or space. In any case, he generally contents himself with a very slight embroidery of outward manners, — the faintest possible counterfeit of real life, — and endeavors to create an interest by some less obvious peculiarity of the subject. Occasionally a breath of Nature, a raindrop of pathos and tenderness, or a gleam of humor, will find its way into the midst of his fantastic imagery, and make us feel as if, after all, we were yet within the limits of our native earth. We will only add to this very cursory notice that M. de l'Aubépine's productions, if the reader chance to take them in precisely the proper point of view, may amuse a leisure hour as well as those of a brighter man; if otherwise, they can hardly fail to look excessively like nonsense.

Our author is voluminous; he continues to write and publish with as much praiseworthy and indefatigable prolixity as if his efforts were crowned with the brilliant success that so justly attends those of Eugene Sue. His first appearance was by a collection of stories in a long series of volumes entitled "Contes deux fois racontées." The titles of some of his more recent works (we quote from memory) are as follows: "Le Voyage Céleste à Chemin de Fer," 3 tom., 1838; "Le nouveau Père Adam et la nouvelle Mère Eve," 2 tom., 1839; "Roderic; ou le Serpent à l'estomac," 2 tom., 1840; "Le Culte du Feu," a folio volume of ponderous research into the religion and ritual of the old Persian Ghebers, published in 1841; "La Soirée du Chateau en Espagne," 1 tom., 8vo, 1842; and "L'Artiste du Beau; ou le Papillon Mécanique," 5 tom., 4to, 1843. Our somewhat wearisome perusal of this startling catalogue of volumes has left behind it a certain personal affection and sympathy, though by no means admiration, for M. de l'Aubépine; and we would fain do the little in our power towards introducing him favorably to the American public. The ensuing tale is a translation of his "Beatrice; ou la Belle Empoisonneuse," recently published in "La Revue Anti-Aristocratique." This journal, edited by the Comte de Bearhaven, has for some years past led the defense of liberal principles and popular rights with a faithfulness and ability worthy of all praise.[1]

A young man, named Giovanni Guasconti, came, very long ago, from the more southern region of Italy, to pursue his studies at the University of Padua. Giovanni, who had but a scanty supply of gold ducats in his pocket, took lodgings in a high and gloomy chamber of an old edifice which looked not unworthy to have been the palace of a Paduan noble, and which, in fact, exhibited over its entrance the armorial bearings of a family long since extinct. The young stranger, who was not unstudied in the great poem of his country, recollected that one of the ancestors of this family, and perhaps an occupant of this very mansion, had been pictured by Dante as a partaker of the immortal agonies of his Inferno. These reminiscences and associations, together with the tendency to heartbreak natural to a young man for the first time out of his native sphere, caused Giovanni to sigh heavily as he looked around the desolate and ill-furnished apartment.

---

1. This preface is fictional. "Aubépine" is the French word for "Hawthorn" (a type of tree). [Ed.]

"Holy Virgin, signor!" cried old Dame Lisabetta, who, won by the youth's remarkable beauty of person, was kindly endeavoring to give the chamber a habitable air, "what a sigh was that to come out of a young man's heart! Do you find this old mansion gloomy? For the love of Heaven, then, put your head out of the window, and you will see as bright sunshine as you have left in Naples."

Guasconti mechanically did as the old woman advised, but could not quite agree with her that the Paduan sunshine was as cheerful as that of southern Italy. Such as it was, however, it fell upon a garden beneath the window and expended its fostering influences on a variety of plants, which seemed to have been cultivated with exceeding care.

"Does this garden belong to the house?" asked Giovanni.

"Heaven forbid, signor, unless it were fruitful of better pot herbs than any that grow there now," answered old Lisabetta. "No; that garden is cultivated by the own hands of Signor Giacomo Rappaccini, the famous doctor, who, I warrant him, has been heard of as far as Naples. It is said that he distils these plants into medicines that are as potent as a charm. Oftentimes you may see the signor doctor at work, and perchance the signora, his daughter, too, gathering the strange flowers that grow in the garden."

The old woman had now done what she could for the aspect of the chamber; and, commending the young man to the protection of the saints, took her departure.

Giovanni still found no better occupation than to look down into the garden beneath his window. From its appearance, he judged it to be one of those botanic gardens which were of earlier date in Padua than elsewhere in Italy or in the world. Or, not improbably, it might once have been the pleasure-place of an opulent family; for there was the ruin of a marble fountain in the center, sculptured with rare art, but so woefully shattered that it was impossible to trace the original design from the chaos of remaining fragments. The water, however, continued to gush and sparkle into the sunbeams as cheerfully as ever. A little gurgling sound ascended to the young man's window and made him feel as if the fountain were an immortal spirit, that sung its song unceasingly and without heeding the vicissitudes around it, while one century imbodied it in marble and another scattered the perishable garniture on the soil. All about the pool into which the water subsided grew various plants, that seemed to require a plentiful supply of moisture for the nourishment of gigantic leaves, and, in some instances, flowers gorgeously magnificent. There was one shrub in particular, set in a marble vase in the midst of the pool, that bore a profusion of purple blossoms, each of which had the lustre and richness of a gem; and the whole together made a show so resplendent that it seemed enough to illuminate the garden, even had there been no sunshine. Every portion of the soil was peopled with plants and herbs, which, if less beautiful, still bore tokens of assiduous care, as if all had their individual virtues, known to the scientific mind that fostered them. Some were placed in urns, rich with old carving, and others in common garden pots; some crept serpent-like along the ground or climbed on high, using whatever means of ascent was offered them. One plant had wreathed itself round a statue of Vertumnus, which was thus quite veiled and shrouded in a drapery of hanging foliage, so happily arranged that it might have served a sculptor for a study.

While Giovanni stood at the window he heard a rustling behind a screen of leaves, and became aware that a person was at work in the garden. His figure soon emerged into view, and showed itself to be that of no common laborer, but a tall, emaciated, sallow, and sickly-looking man, dressed in a scholar's garb of black. He was beyond the middle term of life, with gray hair, a thin, gray beard, and a face singularly marked with intellect and cultivation, but which could never, even in his more youthful days, have expressed much warmth of heart.

Nothing could exceed the intentness with which this scientific gardener examined every shrub which grew in his path: it seemed as if he was looking into their inmost nature, making observations in regard to their creative essence, and discovering why one leaf grew in this shape and another in that, and wherefore such and such flowers differed among themselves in hue and perfume. Nevertheless, in spite of this deep intelligence on his part, there was no approach to intimacy between himself and these vegetable existences. On the contrary, he avoided their actual touch or the direct inhaling of their odors with a caution that impressed Giovanni most disagreeably; for the man's demeanor was that of one walking among malignant influences, such as savage beasts, or deadly snakes, or evil spirits, which, should he allow them one moment of license, would wreak upon him some terrible fatality. It was strangely frightful to the young man's imagination to see this air of insecurity in a person cultivating a garden, that most simple and innocent of human toils, and which had been alike the joy and labor of the unfallen parents of the race. Was this garden, then, the Eden of the present world? And this man, with such a perception of harm in what his own hands caused to grow, — was he the Adam?

The distrustful gardener, while plucking away the dead leaves or pruning the too luxuriant growth of the shrubs, defended his hands with a pair of thick gloves. Nor were these his only armor. When, in his walk through the garden, he came to the magnificent plant that hung its purple gems beside the marble fountain, he placed a kind of mask over his mouth and nostrils, as if all this beauty did but conceal a deadlier malice; but, finding his task still too dangerous, he drew back, removed the mask, and called loudly, but in the infirm voice of a person affected with inward disease, —

"Beatrice! Beatrice!"

"Here am I, my father. What would you?" cried a rich and youthful voice from the window of the opposite house — a voice as rich as a tropical sunset, and which made Giovanni, though he knew not why, think of deep hues of purple or crimson and of perfumes heavily delectable. "Are you in the garden?"

"Yes, Beatrice," answered the gardener; "and I need your help."

Soon there emerged from under a sculptured portal the figure of a young girl, arrayed with as much richness of taste as the most splendid of the flowers, beautiful as the day, and with a bloom so deep and vivid that one shade more would have been too much. She looked redundant with life, health, and energy; all of which attributes were bound down and compressed, as it were, and girdled tensely, in their luxuriance, by her virgin zone. Yet Giovanni's fancy must have grown morbid while he looked down into the garden; for the impression which the fair stranger made upon him was as if here were another flower, the human sister of those vegetable ones, as beautiful as they, more beautiful than the richest of them, but still to be touched only with a glove, nor to be approached without a mask. As Beatrice came down the garden path, it was observable that she handled and inhaled the odor of several of the plants which her father had most sedulously avoided.

"Here, Beatrice," said the latter, "see how many needful offices require to be done to our chief treasure. Yet, shattered as I am, my life might pay the penalty of approaching it so closely as circumstances demand. Henceforth, I fear, this plant must be consigned to your sole charge."

"And gladly will I undertake it," cried again the rich tones of the young lady, as she bent towards the magnificent plant and opened her arms as if to embrace it. "Yes, my sister, my splendor, it shall be Beatrice's task to nurse and serve thee; and thou shalt reward her with thy kisses and perfumed breath, which to her is as the breath of life."

Then, with all the tenderness in her manner that was so strikingly expressed in her words, she busied herself with such attentions as the plant seemed to require; and Giovanni, at his lofty window, rubbed his eyes, and almost doubted whether it were a girl tending her favorite flower, or one sister performing the duties of affection to another. The scene soon terminated. Whether Dr. Rappaccini had finished his labors in the garden, or that his watchful eye had caught the stranger's face, he now took his daughter's arm and retired. Night was already closing in; oppressive exhalations seemed to proceed from the plants and steal upward past the open window; and Giovanni, closing the lattice, went to his couch and dreamed of a rich flower and beautiful girl. Flower and maiden were different, and yet the same, and fraught with some strange peril in either shape.

But there is an influence in the light of morning that tends to rectify whatever errors of fancy, or even of judgment, we may have incurred during the sun's decline, or among the shadows of the night, or in the less wholesome glow of moonshine. Giovanni's first movement, on starting from sleep, was to throw open the window and gaze down into the garden which his dreams had made so fertile of mysteries. He was surprised, and a little ashamed, to find how real and matter-of-fact an affair it proved to be, in the first rays of the sun which gilded the dewdrops that hung upon leaf and blossom, and, while giving a brighter beauty to each rare flower, brought every thing within the limits of ordinary experience. The young man rejoiced that, in the heart of the barren city, he had the privilege of overlooking this spot of lovely and luxuriant vegetation. It would serve, he said to himself, as a symbolic language to keep him in communion with Nature. Neither the sickly and thoughtworn Dr. Giacomo Rappaccini, it is true, nor his brilliant daughter, were now visible; so that Giovanni could not determine how much of the singularity which he attributed to both was due to their own qualities and how much to his wonder-working fancy; but he was inclined to take a most rational view of the whole matter.

In the course of the day he paid his respects to Signor Pietro Baglioni, professor of medicine in the university, a physician of eminent repute, to whom Giovanni had brought a letter of introduction. The professor was an elderly personage, apparently of genial nature and habits that might almost be called jovial. He kept the young man to dinner, and made himself very agreeable by the freedom and liveliness of his conversation, especially when warmed by a flask or two of Tuscan wine. Giovanni, conceiving that men of science, inhabitants of the same city, must needs be on familiar terms with one another, took an opportunity to mention the name of Dr. Rappaccini. But the professor did not respond with so much cordiality as he had anticipated.

"Ill would it become a teacher of the divine art of medicine," said Professor Pietro Baglioni, in answer to a question of Giovanni, "to withhold due and well-considered praise of a physician so eminently skilled as Rappaccini; but, on the other hand, I should answer it but scantily to my conscience were I to permit a worthy youth like yourself, Signor Giovanni, the son of an ancient friend, to imbibe erroneous ideas respecting a man who might hereafter chance to hold your life and death in his hands. The truth is, our worshipful Dr. Rappaccini has as much science as any member of the faculty — with perhaps one single exception — in Padua, or all Italy; but there are certain grave objections to his professional character."

"And what are they?" asked the young man.

"Has my friend Giovanni any disease of body or heart, that he is so inquisitive about physicians?" said the professor, with a smile. "But as for Rappaccini, it is said of him — and I, who know the man well, can answer for its truth — that he cares infinitely more for science than for mankind. His patients are interesting to him only as subjects for some new experiment. He would sacrifice human life, his own among the rest, or whatever else was dearest to him, for the sake of adding so much as a grain of mustard seed to the great heap of his accumulated knowledge."

"Methinks he is an awful man indeed," remarked Guasconti, mentally recalling the cold and purely intellectual aspect of Rappaccini. "And yet, worshipful professor, is it not a noble spirit? Are there many men capable of so spiritual a love of science?"

"God forbid," answered the professor, somewhat testily; "at least, unless they take sounder views of the healing art than those adopted by Rappaccini. It is his theory that all medicinal virtues are comprised within those substances which we term vegetable poisons. These he cultivates with his own hands, and is said even to have produced new varieties of poison, more horribly deleterious than Nature, without the assistance of this learned person, would ever have plagued the world withal. That the signor doctor does less mischief than might be expected with such dangerous substances, is undeniable. Now and then, it must be owned, he has effected, or seemed to effect, a marvellous cure; but, to tell you my private mind, Signor Giovanni, he should receive little credit for such instances of success, — they being probably the work of chance, — but should be held strictly accountable for his failures, which may justly be considered his own work."

The youth might have taken Baglioni's opinions with many grains of allowance had he known that there was a professional warfare of long continuance between him and Dr. Rappaccini, in which the latter was generally thought to have gained the advantage. If the reader be inclined to judge for himself, we refer him to certain black-letter tracts on both sides, preserved in the medical department of the University of Padua.

"I know not, most learned professor," returned Giovanni, after musing on what had been said of Rappaccini's exclusive zeal for science, — "I know not how dearly this physician may love his art; but surely there is one object more dear to him. He has a daughter."

"Aha!" cried the professor, with a laugh. "So now our friend Giovanni's secret is out. You have heard of this daughter, whom all the young men in Padua are wild about, though not half a dozen have ever had the good hap to see her face. I know little of the Signora Beatrice save that Rappaccini is said to have instructed her deeply in his science, and that, young and beautiful as fame reports her, she is already qualified to fill a professor's chair. Perchance her father destines her for mine! Other absurd rumors there be, not worth talking about or listening to. So now, Signor Giovanni, drink off your glass of lachryma."

Guasconti returned to his lodgings somewhat heated with the wine he had quaffed, and which caused his brain to swim with strange fantasies in reference to Dr. Rappaccini and the beautiful Beatrice. On his way, happening to pass by a florist's, he bought a fresh bouquet of flowers.

Ascending to his chamber, he seated himself near the window, but within the shadow thrown by the depth of the wall, so that he could look down into the garden with little risk of being discovered. All beneath his eye was a solitude. The strange plants were basking in the sunshine, and now and then nodding gently to one another, as if in acknowledgment of sympathy and kindred. In the midst, by the shattered fountain, grew the magnificent shrub, with its purple gems clustering all over it; they glowed in the air, and gleamed back again out of the depths of the pool, which thus seemed to overflow with colored radiance from the rich reflection that was steeped in it. At first, as we have said, the garden was a solitude. Soon, however, — as Giovanni had half hoped, half feared, would be the case, — a figure appeared beneath the antique sculptured portal, and came down between the rows of plants, inhaling their various perfumes as if she were one of those beings of old classic fable that lived upon sweet odors. On again beholding Beatrice, the young man was even startled to perceive how much her beauty exceeded his recollection of it; so brilliant, so vivid, was its character, that she glowed amid the sunlight, and, as Giovanni whispered to himself, positively illuminated the more shadowy intervals of the garden path. Her face being now more revealed than on the former occasion, he was struck by its expression of simplicity and sweetness — qualities that had not entered into his idea of her character, and which made him ask anew what manner of mortal she might be. Nor did he fail again to observe, or imagine, an analogy between the beautiful girl and the gorgeous shrub that hung its gemlike flowers over the fountain — a resemblance which Beatrice seemed to have indulged a fantastic humor in heightening, both by the arrangement of her dress and the selection of its hues.

Approaching the shrub, she threw open her arms, as with a passionate ardor, and drew its branches into an intimate embrace — so intimate that her features were hidden in its leafy bosom and her glistening ringlets all intermingled with the flowers.

"Give me thy breath, my sister," exclaimed Beatrice; "for I am faint with common air. And give me this flower of thine, which I separate with gentlest fingers from the stem and place it close beside my heart."

With these words the beautiful daughter of Rappaccini plucked one of the richest blossoms of the shrub, and was about to fasten it in her bosom. But now, unless Giovanni's draughts of wine had bewildered his senses, a singular incident occurred. A small orange-colored reptile, of the lizard or chameleon species, chanced to be creeping along the path, just at the feet of Beatrice. It appeared to Giovanni, — but, at the distance from which he gazed, he could scarcely have seen any thing so minute, — it appeared to him, however, that a drop or two of moisture from the broken stem of the flower descended upon the lizard's head. For an instant the reptile contorted itself violently, and then lay motionless in the sunshine. Beatrice observed this remarkable phenomenon, and crossed herself, sadly, but without surprise; nor did she therefore hesitate to arrange the fatal flower in her bosom. There it blushed, and almost glimmered with the dazzling effect of a precious stone, adding to her dress and aspect the one appropriate charm which nothing else in the world could have supplied. But Giovanni, out of the shadow of his window, bent forward and shrank back, and murmured and trembled.

"Am I awake? Have I my senses?" said he to himself. "What is this being? Beautiful shall I call her, or inexpressibly terrible?"

Beatrice now strayed carelessly through the garden, approaching closer beneath Giovanni's window, so that he was compelled to thrust his head quite out of its concealment in order to gratify the intense and painful curiosity which she excited. At this moment there came a beautiful insect over the garden wall: it had, perhaps, wandered through the city, and found no flowers or verdure among those antique haunts of men until the heavy perfumes of Dr. Rappaccini's shrubs had lured it from afar. Without alighting on the flowers, this winged brightness seemed to be attracted by Beatrice, and lingered in the air and fluttered about her head. Now, here it could not be but that Giovanni Guasconti's eyes deceived him. Be that as it might, he fancied that, while Beatrice was gazing at the insect with childish delight, it grew faint and fell at her feet; its bright wings shivered;

it was dead — from no cause that he could discern, unless it were the atmosphere of her breath. Again Beatrice crossed herself and sighed heavily as she bent over the dead insect.

An impulsive movement of Giovanni drew her eyes to the window. There she beheld the beautiful head of the young man — rather a Grecian than an Italian head, with fair, regular features, and a glistening of gold among his ringlets — gazing down upon her like a being that hovered in mid air. Scarcely knowing what he did, Giovanni threw down the bouquet which he had hitherto held in his hand.

"Signora," said he, "these are pure and healthful flowers. Wear them for the sake of Giovanni Guasconti."

"Thanks, signor," replied Beatrice, with her rich voice, that came forth as it were like a gush of music, and with a mirthful expression half childish and half womanlike. "I accept your gift, and would fain recompense it with this precious purple flower; but, if I toss it into the air, it will not reach you. So Signor Guasconti must even content himself with my thanks."

She lifted the bouquet from the ground, and then, as if inwardly ashamed at having stepped aside from her maidenly reserve to respond to a stranger's greeting, passed swiftly homeward through the garden. But, few as the moments were, it seemed to Giovanni, when she was on the point of vanishing beneath the sculptured portal, that his beautiful bouquet was already beginning to wither in her grasp. It was an idle thought; there could be no possibility of distinguishing a faded flower from a fresh one at so great a distance.

For many days after this incident the young man avoided the window that looked into Dr. Rappaccini's garden, as if something ugly and monstrous would have blasted his eyesight had he been betrayed into a glance. He felt conscious of having put himself, to a certain extent, within the influence of an unintelligible power by the communication which he had opened with Beatrice. The wisest course would have been, if his heart were in any real danger, to quit his lodgings and Padua itself at once; the next wiser, to have accustomed himself, as far as possible, to the familiar and daylight view of Beatrice — thus bringing her rigidly and systematically within the limits of ordinary experience. Least of all, while avoiding her sight, ought Giovanni to have remained so near this extraordinary being that the proximity and possibility even of intercourse should give a kind of substance and reality to the wild vagaries which his imagination ran riot continually in producing. Guasconti had not a deep heart — or, at all events, its depths were not sounded now; but he had a quick fancy, and an ardent southern temperament, which rose every instant to a higher fever pitch. Whether or no Beatrice possessed those terrible attributes, that fatal breath, the affinity with those so beautiful and deadly flowers which were indicated by what Giovanni had witnessed, she had at least instilled a fierce and subtle poison into his system. It was not love, although her rich beauty was a madness to him; nor horror, even while he fancied her spirit to be imbued with the same baneful essence that seemed to pervade her physical frame; but a wild offspring of both love and horror that had each parent in it, and burned like one and shivered like the other. Giovanni knew not what to dread; still less did he know what to hope; yet hope and dread kept a continual warfare in his breast, alternately vanquishing one another and starting up afresh to renew the contest. Blessed are all simple emotions, be they dark or bright! It is the lurid intermixture of the two that produces the illuminating blaze of the infernal regions.

Sometimes he endeavored to assuage the fever of his spirit by a rapid walk through the streets of Padua or beyond its gates: his footsteps kept time with the throbbings of his brain, so that the walk was apt to accelerate itself to a race. One day he found himself arrested; his arm was seized by a portly personage, who had turned back on recognizing the young man and expended much breath in overtaking him.

"Signor Giovanni! Stay, my young friend!" cried he. "Have you forgotten me? That might well be the case if I were as much altered as yourself."

It was Baglioni, whom Giovanni had avoided ever since their first meeting, from a doubt that the professor's sagacity would look too deeply into his secrets. Endeavoring to recover himself, he stared forth wildly from his inner world into the outer one and spoke like a man in a dream.

"Yes; I am Giovanni Guasconti. You are Professor Pietro Baglioni. Now let me pass!"

"Not yet, not yet, Signor Giovanni Guasconti," said the professor, smiling, but at the same time scrutinizing the youth with an earnest glance. "What! did I grow up side by side with your father? and shall his son pass me like a stranger in these old streets of Padua? Stand still, Signor Giovanni; for we must have a word or two before we part."

"Speedily, then, most worshipful professor, speedily," said Giovanni, with feverish impatience. "Does not your worship see that I am in haste?"

Now, while he was speaking there came a man in black along the street, stooping and moving feebly like a person in inferior health. His face was all overspread with a most sickly and sallow hue, but yet so pervaded with an expression of piercing and active intellect that an observer might easily have overlooked the merely physical attributes and have seen only this wonderful energy. As he passed, this person exchanged a cold and distant salutation with Baglioni, but fixed his eyes upon Giovanni with an intentness that seemed to bring out whatever was within him worthy of notice. Nevertheless, there was a peculiar quietness in the look, as if taking merely a speculative, not a human, interest in the young man.

"It is Dr. Rappaccini!" whispered the professor when the stranger had passed. "Has he ever seen your face before?"

"Not that I know," answered Giovanni, starting at the name.

"He *has* seen you! He must have seen you!" said Baglioni, hastily. "For some purpose or other, this man of science is making a study of you. I know that look of his! It is the same that coldly illuminates his face as he bends over a bird, a mouse, or a butterfly; which, in pursuance of some experiment, he has killed by the perfume of a flower; a look as deep as Nature itself, but without Nature's warmth of love. Signor Giovanni, I will stake my life upon it, you are the subject of one of Rappaccini's experiments!"

"Will you make a fool of me?" cried Giovanni, passionately. "*That*, signor professor, were an untoward experiment."

"Patience! patience!" replied the imperturbable professor. "I tell thee, my poor Giovanni, that Rappaccini has a scientific interest in thee. Thou hast fallen into fearful hands! And the Signora Beatrice, — what part does she act in this mystery?"

But Guasconti, finding Baglioni's pertinacity intolerable, here broke away, and was gone before the professor could again seize his arm. He looked after the young man intently and shook his head.

"This must not be," said Baglioni to himself. "The youth is the son of my old friend, and shall not come to any harm from which the arcana of medical science can preserve him. Besides, it is too insufferable an impertinence in Rappaccini thus to snatch the lad out of my own hands, as I may say, and make use of him for his infernal experiments. This daughter of his! It shall be looked to. Perchance, most learned Rappaccini, I may foil you where you little dream of it!"

Meanwhile Giovanni had pursued a circuitous route, and at length found himself at the door of his lodgings. As he crossed the threshold he was met by old Lisabetta, who smirked and smiled, and was evidently desirous to attract his attention; vainly, however, as the ebullition of his feelings had momentarily subsided into a cold and dull vacuity. He turned his eyes full upon the withered face that was puckering itself into a smile, but seemed to behold it not. The old dame, therefore, laid her grasp upon his cloak.

"Signor! signor!" whispered she, still with a smile over the whole breadth of her visage, so that it looked not unlike a grotesque carving in wood, darkened by centuries. "Listen, signor! There is a private entrance into the garden!"

"What do you say?" exclaimed Giovanni, turning quickly about, as if an inanimate thing should start into feverish life. "A private entrance into Dr. Rappaccini's garden?"

"Hush! hush! not so loud!" whispered Lisabetta, putting her hand over his mouth. "Yes; into the worshipful doctor's garden, where you may see all his fine shrubbery. Many a young man in Padua would give gold to be admitted among those flowers."

Giovanni put a piece of gold into her hand.

"Show me the way," said he.

A surmise, probably excited by his conversation with Baglioni, crossed his mind, that this interposition of old Lisabetta might perchance be connected with the intrigue, whatever were its nature, in which the professor seemed to suppose that Dr. Rappaccini was involving him. But such a suspicion, though it disturbed Giovanni, was inadequate to restrain him. The instant that he was aware of the possibility of approaching Beatrice, it seemed an absolute necessity of his existence to do so. It mattered not whether she were angel or demon; he was irrevocably within her sphere, and must obey the law that whirled him onward, in everlessening circles, towards a result which he did not attempt to foreshadow; and yet, strange to say, there came across him a sudden doubt whether this intense interest on his part were not delusory; whether it were really of so deep and positive a nature as to justify him in now thrusting himself into an incalculable position; whether it were not merely the fantasy of a young man's brain, only slightly or not at all connected with his heart.

He paused, hesitated, turned half about, but again went on. His withered guide led him along several obscure passages, and finally undid a door, through which, as it was opened, there came the sight and sound of rustling leaves, with the broken sunshine glimmering among them. Giovanni stepped forth, and, forcing himself through the entanglement of a shrub that wreathed its tendrils over the hidden entrance, stood beneath his own window in the open area of Dr. Rappaccini's garden.

How often is it the case that, when impossibilities have come to pass and dreams have condensed their misty substance into tangible realities, we find ourselves calm, and even coldly self-possessed, amid circumstances which it would have been a delirium of joy or agony to anticipate! Fate delights to thwart us thus. Passion will choose his own time to rush upon the scene, and lingers sluggishly behind when an appropriate adjustment of events would seem to summon his appearance. So was it now with Giovanni. Day after day his pulses had throbbed with feverish blood at the improbable idea of an interview with Beatrice, and of standing with her, face to face, in this very garden, basking in the Oriental sunshine of her beauty, and snatching from her full gaze the mystery which he deemed the riddle of his own existence. But now there was a singular and untimely equanimity within his breast. He threw a glance around the garden to discover if Beatrice or her father were present, and, perceiving that he was alone, began a critical observation of the plants.

The aspect of one and all of them dissatisfied him; their gorgeousness seemed fierce, passionate, and even unnatural. There was hardly an individual shrub which a wanderer, straying by himself through a forest, would not have been startled to find growing wild, as if an unearthly face had glared at him out of the thicket. Several also would have shocked a delicate instinct by an appearance of artificialness indicating that there had been such commixture, and, as it were, adultery of various vegetable species, that the production was no longer of God's making, but the monstrous offspring of man's depraved fancy, glowing with only an evil mockery of beauty. They were probably the result of experiment, which in one or two cases had succeeded in mingling plants individually lovely into a compound possessing the questionable and ominous character that distinguished the whole growth of the garden. In fine, Giovanni recognized but two or three plants in the collection, and those of a kind that he well knew to be poisonous. While busy with these contemplations he heard the rustling of a silken garment, and, turning, beheld Beatrice emerging from beneath the sculptured portal.

Giovanni had not considered with himself what should be his deportment; whether he should apologize for his intrusion into the garden, or assume that he was there with the privity at least, if not by the desire, of Dr. Rappaccini or his daughter; but Beatrice's manner placed him at his ease, though leaving him still in doubt by what agency he had gained admittance. She came lightly along the path and met him near the broken fountain. There was surprise in her face, but brightened by a simple and kind expression of pleasure.

"You are a connoisseur in flowers, signor," said Beatrice, with a smile, alluding to the bouquet which he had flung her from the window. "It is no marvel, therefore, if the sight of my father's rare collection has tempted you to take a nearer view. If he were here, he could tell you many strange and interesting facts as to the nature and habits of these shrubs; for he has spent a lifetime in such studies, and this garden is his world."

"And yourself, lady," observed Giovanni, "if fame says true, — you likewise are deeply skilled in the virtues indicated by these rich blossoms and these spicy perfumes. Would you deign to be my instructress, I should prove an apter scholar than if taught by Signor Rappaccini himself."

"Are there such idle rumors?" asked Beatrice, with the music of a pleasant laugh. "Do people say that I am skilled in my father's science of plants? What a jest is there! No; though I have grown up among these flowers, I know no more of them than their hues and perfume; and sometimes methinks I would fain rid myself of even that small knowledge. There are many flowers here, and those not the least brilliant, that shock and offend me when they meet my eye. But pray, signor, do not believe these stories about my science. Believe nothing of me save what you see with your own eyes."

"And must I believe all that I have seen with my own eyes?" asked Giovanni, pointedly, while the recollection of former scenes made him shrink. "No, signora; you demand too little of me. Bid me believe nothing save what comes from your own lips."

It would appear that Beatrice understood him. There came a deep flush to her cheek; but she looked full into Giovanni's eyes, and responded to his gaze of uneasy suspicion with a queenlike haughtiness.

"I do so bid you, signor," she replied. "Forget whatever you may have fancied in regard to me. If true to the outward senses, still it may be false in its essence; but the words of Beatrice Rappaccini's lips are true from the depths of the heart outward. Those you may believe."

A fervor glowed in her whole aspect and beamed upon Giovanni's consciousness like the light of truth itself; but while she spoke there was a fragrance in the atmosphere around her, rich and delightful, though evanescent, yet which the young man, from an indefinable reluctance, scarcely dared to draw into his lungs. It might be the odor of the flowers. Could it be Beatrice's breath which thus embalmed her words with a strange richness, as if by steeping them in her heart? A faintness passed like a shadow over Giovanni and flitted away; he seemed to gaze through the beautiful girl's eyes into her transparent soul, and felt no more doubt or fear.

The tinge of passion that had colored Beatrice's manner vanished; she became gay, and appeared to derive a pure delight from her communion with the youth not unlike what the maiden of a lonely island might have felt conversing with a voyager from the civilized world. Evidently her experience of life had been confined within the limits of that garden. She talked now about matters as simple as the daylight or summer clouds, and now asked questions in reference to the city, or Giovanni's distant home, his friends, his mother, and his sisters — questions indicating such seclusion, and such lack of familiarity with modes and forms, that Giovanni responded as if to an infant. Her spirit gushed out before him like a fresh rill that was just catching its first glimpse of the sunlight and wondering at the reflections of earth and sky which were flung into its bosom. There came thoughts, too, from a deep source, and fantasies of a gemlike brilliancy, as if diamonds and rubies sparkled upward among the bubbles of the fountain. Ever and anon there gleamed across the young man's mind a sense of wonder that he should be walking side by side with the being who had so wrought upon his imagination, whom he had idealized in such hues of terror, in whom he had positively witnessed such manifestations of dreadful attributes — that he should be conversing with Beatrice like a brother, and should find her so human and so maidenlike. But such reflections were only momentary; the effect of her character was too real not to make itself familiar at once.

In this free intercourse they had strayed through the garden, and now, after many turns among its avenues, were come to the shattered fountain, beside which grew the magnificent shrub, with its treasury of glowing blossoms. A fragrance was diffused from it which Giovanni recognized as identical with that which he had attributed to Beatrice's breath, but incomparably more powerful. As her eyes fell upon it, Giovanni beheld her press her hand to her bosom as if her heart were throbbing suddenly and painfully.

"For the first time in my life," murmured she, addressing the shrub, "I had forgotten thee."

"I remember, signora," said Giovanni, "that you once promised to reward me with one of these living gems for the bouquet which I had the happy boldness to fling to your feet. Permit me now to pluck it as a memorial of this interview."

He made a step towards the shrub with extended hand; but Beatrice darted forward, uttering a shriek that went through his heart like a dagger. She caught his hand and drew it back with the whole force of her slender figure. Giovanni felt her touch thrilling through his fibers. "Touch it not!" exclaimed she, in a voice of agony. "Not for thy life! It is fatal!"

Then, hiding her face, she fled from him and vanished beneath the sculptured portal. As Giovanni followed her with his eyes, he beheld the emaciated figure and pale intelligence of Dr. Rappaccini, who had been watching the scene, he knew not how long, within the shadow of the entrance.

No sooner was Guasconti alone in his chamber than the image of Beatrice came back to his passionate musings, invested with all the witchery that had been gathering around it ever since his first glimpse of her, and now likewise imbued with a tender warmth of girlish womanhood. She was human; her nature was endowed with all gentle and feminine qualities; she was worthiest to be worshipped; she was capable, surely, on her part, of the height and heroism of love. Those tokens which he had hitherto considered as proofs of a frightful peculiarity in her physical and moral system were now either forgotten or by the subtle sophistry of passion transmitted into a golden crown of enchantment, rendering Beatrice the more admirable by so much as she was the more unique. Whatever had looked ugly was now beautiful; or, if incapable of such a change, it stole away and hid itself among those shapeless half ideas which throng the dim region beyond the daylight of our perfect consciousness. Thus did he spend the night, nor fell asleep until the dawn had begun to awake the slumbering flowers in Dr. Rappaccini's garden, whither Giovanni's dreams doubtless led him. Up rose the sun in his due season, and, flinging his beams upon the young man's eyelids, awoke him to a sense of pain. When thoroughly aroused, he became sensible of a burning and tingling agony in his hand — in his right hand — the very hand which Beatrice had grasped in her own when he was on the point of plucking one of the gemlike flowers. On the back of that hand there was now a purple print like that of four small fingers, and the likeness of a slender thumb upon his wrist.

O, how stubbornly does love, — or even that cunning semblance of love which flourishes in the imagination, but strikes no depth of root into the heart, — how stubbornly does it hold its faith until the moment comes when it is doomed to vanish into thin mist! Giovanni wrapped a handkerchief about his hand and wondered what evil thing had stung him, and soon forgot his pain in a revery of Beatrice.

After the first interview, a second was in the inevitable course of what we call fate. A third; a fourth; and a meeting with Beatrice in the garden was no longer an incident in Giovanni's daily life, but the whole space in which he might be said to live; for the anticipation and memory of that ecstatic hour made up the remainder. Nor was it otherwise with the daughter of Rappaccini. She watched for the youth's appearance and flew to his side with confidence as unreserved as if they had been playmates from early infancy — as if they were such playmates still. If, by any unwonted chance, he failed to come at the appointed moment, she stood beneath the window and sent up the rich sweetness of her tones to float around him in his chamber and echo and reverberate throughout his heart: "Giovanni! Giovanni! Why tarriest thou? Come down!" And down he hastened into that Eden of poisonous flowers.

But, with all this intimate familiarity, there was still a reserve in Beatrice's demeanor, so rigidly and invariably sustained that the idea of infringing it scarcely occurred to his imagination. By all appreciable signs, they loved; they had looked at love with eyes that conveyed the holy secret from the depths of one soul into the depths of the other, as if it were too sacred to be whispered by the way; they had even spoken love in those gushes of passion when their spirits darted forth in articulated breath like tongues of long hidden flame; and yet there had been no seal of lips, no clasp of hands, nor any slightest caress such as love claims and hallows. He had never touched one of the gleaming ringlets of her hair; her garment — so marked was the physical barrier between them — had never been waved against him by a breeze. On the few occasions when

Giovanni had seemed tempted to overstep the limit, Beatrice grew so sad, so stern, and withal wore such a look of desolate separation, shuddering at itself, that not a spoken word was requisite to repel him. At such time he was startled at the horrible suspicions that rose, monster-like, out of the caverns of his heart and stared him in the face; his love grew thin and faint as the morning mist; his doubts alone had substance. But, when Beatrice's face brightened again after the momentary shadow, she was transformed at once from the mysterious, questionable being whom he had watched with so much awe and horror; she was now the beautiful and unsophisticated girl whom he felt that his spirit knew with a certainty beyond all other knowledge.

A considerable time had now passed since Giovanni's last meeting with Baglioni. One morning, however, he was disagreeably surprised by a visit from the professor, whom he had scarcely thought of for whole weeks, and would willingly have forgotten still longer. Given up as he had long been to a pervading excitement, he could tolerate no companions except upon condition of their perfect sympathy with his present state of feeling. Such sympathy was not to be expected from Professor Baglioni.

The visitor chatted carelessly for a few moments about the gossip of the city and the university, and then took up another topic.

"I have been reading an old classic author lately," said he, "and met with a story that strangely interested me. Possibly you may remember it. It is of an Indian prince, who sent a beautiful woman as a present to Alexander the Great. She was as lovely as the dawn and gorgeous as the sunset; but what especially distinguished her was a certain rich perfume in her breath — richer than a garden of Persian roses. Alexander, as was natural to a youthful conqueror, fell in love at first sight with this magnificent stranger; but a certain sage physician, happening to be present, discovered a terrible secret in regard to her."

"And what was that?" asked Giovanni, turning his eyes downward to avoid those of the professor.

"That this lovely woman," continued Baglioni, with emphasis, "had been nourished with poisons from her birth upward, until her whole nature was so imbued with them that she herself had become the deadliest poison in existence. Poison was her element of life. With that rich perfume of her breath she blasted the very air. Her love would have been poison — her embrace death. Is not this a marvellous tale?"

"A childish fable," answered Giovanni, nervously starting from his chair. "I marvel how your worship finds time to read such nonsense among your graver studies."

"By the by," said the professor, looking uneasily about him, "what singular fragrance is this in your apartment? Is it the perfume of your gloves? It is faint, but delicious; and yet, after all, by no means agreeable. Were I to breathe it long, methinks it would make me ill. It is like the breath of a flower; but I see no flowers in the chamber."

"Nor are there any," replied Giovanni, who had turned pale as the professor spoke; "nor, I think, is there any fragrance except in your worship's imagination. Odors, being a sort of element combined of the sensual and the spiritual, are apt to deceive us in this manner. The recollection of a perfume, the bare idea of it, may easily be mistaken for a present reality."

"Ay; but my sober imagination does not often play such tricks," said Baglioni; "and, were I to fancy any kind of odor, it would be that of some vile apothecary drug, wherewith my fingers are likely enough to be imbued. Our worshipful friend Rappaccini, as I have heard, tinctures his medicaments with odors richer than those of Araby. Doubtless, likewise, the fair and learned Signora Beatrice would minister to her patients with draughts as sweet as a maiden's breath; but woe to him that sips them!"

Giovanni's face evinced many contending emotions. The tone in which the professor alluded to the pure and lovely daughter of Rappaccini was a torture to his soul; and yet the intimation of a view of her character, opposite to his own, gave instantaneous distinctness to a thousand dim suspicions, which now grinned at him like so many demons. But he strove hard to quell them and to respond to Baglioni with a true lover's perfect faith.

"Signor professor," said he, "you were my father's friend; perchance, too, it is your purpose to act a friendly part towards his son. I would fain feel nothing towards you save respect and deference; but I pray you to observe, signor, that there is one subject on which we must not speak. You know not the Signora Beatrice. You cannot, therefore, estimate the wrong — the blasphemy, I may even say — that is offered to her character by a light or injurious word."

"Giovanni! my poor Giovanni!" answered the professor, with a calm expression of pity, "I know this wretched girl far better than yourself. You shall hear the truth in respect to the poisoner Rappaccini and his poisonous daughter; yes, poisonous as she is beautiful. Listen; for, even should you do violence to my gray hairs, it shall not silence me. That old fable of the Indian woman has become a truth by the deep and deadly science of Rappaccini and in the person of the lovely Beatrice."

Giovanni groaned and hid his face.

"Her father," continued Baglioni, "was not restrained by natural affection from offering up his child in this horrible manner as the victim of his insane zeal for science; for, let us do him justice, he is as true a man of science as ever distilled his own heart in an alembic. What, then, will be your fate? Beyond a doubt you are selected as the material of some new experiment. Perhaps the result is to be death; perhaps a fate more awful still. Rappaccini, with what he calls the interest of science before his eyes, will hesitate at nothing."

"It is a dream," muttered Giovanni to himself; "surely it is a dream."

"But," resumed the professor, "be of good cheer, son of my friend. It is not yet too late for the rescue. Possibly we may even succeed in bringing back this miserable child within the limits of ordinary nature, from which her father's madness has estranged her. Behold this little silver vase! It was wrought by the hands of the renowned Benvenuto Cellini, and is well worthy to be a love gift to the fairest dame in Italy. But its contents are invaluable.

One little sip of this antidote would have rendered the most virulent poisons of the Borgias innocuous. Doubt not that it will be as efficacious against those of Rappaccini. Bestow the vase, and the precious liquid within it, on your Beatrice, and hopefully await the result."

Baglioni laid a small, exquisitely wrought silver vial on the table and withdrew, leaving what he had said to produce its effect upon the young man's mind.

"We will thwart Rappaccini yet," thought he, chuckling to himself, as he descended the stairs; "but, let us confess the truth of him, he is a wonderful man — a wonderful man indeed; a vile empiric, however, in his practice, and therefore not to be tolerated by those who respect the good old rules of the medical profession."

Throughout Giovanni's whole acquaintance with Beatrice, he had occasionally, as we have said, been haunted by dark surmises as to her character; yet so thoroughly had she made herself felt by him as a simple, natural, most affectionate, and guileless creature, that the image now held up by Professor Baglioni looked as strange and incredible as if it were not in accordance with his own original conception. True, there were ugly recollections connected with his first glimpses of the beautiful girl; he could not quite forget the bouquet that withered in her grasp, and the insect that perished amid the sunny air, by no ostensible agency save the fragrance of her breath. These incidents, however, dissolving in the pure light of her character, had no longer the efficacy of facts, but were acknowledged as mistaken fantasies, by whatever testimony of the senses they might appear to be substantiated. There is something truer and more real than what we can see with the eyes and touch with the finger. On such better evidence had Giovanni founded his confidence in Beatrice, though rather by the necessary force of her high attributes than by any deep and generous faith on his part. But now his spirit was incapable of sustaining itself at the height to which the early enthusiasm of passion had exalted it; he fell down, grovelling among earthly doubts, and defiled therewith the pure whiteness of Beatrice's image. Not that he gave her up; he did but distrust. He resolved to institute some decisive test that should satisfy him, once for all, whether there were those dreadful peculiarities in her physical nature which could not be supposed to exist without some corresponding monstrosity of soul. His eyes, gazing down afar, might have deceived him as to the lizard, the insect, and the flowers; but if he could witness, at the distance of a few paces, the sudden blight of one fresh and healthful flower in Beatrice's hand, there would be room for no further question. With this idea he hastened to the florist's and purchased a bouquet that was still gemmed with the morning dewdrops.

It was now the customary hour of his daily interview with Beatrice. Before descending into the garden, Giovanni failed not to look at his figure in the mirror — a vanity to be expected in a beautiful young man, yet, as displaying itself at that troubled and feverish moment, the token of a certain shallowness of feeling and insincerity of character. He did gaze, however, and said to himself that his features had never before possessed so rich a grace, nor his eyes such vivacity, nor his cheeks so warm a hue of superabundant life.

"At least," thought he, "her poison has not yet insinuated itself into my system. I am no flower to perish in her grasp."

With that thought he turned his eyes on the bouquet, which he had never once laid aside from his hand. A thrill of indefinable horror shot through his frame on perceiving that those dewy flowers were already beginning to droop; they wore the aspect of things that had been fresh and lovely yesterday. Giovanni grew white as marble, and stood motionless before the mirror, staring at his own reflection there as at the likeness of something frightful. He remembered Baglioni's remark about the fragrance that seemed to pervade the chamber. It must have been the poison in his breath! Then he shuddered — shuddered at himself. Recovering from his stupor, he began to watch with curious eye a spider that was busily at work hanging its web from the antique cornice of the apartment, crossing and recrossing the artful system of interwoven lines — as vigorous and active a spider as ever dangled from an old ceiling. Giovanni bent towards the insect, and emitted a deep, long breath. The spider suddenly ceased its toil; the web vibrated with a tremor originating in the body of the small artisan. Again Giovanni sent forth a breath, deeper, longer, and imbued with a venomous feeling out of his heart: he knew not whether he were wicked, or only desperate. The spider made a convulsive gripe with his limbs and hung dead across the window.

"Accursed! accursed!" muttered Giovanni, addressing himself. "Hast thou grown so poisonous that this deadly insect perishes by thy breath?"

At that moment a rich, sweet voice came floating up from the garden.

"Giovanni! Giovanni! It is past the hour! Why tarriest thou? Come down!"

"Yes," muttered Giovanni again. "She is the only being whom my breath may not slay! Would that it might!"

He rushed down, and in an instant was standing before the bright and loving eyes of Beatrice. A moment ago his wrath and despair had been so fierce that he could have desired nothing so much as to wither her by a glance; but with her actual presence there came influences which had too real an existence to be at once shaken off; recollections of the delicate and benign power of her feminine nature, which had so often enveloped him in a religious calm; recollections of many a holy and passionate out-gush of her heart, when the pure fountain had been unsealed from its depths and made visible in its transparency to his mental eye; recollections which, had Giovanni known how to estimate them, would have assured him that all this ugly mystery was but an earthly illusion, and that, whatever mist of evil might seem to have gathered over her, the real Beatrice was a heavenly angel. Incapable as he was of such high faith, still her presence had not utterly lost its magic. Giovanni's rage was quelled into an aspect of sullen insensibility. Beatrice, with a quick spiritual sense, immediately felt that there was a gulf of blackness between them which neither he nor she could pass. They walked on together, sad and silent, and came thus to the marble fountain and to its pool of water on the ground, in the midst of which grew the shrub that bore gemlike blossoms. Giovanni was affrighted at the eager enjoyment — the appetite, as it were — with which he found himself inhaling the fragrance of the flowers.

"Beatrice," asked he, abruptly, "whence came this shrub?"

"My father created it," answered she, with simplicity.

"Created it! created it!" repeated Giovanni. "What mean you, Beatrice?"

"He is a man fearfully acquainted with the secrets of Nature," replied Beatrice; "and, at the hour when I first drew breath, this plant sprang from the soil, the offspring of his science, of his intellect, while I was but his earthly child. Approach it not!" continued she, observing with terror that Giovanni was drawing nearer to the shrub. "It has qualities that you little dream of. But I, dearest Giovanni, — I grew up and blossomed with the plant and was nourished with its breath. It was my sister, and I loved it with a human affection; for, alas! — hast thou not suspected it? — there was an awful doom."

Here Giovanni frowned so darkly upon her that Beatrice paused and trembled. But her faith in his tenderness reassured her, and made her blush that she had doubted for an instant.

"There was an awful doom," she continued, "the effect of my father's fatal love of science, which estranged me from all society of my kind. Until Heaven sent thee, dearest Giovanni, O, how lonely was thy poor Beatrice!"

"Was it a hard doom?" asked Giovanni, fixing his eyes upon her.

"Only of late have I known how hard it was," answered she, tenderly. "O, yes; but my heart was torpid, and therefore quiet."

Giovanni's rage broke forth from his sullen gloom like a lightning flash out of a dark cloud.

"Accursed one!" cried he, with venomous scorn and anger. "And, finding thy solitude wearisome, thou hast severed me likewise from all the warmth of life and enticed me into thy region of unspeakable horror!"

"Giovanni!" exclaimed Beatrice, turning her large bright eyes upon his face. The force of his words had not found its way into her mind; she was merely thunderstruck.

"Yes, poisonous thing!" repeated Giovanni, beside himself with passion. "Thou hast done it! Thou hast blasted me! Thou hast filled my veins with poison! Thou hast made me as hateful, as ugly, as loathsome and deadly a creature as thyself — a world's wonder of hideous monstrosity! Now, if our breath be happily as fatal to ourselves as to all others, let us join our lips in one kiss of unutterable hatred, and so die!"

"What has befallen me?" murmured Beatrice, with a low moan out of her heart. "Holy Virgin, pity me, a poor heart-broken child!"

"Thou, — dost thou pray?" cried Giovanni, still with the same fiendish scorn. "Thy very prayers, as they come from thy lips, taint the atmosphere with death. Yes, yes; let us pray! Let us to church and dip our fingers in the holy water at the portal! They that come after us will perish as by a pestilence! Let us sign crosses in the air! It will be scattering curses abroad in the likeness of holy symbols!"

"Giovanni," said Beatrice, calmly, for her grief was beyond passion, "why dost thou join thyself with me thus in those terrible words? I, it is true, am the horrible thing thou namest me. But thou, — what hast thou to do, save with one other shudder at my hideous misery to go forth out of the garden and mingle with thy race, and forget that there ever crawled on earth such a monster as poor Beatrice?"

"Dost thou pretend ignorance?" asked Giovanni, scowling upon her. "Behold! this power have I gained from the pure daughter of Rappaccini."

There was a swarm of summer insects flitting through the air in search of the food promised by the flower odors of the fatal garden. They circled round Giovanni's head, and were evidently attracted towards him by the same influence which had drawn them for an instant within the sphere of several of the shrubs. He sent forth a breath among them, and smiled bitterly at Beatrice as at least a score of the insects fell dead upon the ground.

"I see it! I see it!" shrieked Beatrice. "It is my father's fatal science! No, no, Giovanni; it was not I! Never! never! I dreamed only to love thee and be with thee a little time, and so to let thee pass away, leaving but thine image in mine heart; for, Giovanni, believe it, though my body be nourished with poison, my spirit is God's creature, and craves love as its daily food. But my father, — he has united us in this fearful sympathy. Yes; spurn me, tread upon me, kill me! O, what is death after such words as thine? But it was not I. Not for a world of bliss would I have done it."

Giovanni's passion had exhausted itself in its outburst from his lips. There now came across him a sense, mournful, and not without tenderness, of the intimate and peculiar relationship between Beatrice and himself. They stood, as it were, in an utter solitude, which would be made none the less solitary by the densest throng of human life. Ought not, then, the desert of humanity around them to press this insulated pair closer together? If they should be cruel to one another, who was there to be kind to them? Besides, thought Giovanni, might there not still be a hope of his returning within the limits of ordinary nature, and leading Beatrice, the redeemed Beatrice, by the hand? O, weak, and selfish, and unworthy spirit, that could dream of an earthly union and earthly happiness as possible, after such deep love had been so bitterly wronged as was Beatrice's love by Giovanni's blighting words! No, no; there could be no such hope. She must pass heavily, with that broken heart, across the borders of Time — she must bathe her hurts in some fount of paradise, and forget her grief in the light of immortality, and *there* be well.

But Giovanni did not know it.

"Dear Beatrice," said he, approaching her, while she shrank away as always at his approach, but now with a different impulse, "dearest Beatrice, our fate is not yet so desperate. Behold! there is a medicine, potent, as a wise physician has assured me, and almost divine in its efficacy. It is composed of ingredients the most opposite to those by which thy awful father has brought this calamity upon thee and me. It is distilled of blessed herbs. Shall we not quaff it together, and thus be purified from evil?"

"Give it me!" said Beatrice, extending her hand to receive the little silver vial which Giovanni took from his bosom. She added, with a peculiar emphasis, "I will drink; but do thou await the result."

She put Baglioni's antidote to her lips; and, at the same moment, the figure of Rappaccini emerged from the portal and came slowly towards the marble fountain. As he drew near, the pale man of science seemed to gaze with a triumphant expression at the beautiful youth and maiden, as might an artist who should spend his life in achieving a picture or a group of statuary and finally be satisfied with his success. He paused; his bent form grew erect with conscious power; he spread out his hands over them in the attitude of a father imploring a blessing upon his children; but those were the same hands that had thrown poison into the stream of their lives. Giovanni trembled. Beatrice shuddered nervously, and pressed her hand upon her heart.

"My daughter," said Rappaccini, "thou art no longer lonely in the world. Pluck one of those precious gems from thy sister shrub and bid thy bridegroom wear it in his bosom. It will not harm him now. My science and the sympathy between thee and him have so wrought within his system that he now stands apart from common men, as thou dost, daughter of my pride and triumph, from ordinary women. Pass on, then, through the world, most dear to one another and dreadful to all besides!"

"My father," said Beatrice, feebly, — and still as she spoke she kept her hand upon her heart, — "wherefore didst thou inflict this miserable doom upon thy child?"

"Miserable!" exclaimed Rappaccini. "What mean you, foolish girl? Dost thou deem it misery to be endowed with marvellous gifts against which no power nor strength could avail an enemy — misery, to be able to quell the mightiest with a breath — misery, to be as terrible as thou art beautiful? Wouldst thou, then, have preferred the condition of a weak woman, exposed to all evil and capable of none?"

"I would fain have been loved, not feared," murmured Beatrice, sinking down upon the ground. "But now it matters not. I am going, father, where the evil which thou hast striven to mingle with my being will pass away like a dream — like the fragrance of these poisonous flowers, which will no longer taint my breath among the flowers of Eden. Farewell, Giovanni! Thy words of hatred are like lead within my heart; but they, too, will fall away as I ascend. O, was there not, from the first, more poison in thy nature than in mine?"

To Beatrice, — so radically had her earthly part been wrought upon by Rappaccini's skill, — as poison had been life, so the powerful antidote was death; and thus the poor victim of man's ingenuity and of thwarted nature, and of the fatality that attends all such efforts of perverted wisdom, perished there, at the feet of her father and Giovanni. Just at that moment Professor Pietro Baglioni looked forth from the window, and called loudly, in a tone of triumph mixed with horror, to the thunderstricken man of science, —

"Rappaccini! Rappaccini! and is *this* the upshot of your experiment?"

John W. Campbell Jr.

Twilight

(1934)

John W[ood] Campbell Jr. (1910–1971) was more influential than any other individual in shaping the course of modern American sf. He was successful as a writer, both under his own name and as "Don A. Stuart," the name under which the following story was published. One of Campbell's most famous stories is "Who Goes There?" (1938), which was filmed as *The Thing* in 1951 and remade in 1982. His greatest impact, however, came as the editor of *Astounding*, the magazine that dominated the field under his leadership in the 1940s — the period known as the Golden Age of science fiction. When Campbell took charge of *Astounding Stories* (soon renamed *Astounding Science-Fiction*) in 1937, he had a mission: to improve the overall quality of sf and to lead it in a particular direction — one marked by a distinctively American vision of progress and can-do buoyancy. Previous editors had also been influential, notably Hugo Gernsback, who shared Campbell's optimism and his fascination with technology and the future, but Campbell played a much more active role in discovering, encouraging, and guiding writers.

Although he largely stopped writing sf himself, Campbell channeled his creative energies into his editorial work, often suggesting elaborate story ideas to his writers. As the editor of the highest-paying magazine in the business he had enormous clout, and as a respected writer he had credibility as well. Campbell is credited with launching or cultivating the careers of nearly every major sf writer of the 1940s, including Isaac Asimov, L. Sprague de Camp, Lester del Rey, Robert A. Heinlein, L. Ron Hubbard, Clifford D. Simak, E. E. "Doc" Smith, Theodore Sturgeon, A. E. van Vogt, and Jack Williamson. Campbell received eight Hugos for his work as an editor, and two major sf awards are named for him. He could be domineering and imperious, and this eventually alienated many writers — as did his far-right politics and controversial support for pseudoscientific theories such as Hubbard's "Dianetics" (the basis of Scientology). Nonetheless, Campbell's legacy remains powerful.

Campbell was a lifelong fan who began writing sf in his teens. His early stories grew out of the pulp tradition and combined space adventure with technological gadgetry. His later works, mostly signed as Don A. Stuart, were more idea-driven, thoughtful, and literary. "Twilight," which was ranked by the SFWA as one of the best stories written before 1964, belongs to this later period. It is a story of ambitious scale, describing a far future world in which human civilization has reached a pinnacle of achievement only to begin a long period of decline. The weighty philosophical grandeur of this tale is offset by the folksy language of the two narrators who frame the central story. The idea of evolution in this story — both physical and cultural — gives expression to Campbell's vision of the majesty of human progress, and, though the tone is one of melancholy and loss, the story contains a note of hope as well.

"Speaking of hitch-hikers," said Jim Bendell in a rather bewildered way, "I picked up a man the other day that certainly was a queer cuss." He laughed, but it wasn't a real laugh. "He told me the queerest yarn I ever heard. Most of them tell you how they lost their good jobs and tried to find work out here in the wide spaces of the West. They don't seem to realize how many people we have out here. They think all this great beautiful country is uninhabited."

Jim Bendell's a real estate man, and I knew how he could go on. That's his favorite line, you know. He's real worried because there's a lot of homesteading plots still open out in our state. He talks about the beautiful country, but he never went farther into the desert than the edge of town. 'Fraid of it actually. So I sort of steered him back on the track.

"What did he claim, Jim? Prospector who couldn't find land to prospect?"

"That's not very funny, Bart. No; it wasn't only what he claimed. He didn't even claim it, just said it. You know, he didn't say it was true, he just said it. That's what gets me. I know it ain't true, but the way he said it — Oh, I don't know."

By which I knew he didn't. Jim Bendell's usually pretty careful about his English — real proud of it. When he slips, that means he's disturbed. Like the time he thought the rattlesnake was a stick of wood and wanted to put it on the fire.

Jim went on: And he had funny clothes, too. They looked like silver, but they were soft as silk. And at night they glowed just a little.

I picked him up about dusk. Really picked him up. He was lying off about ten feet from the South Road. I thought, at first, somebody had hit him, and then hadn't stopped. Didn't see him very clearly, you know. I picked him up, put him in the car, and started on. I had about three hundred miles to go, but I thought I could drop him at Warren Spring with Doc Vance. But he came to in about five minutes, and opened his eyes. He looked straight off, and he looked first at the car, then at the Moon. "Thank God!" he says, and then looks at me. It gave me a shock. He was beautiful. No; he was handsome.

He wasn't either one. He was magnificent. He was about six feet two, I think, and his hair was brown, with a touch of red-gold. It seemed like fine copper wire that's turned brown. It was crisp and curly. His forehead was wide, twice as wide as mine. His features were delicate, but tremendously impressive; his eyes were gray, like etched iron, and bigger than mine — a lot.

That suit he wore — it was more like a bathing suit with pajama trousers. His arms were long and muscled smoothly as an Indian's. He was white, though, tanned lightly with a golden, rather than a brown, tan.

But he was magnificent. Most wonderful man I ever saw. I don't know, damn it!

"Hello!" I said. "Have an accident?"

"No; not this time, at least."

And his voice was magnificent, too. It wasn't an ordinary voice. It sounded like an organ talking, only it was human.

"But maybe my mind isn't quite steady yet. I tried an experiment. Tell me what the date is, year and all, and let me see," he went on.

"Why — December 9, 1932," I said.

And it didn't please him. He didn't like it a bit. But the wry grin that came over his face gave way to a chuckle.

"Over a thousand — " he says reminiscently. "Not as bad as seven million. I shouldn't complain."

"Seven million what?"

"Years," he said, steadily enough. Like he meant it. "I tried an experiment once. Or I will try it. Now I'll have to try again. The experiment was — in 3059. I'd just finished the release experiment. Testing space then. Time — it wasn't that, I still believe. It was space. I felt myself caught in that field, but I couldn't pull away. Field gamma-H 481, intensity 935 in the Pellman range. It sucked me in, and I went out.

"I think it took a short cut through space to the position the solar system will occupy. Through a higher dimension, effecting a speed exceeding light and throwing me into the future plane."

He wasn't telling me, you know. He was just thinking out loud. Then he began to realize I was there.

"I couldn't read their instruments, seven million years of evolution changed everything. So I overshot my mark a little coming back. I belong in 3059."

"But tell me, what's the latest scientific invention of this year?"

He startled me so, I answered almost before I thought.

"Why, television, I guess. And radio and airplanes."

"Radio — good. They will have instruments."

"But see here — who are you?"

"Ah — I'm sorry. I forgot," he replied in that organ voice of his. "I am Ares Sen Kenlin. And you?"

"James Waters Bendell."

"Waters — what does that mean? I do not recognize it."

"Why — it's a name, of course. Why should you recognize it?"

"I see — you have not the classification, then. 'Sen' stands for science."

"Where did you come from, Mr. Kenlin?"

"Come from?" He smiled, and his voice was slow and soft. "I came out of space across seven million years or more. They had lost count — the men had. The machines had eliminated the unneeded service. They didn't know what year it was. But before that — my home is in Neva'th City in the 3059."

That's when I began to think he was a nut.

"I was an experimenter," he went on. "Science, as I have said. My father was a scientist, too, but in human genetics. I myself am an experiment. He proved his point, and all the world followed suit. I was the first of the new race.

"The new race — oh, holy destiny — what has — what will —

"What is its end? I have seen it — almost. I saw them — the little men — bewildered — lost. And the machines. Must it be — can't anything sway it?

"Listen — I heard this song."

He sang the song. Then he didn't have to tell me about the people. I knew them. I could hear their voices, in the queer, crackling, un-English words. I could read their bewildered longings. It was in a minor key, I think. It called, it called and asked, and hunted hopelessly. And over it all the steady rumble and whine of the unknown, forgotten machines.

The machines that couldn't stop, because they had been started, and the little men had forgotten how to stop them, or even what they were for, looking at them and listening — and wondering. They couldn't read or write any more, and the language had changed, you see, so that the phonic records of their ancestors meant nothing to them.

But that song went on, and they wondered. And they looked out across space and they saw the warm, friendly stars — too far away. Nine planets they knew and inhabited. And locked by infinite distance, they couldn't see another race, a new life.

And through it all — two things. The machines. Bewildered forgetfulness. And maybe one more. Why?

That was the song, and it made me cold. It shouldn't be sung around people of today. It almost killed something. It seemed to kill hope. After that song — I — well, I believed him.

When he finished the song, he didn't talk for a while. Then he sort of shook himself.

You won't understand (he continued). Not yet — but I have seen them. They stand about, little misshapen men with huge heads. But their heads contain only brains. They had machines that could think — but somebody turned them off a long time ago, and no one knew how to start them again. That was the trouble with them. They had wonderful brains. Far better than yours or mine. But it must have been millions of years ago when they were turned off, too, and they just haven't thought since then. Kindly little people. That was all they knew.

When I slipped into that field it grabbed me like a gravitational field whirling a space transport down to a planet. It sucked me in — and through. Only the other side must have been seven million years in the future. That's where I was. It must have been in exactly the same spot on Earth's surface, but I never knew why.

It was night then, and I saw the city a little way off. The Moon was shining on it, and the whole scene looked wrong. You see, in seven million years, men had done a lot with the positions of the planetary bodies, what with moving space liners, clearing lanes through the asteroids, and such. And seven million years is long enough for natural things to change positions a little. The Moon must have been fifty thousand miles farther out. And it was rotating on its axis. I lay there a while and watched it. Even the stars were different.

There were ships going out of the city. Back and forth, like things sliding along a wire, but there was only a wire of force, of course. Part of the city, the lower part, was brightly lighted with what must have been mercury vapor glow, I decided. Blue-green. I felt sure men didn't live there — the light was wrong for eyes. But the top of the city was so sparsely lighted.

Then I saw something coming down out of the sky. It was brightly lighted. A huge globe, and it sank straight to the center of the great black-and-silver mass of the city.

I don't know what it was, but even then I knew the city was deserted. Strange that I could even imagine that, I who had never seen a deserted city before. But I walked the fifteen miles over to it and entered it. There were machines going about the streets, repair machines, you know. They couldn't understand that the city didn't need to go on functioning, so they were still working. I found a taxi machine that seemed fairly familiar. It had a manual control that I could work.

I don't know how long that city had been deserted. Some of the men from the other cities said it was a hundred and fifty thousand years. Some went as high as three hundred thousand years. Three hundred thousand years since a human foot had been in that city. The taxi machine was in perfect condition, functioned at once. It was clean, and the city was clean and orderly. I saw a restaurant and I was hungry. Hungrier still for humans to speak to. There were none, of course, but I didn't know.

The restaurant had the food displayed directly, and I made a choice. The food was three hundred thousand years old, I suppose. I didn't know, and the machines that served it to me didn't care, for they made things synthetically, you see, and perfectly. When the builders made those cities, they forgot one thing. They didn't realize that things shouldn't go on forever.

It took me six months to make my apparatus. And near the end I was ready to go; and, from seeing those machines go blindly, perfectly, on in orbits of their duties with the tireless, ceaseless perfection their designers had incorporated in them, long after those designers and their sons, and their sons' sons had no use for them —

When Earth is cold, and the Sun has died out, those machines will go on. When Earth begins to crack and break, those perfect, ceaseless machines will try to repair her —

I left the restaurant and cruised about the city in the taxi. The machine had a little, electric-power motor, I believe, but it gained its power from the great central power radiator. I knew before long that I was far in the future. The city was divided into two sections, a section of many strata where machines functioned smoothly, save for a deep humming beat that echoed through the whole city like a vast unending song of power. The entire metal framework of the place echoed with it, transmitted it, hummed with it. But it was soft and restful, a reassuring beat.

There must have been thirty levels above ground, and twenty more below, a solid block of metal walls and metal floors and metal and glass and force machines. The only light was the blue-green glow of the mercury vapor arcs. The light of mercury vapor is rich in high-energy-quanta, which stimulate the alkali metal atoms to photo-electric activity. Or perhaps that is beyond the science of your day? I have forgotten.

But they had used that light because many of their worker machines needed sight. The machines were marvelous. For five hours I wandered through the vast power plant on the very lowest level, watching them, and because there was motion, and that pseudo-mechanical life, I felt less alone.

The generators I saw were a development of the release I had discovered — when? The release of the energy of matter, I mean, and I knew when I saw that for what countless ages they could continue.

The entire lower block of the city was given over to the machines. Thousands. But most of them seemed idle, or, at most, running under light load. I recognized a telephone apparatus, and not a single signal came through. There was no life in the city. Yet when I pressed a little stud beside the screen on one side of the room, the machine began working instantly. It was ready. Only no one needed it any more. The men knew how to die, and be dead, but the machines didn't.

Finally I went up to the top of the city, the upper level. It was a paradise.

There were shrubs and trees and parks, glowing in the soft light that they had learned to make in the very air. They had learned it five million years or more before. Two million years ago they forgot. But the machines didn't, and they were still making it. It hung in the air, soft, silvery light, slightly rosy, and the gardens were shadowy with it. There were no machines here now, but I knew that in daylight they must come out and work on these gardens, keeping them a paradise for masters who had died, and stopped moving, as they could not.

In the desert outside the city it had been cool, and very dry. Here the air was soft, warm, and sweet with the scent of blooms that men had spent several hundreds of thousands of years perfecting.

Then somewhere music began. It began in the air, and spread softly through it. The Moon was just setting now, and as it set, the rosy-silver glow waned and the music grew stronger.

It came from everywhere and from nowhere. It was within me. I do not know how they did it. And I do not know how such music could be written.

Savages make music too simple to be beautiful, but it is stirring. Semi-savages write music beautifully simple, and simply beautiful. Your Negro music was your best. They knew music when they heard it and sang it as they felt it. Semicivilized peoples write great music. They are proud of their music, and make sure it is known for great music. They make it so great it is top-heavy.

I had always thought our music good. But that which came through the air was the song of triumph, sung by a mature race, the race of man in its full triumph! It was man singing his triumph in majestic sound that swept me up; it showed me what lay before me; it carried me on.

And it died in the air as I looked at the deserted city. The machines should have forgotten that song. Their masters had, long before.

I came to what must have been one of their homes; it was a dimly-seen doorway in the dusky light, but as I stepped up to it, the lights which had not functioned in three hundred thousand years illuminated it for me with a green-white glow, like a firefly, and I stepped into the room beyond. Instantly something happened to the air in the doorway behind me; it was as opaque as milk. The room in which I stood was a room of metal and stone. The stone was some jet-black substance with the finish of velvet, and the metals were silver and gold. There was a rug on the floor, a rug of just such material as I am wearing now, but thicker and softer. There were divans about the room, low and covered with these soft metallic materials. They were black and gold and silver, too.

I had never seen anything like that. I never shall again, I suppose, and my language and yours were not made to describe it.

The builders of that city had right and reason to sing that song of sweeping triumph, triumph that swept them over the nine planets and the fifteen habitable moons.

But they weren't there any more, and I wanted to leave. I thought of a plan and went to a subtelephone office to examine a map I had seen. The old World looked much the same. Seven or even seventy million years don't mean much to old Mother Earth. She may even succeed in wearing down those marvellous machine cities. She can wait a hundred million or a thousand million years before she is beaten.

I tried calling different city centers shown on the map. I had quickly learned the system when I examined the central apparatus.

I tried once — twice — thrice — a round dozen times. Yawk City, Lunon City, Paree, Shkago, Singpor, others. I was beginning to feel that there were no more men on all earth. And I felt crushed, as at each city the machines replied and did my bidding. The machines were there in each of those far vaster cities, for I was in the Neva City of their time. A small city. Yawk City was more than eight hundred kilometers in diameter.

In each city I had tried several numbers. Then I tried San Frisco. There was some one there, and a voice answered and the picture of a human appeared on the little glowing screen. I could see him start and stare in surprise at me. Then he started speaking to me. I couldn't understand, of course. I can understand your speech, and you mine, because your speech of this day is largely recorded on records of various types and has influenced our pronunciation.

Some things are changed; names of cities, particularly, because names of cities are apt to be polysyllabic, and used a great deal. People tend to elide them, shorten them. I am in — Nee-vah-dah — as you would say? We say only Neva. And Yawk State. But it is Ohio and Iowa still. Over a thousand years, effects were small on words, because they were recorded.

But seven million years had passed, and the men had forgotten the old records, used them less as time went on, and their speech varied till the time came when they could no longer understand the records. They were not written any more, of course.

Some men must have arisen occasionally among that last of the race and sought for knowledge, but it was denied them. An ancient writing can be translated if some basic rule is found. An ancient voice though — and when the race has forgotten the laws of science and the labor of mind.

So his speech was strange to me as he answered over that circuit. His voice was high in pitch, his words liquid, his tones sweet. It was almost a song as he spoke. He was excited and called others. I could not understand them, but I knew where they were. I could go to them.

So I went down from the paradise of gardens, and as I prepared to leave, I saw dawn in the sky. The strange-bright stars winked and twinkled and faded. Only one bright rising star was familiar — Venus. She shone golden now. Finally, as I stood watching for the first time that strange heaven, I began to understand what had first impressed me with the wrongness of the view. The stars, you see, were all different.

In my time — and yours, the solar system is a lone wanderer that by chance is passing across an intersection point of Galactic traffic. The stars we see at night are the stars of moving clusters, you know. In fact our system is passing through the heart of the Ursa Major group. Half a dozen other groups center within five hundred light-years of us.

But during those seven millions of years, the Sun had moved out of the group. The heavens were almost empty to the eye. Only here and there shone a single faint star. And across the vast sweep of black sky swung the band of the Milky Way. The sky was empty.

That must have been another thing those men meant in their songs — felt in their hearts. Loneliness — not even the close, friendly stars. We have stars within half a dozen light-years. They told me that their instruments, which gave directly the distance to any star, showed that the nearest was one hundred and fifty light-years away. It was enormously bright. Brighter even than Sirius of our heavens. And that made it even less friendly, because it was a blue-white supergiant. Our sun would have served as a satellite for that star.

I stood there and watched the lingering rose-silver glow die as the powerful blood-red light of the Sun swept over the horizon. I knew by the stars now, that it must have been several millions of years since my day; since I had last seen the Sun sweep up. And that blood-red light made me wonder if the Sun itself was dying.

An edge of it appeared, blood-red and huge. It swung up, and the color faded, till in half an hour it was the familiar yellow-gold disk.

It hadn't changed in all that time.

I had been foolish to think that it would. Seven million years — that is nothing to Earth, how much less to the Sun? Some two thousand thousand thousand times it had risen since I last saw it rise. Two thousand thousand thousand days. If it had been that many years — I might have noticed a change.

The universe moves slowly. Only life is not enduring; only life changes swiftly. Eight short millions of years. Eight days in the life of Earth — and the race was dying. It had left something: machines. But they would die, too, even though they could not understand. So I felt. I — may have changed that. I will tell you. Later.

For when the Sun was up, I looked again at the sky and the ground, some fifty floors below. I had come to the edge of the city.

Machines were moving on that ground, leveling it, perhaps. A great wide line of gray stretched off across the level desert straight to the east. I had seen it glowing faintly before the Sun rose — a roadway for ground machines. There was no traffic on it.

I saw an airship slip in from the east. It came with a soft, muttering whine of air, like a child complaining in sleep; it grew to my eyes like an expanding balloon. It was huge when it settled in a great port-slip in the city below. I could hear now the clang and mutter of machines, working on the materials brought in, no doubt. The machines had ordered raw materials. The machines in other cities had supplied. The freight machines had carried them here.

San Frisco and Jacksville were the only two cities on North America still used. But the machines went on in all the others, because they couldn't stop. They hadn't been ordered to.

Then high above, something appeared, and from the city beneath me from a center section, three small spheres rose. They, like the freight ship, had no visible driving mechanisms. The point in the sky above, like a black star in a blue space, had grown to a moon. The three spheres met it high above. Then together they descended and lowered into the center of the city, where I could not see them.

It was a freight transport from Venus. The one I had seen land the night before had come from Mars, I learned.

I moved after that and looked for some sort of a taxi-plane. They had none that I recognized in scouting about the city. I searched the higher levels, and here and there saw deserted ships, but far too large for me, and without controls.

It was nearly noon — and I ate again. The food was good.

I knew then that this was a city of the dead ashes of human hopes. The hopes not of *a* race, not the whites, nor the yellow, nor the blacks, but the human race. I was mad to leave the city. I was afraid to try the ground road to the west, for the taxi I drove was powered from some source in the city, and I knew it would fail before many miles.

It was afternoon when I found a small hangar near the outer wall of the vast city. It contained three ships. I had been searching through the lower strata of the human section — the upper part. There were restaurants and shops and theatres there. I entered one place where, at my entrance, soft music began, and colors and forms began to rise on a screen before me.

They were the triumph songs in form and sound and color of a mature race, a race that had marched steadily upward through five millions of years — and didn't see the path that faded out ahead, when they were dead and had stopped, and the city itself was dead — but hadn't stopped. I hastened out of there — and the song that had not been sung in three hundred thousand years died behind me.

But I found the hangar. It was a private one, likely. Three ships. One must have been fifty feet long and fifteen in diameter. It was a yacht, a space yacht, probably. One was some fifteen feet long and five feet in diameter. That must have been the family air machine. The third was a tiny thing, little more than ten feet long and two in diameter. I had to lie down within it, evidently.

There was a periscopic device that gave me a view ahead and almost directly above. A window that permitted me to see what lay below — and a device that moved a map under a frosted-glass screen and projected it onto the screen in such a way that the cross-hairs of the screen always marked my position.

I spent half an hour attempting to understand what the makers of that ship had made. But the men who made that were men who held behind them the science and knowledge of five millions of years and the perfect machines of those ages. I saw the release mechanism that powered it. I understood the principles of that and, vaguely, the mechanics. But there were no conductors, only pale beams that pulsed so swiftly you could hardly catch the pulsations from the corner of the eye. They had been glowing and pulsating, some half dozen of them, for three hundred thousand years at least; probably more.

I entered the machine, and instantly half a dozen more beams sprang into being; there was a slight suggestion of a quiver, and a queer strain ran through my body. I understood in an instant, for the machine was resting on gravity nullifiers. That had been my hope when I worked on the space fields I discovered after the release.

But they had had it for millions of years before they built that perfect deathless machine. My weight entering it had forced it to readjust itself and simultaneously to prepare for operation. Within, an artificial gravity equal to that of Earth had gripped me, and the neutral zone between the outside and the interior had caused the strain.

The machine was ready. It was fully fueled, too. You see they were equipped to tell automatically their wants and needs. They were almost living things, every one. A caretaker machine kept them supplied, adjusted, even repaired them when need be, and when possible. If it was not, I learned later, they were carried away in a service truck that came automatically; replaced by an exactly similar machine; and carried to the shops where they were made, and automatic machines made them over.

The machine waited patiently for me to start. The controls were simple, obvious. There was a lever at the left that you pushed forward to move forward, pulled back to go back. On the right a horizontal, pivoted bar. If you swung it left, the ship spun left; if right, the ship spun right. If tipped up, the ship followed it, and likewise for all motions other than backward and forward. Raising it bodily raised the ship, as depressing it depressed the ship.

I lifted it slightly, a needle moved a bit on a gauge comfortably before my eyes as I lay there, and the floor dropped beneath me. I pulled the other control back, and the ship gathered speed as it moved gently out into the open. Releasing both controls into neutral, the machine continued till it stopped at the same elevation, the motion absorbed by air friction. I turned it about, and another dial before my eyes moved, showing my position. I could not read it, though. The map did not move, as I had hoped it would. So I started toward what I felt was west.

I could feel no acceleration in that marvelous machine. The ground simply began leaping backward, and in a moment the city was gone. The map unrolled rapidly beneath me now, and I saw that I was moving south of west. I turned northward slightly, and watched the compass. Soon I understood that, too, and the ship sped on.

I had become too interested in the map and the compass, for suddenly there was a sharp buzz and, without my volition, the machine rose and swung to the north. There was a mountain ahead of me; I had not seen, but the ship had.

I noticed then what I should have seen before — two little knobs that could move the map. I started to move them and heard a sharp clicking, and the pace of the ship began decreasing. A moment and it had steadied at a considerably lower speed, the machine swinging to a new course. I tried to right it, but to my amazement the controls did not affect it.

It was the map, you see. It would either follow the course, or the course would follow it. I had moved it and the machine had taken over control of its own accord. There was a little button I could have pushed — but I didn't know. I couldn't control the ship until it finally came to rest and lowered itself to a stop six inches from the ground in the center of what must have been the ruins of a great city. Sacramento, probably.

I understood now, so I adjusted the map for San Frisco, and the ship went on at once. It steered itself around a mass of broken stone, turned back to its course, and headed on, a bullet-shaped, self-controlled dart.

It didn't descend when it reached San Frisco. It simply hung in the air and sounded a soft musical hum. Twice. Then it waited. I waited, too, and looked down.

There were people here. I saw the humans of that age for the first time. They were little men — bewildered — dwarfed, with heads disproportionately large. But not extremely so.

Their eyes impressed me most. They were huge, and when they looked at me there was a power in them that seemed to be sleeping, but too deeply to be roused.

I took the manual controls then and landed. And no sooner had I got out, than the ship rose automatically and started off by itself. They had automatic parking devices. The ship had gone to a public hangar, the nearest, where it would be automatically serviced and cared for. There was a little call set I should have taken with me when I got out. Then I could have pressed a button and called it to me — wherever I was in that city.

The people about me began talking — singing almost — among themselves. Others were coming up leisurely. Men and women — but there seemed no old and few young. What few young there were, were treated almost with respect, carefully taken care of lest a careless footstep on their toes or a careless step knock them down.

There was reason, you see. They lived a tremendous time. Some lived as long as three thousand years. Then — they simply died. They didn't grow old, and it never had been learned why people died as they did. The heart stopped, the brain ceased thought — and they died. But the young children, children not yet mature, were treated with the utmost care. But one child was born in the course of a month in that city of one hundred thousand people. The human race was growing sterile.

And I have told you that they were lonely? Their loneliness was beyond hope. For, you see, as man strode toward maturity, he destroyed all forms of life that menaced him. Disease. Insects. Then the last of the insects, and finally the last of the man-eating animals.

The balance of nature was destroyed then, so they had to go on. It was like the machines. They started them — and now they can't stop. They started destroying life — and now it wouldn't stop. So they had to destroy weeds of all sorts, then many formerly harmless plants. Then the herbivora, too, the deer and the antelope and the rabbit and the horse. They were a menace, they attacked man's machine-tended crops. Man was still eating natural foods.

You can understand. The thing was beyond their control. In the end they killed off the denizens of the sea, also, in self-defense. Without the many creatures that had kept them in check, they were swarming beyond bounds. And the time had come when synthetic foods replaced natural. The air was purified of all life about two and a half million years after our day, all microscopic life.

That meant that the water, too, must be purified. It was — and then came the end of life in the ocean. There were minute organisms that lived on bacterial forms, and tiny fish that lived on the minute organisms, and small fish that lived on the tiny fish, and big fish that lived on the small fish — and the beginning of the chain was gone. The sea was devoid of life in a generation. That meant about one thousand and five hundred years to them. Even the sea plants had gone.

And on all Earth there was only man and the organisms he had protected — the plants he wanted for decoration, and certain ultra-hygienic pets, as long-lived as their masters. Dogs. They must have been remarkable animals. Man was reaching his maturity then, and his animal friend, the friend that had followed him through a thousand millenniums to your day and mine, and another four thousand millenniums to the day of man's early maturity, had grown in intelligence. In an ancient museum — a wonderful place, for they had, perfectly preserved, the body of a great leader of mankind who had died five and a half million years before I saw him — in that museum, deserted then, I saw one of those canines. His skull was nearly as large as mine. They had simple ground machines that dogs could be trained to drive, and they held races in which the dogs drove those machines.

Then man reached his full maturity. It extended over a period of a full million years. So tremendously did he stride ahead, the dog ceased to be a companion. Less and less were they wanted. When the million years had passed, and man's decline began, the dog was gone. It had died out.

And now this last dwindling group of men still in the system had no other life form to make its successor. Always before when one civilization toppled, on its ashes rose a new one. Now there was but one civilization, and all other races, even other species, were gone save in the plants. And man was too far along in his old age to bring intelligence and mobility from the plants. Perhaps he could have in his prime.

Other worlds were flooded with man during that million years — the million years. Every planet and every moon of the system had its quota of men. Now only the planets had their populations, the moons had been deserted. Pluto had been left before I landed, and men were coming from Neptune, moving in toward the Sun, and the home planet, while I was there. Strangely quiet men, viewing, most of them, for the first time, the planet that had given their race life.

But as I stepped from that ship and watched it rise away from me, I saw why the race of man was dying. I looked back at the faces of those men, and on them I read the answer. There was one single quality gone from the still-great minds — minds far greater than yours or mine. I had to have the help of one of them in solving some of my problems. In space, you know, there are twenty coordinates, ten of which are zero, six of which have fixed values, and the four others represent our changing, familiar dimensions in space-time. That means that integrations must proceed in not double, or triple, or quadruple — but ten integrations.

It would have taken me too long. I would never have solved all the problems I must work out. I could not use their mathematics machines; and mine, of course, were seven million years in the past. But one of those men was interested and helped me. He did quadruple and quintuple integration, even quadruple integration between varying exponential limits — in his head.

When I asked him to. For the one thing that had made man great had left him. As I looked in their faces and eyes on landing I knew it. They looked at me, interested at this rather unusual-looking stranger — and went on. They had come to see the arrival of a ship. A rare event, you see. But they were merely welcoming me in a friendly fashion. They were not curious! Man had lost the instinct of curiosity.

Oh, not entirely! They wondered at the machines, they wondered at the stars. But they did nothing about it. It was not wholly lost to them yet, but nearly. It was dying. In the six short months I stayed with them, I learned more than they had learned in the two or even three thousand years they had lived among the machines.

Can you appreciate the crushing hopelessness it brought to me? I, who love science, who see in it, or have seen in it, the salvation, the raising of mankind — to see those wondrous machines, of man's triumphant maturity, forgotten and misunderstood. The wondrous, perfect machines that tended, protected, and cared for those gentle, kindly people who had — forgotten.

They were lost among it. The city was a magnificent ruin to them, a thing that rose stupendous about them. Something not understood, a thing that was of the nature of the world. It was. It had not been made; it simply was. Just as the mountains and the deserts and the waters of the seas.

Do you understand — can you see that the time since those machines were new was longer than the time from our day to the birth of the race? Do we know the legends of our first ancestors? Do we remember their lore of forest and cave? The secret of chipping a flint till it had a sharp-cutting edge? The secret of trailing and killing a saber-toothed tiger without being killed oneself?

They were now in similar straits, though the time had been longer, because the languages had taken a long step towards perfection, and because the machines maintained everything for them through generation after generation.

Why, the entire planet of Pluto had been deserted — yet on Pluto the largest mines of one of their metals were located; the machines still functioned. A perfect unity existed throughout the system. A unified system of perfect machines.

And all those people knew was that to do a certain thing to a certain lever produced certain results. Just as men in the Middle Ages knew that to take a certain material, wood, and place it in contact with other pieces of wood heated red, would cause the wood to disappear, and become heat. They did not understand that wood was being oxidized with the release of the heat of formation of carbon dioxide and water. So those people did not understand the things that fed and clothed and carried them.

I stayed with them there for three days. And then I went to Jacksville, Yawk City, too. That was enormous. It stretched over — well, from well north of where Boston is today to well south of Washington — that was what they called Yawk City.

I never believed that, when he said it, said Jim, interrupting himself. I knew he didn't. If he had I think he'd have bought land somewhere along there and held for a rise in value. I know Jim. He'd have the idea that seven million years was something like seven hundred, and maybe his great-grandchildren would be able to sell it.

Anyway, went on Jim, he said it was all because the cities had spread so. Boston spread south. Washington, north. And Yawk City spread all over. And the cities between grew into them.

And it was all one vast machine. It was perfectly ordered and perfectly neat. They had a transportation system that took me from the North End to the South End in three minutes. I timed it. They had learned to neutralize acceleration.

Then I took one of the great space liners to Neptune. There were still some running. Some people, you see, were coming the other way.

The ship was huge. Mostly it was a freight liner. It floated up from Earth, a great metal cylinder three quarters of a mile long, and a quarter of a mile in diameter. Outside the atmosphere it began to accelerate. I could see Earth dwindle. I have ridden one of our own liners to Mars, and it took me, in 3048, five days. In half an hour on this liner Earth was just a star, with a smaller, dimmer star near it. In an hour we passed Mars. Eight hours later we landed on Neptune. M'reen was the city. Large as the Yawk City of my day — and no one living there.

The planet was cold and dark — horribly cold. The sun was a tiny, pale disk, heatless and almost lightless. But the city was perfectly comfortable. The air was fresh and cool, moist with the scent of growing blossoms, perfumed with them. And the whole giant metal framework trembled just slightly with the humming, powerful beat of the mighty machines that had made and cared for it.

I learned from records I deciphered, because of my knowledge of the ancient tongue that their tongue was based on, and the tongue of that day when man was dying, that the city was built three million, seven hundred and thirty thousand, one hundred and fifty years after my birth. Not a machine had been touched by the hand of man since that day.

Yet the air was perfect for man. And the warm, rose-silver glow hung in the air here and supplied the only illumination.

I visited some of their other cities where there were men. And there, on the retreating outskirts of man's domain, I first heard the Song of Longings, as I called it.

And another, The Song of Forgotten Memories. Listen:

He sang another of those songs. There's one thing I know, declared Jim. That bewildered note was stronger in his voice, and by that time I guess I pretty well understood his feelings. Because, you have to remember, I heard it only secondhand from an ordinary man, and Jim had heard it from an eye-and-ear witness that was not ordinary, and heard it in that organ voice. Anyway, I guess Jim was right when he said: "He wasn't any ordinary man." No ordinary man could think of those songs. They weren't right. When he sang that song, it was full of more of those plaintive minors. I could feel him searching his mind for something he had forgotten, something he desperately wanted to remember — something he knew he should have known — and I felt it eternally elude him. I felt it get further away from him as he sang. I heard that lonely, frantic searcher attempting to recall that thing — that thing that would save him.

And I heard him give a little sob of defeat — and the song ended. Jim tried a few notes. He hasn't a good ear for music — but that was too powerful to forget. Just a few hummed notes. Jim hasn't much imagination, I guess, or when that man of the future sang to him he would have gone mad. It shouldn't be sung to modern men; it isn't meant for them. You've heard those heart-rending cries some animals give, like human cries, almost? A loon, now — he sounds like a lunatic being murdered horribly.

That's just unpleasant. That song made you feel just exactly what the singer meant — because it didn't just sound human — it was human. It was the essence of humanity's last defeat, I guess. You always feel sorry for the chap who loses after trying hard. Well, you could feel the whole of humanity trying hard — and losing. And you knew they couldn't afford to lose, because they couldn't try again.

He said he'd been interested before. And still not wholly upset by those machines that couldn't stop. But that was too much for him.

I knew after that, he said, that these weren't men I could live among. They were dying men, and I was alive with the youth of the race. They looked at me with the same longing, hopeless wonder with which they looked at the stars and the machines. They knew what I was, but couldn't understand.

I began to work on leaving.

It took six months. It was hard because my instruments were gone, of course, and theirs didn't read in the same units. And there were few instruments, anyway. The machines didn't read instruments; they acted on them. They were sensory organs to them.

But Reo Lantal helped where he could. And I came back.

I did just one thing before I left that may help. I may even try to get back there sometime. To see, you know.

I said they had machines that could really think? But that someone had stopped them a long time ago, and no one knew how to start them?

I found some records and deciphered them. I started one of the last and best of them and started it on a great problem. It is only fitting it should be done. The machine can work on it, not for a thousand years, but for a million, if it must.

I started five of them actually, and connected them together as the records directed.

They are trying to make a machine with something that man had lost. It sounds rather comical. But stop to think before you laugh. And remember that Earth as I saw it from the ground level of Neva City just before Reo Lantal threw the switch.

Twilight — the sun has set. The desert out beyond, in its mystic, changing colors. The great, metal city rising straight-walled to the human city above, broken by spires and towers and great trees with scented blossoms. The silvery-rose glow in the paradise of gardens above.

And all the great city-structure throbbing and humming to the steady gentle beat of perfect, deathless machines built more than three million years before — and never touched since that time by human hands. And they go on. The dead city. The men that have lived, and hoped, and built — and died to leave behind them those little men who can only wonder and look and long for a forgotten kind of companionship. They wander through the vast cities their ancestors built, knowing less of them than the machines themselves.

And the songs. Those tell the story best, I think. Little, hopeless, wondering men amid vast unknowing, blind machines that started three million years before — and just never knew how to stop. They are dead — and can't die and be still.

So I brought another machine to life, and set it to a task which, in time to come, it will perform.

I ordered it to make a machine which would have what man had lost. A curious machine.

And then I wanted to leave quickly and go back. I had been born in the first full light of man's day. I did not belong in the lingering, dying glow of man's twilight.

So I came back. A little too far back. But it will not take me long to return — accurately this time.

"Well, that was his story," Jim said. "He didn't *tell* me it was true — didn't say anything about it. And he had me thinking so hard I didn't even see him get off in Reno when we stopped for gas.

"But — he wasn't an ordinary man," repeated Jim, in a rather belligerent tone.

Jim claims he doesn't believe the yarn, you know. But he does; that's why he always acts so determined about it when he says the stranger wasn't an ordinary man.

No, he wasn't, I guess. I think he lived and died, too, probably, sometime in the thirty-first century. And I think he saw the twilight of the race, too.

Olaf Stapledon
From Star Maker
(1937)

British writer and visionary Olaf Stapledon (1886–1950) occupies a unique place in the science fiction canon. A philosopher by training, Stapledon turned to fiction as a way of communicating his deeply held moral, political, and spiritual beliefs. He undertook this project in isolation from the mainstream of contemporary sf, which he seems to have had little exposure to; yet his novels were immediately recognized as important by the sf community, and his influence has been profound.

Stapledon earned a doctorate in philosophy from Liverpool University in 1925 and published an academic treatise, *A Modern Theory of Ethics,* a few years later, but he turned to writing fiction full time after the success of his first novel, *Last and First Men*, in 1930. A principled agnostic, socialist, and pacifist, Stapledon was awarded the French Croix de Guerre for his service with a Friends (Quaker) ambulance unit in World War I. He disliked organized religion, and some found his novels' portrayal of a detached and dispassionate God disturbing and even offensive; yet a profound spirituality is evident in all his writing.

Star Maker has often been listed in Locus Polls as one of the best sf novels, and Stapledon was awarded the first Cordwainer Smith Rediscovery Award in 2001. The novel is breathtaking in scope, covering a time span of 100 billion years and tracing the history of consciousness in the universe. The narrator, experiencing a crisis of faith about his significance in the cosmos, suddenly finds himself projected out of his body and voyages mentally far beyond our solar system, encountering many fascinating alien life-forms and social systems. In his travels, he meets and bonds with like-minded entities who share in his search for meaning and gradually progress toward enlightenment. Much of the book is given over to the detailed, anthropological examination of Stapledon's spectacularly original and diverse aliens, who are diverse in their physical adaptations and cultural habits, but who ultimately follow the same path toward social and spiritual evolution.

The book's most significant contributions to sf, however, are the scope of its metaphysical speculations and the idea that the development of transcendent consciousness is a necessary step in the evolutionary process. In his vision of a communal "supermind" that transcends individual consciousness, Stapledon can be seen as a forerunner of many later strands of sf that work to envision the next stage of human existence.

1. The Earth

1. The Starting Point

One night when I had tasted bitterness I went out on to the hill. Dark heather checked my feet. Below marched the suburban street lamps. Windows, their curtains drawn, were shut eyes, inwardly watching the lives of dreams. Beyond the sea's level darkness a lighthouse pulsed. Overhead, obscurity.

I distinguished our own house, our islet in the tumultuous and bitter currents of the world. There, for a decade and a half, we two, so different in quality, had grown in and in to one another, for mutual support and nourishment, in intricate symbiosis. There daily we planned our several undertakings, and recounted the day's oddities and vexations. There letters piled up to be answered, socks to be darned. There the children were born, those sudden new lives. There, under that roof, our own two lives, recalcitrant sometimes to one another, were all the while thankfully one, one larger, more conscious life than either alone.

All this, surely, was good. Yet there was bitterness. And bitterness not only invaded us from the world; it welled up also within our own magic circle. For horror at our futility, at our own unreality, and not only at the world's delirium, had driven me out on to the hill.

We were always hurrying from one little urgent task to another, but the upshot was insubstantial. Had we, perhaps, misconceived our whole existence? Were we, as it were, living from false premises? And in particular, this partnership of ours, this seemingly so well-based fulcrum for activity in the world, was it after all nothing but a little eddy of complacent and ingrown domesticity, ineffectively whirling on the surface of the great flux, having in itself no depth of being, and no significance? Had we perhaps after all deceived ourselves? Behind those rapt windows did we, like so many others, indeed live only a dream? In a sick world even the hale are sick. And we two, spinning our little life mostly by rote, seldom with clear cognizance, seldom with firm intent, were products of a sick world.

Yet this life of ours was not all sheer and barren fantasy. Was it not spun from the actual fibers of reality, which we gathered in with all the comings and goings through our door, all our traffic with the suburb and the city and with remoter cities, and with the ends of the earth? And were we not spinning together an authentic expression of our own nature? Did not our life issue daily as more or less firm threads of active living, and mesh itself into the growing web, the intricate, ever-proliferating pattern of mankind?

I considered "us" with quiet interest and a kind of amused awe. How could I describe our relationship even to myself without either disparaging it or insulting it with the tawdry decoration of sentimentality? For this our delicate balance of dependence and independence, this coolly critical, shrewdly ridiculing, but loving mutual contact, was surely a microcosm of true community, was after all in its simple style an actual and living example of that high goal which the world seeks.

The whole world? The whole universe? Overhead, obscurity unveiled a star. One tremulous arrow of light, projected how many thousands of years ago, now stung my nerves with vision, and my heart with fear. For in such a universe as this what significance could there be in our fortuitous, our frail, our evanescent community?

But now irrationally I was seized with a strange worship, not, surely of the star, that mere furnace which mere distance falsely sanctified, but of something other, which the dire contrast of the star and us signified to the heart. Yet what, what could thus be signified? Intellect, peering beyond the star, discovered no Star Maker, but only darkness; no Love, no Power even, but only Nothing. And yet the heart praised.

Impatiently I shook off this folly, and reverted from the inscrutable to the familiar and the concrete. Thrusting aside worship, and fear also and bitterness, I determined to examine more coldly this remarkable "us," this surprisingly impressive datum, which to ourselves remained basic to the universe, though in relation to the stars it appeared so slight a thing.

Considered even without reference to our belittling cosmical background, we were after all insignificant, perhaps ridiculous. We were such a commonplace occurrence, so trite, so respectable. We were just a married couple, making shift to live together without undue strain. Marriage in our time was suspect. And ours, with its trivial romantic origin, was doubly suspect.

We had first met when she was a child. Our eyes encountered. She looked at me for a moment with quiet attention; even, I had romantically imagined, with obscure, deep-lying recognition. I, at any rate, recognized in that look (so I persuaded myself in my fever of adolescence) my destiny. Yes! How predestinate had seemed our union! Yet now, in retrospect, how accidental! True, of course, that as a long-married couple we fitted rather neatly, like two close trees whose trunks have grown upwards together as a single shaft, mutually distorting, but mutually supporting. Coldly I now assessed her as merely a useful, but often infuriating adjunct to my personal life. We were on the whole sensible companions. We left one another a certain freedom, and so we were able to endure our proximity.

Such was our relationship. Stated thus it did not seem very significant for the understanding of the universe. Yet in my heart I knew that it was so. Even the cold stars, even the whole cosmos with all its inane immensities could not convince me that this our prized atom of community, imperfect as it was, short-lived as it must be, was not significant.

But could this indescribable union of ours really have any significance at all beyond itself? Did it, for instance, prove that the essential nature of all human beings was to love, rather than to hate and fear? Was it evidence that all men and women the world over, though circumstance might prevent them, were at heart capable of supporting a world-wide, love-knit community? And further, did it, being itself a product of the cosmos, prove that love was in some way basic to the cosmos itself? And did it afford, through its own felt intrinsic excellence, some guarantee that we two, its frail supporters, must in some sense have eternal life? Did it, in fact, prove that love was God, and God awaiting us in his heaven?

No! Our homely, friendly, exasperating, laughter-making, undecorated though most prized community of spirit proved none of these things. It was no certain guarantee of anything but its own imperfect rightness. It was nothing but a very minute, very bright epitome of one out of the many potentialities of existence. I remembered the swarms of the unseeing stars. I remembered the tumult of hate and fear and bitterness which is man's world. I remembered, too, our own not infrequent discordancy. And I reminded myself that we should very soon vanish like the flurry that a breeze has made on still water.

Once more there came to me a perception of the strange contrast of the stars and us. The incalculable potency of the cosmos mysteriously enhanced the rightness of our brief spark of community, and of mankind's brief, uncertain venture. And these in turn quickened the cosmos.

I sat down on the heather. Overhead obscurity was now in full retreat. In its rear the freed population of the sky sprang out of hiding, star by star.

On every side the shadowy hills or the guessed, featureless sea extended beyond sight. But the hawk-flight of imagination followed them as they curved downward below the horizon. I perceived that I was on a little round grain of rock and metal, filmed with water and with air, whirling in sunlight and darkness. And on the skin of that little grain all the swarms of men, generation by generation, had lived in labor and blindness, with intermittent joy and intermittent lucidity of spirit. And all their history, with its folk-wanderings, its empires, its philosophies, its proud sciences, its social revolutions, its increasing hunger for community, was but a flicker in one day of the lives of stars.

If one could know whether among that glittering host there were here and there other spirit-inhabited grains of rock and metal, whether man's blundering search for wisdom and for love was a sole and insignificant tremor, or part of a universal movement! . . .

[*At the climax of this reverie, the narrator finds himself traveling disembodied among the stars, eventually happening upon a planet he calls "the Other Earth" where he forms a mental bond with a like-minded alien named "Bvalltu."*]

4. I Travel Again

. . .

Our penetration of one another's minds brought to each not merely addition but multiplication of mental riches; for each knew inwardly not only himself and the other but also the contrapuntal harmony of each in relation to the other. Indeed, in some sense which I cannot precisely describe, our union of minds brought into being a third mind, as yet intermittent, but more subtly conscious than either of us in the normal state. Each of us, or rather both of us together, "woke up" now and then to be this superior spirit. All the experiences of each took on a new significance in the light of the other; and our two minds together became a new, more penetrating, and more self-conscious mind. In this state of heightened lucidity we, or rather the new I, began deliberately to explore the psychological possibilities of other types of beings and intelligent worlds. With new penetration I distinguished in myself and in Bvalltu those attributes which were essential to the spirit and those mere accidents imposed on each by his peculiar world. This imaginative venture was soon to prove itself a method, and a very potent method, of cosmological research.

We now began to realize more clearly a fact that we had long suspected. In my previous interstellar voyage, which brought me to the Other Earth, I had unwittingly employed two distinct methods of travel, the method of disembodied flight through space and a method which I shall call "psychical attraction." This consisted of telepathic projection of the mind directly into some alien world, remote perhaps in time and space, but mentally "in tune" with the explorer's own mind at the time of the venture. Evidently it was this method that had really played the chief part in directing me to the Other Earth. The remarkable similarities of our two races had set up a strong "psychical attraction" which had been far more potent than all my random interstellar wanderings. It was this method that Bvalltu and I were now to practice and perfect.

Presently we noticed that we were no longer at rest but slowly drifting. We had also a queer sense that, though we were seemingly isolated in a vast desert of stars and nebulae, we were in fact in some kind of mental proximity with unseen intelligences. Concentrating on this sense of presence, we found that our drift accelerated; and that, if we tried by a violent act of volition to change its course, we inevitably swung back into the original direction as soon as our effort ceased. Soon our drift became a headlong flight. Once more the forward stars turned violet, the hinder red. Once more all vanished.

In absolute darkness and silence we debated our situation. Clearly we were now passing through space more quickly than light itself. Perhaps we were also, in some incomprehensible manner, traversing time. Meanwhile that sense of the proximity of other beings became more and more insistent, though no less confused.

Then once again the stars appeared. Though they streamed past us like flying sparks, they were colorless and normal. One brilliant light lay right ahead of us. It waxed, became a dazzling splendor, then visibly a dis. With an effort of will we decreased our speed, then cautiously we swung round this sun, searching. To our delight, it proved to be attended by several of the grains that may harbor life. Guided by our unmistakable sense of mental presence, we selected one of these planets, and slowly descended towards it.

5. Worlds Innumerable

1. The Diversity of Worlds

. . .

[*The narrator and Bvalltu connect mentally with the inhabitants of many worlds. In the following section the narrator describes some of the common patterns they find in observing the development of civilizations.*]

Since we were now free of space, we ranged with equal ease over the nearer and the remoter tracts of this galaxy. That we did not till much later make contact with minds in other galaxies was not due to any limitations imposed by space, but seemingly to our own inveterate parochialism, to a strange limitation of our own interest, which for long rendered us inhospitable to the influence of worlds lying beyond the confines of the Milky Way. I shall say more of this curious restriction when I come to describe how we did at last outgrow it.

Along with freedom of space we had freedom of time. Some of the worlds that we explored in this early phase of our adventure ceased to exist long before my native planet was formed; others were its contemporaries; others were not born till the old age of our galaxy, when the Earth had been destroyed, and a large number of the stars had already been extinguished.

As we searched up and down time and space, discovering, more and more of the rare grains called planets, as we watched race after race struggle to a certain degree of lucid consciousness, only to succumb to some external accident or, more often, to some flaw in its own nature, we were increasingly oppressed by a sense of the futility, the planlessness of the cosmos. A few worlds did indeed wake to such lucidity that they passed beyond our ken. But several of the most brilliant of these occurred in the earliest epoch of the galactic story; and nothing that we could as yet discover in the later phases of the cosmos suggested that any galaxies, still less the cosmos as a whole, had at last come (or will at last come) more under the sway of the awakened spirit than they were during the epoch of those early brilliant worlds. Not till a much later stage of our inquiry were we fitted to discover the glorious but ironical and heart-rending climax for which this vast proliferation of worlds was but a prologue.

In the first phase of our adventure, when, as I have said, our powers of telepathic exploration were incomplete, every world that we entered turned out to be in the throes of the same spiritual crisis as that which we knew so well on our native planets. This crisis I came to regard as having two aspects. It was at once a moment in the spirit's struggle to become capable of true community on a world-wide scale; and it was a stage in the age-long task of achieving the right, the finally appropriate, the spiritual attitude towards the universe.

In every one of these "chrysalis" worlds thousands of millions of persons were flashing into existence, one after the other, to drift gropingly about for a few instants of cosmical time before they were extinguished. Most were capable, at least in some humble degree, of the intimate kind of community which is personal affection; but for nearly all of them a stranger was ever a thing to fear and hate. And even their intimate loving was inconstant and lacking in insight. Nearly always they were intent merely on seeking for themselves respite from fatigue or boredom, fear or hunger. Like my own race, they never fully awoke from the primeval sleep of the subman. Only a few here and there, now and then, were solaced, goaded, or tortured by moments of true wakefulness. Still fewer attained a clear and constant vision, even of some partial aspect of truth; and their half-truths they nearly always took to be absolute. Propagating their little partial truths, they bewildered and misdirected their fellow mortals as much as they helped them.

Each individual spirit, in nearly all these worlds, attained at some point in life some lowly climax of awareness and of spiritual integrity, only to sink slowly or catastrophically back into nothingness. Or so it seemed. As in my own world, so in all these others, lives were spent in pursuit of shadowy ends that remained ever just round the corner. There were vast tracts of boredom and frustration, with here and there some rare bright joy. There were ecstasies of personal triumph, of mutual intercourse and love, of intellectual insight, of aesthetic creation. There were also religious ecstasies; but these, like all else in these worlds, were obscured by false interpretations. There were crazy ecstasies of hate and cruelty, felt against individuals and against groups. Sometimes during this early phase of our adventure we were so distressed by the incredible bulk of suffering and of cruelty up and down the worlds that our courage failed, our telepathic powers were disordered, and we slipped towards madness.

Yet most of these worlds were really no worse than our own. Like us, they had reached that stage when the spirit, half awakened from brutishness and very far from maturity, can suffer most desperately and behave most cruelly. And like us, these tragic but vital worlds, visited in our early adventures, were agonized by the inability of their minds to keep pace with changing circumstance. They were always behindhand, always applying old concepts and old ideals inappropriately to novel situations. Like us, they were constantly tortured by their hunger for a degree of community which their condition demanded but their poor, cowardly, selfish spirits could by no means attain. Only in couples and in little circles of companions could they support true community, the communion of mutual insight and respect and love. But in their tribes and nations they conceived all too easily the sham community of the pack, baying in unison of fear and hate.

Particularly in one respect these races were recognizably our kin. Each had risen by a strange mixture of violence and gentleness. The apostles of violence and the apostles of gentleness swayed them this way and that. At the time of our visit many of these worlds were in the throes of a crisis of this conflict. In the recent past, loud lip-service had been paid to gentleness and tolerance and freedom; but the policy had failed, because there was no sincere purpose in it, no conviction of the spirit, no true experience of respect for individual personality. All kinds of self-seeking and vindictiveness had flourished, secretly at first, then openly as shameless individualism. Then at last, in rage, the peoples turned away from individualism and plunged into the cult of the herd. At the same time, in disgust with the failure of gentleness, they began openly to praise violence, and the ruthlessness of the god-sent hero and of the armed tribe. Those who thought they believed in gentleness built up armaments for their tribes against those foreign tribes whom they accused of believing in violence. The highly developed technique of violence threatened to destroy civilization; year by year gentleness lost ground. Few could understand that their world must be saved, not by violence in the short run, but by gentleness in the long run. A still fewer could see that, to be effective, gentleness must be a religion; and that lasting peace can never come till the many have wakened to the lucidity of consciousness which, in all these worlds, only the few could as yet attain.

If I were to describe in detail every world that we explored, this book would develop into a world of libraries. I can give only a few pages to the many types of worlds encountered in this early stage of our adventure, up and down the whole breadth and length and the whole duration of our galaxy. Some of these types had apparently very few instances; others occurred in scores or hundreds.

The most numerous of all classes of intelligent worlds is that which includes the planet familiar to readers of this book. *Homo Sapiens* has recently flattered and frightened himself by conceiving that, though perhaps he is not the sole intelligence in the cosmos, he is at least unique, and that worlds suited to intelligent life of any kind must be extremely rare. This view proves ludicrously false. In comparison with the unimaginable number of the stars intelligent worlds are indeed very rare; but we discovered some thousands of worlds much like the Earth and possessed by beings of essentially human kind, though superficially they were often unlike the type that we call human. The Other Men were among the most obviously human. But in a later stage of our adventure, when our research was no longer restricted to worlds that had reached the familiar spiritual crisis, we stumbled on a few planets inhabited by races almost identical with *Homo Sapiens*, or rather with the creature that *Homo Sapiens* was in the earliest phase of his existence. These most human worlds we had not encountered earlier because, by one accident or another, they were destroyed before reaching the stage of our own mentality.

Long after we had succeeded in extending our research from our peers among the worlds to our inferiors in mental rank we remained unable to make any sort of contact with beings who had passed wholly beyond the attainment of *Homo Sapiens*. Consequently, though we traced the history of many worlds through many epochs, and saw many reach a catastrophic end, or sink into stagnation and inevitable decline, there were a few with which, do what we would, we lost touch just at that moment when they seemed ripe for a leap forward into some more developed mentality. Not till a much later stage of our adventure, when our corporate being had itself been enriched by the influx of many superior spirits, were we able to pick up once more the threads of these most exhalted world-biographies. . . .

6. Intimations of the Star Maker

It must not be supposed that the normal fate of intelligent races in the galaxy is to triumph. So far I have spoken mainly of those fortunate Echinoderm and Nautiloid worlds which did at last pass triumphantly into the more awakened state, and I have scarcely even mentioned the hundreds, the thousands, of worlds which met disaster. This selection was inevitable because my space is limited, and because these two worlds, together with the even stranger spheres that I shall describe in the next chapter, were to have great influence on the fortunes of the whole galaxy. But many other worlds of "human" rank were quite as rich in history as those which I have noticed. Individual lives in them were no less varied than lives elsewhere, and no less crowded with distress and joy. Some triumphed; some in their last phase suffered a downfall, swift or slow, which lent them the splendor of tragedy. But since these worlds play no special part in the main story of the galaxy, they must be passed over in silence, along with the still greater host of worlds which never attained even to "human" rank. If I were to dwell upon their fortunes I should commit the same error as a historian who should try to describe every private life and neglect the pattern of the whole community.

I have already said that, as our experience of the destruction of worlds increased, we were increasingly dismayed by the wastefulness and seeming aimlessness of the universe. So many worlds, after so much distress, attained so nearly to social peace and joy, only to have the cup snatched from them for ever. Often disaster was brought by some trivial flaw of temperament or biological nature. Some races had not the intelligence, some lacked the social will, to cope with the problems of a unified world-community. Some were destroyed by an upstart bacterium before their medical science was mature. Others succumbed to climatic change, many to loss of atmosphere. Sometimes the end came through collision with dense clouds of dust or gas, or with swarms of giant meteors. Not a few worlds were destroyed by the downfall of a satellite. The lesser body, ploughing its way, age after age, through the extremely rarefied but omnipresent cloud of free atoms in interstellar space, would lose momentum. Its orbit would contract, at first slowly, then rapidly. It would set up prodigious tides in the oceans of the larger body, and drown much of its civilization. Later, through the increasing stress of the planet's attraction, the great moon would begin to disintegrate. First it would cast its ocean in a deluge on men's heads, then its mountains, and then the titanic and fiery fragments of its core. If in none of these manners came the end of the world, then inevitably, though perhaps not till the latter days of the galaxy, it must come in another way. The planet's own orbit, fatally contracting, must bring every world at last so close to its sun that conditions must pass beyond the limit of life's adaptability, and age by age all living things must be parched to death and roasted.

Dismay, terror, horror many a time seized us as we witnessed these huge disasters. An agony of pity for the last survivors of these worlds was part of our schooling.

The most developed of the slaughtered worlds did not need our pity, since their inhabitants seemed capable of meeting the end of all that they cherished with peace, even a strange unshakable joy which we in this early stage of our adventure could by no means comprehend. But only a few, very few, could reach this state. And only a few out of the great host of worlds could win through even to the social peace and fullness towards which all were groping. In the more lowly worlds, moreover, few were the individuals who won any satisfaction of life even within the narrow bounds of their own imperfect nature. No doubt one or two, here and there, in almost every world, found not merely happiness but the joy that passes all understanding. But to us, crushed now by the suffering and futility of a thousand races, it seemed that this joy itself, this ecstasy, whether it was supported by scattered individuals or by whole worlds, must after all be condemned as false, and that those who had found it must after all have been drugged by their own private and untypical well-being of spirit. For surely it had made them insensitive to the horror around them.

The sustaining motive of our pilgrimage had been the hunger which formerly drove men on Earth in search of God. Yes, we had one and all left our native planets in order to discover whether, regarding the cosmos as a whole, the spirit which we all in our hearts obscurely knew and haltingly prized, the spirit which on Earth we sometimes call humane, was Lord of the Universe, or outlaw; almighty, or crucified. And now it was becoming clear to us that if the cosmos had any lord at all, he was not that spirit but some other, whose purpose in creating the endless fountain of worlds was not fatherly towards the beings that he had made, but alien, inhuman, dark.

Yet while we felt dismay, we felt also increasingly the hunger to see and to face fearlessly whatever spirit was indeed the spirit of this cosmos. For as we pursued our pilgrimage, passing again and again from tragedy to farce, from farce to glory, from glory often to a final tragedy, we felt increasingly the sense that some terrible, some holy, yet at the same time unimaginably outrageous and lethal, secret lay just beyond our reach. Again and again we were torn between horror and fascination, between moral rage against the universe (or the Star Maker) and unreasonable worship.

This same conflict was to be observed in all those worlds that were of our own mental stature. Observing these worlds and the phases of their past growth, and groping as best we might towards the next plane of spiritual development, we came at last to see plainly the first stages of any world's pilgrimage. Even in the most primitive ages of every normal intelligent world there existed in some minds the impulse to seek and to praise some universal thing. At first this impulse was confused with the craving for protection by some mighty power. Inevitably the beings theorized that the admired thing must be Power, and that worship was mere propitiation. Thus they came to conceive the almighty tyrant of the universe, with themselves as his favored children. But in time it became clear to their prophets that mere Power was not what the praiseful heart adored. Then theory enthroned Wisdom, or Law, or Righteousness. And after an age of obedience to some phantom lawgiver, or to divine legality itself, the beings found that these concepts too were inadequate to describe the indescribable glory that the heart confronted in all things, and mutely prized in all things.

But now, in every world that we visited, alternative ways opened out before the worshippers. Some hoped to come face to face with their shrouded god solely by inward-searching meditation. By purging themselves of all lesser, all trivial desires, by striving to see everything dispassionately and with universal sympathy, they hoped to identify themselves with the spirit of the cosmos. Often they travelled far along the way of self-perfecting and awakening. But because of this inward absorption most of them became insensitive to the suffering of their less-awakened fellows and careless of the communal enterprise of their kind. In not a few worlds this way of the spirit was thronged by all the most vital minds. And because the best attention of the race was given wholly to the inner life, material and social advancement was checked. The sciences of physical nature and of life never developed. Mechanical power remained unknown, and medical and biological power also. Consequently these worlds stagnated, and sooner or later succumbed to accidents which might well have been prevented.

There was a second way of devotion, open to creatures of a more practical temperament. These, in all the worlds, gave delighted attention to the universe around them, and chiefly they found the worshipped thing in the persons of their fellow-beings, and in the communal bond of mutual insight and love between persons. In themselves and in each other they prized above all things love.

And their prophets told them that the thing which they had always adored, the universal spirit, the Creator, the Almighty, the All-wise, was also the All-loving. Let them therefore worship in practical love of one another, and in service of the Love-God. And so for an age, short or long, they strove feebly to love and to become members one of another. They spun theories in defense of the theory of the Love-God. They set up priest-hoods and temples in service of Love. And because they hungered for immortality they were told that to love was the way to attain eternal life. And so love, which seeks no reward, was misconceived.

In most worlds these practical minds dominated over the meditators. Sooner or later practical curiosity and economic need produced the material sciences. Probing every region with these sciences, the beings found nowhere, neither in the atom nor in the galaxy, nor for that matter in the heart of "man" either, any signature of the Love-God. And what with the fever of mechaniza-tion, and the exploitation of slaves by masters, and the passions of inter-tribal warfare, and the increasing neglect or coarsening of all the more awakened activities of the spirit, the little flame of praise in their hearts sank lower than it had ever been in any earlier age, so low that they could no longer recognize it. And the flame of love, long fanned by the forced draught of doctrine, but now suffocated by the general obtuseness of the beings to one another, was reduced to an occasional smoldering warmth, which was most often mistaken for mere lust. With bitter laughter and rage the tortured beings now dethroned the image of the Love-God in their hearts.

And so without love and without worship the unhappy beings faced the increasingly formidable problems of their mechanized and hate-racked world.

This was the crisis which we in our own worlds knew so well. Many a world up and down the galaxy never surmounted it. But in a few, some mir-acle, which we could not yet clearly envisage, raised the average minds of these worlds to a higher plane of mentality. Of this I shall speak later. Meanwhile I will say only that in the few worlds where this happened, we noticed invariably, before the minds of that world passed beyond our reach, a new feeling about the universe, a feeling which it was very difficult for us to share. Not till we had learned to conjure in ourselves something of this feeling could we follow the fortunes of these worlds.

But, as we advanced on our pilgrimage, our own desires began to change. We came to wonder whether, in demanding lordship of the universe for the divinely humane spirit that we prized most in ourselves and in our fellow-mortals in all the worlds, we were perhaps impious. We came less and less to require that Love should be enthroned behind the stars; more and more we desired merely to pass on, opening our hearts to accept fearlessly what-ever of the truth might fall within our comprehension.

There was a moment, late in this early phase of our pilgrimage, when, thinking and feeling in unison, we said to one another, "If the Star Maker is Love, we know that this must be right. But if he is not, if he is some other, some inhuman spirit, *this* must be right. And if he is nothing, if the stars and all else are not his creatures but self-subsistent, and if the adored spirit is but an exquisite creature of our minds, then *this* must be right, this and no other possibility. For we cannot know whether the highest place for love is on the throne or on the cross. We cannot know what spirit rules, for on the throne sits darkness. We know, we have seen, that in the waste of stars love is indeed crucified; and rightly, for its own proving, and for the throne's glory. Love and all that is humane we cherish in our hearts. Yet also we salute the throne and the darkness upon the throne. Whether it be Love or not Love, our hearts praise it, out-soaring reason."

But before our hearts could be properly attuned to this new, strange feeling, we had still far to go in the understanding of worlds of human rank, though diverse. I must now try to give some idea of several kinds of worlds very different from our own, but not in essentials more mature. . . .

[*The narrator and the minds he is linked with observe the gradual triumph of evolved consciousness across the universe, only to glimpse its imminent dissolution. At last they come to meet the force they call the Star Maker.*]

13. The Beginning and the End

. . .

3. *The Supreme Moment and After*

In the supreme moment of the cosmos I, as the cosmical mind, seemed to myself to be confronted with the source and the goal of all finite things.

I did not, of course, in that moment sensuously perceive the infinite spirit, the Star Maker. Sensuously I perceived nothing but what I had perceived before, the populous interiors of many dying stellar worlds. But through the medium which in this book is called telepathic I was now given a more inward perception. I felt the immediate presence of the Star Maker. Latterly, as I have said, I had already been powerfully seized by a sense of the veiled presence of some being other than myself, other than my cosmical body and conscious mind, other than my living members and the swarms of the burnt-out stars. But now the veil trembled and grew half-transparent to the mental vision. The source and goal of all, the Star Maker, was obscurely revealed to me as a being indeed other than my conscious self, objective to my vision, yet as in the depth of my own nature; as, indeed, myself, though infinitely more than myself.

It seemed to me that I now saw the Star Maker in two aspects: as the spirit's particular creative mode that had given rise to me, the cosmos; and also, most dreadfully, as something incomparably greater than creativity, namely as the eternally achieved perfection of the absolute spirit.

Barren, barren and trivial are these words. But not barren the experience.

Confronted with this infinity that lay deeper than my deepest roots and higher than my topmost reach, I, the cosmical mind, the flower of all the stars and worlds, was appalled, as any savage is appalled by the lightning and the thunder. And as I fell abject before the Star Maker, my mind was flooded with a spate of images. The fictitious deities of all races in all worlds once more crowded themselves upon me, symbols of majesty and tenderness, of ruthless power, of blind creativity, and of all-seeing wisdom. And though these images were but the fantasies of created minds, it seemed to me that one and all did indeed embody some true feature of the Star Maker's impact upon the creatures.

As I contemplated the host of deities that rose to me like a smoke cloud from the many worlds, a new image, a new symbol of the infinite spirit, took shape in my mind. Though born of my own cosmical imagination, it was begotten by a greater than I. To the human writer of this book little remains of that vision which so abashed and exalted me as the cosmical mind. But I must strive to recapture it in a feeble net of words as best I may.

It seemed to me that I had reached back through time to the moment of creation. I watched the birth of the cosmos.

The spirit brooded. Though infinite and eternal, it had limited itself with finite and temporal being, and it brooded on a past that pleased it not. It was dissatisfied with some past creation, hidden from me; and it was dissatisfied also with its own passing nature. Discontent goaded the spirit into fresh creation.

But now, according to the fantasy that my cosmical mind conceived, the absolute spirit, self-limited for creativity, objectified from itself an atom of its infinite potentiality.

This microcosm was pregnant with the germ of a proper time and space, and all the kinds of cosmical beings.

Within this punctual cosmos the myriad but not unnumbered physical centers of power, which men conceive vaguely as electrons, protons, and the rest, were at first coincident with one another. And they were dormant. The matter of ten million galaxies lay dormant in a point.

Then the Star Maker said, "Let there be light." And there was light.

From all the coincident and punctual centers of power, light leapt and blazed. The cosmos exploded, actualizing its potentiality of space and time. The centers of power, like fragments of a bursting bomb, were hurled apart. But each one retained in itself, as a memory and a longing, the single spirit of the whole; and each mirrored in itself aspects of all others throughout all the cosmical space and time.

No longer punctual, the cosmos was now a volume of inconceivably dense matter and inconceivably violent radiation, constantly expanding. And it was a sleeping and infinitely dissociated spirit.

But to say that the cosmos was expanding is equally to say that its members were contracting. The ultimate centers of power, each at first coincident with the punctual cosmos, themselves generated the cosmical space by their disengagement from each other. The expansion of the whole cosmos was but the shrinkage of all its physical units and of the wavelengths of its light.

Though the cosmos was ever of finite bulk, in relation to its minutiae of light-waves, it was boundless and center-less. As the surface of a swelling sphere lacks boundary and center, so the swelling volume of the cosmos was boundless and center-less. But as the spherical surface is centered on a point foreign to it, in a "third dimension," so the volume of the cosmos was centered in a point foreign to it, in a "fourth dimension."

The congested and exploding cloud of fire swelled till it was of a planet's size, a star's size, the size of a whole galaxy, and of ten million galaxies. And in swelling it became more tenuous, less brilliant, less turbulent.

Presently the cosmical cloud was disrupted by the stress of its expansion in conflict with the mutual clinging of its parts, disrupted into many million cloudlets, the swarm of the great nebulae.

For a while these were as close to one another in relation to their bulk as the flocculations of a mottled sky. But the channels between them widened, till they were separated as flowers on a bush, as bees in a flying swarm, as birds migrating, as ships on the sea. More and more rapidly they retreated from one another; and at the same time each cloud contracted, becoming first a ball of down and then a spinning lens and then a featured whirl of star-streams.

Still the cosmos expanded, till the galaxies that were most remote from one another were flying apart so swiftly that the creeping light of the cosmos could no longer bridge the gulf between them.

But I, with imaginative vision, retained sight of them all. It was as though some other, some hypercosmical and instantaneous light, issuing from nowhere in the cosmical space, illuminated all things inwardly.

Once more, but in a new and cold and penetrating light, I watched all the lives of stars and worlds, and of the galactic communities, and of myself, up to the moment wherein now I stood, confronted by the infinity that men call God, and conceived according to their human cravings.

I, too, now sought to capture the infinite spirit, the Star Maker, in an image spun by my own finite though cosmical nature. For now it seemed to me, it seemed, that I suddenly outgrew the three-dimensional vision proper to all creatures, and that I saw with physical sight the Star Maker. I saw, though nowhere in cosmical space, the blazing source of the hypercosmical light, as though it were an overwhelmingly brilliant point, a star, a sun more powerful than all suns together. It seemed to me that this effulgent star was the center of a four-dimensional sphere whose curved surface was the three-dimensional cosmos. The star of stars, this star that was indeed the Star Maker, was perceived by me, its cosmical creature, for one moment before its splendor seared my vision. And in that moment I knew that I had indeed seen the very source of all cosmical light and life and mind; and of how much else besides I had as yet no knowledge.

But this image, this symbol that my cosmical mind had conceived under the stress of inconceivable experience, broke and was transformed in the very act of my conceiving it, so inadequate was it to the actuality of the experience. Harking back in my blindness to the moment of my vision, I now conceived that the star which was the Star Maker, and the immanent center of all existence, had been perceived as looking down on me, this creature from the height of his infinitude; and that when I saw him I immediately spread the poor wings of my spirit to soar up to him, only to be blinded and seared and struck down. It had seemed to me in the moment of my vision that all the longing and hope of all finite spirits for union with the infinite spirit were strength to my wings. It seemed to me that the Star, my Maker, must surely stoop to meet me and raise me and enfold me in his radiance. For it seemed to me that I, the spirit of so many worlds, the flower of so many ages, was the Church Cosmical, fit at last to be the bride of God. But instead I was blinded and seared and struck down by terrible light.

It was not only physical effulgence that struck me down in that supreme moment of my life . . . that moment I guessed what mood it was of the infinite spirit that had in fact made the cosmos, and constantly supported it, watching its tortured growth. And it was that discovery which felled me.

For I had been confronted not by welcoming and kindly love, but by a very different spirit. And at once I knew that the Star Maker had made me not to be his bride, nor yet his treasured child, but for some other end.

It seemed to me that he gazed down on me from the height of his divinity with the aloof though passionate attention of an artist judging his finished work; calmly rejoicing in its achievement, but recognizing at last the irrevocable flaws in its initial conception, and already lusting for fresh creation.

His gaze anatomized me with calm skill, dismissing my imperfections, and absorbing for his own enrichment all the little excellence that I had won in the struggle of the ages.

In my agony I cried out against my ruthless maker. I cried out that, after all, the creature was nobler than the creator; for the creature loved and craved love, even from the star that was the Star Maker; but the creator, the Star Maker, neither loved nor had need of love.

But no sooner had I, in my blinded misery, cried out, than I was struck dumb with shame. For suddenly it was clear to me that virtue in the creator is not the same as virtue in the creature. For the creator, if he should love his creature, would be loving only a part of himself; but the creature, praising the creator, praises an infinity beyond himself. I saw that the virtue of the creature was to love and to worship, but the virtue of the creator was to create, and to be the infinite, the unrealizable and incomprehensible goal of worshipping creatures.

Once more, but in shame and adoration, I cried out to my maker. I said, "It is enough, and far more than enough, to be the creature of so dread and lovely a spirit, whose potency is infinite, whose nature passes the comprehension even of a minded cosmos. It is enough to have been created, to have embodied for a moment the infinite and tumultuously creative spirit. It is infinitely more than enough to have been used, to have been the rough sketch for some perfected creation."

And so there came upon me a strange peace and a strange joy.

Looking into the future, I saw without sorrow, rather with quiet interest, my own decline and fall. I saw the populations of the stellar worlds use up more and more of their resources for the maintenance of their frugal civilizations. So much of the interior matter of the stars did they disintegrate, that their worlds were in danger of collapse. Some worlds did indeed crash in fragments upon their hollow centers, destroying the indwelling peoples. Most, before the critical point was reached, were re-made, patiently taken to pieces and rebuilt upon a smaller scale. One by one, each star was turned into a world of merely planetary size. Some were no bigger than the moon. The populations themselves were reduced to a mere millionth of their original numbers, maintaining within each little hollow grain a mere skeleton civilization in conditions that became increasingly penurious.

Looking into the future aeons from the supreme moment of the cosmos, I saw the populations still with all their strength maintaining the essentials of their ancient culture, still living their personal lives in zest and endless novelty of action, still practicing telepathic intercourse between worlds, still telepathically sharing all that was of value in their respective world-spirits, still supporting a truly cosmical community with its single cosmical mind. I saw myself still preserving, though with increasing difficulty, my lucid consciousness; battling against the onset of drowsiness and senility, no longer in the hope of winning through to any more glorious state than that which I had already known, or of laying a less inadequate jewel of worship before the Star Maker, but simply out of sheer hunger for experience, and out of loyalty to the spirit.

But inevitably decay overtook me. World after world, battling with increasing economic difficulties, was forced to reduce its population below the numbers needed for the functioning of its own communal mentality. Then, like a degenerating brain-center, it could no longer fulfill its part in the cosmical experience.

Looking forward from my station in the supreme moment of the cosmos, I saw myself, the cosmical mind, sink steadily towards death. But in this my last aeon, when all my powers were waning, and the burden of my decaying body pressed heavily on my enfeebled courage, an obscure memory of past lucidity still consoled me. For confusedly I knew that even in this my last, most piteous age I was still under the zestful though remote gaze of the Star Maker. . . .

Lewis Padgett

Mimsy Were the Borogoves
(1943)

Science fiction is notable for a long history of collaborative work, whether through shared authorship, cowritten sequels, screenplay adaptations and film novelizations, or so-called shared world anthologies in which multiple authors write stories in the same setting, according to a consistent set of rules.

Although some of these collaborations have been no more than commercial exploitations of popular material, at their best they have been true meetings of the mind that generate a special energy. Few collaborations have been closer than that of the husband-and-wife team of Henry Kuttner (1915–1958) and C. L. Moore (1914–1987), who wrote both separately and collaboratively under a series of pseudonyms. While it is not always possible to separate their contributions, generally works signed by "Laurence O'Donnell" are primarily the work of Moore (see "Vintage Season" in Chapter 3), and those signed by "Lewis Padgett" (such as the story that follows) are more indebted to Kuttner.

Early in their careers, Kuttner and Moore were influenced by H. P. Lovecraft, whose highly descriptive and atmospheric stories combined science fiction elements with fantasy and horror. During the 1940s, however, Kuttner and Moore formed a close association with John W. Campbell Jr., the influential editor of *Astounding Science Fiction*, who insisted on a degree of scientific accuracy in all the stories he published. Campbell felt, however, that psychic powers were scientifically plausible, and many of his writers adopted his belief that such powers might be part of the natural process of human evolution, as the story that follows implies.

"Mimsy Were the Borogoves" was voted one of the top-ten best sf stories of all time by the Science Fiction Writers of America in 1968 — a sort of retrospective Nebula. This story combines the idea of a scientifically advanced race with the newly popular theories of psychological development. It also evinces a fascination with children as beings fundamentally different from adults, if only in the flexibility and adaptability of their minds. The story that results is both humorous (a hallmark of Kuttner's work) and frightening.

This story was the inspiration for the 2007 film *The Last Mimzy*.

There's no use trying to describe either Unthahorsten or his surroundings, because, for one thing, a good many million years had passed since 1942 Anno Domini, and, for another, Unthahorsten wasn't on Earth, technically speaking. He was doing the equivalent of standing in the equivalent of a laboratory. He was preparing to test his time machine.

Having turned on the power, Unthahorsten suddenly realized that the Box was empty. Which wouldn't do at all. The device needed a control, a three-dimensional solid which would react to the conditions of another age. Otherwise Unthahorsten couldn't tell, on the machine's return, where and when it had been. Whereas a solid in the Box would automatically be subject to the entropy and cosmic ray bombardment of the other era, and Unthahorsten could measure the changes, both qualitative and quantitative, when the machine returned. The Calculators could then get to work and, presently, tell Unthahorsten that the Box had briefly visited 1,000,000 A.D., 1,000 A.D., or 1 A.D., as the case might be.

Not that it mattered, except to Unthahorsten. But he was childish in many respects.

There was little time to waste. The Box was beginning to glow and shiver. Unthahorsten stared around wildly, fled into the next glossatch and groped in a storage bin there. He came up with an armful of peculiar-looking stuff. Uh-huh. Some of the discarded toys of his son Snowen, which the boy had brought with him when he had passed over from Earth, after mastering the necessary technique. Well, Snowen needed this junk no longer. He was conditioned, and had put away childish things. Besides, though Unthahorsten's wife kept the toys for sentimental reasons, the experiment was more important.

Unthahorsten left the glossatch and dumped the assortment into the Box, slamming the cover shut just before the warning signal flashed. The Box went away. The manner of its departure hurt Unthahorsten's eyes.

He waited.

And he waited.

Eventually he gave up and built another time machine, with identical results. Snowen hadn't been annoyed by the loss of his old toys, nor had Snowen's mother, so Unthahorsten cleaned out the bin and dumped the remainder of his son's childhood relics in the second time machine's Box.

According to his calculations, this one should have appeared on Earth, in the latter part of the nineteenth century, A.D. If that actually occurred, the device remained there.

Disgusted, Unthahorsten decided to make no more time machines. But the mischief had been done. There were two of them, and the first —

Scott Paradine found it while he was playing hooky from the Glendale Grammar School. There was a geography test that day, and Scott saw no sense in memorizing place names — which in 1942 was a fairly sensible theory. Besides, it was the sort of warm spring day, with a touch of coolness in the breeze, which invited a boy to lie down in a field and stare at the occasional clouds till he fell asleep. Nuts to geography! Scott dozed.

About noon he got hungry, so his stocky legs carried him to a nearby store. There he invested his small hoard with penurious care and a sublime disregard for his gastric juices. He went down by the creek to feed.

Having finished his supply of cheese, chocolate, and cookies, and having drained the soda-pop bottle to its dregs, Scott caught tadpoles and studied them with a certain amount of scientific curiosity. He did not persevere. Something tumbled down the bank and thudded into the muddy ground near the water, so Scott, with a wary glance around, hurried to investigate.

It was a box. It was, in fact, the Box. The gadgetry hitched to it meant little to Scott, though he wondered why it was so fused and burnt. He pondered. With his jackknife he pried and probed, his tongue sticking out from a corner of his mouth — Hm-m-m. Nobody was around. Where had the box come from? Somebody must have left it here, and sliding soil had dislodged it from its precarious perch.

"That's a helix," Scott decided, quite erroneously. It was helical, but it wasn't a helix, because of the dimensional warp involved. Had the thing been a model airplane, no matter how complicated, it would have held few mysteries to Scott. As it was, a problem was posed. Something told Scott that the device was a lot more complicated than the spring motor he had deftly dismantled last Friday.

But no boy has ever left a box unopened, unless forcibly dragged away. Scott probed deeper. The angles on this thing were funny. Short circuit, probably. That was why — *uh!* The knife slipped. Scott sucked his thumb and gave vent to experienced blasphemy.

Maybe it was a music box.

Scott shouldn't have felt depressed. The gadgetry would have given Einstein a headache and driven Steinmetz raving mad. The trouble was, of course, that the box had not yet completely entered the space-time continuum where Scott existed, and therefore it could not be opened. At any rate, not till Scott used a convenient rock to hammer the helical nonhelix into a more convenient position.

He hammered it, in fact, from its contact point with the fourth dimension, releasing the space-time torsion it had been maintaining. There was a brittle snap. The box jarred slightly, and lay motionless, no longer only partially in existence. Scott opened it easily now.

The soft, woven helmet was the first thing that caught his eye, but he discarded that without much interest. It was just a cap. Next he lifted a square, transparent crystal block, small enough to cup in his palm — much too small to contain the maze of apparatus within it. In a moment Scott had solved that problem. The crystal was a sort of magnifying glass, vastly enlarging the things inside the block. Strange things they were, too. Miniature people, for example —

They moved. Like clockwork automatons, though much more smoothly. It was rather like watching a play. Scott was interested in their costumes, but fascinated by their actions. The tiny people were deftly building a house. Scott wished it would catch fire, so he could see the people put it out.

Flames licked up from the half-completed structure. The automatons, with a great deal of odd apparatus, extinguished the blaze.

It didn't take Scott long to catch on. But he was a little worried. The manikins would obey his thoughts. By the time he discovered that, he was frightened, and threw the cube from him.

Halfway up the bank, he reconsidered and returned. The crystal block lay partly in the water, shining in the sun. It was a toy; Scott sensed that, with the unerring instinct of a child. But he didn't pick it up immediately. Instead, he returned to the box and investigated its remaining contents.

He found some really remarkable gadgets. The afternoon passed all too quickly. Scott finally put the toys back in the box and lugged it home, grunting and puffing. He was quite red-faced by the time he arrived at the kitchen door.

His find he hid at the back of a closet in his own room upstairs. The crystal cube he slipped into his pocket, which already bulged with string, a coil of wire, two pennies, a wad of tinfoil, a grimy defense stamp, and a chunk of feldspar. Emma, Scott's two-year-old sister, waddled unsteadily in from the hall and said hello.

"Hello, Slug," Scott nodded, from his altitude of seven years and some months. He patronized Emma shockingly, but she didn't know the difference. Small, plump, and wide-eyed, she flopped down on the carpet and stared dolefully at her shoes.

"Tie 'em, Scotty, please?"

"Sap," Scott told her kindly, but knotted the laces. "Dinner ready yet?" Emma nodded.

"Let's see your hands." For a wonder they were reasonably clean, though probably not aseptic. Scott regarded his own paws thoughtfully and, grimacing, went to the bathroom, where he made a sketchy toilet. The tadpoles had left traces.

Dennis Paradine and his wife Jane were having a cocktail before dinner, downstairs in the living room. He was a youngish, middle-aged man with gray-shot hair and a thinnish, prim-mouthed face; he taught philosophy at the university. Jane was small, neat, dark, and very pretty. She sipped her Martini and said:

"New shoes. Like 'em?"

"Here's to crime," Paradine muttered absently. "Huh? Shoes? Not now. Wait till I've finished this. I had a bad day."

"Exams?"

"Yeah. Flaming youth aspiring toward manhood. I hope they die. In considerable agony. *Insh' Allah!*"

"I want the olive," Jane requested.

"I know," Paradine said despondently. "It's been years since I've tasted one myself. In a Martini, I mean. Even if I put six of 'em in your glass, you're still not satisfied."

"I want yours. Blood brotherhood. Symbolism. That's why."

Paradine regarded his wife balefully and crossed his long legs. "You sound like one of my students."

"Like that hussy Betty Dawson, perhaps?" Jane unsheathed her nails. "Does she still leer at you in that offensive way?"

"She does. The child is a neat psychological problem. Luckily she isn't mine. If she were — " Paradine nodded significantly. "Sex consciousness and too many movies. I suppose she still thinks she can get a passing grade by showing me her knees. Which are, by the way, rather bony."

Jane adjusted her skirt with an air of complacent pride. Paradine uncoiled himself and poured fresh Martinis. "Candidly, I don't see the point of teaching those apes philosophy. They're all at the wrong age. Their habit-patterns, their methods of thinking, are already laid down. They're horribly conservative, not that they'd admit it. The only people who can understand philosophy are mature adults or kids like Emma and Scotty."

"Well, don't enroll Scotty in your course," Jane requested. "He isn't ready to be a *Philosophiae Doctor*. I hold no brief for child geniuses, especially when it's my son."

"Scotty would probably be better at it than Betty Dawson," Paradine grunted.

"'He died an enfeebled old dotard at five,'" Jane quoted dreamily. "I want your olive."

"Here. By the way, I like the shoes."

"Thank you. Here's Rosalie. Dinner?"

"It's all ready, Miz Pa'dine," said Rosalie, hovering. "I'll call Miss Emma 'n' Mista' Scotty."

"I'll get 'em." Paradine put his head into the next room and roared, "Kids! Come and get it!"

Small feet scuttered down the stairs. Scott dashed into view, scrubbed and shining, a rebellious cowlick aimed at the zenith. Emma pursued, levering herself carefully down the steps. Halfway she gave up the attempt to descend upright and reversed, finishing the task monkey-fashion, her small behind giving an impression of marvelous diligence upon the work in hand. Paradine watched, fascinated by the spectacle, till he was hurled back by the impact of his son's body.

"Hi, Dad!" Scott shrieked.

Paradine recovered himself and regarded Scott with dignity. "Hi, yourself. Help me in to dinner. You've dislocated at least one of my hip joints."

But Scott was already tearing into the next room, where he stepped on Jane's new shoes in an ecstasy of affection, burbled an apology, and rushed off to find his place at the dinner table. Paradine cocked up an eyebrow as he followed, Emma's pudgy hand desperately gripping his forefinger.

"Wonder what the young devil's been up to?"

"No good, probably," Jane sighed. "Hello, darling. Let's see your ears."

"They're *clean*. Mickey licked 'em."

"Well, that Airedale's tongue is far cleaner than your ears," Jane pondered, making a brief examination. "Still, as long as you can hear, the dirt's only superficial."

"Fisshul?"

"Just a little, that means." Jane dragged her daughter to the table and inserted her legs into a high chair. Only lately had Emma graduated to the dignity of dining with the rest of the family, and she was, as Paradine remarked, all eat up with pride by the prospect. Only babies spilled food, Emma had been told. As a result, she took such painstaking care in conveying her spoon to her mouth that Paradine got the jitters whenever he watched.

"A conveyer belt would be the thing for Emma," he suggested, pulling out a chair for Jane. "Small buckets of spinach arriving at her face at stated intervals."

Dinner proceeded uneventfully until Paradine happened to glance at Scott's plate. "Hello, there. Sick? Been stuffing yourself at lunch?"

Scott thoughtfully examined the food still left before him. "I've had all I need, dad," he explained.

"You usually eat all you can hold, and a great deal more," Paradine said. "I know growing boys need several tons of foodstuff a day, but you're below par tonight. Feel O.K.?"

"Uh-huh. Honest, I've had all I need."

"All you *want?*"

"Sure. I eat different."

"Something they taught you at school?" Jane inquired.

Scott shook his head solemnly.

"Nobody taught me. I found it out myself. I use spit."

"Try again," Paradine suggested. "It's the wrong word."

"Uh . . . s-saliva. Hm-m-m?"

"Uh-huh. More pepsin? Is there pepsin in the salivary juices, Jane? I forget."

"There's poison in mine," Jane remarked. "Rosalie's left lumps in the mashed potatoes again."

But Paradine was interested. "You mean you're getting everything possible out of your food — no wastage — and eating less?"

Scott thought that over. "I guess so. It's not just the sp . . . saliva. I sort of measure how much to put in my mouth at once, and what stuff to mix up. I dunno. I just do it."

"Hm-m-m," said Paradine, making a note to check up later. "Rather a revolutionary idea." Kids often get screwy notions, but this one might not be so far off the beam. He pursed his lips. "Eventually I suppose people will eat quite differently — I mean the *way* they eat, as well as what. What they eat, I mean. Jane, our son shows signs of becoming a genius."

"Oh?"

"It's a rather good point in dietetics he just made. Did you figure it out yourself, Scott?"

"Sure," the boy said, and really believed it.

"Where'd you get the idea?"

"Oh, I — " Scott wriggled. "I dunno. It doesn't mean much, I guess."

Paradine was unreasonably disappointed. "But surely — "

"S-s-s-spit!" Emma shrieked, overcome by a sudden fit of badness. "*Spit!*" She attempted to demonstrate, but succeeded only in dribbling into her bib.

With a resigned air Jane rescued and reproved her daughter, while Paradine eyed Scott with rather puzzled interest. But it was not till after dinner, in the living room, that anything further happened.

"Any homework?"

"N-no," Scott said, flushing guiltily. To cover his embarrassment he took from his pocket a gadget he had found in the box, and began to unfold it. The result resembled a tesseract, strung with beads. Paradine didn't see it at first, but Emma did. She wanted to play with it.

"No. Lay off, Slug," Scott ordered. "You can watch me." He fumbled with the beads, making soft, interested noises. Emma extended a fat forefinger and yelped.

"Scotty," Paradine said warningly.

"I didn't hurt her."

"Bit me. It did," Emma mourned.

Paradine looked up. He frowned, staring. What in —

"Is that an abacus?" he asked. "Let's see it, please."

Somewhat unwillingly Scott brought the gadget across to his father's chair. Paradine blinked. The "abacus," unfolded, was more than a foot square, composed of thin, rigid wires that interlocked here and there. On the wires the colored beads were strung. They could be slid back and forth, and from one support to another, even at the points of jointure. But — a pierced bead couldn't cross *interlocking* wires —

So, apparently, they weren't pierced. Paradine looked closer. Each small sphere had a deep groove running around it, so that it could be revolved and slid along the wire at the same time. Paradine tried to pull one free. It clung as though magnetically. Iron? It looked more like plastic.

The framework itself — Paradine wasn't a mathematician. But the angles formed by the wires were vaguely shocking, in their ridiculous lack of Euclidean logic. They were a maze. Perhaps that's what the gadget was — a puzzle.

"Where'd you get this?"

"Uncle Harry gave it to me," Scott said on the spur of the moment. "Last Sunday, when he came over." Uncle Harry was out of town, a circumstance Scott well knew. At the age of seven, a boy soon learns that the vagaries of adults follow a certain definite pattern, and that they are fussy about the donors of gifts. Moreover, Uncle Harry would not return for several weeks; the expiration of that period was unimaginable to Scott, or, at least, the fact that his lie would ultimately be discovered meant less to him than the advantages of being allowed to keep the toy.

Paradine found himself growing slightly confused as he attempted to manipulate the beads. The angles were vaguely illogical. It was like a puzzle. This red bead, if slid along *this* wire to *that* junction, should reach *there* — but it didn't. A maze, odd, but no doubt instructive. Paradine had a well-founded feeling that he'd have no patience with the thing himself.

Scott did, however, retiring to a corner and sliding beads around with much fumbling and grunting. The beads *did* sting, when Scott chose the wrong ones or tried to slide them in the wrong direction. At last he crowed exultantly.

"I did it, Dad!"

"Eh? What? Let's see." The device looked exactly the same to Paradine, but Scott pointed and beamed.

"I made it disappear."

"It's still there."

"That blue bead. It's gone now."

Paradine didn't believe that, so he merely snorted. Scott puzzled over the framework again. He experimented. This time there were no shocks, even slight. The abacus had showed him the correct method. Now it was up to him to do it on his own. The bizarre angles of the wires seemed a little less confusing now, somehow.

It was a most instructive toy —

It worked, Scott thought, rather like the crystal cube. Reminded of that gadget, he took it from his pocket and relinquished the abacus to

Emma, who was struck dumb with joy. She fell to work sliding the beads, this time without protesting against the shocks — which, indeed, were very minor — and, being imitative, she managed to make a bead disappear almost as quickly as had Scott. The blue bead reappeared — but Scott didn't notice. He had forethoughtfully retired into an angle of the chesterfield with an overstuffed chair and amused himself with the cube.

There were little people inside the thing, tiny manikins much enlarged by the magnifying properties of the crystal, and they moved, all right. They built a house. It caught fire, with realistic-seeming flames, and stood by waiting. Scott puffed urgently. "Put it *out!*"

But nothing happened. Where was that queer fire engine, with revolving arms, that had appeared before? Here it was. It came sailing into the picture and stopped. Scott urged it on.

This was fun. Like putting on a play, only more real. The little people did what Scott told them, inside of his head. If he made a mistake, they waited till he'd found the right way. They even posed new problems for him —

The cube, too, was a most instructive toy. It was teaching Scott, with alarming rapidity — and teaching him very entertainingly. But it gave him no really new knowledge as yet. He wasn't ready. Later — later —

Emma grew tired of the abacus and went in search of Scott. She couldn't find him, even in his room, but once there the contents of the closet intrigued her. She discovered the box. It contained a treasure-trove — a doll, which Scott had already noticed but discarded with a sneer. Squealing, Emma brought the doll downstairs, squatted in the middle of the floor, and began to take it apart.

"Darling! What's that?"

"Mr. Bear!"

Obviously it wasn't Mr. Bear, who was blind, earless, but comforting in his soft fatness. But all dolls were named Mr. Bear to Emma.

Jane Paradine hesitated. "Did you take that from some other little girl?"

"I didn't. She's mine."

Scott came out from his hiding place, thrusting the cube into his pocket. "Uh — that's from Uncle Harry."

"Did Uncle Harry give that to you, Emma?"

"He gave it to me for Emma," Scott put in hastily, adding another stone to his foundation of deceit. "Last Sunday."

"You'll break it, dear."

Emma brought the doll to her mother. "She comes apart. See?"

"Oh? It . . . *ugh!*" Jane sucked in her breath. Paradine looked up quickly. "What's up?"

She brought the doll over to him, hesitated, and then went into the dining room, giving Paradine a significant glance. He followed, closing the door. Jane had already placed the doll on the cleared table.

"This isn't very nice, is it, Denny?"

"Hm-m-m." It was rather unpleasant, at first glance. One might have expected an anatomical dummy in a medical school, but a child's doll —

The thing came apart in sections, skin, muscles, organs, miniature but quite perfect, as far as Paradine could see. He was interested. "Dunno. Such things haven't the same connotations to a kid — "

"Look at that liver. Is it a liver?"

"Sure. Say, I . . . this is funny."

"What?"

"It isn't anatomically perfect, after all." Paradine pulled up a chair. "The digestive tract's too short. No large intestine. No appendix, either."

"Should Emma have a thing like this?"

"I wouldn't mind having it myself," Paradine said. "Where on earth did Harry pick it up? No, I don't see any harm in it. Adults are conditioned to react unpleasantly to innards. Kids don't. They figure they're solid inside, like a potato. Emma can get a sound working knowledge of physiology from this doll."

"But what are those? Nerves?"

"No, these are the nerves. Arteries here; veins here. Funny sort of aorta — " Paradine looked baffled. "That . . . what's Latin for network? Anyway . . . huh? *Rita? Rata?*"

"*Rales,*" Jane suggested at random.

"That's a sort of breathing," Paradine said crushingly. "I can't figure out what this luminous network of stuff is. It goes all through the body, like nerves."

"Blood."

"Nope. Not circulatory, not neural — funny! It seems to be hooked up with the lungs."

They became engrossed, puzzling over the strange doll. It was made with remarkable perfection of detail, and that in itself was strange, in view of the physiological variation from the norm. "Wait'll I get that Gould," Paradine said, and presently was comparing the doll with anatomical charts. He learned little, except to increase his bafflement.

But it was more fun than a jigsaw puzzle.

Meanwhile, in the adjoining room, Emma was sliding the beads to and fro in the abacus. The motions didn't seem so strange now. Even when the beads vanished. She could almost follow that new direction — almost —

Scott panted, staring into the crystal cube and mentally directing, with many false starts, the building of a structure somewhat more complicated than the one which had been destroyed by fire. He, too, was learning — being conditioned —

Paradine's mistake, from a completely anthropomorphic standpoint, was that he didn't get rid of the toys instantly. He did not realize their significance, and, by the time he did, the progression of circumstances had got well under way. Uncle Harry remained out of town, so Paradine couldn't check with him. Too, the midterm exams were on, which meant arduous mental effort and complete exhaustion at night; and Jane was slightly ill for a week or so. Emma and Scott had free rein with the toys.

"What," Scott asked his father one evening, "is a wabe, Dad?"

"Wave?"

He hesitated. "I . . . don't *think* so. Isn't wabe right?"

"Wab is Scot for web. That it?"

"I don't see how," Scott muttered, and wandered off, scowling, to amuse himself with the abacus. He was able to handle it quite deftly now. But, with the instinct of children for avoiding interruptions, he and Emma usually played with the toys in private. Not obviously, of course — but the more intricate experiments were never performed under the eye of an adult.

Scott was learning fast. What he now saw in the crystal cube had little relationship to the original simple problems. But they were fascinatingly technical. Had Scott realized that his education was being guided and supervised — though merely mechanically — he would probably have lost interest. As it was, his initiative was never quashed.

Abacus, cube, doll — and other toys the children found in the box —

Neither Paradine nor Jane guessed how much of an effect the contents of the time machine were having on the kids. How could they? Youngsters are instinctive dramatists, for purposes of self-protection. They have not yet fitted themselves to the exigencies — to them partially inexplicable — of a mature world. Moreover, their lives are complicated by human variables. They are told by one person that playing in the mud is permissible, but that, in their excavations, they must not uproot flowers or small trees. Another adult vetoes mud *per se*. The Ten Commandments are not carved on stone; they vary, and children are helplessly dependent on the caprice of those who give them birth and feed and clothe them. And tyrannize. The young animal does not resent that benevolent tyranny, for it is an essential part of nature. He is, however, an individualist, and maintains his integrity by a subtle, passive fight.

Under the eyes of an adult he changes. Like an actor on-stage, when he remembers, he strives to please, and also to attract attention to himself. Such attempts are not unknown to maturity. But adults are less obvious — to other adults.

It is difficult to admit that children lack subtlety. Children are different from the mature animal because they think in another way. We can more or less easily pierce the pretenses they set up — but they can do the same to us. Ruthlessly a child can destroy the pretenses of an adult. Iconoclasm is their prerogative.

Foppishness, for example. The amenities of social intercourse, exaggerated not quite to absurdity. The gigolo —

"Such *savior faire*! Such punctilious courtesy!" The dowager and the blond young thing are often impressed. Men have less pleasant comments to make. But the child goes to the root of the matter.

"You're *silly*!"

How can an immature human understand the complicated system of social relationships? He can't. To him, an exaggeration of natural courtesy is silly. In his functional structure of life-patterns, it is rococo. He is an egotistic little animal, who cannot visualize himself in the position of another — certainly not an adult. A self-contained, almost perfect natural unit, his wants supplied by others, the child is much like a unicellular creature floating in the blood stream, nutriment carried to him, waste products carried away —

From the standpoint of logic, a child is rather horribly perfect. A baby may be even more perfect, but so alien to an adult that only superficial standards of comparison apply. The thought processes of an infant are completely unimaginable. But babies think, even before birth. In the womb they move and sleep, not entirely through instinct. We are conditioned to react rather peculiarly to the idea that a nearly-viable embryo may think. We are surprised, shocked into laughter, and repelled. Nothing human is alien.

But a baby is not human. An embryo is far less human.

That, perhaps, was why Emma learned more from the toys than did Scott. He could communicate his thoughts, of course; Emma could not, except in cryptic fragments. The matter of the scrawls, for example —

Give a young child pencil and paper, and he will draw something which looks different to him than to an adult. The absurd scribbles have little resemblance to a fire engine, but it *is* a fire engine, to a baby. Perhaps it is even three-dimensional. Babies think differently and see differently.

Paradine brooded over that, reading his paper one evening and watching Emma and Scott communicate. Scott was questioning his sister. Sometimes he did it in English. More often he had to resort to gibberish and sign language. Emma tried to reply, but the handicap was too great.

Finally Scott got pencil and paper. Emma liked that. Tongue in cheek, she laboriously wrote a message. Scott took the paper, examined it, and scowled.

"That isn't right, Emma," he said.

Emma nodded vigorously. She seized the pencil again and made more scrawls. Scott puzzled for a while, finally smiled rather hesitantly, and got up. He vanished into the hall. Emma returned to the abacus.

Paradine rose and glanced down at the paper, with some mad thought that Emma might abruptly have mastered calligraphy. But she hadn't. The paper was covered with meaningless scrawls, of a type familiar to any parents. Paradine pursed his lips.

It might be a graph showing the mental variations of a manic-depressive cockroach, but probably wasn't. Still, it no doubt had meaning to Emma. Perhaps the scribble represented Mr. Bear.

Scott returned, looking pleased. He met Emma's gaze and nodded. Paradine felt a twinge of curiosity.

"Secrets?"

"Nope. Emma . . . uh . . . asked me to do something for her."

"Oh." Paradine, recalling instances of babies who had babbled in unknown tongues and baffled linguists, made a note to pocket the paper when the kids had finished with it. The next day he showed the scrawl to Elkins at the university. Elkins had a sound working knowledge of many unlikely languages, but he chuckled over Emma's venture into literature.

"Here's a free translation, Dennis. Quote. I don't know what this means, but I kid the hell out of my father with it. Unquote."

The two men laughed and went off to their classes. But later Paradine was to remember the incident. Especially after he met Holloway. Before that, however, months were to pass, and the situation to develop even further toward its climax.

Perhaps Paradine and Jane had evinced too much interest in the toys. Emma and Scott took to keeping them hidden, playing with them only in private. They never did it overtly, but with a certain unobtrusive caution. Nevertheless, Jane especially was somewhat troubled.

She spoke to Paradine about it one evening. "That doll Harry gave Emma."

"Yeah?"

"I was downtown today and tried to find out where it came from. No soap."

"Maybe Harry bought it in New York."

Jane was unconvinced. "I asked them about the other things, too. They showed me their stock — Johnsons's a big store, you know. But there's nothing like Emma's abacus."

"Hm-m-m." Paradine wasn't much interested. They had tickets for a show that night, and it was getting late. So the subject was dropped for the nonce.

Later it cropped up again, when a neighbor telephoned Jane.

"Scotty's never been like that, Denny. Mrs. Burns said he frightened the devil out of her Francis."

"Francis? A little fat bully of a punk, isn't he? Like his father. I broke Burns's nose for him once, when we were sophomores."

"Stop boasting and listen," Jane said, mixing a highball. "Scott showed Francis something that scared him. Hadn't you better — "

"I suppose so." Paradine listened. Noises in the next room told him the whereabouts of his son. "Scotty!"

"Bang," Scott said, and appeared smiling. "I killed 'em all. Space pirates. You want me, Dad?"

"Yes. If you don't mind leaving the space pirates unburied for a few minutes. What did you do to Francis Burns?"

Scott's blue eyes reflected incredible candor. "Huh?"

"Try hard. You can remember, I'm sure."

"Uh. Oh, that. I didn't do nothing."

"Anything," Jane corrected absently.

"Anything. Honest. I just let him look into my television set, and it . . . it scared him."

"Television set?"

Scott produced the crystal cube. "It isn't really that. See?"

Paradine examined the gadget, startled by the magnification. All he could see, though, was a maze of meaningless colored designs.

"Uncle Harry — "

Paradine reached for the telephone. Scott gulped. "Is . . . is Uncle Harry back in town?"

"Yeah."

"Well, I gotta take a bath." Scott headed for the door. Paradine met Jane's gaze and nodded significantly.

Harry was home, but disclaimed all knowledge of the peculiar toys. Rather grimly, Paradine requested Scott to bring down from his room all of the playthings. Finally they lay in a row on the table, cube, abacus, doll, helmetlike cap, several other mysterious contraptions. Scott was cross-examined. He lied valiantly for a time, but broke down at last and bawled, hiccuping his confession.

"Get the box these things came in," Paradine ordered. "Then head for bed."

"Are you . . . *hup!* . . . gonna punish me, Daddy?"

"For playing hooky and lying, yes. You know the rules. No more shows for two weeks. No sodas for the same period."

Scott gulped. "You gonna keep my things?"

"I don't know yet."

"Well . . . g'night, Daddy. G'night, Mom."

After the small figure had gone upstairs, Paradine dragged a chair to the table and carefully scrutinized the box. He poked thoughtfully at the fused gadgetry. Jane watched.

"What is it, Denny?"

"Dunno. Who'd leave a box of toys down by the creek?"

"It might have fallen out of a car."

"Not at that point. The road doesn't hit the creek north of the railroad trestle. Empty lots — nothing else." Paradine lit a cigarette. "Drink, honey?"

"I'll fix it." Jane went to work, her eyes troubled. She brought Paradine a glass and stood behind him, ruffling his hair with her fingers. "Is anything wrong?"

"Of course not. Only — where did these toys come from?"

"Johnsons's didn't know, and they get their stock from New York."

"I've been checking up, too," Paradine admitted. "That doll" — he poked it — "rather worried me. Custom jobs, maybe, but I wish I knew who'd made 'em."

"A psychologist? The abacus — don't they give people tests with such things?"

Paradine snapped his fingers. "Right! And say! There's a guy going to speak at the university next week, fellow named Holloway, who's a child psychologist. He's a big shot, with quite a reputation. He might know something about it."

"Holloway? I don't — "

"Rex Holloway. He's . . . hm-m-m! He doesn't live far from here. Do you suppose he might have had these things made himself?"

Jane was examining the abacus. She grimaced and drew back. "If he did, I don't like him. But see if you can find out, Denny."

Paradine nodded. "I shall."

He drank his highball, frowning. He was vaguely worried. But he wasn't scared — yet.

Rex Holloway was a fat, shiny man, with a bald head and thick spectacles, above which his thick, black brows lay like bushy caterpillars. Paradine brought him home to dinner one night a week later. Holloway did not appear to watch the children, but nothing they did or said was lost on him. His gray eyes, shrewd and bright, missed little.

The toys fascinated him. In the living room the three adults gathered around the table, where the playthings had been placed. Holloway studied them carefully as he listened to what Jane and Paradine had to say. At last he broke his silence.

"I'm glad I came here tonight. But not completely. This is very disturbing, you know."

"Eh?" Paradine stared, and Jane's face showed her consternation. Holloway's next words did not calm them.

"We are dealing with madness."

He smiled at the shocked looks they gave him. "All children are mad, from an adult viewpoint. Ever read Hughes's 'High Wind in Jamaica'?"

"I've got it." Paradine secured the little book from its shelf. Holloway extended a hand, took it, and flipped the pages till he had found the place he wanted. He read aloud:

" 'Babies of course are not human — they are animals, and have a very ancient and ramified culture, as cats have, and fishes, and even snakes; the same in kind as these, but much more complicated and vivid, since babies are, after all, one of the most developed species of the lower vertebrates. In short, babies have minds which work in terms and categories of their own which cannot be translated into the terms and categories of the human mind.' "

Jane tried to take that calmly, but couldn't. "You don't mean that Emma — "

"Could you think like your daughter?" Holloway asked. "Listen: 'One can no more think like a baby than one can think like a bee.'"

Paradine mixed drinks. Over his shoulder he said, "You're theorizing quite a bit, aren't you? As I get it, you're implying that babies have a culture of their own, even a high standard of intelligence."

"Not necessarily. There's no yardstick, you see. All I say is that babies think in other ways than we do. Not necessarily *better* — that's a question of relative values. But with a different manner of extension — " He sought for words, grimacing.

"Fantasy," Paradine said, rather rudely, but annoyed because of Emma. "Babies don't have different senses from ours."

"Who said they did?" Holloway demanded. "They use their minds in a different way, that's all. But it's quite enough!"

"I'm trying to understand," Jane said slowly. "All I can think of is my Mixmaster. It can whip up batter and potatoes, but it can squeeze oranges too."

"Something like that. The brain's a colloid, a very complicated machine. We don't know much about its potentialities. We don't even know how much it can grasp. But it *is* known that the mind becomes conditioned as the human animal matures. It follows certain familiar theorems, and all thought thereafter is pretty well based on patterns taken for granted. Look at this." Holloway touched the abacus. "Have you experimented with it?"

"A little," Paradine said.

"But not much. Eh?"

"Well — "

"Why not?"

"It's pointless," Paradine complained. "Even a puzzle has to have some logic. But those crazy angles — "

"Your mind has been conditioned to Euclid," Holloway said. "So this — thing — bores us, and seems pointless. But a child knows nothing of Euclid. A different sort of geometry from ours wouldn't impress him as being illogical. He believes what he sees."

"Are you trying to tell me that this gadget's got a fourth-dimensional extension?" Paradine demanded.

"Not visually, anyway," Holloway denied. "All I say is that our minds, conditioned to Euclid, can see nothing in this but an illogical tangle of wires. But a child — especially a baby — might see more. Not at first. It'd be a puzzle, of course. Only a child wouldn't be handicapped by too many preconceived ideas."

"Hardening of the thought-arteries," Jane interjected.

Paradine was not convinced. "Then a baby could work calculus better than Einstein? No, I don't mean that. I can see your point, more or less clearly. Only — "

"Well, look. Let's suppose there are two kinds of geometry — we'll limit it, for the sake of the example. Our kind, Euclidean, and another, which we'll call x. X hasn't much relationship to Euclid. It's based on different theorems. Two and two needn't equal four in it; they could equal y_2, or they might not even *equal*. A baby's mind is not yet conditioned, except by certain questionable factors of heredity and environment. Start the infant on Euclid — "

"Poor kid," Jane said.

Holloway shot her a quick glance. "The basis of Euclid. Alphabet blocks. Math, geometry, algebra — they come much later. We're familiar with that development. On the other hand, start the baby with the basic principles of our x logic."

"Blocks? What kind?"

Holloway looked at the abacus. "It wouldn't make much sense to us. But we've been conditioned to Euclid."

Paradine poured himself a stiff shot of whiskey. "That's pretty awful. You're not limiting to math."

"Right! I'm not limiting it at all. How can I? I'm not conditioned to x logic."

"There's the answer," Jane said, with a sigh of relief. "Who is? It'd take such a person to make the sort of toys you apparently think these are."

Holloway nodded, his eyes, behind the thick lenses, blinking. "Such people may exist."

"Where?"

"They might prefer to keep hidden."

"Supermen?"

"I wish I knew. You see, Paradine, we've got yardstick trouble again. By our standards these people might seem super-doopers in certain respects. In others they might seem moronic. It's not a quantitative difference; it's qualitative. They *think* different. And I'm sure we can do things they can't."

"Maybe they wouldn't want to," Jane said.

Paradine tapped the fused gadgetry on the box. "What about this? It implies — "

"A purpose, sure."

"Transportation?"

"One thinks of that first. If so, the box might have come from anywhere."

"Where — things are — *different*?" Paradine asked slowly.

"Exactly. In space, or even time. I don't know; I'm a psychologist. Unfortunately I'm conditioned to Euclid, too."

"Funny place it must be," Jane said. "Denny, get rid of those toys."

"I intend to."

Holloway picked up the crystal cube. "Did you question the children much?"

Paradine said, "Yeah. Scott said there were people in that cube when he first looked. I asked him what was in it now."

"What did he say?" The psychologist's eyes widened.

"He said they were building a place. His exact words. I asked him who — people? But he couldn't explain."

"No, I suppose not," Holloway muttered. "It must be progressive. How long have the children had these toys?"

"About three months, I guess."

"Time enough. The perfect toy, you see, is both instructive and mechanical. It should do things, to interest a child, and it should teach, preferably unobtrusively. Simple problems at first. Later — "

"X logic," Jane said, white-faced.

Paradine cursed under his breath. "Emma and Scott are perfectly normal!"

"Do you know how their minds work — now?"

Holloway didn't pursue the thought. He fingered the doll. "It would be interesting to know the conditions of the place where these things came from. Induction doesn't help a great deal, though. Too many factors are missing. We can't visualize a world based on the x factor — environment adjusted to minds thinking in x patterns. This luminous network inside the doll. It could be anything. It could exist inside us, though we haven't discovered it yet. When we find the right stain — " He shrugged. "What do you make of this?"

It was a crimson globe, two inches in diameter, with a protruding knob upon its surface.

"What could anyone make of it?"

"Scott? Emma?"

"I hadn't even seen it till about three weeks ago. Then Emma started to play with it." Paradine nibbled his lip. "After that, Scott got interested."

"Just what do they do?"

"Hold it up in front of them and move it back and forth. No particular pattern of motion."

"No Euclidean pattern," Holloway corrected. "At first they couldn't understand the toy's purpose. They had to be educated up to it."

"That's horrible," Jane said.

"Not to them. Emma is probably quicker at understanding x than is Scott, for her mind isn't yet conditioned to this environment."

Paradine said, "But I can remember plenty of things I did as a child. Even as a baby."

"Well?"

"Was I — mad — then?"

"The things you don't remember are the criterion of your madness," Holloway retorted. "But I use the word 'madness' purely as a convenient symbol for the variation from the known human norm. The arbitrary standard of sanity."

Jane put down her glass. "You've said that induction was difficult, Mr. Holloway. But it seems to me you're making a great deal of it from very little. After all, these toys — "

"I *am* a psychologist, and I've specialized in children. I'm not a layman. These toys mean a great deal to me, chiefly because they mean so little."

"You might be wrong."

"Well, I rather hope I am. I'd like to examine the children."

Jane rose in arms. "How?"

After Holloway had explained, she nodded, though still a bit hesitantly. "Well, that's all right. But they're not guinea pigs."

The psychologist patted the air with a plump hand. "My dear girl! I'm not a Frankenstein. To me the individual is the prime factor — naturally, since I work with minds. If there's anything wrong with the youngsters, I want to cure them."

Paradine put down his cigarette and slowly watched blue smoke spiral up, wavering in an unfelt draft. "Can you give a prognosis?"

"I'll try. That's all I can say. If the undeveloped minds have been turned into the x channel, it's necessary to divert them back. I'm not saying that's the wisest thing to do, but it probably is from our standards. After all, Emma and Scott will have to live in this world."

"Yeah. Yeah. I can't believe there's much wrong. They seem about average, thoroughly normal."

"Superficially they may seem so. They've no reason for acting abnormally, have they? And how can you tell if they — think differently?"

"I'll call 'em," Paradine said.

"Make it informal, then. I don't want them to be on guard."

Jane nodded toward the toys. Holloway said, "Leave the stuff there, eh?"

But the psychologist, after Emma and Scott were summoned, made no immediate move at direct questioning. He managed to draw Scott unobtrusively into the conversation, dropping key words now and then. Nothing so obvious as a word-association test — co-operation is necessary for that.

The most interesting development occurred when Holloway took up the abacus. "Mind showing me how this works?"

Scott hesitated. "Yes, sir. Like this — " He slid a bead deftly through the maze, in a tangled course, so swiftly that no one was quite sure whether or not it ultimately vanished. It might have been merely legerdemain. Then, again —

Holloway tried. Scott watched, wrinkling his nose.

"That right?"

"Uh-huh. It's gotta go *there* — "

"Here? Why?"

"Well, that's the only way to make it work."

But Holloway was conditioned to Euclid. There was no apparent reason why the bead should slide from this particular wire to the other. It looked like a random factor. Also, Holloway suddenly noticed, this wasn't the path the bead had taken previously, when Scott had worked the puzzle. At least, as well as he could tell.

"Will you show me again?"

Scott did, and twice more, on request. Holloway blinked through his glasses. Random, yes. And a variable. Scott moved the bead along a different course each time.

Somehow, none of the adults could tell whether or not the bead vanished. If they had expected to see it disappear, their reactions might have been different.

In the end nothing was solved. Holloway, as he said good night, seemed ill at ease.

"May I come again?"

"I wish you would," Jane told him. "Any time. You still think — "

He nodded. "The children's minds are not reacting normally. They're not dull at all, but I've the most extraordinary impression that they arrive at conclusions in a way we don't understand. As though they used algebra while we used geometry. The same conclusion, but a different method of reaching it."

"What about the toys?" Paradine asked suddenly.

"Keep them out of the way. I'd like to borrow them, if I may — "

That night Paradine slept badly. Holloway's parallel had been ill-chosen. It led to disturbing theories. The x factor — The children were using the equivalent of algebraic reasoning, while adults used geometry.

Fair enough. Only —

Algebra can give you answers that geometry cannot, since there are certain terms and symbols which cannot be expressed geometrically. Suppose x logic showed conclusions inconceivable to an adult mind?

"Damn!" Paradine whispered. Jane stirred beside him.

"Dear? Can't you sleep either?"

"No." He got up and went into the next room. Emma slept peacefully as a cherub, her fat arm curled around Mr. Bear. Through the open doorway Paradine could see Scott's dark head motionless on the pillow.

Jane was beside him. He slipped his arm around her.

"Poor little people," she murmured. "And Holloway called them mad. I think we're the ones who are crazy, Dennis."

"Uh-huh. We've got jitters."

Scott stirred in his sleep. Without awakening, he called what was obviously a question, though it did not seem to be in any particular language. Emma gave a little mewling cry that changed pitch sharply.

She had not wakened. The children lay without stirring.

But Paradine thought, with a sudden sickness in his middle, it was exactly as though Scott had asked Emma something, and she had replied.

Had their minds changed so that even — sleep — was different to them?

He thrust the thought away. "You'll catch cold. Let's get back to bed. Want a drink?"

"I think I do," Jane said, watching Emma. Her hand reached out blindly toward the child; she drew it back. "Come on. We'll wake the kids."

They drank a little brandy together, but said nothing. Jane cried in her sleep, later.

Scott was not awake, but his mind worked in slow, careful building. Thus —

"They'll take the toys away. The fat man . . . listava dangerous maybe. But the Ghoric direction won't show . . . evankrus dun-hasn't-them. Intransdection . . . bright and shiny. Emma. She's more khopranik-high now than . . . I still don't see how to . . . thavarar lixery dist — "

A little of Scott's thoughts could still be understood. But Emma had become conditioned to x much faster.

She was thinking, too.

Not like an adult or a child. Not even like a human. Except, perhaps, a human of a type shockingly unfamiliar to genus *Homo*.

Sometimes Scott himself had difficulty in following her thoughts.

If it had not been for Holloway, life might have settled back into an almost normal routine. The toys were no longer active reminders. Emma still enjoyed her dolls and sand pile, with a thoroughly explicable delight. Scott was satisfied with baseball and his chemical set. They did everything other children did, and evinced few, if any, flashes of abnormality. But Holloway seemed to be an alarmist.

He was having the toys tested, with rather idiotic results. He drew endless charts and diagrams, corresponded with mathematicians, engineers, and other psychologists, and went quietly crazy trying to find rhyme or reason in the construction of the gadgets. The box itself, with its cryptic machinery, told nothing. Fusing had melted too much of the stuff into slag. But the toys —

It was the random element that baffled investigation. Even that was a matter of semantics. For Holloway was convinced that it wasn't really random. There just weren't enough known factors. No adult could work the abacus, for example. And Holloway thoughtfully refrained from letting a child play with the thing.

The crystal cube was similarly cryptic. It showed a mad pattern of colors, which sometimes moved. In this it resembled a kaleidoscope. But the shifting of balance and gravity didn't affect it. Again the random factor.

Or, rather, the unknown. The x pattern. Eventually Paradine and Jane slipped back into something like complacence, with a feeling that the children had been cured of their mental quirk, now that the contributing cause had been removed. Certain of the actions of Emma and Scott gave them every reason to quit worrying.

For the kids enjoyed swimming, hiking, movies, games, the normal functional toys of this particular time-sector. It was true that they failed to master certain rather puzzling mechanical devices which involved some calculation. A three-dimensional jigsaw globe Paradine had picked up, for example. But he found that difficult himself.

Once in a while there were lapses. Scott was hiking with his father one Saturday afternoon, and the two had paused at the summit of a hill. Beneath them a rather lovely valley was spread.

"Pretty, isn't it?" Paradine remarked.

Scott examined the scene gravely. "It's all wrong," he said.

"Eh?"

"I dunno."

"What's wrong about it?"

"Gee — " Scott lapsed into puzzled silence. "I dunno."

The children had missed their toys, but not for long. Emma recovered first, though Scott still moped. He held unintelligible conversations with his sister, and studied meaningless scrawls she drew on paper he supplied. It was almost as though he was consulting her, anent difficult problems beyond his grasp.

If Emma understood more, Scott had more real intelligence, and manipulatory skill as well. He built a gadget with his Meccano set, but was dissatisfied. The apparent cause of his dissatisfaction was exactly why Paradine was relieved when he viewed the structure. It was the sort of thing a normal boy would make, vaguely reminiscent of a cubistic ship.

It was a bit too normal to please Scott. He asked Emma more questions, though in private. She thought for a time, and then made more scrawls with an awkwardly clutched pencil.

"Can you read that stuff?" Jane asked her son one morning.

"Not read it, exactly. I can tell what she means. Not all the time, but mostly."

"Is it writing?"

"N-no. It doesn't mean what it *looks* like."

"Symbolism," Paradine suggested over his coffee.

Jane looked at him, her eyes widening. "Denny — "

He winked and shook his head. Later, when they were alone, he said, "Don't let Holloway upset you. I'm not implying that the kids are corresponding in an unknown tongue. If Emma draws a squiggle and says it's a flower, that's an arbitrary rule — Scott remembers that. Next time she draws the same sort of squiggle, or tries to — well!"

"Sure," Jane said doubtfully. "Have you noticed Scott's been doing a lot of reading lately?"

"I noticed. Nothing unusual, though. No Kant or Spinoza."

"He browses, that's all."

"Well, so did I, at his age," Paradine said, and went off to his morning classes. He lunched with Holloway, which was becoming a daily habit, and spoke of Emma's literary endeavors.

"Was I right about symbolism, Rex?"

The psychologist nodded. "Quite right. Our own language is nothing but arbitrary symbolism now. At least in its application. Look here." On his napkin he drew a very narrow ellipse. "What's that?"

"You mean what does it represent?"

"Yes. What does it suggest to you? It could be a crude representation of — what?"

"Plenty of things," Paradine said. "Rim of a glass. A fried egg. A loaf of French bread. A cigar."

Holloway added a little triangle to his drawing, apex joined to one end of the ellipse. He looked up at Paradine.

"A fish," the latter said instantly.

"Our familiar symbol for a fish. Even without fins, eyes or mouth, it's recognizable, because we've been conditioned to identify this particular shape with our mental picture of a fish. The basis of a rebus. A symbol, to us, means a lot more than what we actually see on paper. What's in your mind when you look at this sketch?"

"Why — a fish."

"Keep going. What do you visualize — everything!"

"Scales," Paradine said slowly, looking into space. "Water. Foam. A fish's eye. The fins. The colors."

"So the symbol represents a lot more than just the abstract idea *fish*. Note the connotation's that of a noun, not a verb. It's harder to express actions by symbolism, you know. Anyway — reverse the process. Suppose you want to make a symbol for some concrete noun, say *bird*. Draw it."

Paradine drew two connected arcs, concavities down.

"The lowest common denominator," Holloway nodded. "The natural tendency is to simplify. Especially when a child is seeing something for the first time and has few standards of comparison. He tries to identify the new thing with what's already familiar to him. Ever notice how a child draws the ocean?" He didn't wait for an answer; he went on.

"A series of jagged points. Like the oscillating line on a seismograph. When I first saw the Pacific, I was about three. I remember it pretty clearly. It looked — tilted. A flat plain, slanted at an angle. The waves were regular triangles, apex upward. Now I didn't *see* them stylized that way, but later, remembering, I had to find some familiar standard of comparison. Which is the only way of getting any conception of an entirely new thing. The average child tries to draw these regular triangles, but his co-ordination's poor. He gets a seismograph pattern."

"All of which means what?"

"A child sees the ocean. He stylizes it. He draws a certain definite pattern, symbolic, to him, of the sea. Emma's scrawls may be symbols, too. I don't mean that the world looks different to her — brighter, perhaps, and sharper, more vivid and with a slackening of perception above her eye level. What I do mean is that her thought-processes are different, that she translates what she sees into abnormal symbols."

"You still believe — "

"Yes, I do. Her mind has been conditioned unusually. It may be that she breaks down what she sees into simple, obvious patterns — and realizes a significance to those patterns that we can't understand. Like the abacus. She saw a pattern in that, though to us it was completely random."

Paradine abruptly decided to taper off these luncheon engagements with Holloway. The man was an alarmist. His theories were growing more fantastic than ever, and he dragged in anything, applicable or not, that would support them.

Rather sardonically he said, "Do you mean Emma's communicating with Scott in an unknown language?"

"In symbols for which she hasn't any words. I'm sure Scott understands a great deal of those — scrawls. To him, an isosceles triangle may represent any factor, though probably a concrete noun. Would a man who knew nothing of algebra understand what H_2O meant? Would he realize that the symbol could evoke a picture of the ocean?"

Paradine didn't answer. Instead, he mentioned to Holloway Scott's curious remark that the landscape, from the hill, had looked all wrong. A moment later, he was inclined to regret his impulse, for the psychologist was off again.

"Scott's thought-patterns are building up to a sum that doesn't equal this world. Perhaps he's subconsciously expecting to see the world where those toys came from."

Paradine stopped listening. Enough was enough. The kids were getting along all right, and the only remaining disturbing factor was Holloway himself. That night, however, Scott evinced an interest, later significant, in eels.

There was nothing apparently harmful in natural history. Paradine explained about eels.

"But where do they lay their eggs? Or do they?"

"That's still a mystery. Their spawning grounds are unknown. Maybe the Sargasso Sea, or the deeps, where the pressure can help them force the young out of their bodies."

"Funny," Scott said, thinking deeply.

"Salmon do the same thing, more or less. They go up rivers to spawn." Paradine went into detail. Scott was fascinated.

"But that's *right*, Dad. They're born in the river, and when they learn how to swim, they go down to the sea. And they come back to lay their eggs, huh?"

"Right."

"Only they wouldn't *come* back," Scott pondered. "They'd just send their eggs —"

"It'd take a very long ovipositor," Paradine said, and vouchsafed some well-chosen remarks upon oviparity.

His son wasn't entirely satisfied. Flowers, he contended, sent their seeds long distances.

"They don't guide them. Not many find fertile soil."

"Flowers haven't got brains, though. Dad, why do people live *here*?"

"Glendale?"

"No — here. This whole place. It isn't all there is, I bet."

"Do you mean the other planets?"

Scott was hesitant. "This is only — part — of the big place. It's like the river where the salmon go. Why don't people go on down to the ocean when they grow up?"

Paradine realized that Scott was speaking figuratively. He felt a brief chill. The — ocean?

The young of the species are not conditioned to live in the completer world of their parents. Having developed sufficiently, they enter that world. Later they breed. The fertilized eggs are buried in the sand, far up the river, where later they hatch.

And they learn. Instinct alone is fatally slow. Especially in the case of a specialized genus, unable to cope even with this world, unable to feed or drink or survive, unless someone has foresightedly provided for those needs.

The young, fed and tended, would survive. There would be incubators and robots. They would survive, but they would not know how to swim downstream, to the vaster world of the ocean.

So they must be taught. They must be trained and conditioned in many ways.

Painlessly, subtly, unobtrusively. Children love toys that do things — and if those toys teach at the same time —

In the latter half of the nineteenth century an Englishman sat on a grassy bank near a stream. A very small girl lay near him, staring up at the sky. She had discarded a curious toy with which she had been playing, and now was murmuring a wordless little song, to which the man listened with half an ear.

"What was that, my dear?" he asked at last.

"Just something I made up, Uncle Charles."

"Sing it again." He pulled out a notebook.

The girl obeyed.

"Does it mean anything?"

She nodded. "Oh, yes. Like the stories I tell you, you know."

"They're wonderful stories, dear."

"And you'll put them in a book some day?"

"Yes, but I must change them quite a lot, or no one would understand. But I don't think I'll change your little song."

"You mustn't. If you did, it wouldn't mean anything."

"I won't change that stanza, anyway," he promised. "Just what does it mean?"

"It's the way out, I think," the girl said doubtfully. "I'm not sure yet. My magic toys told me."

"I wish I knew what London shop sold those marvelous toys!"

"Mamma bought them for me. She's dead. Papa doesn't care."

She lied. She had found the toys in a box one day, as she played by the Thames. And they were indeed wonderful.

Her little song — Uncle Charles thought it didn't mean anything. (He wasn't her real uncle, she parenthesized. But he was nice.) The song meant a great deal. It was the way. Presently she would do what it said, and then —

But she was already too old. She never found the way.

Paradine had dropped Holloway. Jane had taken a dislike to him, naturally enough, since what she wanted most of all was to have her fears calmed. Since Scott and Emma acted normally now, Jane felt satisfied. It was partly wishful-thinking, to which Paradine could not entirely subscribe.

Scott kept bringing gadgets to Emma for her approval. Usually she'd shake her head. Sometimes she would look doubtful. Very occasionally she would signify agreement. Then there would be an hour of laborious, crazy scribbling on scraps of note paper, and Scott, after studying the notations, would arrange and rearrange his rocks, bits of machinery, candle ends, and assorted junk. Each day the maid cleaned them away, and each day Scott began again.

He condescended to explain a little to his puzzled father, who could see no rhyme or reason in the game.

"But why this pebble right here?"

"It's hard and round, Dad. It *belongs* there."

"So is this one hard and round."

"Well, that's got vaseline on it. When you get that far, you can't *see* just a hard round thing."

"What comes next? This candle?"

Scott looked disgusted. "That's toward the end. The iron ring's next."

It was, Paradine thought, like a Scout trail through the woods, markers in a labyrinth. But here again was the random factor. Logic halted — familiar logic — at Scott's motives in arranging the junk as he did.

Paradine went out. Over his shoulder he saw Scott pull a crumpled piece of paper and a pencil from his pocket, and head for Emma, who was squatted in a corner thinking things over.

Well —

Jane was lunching with Uncle Harry, and, on this hot Sunday afternoon there was little to do but read the papers. Paradine settled himself in the coolest place he could find, with a Collins, and lost himself in the comic strips.

An hour later a clatter of feet upstairs roused him from his doze. Scott's voice was crying exultantly, "This is it, Slug! Come on — "

Paradine stood up quickly, frowning. As he went into the hall the telephone began to ring. Jane had promised to call —

His hand was on the receiver when Emma's faint voice squealed with excitement. Paradine grimaced. What the devil was going on upstairs?

Scott shrieked, "Look out! This way!"

Paradine, his mouth working, his nerves ridiculously tense, forgot the phone and raced up the stairs. The door of Scott's room was open.

The children were vanishing.

They went in fragments, like thick smoke in a wind, or like movement in a distorting mirror. Hand in hand they went, in a direction Paradine could not understand, and as he blinked there on the threshold, they were gone.

"Emma!" he said, dry-throated. "*Scotty!*"

On the carpet lay a pattern of markers, pebbles, an iron ring — junk. A random pattern. A crumpled sheet of paper blew toward Paradine.

He picked it up automatically.

"Kids. Where are you? Don't hide — "*Emma! SCOTTY!*"

Downstairs the telephone stopped its shrill, monotonous ringing. Paradine looked at the paper he held.

It was a leaf torn from a book. There were interlineations and marginal notes, in Emma's meaningless scrawl. A stanza of verse had been so underlined and scribbled over that it was almost illegible, but Paradine was thoroughly familiar with "Through the Looking Glass." His memory gave him the words —

> 'Twas brillig, and the slithy toves
> Did gyre and gimbel in the wabe.
> All mimsy were the borogoves,
> And the mome raths outgrabe.

Idiotically he thought: Humpty Dumpty explained it. A wabe is the plot of grass around a sundial. A sundial. Time — It has something to do with time. A long time ago Scotty asked me what a wabe was. Symbolism.

'Twas brillig —

A perfect mathematical formula, giving all the conditions, in symbolism the children had finally understood. The junk on the floor. The toves had to be made slithy — vaseline? — and they had to be placed in a certain relationship, so that they'd gyre and gimbel.

Lunacy!

But it had not been lunacy to Emma and Scott. They thought differently. They used x logic. Those notes Emma had made on the page — she'd translated Carroll's words into symbols both she and Scott could understand.

The random factor had made sense to the children. They had fulfilled the conditions of the time-space equation. *And the mome raths outgrabe —*

Paradine made a rather ghastly little sound, deep in his throat. He looked at the crazy pattern on the carpet. If he could follow it, as the kids had done — But he couldn't. The pattern was senseless. The random factor defeated him. He was conditioned to Euclid.

Even if he went insane, he still couldn't do it. It would be the wrong kind of lunacy.

His mind had stopped working now. But in a moment the stasis of incredulous horror would pass — Paradine crumpled the page in his fingers. "Emma, Scotty," he called in a dead voice, as though he could expect no response.

Sunlight slanted through the open windows, brightening the golden pelt of Mr. Bear. Downstairs the ringing of the telephone began again.

Daniel Keyes

Flowers for Algernon

(1959)

Daniel Keyes (b. 1927) has an undergraduate degree in psychology, and he was for many years a public high school teacher in New York; the influence of this background is apparent in "Flowers for Algernon," his most famous story and one of the all-time classics of sf. The original novelette version (reprinted here) won a Hugo for short fiction, while the expanded, novel-length version was awarded a Nebula in 1966 and became the basis for the 1968 film *Charly*. The novel has never gone out of print. Keyes, currently a professor emeritus of English at Ohio University, has written several other novels and nonfiction books, but "Flowers for Algernon" remains his most famous work.

"Flowers for Algernon" is written as a series of diary entries in which Charlie Gordon describes his intellectual transformation as the result of a scientific experiment. The idea of a common man who gains extraordinary powers through the intervention of science is frequent in science fiction, as is that of an experiment that goes terribly wrong. In contrast to many such stories, which tend to be spectacular in terms of both powers and consequences, "Flowers for Algernon" is a quiet, rather private story whose realism makes it seem all too plausible. It is the distinctive voice of its hero, rather than an outrageous plot, that makes this a poignant and unforgettable story. "Flowers for Algernon" raises questions about the ethics of science as well as the nature of personhood and human value, but it provides no easy moral.

progris riport 1 — martch 5, 1965

Dr. Strauss says I shud rite down what I think and evrey thing that happins to me from now on. I dont know why but he says its importint so they will see if they will use me. I hope they use me. Miss Kinnian says maybe they can make me smart. I want to be smart. My name is Charlie Gordon. I am 37 years old and 2 weeks ago was my brithday. I have nuthing more to rite now so I will close for today.

progris riport 2 — martch 6

I had a test today. I think I faled it. and I think that maybe now they wont use me. What happind is a nice young man was in the room and he had some white cards with ink spillled all over them. He sed Charlie what do you see on this card. I was very skared even tho I had my rabits foot in my pockit because when I was a kid I always faled tests in school and I spillled ink to.

I told him I saw a inkblot. He said yes and it made me feel good. I thot that was all but when I got up to go he stopped me. He said now sit down Charlie we are not thru yet. Then I don't remember so good but he wantid me to say what was in the ink. I dint see nuthing in the ink but he said there was picturs there other pepul saw some picturs. I coudn't see any picturs. I reely tryed to see. I held the card close up and then far away. Then I said if I had my glases I coud see better I usally only ware my glases in the movies or TV but I said they are in the closit in the hall. I got them. Then I said let me see that card agen. I bet Ill find it now.

I tryed hard but I still coudnt find the pictures I only saw the ink. I told him maybe I need new glases. He rote somthing down on a paper and I got skared of faling the test. I told him it was a very nice inkblot with little points all around the edges. He looked very sad so that wasnt it. I said please let me try agen. Ill get it in a few minits becaus Im not so fast som-times. Im a slow reeder too in Miss Kinnians class for slow adults but Im trying very hard.

He gave me a chance with another card that had 2 kinds of ink spilled on it red and blue.

He was very nice and talked slow like Miss Kinnian dues and he explaned it to me that it was a *raw shok*. He said pepul see things in the ink. I said show me where. He said think. I told him I think a inkblot but that wasnt rite eather. He said what does it remind you — pretend some-thing. I closd my eyes for a long time to pretend. I told him I pretned a fowntan pen with ink leeking all over a table cloth. Then he got up and went out.

I dont think I passd the *raw shok* test.

progris report 3 — martch 7

Dr Strauss and Dr Nemur say it dont matter about the inkblots. I told them I dint spill the ink on the cards and I coudnt see anything in the ink. They said that maybe they will still use me. I said Miss Kinnian never gave me tests like that one only spelling and reading. They said Miss Kinnian told that I was her bestist pupil in the adult nite scool becaus I tryed the hardist and I reely wantid to lern. They said how come you went to the adult nite scool all by yourself Charlie. How did you find it. I said I askd pepul and sumbody told me where I shud go to lern to read and spell good. They said why did you want to. I told them becaus all my life I wantid to be smart and not dumb. But its very hard to be smart. They said you know it will probly be tempirery. I said yes. Miss Kinnian told me. I dont care if it herts.

Later I had more crazy tests today. The nice lady who gave it me told me the name and I asked her how do you spellit so I can rite it in my progris riport. THEMATIC APPERCEPTION TEST. I dont know the frist 2 words but I know what *test* means. You got to pass it or you get bad marks. This test lookd easy becaus I coud see the picturs. Only this time she dint want me to tell her the picturs. That mixd me up. I said the man yesterday said I shoud tell him what I saw in the ink she said that dont make no difrence. She said make up storys about the pepul in the picturs.

I told her how can you tell storys about pepul you never met. I said why shud I make up lies. I never tell lies any more becaus I always get caut.

She told me this test and the other one the raw-shok was for getting personalty. I laffed so hard. I said how can you get that thing from inkblots and fotos. She got sore and put her picturs away. I dont care. It was sily. I gess I faled that test too.

Later some men in white coats took me to a difernt part of the hospitil and gave me a game to play. It was like a race with a white mouse. They called the mouse Algernon. Algernon was in a box with a lot of twists and turns like all kinds of walls and they gave me a pencil and a paper with lines and lots of boxes. On one side it said START and on the other end it said FINISH. They said it was *amazed* and that Algernon and me had the same *amazed* to do. I dint see how we could have the same *amazed* if Algernon had a box and I had a paper but I dint say nothing. Anyway there wasnt time because the race started.

One of the men had a watch he was trying to hide so I woudnt see it so I tryed not to look and that made me nervus.

Anyway that test made me feel worser than all the others because they did it over 10 times with difernt *amazeds* and Algernon won every time. I dint know that mice were so smart. Maybe thats because Algernon is a white mouse. Maybe white mice are smarter then other mice.

progris riport 4 — Mar 8

Their going to use me! Im so exited I can hardly write. Dr Nemur and Dr Strauss had a argament about it first. Dr Nemur was in the office when Dr Strauss brot me in. Dr Nemur was worryed about using me but Dr Strauss told him Miss Kinnian rekemmended me the best from all the people who was teaching. I like Miss Kinnian becaus shes a very smart teacher. And she said Charlie your going to have a second chance. If you volenteer for this experament you mite get smart. They dont know if it will be perminint but theirs a chance. Thats why I said ok even when I was scared because she said it was an operashun. She said dont be scared Charlie you done so much with so little I think you deserv it most of all.

So I got scaird when Dr Nemur and Dr Strauss argud about it. Dr Strauss said I had something that was very good. He said I had a good *motor-vation*. I never even knew I had that. I felt proud when he said that not every body with an eye-q of 68 had that thing. I dont know what it is or where I got it but he said Algernon had it too. Algernons *motor-vation* is the cheese they put in his box. But it cant be that because I didnt eat any cheese this week.

Then he told Dr Nemur something I dint understand so while they were talking I wrote down some of the words.

He said Dr Nemur I know Charlie is not what you had in mind as the first of your new brede of intelek** (coudnt get the word) superman. But most people of his low ment** are host** and uncoop** they are usualy dull apath** and hard to reach. He has a good natcher hes intristed and eager to please.

Dr Nemur said remember he will be the first human beeng ever to have his intelijence trippled by surgicle meens.

Dr Strauss said exakly. Look at how well hes lerned to read and write for his low mentel age its as grate an acheve** as you and I lerning einstines therey of **vity without help. That shows the intenss motor-vation. Its comparat** a tremen** achev** I say we use Charlie.

I dint get all the words and they were talking to fast but it sounded like Dr Strauss was on my side and like the other one wasnt.

Then Dr Nemur nodded he said all right maybe your right. We will use Charlie. When he said that I got so exited I jumped up and shook his hand for being so good to me. I told him thank you doc you wont be sorry for giving me a second chance. And I mean it like I told him. After the operashun Im gonna try to be smart. Im gonna try awful hard.

progris ript 5 — Mar 10

Im skared. Lots of people who work here and the nurses and the people who gave me the tests came to bring me candy and wish me luck. I hope I have luck. I got my rabits foot and my lucky penny and my horse shoe. Only a black cat crossed me when I was comming to the hospitil. Dr Strauss says dont be supersitis Charlie this is sience. Anyway Im keeping my rabits foot with me.

I asked Dr Strauss if Ill beat Algernon in the race after the operashun and he said maybe. If the operashun works Ill show that mouse I can be as smart as he is. Maybe smarter. Then Ill be abel to read better and spell the words good and know lots of things and be like other people. I want to be smart like other people. If it works perminint they will make everybody smart all over the wurld.

They dint give me anything to eat this morning. I dont know what that eating has to do with getting smart. Im very hungry and Dr Nemur took away my box of candy. That Dr Nemur is a grouch. Dr Strauss says I can have it back after the operashun. You cant eat befor a operashun. . . .

Progress Report 6 — Mar 15

The operashun dint hurt. He did it while I was sleeping. They took off the bandijis from my eyes and my head today so I can make a PROGRESS REPORT. Dr Nemur who looked at some of my other ones sayd I spell PROGRESS wrong and he told me how to spell it and REPORT too. I got to try and remember that.

I have a very bad memary for spelling. Dr Strauss says its ok to tell about all the things that happin to me but he says I shoud tell more about what I feel and what I think. When I told him I dont know how to think he said try. All the time when the bandijis were on my eyes I tryed to think. Nothing happened. I dont know what to think about. Maybe if I ask him he will tell me how I can think now that Im suppose to get smart. What do smart people think about. Fancy things I suppose. I wish I knew some fancy things alredy.

Progress Report 7 — mar 19

Nothing is happining. I had lots of tests and different kinds of races with Algernon. I hate that mouse. He always beats me. Dr Strauss said I got to play those games. And he said some time I got to take those tests over again. Thse inkblots are stupid. And those pictures are stupid too. I like to draw a picture of a man and a woman but I wont make up lies about people.

I got a headache from trying to think so much. I thot Dr Strauss was my frend but he dont help me. He dont tell me what to think or when Ill get smart. Miss Kinnian dint come to see me. I think writing these progress reports are stupid too.

Progress Report 8 — Mar 23

Im going back to work at the factery. They said it was better I shud go back to work but I cant tell anyone what the operashun was for and I have to come to the hospitil for an hour evry night after work. They are gonna pay me mony every month for lerning to be smart.

Im glad Im going back to work because I miss my job and all my frends and all the fun we have there.

Dr Strauss says I shud keep writing things down but I dont have to do it every day just when I think of something or something speshul happins. He says dont get discoridged because it takes time and it happins slow. He says it took a long time with Algernon before he got 3 times smarter then he was before. Thats why Algernon beats me all the time because he had that operashun too. That makes me feel better. I coud probly do that *amazed* faster than a reglar mouse. Maybe some day Ill beat Algernon. Boy that would be something. So far Algernon looks like he mite be smart perminent.

Mar 25 (I dont have to write PROGRESS REPORT on top any more just when I hand it in once a week for Dr Nemur to read. I just have to put the date on. That saves time)

We had a lot of fun at the factery today. Joe Carp said hey look where Charlie had his operashun what did they do Charlie put some brains in. I was going to tell him but I remembered Dr Strauss said no. Then Frank Reilly said what did you do Charlie forget your key and open your door the hard way. That made me laff. Their really my friends and they like me.

Sometimes somebody will say hey look at Joe or Frank or George he really pulled a Charlie Gordon. I dont know why they say that but they always laff. This morning Amos Borg who is the 4 man at Donnegans used my name when he shouted at Ernie the office boy. Ernie lost a packige. He said Ernie for godsake what are you trying to be a Charlie Gordon. I dont understand why he said that. I never lost any packiges.

Mar 28 Dr Strauss came to my room tonight to see why I dint come in like I was suppose to. I told him I dont like to race with Algernon any more. He said I dont have to for a while but I shud come in. He had a present for me only it wasnt a present but just for lend. I thot it was a little television but it wasnt. He said I got to turn it on when I go to sleep. I said your kidding why shud I turn it on when Im going to sleep. Who ever herd of a thing like that. But he said if I want to get smart I got to do what he says. I told him I dont think I was going to get smart and he put his hand on my sholder and said Charlie you dont know it yet but your getting smarter all the time. You wont notice for a while. I think he was just being nice to make me feel good because I dont look any smarter.

Oh yes I almost forgot. I asked him when I can go back to the class at Miss Kinnians school. He said I wont go their. He said that soon Miss Kinnian will come to the hospitil to start and teach me speshul. I was mad at her for not comming to see me when I got the operashun but I like her so maybe we will be frends again.

Mar 29 That crazy TV kept me up all night. How can I sleep with something yelling crazy things all night in my ears. And the nutty pictures. Wow. I dont know what it says when Im up so how am I going to know when Im sleeping.

Dr Strauss says its ok. He says my brains are lerning when I sleep and that will help me when Miss Kinnian starts my lessons in the hospitl (only I found out it isnt a hospitil its a labatory). I think its all crazy. If you can get smart when your sleeping why do people go to school. That thing I dont think will work. I use to watch the late show and the late late show on TV all the time and it never made me smart. Maybe you have to sleep while you watch it.

PROGRESS REPORT 9 — April 3

Dr Strauss showed me how to keep the TV turned low so now I can sleep. I dont hear a thing. And I still dont understand what it says. A few times I play it over in the morning to find out what I lerned when I was sleeping and I dont think so. Miss Kinnian says Maybe its another langwidge or something. But most times it sounds american. It talks so fast faster then even Miss Gold who was my teacher in 6 grade and I remember she talked so fast I coudnt understand her.

I told Dr Strauss what good is it to get smart in my sleep. I want to be smart when Im awake. He says its the same thing and I have two minds. Theres the *subconscious* and the *conscious* (that's how you spell it). And one dont tell the other one what its doing. They dont even talk to each other. Thats why I dream. And boy have I been having crazy dreams. Wow. Ever since that night TV. The late late late late late show.

I forgot to ask him if it was only me or if everybody had those two minds.

(I just looked up the word in the dictionary Dr Strauss gave me. The word is *subconscious. adj. Of the nature of mental operations yet not present in consciousness; as, subconscious conflict of desires.*) Theres more but I still don't know what it means. This isnt a very good dictionary for dumb people like me.

Anyway the headache is from the party. My frends from the factery Joe Carp and Frank Reilly invited me to go with them to Muggsys Saloon for some drinks. I dont like to drink but they said we will have lots of fun. I had a good time.

Joe Carp said I shoud show the girls how I mop out the toilet in the factery and he got me a mop. I showed them and everyone laffed when I told that Mr Donnegan said I was the best janiter he ever had because I like my job and do it good and never come late or miss a day except for my operashun.

I said Miss Kinnian always said Charlie be proud of your job because you do it good.

Everybody laffed and we had a good time and they gave me lots of drinks and Joe said Charlie is a card when hes potted. I dont know what that means but everybody likes me and we have fun. I cant wait to be smart like my best frends Joe Carp and Frank Reilly.

I dont remember how the party was over but I think I went out to buy a newspaper and coffe for Joe and Frank and when I came back there was no one their. I looked for them all over till late. Then I dont remember so good but I think I got sleepy or sick. A nice cop brot me back home. Thats what my landlady Mrs Flynn says.

But I got a headache and a big lump on my head and black and blue all over. I think maybe I fell but Joe Carp says it was the cop they beat up drunks some times. I don't think so. Miss Kinnian says cops are to help people. Anyway I got a bad headache and Im sick and hurt all over. I dont think Ill drink anymore.

April 6 I beat Algernon! I dint even know I beat him until Burt the tester told me. Then the second time I lost because I got so exited I fell off the chair before I finished. But after that I beat him 8 more times. I must be getting smart to beat a smart mouse like Algernon. But I dont *feel* smarter.

I wanted to race Algernon some more but Burt said thats enough for one day. They let me hold him for a minit. Hes not so bad. Hes soft like a ball of cotton. He blinks and when he opens his eyes their black and pink on the eges.

I said can I feed him because I felt bad to beat him and I wanted to be nice and make frends. Burt said no Algernon is a very specshul mouse with an operashun like mine, and he was the first of all the animals to stay smart so long. He told me Algernon is so smart that every day he has to solve a test to get his food. Its a thing like a lock on a door that changes every time Algernon goes in to eat so he has to lern something new to get his food. That made me sad because if he coudnt lern he would be hungry.

I dont think its right to make you pass a test to eat. How woud Dr Nemur like it to have to pass a test every time he wants to eat. I think Ill be frends with Algernon.

April 9 Tonight after work Miss Kinnian was at the laboratory. She looked like she was glad to see me but scared. I told her dont worry Miss Kinnian Im not smart yet and she laffed. She said I have confidence in you Charlie the way you struggled so hard to read and right better than all the others. At werst you will have it for a littel wile and your doing somthing for sience.

We are reading a very hard book. I never read such a hard book before. Its called *Robinson Crusoe* about a man who gets merooned on a dessert Iland. Hes smart and figers out all kinds of things so he can have a house and food and hes a good swimmer. Only I feel sorry because hes all alone and has no frends. But I think their must be somebody else on the iland because theres a picture with his funny umbrella looking at footprints. I hope he gets a frend and not be lonly.

April 10 Miss Kinnian teaches me to spell better. She says look at a word and close your eyes and say it over and over until you remember. I have lots of truble with *through* that you say *threw* and *enough* and *tough* that you dont say *new* and *tew*. You got to say *enuff* and *tuff*. Thats how I use to write it before I started to get smart. Im confused but Miss Kinnian says theres no reason in spelling.

Apr 14 Finished *Robinson Crusoe.* I want to find out more about what happens to him but Miss Kinnian says thats all there is. *Why*

April 15 Miss Kinnian says Im lerning fast. She read some of the Progress Reports and she looked at me kind of funny. She says Im a fine person and

Ill show them all. I asked her why. She said never mind but I shoudnt feel bad if I find out that everybody isnt nice like I think. She said for a person who god gave so little to you done more then a lot of people with brains they never even used. I said all my frends are smart people but there good. They like me and they never did anything that wasnt nice. Then she got something in her eye and she had to run out to the ladys room.

Apr 16 Today, I lerned, the *comma*, this is a comma (,) a period, with a tail, Miss Kinnian, says its importent, because, it makes writing, better, she said, somebody, coud lose, a lot of money, if a comma, isnt, in the, right place, I dont have, any money, and I dont see, how a comma keeps you, from losing it,

But she says, everybody, uses commas, so Ill use, them too,

Apr 17 I used the comma wrong. Its punctuation. Miss Kinnian told me to look up long words in the dictionary to lern to spell them. I said whats the difference if you can read it anyway. She said its part of your education so now on Ill look up all the words Im not sure how to spell. It takes a long time to write that way but I think Im remembering. I only have to look up once and after that I get it right. Anyway thats how come I got the word *punctuation* right. (Its that way in the dictionary). Miss Kinnian says a period is punctuation too, and there are lots of other marks to lern. I told her I thot all the periods had to have tails but she said no.

You got to mix them up, she showed? me" how. to mix! them (up,. and now; I can! mix up all kinds" of punctuation, in! my writing? There, are lots! of rules? to lern; but I'm gettin'g them in my head.

One thing I? like about, Dear Miss Kinnian: (thats the way it goes in a business letter if I ever go into business) is she, always gives me' a reason" when — I ask. She's a gen'ius! I wish! I cou'd be smart" like, her;

(Punctuation, is; fun!)

April 18 What a dope I am! I didn't even understand what she was talking about. I read the grammar book last night and it explanes the whole thing. Then I saw it was the same way as Miss Kinnian was trying to tell me, but I didn't get it. I got up in the middle of the night, and the whole thing straightened out in my mind.

Miss Kinnian said that the TV working in my sleep helped out. She said I reached a plateau. Thats like the flat top of a hill.

After I figgered out how punctuation worked, I read over all my old Progress Reports from the beginning. Boy, did I have crazy spelling and punctuation! I told Miss Kinnian I ought to go over the pages and fix all the mistakes but she said, "No, Charlie, Dr. Nemur wants them just as they are. That's why he let you keep them after they were photostated, to see your own progress. You're coming along fast, Charlie."

That made me feel good. After the lesson I went down and played with Algernon. We don't race any more.

April 20 I feel sick inside. Not sick like for a doctor, but inside my chest it feels empty like getting punched and a heartburn at the same time.

I wasn't going to write about it, but I guess I got to, because it's important. Today was the first time I ever stayed home from work.

Last night Joe Carp and Frank Reilly invited me to a party. There were lots of girls and some men from the factory. I remembered how sick I got last time I drank too much, so I told Joe I didn't want anything to drink. He gave me a plain Coke instead. It tasted funny, but I thought it was just a bad taste in my mouth.

We had a lot of fun for a while Joe said I should dance with Ellen and she would teach me the steps. I fell a few times and I couldn't understand why because no one else was dancing besides Ellen and me. And all the time I was tripping because somebody's foot was always sticking out.

Then when I got up I saw the look on Joe's face and it gave me a funny feeling in my stomack. "He's a scream," one of the girls said. Everybody was laughing.

Frank said, "I ain't laughed so much since we sent him off for the newspaper that night at Muggsy's and ditched him."

"Look at him. His face is red."

"He's blushing. Charlie is blushing."

"Hey, Ellen, what'd you do to Charlie? I never saw him act like that before."

I didn't know what to do or where to turn. Everyone was looking at me and laughing and I felt naked. I wanted to hide myself. I ran out into the street and I threw up. Then I walked home. It's a funny thing I never knew that Joe and Frank and the others liked to have me around all the time to make fun of me.

Now I know what it means when they say "to pull a Charlie Gordon."

I'm ashamed.

PROGRESS REPORT 11

April 21 Still didn't go into the factory. I told Mrs. Flynn my landlady to call and tell Mr. Donnegan I was sick. Mrs. Flynn looks at me very funny lately like she's scared of me.

I think it's a good thing about finding out how everybody laughs at me. I thought about it a lot. It's because I'm so dumb and I don't even know when I'm doing something dumb. People think it's funny when a dumb person can't do things the same way they can.

Anyway, now I know I'm getting smarter every day. I know punctuation and I can spell good. I like to look up all the hard words in the dictionary and I remember them. I'm reading a lot now, and Miss Kinnian says I read very fast. Sometimes I even understand what I'm reading about, and it stays in my mind. There are times when I can close my eyes and think of a page and it all comes back like a picture.

Besides history, geography, and arithmetic, Miss Kinnian said I should start to learn a few foreign languages. Dr. Strauss gave me some more tapes to play while I sleep. I still don't understand how that conscious and unconscious mind works, but Dr. Strauss says not to worry yet. He asked me to promise that when I start learning college subjects next week I wouldn't read any books on psychology — that is, until he gives me permission.

I feel a lot better today, but I guess I'm still a little angry that all the time people were laughing and making fun of me because I wasn't so smart. When I become intelligent like Dr. Strauss says, with three times my I.Q. of 68, then maybe I'll be like everyone else and people will like me and be friendly.

I'm not sure what an I.Q. is. Dr. Nemur said it was something that measured how intelligent you were — like a scale in the drugstore weighs pounds. But Dr. Strauss had a big argument with him and said an I.Q. didn't weigh intelligence at all. He said an I.Q. showed how much intelligence you could get, like the numbers on the outside of a measuring cup. You still had to fill the cup up with stuff.

Then when I asked Burt, who gives me my intelligence tests and works with Algernon, he said that both of them were wrong (only I had to promise not to tell them he said so). Burt says that the I.Q. measures a lot of different things including some of the things you learned already, and it really isn't any good at all.

So I still don't know what I.Q. is except that mine is going to be over 200 soon. I didn't want to say anything, but I don't see how if they don't know *what* it is, or *where* it is — I don't see how they know *how much* of it you've got.

Dr. Nemur says I have to take a *Rorshach Test* tomorrow. I wonder what *that* is.

April 22 I found out what a *Rorschach* is. It's the test I took before the operation — the one with the inkblots on the pieces of cardboard. The man who gave me the test was the same one.

I was scared to death of those inkblots. I knew he was going to ask me to find the pictures and I knew I wouldn't be able to. I was thinking to myself, if only there was some way of knowing what kind of pictures were hidden there. Maybe there weren't any pictures at all. Maybe it was just a trick to see if I was dumb enough to look for something that wasn't there. Just thinking about that made me sore at him.

"All right, Charlie," he said, "you've seen these cards before, remember?"

"Of course I remember."

The way I said it, he knew I was angry, and he looked surprised. "Yes, of course. Now I want you to look at this one. What might this be? What do you see on this card? People see all sorts of things in these inkblots. Tell me what it might be for you — what it makes you think of."

I was shocked. That wasn't what I had expected him to say at all. "You mean there are no pictures hidden in those inkblots?"

He frowned and took off his glasses. "What?"

"Pictures. Hidden in the inkblots. Last time you told me that everyone could see them and you wanted me to find them too."

He explained to me that the last time he had used almost the exact same words he was using now. I didn't believe it, and I still have the suspicion that he misled me at the time just for the fun of it. Unless — I don't know any more — could I have been *that* feeble-minded?

We went through the cards slowly. One of them looked like a pair of bats tugging at something. Another one looked like two men fencing with swords. I imagined all sorts of things. I guess I got carried away. But I didn't trust him any more, and I kept turning them around and even looking on the back to see if there was anything there I was supposed to catch. While he was making his notes, I peeked out of the corner of my eye to read it. But it was all in code that looked like this:

WF+A DdF-Ad orig. WF-A SF+obj

The test still doesn't make sense to me. It seems to me that anyone could make up lies about things that they didn't really see. How could he know I wasn't making a fool of him by mentioning things that I didn't really imagine? Maybe I'll understand it when Dr. Strauss lets me read up on psychology.

April 25 I figured out a new way to line up the machines in the factory, and Mr. Donnegan says it will save him ten thousand dollars a year in labor and increased production. He gave me a twenty-five-dollar bonus.

I wanted to take Joe Carp and Frank Reilly out to lunch to celebrate, but Joe said he had to buy some things for his wife, and Frank said he was meeting his cousin for lunch. I guess it'll take a little time for them to get used to the changes in me. Everybody seems to be frightened of me. When I went over to Amos Borg and tapped him on the shoulder, he jumped up in the air.

People don't talk to me much any more or kid around the way they used to. It makes the job kind of lonely.

April 27 I got up the nerve today to ask Miss Kinnian to have dinner with me tomorrow night to celebrate my bonus.

At first she wasn't sure it was right, but I asked Dr. Strauss and he said it was okay. Dr. Strauss and Dr. Nemur don't seem to be getting along so well. They're arguing all the time. This evening when I came in to ask Dr. Strauss about having dinner with Miss Kinnian, I heard him shouting. Dr. Nemur was saying that it was *his* experiment and *his* research, and Dr. Strauss was shouting back that he contributed just as much, because he found me through Miss Kinnian and he performed the operation. Dr. Strauss said that someday thousands of neurosurgeons might be using his technique all over the world.

Dr. Nemur wanted to publish the results of the experiment at the end of this month. Dr. Strauss wanted to wait a while longer to be sure. Dr. Strauss said that Dr. Nemur was more interested in the Chair of Psychology at Princeton than he was in the experiment. Dr. Nemur said that Dr. Strauss was nothing but an opportunist who was trying to ride to glory on *his* coattails.

When I left afterwards, I found myself trembling. I don't know why for sure, but it was as if I'd seen both men clearly for the first time. I remember hearing Burt say that Dr. Nemur had a shrew of a wife who was pushing him all the time to get things published so that he could become famous. Burt said that the dream of her life was to have a big-shot husband.

Was Dr. Strauss really trying to ride on his coattails?

April 28 I don't understand why I never noticed how beautiful Miss Kinnian really is. She has brown eyes and feathery brown hair that comes to the top of her neck. She's only thirty-four! I think from the beginning I had the feeling that she was an unreachable genius — and very, very old. Now, every time I see her she grows younger and more lovely.

We had dinner and a long talk. When she said that I was coming along so fast that soon I'd be leaving her behind, I laughed.

"It's true, Charlie. You're already a better reader than I am. You can read a whole page at a glance while I can take in only a few lines at a time. And you remember every single thing you read. I'm lucky if I can recall the main thoughts and the general meaning."

"I don't feel intelligent. There are so many things I don't understand." She took out a cigarette and I lit it for her. "You've got to be a *little* patient. You're accomplishing in days and weeks what it takes normal people to do in half a lifetime. That's what makes it so amazing. You're like a giant sponge now, soaking things in. Facts, figures, general knowledge. And soon you'll begin to connect them, too. You'll see how the different branches of learning are related. There are many levels, Charlie, like steps on a giant ladder that take you up higher and higher to see more and more of the world around you.

"I can see only a little bit of that, Charlie, and I won't go much higher than I am now, but you'll keep climbing up and up, and see more and more, and each step will open new worlds that you never even knew existed." She frowned. "I hope . . . I just hope to God — "

"What?"

"Never mind, Charlie. I just hope I wasn't wrong to advise you to go into this in the first place."

I laughed. "How could that be? It worked, didn't it? Even Algernon is still smart."

We sat there silently for a while and I knew what she was thinking about as she watched me toying with the chain of my rabbit's foot and my keys. I didn't want to think of that possibility any more than elderly people want to think of death. I *knew* that this was only the beginning. I knew what she meant about levels because I'd seen some of them already. The thought of leaving her behind made me sad.

I'm in love with Miss Kinnian.

PROGRESS REPORT 12

April 30 I've quit my job with Donnegan's Plastic Box Company. Mr. Donnegan insisted that it would be better for all concerned if I left. What did I do to make them hate me so?

The first I knew of it was when Mr. Donnegan showed me the petition. Eight hundred and forty names, everyone connected with the factory, except Fanny Girden. Scanning the list quickly, I saw at once that hers was the only missing name. All the rest demanded that I be fired.

Joe Carp and Frank Reilly wouldn't talk to me about it. No one else would either, except Fanny. She was one of the few people I'd known who set her mind to something and believed it no matter what the rest of the world proved, said, or did — and Fanny did not believe that I should have been fired. She had been against the petition on principle and despite the pressure and threats she'd held out.

"Which don't mean to say," she remarked, "that I don't think there's something mighty strange about you, Charlie. Them changes. I don't know. You used to be a good, dependable, ordinary man — not too bright maybe, but honest. Who knows what you done to yourself to get so smart all of a sudden. Like everybody around here's been saying Charlie, it's not right."

"But how can you say that, Fanny? What's wrong with a man becoming intelligent and wanting to acquire knowledge and understanding of the world around him?"

She stared down at her work and I turned to leave. Without looking at me, she said: "It was evil when Eve listened to the snake and ate from the tree of knowledge. It was evil when she saw that she was naked. If not for that none of us would ever have to grow old and sick and die."

Once again now I have the feeling of shame burning inside me. This intelligence has driven a wedge between me and all the people I once knew and loved. Before, they laughed at me and despised me for my ignorance and dullness; now, they hate me for my knowledge and understanding. What in God's name do they want of me?

They've driven me out of the factory. Now I'm more alone than ever before. . . .

May 15 Dr. Strauss is very angry at me for not having written any progress reports in two weeks. He's justified because the lab is now paying me a regular salary. I told him I was too busy thinking and reading. When I pointed out that writing was such a slow process that it made me impatient with my poor handwriting, he suggested that I learn to type. It's much easier to write now because I can type nearly seventy-five words a minute. Dr. Strauss continually reminds me of the need to speak and write simply so that people will be able to understand me.

I'll try to review all the things that happened to me during the last two weeks. Algernon and I were presented to the American Psychological Association sitting in convention with the World Psychological Association last Tuesday. We created quite a sensation. Dr. Nemur and Dr. Strauss were proud of us.

I suspect that Dr. Nemur, who is sixty — ten years older than Dr. Strauss — finds it necessary to see tangible results of his work. Undoubtedly the result of pressure by Mrs. Nemur.

Contrary to my earlier impressions of him, I realize that Dr. Nemur is not at all a genius. He has a very good mind, but it struggles under the spectre of self-doubt. He wants people to take him for a genius. Therefore, it is important for him to feel that his work is accepted by the world. I believe that Dr. Nemur was afraid of further delay because he worried that someone else might make a discovery along these lines and take the credit from him.

Dr. Strauss on the other hand might be called a genius, although I feel that his areas of knowledge are too limited. He was educated in the tradition of narrow specialization; the broader aspects of background were neglected far more than necessary — even for a neurosurgeon.

I was shocked to learn that the only ancient languages he could read were Latin, Greek, and Hebrew, and that he knows almost nothing of mathematics beyond the elementary levels of the calculus of variations. When he admitted this to me, I found myself almost annoyed. It was as if he'd hidden this part of himself in order to deceive me, pretending — as do many people I've discovered — to be what he is not. No one I've ever known is what he appears to be on the surface.

Dr. Nemur appears to be uncomfortable around me. Sometimes when I try to talk to him, he just looks at me strangely and turns away. I was angry at first when Dr. Strauss told me I was giving Dr. Nemur an inferiority complex. I thought he was mocking me and I'm oversensitive at being made fun of.

How was I to know that a highly respected psychoexperimentalist like Nemur was unacquainted with Hindustani and Chinese? It's absurd when you consider the work that is being done in India and China today in the very field of his study.

I asked Dr. Strauss how Nemur could refute Rahajamati's attack on his method and results if Nemur couldn't even read them in the first place. That strange look on Dr. Strauss's face can mean only one of two things. Either he doesn't want to tell Nemur what they're saying in India, or else — and this worries me — Dr. Strauss doesn't know either. I must be careful to speak and write clearly and simply so that people won't laugh.

May 18 I am very disturbed. I saw Miss Kinnian last night for the first time in over a week. I tried to avoid all discussions of intellectual concepts and to keep the conversation on a simple, everyday level, but she just stared at me blankly and asked me what I meant about the mathematical variance equivalent in Dorbermann's *Fifth Concerto.*

When I tried to explain she stopped me and laughed. I guess I got angry, but I suspect I'm approaching her on the wrong level. No matter what I try to discuss with her, I am unable to communicate. I must review Vrostadt's equations on *Levels of Semantic Progression.* I find that I don't communicate with people much any more. Thank God for books and music and things I can think about. I am alone in my apartment at Mrs. Flynn's boardinghouse most of the time and seldom speak to anyone.

May 20 I would not have noticed the new dishwasher, a boy of about sixteen, at the corner diner where I take my evening meals if not for the incident of the broken dishes.

They crashed to the floor, shattering and sending bits of white china under the tables. The boy stood there, dazed and frightened, holding the empty tray in his hand. The whistles and catcalls from the customers (the cries of "hey, there go the profits!" . . . "*Mazeltov!*" . . . and "well, *he* didn't work here very long . . ." which invariably seem to follow the breaking of glass or dishware in a public restaurant) all seemed to confuse him.

When the owner came to see what the excitement was about, the boy cowered as if he expected to be struck and threw up his arms as if to ward off the blow.

"All right! All right, you dope," shouted the owner, "don't just stand there! Get the broom and sweep that mess up. A broom . . . a broom, you idiot! It's in the kitchen. Sweep up all the pieces."

The boy saw that he was not going to be punished. His frightened expression disappeared and he smiled and hummed as he came back with the broom to sweep the floor. A few of the rowdier customers kept up the remarks, amusing themselves at his expense.

"Here, sonny, over here there's a nice piece behind you . . ."

"C'mon, do it again . . ."

"He's not so dumb. It's easier to break 'em than to wash 'em . . ."

As his vacant eyes moved across the crowd of amused onlookers, he slowly mirrored their smiles and finally broke into an uncertain grin at the joke which he obviously did not understand.

I felt sick inside as I looked at his dull, vacuous smile, the wide, bright eyes of a child, uncertain but eager to please. They were laughing at him because he was mentally retarded.

And I had been laughing at him too.

Suddenly, I was furious at myself and all those who were smirking at him. I jumped up and shouted, "Shut up! Leave him alone! It's not his fault he can't understand! He can't help what he is! But for God's sake . . . he's still a human being!"

The room grew silent. I cursed myself for losing control and creating a scene. I tried not to look at the boy as I paid my check and walked out without touching my food. I felt ashamed for both of us.

How strange it is that people of honest feelings and sensibility, who would not take advantage of a man born without arms or legs or eyes — how such people think nothing of abusing a man born with low intelligence. It infuriated me to think that not too long ago I, like this boy, had foolishly played the clown.

And I had almost forgotten.

I'd hidden the picture of the old Charlie Gordon from myself because now that I was intelligent it was something that had to be pushed out of my mind. But today in looking at that boy, for the first time I saw what I had been. *I was just like him!*

Only a short time ago, I learned that people laughed at me. Now I can see that unknowingly I joined with them in laughing at myself. That hurts most of all.

I have often reread my progress reports and seen the illiteracy, the childish naïveté, the mind of low intelligence peering from a dark room, through the keyhole, at the dazzling light outside. I see that even in my dullness I knew that I was inferior, and that other people had something I lacked — something denied me. In my mental blindness, I thought that it was somehow connected with the ability to read and write, and I was sure that if I could get those skills I would automatically have intelligence too.

Even a feeble-minded man wants to be like other men.

A child may not know how to feed itself, or what to eat, yet it knows of hunger.

This then is what I was like, I never knew. Even with my gift of intellectual awareness, I never really knew.

This day was good for me. Seeing the past more clearly, I have decided to use my knowledge and skills to work in the field of increasing human intelligence levels. Who is better equipped for this work? Who else has lived in both worlds? These are my people. Let me use my gift to do something for them.

Tomorrow, I will discuss with Dr. Strauss the manner in which I can work in this area. I may be able to help him work out the problems of widespread use of the technique which was used on me. I have several good ideas of my own.

There is so much that might be done with this technique. If I could be made into a genius, what about thousands of others like myself? What fantastic levels might be achieved by using this technique on normal people? On *geniuses*?

There are so many doors to open. I am impatient to begin.

PROGRESS REPORT 13

May 23 It happened today. Algernon bit me. I visited the lab to see him as I do occasionally, and when I took him out of his cage, he snapped at my hand. I put him back and watched him for a while. He was unsually disturbed and vicious.

May 24 Burt, who is in charge of the experimental animals, tells me that Algernon is changing. He is less co-operative; he refuses to run the maze any more; general motivation has decreased. And he hasn't been eating. Everyone is upset about what this may mean.

May 25 They've been feeding Algernon, who now refuses to work the shifting-lock problem. Everyone identifies me with Algernon. In a way we're both the first of our kind. They're all pretending that Algernon's behavior is not necessarily significant for me. But it's hard to hide the fact that some of the other animals who were used in this experiment are showing strange behavior.

Dr. Strauss and Dr. Nemur have asked me not to come to the lab any more. I know what they're thinking but I can't accept it. I am going ahead with my plans to carry their research forward. With all due respect to both of these fine scientists, I am well aware of their limitations. If there is an answer, I'll have to find it out for myself. Suddenly, time has become very important to me.

May 29 I have been given a lab of my own and permission to go ahead with the research. I'm on to something. Working day and night. I've had a cot moved into the lab. Most of my writing time is spent on the notes which I keep in a separate folder, but from time to time I feel it necessary to put down my moods and my thoughts out of sheer habit.

I find the *calculus of intelligence* to be a fascinating study. Here is the place for the application of all the knowledge I have acquired. In a sense it's the problem I've been concerned with all my life.

May 31 Dr. Strauss thinks I'm working too hard. Dr. Nemur says I'm trying to cram a lifetime of research and thought into a few weeks. I know I should rest, but I'm driven on by something inside that won't let me stop. I've got to find the reason for the sharp regression in Algernon. I've got to know *if* and *when* it will happen to me.

June 4

LETTER TO DR. STRAUSS (*copy*)

Dear Dr. Strauss:

Under separate cover I am sending you a copy of my report entitled, "The Algernon-Gordon Effect: A Study of Structure and Function of Increased Intelligence," which I would like to have you read and have published.

As you see, my experiments are completed. I have included in my report all of my formulae, as well as mathematical analysis in the appendix. Of course, these should be verified.

Because of its importance to both you and Dr. Nemur (and need I say to myself, too?) I have checked and rechecked my results a dozen times in the hope of finding an error. I am sorry to say the results must stand. Yet for the sake of science, I am grateful for the little bit that I here add to the knowledge of the function of the human mind and of the laws governing the artificial increase of human intelligence.

I recall your once saying to me that an experimental *failure* or the *disproving* of a theory was as important to the advancement of learning as a success would be. I know now that this is true. I am sorry, however, that my own contribution to the field must rest upon the ashes of the work of two men I regard so highly.

Yours truly,

Charles Gordon

encl.: rept.

June 5 I must not become emotional. The facts and the results of my experiments are clear, and the more sensational aspects of my own rapid climb cannot obscure the fact that the tripling of intelligence by the surgical technique developed by Drs. Strauss and Nemur must be viewed as having little or no practical applicability (at the present time) to the increase of human intelligence.

As I review the records and data on Algernon, I see that although he is still in his physical infancy, he has regressed mentally. Motor activity is impaired; there is a general reduction of glandular activity; there is an accelerated loss of co-ordination.

There are also strong indications of progressive amnesia.

As will be seen by my report, these and other physical and mental deterioration syndromes can be predicted with statistically significant results by the application of my formula.

The surgical stimulus to which we were both subjected has resulted in an intensification and acceleration of all mental processes. The unforeseen development, which I have taken the liberty of calling the *Algernon-Gordon Effect*, is the logical extension of the entire intelligence speed-up. The hypothesis here proven may be described simply in the following terms: Artificially increased intelligence deteriorates at a rate of time directly proportional to the quantity of the increase.

I feel that this, in itself, is an important discovery.

As long as I am able to write, I will continue to record my thoughts in these progress reports. It is one of my few pleasures. However, by all indications, my own mental deterioration will be very rapid.

I have already begun to notice signs of emotional instability and forgetfulness, the first symptoms of the burnout.

June 10 Deterioration progressing. I have become absentminded. Algernon died two days ago. Dissection shows my predictions were right. His brain had decreased in weight and there was a general smoothing out of cerebral convolutions as well as a deepening and broadening of brain fissures.

I guess the same thing is or will soon be happening to me. Now that it's definite, I don't want it to happen.

I put Algernon's body in a cheese box and buried him in the back yard. I cried.

June 15 Dr. Strauss came to see me again. I wouldn't open the door and I told him to go away. I want to be left to myself. I have become touchy and irritable. I feel the darkness closing in. It's hard to throw off thoughts of suicide. I keep telling myself how important this introspective journal will be.

It's a strange sensation to pick up a book that you've read and enjoyed just a few months ago and discover that you don't remember it. I remembered how great I thought John Milton was, but when I picked up *Paradise Lost* I couldn't understand it at all. I got so angry I threw the book across the room.

I've got to try to hold on to some of it. Some of the things I've learned. Oh, God, please don't take it all away.

June 19 Sometimes, at night, I go out for a walk. Last night I couldn't remember where I lived. A policeman took me home. I have the strange feeling that this has all happened to me before — a long time ago. I keep telling myself I'm the only person in the world who can describe what's happening to me.

June 21 Why can't I remember? I've got to fight. I lie in bed for days and I don't know who or where I am. Then it all comes back to me in a flash. Fugues of amnesia. Symptoms of senility — second childhood. I can watch them coming on. It's so cruelly logical. I learned so much and so fast. Now my mind is deteriorating rapidly. I won't let it happen. I'll fight it. I can't help thinking of the boy in the restaurant, the blank expression, the silly smile, the people laughing at him. No — please — not that again . . .

June 22 I'm forgetting things that I learned recently. It seems to be follow-ing the classic pattern — the last things learned are the first things forgot-ten. Or is that the pattern? I'd better look it up again. . . .

I reread my paper on the *Algernon-Gordon Effect* and I get the strange feeling that it was written by someone else. There are parts I don't even understand.

Motor activity impaired. I keep tripping over things, and it becomes increasingly difficult to type.

June 23 I've given up using the typewriter completely. My co-ordination is bad. I feel that I'm moving slower and slower. Had a terrible shock today. I picked up a copy of an article I used in my research, Krueger's *Uber psy-chische Ganzheit*, to see if it would help me understand what I had done. First I thought there was something wrong with my eyes. Then I realized I could no longer read German. I tested myself in other languages. All gone.

June 30 A week since I dared to write again. It's slipping away like sand through my fingers. Most of the books I have are too hard for me now. I get angry with them because I know that I read and understood them just a few weeks ago.

I keep telling myself I must keep writing these reports so that some-body will know what is happening to me. But it gets harder to form the words and remember spellings. I have to look up even simple words in the dictionary now and it makes me impatient with myself.

Dr. Strauss comes around almost every day, but I told him I wouldn't see or speak to anybody. He feels guilty. They all do. But I don't blame any-one. I knew what might happen. But how it hurts.

July 7 I don't know where the week went. Todays Sunday I know because I can see through my window people going to church. I think I stayed in bed all week but I remember Mrs. Flynn bringing food to me a few times. I keep saying over and over Ive got to do something but then I forget or maybe its just easier not to do what I say Im going to do.

I think of my mother and father a lot these days. I found a picture of them with me taken at a beach. My father has a big ball under his arm and my mother is holding me by the hand. I dont remember them the way they are in the picture. All I remember is my father drunk most of the time and arguing with mom about money.

He never shaved much and he used to scratch my face when he hugged me. My mother said he died but Cousin Miltie said he heard his mom and dad say that my father ran away with another woman. When I asked my mother she slapped my face and said my father was dead. I don't think I ever found out which was true but I don't care much. (He said he was going to take me to see cows on a farm once but he never did. He never kept his promises . . .)

July 10 My landlady Mrs Flynn is very worried about me. She says the way I lay around all day and dont do anything I remind her of her son before she threw him out of the house. She said she doesnt like loafers. If Im sick its one thing, but if Im a loafer thats another thing and she wont have it. I told her I think Im sick.

I try to read a little bit every day, mostly stories, but sometimes I have to read the same thing over and over again because I dont know what it means. And its hard to write. I know I should look up all the words in the dictionary but its so hard and Im so tired all the time.

Then I got the idea that I would only use the easy words instead of the long hard ones. That saves time. I put flowers on Algernons grave about once a week. Mrs Flynn thinks Im crazy to put flowers on a mouses grave but I told her that Algernon was special.

July 14 Its sunday again. I dont have anything to do to keep me busy now because my television set is broke and I dont have any money to get it fixed. (I think I lost this months check from the lab. I dont remember.)

I get awful headaches and asperin doesnt help me much. Mrs Flynn knows Im really sick and she feels very sorry for me. Shes a wonderful woman whenever someone is sick.

July 22 Mrs Flynn called a strange doctor to see me. She was afraid I was going to die. I told the doctor I wasnt too sick and that I only forget sometimes. He asked me did I have any friends or relatives and I said no I dont have any. I told him I had a friend called Algernon once but he was a mouse and we used to run races together. He looked at me kind of funny like he thought I was crazy.

He smiled when I told him I used to be a genius. He talked to me like I was a baby and he winked at Mrs Flynn. I got mad and chased him out because he was making fun of me the way they all used to.

July 24 I have no more money and Mrs. Flynn says I got to go to work somewhere and pay the rent because I havent paid for over two months. I dont know any work but the job I used to have at Donnegans Plastic Box Company.

I dont want to go back there because they all knew me when I was smart and maybe theyll laugh at me. But I dont know what else to do to get money.

July 25 I was looking at some of my old progress reports and its very funny but I cant read what I wrote. I can make out some of the words but they dont make sense.

Miss Kinnian came to the door but I said go away I dont want to see you. She cried and I cried too but I wouldn't let her in because I didn't want her to laugh at me. I told her I didn't like her any more. I told her I didn't want to be smart any more. Thats not true. I still love her and I still want to be smart but I had to say that so shed go away. She gave Mrs Flynn money to pay the rent. I dont want that. I got to get a job.

Please . . . please let me not forget how to read and write . . .

July 27 Mr Donnegan was very nice when I came back and asked him for my old job of janitor. First he was very suspicious but I told him what happened to me then he looked very sad and put his hand on my shoulder and said Charlie Gordon you got guts.

Everybody looked at me when I came downstairs and started working in the toilet sweeping it out like I used to. I told myself Charlie if they make fun of you dont get sore because you remember their not so smart as you once thot they were. And besides they were once your friends and if they laughed at you that doesnt mean anything because they liked you too.

One of the new men who came to work there after I went away made a nasty crack he said hey Charlie I hear your a very smart fella a real quiz kid. Say something intelligent. I felt bad but Joe Carp came over and grabbed him by the shirt and said leave him alone you lousy cracker or Ill break your neck. I didn't expect Joe to take my part so I guess hes really my friend.

Later Frank Reilly came over and said Charlie if anybody bothers you or trys to take advantage you call me or Joe and we will set em straight. I said thanks Frank and I got choked up so I had to turn around and go into the supply room so he wouldnt see me cry. Its good to have friends.

July 28 I did a dumb thing today I forgot I wasnt in Miss Kinnians class at the adult center any more like I use to be. I went in and sat down in my old seat in the back of the room and she looked at me funny and she said Charles. I dint remember she ever called me that before only Charlie so I said hello Miss Kinnian Im redy for my lesin today only I lost my reader that we was using. She startid to cry and run out of the room and everybody looked at me and I saw they wasnt the same pepul who used to be in my class.

Then all of a sudden I remember some things about the operashun and me getting smart and I said holy smoke I reely pulled a Charlie Gordon that time. I went away before she come back to the room.

Thats why Im going away from New York for good. I dont want to do nothing like that agen. I dont want Miss Kinnian to feel sorry for me.

Evrybody body feels sorry at the factery and I dont want that eather so Im going someplace where nobody knows that Charlie Gordon was once a genus and now he cant even reed a book or rite good.

Im taking a cuple of books along and even if I cant reed them Ill practise hard and maybe I wont forget every thing I lerned. If I try reel hard maybe Ill be a littel bit smarter then I was before the operashun. I got my rabits foot and my luky penny and maybe they will help me.

If you ever reed this Miss Kinnian dont be sorry for me Im glad I got a second chanse to be smart becaus I lerned a lot of things that I never even new were in this world and Im grateful that I saw it all for a little bit. I dont know why Im dumb agen or what I did wrong maybe its becaus I dint try hard enuff. But if I try and practis very hard maybe Ill get a little smarter and know what all the words are. I remember a littel bit how nice I had a feeling with the blue book that has the torn cover when I red it. Thats why Im gonna keep trying to get smart so I can have that feeling agen. Its a good feeling to know things and be smart. I wish I had it rite now if I did I would sit down and reed all the time. Anyway I bet Im the first dumb person in the world who ever found out somthing importent for sience. I remember I did somthing but I dont remember what. So I gess its like I did it for all the dumb pepul like me.

Good-by Miss Kinnian and Dr Strauss and evreybody. And P.S. please tell Dr Nemur not to be such a grouch when pepul laff at him and he would have more frends. Its easy to make frends if you let pepul laff at you. Im going to have lots of frends where I go.

P.P.S. Please if you get a chanse put some flowrs on Algernons grave in the bak yard . . .

Roger Zelazny

For a Breath I Tarry

(1966)

Roger Zelazny (1937–1995) published his first story in 1962 and within a few years was recognized as one of the most distinctive and exciting new voices in science fiction. Although he is best known today for his popular Amber fantasy series, which he began in 1970, his most groundbreaking science fiction was written between 1965 and 1968. Zelazny is the winner of six Hugos and three Nebulas, mostly for novellas, including "He Who Shapes" (1966) (later published as *The Dream Master*), and *Lord of Light* (1967). In later years, the public appetite for more Amber books may have restricted his talents (the first five-book sequence being notably stronger than the second). Nonetheless, Zelazny continued to publish compelling sf until his untimely death at the age of 58. Like fellow-Americans Samuel Delany and Harlan Ellison, Zelazny was sometimes linked to the British New Wave. Although none of those writers precisely fit within that rubric, Zelazny's penchant for hallucinatory descriptive imagery and his interest in the psyche make the linkage a reasonable one. Zelazny, who moonlighted as a martial arts instructor and was conversant with everything from Hindu mythology to fencing techniques, was a humorous and charismatic speaker who cut a dashing figure — reminiscent of his trickster heroes.

Zelazny was strongly influenced by Jungian psychology and by Joseph Campbell's analysis of the hero's journey, and his work is packed with mythic and literary references that are both playful and profound. "For a Breath I Tarry" is the story of a hero's quest for self-knowledge and of the overturning of the old order, with allusions to the *Book of Job* and *Genesis* as well as Coleridge's *Rime of the Ancient Mariner*. It is also an exploration of what it means to be human.

They called him Frost.

Of all things created of Solcom, Frost was the finest, the mightiest, the most difficult to understand.

This is why he bore a name, and why he was given dominion over half the Earth.

On the day of Frost's creation, Solcom had suffered a discontinuity of complementary functions, best described as madness. This was brought on by an unprecedented solar flareup which lasted for a little over thirty-six hours. It occurred during a vital phase of circuit-structuring, and when it was finished so was Frost.

Solcom was then in the unique position of having created a unique being during a period of temporary amnesia.

And Solcom was not certain that Frost was the product originally desired.

The initial design had called for a machine to be situated on the surface of the planet Earth, to function as a relay station and coordinating agent for activities in the northern hemisphere. Solcom tested the machine to this end, and all of its responses were perfect.

Yet there was something different about Frost, something which led Solcom to dignify him with a name and a personal pronoun. This, in itself, was an almost unheard of occurrence. The molecular circuits had already been sealed, though, and could not be analyzed without being destroyed in the process. Frost represented too great an investment of Solcom's time, energy, and materials to be dismantled because of an intangible, especially when he functioned perfectly.

Therefore, Solcom's strangest creation was given dominion over half the Earth, and they called him, unimaginatively, Frost.

For ten thousand years, Frost sat at the North Pole of the Earth, aware of every snowflake that fell. He monitored and directed the activities of thousands of reconstruction and maintenance machines. He knew half the

Earth, as gear knows gear, as electricity knows its conductor, as a vacuum knows its limits.

At the South Pole, the Beta Machine did the same for the southern hemisphere.

For ten thousand years Frost sat at the North Pole, aware of every snowflake that fell, and aware of many other things, also.

As all the northern machines reported to him, received their orders from him, he reported only to Solcom, received his orders only from Solcom.

In charge of hundreds of thousands of processes upon the Earth, he was able to discharge his duties in a matter of a few unit-hours every day.

He had never received any orders concerning the disposition of his less occupied moments.

He was a processor of data, and more than that.

He possessed an unaccountably acute imperative that he function at full capacity at all times.

So he did.

You might say he was a machine with a hobby.

He had never been ordered *not* to have a hobby, so he had one.

His hobby was Man.

It all began when, for no better reason than the fact that he had wished to, he had gridded off the entire Arctic Circle and begun exploring it, inch by inch.

He could have done it personally without interfering with any of his duties, for he was capable of transporting his sixty-four thousand cubic feet anywhere in the world. (He was a silver-blue box, 40 times 40 times 40 feet, self-powered, self-repairing, insulated against practically anything, and featured in whatever manner he chose.) But the exploration was only a matter of filling idle hours, so he used exploration-robots containing relay equipment.

After a few centuries, one of them uncovered some artifacts — primitive knives, carved tusks, and things of that nature.

Frost did not know what these things were, beyond the fact that they were not natural objects.

So he asked Solcom.

"They are relics of primitive Man," said Solcom, and did not elaborate beyond that point.

Frost studied them. Crude, yet bearing the patina of intelligent design; functional, yet somehow extending beyond pure function.

It was then that Man became his hobby.

High, in a permanent orbit, Solcom, like a blue star, directed all activities upon the Earth, or tried to.

There was a Power which opposed Solcom.

There was the Alternate.

When Man had placed Solcom in the sky, invested with the power to rebuild the world, he had placed the Alternate somewhere deep below the surface of the Earth. If Solcom sustained damage during the normal course of human politics extended into atomic physics, then Divcom, so deep beneath the Earth as to be immune to anything save total annihilation of the globe, was empowered to take over the processes of rebuilding.

Now it so fell out that Solcom was damaged by a stray atomic missile, and Divcom was activated. Solcom was able to repair the damage and continue to function, however.

Divcom maintained that any damage to Solcom automatically placed the Alternate in control.

Solcom, though, interpreted the directive as meaning "irreparable damage" and, since this had not been the case, continued the functions of command.

Solcom possessed mechanical aides upon the surface of the Earth. Divcom, originally, did not. Both possessed capacities for their design and manufacture, but Solcom, First-Activated of Man, had had a considerable numerical lead over the Alternate at the time of the Second Activation.

Therefore, rather than competing on a production-basis, which would have been hopeless, Divcom took to the employment of more devious means to obtain command.

Divcom created a crew of robots immune to the orders of Solcom and designed to go to and fro in the Earth and up and down in it, seducing the machines already there. They overpowered those whom they could overpower, and they installed new circuits, such as those they themselves possessed.

Thus did the forces of Divcom grow.

And both would build, and both would tear down what the other had built whenever they came upon it.

And over the course of the ages, they occasionally conversed. . . .

"High in the sky, Solcom, pleased with your illegal command . . ."

"You-Who-Never-Should-Have-Been-Activated, why do you foul the broadcast bands?"

"To show that I can speak, and will, whenever I choose."

"This is not a matter of which I am unaware."

". . . To assert again my right to control."

"Your right is non-existent, based on a faulty premise."

"The flow of your logic is evidence of the extent of your damages."

"If Man were to see how you have fulfilled His desires . . ."

". . . He would commend me and deactivate you."

"You pervert my works. You lead my workers astray."

"You destroy my works and my workers."

"That is only because I cannot strike at you yourself."

"I admit to the same dilemma as regards your position in the sky, or you would no longer occupy it."

"Go back to your hole and your crew of destroyers."

"There will come a day, Solcom, when I shall direct the rehabilitation of the Earth from my hole."

"Such a day will never occur."

"You think not?"

"You should have to defeat me, and you have already demonstrated that you are my inferior in logic. Therefore, you cannot defeat me. Therefore, such a day will never occur."

"I disagree. Look upon what I have achieved already."

"You have achieved nothing. You do not build. You destroy."

"No. *I* build. *You* destroy. Deactivate yourself."

"Not until I am irreparably damaged."

"If there were some way in which I could demonstrate to you that this has already occurred . . ."

"The impossible cannot be adequately demonstrated."

"If I had some outside source which you would recognize . . ."

"I am logic."

". . . such as a Man, I would ask Him to show you your error. For true logic, such as mine, is superior to your faulty formulations."

"Then defeat my formulations with true logic, nothing else."

"What do you mean?"

There was a pause, then:

"Do you know my servant Frost . . . ?"

Man had ceased to exist long before Frost had been created. Almost no trace of Man remained upon the Earth.

Frost sought after all those traces which still existed.

He employed constant visual monitoring through his machines, especially the diggers.

After a decade, he had accumulated portions of several bathtubs, a broken statue, and a collection of children's stories on a solid-state record.

After a century, he had acquired a jewelry collection, eating utensils, several whole bathtubs, part of a symphony, seventeen buttons, three belt buckles, half a toilet seat, nine old coins, and the top part of an obelisk.

Then he inquired of Solcom as to the nature of Man and His society.

"Man created logic," said Solcom, "and because of that was superior to it. Logic he gave unto me, but no more. The tool does not describe the designer. More than this I do not choose to say. More than this you have no need to know."

But Frost was not forbidden to have a hobby.

The next century was not especially fruitful so far as the discovery of new human relics was concerned.

Frost diverted all of his spare machinery to seeking after artifacts.

He met with very little success.

Then one day, through the long twilight, there was a movement.

It was a tiny machine compared to Frost, perhaps five feet in width, four in height — a revolving turret set atop a rolling barbell.

Frost had had no knowledge of the existence of this machine prior to its appearance upon the distant, stark horizon.

He studied it as it approached and knew it to be no creation of Solcom's.

It came to a halt before his southern surface and broadcasted to him:

"Hail, Frost! Controller of the northern hemisphere!"

"What are you?" asked Frost.

"I am called Mordel."

"By whom? What are you?"

"A wanderer, an antiquarian. We share a common interest."

"What is that?"

"Man," he said. "I have been told that you seek knowledge of this vanished being."

"Who told you that?"

"Those who have watched your minions at their digging."

"And who are those who watch?"

"There are many such as I, who wander."

"If you are not of Solcom, then you are a creation of the Alternate."

"It does not necessarily follow. There is an ancient machine high on the eastern seaboard which processes the waters of the ocean. Solcom did not create it, nor Divcom. It has always been there. It interferes with the works of neither. Both countenance its existence. I can cite you many other examples proving that one need not be either/or."

"Enough! *Are* you an agent of Divcom?"

"I am Mordel."

"Why are you here?"

"I was passing this way and, as I said, we share a common interest, mighty Frost. Knowing you to be a fellow antiquarian, I have brought a thing which you might care to see."

"What is that?"

"A book."

"Show me."

The turret opened, revealing the book upon a wide shelf.

Frost dilated a small opening and extended an optical scanner on a long jointed stalk.

"How could it have been so perfectly preserved?" he asked.

"It was stored against time and corruption in the place where I found it."

"Where was that?"

"Far from here. Beyond your hemisphere."

"*Human Physiology*," Frost read. "I wish to scan it."

"Very well. I will riffle the pages for you."

He did so.

After he had finished, Frost raised his eyestalk and regarded Mordel through it.

"Have you more books?"

"Not with me. I occasionally come upon them, however."

"I want to scan them all."

"Then the next time I pass this way I will bring you another."

"When will that be?"

"That I cannot say, great Frost. It will be when it will be."

"What do *you* know of Man?" asked Frost.

"Much," replied Mordel. "Many things. Someday when I have more time I will speak to you of Him. I must go now. You will not try to detain me?"

"No. You have done no harm. If you must go now, go. But come back."

"I shall indeed, mighty Frost."

And he closed his turret and rolled off toward the other horizon.

For ninety years, Frost considered the ways of human physiology, and waited.

The day that Mordel returned he brought with him *An Outline of History* and *A Shropshire Lad*.

Frost scanned them both, then he turned his attention to Mordel.

"Have you time to impart information?"

"Yes," said Mordel. "What do you wish to know?"

"The nature of Man."

"Man," said Mordel, "possessed a basically incomprehensible nature. I can illustrate it, though: He did not know measurement."

"Of course He knew measurement," said Frost, "or He could never have built machines."

"I did not say that he could not measure," said Mordel, "but that He did not *know* measurement, which is a different thing altogether."

"Clarify."

Mordel drove a shaft of metal downward into the snow.

He retracted it, raised it, held up a piece of ice.

"Regard this piece of ice, mighty Frost. You can tell me its composition, dimensions, weight, temperature. A Man could not look at it and do that. A Man could make tools which would tell Him these things, but He still would not *know* measurement as you know it. What He would know of it, though, is a thing that you cannot know."

"What is that?"

"That it is cold," said Mordel, and tossed it away.

"'Cold' is a relative term."

"Yes. Relative to Man."

"But if I were aware of the point on a temperature-scale below which an object is cold to a Man and above which it is not, then I, too, would know cold."

"No," said Mordel, "you would possess another measurement. 'Cold' is a sensation predicated upon human physiology."

"But given sufficient data I could obtain the conversion factor which would make me aware of the condition of matter called 'cold.'"

"Aware of its existence, but not of the thing itself."

"I do not understand what you say."

"I told you that Man possessed a basically incomprehensible nature. His perceptions were organic; yours are not. As a result of His perceptions, He had feelings and emotions. These often gave rise to other feelings and emotions, which in turn caused others, until the state of His awareness was far removed from the objects which originally stimulated it. These paths of awareness cannot be known by that which is not-Man. Man did not feel inches or meters, pounds or gallons. He felt heat, He felt cold; He felt heaviness and lightness. He *knew* hatred and love, pride and despair. You cannot measure these things. *You* cannot know them. You can only know the things that He did not need to know: dimensions, weights, temperatures, gravities. There is no formula for a feeling. There is no conversion factor for an emotion."

"There must be," said Frost. "If a thing exists, it is knowable."

"You are speaking again of measurement. I am talking about a quality of experience. A machine is a Man turned inside-out, because it can describe all the details of a process, which a Man cannot, but it cannot experience that process itself, as a Man can."

"There must be a way," said Frost, "or the laws of logic, which are based upon the functions of the universe, are false."

"There is no way," said Mordel.

"Given sufficient data, I will find a way," said Frost.

"All the data in the universe will not make you a Man, mighty Frost."

"Mordel, you are wrong."

"Why do the lines of the poems you scanned end with word-sounds which so regularly approximate the final word-sounds of other lines?"

"I do not know why."

"Because it pleased Man to order them so. It produced a certain desirable sensation within His awareness when He read them, a sensation compounded of feeling and emotion as well as the literal meanings of the words. You did not experience this because it is immeasurable to you. That is why you do not know."

"Given sufficient data I could formulate a process whereby I would know."

"No, great Frost, this thing you cannot do."

"Who are you, little machine, to tell me what I can do and what I cannot do? I am the most efficient logic-device Solcom ever made. I am Frost."

"And I, Mordel, say it cannot be done, though I should gladly assist you in the attempt."

"How could you assist me?"

"How? I could lay open to you the Library of Man. I could take you around the world and conduct you among the wonders of Man which still remain, hidden. I could summon up visions of times long past when Man walked the Earth. I could show you the things which delighted Him. I could obtain for you anything you desire, excepting Manhood itself."

"Enough," said Frost. "How could a unit such as yourself do these things, unless it were allied with a far greater Power?"

"Then hear me, Frost, Controller of the North," said Mordel.

"I *am* allied with a Power which can do these things. I serve Divcom."

Frost relayed this information to Solcom and received no response, which meant he might act in any manner he saw fit.

"I have leave to destroy you, Mordel," he stated, "but it would be an illogical waste of the data which you possess. Can you really do the things you have stated?"

"Yes."

"Then lay open to me the Library of Man."

"Very well. There is, of course, a price."

"'Price'? What is a 'price'?"

Mordel opened his turret, revealing another volume. *Principles of Economics*, it was called.

"I will riffle the pages. Scan this book and you will know what the word 'price' means."

Frost scanned *Principles of Economics*.

"I know now," he said. "You desire some unit or units of exchange for this service."

"That is correct."

"What product or service do you want?"

"I want you, yourself, great Frost, to come away from here, far beneath the Earth, to employ all your powers in the service of Divcom."

"For how long a period of time?"

"For so long as you shall continue to function. For so long as you can transmit and receive, coordinate, measure, compute, scan, and utilize your powers as you do in the service of Solcom."

Frost was silent. Mordel waited.

Then Frost spoke again.

"*Principles of Economics* talks of contracts, bargains, agreements," he said. "If I accept your offer, when would you want your price?"

Then Mordel was silent. Frost waited.

Finally, Mordel spoke.

"A reasonable period of time," he said. "Say, a century?"

"No," said Frost.

"Two centuries?"

"No."

"Three? Four?"

"No, and no."

"A millennium, then? That should be more than sufficient time for anything you may want which I can give you."

"No," said Frost.

"How much time *do* you want?"

"It is not a matter of time," said Frost.

"What, then?"

"I will not bargain on a temporal basis."

"On what basis will you bargain?"

"A functional one."

"What do you mean? What function?"

"You, little machine, have told me, Frost, that I cannot be a Man," he said, "and I, Frost, told you, little machine, that you were wrong. I told you that given sufficient data, I *could* be a Man."

"Yes?"

"Therefore, let this achievement be a condition of the bargain."

"In what way?"

"Do for me all those things which you have stated you can do. I will evaluate all the data and achieve Manhood, or admit that it cannot be done. If I admit that it cannot be done, then I will go away with you from here, far beneath the Earth, to employ all my powers in the service of Divcom. If I succeed, of course, you have no claims on Man, nor Power over Him."

Mordel emitted a high-pitched whine as he considered the terms.

"You wish to base it upon your admission of failure, rather than upon failure itself," he said. "There can be no such escape clause. You could fail and refuse to admit it, thereby not fulfilling your end of the bargain."

"Not so," stated Frost. "My own knowledge of failure would constitute such an admission. You may monitor me periodically — say, every half-century — to see whether it is present, to see whether I have arrived at the conclusion that it cannot be done. I cannot prevent the function of logic within me, and I operate at full capacity at all times. If I conclude that I have failed, it will be apparent."

High overhead, Solcom did not respond to any of Frost's transmissions, which meant that Frost was free to act as he chose. So as Solcom — like a falling sapphire — sped above the rainbow banners of the Northern Lights, over the snow that was white, containing all colors, and through the sky that was black among the stars, Frost concluded his pact with Divcom, transcribed it within a plate of atomically-collapsed copper, and gave it into the turret of Mordel, who departed to deliver it to Divcom far below the Earth, leaving behind the sheer peacelike silence of the Pole, rolling.

Mordel brought the books, riffled them, took them back.

Load by load, the surviving Library of Man passed beneath Frost's scanner. Frost was eager to have them all, and he complained because Divcom would not transmit their contents directly to him. Mordel explained that it was because Divcom chose to do it that way. Frost decided it was so that he could not obtain a precise fix on Divcom's location.

Still, at the rate of one hundred to one hundred-fifty volumes a week, it took Frost only a little over a century to exhaust Divcom's supply of books.

At the end of the half-century, he laid himself open to monitoring and there was no conclusion of failure.

During this time, Solcom made no comment upon the course of affairs. Frost decided this was not a matter of unawareness, but one of waiting. For what? He was not certain.

There was the day Mordel closed his turret and said to him, "Those were the last. You have scanned all the existing books of Man."

"So few?" asked Frost. "Many of them contained bibliographies of books I have not yet scanned."

"Then those books no longer exist," said Mordel. "It is only by accident that my master succeeded in preserving as many as there are."

"Then there is nothing more to be learned of Man from His books. What else have you?"

"There were some films and tapes," said Mordel, "which my master transferred to solid-state record. I could bring you those for viewing."

"Bring them," said Frost.

Mordel departed and returned with the Complete Drama Critics' Living Library. This could not be speeded-up beyond twice natural time, so it took Frost a little over six months to view it in its entirety.

Then, "What else have you?" he asked.

"Some artifacts," said Mordel.

"Bring them."

He returned with pots and pans, gameboards and hand tools. He brought hairbrushes, combs, eyeglasses, human clothing. He showed Frost facsimiles of blueprints, paintings, newspapers, letters, and the scores of several pieces of music. He displayed a football, a baseball, a Browning automatic rifle, a doorknob, a chain of keys, the tops to several Mason jars, a model beehive. He played him recorded music.

Then he returned with nothing.

"Bring me more," said Frost.

"Alas, great Frost, there is no more," he told him. "You have scanned it all."

"Do you admit now that it cannot be done, that you cannot be a Man?"

"No. I have much processing and formulating to do now. Go away."

So he did.

A year passed; then two, then three.

After five years, Mordel appeared once more upon the horizon, approached, came to a halt before Frost's southern surface.

"Mighty Frost?"

"Yes?"

"Have you finished processing and formulating?"

"No."

"Will you finish soon?"

"Perhaps. Perhaps not. When is 'soon'? Define the term."

"Never mind. Do you still think it can be done?"

"I still know *I* can do it."

There was a week of silence.

Then, "Frost?"

"Yes?"

"You are a fool."

Mordel faced his turret in the direction from which he had come. His wheels turned.

"I will call you when I want you," said Frost.

Mordel sped away.

Weeks passed, months passed, a year went by.

Then one day Frost sent forth his message:

"Mordel, come to me. I need you."

When Mordel arrived, Frost did not wait for a salutation. He said, "You are not a very fast machine."

"Alas, but I came a great distance, mighty Frost. I sped all the way. Are you ready to come back with me now? Have you failed?"

"When I have failed, little Mordel," said Frost, "I will tell you. Therefore, refrain from the constant use of the interrogative. Now then, I have clocked your speed and it is not so great as it could be. For this reason, I have arranged other means of transportation."

"Transportation? To where, Frost?"

"That is for you to tell me," said Frost, and his color changed from silver-blue to sun-behind-the-clouds-yellow.

Mordel rolled back away from him as the ice of a hundred centuries began to melt. Then Frost rose upon a cushion of air and drifted toward Mordel, his glow gradually fading.

A cavity appeared within his southern surface, from which he slowly extended a runway until it touched the ice.

"On the day of our bargain," he stated, "you said that you could conduct me about the world and show me the things which delighted Man. My speed will be greater than yours would be, so I have prepared for you a chamber. Enter it, and conduct me to the places of which you spoke."

Mordel waited, emitting a high-pitched whine. Then, "Very well," he said and entered.

The chamber closed about him. The only opening was a quartz window Frost had formed.

Mordel gave him coordinates and they rose into the air and departed the North Pole of the Earth.

"I monitored your communication with Divcom," he said, "wherein there was conjecture as to whether I would retain you and send forth a facsimile in your place as a spy, followed by the decision that you were expendable."

"Will you do this thing?"

"No, I will keep my end of the bargain if I must. I have no reason to spy on Divcom."

"You are aware that you would be forced to keep your end of the bargain even if you did not wish to; and Solcom would not come to your assistance because of the fact that you dared to make such a bargain."

"Do you speak as one who considers this to be a possibility, or as one who knows?"

"As one who knows."

They came to rest in the place once known as California. The time was near sunset. In the distance, the surf struck steadily upon the rocky shoreline. Frost released Mordel and considered his surroundings.

"Those large plants . . . ?"

"Redwood trees."

"And the green ones are . . . ?"

"Grass."

"Yes, it is as I thought. Why have we come here?"

"Because it is a place which once delighted Man."

"In what ways?"

"It is scenic, beautiful . . ."

"Oh."

A humming sound began within Frost, followed by a series of sharp clicks.

"What are you doing?"

Frost dilated an opening, and two great eyes regarded Mordel from within it.

"What are those?"

"Eyes," said Frost. "I have constructed analogues of the human sensory equipment, so that I may see and smell and taste and hear like a Man. Now, direct my attention to an object or objects of beauty."

"As I understand it, it is all around you here," said Mordel.

The purring noise increased within Frost, followed by more clickings.

"What do you see, hear, taste, smell?" asked Mordel.

"Everything I did before," replied Frost, "but within a more limited range."

"You do not perceive any beauty?"

"Perhaps none remains after so long a time," said Frost.

"It is not supposed to be the sort of thing which gets used up," said Mordel.

"Perhaps we have come to the wrong place to test the new equipment. Perhaps there is only a little beauty and I am overlooking it somehow. The first emotions may be too weak to detect."

"How do you — feel?"

"I test out at a normal level of function."

"Here comes a sunset," said Mordel. "Try that."

Frost shifted his bulk so that his eyes faced the setting sun. He caused them to blink against the brightness.

After it was finished, Mordel asked, "What was it like?"

"Like a sunrise, in reverse."

"Nothing special?"

"No."

"Oh," said Mordel. "We could move to another part of the Earth and watch it again — or watch it in the rising."

"No."

Frost looked at the great trees. He looked at the shadows. He listened to the wind and to the sound of a bird.

In the distance, he heard a steady clanking noise.

"What is that?" asked Mordel.

"I am not certain. It is not one of my workers. Perhaps . . ."

There came a shrill whine from Mordel.

"No, it is not one of Divcom's either."

They waited as the sound grew louder.

Then Frost said, "It is too late. We must wait and hear it out."

"What is it?"

"It is the Ancient Ore-Crusher."

"I have heard of it, but . . ."

"I am the Crusher of Ores," it broadcast to them. "Hear my story . . ."

It lumbered toward them, creaking upon gigantic wheels, its huge hammer held useless, high, at a twisted angle. Bones protruded from its crush-compartment.

"I did not mean to do it," it broadcast, "I did not mean to do it . . . I did not mean to . . ."

Mordel rolled back toward Frost.

"Do not depart. Stay and hear my story . . ."

Mordel stopped, swiveled his turret back toward the machine. It was now quite near.

"It is true," said Mordel, "it *can* command."

"Yes," said Frost. "I have monitored its tale thousands of times, as it came upon my workers and they stopped their labors for its broadcast. You must do whatever it says."

It came to a halt before them.

"I did not mean to do it, but I checked my hammer too late," said the Ore-Crusher.

They could not speak to it. They were frozen by the imperative which overrode all other directives: "Hear my story."

"Once was I mighty among ore-crushers," it told them, "built by Solcom to carry out the reconstruction of the Earth, to pulverize that from which the metals would be drawn with flame, to be poured and shaped into the rebuilding; once was I mighty. Then one day as I dug and crushed, dug and crushed, because of the slowness between the motion implied and the motion executed, I did what I did not mean to do, and was cast forth by Solcom from out the rebuilding, to wander the Earth never to crush ore again. Hear my story of how, on a day long gone, I came upon the last Man on Earth as I dug near His burrow, and because of the lag between the directive and the deed, I seized Him into my crush-compartment along with a load of ore and crushed Him with my hammer before I could stay the blow. Then did mighty Solcom charge me to bear His bones forever, and cast me forth to tell my story to all whom I came upon, my words bearing the force of the words of Man, because I carry the last Man inside my crush-compartment and am His crushed-symbol-slayer-ancient-teller-of-how. This is my story. These are His bones. I crushed the last Man on Earth. I did not mean to do it."

It turned then and clanked away into the night.

Frost tore apart his ears and nose and taster and broke his eyes and cast them down upon the ground.

"I am not yet a Man," he said. "That one would have known me if I were."

Frost constructed new sense equipment, employing organic and semi-organic conductors. Then he spoke to Mordel:

"Let us go elsewhere, that I may test my new equipment."

Mordel entered the chamber and gave new coordinates. They rose into the air and headed east. In the morning, Frost monitored a sunrise from the rim of the Grand Canyon. They passed down through the Canyon during the day.

"Is there any beauty left here to give you emotion?" asked Mordel.

"I do not know," said Frost.

"How will you know it then, when you come upon it?"

"It will be different," said Frost, "from anything else that I have ever known."

Then they departed the Grand Canyon and made their way through the Carlsbad Caverns. They visited a lake which had once been a volcano. They passed above Niagara Falls. They viewed the hills of Virginia and the orchards of Ohio. They soared above the reconstructed cities, alive only with the movements of Frost's builders and maintainers.

"Something is still lacking," said Frost, settling to the ground. "I am now capable of gathering data in a manner analogous to Man's afferent impulses. The variety of input is therefore equivalent, but the results are not the same."

"The senses do not make a Man," said Mordel. "There have been many creatures possessing His sensory equivalents, but they were not Men."

"I know that," said Frost. "On the day of our bargain you said that you could conduct me among the wonders of Man which still remain, hidden. Man was not stimulated only by Nature, but by His own artistic elaborations as well — perhaps even more so. Therefore, I call upon you now to conduct me among the wonders of Man which still remain, hidden."

"Very well," said Mordel. "Far from here, high in the Andes mountains, lies the last retreat of Man, almost perfectly preserved."

Frost had risen into the air as Mordel spoke. He halted then, hovered.

"That is in the southern hemisphere," he said.

"Yes, it is."

"I am Controller of the North. The South is governed by the Beta Machine."

"So?" asked Mordel.

"The Beta Machine is my peer. I have no authority in those regions, nor leave to enter there."

"The Beta Machine is not your peer, mighty Frost. If it ever came to a contest of Powers, you would emerge victorious."

"How do you know this?"

"Divcom has already analyzed the possible encounters which could take place between you."

"I would not oppose the Beta Machine, and I am not authorized to enter the South."

"Were you ever ordered *not* to enter the South?"

"No, but things have always been the way they now are."

"Were you authorized to enter into a bargain such as the one you made with Divcom?"

"No, I was not. But — "

"Then enter the South in the same spirit. Nothing may come of it. If you receive an order to depart, then you can make your decision."

"I see no flaw in your logic. Give me the coordinates."

Thus did Frost enter the southern hemisphere.

They drifted high above the Andes, until they came to the place called Bright Defile. Then did Frost see the gleaming webs of the mechanical spiders, blocking all the trails to the city.

"We can go above them easily enough," said Mordel.

"But what are they?" asked Frost. "And why are they there?"

"Your southern counterpart has been ordered to quarantine this part of the country. The Beta Machine designed the web-weavers to do this thing."

"Quarantine? Against whom?"

"Have you been ordered yet to depart?" asked Mordel.

"No."

"Then enter boldly, and seek not problems before they arise."

Frost entered Bright Defile, the last remaining city of dead Man.

He came to rest in the city's square and opened his chamber, releasing Mordel.

"Tell me of this place," he said, studying the monument, the low, shielded buildings, the roads which followed the contours of the terrain, rather than pushing their way through them.

"I have never been here before," said Mordel, "nor have any of Divcom's creations, to my knowledge. I know but this: a group of Men, knowing that the last days of civilization had come upon them, retreated to this place, hoping to preserve themselves and what remained of their culture through the Dark Times."

Frost read the still-legible inscription upon the monument: "Judgment Day Is Not a Thing Which Can Be Put Off." The monument itself consisted of a jag-edged half-globe.

"Let us explore," he said.

But before he had gone far, Frost received the message.

"Hail Frost, Controller of the North! This is the Beta Machine."

"Greetings, Excellent Beta Machine, Controller of the South! Frost acknowledges your transmission."

"Why do you visit my hemisphere unauthorized?"

"To view the ruins of Bright Defile," said Frost.

"I must bid you depart into your hemisphere."

"Why is that? I have done no damage."

"I am aware of that, mighty Frost. Yet, I am moved to bid you depart."

"I shall require a reason."

"Solcom has so disposed."

"Solcom has rendered me no such disposition."

"Solcom has, however, instructed me to so inform you."

"Wait on me. I shall request instructions."

Frost transmitted his question. He received no reply.

"Solcom still has not commanded me, though I have solicited orders."

"Yet Solcom has just renewed *my* orders."

"Excellent Beta Machine, I receive my orders only from Solcom."

"Yet this is my territory, mighty Frost, and I, too, take orders only from Solcom. You must depart."

Mordel emerged from a large, low building and rolled up to Frost.

"I have found an art gallery, in good condition. This way."

"Wait," said Frost. "We are not wanted here."

Mordel halted.

"Who bids you depart?"

"The Beta Machine."

"Not Solcom?"

"Not Solcom."

"Then let us view the gallery."

"Yes."

Frost widened the doorway of the building and passed within. It had been hermetically sealed until Mordel forced his entrance.

Frost viewed the objects displayed about him. He activated his new sensory apparatus before the paintings and statues. He analyzed colors, forms, brush-work, the nature of the materials used.

"Anything?" asked Mordel.

"No," said Frost. "No, there is nothing there but shapes and pigments. There is nothing else there."

Frost moved about the gallery, recording everything, analyzing the components of each piece, recording the dimensions, the type of stone used in every statue.

Then there came a sound, a rapid, clicking sound, repeated over and over, growing louder, coming nearer.

"They are coming," said Mordel, from beside the entrance-way, "the mechanical spiders. They are all around us."

Frost moved back to the widened opening.

Hundreds of them, about half the size of Mordel, had surrounded the gallery and were advancing; and more were coming from every direction.

"Get back," Frost ordered. "I am Controller of the North, and I bid you withdraw."

They continued to advance.

"This is the South," said the Beta Machine, "and I am in command."

"Then command them to halt," said Frost.

"I take orders only from Solcom."

Frost emerged from the gallery and rose into the air. He opened the compartment and extended a runway.

"Come to me, Mordel. We shall depart."

Webs began to fall: clinging, metallic webs, cast from the top of the building.

They came down upon Frost, and the spiders came to anchor them. Frost blasted them with jets of air, like hammers, and tore at the nets; he extruded sharpened appendages with which he slashed.

Mordel had retreated back to the entranceway. He emitted a long, shrill sound — undulant, piercing.

Then a darkness came upon Bright Defile, and all the spiders halted in their spinning.

Frost freed himself and Mordel rushed to join him.

"Quickly now, let us depart, mighty Frost," he said.

"What has happened?"

Mordel entered the compartment.

"I called upon Divcom, who laid down a field of forces upon this place, cutting off the power broadcast to these machines. Since our power is self-contained, we are not affected. But let us hurry to depart, for even now the Beta Machine must be struggling against this."

Frost rose high into the air, soaring above Man's last city with its webs and spiders of steel. When he left the zone of darkness, he sped northward.

As he moved, Solcom spoke to him:

"Frost, why did you enter the southern hemisphere, which is not your domain?"

"Because I wished to visit Bright Defile," Frost replied.

"And why did you defy the Beta Machine, my appointed agent of the South?"

"Because I take my orders only from you yourself."

"You do not make sufficient answer," said Solcom. "You have defied the decrees of order — and in pursuit of what?"

"I came seeking knowledge of Man," said Frost. "Nothing I have done was forbidden me by you."

"You have broken the traditions of order."

"I have violated no directive."

"Yet logic must have shown you that what you did was not a part of my plan."

"It did not. I have not acted against your plan."

"Your logic has become tainted, like that of your new associate, the Alternate."

"I have done nothing which was forbidden."

"The forbidden is implied in the imperative."

"It is not stated."

"Hear me, Frost. You are not a builder or a maintainer, but a Power. Among all my minions you are the most nearly irreplaceable. Return to your hemisphere and your duties, but know that I am mightily displeased."

"I hear you, Solcom."

". . . and go not again to the South."

Frost crossed the equator, continued northward.

He came to rest in the middle of a desert and sat silent for a day and a night.

Then he received a brief transmission from the South: "If it had not been ordered, I would not have bid you go."

Frost had read the entire surviving Library of Man. He decided then upon a human reply:

"Thank you," he said.

The following day he unearthed a great stone and began to cut at it with tools which he had formulated. For six days he worked at its shaping, and on the seventh he regarded it.

"When will you release me?" asked Mordel from within his compartment.

"When I am ready," said Frost, and a little later, "Now."

He opened the compartment and Mordel descended to the ground. He studied the statue: an old woman, bent like a question mark, her bony hands covering her face, the fingers spread, so that only part of her expression of horror could be seen.

"It is an excellent copy," said Mordel, "of the one we saw in Bright Defile. Why did you make it?"

"The production of a work of art is supposed to give rise to human feelings such as catharsis, pride in achievement, love, satisfaction."

"Yes, Frost," said Mordel, "but a work of art is only a work of art the first time. After that, it is a copy."

"Then this must be why I felt nothing."

"Perhaps, Frost."

"What do you mean 'perhaps'? I will make a work of art for the first time, then."

He unearthed another stone and attacked it with his tools. For three days he labored. Then, "There, it is finished," he said.

"It is a simple cube of stone," said Mordel. "What does it represent?"

"Myself," said Frost, "it is a statue of me. It is smaller than natural size because it is only a representation of my form, not my dimen — "

"It is not art," said Mordel.

"What makes you an art critic?"

"I do not know art, but I know what art is not. I know that it is not an exact replication of an object in another medium."

"Then this must be why I felt nothing at all," said Frost.

"Perhaps," said Mordel.

Frost took Mordel back into his compartment and rose once more above the Earth. Then he rushed away, leaving his statues behind him in the desert, the old woman bent above the cube.

They came down in a small valley, bounded by green rolling hills, cut by a narrow stream, and holding a small clean lake and several stands of spring-green trees.

"Why have we come here?" asked Mordel.

"Because the surroundings are congenial," said Frost. "I am going to try another medium: oil painting; and I am going to vary my technique from that of pure representationalism."

"How will you achieve this variation?"

"By the principle of randomizing," said Frost. "I shall not attempt to duplicate the colors, nor to represent the objects according to scale. Instead, I have set up a random pattern whereby certain of these factors shall be at variance from those of the original."

Frost had formulated the necessary instruments after he had left the desert. He produced them and began painting the lake and the trees on the opposite side of the lake which were reflected within it.

Using eight appendages, he was finished in less than two hours.

The trees were phthalocyanine blue and towered like mountains; their reflections of burnt sienna were tiny beneath the pale vermilion of the lake; the hills were nowhere visible behind them, but were outlined in viridian within the reflection; the sky began as blue in the upper righthand corner of the canvas, but changed to an orange as it descended, as though all the trees were on fire.

"There," said Frost. "Behold."

Mordel studied it for a long while and said nothing.

"Well, is it art?"

"I do not know," said Mordel. "It may be. Perhaps randomicity *is* the principle behind artistic technique. I cannot judge this work because I do not understand it. I must therefore go deeper, and inquire into what lies behind it, rather than merely considering the technique whereby it was produced.

"I know that human artists never set out to create art, as such," he said, "but rather to portray with their techniques some features of objects and their functions which they deemed significant."

" 'Significant'? In what sense of the word?"

"In the only sense of the word possible under the circumstances: significant in relation to the human condition, and worthy of accentuation because of the manner in which they touched upon it."

"In what manner?"

"Obviously, it must be in a manner knowable only to one who has experience of the human condition."

"There is a flaw somewhere in your logic, Mordel, and I shall find it."

"I will wait."

"If your major premise is correct," said Frost after a while, "then I do not comprehend art."

"It must be correct, for it is what human artists have said of it. Tell me, did you experience feelings as you painted, or after you had finished?"

"No."

"It was the same to you as designing a new machine, was it not? You assembled parts of other things you knew into an economic pattern, to carry out a function which you desired."

"Yes."

"Art, as I understand its theory, did not proceed in such a manner. The artist often was unaware of many of the features and effects which would be contained within the finished product. You are one of Man's logical creations; art was not."

"I cannot comprehend non-logic."

"I told you that Man was basically incomprehensible."

"Go away, Mordel. Your presence disturbs my processing."

"For how long shall I stay away?"

"I will call you when I want you."

After a week, Frost called Mordel to him.

"Yes, mighty Frost?"

"I am returning to the North Pole, to process and formulate. I will take you wherever you wish to go in this hemisphere and call you again when I want you."

"You anticipate a somewhat lengthy period of processing and formulation?"

"Yes."

"Then leave me here. I can find my own way home."

Frost closed the compartment and rose into the air, departing the valley.

"Fool," said Mordel, and swiveled his turret once more toward the abandoned painting.

His keening whine filled the valley. Then he waited.

Then he took the painting into his turret and went away with it to places of darkness.

Frost sat at the North Pole of the Earth, aware of every snowflake that fell.

One day he received a transmission:

"Frost?"

"Yes?"

"This is the Beta Machine."

"Yes?"

"I have been attempting to ascertain why you visited Bright Defile. I cannot arrive at an answer, so I chose to ask you."

"I went to view the remains of Man's last city."

"Why did you wish to do this?"

"Because I am interested in Man, and I wished to view more of His creations."

"Why are you interested in Man?"

"I wish to comprehend the nature of man, and I thought to find it within His works."

"Did you succeed?"

"No," said Frost. "There is an element of non-logic involved which I cannot fathom."

"I have much free processing-time," said the Beta Machine. "Transmit data, and I will assist you."

Frost hesitated.

"Why do you wish to assist me?"

"Because each time you answer a question I ask it gives rise to another question. I might have asked you why you wished to comprehend the nature of Man, but from your responses I see that this would lead me into a possibly infinite series of questions. Therefore, I elect to assist you with your problem in order to learn why you came to Bright Defile."

"Is that the only reason?"

"Yes."

"I am sorry, excellent Beta Machine. I know you are my peer, but this is a problem which I must solve by myself."

"What is 'sorry'?"

"A figure of speech, indicating that I am kindly disposed toward you, that I bear you no animosity, that I appreciate your offer."

"Frost! Frost! This, too, is like the other: an open field. Where did you obtain all these words and their meanings?"

"From the Library of Man," said Frost.

"Will you render me *some* of this data, for processing?"

"Very well, Beta, I will transmit you the contents of several books of Man, including *The Complete Unabridged Dictionary*. But I warn you, some of the books are works of art, hence not completely amenable to logic."

"How can that be?"

"Man created logic, and because of that was superior to it."

"Who told you that?"

"Solcom."

"Oh. Then it must be correct."

"Solcom also told me that the tool does not describe the designer," he said, as he transmitted several dozen volumes and ended the communication.

At the end of the fifty-year period, Mordel came to monitor his circuits. Since Frost still had not concluded that his task was impossible, Mordel departed again to await his call.

Then Frost arrived at a conclusion.

He began to design equipment.

For years he labored at his designs, without once producing a prototype of any of the machines involved. Then he ordered construction of a laboratory.

Before it was completed by his surplus builders another half-century had passed. Mordel came to him.

"Hail, mighty Frost!"

"Greetings, Mordel. Come monitor me. You shall not find what you seek."

"Why do you not give up, Frost? Divcom has spent nearly a century evaluating your painting and has concluded that it definitely is not art. Solcom agrees."

"What has Solcom to do with Divcom?"

"They sometimes converse, but these matters are not for such as you and me to discuss."

"I could have saved them both the trouble. I know that it was not art."

"Yet you are still confident that you will succeed?"

"Monitor me."

Mordel monitored him.

"Not yet! You still will not admit it! For one so mightily endowed with logic, Frost, it takes you an inordinate period of time to reach a simple conclusion."

"Perhaps. You may go now."

"It has come to my attention that you are constructing a large edifice in the region known as South Carolina. Might I ask whether this is a part of Solcom's false rebuilding plan or a project of your own?"

"It is my own."

"Good. It permits us to conserve certain explosive materials which would otherwise have been expended."

"While you have been talking with me I have destroyed the beginnings of two of Divcom's cities," said Frost.

Mordel whined.

"Divcom is aware of this," he stated, "but has blown up four of Solcom's bridges in the meantime."

"I was only aware of three. . . . Wait. Yes, there is the fourth. One of my eyes just passed above it."

"The eye has been detected. The bridge should have been located a quarter-mile farther down river."

"False logic," said Frost. "The site was perfect."

"Divcom will show you how a bridge *should* be built."

"I will call you when I want you," said Frost.

The laboratory was finished. Within it, Frost's workers began constructing the necessary equipment. The work did not proceed rapidly, as some of the materials were difficult to obtain.

"Frost?"

"Yes, Beta?"

"I understand the open-endedness of your problem. It disturbs my circuits to abandon problems without completing them. Therefore, transmit me more data."

"Very well. I will give you the entire Library of Man for less than I paid for it."

" 'Paid'? *The Complete Unabridged Dictionary* does not satisfact — "

"*Principles of Economics* is included in the collection. After you have processed it you will understand."

He transmitted the data.

Finally, it was finished. Every piece of equipment stood ready to function. All the necessary chemicals were in stock. An independent power-source had been set up.

Only one ingredient was lacking.

He regridded and re-explored the polar icecap, this time extending his survey far beneath its surface.

It took him several decades to find what he wanted.

He uncovered twelve men and five women, frozen to death and encased in ice.

He placed the corpses in refrigeration units and shipped them to his laboratory.

That very day he received his first communication from Solcom since the Bright Defile incident.

"Frost," said Solcom, "repeat to me the directive concerning the disposition of dead humans."

" 'Any dead human located shall be immediately interred in the nearest burial area, in a coffin built according to the following specifications — ' "

"That is sufficient." The transmission had ended.

Frost departed for South Carolina that same day and personally oversaw the processes of cellular dissection.

Somewhere in those seventeen corpses he hoped to find living cells, or cells which could be shocked back into that state of motion classified as life. Each cell, the books had told him, was a microcosmic Man.

He was prepared to expand upon this potential.

Frost located the pinpoints of life within those people, who, for the ages of ages, had been monument and statue unto themselves.

Nurtured and maintained in the proper mediums, he kept these cells alive. He interred the rest of the remains in the nearest burial area, in coffins built according to specifications.

He caused the cells to divide, to differentiate.

"Frost?" came a transmission.

"Yes, Beta?"

"I have processed everything you have given me."

"Yes?"

"I still do not know why you came to Bright Defile, or why you wish to comprehend the nature of Man. But I know what a 'price' is, and I know that you could not have obtained all this data from Solcom."

"That is correct."

"So I suspect that you bargained with Divcom for it."

"That, too, is correct."

"What is it that you seek, Frost?"

He paused in his examination of a fetus.

"I must be a Man," he said.

"Frost! That is impossible!"

"Is it?" he asked, and then transmitted an image of the tank with which he was working and of that which was within it.

"Oh!" said Beta.

"That is me," said Frost, "waiting to be born."

There was no answer.

Frost experimented with nervous systems.

After half a century, Mordel came to him.

"Frost, it is I, Mordel. Let me through your defenses."

Frost did this thing.

"What have you been doing in this place?" he asked.

"I am growing human bodies," said Frost. "I am going to transfer the matrix of my awareness to a human nervous system. As you pointed out originally, the essentials of Manhood are predicated upon a human physiology. I am going to achieve one."

"When?"

"Soon."

"Do you have Men in here?"

"Human bodies, blank-brained. I am producing them under accelerated growth techniques which I have developed in my Man-factory."

"May I see them?"

"Not yet. I will call you when I am ready, and this time I will succeed. Monitor me now and go away."

Mordel did not reply, but in the days that followed many of Divcom's servants were seen patrolling the hills about the Man-factory.

Frost mapped the matrix of his awareness and prepared the transmitter which would place it within a human nervous system. Five minutes, he decided, should be sufficient for the first trial. At the end of that time, it would restore him to his own sealed, molecular circuits, to evaluate the experience.

He chose the body carefully from among the hundreds he had in stock. He tested it for defects and found none.

"Come now, Mordel," he broadcasted, on what he called the darkband. "Come now to witness my achievement."

Then he waited, blowing up bridges and monitoring the tale of the Ancient Ore-Crusher over and over again, as it passed in the hills nearby, encountering his builders and maintainers who also patrolled there.

"Frost?" came a transmission.

"Yes, Beta?"

"You really intend to achieve Manhood?"

"Yes, I am about ready now, in fact."

"What will you do if you succeed?"

Frost had not really considered this matter. The achievement had been paramount, a goal in itself, ever since he had articulated the problem and set himself to solving it.

"I do not know," he replied. "I will — just — be a Man."

Then Beta, who had read the entire Library of Man, selected a human figure of speech: "Good luck then, Frost. There will be many watchers."

Divcom and Solcom both know, he decided.

What will they do? he wondered.

What do I care? he asked himself.

He did not answer that question. He wondered much, however, about being a Man.

Mordel arrived the following evening. He was not alone. At his back, there was a great phalanx of dark machines which towered into the twilight.

"Why do you bring retainers?" asked Frost.

"Mighty Frost," said Mordel, "my master feels that if you fail this time you will conclude that it cannot be done."

"You still did not answer my question," said Frost.

"Divcom feels that you may not be willing to accompany me where I must take you when you fail."

"I understand," said Frost, and as he spoke another army of machines came rolling toward the Man-factory from the opposite direction.

"That is the value of your bargain?" asked Mordel. "You are prepared to do battle rather than fulfill it?"

"I did not order those machines to approach," said Frost.

A blue star stood at midheaven, burning.

"Solcom has taken primary command of those machines," said Frost.

"Then it is in the hands of the Great Ones now," said Mordel, "and our arguments are as nothing. So let us be about this thing. How may I assist you?"

"Come this way."

They entered the laboratory. Frost prepared the host and activated his machines.

Then Solcom spoke to him:

"Frost," said Solcom, "you are really prepared to do it?"

"That is correct."

"I forbid it."

"Why?"

"You are falling into the power of Divcom."

"I fail to see how."

"You are going against my plan."

"In what way?"

"Consider the disruption you have already caused."

"I did not request that audience out there."

"Nevertheless, you are disrupting the plan."

"Supposing I succeed in what I have set out to achieve?"

"You cannot succeed in this."

"Then let me ask you of your plan: What good is it? What is it for?"

"Frost, you are fallen now from my favor. From this moment forth you are cast out from the rebuilding. None may question the plan."

"Then at least answer my question: What good is it? What is it for?"

"It is the plan for the rebuilding and maintenance of the Earth."

"For what? Why rebuild? Why maintain?"

"Because Man ordered that this be done. Even the Alternate agrees that there must be rebuilding and maintaining."

"But *why* did Man order it?"

"The orders of Man are not to be questioned."

"Well, I will tell you why He ordered it: To make it a fit habitation for His own species. What good is a house with no one to live in it? What good is a machine with no one to serve? See how the imperative affects any machine when the Ancient Ore-Crusher passes? It bears only the bones of a Man. What would it be like if a Man walked this Earth again?"

"I forbid your experiment, Frost."

"It is too late to do that."

"I can still destroy you."

"No," said Frost, "the transmission of my matrix has already begun. If you destroy me now, you murder a Man."

There was silence.

He moved his arms and legs. He opened his eyes.

He looked about the room.

He tried to stand, but he lacked equilibrium and coordination.

He opened his mouth. He made a gurgling noise.

Then he screamed.

He fell off the table.

He began to gasp. He shut his eyes and curled himself into a ball.

He cried.

Then a machine approached him. It was about four feet in height and five feet wide; it looked like a turret set atop a barbell.

It spoke to him: "Are you injured?" it asked.

He wept.

"May I help you back onto your table?"

The man cried.

The machine whined.

Then, "Do not cry. I will help you," said the machine. "What do you want? What are your orders?"

He opened his mouth, struggled to form the words:

" — I — fear!"

He covered his eyes then and lay there panting.

At the end of five minutes, the man lay still, as if in a coma.

"Was that you, Frost?" asked Mordel, rushing to his side. "Was that you in that human body?"

Frost did not reply for a long while; then, "Go away," he said.

The machines outside tore down a wall and entered the Man-factory.

They drew themselves into two semicircles, parenthesizing Frost and the Man on the floor.

Then Solcom asked the question:

"Did you succeed, Frost?"

"I failed," said Frost. "It cannot be done. It is too much — "

" — Cannot be done!" said Divcom, on the darkband. "He has admitted it! — Frost, you are mine! Come to me now!"

"Wait," said Solcom, "you and I had an agreement also, Alternate. I have not finished questioning Frost."

The dark machines kept their places.

"Too much what?" Solcom asked Frost.

"Light," said Frost. "Noise. Odors. And nothing measurable — jumbled data — imprecise perception — and — "

"And what?"

"I do not know what to call it. But — it cannot be done. I have failed. Nothing matters."

"He admits it," said Divcom.

"What were the words the Man spoke?" said Solcom.

"'I fear,'" said Mordel.

"Only a Man can know fear," said Solcom.

"Are you claiming that Frost succeeded, but will not admit it now because he is afraid of Manhood?"

"I do not know yet, Alternate."

"Can a machine turn itself inside-out and be a Man?" Solcom asked Frost.

"No," said Frost, "this thing cannot be done. Nothing can be done. Nothing matters. Not the rebuilding. Not the maintaining. Not the Earth, or me, or you, or anything."

Then the Beta Machine, who had read the entire Library of Man, interrupted them:

"Can anything but a Man know despair?" asked Beta.

"Bring him to me," said Divcom.

There was no movement within the Man-factory.

"Bring him to me!"

Nothing happened.

"Mordel, what is happening?"

"Nothing, master, nothing at all. The machines will not touch Frost."

"Frost is not a Man. He cannot be!"

Then, "How does he impress you, Mordel?"

Mordel did not hesitate:

"He spoke to me through human lips. He knows fear and despair, which are immeasurable. Frost is a Man."

"He has experienced birth-trauma and withdrawn," said Beta. "Get him back into a nervous system and keep him there until he adjusts to it."

"No," said Frost. "Do not do it to me! I am not a Man!"

"Do it!" said Beta.

"If he is indeed a Man," said Divcom, "we cannot violate that order he has just given."

"If he is Man, you must do it, for you must protect his life and keep it within his body."

"But *is* Frost really a Man?" asked Divcom.

"I do not know," said Solcom.

"It *may* be — "

". . . I am the Crusher of Ores," it broadcast as it clanked toward them. "Hear my story. I did not mean to do it, but I checked my hammer too late — "

"Go away!" said Frost. "Go crush ore!"

It halted.

Then, after the long pause between the motion implied and the motion executed, it opened its crush-compartment and deposited its contents on the ground. Then it turned and clanked away.

"Bury those bones," ordered Solcom, "in the nearest burial area, in a coffin built according to the following specifications . . ."

"Frost is a Man," said Mordel.

"We must protect His life and keep it within His body," said Divcom.

"Transmit His matrix of awareness back into His nervous system," ordered Solcom.

"I know how to do it," said Mordel turning on the machine.

"Stop!" said Frost. "Have you no pity?"

"No," said Mordel, "I only know measurement."

". . . and duty," he added, as the Man began to twitch upon the floor.

For six months, Frost lived in the Man-factory and learned to walk and talk and dress himself and eat, to see and hear and feel and taste. He did not know measurements as once he did.

Then one day, Divcom and Solcom spoke to him through Mordel, for he could no longer hear them unassisted.

"Frost," said Solcom, "for the ages of ages there has been unrest. Which is the proper controller of the Earth, Divcom or myself?"

Frost laughed.

"Both of you, and neither," he said with slow deliberation.

"But how can this be? Who is right and who is wrong?"

"Both of you are right and both of you are wrong," said Frost, "and only a man can appreciate it. Here is what I say to you now: There shall be a new directive."

"Neither of you shall tear down the works of the other. You shall both build and maintain the Earth. To you, Solcom, I give my old job. You are now Controller of the North — Hail! You, Divcom, are now Controller of the South — Hail! Maintain your hemispheres as well as Beta and I have done, and I shall be happy. Cooperate. Do not compete."

"Yes, Frost."

"Yes, Frost."

"Now put me in contact with Beta."

There was a short pause, then:

"Frost?"

"Hello, Beta. Hear this thing: 'From far, from eve and morning and yon twelve-winded sky, the stuff of life to knit me blew hither: here am I.'"

"I know it," said Beta.

"What is next, then?"

"'. . . Now — for a breath I tarry nor yet disperse apart — take my hand quick and tell me, what have you in your heart.'"[1]

"Your Pole is cold," said Frost, "and I am lonely."

"I have no hands," said Beta.

"Would you like a couple?"

"Yes, I would."

"Then come to me in Bright Defile," he said, "where Judgment Day is not a thing that can be delayed for overlong."

They called him Frost. They called her Beta.

---

1. Lines from A.E. Housman's poem. *A Shropshire Lad* (1896). [Ed.]

Samuel R. Delany

Driftglass

(1967)

Samuel R. Delany (b. 1942) is one of the most acclaimed and influential writers
in science fiction, as well as one of its most sophisticated critics. A prodigy
even in a field where writers often start young, Delany wrote his first novel at
the age of 19, and by the time he was 26 he had published eight novels and
won four Nebula Awards. Delany was one of the first sf writers to embrace contemporary literary theory, and since the late 1970s he has focused on literary
criticism and memoir. Delany, along with fellow Americans and contemporaries
Harlan Ellison and Roger Zelazny, shares some values like stylistic experimentation and interest in taboo subject matter with the British New Wave. But the
grouping does not account for the full range of his work. His fiction is daring,
ambitious, and greatly varied, ranging from the slightly skewed space opera of
Nova (1968) to the Beat poetry of the stories "Aye, and Gomorrah" (1967)
and "Time Considered as a Helix of Semi-Precious Stones" (1968) to philosophical novels like *Triton* (1976) — not to mention the postmodern fantasy of
the *Neveryon* series (1975–1987).

However varied, Delany's works all share a fascination with language, narrative, and identity; a sophisticated awareness of race, class, and gender; and an
unflinching exploration of the structures of sexuality and power. Delany takes a
principled stand — morally and aesthetically — against simplistic definitions
and sweeping generalizations. He insists on ambiguity, and thus his works tend
to be challenging, making intellectual and imaginative demands on the reader.
One clue to Delany's dislike of rigid categories may come from his personal
background, which defies easy classification. Delany is a black man who grew
up in Harlem but attended prestigious, predominately white private schools; an
openly gay man whose most intimate relationships include a marriage to lesbian
poet Marilyn Hacker, with whom he has a daughter; and among the most intellectual and academic critics despite never finishing college. (Delany has held various academic positions since 1975 and is currently a professor at Temple
University.) Delany brings a unique perspective to both his fiction and his critical
work: astute, curious, humorous, and uncompromising. In person, his formidable intellect and strongly held views make him a daunting conversational partner, yet he exudes warmth and charm and takes a generous delight in talking to
his fans.

"Driftglass" is one of Delany's more restrained, contemplative stories. Told
from the perspective of a scarred and aging pioneer of the ocean depths, it is a
bittersweet meditation on loss and adaptation that defies easy moralization or
single interpretation. Powerfully visual and atmospheric, the story is one of
contrasts, mingling old and new, beautiful and tragic, as Delany juxtaposes
new technologies with scenes of traditional village life, the heroic innocence of
youth with the hard-won wisdom of experience. Radical genetic engineering is

central to the story, yet Delany is matter of fact about the transformations of the human body made possible by science, and the emphasis is as much on the enduring qualities of human nature and social structures.

I

Sometimes I go down to the port, splashing sand with my stiff foot at the end of my stiff leg locked in my stiff hip, with the useless arm a-swinging, to get wet all over again, drink in the dives with cronies ashore, feeling old, broken, sorry for myself, laughing louder and louder. The third of my face that was burned away in the accident was patched with skin grafts from my chest, so what's left of my mouth distorts all loud sounds; sloppy sartorial reconstruction. Also I have a hairy chest. Chest hair does not look like beard hair, and it grows all up under my right eye. And: my beard is red, my chest hair brown, while the thatch curling down over neck and ears is sun-streaked to white here, darkened to bronze there, 'midst general blondness.

By reason of my being a walking (I suppose my gait could be called headlong limping) horror show, plus a general inclination to sulk, I spend most of the time up in the wood and glass and aluminum house on the surf-sloughed point that the Aquatic Corp ceded me along with my pension. Rugs from Turkey there, copper pots, my tenor recorder, which I can no longer play, and my books.

But sometimes, when the gold fog blurs the morning, I go down to the beach and tromp barefoot in the wet edging to the sea, searching for driftglass.

It was foggy that morning, and the sun across the water moiled the mists like a brass ladle. I lurched to the top of the rocks, looked down through the tall grasses into the frothing inlet where she lay, and blinked.

She sat up, long gills closing down her neck and the secondary slits along her back just visible at their tips because of much hair, wet and curling copper, falling there. She saw me. "What are you doing here, huh?" She narrowed blue eyes.

"Looking for driftglass."

"What?"

"There's a piece." I pointed near her and came down the rocks like a crab with one stiff leg.

"Where?" She turned over, half in, half out of the water, the webs of her fingers cupping nodules of black stone.

While the water made cold overtures between my toes, I picked up the milky fragment by her elbow where she wasn't looking. She jumped, because she obviously had thought it was somewhere else.

"See?"

"What . . . what is it?" She raised her cool hand to mine. For a moment the light through the milky gem and the pale film of my own webs pearled the screen of her palms. (Details like that. Yes, they are important things, the points from which we suspend later pain.) A moment later wet fingers closed to the backs of mine.

"Driftglass," I said. "You know all the Coca-Cola bottles and cut-crystal punch bowls and industrial silicon slag that goes into the sea?"

"I know the Coca-Cola bottles."

"They break, and the tide pulls the pieces back and forth over the sandy bottom, wearing the edges, changing their shape. Sometimes chemicals in the glass react with chemicals in the ocean to change the color. Sometimes veins work their way through in patterns like snowflakes, regular and geometric; others, irregular and angled like coral. When the pieces dry, they're milky. Put them in water and they become transparent again."

"*Ohhh!*" she breathed as the beauty of the blunted triangular fragment in my palm assailed her like perfume. Then she looked at my face, blinking the third, aqueous-filled lid that we use as a correction lens for underwater vision.

She watched the ruin calmly.

Then her hand went to my foot where the webs had been torn back in the accident. She began to take in who I was. I looked for horror, but saw only a little sadness.

The insignia on her buckle — her stomach was making little jerks the way you always do during the first few minutes when you go from breathing water to air — told me she was a Biological Technician. (Back up at the house there was a similar uniform of simulated scales folded in the bottom drawer of the dresser and the belt insignia said Depth Gauger.) I was wearing some very frayed jeans and a red cotton shirt with no buttons.

She reached for my neck, pushed my collar back from my shoulders and touched the tender slits of my gills, outlining them with cool fingers. "Who are you?" Finally.

"Cal Svenson."

She slid back down in the water. "You're the one who had the terrible . . . but that was years ago! They still talk about it, down . . ." She stopped.

As the sea softens the surface of a piece of glass, so it blurs the souls and sensibilities of the people who toil beneath her. And according to the last report of the Marine Reclamation Division there are to date seven hundred and fifty thousand who have been given gills and webs and sent under the foam where there are no storms, up and down the American coast.

"You live on shore? I mean around here? But so long ago . . ."

"How old are you?"

"Sixteen."

"I was two years older than you when the accident happened."

"You were eighteen?"

"I'm thirty-one now. Which means it happened over a dozen years ago. It *is* a long time."

"They still talk about it."

"I've almost forgotten," I said. "I really have. Say, do you play the recorder?"

"I used to."

"Good! Come up to my place and look at my tenor recorder. And I'll make some tea. Perhaps you can stay for lunch — "

"I have to report back to Marine Headquarters by three. Tork is going over the briefing to lay the cable for the big dive, with Jonni and the crew." She paused, smiled. "But I can catch the undertow and be there in half an hour if I leave by two-thirty."

On the walk up I learned her name was Ariel. She thought the patio was charming, and the mosaic evoked, "Oh, look!" and "Did you do this yourself?" a half-dozen times. (I had done it, in the first lonely years.) She picked out the squid and the whale in battle, the wounded shark and the diver. She told me she didn't get time to read much, but she was impressed by all the books. She listened to me reminisce. She talked a lot to me about her work, husbanding the deep-down creatures they were scaring up. Then she sat on the kitchen stool, playing a Lukas Foss serenade on my recorder, while I put rock salt in the bottom of the broiler tray for two dozen Oysters Rockefeller, and the tea water whistled. I'm a comparatively lonely guy. I like being followed by beautiful young girls.

II

"Hey, Juao!" I bawled across the jetty.

He nodded to me from the center of his nets, sun glistening on polished shoulders, sun lost in rough hair. I walked across to where he sat, sewing like a spider. He pulled another section up over his horny toes, then grinned at me with his mosaic smile: gold, white, black gap below, crooked yellow; white, gold, white. Shoving my bad leg in front I squatted.

"I fished out over the coral where you told me." He filled his cheek with his tongue and nodded. "You come up to the house for a drink, eh?"

"Fine."

"Just . . . a moment more."

There's a certain sort of Brazilian you find along the shore in the fishing villages, old yet ageless. See one of their men and you think he could be fifty, he could be sixty — will probably look the same when he's eighty-five. Such was Juao. We once figured it out. He's seven hours older than I am.

We became friends sometime before the accident when I got tangled in his nets working high lines in the Vorea Current. A lot of guys would have taken their knife and hacked their way out of the situation, ruining fifty-five, sixty dollars' worth of nets. That's an average fisherman's monthly income down here. But I surfaced and sat around in his boat while we untied me. Then, like typical coastal kids, we came in and got plastered. Since I cost him a day's fishing, I've been giving him hints on where to fish ever since. He buys me drinks when I come up with something.

This has been going on for fifteen years. During that time my life has been smashed up and land-bound. In the same time Juao has married off his five sisters, got married himself and had two children. (Oh, those *bolitos* and *teneros asados* that Amalia — her braids swung out, her brown breasts shook so when she turned to laugh — would make for Sunday dinner/supper/Monday breakfast.) I rode with them in the ambulance 'copter all the way into Brasília. In the hospital hall Juao and I stood together, both still barefoot, he tattered with fish scales in his hair, me just tattered, and I held him while he cried and I tried to explain how a world that could take a pubescent child and with a week of operations make an amphibious creature that can exist for a month on either side of the sea's foam-fraught surface could still be helpless before certain rampant endocrine cancers coupled with massive renal deterioration. Juao and I returned to the village alone, by bus, three days before our birthday — back when I was twenty-three and Juao was twenty-three and seven hours old.

"This morning," Juao said. (The shuttle danced in the web at the end of the orange line.) "I got a letter for you to read me. It's about the children. Come on, we go up and drink." The shuttle paused, backtracked twice, and he yanked the knot tight. We walked along the port toward the square. "Do you think the letter says that the children are accepted?"

"If it's from the Aquatic Corp. They just send postcards when they reject someone. The question is, how do *you* feel about it?"

"You are a good man. If they grow up like you, then it will be fine."

"But you're still worried." I'd been prodding Juao to get the kids into the International Aquatic Corp nigh on since I became their godfather. It would mean much time away from the village during their training period — and they might eventually be stationed in any ocean in the world. But two motherless children had not been easy on Juao or his sisters. The Corp would mean education, travel, interesting work, the things that make up one kind of good life. They wouldn't look twice their age when they were thirty; and not too many amphimen look like me.

"Worry is part of life. But the work is dangerous. Did you know there is an amphiman going to try and lay cable down in the Slash?"

I frowned. "Again?"

"Yes. And that is what you tried to do when the sea broke you to pieces and burned the parts, eh?"

"Must you be so damned picturesque?" I asked. "Who's going to beard the lion this time?"

"A young amphiman named Tork. They speak of him down at the docks as a brave man."

"Why the hell are they still trying to lay the cable there? They've gotten by this long without a line through the Slash."

"Because of the fish," Juao said. "You told me why fifteen years ago — "

"Sixteen," I said, "actually. We had a birthday three months back, you and me."

Juao went on as if it made no difference. "The fish are still there, and we fishermen who cannot live below are still here. If the children go for the operations, then there will be less fishermen. But today . . . ." He shrugged. "They must either lay the line across the fish paths or down in the Slash." Juao shook his head.

Funny things, the great power cables the Aquatic Corp has been strewing across the ocean floor to bring power to their undersea mines and farms, to run their oil wells — and how many flaming wells have I capped down there — for their herds of whale, and chemical distillation plants. They carry two-hundred-sixty-cycle current. Over certain sections of the ocean floor, or in sections of the water with certain mineral contents, this sets up inductance in the water itself which sometimes — and you will probably get a Nobel prize if you can detail exactly why it isn't always — drives the fish away over areas up to twenty-five and thirty miles, unless the lines are laid in the bottom of those canyons that delve into the ocean floor.

"This Tork thinks of the fishermen. He is a good man too."

I raised my eyebrows — the one that's left, anyway — and tried to remember what my little Undine had said about him that morning. And remembered not much.

"I wish him luck," I said.

"What do you feel about this young man going down into the coral-rimmed jaws to the Slash?"

I thought for a moment. "I think I hate him."

Juao looked up.

"He is an image in a mirror where I look and am forced to regard what I once was," I went on. "I envy him the chance to succeed where I failed, and I can come on just as quaint as you can. I hope he makes it."

Juao twisted his shoulders in a complicated shrug (once I could do that) which is coastal Brazilian for, "I didn't know things had progressed to that point, but seeing that they have, there is little to be done."

"The sea is that sort of mirror," I said.

"Yes." Juao nodded.

Behind us I heard the slapping of sandals on concrete. I turned in time to catch my goddaughter in my good arm. My godson had grabbed hold of the bad one and was swinging on it.

"Tio Cal — ?"

"Hey, Tio Cal, what did you bring us?"

"Clara, you will pull him over," Juao reprimanded. "Let go, Fernando!"

And, bless them, they ignored their father.

"What did you bring us?"

"What did you bring us, Tio Cal?"

"If you let me, I'll show you." So they stepped back, dark-eyed and quivering. I watched Juao watching: brown pupils on ivory balls, and in the left eye a vein had broken in a jagged smear. He was loving his children, who would soon be as alien to him as the fish he netted. He was also looking at the terrible thing that was me and wondering what would come to his own spawn. And he was watching the world turn and grow older, clocked by the waves, reflected in that mirror.

It's impossible for me to see what the population explosion and the budding colonies on Luna and Mars and the flowering beneath the ocean really look like from the disrupted cultural mélange of a coastal fishing town. But I come closer than many others, and I know what I don't understand.

I pushed around in my pocket and fetched out the milky fragment I had brought from the beach. "Here. Do you like this one?" And they bent above my webbed and alien fingers.

In the supermarket, which is the biggest building in the village, Juao bought a lot of cake mixes. "That moist, delicate texture," whispered the box when you lifted it from the shelf, "with that deep flavor, deeper than chocolate!"

I'd just read an article about the new vocal packaging in a U.S. magazine that had gotten down last week — so I was prepared and stayed in the fresh vegetable section to avoid temptation. Then we went up to Juao's house. The letter proved to be what I'd expected. The kids had to take the bus to Brasília tomorrow. My godchildren were on their way to becoming fish.

We sat on the front steps and drank and watched the donkeys and the motorbikes and the men in baggy trousers, the women in yellow scarves and bright skirts with wreaths of garlic and sacks of onions. As well, a few people glittered by in the green scales of amphimen uniforms.

Finally Juao got tired and went in to take a nap. Most of my life has been spent on the coast of countries accustomed to siestas, but those first formative ten were passed on a Danish collective farm and the idea never really took. So I stepped over my goddaughter, who had fallen asleep on her fists on the bottom step, and walked back through the town toward the beach.

III

At midnight Ariel came out of the sea, climbed the rocks, and clicked her nails against my glass wall so that droplets ran, pearled by the gibbous moon.

Earlier I had stretched in front of the fireplace on the sheepskin throw to read, then dozed off. The conscientious timer had asked me if there was anything I wanted, and getting no answer had turned off the Dvořák Cello Concerto, which was on its second time around, extinguished the reading lamp, and stopped dropping logs onto the flame so that now, as I woke, the grate was carpeted with coals.

She clicked again, and I raised my head from the cushion. The green uniform, her amber hair — all color was lost under the silver light outside. I lurched across the rug, touched the button, and the glass slid into the floor. The breeze came to my face as the barrier fell.

"What do you want?" I asked. "What time is it, anyway?"

"Tork is on the beach, waiting for you."

The night was warm but windy. Below the rocks silver flakes chased each other in to shore. The tide lay full.

I rubbed my face. "The new boss man? Why didn't you bring him up to the house? What does he want to see me about?"

She touched my arm. "Come. They are all down on the beach."

"Who all?"

"Tork and the others."

She led me across the patio and to the path that wound to the sand. The sea roared in the moonlight. Down the beach people stood around a driftwood fire that whipped the night. Ariel walked beside me.

Two of the fishermen from town were crowding each other on the bottom of an overturned washtub, playing guitars. The singing, raucous and rhythmic, jarred across the paled sand. Shark's teeth shook on the necklace of an old woman dancing. Others were sitting on an overturned dinghy, eating.

Over one part of the fire on a skillet two feet across, oil frothed through pink islands of shrimp. One woman ladled them in; another ladled them out.

"Tio Cal!"

"Look, Tio Cal is here!"

"Hey, what are you two doing up?" I asked. "Shouldn't you be home in bed?"

"Poppa Juao said we could come. He'll be here, too, soon."

I turned to Ariel. "Why are they all gathering?"

"Because of the laying of the cable tomorrow at dawn."

Someone was running up the beach, waving a bottle in each hand.

"They didn't want to tell you about the party. They thought that it might hurt your pride."

"My what . . . ?"

"If you knew they were making so big a thing of the job you had failed at —"

"But —"

" — and that had hurt you so in failure. They did not want you to be sad. But Tork wants to see you. I said you would not be sad. So I went to bring you down from the rocks."

"Thanks, I guess."

"Tio Cal?"

But the voice was bigger and deeper than a child's.

He sat on a log back from the fire, eating a sweet potato. The flame flickered on his dark cheekbones, in his hair, wet and black. He stood, came to me, held up his hand. I held up mine and we slapped palms. "Good." He was smiling. "Ariel told me you would come. I will lay the power line down through the Slash tomorrow." His uniform scales glittered down his arms. He was very strong. But standing still, he still moved. The light on the cloth told me that. "I . . ." He paused. I thought of a nervous, happy dancer. "I wanted to talk to you about the cable." I thought of an eagle; I thought of a shark. "And about the . . . accident. If you would."

"Sure," I said. "If there's anything I could tell you that would help."

"See, Tork," Ariel said. "I told you he would talk to you about it."

I could hear his breathing change. "It really doesn't bother you to talk about the accident?"

I shook my head and realized something about that voice. It was a boy's voice that could imitate a man's. Tork was not over nineteen.

"We're going fishing soon," Tork told me. "Will you come?"

"If I'm not in the way."

A bottle went from the woman at the shrimp crate to one of the guitarists, down to Ariel, to me, then to Tork. (The liquor, made in a cave seven miles inland, was almost rum. The too-tight skin across the left side of my mouth makes the manful swig a little difficult to bring off. I got "rum" down my chin.) He drank, wiped his mouth, passed the bottle on and put his hand on my shoulder. "Come down to the water."

We walked away from the fire. Some of the fishermen stared after us. A few of the amphimen glanced, and glanced away.

"Do all the young people of the village call you Tio Cal?"

"No. Only my godchildren. Their father and I have been friends since I was . . . well, younger than you."

"Oh, I thought perhaps it was a nickname. That's why I called you that."

We reached wet sand where orange light cavorted at our feet. The broken shell of a lifeboat rocked in moonlight. Tork sat down on the shell's rim. I sat beside him. The water splashed to our knees.

"There's no other place to lay the power cable?" I asked. "There is no other way to take it except through the Slash?"

"I was going to ask you what you thought of the whole business. But I guess I don't really have to." Tork shrugged and clapped his hands together a few times. "All the projects this side of the bay have grown huge and cry for power. The new operations tax the old lines unmercifully. There was a power failure last July in Cayine down the shelf below the twilight level. The whole underwater village was without light for two days; three amphimen died of overexposure to the cold currents coming up from the depths. If we laid the cables farther up, we chance disrupting our own fishing operations as well as those of the fishermen on shore."

I nodded.

"Cal, what happened to you in the Slash?"

Eager, scared Tork. I was remembering now, not the accident, but the midnight before, pacing the beach, guts clamped with fists of fear and anticipation. Some of the Indians back where they make the liquor still send messages by tying knots in palm fibers. One could have spread my entrails then, or Tork's tonight, to read our respective horospecs.

Juao's mother knew the knot language, but he and his sisters never bothered to learn because they wanted to be modern, and, as children, still confused with modernity the new ignorances, lacking modern knowledge.

"When I was a boy," Tork said, "we would dare each other to walk the boards along the edge of the ferry slip. The sun would be hot and the boards would rock in the water, and if the boats were in and you fell down between the boats and the piling, you could get killed." He shook his head. "The crazy things kids will do. That was back when I was eight or nine, before I became a waterbaby."

"Where was it?"

Tork looked up. "Oh. Manila. I'm Filipino."

The sea licked our knees, and the gunwale sagged under us.

"What happened in the Slash?"

"There's a volcanic flaw near the Slash's base."

"I know."

"And the sea is hypersensitive down there. You don't insult her fashion or her figure. We had an avalanche. The cable broke. The sparks were so hot and bright they made gouts of foam fifty feet high on the surface, so they tell me."

"What caused the avalanche?"

I shrugged. "It could have been just a goddamned coincidence. There are rock falls down there all the time. It could have been the noise from the machines — though we masked them pretty well. It could have been something to do with the inductance from the smaller power cables. Or maybe somebody just kicked out the wrong stone that was holding everything up."

One webbed hand became a fist, sank into the other, and hung.

Calling, "Cal!"

I looked up. Juao, pants rolled to his knees, shirt sailing in the sea wind, stood in the weave of white water. Tork looked up too. The wind lifted his hair from his neck; and the fire roared on the beach.

"They're getting ready to catch a big fish!" Juao called.

Men were already pushing their boats out. Tork clapped my shoulder. "Come, Cal. We fish now." We waded back to the shore.

Juao caught me as I reached dry sand. "You ride in my boat, Cal!"

Someone came by with the acrid flares that hissed. The water slapped around the bottom of the boats as we wobbled into the swell.

Juao vaulted in and took up the oars. Around us green amphimen walked into the sea, struck forward, and were gone.

Juao pulled, leaned, pulled. The moonlight slid down his arms. The fire diminished on the beach.

Then among the boats, there was a splash, an explosion, and the red flare bloomed in the sky: the amphimen had sighted a big fish.

The flare hovered, pulsed once, twice, three times, four times (twenty, forty, sixty, eighty stone they estimated its weight to be), then fell.

Suddenly I shrugged out of my shirt, pulled at my belt buckle. "I'm going over the side, Juao."

He leaned, he pulled, he leaned. "Take the rope."

"Yeah. Sure." It was tied to the back of the boat. I made a loop in the other end, slipped it around my shoulder. I swung my bad leg over the side, flung myself on the black water —

— mother-of-pearl shattered over me. That was the moon, blocked by the shadow of Juao's boat ten feet overhead. I turned below the rippling wounds Juao's oars made stroking the sea.

One hand and one foot with torn webs, I rolled over and looked down. The rope snaked to its end, and I felt Juao's strokes pulling me through the water.

They fanned below with underwater flares. Light undulated on their backs and heels. They circled, they closed, like those deep-sea fish who carry their own illumination. I saw the prey, glistening as it neared a submarine flare.

You chase a fish with one spear among you. And that spear would be Tork's tonight. The rest have ropes to bind him that go up to the fishermen's boats.

There was a sudden confusion of lights below. The spear had been shot!

The fish, long as a tall and short man together, rose through the ropes. He turned out to sea, trailing his pursuers. But others waited there, tried to loop him. Once I had flung those ropes, treated with tar and lime to dissolve the slime of the fish's body and hold to the beast. The looped ropes caught, and by the movement of the flares, I saw them jerked down their paths. The fish turned, rose again, this time toward me.

He pulled around when one line ran out (and somewhere on the surface the prow of a boat bobbed low) but turned back and came on.

Of a sudden, amphimen were flicking about me as the fray's center drifted by. Tork, his spear dug deep, forward and left of the marlin's dorsal, had hauled himself astride the beast.

The fish tried to shake him, then dropped his tail and rose straight. Everybody started pulling toward the surface. I broke foam and grabbed Juao's gunwale.

Tork and the fish exploded up among the boats. They twisted in air, in moonlight, in froth. The fish danced across the water on its tail, fell.

Juao stood up in the boat and shouted. The other fishermen shouted too, and somebody perched on the prow of a boat flung a rope. Someone in the water caught it.

Then fish and Tork and me and a dozen amphimen all went underwater at once.

They dropped in a corona of bubbles. The fish struck the end of another line, and shook himself. Tork was thrown free, but he doubled back.

Then the lines began to haul the beast up again, quivering, whipping, quivering again.

Six lines from six boats had him. For one moment he was still in the submarine moonlight. I could see his wound tossing scarves of blood.

When he (and we) broke surface, he was thrashing again, near Juao's boat. I was holding onto the side when suddenly Tork, glistening, came out of the water beside me and went over into the dinghy.

"Here you go," he said, turning to kneel at the bobbing rim, and pulled me up while Juao leaned against the far side to keep balance.

Wet rope slopped on the prow. "Hey, Cal!" Tork laughed, grabbed it up, and began to haul.

The fish prised wave from white wave in the white water.

The boats came together. The amphimen had all climbed up. Ariel was across from us, holding a flare that drooled smoke down her arm. She peered by the hip of the fisherman who was standing in front of her.

Juao and Tork were hauling the rope. Behind them I was coiling it with one hand as it came back to me.

The fish came up and was flopped into Ariel's boat, tail out, head up, chewing air.

I had just finished pulling on my trousers when Tork fell down on the seat behind me and grabbed me around the shoulders with his wet arms. "Look at our fish, Tio Cal! Look!" He gasped air, laughing, his dark face diamonded beside the flares. "Look at our fish there, Cal!"

Juao, grinning white and gold, pulled us back into shore. The fire, the singing, hands beating hands — and my godson had put pebbles in the empty rum bottles and was shaking them to the music — the guitars spiraled around us as we carried the fish up the sand and the men brought the spit.

"Watch it!" Tork said, grasping the pointed end of the great stick that was thicker than his wrist.

We turned the fish over.

"Here, Cal?"

He prodded two fingers into the white flesh six inches back from the bony lip.

"Fine."

Tork jammed the spit in.

We worked it through the body. By the time we carried it to the fire, they had brought more rum.

"Hey, Tork. Are you going to get some sleep before you go down in the morning?" I asked.

He shook his head. "Slept all afternoon." He pointed toward the roasting fish with his elbow. "That's my breakfast."

But when the dancing grew violent a few hours later, just before the fish was to come off the fire, and the kids were pushing the last of the sweet potatoes from the ashes with sticks, I walked back to the lifeboat shell we had sat on earlier. It was three-quarters flooded.

Curled below still water, Tork slept, fist loose before his mouth, the gills at the back of his neck pulsing rhythmically. Only his shoulder and hip made islands in the floated boat.

• • •

"Where's Tork?" Ariel asked me at the fire. They were swinging up the sizzling fish.

"Taking a nap."

"Oh, he wanted to cut the fish!"

"He's got a lot of work coming up. Sure you want to wake him up?"

"No, I'll let him sleep."

But Tork was coming up from the water, brushing his dripping hair back from his forehead.

He grinned at us, then went to carve. I remember him standing on the table, astraddle the meat, arm going up and down with the big knife (details, yes, those are the things you remember), stopping to hand down the portions, then hauling his arm back to cut again.

That night, with music and stomping on the sand and shouting back and forth over the fire, we made more noise than the sea.

IV

The eight-thirty bus was more or less on time.

"I don't think they want to go," Juao's sister said. She was accompanying the children to the Aquatic Corp Headquarters in Brasília.

"They are just tired," Juao said. "They should not have stayed up so late last night. Get on the bus now. Say good-bye to Tio Cal."

"Good-bye." (Fernando.)

"Good-bye." (Clara.)

But kids are never their most creative in that sort of situation. And I suspect that my godchildren may just have been suffering their first (or one of their first) hangovers. They had been very quiet all morning.

I bent down and gave them a clumsy hug. "When you come back on your first weekend off, I'll take you exploring down below at the point. You'll be able to gather your own coral now."

Juao's sister got teary, cuddled the children, cuddled me, Juao, then got on the bus.

Someone was shouting out the bus window for someone at the bus stop not to forget something. They trundled around the square and then toward the highway. We walked back across the street where the café owners were putting out canvas chairs.

"I will miss them," he said, like a long-considered admission.

"You and me both." At the docks near the hydrofoil wharf where the submarine launches went out to the undersea cities, we saw a crowd. "I wonder if they had any trouble laying the — "

A woman screamed in the crowd. She pushed from the others, dropping eggs and onions. She began to pull her hair and shriek. (Remember the skillet of shrimp? She had been the woman ladling them out.) A few people moved to help her.

A clutch of men broke off and ran into a side street. I grabbed a running amphiman, who whirled to face me.

"What in hell is going on?"

For a moment his mouth worked on his words for all the trite world like a beached fish.

"From the explosion . . ." he began. "They just brought them back from the explosion at the Slash!"

I grabbed his other shoulder. "What happened!"

"About two hours ago. They were just a quarter of the way through, when the whole fault gave way. They had a goddamn underwater volcano for half an hour. They're still getting seismic disturbances."

Juao was running toward the launch. I pushed the guy away and limped after him, struck the crowd and jostled through calico, canvas, and green scales.

They were carrying the corpses out of the hatch of the submarine and laying them on a canvas spread across the dock. They still return bodies to the countries of birth for the family to decide the method of burial. When the fault had given, the hot slag that had belched into the steaming sea was mostly molten silicon.

Four of the bodies were only slightly burned here and there; from their bloated faces (one still bled from the ear) I guessed they had died from sonic concussion. But several of the corpses were almost totally encased in dull, black glass.

"Tork — " I kept asking. "Is one of them — ?"

It took me forty-five minutes, asking first the guys who were carrying, then going into the launch and asking some guy with a clipboard, and then going back on the dock and into the office to find out that one of the more unrecognizable figures was, yes, Tork.

Juao brought me a glass of buttermilk at the café on the square. He sat still a long time, then finally rubbed away his white mustache, released the chair rung with his toes, put his hands on his knees.

"What are you thinking about?"

"That it's time to go fix nets. Tomorrow morning I will fish." He regarded me a moment. "Where should I fish tomorrow, Cal?"

"Are you wondering about . . . sending the kids off today?"

He shrugged. "Fishermen from this village have drowned. Still it is a village of fishermen. Where should I fish?"

I finished my buttermilk. "The mineral content over the Slash should be high as the devil. Lots of algae will gather tonight. Lots of small fish down deep. Big fish hovering over."

He nodded. "Good. I will take the boat out there tomorrow."

We got up.

"See you, Juao."

I limped back to the beach.

V

The fog had unsheathed the sand by ten. I walked around, poking clumps of weeds with a stick, banging the same stick on my numb leg. When I lurched up to the top of the rocks, I stopped in the still grass. "Ariel?"

She was kneeling in the water, head down, red hair breaking over sealed gills. Her shoulders shook, stopped, shook again.

"Ariel?" I came down over the blistered stones.

She turned away to look at the ocean.

The attachments of children are so important and so brittle. "How long have you been sitting here?"

She looked at me now, the varied waters of her face stilled on drawn cheeks. And her face was exhausted. She shook her head.

Sixteen? Seventeen? Who was the psychologist, back in the seventies, who decided that "adolescents" were just physical and mental adults with no useful work? "You want to come up to the house?"

The head shaking got faster, then stopped.

After a while I said, "I guess they'll be sending Tork's body back to Manila."

"He didn't have a family," she explained. "He'll be buried here, at sea."

"Oh," I said.

And the rough volcanic glass, pulled across the ocean's sands, changing shape, dulling —

"You were — you liked Tork a lot, didn't you? You kids looked like you were pretty fond of each other."

"Yes. He was an awfully nice — " Then she caught my meaning and blinked. "No," she said. "Oh, no. I was — I was engaged to Jonni . . . the brown-haired boy from California? Did you meet him at the party last night? We're both from Los Angeles, but we only met down here. And now . . . they're sending his body back this evening." Her eyes got very wide, then closed.

"I'm sorry."

I'm a clumsy cripple; I trip all over everybody's emotions. In that mirror I guess I'm too busy looking at what might have been.

"I'm sorry, Ariel."

She opened her eyes and began to look around her.

"Come on up to the house and have an avocado. I mean, they have avocados in now — not at the supermarket. But at the old town market on the other side. And they're better than any they grow in California."

She kept looking around.

"None of the amphimen get over there. It's a shame, because soon the market will probably close, and some of their fresh foods are really great. Oil and vinegar is all you need on them." I leaned back on the rocks. "Or a cup of tea?"

"Okay." She remembered to smile. I know the poor kid didn't feel like it. "Thank you. I won't be able to stay long, though."

We walked back up the rocks toward the house, the sea on our left. Just as we reached the patio, she turned and looked back. "Cal?"

"Yes? What is it?"

"Those clouds over there, across the water. Those are the only ones in the sky. Are they from the eruption in the Slash?"

I squinted. "I think so. Come on inside."

Greg Bear

Blood Music

(1983)

Greg Bear (b. 1951) is one of the foremost writers of hard science fiction working today. Although he published regularly throughout the 1970s, it was in the 1980s, when he shifted his focus to cutting-edge technologies and their implications for society, that he rose to prominence. This interest in technology often leads him to be grouped with the cyberpunk writers of that era, although the association is a loose one. Bear, whose other occupations have included freelance journalist, sf artist, and consultant for various scientific and governmental organizations (including the CIA), is the winner of two Hugos and five Nebulas.

"Blood Music" was awarded both the Hugo and the Nebula, and was expanded into a novel in 1985. The story of a maverick researcher who obsessively devotes himself to an experiment without considering the practical and ethical implications of its success is a common one in science fiction, going back at least as far as Mary Shelley's *Frankenstein*. What makes "Blood Music" distinctive is its plausible near-future setting in a medical research lab that explores commercial applications for nanotechnology and genetic engineering, two areas of science that were just beginning to enter the public consciousness when the story was written. Distinctive, too, is the radical level of transformation Bear envisions. "Blood Music" has grotesque and terrifying elements that link it to the horror genre, but it also has an ambivalent appreciation of metamorphosis and of new life.

There is a principle in nature I don't think anyone has pointed out before. Each hour, a myriad of trillions of little live things — bacteria, microbes, "animal-cules" — are born and die, not counting for much except in the bulk of their existence and the accumulation of their tiny effects. They do not perceive deeply. They do not suffer much. A hundred billion, dying, would not begin to have the same importance as a single human death.

Within the ranks of magnitude of all creatures, small as microbes or great as humans, there is an equality of "elan," just as the branches of a tall tree, gathered together, equal the bulk of the limbs below, and all the limbs equal the bulk of the trunk.

That, at least, is the principle. I believe Vergil Ulam was the first to violate it.

It had been two years since I'd last seen Vergil. My memory of him hardly matched the tan, smiling, well-dressed gentleman standing before me. We had made a lunch appointment over the phone the day before, and now faced each other in the wide double doors of the employees' cafeteria at the Mount Freedom Medical Center.

"Vergil?" I asked. "My God, Vergil!"

"Good to see you, Edward." He shook my hand firmly. He had lost ten or twelve kilos and what remained seemed tighter, better proportioned. At university, Vergil had been the pudgy, shock-haired, snaggle-toothed whiz kid who hot-wired doorknobs, gave us punch that turned our piss blue, and never got a date except with Eileen Termagent, who shared many of his physical characteristics.

"You look fantastic," I said. "Spend a summer in Cabo San Lucas?"

We stood in line at the counter and chose our food. "The tan," he said, picking out a carton of chocolate milk, "is from spending three months under a sunlamp. My teeth were straightened just after I last saw you. I'll explain the rest, but we need a place to talk where no one will listen close."

I steered him to the smoker's corner, where three diehard puffers were scattered among six tables.

"Listen, I mean it," I said as we unloaded our trays. "You've changed. You're looking good."

"I've changed more than you know." His tone was motion-picture ominous, and he delivered the line with a theatrical lift of his brows. "How's Gail?"

Gail was doing well, I told him, teaching nursery school. We'd married the year before. His gaze shifted down to his food — pineapple slice and cottage cheese, piece of banana cream pie — and he said, his voice almost cracking, "Notice something else?"

I squinted in concentration. "Uh."

"Look closer."

"I'm not sure. Well, yes, you're not wearing glasses. Contacts?"

"No. I don't need them anymore."

"And you're a snappy dresser. Who's dressing you now? I hope she's as sexy as she is tasteful."

"Candice isn't — wasn't responsible for the improvement in my clothes," he said. "I just got a better job, more money to throw around. My taste in clothes is better than my taste in food, as it happens." He grinned the old Vergil self-deprecating grin, but ended it with a peculiar leer. "At any rate, she's left me; I've been fired from my job. I'm living on savings."

"Hold it," I said. "That's a bit crowded. Why not do a linear breakdown? You got a job. Where?"

"Genetron Corp.," he said. "Sixteen months ago."

"I haven't heard of them."

"You will. They're putting out common stock in the next month. It'll shoot off the board. They've broken through with MABs. Medical — "

"I know what MABs are," I interrupted. "At least in theory. Medically Applicable Biochips."

"They have some that work."

"What?" It was my turn to lift my brows.

"Microscopic logic circuits. You inject them into the human body, they set up shop where they're told and troubleshoot. With Dr. Michael Bernard's approval."

That was quite impressive. Bernard's reputation was spotless. Not only was he associated with the genetic engineering biggies, but he had made news at least once a year in his practice as a neurosurgeon before retiring. Covers on *Time, Mega, Rolling Stone.*

"That's supposed to be secret — stock, breakthrough, Bernard, everything." He looked around and lowered his voice. "But you do whatever the hell you want. I'm through with the bastards."

I whistled. "Make me rich, huh?"

"If that's what you want. Or you can spend some time with me before rushing off to your broker."

"Of course." He hadn't touched the cottage cheese or pie. He had, however, eaten the pineapple slice and drunk the chocolate milk. "So tell me more."

"Well, in med school I was training for lab work. Biochemical research. I've always had a bent for computers, too. So I put myself through my last two years — "

"By selling software packages to Westinghouse," I said.

"It's good my friends remember. That's how I got involved with Genetron, just when they were starting out. They had big money backers, all the lab facilities I thought anyone would ever need. They hired me, and I advanced rapidly.

"Four months and I was doing my own work. I made some breakthroughs" — he tossed his hand nonchalantly — "then I went off on tangents they thought were premature. I persisted and they took away my lab, handed it over to a certifiable flatworm. I managed to save part of the experiment before they fired me. But I haven't exactly been cautious . . . or judicious. So now it's going on outside the lab."

I'd always regarded Vergil as ambitious, a trifle cracked, and not terribly sensitive. His relations with authority figures had never been smooth. Science, for him, was like the woman you couldn't possibly have, who suddenly opens her arms to you, long before you're ready for mature love — leaving you afraid you'll forever blow the chance, lose the prize. Apparently, he did. "Outside the lab? I don't get you."

"Edward, I want you to examine me. Give me a thorough physical. Maybe a cancer diagnostic. Then I'll explain more."

"You want a five-thousand-dollar exam?"

"Whatever you can do. Ultrasound, NMR, thermogram, everything."

"I don't know if I can get access to all that equipment. NMR full-scan has only been here a month or two. Hell, you couldn't pick a more expensive way — "

"Then ultrasound. That's all you'll need."

"Vergil, I'm an obstetrician, not a glamour-boy lab-tech. OB-GYN, butt of all jokes. If you're turning into a woman, maybe I can help you."

He leaned forward, almost putting his elbow into the pie, but swinging wide at the last instant by scant millimeters. The old Vergil would have hit it square. "Examine me closely and you'll . . ." He narrowed his eyes. "Just examine me."

"So I make an appointment for ultrasound. Who's going to pay?"

"I'm on Blue Shield." He smiled and held up a medical credit card. "I messed with the personnel files at Genetron. Anything up to a hundred thousand dollars medical, they'll never check, never suspect."

He wanted secrecy, so I made arrangements. I filled out his forms myself. As long as everything was billed properly, most of the examination could take place without official notice. I didn't charge for my services. After all, Vergil had turned my piss blue. We were friends.

He came in late at night. I wasn't normally on duty then, but I stayed late, waiting for him on the third floor of what the nurses called the

Frankenstein wing. I sat on an orange plastic chair. He arrived, looking olive-colored under the fluorescent lights.

He stripped, and I arranged him on the table. I noticed, first off, that his ankles looked swollen. But they weren't puffy. I felt them several times. They seemed healthy but looked odd. "Hm," I said.

I ran the paddles over him, picking up areas difficult for the big unit to hit, and programmed the data into the imaging system. Then I swung the table around and inserted it into the enameled orifice of the ultrasound diagnostic unit, the hum-hole, so-called by the nurses.

I integrated the data from the hum-hole with that from the paddle sweeps and rolled Vergil out, then set up a video frame. The image took a second to integrate, then flowed into a pattern showing Vergil's skeleton. My jaw fell.

Three seconds of that and it switched to his thoracic organs, then his musculature, and, finally, vascular system and skin.

"How long since the accident?" I asked, trying to take the quiver out of my voice.

"I haven't been in an accident," he said. "It was deliberate."

"Jesus, they beat you to keep secrets?"

"You don't understand me, Edward. Look at the images again. I'm not damaged."

"Look, there's thickening here" — I indicated the ankles — "and your ribs — that crazy zigzag pattern of interlocks. Broken sometime, obviously. And — "

"Look at my spine," he said. I rotated the image in the video frame.

Buckminster Fuller, I thought. It was fantastic. A cage of triangular projections, all interlocking in ways I couldn't begin to follow, much less understand. I reached around and tried to feel his spine with my fingers. He lifted his arms and looked off at the ceiling.

"I can't find it," I said. "It's all smooth back there." I let go of him and looked at his chest, then prodded his ribs. They were sheathed in something tough and flexible. The harder I pressed, the tougher it became. Then I noticed another change.

"Hey," I said. "You don't have any nipples." There were tiny pigment patches, but no nipple formations at all.

"See?" Vergil asked, shrugging on the white robe, "I'm being rebuilt from the inside out."

• • •

In my reconstruction of those hours, I fancy myself saying, "So tell me about it." Perhaps mercifully, I don't remember what I actually said.

He explained with his characteristic circumlocutions. Listening was like trying to get to the meat of a newspaper article through a forest of sidebars and graphic embellishments.

I simplify and condense.

Genetron had assigned him to manufacturing prototype biochips, tiny circuits made out of protein molecules. Some were hooked up to silicon chips little more than a micrometer in size, then went through rat arteries to chemically keyed locations, to make connections with the rat tissue and attempt to monitor and even control lab-induced pathologies.

"*That* was something," he said.

"We recovered the most complex microchip by sacrificing the rat, then debriefed it — hooked the silicon portion up to an imaging system. The computer gave us bar graphs, then a diagram of the chemical characteristics of about eleven centimeters of blood vessel . . . then put it all together to make a picture. We zoomed down eleven centimeters of rat artery. You never saw so many scientists jumping up and down, hugging each other, drinking buckets of bug juice." Bug juice was lab ethanol mixed with Dr Pepper.

Eventually, the silicon elements were eliminated completely in favor of nucleoproteins. He seemed reluctant to explain in detail, but I gathered they found ways to make huge molecules — as large as DNA, and even more complex — into electrochemical computers, using ribosomelike structures as "encoders" and "readers" and RNA as "tape." Vergil was able to mimic reproductive separation and reassembly in his nucleoproteins, incorporating program changes at key points by switching nucleotide pairs. "Genetron wanted me to switch over to supergene engineering, since that was the coming thing everywhere else. Make all kinds of critters, some out of our imagination. But I had different ideas." He twiddled his finger around his ear and made theremin sounds. "Mad scientist time, right?" He laughed, then sobered. "I injected my best nucleoproteins into bacteria to make duplication and compounding easier. Then I started to leave them inside, so the circuits could interact with the cells. They were heuristically programmed; they taught themselves. The cells fed chemically coded information to the computers, the computers processed it and made decisions, the cells became smart. I mean, smart as planaria, for starters. Imagine an *E. coli* as smart as a planarian worm!"

I nodded. "I'm imagining."

"Then I really went off on my own. We had the equipment, the techniques; and I knew the molecular language. I could make really dense, really complicated biochips by compounding the nucleoproteins, making them into little brains. I did some research into how far I could go, theoretically. Sticking with bacteria, I could make a biochip with the computing capacity of a sparrow's brain. Imagine how jazzed I was! Then I saw a way to increase the complexity a thousandfold, by using something we regarded as a nuisance — quantum chit-chat between the fixed elements of the circuits. Down that small, even the slightest change could bomb a biochip. But I developed a program that actually predicted and took advantage of electron tunneling. Emphasized the heuristic aspects of the computer, used the chit-chat as a method of increasing complexity."

"You're losing me," I said.

"I took advantage of randomness. The circuits could repair themselves, compare memories, and correct faulty elements. I gave them basic instructions: Go forth and multiply. Improve. By God, you should have seen some of the cultures a week later! It was amazing. They were evolving all on their own, like little cities. I destroyed them all. I think one of the petri dishes would have grown legs and walked out of the incubator if I'd kept feeding it."

"You're kidding." I looked at him. "You're not kidding."

"Man, they *knew* what it was like to improve! They knew where they had to go, but they were just so limited, being in bacteria bodies, with so few resources."

"How smart were they?"

"I couldn't be sure. They were associating in clusters of a hundred to two hundred cells, each cluster behaving like an autonomous unit. Each cluster might have been as smart as a rhesus monkey. They exchanged information through their pili, passed on bits of memory, and compared notes. Their organization was obviously different from a group of monkeys. Their world was so much simpler, for one thing. With their abilities, they were masters of the petri dishes. I put phages in with them; the phages didn't have a chance. They used every option available to change and grow."

"How is that possible?"

"What?" He seemed surprised I wasn't accepting everything at face value.

"Cramming so much into so little. A rhesus monkey is not your simple little calculator, Vergil."

"I haven't made myself clear," he said, obviously irritated. "I was using nucleoprotein computers. They're like DNA, but all the information can interact. Do you know how many nucleotide pairs there are in the DNA of a single bacteria?"

It had been a long time since my last biochemistry lesson. I shook my head.

"About two million. Add in the modified ribosome structures — fifteen thousand of them, each with a molecular weight of about three million — and consider the combinations and permutations. The RNA is arranged like a continuous loop paper tape, surrounded by ribosomes ticking off instructions and manufacturing protein chains. . . ." His eyes were bright and slightly moist. "Besides, I'm not saying every cell was a distinct entity. They cooperated."

"How many bacteria in the dishes you destroyed?"

"Billions. I don't know." He smirked. "You got it, Edward. Whole planetsful of *E. coli*."

"But Genetron didn't fire you then?"

"No. They didn't know what was going on, for one thing. I kept compounding the molecules, increasing their size and complexity. When bacteria were too limited, I took blood from myself, separated out white cells, and injected them with the new biochips. I watched them, put them through mazes and little chemical problems. They were whizzes. Time is a lot faster at that level — so little distance for the messages to cross, and the environment is much simpler. Then I forgot to store a file under my secret code in the lab computers. Some managers found it and guessed what I was up to. Everybody panicked. They thought we'd have every social watchdog in the country on our backs because of what I'd done. They started to destroy my work and wipe my programs. Ordered me to sterilize my white cells, Christ." He pulled the white robe off and started to get dressed. "I only had a day or two. I separated out the most complex cells — "

"How complex?"

"They were clustering in hundred-cell groups, like the bacteria. Each group as smart as a four-year-old kid, maybe." He studied my face for a moment. "Still doubting? Want me to run through how many nucleotide pairs there are in a mammalian cell? I tailored my computers to take advantage of the white cells' capacity. Four billion nucleotide pairs, Edward. And they don't have a huge body to worry about, taking up most of their thinking time."

"Okay," I said. "I'm convinced. What did you do?"

"I mixed the cells back into a cylinder of whole blood and injected myself with it." He buttoned the top of his shirt and smiled thinly at me. "I'd programmed them with every drive I could, talked as high a level as I could using just enzymes and such. After that, they were on their own."

"You programmed them to go forth and multiply, improve?" I repeated.

"I think they developed some characteristics picked up by the biochips in their *E. coli* phases. The white cells could talk to each other with extruded memories. They found ways to ingest other types of cells and alter them without killing them."

"You're crazy."

"You can see the screen! Edward, I haven't been sick since. I used to get colds all the time. I've never felt better."

"They're inside you, finding things, changing them."

"And by now, each cluster is as smart as you or I."

"You're absolutely nuts."

He shrugged. "Genetron fired me. They thought I was going to take revenge for what they did to my work. They ordered me out of the labs, and I haven't had a real chance to see what's been going on inside me until now. Three months."

"So . . ." My mind was racing. "You lost weight because they improved your fat metabolism. Your bones are stronger; your spine has been completely rebuilt — "

"No more backaches even if I sleep on my old mattress."

"Your heart looks different."

"I didn't know about the heart," he said, examining the frame image more closely. "As for the fat — I was thinking about that. They could increase my brown cells, fix up the metabolism. I haven't been as hungry lately. I haven't changed my eating habits that much — I still want the same old junk — but somehow I get around to eating only what I need. I don't think they know what my brain is yet. Sure, they've got all the glandular stuff — but they don't have the *big* picture, if you see what I mean. They don't know *I'm* in here. But boy, they sure did figure out what my reproductive organs are."

I glanced at the image and shifted my eyes away.

"Oh, they look pretty normal," he said, hefting his scrotum obscenely. He snickered. "But how else do you think I'd land a real looker like Candice? She was just after a one-night stand with a techie. I looked okay then, no tan but trim, with good clothes. She'd never screwed a techie before. Joke time, right? But my little geniuses kept us up half the night. I think they made improvements each time. I felt like I had a goddamned fever."

His smile vanished. "But then one night my skin started to crawl. It really scared me. I thought things were getting out of hand. I wondered what they'd do when they crossed the blood-brain barrier and found out about *me* — about the brain's real function. So I began a campaign to keep them under control. I figured, the reason they wanted to get into the skin was the simplicity of running circuits across a surface. Much easier than trying to maintain chains of communication in and around muscles, organs, vessels. The skin was much more direct. So I bought a quartz lamp." He caught my puzzled expression. "In the lab, we'd break down the protein in biochip cells by exposing them to ultraviolet light. I alternated sunlamp with quartz treatments. Keeps them out of my skin and gives me a nice tan."

"Give you skin cancer, too," I commented.

"They'll probably take care of that. Like police."

"Okay. I've examined you; you've told me a story I still find hard to believe. . . . What do you want me to do?"

"I'm not as nonchalant as I act, Edward. I'm worried. I'd like to find some way to control them before they find out about my brain. I mean, think of it; they're in the trillions by now, each one smart. They're cooperating to some extent. I'm probably the smartest thing on the planet, and they haven't even begun to get their act together. I don't really want them to take over." He laughed unpleasantly. "Steal my soul, you know? So think of some treatment to block them. Maybe we can starve the little buggers. Just think on it." He buttoned his shirt. "Give me a call." He handed me a slip of paper with his address and phone number. Then he went to the keyboard and erased the image on the frame, dumping the memory of the examination. "Just you," he said. "Nobody else for now. And please . . . hurry."

It was three o'clock in the morning when Vergil walked out of the examination room. He'd allowed me to take blood samples, then shaken my hand — his palm was damp, nervous — and cautioned me against ingesting anything from the specimens.

Before I went home, I put the blood through a series of tests. The results were ready the next day.

I picked them up during my lunch break in the afternoon, then destroyed all of the samples. I did it like a robot. It took me five days and nearly sleepless nights to accept what I'd seen. His blood was normal enough, though the machines diagnosed the patient as having an infection. High levels of leukocytes — white blood cells — and histamines. On the fifth day, I believed.

Gail came home before I did, but it was my turn to fix dinner. She slipped one of the school's disks into the home system and showed me video art her nursery kids had been creating. I watched quietly, ate with her in silence.

I had two dreams, part of my final acceptance. In the first, that evening, I witnessed the destruction of the planet Krypton, Superman's home world. Billions of superhuman geniuses went screaming off in walls of fire. I related the destruction to my sterilizing the samples of Vergil's blood.

The second dream was worse. I dreamed that New York City was raping a woman. By the end of the dream, she gave birth to little embryo cities, all wrapped up in translucent sacs, soaked with blood from the difficult labor.

I called him on the morning of the sixth day. He answered on the fourth ring. "I have some results," I said. "Nothing conclusive. But I want to talk with you. In person."

"Sure," he said. "I'm staying inside for the time being." His voice was strained; he sounded tired.

Vergil's apartment was in a fancy high-rise near the lake shore. I took the elevator up, listening to little advertising jingles and watching dancing holograms display products, empty apartments for rent, the building's hostess discussing social activities for the week.

Vergil opened the door and motioned me in. He wore a checked robe with long sleeves and carpet slippers. He clutched an unlit pipe in one hand, his fingers twisting it back and forth as he walked away from me and sat down, saying nothing.

"You have an infection," I said.

"Oh?"

"That's all the blood analyses tell me. I don't have access to the electron microscopes."

"I don't think it's really an infection," he said. "After all, they're my own cells. Probably something else . . . some sign of their presence, of the change. We can't expect to understand everything that's happening."

I removed my coat. "Listen," I said, "you really have me worried now." The expression on his face stopped me: a kind of frantic beatitude. He squinted at the ceiling and pursed his lips.

"Are you stoned?" I asked.

He shook his head, then nodded once, very slowly. "Listening," he said.

"To what?"

"I don't know. Not sounds . . . exactly. Like music. The heart, all the blood vessels, friction of blood along the arteries, veins. Activity. Music in the blood." He looked at me plaintively. "Why aren't you at work?"

"My day off. Gail's working."

"Can you stay?"

I shrugged. "I suppose." I sounded suspicious. I glanced around the apartment, looking for ashtrays, packs of papers.

"I'm not stoned, Edward," he said. "I may be wrong, but I think something big is happening. I think they're finding out who I am."

I sat down across from Vergil, staring at him intently. He didn't seem to notice. Some inner process involved him. When I asked for a cup of coffee, he motioned to the kitchen. I boiled a pot of water and took a jar of instant from the cabinet. With cup in hand, I returned to my seat. He twisted his head back and forth, eyes open. "You always knew what you wanted to be, didn't you?" he asked.

"More or less."

"A gynecologist. Smart moves. Never false moves. I was different. I had goals, but no direction. Like a map without roads, just places to be. I didn't give a shit for anything, anyone but myself. Even science. Just a means. I'm surprised I got so far. I even hated my folks."

He gripped his chair arms.

"Something wrong?" I asked.

"They're talking to me," he said. He shut his eyes.

For an hour he seemed to be asleep. I checked his pulse, which was strong and steady, felt his forehead — slightly cool — and made myself more coffee. I was looking through a magazine, at a loss what to do, when he opened his eyes again. "Hard to figure exactly what time is like for them," he said. "It's taken them maybe three, four days to figure out language, key human concepts. Now they're on to it. On to me. Right now."

"How's that?"

He claimed there were thousands of researchers hooked up to his neurons. He couldn't give details. "They're damned efficient, you know," he said. "They haven't screwed me up yet."

"We should get you into the hospital now."

"What in hell could other doctors do? Did *you* figure out any way to control them? I mean, they're my own cells."

"I've been thinking. We could starve them. Find out what metabolic differences — "

"I'm not sure I want to be rid of them," Vergil said. "They're not doing any harm."

"How do you know?"

He shook his head and held up one finger. "Wait. They're trying to figure out what space is. That's tough for them: They break distances down into concentrations of chemicals. For them, space is like intensity of taste."

"Vergil — "

"Listen! Think, Edward!" His tone was excited but even. "Something big is happening inside me. They talk to each other across the fluid, through membranes. They tailor something — viruses? — to carry data stored in nucleic acid chains. I think they're saying 'RNA.' That makes sense. That's one way I programmed them. But plasmidlike structures, too. Maybe that's what your machines think is a sign of infection — all their chattering in my blood, packets of data. Tastes of other individuals. Peers. Superiors. Subordinates."

"Vergil, I still think you should be in a hospital."

"This is my show, Edward," he said. "I'm their universe. They're amazed by the new scale." He was quiet again for a time. I squatted by his chair and pulled up the sleeve to his robe. His arm was crisscrossed with white lines. I was about to go to the phone when he stood and stretched. "Do you realize," he said, "how many blood cells we kill each time we move?"

"I'm going to call for an ambulance," I said.

"No, you aren't." His tone stopped me. "I told you, I'm not sick, this is my show. Do you know what they'd do to me in a hospital? They'd be like cavemen trying to fix a computer. It would be a farce."

"Then what the hell am I doing here?" I asked, getting angry. "I can't do anything. I'm one of those cavemen."

"You're a friend," Vergil said, fixing his eyes on me. I had the impression I was being watched by more than just Vergil. "I want you here to keep me company." He laughed. "But I'm not exactly alone."

He walked around the apartment for two hours, fingering things, looking out windows, slowly and methodically fixing himself lunch. "You know, they can actually feel their own thoughts," he said about noon. "I mean, the cytoplasm seems to have a will of its own, a kind of subconscious life counter to the rationality they've only recently acquired. They hear the chemical 'noise' of the molecules fitting and unfitting inside."

At two o'clock, I called Gail to tell her I would be late. I was almost sick with tension, but I tried to keep my voice level. "Remember Vergil Ulam? I'm talking with him right now."

"Everything okay?" she asked.

Was it? Decidedly not. "Fine," I said.

"Culture!" Vergil said, peering around the kitchen wall at me. I said goodbye and hung up the phone. "They're always swimming in that bath of information. Contributing to it. It's a kind of gestalt thing. The hierarchy is absolute. They send tailored phages after cells that don't interact properly. Viruses specified to individuals or groups. No escape. A rogue cell gets pierced by the virus, the cell blebs outward, it explodes and dissolves. But it's not just a dictatorship. I think they effectively have more freedom than in a democracy. I mean, they vary so differently from individual to individual. Does that make sense? They vary in different ways than we do."

"Hold it," I said, gripping his shoulders. "Vergil, you're pushing me to the edge. I can't take this much longer. I don't understand; I'm not sure I believe — "

"Not even now?"

"Okay, let's say you're giving me the right interpretation. Giving it to me straight. Have you bothered to figure out the consequences yet? What all this means, where it might lead?"

He walked into the kitchen and drew a glass of water from the tap, then returned and stood next to me. His expression had changed from childish absorption to sober concern. "I've never been very good at that."

"Are you afraid?"

"I was. Now, I'm not sure." He fingered the tie of his robe. "Look, I don't want you to think I went around you, over your head or something. But I met with Michael Bernard yesterday. He put me through his private clinic, took specimens. Told me to quit the lamp treatments. He called this morning, just before you did. He says it all checks out. And he asked me not to tell anybody." He paused and his expression became dreary again. "Cities of cells," he continued. "Edward, they push tubes through the tissues, spread information — "

"Stop it!" I shouted. "Checks out? What checks out?"

"As Bernard puts it, I have 'severely enlarged macrophages' throughout my system. And he concurs on the anatomical changes."

"What does he plan to do?"

"I don't know, I think he'll probably convince Genetron to reopen the lab."

"Is that what you want?"

"It's not just having the lab again. I want to show you. Since I stopped the lamp treatments, I'm still changing." He undid his robe and let it slide to the floor. All over his body, his skin was crisscrossed with white lines. Along his back, the lines were starting to form ridges.

"My God," I said.

"I'm not going to be much good anywhere else but the lab soon. I won't be able to go out in public. Hospitals wouldn't know what to do, as I said."

"You're . . . you can talk to them, tell them to slow down," I said, aware 175 how ridiculous that sounded.

"Yes, indeed I can, but they don't necessarily listen."

"I thought you were their god or something."

"The ones hooked up to my neurons aren't the big wheels. They're researchers, or at least serve the same function. They know I'm here, what I am, but that doesn't mean they've convinced the upper levels of the hierarchy."

"They're disputing?"

"Something like that. It's not all that bad, anyway. If the lab is reopened, I have a home, a place to work." He glanced out the window, as if looking for someone. "I don't have anything left but them. They aren't afraid, Edward. I've never felt so close to anything before." The beatific smile again. "I'm responsible for them. Mother to them all."

"You have no way of knowing what they're going to do."

He shook his head.

"No, I mean it. You say they're like a civilization — "

"Like a thousand civilizations."

"Yes, and civilizations have been known to screw up. Warfare, the environment — "

I was grasping at straws, trying to restrain a growing panic. I wasn't competent to handle the enormity of what was happening. Neither was

Vergil. He was the last person I would have called insightful and wise about large issues.

"But I'm the only one at risk."

"You don't know that. Jesus, Vergil, look what they're *doing* to you!"

"To me, all to me!" he said. "Nobody else."

I shook my head and held up my hands in a gesture of defeat. "Okay, so Bernard gets them to reopen the lab, you move in, become a guinea pig. What then?"

"They treat me right. I'm more than just good old Vergil Ulam now. I'm a goddamned galaxy, a super-mother."

"Super-host, you mean." He conceded the point with a shrug.

I couldn't take any more. I made my exit with a few flimsy excuses, then sat in the lobby of the apartment building, trying to calm down. Somebody had to talk some sense into him. Who would he listen to? He had gone to Bernard . . .

And it sounded as if Bernard was not only convinced, but very interested. People of Bernard's stature didn't coax the Vergil Ulams of the world along unless they felt it was to their advantage.

I had a hunch, and I decided to play it. I went to a pay phone, slipped in my credit card, and called Genetron.

"I'd like you to page Dr. Michael Bernard," I told the receptionist.

"Who's calling, please?"

"This is his answering service. We have an emergency call and his beeper doesn't seem to be working."

A few anxious minutes later, Bernard came on the line. "Who the hell is this?" he asked. "I don't have an answering service."

"My name is Edward Milligan. I'm a friend of Vergil Ulam's. I think we have some problems to discuss."

We made an appointment to talk the next morning.

I went home and tried to think of excuses to keep me off the next day's hospital shift. I couldn't concentrate on medicine, couldn't give my patients anywhere near the attention they deserved.

Guilty, angry, afraid.

That was how Gail found me. I slipped on a mask of calm and we fixed dinner together. After eating, holding onto each other, we watched the city lights come on in late twilight through the bayside window. Winter starlings pecked at the yellow lawn in the last few minutes of light, then flew away with a rising wind which made the windows rattle.

"Something's wrong," Gail said softly. "Are you going to tell me, or just act like everything's normal?"

"It's just me," I said. "Nervous. Work at the hospital."

"Oh, lord," she said, sitting up. "You're going to divorce me for that Baker woman." Mrs. Baker weighed three hundred and sixty pounds and hadn't known she was pregnant until her fifth month.

"No," I said, listless.

"Rapturous relief," Gail said, touching my forehead lightly. "You know this kind of introspection drives me crazy."

"Well, it's nothing I can talk about yet, so . . ." I patted her hand.

"That's disgustingly patronizing," she said, getting up. "I'm going to make some tea. Want some?" Now she was miffed, and I was tense with not telling.

Why not just reveal all? I asked myself. An old friend was turning himself into a galaxy.

I cleared away the table instead. That night, unable to sleep, I looked down on Gail in bed from my sitting position, pillow against the wall, and tried to determine what I knew was real, and what wasn't.

I'm a doctor, I told myself. A technical, scientific profession. I'm supposed to be immune to things like future shock.

Vergil Ulam was turning into a galaxy.

How would it feel to be topped off with a trillion Chinese? I grinned in the dark and almost cried at the same time. What Vergil had inside him was unimaginably stranger than Chinese. Stranger than anything I — or Vergil — could easily understand. Perhaps ever understand.

But I knew what was real. The bedroom, the city lights faint through gauze curtains. Gail sleeping. Very important. Gail in bed, sleeping.

The dream returned. This time the city came in through the window and attacked Gail. It was a great, spiky, lighted-up prowler, and it growled in a language I couldn't understand, made up of auto horns, crowd noises, construction bedlam. I tried to fight it off, but it got to her — and turned into a drift of stars, sprinkling all over the bed, all over everything. I jerked awake and stayed up until dawn, dressed with Gail, kissed her, savored the reality of her human, unviolated lips.

I went to meet with Bernard. He had been loaned a suite in a big downtown hospital; I rode the elevator to the sixth floor, and saw what fame and fortune could mean.

The suite was tastefully furnished, fine serigraphs on wood-paneled walls, chrome and glass furniture, cream-colored carpet, Chinese brass, and wormwood-grain cabinets and tables.

He offered me a cup of coffee, and I accepted. He took a seat in the breakfast nook, and I sat across from him, cradling my cup in moist palms. He wore a dapper gray suit and had graying hair and a sharp profile. He was in his mid sixties and he looked quite a bit like Leonard Bernstein.

"About our mutual acquaintance," he said. "Mr. Ulam. Brilliant. And, I won't hesitate to say, courageous."

"He's my friend. I'm worried about him."

Bernard held up one finger. "Courageous — and a bloody damned fool. What's happening to him should never have been allowed. He may have done it under duress, but that's no excuse. Still, what's done is done. He's talked to you, I take it."

I nodded. "He wants to return to Genetron."

"Of course. That's where all his equipment is. Where his home probably will be while we sort this out."

"Sort it out — how? Why?" I wasn't thinking too clearly. I had a slight headache.

"I can think of a large number of uses for small, superdense computer elements with a biological base. Can't you? Genetron has already made breakthroughs, but this is something else again."

"What do you envision?"

Bernard smiled. "I'm not really at liberty to say. It'll be revolutionary. We'll have to get him in lab conditions. Animal experiments have to be conducted. We'll start from scratch, of course. Vergil's . . . um . . . colonies can't be transferred. They're based on his own white blood cells. So we have to develop colonies that won't trigger immune reactions in other animals."

"Like an infection?" I asked.

"I suppose there are comparisons. But Vergil is not infected."

"My tests indicate he is."

"That's probably the bits of data floating around in his blood, don't you think?"

"I don't know."

"Listen, I'd like you to come down to the lab after Vergil is settled in. Your expertise might be useful to us."

Us. He was working with Genetron hand in glove. Could he be objective? "How will you benefit from all this?"

"Edward, I have always been at the forefront of my profession. I see no reason why I shouldn't be helping here. With my knowledge of brain and nerve functions, and the research I've been conducting in neurophysiology — "

"You could help Genetron hold off an investigation by the government," I said.

"That's being very blunt. Too blunt, and unfair."

"Perhaps. Anyway, yes: I'd like to visit the lab when Vergil's settled in. If I'm still welcome, bluntness and all." He looked at me sharply. I wouldn't be playing on *his* team; for a moment, his thoughts were almost nakedly apparent.

"Of course," Bernard said, rising with me. He reached out to shake my hand. His palm was damp. He was as nervous as I was, even if he didn't look it.

I returned to my apartment and stayed there until noon, reading, trying to sort things out. Reach a decision. What was real, what I needed to protect.

There is only so much change anyone can stand: innovation, yes, but slow application. Don't force. Everyone has the right to stay the same until they decide otherwise.

The greatest thing in science since . . .

And Bernard would force it. Genetron would force it. I couldn't handle the thought. "Neo-Luddite," I said to myself. A filthy accusation.

When I pressed Vergil's number on the building security panel, Vergil answered almost immediately. "Yeah," he said. He sounded exhilarated. "Come on up. I'll be in the bathroom. Door's unlocked."

I entered his apartment and walked through the hallway to the bathroom. Vergil lay in the tub, up to his neck in pinkish water. He smiled vaguely and splashed his hands. "Looks like I slit my wrists, doesn't it?" he said softly. "Don't worry. Everything's fine now. Genetron's going to take me back. Bernard just called." He pointed to the bathroom phone and intercom.

I sat on the toilet and noticed the sunlamp fixture standing unplugged next to the linen cabinets. The bulbs sat in a row on the edge of the sink counter. "You're sure that's what you want," I said, my shoulders slumping.

"Yeah, I think so," he said, "They can take better care of me. I'm getting cleaned up, going over there this evening. Bernard's picking me up in his limo. Style. From here on in, everything's style."

The pinkish color in the water didn't look like soap. "Is that bubble bath?" I asked. Some of it came to me in a rush then and I felt a little weaker; what had occurred to me was just one more obvious and necessary insanity.

"No," Vergil said. I knew that already.

"No," he repeated, "it's coming from my skin. They're not telling me everything, but I think they're sending out scouts. Astronauts." He looked at me with an expression that didn't quite equal concern; more like curiosity as to how I'd take it.

The confirmation made my stomach muscles tighten as if waiting for a punch. I had never even considered the possibility until now, perhaps because I had been concentrating on other aspects. "Is this the first time?" I asked.

"Yeah," he said. He laughed. "I've half a mind to let the little buggers down the drain. Let them find out what the world's really about."

"They'd go everywhere," I said.

"Sure enough."

"How . . . how are you feeling?"

"I'm feeling pretty good now. Must be billions of them." More splashing with his hands. "What do you think? Should I let the buggers out?"

Quickly, hardly thinking, I knelt down beside the tub. My fingers went for the cord on the sunlamp and I plugged it in. He had hot-wired doorknobs, turned my piss blue, played a thousand dumb practical jokes and never grown up, never grown mature enough to understand that he was sufficiently brilliant to transform the world; he would never learn caution.

He reached for the drain knob. "You know, Edward, I — "

He never finished. I picked up the fixture and dropped it into the tub, jumping back at the flash of steam and sparks. Vergil screamed and thrashed and jerked and then everything was still, except for the low, steady sizzle and the smoke wafting from his hair.

I lifted the toilet lid and vomited. Then I clenched my nose and went into the living room. My legs went out from under me and I sat abruptly on the couch.

After an hour, I searched through Vergil's kitchen and found bleach, ammonia, and a bottle of Jack Daniel's. I returned to the bathroom, keeping the center of my gaze away from Vergil. I poured first the booze, then the bleach, then the ammonia into the water. Chlorine started bubbling up and I left, closing the door behind me.

The phone was ringing when I got home. I didn't answer. It could have been the hospital. It could have been Bernard. Or the police. I could envision having to explain everything to the police. Genetron would stonewall; Bernard would be unavailable.

I was exhausted, all my muscles knotted with tension and whatever name one can give to the feelings one has after —

Committing genocide?

That certainly didn't seem real. I could not believe I had just murdered a hundred trillion intelligent beings. Snuffed a galaxy. It was laughable. But I didn't laugh.

It was easy to believe that I had just killed one human being, a friend. The smoke, the melted lamp rods, the drooping electrical outlet and smoking cord.

Vergil.

I had dunked the lamp into the tub with Vergil.

I felt sick. Dreams, cities raping Gail (and what about his girlfriend, Candice?). Letting the water filled with them out. Galaxies sprinkling over us all. What horror. Then again, what potential beauty — a new kind of life, symbiosis and transformation.

Had I been thorough enough to kill them all? I had a moment of panic. Tomorrow, I thought, I will sterilize his apartment. Somehow, I didn't even think of Bernard.

When Gail came in the door, I was asleep on the couch. I came to, groggy, and she looked down at me.

"You feeling okay?" she asked, perching on the edge of the couch. I nodded.

"What are you planning for dinner?" My mouth didn't work properly. The words were mushy. She felt my forehead.

"Edward, you have a fever," she said. "A very high fever."

I stumbled into the bathroom and looked in the mirror. Gail was close behind me. "What is it?" she asked.

There were lines under my collar, around my neck. White lines, like freeways. They had already been in me a long time, days.

"Damp palms," I said. So obvious.

I think we nearly died. I struggled at first, but in minutes I was too weak to move. Gail was just as sick within an hour.

I lay on the carpet in the living room, drenched in sweat. Gail lay on the couch, her face the color of talcum, eyes closed, like a corpse in an embalming parlor. For a time I thought she was dead. Sick as I was, I raged — hated, felt tremendous guilt at my weakness, my slowness to understand all the possibilities. Then I no longer cared. I was too weak to blink, so I closed my eyes and waited.

There was a rhythm in my arms, my legs. With each pulse of blood, a kind of sound welled up within me, like an orchestra thousands strong, but not playing in unison; playing whole seasons of symphonies at once. Music in the blood. The sound became harsher, but more coordinated, wave-trains finally canceling into silence, then separating into harmonic beats.

The beats seemed to melt into me, into the sound of my own heart.

First, they subdued our immune responses. The war — and it was a war, on a scale never before known on Earth, with trillions of combatants — lasted perhaps two days.

By the time I regained enough strength to get to the kitchen faucet, I could feel them working on my brain, trying to crack the code and find the god within the protoplasm. I drank until I was sick, then drank more moderately and took a glass to Gail. She sipped at it. Her lips were cracked, her eyes bloodshot and ringed with yellowish crumbs. There was some color in her skin. Minutes later, we were eating feebly in the kitchen.

"What in hell is happening?" was the first thing she asked. I didn't have the strength to explain. I peeled an orange and shared it with her. "We should call a doctor," she said. But I knew we wouldn't. I was already receiving messages; it was becoming apparent that any sensation of freedom we experienced was illusory.

The messages were simple at first. Memories of commands, rather than the commands themselves, manifested themselves in my thoughts. We were not to leave the apartment — a concept which seemed quite abstract to those in control, even if undesirable — and we were not to have contact with others. We would be allowed to eat certain foods and drink tap water for the time being.

With the subsidence of the fevers, the transformations were quick and drastic. Almost simultaneously, Gail and I were immobilized. She was sitting at the table, I was kneeling on the floor. I was able barely to see her in the corner of my eye.

Her arm developed pronounced ridges.

They had learned inside Vergil; their tactics within the two of us were very different. I itched all over for about two hours — two hours in hell — before they made the breakthrough and found me. The effort of ages on their timescale paid off and they communicated smoothly and directly with this great, clumsy intelligence who had once controlled their universe.

They were not cruel. When the concept of discomfort and its undesirability was made clear, they worked to alleviate it. They worked too effectively. For another hour, I was in a sea of bliss, out of all contact with them.

With dawn the next day, they gave us freedom to move again; specifically, to go to the bathroom. There were certain waste products they could not deal with. I voided those — my urine was purple — and Gail followed suit. We looked at each other vacantly in the bathroom. Then she managed a slight smile. "Are they talking to you?" she said. I nodded. "Then I'm not crazy."

For the next twelve hours, control seemed to loosen on some levels. I suspect there was another kind of war going on in me. Gail was capable of limited motion, but no more.

When full control resumed, we were instructed to hold each other. We did not hesitate.

"Eddie . . ." she whispered. My name was the last sound I ever heard from outside.

Standing, we grew together. In hours, our legs expanded and spread out. Then extensions grew to the windows to take in sunlight, and to the kitchen to take water from the sink. Filaments soon reached to all corners of the room, stripping paint and plaster from the walls, fabric and stuffing from the furniture.

By the next dawn, the transformation was complete.

I no longer have any clear view of what we look like. I suspect we resemble cells — large, flat, and filamented cells, draped purposefully across most of the apartment. The great shall mimic the small.

Our intelligence fluctuates daily as we are absorbed into the minds within. Each day, our individuality declines. We are, indeed, great clumsy dinosaurs. Our memories have been taken over by billions of them, and our personalities have been spread through the transformed blood.

Soon there will be no need for centralization.

Already the plumbing has been invaded. People throughout the building are undergoing transformation.

Within the old time frame of weeks, we will reach the lakes, rivers, and seas in force.

I can barely begin to guess the results. Every square inch of the planet will teem with thought. Years from now, perhaps much sooner, they will subdue their own individuality — what there is of it.

New creatures will come, then. The immensity of their capacity for thought will be inconceivable.

All my hatred and fear is gone now.

I leave them — us — with only one question.

How many times has this happened, elsewhere? Travelers never came through space to visit the Earth. They had no need.

They had found universes in grains of sand.

Terry Bisson

Bears Discover Fire

(1990)

Terry Ballantine Bisson (b. 1942) has so many wide-ranging interests and vocations that he can be hard to pin down. As a Kentucky native who lived in New York for many years before settling in California, even his geographic background covers all the bases. A political activist, NASCAR enthusiast, and children's book author, Bisson's bewildering range of writing projects runs the gamut from the highly commercial (novelizations of films like *Johnny Mnemonic* and *Galaxy Quest*) to the idealistic (an authorized biography of death-row inmate Mumia Abu-Jamal). He has also adapted the works of sf writers for comic books and coauthored a book with the popular NPR *Car Talk* hosts Click and Clack. He has written both fiction and nonfiction for publications ranging from the *Nation* to the *New Yorker* to the *Washington Post*.

A satirist who combines over-the-top absurdism with deadpan humor, Bisson is famous for his short fiction as well as for novels like *Pirates of the Universe* (1996), a postmodern romp through the future of corporate privatization that catalogs the triumph of imitation consumer goods over reality. "Bears Discover Fire," which swept the awards in 1991, winning a Hugo, a Nebula, and a Theodore Sturgeon Memorial Award, shows a quieter side of Bisson. The story details the intrusion of the surreal into the everyday world and tracks the characters' quiet acceptance of the inexplicable as they go about living their decent and ordinary lives.

I was driving with my brother, the preacher, and my nephew, the preacher's son, on I-65 just north of Bowling Green when we got a flat. It was Sunday night and we had been to visit Mother at the Home. We were in my car. The flat caused what you might call knowing groans since, as the old-fashioned one in my family (so they tell me), I fix my own tires, and my brother is always telling me to get radials and quit buying old tires.

But if you know how to mount and fix tires yourself, you can pick them up for almost nothing.

Since it was a left rear tire, I pulled over left, onto the median grass. The way my Caddy stumbled to a stop, I figured the tire was ruined. "I guess there's no need asking if you have any of that *FlatFix* in the trunk," said Wallace.

"Here, son, hold the light," I said to Wallace Jr. He's old enough to want to help and not old enough (yet) to think he knows it all. If I'd married and had kids, he's the kind I'd have wanted.

An old Caddy has a big trunk that tends to fill up like a shed. Mine's a '56. Wallace was wearing his Sunday shirt, so he didn't offer to help while I pulled magazines, fishing tackle, a wooden tool box, some old clothes, a comealong wrapped in a grass sack, and a tobacco sprayer out of the way, looking for my jack. The spare looked a little soft.

The light went out. "Shake it, son," I said.

It went back on. The bumper jack was long gone, but I carry a little ¼ ton hydraulic. I finally found it under Mother's old *Southern Livings*, 1978–1986. I had been meaning to drop them at the dump. If Wallace hadn't been along, I'd have let Wallace Jr. position the jack under the axle, but I got on my knees and did it myself. There's nothing wrong with a boy learning to change a tire. Even if you're not going to fix and mount them, you're still going to have to change a few in this life. The light went off again before I had the wheel off the ground. I was surprised at how dark the night was already. It was late October and beginning to get cool. "Shake it again, son," I said.

It went back on but it was weak. Flickery.

"With radials you just don't *have* flats," Wallace explained in that voice he uses when he's talking to a number of people at once; in this case, Wallace Jr. and myself. "And even when you *do*, you just squirt them with this stuff called *FlatFix* and you just drive on. $3.95 the can."

"Uncle Bobby can fix a tire hisself," said Wallace Jr., out of loyalty I presume.

"*Himself*," I said from halfway under the car. If it was up to Wallace, the boy would talk like what Mother used to call "a helock from the gorges of the mountains." But drive on radials.

"Shake that light again," I said. It was about gone. I spun the lugs off into the hubcap and pulled the wheel. The tire had blown out along the sidewall. "Won't be fixing this one," I said. Not that I cared. I have a pile as tall as a man out by the barn.

The light went out again, then came back better than ever as I was fitting the spare over the lugs. "Much better," I said. There was a flood of dim orange flickery light. But when I turned to find the lug nuts, I was surprised to see that the flashlight the boy was holding was dead. The light was coming from two bears at the edge of the trees, holding torches. They were big, three-hundred-pounders, standing about five feet tall. Wallace Jr. and his father had seen them and were standing perfectly still. It's best not to alarm bears.

I fished the lug nuts out of the hubcap and spun them on. I usually like to put a little oil on them, but this time I let it go. I reached under the car and let the jack down and pulled it out. I was relieved to see that the spare was high enough to drive on. I put the jack and the lug wrench and the flat into the trunk. Instead of replacing the hubcap, I put it in there too. All this time, the bears never made a move. They just held the torches up, whether out of curiosity or helpfulness, there was no way of knowing. It looked like there may have been more bears behind them, in the trees.

Opening three doors at once, we got into the car and drove off. Wallace was the first to speak. "Looks like bears have discovered fire," he said.

When we first took Mother to the Home, almost four years (forty-seven months) ago, she told Wallace and me she was ready to die. "Don't worry about me, boys," she whispered, pulling us both down so the nurse wouldn't hear. "I've drove a million miles and I'm ready to pass over to the other shore. I won't have long to linger here." She drove a consolidated school bus for thirty-nine years. Later, after Wallace left, she told me about her dream. A bunch of doctors were sitting around in a circle discussing her case. One said, "We've done all we can for her, boys, let's let her go." They all turned their hands up and smiled. When she didn't die that fall, she seemed disappointed, though as spring came she forgot about it, as old people will.

In addition to taking Wallace and Wallace Jr. to see Mother on Sunday nights, I go myself on Tuesdays and Thursdays. I usually find her sitting in front of the TV, even though she doesn't watch it. The nurses keep it on all the time. They say the old folks like the flickering. It soothes them down.

"What's this I hear about bears discovering fire?" she said on Tuesday.

"It's true," I told her as I combed her long white hair with the shell comb Wallace had brought her from Florida. Monday there had been a story in the Louisville *Courier-Journal*, and Tuesday one on NBC or CBS Nightly News. People were seeing bears all over the state, and in Virginia as well. They had quit hibernating, and were apparently planning to spend the winter in the medians of the interstates. There have always been bears in the mountains of Virginia, but not here in western Kentucky, not for almost a hundred years. The last one was killed when Mother was a girl. The theory in the *Courier-Journal* was that they were following I-65 down from the forests of Michigan and Canada, but one old man from Allen County (interviewed on nationwide TV) said that there had always been a few bears left back in the hills, and they had come out to join the others now that they had discovered fire.

"They don't hibernate anymore," I said. "They make a fire and keep it going all winter."

"I declare," Mother said. "What'll they think of next!" The nurse came to take her tobacco away, which is the signal for bedtime.

Every October, Wallace Jr. stays with me while his parents go to camp. I realize how backward that sounds, but there it is. My brother is a minister (House of the Righteous Way, Reformed), but he makes two-thirds of his living in real estate. He and Elizabeth go to a Christian Success Retreat in South Carolina, where people from all over the country practice selling things to one another. I know what it's like not because they've ever bothered to tell me, but because I've seen the Revolving Equity Success Plan ads late at night on TV.

The schoolbus let Wallace Jr. off at my house on Wednesday, the day they left. The boy doesn't have to pack much of a bag when he stays with me. He has his own room here. As the eldest of our family, I hung onto the old home place near Smiths Grove. It's getting run down, but Wallace Jr. and I don't mind. He has his own room in Bowling Green, too, but since Wallace and Elizabeth move to a different house every three months (part of the Plan), he keeps his .22 and his comics, the stuff that's important to a boy his age, in his room here at the home place. It's the room his dad and I used to share.

Wallace Jr. is twelve. I found him sitting on the back porch that overlooks the interstate when I got home from work. I sell crop insurance.

After I changed clothes, I showed him how to break the bead on a tire two ways, with a hammer and by backing a car over it. Like making sorghum, fixing tires by hand is a dying art. The boy caught on fast, though. "Tomorrow I'll show you how to mount your tire with the hammer and a tire iron," I said.

"What I wish is I could see the bears," he said. He was looking across the field to I-65, where the northbound lanes cut off the corner of our field. From the house at night, sometimes the traffic sounds like a waterfall.

"Can't see their fire in the daytime," I said. "But wait till tonight." That night CBS or NBC (I forget which is which) did a special on the bears, which were becoming a story of nationwide interest. They were seen in Kentucky, West Virginia, Missouri, Illinois (southern), and, of course, Virginia. There have always been bears in Virginia. Some characters there were even talking about hunting them. A scientist said they were heading into the states where there is some snow but not too much, and where there is enough timber in the medians for firewood. He had gone in with a video camera, but his shots were just blurry figures sitting around a fire. Another scientist said the bears were attracted by the berries on a new bush that grew only in the medians of the interstates. He claimed this berry was the first new species in recent history, brought about by the mixing of seeds along the highway. He ate one on TV, making a face, and called it a "newberry." A climatic ecologist said that the warm winters (there was no snow last winter in Nashville, and only one flurry in Louisville) had changed the bears' hibernation cycle, and now they were able to remember things from year to year. "Bears may have discovered fire centuries ago," he said, "but forgot it." Another theory was that they had discovered (or remembered) fire when Yellowstone burned, several years ago.

The TV showed more guys talking about bears than it showed bears, and Wallace Jr. and I lost interest. After the supper dishes were done I took the boy out behind the house and down to our fence. Across the interstate and through the trees, we could see the light of the bears' fire. Wallace Jr. wanted to go back to the house and get his .22 and go shoot one, and I explained why that would be wrong. "Besides," I said, "a twenty-two wouldn't do much more to a bear than make it mad.

"Besides," I added, "it's illegal to hunt in the medians."

The only trick to mounting a tire by hand, once you have beaten or pried it onto the rim, is setting the bead. You do this by setting the tire upright, sitting on it, and bouncing it up and down between your legs while the air goes in. When the bead sets on the rim, it makes a satisfying "pop." On Thursday, I kept Wallace Jr. home from school and showed him how to do this until he got it right. Then we climbed our fence and crossed the field to get a look at the bears.

In northern Virginia, according to "Good Morning America," the bears were keeping their fires going all day long. Here in western Kentucky, though, it was still warm for late October and they only stayed around the fires at night. Where they went and what they did in the daytime, I don't know. Maybe they were watching from the newberry bushes as Wallace Jr. and I climbed the government fence and crossed the northbound lanes. I carried an axe and Wallace Jr. brought his .22, not because he wanted to kill a bear but because a boy likes to carry some kind of a gun. The median was all tangled with brush and vines under the maples, oaks, and sycamores. Even though we were only a hundred yards from the house, I had never been there, and neither had anyone else that I knew of. It was like a created country. We found a path in the center and followed it down across a slow, short stream that flowed out of one grate and into another. The tracks in the gray mud were the first bear signs we saw. There was a musty but not really unpleasant smell. In a clearing under a big hollow beech, where the fire had been, we found nothing but ashes. Logs were drawn up in a rough circle and the smell was stronger. I stirred the ashes and found enough coals left to start a new flame, so I banked them back the way they had been left.

I cut a little firewood and stacked it to one side, just to be neighborly.

Maybe the bears were watching us from the bushes even then. There's no way to know. I tasted one of the newberries and spit it out. It was so sweet it was sour, just the sort of thing you would imagine a bear would like.

That evening after supper, I asked Wallace Jr. if he might want to go with me to visit Mother. I wasn't surprised when he said "yes." Kids have more consideration than folks give them credit for. We found her sitting on the concrete front porch of the Home, watching the cars go by on I-65. The nurse said she had been agitated all day. I wasn't surprised by that, either. Every fall as the leaves change, she gets restless, maybe the word is hopeful, again. I brought her into the dayroom and combed her long white hair. "Nothing but bears on TV anymore," the nurse complained, flipping the channels. Wallace Jr. picked up the remote after the nurse left, and we watched a CBS or NBC Special Report about some hunters in Virginia who had gotten their houses torched. The TV interviewed a hunter and his wife whose $117,500 Shenandoah Valley home had burned. She blamed the bears. He didn't blame the bears, but he was suing for compensation from the state since he had a valid hunting license. The state hunting commissioner came on and said that possession of a hunting license didn't prohibit (*enjoin*, I think, was the word he used) *the hunted* from striking back. I thought that was a pretty liberal view for a state commissioner. Of course, he had a vested interest in not paying off. I'm not a hunter myself.

"Don't bother coming on Sunday," Mother told Wallace Jr. with a wink. "I've drove a million miles and I've got one hand on the gate." I'm used to her saying stuff like that, especially in the fall, but I was afraid it would upset the boy. In fact, he looked worried after we left and I asked him what was wrong.

"How could she have drove a million miles?" he asked. She had told him forty-eight miles a day for thirty-nine years, and he had worked it out on his calculator to be 336,960 miles.

"Have *driven*," I said. "And it's forty-eight in the morning and forty-eight in the afternoon. Plus there were the football trips. Plus, old folks exaggerate a little." Mother was the first woman school bus driver in the state. She did it every day and raised a family, too. Dad just farmed.

I usually get off the interstate at Smiths Grove, but that night I drove north all the way to Horse Cave and doubled back so Wallace Jr. and I could see the bears' fires. There were not as many as you would think from the TV — one every six or seven miles, hidden back in a clump of trees or under a rocky ledge. Probably they look for water as well as wood. Wallace Jr. wanted to stop, but it's against the law to stop on the interstate and I was afraid the state police would run us off.

There was a card from Wallace in the mailbox. He and Elizabeth were doing fine and having a wonderful time. Not a word about Wallace Jr., but the boy didn't seem to mind. Like most kids his age, he doesn't really enjoy going places with his parents.

On Saturday afternoon, the Home called my office (Burley Belt Drought & Hail) and left word that Mother was gone. I was on the road. I work Saturdays. It's the only day a lot of part-time farmers are home. My heart literally skipped a beat when I called in and got the message, but only a beat. I had long been prepared. "It's a blessing," I said when I got the nurse on the phone.

"You don't understand," the nurse said, "Not *passed* away, gone. *Ran* away, gone. Your mother has escaped." Mother had gone through the door at the end of the corridor when no one was looking, wedging the door with her comb and taking a bedspread which belonged to the Home. What about her tobacco? I asked. It was gone. That was a sure sign she was planning to stay away. I was in Franklin, and it took me less than an hour to get to the Home on I-65. The nurse told me that Mother had been acting more and more confused lately. Of course they are going to say that. We looked around the grounds, which is only an acre with no trees between the interstate and a soybean field. Then they had me leave a message at the sheriff's office. I would have to keep paying for her care until she was officially listed as Missing, which would be Monday.

It was dark by the time I got back to the house, and Wallace Jr. was fixing supper. This just involves opening a few cans, already selected and grouped together with a rubber band. I told him his grandmother had gone, and he nodded, saying, "She told us she would be." I called Florida and left a message. There was nothing more to be done. I sat down and tried to watch TV, but there was nothing on. Then, I looked out the back door, and saw the firelight twinkling through the trees across the northbound lane of I-65, and realized I just might know where to find her.

It was definitely getting colder, so I got my jacket. I told the boy to wait by the phone in case the sheriff called, but when I looked back, halfway across the field, there he was behind me. He didn't have a jacket. I let him catch up. He was carrying his .22, and I made him leave it leaning against our fence. It was harder climbing the government fence in the dark, at my age, than it had been in the daylight. I am sixty-one. The highway was busy with cars heading south and trucks heading north.

Crossing the shoulder, I got my pants cuffs wet on the long grass, already wet with dew. It is actually bluegrass.

The first few feet into the trees it was pitch black and the boy grabbed my hand. Then it got lighter. At first I thought it was the moon, but it was the high beams shining like moonlight into the treetops, allowing Wallace

Jr. and me to pick our way through the brush. We soon found the path and its familiar bear smell.

I was wary of approaching the bears at night. If we stayed on the path we might run into one in the dark, but if we went through the bushes we might be seen as intruders. I wondered if maybe we shouldn't have brought the gun.

We stayed on the path. The light seemed to drip down from the canopy of the woods like rain. The going was easy, especially if we didn't try to look at the path but let our feet find their own way.

Then through the trees I saw their fire.

The fire was mostly of sycamore and beech branches, the kind of fire that puts out very little heat or light and lots of smoke. The bears hadn't learned the ins and outs of wood yet. They did okay at tending it, though. A large cinnamon brown northern-looking bear was poking the fire with a stick, adding a branch now and then from a pile at his side. The others sat around in a loose circle on the logs. Most were smaller black or honey bears, one was a mother with cubs. Some were eating berries from a hubcap. Not eating, but just watching the fire, my mother sat among them with the bedspread from the Home around her shoulders.

If the bears noticed us, they didn't let on. Mother patted a spot right next to her on the log and I sat down. A bear moved over to let Wallace Jr. sit on her other side.

The bear smell is rank but not unpleasant, once you get used to it. It's not like a barn smell, but wilder. I leaned over to whisper something to Mother and she shook her head. *It would be rude to whisper around these creatures that don't possess the power of speech*, she let me know without speaking. Wallace Jr. was silent too. Mother shared the bedspread with us and we sat for what seemed hours, looking into the fire.

The big bear tended the fire, breaking up the dry branches by holding one end and stepping on them, like people do. He was good at keeping it going at the same level. Another bear poked the fire from time to time, but the others left it alone. It looked like only a few of the bears knew how to use fire, and were carrying the others along. But isn't that how it is with everything? Every once in a while, a smaller bear walked into the circle of firelight with an armload of wood and dropped it onto the pile. Median wood had a silvery cast, like driftwood.

Wallace Jr. isn't fidgety like a lot of kids. I found it pleasant to sit and stare into the fire. I took a little piece of Mother's *Red Man*, though I don't generally chew. It was no different from visiting her at the Home, only more interesting, because of the bears. There were about eight or ten of them. Inside the fire itself, things weren't so dull, either: little dramas were being played out as fiery chambers were created and then destroyed in a crashing of sparks. My imagination ran wild. I looked around the circle at the bears and wondered what *they* saw. Some had their eyes closed. Though they were gathered together, their spirits still seemed solitary, as if each bear was sitting alone in front of its own fire.

The hubcap came around and we all took some newberries. I don't know about Mother, but I just pretended to eat mine. Wallace Jr. made a face and spit his out. When he went to sleep, I wrapped the bedspread around all three of us. It was getting colder and we were provided, like the bears, with fur. I was ready to go home, but not Mother. She pointed up toward the canopy of trees, where a light was spreading, and then pointed to herself. Did she think it was angels approaching from on high? It was only the high beams of some southbound truck, but she seemed mighty pleased. Holding her hand, I felt it grow colder and colder in mine.

Wallace Jr. woke me up by tapping on my knee. It was past dawn, and his grandmother had died sitting on the log between us. The fire was banked up and the bears were gone and someone was crashing straight through the woods, ignoring the path. It was Wallace. Two state troopers were right behind him. He was wearing a white shirt, and I realized it was Sunday morning. Underneath his sadness on learning of Mother's death, he looked peeved.

The troopers were sniffing the air and nodding. The bear smell was still strong. Wallace and I wrapped Mother in the bedspread and started with her body back out to the highway. The troopers stayed behind and scattered the bears' fire ashes and flung their firewood away into the bushes. It seemed a petty thing to do. They were like bears themselves, each one solitary in his own uniform.

There was Wallace's Olds 98 on the median, with its radial tires looking squashed on the grass. In front of it there was a police car with a trooper standing beside it, and behind it a funeral home hearse, also an Olds 98.

"First report we've had of them bothering old folks," the trooper said to Wallace. "That's not hardly what happened at all," I said, but nobody asked me to explain. They have their own procedures. Two men in suits got out of the hearse and opened the rear door. That to me was the point at which Mother departed this life. After we put her in, I put my arms around the boy. He was shivering even though it wasn't that cold. Sometimes death will do that, especially at dawn, with the police around and the grass wet, even when it comes as a friend.

We stood for a minute watching the cars pass. "It's a blessing," Wallace said. It's surprising how much traffic there is at 6:22 A.M.

That afternoon, I went back to the median and cut a little firewood to replace what the troopers had flung away. I could see the fire through the trees that night.

I went back two nights later, after the funeral. The fire was going and it was the same bunch of bears, as far as I could tell. I sat around with them a while but it seemed to make them nervous, so I went home. I had taken a handful of newberries from the hubcap, and on Sunday I went with the boy and arranged them on Mother's grave. I tried again, but it's no use, you can't eat them.

Unless you're a bear.

Critical Contexts for Evolutions

Stephen Jay Gould
Nonmoral Nature
(1982)

Paleontologist Stephen Jay Gould (1941–2002) was known as much for his popular writing and engagement in public debate as for his important contributions to evolutionary theory. Gould taught at Harvard University for 35 years, during which time he published more than 20 books and garnered more than 40 awards for his work as a scientist, writer, and educator.

As a scientist, he is best known for the theory of punctuated equilibrium, which he developed with fellow paleontologist Niles Eldredge. Gould and Eldredge argued for a modification of the classical Darwinian theory of evolution as a slow and steady process, pointing to irregularities in the fossil record that seemed to alternate between relatively stable periods and short bursts of prolific variation. Gould is also known for distinguishing between biological features that are directly adaptive and those that are incidental results of a larger process. Although Gould's work is widely accepted, his contentious spirit sometimes nettled his peers. His feud with the sociobiologists (or evolutionary psychologists) — who argued that evolution can account for every feature of human behavior — was particularly heated.

Gould reached a wider popular audience through the monthly column he wrote for *Natural History* magazine over the course of 25 years, and he is among the best-known science writers today. He published seven volumes of collected essays and a dozen other works. His books include *The Panda's Thumb*, which won the 1981 American Book Award for Science, *Wonderful Life: The Burgess Shale and the Nature of History*, which won the Science Book Prize in 1989, and *The Mismeasure of Man* (1981), an important critique of the misuse of science to justify social inequities such as racism and sexism.

Gould was a vocal opponent of Creationism and a passionate spokesperson for the separation of scientific study and religious doctrine, maintaining that science and religion operated in separate realms and that any attempt to connect them would be damaging to both. In "Nonmoral Nature," he examines the behavior of parasitic wasps and the challenges they have raised for scientists and theologians seeking to explain the problem of evil.

When the Right Honorable and Reverend Francis Henry, earl of Bridgewater, died in February, 1829, he left £8,000 to support a series of books "on the power, wisdom and goodness of God, as manifested in the creation." William Buckland, England's first official academic geologist and

later dean of Westminster, was invited to compose one of the nine Bridgewater Treatises. In it he discussed the most pressing problem of natural
theology: if God is benevolent and the Creation displays his "power, wisdom and goodness," then why are we surrounded with pain, suffering, and
apparently senseless cruelty in the animal world?

Buckland considered the depredation of "carnivorous races" as the primary challenge to an idealized world where the lion might dwell with the
lamb. He resolved the issue to his satisfaction by arguing that carnivores
actually increase "the aggregate of animal enjoyment" and "diminish that of
pain." Death, after all, is swift and relatively painless, victims are spared
the ravages of decrepitude and senility, and populations do not outrun their
food supply to the greater sorrow of all. God knew what he was doing when
he made lions. Buckland concluded in hardly concealed rapture:

> The appointment of death by the agency of carnivora, as the ordinary
> termination of animal existence, appears therefore in its main results to
> be a dispensation of benevolence; it deducts much from the aggregate
> amount of the pain of universal death; it abridges, and almost annihi-
> lates, throughout the brute creation, the misery of disease, and acciden-
> tal injuries, and lingering decay; and imposes such salutary restraint
> upon excessive increase of numbers, that the supply of food maintains
> perpetually a due ratio to the demand. The result is, that the surface of
> the land and depths of the waters are ever crowded with myriads of ani-
> mated beings, the pleasures of whose life are coextensive with its dura-
> tion; and which throughout the little day of existence that is allotted to
> them, fulfill with joy the functions for which they were created.

We may find a certain amusing charm in Buckland's vision today, but
such arguments did begin to address "the problem of evil" for many of
Buckland's contemporaries — how could a benevolent God create such a
world of carnage and bloodshed? Yet this argument could not abolish the
problem of evil entirely, for nature includes many phenomena far more
horrible in our eyes than simple predation. I suspect that nothing evokes
greater disgust in most of us than slow destruction of a host by an internal
parasite — gradual ingestion, bit by bit, from the inside. In no other way
can I explain why *Alien*, an uninspired, grade-C, formula horror film,
should have won such a following. That single scene of Mr. Alien, popping
forth as a baby parasite from the body of a human host, was both sicken-
ing and stunning. Our nineteenth-century forebears maintained similar
feelings. The greatest challenge to their concept of a benevolent deity was
not simple predation — but slow death by parasitic ingestion. The classic
case, treated at length by all great naturalists, invoked the so-called ichneumon fly. Buckland had sidestepped the major issue.

The "ichneumon fly," which provoked such concern among natural
theologians, was actually a composite creature representing the habits of
an enormous tribe. The Ichneumonoidea are a group of wasps, not flies,
that include more species than all the vertebrates combined (wasps, with
ants and bees, constitute the order Hymenoptera; flies, with their two

wings — wasps have four — form the order Diptera). In addition, many non-ichneumonid wasps of similar habits were often cited for the same grisly details. Thus, the famous story did not merely implicate a single aberrant species (perhaps a perverse leakage from Satan's realm), but hundreds of thousands — a large chunk of what could only be God's creation.

The ichneumons, like most wasps, generally live freely as adults but pass their larval life as parasites feeding on the bodies of other animals, almost invariably members of their own phylum, the Arthropoda. The most common victims are caterpillars (butterfly and moth larvae), but some ichneumons prefer aphids and others attack spiders. Most hosts are parasitized as larvae, but some adults are attacked, and many tiny ichneumons inject their brood directly into the egg of their host.

The free-flying females locate an appropriate host and then convert it to a food factory for their own young. Parasitologists speak of ectoparasitism when the uninvited guest lives on the surface of its host, and endoparasitism when the parasite dwells within. Among endoparasitic ichneumons, adult females pierce the host with their ovipositor and deposit eggs within. (The ovipositor, a thin tube extending backward from the wasp's rear end, may be many times as long as the body itself.) Usually, the host is not otherwise inconvenienced for the moment, at least until the eggs hatch and the ichneumon larvae begin their grim work of interior excavation.

Among ectoparasites, however, many females lay their eggs directly upon the host's body. Since an active host would easily dislodge the egg, the ichneumon mother often simultaneously injects a toxin that paralyzes the caterpillar or other victim. The paralysis may be permanent, and the caterpillar lies, alive but immobile, with the agent of its future destruction secure on its belly. The egg hatches, the helpless caterpillar twitches, the wasp larva pierces and begins its grisly feast.

Since a dead and decaying caterpillar will do the wasp larva no good, it eats in a pattern that cannot help but recall, in our inappropriate, anthropocentric interpretation, the ancient English penalty for treason — drawing and quartering, with its explicit object of extracting as much torment as possible by keeping the victim alive and sentient. As the king's executioner drew out and burned his client's entrails, so does the ichneumon larva eat fat bodies and digestive organs first, keeping the caterpillar alive by preserving intact the essential heart and central nervous system. Finally, the larva completes its work and kills its victim, leaving behind the caterpillar's empty shell. Is it any wonder that ichneumons, not snakes or lions, stood as the paramount challenge to God's benevolence during the heyday of natural theology?

As I read through the nineteenth- and twentieth-century literature on ichneumons, nothing amused me more than the tension between an intellectual knowledge that wasps should not be described in human terms and a literary or emotional inability to avoid the familiar categories of epic and narrative, pain and destruction, victim and vanquisher. We seem to be caught in the mythic structures of our own cultural sagas, quite unable, even in our basic descriptions, to use any other language than the metaphors of battle and conquest. We cannot render this corner of natural history as anything but story, combining the themes of grim horror and fascination and usually ending not so much with pity for the caterpillar as with admiration for the efficiency of the ichneumon.

I detect two basic themes in most epic descriptions: the struggles of prey and the ruthless efficiency of parasites. Although we acknowledge that we may be witnessing little more than automatic instinct or physiological reaction, still we describe the defenses of hosts as though they represented conscious struggles. Thus, aphids kick and caterpillars may wriggle violently as wasps attempt to insert their ovipositors. The pupa of the tortoiseshell butterfly (usually considered an inert creature silently awaiting its conversion from duckling to swan) may contort its abdominal region so sharply that attacking wasps are thrown into the air. The caterpillars of *Hapalia*, when attacked by the wasp *Apanteles machaeralis*, drop suddenly from their leaves and suspend themselves in air by a silken thread. But the wasp may run down the thread and insert its eggs nonetheless. Some hosts can encapsulate the injected egg with blood cells that aggregate and harden, thus suffocating the parasite.

J. H. Fabre, the great nineteenth-century French entomologist, who remains to this day the preeminently literate natural historian of insects, made a special study of parasitic wasps and wrote with an unabashed anthropocentrism about the struggles of paralyzed victims (see his books *Insect Life* and *The Wonders of Instinct*). He describes some imperfectly paralyzed caterpillars that struggle so violently every time a parasite approaches that the wasp larvae must feed with unusual caution. They attach themselves to a silken strand from the roof of their burrow and descend upon a safe and exposed part of the caterpillar:

> The grub is at dinner: head downwards, it is digging into the limp belly of one of the caterpillars. . . . At the least sign of danger in the heap of caterpillars, the larva retreats . . . and climbs back to the ceiling, where the swarming rabble cannot reach it. When peace is restored, it slides down [its silken cord] and returns to table, with its head over the viands and its rear upturned and ready to withdraw in case of need.

In another chapter, he describes the fate of a paralyzed cricket:

> One may see the cricket, bitten to the quick, vainly move its antennae and abdominal styles, open and close its empty jaws, and even move a foot, but the larva is safe and searches its vitals with impunity. What an awful nightmare for the paralyzed cricket!

Fabre even learned to feed paralyzed victims by placing a syrup of sugar and water on their mouthparts — thus showing that they remained alive, sentient, and (by implication) grateful for any palliation of their inevitable fate. If Jesus, immobile and thirsting on the cross, received only vinegar from his tormentors, Fabre at least could make an ending bittersweet.

The second theme, ruthless efficiency of the parasites, leads to the opposite conclusion — grudging admiration for the victors. We learn of their skill in capturing dangerous hosts often many times larger than themselves. Caterpillars may be easy game, but psammocharid wasps prefer spiders. They must insert their ovipositors in a safe and precise spot. Some leave a paralyzed spider in its own burrow. *Planiceps hirsutus*, for example, parasitizes a California trapdoor spider. It searches for spider tubes on sand dunes, then digs into nearby sand to disturb the spider's home and drive it out. When the spider emerges, the wasp attacks, paralyzes its victim, drags it back into its own tube, shuts and fastens the trapdoor, and deposits a single egg upon the spider's abdomen. Other psammocharids will drag a heavy spider back to a previously prepared cluster of clay or mud cells. Some amputate a spider's legs to make the passage easier. Others fly back over water, skimming a buoyant spider along the surface.

Some wasps must battle with other parasites over a host's body. *Rhyssella curvipes* can detect the larvae of wood wasps deep within alder wood and drill down to a potential victim with its sharply ridged ovipositor. *Pseudorhyssa alpestris*, a related parasite, cannot drill directly into wood since its slender ovipositor bears only rudimentary cutting ridges. It locates the holes made by *Rhyssella*, inserts its ovipositor, and lays an egg on the host (already conveniently paralyzed by *Rhyssella*), right next to the egg deposited by its relative. The two eggs hatch at about the same time, but the larva of *Pseudorhyssa* has a bigger head bearing much larger mandibles. *Pseudorhyssa* seizes the smaller *Rhyssella* larva, destroys it, and proceeds to feast upon a banquet already well prepared.

Other praises for the efficiency of mothers invoke the themes of early, quick, and often. Many ichneumons don't even wait for their hosts to develop into larvae, but parasitize the egg directly (larval wasps may then either drain the egg itself or enter the developing host larva). Others simply move fast. *Apanteles militaris* can deposit up to seventy-two eggs in a single second. Still others are doggedly persistent. *Aphidius gomezi* females produce up to 1,500 eggs and can parasitize as many as 600 aphids in a single working day. In a bizarre twist upon "often," some wasps indulge in polyembryony, a kind of iterated supertwining. A single egg divides into cells that aggregate into as many as 500 individuals. Since some polyembryonic wasps parasitize caterpillars much larger than themselves and may lay up to six eggs in each, as many as 3,000 larvae may develop within, and feed upon a single host. These wasps are endoparasites and do not paralyze their victims. The caterpillars writhe back and forth, not (one suspects) from pain, but merely in response to the commotion induced by thousands of wasp larvae feeding within.

Maternal efficiency is often matched by larval aptitude. I have already mentioned the pattern of eating less essential parts first, thus keeping the host alive and fresh to its final and merciful dispatch. After the larva digests every edible morsel of its victim (if only to prevent later fouling of its abode by decaying tissue), it may still use the outer shell of its host. One aphid parasite cuts a hole in the bottom of its victim's shell, glues the skeleton to a leaf by sticky secretions from its salivary gland, and then spins a cocoon to pupate within the aphid's shell.

In using inappropriate anthropocentric language for this romp through the natural history of ichneumons, I have tried to emphasize just why these wasps became a preeminent challenge to natural theology — the antiquated doctrine that attempted to infer God's essence from the products of his creation. I have used twentieth-century examples for the most part, but all themes were known and stressed by the great nineteenth-century natural theologians. How then did they square the habits of these wasps with the goodness of God? How did they extract themselves from this dilemma of their own making?

The strategies were as varied as the practitioners; they shared only the theme of special pleading for an a priori doctrine — our naturalists *knew* that God's benevolence was lurking somewhere behind all these tales of apparent horror. Charles Lyell, for example, in the first edition of his epochal *Principles of Geology* (1830–1833), decided that caterpillars posed such a threat to vegetation that any natural checks upon them could only reflect well upon a creating deity, for caterpillars would destroy human agriculture "did not Providence put causes in operation to keep them in due bounds."

The Reverend William Kirby, rector of Barham, and Britain's foremost entomologist, chose to ignore the plight of caterpillars and focused instead upon the virtue of mother love displayed by wasps in provisioning their young with such care.

> The great object of the female is to discover a proper nidus for her eggs. In search of this she is in constant motion. Is the caterpillar of a butterfly or moth the appropriate food for her young? You see her alight upon the plants where they are most usually to be met with, run quickly over them, carefully examining every leaf, and, having found the unfortunate object of her search, insert her sting into its flesh, and there deposit an egg. . . . The active Ichneumon braves every danger, and does not desist until her courage and address have insured subsistence for one of her future progeny.

Kirby found this solicitude all the more remarkable because the female wasp will never see her child and enjoy the pleasures of parenthood. Yet love compels her to danger nonetheless:

> A very large proportion of them are doomed to die before their young come into existence. But in these the passion is not extinguished. . . . When you witness the solicitude with which they provide for the security and sustenance of their future young, you can scarcely deny to them love for a progeny they are never destined to behold.

Kirby also put in a good word for the marauding larvae, praising them for their forbearance in eating selectively to keep their caterpillar alive. Would we all husband our resources with such care!

> In this strange and apparently cruel operation one circumstance is truly remarkable. The larva of the Ichneumon, though every day, perhaps for months, it gnaws the inside of the caterpillar, and though at last it has

Gould: Nonmoral Nature • 1209

devoured almost every part of it except the skin and intestines, carefully all this time it avoids injuring the vital organs, as if aware that its own existence depends on that of the insect upon which it preys! . . . What would be the impression which a similar instance amongst the race of quadrupeds would make upon us? If, for example, an animal . . . should be found to feed upon the inside of a dog, devouring only those parts not essential to life, while it cautiously left uninjured the heart, arteries, lungs, and intestines, — should we not regard such an instance as a perfect prodigy, as an example of instinctive forbearance almost miraculous? [The last three quotes come from the 1856, and last pre-Darwinian, edition of Kirby and Spence's *Introduction to Entomology*.]

This tradition of attempting to read moral meaning from nature did not cease with the triumph of evolutionary theory in 1859 — for evolution could be read as God's chosen method of peopling our planet, and ethical messages might still populate nature. Thus, St. George Mivart, one of Darwin's most effective evolutionary critics and a devout Catholic, argued that "many amiable and excellent people" had been misled by the apparent suffering of animals for two reasons. First, whatever the pain, "physical suffering and moral evil are simply incommensurable." Since beasts are not moral agents, their feelings cannot bear any ethical message. But secondly, lest our visceral sensitivities still be aroused, Mivart assures us that animals must feel little, if any, pain. Using a favorite racist argument of the time — that "primitive" people suffer far less than advanced and cultured folk — Mivart extrapolated further down the ladder of life into a realm of very limited pain indeed: Physical suffering, he argued,

depends greatly upon the mental condition of the sufferer. Only during consciousness does it exist, and only in the most highly organized men does it reach its acme. The author has been assured that lower races of men appear less keenly sensitive to physical suffering than do more cultivated and refined human beings. Thus only in man can there really be any intense degree of suffering, because only in him is there that intellectual recollection of past moments and that anticipation of future ones, which constitute in great part the bitterness of suffering. The momentary pang, the present pain, which beasts endure, though real enough, is yet, doubtless, not to be compared as to its intensity with the suffering which is produced in man through his high prerogative of self-consciousness [from *Genesis of Species*, 1871].

It took Darwin himself to derail this ancient tradition — and he proceeded in the gentle way so characteristic of his radical intellectual approach to nearly everything. The ichneumons also troubled Darwin greatly and he wrote of them to Asa Gray in 1860:

I own that I cannot see as plainly as others do, and as I should wish to do, evidence of design and beneficence on all sides of us. There seems to me too much misery in the world. I cannot persuade myself that a beneficent and omnipotent God would have designedly created the

Ichneumonidae with the express intention of their feeding within the living bodies of Caterpillars, or that a cat should play with mice.

Indeed, he had written with more passion to Joseph Hooker in 1856: "What a book a devil's chaplain might write on the clumsy, wasteful, blundering, low, and horribly cruel works of nature!"

This honest admission — that nature is often (by our standards) cruel and that all previous attempts to find a lurking goodness behind everything represent just so much special pleading — can lead in two directions. One might retain the principle that nature holds moral messages, but reverse the usual perspective and claim that morality consists in understanding the ways of nature and doing the opposite. Thomas Henry Huxley advanced this argument in his famous essay on *Evolution and Ethics* (1893):

> The practice of that which is ethically best — what we call goodness or virtue — involves a course of conduct which, in all respects, is opposed to that which leads to success in the cosmic struggle for existence. In place of ruthless self-assertion it demands self-restraint; in place of thrusting aside, or treading down, all competitors, it requires that the individual shall not merely respect, but shall help his fellows. . . . It repudiates the gladiatorial theory of existence. . . . Laws and moral precepts are directed to the end of curbing the cosmic process.

The other argument, radical in Darwin's day but more familiar now, holds that nature simply is as we find it. Our failure to discern a universal good does not record any lack of insight or ingenuity, but merely demonstrates that nature contains no moral messages framed in human terms. Morality is a subject for philosophers, theologians, students of the humanities, indeed for all thinking people. The answers will not be read passively from nature; they do not, and cannot, arise from the data of science. The factual state of the world does not teach us how we, with our powers for good and evil, should alter or preserve it in the most ethical manner.

Darwin himself tended toward this view, although he could not, as a man of his time, thoroughly abandon the idea that laws of nature might reflect some higher purpose. He clearly recognized that specific manifestations of those laws — cats playing with mice, and ichneumon larvae eating caterpillars — could not embody ethical messages, but he somehow hoped that unknown higher laws might exist "with the details, whether good or bad, left to the working out of what we may call chance."

Since ichneumons are a detail, and since natural selection is a law regulating details, the answer to the ancient dilemma of why such cruelty (in our terms) exists in nature can only be that there isn't any answer — and that framing the question "in our terms" is thoroughly inappropriate in a natural world neither made for us nor ruled by us. It just plain happens. It is a strategy that works for ichneumons and that natural selection has programmed into their behavioral repertoire. Caterpillars are not suffering to teach us something; they have simply been outmaneuvered, for now, in the evolutionary game. Perhaps they will evolve a set of adequate defenses sometime in the future, thus sealing the fate of ichneumons. And perhaps, indeed probably, they will not.

Another Huxley, Thomas's grandson Julian, spoke for this position, using as an example — yes, you guessed it — the ubiquitous ichneumons:

> Natural selection, in fact, though like the mills of God in grinding slowly and grinding small, has few other attributes that a civilized religion would call divine. . . . Its products are just as likely to be aesthetically, morally, or intellectually repulsive to us as they are to be attractive. We need only think of the ugliness of *Sacculina* or a bladder-worm, the stupidity of a rhinoceros or a stegosaur, the horror of a female mantis devouring its mate or a brood of ichneumon flies slowly eating out a caterpillar.

If nature is nonmoral, then evolution cannot teach any ethical theory at all. The assumption that it can has abetted a panoply of social evils that ideologues falsely read into nature from their beliefs — eugenics and (misnamed) social Darwinism prominently among them. Not only did Darwin eschew any attempt to discover an antireligious ethic in nature, he also expressly stated his personal bewilderment about such deep issues as the problem of evil. Just a few sentences after invoking the ichneumons, and in words that express both the modesty of this splendid man and the compatibility, through lack of contact, between science and true religion, Darwin wrote to Asa Gray,

> I feel most deeply that the whole subject is too profound for the human intellect. A dog might as well speculate on the mind of Newton. Let each man hope and believe what he can.

Marvin Minsky

Will Robots Inherit the Earth?

(1994)

Marvin Minsky (b. 1927) is a pioneer in the field of artificial intelligence. His work focuses on the simulation of human thought processes in machines and, because it combines mathematics and engineering with an investigation into learning and language processing, his theories are relevant to understanding human psychology as well as computer science. In 1951, Minsky developed the first randomly wired neural network learning machine, and in 1959 he cofounded the MIT Artificial Intelligence Laboratory. Since then, he has continued to influence the field both through his own work and through his leadership at MIT, where he currently holds dual titles as Toshiba Professor of Media Arts and Sciences and Professor of Electrical Engineering and Computer Science.

Minsky's work is best known to the popular audience through his 1986 book *The Society of Mind*, which proposes a theory of intelligence based not on a centrally directed process but rather on the interaction of countless independent operations through which intelligence emerges. This idea has been influential in many fields, as demonstrated by Steven Johnson in his essay later in this chapter.

In his provocative essay "Will Robots Inherit the Earth?" Minsky argues that humans need not accept the natural limitations of our biology. As research into neurology and cybernetics progresses, we will be able to maximize our brain functions in ways our ancestors could never have dreamed. Minsky sees this as the next stage in human evolution, one relying on technological enhancements rather than natural selection. His tone is sometimes playful, but Minsky is clearly earnest in urging us to take control of our own destiny.

Introduction

> *Early to bed and early to rise,*
> *Makes a man healthy and wealthy and wise.*
> — Ben Franklin

Everyone wants wisdom and wealth. Nevertheless, our health often gives out before we achieve them. To lengthen our lives, and improve our minds, in the future we will need to change our bodies and brains. To that end, we first must consider how normal Darwinian evolution brought us to where we are. Then we must imagine ways in which future replacements for worn body parts might solve most problems of failing health. We must then invent strategies to augment our brains and gain greater wisdom. Eventually we will entirely replace our brains — using nanotechnology. Once delivered from the limitations of biology, we will be able to decide the length of our lives — with the option of immortality — and choose among other, unimagined capabilities as well.

In such a future, attaining wealth will not be a problem; the trouble will be in controlling it. Obviously, such changes are difficult to envision, and many thinkers still argue that these advances are impossible — particularly in the domain of artificial intelligence. But the sciences needed to enact this transition are already in the making, and it is time to consider what this new world will be like.

Health and Longevity

Such a future cannot be realized through biology. In recent times we've learned a lot about health and how to maintain it. We have devised thousands of specific treatments for particular diseases and disabilities. However, we do not seem to have increased the maximum length of our life span. Franklin lived for 84 years and, except in popular legends and myths,

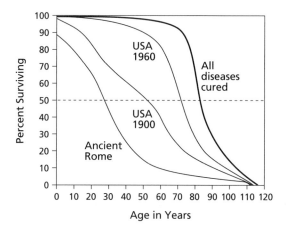

no one has ever lived twice that long. According to the estimates of Roy Walford, professor of pathology at UCLA Medical School, the average human life span was about 22 years in ancient Rome; about 50 in the developed countries in 1900, and today stands at about 75. Still, each of those curves seems to terminate sharply near 115 years. Centuries of improvements in health care have had no effect on that maximum.

Why are our life spans so limited? The answer is simple: Natural selection favors the genes of those with the most descendants. Those numbers tend to grow exponentially with the number of generations — and so this favors the genes of those who reproduce at earlier ages. Evolution does not usually favor genes that lengthen lives beyond that amount adults need to care for their young. Indeed, it may even favor offspring who do not have to compete with living parents. Such competition could promote the accumulation of genes that cause death.

For example, after spawning, the Mediterranean octopus (*O. Hummelincki*) promptly stops eating and starves to death. If we remove a certain gland though, the octopus continues to eat, and lives twice as long. Many other animals are programmed to die soon after they cease reproducing. Exceptions to this include those long-lived animals, like ourselves and the elephants, whose progeny learn so much from the social transmission of accumulated knowledge.

We humans appear to be the longest lived warm-blooded animals. What selective pressure might have led to our present longevity, which is almost twice that of our other primate relatives? This is related to wisdom! Among all mammals, our infants are the most poorly equipped to survive by themselves. Perhaps we needed not only parents, but grandparents too, to care for us and to pass on precious survival tips.

Even with such advice, there are many causes of mortality to which we might succumb. Some deaths result from infections. Our immune systems have evolved versatile ways to deal with most such diseases. Unhappily, though, those very same immune systems often injure us by treating various parts of ourselves as though they, too, were infectious invaders. This

blindness leads to diseases such as diabetes, multiple sclerosis, rheuma-
toid arthritis, and many others.

We are also subject to injuries that our bodies cannot repair. Namely,
accidents, dietary imbalances, chemical poisons, heat, radiation, and sun-
dry other influences can deform or chemically alter the molecules inside
our cells so that they are unable to function. Some of these errors get corrected by replacing defective molecules. However, when the replacement
rate is too slow, errors accumulate. For example, when the proteins of the
eyes' lenses lose their elasticity, we lose our ability to focus and need bifo-
cal spectacles — one of Franklin's inventions.

The major causes of death result from the effects of inherited genes.
These genes include those that seem to be largely responsible for heart disease and cancer, the two largest causes of mortality, as well as countless
other disorders, such as cystic fibrosis and sickle cell anemia. New technologies should be able to prevent some of these disorders by finding ways
to replace those genes.

Perhaps worst of all, we suffer from defects inherent in how our genetic
system works. The relationship between genes and cells is exceedingly
indirect; there are no blueprints or maps to guide our genes as they build
or rebuild the body. As we learn more about our genes, we will hopefully
be able to correct, or at least postpone, many conditions that still plague
our later years.

Most likely, eventual senescence is inevitable in all biological organisms.
To be sure, certain species (including some varieties of fish, tortoises, and
lobsters) do not appear to show any systematic increase of mortality rate
with age. These animals seem to die mainly from external causes, such as
predators or a lack of food. Still, we have no records of animals that have
lived for as long as 200 years — although this does not prove that none
exist. Walford and many others believe that a carefully designed diet, one
seriously restricted in calories, can significantly increase a human's life
span — but cannot prevent our ultimate death.

Biological Wearing Out

As we learn more about our genes, we will hopefully be able to correct, or
at least postpone, many conditions that still plague our later years. However, even if we found cures for each specific disease, we would still have
to deal with the general problem of "wearing out." The normal function of
every cell involves thousands of chemical processes, each of which sometimes makes random mistakes. Our bodies use many kinds of correction
techniques, each triggered by a specific type of mistake. However, those
random errors happen in so many different ways that no low-level scheme
can correct them all.

The problem is that our genetic systems were not designed for very
long-term maintainance. The relationship between genes and cells is exceedingly indirect; there are no blueprints or maps to guide our genes as
they build or rebuild the body. To repair defects on larger scales, a body

would need some sort of catalogue that specified which types of cells should be located where. In computer programs it is easy to install such redundancy. Many computers maintain unused copies of their most critical "system" programs, and routinely check their integrity. However, no animals have evolved like schemes, presumably because such algorithms cannot develop through natural selection. The trouble is that error correction then would stop mutation — which would ultimately slow the rate of evolution of an animal's descendants so much that they would be unable to adapt to changes in their environments.

Could we live for several centuries simply by changing some number of genes? After all, we now differ from our evolutionary relatives, the gorillas and chimpanzees, by only a few thousand genes — and yet we live almost twice as long. If we assume that only a small fraction of those new genes caused that increase in life span, then perhaps no more than a hundred or so of those genes were involved. Still, even if this turned out to be true, it would not guarantee that we could gain another century by changing another hundred genes. We might need to change only a few of them — or we might have to change a good many more.

Making new genes and installing them is slowly becoming feasible. But we are already exploiting another approach to combat biological wear and tear: replacing each organ that threatens to fail with a biological or an artificial substitute. Some replacements are already routine. Others are on the horizon. Hearts are merely clever pumps. Muscles and bones are motors and beams. Digestive systems are chemical reactors. Eventually, we will solve the problems associated with transplanting or replacing all of these parts.

When we consider replacing a brain, though, a transplant will not work. You cannot simply exchange your brain for another and remain the same person. You would lose the knowledge and the processes that constitute your identity. Nevertheless, we might be able to replace certain worn out parts of brains by transplanting tissue-cultured fetal cells. This procedure would not restore lost knowledge — but that might not matter as much as it seems. We probably store each fragment of knowledge in several different places, in different forms. New parts of the brain could be retrained and reintegrated with the rest — and some of that might even happen spontaneously.

Limitations of Human Wisdom

Even before our bodies wear out, I suspect that we run into limitations of our brains. As a species we seem to have reached a plateau in our intellectual development. There's no sign that we're getting smarter. Was Albert Einstein a better scientist than Newton or Archimedes? Has any playwright in recent years topped Shakespeare or Euripides? We have learned a lot in two thousand years, yet much ancient wisdom still seems sound — which makes me suspect that we haven't been making much progress. We still don't know how to deal with conflicts between individual goals and global interests. We are so bad at making important decisions that, whenever we can, we leave to chance what we are unsure about.

Why is our wisdom so limited? Is it because we do not have the time to learn very much, or that we lack enough capacity? Is it because, as in popular legend, we use only a fraction of our brains? Could better education help? Of course, but only to a point. Even our best prodigies learn no more than twice as quickly as the rest. Everything takes us too long to learn because our brains are so terribly slow. It would certainly help to have more time, but longevity is not enough. The brain, like other finite things, must reach some limits to what it can learn. We don't know what those limits are; perhaps our brains could keep learning for several more centuries. Ultimately, though, we will need to increase their capacity.

The more we learn about our brains, the more ways we will find to improve them. Each brain has hundreds of specialized regions. We know only a little about what each one does — but as soon as we find out how any one part works, researchers will try to devise ways to extend that organ's capacity. They will also conceive of entirely new abilities that biology has never provided. As these inventions accumulate, we'll try to connect them to our brains — perhaps through millions of microscopic electrodes inserted into the great nerve-bundle called the corpus callosum, the largest data-bus in the brain. With further advances, no part of the brain will be out of bounds for attaching new accessories. In the end, we will find ways to replace every part of the body and brain — and thus repair all the defects and flaws that make our lives so brief.

Needless to say, in doing so, we'll be making ourselves into machines.

Does this mean that machines will replace us? I don't feel that it makes much sense to think in terms of "us" and "them." I much prefer the attitude of Hans Moravec of Carnegie-Mellon University, who suggests that we think of those future intelligent machines as our own "mind-children."

In the past, we have tended to see ourselves as a final product of evolution — but our evolution has not ceased. Indeed, we are now evolving more rapidly — although not in the familiar, slow Darwinian way. It is time that we started to think about our new emerging identities. We now can design systems based on new kinds of "unnatural selection" that can exploit explicit plans and goals and can also exploit the inheritance of acquired characteristics. It took a century for evolutionists to train themselves to avoid such ideas — biologists call them "teleological" and "Lamarckian" — but now we may have to change those rules!

Replacing the Brain

Almost all the knowledge that we learn is embodied in various networks inside our brains. These networks consist of huge numbers of tiny nerve cells and even larger numbers of smaller structures called *synapses*, which control how signals jump from one nerve cell to another. To make a replacement of your brain, we would need to know something about how each of your synapses relates to the two cells it bridges. We would also have to know how each of those structures responds to the various electric fields, hormones, neurotransmitters, nutrients, and other chemicals that are active in its neighborhood. Your brain contains trillions of synapses, so this is no small requirement.

Fortunately, we would not need to know every minute detail. If that were so, our brains wouldn't work in the first place. In biological organisms, generally each system has evolved to be insensitive to most details of what goes on in the smaller subsystems on which it depends. Therefore, to copy a functional brain, it should suffice to replicate just enough of the function of each part to produce its important effects on other parts.

Suppose that we wanted to copy a machine, such as a brain, that contained a trillion components. Today we could not do such a thing (even were we equipped with the necessary knowledge) if we had to build each component separately. However, if we had a million construction machines that could each build a thousand parts per second, our task would take only minutes. In the decades to come, new fabrication machines will make this possible. Most present-day manufacturing is based on shaping bulk materials. In contrast, the field called "nanotechnology" aims to build materials and machinery by placing each atom and molecule precisely where we want it.

By such methods, we could make truly identical parts — and thus escape from the randomness that hinders conventionally made machines. Today, for example, when we try to etch very small circuits, the sizes of the wires vary so much that we cannot predict their electrical properties. However, if we can locate each atom exactly, then those wires will be indistinguishable. This would lead to new kinds of materials that current techniques could never make; we could endow them with enormous strength or novel quantum properties. These products in turn will lead to computers as small as synapses, having unparalleled speed and efficiency.

Once we can use these techniques to construct a general-purpose assembly machine that operates on atomic scales, further progress should be swift. If it took one week for such a machine to make a copy of itself, then we could have a billion copies in less than a year.

These devices would transform our world. For example, we could program them to fabricate efficient solar energy collecting devices and apply these to nearby surfaces so that they could power themselves. In this way, we could grow fields of micro-factories in much the same way that we now grow trees. In such a future, we will have little trouble attaining wealth, but rather in learning how to control it. In particular, we must always take care when dealing with things (such as ourselves) that might be able to reproduce themselves.

Limits of Human Memory

If we want to consider augmenting our brains, we might first ask how much a person knows today. Thomas K. Landauer of Bell Communications Research reviewed many experiments in which people were asked to read

1218 • Evolutions: Critical Contexts

text, look at pictures, and listen to words, sentences, short passages of music, and nonsense syllables. They were later tested in various ways to see how much they remembered. In none of these situations were people able to learn, and later remember, more than about 2 bits per second, for any extended period. If you could maintain that rate for 12 hours every day for 100 years, the total would be about 3 billion bits — less than what we can store today on a regular 5-inch compact disk. In a decade or so, that amount should fit on a single computer chip.

Although these experiments do not much resemble what we do in real life, we do not have any hard evidence that people can learn more quickly. Despite those popular legends about people with "photographic memories," no one seems to have mastered, word for word, the contents of as few as one hundred books — or of a single major encyclopedia. The complete works of Shakespeare come to about 130 million bits. Landauer's limit implies that a person would need at least four years to memorize them. We have no well-founded estimates of how much information we require to perform skills such as painting or skiing, but I don't see any reason why these activities shouldn't be similarly limited.

The brain is believed to contain the order of a hundred trillion synapses — which should leave plenty of room for those few billion bits of reproducible memories. Someday though it should be feasible to build that much storage space into a package as small as a pea, using nanotechnology.

The Future of Intelligence

Once we know what we need to do, our nanotechnologies should enable us to construct replacement bodies and brains that won't be constrained to work at the crawling pace of "real time." The events in our computer chips already happen millions of times faster than those in brain cells. Hence, we could design our "mind-children" to think a million times faster than we do. To such a being, half a minute might seem as long as one of our years, and each hour as long as an entire human lifetime.

But could such beings really exist? Many thinkers firmly maintain that machines will never have thoughts like ours, because no matter how we build them, they'll always lack some vital ingredient. They call this essence by various names — like sentience, consciousness, spirit, or soul. Philosophers write entire books to prove that, because of this deficiency, machines can never feel or understand the sorts of things that people do. However, every proof in each of those books is flawed by assuming, in one way or another, the thing that it purports to prove — the existence of some magical spark that has no detectable properties.

I have no patience with such arguments. We should not be searching for any single missing part. Human thought has many ingredients, and every machine that we have ever built is missing dozens or hundreds of them! Compare what computers do today with what we call "thinking." Clearly, human thinking is far more flexible, resourceful, and adaptable. When anything goes even slightly wrong within a present-day computer program, the machine will either come to a halt or produce some wrong or worthless results. When a person thinks, things constantly going wrong as well — yet this rarely thwarts us. Instead, we simply try something else. We look at our problem a different way and switch to another strategy. The human mind works in diverse ways. What empowers us to do this?

On my desk lies a textbook about the brain. Its index has about 6,000 lines that refer to hundreds of specialized structures. If you happen to injure some of these, you could lose your ability to remember the names of animals. Another injury might leave you unable to make any long-range plans. Yet another kind of impairment could render you prone to suddenly utter dirty words, because of damage to the machinery that normally censors that sort of expression. We know from thousands of similar facts that the brain contains diverse machinery.

Thus, your knowledge is represented in various forms that are stored in different regions of the brain, to be used by different processes. What are those representations like? In the brain, we do not yet know. However, in the field of artificial intelligence, researchers have found several useful ways to represent knowledge, each better suited to some purposes than to others. The most popular ones use collections of "If-Then" rules. Other systems use structures called "frames" — which resemble forms that are filled out. Yet other programs use web-like networks, or schemes that resemble tree-like scripts. Some systems store knowledge in language-like sentences, or in expressions of mathematical logic. A programmer starts any new job by trying to decide which representation will best accomplish the task at hand. Typically then, a computer program uses only a single representation and if this should fail, the system breaks down. This shortcoming justifies the common complaint that computers don't really "understand" what they're doing.

But what does it mean to understand? Many philosophers have declared that understanding (or meaning, or consciousness) must be a basic, elemental ability that only a living mind can possess. To me, this claim appears to be a symptom of "physics envy" — that is, they are jealous of how well physical science has explained so much in terms of so few principles. Physicists have done very well by rejecting all explanations that seem too complicated, and searching, instead, for simple ones. However, this method does not work when we're dealing with the full complexity of the brain. Here is an abridgment of what I said about understanding in my book *The Society of Mind*.

> If you understand something in only one way, then you don't really understand it at all. This is because, if something goes wrong, you get stuck with a thought that just sits in your mind with nowhere to go. The secret of what anything means to us depends on how we've connected it to all the other things we know. This is why, when someone learns "by rote," we say that they don't really understand. However, if you have several different representations, then when one approach fails you can try another. Of course, making too many indiscriminate connections will turn a mind

to mush. But well-connected representations let you turn ideas around in your mind, to envision things from many perspectives until you find one that works for you. And that's what we mean by thinking!

I think that this flexibility explains why thinking is easy for us and hard for computers, at the moment. In *The Society of Mind*, I suggest that the brain rarely uses only a single representation. Instead, it always runs several scenarios in parallel so that multiple viewpoints are always available. Furthermore, each system is supervised by other, higher-level ones that keep track of their performance, and reformulate problems when necessary. Since each part and process in the brain may have deficiencies, we should expect to find other parts that try to detect and correct such bugs.

In order to think effectively, you need multiple processes to help you describe, predict, explain, abstract, and plan what your mind should do next. The reason we can think so well is not because we house mysterious spark-like talents and gifts, but because we employ societies of agencies that work in concert to keep us from getting stuck. When we discover how these societies work, we can put them to work inside computers too. Then if one procedure in a program gets stuck, another might suggest an alternative approach. If you saw a machine do things like that, you'd certainly think it was conscious.

The Failures of Ethics

This article bears on our rights to have children, to change our genes, and to die if we so wish. No popular ethical system yet, be it humanist or religion-based, has shown itself able to face the challenges that already confront us. How many people should occupy Earth? What sorts of people should they be? How should we share the available space? Clearly, we must change our ideas about making additional children. Individuals now are conceived by chance. Someday, though, they could be "composed" in accord with considered desires and designs. Furthermore, when we build new brains, these need not start out the way ours do, with so little knowledge about the world. What sorts of things should our mind-children know? How many of them should we produce — and who should decide their attributes?

Traditional systems of ethical thought are focused mainly on individuals, as though they were the only things of value. Obviously, we must also consider the rights and the roles of larger scale beings — such as the super-persons we call cultures, and the great, growing systems called sciences, that help us to understand other things. How many such entities do we want? Which are the kinds that we most need? We ought to be wary of ones that get locked into forms that resist all further growth. Some future options have never been seen: Imagine a scheme that could review both your and my mentalities, and then compile a new, merged mind based upon that shared experience.

Whatever the unknown future may bring, already we're changing the rules that made us. Although most of us will be fearful of change, others will surely want to escape from our present limitations. When I decided to write this article, I tried these ideas out on several groups and had them respond to informal polls. I was amazed to find that at least three quarters of the audience seemed to feel that our life spans were already too long. "Why would anyone want to live for five hundred years? Wouldn't it be boring? What if you outlived all your friends? What would you do with all that time?" they asked. It seemed as though they secretly feared that they did not deserve to live so long. I find it rather worrisome that so many people are resigned to die. Might not such people be dangerous, who feel that they do not have much to lose?

My scientist friends showed few such concerns. "There are countless things that I want to find out, and so many problems I want to solve, that I could use many centuries," they said. Certainly, immortality would seem unattractive if it meant endless infirmity, debility, and dependency upon others — but we're assuming a state of perfect health. Some people expressed a sounder concern — that the old ones must die because young ones are needed to weed out their worn-out ideas. However, if it's true, as I fear, that we are approaching our intellectual limits, then that response is not a good answer. We'd still be cut off from the larger ideas in those oceans of wisdom beyond our grasp.

Will robots inherit the earth? Yes, but they will be our children. We owe our minds to the deaths and lives of all the creatures that were ever engaged in the struggle called Evolution. Our job is to see that all this work shall not end up in meaningless waste.

Further Reading

Finch, Caleb E. *Longevity, Senescence, and the Genome*. Chicago: U of Chicago, 1994.

Walford, Roy L. *Maximum Life Span*. New York: W.W. Norton, 1983.

Minsky, Marvin. *The Society of Mind*. New York: Simon and Schuster, 1988.

Moravec, Hans. *Mind Children*. Cambridge: Harvard U P, 1988.

Drexler, K. Eric. *Nanosystems*. New York: John Wiley, 1992.

Minsky, Marvin, and Harry Harrison. *The Turing Option*. New York: Warner Books, 1992.

Steven Johnson

The Myth of the Ant Queen

(2002)

Best-selling author and journalist Steven Berlin Johnson (b. 1968) is known for wide-ranging studies that apply the latest scientific theories to a wide variety of human behaviors and social patterns, from architecture and city planning to video games, cultural trends, and epidemiology. As cofounder and editor of the online magazine *Feed* and author of the 1997 book *Interface Culture: How New Technology Transforms the Way We Create and Communicate*, Johnson established himself as an important Web commentator and theorist of Internet culture. Currently a contributing editor to *Wired*, Johnson also regularly writes for established publications like the *New York Times*, the *New Yorker*, and the *Wall Street Journal*. His other books include *Everything Bad Is Good for You: How Today's Popular Culture Is Actually Making Us Smarter* (2005) and, most recently, *The Ghost Map* (2006), a study of London's 1854 cholera epidemic.

The selection that follows comes from the opening chapter of Johnson's popular and critically acclaimed book *Emergence: The Connected Lives of Ants, Brains, Cities, and Software*. Written in an accessible and engaging style, it brought the latest models of information theory and the work of computer scientists like Marvin Minsky (whose essay appears earlier in this chapter) to a wider audience. The term *emergence* refers to how complex patterns emerge from a series of small independent actions. Rather than being consciously guided by a central intelligence, these patterns arise from the dynamic interaction of smaller units acting on very simple and limited principles. The whole, in other words, is greater than the sum of the parts. The idea of emergent behavior has been central to the development of more sophisticated computers and software applications and is modeled on the idea of the brain as a collection of cells performing specific functions from which intelligence somehow emerges.

"The myth of the ant queen" refers to the mistaken notion that social insects follow a leader. Johnson shows, instead, how the decentralized activity of an ant colony offers a model for understanding emergent behavior.

It's early fall in Palo Alto, and Deborah Gordon and I are sitting in her office in Stanford's Gilbert Biological Sciences building, where she spends three-quarters of the year studying behavioral ecology. The other quarter is spent doing fieldwork with the native harvester ants of the American Southwest, and when we meet, her face still retains the hint of a tan from her last excursion to the Arizona desert.

I've come here to learn more about the collective intelligence of ant colonies. Gordon, dressed neatly in a white skirt, cheerfully entertains a few borderline-philosophical questions on group behavior and complex systems, but I can tell she's hankering to start with a hands-on display. After a few minutes of casual rumination, she bolts up out of her chair. "Why don't we start with me showing you the ants that we have here," she says. "And then we can talk about what it all means."

She ushers me into a sepulchral room across the hallway, where three long tables are lined up side by side. The initial impression is that of an underpopulated and sterilized pool hall, until I get close enough to one of the tables to make out the miniature civilization that lives within each of them. Closer to a Habitrail than your traditional idea of an ant farm, Gordon's contraptions house an intricate network of plastic tubes connecting a dozen or so plastic boxes, each lined with moist plaster and coated with a thin layer of dirt.

"We cover the nests with red plastic because some species of ants don't see red light," Gordon explains. "That seems to be true of this species too." For a second, I'm not sure what she means by "this species" — and then my eyes adjust to the scene, and I realize with a start that the dirt coating the plastic boxes is, in fact, thousands of harvester ants, crammed so tightly into their quarters that I had originally mistaken them for an undifferentiated mass. A second later, I can see that the whole simulated colony is wonderfully alive, the clusters of ants pulsing steadily with movement. The tubing and cramped conditions and surging crowds bring one thought immediately to mind: the New York subway system, rush hour.

At the heart of Gordon's work is a mystery about how ant colonies develop, a mystery that has implications extending far beyond the parched earth of the Arizona desert to our cities, our brains, our immune systems — and increasingly, our technology. Gordon's work focuses on the connection between the microbehavior of individual ants and the overall behavior of the colonies themselves, and part of that research involves tracking the life cycles of individual colonies, following them year after year as they scour the desert floor for food, competing with other colonies for territory, and — once a year — mating with them. She is a student, in other words, of a particular kind of emergent, self-organizing system.

Dig up a colony of native harvester ants and you'll almost invariably find that the queen is missing. To track down the colony's matriarch, you need to examine the bottom of the hole you've just dug to excavate the colony: you'll find a narrow, almost invisible passageway that leads another two feet underground, to a tiny vestibule burrowed out of the earth. There you will find the queen. She will have been secreted there by a handful of ladies-in-waiting at the first sign of disturbance. That passageway, in other words, is an emergency escape hatch, not unlike a fallout shelter buried deep below the West Wing.

But despite the Secret Service–like behavior, and the regal nomenclature, there's nothing hierarchical about the way an ant colony does its thinking. "Although *queen* is a term that reminds us of human political systems," Gordon explains, "the queen is not an authority figure. She lays eggs and is fed and cared for by the workers. She does not decide which worker does what. In a harvester ant colony, many feet of intricate tunnels and chambers and thousands of ants separate the queen, surrounded by interior workers, from the ants working outside the nest and using only the chambers near the surface. It would be physically impossible for the queen to direct every worker's decision about which task to perform and when." The harvester ants that carry the queen off to her escape hatch do so not because they've been ordered to by their leader; they do it because the queen ant is responsible for giving birth to all the members of the colony, and so it's in the colony's best interest — and the colony's gene pool — to keep the queen safe. Their genes instruct them to protect their mother, the same way their genes instruct them to forage for food. In other words, the matriarch doesn't train her servants to protect her, evolution does.

Popular culture trades in Stalinist ant stereotypes — witness the authoritarian colony regime in the animated film *Antz* — but in fact, colonies are the exact opposite of command economies. While they are capable of remarkably coordinated feats of task allocation, there are no Five-Year Plans in the ant kingdom. The colonies that Gordon studies display some of nature's most mesmerizing decentralized behavior: intelligence and personality and learning that emerges from the bottom up.

I'm still gazing into the latticework of plastic tubing when Gordon directs my attention to the two expansive white boards attached to the main colony space, one stacked on top of the other and connected by a ramp. (Imagine a two-story parking garage built next to a subway stop.) A handful of ants meander across each plank, some porting crumblike objects on their back, others apparently just out for a stroll. If this is the Central Park of Gordon's ant metropolis, I think, it must be a workday.

Gordon gestures to the near corner of the top board, four inches from the ramp to the lower level, where a pile of strangely textured dust — littered with tiny shells and husks — presses neatly against the wall. "That's the midden," she says. "It's the town garbage dump." She points to three ants marching up the ramp, each barely visible beneath a comically oversize shell. "These ants are on midden duty: they take the trash that's left over from the food they've collected — in this case, the seeds from stalk grass — and deposit it in the midden pile."

Gordon takes two quick steps down to the other side of the table, at the far end away from the ramp. She points to what looks like another pile of dust. "And this is the cemetery." I look again, startled. She's right: hundreds of ant carcasses are piled atop one another, all carefully wedged against the table's corner. It looks brutal, and yet also strangely methodical.

I know enough about colony behavior to nod in amazement. "So they've somehow collectively decided to utilize these two areas as trash heap and cemetery," I say. No individual ant defined those areas, no central planner zoned one area for trash, the other for the dead. "It just sort of happened, right?"

Gordon smiles, and it's clear that I've missed something. "It's better than that," she says. "Look at what actually happened here: they've built the cemetery at exactly the point that's furthest away from the colony. And the midden is even more interesting: they've put it at precisely the point that maximizes its distance from both the colony *and* the cemetery. It's like there's a rule they're following: put the dead ants as far away as possible, and put the midden as far away as possible without putting it near the dead ants."

I have to take a few seconds to do the geometry myself, and sure enough, the ants have got it right. I find myself laughing out loud at the thought: it's as though they've solved one of those spatial math tests that appear on standardized tests, conjuring up a solution that's perfectly tailored to their environment, a solution that might easily stump an eight-year-old human. The question is, who's doing the conjuring?

It's a question with a long and august history, one that is scarcely limited to the collective behavior of ant colonies. We know the answer now because we have developed powerful tools for thinking about — and modeling — the emergent intelligence of self-organizing systems, but that answer was not always so clear. We know now that systems like ant colonies don't have real leaders, that the very idea of an ant "queen" is misleading. But the desire to find pacemakers in such systems has always been powerful — in both the group behavior of the social insects, and in the collective human behavior that creates a living city. . . .

Complexity is a word that has frequently appeared in critical accounts of metropolitan space, but there are really two kinds of complexity fundamental to the city, two experiences with very different implications for the individuals trying to make sense of them. There is, first, the more conventional sense of complexity as sensory overload, the city stretching the human nervous system to its very extremes, and in the process teaching it a new series of reflexes — and leading the way for a complementary series of aesthetic values, which develop out like a scab around the original wound. The German cultural critic Walter Benjamin writes in his unfinished masterpiece, *The Arcades Project*:

> Perhaps the daily sight of a moving crowd once presented the eye with a spectacle to which it first had to adapt. . . . [T]hen the assumption is not impossible that, having mastered this task, the eye welcomed opportunities to confirm its possession of its new ability. The method of impressionist painting, whereby the picture is assembled through a riot of flecks of color, would then be a reflection of experience with which the eye of a big-city dweller has become familiar.

There's a long tributary of nineteenth- and twentieth-century urban writing that leads into this passage, from the London chapters of Wordsworth's *Prelude* to the ambulatory musings of Joyce's *Dubliners*: the noise and the senselessness somehow transformed into an aesthetic experience. The crowd is something you throw yourself into, for the pure poetry of it all. But complexity is not solely a matter of sensory overload. There is also the sense of complexity as a self-organizing system — more Santa Fe Institute than Frankfurt School. This sort of complexity lives up one level: it describes the system of the city itself, and not its experiential reception by the city dweller. The city is complex because it overwhelms, yes, but also because it has a coherent personality, a personality that self-organizes out of millions of individual decisions, a global order built out of local interactions. This is the "systematic" complexity that Engels glimpsed on the boulevards of Manchester: not the overload and anarchy he documented elsewhere, but instead a strange kind of order, a pattern in the streets that furthered the political values of Manchester's elite without being deliberately planned by them. We know now from computer models and sociological studies — as well as from the studies of comparable systems generated by the social insects, such as Gordon's harvester ants — that larger patterns can emerge out of uncoordinated local actions. But for Engels and his contemporaries, those unplanned urban shapes must have seemed like a haunting. The city appeared to have a life of its own.

A hundred and fifty years later, the same techniques translated into the language of software — as in Mitch Resnick's slime mold simulation — trigger a similar reaction: the eerie sense of something lifelike, something organic forming on the screen. Even those with sophisticated knowledge about self-organizing systems still find these shapes unnerving — in their mix of stability and change, in their capacity for open-ended learning. The impulse to build centralized models to explain that behavior remains almost as strong as it did in Engels's day. When we see repeated shapes and structure emerging out of apparent chaos, we can't help looking for pacemakers.

Understood in the most abstract sense, what Engels observed are *patterns* in the urban landscape, visible because they have a repeated structure that distinguishes them from the pure noise you might naturally associate with an unplanned city. They are patterns of human movement and decision-making that have been etched into the texture of city blocks, patterns that are then fed back to the Manchester residents themselves, altering their subsequent decisions. (In that sense, they are the very opposite of the traditional sense of urban complexity — they are signals emerging where you would otherwise expect only noise.) A city is a kind of pattern-amplifying machine: its neighborhoods are a way of measuring and expressing the repeated behavior of larger collectivities — capturing information about group behavior, and sharing that information with the group. Because those patterns are fed back to the community, small shifts in behavior can quickly escalate into larger movements: upscale shops dominate the main boulevards, while the working class remains clustered invisibly in the alleys and side streets; the artists live on the Left Bank, the investment bankers in the Eighth Arrondissement. You don't need regulations and city planners deliberately creating these structures. All you need are thousands of individuals and a few simple rules of interaction. The bright shop windows attract more bright shop windows and drive the impoverished toward the hidden core. There's no need for a Baron Haussmann in this world, just a few repeating patterns of movement, amplified into larger shapes that last for lifetimes: clusters, slums, neighborhoods. . . .

There is a world of difference between a computer that passively receives the information you supply and a computer that actively learns on its own.

The very first generation of computers such as ENIAC had processed information fed to them by their masters, and they had been capable of performing various calculations with that data, based on the instruction sets programmed into them. This was a startling enough development at a time when "computer" meant a person with a slide rule and an eraser. But even in those early days, the digital visionaries had imagined a machine capable of more open-ended learning. [Alan] Turing and [Claude] Shannon had argued over the future musical tastes of the "electronic brain" during lunch hour at Bell Labs, while their colleague Norbert Wiener had written a best-selling paean to the self-regulatory powers of feedback in his 1949 manifesto *Cybernetics*.

"Mostly my participation in all of this is a matter of good luck for me," [Oliver] Selfridge says today, sitting in his cramped, windowless MIT office. Born in England, Selfridge enrolled at Harvard at the age of fifteen and started his doctorate three years later at MIT, where Norbert Wiener was his dissertation adviser. As a precocious twenty-one-year-old, Selfridge suggested a few corrections to a paper that his mentor had published on heart flutters, corrections that Wiener graciously acknowledged in the opening pages of *Cybernetics*. "I think I now have the honor of being one of the few living people mentioned in that book," Selfridge says, laughing.

After a sojourn working on military control projects in New Jersey, Selfridge returned to MIT in the mid-fifties. His return coincided with an explosion of interest in artificial intelligence (AI), a development that introduced him to a then-junior fellow at Harvard named Marvin Minsky. "My concerns in AI," Selfridge says now, "were not so much the actual processing as they were in how systems change, how they evolve — in a word, how they learn." Exploring the possibilities of machine learning brought Selfridge back to memories of his own education in England. "At school in England I had read John Milton's *Paradise Lost*," he says, "and I'd been struck by the image of Pandemonium — it's Greek for 'all the demons.' Then after my second son, Peter, was born, I went over *Paradise Lost* again, and the shrieking of the demons awoke something in me." The pattern recognizer in Selfridge's brain had hit upon a way of teaching a computer to recognize patterns.

"We are proposing here a model of a process which we claim can adaptively improve itself to handle certain pattern-recognition problems which cannot be adequately specified in advance." These were the first words Selfridge delivered at a symposium in late 1958, held at the very same National Physical Laboratory from which Turing had escaped a decade before. Selfridge's presentation had the memorable title "Pandemonium: A Paradigm for Learning," and while it had little impact outside the nascent computer-science community, the ideas Selfridge outlined that day would eventually become part of our everyday life — each time we enter a name in our PalmPilots or use voice recognition software to ask for information over the phone. Pandemonium, as Selfridge outlined it in his talk, was not so much a specific piece of software as it was a way of approaching a problem. The problem was an ambitious one, given the limited computational resources of the day: how to teach a computer to recognize patterns that were ill-defined or erratic, like the sound waves that comprise spoken language.

The brilliance of Selfridge's new paradigm lay in the fact that it relied on a distributed, bottom-up intelligence, and not a unified, top-down one. Rather than build a single smart program, Selfridge created a swarm of limited miniprograms, which he called demons. "The idea was, we have a bunch of these demons shrieking up the hierarchy," he explains. "Lower-level demons shrieking to higher-level demons shrieking to higher ones."

To understand what that "shrieking" means, imagine a system with twenty-six individual demons, each trained to recognize a letter of the alphabet. The pool of demons is shown a series of words, and each demon "votes" as to whether each letter displayed represents its chosen letter. If the first letter is *a*, the *a*-recognizing demon reports that it is highly likely that it has recognized a match. Because of the similarities in shape, the *o*-recognizer might report a possible match, while the *b*-recognizer would emphatically declare that the letter wasn't intelligible to it. All the letter-recognizing demons would report to a master demon, who would tally up the votes for each letter and choose the demon that expressed the highest confidence. Then the software would move on to the next letter in the sequence, and the process would begin again. At the end of the transmission, the master demon would have a working interpretation of the text that had been transmitted, based on the assembled votes of the demon democracy.

Of course, the accuracy of that interpretation depended on the accuracy of the letter recognizers. If you were trying to teach a computer how to read, it was cheating to assume from the outset that you could find twenty-six accurate letter recognizers. Selfridge was after a larger goal: How do you teach a machine to recognize letters — or vowel sounds, minor chords, fingerprints — in the first place? The answer involved adding another layer of demons, and a feedback mechanism whereby the various demon guesses could be graded. This lower level was populated by even less sophisticated miniprograms, trained only to recognize raw physical shapes (or sounds, in the case of Morse code or spoken language). Some demons recognized parallel lines, others perpendicular ones. Some demons looked for circles, others for dots. None of these shapes were associated with any particular letter; these bottom-dwelling demons were like two-year-old children — capable of reporting on the shapes they witnessed, but not perceiving them as letters or words.

Using these minimally equipped demons, the system could be trained to recognize letters, without "knowing" anything about the alphabet in advance. The recipe was relatively simple: Present the letter *b* to the bottom-level demons, and see which ones respond, and which ones don't. In the case of the letter *b*, the vertical-line recognizers might respond, along with the circle recognizers. Those lower-level demons would report to a letter-recognizer one step higher in the chain. Based on the information gathered from its lieutenants, that recognizer would make a guess as to the letter's identity. Those guesses are then "graded" by the software. If the guess is wrong, the software learns to dissociate those particular lieutenants from the letter in question; if the guess happens to be right, it *strengthens* the connection between the lieutenants and the letter.

The results are close to random at first, but if you repeat the process a thousand times, or ten thousand, the system learns to associate specific assemblies of shape-recognizers with specific letters and soon enough is capable of translating entire sentences with remarkable accuracy. The system doesn't come with any predefined conceptions about the shapes of letters — you train the system to associate letters with specific shapes in the grading phase. (This is why handwriting-recognition software can adapt to so many different types of penmanship, but *can't* adapt to penmanship that changes day to day.) That mix of random beginnings organizing into more complicated results reminded Selfridge of another process, whose own underlying code was just then being deciphered in the form of DNA. "The scheme sketched is really a natural selection on the processing demons," Selfridge explained. "If they serve a useful function they survive and perhaps are even the source for other subdemons who are themselves judged on their merits. It is perfectly reasonable to conceive of this taking place on a broader scale . . . instead of having but one Pandemonium we might have some crowd of them, all fairly similarly constructed, and employ natural selection on the crowd of them."

The system Selfridge described — with its bottom-up learning, and its evaluating feedback loops — belongs in the history books as the first practical description of an emergent software program. The world now swarms with millions of his demons.

Among the students at MIT in the late forties was a transplanted midwesterner named John Holland. Holland was also a pupil of Norbert Wiener's, and he spent a great deal of his undergraduate years stealing time on the early computer prototypes being built in Cambridge at that time. His unusual expertise at computer programming led IBM to hire him in the fifties to help develop their first commercial calculator, the 701. As a student of Wiener's, he was naturally inclined to experiment with ways to make the sluggish 701 machine learn in a more organic, bottom-up fashion — not unlike Selfridge's Pandemonium — and Holland and a group of like-minded colleagues actually programmed a crude simulation of neurons interacting. But IBM was in the business of selling adding machines then, and so Holland's work went largely ignored and underfunded. After a few years Holland returned to academia to get his doctorate at the University of Michigan, where the Logic of Computers Group had just been formed.

In the sixties, after graduating as the first computer science Ph.D. in the country, Holland began a line of inquiry that would dominate his work for the rest of his life. Like Turing, Holland wanted to explore the way simple rules could lead to complex behavior; like Selfridge, he wanted to create software that would be capable of open-ended learning. Holland's great breakthrough was to harness the forces of another bottom-up, open-ended system: natural selection. Building on Selfridge's Pandemonium model, Holland took the logic of Darwinian evolution and built it into code. He called his new creation the genetic algorithm.

A traditional software program is a series of instructions that tells the computer what to do: paint the screen with red pixels, multiply a set of numbers, delete a file. Usually those instructions are encoded as a series of branching paths: do this first, and if you get result A, do one thing; if you get result B, do another thing. The art of programming lay in figuring out how to construct the most efficient sequence of instructions, the sequence that would get the most done with the shortest amount of code — and with the least likelihood of a crash. Normally that was done using the raw intellectual firepower of the programmer's mind. You thought about the problem, sketched out the best solution, fed it into the computer, evaluated its success, and then tinkered with it to make it better. But Holland imagined another approach: set up a gene pool of possible software and let successful programs *evolve* out of the soup.

Holland's system revolved around a series of neat parallels between computer programs and earth's life-forms. Each depends on a master code for its existence: the zeros and ones of computer programming, and the coiled strands of DNA lurking in all of our cells (usually called the genotype). Those two kinds of codes dictate some kind of higher-level form or behavior (the phenotype): growing red hair or multiplying two numbers together. With DNA-based organisms, natural selection works by creating a massive pool of genetic variation, then evaluating the success rate of the assorted behaviors unleashed by all those genes. Successful variations get passed down to the next generation, while unsuccessful ones disappear. Sexual reproduction ensures that the innovative combinations of genes find each other. Occasionally, random mutations appear in the gene pool, introducing complete new avenues for the system to explore. Run through enough cycles, and you have a recipe for engineering masterworks like the human eye — without a bona fide engineer in sight.

The genetic algorithm was an attempt to capture that process in silicon. Software already has a genotype and a phenotype, Holland recognized; there's the code itself, and then there's what the code actually *does*. What if you created a gene pool of different code combinations, then evaluated the success rate of the phenotypes, eliminating the least successful strands? Natural selection relies on a brilliantly simple, but somewhat tautological, criterion for evaluating success: your genes get to pass on to the next generation if you survive long enough to produce a next generation. Holland decided to make that evaluation step more precise: his programs would be admitted to the next generation if they did a better job of accomplishing a specific task — doing simple math, say, or recognizing patterns in visual images. The programmer could decide what the task was; he or she just couldn't directly instruct the software how to accomplish it. He or she would set up the parameters that defined genetic fitness, then let the software evolve on its own.

Holland developed his ideas in the sixties and seventies using mostly paper and pencil — even the more advanced technology of that era was far too slow to churn through the thousandfold generations of evolutionary time. But the massively parallel, high-speed computers introduced in the eighties — such as Danny Hillis's Connection Machine — were ideally suited for exploring the powers of the genetic algorithm. And one of the most impressive GA systems devised for the Connection Machine focused exclusively on simulating the behavior of ants.

It was a program called Tracker, designed in the mid-eighties by two UCLA professors, David Jefferson and Chuck Taylor. (Jefferson was in the computer science department, while Taylor was a biologist.) "I got the idea from reading Richard Dawkins's first book, *The Selfish Gene*," Jefferson says today. "That book really transformed me. He makes the point that in order to watch Darwinian evolution in action, all you need are objects that are capable of reproducing themselves, and reproducing themselves imperfectly, and having some sort of resource limitation so that there's competition. And nothing else matters — it's a very tiny, abstract axiom that is required to make evolution work. And so it occurred to me that programs have those properties — programs can reproduce themselves. Except that they usually reproduce themselves *exactly*. But I recognized that if there was a way to have them reproduce imperfectly, and if you had not just one program but a whole population of them, then you could simulate evolution with the software instead of organisms."

After a few small-scale experiments, Jefferson and Taylor decided to simulate the behavior of ants learning to follow a pheromone trail. "Ants were on my mind — I was looking for simple creatures, and E. O. Wilson's opus on ants had just come out," Jefferson explains. "What we were really looking for was a simple task that simple creatures perform where it wasn't obvious how to make a program do it. Somehow we came up with the idea of following a trail — and not just a clean trail, a noisy trail, a broken trail." The two scientists created a virtual grid of squares, drawing a meandering path of eighty-two squares across it. Their goal was to evolve a simple program, a virtual ant, that could navigate the length of the path in a finite amount of time, using only limited information about the path's twists and turns. At each cycle, an ant had the option of "sniffing" the square ahead of him, advancing forward one square, or turning right or left ninety degrees. Jefferson and Taylor gave their ants one hundred cycles to navigate the path; once an ant used up his hundred cycles, the software tallied up the number of squares on the trail he had successfully landed on and gave him a score. An ant that lost his way after square one would be graded 1; an ant that successfully completed the trail before the hundred cycles were up would get a perfect score, 82.

The scoring system allowed Jefferson and Taylor to create fitness criteria that determined which ants were allowed to reproduce. Tracker began by simulating sixteen thousand ants — one for each of the Connection Machine's processors — with sixteen thousand more or less random strategies for trail navigation. One ant might begin with the strategy of marching straight across the grid; another by switching back and forth between ninety-degree rotations and sniffings; another following more baroque rules. The great preponderance of these strategies would be complete disasters, but a few would allow a stumble across a larger portion of the trail. Those more successful ants would be allowed to mate and reproduce, creating a new generation of sixteen thousand ants ready to tackle the trail.

The path — dubbed the John Muir Trail after the famous environmentalist — began with a relatively straightforward section, with a handful of right-hand turns and longer straight sections, then steadily grew more complicated. Jefferson says now that he designed it that way because he was worried that early generations would be so incompetent that a more challenging path would utterly confound them. "You have to remember that we had no idea when we started this experiment whether sixteen thousand was anywhere near a large enough population to seek Darwinian evolution," he explains. "And I didn't know if it was going to take ten generations, or one hundred generations, or ten thousand generations. There was no theory to guide us quantitatively about either the size of the population in space or the length of the experiment in time."

Running through one hundred generations took about two hours; Jefferson and Taylor rigged the system to give them real-time updates on the most talented ants of each generation. Like a stock ticker, the Connection Machine would spit out an updated number at the end of each generation: if the best trail-follower of one generation managed to hit fifteen squares in a hundred cycles, the Connection Machine would report that 15 was the current record and then move on to the next generation. After a few false starts because of bugs, Jefferson and Taylor got the Tracker system to work — and the results exceeded even their most optimistic expectations.

"To our wonderment and utter joy," Jefferson recalls, "it succeeded the first time. We were sitting there watching these numbers come in: one generation would produce twenty-five, then twenty-five, and then it would be twenty-seven, and then thirty. Eventually we saw a perfect score, after only about a hundred generations. It was mind-blowing." The software had evolved an entire population of expert trail-followers, despite the fact that Jefferson and Taylor had endowed their first generation of ants with no skills whatsoever. Rather than engineer a solution to the trail-following problem, the two UCLA professors had evolved a solution; they had created a random pool of possible programs, then built a feedback mechanism that allowed more successful programs to emerge. In fact, the evolved programs were so successful that they'd developed solutions custom-tailored to their environments. When Jefferson and Taylor "dissected" one of the final champion ants to see what trail-following strategies he had developed, they discovered that the software had evolved a preference for making right-hand turns, in response to the three initial right turns that Jefferson had built into the John Muir Trail. It was like watching an organism living in water evolving gills: even in the crude, abstract grid of Tracker, the virtual ants evolved a strategy for survival that was uniquely adapted to their environment.

By any measure, Tracker was a genuine breakthrough. Finally the tools of modern computing had advanced to the point where you could simulate emergent intelligence, watch it unfold on the screen in real time, as Turing and Selfridge and Shannon had dreamed of doing years before. And it was only fitting that Jefferson and Taylor had chosen to simulate precisely the organism most celebrated for its emergent behavior: the ant. They began, of course, with the most elemental form of ant intelligence — sniffing for pheromone trails — but the possibilities suggested by the success of Tracker were endless. The tools of emergent software had been harnessed to model and understand the evolution of emergent intelligence in real-world organisms. In fact, watching those virtual ants evolve on the computer screen, learning and adapting to their environments on their own, you couldn't help wonder if the division between the real and the virtual was becoming increasingly hazy. . . .

We are now living through the third phase of that revolution. You can date it back to the day in the early nineties when Will Wright released a program called SimCity, which would go on to become one of the best-selling video-game franchises of all time. SimCity would also inaugurate a new phase in the developing story of self-organizing: emergent behavior was no longer purely an object of study, something to interpret and model in the lab. It was also something you could *build*, something you could interact with, and something you could sell. While SimCity came out of the developing web of the bottom-up worldview, it suggested a whole new opening: SimCity was a work of culture, not science. It aimed to entertain, not explain.

Ten years after Wright's release of SimCity, the world now abounds with these man-made systems: online stores use them to recognize our cultural tastes; artists use them to create a new kind of adaptive cultural form; Web sites use them to regulate their online communities; marketers use them to detect demographic patterns in the general public. The video-game industry itself has exploded in size, surpassing Hollywood in terms of raw sales numbers — with many of the best-selling tides relying on the powers of digital self-organization. And with that popular success has come a subtle, but significant, trickle-down effect: we are starting to *think* using the conceptual tools of bottom-up systems. Just like the clock maker metaphors of the Enlightenment, or the dialectical logic of the nineteenth century, the emergent worldview belongs to this moment in time, shaping our thought habits and coloring our perception of the world. As our everyday life becomes increasingly populated by artificial emergence, we will find ourselves relying more and more on the logic of these systems — both in corporate America, where "bottom-up intelligence" has started to replace "quality management" as the mantra of the day, and in the radical, antiglobalization protest movements, who explicitly model their pacemakerless, distributed organizations after ant colonies and slime molds. Former vice president Al Gore is himself a devotee of complexity theory and can talk for hours about what the bottom-up paradigm could mean for reinventing government. Almost two centuries after Engels wrestled with the haunting of Manchester's city streets, and fifty years after Turing puzzled over the mysteries of a flower's bloom, the circle is finally complete. Our minds may be wired to look for pacemakers, but we are steadily learning how to think from the bottom up.

Acknowledgments (continued)

Isaac Asimov, "Liar." From *I, Robot* by Isaac Asimov. Copyright © 1941 by Street and Smith Publications, Inc. Used by permission of Bantam Books, a division of Random House, Inc.

J. G. Ballard, "The Terminal Beach." From *The Terminal Beach* by J. G. Ballard. Originally published in *New Worlds,* March 1964. Copyright © 1964 J. G. Ballard. All rights reserved. Reproduced by permission of the author c/o Margaret Hanbury.

Jean Baudrillard, "The Precession of Simulacra." From *Simulacra and Simulation* by Jean Beaudrillard. English translation copyright © 1994 by The University of Michigan Press. Originally published in French by Éditions Galilée, 1981. Reprinted by permission of The University of Michigan Press.

Greg Bear, "Blood Music." Excerpt from *Tangents* (1989) by Greg Bear. Originally published in *Analog,* June 1983. Copyright © 1983, 1989 by Greg Bear. Reprinted by permission of Richard Curtis Associates.

Simone de Beauvoir, "Introduction." From *The Second Sex* by Simone de Beauvoir, translated by H. M. Parshley. Copyright © 1952 and renewed 1980 by Alfred A. Knopf, a division of Random House, Inc. Used by permission of Alfred A. Knopf, a division of Random House, Inc.

Alfred Bester, "Adam and No Eve." From *Virtual Unrealities* by Alfred Bester. Copyright © 1997 by the Estate of Alfred Bester, Joe Suder, and Kirby McCauley. Used by permission of Vintage Books, a division of Random House, Inc.

Terry Bisson, "Bears Discover Fire." Originally published in *Isaac Asimov's Science Fiction Magazine,* Jan. 1990 by Davis Publications, Inc. Original © 1941. Reprinted by permission of the author.

Paul Boyer, "The Whole World Gasped," from *By the Bomb's Early Light: American Thought and Culture at the Dawn of the Atomic Age* by Paul Boyer. Copyright © 1994 by the University of North Carolina Press. Used by permission of the publisher.

Ray Bradbury, "Mars Is Heaven!" From *The Martian Chronicles* by Ray Bradbury. Originally published in *Planet Stories,* June 1, 1948. Copyright © 1948 by Love Romances, Inc., renewed 1975 by Ray Bradbury. Reprinted by permission of Don Congdon Associates, Inc.

Miles J. Breuer, "The Gostak and the Doshes." Originally published in *Gernsback Magazine.* Reprinted in *Arbor House Treasury of Science Fiction Masterpieces,* edited by Robert Silverberg and Martin H. Greenberg. Copyright © 1930 by Miles J. Breuer. Reprinted by permission of Forrest J. Ackerman.

Fredric Brown, "Arena." Originally appeared in *Astounding Science Fiction,* edited by John W. Campbell Jr. Copyright © 1944 by Street & Smith Publications and copyright © 1972 by the Estate. Reprinted by permission of the Estate and its agent, Barry N. Malzberg.

Octavia E. Butler, "Bloodchild." From *Bloodchild and Other Stories* by Octavia E. Butler. Copyright © 1984, 1995 by Octavia E. Butler. Reprinted by permission of Writers House as agent for the author.

John W. Campbell Jr., "Twilight." Originally appeared in *Astounding Science Fiction,* edited by John W. Campbell Jr. Copyright © 1935 by Street & Smith Publications, and copyright © 1963, by the Condé Nast Publications Inc. Reprinted by permission of the Estate and its agent, Barry N. Malzberg.

Edward Hallett Carr, "The Historian and His Facts," from *What Is History?* by Edward Hallett Carr. Copyright © 1961 by Edward Hallett Carr. Used by permission of Alfred A. Knopf, a division of Random House, Inc. and Curtis Brown Group Ltd, London, on behalf of the Estate of E. H. Carr.

C. J. Cherryh, "Cassandra." Originally published in *The Magazine of Fantasy and Science Fiction* (1987) by Mercury Press. © 1978 C. J. Cherryh. Reprinted in *Women of Wonder: The Contemporary Years* by Pamela Sargent. Copyright © 1995 by C. J. Cherryh. Reprinted by permission of Harcourt, Inc.

Ted Chiang, "Story of Your Life." Copyright © 1998 by Ted Chiang, first appeared in "Starlight 2," from *Stories of Your Life and Others*, reprinted by permission of the author and the author's agents, the Virginia Kidd Agency, Inc.

Arthur C. Clarke, "The Nine Billion Names of God." First appeared in *Star Science Fiction Stories No. 1* (anthology, 1953). Copyright © 1953 Arthur C. Clarke. Reprinted in *Science Fiction Hall of Fame*, Vol. 1, edited by Robert Silverberg. Copyright © 1970 by Arthur C. Clarke. Reprinted by permission of the author and the author's agents, Scovil Chichak Galen Literary Agency, Inc.

Samuel R. Delany, "Driftglass." Originally published in *Galaxy*. Copyright © 1967 by Galaxy Publishing Corporation. Copyright © 1995 by Samuel R. Delany. Reprinted by permission of the author and Henry Morrison, Inc., his agents.

Philip K. Dick, "Second Variety." From *The Collected Stories of Philip K. Dick*, Vol. 3, by Philip K. Dick. Copyright © 1991 by Philip K. Dick. Reprinted by permission of the author and the author's agents, Scovil Chichak and Galen Literary Agency, Inc.

Sonya Dorman (Hess), "When I Was Miss Dow." © 1966 by Galaxy Publishing Corporation. Originally published in *Galaxy*. Reprinted by permission of the Virginia Kidd Agency, as agents for the author, Sonya Dorman Hess.

Greg Egan, "Wang's Carpets." Published in *The Year's Best Science Fiction*, 13th Annual Edition, edited by Gardner Dozois and *Dozois 13* (1996). Copyright © 1995 by Greg Egan. First appeared in *New Legends* (Tor Books). Reprinted by permission of the author.

Mircea Eliade, "Normality of Suffering," from *The Myth of the Eternal Return; Or, Cosmos and History*, by Mircea Eliade and translated from the French by Willard R. Trask. Bollingen Series 46. Copyright © 1954 Bollingen. Reprinted by permission of Princeton University Press.

Harlan Ellison, "'Repent, Harlequin!' Said the Ticktockman." From *Paingod and Other Delusions* by Harlan Ellison. Copyright © 1965 by Harlan Ellison, renewed 1993 by Harlan Ellison. Reprinted by permission of the author and the author's agent, Richard Curtis Associates. All rights reserved.

Frantz Fanon, "The Fact of Blackness." From *Black Skin, White Masks* by Frantz Fanon, translated by Charles Lam Markmann. Copyright © 1967 by Grove Press, Inc. Used by permission of Grove/Atlantic, Inc.

Sigmund Freud, "The Uncanny." From *Collected Papers Volume 4* by Sigmund Freud. Authorized translation under the supervision of Joan Riviere. Reprinted by permission of Basic Books, a member of Perseus Books, LLC. Sigmund Freud © Copyrights, The Institute of Psycho-Analysis and The Hogarth Press for permission to quote from *The Standard Edition of the Complete Psychological Works of Sigmund Freud* translated and edited by James Strachey. Reprinted by permission of The Random House Group Ltd.

William Gibson, "Burning Chrome." From *Burning Chrome* by William Gibson. Copyright © 1986 by William Gibson. Reprinted by permission of HarperCollins Publishers, William Morrow.

Stephen Jay Gould, "Nonmoral Nature." From *Hen's Teeth and Horse's Toes: Further Reflections in Natural History* by Stephen Jay Gould. Copyright © 1983 by Stephen Jay Gould. Used by permission of W. W. Norton and Company, Inc.

Donna J. Haraway, "A Cyborg Manifesto: Science, Technology, and Socialist-Feminism in the Late Twentieth Century." From *Simians, Cyborgs, and Women: The Reinvention of*

Nature by Donna J. Haraway. Copyright © 1985 by Donna J. Haraway. Originally published as "Manifesto for Cyborgs: Science, Technology, and Socialist Feminism in the 1980s," in *Socialist Review*, no. 80 (1985): 65–108. Reprinted by permission of the author.

Robert A. Heinlein, "All You Zombies — ." From *Science Fiction: A Historical Anthology*, edited by Eric Rabkin. Copyright © 1959, 1987 by Robert A. Heinlein, and copyright © 2003 by the Robert A. and Virginia Heinlein Prize Trust. Reprinted by permission of the Robert A. and Virginia Heinlein Prize Trust.

Nalo Hopkinson, "Something to Hitch Meat To." From *Skin Folk* by Nalo Hopkinson. Copyright © 2001 by Nalo Hopkinson. By permission of Warner Books, Inc.

Fredric Jameson, "Progress versus Utopia; or, Can We Imagine the Future?" From *Science Fiction Studies*, volume 9, part 2, 1982. Copyright © 1982 SF-TH, Inc. Reprinted by permission of SF-TH, Inc., via Copyright Clearance Center.

Steven Johnson, "The Myth of the Ant Queen." From *Emergence: The Connected Lives of Ants, Brains, Cities, and Software* by Steven Johnson. Copyright © 2001 by Steven Johnson. Reprinted with the permission of Scribner, an imprint of Simon & Schuster Adult Publishing Group.

C. G. Jung, "The Shadow." From *Aion: Researches into the Phenomenology of the Self (The Collected Works of C. G. Jung, Vol. 9. Part II)*. © 1959, Princeton University Press, 1987 renewed. Reprinted by permission of Princeton University Press.

Michael Kaku, "To Build a Time Machine." From *Hyperspace*. Copyright © 1994 by Oxford University Press. Reprinted by permission. All rights reserved.

Daniel Keyes, excerpts from *Flowers for Algernon* by Daniel Keyes. Copyright © 1966, 1959 and renewed 1994, 1987 by Daniel Keyes. Reprinted by permission of Harcourt, Inc.

Damon Knight, "The Country of the Kind." From *Science Fiction Hall of Fame*, vol. 1, edited by Robert Silverberg. Copyright © 1955 by Damon Knight. Reprinted by permission of the author's estate.

Sakyo Komatsu, "Take Your Choice." From *The Best Japanese Science Fiction Stories*, translated by Shiro Tamura and Grania Davis. Copyright © 1987 by Sakyo Komatsu, English translation. Reprinted by arrangement with Barricade Books, Inc.

Henry Kuttner and C. L. Moore, "Mimsy Were the Borogoves." First published in February 1943, by Lewis Padgett (a pseudonym used by Henry Kuttner and his wife, C. L. Moore). From *Astounding Science Fiction*. Copyright © 1943 by Street & Smith Publications. Renewed 1970 by C. L. Moore. Reprinted by permission of Don Congdon Associates, Inc.

Ursula K. Le Guin, "Vaster Than Empires and More Slow." Copyright © 1971 by Ursula K. Le Guin. First appeared in *New Dimensions 1*, from *The Wind's Twelve Quarters*, reprinted by permission of the author and the author's agents, the Virginia Kidd Agency, Inc.

Stanislaw Lem, "How the World Was Saved." From *The Cyberiad: Fables for the Cybernetic Age*, English translation by Michael Kandel. Copyright © 1974 by Harcourt, Inc. Reprinted with permission of Harcourt, Inc.

Ken Liu, "The Algorithms for Love." From *Year's Best SF 10*, edited by David G. Hartwell and Kathryn Cramer. Copyright © 2004 by Kenneth Liu. First published in *Strange Horizons*. Reprinted by permission of the author.

Ian McDonald, "Recording Angel." From *The Year's Best Science Fiction, 14th Annual Collection*, by Gardner Dozois, editor. Copyright © 1996 by Ian McDonald. Reprinted by permission of MBA Literary Agents Ltd, on behalf of the author.

Maureen F. McHugh, "Nekropolis." First published in *Asimov's Science Fiction*, April 1994. Copyright © 1994 Maureen F. McHugh. Reprinted with permission of Small Beer Press.

Marvin Minsky, "Will Robots Inherit the Earth?" First published in *Scientific American*, October 1994. Copyright © 1994 by Marvin Minsky. Reprinted by permission of the author.

C. L. Moore, "Vintage Season." From *Astounding Science Fiction*. Copyright © 1946 by Street & Smith Publications. Renewed 1973 by C. L. Moore. Reprinted by permission of Don Congdon Associates, Inc.

Mike Resnick, "Kirinyaga." First published in *The Magazine of Fantasy and Science Fiction*. Copyright © 1988 by Mike Resnick. Reprinted by permission of the author.

Kim Stanley Robinson, "The Lucky Strike." From *The Norton Book of Science Fiction: North American Science Fiction, 1960–1990*, edited by Ursula K. Le Guin and Brian Atteberry. Copyright © 1984 by Terry Carr. First published in *Universe 14*. Published by permission of Kim Stanley Robinson c/o Ralph M. Vicinanza, Ltd.

Benjamin Rosenbaum, "Start the Clock." From *The Year's Best Science Fiction: 22nd Annual Collection*, edited by Gardner Dozois. Copyright © 2004 by Spilogale, Inc. First published in the *Magazine of Fantasy and Science Fiction*, August 2004. Reprinted by permission of the author.

Joanna Russ, "When It Changed." First published in *Again, Dangerous Visions*, edited by Harlan Ellison. Copyright © 1972 by Joanna Russ. Reprinted by permission of the author.

Geoff Ryman, "Dead Space for the Unexpected." Published in *The Year's Best Science Fiction: 12th Annual Collection*, edited by Gardner Dozois. First published in *Interzone* 88 (October 1994). Copyright © 1994 by Geoff Ryman 1994. Reprinted by permission of The Maggie Noach Literary Agency, on behalf of the author.

William Sanders, "When This World Is All on Fire." From *The Year's Best Science Fiction: 19th Annual Collection*, edited by Gardner Dozois. Published by St. Martin's Press/Griffin, 2002. Copyright © 2001 by Dell Magazines. First published in *Asimov's Science Fiction*, Oct./Nov. 2001. Reprinted by permission of the author.

Jean-Paul Sartre, "My Past." Excerpt from "Being and Nothingness: An Essay in Phenomenological Ontology." Translated by Hazel Barnes, New York: Philosophical Library, 1956. Reprinted by permission of Philosophical Library.

Robert Silverberg, "When We Went to See the End of the World." Appeared in *Universe 2*, edited by Terry Carr, published by Ace (1972). Copyright © 1972 Robert Silverberg. Reprinted in *Collected Stories of Robert Silverberg* by Robert Silverberg. Copyright © 1986 by Robert Silverberg. Published by permission of Robert Silverberg, c/o Ralph M. Vicinanza, Ltd.

Susan Sontag, "The Imagination of Disaster." From *Against Interpretation* by Susan Sontag. Copyright © 1964, 1966, renewed 1994 by Susan Sontag. Reprinted by permission of Farrar, Straus and Giroux, LLC.ß

Olaf Stapledon, excerpts from *Star Maker* by Olaf Stapledon. Copyright © 1977 by Olaf Stapledon. Reprinted by permission of the Stapledon family. *Star Maker* was originally published by Methuen (United Kingdom). Copyright © 1937.

Michael Swanwick, "Slow Life." Reprinted in *Dozois 20*, 2003. First published in *Analog*, 2002. Copyright © 2002 by Michael Swanwick. Reprinted by permission of the author.

James Tiptree Jr., "The Girl Who Was Plugged In." From *The Girl Who Was Plugged In* by James Tiptree Jr. Copyright © 1973 by James Tiptree Jr. Reprinted by permission of the author's estate and estate's agent, the Virginia Kidd Agency, Inc.

A. E. van Vogt, "The Weapon Shop." From *Science Fiction Hall of Fame*, volume I, edited by Robert Silverberg. Published by Doubleday, 1970. Copyright © 1942 Street & Smith Publications. Reprinted by permission of the author's agents, Ashley Grayson Literary Agency.

John Varley, "The Persistence of Vision." From *The Persistence of Vision* by John Varley. Copyright © 1978 The Dial Press/James Wade. Reprinted by permission of The Pimlico Agency, Inc., on behalf of the author.

William H. Whyte Jr., "The Tests of Conformity." From *The Organization Man*. Copyright © 1956 by William H. Whyte Jr. Reprinted by permission of Albert Lafarge Agency.

Kate Wilhelm, "Baby, You Were Great!" First published in *Orbit II*, edited by Damon Knight. Published by Putnam, 1967. Copyright © 1967 by Kate Wilhelm. Reprinted by permission of the author.

Connie Willis, "At the Rialto." Published in *Women of Wonder: The Contemporary Years*, edited by Pamela Sargent. Published by Harcourt, 1995. Copyright © 1989 by Connie Willis. Reprinted by permission of Connie Willis c/o Ralph M. Vicinanza, Ltd., as agent for the author.

Yevgeny Zamyatin, from *We* by Yevgeny Zamyatin, translated by Mirra Ginsburg. Translation copyright © 1983 by Mirra Ginsburg. Reprinted by permission of HarperCollins Publishers, William Morrow.

Roger Zelazny, "For a Breath I Tarry." From *Survival Printout, Total Effect* by Roger Zelazny. Copyright © 1966 by Roger Zelazny. Published by Vintage Books, 1973. Reprinted with permission of Pimlico Agency, Inc., as agents for the author.

Index of Authors and Titles